EVERYMAN,
I WILL GO WITH THEE,
AND BE THY GUIDE,
IN THY MOST NEED
TO GO BY THY SIDE

NAGUIB MAHFOUZ

The Cairo Trilogy

Palace Walk   Palace of Desire   Sugar Street

Translated by William Maynard Hutchins,
Olive E. Kenny, Lorne M. Kenny
and Angele Botros Samaan
with an Introduction by Sabry Hafez

EVERYMAN'S   LIBRARY

Alfred A. Knopf New York London Toronto

248

THIS IS A BORZOI BOOK
PUBLISHED BY ALFRED A. KNOPF

First included in Everyman's Library, 2001
Palace Walk was originally published in Arabic in 1956
under the title *Bayn-al-Qasrayn*.
Copyright © 1956 by Naguib Mahfouz
Palace of Desire was originally published in Arabic in 1957
under the title *Qasr al-Shawq*.
Copyright © 1957 by Naguib Mahfouz
Sugar Street was originally published in Arabic in 1957
under the title *al-Sukkariyya*.
Copyright © 1957 by Naguib Mahfouz

Palace Walk: English-language translation by William Maynard Hutchins and
Olive E. Kenny copyright © 1990 by The American University in Cairo Press
Palace of Desire: English-language translation by William Maynard Hutchins,
Lorne M. Kenny and Olive E. Kenny copyright © 1991 by The American
University in Cairo Press
Sugar Street: English-language translation by William Maynard Hutchins and
Angele Botros Samaan copyright © 1992 by The American University
in Cairo Press
Originally published in the United States by Doubleday in 1990 (*Palace Walk*),
1991 (*Palace of Desire*), and 1992 (*Sugar Street*).
This edition is published by arrangement with Doubleday, a division of
Random House, Inc.

Introduction, Bibliography and Chronology copyright © 2001
by Everyman's Library
Typography by Peter B. Willberg
Third printing (US)

US website: www.randomhouse/everymans

ISBN: 0-375-41331-6 (US)
1-85715-248-4 (UK)

A CIP catalogue reference for this book is available from the
British Library

Book design by Barbara de Wilde and Carol Devine Carson

Printed and bound in Germany by GGP Media, Germany

CONTENTS

INTRODUCTION

Naguib Mahfouz is the first and, as yet, the only Arab writer to win the Nobel Prize for literature, and one cannot think of a better text than his magisterial *Cairo Trilogy* to be the first modern Arabic literary work to appear in Everyman's Library. This superb narrative matches the great masters of the European tradition, invoking echoes of Balzac, Tolstoy, Thomas Mann, Dickens and even Dostoevsky. Its scope, richness, literary value, philosophical weight, dexterity of style, originality of insight, variety of characterization, tragic intensity, humour and vitality are unmatched by any other Arabic novel.

The Trilogy is also one of those rare works which provides its reader with a deep insight into the culture which produced it. Reading this monumental yet highly enjoyable book enriches one more than any number of textbooks about Egypt's modern history, society and culture. It inscribes the physical appearance, atmosphere and the vibrant rhythms of Cairo's life into the very texture of its narrative.

*

In 1911 two unconnected events took place and proved to be crucial for the future of the Arabic novel: one in the *Quartier Latin* in the heart of Paris, the other in the popular al-Gamaliya quarter of old Cairo. In Paris, while studying for his doctorate in law, Muhammad Husain Haykal (1888–1956) completed *Zaynab*, the book considered by many to mark the birth of the Arabic novel. In al-Gamaliya, in the heart of Cairo, Naguib Mahfouz was born on 11 December. Later he would overlook the last three weeks of the year and claim that he was born in 1912, the year of *Zaynab*'s publication. *Zaynab* presented the rural aspects of the Egyptian character and opened the way for many stories about the countryside. Mahfouz's upbringing in the culturally rich and densely populous commercial district of al-Gamaliya qualified him to shift the fictional emphasis from the country to the city, to construct Egypt's urban novel, and to bring this emerging genre to full maturity. Furthermore, he succeeded in putting this new type of fiction on the world literary map.

Mahfouz came from a middle-class background. His father was a high-ranking civil servant, and his family lived in comfort. As the youngest of six – four sisters and two brothers – Mahfouz enjoyed the attention and affection of everyone and relished his happy childhood in al-Gamaliya. His vivid recollections of old Cairo were an everlasting source of inspiration for his work, from his early novels up to his last one, *Echoes of an Autobiography* (1995).

The novel as a genre is considered by many to be the epic of the urban middle class. Mahfouz's Cairene origins thus equipped him to be scribe of this teeming metropolis, to which he devoted his life and prodigious work. As a young boy Mahfouz witnessed the 1919 revolution whose major events took place in Cairo, some of its confrontations with the British in the very square in which he lived. The common association between the rise of national fiction and the awakening of national consciousness made his experience of this revolution one of the vital developments of his literary education, and a rich source of inspiration for his Trilogy.

Mahfouz's literary education was not attained at home where there was no library or literary culture; it was acquired through the popular storytelling of the bard in the coffee-house next to their house. When Mahfouz went to Cairo University in 1930 he studied philosophy and read avidly. His university years coincided with the economic crisis and political repression of the unstable minority governments in Egypt at that time. The University was a hive of political activity and Mahfouz was a liberal Wafdist – the Wafd was the majority party – working to end British occupation of the country, but he was aware of other political movements, particularly the Leftists and Muslim Brothers, whose exponents appear in many of his novels.

On graduation in 1934 he worked for the University, contemplated postgraduate study and even registered for a PhD in philosophy with Sufism in Islamic philosophy as the topic of his research. His first publications were philosophical essays in cultural journals, but he soon abandoned academic endeavour and embarked on a literary career. Yet philosophical concepts and spiritual preoccupations pervade his work. One of the marginal but memorable characters of *The Cairo Trilogy* is Mutawalli Abd al-Samad, the clown of the piece in the Shakespearean sense. He is a perpetual voice of calm and premonition in the best tradition of Sufism, representing the timeless spirituality that dwells in the worldliness of al-Gamaliya.

Novels were unknown in Arabic literature before the twentieth century. This is rather ironic in a culture that produced one of the most fascinating and influential narrative texts, *The Arabian Nights*. But, for centuries, this narrative gem, which is a potent arch-text in the work of contemporary writers such as Borges, Márquez, Rushdie, Barth and Eco, was relegated to the ranks of popular culture. That did not prevent it from firing the imagination of the young Mahfouz and inspiring him to become the new Shahrazad of Arabic narrative. The thirty years between the birth of the Arabic novel and Mahfouz's first work can be seen retrospectively as preparing the ground for the arrival of the master par excellence of this genre in Arabic literature.

The intervening works of Taha Husain (1889–1973), Ibrahim al-Mazini (1890–1949), Mahmud Tahir Lashin (1894–1954) and Tawfiq al-Hakim (1898–1987), significant as they may be, succeeded only in rooting the conventions of the genre in Arabic culture and acquainting the readers with its rubrics. They were all works of limited scope, though their role in establishing the new genres (the novel, drama and the short story) cannot be overlooked. They convinced the reading public of their relevance, value and significance. Aware of the pioneering nature of their work, these writers diversified their literary endeavour and, with the exception of Lashin, did not dedicate themselves to one genre. In contrast, Mahfouz concentrated for much of his career almost entirely on the novel. After a few years of what may be considered apprenticeship in writing short stories, he devoted himself to the novel for twenty-five years, before dividing his energy between the two genres. In his prolific writing life, he published more than thirty novels and fifteen collections of stories.

Mahfouz's literary career began soon after his graduation.

THE CAIRO TRILOGY

In 1938, he published his first book, *Hams al-Junun* (*Whispers of Madness*), a collection of short stories. In 1939 he left the world of academia, opted for an undemanding civil service job and published his first novel, *'Abath al-Aqdar* (*Absurd Fates*). This and the following two novels were historical works written as part of a grand project to employ the narrative genre in relating the history of Egypt from the time of the pharaohs to the present, a lifetime project of forty novels. Since studying *Ivanhoe* as part of the English curriculum at secondary school, Mahfouz had been fascinated by the historical novels of Walter Scott and embarked on this project under his influence. But Scott was not the only model, for by the time he had completed his education and started writing, several Arabic historical novels had appeared. Mahfouz's historical novels were clearly different from their predecessors in the genre. Although they had romantic overtones, they were marked by structural coherence and high artistic standards.

The setting aimed to root the work in Egyptian history, but beneath the historical structure Mahfouz was clearly concerned with contemporary national issues. Aware of his nation's historical amnesia, he mirrors the present in the past in order to enable the nation to draw support and guidance from its own history. The past is clearly used to shape the imagined community and to bolster bruised national identity. The events narrated in these novels are mainly metaphoric representations of aspects of the national condition: the quest for independence, and the need to develop the national character and the individual's awareness of his role in society. After writing three such novels, two of which won important literary prizes, Mahfouz abandoned this genre, and turned his attention to the present. He realized that he had not made a dent in the vast history of Egypt, for he was still in the early pharaonic period.

Three factors played an important role in this change of direction: reading nineteenth-century European novels, the outbreak of World War II and its impact on Egypt, and Mahfouz's urban life. When Mahfouz was introduced to the novels of Zola, Balzac, Flaubert, Thomas Mann and Dickens, he began to doubt the ability of the historical novel to deal with the rapidly changing reality of his time and the urgent issues of his community. The turbulent years of the war were characterized by protracted social, national and moral crises in Egypt, and Mahfouz became increasingly aware of the need to avoid historical metaphor and deal directly with burning social issues. He began to understand that his lack of first-hand experience and knowledge of the countryside militated against his historical project.

The title of his first 'realistic' novel, *al-Qahirah al-Jadidah* (*New Cairo*), written in the first year of the war but not published until 1943, sums up his objective: to articulate the new reality of a changing city. During the remaining years of World War II he wrote three more novels surveying the socio-historical reality of Egypt from the beginning of the twentieth century up to the war. These novels are concerned with the transformation of Cairo, physical and cultural. The urban space of old and new Cairo is both the setting and the symbol of the clashes of cultural values which affect many of the inhabitants of this teeming third-world metropolis. The novels of this phase of Mahfouz's literary career reflect the trauma of change and its social, human and political consequences. They shift the focus of the Arabic novel from the country to the city, from the past to the present; they force it to deal with the problems of change and the conflict between the old and the new, between tradition and modernity.

One of these novels, *Midaq Alley* (1946), skilfully demonstrates the intriguing but frequently tragic transformation of a society whose aspirations extend beyond its ability to realize them. The juxtaposition of the old alley and its desire for modernity and progress, with modern Cairo in which the colonial presence provides modernity with subordination, gives the novel potency and relevance. Its tragic heroine, Hamidah, is often perceived as a 'metaphor' for Egypt in her naïve but just quest to improve her life and ameliorate her difficult situation. The novel shows the deterioration of Hamidah's strong character from the desirable belle of the old quarter to the cheap strumpet of the colonized city, overwhelmed by the dictates of the war. It demonstrates the inevitability of Hamidah prostituting herself in a city controlled by the forces of colonialism.

THE CAIRO TRILOGY

The four realistic novels create in their richly textured canvas a literary typography of the Cairene urban scene. They eloquently express the predicament of its inhabitants who are caught in the web of tradition and unable to cope with the ramifications of the city's rapid transformation. But Mahfouz's realistic project was not to be fully realized until he wrote *The Cairo Trilogy*, the work that culminates this phase.

The Trilogy is the *magnum opus* of the Cairene urban chronicles, a grand narrative project that took over six years (1946–52) to accomplish. Its completion coincided with the final collapse of the old regime. Inspired by John Galsworthy's *The Forsyte Saga*, and Thomas Mann's *Buddenbrooks*, it was the first family saga in modern Arabic literature. Many others have followed, but it remains unique in scope and profundity. In the 1940s, Egypt was at a crossroads of conflicting visions and projects and needed a stocktaking narrative to elaborate its identity and articulate its choices. Mahfouz was also at a personal political crossroads. He had lost faith in, or at least harboured doubts about, his old Wafdist ideology after the Wafd was discredited for agreeing in 1942 to form a government at the request of the British. New ideologies and different narratives were springing up and he needed to examine them.

Thus, the Trilogy was the result of his search for a sense of direction and of personal and national history. It is a multi-stranded narrative that records the socio-political transformation of modern Egypt in its quest for national identity and a role in the modern world. It also sketches the topography of the urban scene with its rich cultural heritage and elaborate network of human relations. It is a valuable document of social history and of cultural anthropology as well as a literary masterpiece. It should be read both as a realistic representation of its society and as an allegorical rendering of Egypt's quest for nationhood and modernity because of its intricate viewing of the nation from multiple narrative and ideological positions.

The Cairo Trilogy, which appears in this edition for the first time as one book, was originally conceived as a single novel, and not as three separate works. When Mahfouz finished what he considered his best achievement yet, he took the manuscript, over a thousand hand-written foolscap pages, to his publisher, Said al-Sahhar, who looked at the book and said without reading it: 'What sort of a calamity is this?' Sahhar returned the novel to Mahfouz and refused to publish it on the grounds of cost, despite the fact that the story was hailed by Taha Husain, the doyen of Arabic literature, as a great novel. Mahfouz was depressed and on the verge of a nervous breakdown.

What saved the author and his novel was a lucky coincidence. Yusuf al-Siba'i, the literary commissar of the new regime, was launching a monthly review, *al-Risalah al-Jadidah*, and looking, as was the custom in Egypt at the time, for a new novel to serialize. When he asked Mahfouz if he had a manuscript, Mahfouz told him the story of his rejected novel. Al-Siba'i was encouraged, rather than discouraged, by the length of the book. It would keep his review going for some time. In 1955, the serialization of *Bayn al-Qasrayn (Palace Walk)*, as the whole novel was originally entitled, started in *al-Risalah al-Jadidah*, but the book was much longer than the short-lived *al-Risalah al-Jadidah* could sustain.

As soon as its early chapters were published, readers and critics alike realized that Mahfouz had produced a major literary work. However, Sahhar was still reluctant to publish the whole novel, though he agreed, in 1956, to bring out the serialized portion in book form, which became known as *Palace Walk*. When this was successful, he asked Mahfouz to give him another manageable portion of the novel to publish. That is when Mahfouz divided his work into three parts, with the inevitable revision to its narrative structure, giving the other two novels, published in 1957, the respective titles of *Qasr al-Shawq (Palace of Desire)* and *al-Sukkariyyah (Sugar Street)*. The three titles are taken from actual street names in the district of al-Gamaliya.

The Trilogy is the great family saga of modern Arabic literature and the work that enshrines middle class morality and culture. It places the Egyptian family at the heart of its narrative and follows its ups and downs over three different generations. Unlike many European novels of its ilk, it does not take the adventure or education of the individual as its core, but gives the central role to the family and the collective.

It also makes the mother the unsung heroine of the family, despite the ostensible authority of the father. The mother is not only the hub of family life, 'the queen with no rival to her sovereignty'; she is also the one who provides the children, male and female alike, with comfort, confidence and support. More important for the novel is the fact that she is the one who sets the pace and controls the space of the narrative.

Beneath the conventional patriarchal power structure of the story there is a subtle layer of narrative that steadily subverts patriarchal authority. This makes the novel an elegy charting the dwindling of patriarchy in Egypt's painful path to modernity. As such it is both a realistic family saga and a national allegory and each enriches the other, though the success of its realistic dimension often masks its allegorical one. The dual genealogy of the Trilogy is responsible for these two layers in its structure. Mahfouz's reading of the European realistic novel and his desire to create an Egyptian family saga inspires the realistic layer, while the allegorical dimension is a result of his awareness of an Egyptian tradition that uses the novel to mirror national reality and his need to circumvent political authoritarian control and challenge the prevailing establishment.

The Trilogy spans a long and decisive period of Egypt's modern history. *Palace Walk* begins during World War I in 1917 with the bombardment that discredited the Ottomans and ends with the outbreak of the 1919 nationalist revolution. *Palace of Desire* starts five years later in 1924 with the British negotiation with Sa'd Zaghlul, the charismatic leader of the Wafd, and ends with his death in 1927. *Sugar Street* begins in 1935 with Mustafa al-Nahhas, Zaghlul's successor, addressing a Wafd Party conference and ends with the mass arrest of political activists in 1944. But these political and historical events are mere temporal markers of the internal historical memory of the text and are inseparable from its spatial presentation.

The novel is mainly concerned with the family and mediates political events through its various members. In *Palace Walk*, the Jawad family home is the locus of the narrative and the traditional quarter of al-Gamaliya is the main space of the novel. The novel's world is in the grip of historical transition. As the title *Bayn al-Qasrayn* indicates, literally 'between two palaces' and not *Palace Walk*, Egypt was in a liminal space between two political orders: the Ottoman Caliphate with its waning traditional legitimacy and the new independent nation whose difficult birth requires the sacrificial blood of Fahmy.

If the Jawads' household dwells between these two orders, the Shaddads' mansion in *Palace of Desire*, is firmly lodged in the new state, where Egypt makes a conscious decision to emphasize its link with European culture and western life-styles. It is the opposite of the Jawads' in every respect, as the new district of al-Abbasiya is distinctly different to that of al-Gamaliya. In *Sugar Street*, with its social polarization and conflicting ideologies, opposites and doubles of the Jawad family house emerge. These include contrasts – such as Professor Forster's villa in al-Ma'adi and Abd al-Rahim Pasha's palace in Helwan – and doubles, in the form of the Sugar Street house and Sawsan Hammad's basement flat.

All these loci are inseparable from their times in the narrative. The expansion of space accompanies the augmentation of time from one novel to the next, but this is ironically marked by the shrinking of narrative. *Palace Walk* covers two years in 533 pages, *Palace of Desire* four years in 448 pages, and *Sugar Street* ten years in 330 pages. *Palace Walk* establishes the traditional time with its slow rhythm and static continuity, the rituals and daily chores mark the cyclical time. The eruption of the revolution that brings this first part to a close with the tragic death of Fahmy dislodges the eternal timelessness from its harmony, stability and static continuity.

Palace of Desire opens five years later with al-Sayyid 'extracting from his caftan the gold watch', the emblem of chronometric time, as a clear indication of a new perception. *Sugar Street* demonstrates how this new time and the vicissitudes of life have taken their toll on the old cohesive family, and is characterized by its fast pace of change and drama. This reflects the change from the pre-modern condition, with its timeless simultaneity of past and future in an instantaneous present, its slow rhythm and static rituals, to modern, heterogeneous, empty time, the time of dynamic transformation and rapid change. As Benedict Anderson convincingly argues in his *Imagined Communities*, this change in the concept of time is vital for the birth of the imagined community of the nation. The very structure of Mahfouz's narrative shows the dynamics and pains of this change in the life of both the family and the nation.

What Bakhtin called the chronotopic presentation of narrative creates constant interaction between time and space throughout the text, which redefines relationships of power and develops its meaning and trajectories. The Trilogy starts with the mother, Amina, waking up at night and ends with her death, as though she were the *raison d'être* of the narrative. In the first half of *Palace Walk*, she is inseparable from our perception of the novel's time and space. Chronotopic dialectics permeate the texture of the narrative. The greater the gap between the time of the narrative and the present, the greater the need to employ detailed social codes in order to reproduce the socio-cultural milieu and make it vivid, authentic and lively. Hence the narrative needs more time and space to develop a sense of reality regarding the years between 1917–19 than it does for the more recent years of the 1940s.

Culinary and other social rituals punctuate life in the Jawad family household. At dawn, the day starts with the kneading of dough in the baking room on the ground floor. Although, chronologically, the kneading takes place after the mother performs the dawn prayer, narrative order reverses this, making it the marker of the beginning of the day. This change is reinforced by describing the kneading and the subsequent baking in detail while mentioning the prayer only in reported narrative. Another indication of Amina's importance is the narrative subversion of the established order. The allocation of space in the house is hierarchically designated. The patriarch occupies the top floor, the mother and the male children the middle floor, the other females the ground floor, and the baking room is banished to the courtyard. But the temporal arrangement of the narrative brings the baking room, the domain of the mother and her domestic activities, forward. This narrative inversion of the realistic order subverts reality and rebalances a social hierarchy that diminishes the status of women by giving them narrative precedence over the world of men.

The elaborate description of the baking room, with its active females as the source of life and many of its delicious pleasures, gives it a highly significant role in punctuating the day and marking seasonal events, such as Ramadan, two annual feasts, and various other social occasions. No wonder, for it is also the kitchen and the incontestable realm of the mother where she reigns supreme over the domestic life of her family. The room is presented not only as the internal clock of the house, the source of its nourishment (it backs on to the larder and storeroom), but also as the testing ground for its women. It harbours special recipes for fattening birds and animals for domestic consumption, and women for prospective suitors. The warmth and intimacy of the room contrast with other areas of the house.

Once breakfast is prepared, the mother takes it on a brass tray to the dining room and oversees its serving and consumption. Here again Mahfouz uses food to communicate a host of significant messages. Breakfast is singled out because it is the only meal in which the boys eat with their father, the nearest thing to a family gathering. The dishes eaten reveal the social background of the family and even its national identity. Eggs, brown beans, cheese, pickled lemons and peppers and hot loaves of flat round bread for breakfast put the family into the upper stratum of the middle class, while the presence of fried beans makes it unmistakably Egyptian, for fried brown beans are as Egyptian as bacon and eggs are British. The eating of the meal on a low table around which cushions are placed for seating further identifies the social setting as one of a family rising to the upper level of the middle class rather than falling into it from a higher one. The latter would cling to a normal dining table and chairs. The interaction between the father and his three boys, the only members of the family allowed to eat with him, reveals further information about his character, his educational and cultural background and his relationship with his children.

Although the mother is not allowed to eat with them, her job does not end with the bringing of the breakfast tray. She stands in the room by the water jug waiting to obey any command. The mother who reigns supreme downstairs is reduced to a voiceless marginal existence upstairs. Yet her silent presence during the ritual confers on her a kind of hieromancy which is not available to the other female members of the family. The three boys, though famished, restrain themselves and wait until their father starts, then they follow in order of seniority: Yasin, Fahmy and then Kamal. This shows their highly formal response to paternal authority and the degree of hierarchical interaction within the family, which is reinforced when the author changes the narrative point of view and describes the progression of the meal from the standpoint of the youngest son, Kamal. He fears his father the most, eats cautiously and nervously and is concerned about his inability to compete for his share of food with his two energetic elder brothers, particularly after his father leaves the table. The departure of the father, followed by the mother, leads to the collapse of the eating order and transforms the formalized hierarchical space into a democratic one. Now the three boys fight for the food in a completely different setting. This very transformation is a further indication of the inner dynamics of the family.

The early departure of the father prepares the reader for the finale of his breakfast, when he goes to his room and the mother follows him with a cup containing three raw eggs mixed with milk and honey. Here the narrative opens on the world of different concoctions and tonics; some are prepared for the father to stimulate his appetite or for their aphrodisiac effect, while others are cooked for the daughters to make them plump and attractive. It also introduces the reader to the two contrasting concerns of men and women in this domain. While the mother is versed in the dietary aspects of such tonics, the father introduces us, through his train of thought, to the narcotic variations on the theme.

There is another significant contrast between the family gathering over which the father prevails, the breakfast, and that over which the mother presides, the coffee hour, soon before sunset. In the latter, a democratic matriarchal interaction replaces the oppressive patriarchal order. Unlike breakfast, which takes place on the top floor and is confined to the male members of the family, the coffee hour takes place on the first floor and is open to everyone, bar the absent father who, after work, goes on his nocturnal exploits. Although not every member of the family is allowed to drink coffee, everyone plays a role in the social ritual, which brings them together and allows for the realization of their different needs. The breakfast scene with its rigidly hierarchic order is presented from a unitary viewpoint. When the author changes the narrative perspective to relate the rest of the scene from Kamal's point of view, this is done mainly to demonstrate the power of the hierarchical control. The coffee-hour scene allows for a polyphony of voices and a multidimensional narrative.

Family politics in the Trilogy are revealed in the daily rituals of eating and drinking coffee as well as in the symbolism of the distribution of space for each activity. The breakfast takes place on the top floor, which is the sole domain of the father. Everyone comes to *his* ground and behaves according to *his* rules. The same can be said about the ground floor, the incontestable kingdom of the mother, and even about the first floor during the coffee hour. But since time and change are the two invisible heroes of the Trilogy the ordering of space changes and with it the significance of meals and refreshments that take place there.

In *Palace of Desire*, the move of the coffee hour from the first floor to the ground floor after the death of Fahmy and the marriage of the two daughters shows how these two major blows to the mother's world have almost eradicated the main source of her social pleasure. The devastating blow to the harmony of this home comes from the counter-space of the Shaddad mansion. The trappings of modernity in Aïda's house are as significant as the different food she brings to the picnic at the Pyramids, where secularism and pharaonicism are brought together. Food can clearly indicate social class, cultural background and even temporal changes in modes of behavior and taste, but it can also herald a conceptual change in Kamal's life.

In *Sugar Street*, the return of the coffee hour to the first floor is used as an indicator of a major relational change. The series of disasters afflicting the beautiful younger daughter, Aisha, gives her certain liberties earned through suffering, including smoking openly and participating fully in the coffee hour with the male members of the family. The coffee hour now brings the women from the ground floor to the first, hence establishing at least a quasi-parity between all members of the family. This is possible because of the deteriorating health of the patriarch, which forces him to come down from the top to the first floor. Now he eats his supper, which consists of yoghurt and an orange, at home. No longer can he partake of the delights of night parties and the food and drink associated with them. When he becomes frail, al-Sayyid is brought down to the ground floor and ends up bedridden and totally dependent on his wife, thus completing his descent, while Amina stays in her first-floor room until the end. Later on the absence of the coffee hour becomes as significant as its presence.

The spatial rise of the mother is inseparable from the fall of the patriarch. While Amina appears to be submissive and docile her remarkable character and pragmatic conduct speak of a strong, practical woman. In contrast, al-Sayyid is an authoritarian man and a product of an authoritarian society. Ironically both the demonstration and concealment of his virility and debauchery are quintessential to his patriarchy. Hence his character is the locus for sharp contradictions, for he is honest and hypocritical, harsh and tender, stern and joyful, pious and libertine, strong and weak. The seeds of his downfall are carefully implanted in the narrative: from the early scene of Yasin's discovery of his lascivious activities; to Fahmy's refusal to pledge to sever his links with the patriotic movement; to Kamal's unwillingness to follow his advice and study law; to his humiliation by the British in front of his son; to Zanuba's rejection of his advances. Similarly, the rise of the mother is as carefully implanted in the text, from the time when the children plot to demand her return after she is banished from the house as a result of her egregious act of disobedience and visit to the shrine of al-Husayn, until the time she reigns supreme in her household.

In these examples concerning the daily rituals, the mundane and the quotidian, one glimpses certain aspects of the politics of narrative presentation which Mahfouz employs in the Trilogy, politics of gender and power. Simple rituals are depicted as repositories of cultural values and power relationships as microcosms of political ones. We see how the life of the family is inseparable from the vicissitudes of the times and of politics in the country, and how spatial presentations shift to suit temporal changes. But nowhere in the Trilogy are the realistic and the allegorical so closely intertwined as in the central love story of the novel, that of Kamal and Aïda.

The story is played out on several levels, the most significant of which is the allegorical one as an embodiment of the internal war of the body politic. When Kamal falls for Aïda, it is not her class that attracts him, but her culture, European sensibility and secular orientation. She is unfettered by archaic tradition and is free to determine her future, qualities of the Egypt of his dreams. 'Aïda could have been on his mind when he said of Egypt, "Has she dismissed the one man she could trust at a time when he was busy defending her rights?"' As a result of seeing her in these terms, he sees himself vis-à-vis his rival as a sincere man accorded the unjust treatment given to Sa'd Zaghlul at the hands of his rival, Ziwar Pasha, who replaces Zaghlul as Prime Minister. The failure of Kamal's affair with Aïda is seen as a betrayal, and heralds the end of the middle novel of the Trilogy with the cataclysmic historical event of the death of Zaghlul.

The Trilogy has an internal historical memory whereby certain repetitions demonstrate the impact of time and cruelty of change, and this widens the scope of its interpretation. It makes effective use of the narrative device of mirroring views, events and characters on each other as if one were continually in a hall of mirrors. Yasin's interest in Maryam echoes his late brother's desire to marry her. Al-Sayyid's lust for Zanuba recalls her past affair with his son, and her future marriage to Yasin is a constant reminder of this past. Kamal attempts to recapture his love for Aïda by chasing her younger sister, Budur. Ahmad's short love affair with Alawiya Sabri conjures up Kamal's protracted passion for Aïda, and contrasts with it at the same time. These all mirror the present in the past and demonstrate how things have changed.

We have seen how each house in the Trilogy has its opposite and its double. The same process extends to the main characters where a constant process of mirroring, of contrast and similarity takes place. Al-Sayyid has both Shaddad Bey as his complete opposite and his own friends Iffat and al-Far as his doubles. Amina has both Haniya, Yasin's mother, and Bahija, Maryam's mother, as her opposites and her daughter Khadija and even Zanuba as her doubles. Kamal has Fuad al-Hamzawi as his opposite, has both similarity and contrast with his own brother, Yasin, and his friend, Riyad Qaldas, and has his nephew, Ahmad, as his double. Kamal, a Hamlet-like figure who is perfectly at home with radicalism and conservatism, has long been interpreted as bearing many autobiographical elements of Mahfouz's persona, but the author has as many autobiographical affinities with Kamal as with his nephew Ahmad.

Mahfouz has said that his narrative is concerned more with architecture and less with interior decoration. The Trilogy succeeds in becoming both a political allegory and a reservoir of social customs, folk tales and songs, popular tunes, common proverbs and the whole undercurrent of urban culture in Egypt in the first half of this century. It reflects the cultural and political development of a society in turmoil under the pressures of the British occupation, and draws a highly detailed map of Egypt's political orientations. As a family saga it succeeds in enshrining major social stereotypes of relationships, emotions and role-playing to the extent that its hero, Ahmad Abd al-Jawad, has become the Egyptian patriarch par excellence. Even today, when the Trilogy is serialized on television, both men and women throughout the Arab world view this archetypal and larger-than-life patriarch with melancholic nostalgia and admiration. This is so because the author portrayed him with similar sentiments for he was based on Mahfouz's own father. It is ironic that the most memorable patriarch in modern Arabic literature is the one who portrays the decline of patriarchy and its distinction and stature.

The novel also has its prophetic vision and warning for the future. Every novel in the Trilogy ends with a death and a birth, but the death and birth of the final novel, *Sugar Street*, are oracular. The novel ends with the death of Amina, and the imprisonment of her two grandchildren Ahmad and Abd al-Mun'im, the Communist and the Muslim Brother. The two exponents of the conflicting ideologies of progress and regres-

INTRODUCTION

sion emerged from the same house on Sugar Street, and are at the end incarcerated in the same cell. But the birth in this final novel is especially significant, for the new-born is the son of the Islamicist, a portent that is still relevant to the Arab reality of the present day.

Sabry Hafez

SABRY HAFEZ is Professor of modern Arabic and comparative literature in the School of Oriental and African Studies, University of London. He has known Mahfouz since 1960 and published numerous articles and two books on him in Arabic. He has written extensively on modern Arabic literature and literary theory in both Arabic and English. His most recent book in English is *The Genesis of Arabic Narrative Discourse: A Study in the Sociology of Modern Arabic Literature.*

SELECT BIBLIOGRAPHY

This bibliography is confined to works available in English.

MEHAHEM MILSON, *Naguib Mahfouz: The Novelist-Philosopher of Cairo*, St Martin Press, New York, 1998.

RASHEED EL-ENANY, *Naguib Mahfouz: The Pursuit of Meaning*, Routledge, London and New York, 1993.

MICHAEL BEARD and ADNAN HAYDAR, eds, *Naguib Mahfouz: From Regional Fame to Global Recognition*, Syracuse University Press, Syracuse, 1993.

TREVOR LE GASSICK, ed., *Critical Perspectives on Naguib Mahfouz*, Three Continents Press, Washington DC, 1991.

HAIM GORDON, *Naguib Mahfouz's Egypt: Existential Themes in his Writings*, Greenwood Press, New York, 1990.

M. M. ENANI, ed., *Egyptian Perspectives on Naguib Mahfouz: A Collection of Critical Essays*, General Egyptian Book Organization, Cairo, 1989.

MATTITYAHU PELED, *Religion My Own: the Literary Works of Najib Mahfuz*, Transaction Books, New Brunswick, 1983.

SASSON SOMEKH, *The Changing Rhythm: A Study of Najib Mahfuz's Novels*, E. J. Brill, Leiden, 1973.

E. M. FORSTER, *Alexandria: A History and a Guide*, Whitehead Morris Limited, Alexandria, 1922.

MATTI MOOSA, *The Origins of Modern Arabic Fiction*, Three Continents Press, Washington, DC, 1983.

ALI B. JAD, *Form and Technique in the Egyptian Novel (1912–1971)*, Ithaca Press, London, 1983.

ROGER ALLEN, *The Arabic Novel: An Historical and Critical Introduction*, Syracuse University Press, Syracuse, 1982.

HILARY KILPATRICK, *The Modern Egyptian Novel: a Study in Social Criticism*, Ithaca Press, London, 1974.

HAMDI SAKKUT, *The Egyptian Novel and its Main Trends (1913–1952)*, The American University in Cairo Press, Cairo, 1971.

J. BRUGMAN, *An Introduction to the History of Modern Arabic Literature in Egypt*, E. J. Brill, Leiden, 1984.

CHARLES D. SMITH, *Islam and the Search for Social Order in Modern Egypt: A Biography of Muhammad Husayn Haykal*, State University of New York, Albany, 1983.

MARINA STAGH, *The Limits of Freedom of Speech: Prose Literature and Prose Writers in Egypt under Nasser and Sadat*, Acta Universitatis Stockholmiensis, Stockholm, 1994.

H. A. R. GIBB, *Arabic Literature*, Oxford University Press, Oxford, 1963.
ALBERT HOURANI, *Arabic Thought in the Liberal Age: 1798–1939*, Oxford University Press, Oxford, 1962.
P. J. VATIKIOTIS, *The History of Egypt*, Johns Hopkins University Press, Baltimore, 1985.

CHRONOLOGY

DATE	AUTHOR'S LIFE	LITERARY CONTEXT
1911	On Monday 11 December, birth of Naguib Mahfouz to 'Abd al-'Aziz Ibrahim Ahmad al-Basha and Fatimah Ibrahim Mustafa, in Cairo, in the old district of al-Gamaliya.	Muhammad Husain Haykal (1888–1956) completes the writing of *Zaynab* in Paris. Conrad: *Under Western Eyes*.
1912		Publication of *Zaynab*, the first Arabic novel, in Cairo, under the pseudonym Misri Fallah (Egyptian Peasant).
1913		Proust: *Swann's Way*. Lawrence: *Sons and Lovers*.
1914		Death of Jurji Zaydan (1861–1914), founder of the historical novel in Arabic. Joyce: *A Portrait of the Artist as a Young Man* (to 1915).
1916	Goes to traditional *Kuttab* school.	Bely: *Petersburg*.
1917 1918	Goes to primary school.	
1919	Participates in demonstrations during the 1919 revolution.	Woolf: *Night and Day*. Shaw: *Heartbreak House*.
1922		Joyce: *Ulysses*. Eliot: *The Waste Land*. Galsworthy: *The Forsyte Saga*. The discovery of the tomb and treasures of Tutankhamen becomes a source of national pride and fosters great interest in Egypt's Pharaonic past.
1923	Begins his secondary school education.	Huda Sha'rawi (1879–1947) establishes the first Feminist Union of Egypt. Svevo: *Zeno's Conscience*.
1924		Forster: *A Passage to India*. Mann: *The Magic Mountain*. Ford: *Parade's End* (to 1928).

Egypt under protectorate. Mustafa Kamil's Patriotic Quest for Independence. Agadir crisis.

Sinking of the *Titanic*. Scott's Antarctic expedition.

Outbreak of World War I.

Easter Rising in Dublin.

October Revolution in Russia.
Armistice. Egypt demands the fulfilment of Britain's promise to evacuate Egypt after the end of the war.
The outbreak of the 1919 revolution and the formation of the Wafd party with its liberal nationalism.
End of protectorate and first declaration of Independence. Establishment of USSR. Mussolini forms government in Italy.

First Constitution of 1923. Munich putsch by Nazis. German financial crisis.

Zaghlul forms the first Wafd government. The foundation of the first Communist party in Egypt. First Labour government in Britain.

DATE	AUTHOR'S LIFE	LITERARY CONTEXT
1925		The launch of *al-Fajr,* a literary journal devoted to the promotion of new narrative genres. Ali Abd al-Raziq (1887–1966): *Islam and the Rules of Government.* Kafka: *The Trial.* Fitzgerald: *The Great Gatsby.*
1926		Taha Husain publishes *Fi al-Shi'r al-Jahili* (*On Pre-Islamic Poetry*). The book is banned and the author is tried but acquitted.
1927		Tawfiq al-Hakim (1899–1987) writes his novel *Awdar al-Ruh* (*The Return of the Spirit*) in Paris. Taha Husain publishes *al-Ayyam* (*An Egyptian Childhood*). Haykal starts a national debate on the pages of *Al-Siyasah* on the need for the creation of a national literature. Proust: *In Search of Lost Time.* Woolf: *To the Lighthouse.*
1928		Introduction of mixed university education. Salama Musa (1887–1958) and his progressive journal, *Al-Majallah al-Jadidah,* play key role in the dissemination of left-wing ideas.
1929		Faulkner: *The Sound and the Fury.* Hemingway: *A Farewell to Arms.*
1930	Begins his university education. Publishes his first article on Fabian Socialism in *Al-Majallah al-Jadidah.*	Musil: *The Man Without Qualities* (vol. 1). Faulkner: *As I Lay Dying.*
1932	Translates from English a short book on Ancient Egypt. Supports the schism in the Wafd for some time, then returns to the main Wafd.	Publication of *The Return of the Spirit* in Cairo. Death of two major poets: Ahmad Sawqi (b. 1868) and Hafiz Ibrahim (b. 1872). Huxley: *Brave New World.*

CHRONOLOGY

HISTORICAL EVENTS

General Strike in Britain.

Death of Sa'd Zaghlul.

The religio-political movement, the Muslim Brethren, is founded by Hasan al-Banna.

Wall Street Crash.

Isma'il Sidqi becomes Prime Minister of Egypt, abrogates the 1923 Constitution and replaces it with 1930 Constitution. World economic crisis.

Egypt suffers the impact of the 1930s economic crisis. Schism in Wafd party and formation of Sa'dis party.

THE CAIRO TRILOGY

DATE	AUTHOR'S LIFE	LITERARY CONTEXT
1933	Contemplates becoming a musician, joins the Institute for Oriental Music for one year, then goes back to complete his degree in philosophy.	Hemingway: *Winner Take Nothing*.
1934	Graduates from Fu'ad I University (later Cairo University) with degree in philosophy. Obtains his first job in the university administration. His first short story appears in *Al-Majallah al-Jadidah*. Starts postgraduate studies in philosophy with the intention of writing a thesis on 'Aesthetics in Islamic philosophy' with his mentor, Mustafa Abd al-Raziq (1885–1947).	Waugh: *A Handful of Dust*. Fitzgerald: *Tender is the Night*.
1936	Under the influence of Salama Musa, decides to abandon postgraduate study and devote his time to writing fiction. Starts an intensive programme of reading the classics of world literature, particularly the novel.	The promise of independence gives rise to cultural euphoria. Huxley: *Eyeless in Gaza*.
1937	Death of his father. He continues to live with his mother. Continues his intensive reading programme.	Woolf: *The Years*.
1938	Publication of first collection of short stories, *Hams al-Junun* (Whispers of Madness).	The publication of Taha Husain's *Mustaqbal al-Thaqafa fi Misr* (Future of Culture in Egypt). Dos Passos: *USA*.
1939	Appointed Parliamentary Secretary to Mustafa Abd al-Raziq, the Minister of *Awqaf* (Religious Endowments). *'Abath al-Aqdar* (Vicissitudes of Fate) is published.	Steinbeck: *The Grapes of Wrath*. Joyce: *Finnegans Wake*.
1940		Hemingway: *For Whom the Bell Tolls*. Stead: *The Man Who Loved Children*. Greene: *The Power and the Glory*.
1941		Brecht: *Mother Courage*.

CHRONOLOGY

Ahmad Husain founds Young Egypt, an extreme Egyptian nationalist movement with its Green Shirts.

Hitler becomes German Chancellor.

Death of King Fu'ad; his young son, Farouk, ascends the throne. Italian forces occupy Abyssinia. Aware of the mounting Axis threat in Europe, Britain signs a conciliatory treaty with Egypt. Outbreak of Spanish Civil War (to 1939). Stalin's 'Great Purge' of the Communist Party (to 1938).

Japanese invasion of China.

Germany annexes Austria; Munich crisis.

World War II.

France surrenders to Germany. Battle of Britain.

US enters war.

DATE	AUTHOR'S LIFE	LITERARY CONTEXT
1942	As a Wafdist, Mahfouz is dismayed and disillusioned by his party's agreement to form a government at the request of its arch-enemy, the British.	Camus: *The Outsider*.
1943	*Radubis* wins the literary prize of the philanthopist Qut al-Qulub al-Dimirdashiyyah (1892–1968).	
1944	*Kifah Tibah* (The Struggle of Thebes) is published and wins the literary prize of the Arabic Academy.	Borges: *Ficciones*. Waugh: *Brideshead Revisited*.
1945	*Al-Qahira al-Jadidah* (New Cairo) is published.	Publication of Yahya Haqqi's (1905–94) *Qindil Umm Hashim*, (*The Saint's Lamp*). Sartre: *The Roads to Freedom* (to 1947). Orwell: *Animal Farm*.
1946	*Khan al-Khalili* is published and wins the literary prize of the Ministry of Education.	Many left-wing writers and intellectuals arrested. Tanizaki: *The Makioka Sisters* (to 1948).
1947	Abd al-Raziq becomes Minister of *Awqaf* and appoints Mahfouz as his Parliamentary Secretary. *Zuqaq al-Midaqq* (*Midaq Alley*) is published and is rejected by the committee of the literary prize of the Ministry of Education. Writes his first screenplay, *Antar wa Ablah* (Antar and Ablah): the film is directed by Salah Abu-Saif. This marks the beginning of a secondary career as screenplay writer. (He was to script more than twelve films.) The beginning of a long friendship with Tawfiq Al-Hakim.	Camus: *The Plague*. Mann: *Doctor Faustus*. Levi: *If This is a Man*.
1948	*Al-Sarab* (Mirage) is published and is rejected by the committee of the literary prize of the Ministry of Education for its eroticism.	Greene: *The Heart of the Matter*.

CHRONOLOGY

HISTORICAL EVENTS

The German army threatens to overrun Egypt; demonstrations chant,
'Forward Rommel!', and the British are unable to secure their supply lines.
British tanks surround the palace and force the king on 4 February to
appoint a Wafd government to control the masses. Rommel is defeated at
El Alamein.
Allied forces invade Italy.

D-Day landings in Normandy.

WWII ends. Atomic bombs dropped on Japan. United Nations founded.

Massive demonstrations of students and workers against the British. USSR
extends influence in eastern Europe: beginning of the Cold War.

Marshall Plan begins in Europe.

The Nakbah, the loss of Palestine and the foundation of the state of Israel
on Arab territories. Apartheid introduced in South Africa.

THE CAIRO TRILOGY

DATE	AUTHOR'S LIFE	LITERARY CONTEXT
1949	*Bidayah wa Nihayah (The Beginning and the End)* is published.	Publication of Taha Husain's *al-Mu'adhdhbun fi al-Ard (The Wretched of the Earth)* gives tremendous boost to realistic narrative. Orwell: *Nineteen Eighty-Four.*
1952	The writing of *The Cairo Trilogy* is completed. As a Wafdist, Mahfouz is completely surprised by the army takeover.	Beckett: *Waiting for Godot.* Waugh: *Men at Arms.*
1953	Yahya Haqqi is given the role of establishing a new Department for the Arts; this becomes the nucleus of the later Ministry of Culture. He appoints Mahfouz as his assistant.	More arrests of left-wing intellectuals. Bellow: *The Adventures of Augie March.*
1954	The serialization of the Trilogy in *al-Risalah al-Jadidah.* Marries Atiyyatallah Ibrahim from Alexandria. The peak of his cinema activities until end of 1950s.	The publication of Yusuf Idris' *Arkhas Layali (Cheapest Nights)* and Abd al-Rahman al-Sharqawi's *al-Ard (The Egyptian Earth).*
1955		Nabokov: *Lolita.* Kemal: *Memed, My Hawk.*
1956	*Bayn al-Qasrain (Palace Walk)* is published in book form.	Performance of Nu'man 'Ashour's *Al-Nas illi That (People Downstairs).* Mishima: *The Temple of the Golden Pavilion.* Osborne: *Look Back in Anger.*
1957	The two other parts of the *Cairo Trilogy, Qasr al-Shawq (Palace of Desire)* and *al-Sukkariyyah (Sugar Street)* are published. Obtains the State Literary Prize for the Novel.	Pasternak: *Doctor Zhivago.*
1958	Becomes Head of Cinema in the Arts Department and Chair of Board of Censorship.	Performance of Al-Hakim's *al-Sultan al-Ha'r (Sultan's Dilemma).* Lampedusa: *The Leopard.*
1959	*Awlad Haratina (Children of Gebelawi)* is serialized in *al-Ahram,* but the Azhar, the central religious establishment, objects to it and it does not appear in book form in Egypt.	Further arrests of left-wing intellectuals. Grass: *The Tin Drum.*

CHRONOLOGY

DATE	AUTHOR'S LIFE	LITERARY CONTEXT
1960	Diagnosed as diabetic he imposes a strict health programme on his life. *Al-Liss wa'l-Kilab* (*The Thief and the Dogs*) is serialized in *al-Ahram*.	Performance of Yusuf Idris' *Al-Farafir* (Flip-Flap). Updike: *Rabbit, Run*.
1961	Becomes adviser to the Minister of Culture. *Al-Liss wa'l-Kilab* is published in book form. *Al-Simman wa'l-Kharif (Autumn Quail)* is serialized in *al-Ahram*.	Heller: *Catch-22*. Naipaul: *A House for Mr Biswas*.
1962	*Al-Simman wa'l-Kharif* is published in book form. *Dunya Allah (God's World)**, his first collection of short stories in 25 years.	Solzhenitsyn: *One Day in the Life of Ivan Denisovich*. Bassani: *The Garden of the Finzi-Contini*. Nabokov: *Pale Fire*.
1963	*Al-Tariq (The Search)* is serialized in *al-Ahram*.	Levi: *The Truce*.
1964	Becomes the Head of the Cinema Organization, Ministry of Culture. *Al-Tariq* is published in book form. *Al-Shahhadh (The Beggar)* is serialized in *al-Ahram*.	Bellow: *Herzog*.
1965	*Al-Shahhadh* is published in book form. *Tharthara Fawq al-Nil (Adrift in the Nile)* is serialized and Amer, Nasser's second-in-command, threatens Mahfouz with imprisonment. Nasser intervenes and Mahfouz is saved from arrest. *Bayt Sayyi' al-Sum'ah* (A House of Ill Repute)* is published.	Calvino: *Cosmicomics*.
1966	*Tharthara al-Nil* is published in book form. *Awlad Haratina* is published in book form in Beirut for the first time. *Miramar (Miramar)* is serialized in *al-Ahram*.	Bulgakov: *The Master and Magarita*. Nabokov: *Speak, Memory*.
1967	*Miramar* is published in book form.	Márquez: *One Hundred Years of Solitude*.
1968	Awarded the State Emeritus Prize, the highest literary prize in Egypt. Death of his mother.	Solzhenitsyn: *Cancer Ward*.
1969	*Khammarat al-Qitt al-Aswad* (Black Cat Bar)* is published.	

CHRONOLOGY

HISTORICAL EVENTS

The first 'socialist' five-year plan and the nationalization of foreign economic interests in the country.

Syria secedes from its union with Egypt. Erection of Berlin Wall. Yuri Gagarin becomes first man in space.

Army officers in Yemen overthrow the Imam. Egyptian involvement in the ensuing war begins. Cuban missile crisis.

Assasination of President Kennedy.

Khrushchev deposed in USSR and replaced by Brezhnev. Mandela imprisoned in South Africa (to 1990).

Mao launches 'Cultural Revolution' in China.

June war with Israel which results in the occupation of the rest of Palestine as well as the Egyptian Sinai peninsula and the Syrian Golan Heights. A war of attrition between Egypt and Israel along the Suez Canal begins. Student unrest throughout Europe and USA. Soviet-led invasion of Czechoslovakia. Assassination of Martin Luther King. Nixon US President. Americans land first man on the moon.

DATE	AUTHOR'S LIFE	LITERARY CONTEXT
1970	Re-appointed adviser to the Minister of Culture. *Taht al Mizallah* (In a Bus Stop)* is published.	Mandelstam: *Hope Against Hope.*
1971	Officially retires from government. Accepts a new post as 'writer in residence' for *al-Ahram* newspaper. *Al-Ahram* refuses to serialize his novel *al-Maraya* (*Mirrors*), and it is serialized in the weekly *Radio and Television*. *Shahr al-'Asal* (Honeymoon)* is published.	Böll: *Group Portrait with Lady.*
1972	*Maraya* appears in book form. *Al-Ahram* refuses to serialize his novel *Hubb Taht al-Matar* (Love in the Rain); it appears in the weekly *Al-Shabab*. *Hikayah Bila Bidayah wala Nihayah* (A Tale without a Beginning or an End)* is published.	Tawfiq al-Hakim initiates a petition in protest against the lack of action to regain the occupied lands. It is signed by a large number of intellectuals including Mahfouz. Sadat dismisses most signatories of the petition from their jobs and bans Hakim and Mahfouz from publication.
1973	*Hubb Taht al-Matar* appears in book form. *Al-Jarimah* (The Crime)* is published.	Pynchon: *Gravity's Rainbow.*
1974	*Al-Ahram* refuses to publish *Al-Karnak* (*Karnak*), and it is published in book form. Mahfouz is sued for exposing atrocities in political prisons.	
1975	*Hadrat al-Muhtaram* (*Respected Sir*) is published. *Hikayat Haratina* (*Tales of Our Alley*) is published.	Levi: *The Periodic Table.* Fuentes: *Terra Nostra.*
1976	*Qalb al-Layl* (The Heart of the Night) is published.	
1977	*Malhamat al-Harafish* (*Harafish*) is published.	Morrison: *Song of Solomon.*
1979	*Al-Habb fawq Hadabat al-Haram* (Love on the Pyramids' Plateau)* is published. *Al-Shaytan Ya'iz* (The Devil Preaches)* is published. Mahfouz's work is banned in most Arab countries after his support of Sadat's Camp David Accord.	Calvino: *If on a winter's night a traveler.*

CHRONOLOGY

DATE	AUTHOR'S LIFE	LITERARY CONTEXT
1980	*'Asr al-Hubb* (The Age of Love) is published.	Burgess: *Earthly Powers.*
1981	*Afrah al-Qubbah* (*Wedding Song*) is published.	Rushdie: *Midnight's Children.*
1982	*Layali Alf Laylah (Arabian Nights and Days)* is published. *Ra'ayt fima Yara al-Na'im* (I saw a Dream)* is published. *Al-Baqi min al-Zaman Sa'ah* (There Only Remains One Hour) is published.	Levi: *If Not Now, When?*. Vargas Llosa: *Aunt Julia and the Scriptwriter.*
1983	*Rihlat Ibn Fattumah* (*The Journey of Ibn Fattuma*) is published. *Amam al-'Arsh* (Before the Throne) is published.	
1984	*Al-Tanzim al-Sirri* (Secret Organization)* is published.	Márquez: *Love in the Time of Cholera.* Kundera: *The Unbearable Lightness of Being.*
1985	*Yawm Qutil al-Za'im* (*The Day the Leader Was Killed*) is published.	Grossman: *Life and Fate.*
1987	*Hadith al-Sabah wa'l-Masa'* (Tales of Mornings and Evenings) is published. *Sabah al-Ward* (A Very Good Morning)* is published.	Morrison: *Beloved.*
1988	Award of the Nobel Prize for Literature. The Swedish Academy mentions both *The Cairo Trilogy* and *Children of Gebelawi. Qushtumur* (Qushtumur) is published.	Rushdie: *The Satanic Verses.*
1989	The citation of *Children of Gebelawi* in the Nobel Committee decision leads a Muslim Fundamentalist leader, Omar Abd al-Rahman, to issue a *Fatwa* for his death. Mahfouz defies the *Fatwa* and refuses government protection. *Al-Fajr al-Kadhib* (False Dawn)* is published.	Barnes: *A History of the World in 10 $\frac{1}{2}$ Chapters.* M. Amis: *London Fields.*
1990	Three collections of his journalistic essays are published: *Hawl al-Din wa'l-Dimoqratiyyah* (On Religion and Democracy), *Hawl al-Thaqafah wa'l-Ta'lim* (On Culture and Education), and *Hawl al-Shabab wa'l-Hurriyah* (On Youth and Freedom).	Updike: *Rabbit at Rest.*

CHRONOLOGY

Solidarity union formed in Poland.

Assassination of Sadat by a group of army officers. Mubarak succeeds him.
Reagan becomes US President.
Israel invades Lebanon and the Palestinians are driven into the sea. The
massacres of Sabra and Shatila take place following Israel's occupation of
Beirut. Falklands war.

Famine in Ethiopia.

Gorbachev comes to power in USSR.

The eruption of *intifada* (uprising) in the occupied Palestinian territories.

Collapse of Communist empire in eastern Europe. Fall of the Berlin Wall.
Tienanmen Square massacre in China. De Klerk becomes President of
South Africa.

Saddam Husain invades Kuwait.

DATE	AUTHOR'S LIFE	LITERARY CONTEXT
1991		
1992		
1994	A Muslim Fundamentalist plunges a knife into his neck. He survives, but is left partly paralysed in his right arm.	Aksyonov: *Generations of Winter.*
1995	*Asda' al-Sirah al-Dhatiyyah* (*Echoes of an Autobiography*) is published.	M. Amis: *The Information.* P. Fitzgerald: *The Blue Flower.*
1996	*Al-Qarar al-Akhir* (The Final Decision)* is published.	
1998		
2000	*Kitab al-Qarn* (The Book of the Century)* is published.	

Titles of Mahfouz's works are given in transliterated form, followed by a translation of the title in parentheses. Where the work is available in English, the title in parentheses is that of the English translation, and is therefore italicized. An asterisk indicates a collection of short stories.

CHRONOLOGY

The Gulf war takes place. American and Allied troops liberate Kuwait from
the Iraqis, but Iraq is completely devastated.
Clinton elected US President. Civil war in former Yugoslavia.

Assassination of Israeli Prime Minister, Yitzhak Rabin.

President Clinton re-elected.

Clinton orders air-strikes against Iraq.
The eruption of the second *intifada* and student demonstrations in Egypt.
Putin succeeds Yeltsin as Russian President. Violence in Chechnya.
Milosevic's regime in the former Yugoslavia collapses; Vojislav Kostunica
elected President.

THE CAIRO TRILOGY

With appreciation to David Morse

— THE EDITOR

PALACE WALK

1

SHE WOKE at midnight. She always woke up then without having
to rely on an alarm clock. A wish that had taken root in her awoke
her with great accuracy. For a few moments she was not sure she
was awake. Images from her dreams and perceptions mixed
together in her mind. She was troubled by anxiety before opening
her eyes, afraid sleep had deceived her. Shaking her head gently,
she gazed at the total darkness of the room. There was no clue by
which to judge the time. The street noise outside her room would
continue until dawn. She could hear the babble of voices from the
coffeehouses and bars, whether it was early evening, midnight, or
just before daybreak. She had no evidence to rely on except her
intuition, like a conscious clock hand, and the silence encompassing the house, which revealed that her husband had not yet rapped
at the door and that the tip of his stick had not yet struck against the
steps of the staircase.

Habit woke her at this hour. It was an old habit she had developed when young and it had stayed with her as she matured. She
had learned it along with the other rules of married life. She woke
up at midnight to await her husband's return from his evening's
entertainment. Then she would serve him until he went to sleep.
She sat up in bed resolutely to overcome the temptation posed by
sleep. After invoking the name of God, she slipped out from under
the covers and onto the floor. Groping her way to the door, she
guided herself by the bedpost and a panel of the window. As she
opened the door, faint rays of light filtered in from a lamp set on a
bracketed shelf in the sitting room. She went to fetch it, and the
glass projected onto the ceiling a trembling circle of pale light
hemmed in by darkness. She placed the lamp on the table by the
sofa. The light shone throughout the room, revealing the large,
square floor, high walls, and ceiling with parallel beams. The
quality of the furnishings was evident: the Shiraz carpet, large
brass bed, massive armoire, and long sofa draped with a small rug
in a patchwork design of different motifs and colors.

The woman headed for the mirror to look at herself. She noted that her brown scarf was wrinkled and pushed back. Strands of chestnut hair had crept down over her forehead. Grasping the knot with her fingers, she untied it. She smoothed the scarf around her hair and retied the two ends slowly and carefully. She wiped the sides of her face with her hands as though trying to erase any last vestiges of sleep. In her forties and of medium build, she looked slender, although her body's soft skin was filled out to its narrow limits in a charmingly harmonious and symmetrical way. Her face was oblong, with a high forehead and delicate features. She had beautiful, small eyes with a sweet dreamy look. Her nose was petite and thin, flaring out a little at the nostrils. Beneath her tender lips, a tapered chin descended. The pure, fair skin of her cheek revealed a beauty spot of intensely pure black. She seemed to be in a hurry as she wrapped her veil about her and headed for the door to the balcony. Opening it, she entered the closed cage formed by the wooden latticework and stood there, turning her face right and left while she peeked out through the tiny, round openings of the latticework panels that protected her from being seen from the street.

The balcony overlooked the ancient building housing a cistern downstairs and a school upstairs which was situated in the middle of Palace Walk, or Bayn al-Qasrayn. Two roads met there: al-Nahhasin, or Coppersmiths Street, going south and Palace Walk, which went north. To her left, the street appeared narrow and twisting. It was enveloped in a gloom that was thicker overhead where the windows of the sleeping houses looked down, and less noticeable at street level, because of the light coming from the handcarts and from the vapor lamps of the coffeehouses and the shops that stayed open until dawn. To her right, the street was engulfed in darkness. There were no coffeehouses in that direction, only large stores, which closed early. There was nothing to attract the eye except the minarets of the ancient seminaries of Qala'un and Barquq, which loomed up like ghostly giants enjoying a night out by the light of the gleaming stars. It was a view that had grown on her over a quarter of a century. She never tired of it. Perhaps boredom was an irrelevant concept for a life as monotonous as hers. The view had been a companion for her in her solitude and a friend in her loneliness during a long period when she was deprived of friends and companions before her children were born, when for most of the day and night she had been the sole occupant of this large house with its two stories of spacious rooms with high ceilings, its dusty courtyard and deep well.

She had married before she turned fourteen and had soon found herself the mistress of the big house, following the deaths of her husband's parents. An elderly woman had assisted her in looking after it but deserted her at dusk to sleep in the oven room in the courtyard, leaving her alone in a nocturnal world teeming with spirits and ghosts. She would doze for an hour and lie awake the next, until her redoubtable husband returned from a long night out.

To set her mind at rest she had gotten into the habit of going from room to room, accompanied by her maid, who held the lamp for her, while she cast searching, frightened glances through the rooms, one after the other. She began with the first floor and continued with the upper story, reciting the Qur'an suras she knew in order to ward off demons. She would conclude with her room, lock the door, and get into bed, but her recitations would continue until she fell asleep.

She had been terrified of the night when she first lived in this house. She knew far more about the world of the jinn than that of mankind and remained convinced that she was not alone in the big house. There were demons who could not be lured away from these spacious, empty old rooms for long. Perhaps they had sought refuge there before she herself had been brought to the house, even before she saw the light of day. She frequently heard their whispers. Time and again she was awakened by their warm breath. When she was left alone, her only defense was reciting the opening prayer of the Qur'an and sura one hundred and twelve from it, about the absolute supremacy of God, or rushing to the latticework screen at the window to peer anxiously through it at the lights of the carts and the coffeehouses, listening carefully for a laugh or cough to help her regain her composure.

Then the children arrived, one after the other. In their early days in the world, though, they were tender sprouts unable to dispel her fears or reassure her. On the contrary, her fears were multiplied by her troubled soul's concern for them and her anxiety that they might be harmed. She would hold them tight, lavish affection on them, and surround them, whether awake or asleep, with a protective shield of Qur'an suras, amulets, charms, and incantations. True peace of mind she would not achieve until her husband returned from his evening's entertainment.

It was not uncommon for her, while she was alone with an infant, rocking him to sleep and cuddling him, to clasp him to her breast suddenly. She would listen intently with dread and alarm and then call out in a loud voice, as though addressing someone in the room, "Leave us alone. This isn't where you belong. We are Muslims and believe in the one God." Then she would quickly and fervently recite the one hundred and twelfth sura of the Qur'an about the uniqueness of God. Over the course of time as she gained more experience living with the spirits, her fears diminished a good deal. She was calm enough to jest with them without being frightened. If she happened to sense one of them prowling about, she would say in an almost intimate tone, "Have you no respect for those who worship God the Merciful? He will protect us from you, so do us the favor of going away." But her mind was never completely at rest until her husband returned. Indeed, the mere fact of his presence in the house, whether awake or asleep, was enough to make her feel secure. Then it did not matter whether the doors were open or locked, the lamp burning brightly or extinguished.

It had occurred to her once, during the first year she lived with him, to venture a polite objection to his repeated nights out. His response had been to seize her by the ears and tell her peremptorily in a loud voice, "I'm a man. I'm the one who commands and forbids. I will not accept any criticism of my behavior. All I ask of you is to obey me. Don't force me to discipline you."

She learned from this, and from the other lessons that followed, to adapt to everything, even living with the jinn, in order to escape the glare of his wrathful eye. It was her duty to obey him without reservation or condition. She yielded so wholeheartedly that she even disliked blaming him privately for his nights out. She became convinced that true manliness, tyranny, and staying out till after midnight were common characteristics of a single entity. With the passage of time she grew proud of whatever he meted out, whether it pleased or saddened her. No matter what happened, she remained a loving, obedient, and docile wife. She had no regrets at all about reconciling herself to a type of security based on surrender.

Whenever she thought back over her life, only goodness and happiness came to mind. Fears and sorrows seemed meaningless ghosts to her, worth nothing more than a smile of pity. Had she not lived with this husband and his shortcomings for a quarter century and been rewarded by children who were the apples of her eye, a home amply provided with comforts and blessings, and a happy, adult life? Of course she had. Being surrounded by the jinn had been bearable, just as each evening was bearable. None of them had attempted to hurt her or the children. They had only played some harmless pranks to tease her. Praise God, the merit was all God's. He calmed her heart and with His mercy brought order to her life.

She even profoundly loved this hour of waiting up, though it interrupted a pleasant sleep and forced her to do chores that should have ceased with the end of the day. Not only had it become an integral part of her life, tied to many of her memories, but it continued to be the living symbol of her affection for her spouse, of her wholehearted dedication to making him happy, which she revealed to him night after night. For this reason, she was filled with contentment as she stood in the balcony peering through the openings toward Palace Walk and al-Khurunfush streets and then towards Hammam al Sultan or the various minarets.

She let her eyes wander over the houses bunched together untidily on both sides of the road like a row of soldiers standing at ease, relaxing from harsh discipline. She smiled at the beloved view of this road, which stayed awake until the break of dawn, while the other streets, lanes, and alleys slept. It distracted her from her sleeplessness and kept her company when she was lonely, dispelling her fears. Night changed nothing save to envelop the surrounding areas with a profound silence that provided a setting in which the street's sounds could ring out clearly, like the shadows at the edges of a painting that give the work depth and clarity. A laugh would resound as though bursting out in her room, and a remark made in a normal tone of voice could be heard distinctly. She could listen to a cough rattle on until it ended in a kind of moan. A waiter's voice would ring out like the call of a muezzin: "Another ball of tobacco for the pipe," and she would merrily ask herself, "By God, are these people ordering a refill at this hour?"

They reminded her of her absent husband. She would wonder, "Where do you suppose he is now? What is he doing? . . . May he be safe and sound whatever he does."

It was suggested to her once that a man like Mr. Ahmad Abd al-Jawad, so wealthy, strong, and handsome, who stayed out night after night, must have other women in his life. At that time, her life was poisoned by jealousy, and intense sorrow overcame her. Her courage was not up to speaking to him about it, but she confided her grief to her mother, who sought as best she could to soothe her mind with fine words, telling her, "He married you after divorcing his first wife. He could have kept her too, if he'd wanted, or taken second, third, and fourth wives. His father had many wives. Thank our Lord that you remain his only wife."

Although her mother's words did not help much then, she eventually accepted their truth and validity. Even if the rumor was accurate, perhaps that was another characteristic of manliness, like late nights and tyranny. At any rate, a single evil was better than many. It would be a mistake to allow suspicion to wreck her good life filled with happiness and comfort. Moreover, in spite of everything, perhaps the rumor was idle speculation or a lie. She discovered that jealousy was no different from the other diffi-culties troubling her life. To accept them was an inevitable and binding decree. Her only means of combating them was, she found, to call on patience and rely on her inner strength, the one resource in the struggle against disagreeable things. Jealousy and its motivation became something she put up with like her husband's other troubling characteristics or living with the jinn.

She continued to watch the road and listen to the people chat until she heard a horse's hoofbeats. She turned her head toward al-Nahhasin Street and saw a carriage slowly approaching, its lamps shining in the darkness. She sighed with relief and murmured, "Finally . . ." It was the carriage of one of his friends, bringing him to the door of his house after their evening out before continuing on as usual to al-Khurunfush with the owner and some other friends who lived there. The carriage stopped in front of the house, and her husband's voice rang out cheerfully: "May God keep you."

She would listen lovingly and with amazement to her husband's voice when he said good night to his friends. If she had not heard him every night at about this hour, she would not have believed it.

She and the children were accustomed to nothing but prudence, dignity, and gravity from him. How did he come by these joyful, jesting sounds, which flowed out so merrily and graciously?

The owner of the carriage teased her husband, asking, "Did you hear what the horse said to himself when you got out? He commented it's a pity I bring a man like you home every night when all you deserve is an ass."

The men in the vehicle exploded with laughter. Her husband waited for them to quiet down. Then he replied, "Didn't you hear the answer? He said in that case I'd be riding you."

The men burst out laughing once more. The vehicle's owner said, "We'll save the rest for tomorrow night."

The carriage proceeded along Palace Walk, and her husband headed for their door. She left the balcony for the bedroom. Picking up the lamp, she went to the sitting room and then to the hall to stand at the top of the stairs. She could hear the outside door being slammed shut and the bolt sliding into place. She imagined his tall figure crossing the courtyard as he donned awesome dignity and shed the mirthfulness which, had she not overheard it, she would have never thought possible. Hearing the tip of his walking stick strike the steps of the stairway, she held the lamp out over the banister to light his way.

2

THE MAN made his way toward her. She went on ahead of him, holding the lamp aloft. He followed, mumbling, "Good evening, Amina."

She replied in a low voice, both polite and deferential, "Good evening, sir."

When they reached the bedroom, Amina went to put the lamp on the table, while her husband hung his stick on the edge of the bedstead. He took off his fez, which he placed on the cushion at the center of the sofa, and then his wife approached to help him remove his clothes. He looked tall and broad-shouldered standing there. He had a massive body with a large, firm belly, covered smartly and comfortably by a cloak and a caftan that showed both his good taste and his wealth. His spread of neatly combed and parted black hair, his ring with its large diamond, and his gold watch only served to emphasize his refinement and affluence. His long face was expressive, with firm skin and clean-cut features. Taken as a whole, it revealed his strong personality and good looks. He had wide, blue eyes and a large, proud nose which, despite its size, was well proportioned for the expanse of his face. His lips were full and the ends of his thick, black mustache were twisted with extraordinary care.

When his wife came near him, he spread his arms out. She removed his cloak and folded it carefully before placing it on the sofa. Turning back to him, she loosened the sash of his caftan, removed it, and folded it up with similar care to lay it on top of the cloak. Her husband took his house shirt and then his white skull-cap, putting on each in turn. Yawning, he stretched and sat down on the sofa. He spread out his legs and leaned his head against the wall. After his wife finished arranging his clothes, she sat beside his extended feet and began to remove his shoes and socks. When his right foot was bared, the first defect of this handsome, powerful body was revealed. His little toe had been eaten away by successive scrapings of a razor attacking a chronic corn.

Amina left the room for a few minutes and returned with a basin and pitcher. Placing the basin by her husband's feet, she stood ready and waiting with the pitcher in her hand. Her husband straightened up and held his hands out to her. She poured the water for him. He washed his face, rubbed his head, and rinsed thoroughly. Then he took the towel from the sofa cushion and set about drying his head, face, and hands, while his wife carried the basin to the bath. This task was the last of the many duties she performed in the big house. For a quarter of a century she had continued to discharge it with an ardor undimmed by ennui. To the contrary, she did it with pleasure and delight and with the same enthusiasm that spurred her on to undertake the other household chores from just before sunrise until sunset. For this reason she was called "the bee" by women in her neighborhood, in recognition of her incessant perseverance and energy.

She returned to the room, closed the door, and pulled a pallet out from under the bed. She placed it in front of the sofa and sat cross-legged on it. In good conscience she did not think she had any right to sit beside him. Time passed without her speaking. She waited until he invited her to speak; then she would. Her husband slumped back against the sofa cushion. After a long evening of partying he looked tired. His eyelids, which were red at the edges from his drinking, drooped. He was breathing heavily as if inebriated. Although he was in the habit of drinking to the point of intoxication every night, he postponed his return home until the effects of the wine had worn off and he had regained control of himself. He wished to protect his dignity and image at home. His wife was the only member of his family allowed to see him after he had been out carousing. The only effect of the drinking she could remark was the smell.

She had never encountered any alarming or perverse conduct from him, except when they were first married, and she had chosen to overlook that. Paradoxically, by keeping him company at this hour, she reaped a chattiness and expansiveness in his conversation she could rarely gain when he was completely sober. She well remembered how distressed she had been when she first noticed he was coming home drunk from his evening escapades. To her mind, wine had always suggested brutality and craziness and, most shocking of all, an offense against religion. She had been disgusted and scared. Whenever he came home, she had

suffered unbearable torments. In time, experience had revealed
that on his return from his partying he was more gentle than on
any other occasion and not so stern. His look was more tender and
he was much more talkative. She grew to enjoy his company and
stopped worrying, although she never forgot to implore God to
pardon his sin and forgive him. She dearly wished he would be
that good-humored when he was sober and in his right mind.
She was thoroughly amazed that this sin made him more amiable.
She was torn for a long time between her hatred for it, based
on her religious training, and the comfort and peace she
gained from it. She buried her thoughts deep inside her, however,
and concealed them as though unable even to admit them to
herself.

Her husband spared no effort to safeguard his dignity and
authority. His moments of tenderness were fleeting and accidental. As he sat there, a broad smile might appear on his lips at a
memory that cropped up from his happy evening. At once he
would get control of himself and press his lips together while
stealing a glance at his wife. He would find her as usual, in front
of him, with her eyes lowered. Reassured, he would return to his
memories and his heart that cherished them as though from an
unquenchable thirst for the pleasures of life. It seemed he could
still see the party, composed of a select group of his favorite friends
and chums. In the midst of them was one of those moonlike
beauties who shone in his life from time to time. He could still
hear the jokes, wisecracks, and witty comments for which he had
such a talent, stringing one after the other, when he was animated
by wine and music. He recalled his clever remarks with a care and
attention accented by wonder and self-satisfaction. He remembered their effect on people and the success and delight they
occasioned, making him everyone's best friend.

It was hardly surprising. He often felt the role he played at these
parties was so significant that it was practically the ultimate anyone
could hope for in life. His career as a whole was a necessary task he
performed in order to gain some hours filled with drink, laughter,
song, and flirtation to be spent in the chummy company of his pals.
Now and then some of the sweet, catchy tunes that were sung at
their happy parties ran through his head. He abandoned himself to
them and sighed, as they drifted away from him, "God is most
great." He loved the singing as much as the drink, laughter,

companions, and pretty girls. He would not tolerate a party without song.

It was nothing for him to journey a long way, to the outskirts of Cairo, in order to hear a renowned male vocalist like al-Hamuli, Muhammad Uthman, or al-Manilawi, wherever he resided. Thus their tunes found shelter in his hospitable soul, like nightingales in a leafy tree. He became a music expert and an acknowledged authority on lyrics, tunes, and music appreciation. He loved song with both his soul and his body. Spiritually he was transported and overwhelmed. Physically his senses were strongly aroused, setting him dancing, particularly his head and hands. For this reason, he had unforgettable spiritual and physical associations with lines from songs like: "So why do you torment me and shun me?" or "What will we know tomorrow? . . . What will we see the following day?" and "Listen, then, and pay attention to what I'm telling you." Any one of these tunes with its associated family of memories would suffice to bring his intoxication to a boil.

Transported by the music, he would nod his head, smile lasciviously, snap his fingers, and sing along when alone. Singing, however, was not an isolated pleasure attracting him for itself. It was a flower in a bouquet, gaining beauty from the setting and contributing to it. How welcome it was in the company of a close friend and loyal comrade when combined with vintage wine and pleasant conversation. To devote himself to it alone, to listen to it at home played on a phonograph, however fine and agreeable that might be, lacked the appropriate atmosphere, ambiance, and environment. How preposterous to think his heart should be satisfied with that! What he liked was to interpose a witty remark between one tune and the next to set everyone laughing, to take a sip from a full glass before starting the music again, and to observe its effect in the face of a friend or the eye of a chum. Then they would all join in expressing their admiration by saying, "Praise the Lord."

The creation of memories was not the only result of his partying. Another of its other virtues was the tendency it produced in him to be kind to his obedient, submissive wife. It was what she longed for when she was with him. He was companionable and talkative. He would tell her his innermost thoughts, thus making her feel, if only for the moment, that she was not just his servant but also a partner in his life. He proceeded to discuss household matters with her. He told her he had directed a merchant he knew to buy up a reserve of clarified butter, wheat, and cheese for the house. He attacked the rise in prices and the scarcity of necessary commodities caused by this war, which had been giving the world a pounding for the past three years. As always when he mentioned the war, he began cursing the Australian troops who had spread through the city like locusts, destroying the land.

The truth was that he had a special reason for resenting the Australians. Their tyranny separated him from the Ezbekiya Garden entertainment district, which he had abandoned in defeat, except for the few rare opportunities he could snatch. He could not stand to expose himself to soldiers who openly plundered people of their possessions and took pleasure in abusing and insulting them without restraint.

He began to ask after the "children," as he called them, making no distinction between the eldest of them, a clerk in al-Nahhasin School, and the youngest, who was a pupil in Khalil Agha Elementary School. Then he inquired suspiciously, "And Kamal? You better not be covering up his mischief."

The woman thought of her young son, whose innocent pranks she did in fact conceal. Her husband did not recognize that there could be innocent games or amusements. She replied meekly, "He respects his father's commands."

Her husband was silent for a moment. His thoughts seemed to be wandering. Once more he was harvesting memories from his happy evening. Then his memory slipped back to the events of the day before the party. He remembered all at once that it had been a momentous day. In his condition, he did not feel like keeping from her anything that floated to consciousness. He said as though addressing himself, "What a fine man Prince Kamal al-Din Husayn is! Do you know what he did? He refused to ascend the throne of his late father so long as the British are in charge."

The woman had heard the day before of the death of Sultan Husayn Kamal, but this was the first time she heard the name of his son. She could not find anything to say, but moved by her feelings of veneration for the speaker and afraid not to comment on something he said, she responded, "May God have mercy on the Sultan and bless his son."

Her husband continued his remarks: "Prince Ahmad Fuad, or Sultan Fuad as he will be known from now on, accepted the throne. The celebration came to a climax today with his investiture. Then he went in a procession from Bustan Castle to Abdin Palace. Praise to God, the Everlasting."

Amina listened to him with interest and delight. She was interested in any news of the outside world, about which she knew almost nothing. Her delight was inspired by the affectionate attention she could boast of because her husband had spoken to her of such weighty matters. Moreover, the knowledge represented by the conversation gave her pleasure, because she could repeat it to her children, especially her two daughters, who were as totally ignorant of the outside world as she. She could think of nothing better to repay him for his generous sentiments than to repeat in his hearing the prayer she knew he heartily endorsed. She was also expressing her own sincere emotions when she said, "Our Lord can return our sovereign Abbas to us."

The man shook his head and murmured, "When? . . . When? Only the Lord knows. All we read about in the papers are British victories. Will they really win or will the Germans and Turks be victorious in the end? Answer our prayer, O God."

The man closed his eyes from fatigue and yawned. He stretched out, saying, "Take the lamp back to the sitting room."

The woman got to her feet and took the lamp from the table. Before she left the room, she heard her husband belch. She stammered, "Health and strength."

3

THROUGH THE stillness of the early morning, when the dark dawn sky was transfixed by arrows of light, there rose from the courtyard oven room the sound of dough being kneaded rhythmically, like the beating of a drum. Amina had been up for about half an hour. She had finished her ablutions and prayed before going down to the oven room to rouse Umm Hanafi, the servant, who was in her forties and had been a maid in the house when she was a girl. She had left the house to marry and had returned after her divorce. While Umm Hanafi worked the dough, Amina busied herself preparing breakfast.

The house had a wide courtyard with a well at the far right. The well's opening had been fitted with a wooden cover once children's feet began pattering across the ground. That was followed by the installation of water pipes. On the far left, by the entrance to the women's quarters, were two large chambers. The oven occupied one, devoted to baking, and the other served as a storeroom.

The oven room, although isolated, had a special claim on Amina's affections. If the hours she had passed inside it were added up, they would be a lifetime. Moreover, the room came alive with the delights of each holiday in its season, when hearts, merry with the joys of life, kept an anxious watch. Appetites were whetted by all the delicious foods prepared there for each holiday in turn, like the sweet fruit compotes and doughnuts for Ramadan or the cake and pastries for Id al-Fitr marking the end of Ramadan. For Id al-Adha, the Feast of the Sacrifice, there was the lamb that was fattened up and pampered only to be slaughtered while the children watched. Thus the universal rejoicing was not without a mournful tear. The blaze of the fire gleamed from the depths of the oven through the arched opening, like a flaming firebrand of joy in the secret recesses of the heart. It seemed both one of the ornaments of each festival and its harbinger.

If Amina, in the upper stories, felt she was a deputy or representative of the ruler, lacking any authority of her own, here she was the queen, with no rival to her sovereignty. The oven lived and died at her command. The fate of the coal and wood, piled in the right-hand corner, rested on a word from her. The stove that occupied the opposite corner, beneath shelves with pots, plates, and the copper serving tray, slept or hissed with flame at a gesture from her. Here she was the mother, wife, teacher, and artist everyone respected. They had full confidence in everything she produced. The only praise she ever succeeded in eliciting from her husband, if he did favor her with praise, was for a type of food she prepared and cooked to perfection.

Umm Hanafi was the right arm of this small empire, whether Amina directed the work herself or allowed one of her daughters to practice this craft under her supervision. Umm Hanafi was a stout woman who was shapeless and formless. The single goal governing her ample increase in flesh had been corpulence. Considerations of beauty had been ignored. She was totally satisfied, for she reckoned corpulence to be beauty of the finest sort. No wonder, then, that all her household chores seemed almost secondary to her in comparison with her primary duty, which was to fatten up the family, or more specifically the females, with miraculous remedies that were not only charms to produce beauty but its secret essence. Although these potions did not always do the trick, they had proved their value more than once and deserved the hopes and dreams invested in them. It was not surprising that Umm Hanafi should grow plump in these circumstances. But her weight in no way diminished her vigor. The moment her mistress woke her, she rose, ready to get to work. She hastened to the bread basin, and soon there rang out the sound of the kneading, which served as an alarm clock in this house. It reached the children on the first floor and the father on the top floor, notifying everyone that it was time to rise.

Mr. Ahmad Abd al-Jawad rolled over on his side and opened his eyes. He scowled at once, furious at the sound that had disturbed his sleep. He suppressed his anger, however, since he knew he had to wake up. Normally his first sensation after regaining consciousness was of his hangover. He struggled against it forcefully and sat up in bed, although still dominated by a desire to go back to sleep. His boisterous nights were not able to make him forget his daytime duties.

He would awake at this early hour, no matter how late he had been in getting to bed, in order to leave for his shop a little before eight. During his siesta he would have ample time to make up for his lost sleep and to restore his energy for another night on the town. Thus the moment he awoke was the worst of his whole day. He would leave his bed, swaying from exhaustion and dizziness. He encountered a life devoid of any sweet memories or warm feelings. They seemed to have changed into a pounding in his brain and eyelids.

The blows of the dough went on relentlessly. Fahmy was one of the earliest of those awakened on the first floor. He was easy to rouse, even though he stayed up late concentrating on his law books. The first image that came to him on waking was of a round face with black eyes at the center of its ivory surface. He whispered to himself, "Maryam." Had he yielded to the temptation, he would have remained under the covers for a long time to be alone with the phantom visitor who came to keep him company with the tenderest affection. He would gaze at her to his heart's content, converse with her, and reveal one secret after another to her while drawing close to her with a daring not imaginable except in this warm repose early in the morning. As usual, however, he postponed this reverie until Friday morning and sat up in bed. He turned to look at his brother sleeping in the adjoining bed and shouted, "Yasin, Yasin! Wake up."

The youth's snoring was cut short. He snorted in annoyance and muttered rather nasally, "I'm awake. I woke up before you."

Fahmy waited, smiling, till the other began snoring again. Then he yelled at him, "Wake up!"

Grumbling, Yasin rolled over in bed. The covers slipped off one side of his body, which resembled his father's in size and bulk. He opened his bloodshot eyes, which gazed vacantly beneath a brow contracted in a disgruntled frown. "Phooey . . . how did it get to be morning so fast? Why can't we sleep till we've had enough? Discipline, always discipline. We might as well be in the army." He reared up, supporting himself on his hands and knees. He shook his head to expel its drowsiness. He happened to look over at the third bed, where Kamal lay sleeping. No one would wrench him out of his sleep for half an hour. Yasin said enviously, "The lucky kid!" As his head cleared a little, he sat up with his legs crossed under him on the bed. He rested his head in his hands. He wished it was filled with the sweet thoughts that brighten day-dreams, but he, like his father, awoke with enough of a hangover to keep dreams at bay. He saw the musician Zanuba in his imagination, though not with his normal delight. All the same, his lips parted in a smile.

In the adjoining room, Khadija had gotten out of bed without having to use the dough alarm. She, of all the family, most resembled her mother in her energy and early rising. Aisha generally was awakened by the movement of the bed when her sister sat up and jumped to the floor. Khadija intentionally rocked the bed and thus started a quarrel and exchange of insults, which through repetition had become a coarse kind of joke. Although Aisha remained awake, she did not rise after she had stopped bickering but surrendered to one of her long happy daydreams.

Life stirred and activity spread throughout the first floor. Windows were opened and light poured in. Close behind came a draft of air, bringing with it the grinding of the wheels of the mule-drawn Suarès omnibus, the voices of workmen, and the cry of the hot-cereal vendor. Movement continued between the two bedrooms and the bath. Yasin appeared, his stocky body in a loose-fitting house shirt, along with Fahmy, who was tall and slim, resembling, except for this slenderness, his father. The two girls went down to the courtyard to join their mother in the oven room. Rarely will two such dissimilar people belong to one family. That Khadija was a brunette was not a flaw, but the features of her face were noticeably out of proportion with each other. Aisha, on the other hand, was a blonde who radiated a halo of beauty and good looks.

Although their father was alone on the top floor, Amina had arranged everything so he would need no assistance. On the table he found a cup filled with fenugreek tea, which he used to freshen his mouth. When he went to the bath he inhaled the fragrance of sweet incense and found clean clothes carefully arranged on the chair. He washed in cold water, as he did every morning, summer or winter. Then he returned to his room with renewed vitality and energy. He took the prayer rug, which had been folded and placed on the back of the sofa, and spread it out to perform the morning prayer. When he prayed, his face was humble, not the smiling, merry face his friends encountered or the stern, resolute one his family knew. This was a responsive face. Piety, love, and hope shone from its relaxed features, which were molded by a wish to ingratiate, cajole, and seek forgiveness. He did not pray in a mechanical way limited to recitation, standing, and prostration. His prayer was based on affection, emotion, and feelings. He performed it with the same enthusiasm he invested in every aspect of life, pouring himself into each. When he worked, he put his whole heart into it. If he befriended someone, he was exception-ally affectionate. When he fell in love, he was swept off his feet. He did not drink without getting drunk. He was earnest and sincere in everything. Thus for him the mandatory prayer became a spiritual pilgrimage in which he traversed the expansive realms of the Master. Even after he had finished praying he would sit cross-legged with palms outstretched and implore God to watch over him carefully, forgive him, and bless his offspring and business.

When the mother had finished preparing the food for breakfast, she allowed the girls to arrange it on the tray. She went to the brothers' room, where she discovered Kamal still sound asleep. Smiling, she approached him and placed the palm of her hand on his forehead to recite the opening prayer of the Qur'an. Then she began calling him, shaking him gently. She did not leave him until he was out of bed. Fahmy came in. Seeing her there, he smiled and wished her good morning. She responded, with a look of love sparkling in her eyes, "Light of my eyes, may your morning be bright."

She greeted her stepson Yasin with the same tenderness. He replied with the affection due a woman who was like a real mother to him.

When Khadija returned from the oven room, Fahmy and Yasin, particularly Yasin, greeted her with some of the taunts they often used against her. Their jests were aimed at her disagreeable appear-ance or her sharp tongue. Nevertheless, she exerted considerable influence over the two brothers, since she looked after their concerns with an outstanding skill seldom volunteered by Aisha, who shone in the family as the beautiful but useless personification of good looks and charm.

Yasin accosted Khadija: "We were talking about you. We were saying that if every woman looked like you, men would be spared all heartaches."

She shot back, "And if all men were like you, they would never get headaches from thinking."

At that their mother called out, "Breakfast is ready, gentlemen."

4

THE DINING room was on the top floor along with the parents' bedroom. On this story were also located a sitting room and a fourth chamber, which was empty except for a few toys Kamal played with when he had time.

The cloth had been spread on the low table and the cushions arranged around it. The head of the household came and sat down cross-legged in the principal place. The three brothers filed in. Yasin sat on his father's right, Fahmy at his left, and Kamal opposite him. The brothers took their places politely and deferentially, with their heads bowed as though at Friday prayers. There was no distinction in this between the secretary from al-Nahhasin School, the law student, and the pupil from Khalil Agha. No one dared look directly at their father's face. When they were in his presence they would not even look at each other, for fear of being overcome by a smile. The guilty party would expose himself to a dreadful scolding.

Breakfast was the only time of day they were together with their father. When they came home in the afternoon, he would already have left for his shop after taking his lunch and a nap. He would not return again until after midnight. Sitting with him, even for such a short period, was extremely taxing for them. They were forced to observe military discipline all the time. Their fear itself made them more nervous and prone to the very errors they were trying so hard to avoid. The meal, moreover, was consumed in an atmosphere that kept them from relishing or enjoying the food. It was common for their father to inspect the boys during the short interval before the mother brought the tray of food. He examined them with a critical eye until he could discover some failing, however trivial, in a son's appearance or a spot on his clothes. Then a torrent of censure and abuse would pour forth.

He might ask Kamal gruffly, "Have you washed your hands?" If Kamal answered in the affirmative, he would order him, "Show me!" Terrified, the boy would spread his palms out. Instead of commending him for cleanliness, the father would threaten him. "If you ever forget to wash them before eating, I'll cut them off to spare you the trouble of looking after them." Sometimes he would ask Fahmy, "Is that son of a bitch studying his lessons or not?" Fahmy knew whom he meant, for "son of a bitch" was the epithet their father reserved for Kamal.

Fahmy's answer was that Kamal memorized his lessons very well. The truth was that the boy had to be clever to escape his father's fury. His quick mind spared him the need to be serious and diligent, although his superior achievement implied he was both. The father demanded blind obedience from his sons, and that was hard to bear for a boy who loved playing more than eating.

Remembering Kamal's playfulness, al-Sayyid Ahmad commented angrily, "Manners are better than learning." Then turning toward Kamal, he continued sharply: "Hear that, you son of a bitch."

The mother carried in the large tray of food and placed it on the cloth. She withdrew to the side of the room near a table on which stood a water jug. She waited there, ready to obey any command. In the center of the gleaming copper tray was a large oval dish filled with fried beans and eggs. On one side hot loaves of flat bread were piled. On the other side were arranged small plates with cheese, pickled lemons and peppers, as well as salt and cayenne and black pepper. The brothers' bellies were aflame with hunger, but they restrained themselves and pretended not to see the delightful array, as though it meant nothing to them, until their father put out his hand to take a piece of bread. He split it open while muttering, "Eat." Their hands reached for the bread in order of seniority: Yasin, Fahmy, and then Kamal. They set about eating without forgetting their manners or reserve.

Their father devoured his food quickly and in great quantities as though his jaws were a mechanical shredding device working non-stop at full speed. He lumped together into one giant mouthful a wide selection of the available dishes – beans, eggs, cheese, pepper and lemon pickles – which he proceeded to pulverize with dispatch while his fingers prepared the next helping. His sons ate with deliberation and care, no matter what it cost them and how incompatible it was with their fiery temperaments. They were painfully aware of the severe remark or harsh look they would receive should one of them be remiss or weak and forget himself and thus neglect the obligatory patience and manners.

Kamal was the most uneasy, because he feared his father the most. The worst punishment either of his two brothers would receive was a rebuke or a scolding. The least he could expect was a kick or a slap. For this reason, he consumed his food cautiously and nervously, stealing a glance from time to time at what was left. The food's quick disappearance added to his anxiety. He waited apprehensively for a sign that his father was finished eating. Then he would have a chance to fill his belly. Kamal knew that although his father devoured his food quickly, taking huge helpings selected from many different dishes, the ultimate threat to the food, and therefore to him, came from his two brothers. His father ate quickly and got full quickly. His two brothers only began the battle in earnest once their father left the table. They did not give up until the plates were empty of anything edible.

Therefore, no sooner had his father risen and departed than Kamal rolled up his sleeves and attacked the food like a madman. He employed both his hands, one for the large dish and the other for the small ones. All the same, his endeavor seemed futile, given his brothers' energetic efforts. So Kamal fell back on a trick he resorted to when his welfare was threatened in circumstances like these. He deliberately sneezed on the food. His two brothers recoiled, looking at him furiously, but left the table, convulsed with laughter. Kamal's dream for the morning was realized. He found himself alone at the table.

The father returned to his room after washing his hands. Amina followed him there, bringing a cup containing three raw eggs mixed with a little milk, which she handed to him. After swallowing the concoction, he sat down to sip his morning coffee. The rich egg drink was the finale of his breakfast. It was one of a number of tonics he used regularly after meals or between them – like cod-liver oil and sugared walnuts, almonds, and hazelnuts – to safeguard the health of his huge body. They helped compensate for the wear and tear occasioned by his passions. He also limited his diet to meat and varieties of foods known for their richness. Indeed, he scorned light and even normal meals as a waste of time not befitting a man of his stature.

Hashish had been prescribed for him to stimulate his appetite, in addition to its other benefits. Although he had tried it, he had never been comfortable with it and had abandoned it without regret. He disliked it because it induced in him a stupor, both somber and still, and a predisposition toward silence as well as a feeling of isolation even when he was with his best friends. He disliked these symptoms that were in rude contrast to his normal disposition aflame with youthful outbursts of mirth, elated excitement, intimate delights, and bouts of jesting and laughter. For fear of losing the qualities required of an exceptionally virile lover, he dosed himself with an expensive narcotic for which Muhammad Ajami, the couscous vendor by the façade of the seminary of al-Salih Ayyub in the vicinity of the Goldsmiths Bazaar, was renowned. The vendor prepared it as a special favor for his most honored clients among the merchants and local notables. Al-Sayyid Ahmad was not addicted to the drug, but he would take some from time to time whenever he encountered a new love, particularly if the object of his passion was a woman experienced with men and their ways.

He finished sipping his coffee. He got up to look in the mirror and began putting on the garments Amina handed to him one at a time. He cast a searching look at his attire. He combed his hair, which hung down on both sides of his head. Then he smoothed and twisted his mustache. He scrutinized the appearance of his face and turned slowly to the right to inspect the left side and then to the left to study the right. When at last he was satisfied with what he saw, he stretched out his hand to his wife for the bottle of cologne Uncle Hasanayn, the barber, prepared for him. He cleansed his hands and face and moistened the chest of his caftan and his handkerchief with it. Then he put on his fez, took his walking stick, and left the room, spreading a pleasant fragrance before and after him. The whole family knew the scent, distilled from assorted flowers. Whenever they inhaled it, the image of the head of the house with his resolute, solemn face would come to mind. It would inspire in the heart, along with love, both awe and fear. At this hour of the morning, however, the fragrance was an announcement of their father's departure. Everyone greeted it with a relief that was innocent rather than reprehensible, like a prisoner's satisfaction on hearing the clatter of chains being unfastened from his hands and feet. Each knew he would shortly regain his liberty to talk, laugh, sing, and do many other things free from danger.

Yasin and Fahmy had finished putting on their clothes. Kamal rushed to the father's room, immediately after he left, to satisfy a desire to imitate his father's gestures that he had stealthily observed from the edge of the door, which was ajar. He stood in front of the mirror looking at himself with care and pleasure. Then he barked in a commanding tone of voice to his mother, "The cologne, Amina." He knew she would not honor this demand but proceeded to wipe his hands on his face, jacket, and short pants, as if moistening them with cologne. Although his mother was struggling not to laugh, he zealously kept up the pretense of being in deadly earnest. He proceeded to review his face in the mirror from the right side to the left. He went on to smooth his imaginary mustache and twist its ends. After that he turned away from the mirror and belched. He looked at his mother and, when he got no response from her except laughter, remonstrated with her: "You're supposed to wish me health and strength."

The woman laughingly mumbled, "Health and strength, sir." Then he left the room mimicking his father's gait and holding his hand as though leaning on a stick.

The mother and her two girls went at once to the balcony. They stood at the window overlooking al-Nahhasin Street to observe through the holes of its wooden grille the men of the family on the street. The father could be seen moving in a slow and dignified fashion. He projected an aura of grandeur and good looks, raising his hands in greeting from time to time. Uncle Hasanayn, the barber, Hajj Darwish, who sold beans, al-Fuli, the milkman, and al-Bayumi, the drinks vendor, all rose to greet him. The women watched him with eyes filled with love and pride. Fahmy followed behind him with hasty steps and then Yasin with the body of a bull and the elegance of a peacock. Finally Kamal made his appearance. He had scarcely taken two steps when he turned around and looked up at the window where he knew his mother and sisters were concealed. He smiled and then went on his way, clutching his book bag under his arm and searching the ground for a pebble to kick.

This moment was one of the happiest of the mother's day. All the same, her anxiety that her men might be harmed by the evil eye knew no limits. She continued reciting the Qur'anic verse "And from the mischief of the envious person in his envy" (113:5) until they were out of sight.

THE MOTHER left the balcony followed by Khadija, but Aisha tarried there till she was alone. Then she went to the side of the balcony overlooking Palace Walk. She peered out through the holes of the grille with interest and longing. The gleam in her eyes and the way she bit her lip showed she was expecting something to happen. She did not have long to wait, for a young police officer appeared from the corner of al-Khurunfush Street. He came closer, slowly making his way toward the Gamaliya police station. At that, the girl quickly left the balcony for the sitting room and headed for the side window. She turned the knob and opened the two panels a crack. She stood there, her heart pounding with a violence provoked by both fear and affection. When the officer neared the house, he raised his eyes cautiously but not his head, for in Egypt in those days it was not considered proper to raise your head in such circumstances. His face shone with the light of a hidden smile that was reflected on the girl's face as a shy radiance.

She sighed and closed the window, fastening it nervously as though hiding evidence of a bloody crime. She retreated, her eyes closed from the intensity of the emotion. She let herself sink into a chair and leaned her head on her hand. She roamed through the space of her infinite sensations, experiencing neither sheer happiness or total fear. Her heart was divided between the two emotions, each mercilessly trying to attract it. If she succumbed to the intoxication and enchantment of happiness, fear's hammer struck her heart, warning and threatening her. She did not know whether it would be better for her to abandon her adventure or to continue obeying her heart. Her love and fear were both intense. She lingered in her drowsy conflict for some time. Then the voices of fear and censure subsided, and during this truce she enjoyed an intoxicating dream.

She recalled with her usual delight how she had been shaking dust from the window curtain one day when she chanced to look at the street through the window, which was halfway open to let the dust fly out. Her glance had fallen on him as he looked up at her face with astonished admiration. She had drawn back in apparent alarm, but before he disappeared from sight he had made an unforgettable impression on her imagination with his gold star and red stripe. A vision to enchant the mind and ravish the imagination, it hovered before her eyes for a long time.

At the same hour the next day and for days after, she had gone to stand by the slit, where he could not see her. She would observe with triumphant happiness how he looked up at the closed window with concern and longing and then how his features were illumined by the light of joy as he began to discern her figure at the crack. Her heart, on fire and reaching out, awake for the first time, looked forward impatiently to this moment, savoring it happily and then dreamily bidding it adieu as it ended.

A month had passed and once more it had been time to dust the curtains. She had set about shaking them, deliberately leaving the window halfway open so she could be seen. In this manner, days and months had passed until her thirst for even more romance conquered her oppressive fear and she had taken an insane step. She had opened the two panels of the window and stood there, her heart beating violently from affection and fear. She might as well have proclaimed her love to him. She seemed to be a person throwing herself down from a vast height to escape a searing fire all around her.

The sentiments of fear and censure having subsided enough for a truce to be proclaimed, she enjoyed the intoxication of her dream. She awoke determined to shut out the fear troubling her serenity. In order to soothe her conscience she started to tell herself, "The earth didn't shake. Everything went off peacefully. No one saw me, and no one will. Moreover, I didn't do anything wrong!" She stood up and, to make herself think she had a clear conscience, sang in a sweet voice, "You there with the red stripe, you who have taken me prisoner, have pity on my humiliation." She sang it repeatedly, until her sister Khadija's voice reached her from the dining room.

Khadija shouted sarcastically, "Diva Munira al-Mahdiya, you renowned prima donna, please do us the favor of eating. Your servant has set the table for you."

This voice brought her back to her senses as though Khadija had shaken her. She fell from the Platonic world of ideal forms to reality, feeling somewhat frightened for no clear reason, since everything had passed peacefully, as she told herself. All the same, her sister's voice, objecting to her singing and to her images in particular, alarmed her, possibly because Khadija was so critical toward her. Nevertheless, she set aside this momentary anxiety and responded with a brief laugh. She ran to the dining room and found that the cloth had indeed been spread and that her mother was bringing in the tray of food.

Khadija said to her sharply the moment she entered, "You loll about, off by yourself, while I prepare everything. We've had enough singing."

Although Aisha usually spoke tenderly to Khadija to protect herself from Khadija's sharp tongue, the latter's insistence on reprimanding her whenever an opportunity arose occasionally made Aisha wish to rile her. Pretending to be in earnest, she said, "Didn't we agree to divide the work in the house between us? So you do the chores and I'll do the singing."

Khadija looked at her mother and said mockingly of her sister, "Perhaps she intends to become a professional."

Aisha did not get angry. To the contrary, she said, again with affected seriousness, "Why not! My voice is like a bird's, like a curlew's."

Although Aisha's previous words had not stirred Khadija's rage, since they were in jest, this last statement did, both because it was obviously true and because Khadija envied her the beauty of her voice along with her other attractions. So she attacked her: "Listen, madam, this is the home of an honorable man. There would be nothing wrong with his daughters having voices like donkeys, but it's a disgrace for them to be nothing but pretty pictures of no use or value."

"If your voice were beautiful like mine you wouldn't say that."

"Of course! We'd sing duets together. You'd say, 'You there with the red stripe, you who' – and I'd continue – 'have taken me prisoner, have pity on my humiliation.' We'll let the lady" – pointing toward her mother – "do the sweeping, scrubbing, and cooking."

The mother, who was accustomed to this bickering, had taken her place and implored them, "Trust in God. Sit down. Let's eat our breakfast in peace."

They came over and sat down. Khadija observed, "Mother, you're not fit to raise anyone."

Her mother muttered calmly, "God forgive you. I'll leave the child rearing to you, so long as you don't forget your own manners." She stretched her hand out to the tray of food, reciting, "In the name of God the Merciful, the Compassionate."

Khadija was twenty and the eldest, except for Yasin, her half brother, who was about twenty-one. She was strong and plump, thanks to Umm Hanafi, although a trifle short. Her face had acquired its features from her parents but in a combination lacking in harmony or charm. She had inherited her mother's small, beautiful eyes and her father's huge nose, or a smaller version of it, although not small enough to be excused. While this nose on her father's face, where it fit, lent his face a noticeable majesty, it added nothing to the girl's looks.

Aisha was in her prime at sixteen. She was the very picture of beauty. She was of slender build and figure, but in her family circle this was considered a defect to be remedied by the ministrations of Umm Hanafi. Her face was as beautiful as the moon. She had a white complexion suffused with rosy highlights and her father's blue eyes, which went well with her mother's small nose. Unlike all the others, she had golden hair, inherited from her paternal grandmother, thanks to the laws of genetics.

It was natural that Khadija should grasp the differences between her and her sister. Neither her extraordinary proficiency in running the house and doing embroidery or her indefatigable vigor, which never dimmed or dulled, gained her anything. On the whole, Khadija felt a jealousy toward Aisha she did not bother to hide, thereby causing the beautiful girl to be upset with her frequently. Fortunately, this natural jealousy did not leave any negative residue deep in her soul. She was content to vent it through the sarcastic sauciness of her tongue. Moreover, she was a girl who, despite the handicaps nature had given her, had a heart full of affection for her family, even though she did not spare them her bitter mockery. Regardless of how long her jealousy lasted, it did not warp her disposition or become hatred or loathing.

Although her sarcasm was humorous when aimed at a member of her family, she was a scold of the first degree with regard to their neighbors and acquaintances. Her eyes, like the needle of a compass always attracted to the magnetic pole, lit first on people's imperfections. If their shortcomings were cloaked, she contrived to uncover and enlarge them. Then she applied epithets to her victims to match their defects. They were usually known by these in the family circle.

She called the widow of the late Mr. Shawkat, the oldest friend of her parents, "the machine gun," because of the way her spittle flew when she talked. Umm Maryam, their next-door neighbor, she named "Could you spare?" because she borrowed household utensils from them now and then. The teacher at the Qur'an school of Palace Walk was the "evilest of creation" because when he taught he frequently recited this verse from the Qur'an (113:2) along with the rest of the sura and because of his ugly face. The cooked-beans vendor was "baldy" because he had no hair, the milkman "one-eye" because his vision was impaired. The nicknames she gave the members of her family were less virulent. Her mother was "the muezzin" because she rose so early, Fahmy "the bedpost" because he was slender, and Aisha "the reed" for the same reason. Yasin she called "Bamba Kashar" after a notorious chanteuse of the day, since he was both plump and fastidious.

Her outspokenness was not merely satirical. There was truly no limit to her harshness if someone got in her family's way. Then her criticism of people was violent and devoid of tolerance and forgiveness. She showed a pronounced lack of interest in the sorrows that trouble people from day to day. This harshness was displayed domestically in her unparalleled treatment of Umm Hanafi and even in her handling of the domestic animals, such as the cats, which were pampered by Aisha in ways beyond description. Her rudeness to Umm Hanafi was a subject of controversy between her and her mother. The mother treated her servants exactly like part of her family. She thought everyone was an angel and did not know how to think ill of anyone. Khadija, on the other hand, was disposed to suspect the woman, since it was her nature to be suspicious of everyone. She did not hide her fear that the servant slept too close to the storeroom. She asked her mother, "How did she get so fat? From the remedies she concocts? We all consume those and we haven't gotten fat like her. It's the butter and honey she skims off without measure when we're asleep."

The mother defended Umm Hanafi as best she could. When her daughter's insistence got on her nerves, she said, "Let her eat what she wants. We have lots, and her belly has limits that cannot be exceeded. We'll not go hungry in any case."

Khadija was not pleased by this remark. She began to examine the tins of butter and jars of honey every morning. Umm Hanafi observed this behavior with a smile. She loved the whole family for the sake of her excellent mistress.

Khadija did not behave like this with members of her family. If one of them was indisposed, she was filled with tenderness and knew no rest. When Kamal came down with measles, she insisted on sharing his bed. She could not stand for even Aisha to be afflicted by the slightest misfortune. Her heart had no equal both in coldness and in compassion.

When she sat down to eat she abandoned her quarrel with Aisha. She attacked the beans and eggs with an appetite that was proverbial in the family. For all of them, food, in addition to its nutritional value, ultimately served an aesthetic goal, because it was the natural foundation for becoming well rounded. They ate deliberately and painstakingly. They did their very best to chew their food thoroughly. They did not even slow down when they were full. They kept on eating until they were stuffed, each according to her capacity. The mother was the first to finish, followed by Aisha. Khadija was left alone with the remaining food. She did not quit until all the dishes were wiped clean.

Aisha's slenderness did not correspond to the diligence with which she ate. The magic of the fattening potions failed on her. Khadija was moved to make fun of her, suggesting that evil machinations had caused her to be soil unfit for the good seed sowed in her. She also liked to ascribe Aisha's slenderness to the weakness of her faith. She would tell her, "We all fast during Ramadan except you. You pretend to fast and then slip into the storeroom like a mouse to fill your tummy with walnuts, almonds, and hazelnuts. Then you break your fast with us so ravenously that those who have been fasting envy your appetite. But God won't bless you."

The breakfast hour was one of the rare times when the three women were alone. Thus it was the most appropriate occasion for them to disclose and air secrets, especially about matters they would be embarrassed to discuss when the men of the family were present. Khadija had something she wanted to say, even though she was busy eating. She remarked in a calm voice, totally different from the yell she had recently employed, "Mother, I had a strange dream."

In deference to her intimidating daughter, the mother replied, even before she swallowed the morsel in her mouth, "A good dream, daughter, God willing."

Khadija said with increased concern, "I seemed to be walking on the wall of a roof terrace. Perhaps it was the roof of our house, or another. Then an unknown person pushed me off and I fell screaming."

Aisha's interest was serious enough to cause her to stop eating, but her sister was silent for a short time to create the greatest possible impression. Their mother murmured, "God grant it's for the best."

Trying not to smile, Aisha asked, "Wasn't I the unknown person who pushed you? Isn't that so?"

Khadija was afraid the mood would be ruined by this joke. She shouted at her, "It's a dream, not a game. Stop your foolishness." Then, addressing her mother, she said, "I fell screaming, but I didn't hit the ground as I expected. Instead I landed on a horse that carried me off and flew away."

Amina sighed with relief as though she had grasped the meaning of the dream and was reassured by it. She smiled and resumed eating. Then she said, "Who knows, Khadija? . . . Perhaps it's your bridegroom!"

Talk about bridegrooms was permitted only on an occasion like this and then only in the form of a terse allusion. The girl's heart throbbed. She was apprehensive about marriage in a way she was about nothing else. She believed in her dream and the interpretation. Therefore she was overjoyed by her mother's words. All the same, she wanted to disguise her embarrassment with irony as usual, even if it was at her own expense, and said, "You think the horse is a bridegroom? My bridegroom will have to be an ass."

Aisha laughed till bits of food flew from her mouth. Fearing Khadija would misinterpret her laughter, she said, "You put yourself down too much, Khadija. You're just fine."

Khadija cast her a glance full of suspicion and doubt. Then their mother started to speak: "You're an extraordinary girl. Who can match your skill or energy? Or your quick wit and pretty face? What more can you ask for?"

The girl touched the tip of her nose with her finger and asked with a laugh, "Doesn't this stand in the way of marriage?"

Smiling, her mother replied, "Nonsense . . . you're still young, daughter."

Khadija was distressed to have youth mentioned, since she did not consider herself young compared with the age most girls were when they married. She said to her mother, "You married, Mother, before you turned fourteen."

The mother, who was actually no less apprehensive than her daughter, replied, "Nothing comes early or late except as God grants."

Aisha sincerely wished: "May our Lord soon allow us to celebrate your wedding."

Khadija looked at her skeptically, remembering how one of the neighbor women had asked to marry Aisha to her son. Their father had refused to let the younger sister marry before the elder. She asked, "Do you really want me to marry, or do you hope it will leave the way clear for you to marry?"

Aisha answered with a laugh, "Both."

6

WHEN THEY had finished breakfast, the mother said, "Aisha, you do the laundry today and Khadija will clean the house. Afterward meet me in the oven room."

Amina divided the work between them right after breakfast. They were content to be ruled by her, and Aisha would not question her assignment. Khadija would take the trouble to make a few comments, either to show her worth or to start a quarrel. Thus she said, "I'll let you clean the house if you think washing the clothes is too much. But if you make a fuss over the washing so you can stay in the bathroom till all the work in the kitchen is finished, that's an excuse that can be rejected in advance."

Aisha ignored her remark and went off to the bath humming. Khadija commented sarcastically, "Lucky for you that sound reverberates in the bathroom like a phonograph speaker. So sing and let the neighbors hear it."

Their mother left the room and went through the hall to the stairs. She climbed to the roof to make her morning rounds there before descending to the oven room. The bickering between her daughters was nothing new to her. Over the course of time it had turned into a customary way of life when the father was not at home and no one could think of anything pleasant to say. She had tried to stop it by using entreaty, humor, and tenderness. That was the only type of discipline she employed with her children. It fit her nature, which could not stand anything stronger. She lacked the firmness that rearing children occasionally requires. Perhaps she would have liked to be firm but was not able to. Perhaps she had attempted to be firm but had been overcome by her emotions and weakness. It seemed she could not bear for the ties between her and her children to be anything but love and affection. She let the father or his shadow, which dominated the children from afar, straighten them out and lay down the law. Thus their silly quarrel did not weaken her admiration for her two girls or her satisfaction with them. Even Aisha, who was insanely fond of singing and standing in front of the mirror, her laziness notwithstanding, was no less skillful and organized than Khadija.

Amina would have been justified in allowing herself long periods of relaxation, but she was prevented by a natural tendency that was almost a disease. She insisted on supervising everything in the house, no matter how small. When the girls finished their work, she would go around energetically inspecting the rooms, living areas, and halls, with a broom in one hand and a feather duster in the other. She searched the corners, walls, curtains, and all the furnishings to eliminate an overlooked speck of dust, finding as much pleasure and satisfaction in that as in removing a speck from her eye. She was by nature such a perfectionist that she examined the clothes about to be laundered. If she discovered a piece of clothing that was unusually dirty, she would not spare the owner a gentle reminder of his duty, whether it was Kamal, who was going on ten, or Yasin, who had two clear and contradictory approaches to caring for himself. He was excessively fastidious about his external appearance – his suit, fez, shirt, necktie, and shoes – but shockingly neglectful of his underwear.

Naturally this comprehensive concern of hers did not exclude the roof and the pigeons and chickens that inhabited it. In fact, the time she spent on the roof was filled with love and delight from the opportunities it presented for work, not to mention the joys of play and merriment she found there. No wonder, for the roof was a new world she had discovered. The big house had known nothing of it until she joined the family. She had created it afresh through the force of her spirit, back when the house retained the appearance it had always had since being built ages before. It was her idea to have these cages with the cooing pigeons put on some of the high walls. She had arranged these wooden chicken coops where the hens clucked as they foraged for food. How much joy she got from scattering grain for them or putting the water container on the ground as the hens raced for it, preceded by their rooster. Their beaks fell on the grain quickly and regularly, like sewing-machine needles, leaving little indentations in the dust like the pockmarks from a drizzle. How good she felt when she saw them gazing at her with clear little eyes, inquisitive and questioning, while they cackled and clucked with a shared affection that filled her heart with tenderness.

She loved the chickens and pigeons as she loved all of God's creatures. She made little noises to them, thinking they understood and responded. Her imagination had bestowed conscious, intelligent life on all animals and occasionally even on inanimate objects. She was quite certain that these beings praised her Lord and were in contact, by various means, with the spirit world. Her world with its earth and sky, animals and plants, was a living, intelligent one. Its merits were not confined to the blessing of life. It found its completion in worship. It was not strange, then, that, relying on one excuse or another, she prolonged the lives of the roosters and hens. One hen was full of life, another a good layer. This rooster woke her in the morning with his crowing. Perhaps if it had been left entirely to her, she would never have consented to put her knife to their throats. If circumstances did force her to slaughter one, she selected a chicken or pigeon with a feeling close to anguish. She would give it a drink, seek God's mercy for it, invoke God's name, ask forgiveness, and then slaughter it. Her consolation was that she was exercising a right that God the Benefactor had granted to all those who serve Him.

The most amazing aspect of the roof was the southern half overlooking al-Nahhasin Street. There in years past she had planted a special garden. There was not another one like it in the whole neighborhood on any of the other roofs, which were usually covered with chicken droppings. She had first begun with a small number of pots of carnations and roses. They had increased year by year and were arranged in rows parallel to the sides of the walls. They grew splendidly, and she had the idea of putting a trellis over the top. She got a carpenter to install it. Then she planted both jasmine and hyacinth bean vines. She attached them to the trellis and around the posts. They grew tall and spread out until the area was transformed into an arbor garden with a green sky from which jasmine flowed down. An enchanting, sweet fragrance was diffused throughout.

This roof, with its inhabitants of chickens and pigeons and its arbor garden, was her beautiful, beloved world and her favorite place for relaxation out of the whole universe, about which she knew nothing. As usual at this hour, she set about caring for it. She swept it, watered the plants, fed the chickens and pigeons. Then for a long time, with smiling lips and dreamy eyes, she enjoyed the scene surrounding her. She went to the end of the garden and

stood behind the interwoven, coiling vines, to gaze out through
the openings at the limitless space around her.

She was awed by the minarets which shot up, making a profound impression on her. Some were near enough for her to see
their lamps and crescent distinctly, like those of Qala'un and
Barquq. Others appeared to her as complete wholes, lacking
details, like the minarets of the mosques of al-Husayn, al-Ghuri,
and al-Azhar. Still other minarets were at the far horizon and
seemed phantoms, like those of the Citadel and Rifa'i mosques.
She turned her face toward them with devotion, fascination,
thanksgiving, and hope. Her spirit soared over their tops, as
close as possible to the heavens. Then her eyes would fix on the
minaret of the mosque of al-Husayn, the dearest one to her
because of her love for its namesake. She looked at it affectionately, and her yearnings mingled with the sorrow that pervaded
her every time she remembered she was not allowed to visit the
son of the Prophet of God's daughter, even though she lived only
minutes away from his shrine.

She sighed audibly and that broke the spell. She began to amuse
herself by looking at the roofs and streets. The yearnings would
not leave her. She turned her back on the wall. Looking at the
unknown had overwhelmed her: both what is unknown to most
people, the invisible spirit world, and the unknown with respect
to her in particular, Cairo, even the adjacent neighborhood, from
which voices reached her. What could this world of which she saw
nothing but the minarets and roofs be like? A quarter of a century
had passed while she was confined to this house, leaving it only on
infrequent occasions to visit her mother in al-Khurunfush. Her
husband escorted her on each visit in a carriage, because he could
not bear for anyone to see his wife, either alone or accompanied
by him.

She was neither resentful nor discontented, quite the opposite.
All the same, when she peeked through the openings between the
jasmine and the hyacinth bean vines, off into space, at the minarets
and rooftops, her delicate lips would rise in a tender, dreamy smile.
Where might the law school be where Fahmy was sitting at this
moment? Where was the Khalil Agha School, which Kamal
assured her was only a minute's trip from the mosque of al-
Husayn? Before leaving the roof, she spread her hands out in
prayer and called on her Lord: "God, I ask you to watch over

my husband and children, my mother and Yasin, and all the people: Muslims and Christians, even the English, my Lord, but drive them from our land as a favor to Fahmy, who does not like them."

7

WHEN AL-SAYYID Ahmad Abd al-Jawad reached his store, situated in front of the mosque of Barquq on al-Nahhasin Street, his assistant, Jamil al-Hamzawi, had already opened and readied it for their customers. The proprietor greeted him courteously and, smiling sweetly, headed for his desk. Al-Hamzawi was fifty. He had spent thirty of these years in this shop as an assistant to the founder, al-Hajj Abd al-Jawad, and then to al-Sayyid Ahmad after the father's death. He remained loyal to his master both for the sake of his job and out of devotion. He revered and loved him the way everyone did who had any dealings with him, whether of business or friendship.

The truth was that he was dreaded and feared only in his own family. With everyone else – friends, acquaintances, and customers – he was a different person. He received his share of respect and esteem but above all else was loved. He was loved for the charm of his personality more than for any of his many other fine characteristics. His acquaintances did not know what he was like at home. The members of his family did not know him as others did.

His store was of medium size. Containers of coffee beans, rice, nuts, dried fruit, and soap were crammed on the shelves and piled by the walls. The owner's desk with its ledgers, papers, and telephone stood on the left opposite the entrance. To the right of where he sat there was a green safe mounted in the wall. It looked reassuringly solid, and its color was reminiscent of bank notes. In the center of the wall over the desk hung an ebony frame containing an Arabic inscription illuminated in gold that read: "In the name of God."

Business was light early in the morning. The proprietor began to review the accounts of the previous day with a zeal inherited from his father but preserved with his own abundant vitality. Meanwhile al-Hamzawi stood by the entrance, his arms folded against his chest. He was reciting to himself the Qur'an verses he knew best. His voice could not be heard, but the continual motion of his lips gave him away. From time to time a faint whisper slipped out from a sibilant *s* sound. He continued his recitation until the arrival of the blind shaykh who had been retained to recite the Qur'an every morning.

Al-Sayyid Ahmad would raise his head from his ledger every so often to listen to the recitation or look out at the street and the endless flow of passersby, hand and horse carts, and the Suarès omnibus, which was so big and heavy it could scarcely wobble along. There were singing vendors who chanted jingles about their tomatoes, mallow greens, and okra, each in his own style. The commotion did not interfere with the proprietor's concentration. He had grown accustomed to it over a period of more than thirty years. He was so lulled by the noise that he was disturbed if it ceased.

A customer came in and al-Hamzawi waited on him. Some friends and neighbors who were merchants stopped by. They liked to visit with al-Sayyid Ahmad, even if only for a short time. They would exchange greetings and enjoy one of his pleasantries or witty sayings. They made him feel proud of his skill as a gifted storyteller. His conversation had brilliant touches relating to the popular culture that he had absorbed not from schooling, since he had never finished primary school, but from reading newspapers and befriending an elite group of gentry, government officials, and attorneys. His native wit, graciousness, charm, and status as a prosperous merchant qualified him to associate with them on an equal footing. He had molded a mentality for himself different from the limited mercantile one. The love, respect, and honor these fine people bestowed on him doubled his pride. When one of them sincerely and truthfully told him, "If you had had the opportunity to study law, you would have been an exceptionally eloquent attorney," this statement inflated his ego. All the same, he was good at hiding his pride with his charm, modesty, and affability. None of these visitors stayed long. They went off one after the other, and the pace of work increased in the shop.

All at once a man rushed in as though propelled by a powerful hand. He stood in the middle of the store, squinting his narrow eyes to see better. He aimed them at the owner's desk. Although he was no more than three meters away, his efforts to make him out were to no avail. So he called out, "Is al-Sayyid Ahmad Abd al-Jawad here?"

The proprietor replied with a smile, "Welcome, Shaykh Mutawalli Abd al-Samad. Have a seat. You bless us with your presence."

The man bent his head. It so happened that as al-Hamzawi approached to greet him, the visitor, who did not notice his outstretched hand, sneezed unexpectedly. Al-Hamzawi drew back and took out his handkerchief. A smile and a frown collided on his face. The shaykh plunged toward the desk, muttering, "Praise God, Lord of the universe." He raised the edge of his cloak and wiped his face with it. He sat down on the chair his host offered him.

The shaykh appeared to be in enviable health for his age, which was over seventy-five. If it had not been for his weak eyes, his eyelids that were inflamed at the edges, and his sunken mouth, he would have had nothing to complain of. He was wrapped in a faded, threadbare cloak. Although he could have exchanged it for a better one through the donations of benefactors, he clung to it. He said that al-Husayn had blessed him in a dream and thus had given the cloak he wore an excellence that would not fade away. The shaykh had performed miracles by penetrating the barriers of normal human knowledge to the invisible realm. He was known equally for his healing prayers, amulets, candor, and wit. He was at home with humor and mirth and that especially endeared him to al-Sayyid Ahmad. Although a resident of the quarter, he did not burden any of his disciples with his visits. Months might pass without anyone knowing where he was. When he dropped by after an absence, he received a warm welcome and presents.

The owner gestured to his assistant to prepare the usual present of rice, coffee, and soap for the shaykh. Then he said to welcome him, "We've missed you, Shaykh Mutawalli. We haven't had the pleasure of seeing you since the holiday of Ashura."

The man replied bluntly, "I'm absent when I think fit and present when I choose. You should not ask why."

The proprietor, who was used to his style, stammered, "Even when you are absent, your blessing is present."

The shaykh did not seem touched by this praise. On the contrary, he shook his head in a way that showed his patience was exhausted. He said gruffly, "Haven't I warned you more than once not to speak to me until I address you? You should be silent."

Feeling an urge to vex him, the proprietor said, "Sorry, Shaykh Abd al-Samad. I forgot your warning. My excuse is that I forgot it because you have been absent so long."

The shaykh struck his hands together and shouted, "An excuse is worse than a sin." Pointing his index finger in a threatening way, he continued: "If you persist in disobeying me, I'll be unable to accept your gift."

The proprietor sealed his lips and spread out his hands in submission, constraining himself to be quiet this time. Shaykh Mutawalli waited to be sure of his obedience. After clearing his throat he said, "I commence with a prayer in honor of Muham-mad, the beloved master of creation."

The proprietor responded from his depths, "God's blessing and peace on him."

"I praise your father as he deserves; may God have plentiful compassion for him and grant him a spacious abode in His paradise. I can almost see him sitting where you are. The difference between the two of you being that your late father retained the turban and you have traded it in for this fez."

The proprietor murmured with a smile, "May God forgive us."

The shaykh yawned till tears came to his eyes. Then he spoke again: "I pray to God that He may grant your children prosperity and piety: Yasin, Khadija, Fahmy, Aisha, and Kamal and their mother. Amen."

Hearing the shaykh pronounce the names Khadija and Aisha sounded odd to al-Sayyid Ahmad, even though he was the one who had told him their names a long time ago, so he could write amulet inscriptions for them. It was not the first time the shaykh had pronounced their names, nor would it be the last, but never would the name of any of his women be mentioned outside their chambers, even on the tongue of Shaykh Mutawalli, without its having a strange and unpleasant impact on him, even if only for a short time. All the same, he muttered, "Amen, O Lord of the universe."

The shaykh said with a sigh, "Then I ask God the Benefactor to return to us our leader Abbas, backed by one of the caliph's armies, which are without beginning or end."

"We so ask Him and it would not be difficult for Him."

The shaykh's voice rose as he said angrily, "And that He afflict

the English and their allies with a shocking defeat, leaving them
without a leg to stand on."

"May our Lord carry them all off."

The shaykh shook his head sorrowfully. He said with anguish,
"Yesterday I was walking in the Muski when two Australian
soldiers blocked my way. They told me to hand over everything
I had. So I emptied my pockets for them and brought out the one
thing I had, an ear of corn. One of them took it and kicked it like a
ball. The other snatched my turban. He unwound the cloth from
it, ripped it, and flung it in my face."

The proprietor listened closely, fighting off the temptation to
smile. He quickly disguised it by an exaggerated display of disapproval. He shouted in condemnation, "May God destroy and
annihilate them."

The other man concluded his account: "I raised my hand to the
sky and called out, 'Almighty God, rip their nation to shreds the
way they ripped my turban cloth.'"

"Your prayer will be answered, God willing."

The shaykh leaned back and closed his eyes to rest a little.
Meanwhile the proprietor scrutinized his face and smiled. Then
the religious guide opened his eyes and addressed him in a calm
voice and a new tone, giving warning of a new subject. He said,
"What an astute and gallant man you are, Ahmad, you son of Abd
al-Jawad."

The proprietor smiled with pleasure. He responded in a low
voice, "I ask God's forgiveness, Shaykh Abd al-Samad . . ."

The shaykh interrupted him, saying, "Not so fast. I'm the sort of
person who praises only to clear the way to speak the truth, for the
sake of encouragement, son of Abd al-Jawad."

A wary circumspection was evident in the eyes of the proprietor. He muttered, "May our Lord be gracious to us."

The shaykh gestured at him with his gnarled forefinger and
asked him threateningly, "What do you have to say as a devout
Muslim concerning your lust for women?"

The proprietor was accustomed to his candor. Thus he was not
troubled by his assault. After a brief laugh he replied, "How can
you fault me for that? Didn't the Messenger of God (the blessing
and peace of God upon him) speak of his love for perfume and
women?"

The shaykh frowned and looked even grimmer in protest

against the proprietor's logic, which he did not like. He countered, "Licit acts are not the same as forbidden ones, you son of Abd al-Jawad. Marriage is not the same as chasing after hussies."

The proprietor stared at nothing in particular and said in a serious tone, "I have never allowed myself to offend against honor or dignity at all. Praise God for that."

The shaykh struck his hands on his knees and exclaimed with astonishment and disgust, "A weak excuse fit only for a weak person. Immorality is damnable even if it is with a debauched woman. Your father, may God have mercy on him, was crazy about women. He married twenty times. Why don't you follow his path and shun the sinner's?"

The proprietor laughed out loud. He asked, "Are you one of God's saints or a nuptial official? My father was almost sterile; so he married many times. Even though I was his only child, his property was split up between me and his last four wives, not to mention what he lost during his lifetime in divorce settlements. Now I'm the father of three males and two females. It wouldn't be proper for me to slip into more marriages and have to divide the wealth that God has bestowed on us. Don't forget, Shaykh Mutawalli, that the professional women entertainers of today are the slave girls of yesterday, whose purchase and sale God made legal. More than anything else, God is forgiving and merciful."

The shaykh moaned. Shaking his torso right and left, he said, "How adept you are, you sons of Adam, in embellishing evil. By God, you son of Abd al-Jawad, were it not for my love of you, I would not suffer you to speak to me, you fornicator."

The proprietor spread out his hands and said with a smile, "God grant . . ."

The shaykh snorted in annoyance and yelled, "If it weren't for your jokes, you'd be the most perfect of men."

"Perfection is God's alone."

The shaykh turned toward him and motioned with his hand as if to say, "Let's put this aside." Then he asked in the tone of an interrogator tightening his grip around his victim's throat, "And wine? What do you say about that?"

Suddenly the proprietor's spirits flagged. His discomfort was apparent in his eyes. He remained silent for some time. The shaykh sensed submission in his silence. He shouted in triumph,

"Isn't it forbidden? No one would succumb to it who strives to obey and love God."

The proprietor interrupted with the zeal of a man fending off a veritable disaster: "I certainly strive to obey and love Him."

"By word or deed?"

Although he had an answer ready, he took some time to think about it before replying. He was not accustomed to busying himself with introspection or self-analysis. In this way he was like most people who are rarely alone. His mind did not swing into action until some external force required it: a man or woman or some element of his material life. He had surrendered himself to the busy current of his life, submerging himself totally in it. All he saw of himself was his reflection on the surface of the stream. Moreover, his zest for life had not diminished as he grew older. He was forty-five and still enjoyed an ardent and exuberant vigor like that of an adolescent youth. His life was composed of a diversity of mutually contradictory elements, wavering between piety and depravity. Contradictory though they were, they all met with his satisfaction, without needing to be propped up by any pillar of personal philosophy or hypocritical rationalization. His conduct issued directly from his special nature. Having a clear conscience, he was good-hearted and sincere in everything he did. His breast was not shaken by storms of doubt, and he passed his nights peacefully. His faith was deep. It was true that he had inherited it and that there was no room for innovation in it. All the same, his sensitivity, discernment, and sincerity had added an elevated, refined feeling to it, which prevented it from being a blind traditionalism or a ritualism inspired by nothing but desire or fear. The most striking characteristic of his faith as a whole was its pure, fertile love. Using it, he set about performing all his duties to God, like prayer, fasting, or almsgiving, with love, ease, and happiness; not to mention a clear conscience, a heart abounding in love for people, and a soul that was generous in its gallantry and help for others. These qualities made him a dear friend. People vied to enjoy the pleasures of his friendship.

With the same ardent, overflowing vitality, he opened his breast to the joys and pleasures of life. He delighted in fancy food. He was enchanted by vintage wine. He was crazy about a pretty face. He pursued each of these pleasures with gaiety, joy, and passion. His conscience was not weighed down by guilty feelings or anxious scruples. He was exercising a right granted him by life, as though there was no conflict between the duty life gave his heart and the duty God entrusted to his conscience. At no time in his life had he felt estranged from God or a target for His vengeance. He communed peacefully with Him. Was he two separate people combined into one personality? Was his faith in the divine magnanimity so strong that he could not believe these pleasures really had been forbidden? Even if they were forbidden, should they not be excused so long as no one was harmed? Most probably what happened was that he embraced life with his heart and emotions without resorting to thought or reflection. He found within himself strong instincts, some directed toward God and tamed through worship and others set for pleasure and quenched in play. The integration of all these within him was secure and carefree. His soul was not disturbed by any need to reconcile them. He was not forced to justify them in his thoughts, except under the pressure of criticism like that with which Shaykh Mutawalli Abd al-Samad confronted him. Under such circumstances, he found himself more distressed by thinking than by the accusation itself, not because he shrugged off being accused before God, but because he could not believe that he was actually being accused or that God would truly be angry at him for having a little fun that harmed no one. Thought, however, was a burden and revealed how trivial his knowledge of his religion was. For this reason, he frowned when the other man challengingly asked him whether his obedience was "by word or deed."

He responded in a tone that did not hide his distress, "By word and deed both. By prayer, fasting, and almsgiving. By remembering God whether I am standing or sitting. Why is it wrong for me, after that, to refresh myself with a little fun, harming no one, or for me to overlook one rule? Is nothing forbidden save these two things?"

The shaykh raised his eyebrows and closed his eyes to indicate that he did not agree. Then he muttered, "What a perverse defense!"

The proprietor suddenly went from anxiety to gaiety, as was his wont, and said expansively, "God is clement and merciful, Shaykh Abd al-Samad. I don't picture Him, may He be high and exalted, being in any way spiteful or sullen. Even His vengeance is mercy in disguise. I offer Him love, obedience, reverence, and a good deed is worth ten . . ."

"In the calculus of good deeds, you have the most to gain."

The proprietor motioned to Jamil al-Hamzawi to bring the shaykh's present. He said happily, "God's all we need, along with the favors of His deputy."

The proprietor's assistant brought him the parcel, which he took and presented to the shaykh. "To your health," he said with a laugh.

The shaykh accepted it and said, "May God provide for you generously and forgive you."

The proprietor mumbled, "Amen." Then, smiling, he asked him, "Weren't you well off once, master?"

The shaykh laughed and replied, "May God go easy on you. You're a generous man with a good heart. I take this occasion to caution you against excessive generosity, for it is not compatible with making a living as a merchant."

The proprietor asked in astonishment, "Are you tempting me to withdraw the gift?"

The man rose and replied, "The gift to me is not excessive. Begin somewhere else, you son of Abd al-Jawad. Peace to you and God's mercy."

The shaykh left the store in a hurry and disappeared from sight. The proprietor kept on thinking. He was mulling over the dispute that had flared up between him and the shaykh. Then he spread his hands out in entreaty. He mumbled, "God, forgive me both my bygone and recent sins. God, You are clement and merciful."

8

KAMAL LEFT the Khalil Agha School in the afternoon, bobbing along in the swelling current of pupils who blocked off the road with their flow. They began to scatter, some along al-Darrasa, some on New Street, others on al-Husayn. Meanwhile bands of them encircled the roving vendors stationed to catch them at the ends of the streets that branched out from the school. Their baskets contained melon seeds, peanuts, doum palm fruit, and sweets. At this hour, the street also witnessed fights, which broke out here and there between pupils forced to keep their disagreements quiet during the day to avoid school punishment.

Kamal had only rarely been embroiled in a fight, perhaps not more than twice during the two years he had been at the school. He had avoided fights, not from a lack of disputes, which actually were plentiful, nor because he disliked fighting. Being forced to renounce fighting caused him profound regret, but the over-whelming majority of the other pupils were much older, making him and a few of his companions aliens in the school. They stumbled along in their short pants surrounded by pupils over fifteen, many close to twenty. They plowed through the younger boys pompously and haughtily, sporting their mustaches. One of them would stop him in the school courtyard for no reason and snatch the book from his hand to toss far away like a ball. Another would take a piece of candy from him and pop it in his own mouth, without so much as asking, while carrying on a conversation with someone else.

Kamal's desire to fight did not desert him, but he suppressed it out of fear of the consequences. He responded only when one of his young companions provoked him. He found that attacking them vented his stifled rebellious feelings. It was a way to regain confidence in himself and his strength. Neither fighting nor being forced to refrain was the worst insult the aggressors could inflict. There were the curses and bad language that reached his ears, whether or not intended for him. He understood the meaning of some of the expressions and was cautious with them. Others he did not know and repeated innocently at home, thus stirring up a storm of outrage and indignation. This led to a complaint to the school disciplinarian, who was a friend of his father's.

It was nothing but bad luck which decreed that his adversary in one of his two fights was from a family of known toughs living in al-Darrasa. On the afternoon following the battle, Kamal found waiting for him at the door of the school a gang of youths armed with sticks, forming a ring of terrifying evil. When his adversary gestured to point him out, Kamal grasped the danger lying in wait for him. He fled back to the school and appealed to the disciplinary officer for help. The man tried in vain to dissuade the gang from its objective. They spoke so rudely to him that he was forced to summon a policeman to escort the boy home. The disciplinarian paid a call on Kamal's father at his shop and told him of the danger menacing his son. He advised him to attempt to resolve the matter prudently and diplomatically. The father had recourse to some merchants he knew in al-Darrasa. They went to the home of the toughs to intercede for him. Thus the father made use of his well-known forbearance and sensitivity to soothe their tempers. They not only forgave the boy but swore to protect him like one of their sons. The day was not over before al-Sayyid Ahmad sent someone to them with several presents. Kamal escaped from the sticks of the toughs, but it was like jumping out of the pan into the fire. His father's stick did more to his feet than tens of others would have.

Kamal started home from school. Although the sound of the bell signaling the end of the school day brought a joy to his soul unmatched by any other in those days, still the breeze of freedom he inhaled lightheartedly outside the school gates did not obliterate from his mind the echoes of the last class, which was also his favorite: religion. That day the shaykh had recited to them the Qur'an sura containing: "Say it is revealed unto me that a group of the jinn listened" (72:1). He had explained the passage to them. Kamal had concentrated his attention on it and raised his hand more than once to ask about points he did not understand. Since the teacher was favorably disposed toward him on account of the extraordinary interest he displayed in the lesson as well as his excellent memorization of Qur'an suras, he was much more open to the boy's questions than he usually was with his pupils. The shaykh had undertaken to tell him about the jinn and their different groups, including the Muslim jinn, and in particular the jinn who will gain entry to paradise in the end as an example for their brothers, the human beings. The boy learned by heart every word he said. He kept on turning the lesson around in his mind until he crossed the street to get to the pastry shop.

In addition to his enthusiasm for religious studies, he knew he was not just learning it for himself alone. He would have to repeat what he had grasped to his mother at home, as he had been doing since he was in Qur'anic kindergarten. He would tell her about the lesson and she would review, in the light of this new information, what she had previously learned from her father, a religious scholar trained at al-Azhar mosque university. They would discuss what they knew for a long time. Then he would teach her the new Qur'an suras she had not previously memorized.

He reached the pastry shop and stretched out his hand with the small change he had hung on to since morning. He took a piece of pastry with the total delight he experienced only on such a sweet occasion. It made him frequently dream of owning a candy store one day, not to sell the candy but to eat it. He continued on his way down al-Husayn Street, munching on the pastry with pleasure. He hummed and forgot he had been a prisoner all day long, not allowed to move, not to mention play or have fun. He was a sitting duck to be struck at any moment by the teacher's stick raised threateningly over the pupils' heads. In spite of all this, he did not hate school totally, since his accomplishments within its walls brought him praise and encouragement. His brother Fahmy was impressed because he did so well, but Kamal did not even receive one percent of his brother's appreciation from his father.

On his way, he passed by the tobacco store of Matoussian. He stopped under its sign, as he did every day at this hour, and raised his small eyes to the colored poster of a woman reclining on a divan with a cigarette between her crimson lips, from which rose a curling plume of smoke. She was leaning her arm on the window-sill. The curtain was drawn back to reveal a scene combining a grove of date palms and a branch of the Nile. He privately called the woman Aisha after his sister, since they both had golden hair and blue eyes. Although he was just going on ten, his admiration for the mistress of the poster was limitless. How often he thought of her enjoying life in its most splendid manifestations. How often he imagined himself sharing her carefree days in that luxurious room with its pristine view that offered her, in fact both of them, its earth, palms, water, and sky. He would swim in the green river valley or cross the water in the skiff that appeared ghostlike far off in the picture. He would shake the palm trees till the dates fell around him or sit near the beautiful woman with his eyes gazing at her dreamy ones.

He was not good-looking like his brothers. He was perhaps the one in the family who most resembled his sister Khadija. Like hers, his face combined his mother's small eyes and his father's huge nose, but without the refinements of Khadija's. He had a large head with a forehead that protruded noticeably, making his eyes seem even more sunken than they actually were. Unfortunately, he had first realized how strange he looked when a schoolmate teased him and called him a two-headed boy. Kamal had been enraged, and his anger had gotten him into one of his two fights. Even after he taught the boy a lesson, he was still upset and complained of his unhappiness to his mother. She was upset because he was. She tried to console him, telling him that people with large heads had large brains and that the Prophet (peace upon him) had a large head. To resemble the Prophet was the ultimate that anyone could aspire to.

He tore himself away from the picture of the smoking lady, and gazed this time at the mosque of al-Husayn. He had been taught to revere al-Husayn, and not surprisingly the holy martyr's shrine provided his imagination with countless sensations. Although his high regard for al-Husayn – matching the high status his mother in particular and the family in general accorded him – derived from al-Husayn's relationship to his grandfather, the Prophet, Kamal's knowledge of the Prophet had not provided him with what he knew about al-Husayn and the events of his life, nor did it explain the way his soul always hungered to have the saga of al-Husayn repeated, so he could draw from it the finest stories and the deepest faith. This centuries-old saga had found in Kamal an attentive, passionate, loving, believing, grieving, weeping listener. His suffering response was eased only by the fact that the martyr's head, after being severed from his immaculate body, chose Egypt from all the world for its resting place. Immaculate, it came to Cairo, glorifying God, and settled to the ground where al-Husayn's shrine now stands.

Kamal frequently stood in front of the shrine, dreaming and

thinking. He wished his vision could penetrate it, to see the beautiful face. His mother assured him it had withstood the vicissitudes of time, because of its divine secret being. It had preserved its bloom and beauty, so that it lit up the darkness of its abode. Although unable to fulfill his wish, he stood there for long periods, communing with himself. He expressed his love and told his problems to the Prophet's grandson. These arose from his vivid daydreams about the jinn and his father's threats. He would implore al-Husayn's assistance for his exams, which he had to take every three months. He would usually conclude his private audience with a plea for a visit in his dreams. His custom of passing by the mosque both morning and evening had somewhat lessened its impact on him, but the moment his eyes fell on the shrine he would repeat the opening prayer of the Qur'an, even if he passed by repeatedly in a single day. Indeed, the shrine's familiarity could not rob his breast of his splendid dreams. The sight of the towering walls still evoked a response from his heart and the lofty minaret still called out to his soul, which quickly answered.

Reciting the Qur'anic prayer, he cut across al-Husayn Street and then turned into Khan Ja'far. From there he headed for Bayt al-Quadi Square. Instead of going home by way of al-Nahhasin, he crossed the square to Qirmiz Alley, despite its desolation and the fears it aroused in him, in order to avoid passing by his father's store. His father made him tremble with terror. He could not imagine that a jinni popping out at him would frighten him any more than his father screaming at him in anger. His distress was doubled, because he was never convinced of the appropriateness of the stern commands with which his father pursued him in his attempt to keep the boy from the fun and games he craved. Even if he had seriously wished to yield to his father's wishes and had tried to spend all his free time sitting quietly with his hands folded together, he would not have been able to obey that haughty, tyrannical will. He furtively took his fun behind his father's back whenever he felt like it, at home or in the street. His father knew nothing of this, unless a member of the household, exasperated when Kamal got out of hand and carried things too far, informed on him.

Kamal had gotten a ladder one day and climbed onto the arbor of hyacinth beans and jasmine, high above the roofs. His mother, seeing him there poised between earth and sky, had shrieked in terror until she had forced him to come down. Her concern over the consequences of such dangerous sport had won out over her fear of exposing him to his father's severity. She had told her husband what Kamal had been up to. He had immediately summoned him and ordered him to stretch out his feet. He had beaten them with his stick, paying no attention to Kamal's screams, which filled the house. Then the boy had limped out of the room to join his brothers and sisters in the sitting room. They had been trying not to laugh, except for Khadija. She had taken him in her arms and whispered to him, "You deserved it.... What were you doing, climbing the hyacinth beans and bumping your head against the sky? Did you think you were a zeppelin?" Except for such dangerous games, his mother shielded him and allowed him as much innocent play as he wanted.

He was often amazed to remember that this same father had been sweet and kind to him not so long ago, when he was a small child. Al-Sayyid Ahmad had enjoyed playing with him and from time to time had treated him to various kinds of sweets. He had done his best to lighten Kamal's circumcision day, hideous though it was, by filling his lap with chocolates and candy and smothering him with care and affection. Then how quickly everything had changed. Affection had turned to severity, tender conversation to shouts, and fondling to blows. He had even made circumcision itself a means for terrifying the boy. For a long time Kamal had been confused and had thought it possible they might inflict the same fate on what he had left.

It was not just fear which he felt toward his father. His respect for him was as great as his fear. He admired his strong, imposing appearance, his dignity that swept everyone along with it, the elegance of his clothing, and the ability he believed him to have to do anything. Perhaps it was the way his mother spoke about her husband that put him in such awe of him. He could not imagine that any other man in the world could equal al-Sayyid Ahmad's power, dignity, or wealth. As for love, everyone in the household loved the man to the point of worship. Kamal's small heart absorbed its love for him from this environment, but that love remained a hidden jewel, locked up inside him by fear and terror.

He approached Qirmiz Alley with its vaulted roof, which the jinn used as a theater for their nightly games. Although it frightened him, he preferred going that way to passing by his father's store. When he entered the cavelike space he started reciting, "Say He is the one God" (Qur'an, 112:1), in a loud voice that resounded in the gloom beneath the curves of the roof. His eyes looked eagerly ahead at the distant mouth of the tunnel where light shone from the street. He quickened his steps, still repeating the Qur'an sura to keep from thinking about the jinn, for jinn have no power over anyone who arms himself with God's verses. His father's anger, once it flared up, could not be averted, even if he recited all of God's Book. He left the vaulted section of the alley for the other half. At the end he could see Palace Walk and the entrance of Hammam al-Sultan. Then his eyes fell on his home's dark green wooden grilles and the large door with its bronze knocker. His mouth opened in a happy smile at the wide variety of amusements this place harbored for him. Soon the boys from all the neighboring houses would run to join him in his wide courtyard, with its several chambers, surrounding the oven room. There would be fun and games and sweet potatoes.

At that moment he saw the Suarès omnibus slowly crossing the street heading for Palace Walk. His heart leapt. Pleasure at his own cleverness filled him. At once he tucked his book bag under his left arm and raced to catch it. He jumped on the back steps, but the conductor did not let him enjoy his pleasure for very long. He came and asked the boy for his fare, giving him a suspicious, challenging look. Kamal told him ingratiatingly that he would get off as soon as it stopped but could not while it was moving. The conductor turned from him and yelled to the driver to stop the vehicle. He was angrily scolding Kamal, but when he looked away the boy seized the opportunity to tread on the instep of his foot, take a swing at him, and hop to the ground. He shot off in flight. The conductor's curses that followed him were filthier than balls of mud with stones inside. It had not been a deliberate plan or an original one. He had simply been delighted to see a boy do it that morning. When he got the chance to try it himself, he did.

9

EXCEPT FOR the father, the family gathered shortly before sunset for what they called the coffee hour. The chosen site was the first-floor sitting room surrounded by the children's bedrooms, the parlor, and a fourth small room set aside for studying. Its floor was spread with colored mats. Divans with pillows and cushions stood in the corners. Hanging from the ceiling was a large lantern illuminated by an equally large kerosene lamp. The mother sat on a sofa in the center. In front of her was a large brazier where the coffeepot was half buried in the embers topped by ashes. To her right was a table holding a brass tray with cups lined up on it. The children were seated opposite her, including those permitted to drink coffee with her, like Yasin and Fahmy, and those barred from it by custom and etiquette, like the two sisters and Kamal, who contented themselves with the conversation.

This hour was well loved by them. It was a time to enjoy being together as a family and to have a pleasant chat. They would cluster under their mother's wing with love and all-embracing affection. The very way they sat leaning back with their legs folded under them showed how free and relaxed they felt.

While Khadija and Aisha urged the coffee drinkers to finish so they could read their fortunes in the grounds, Yasin talked for a time and then read a story about two orphan girls from an anthology called *Evening Tales for the People*. He was in the habit of devoting some of his free time to reading stories and poems. It was not because he felt a need for more education, since at that time the primary certificate was no mean achievement. Rather, he loved to be entertained and was infatuated with poetry and good style. He looked, with his massive body in a loose house shirt, like an enormous water skin. Yet, by the standards of the time, his girth did not detract from the good looks of his full brown face with its seductive black eyes, joined eyebrows, and sensuous lips. Despite his youth – he was only twenty-one – his overall appearance revealed a full-fledged manliness.

Kamal clung to Yasin to garner whatever rare stories he would toss him now and again. He kept asking for more, oblivious to the distress his insistence caused his brother. Kamal wanted to satisfy the yearnings that set his imagination on fire at this time every day. How quickly Yasin would be distracted from him by the conversation or get caught up in the reading. From time to time Yasin would favor him, when his urging became intense, with some brief words which, even if they answered one of his questions, were very likely to arouse new questions he could not answer. Kamal kept looking, sadly and jealously, at his brother when he was busy reading. This skill furnished Yasin with the key to a magical world. Kamal's inability to read the story by himself vexed him. How sad it made him to have the book in his hands, to be able to turn the pages to his heart's content, and not be able to decipher the symbols and thus enter the world of visions and dreams. Kamal found in this facet of Yasin a stimulus for his imagination, supplying him with a variety of pleasures but also arousing painful cravings. He would often raise his eyes to his brother and ask him apprehensively, "What happened after that?"

The young man would snort in response: "Don't give me a hard time with your questions. Don't push your luck. If I don't tell you today, then tomorrow." Nothing made Kamal more unhappy than having to wait until the next day. The word "tomorrow" came to be linked in his mind with sadness. It was not unusual for him to turn to his mother after the gathering broke up in hopes that she would tell him what "happened after that," but she did not know the story of the two orphan girls or the others Yasin read. Since it grieved her to turn him away disappointed, she would tell him what stories she remembered about brigands and the jinn. Slowly his imagination would be diverted to these, and he would be partially consoled.

In that coffee hour Kamal frequently felt lost and neglected by his family. Hardly anyone paid attention to him. Their endless conversations made them forget him. He was not above fabricating something to excite their interest, if only briefly. Thus he threw himself into the course of the conversation, daringly interrupting its flow. Like a torpedo going off, he said suddenly in a high-pitched voice, as though he had all at once remembered a momentous event, "What an unforgettable sight I saw on my way home. I saw a boy jump on the steps of the Suarès omnibus. He slapped the conductor and then rushed off at top speed. But the man raced after him till he caught him. He kicked him in the stomach as hard as he could."

Kamal glanced at their faces to judge the impact of his story, but found no interest there. He noticed, rather, a rejection of his news and a determination to continue their conversation. He saw Aisha's hand stretching out to his mother's chin to turn her away from him, after she had begun to listen to him. He even glimpsed a mocking smile spread across Yasin's lips. He had not lifted his head from the book. Obstinately Kamal said in a loud voice, "The boy fell down writhing with pain and people crowded around him. Then what do you know, he had departed from this life."

His mother moved the cup from her lips and asked, "Son, are you saying he died?"

Kamal was gratified by her interest and concentrated his forces on her, like a desperate assailant throwing all his reserves against the weakest section of a forbidding wall. He said, "Yes, he died. With my own eyes I saw his blood pouring out."

Fahmy glanced at him scornfully as if to say, "I know it isn't the first story like this you've told." He asked sarcastically, "Didn't you say the conductor kicked him in the stomach? So where did this blood come from?"

The flame of victory that had been shining in his eyes since he caught his mother's attention went out. Flashes of confusion and exasperation took its place. Then his imagination came to his rescue, and his eyes recovered their lively look. He said, "When the man kicked him in the stomach, he fell on his face and split his head open."

At this, Yasin, without raising his eyes from the two orphan girls, commented, "Or the blood flowed from his mouth. Blood might come from his mouth without any need for an external injury. There is more than one explanation for your fake news, as usual. So have no fear."

Kamal protested against his brother's suggestion that he had made it up. He proceeded to swear the most awesome oaths that it was true, but his protests were lost in the clamorous laughter uniting harmoniously both the deep voices of the men and the high-pitched ones of the women.

Khadija's sarcastic nature was aroused. She remarked, "You certainly have a lot of victims. If the reports you give were true, you'd leave none of the inhabitants of al-Nahhasin alive. What will you tell our Lord if He takes you to account for these reports?"

Kamal found in Khadija a worthy adversary. As usual when he collided with her sarcasm, he began to allude to her nose. He said, "I'll tell Him it's the fault of my sister's snout."

She replied with a laugh, "It's just like yours! Don't we share this affliction?"

At this, Yasin spoke again: "You're telling the truth, sister." She turned toward him, ready to pounce on him, but he forestalled her by saying, "Have I made you angry? Why? All I did was to express openly my agreement with you."

She told him furiously, "Remember your own shortcomings before you allude to the defects of other people."

He raised his eyebrows, pretending to be perplexed. Then he murmured, "By God, the greatest defect is nothing compared to this nose."

Fahmy made a show of being displeased but asked in tones that indicated he was joining the fray, "What are you talking about, brother? A nose or a criminal offense?"

Since Fahmy rarely joined in a quarrel like this, Yasin welcomed his words enthusiastically. He said, "It's both at the same time. Think of the criminal responsibility assumed by the person who presents this bride to her ill-fated bridegroom."

Kamal crowed with laughter like a recurrent whistle. The mother was not happy to have her daughter fall victim to so many assailants. Wanting to bring the conversation back to its original subject, she said quietly, "Your idle chatter has drawn you away from the topic of the conversation, which was whether Mr. Kamal's story was true or not. All the same, I see no reason for doubting him since he has sworn to it. Yes, Kamal would never swear falsely about something."

The boy's pleasure at his revenge faded at once. Although his brothers and sisters continued the joke for a while, he withdrew into a world of his own. He exchanged an earnest glance with his mother and then isolated himself to reflect anxiously and uneasily. He had grasped the seriousness of a lying oath. It could stir the wrath of God and His saints. It distressed him deeply to swear falsely by al-Husayn, in particular, because of his love for him, but he frequently found himself in a serious dilemma, as he had today, from which in his opinion the only escape was a false oath. Drawn unwittingly into making one, he would still be worried and anxious, especially when he remembered his offense. He wished he could pull up his sinful past by the roots or begin with a clean, new page. He thought of al-Husayn and of standing at the base of his minaret that seemed to touch the sky. He entreated the Prophet's grandson to forgive his error. He felt the shame of having committed an unpardonable offense against a loved one. He was plunged in his supplications for some time. Then he began to pay attention to what was going on around him.

He opened his ears to the conversation that was continuing with a combination of old themes and new ones. Little of it interested him. It naturally consisted of a repetition of memories drawn from the family's past, whether recent or distant, of news about what was happening to the neighbors, their joys and sorrows, and of a discussion about the awkward relationship that his two brothers had with their tyrannical father. Khadija would embark on an exposition of this last subject and analyze it in a humorous or malicious fashion. Thus the boy acquired knowledge that developed in his imagination into a strange portrait, deeply indebted to the conflict between the aggressive, mocking spirit of Khadija and the indulgently forgiving spirit of his mother.

Kamal tuned in when Fahmy was telling Yasin, "Hindenburg's last offensive was extremely important. It's quite possible it will be the turning point of the war."

Yasin was sympathetic to his brother's hopes, but in a calm way tinged with indifference. Like his brother, he wished the Germans would win and consequently the Turks too. He wanted the caliphate claimed by the Ottoman sultans to regain its previous might and for Khedive Abbas II and Muhammad Farid to return to Egypt. None of these hopes, however, preoccupied his heart, except when he was talking about them. Shaking his head, he observed, "Four years have passed and we keep saying this same thing. . . ."

Fahmy replied with anxious longing, "Every war has an end. This war has got to end. I don't think the Germans will lose."

"This is what we pray to God will happen, but what will you say if we discover the Germans are just the way the English describe them?"

As the debate caught fire and grew more intense Fahmy raised his voice and said, "The important thing is to rid ourselves of the nightmare of the English and for the caliphate to return to its previous grandeur. Then we will find the way prepared for us."

Khadija interrupted their conversation to ask, "Why do you love the Germans when they're the ones who sent a zeppelin to drop bombs on us?"

Fahmy proceeded to affirm, as he always did, that the Germans had intended their bombs for the English, not the Egyptians. Then the conversation turned to zeppelin airships and what was reported of their huge size, speed, and danger, until Yasin rose and went to his room to change, prior to leaving the house for his usual night on the town. He returned after a brief absence, ready and outfitted. His clothes looked elegant, and he made a handsome appearance. With his large body, sprouting mustache, and mature masculinity he seemed much older than he was. He said goodbye to them and went off.

Kamal gazed after him with a look revealing how much he envied him the enjoyment of his liberty with its enchanting freedom from restrictions. It was no secret to Kamal that his brother, since his appointment as a secretary at al-Nahhasin School, no longer had to account for his comings or goings. He could stay out as late as he wished and return whenever he wanted. How beautiful it was and how blissful. How happy a person would be to be able to come and go as he pleased and stay out nights as long as he desired. He could limit his reading, once he mastered the skills, to novels and poetry.

He suddenly asked his mother, "When I get a job, will I be able to go out nights like Yasin?"

His mother smiled and replied, "Going out nights is not a goal you should be dreaming about now."

He shouted in protest, "But my father goes out at night and so does Yasin." His mother raised her eyebrows in confusion and stammered, "Be patient till you become a man. Then you can get a job. When the time is right, God will grant you opportunities."

Kamal did not seem prepared to wait. He asked, "Why can't I get a job in three years when I have my primary certificate?"

Khadija yelled sarcastically, "You want to get a job before you're fourteen! What will you do if you wet your pants at work?"

Before Kamal could proclaim his outrage at his sister, Fahmy told him derisively, "What a donkey you are. . . . Why don't you think about going into law like me? If it weren't for circumstances beyond his control, Yasin would have gotten his primary certificate before he was twenty. Then he would have completed his education. Lazybones, you don't even know what to wish for."

10

WHEN FAHMY and Kamal climbed to the roof of the house, the sun was about to disappear. It seemed a tranquil, white disk – its vitality faded, heat turned cold, and glow gone out. The garden with its ceiling of hyacinth beans and jasmine was already growing dark. The young man and the boy went to the far side of the roof where nothing barred the sun's last rays.

They headed for the wall adjoining their neighbors' roof. Fahmy brought Kamal to this spot every evening at sunset on the pretext of reviewing his lessons in the fresh air, even though it was chilly by this time of day in November. Fahmy stationed the boy with his back to the wall and stood facing him, in order to observe the neighbors' adjoining roof without having to turn. There, among the clotheslines, a girl appeared, a young woman of about twenty. She was busy gathering the dry clothes and piling them in a large basket. Although Kamal spoke in his usual loud voice, she kept on with her work as though she had not noticed the arrival of the two interlopers.

The hope that brought Fahmy at this hour was of catching a glimpse of her if some errand called her to the roof. Whenever his hope was fulfilled, his face, blushing with surprised delight, revealed how excited it made him. He began to listen to his younger brother absentmindedly while his eyes roamed about furtively.

She was visible one moment and concealed the next, or part of her could be seen while the rest was out of sight, depending on where she was in relation to the clothes and sheets. The girl was of medium build with a clear complexion verging on white. She had black eyes that radiated life, vivacity, and warmth, but her beauty and his surging emotions and feeling of victory at seeing her could not erase the anxiety pervading him, feebly when she was present and strongly when he was by himself, at her being so daring that she showed herself to him. Was he not man enough for a girl to hide from or was she a girl who did not mind showing herself to men? He kept asking himself why she did not turn and flee in alarm as Khadija or Aisha would have if either had found herself in the same situation. What strange spirit caused her to be an exception to commonly observed traditions and revered customs? Would he not have felt calmer if she had shown that customary modesty, even at the expense of his indescribable pleasure at seeing her? All the same, he invented excuses for her, based on the length of time they had been neighbors, her growing up alone, and perhaps affection too. He continued to argue and debate with his soul to encourage and satisfy it.

Since he was not as daring as she, he started to watch the nearby roofs stealthily to make sure that they were free of witnesses. For a young man of eighteen to violate the honor of the neighbors, especially such a good neighbor as al-Sayyid Muhammad Ridwan, was not a matter to be tolerated. For this reason he was always distressed by the gravity of his action. He was afraid news of it would reach his father, with calamitous results. The way love can disregard fears, however, is an age-old wonder. No fear is able to spoil love's development or keep it from dreaming of its appointed hour.

Fahmy watched her appear and disappear until no clothes were left to separate them. She faced him, her small hands rising and falling, her fingers slowly and deliberately grasping and releasing what she held, as though she was dragging out her work on purpose. His heart guessed it was on purpose, although he was torn between doubt and hope. He did not fight his feeling of being liberated to the farthest horizons by his happiness. He was conscious of nothing but dancing melodies. Although she did not glance up at him, her demeanor, the blush on her cheeks, and her avoidance of looking at him all betrayed how intensely conscious she was of his presence, or the impact he had made on her feelings.

Composed and still, she appeared to be very reserved, as though she was not the same girl who spread joy and delight throughout his house when she visited his sister and her voice carried through the house accompanied by her sonorous laughter. He would crouch behind the door of his room with a book in his hand, ready to pretend he was memorizing his lesson if anyone knocked on the door. He would intercept the melodious sounds of her words and laughter by concentrating on separating them from the other voices that blended with hers. His mind was like a magnet attracting to itself only the bits of steel from a mixture of various materials. He might catch a glimpse of her as he crossed the sitting room. Their eyes might meet in a glance which, though fleeting, would be enough to intoxicate him and stun him as though he had received a message with it so momentous it made his head spin.

He nourished his eyes and spirit with glimpses of her face. Even though the looks were furtive and fleeting, they took control of his spirit and senses. They were strong and penetrating. A single one conveyed more than a lengthy gaze or a deep investigation. They were like a burst of lightning glowing for a brief moment, its flash illuminating vast expanses and dazzling the eyes. His heart was drunk with a mysterious and intoxicating joy, even though it was never free of a sorrow which trailed it, like the troublesome Khamsin winds from the sandy desert trailing the advent of spring. He could not stop thinking about the four years it would take to complete his education. During that time, countless hands might stretch out to pluck this ripe fruit. If the atmosphere of the house had not been so suffocating, with his father's iron grip tight around his neck, he would have been able to seek a more direct route to reassure his heart. He was afraid to breathe a word about his hopes and expose them to the harsh rebuke of his father, which would scatter them and send them flying off.

He asked himself what she was thinking as he looked out over his brother's head. Was it really nothing more than taking in the laundry? Had she not yet felt what motivated him to stand here evening after evening? What was her heart's response to these daring steps of his? He imagined himself hopping over the wall that separated the roofs to join her where she stood in the dusk. He imagined her reaction in different ways. She would be waiting for him by appointment or would be surprised at his advance and start to flee. Then he thought about what would come next – the confession, complaint, and censure. In either case, hugging and kissing might follow, but these were mere speculations and flights of the imagination. Fahmy was well grounded in religion and manners and knew how unrealistic and absurd they were.

It was a silent scene, but the silence was electric and could almost speak without a tongue. Even Kamal had an anxious look in his small eyes, as though asking about the meaning of this strange seriousness that excited his curiosity pointlessly. Then, his patience exhausted, he raised his voice to say, "I've memorized the words. Aren't you going to listen to me?"

Fahmy was roused by his voice and took the notebook from him. He proceeded to ask him the meanings of the words while Kamal answered, until Fahmy's eyes fell on a beloved one. He discovered an extraordinary link between it and his present situation. He raised his voice intentionally when he asked what it meant: "Heart?"

The boy answered him and spelled the word, while Fahmy tried to discern her reaction. He raised his voice once more and asked, "Love?"

Kamal was a little disconcerted. Then he said in a voice that showed he was objecting, "This word isn't in the notebook."

Smiling, Fahmy said, "But I've mentioned it to you repeatedly. You ought to know it by heart."

The boy frowned, as though by contracting the arch of his eyebrows he could fish out the fugitive word. His brother, though, did not wait for the results of this attempt. He continued his examination in the same loud voice, saying, "Marriage . . ."

He thought he noticed the semblance of a smile on her lips at that. His heart beat rapidly and feverishly. He was filled with a sense of victory, because he had at last been able to transmit to her a charge of the electricity blazing in his heart. He wondered why it was this word which elicited a reaction from her. Was it because she disapproved of what preceded, or was it the first she heard?

Before he knew it, he heard Kamal protesting, after being unable to remember the answer, "These words are very hard."

His heart affirmed his brother's innocent statement. He reflected on his situation in light of it. His joy at once subsided, or almost. He wanted to speak, but he saw she had bent over the basket. She picked it up and approached the wall adjoining the roof of his house. She placed the basket on top of the wall and began to press the laundry down with the palms of her hands. She was close to him, separated by little more than a meter. Had she wanted to, she could have chosen another place on the wall, but she had deliberately confronted him. She had acted so aggressively that she seemed daring to a degree that frightened and perplexed him. His heartbeats were fast and feverish once more. He felt life was disclosing to him a new variety of treasure he had never experienced before. It was charming, delightful, vital, and enjoyable. She did not stand close to him long, for at once she lifted the basket and turned to go to the door leading down from the roof. She darted away from him and disappeared from sight. He stared at the door for some time, oblivious to his brother, who repeated his complaint about the difficulty of the word.

Fahmy felt a desire to be alone to enjoy this new experience of love. He looked out into space and pretended to be astonished, as though he had just noticed for the first time the darkness marching across the horizon. He muttered, "It's time for us to go in. . . ."

11

KAMAL WAS memorizing his lessons in the sitting room. He had left Fahmy alone in the study in order to be closer to his mother and sisters, who were enjoying a continuation of the coffee party limited to women. Their talk, however trifling, provided them with incomparable delight, and as usual they sat so close to each other they seemed a single body with three heads.

Kamal sat cross-legged on the sofa facing them. He had his book open in his lap. He would read for a while and then close his eyes to try to learn some by heart. At intervals he would amuse himself by looking at them and listening to their conversation. Fahmy only grudgingly agreed to let him study his lessons away from his supervision, but the boy's excellent performance in school provided him with an excuse to choose any place he wanted for studying. In fact, his diligence was his only virtue worth praising and, had it not been for his naughtiness, it would have won encouragement even from his father.

Despite his diligence and superior performance, he got bored at times and felt so disgusted with work and discipline that he envied his mother and sisters their ignorance and the rest and peace they enjoyed. Privately he even wished the destiny of men in this world was like that of women, but these were fleeting moments. He never forgot the advantages he possessed, which inspired him frequently to lord it over them and brag, even for no reason at all. It was not unusual for him to ask them, his voice resounding with challenge, "Who knows the capital of the Cape?" or "How do you say 'boy' in French?"

He would encounter a polite silence from Aisha. Khadija would acknowledge her ignorance, but retort, "Only a person with a head like yours can handle such riddles."

Her mother would comment with innocent self-confidence: "If you'd teach me these things the way you do religious studies, I'd know them as well as you." In spite of her gentleness and humility, she was intensely proud of her general knowledge, which had come down to her from antiquity through successive generations. She did not feel in need of further education or suspect there was any new knowledge worth adding to the religious, historical, and medical information she already possessed. Her faith in her learning was doubled by the fact that she had gotten it straight from her father, or by growing up in his house, and that her father was a shaykh and one of the religious scholars God favored over all creation, because they knew the Qur'an by heart. It was inconceivable that any knowledge could equal his, although, in the interest of keeping the peace, she did not mention this to the others.

She frequently disapproved of things the boys were told in school. She was upset either because of the explanations provided or because young minds were allowed to learn such things. Fortunately, she did not detect a difference worth mentioning between what the boy was told in school about religion and her own knowledge of it. Since the school lesson consisted of little more than recitation of Qur'an suras along with commentaries on them and the first principles of religion, she had found it allowed her scope to narrate the legends she knew and believed to be an inseparable part of the reality and essence of religion. She may even have seen in them an eternal element of religion. Most recounted miracles of the Prophet and prodigies of the Prophet's companions and the saints, along with various spells for defense against the jinn, reptiles, and diseases.

The boy did not doubt these tales and believed in them, because they came from his mother and they did not conflict with what he learned about religion at school. Moreover, the mentality of his religion teacher, as revealed by his casual remarks, did not differ at all from the mother's. Kamal was enthralled by the legends in a way that none of his dry lessons could match. Filled with enjoyment and flights of the imagination, his mother's lesson was one of the happiest hours of his day.

On subjects outside religion, their disputes were not infrequent. For example, they differed once about whether the earth rotates on its own axis in space or stands on the head of an ox. When she found the boy insistent, she backed down and pretended to give in. All the same, she slipped off to Fahmy's room to ask him about the truth of the ox supporting the earth, and whether it still did. The young man thought he should be gentle with her and answer in language she would like. He told her that the earth is held up by the power and wisdom of God. His mother left content with this answer, which pleased her, and the large ox was not erased from her imagination.

Kamal, however, did not choose this gathering for his studies to boast about his learning or because he liked intellectual disputes. The truth was that he loved the women's company with all his heart and did not want to be separated from them even when he was working. Seeing them gave him a pleasure nothing else could equal. He loved his mother more than anything in the world. He could not imagine existing without her even for a moment. Khadija played the role of a second mother in his life, despite the impudence of her tongue and the bite of her temper. Aisha, although she never went out of her way to help anyone, loved him deeply, and he reciprocated her love totally. He would not take a drink of water from the jug without asking her to drink first. Then he would put his lips on the place she had drunk from.

As it did every evening, this gathering lasted until about eight, when the two girls rose, said good night to their mother, and went to their bedroom. At that, the boy hurried to finish reading his lesson. Then he took his religion textbook and moved next to his mother on her sofa. He told her temptingly, "Today we heard a commentary on a fantastic sura you'll really like."

The woman sat up and replied reverently and devoutly, "All the words of our Lord are fantastic."

He was pleased by her interest. A feeling of bliss and power he experienced only during this final lesson of the day coursed through him. Indeed he found in this religion lesson more than one reason to be happy. For at least half of it he had the role of teacher. So far as he was able, he would attempt to recall whatever he could about his teacher's bearing and gestures and the feeling of power and superiority he projected. In the other half of the lesson he would find enjoyment in the memories and legends she related to him. Throughout it all he would have his mother completely to himself.

Kamal looked in the book almost conceitedly. Then he recited, "In the name of God, the Compassionate, the Merciful. Say: It has been revealed to me that a group of the jinn listened in. They said, 'We have heard a wondrous Qur'an. It provides guidance to correct decisions. We declare our belief in it and shall worship our

Lord exclusively.' " (72:1–2.) He recited "The Jinn" through the twenty-eighth verse.

His mother's eyes had an apprehensive and anxious look. She had warned him against uttering the words "jinn" and "afreet" as a precaution against dangers, some of which she mentioned in order to frighten him and others she withheld out of concern and circumspection. She did not know what to do when he recited one of these dangerous names in a holy sura. Indeed, she did not even know what to do to prevent him from memorizing this sura or what she would do if, as usual, he invited her to memorize it with him. The boy detected this anxiety in her face. He was overcome by a crafty pleasure. He recited the passage several times, emphatically pronouncing the dangerous word while he observed her anxiety. He expected she would ultimately express her concern apologetically, but her anxiety was so intense that she took refuge in silence.

He began to repeat the commentary to her the way he had heard it until he suggested, "So you see that some of the jinn listened to the Qur'an and believed in it; perhaps the ones living in our house are some of these Muslim jinn. Otherwise, why have they spared us all this time?"

The woman replied rather uneasily, "Perhaps they are, but it's possible some others are mixed in with them. So it would be best for us not to repeat their names."

"There's nothing to fear in repeating the word. That's what our teacher said."

His mother stared at him critically and said, "The teacher doesn't know everything."

"Even if the name is in a sacred verse?"

Confronted by his question she felt upset but found herself forced to respond, "The word of our Lord is a blessing in its entirety."

Kamal was satisfied and continued with his account of the commentary: "Our shaykh also says their bodies are made of fire!"

Her anxiety became extreme. She implored God's protection and invoked His name a number of times.

Kamal continued talking: "I asked the shaykh if the Muslims among them would enter paradise. He said, 'Yes.' I also asked him how they could, if their bodies are made of fire. He replied sharply that God can do anything."

"May His might be exalted."

He gazed at her with concern and then asked, "If we meet them in paradise, won't their fire burn us?"

The woman smiled and said confidently and devoutly, "There is no harm or fear there."

The boy's eyes wandered dreamily. Then he changed the course of the conversation suddenly by asking, "Will we see God in the next world with our eyes?"

His mother answered with the same confidence and devotion, "This is true. There can be no doubt of it."

Yearnings showed in his dreamy glance like rays of light shining through the darkness. He asked himself when he would see God. In what form would He appear? Abruptly shifting topics once more, he asked his mother, "Is my father afraid of God?"

She was astonished and said incredulously, "What a strange question! Son, your father is a pious man, a believer who fears his Lord."

Perplexed, he shook his head and said in a subdued voice, "I can't imagine my father being afraid of anything."

His mother shouted in censure: "May God forgive you. . . . God forgive you."

He apologized for what he had said with a tender smile. Then he invited her to memorize the new sura. They proceeded to recite it together, verse by verse, and repeat it. When they thought they had accomplished as much as they could, the boy rose to go to his bedroom.

She stayed with him until he had slipped under the covers of his little bed. Placing her hand on his forehead, she recited the Throne Verse from the Qur'an about God's all-encompassing, watchful care (2:255). She leaned over and kissed his cheek. He put his arms around her neck and gave her a long kiss that came from the depths of his small heart.

She always had trouble getting away from him when she said good night. He would use every trick he knew to keep her beside him for the longest time possible, even if he did not get her to stay till he fell asleep in her arms. He had found that the best way to attain his goal was to ask her to recite, when she finished the Throne Verse, a second and a third verse with her hand on his head. If he perceived she was excusing herself with a smile, he would implore her to continue, citing his fear of being alone in the room or the bad dreams he would have unless there was a lengthy recitation of sacred verses. He might go so far in trying to retain her as to pretend to be sick. He found nothing wrong in these stratagems. He was certain that they did not even compensate for a sacred right which had been violated in the most atrocious way the day he was unjustly and forcibly separated from his mother and brought to this solitary bed in his brother's room.

How often he remembered with sorrow the time not so far distant when he and his mother shared a bed. He would fall asleep, his head resting on her arm, while she filled his ear with the sound of her gentle voice recounting stories of the prophets and saints. He would be asleep before his father returned from his night out and wake only after the man had risen to bathe. He would not see anyone else with his mother. The world belonged to him and he had no rival. Then a blind decree that made no sense had separated them. He had looked to her to see what impact his banishment had made on her.

How startled he had been by her encouragement, which implied that she agreed with the decision. She had congratulated him, saying, "Now you've become a man. You have a right to a bed of your own." Who said it would make him happy to become a man or that he craved a bed of his own? Although he had soaked his first private pillow with his tears and warned his mother he would never forgive her so long as he lived, he had never dared slip back into his former bed. He knew that behind that treacherous, tyrannical action crouched his father's unalterable will. How sad he had been. The dregs of sorrow embittered his dreams. How furious he had been with his mother, not just because it was impossible for him to be furious at his father but because she was the last person he thought would disappoint his hopes. She knew, though, how to appease him and gradually cheer him up.

At first she took care not to leave him until sleep made off with him. She would tell him, "We haven't been separated the way you claim. Don't you see that we're together? We'll stay together always. Nothing but sleep will separate us. It did that even when we were in one bed."

Now the sorrow had sunk below the surface of his emotions. He had accepted his new life, although he would not allow her to leave until he had used up all his tricks to make her stay the longest possible time. He held her hand as avidly as a child grasping his toy when other children are trying to snatch it away. She kept on reciting verses from the Qur'an with a hand on his head until sleep took him by surprise.

She bade him good night with a tender smile and went to the next room. She opened the door gently and looked toward the blurred shape of the bed on the right. She asked softly, "Are you both asleep?"

She could hear Khadija's voice reply, "How can I fall asleep when Miss Aisha's snoring fills the room?"

Then Aisha's voice was heard, protesting sleepily, "No one has ever heard me snore. She keeps me awake with her constant chatter."

Their mother said critically, "Have you forgotten my advice to cease your banter when it's time to go to sleep?"

She closed the door again and went to the study. She knocked on the door gently. Then she opened it and poked her head in to ask with a smile, "Do you need anything, sir?"

Fahmy raised his head from the book and thanked her, his face aglow with a charming smile. She closed the door and crossed the sitting room to the outer hall, before climbing the stairs to the top floor, where her husband's bedroom was. The Qur'an verses she was reciting preceded her.

12

WHEN YASIN left the house he naturally knew where he was going, since he went there every evening. He appeared, however, to have no idea where he was heading. He was always like this when walking in the street. He went along slowly in a friendly, complaisant manner. He strutted vainly and proudly, as though never forgetting for a moment his enormous body, his face radiating vitality and manliness, his elegant garments that received more than their fair share of attention, the fly whisk with its ivory handle that never left his hand winter or summer, and his tall fez tilted to the right so it almost touched his eyebrows.

As he walked, he was also in the habit of lifting his eyes but not his head to spy out what might just possibly be hiding behind the windows. By the time he got to the end of a street he would feel dizzy from moving his eyes around so much. His passion for the women he encountered was an incurable malady. He scrutinized them as they approached and gazed after their bodies as they drew away. He would get as agitated as a raging bull and then forget himself. He could no longer conceal his intentions discreetly. In time Uncle Hasanayn, the barber, Hajj Darwish, who sold beans, al-Fuli, the milkman, al-Bayumi, the drinks vendor, Abu Sari', who roasted seeds for snacks, and others like them noticed what was happening. Some of them joked about it, and others criticized him. The fact that Ahmad Abd al-Jawad was a neighbor and highly regarded by them gave them a reason to close their eyes and pardon Yasin.

The young man's vital forces were so powerful that they dominated him if he was otherwise at liberty. At no time did they grant him any relief from their proddings. He continually felt their tongues burning against his senses and consciousness. They were like a jinni on his back, guiding him wherever it wished. All the same it was not a jinni that frightened or upset him. He did not wish to be freed from it. In fact, he might even have desired more like it.

His jinni quickly disappeared and changed into a gentle angel when he approached his father's store. There he kept his eyes to himself and walked normally. He was polite and modest. He walked faster and did not let himself be distracted by anything. When he passed the door of the shop, he looked inside. There were many people present, but his eyes met those of his father, who sat behind his desk. He bowed respectfully and saluted his father politely. The man answered his greeting with a smile. Then Yasin continued on his way as delighted with this smile as though he had received an unparalleled boon.

The fact was that his father's accustomed violence, even though it had undergone a noticeable change since the youth joined the corps of government employees, still remained in Yasin's opinion a form of violence moderated by civility. The bureaucrat had not freed himself from his former fear, which had filled his heart when he was a schoolboy. He had never outgrown his feeling that he was the son and the other man the father. Huge as he was, he could not help feeling tiny in his father's presence, like a sparrow that would tremble if a pebble fell. As soon as he got past his father's store and safely out of sight, Yasin's airs returned. His eyes began to flutter about again, not discriminating between fine ladies and women who sold doum palm fruit and oranges on the street. The jinni controlling him was wild about women in general. It was unassuming and equally fond of refined and humble women. Although they resembled the ground on which they sat in their color and filth, even the women who sold doum palm fruit and oranges occasionally possessed some beautiful feature. They might have rounded breasts or eyes decorated with kohl. What more could his jinni wish for than that?

He headed toward the Goldsmiths Bazaar and then to al-Ghuriya. He turned into al-Sayyid Ali's coffee shop on the corner of al-Sanadiqiya. It resembled a store of medium size and had a door on al-Sanadiqiya and a window with bars overlooking al-Ghuriya. There were some padded benches arranged in the corners. Yasin took his place on the bench under the window. It had been his favorite for weeks. He ordered tea. He sat where he could look out the window easily without arousing suspicion. He could glance up whenever he wished at a small window of a house on the other side of the street. It was quite possibly the only shuttered window that had not been carefully closed. This oversight was not surprising since the window belonged to the residence of Zubayda the chanteuse. Yasin was not ready for the chanteuse herself. He would need to pass patiently and persistently through many more stages of wantonness before he could aspire to her. He was watching for Zanuba to appear. She was Zubayda's foster daughter. She played the lute and was a gleaming star in the troupe.

The period of his employment with the government was a time full of memories and came to him after the long, obligatory asceticism he had endured out of respect for his father and the frightening shadow he cast on his life. Thereafter, he had plunged into the Ezbekiya entertainment district like water down the falls, in spite of the harassment of the soldiers brought to Cairo by the winds of war. Then the Australians appeared on the field, and Yasin had been obliged to forsake his places of amusement to escape their brutality. He had been at his wits' end and had begun to roam the alleys of his neighborhood like a madman. The greatest pleasure he could hope for was a woman selling oranges or a gypsy fortune-teller.

Then one day he had seen Zanuba and, dumbfounded, had followed her home. He had confronted her time after time but had almost nothing to show for it. She was a woman, and to him every woman was desirable. Moreover, she was beautiful and so he was wild about her. Even when his eyes were wide open, love for him was nothing but blind desire. It was the most elevated form of love he knew.

He looked out between the bars at the empty window with such apprehension and anxiety that he forgot what he was doing and drank hot tea without waiting for it to cool. He swallowed some and burned himself. He started to breathe out and put the glass back on the brass tray. He glanced about at the other patrons as though implying that their loud voices had disturbed him so much they were responsible for his accident and the reason that Zanuba had not appeared at the window.

"Where could that cursed woman be?" he wondered. "Is she hiding on purpose? She must certainly know I'm here. She may even have seen me arrive. If she continues to play the coquette right to the very end she'll make today one more day of torture."

He resumed his stealthy looks at the other men sitting there to see whether any of them had noticed. He found they were all immersed in their endless conversations. He was relieved and looked back at his targeted site, but the train of his thoughts was interrupted by memories of the troubles he had encountered during the day at school. The headmaster had questioned the honesty of a meat distributor and had undertaken an investigation in which Yasin, as school secretary, had participated. Then he had appeared a little slack in his work, and the headmaster had scolded him. That had spoiled the remainder of the day for him and made him think of complaining about the man to his father, for the two men were old friends. The only problem was he feared his father might be rougher on him than his boss.

"Get rid of these stupid ideas," he advised himself. "We're done with the school and the headmaster, curses on them. What I'm being put through by that smart-ass bitch, who's too stingy to let me see her, is enough for now."

Dreams of naked women began to swarm through his mind. Such visions frequently played on the stage of his imagination when he was looking at a woman or trying to remember her. They were created by a rash emotion that stripped bodies of their coverings and revealed them naked the way God created them. This emotion did not make an exception for his body either. His visions would progress through all types of fun and games with nothing held back.

He had just sunk into these dreams when the voice of a driver crying "whoa" to his donkey roused him. He looked in that direction and saw a donkey cart standing in front of the singer's house. He asked himself if the wagon might have come to carry the members of the troupe to some wedding. He summoned the waiter and paid him to be ready to leave at a moment's notice. Time passed while he waited and watched.

Then the door of the house opened and one of the women from the troupe emerged, leading a blind man. He was wearing a long shirt, an overcoat, and dark glasses and carried a zitherlike qanun under his arm. The woman climbed into the cart and took the qanun. She grasped the blind man's hand while the driver helped him from the other side till he reached the woman. They sat next to each other at the front of the wagon. They were followed immediately by a second woman carrying a tambourine and a third with a parcel under her arm. The women were concealed in their wraps but their faces were visible. In place of long veils they were wearing short ones embellished with brilliant colors that made them look like the candy bride dolls sold at festivals. And then what? . . . With yearning eyes and throbbing heart he saw the lute emerging from the door in its red case.

Finally Zanuba appeared. The edge of her wrap was placed far back on her head to reveal a crimson kerchief with little tassels. Beneath it there gleamed laughing black eyes with glances full of merriment and deviltry. She approached the wagon and held out the lute to a woman who took it. Zanuba raised a foot over the wheel. Yasin craned his neck and gulped. He caught a glimpse of her stocking, where it was fastened above her knee, and of a stretch of her bare leg. The pleasantly clear skin showed through the fringes of an orange dress.

"If only this bench would sink into the ground with me about a meter. My Lord, her face is brown, but where it doesn't show, her skin is white, really white. So what do her thighs look like? And her belly? Oh my goodness . . ."

Zanuba placed her hands on the top of the wagon and braced herself so she could get her knees on the edge. Then she began crawling onto the wagon on all fours.

"Good God, good gracious . . . Oh, if only I were at the door of her house or even in the shop of Muhammad the fez maker. Look at that son of a bitch staring at her ass with both eyes. After today he ought to call himself Muhammad the Conqueror. O God . . . O Deliverer."

Her back started to straighten and she stood up on the wagon. She opened her wrap and, taking the two ends in her hands, shook it repeatedly as though she were a bird flapping its wings. She draped the black cloth around her skillfully to reveal the details of her body's features and articulations. It especially highlighted her full, gleaming rump. Then she sat down at the rear of the wagon. Under the pressure of her weight, her buttocks were compressed and ballooned out to the right and left, making a fine cushion.

Yasin rose and left the coffee shop. He found that the wagon had moved off. He followed after it slowly, gasping and clenching his teeth in his excitement. The wagon proceeded on its way haltingly, dragging and swaying. The women on board were rocking back and forth. The young man trained his eyes on the lute player's cushion. He followed her motions so closely that after a while he imagined she was dancing. Darkness was engulfing the narrow street. Many of the shops had begun to close their doors.

Most of the people in the street were workers returning to their homes, drained of strength. Between the weary crowds and the darkness Yasin found ample opportunity to devote himself to looking and dreaming in peace and quiet.

"O God, may this street never end. May this dancing movement never cease. What a royal rump combining both arrogance and graciousness. A wretch like me can almost feel its softness and its firmness both, merely by looking. This wonderful crack separating the two halves – you can almost hear the cloth covering it talk about it. And what can't be seen is even better... Now I understand why some men pray four prostrations before bedding a bride. Isn't this a dome? Why, yes, and under the dome lies the shaykh in his tomb. I'm certainly a devotee of this shaykh. Hear me, Shaykh Adawi!"

Yasin cleared his throat as the wagon approached Mutawalli Gate, known as Bab al-Zuwayla. Zanuba turned around. He saw her, and she saw him. It seemed to him he could detect the hint of a smile on her lips when she turned her head away. His heart beat violently, and an intoxicating, fiery pleasure penetrated his consciousness. The wagon went through Mutawalli Gate and then turned left. At that point the young man was forced to stop, since nearby he saw telltale decorations, lights, and a cheering crowd. He drew back a little, his eyes never leaving the lute player. He watched her avidly as she descended to the ground. She tossed a playful look his way and headed for the wedding party. She disappeared through the door in a clamor of joyous ululation. He sighed passionately and was overcome by a furious perplexity. He seemed anxious, as though he did not know which way to turn.

"God curse the Australians! Where are you, Ezbekiya, for me to disperse my care and sorrow in you and draw a little patience from you?"

He turned on his heels, muttering, "To the only consolation left... to Costaki." No sooner had he mentioned the name of the Greek grocer than his head began to perspire, longing for the intoxication of drink. Wine and women in his life were inseparable and complementary. It was in the company of a woman that he had first gotten a taste for wine. By force of habit it had become one of the valued ingredients and sources of pleasure for him. All the same, it was not always granted that the two, wine and women, came together. Many nights were devoid of women, and he had no choice but to relieve his anguish with drink. Over the course of time as the habit became established he seemed almost to have fallen in love with wine for its own sake.

He returned by the route he had come and made his way to the grocery store of Costaki at the head of New Street. It was a large saloon. The front was a grocery store and the inner room a bar; a small door connected the two. He stopped at the entrance, mixing with the customers, while examining the street to see if his father was in the vicinity. Then he headed for the small interior door, but he had scarcely taken a step when he noticed in front of him a man standing by the scales while Mr. Costaki himself weighed a large parcel for him. Involuntarily he turned his head toward the man. Yasin's face immediately became gloomy. A rude tremor shot through his body, making his heart contract with fear and disgust. There was nothing in the man's appearance to inspire these hostile emotions. He was in his sixth decade and was wearing a loose gown and a turban. His mustache was white and gave him a noble, gentle look. Yasin, however, proceeded on in consternation, as though fleeing before the man's eyes could fall on him. He pushed open the door of the bar rather forcefully and went in, as the earth seemed to sway beneath his feet.

13

YASIN THREW himself down on the first chair he found. His strength seemed to have given out and he looked somber. He called the waiter and ordered a carafe of cognac in a tone that showed his patience was exhausted. The bar was just a room with a large lantern hanging from the ceiling. Wooden tables with rattan chairs were lined up along the sides. The patrons sitting there included rustic types, workers, and gentlemen. In the center of the room directly under the lantern, pots of carnations were grouped together.

It was strange that he had not forgotten the man and had recognized him at first glance. When was the last time he had seen him? He could not be sure, but most probably he had set eyes on him only twice during the past twelve years, the second time being the encounter that had just shaken him. The man had changed. There was no doubt about it. He had turned into a dignified, sedate old man. If God had only forbidden the blind coincidence that had brought them together . . . His lips curled in disgust and resentment. He felt he was swallowing a bitter humili-ation. How degrading and demeaning! He would hardly recover, with pain and perseverance, from his anguish before it was resur-rected by some repressed memory or cursed chance encounter like today's. Once again he would be abased, broken . . . lost. In spite of himself, he thought back over the odious past, with all the force of the strife lying behind it.

The darkness drew back to reveal the ugly apparitions that frequently grasped at him like emblems of torment and loathing. Among them he could make out the fruit store at the head of the cul-de-sac called the Palace of Desire, or Qasr al-Shawq. An image with blurred features came to him. It was himself as a boy. He saw the boy hurrying to the shop where that same man greeted him and brought him a bag filled with oranges and apples. Joyfully he took it back to the woman who had sent him and was waiting for him . . . to his mother, not someone else, alas. The memory made him frown with rage and anguish. Then he recalled the image of the man. He asked himself apprehensively whether that man could possibly recognize him if he saw him. Would he recognize in him the small boy he had once known as that woman's son? A tremor of alarm passed through him. His towering, bulky body seemed to fade and dwindle until he sensed it had become nothing at all.

At that point the carafe and glass were brought. He poured out some cognac and drank greedily and nervously. He was in a hurry to reap the drinker's share of refreshment and forgetfulness, but suddenly his mother's face appeared to him from the depths of the past. He could not keep himself from spitting. Which should he curse: fate, which made her his mother, or her beauty, which caused so many men to fall in love with her and enveloped him in disasters? It was beyond his power to change anything destined to befall him. All he could do was submit to the divine decree that mauled his self-esteem. After everything he had endured, it was surely unjust to expect him to make amends for what fate had decreed, as though he were the sinful offender. He did not know why he deserved that curse.

There were many children like him raised by divorced mothers. Unlike many of them, he had found with his mother pure affection, boundless love, and abundant fondling unrestrained by a father's control. He had enjoyed a happy childhood based on love, tenderness, and gentleness. He could still remember many things about the old house in Qasr al-Shawq, like its roof, which overlooked countless other ones. Minarets and domes were visible from it in all directions. Its enclosed balcony looked down on al-Gamaliya Street, where night after night wedding processions passed, lit by candles and flanked by toughs. Most would lead to brawls in which cudgels were wielded and blood flowed.

In that house he had loved his mother in a way that could not be surpassed. In it an obscure doubt had crept into his heart. There the first seeds of a strange aversion had been cast into his breast, the aversion of a son for his mother. These seeds were destined to grow and mature until they changed in time into a hatred like a chronic disease. He had often told himself that if a person had a strong enough will he might be able to carve out more than one future, but no matter how strong his will he could never have more than one inescapable and unavoidable past.

Now he asked himself, as he had frequently before, when he had realized that he and his mother were not alone. It was unlikely that he had known with any certainty. All he could remember was that at one point in his childhood his senses had noted with disdain a new person who intruded on the household from time to time. Perhaps he, Yasin, had looked at him skeptically and somewhat fearfully. The man had probably done everything in his power to amuse and please him.

He gazed back into the past with intense hatred and revulsion but found he could not fight it off. His past was like a boil he wished he could ignore, while his hand could not keep from touching it every now and then. Moreover, there were matters he could not possibly forget. In a certain place, at a time between daylight and darkness, from beneath the upper window or through a dining-room door with red and blue triangles of glass – in that place he remembered he had suddenly beheld, in circumstances corroded by forgetfulness, the intruder assaulting his mother. He had not been able to keep himself from screaming from the depths of his heart. He had howled and wept until the woman came to him, clearly disturbed. She had attempted to put his mind at rest and calm him down.

At that point the train of his thoughts was cut short by his intense resentment. He looked around him despondently. Then he filled his glass from the carafe and drank. When he set the glass back down he noticed a drop of liquid on the edge of his jacket. He thought it was wine and took out his handkerchief. He started patting the spot. Checking on a hunch, he examined the outside of the glass and saw drops of water clinging to it near the bottom. He surmised it was water and not wine that had fallen on his coat and thus regained his composure. But what a deceptive composure it was! His mind's eye had returned to the odious past.

He did not remember when the incident in question had taken place or how old he had been at the time. He did remember quite certainly that the seducer kept on coming to the old house and had frequently tried to ingratiate himself with Yasin by giving him sweet and tasty fruit. After that, he had seen the man in his fruit store at the head of the alley when his mother brought him along with her to run an errand. With childish innocence he had pointed the man out to her. She had dragged him forcefully away and forbidden him to point at the man. Thus Yasin learned to pretend not to know him when his mother was with him on the street. This incident had made the man seem even more mysterious and incomprehensible to him. She had also cautioned him against mentioning the man in the presence of an elderly uncle who was still alive at that time and who visited them occasionally. He had heeded her warning and become even more apprehensive.

Fate had not been satisfied with that. If the man had not visited the house for several days, his mother would send the boy to invite him to come "tonight." The man would receive him graciously and fill a bag with apples and bananas. He would give the boy his acceptance or apologies, as the case might be. It got to the point that when Yasin wanted some tasty fruit he would ask his mother's permission to go to the man to invite him for "tonight." When he remembered this, his forehead broke out in a sweat from shame, and he exhaled in annoyance. Then he poured some cognac and swallowed it.

Slowly the fiery intoxication spread through his system and began to play its magical role in helping him bear his troubles. "I've said a thousand times I've got to leave the past buried in its grave. It's no use. I don't have a mother. My stepmother, who is tender and good, is all the mother I need. Everything's fine except for an old memory I can get rid of. I wonder why I allow it to persist with me and exhume it time after time. Why? It was just bad luck which plunked that man in front of me today. He's destined to die one day. I wish a lot of men would die. He's not the only one."

Although his intellect forbade it, his rebellious imagination continued the journey through his gloomy past. Now he felt more relaxed about it. Indeed, there was not much more to the story itself. The rest of it differed from the beginning, perhaps, and seemed relatively bright after the dark period he had endured as a young child. This improvement came in the few years preceding his transfer to his father's custody. Then his mother had summoned up the courage to tell him openly that the fruit merchant had been visiting her in hopes of marrying her. She had hesitated to accept him and probably would refuse him for Yasin's sake. How much truth was there to what he had been told? It would be absurd to put too much faith in the details of his memories, but he had certainly attempted to understand and comprehend. He had been afflicted with an obscure doubt, revealing itself to the heart rather than the intellect. He had suffered enough distress to scare away the dove of peace and prepare the earth of his soul to receive the seed of the revulsion, which in time had grown to maturity.

When he was nine, he had been transferred to his father's custody. Before that, his father had only seen him a limited number of times, to avoid friction with Yasin's mother. When he came to his father's house as a boy he was ignorant even of the most elementary forms of knowledge and had to make up for the ill effects of his mother's excessive pampering. He hated learning and had little willpower to help him. Had it not been for the ferocity of his father and the pleasant atmosphere of his new home he would not have succeeded in obtaining the primary certificate even when he was over nineteen.

As he grew older and grasped the facts of life, he paraded in review his life in his mother's house and examined it from different perspectives, using his new expertise to cast a glaring light on it. Then the bitter and repugnant realities were revealed to him. Whenever he took a step forward in life, he found the past was like a poisoned weapon attacking him and his dignity from within.

At first his father had tried to ask him about life in his mother's home. Even though he was young, he had abstained from digging up the sad memories. His wounded pride defeated both a desire to arouse his father's interest and the love of chattering characteristic of small boys. He kept silent until he received strange news about his mother's marriage to a coal merchant in the Mubayyada region of al-Gamaliya. Then the boy wept for a long time. His anger was more than he could bear, and he burst out and told his father about the fruit merchant whose offer of marriage his mother had claimed, one day, she had refused for Yasin's sake.

His link to her had been severed at that time, eleven years ago. He knew nothing about her except what his father related from time to time, like her divorce from the coal merchant after two years of marriage to him. Then she had married a master sergeant the year later. After about two years she was divorced again, and so forth and so on.

During the lengthy separation, the woman had frequently endeavored to see him. She would send someone to his father to ask his permission for their son to visit her, but Yasin rejected her invitations with intense distaste and revulsion, even though his father advised him to be conciliatory and forgiving. The truth was that he held a fierce grudge against her that rose from the very core of his wounded heart. He closed the door of forgiveness and pardon on her and barricaded it with anger and hatred. He believed he was not being unjust to her. He had simply set her down at the level to which her activity had lowered her.

"A woman. Yes, she's nothing but a woman. Every woman is a filthy curse. A woman doesn't know what virtue is, unless she's denied all opportunities for adultery. Even my stepmother, who's a fine woman – God only knows what she would be like if it weren't for my father."

His thoughts were interrupted by a man's voice which rang out: "Wine has nothing but benefits. I'll cut off the head of anyone who disagrees. Hashish, dope, and opium are very harmful, but wine is full of benefits."

"What are its benefits?" his companion asked.

"Its benefits! What a strange question!" the man replied incredulously. "Everything about it is beneficial, as I told you. You know this. You believe it. . . ."

The companion said, "But hashish, opium, and other narcotics are also beneficial. You ought to know this and believe it. Everyone says so. Are you going to oppose this popular consensus?"

The first man hesitated a little. Then he observed, "Everything's beneficial, then. Everything. Wine, hashish, opium, narcotics, and whatever comes along."

His companion retorted in a victorious tone, "But wine is forbidden by Islam."

The man said angrily, "Is that all you can come up with? You should give alms righteously, go on pilgrimage, feed the poor. The opportunities for atonement are plentiful, and a good deed is worth ten others."

Yasin smiled with relief. Yes, at last he was able to smile. "Let her go to hell and take the past with her. I'm not responsible for any of it. Every man gets some dirt on him in this life. Anyone who could pull back the curtain would get an eyeful. The only thing that interests me is her real estate: the store on al-Hamzawi, the residence in al-Ghuriya, and the old house in the Palace of Desire. I swear to God that if I inherit all of it one day, I'll have no qualms about praying God to be compassionate to her. . . . Oh . . . Zanuba, I almost forgot about you, and only the devil could make me forget you. It was a woman who tormented me, and it's with a woman that I seek consolation. Oh, Zanuba, I didn't know until today that under your clothes you have such a fair complexion. . . . Ugh, I need to erase this thought from my head. The truth is that my mother's an aching molar that won't stop hurting till it's pulled."

14

AL-SAYYID AHMAD Abd al-Jawad sat behind the desk in his store. The fingers of his left hand were playing with his elegant mustache as they commonly did when he was carried off by the flow of his thoughts. He was staring into space, and the expression on his face suggested that he felt relaxed and contented. He was obviously pleased to feel the love and affection people harbored for him. If he could have discerned some sign of their love every day, that would have made each day happy and splendid in a way no amount of repetition could blunt. Today he had received yet another proof of their love.

The night before, he had been unable to attend a party to which one of his friends had invited him. Immediately after he had taken his seat in the store this morning, the man who had invited him and some comrades who were guests at the party had come to see him. They had reprimanded him for missing it and held him responsible for diminishing their delight and enjoyment. They had said, among other things, that they had not really laughed from the bottom of their hearts the way they did when he was present. They had not found the same pleasure in drinking that they did with him. Their party, as they put it, had lacked its soul.

Now he was joyfully and proudly reviewing their remarks. He was deeply touched by the intensity of their reproaches and the warmth of his own apologies. All the same, he did not escape the reprimands of his conscience, which by its very nature was bent on pleasing his dear friends and thirsty for a fond and sincere drink from the springs of friendship and affection. It might almost have spoiled his good humor, except for the contentment and pride he felt because of the love his friends' revolt against him revealed. Yes, how often the love that attracted him to others and them to him had cheered his heart with unlimited delight and satisfaction. He seemed to have been created for friendship more than for anything else.

He had encountered another manifestation of this love, or of a different type of love, later that morning. Umm Ali the match-maker had called on him. She had told him, after beating around the bush for some time, "You surely know that Madam Nafusa, the widow of al-Hajj Ali al-Dasuqi, owns seven stores in al Mugharbilin?"

Al-Sayyid Ahmad had smiled. He had grasped intuitively what the woman was hinting at, and his heart had told him she was not simply playing the matchmaker this time but was a messenger sworn to secrecy. He had imagined on more than one occasion that Madam Nafusa had come close to announcing her affection for him during her frequent trips to his store to buy groceries. All the same, he had wanted to sound her out, if only to amuse himself. He had replied with apparent interest, "It's your job to find a suitable husband for her. And they're hard to come by!"

Umm Ali had thought she had achieved her objective. She had said, "I've chosen you out of all men. What do you say?"

The proprietor had laughed loudly and merrily, revealing his good humor and self-satisfaction, but had replied decisively, "I've been married twice. I failed the first time. God made me successful with the second. I will not be reckless with the blessing God has granted me."

The truth was that he had often overcome, by the force of his inalterable will, the temptations of another marriage, in spite of the suitable opportunities that came his way. It seemed he had not forgotten the example of his father, who had slipped inadvertently into a succession of marriages that squandered his fortune and caused him many problems. He, his father's only child, had been left with only a negligible amount of money. Now, through his own profits and income, he enjoyed an ample living that furnished his family happiness and comfort and provided him with as much as he wished to spend on his amusements and entertainments. How could he do something that would spoil this excellent and convenient situation that secured for him both honor and freedom? Indeed, he had not amassed a fortune, not from a lack of means of accumulating one, but because of the generosity that was part of his nature. Spending his wealth and enjoying what it brought him were the only reasons he could see for having it. Moreover, a deep faith in God and His benefactions filled his soul with a sense of trust and confidence that protected him from the fear afflicting many people with regard to their possessions and their future.

His rejection of the lures of further matrimony did not prevent him from being pleased and proud whenever a good opportunity came his way. Consequently, he could not overlook the fact that a beautiful woman like Madam Nafusa wanted him to be her husband. This thought dominated his mind now. He began to look at his assistant and the customers with vacant eyes and a dreamy, smiling face. He remembered, again with a smile, how one of his friends had teased him that morning about his elegance and his use of perfume: "Enough of that. Enough for you, old man."

Old man? He actually was forty-five, but what could this critic say about his enormous vitality, robust health, and stream of gleaming black hair? His feeling of youthfulness had not weakened or diminished. His boyish vigor seemed to increase with time, and he had lost none of his charms. Indeed, despite his modesty and complaisance, he was intensely conscious of his looks and secretly both proud and vain. He was enormously fond of praise. His humility and graciousness seemed designed to increase praise and to spur his companions gently on to say more nice things about him. He was so self-confident that he believed himself superior to other men in looks, grace, and elegance, but he was not a bore about it. His modesty also came to him naturally. It was an innate characteristic that arose from a disposition overflowing with good humor, sincerity, and love.

In fact, he made use of this native disposition, without any reservations, to scout for more love. Inspired by this thirst for love, his nature was inclined toward sincerity, faithfulness, serenity, humility: the attributes that attract love and approval the way flowers attract butterflies. Although his modesty seemed to be a skill, it was a natural characteristic. His skill came instinctively and not from any act of will, revealing itself naturally and simply, without any affectation or effort. He preferred to be silent about his good qualities and conceal his pleasing qualities, while joking about his faults and defects, in order to seek love and affection. To make his virtues known and brag about them could easily have incited an envious reaction. His effective and skillful use of modesty drove his admirers to praise what his wisdom and reserve passed over. Without his resorting to any unseemly boasting, his merits were made public in a way he could never have achieved by himself, thus increasing his charm and the affection lavished on him.

He sought guidance from this same intuitive inspiration even when he was clowning around, socializing, and enjoying music. On those occasions, no matter what effect drinking had on his mind, he never lost his skill and adroitness. If he had wanted to, he could easily have overwhelmed his companions with his quick wit, ability to improvise, excellent sense of humor, and scathing sarcasm, but he conducted parties in an expert and generous way, giving everyone present a chance to participate. When someone told a joke, even if it fell flat, he would favor him with his resounding laughter. He had an intense desire to prevent his own jokes from wounding anyone. If a jest required him to attack a companion, he would make up for his attack by encouraging the other man and flattering him, even if he had to make fun of himself. The party would not end until everyone present had stored up delightful and captivating memories.

The benefits of his natural delicacy, or delicate nature, were not limited to the comic side of his life. They also extended to important aspects of his social life and made themselves felt in the most magnificent way in his well-known generosity, whether manifested in the banquets he hosted in the big house from time to time or in the donations he made to needy people linked to him by some business or personal relationship. He was generous and gallant in his assistance to friends and acquaintances, acting as a guardian for them, but in a way imbued with love and trust. They relied on him when they needed advice, mediation, or a service, whether their problems related to work, money, or personal and domestic questions like an engagement, marriage, or divorce. He was happy to undertake these duties for no wage other than love, serving as an agent, marriage official, and referee. No matter how hard these tasks were, he always found that carrying them out filled his life with delight and joy.

A man like this, excelling in so many social graces and then concealing it, as though fearful of substantial harm if people knew, may allow his modesty to dissolve when alone with his thoughts. Such a man is then apt to savor his fine qualities for a long time and succumb to pride and vanity. Thus al-Sayyid Ahmad began to recall both the censure of his devoted friends and the offer of Umm Ali the matchmaker with pleasure, delight, and glee, which mixed together in his heart in an intoxicating but harmless fashion. Yet the sting of sorrow intruded on his reverie, and he started to tell himself, "Madam Nafusa is a lady with many estimable qualities. Many have desired her, but she wants me. All the same, I won't take another wife. That matter is settled. And she's not the kind of woman who would agree to live with a man without getting married. This is the way I am and that's the way she is. So how can we get together? . . . If she had come my way at any time but now when the Australians have us blocked in, it would have been easy. What a pity the roads are barricaded when we need to use them."

A carriage stopped at the entrance to the store then and interrupted his thoughts. He looked out to see what was happening. He saw the vehicle tip toward the store under the weight of a prodigious woman who began to alight from it very slowly, hampered by her folds of flesh and fat. A black maid had gotten down first and held a hand out for her to lean on while she descended. The woman paused for a moment, sighing as though seeking some relief from the arduous descent. Then, like the ceremonial camel litter that each year was a traditional highlight of the procession of pilgrims setting off for Mecca, she made her way into the store, swaying and trembling.

Meanwhile the maid's voice rang out almost oratorically to announce her mistress: "Make way, fellows, you and the other one, for Madam Zubayda, queen of the singers."

A muffled laugh escaped from Madam Zubayda. Addressing the maid in a counterfeit tone of reprimand, she said, "May God forgive you, Jaljal . . . Queen of the singers! That's enough. Haven't you learned the virtue of humility?"

Jamil al-Hamzawi rushed toward her, his mouth hanging open in a wide smile. He said, "Welcome! We should have spread the earth with sand for you."

Al-Sayyid Ahmad rose. He was examining her with a look both astonished and thoughtful. Then, to complete his employee's greeting, he said, "No, with henna and roses, but what can we do when good fortune arrives unannounced?"

The proprietor saw his assistant going to get a chair. He beat him to it with a broad step almost like a jump. The other man moved aside, concealing his smile. The proprietor presented the chair to the visitor himself. He gestured with his hand to invite her to have a seat, but as he did so his hand stretched out to its full extent, perhaps without his being conscious of it. The openings between his fingers spread apart till the hand resembled a fan. This manual expansion was influenced possibly by the effect on his imagination of her prodigious bottom, which would shortly fill the seat of the chair and certainly spill over the sides.

The woman thanked him with a smile. The beauty of her face shone, with no veil to conceal it. She sat down, gleaming in her finery and jewels. Then she turned toward her maid and addressed her, although what she said was not intended solely for her: "Didn't I tell you, Jaljal, there's no reason for us to wander hither and yon to do our shopping when we have this fine store?"

The maid agreed: "You were right as usual, Sultana. Why should we go far away when here we have the noble Mr. Ahmad Abd al-Jawad?"

The lady drew back her head as though shocked by what Jaljal had said. She cast her a disapproving look and then glanced back and forth between the proprietor and the maid so he could see her disapproval. Concealing a smile, she said, "How embarrassing! I was talking to you about the shop, Jaljal, not about al-Sayyid Ahmad."

The proprietor's experienced heart felt the affectionate atmosphere created by the woman's remarks. Guided by his quick instincts, he got into the spirit and murmured with a smile, "The shop and al-Sayyid Ahmad are one and the same, Sultana."

She raised her eyebrows coquettishly and replied with gentle obstinacy, "But we are interested in the store, not al-Sayyid Ahmad."

It seemed that al-Sayyid Ahmad was not the only person to feel the fine atmosphere created by the sultana, for here was Jamil al-Hamzawi, who alternated between haggling with the customers and stealing looks at any part of the singer's body he could get his eyes on, and there were the customers letting their eyes wander from the merchandise to pass over the lady. Indeed it seemed that this propitious visit had even caught the attention of passersby in the street. The proprietor decided to move closer to the sultana and turn his broad back on the door and the people to protect her from the disturbance of intruders. All the same, this did not make him forget where he was in the conversation. He continued with his little joke: "God, may His wisdom be exalted, decreed that inanimate things have better luck at times than man."

She answered suggestively, "I think you're exaggerating. Inanimate goods are no luckier than a man, but frequently they are more useful."

Al-Sayyid Ahmad gave her a piercing look with his blue eyes. Pretending to be astonished, he exclaimed, "More useful!" and then, pointing at the floor, "This store!"

She granted him a short, sweet laugh but said in a tone not without a deliberate harshness, "I want sugar, coffee, rice; the man needs his store for these things." Then she continued with an inflection free of any flirtatiousness: "Moreover, men are much harder on the heart."

The doors of desire had opened for the proprietor. He sensed he was faced with something far more significant than a simple purchase. He objected, "Not all men are the same, Sultana. Who told you that a man's no substitute for rice, sugar, and coffee? It's with a man that you truly find nourishment, sweetness, and satisfaction."

She laughed and asked him, "Are you talking about a man or a kitchen?"

He answered victoriously, "If you look closely, you'll discover an amazing similarity between a man and a kitchen. Each of them fills the belly with life."

The woman lowered her eyes for a time. The proprietor expected her to look up at him with a bright smile, but the glance she directed at him was serious. He sensed at once that she had changed strategy or perhaps was not really comfortable about slipping into a relationship so quickly. She turned away and then he heard her say quietly, "May God help you . . . but all we need today are rice, coffee, and sugar."

The proprietor stepped away from her and tried to look serious. He summoned his assistant and in a loud voice entrusted the lady's orders to him. He gave the impression that he too had decided to refrain from being too affectionate and to get back to business, but it was just a maneuver. Immediately afterward he went on the attack again with his smile and murmured to the sultana, "The store and its proprietor are yours to command."

The maneuver had its effect, for the woman said jokingly,

"I want the store, and you insist on giving yourself."

"I'm no doubt better than my store, or the best thing in it."

She beamed with a mischievous smile and said, "This contradicts what we've heard about the excellence of your merchandise."

The proprietor laughed boisterously and said, "Why do you need sugar when there's all this sweetness on your tongue?"

This verbal battle was followed by a period of silence during which each of them appeared content with himself. Then the performer opened her purse and took out a small mirror with a silver handle. She began to look at herself. The proprietor went back to his desk. He stood, leaning on the edge of it, while he studied her face with interest.

The truth was that when his eyes had first noticed her, his heart had told him that she had not made her visit merely to buy something. Then her warm and responsive conversation had confirmed his suspicions. Now all that remained was for him to decide whether to respond or to bid her a final adieu. It was not the first time he had seen her, for he had frequently run into her at weddings hosted by his friends. He knew from secondhand reports that al-Sayyid Khalil al-Banan had been her lover for a long time but that they had recently separated. Perhaps it was for this reason that she was looking for goods at a new store. She was very beautiful, even though her status as a singer was only secondrate. All the same, he was more interested in her as a woman than as a singer. She certainly was desirable. Her folds of flesh and fat would warm a chilly man during the bitter cold of winter, which was at hand.

His reflections were cut short by al-Hamzawi, who brought the three parcels. The maid took them, and the lady thrust her hand into her purse, apparently to take out some money. Al-Sayyid Ahmad gestured to her not to try to pay: "That would be quite wrong."

The woman pretended to be astonished. "Wrong, Mr. al-Sayyid? How can doing what's right be wrong?"

"This is an auspicious visit. It's our duty to greet it with the honor it deserves. It would be impossible for me to do justice to it."

While he was talking, she stood up. She did not offer any serious resistance to his generosity but warned, "Your generosity will make me hesitate more than once before I come back to you again."

The proprietor laughed boisterously and replied, "Have no fear! I'm generous to a customer the first time, but I make up for my loss later, even if I have to cheat. This is the way merchants operate."

The lady smiled and held out her hand to him. She commented, "When a generous man like you cheats, it isn't really cheating. Thank you, Sayyid Ahmad."

He responded from the depths of his heart, "Don't mention it, Sultana."

He stood watching her strut toward the door and then climb into the carriage. She took her place, and Jaljal sat on the small seat opposite her. The carriage rolled off with its precious cargo and disappeared from sight.

Then here was al-Hamzawi, asking as he turned a page of the ledger, "How can this sum be accounted for?"

The proprietor looked at his assistant with a smile and replied, "Write beside it: 'Goods destroyed by an act of God.'" He murmured to himself as he returned to his desk, "God is beautiful and loves beauty."

15

THAT EVENING al-Sayyid Ahmad closed his store and set off surrounded by respectful glances and diffusing a pleasant fragrance. He proceeded to the Goldsmiths Bazaar and from there to al-Ghuriya till he reached al-Sayyid Ali's coffee shop. As he passed it, he looked at the singer's house and the adjoining buildings. He observed that the string of shops on both sides of it were still open and that the flow of pedestrian traffic was at its height. He continued on to a friend's house, where he passed an hour. Then he excused himself and returned to al-Ghuriya, which was engulfed in darkness and almost deserted.

Confident and relaxed, he approached the house. He knocked on the door and waited, looking carefully at everything around him. The only light came from the window of al-Sayyid Ali's coffee shop and from a kerosene lamp on a handcart at the corner of New Street. The door opened and the form of a young servant girl could be seen. Without any hesitation, in order to inspire in the girl trust and confidence, he asked her in a forceful voice, "Is Madam Zubayda at home?"

The girl looked up at him and asked with the reserve her job required, "Who are you, sir?"

He responded determinedly, "A person who wishes to reach an agreement with her for an evening's entertainment."

The girl was gone for some minutes before returning to invite him in. She stepped aside to allow him to enter. He followed her up the narrow steps of the staircase to a hallway. She opened the door facing him, and he passed through it into a darkened room. He stood there near the entrance, listening to her footsteps as she ran to fetch a lamp. He watched her place it on a table. She moved a chair to the center of the room to stand on while she lit the large lamp hanging from the ceiling. Then she put the chair back where it belonged. She took the small lamp and left the room, saying politely, "Please have a seat, sir."

He went over to a sofa at the front of the room and sat there confidently and calmly, demonstrating that he was accustomed to situations like this and certain the results would be to his liking. He removed his fez and placed it on a cushion at the center of the sofa. He stretched his legs out and made himself comfortable. He saw a room of medium size with sofas and chairs arranged around the sides. The floor was covered with a Persian carpet. In front of each of the three large sofas stood a serving table inlaid with mother-of-pearl. The windows and door were hung with curtains that prevented the aroma of incense he enjoyed from escaping. He amused himself by watching a moth flutter nervously and eagerly around the lamp. While he waited, the servant brought him coffee. It was some time before he heard the rhythmic thump of slippers striking the floor.

He became fully alert and stared at the opening of the door, which was immediately filled by the prodigious body, its pronounced curves sensuously draped in a blue dress. The moment the woman's eyes fell on him she stopped in astonishment and shouted, "In the name of God, the Compassionate, the Merciful! . . . You!"

His eyes ran over her body as quickly and greedily as a mouse on a sack of rice looking for a place to get in. He said admiringly, "In the name of God. God's will be done."

After her pause, she continued to advance, smiling. She said with pretended fear, "Your eye! God protect me from it."

Al-Sayyid Ahmad rose to take her outstretched hand. Sniffing the fragrant incense with his enormous nose, he asked, "Are you afraid of an envious eye even when protected by this incense?"

She freed her hand from his and stepped back to sit on one of the side couches. She replied, "My incense is a boon and a blessing. It's a mixture of various kinds, some Arab and some Indian that I blend myself. It's capable of ridding the body of a thousand and one jinn."

He sat down again and said, waving his hands in despair, "But not my body. My body has a jinni of a different sort. Incense doesn't do any good with him. The matter is more severe and dangerous."

The woman struck her chest like a heaving water skin and shouted, "But I perform at weddings, not exorcisms."

He said hopefully, "We'll see if you have a remedy for what ails me."

They were silent for a time. The sultana started to look at him somewhat reflectively, as though trying to discern the secret of his visit and whether he really had come to ask her to perform at a party, as he had told the servant. Her curiosity got the better of her and she asked, "A wedding or a circumcision?"

Smiling he replied, "Whichever you wish."

"Do you have an uncircumcised boy or a bridegroom?"

"I've got everything."

She gave him a warning look as if to say, "How tiresome you are!" Then she muttered sarcastically, "We'll be happy to serve you, whatever it happens to be."

Al-Sayyid Ahmad raised his hands to the top of his head in a gesture of thanks. He said with a gravity that belied his intentions, "God bless you! All the same, I'm still determined to leave the choice to you."

She sighed with a rage that was half humorous and replied, "I prefer weddings, of course."

"But I'm a married man. I don't need any more wedding processions."

She yelled at him, "What a joker you are ... Then let it be a circumcision."

"So be it."

She asked cautiously, "Your son?"

Twisting his mustache, he answered simply, "Me."

The sultana let out a flowing laugh. She decided to stop thinking about the question of an evening performance. She guessed what kind of performance it would be. She shouted at him, "What a crafty man you are. If my arm were long enough I'd break your back."

He rose and approached, saying, "I won't deprive you of anything you want." He sat down beside her. She started to hit him but hesitated and then stopped. He asked her anxiously, "Why don't you honor me with a beating?"

She shook her head and replied scornfully, "I'm afraid I would have to repeat my ritual ablutions."

He asked longingly, "May I hope we can pray together?" He privately asked God's forgiveness as soon as he had made this joke. Although there were no limits to his impudence when he was intoxicated by his sense of humor, his heart was always troubled and uneasy until he secretly and sincerely asked God's forgiveness for the humorous excesses of his tongue.

The woman asked with ironic coquetry, "Do you mean, reverend sir, the kind of prayer the muezzin says is better than sleep?"

"No, prayer which is a form of sleep."

She could not keep herself from saying with a laugh, "What a man you are! On the outside you are dignified and pious, but inside you're licentious and debauched. Now I really believe what I was told about you."

Al-Sayyid Ahmad sat up with interest and asked, "What were you told? . . . May God spare us the evil of what people say."

"They told me you're a womanizer and a heavy drinker."

He sighed audibly in relief and commented, "I thought it would be criticism of some fault, thank God."

"Didn't I tell you you're a crafty sinner?"

"Here's the evidence, then, that I've won your acceptance, God willing."

The woman raised her head haughtily and replied, "Keep your distance. . . . I'm not like the women you've had. Zubayda is known, if I do say so myself, for her self-respect and good taste."

The man raised his hands to his chest and looked at her in a way both challenging and gentle. He remarked calmly, "It's when a man is tested that he's honored or despised."

"How come you're so cocky when, according to you, you haven't even been circumcised yet?"

Al-Sayyid Ahmad laughed loudly for a long time. Then he said, "You don't believe me, you circumciser. Well, if you're in doubt . . ."

She punched him in the shoulder before he could finish his sentence. He stopped talking, and then they burst out laughing together. He was happy she laughed along with him. He surmised that, given both the veiled and open remarks that had passed between them, her laughter constituted an announcement of her consent. The flirtatious smile, visible in her eyes with their shadow of kohl, served to confirm this idea in his mind. He thought he would greet this flirtation in kind, but she cautioned him, "Don't make me think even worse of you."

Her statement reminded him of her reference to things she had heard. He asked her with interest, "Who's been talking to you about me?"

She replied tersely, giving him an accusing look, "Jalila."

This name took him by surprise. It was like a critic interrupting their tête-à-tête. He smiled in a way that showed he was uncomfortable. Jalila was the famous performer he had loved for such a long time, until they separated after the fire had died in their romance. They continued to like each other but had gone their separate ways. Relying on his experience with women, he thought he had better say, as though he really meant it, "God curse her face and voice!" Then, trying to avoid this topic, he continued: "Let's skip all this and talk seriously."

She asked sarcastically, "Doesn't Jalila deserve a gentler and more gracious comment? Or are you always like this when you talk about a woman you've dumped?"

Al-Sayyid Ahmad felt a little uneasy, but he was awash with the sexual conceit aroused in him when a new lover discussed one of his former girlfriends. He enjoyed the sweet intoxication of triumph for some time. Then he remarked with his customary suavity, "In the presence of beauty like yours, I'm unable to put it aside for memories that are buried and forgotten."

Although the sultana retained her ironic look, she responded to the praise by raising her eyebrows and concealing a faint smile that had stolen across her lips. All the same, she addressed him scornfully: "A merchant is generous with his sweet talk until he gets what he wants."

"We merchants deserve to go to paradise because people are so unfair to us."

She shrugged her shoulders with disdain and then asked him with unconcealed interest, "When were you seeing each other?"

He waved his arm as if to say, "What a long time ago!" Then he muttered, "Ages and ages ago."

She laughed mockingly and said in a tone of revenge, "In the days of your youth, which have passed."

He looked at her reproachfully and said, "I wish I could suck the venom from your tongue."

She continued with what she was saying in the same tone: "She took you in when your flesh was firm and left you nothing but bones."

He gestured with his forefinger to caution her, saying, "I'm one of those hardy men who get married in their sixties."

"Motivated by passion or senility?"

He roared with laughter and said, "Lady, fear God. Let's have a serious talk."

"Serious? . . . You mean about the evening's entertainment you came to arrange?"

"I seek entertainment for a whole lifetime."

"A whole lifetime or just half?"

"May our Lord grant us what is good for us. . . ."

"May our Lord grant us what is pleasant."

He secretly requested God's forgiveness in advance before he asked, "Shall we recite the opening prayer of the Qur'an?"

She jumped up suddenly, ignoring his invitation, and cried out in alarm, "My Lord . . . it's later than I thought. I have an important engagement tonight."

Al-Sayyid Ahmad rose too. He stretched out his hand to take hers. He spread open her palm tinted with henna and looked at it with desire and fascination. He kept on holding it even after she tried repeatedly to withdraw it. Finally she pinched his finger and raised her hand to his mustache. She shouted menacingly to him, "Let go of me or you'll leave my house with only half a mustache."

He saw that her forearm was near his mouth. He abandoned the dispute and slowly brought his lips to her arm until they sank into its soft flesh. A delicious fragrance of carnations wafted from her. He sighed and murmured, "Till tomorrow?"

She escaped from his hand without any resistance this time. She gave him a lengthy look. Then she smiled and recited softly:

> My sparrow, Mother, my little bird,
> I'll play and show him what I have learned.

She repeated these lines several times as she saw him out. Al-Sayyid Ahmad left the room singing the opening of this song in a low voice both dignified and sedate. He seemed to be examining the words for their hidden meaning.

IN THE home of the singer Zubayda there was a room like a hall in the middle of her residence that was dubbed the recital chamber. Actually it was a hall for which new uses had been found. Perhaps the most important of these for her and her troupe was rehearsing their songs and learning new material. It had been chosen because it was far from the public street and separated from it by bedrooms and reception chambers. Its size also made it a suitable location for her private parties, which usually were either exorcisms or recitals to which she would invite her special friends and close acquaintances. The motive for hosting these parties was not simply generosity, for any generosity manifested was almost always that of the guests themselves. The aim was to increase the number of fine friends able to invite her to perform at their parties or to help promote her by praising her in the circles where they were received. It was also from these men that she selected lover after lover.

Now it was al-Sayyid Ahmad Abd al-Jawad's turn to honor the festive hall, accompanied by some of his most distinguished acquaintances. He had displayed boundless energy following the daring meeting that had taken place between them at her house. His messengers had immediately taken her a generous gift of candied nuts and dried fruit, sweets and other presents, in addition to a stove he commissioned which was decorated with silver plate. These gifts were all a token of the affection to follow. Leaving the guest list entirely up to him, the sultana had invited him to a get-acquainted party in honor of their newfound love.

The chamber was remarkable for its attractive, Egyptian look. A row of comfortable sofas with brocade upholstery, suggesting both luxury and dissipation, stretched out on either side of the sultana's divan, which was flanked by mattresses and cushions for her troupe. The long expanse of floor was covered with carpets of many different colors and types. On a table suspended from the right wall, halfway along it, candles were arranged in candelabra where they looked as lovely and intense as a beauty mark on a cheek. There was a huge lamp hanging from the peak of a skylight in the center of the ceiling. The skylight's windows looked out on the roof terrace and were left open on warm evenings, but closed when it was cold.

Zubayda sat cross-legged on the divan. At her right was Zanuba, the lute player, her foster daughter. On her left was Abduh, the blind performer on the zitherlike qanun. The women of the troupe sat on both sides, some clasping tambourines, others stroking their conical drums or playing with finger cymbals. The sultana had selected for al-Sayyid Ahmad the first seat on the right. The other men, his friends, found places for themselves without any hesitation, as though they lived there. This was not odd since there was nothing novel about the situation for them and it was not the first time they had seen the sultana. Al-Sayyid Ahmad presented his friends to the performer, beginning with al-Sayyid Ali, the flour merchant.

Zubayda laughed and said, "Al-Sayyid Ali is no stranger to me. I performed at his daughter's wedding last year."

Then he turned to the copper merchant. One of the men accused him of being a fan of the vocalist Bamba Kashar, and the merchant quickly remarked, "Lady, I've come to repent."

The introductions continued until everyone was presented. Then Jaljal, the maid, brought in glasses of wine and served the guests. The men started to feel a vitality mixed with liberality and mirth. Al-Sayyid Ahmad was undeniably the bridegroom of the party. His friends called him that and he felt it too, deep inside. At first he had been a little uncomfortable in a way rare for him but had concealed his discomfort with an extra amount of laughter and mirth. Once he began drinking, the embarrassment left him spontaneously and his composure returned. He threw himself wholeheartedly into the excitement.

Whenever he felt a surge of desire – and desires are aroused at musical entertainments – he would gaze greedily at the sultana of the soiree. His eyes would linger on the folds of her massive body. He felt good about the blessing fortune had bestowed on him. He congratulated himself on the sweet delights he could look forward to that night and following ones.

" 'It's when a man is tested that he's honored or despised.' I challenged her with this declaration. I've got to live up to my word. I wonder what she's like as a woman and how far she'll go? I'll discover the truth at a suitable time. In any case, I'll play by her rules. To ensure a victory over an opponent, you must assume she's vigilant and strong. I won't deviate from my long-standing practice of making my own pleasure a secondary objective after hers, which is the real goal and climax. In that way my pleasure will be achieved in the most perfect fashion."

Despite his great number of amorous adventures, out of all the different varieties of love, al-Sayyid Ahmad had experienced only lust. All the same, he had progressed in his pursuit of it to its purest and most delicate form. He was not simply an animal. In addition to his sensuality, he was endowed with a delicacy of feeling, a sensitivity of emotion, and an ingrained love for song and music. He had elevated lust to its most exalted type. It was for the sake of this lust alone that he had married the first time and then for the second. Over the course of time, his conjugal love was affected by calm new elements of affection and familiarity, but in essence it continued to be based on bodily desire. When an emotion is of this type, especially when it has acquired a renewed power and exuberant vitality, it cannot be content with only one form of expression. Thus he had shot off in pursuit of all the varieties of love and passion, like a wild bull. Whenever desire called, he answered, deliriously and enthusiastically. No woman was anything more than a body to him. All the same, he would not bow his head before that body unless he found it truly worthy of being seen, touched, smelled, tasted, and heard. It was lust, yes, but not bestial or blind. It had been refined by a craft that was at least partially an art, setting his lust in a framework of delight, humor, and good cheer. Nothing was so like his lust as his body, since both were huge and powerful, qualities that bring to mind roughness and savagery. Yet both concealed within them grace, delicacy, and affection, even though he might intentionally cloak those characteristics at times with sternness and severity. While he was devouring the sultana with his glances he did not limit his active imagination to having sex with her. It also wandered through various dreams of amusing pastimes and tuneful celebrations.

Zubayda felt the warmth of his gaze. Glancing around at the faces of the guests vainly and coquettishly, she told him,

"Bridegroom, control yourself. Aren't you embarrassed in front of your associates?"

"There's no point trying to be chaste in the presence of such a prodigious and voluptuous body."

The songstress released a resounding laugh. Then with great delight she asked the men, "What do you think of your friend?"

They all replied in one breath, "He's excused!"

At this the blind qanun player shook his head to the right and left, his lower lip hanging open. He muttered, "He's excused who gives a warning."

Although the man's proverb was well received, the lady turned on him in mock anger and punched him in the chest, yelling, "You hush and shut your big mouth."

The blind man accepted the blow laughingly. He opened his mouth as though to speak but closed it again to be safe. The woman turned her head toward al-Sayyid Ahmad and told him threateningly, "This is what happens to people who get out of line."

Pretending to be alarmed, he replied, "But I came to learn how to get out of line."

The woman struck her chest with her hand and shouted, "What cheek! . . . Did you all hear what he said?"

More than one of them said at the same time, "It's the best thing we've heard so far."

One of the group added, "You ought to hit him if he doesn't get out of line."

Someone else suggested, "You ought to obey him so long as he stays out of line."

The woman raised her eyebrows to show an astonishment she did not feel and asked, "Do you love being naughty this much?"

Al-Sayyid Ahmad sighed and said, "May our Lord perpetuate our naughtiness."

At that the performer picked up a tambourine and said, "Here's something better for you to listen to."

She struck the tambourine in a rather nonchalant way, but the sound rose above the babbling commotion like an alarm and silenced it. The noise of her tambourine teased their ears. Everyone gradually dropped what he was doing. The members of the troupe got ready to play while the gentlemen drained their glasses.

Then they gazed at the sultana. The room was so silent it almost declared their eagerness to enjoy the music.

The maestra gestured to her troupe and they burst out playing an overture by the composer Muhammad Uthman. Heads started to sway with the music. Al-Sayyid Ahmad surrendered himself to the resonant sound of the qanun, which set his heart on fire. Echoes of many different melodies from a long era filled with nights of musical ecstasy burst into flame within him, as though small drops of gasoline had fallen on a hidden ember. The qanun certainly was his favorite instrument, not only because of the virtuosity of a performer like al-Aqqad, but because of something about the very nature of the strings. Although he knew he was not going to hear a famous virtuoso like al-Aqqad or al-Sayyid Abduh, his enthusiastic heart made up for the defects of the performance with its passion.

The moment the troupe finished the five-part overture, the singer began "The sweetness of your lips intoxicates me." The troupe joined her enthusiastically. The most movingly beautiful part of this song was the harmony between two voices: the blind musician's gruff, expansive one and Zanuba the lutanist's delicate, childlike one. Al-Sayyid Ahmad was deeply touched. He quickly drained his glass to join in the chorus. In his haste to start singing he forgot to clear his throat and at first sounded choked. Others in the group soon plucked up their courage and followed his example. Soon everyone in the room was part of the troupe singing as though with one voice.

When that piece was finished, al-Sayyid Ahmad expected to hear some instrumental solos and vocal improvisation as usual, but Zubayda capped the ending with one of her resounding laughs to demonstrate her pleasure and amazement. She began to congratulate the new members of the troupe jokingly and asked them what they would like to hear. Al-Sayyid Ahmad was secretly distressed and momentarily depressed, since his passion for singing was intense. Few of those around him noticed anything. Then he realized that Zubayda, like most others of her profession, including the famous Bamba Kashar herself, was not capable of doing solo improvisations. He hoped she would pick a light ditty of the kind sung to the ladies at a wedding party. He would prefer that to having her attempt a virtuoso piece and fail to get it right. He tried to spare his ears the suffering he anticipated by suggesting an easy song suitable for the lady's voice. He asked, "What would you all think of 'My sparrow, Mother'?"

He looked at her suggestively, trying to arouse in her an interest in this ditty with which she had crowned their conversation a few days before in the reception room. A voice from the far end of the hall cried out sarcastically, "It would be better to ask your mother for that one."

The suggestion was quickly lost in the outburst of guffaws that spoiled his plan for him. Before he could try again, one group requested "O Muslims, O People of God" and another wanted "Get well, my heart."

Zubayda was wary about favoring one bunch over the other and announced she would sing for them "I'm an accomplice against myself." Her announcement was warmly received. Al-Sayyid Ahmad saw no alternative to resigning himself and seeking his pleasure in wine and dreams about his promising chances for the evening. His lips gleamed with a sincere smile that the gang of inebriates cheerfully perceived. He was touched by the woman's desire to imitate the virtuosi in order to please her knowledgeable listeners, even though her actions were not totally free of the vanity common among singers.

As the troupe was getting ready to sing, one of the men rose and called out enthusiastically, "Give the tambourine to al-Sayyid Ahmad. He's an expert."

Zubayda shook her head in amazement and asked, "Really?"

Al-Sayyid Ahmad moved his fingers quickly and nimbly as if giving her a demonstration of his skill. Zubayda smiled and remarked, "No wonder! You were Jalila's pupil."

The gentlemen laughed uproariously. The laughter continued until Mr. al-Far's voice rose to ask the sultana, "What are you planning to teach him?"

She replied teasingly, "I'll teach him to play the qanun. Wouldn't you like that?"

Al-Sayyid Ahmad implored her, "Teach me internal repetitions, if you will."

Many of them encouraged him to join the musicians and he took the tambourine. Then he rose and removed his outer cloak. In his chestnut caftan he looked so tall and broad that he could have been a charger prancing on its hind legs. He pushed back his sleeves and went to the divan to take his place beside the lady. To make room for him she rose halfway and scooted to the left. Her red dress slipped back to reveal a strong, fleshy leg which was white brushed with pink where she had plucked the hair. The bottom of her leg was adorned with a gold anklet that could barely encompass it.

One of the men who glimpsed that sight shouted in a voice like thunder, "The Ottoman caliphate forever!"

Al-Sayyid Ahmad, who was ogling the woman's breasts, yelled after him, "Say: the Ottoman grand brassiere forever!"

The performer shouted to caution them: "Lower your voices or the English will throw us in jail for the night."

Al-Sayyid Ahmad, whose head was feeling the effects of the wine, yelled, "If you're with me, I'll go for life at hard labor."

More than one voice called out, "Death to anyone who lets you two go there alone."

The woman wanted to end the debate begun by the sight of her leg and handed the tambourine to al-Sayyid Ahmad. She told him, "Show me what you can do."

He took the tambourine and smiled as he rubbed it with the palm of his hand. His fingers began to strike it skillfully and then the other instruments started playing. Zubayda glanced at the eyes fixed on her and sang:

> *I'm an accomplice against myself*
> *When my lover steals my heart.*

Al-Sayyid Ahmad found himself in a wonderfully intoxicating situation. The sultana's breath fluttered toward him each time she turned his way, meeting the vapors which rose to the top of his head with every sip. He quickly forgot the refrains of the famous musicians al-Hamuli, Muhammad Uthman, and al-Manilawi, and lived in the present, happy and content. The inflections of her voice made the strings of his heart vibrate. His energy flared up and he beat the tambourine in a way no professional could match. His intoxication became a burning, titillating, inspiring, raging drunkenness the moment the woman sang:

> *You who are going to see him*
> *Take a kiss from me as a pledge for my*
> *Sweetheart's mouth.*

His companions kept pace with him or surpassed him as the wine made its ultimate impact on them. They were so agitated by desire they seemed trees dancing in the frenzy of a hurricane.

Slowly, gradually the time came for the song to close. Zubayda ended by repeating the same phrase that began it: "I'm an accomplice against myself," but with a spirit that was calm, reflective, and valedictory, and then final. The melodies vanished like an airplane carrying a lover over the horizon. Although the conclusion was greeted by a storm of applause and clapping, silence soon reigned over the hall, for their souls were worn out by all the exertion and emotion. A period passed when nothing was heard except the sound of someone coughing, clearing his throat, striking a match, or uttering a word that required no reply. The guests realized it was time to say good night. Some could be seen looking for articles of clothing they had stripped off in the heat of their musical ecstasy and placed behind them on the cushions. Others were having too good a time to leave until they had sipped every possible drop of this sweet wine.

One of these cried out, "We won't go until we have a wedding procession to present the sultana to al-Sayyid Ahmad."

The suggestion was warmly received and widely supported. Incredulous, the gentleman and the entertainer collapsed with laughter. Before they knew what was happening, several men had surrounded them and dragged them to their feet, gesturing to the troupe to commence the joyous anthem. The couple stood side by side, she like the ceremonial camel litter bound for Mecca and he like the camel. They were giants made less threatening by their good looks. Coquettishly she placed her arm under his and gestured to those surrounding them to clear the way. The woman with the tambourine started playing it, and the troupe along with many of the guests began to sing the wedding song: "Look this way, you handsome fellow." The bridal couple proceeded with deliberate steps, strutting forward, animated by both the music and the wine.

When she saw this sight, Zanuba stopped playing her lute and could not keep from emitting a long, ringing trill or shriek of joy. If it could have taken bodily form, it would have been a twisting tongue of flame splitting the heavens like a shooting star.

Their friends tried to outdo each other in offering their congratulations: "A happy marriage and many sons."

"Healthy children who are good dancers and singers."

One of the men shouted to caution them, "Don't put off until
tomorrow what you can do today."

The troupe kept playing and the friends kept waving their hands
until al-Sayyid Ahmad and the woman disappeared through the
door leading to the interior of the house.

17

AL-SAYYID AHMAD was sitting at his desk in the store when Yasin walked in unexpectedly. The visit was not merely unexpected but extraordinary, since it was unusual for the young man to visit his father at the store. Even at home he avoided him to the best of his ability. Moreover, Yasin looked absentminded and serious. He approached his father, giving him nothing more than a mechanical salute. Seeming to forget himself, he neglected to show the pronounced respect and deference customary when in his father's presence. Then he said in a voice that showed how upset he was, "Greetings, Father. I've come to talk to you about something important."

His father looked up at him quizzically. Although he felt anxious he relied on his willpower to conceal it and asked calmly, "Good news, God willing."

Jamil al-Hamzawi brought Yasin a chair as he welcomed him, and his father ordered him to have a seat. The young man brought the chair closer to the desk and sat down. He seemed to hesitate for a few moments. Then he sighed in exasperation at his own hesitation and said in a quavering voice with touching brevity, "The thing is, my mother's going to get married."

Although al-Sayyid Ahmad was expecting bad news, his forebodings had not wandered in the direction of this outgrown corner of his past. Therefore the announcement caught him off guard. He frowned as he always did when he remembered anything about his first wife. It upset him and he was alarmed because of the direct threat to his son's honor. "Who told you so?" he inquired, asking not to seek information but to escape from an unpleasant reality or provide himself time to deliberate and calm his nerves.

"Her relative Shaykh Hamdi. He visited me at al-Nahhasin School and told me the news. He confirmed it would take place within a month."

The news, then, was a fact beyond doubt, and it was nothing

novel for her. If the past was any guide, it would not be her last marriage either. But what sin had this youth committed to be subjected to this harsh punishment, which hurt him again and again? The man felt pity and affection for his son. It was hard on him that he, to whom people turned in times of trouble, could do nothing to relieve Yasin's pain. He asked himself what he would have done if he had been afflicted with such a mother. He was distressed, and his pity and affection for his son became more intense. Then he wanted to ask about her fiancé but resisted the temptation, because he was worried about making his son's wound worse and could not bring himself to ask. Given the current disaster, curiosity about the woman who had been his wife would not be appropriate.

Yasin, as though reading his mind, volunteered emotionally, "And who's she marrying! A person called Ya'qub Zaynhum who has a bakery in al-Darrasa. He's in his thirties!"

He became even more agitated, and his voice trembled as he spat out the final phrase like a fish bone. His feeling of disgust and aversion passed over to his father, who began repeating to himself: "In his thirties. . . . What a disgrace! It's adultery disguised as marriage." The man was angry because his son was and for his own sake too. He always got angry when news of her private affairs reached him. It appeared to reawaken his sense of responsibility for what she did, since she had once been his wife. He also seemed, even after such a long time, to be hurt by the fact that she had escaped from his discipline and had disobeyed his will. He remembered the days he had lived with her, however few, with the exceptional clarity of a man recalling an illness he has had. It was hardly surprising that a man as sure of himself as he was should see in the mere wish to disobey him an inexcusable crime and crushing defeat.

Moreover, she had been and perhaps still was beautiful and full of feminine attractions. He had enjoyed living with her for a few months until she displayed some resistance to his will, which he imposed on close family members. She saw no harm in enjoying some freedom, even if it was limited to visiting her father from time to time. Al-Sayyid Ahmad had grown angry and had attempted to restrain her, at first by scolding her and then by violent beatings. The spoiled woman had fled to her parents, and anger had blinded the haughty man. He thought the best way to discipline her and bring her back to her senses was to divorce her for a time – naturally just for a time, since he was very attached to her. He did divorce her and pretended to forget about her for a period of days and then weeks, while he waited for a representative of her family to bring him good news. When no one knocked on his door, he swallowed his pride and sent someone to sound out the situation to prepare for a reconciliation. The messenger returned saying they would welcome him on the condition that he would not forbid her to leave the house and would not beat her. He had expected that they would agree without any stipulation or condition. He became violently angry and swore never to marry her again. Thus they had gone their separate ways, and Yasin's fate was to be born away from his father and to suffer humiliation and pain in his mother's house.

Although the woman had married more than once and although, in her son's eyes, marriage was the most honorable of her offenses, this anticipated marriage seemed more outrageous than the previous ones and more calculated to cause pain. The woman was at least forty, and Yasin was now fully grown and aware of his ability to defend his honor from harm and humiliation. He was no longer in his previous situation when, because of his youth, he could only react to the disturbing rumors about his mother with astonishment, alarm, and tears. He now considered himself a responsible adult who should not sit on his hands when humiliated. These thoughts passed through the father's head. He was painfully aware of how serious they were, but he resolved to downplay their significance as best he could in order to spare his eldest son the vexation.

He shook his broad shoulders as though it did not matter very much and said, "Didn't we vow to consider her a person who never existed?"

Yasin replied sadly and despondently, "But she does exist, Father. No matter what we vow, she continues to be my mother so long as God spares her, both in my eyes and in everyone else's."

The young man breathed out heavily. With the handsome, black eyes he had inherited from his mother he gazed at his father in a penetrating plea for help. He seemed to be telling him, "You're my powerful, mighty father. Give me your hand."

Al-Sayyid Ahmad was even more profoundly moved but continued to pretend to be calm and unconcerned. He remarked, "I don't blame you for feeling hurt, but don't exaggerate. I can understand your anger, but if you'll just be reasonable, you'll get over it without too much trouble. Ask yourself calmly how her marriage harms you. . . . A woman gets married? Women get married every day and every hour. In view of her past conduct, she cannot be held responsible for a marriage like this. Perhaps she even ought to be thanked for it. As I've told you repeatedly, your mind won't be at rest till you stop thinking about her and pretend she never existed. Trust in God and don't take it so hard. No matter what people say, you should find consolation in the fact that marriage is a legal relationship sanctioned by religion."

He said these things without meaning them, since they totally contradicted his extreme, innate sensitivity over anything relating to family etiquette. He said it all with such warmth that he seemed to be telling the truth, thanks to the diplomatic skills he had acquired while learning to become a wise arbitrator and beneficent intermediary capable of settling disputes between people. Although his words were not lost on Yasin, since it was inconceivable that any of his children would ignore what he said, the young man's anger was too profound to evaporate all at once. The words affected him like a cup of cold water poured into a boiling pot.

He immediately replied to his father, "It's a legal relationship of course, Father, but at times it seems as far removed as possible from piety or legality. I ask myself: What could motivate this man to marry her?"

Despite the gravity of the situation the father said to himself a bit sarcastically, "You ought to ask what's motivating her!"

Before al-Sayyid Ahmad could answer, Yasin continued: "It's greed and nothing else."

"Or maybe a sincere desire to marry her."

The youth flew into a rage and shouted in a hurt and furious way, "No, it's nothing but greed!"

Although it was a serious situation, al-Sayyid Ahmad could not help noticing the sharpness of the tone with which his son had addressed him. Given his son's condition and grief, he felt uncomfortable simply reaffirming what he had said before. Hearing no further objection, Yasin continued with relative composure: "What makes him marry a woman ten years older is greed for her money and property."

The father shrewdly saw the benefit in shifting the conversation to this topic. It would divert the young man from dwelling on more sensitive and painful matters. Thinking about that man might keep him from examining his mother's motives for getting married. In addition, he realized how well founded his son's opinion probably was regarding this fiancé. He was quickly convinced and embraced his son's fears. Yes, Haniya, Yasin's mother, was well-to-do. Her fortune in real estate had remained intact in spite of her experiments with marriage and love. Although in the past she had been a beautiful young woman with both magic and majesty, to be feared and not feared for, now it was unlikely that she had as much control over herself as she once did, not to mention control over others. Her fortune might well be squandered on the battlefield of love, where she was no longer so competitive. It would be outrageous in the extreme if Yasin emerged from the inferno of this tragedy with both wounded honor and empty hands.

Al-Sayyid Ahmad remarked to his son as though thinking it over by himself, "I see you're right, son, in what you say. A woman her age is an easy mark and could well be a temptation to greedy men. What can we do? Should we seek to contact that man and force him to abandon his adventure? To try to intimidate him, threatening and menacing him, runs contrary to our ethics and what people know we stand for. To attempt to entreat and persuade him would be a humiliation our honor could not bear. That leaves us only the woman herself. I'm not overlooking your break with her that she richly deserved and still does. The truth is, I'd not be comfortable about your reestablishing a link with her, if the new circumstances did not require it. Necessity has its own rules. No matter how difficult it is for you to visit her, it's your own mother you're returning to, after all. Who knows? Perhaps your surprise appearance on her horizon will bring her back to her right mind."

Yasin looked like a hypnotist's subject in the moments preceding the hypnotic suggestion. He was silent and dazed. His state revealed the profound impact his father had on him or indicated that this suggestion had not taken him by surprise. All the same, he stammered, "Isn't there any better solution?"

His father replied forcefully and plainly, "I think it is the best solution."

As though addressing himself, Yasin asked, "How can I go back to her? How can I force myself back into a past I fled and want more than anything to erase from my life? I have no mother . . . no mother at all."

Despite what Yasin appeared to be saying, his father felt he had succeeded in converting him to his opinion. He told him diplomatically, "True, but I think if you appear in front of her, after this long absence, it will have an effect. Perhaps if she sees you before her, a full-grown man, her maternal instincts will be awakened. Then she'll mend her ways and shy away from anything that might damage your honor. Who knows?"

Plunged in thought, Yasin calmed his mind, heedless of his despairing, anguished appearance. He was shuddering from fear of the scandal awaiting him. That was possibly the most heinous thing troubling him, but his fear of losing the fortune he expected to inherit one day was no less appalling. What could he do? No matter how he approached the issue he could find no better solution than the one his father had suggested. Indeed, no matter how shaky he felt, the fact that the idea came from his father lent it, in his opinion, validity and spared him a lot of worry. "So be it," he said to himself. Then, addressing his father, he said, "Just as you wish, Father."

18

WHEN HIS feet brought him to al-Gamaliya Street, he was so choked up he felt he would die. He had not been there for eleven years, eleven years that had passed without his heart yearning for it once. Any memory of the area that had flashed into his mind had been surrounded by a depressing black halo and ornamented with the stuff from which nightmares are woven. The truth was that he had not simply left home but, when the opportunity arose, had fled. Angry and dejected, he had turned his back on it and avoided it completely. It was not a place he sought out or even cut across on the way to some other district.

Yet it remained exactly the way it had been when he was growing up. Nothing had changed. The street was still so narrow a handcart would almost block it when passing by. The protruding balconies of the houses almost touched each other overhead. The small shops resembled the cells of a beehive, they were so close together and crowded with patrons, so noisy and humming. The street was unpaved, with gaping holes full of mud. The boys who swarmed along the sides of the street made footprints in the dirt with their bare feet. There was the same never-ending stream of pedestrian traffic. Uncle Hasan's snack shop and Uncle Sulayman's restaurant too remained just as he had known them. If it had not been for the bitterness of the past and his present suffering, a tender smile, which the child in him wished to display, might well have traced itself on his lips.

The cul-de-sac known as the Palace of Desire or Qasr al-Shawq came into sight. His heart pounded so strongly it almost deafened his ears. At the corner on the right could be seen baskets of oranges and apples arranged on the ground in front of the fruit store. He bit his lip and lowered his eyes in shame. The past was stained with dishonor and buried in the muck of disgrace, constantly emitting a lament of shame and pain. Even so, the past as a whole was not nearly so heavy a burden as this one store, which was a living symbol, enduring through time. Its owner, baskets, fruit, location, and memories seemed a combination of shameless boasting and painful defeat. Since the past was composed of events and memories, by its very nature it was apt to fade away and be forgotten. This store provided physical evidence to restore what had faded and fill in what he had forgotten. With each step he took toward the cul-de-sac he moved several steps away from the present, traveling back through time, in spite of himself.

He could almost see a boy in the store looking up at the proprietor and saying, "Mama invites you to come tonight." He saw him returning home with a bag of fruit, grinning happily. There he was, pointing the man out to his mother as they walked along the street. She was pulling him away by the arm, so he would not attract attention. He was sobbing with tears at the man's savage assault on his mother, which he re-created afresh with his current level of sophistication each time he thought about it, thus turning it into an ultimate manifestation of horror. These searing visions began to pursue him. He strove to flee from them, but no sooner would he escape from the clutches of one than he would be grabbed violently by another, stirring deep inside him a volcano of hatred and anger.

He kept on walking toward his destination but in a miserable state. "How can I enter this dead-end street when that store's at the corner? . . . And the man . . . will he be in his usual spot? I won't look that way. What devilish force is tempting me to look? Will he recognize me if our eyes meet? If he seems to recognize me, I'll kill him. But how could he know me? Not him, not anyone in this neighborhood . . . eleven years. I left here a boy and return a bull . . . with two horns! Don't we have the power to exterminate the poisonous vermin that keep on stinging us?"

He headed into the cul-de-sac, hurrying a little. He imagined people would be looking inquisitively at him and asking, "Where and when have we seen that face?" He went along the alley, which rose unevenly uphill, forcing himself to shake the suffocating dust from his face and head, if only temporarily. To make it easier to carry through with his resolve, he distanced himself from his surroundings, which he began to study. He told himself, "Don't be impatient with this tiresome street. When you were young you really enjoyed sliding down it on a board." All the same, when he could see the wall of the house, he started wondering again, "Where am I going? To my mother! . . . How amazing! I don't

believe it. What will I say to her? How will she receive me?...
I wish...."

He turned right, into a subsidiary cul-de-sac, and approached
the first door on the left. Without the slightest doubt it was the old
house. He crossed the street to it the way he did when he was
young, without any hesitation or reflection, as though he had only
left it the day before, but this time he stormed through the door
with unaccustomed anguish. He climbed the stairs with slow,
heavy steps. Despite his anxiety, he caught himself examining
things carefully to compare them with what he remembered. He
found the stairway a little narrower. It was worn in some places
and small chips had fallen from the edges of the treads where they
protruded over the risers. His memories quickly obscured the
present entirely. In this state he passed the two floors that were
rented out and reached the top one. He stopped for a few
moments to regain his strength, his chest heaving. Then he
shook his shoulders disdainfully and knocked on the door. After
a minute or so, it was opened, revealing a middle-aged servant.
The moment she saw that he was a stranger, she hid behind the
door and asked him politely what he wanted.

Although it was unreasonable to expect the servant to recognize
him, he became agitated and resolutely made his way inside,
heading for the parlor. He said in a commanding voice, "Tell
your mistress Yasin's here."

"What do you suppose the servant thinks of me?" He turned
around and saw her hastening away inside, either because his
imperious tone had cowed her or ... He bit his lip and walked
into the room. In his haste and fury he assumed unconsciously that
it was the parlor, although in different circumstances his memory
would have known every corner of the house without a guide.
Then, dredging up memories, he would have made a tour from
the bath, to which he was carried in tears, on to the enclosed
balcony, where evening after evening he had watched wedding
processions, through the spaces between the wooden spindles.
Was the current furniture in the room the same as in the distant
past?

All he remembered of the old furnishings was a long mirror set
on a gilded basin with openings in the cover, from which sprouted
artificial roses of various colors. There were candelabra attached to
the edges of the mirror. Dangling from their necks were crystal

crescents, which he had frequently enjoyed playing with while he looked through them at the room, which would shimmer in strange disguises. He could remember their fascination even when he could not see them. There was no reason to wonder, for today's furnishings were different and not merely because they were newer. The decor of a frequently married woman was subject to change and renovation, in the same way that his mother had traded in his father, the coal dealer, and the master sergeant. Yasin felt tense and anxious. He perceived that he had not only knocked on the door of his former home but had scraped the scab off an inflamed sore and plunged into its pus.

He did not have long to wait, perhaps even less time than he imagined. He soon heard quick footsteps approaching and a person talking to herself. The voice was loud, but Yasin could not make out the words. Then he sensed she was there, although his back was turned to the doorway. Her shoulder jarred against the second door, which was still closed. He heard her call out breathlessly, "Yasin! My son! . . . How can I believe my eyes? . . . My Lord. . . . You've become a man. . . ."

Blood rushed to his beefy face. He turned toward her anxiously, not knowing how to address her or how their meeting would turn out, but the woman spared him from having to form any plan. She rushed to him and put her arms around him. She embraced him nervously and intensely. She began kissing his chest, the highest part of his tall body her lips could reach. Then she was sobbing and her eyes were bathed in tears. She buried her face against his breast, forgetting herself for a while until she could catch her breath. All that time he had not moved or spoken a word. He felt deeply and painfully the unbearable awkwardness of his rigidity, yet no indication of life, of any life at all, was revealed by him. He remained motionless and dumb. He was profoundly touched, although at first it was not clear to him what kind of emotion it was. Despite the warmth of his reception he experienced no desire to throw himself into her arms or kiss her. He was unable to pluck out the sad memories lodged inside him like a chronic disease afflicting him since childhood.

Although he was resolved and determined to clear the past from the stage of the present and retain control of his mind and his wits, the discarded past threw dark shadows on the surface of his heart, like a fly brushed away from the mouth which has left behind infectious germs. He perceived at that terrifying moment, more than he had throughout his past life, the sad truth that had clouded his heart for a long time: he no longer felt anything for his mother. The woman raised her head, as though beseeching him to bring his face close to hers. He was not able to refuse and leaned over. She kissed him on the cheeks and forehead. As they embraced, their eyes met, and he kissed her forehead, moved by his frustration at being so ill at ease and embarrassed, not by any other sentiment.

Then he heard her murmur, "She told me Yasin was here. I said, 'Yasin! Who could that be? But who else could he be? I only have one Yasin, the person who deprived himself of my house and deprived me of him. So what has happened? How come he's accepted my invitation after such a long time?' I ran here like a madwoman, not believing my ears. Here you are. You, not someone else, praise to God. You left me a boy and have returned a man. I have been dying to see you and you didn't even know I was alive."

She took him by the arm and led him to the sofa. He accompanied her, asking himself when this tumultuous wave of affectionate welcome would roll by so he could see the way clear to achieve his objective. He began to look at her stealthily, with a curiosity mixed with astonishment and anxiety. She seemed not to have changed except that her body had filled out. She still retained her beautiful figure. Her fair, round face and black eyes accentuated with kohl were just as beautiful as ever. He was not comfortable with the makeup he observed on her face and neck. He seemed to have been expecting that the years would have changed her dedication to taking care of herself and her passion for personal adornment even when she was all alone.

They sat side by side while she gazed affectionately at his face for a time and then measured his height and girth with admiring eyes. In a trembling voice she said, "Oh, my Lord. I can hardly believe my eyes. I'm in a dream. This is Yasin! A whole lifetime has gone up in smoke. How often I invited you and begged you. I sent you messenger after messenger. What can I say? . . . Let me ask you why you were so hardhearted to me. How could you turn away from my loving pleas? How could you turn a deaf ear to the cry of my grieving heart? How? . . . How? How could you forget you had a mother secluded here?"

Her final sentence caught his attention. He found it so strange that it invited both his sarcasm and his lamentation. It might well have slipped out because of her bewildered emotional state. Yes, there had been something, things, to remind him morning and evening that he had a mother, but what kind of thing or things?

He looked up anxiously without speaking, and their eyes met for a moment. The woman jumped in, longingly, to ask: "Why don't you speak?"

Yasin overcame his uncertainty with an audible sigh. Then he replied, as though finding no alternative, "I thought about you a lot, but my pain was unbearable."

Before he could complete what he was going to say, the light sparkling in her eyes faded, and a cloud of disappointment and list-lessness, driven by a wind from the depths of the sad past, settled over her pupils. She could not stand to look him in the eye any longer. She glanced down and said in a mournful voice, "I thought you were over the sorrows of the past. God knows they weren't worth the anger you displayed, keeping you away from me for eleven years."

He was amazed and infuriated by her criticism. He found it so reprehensible that it felt like salt poured on his angry wound. He was upset and would have exploded had it not been for the goal of his visit. Did the woman really mean what she said? Did her deeds really seem so insignificant to her? Or did she think he did not know what had happened? Although he controlled his nerves by exerting his will, he replied, "Are you saying my anger was unmerited? What took place merited the utmost anger and even more."

She let her back collapse against the sofa cushion. She cast him a look combining censure with an appeal for affection. She asked, "What's wrong with a woman remarrying after she gets divorced?"

He felt the fires of anger flaming through his veins, but the only apparent effect was the closing and tightening of his lips. She still made it seem so simple when she talked, as though she was convinced of the certainty of her innocence. She asked what was wrong with a woman getting married after she had been divorced. Fine, there was nothing wrong with some woman remarrying after her divorce, but if that woman was his mother, then it was a different story, a very different story. And to which marriage was she referring? There had been a marriage and a divorce, a marriage and a divorce, and then a marriage and a divorce. And there was something even more bitter and calamitous: that fruitmonger. . . . Did she remember him? Should he slap her in the face with those memories? Should he tell her frankly that he was no longer as ignorant as she thought? The intensity of his memories forced him to abandon his moderation this time. With great resentment he said, "Marriage and divorce, marriage and divorce, these are disgraceful affairs that should not have seemed right to you. How often they have shredded my heart, mercilessly."

She folded her arms across her chest in despondent surrender and remarked with mournful tenderness, "It's bad luck and nothing else. I've been unlucky, that's all there is to it."

He cut her off short, contracting his facial muscles and making his neck swell out, saying, as though the words he uttered were repulsive and revolted him, "Don't try to justify your actions. That only hurts me more. It's best if we pull down the curtain on our pains and hide them, since we're unable to wipe them out of existence."

She reluctantly took refuge in silence. Her heart was apprehensive that stormy memories would spoil the happy reunion and the hopes it had inspired in her. She began to observe him anxiously, as though trying to guess what he was concealing in his chest. When she could not stand his silence any longer she said plaintively, "Don't keep on tormenting me. You're my only child."

These words had a strange effect on him as though revealing to him for the first time that he truly was her son and that she was the only mother he had. All the same, it served him as a new incentive for outrage and anxiety. How many men! He turned his face away to conceal from her the traces of revulsion and anger sketched on its surface. He closed his eyes to flee from memories of vile sights.

At that moment he heard her say gently and imploringly, "Let me believe that my present happiness is a reality and not an illusion and that you came to me having rid your heart forever of all the sorrows of the past."

He gave her a long, hard look that revealed the serious nature of his thoughts, but there was nothing then that could have deterred him from trying to achieve his objective or even postponed it for a while. In a voice indicating that the words he spoke were far less important than what they implied, he remarked, "This depends on you. If you wish, you will have everything you want."

An anxious look could be seen in the woman's eyes, revealing the reawakened fear she was suffering. She replied, "I desire your love from the depths of my heart. How often have I yearned and striven for it, only to have you reject me mercilessly."

He was distracted from her affectionate words by the thought disturbing his mind. He continued: "What you crave is within your grasp. It is in your hands alone, if you take wisdom for your guide."

The woman asked with alarm, "What do you mean?"

Her feigned ignorance infuriated him and he said, "The import of my words is plain. You should refrain from doing something which, if the information reaching me is correct, would be a fatal blow for me."

She opened her eyes wide and then frowned with unconcealed despair. She muttered unwittingly, "What do you mean?"

Assuming that she was playing dumb on purpose he responded with rage, "I mean that you should annul the plan to remarry. Don't even consider doing something like this again. I'm not a child anymore. My patience won't stand for any further insults."

She bowed her head with unmistakable sorrow. She kept it down for some time, as though asleep. Then she raised her head slowly. The grief visible in her expression was too profound to measure. In a feeble voice, as though addressing herself, she said, "So you came because of that!"

Without considering what he was saying, he replied, "Yes!"

His answer could just as well have been a burst of gunfire, for everything around him changed and was transformed suddenly. The atmosphere became gloomy. Later, when he was alone, he went back over that conversation. He was comfortable with everything he had said until this final answer. He pondered over it, not knowing whether he had made a mistake or said the right thing.

His mother murmured as she looked around her, "How I wish my ears were deceiving me."

He realized only too late that he had gone too fast. He was angry with himself, furious, and poured his wrath on everything but himself. In an attempt to conceal his error at the expense of an even greater one, without stopping to think, he burst out: "You do just what you want without thinking about the consequences. I've always been the victim who has been hurt for no fault of his own. I would have thought that life would have taught you some lessons. So imagine my surprise when someone tells me you're planning to get married again. What a scandal, and it keeps recurring every few years, without any end in sight."

Her despair was so intense that she listened to him with apparent disinterest. Then she said sorrowfully, "You're a victim and I'm a victim. Each of us becomes a victim when your father and that woman who has taken you under her wing start whispering to you."

He was amazed by this shift in the course of the conversation. It appeared ludicrous to him, but he did not laugh. If anything, he was even angrier and said, "What bearing do my father and his wife have on this matter? Don't try to evade responsibility for your actions by throwing accusations in the faces of innocent people."

She protested in a voice like a groan, "I've never seen a son crueler than you.... Is this what you have to tell me after a separation of eleven years?"

He waved his hand in angry rejection and said sharply and furiously, "A sinful mother is likely to give birth to a cruel son."

"I'm no sinner.... I'm not a sinner. But you are as cruel and hard-hearted as your father."

He snorted with vexation and shouted, "We're back to my father! We have enough to discuss without him. Fear God and retreat from this new scandal . . . I wish to prevent this scandal at any price."

Her despair and sorrow were so intense that her voice sounded cold when she said, "How does it concern you?"

Astonished, he yelled back, "My mother's scandal shouldn't concern me?"

She replied with a sorrow blended with a slight amount of sarcasm, "You have the right to stop thinking of me as your mother."

"What do you mean?"

Ignoring his question, she muttered, "Since you have no feelings for me anymore, the best thing is for you to leave me and my concerns alone."

He shouted angrily, "What's already happened is all I can bear. I will not permit you to soil my reputation again."

Swallowing bitterly, she replied, "With God as my witness, there's nothing about it that will soil anyone's reputation."

He asked her disapprovingly, "Are you determined to go through with this marriage?"

She was silent for a time. Her head was bowed sadly and she was sunk in despair. A deep sigh escaped her. Then she said in a scarcely audible voice, "The matter's settled. The marriage contract has been drawn up. I'm no longer in a position to stop it."

Yasin jumped to his feet. His corpulent body was rigid and his face pale. Boiling with anger, he stared at her bowed head. Then he roared at her. "What a woman you are. . . . You criminal!"

She mumbled in a choked voice revealing her total surrender, "May God forgive you."

At that moment it occurred to him to blast her with what he knew about her past conduct, things she assumed he did not know, like the sinister story of the fruit seller. It would be a bomb he could drop on her head suddenly and blow her to bits, exacting the most hideous revenge. There was a terrifying flash from his eyes, flying out from beneath a frowning, gloomy brow with furrows that seemed threatening suggestions of forthcoming evil. He opened his mouth to drop his bombshell, but his tongue would not move. It stuck to the roof of his mouth as though forced there by his brain, which had not been blinded by his suffering to the calamity that would result. The dreadful instant passed with the speed of a fleeting earthquake during which a person feels death breathing on his face repeatedly for a few moments before everything returns to normal. He groaned but suppressed his anger. He backed down, without regrets. His forehead was dripping with cold sweat. Later, when he remembered various moments of this strange meeting, he recalled how he had acted then and felt relieved that he had held back, even though he was totally amazed by his restraint. What most surprised him was his feeling that he held back out of compassion for himself, not for her. Although he already knew what he would have revealed, he seemed to have been shielding his own honor rather than hers.

He blew off steam by striking his hands together and saying, "Criminal! . . . Scandal incarnate! . . . How I'll laugh at my foolishness every time I remember that I hoped something good might come from this visit. . . ." Then he continued sarcastically: "I'm amazed you can desire my affection after this."

She was distraught and sad. He heard her say, "My soul made me hope we could live together with love, in spite of everything. Your surprise visit inspired warm hopes in my heart that made me imagine I could give you the most exalted form of love my heart possesses . . . unblemished."

He backed away from her, as though fleeing from the tenderness of her words. Nothing could have excited his anger more than that. Filled with anger and despair, he sensed there was no longer anything to be gained from staying on in this hateful atmosphere. Turning around to make his way out, he said, "I wish I could kill you."

She lowered her eyes and said with unconcealed sorrow, "If you do, you'll relieve me of the sufferings of my life."

His anguish reached its peak. He threw her a final look filled with loathing. As he left the place, the floor of the room shook with his footsteps. When he reached the street and began to come to his senses, he remembered for the first time that he had forgotten to discuss the real estate and property. He had not mentioned so much as a word about it. How had he forgotten when it was the main reason for his visit?

19

MRS. AMINA opened the door and stuck her head in, saying with her customary tenderness, "Is there anything I can do for you, sir?"

She heard Fahmy's voice reply, "Come here, Mother. It will only take five minutes."

The woman entered, happy to comply with his request. She found him standing in front of his desk with a serious and concerned expression on his face. He took her hand and led her to a sofa near the door. He seated her and then sat down beside her, asking, "Is everyone asleep?"

The woman realized that she had not been invited to perform some trivial favor; otherwise what need was there for such care or this interest in privacy? His concern was quickly transmitted to her sensitive soul. She answered, "Khadija and Aisha went to their room at their usual time and I just left Kamal in his bed now."

Fahmy had been waiting for this moment since he retired to the study early in the evening. He had not been able to concentrate his attention on the book before him as usual. Off and on he had been following the conversation between his mother and his sisters, worried that they would never stop talking. Then he had listened to his mother and Kamal memorize a section of the seventy-eighth sura of the Qur'an, beginning: "Concerning what are they disputing?" Finally the house had become quiet and his mother had come to say good night. He had invited her to come in, and the tension of waiting had ended for him.

Although his mother was gentle as a dove and he felt no reserve or fear with her, he found it difficult to express what he wanted to say. He was overcome by a shy embarrassment. A long period of silence passed before, twitching his eyelids, he said, "Mother, I've invited you to advise me on a topic of great concern to me."

The woman's anxiety became so intense that her tender heart almost transformed it into fear. She replied, "I'm listening, son."

He breathed deeply to relieve his nerves and said, "What would you think if . . . I mean, isn't it possible that . . ." He came to a hesitant stop. Then he changed his tone and said delicately but anxiously, "I have no one to confide my innermost feelings to except for you . . . ."

"Of course, my son, that's only natural."

Taking courage from this, he said, "What would you think about trying to arrange an engagement between me and Maryam, the daughter of our neighbor al-Sayyid Muhammad Ridwan?"

At first Amina was astonished by his suggestion. Her initial response was a smile revealing more anxiety than joy. Then the fear that had gripped her while she was waiting for him to declare what he had in mind dispersed. Her smile broadened and shone, announcing her unqualified delight. She hesitated for some moments, not knowing what to say, then she burst out: "Is this really what you want? . . . I'll give you my frank opinion. . . . The day I go to arrange an engagement for you with a decent girl will be the happiest day of my life."

The youth blushed and said gratefully, "Thank you, Mother."

His mother gazed at him with a tender smile and remarked wistfully, "What a happy day! I've had to work hard and be patient many times. It's not too much to ask that God reward me for my exertion and patience with a day like this I've been hoping for; indeed with many more like it when I rejoice for you and your sisters Khadija and Aisha."

Her mind wandered off in happy dreams until something occurred to her that suddenly roused her. She drew her head back anxiously like a cat that sees a dog approaching. She muttered sympathetically, "But . . . your father?"

Fahmy smiled angrily and replied, "That's why I'm asking for your advice. . . ."

The woman thought a little. Then she said, as though to herself, "I don't know how he'll react to this request. Your father's a strange man, different from anyone else. What others take for granted, he considers a crime."

Fahmy frowned and said, "There's nothing in the affair to warrant anger or opposition."

"That's what I think."

"It goes without saying that the marriage won't take place until I have completed my studies and found myself a job."

"Of course, of course."

"So what could anyone object to, then?"

She gave him a look that seemed to say, "Who's going to remonstrate with your father if he doesn't care to listen to reason?" After all, her known stance toward him was blind obedience, whether he was right or wrong, just or tyrannical. What she said, however, was: "I hope your request will be blessed by acceptance."

The young man responded enthusiastically, "My father married when he was my age, and I don't even intend to do that. I'm planning to wait till my marriage seems so normal there will be no objection to it from any quarter . . . ."

"May our Lord grant our request."

They were still for a time, looking at each other, united by a single thought, knowing instinctively that they understood each other perfectly. It was not hard for them to read each other's thoughts. Then Fahmy expressed what was preoccupying both of them: "Now we need to think about who ought to raise the topic with him . . . ."

The woman smiled, but anxiety had robbed her smile of its spirit. She realized that her resourceful son was reminding her of a duty only she could perform. She did not object to doing it, since there was no alternative, but she accepted the task reluctantly, as she did many others. She asked God that it would end well. She remarked tenderly and affectionately, "Who should bring it up but me? . . . May our Lord be with us."

"I'm sorry. . . . If I could, I'd do it myself."

"I'll talk to him, and it will be successful, God willing. Maryam's a pretty girl, polite and from a fine family."

She was silent for a moment. Then, as though it had only just occurred to her, she asked, to clarify something, "But isn't she your age or even older?"

The youth replied uneasily, "That doesn't matter to me at all!"

Smiling, she replied, "With God's blessing; may our Lord be with us." Then, as she stood up, she added, "I leave you now in the Master's care. Until tomorrow." She leaned toward him and kissed him, then she left the room, closing the door behind her. She was astonished to find Kamal sitting on a sofa, bent over a notebook. She shouted at him, "What are you doing here?"

Smiling in embarrassment, he rose and replied, "I remembered that I'd left my English notebook. So I came to get it. Then I thought I'd review the words one more time."

Once again she went with him to the bedroom. She did not leave him until he was stretched out under the cover, but he did not fall asleep. The lively thoughts racing through his mind defeated sleep. As soon as he heard his mother's footsteps going upstairs to the top floor, he leapt out of bed. Then he opened the door and ran to his sisters' room. He shoved the door open and went in without shutting it, so the lamp in the hall could illumine some of the darkness blanketing the room. He rushed to the bed and whispered, "Khadija!"

Astonished, the young woman sat up in bed. He jumped up beside her, so excited he was breathless. As though not satisfied with entrusting the secret that had kept him from falling asleep to only one listener, he put his hand on Aisha and shook her. The girl had already noticed his arrival. She threw back the cover and raised her head, half out of curiosity and half in protest. She asked, "What brings you now?"

He paid no attention to her tone of protest, because he was certain that a single word hinting at his secret would be enough to turn them head over heels. His heart jumped with delight and joy at this thought. Then he whispered, as though he was afraid someone else would hear him, "I've got an amazing secret."

Khadija asked him, "What secret? . . . Tell us what you've got and show us how clever you are."

He could not conceal it any longer. He replied, "My brother Fahmy wants to get engaged to Maryam."

At that, Aisha sat up in bed too, with a quick, mechanical motion, as though the revelation was cold water splashed on her face and teeth. The three shadows moved close together in a mound resembling a pyramid in the faint light penetrating the room, which was reflected on the floor near the open door as a trapezoidal panel. Its edges fluctuated with the oscillations of the lamp's wick, which had been exposed to a draft when the door was left open. The breeze reached the hall in gentle whispers, flowing surreptitiously from the small openings of the girls' window.

Khadija asked with great interest, "How do you know that?"

"I got out of bed to fetch my English notebook. When I reached the door of the study I heard my brother's voice. So I stayed there on the sofa." Then he repeated what he had overheard. They listened to him, spellbound, until he finished. At that point Aisha asked, as though she needed further convincing, "Do you believe this, Khadija?"

In a voice that sounded as though she was speaking by telephone from a distant city, her sister replied, "Do you imagine he's invented a long, complicated story like this?"

"You're right." Aisha laughed to relieve her tension and continued: "There's a big difference between the death of the boy in the street and this story."

Paying no attention to Kamal's objection to the insinuation directed at him, Khadija asked, "How do you suppose this came about?"

Aisha laughed and observed, "Didn't I tell you once I doubted it was the hyacinth beans that enticed Fahmy to the roof every day?"

"It's another kind of fragrant vine that's wound itself around his leg."

Aisha sang softly: "You're not to be blamed, my eyes, for loving him."

Khadija chided her: "Hush . . . this isn't the time for singing. . . . Maryam's in her twenties and Fahmy's eighteen. How can Mother agree to that?"

"Mother? . . . Mother's a gentle dove and wouldn't know how to say no. But wait a minute; it's only fair to say that Maryam's beautiful and a fine girl. . . . Moreover, our house is the only one in the neighborhood that hasn't had a wedding yet . . . ."

Both Khadija and Aisha loved Maryam, but love had never been able to hide a loved one's defects from Khadija's eyes, regardless of the circumstances, and when provoked she would not limit herself to criticizing defects. Since the marriage saga stirred her latent fears and jealousy, she turned on her friend without any qualms. Her heart refused to accept her as a wife for her brother. She proceeded to say, "Are you crazy? . . . Maryam's pretty, but she's not nearly good enough for Fahmy. You donkey, Fahmy's getting an advanced degree. He'll be a judge someday. Can you imagine Maryam as the wife of a high-ranking judge? She's like us in most respects. Indeed, in more than one respect she's not as good as we are, and neither of us is ever going to marry a judge."

Aisha asked herself, "Who says a judge is better than an officer?" Then she said to her sister argumentatively, "Why not?"

Without paying attention to her sister's protest, Khadija continued: "Fahmy will be able to marry a girl a hundred times more beautiful than Maryam and at the same time one who's educated, rich, and the daughter of a bey or even a pasha. So why should he be in a hurry to get engaged to Maryam? She's nothing but an illiterate with a sharp tongue. You don't know her as well as I do."

Aisha perceived that in Khadija's eyes Maryam had been transformed into a bundle of faults and defects. All the same, she could not keep from smiling secretly in the dark at the description of Maryam as sharp-tongued, since the epithet was much more suitable for Khadija. She abandoned her protest and said submissively, "Let's leave the matter to God . . . ."

Khadija replied with conviction, "The matter is in God's hands in heaven and in Daddy's here on earth. We'll find out what he thinks about it tomorrow." Then she told Kamal, "It's time for you to go quietly to your bed."

Kamal returned to his room, telling himself, "That only leaves Yasin, and I'll tell him tomorrow."

20

KHADIJA AND AISHA were sitting beside the closed door of their parents' room on the top floor. They were facing each other with their legs crossed beneath them, warily trying not to breathe too loud as they strained with great interest to hear what was being said inside. It was shortly before the afternoon prayer, and their father had risen from his siesta and performed his ablutions. As usual, he was sitting drinking his coffee while he waited for the call to prayer. He would pray and then return to the store. The sisters expected their mother to broach the subject Kamal had told them about, since there would be no more suitable time for this purpose. Their father's loud voice carried to them from inside, discussing ordinary household matters. They listened apprehensively and attentively, exchanging questioning glances, until finally they heard their mother say in an exceptionally polite and submissive way, "Sir, if you will allow me, I'll tell you something Fahmy requested me to bring to your attention."

At that, Aisha gestured with her chin toward the room as though saying, "Here it comes." Meanwhile Khadija was imagining her mother's condition as she prepared to utter the dangerous words. Her heart went out to her and she bit her lip in her intense sympathy.

Then they heard their father's voice asking, "What does he want?"

Silence reigned for a short time, although it seemed long to the eavesdroppers. Then the woman said gently, "Fahmy, sir, is a fine young man. He has gained favor with you through his seriousness, success in school, and good manners, may God protect him from the evil eye. Perhaps he has entrusted his request to me hoping that his status with his father will be an argument on his behalf."

Their father responded in a tone the girls thought showed his pleasure with their mother's proposal so far: "What does he want? . . . Speak."

They leaned their heads against the door. Each of them was staring at the other, but hardly seeing her. They made out the feeble voice saying, "Sir, you know our excellent neighbor Muhammad Ridwan?"

"Naturally."

"He is a fine man like you, sir. It's a good family and they're exceptional neighbors."

"Yes."

She continued after some hesitation: "Fahmy asks, sir, whether his father will allow him . . . to become engaged to Maryam, the daughter of our excellent neighbor, so that she will be under his supervision until he is ready to get married."

The father's voice grew louder and his tone was harsh with anger and disapproval: "Get engaged? . . . What are you saying, woman? . . . He's only a boy! . . . God's will be done. . . . Repeat what you just said."

Khadija imagined that their mother had recoiled in alarm. The trembling voice said, "All he did was ask. It was just a question, sir, with the decision left entirely to you . . . ."

He replied in an explosion of anger: "What is this spineless pampering? I'm not accustomed to it and he shouldn't be either. I don't know what could corrupt a schoolboy to the extent that he would make such an outrageous request. . . . But a mother like you could well ruin her children. If you were the kind of mother you ought to be, he would never have dared discuss such insolent nonsense with you."

The two girls were seized by fear and anxiety, but for Khadija these were mixed with relief. Then they heard their mother say in a trembling, subservient voice, "Don't burden yourself, sir, with the trouble of getting angry. Nothing matters except your anger. I certainly did not intend any offense, nor did my son when he innocently conveyed his request to me. He came to me with the best of intentions; so I thought I would present the matter to you. Since this is what you think, I'll tell him. He will submit to it totally, just as he obeys all your commands."

"He'll obey me whether he wishes to or not. But I want to tell you that you're a weak mother and nothing good can be hoped from you."

"I'm careful to see they do as you command."

"Tell me: What led him to think of making this request?"

The girls listened intently and anxiously. They were surprised by this unexpected question. They did not hear any answer from their mother but imagined she was blinking her eyes in confusion and fear. They felt great sympathy for her.

"What's struck you dumb? . . . Tell me: Has he seen her?"

"Of course not, sir. My son doesn't lift his eyes to look at a neighbor girl or anyone else."

"How can he want to get engaged to her if he hasn't seen her? I didn't know I had sons who were sneaking looks at the respectable women of our neighbors."

"God shelter us, sir. God shelter us. . . . When my son walks in the street he turns neither to the right nor to the left. When he's at home he scarcely leaves his room unless he has to."

"So what made him ask for her, then?"

"Perhaps, sir, he heard his sisters talking about her . . ."

A tremor passed through the bodies of the two girls. Their mouths were gaping open in alarm as they listened.

"Since when are his sisters matchmakers? Glory to God, am I going to have to leave my store and job to squat at home in order to patrol it and rid it of corruption?"

The mother cried out in a sobbing voice, "Your house is the most respectable one of all. By God, sir, if you hadn't got angry so quickly, the matter would be over and done with."

The man yelled in a threatening voice, "Tell him to mind his manners, have some shame, and know his place. The best thing for him would be to concentrate on his studies."

The girls heard some movement inside the room. They rose cautiously and tiptoed away.

Mrs. Amina thought it best to leave the room, according to the policy she followed whenever she accidentally let something slip out that stirred his anger. She would not return unless he summoned her. She had learned from experience that for her to remain when he was angry and try to calm him down with gentle words only made him more furious.

Al-Sayyid Ahmad found himself alone. The observable effects of his anger, like the rage apparent in his eyes, complexion, words, and the gestures of his hands, subsided, but the anger deep within his chest lingered on like dregs at the bottom of a pot.

It was an established fact that he got angry at home for the most trivial reasons and not merely because of his plan for the management of his home. He was also affected by his sharp temper, which was not held in check at home by the brakes of civility that he employed to perfection outside his household. His domestic rage presumably granted him some relief from the effort he exerted with other people, when he suffered in the interest of self-control, tolerance, graciousness, and concern for other people's feelings and affection. Not infrequently he realized he had gotten angry for no reason at all, but even then he did not regret it. He believed that getting angry over a trivial matter would prevent serious offenses, which would truly merit his anger.

All the same, he did not consider what he had heard concerning Fahmy that afternoon to be a minor error. He discerned in it an unseemly turbulence that should not be agitating the soul of a schoolboy from his family. He could not imagine that the world of the emotions had infiltrated the atmosphere of his home, which he vigilantly strove to keep one of stern purity and immaculate innocence. Then it was time for the afternoon prayer, a good opportunity for spiritual exercise. He emerged from his prayers with a calmer heart and a more relaxed mind. He sat on the prayer rug, spread out his hands, and asked God to bless him with both offspring and money. He prayed especially that he have reason for pride in his children's good sense, integrity, and success.

By the time he left the house his frown was merely a device intended to frighten his family. At the store he told some of his friends about the event as though it was a silly prank, not a calamity, because he did not like to bore people with calamities. They made some humorous comments about it of the kind they enjoyed, and before long he was joining in their jokes. When they left, he was roaring with laughter. At his store, the event did not seem as serious to him as it had in his room at home. He was able to laugh about it and even sympathize with the request. He ended up telling himself happily, with a smile, "There's nothing wrong with a kid who takes after his old man."

21

WHEN KAMAL darted out of the door of his house, evening was beginning to darken the streets, alleys, minarets, and domes. His happiness at this unexpected excursion at a time he was rarely allowed out was matched only by his pride in the message Fahmy had entrusted to him. It was not lost on him that Fahmy had chosen him instead of anyone else. That the atmosphere had been one of circumspect secrecy lent the message and therefore Kamal a special importance. His young heart felt it and danced with excitement and pride. He wondered with amazement what had shaken Fahmy enough to plunge him into a sad and anxious state, making him seem a different person, one Kamal had never seen or heard before.

Fahmy was known for his self-control. Their father would explode like a volcano for the most trifling reason. Yasin spoke sweetly but was prone to sudden outbursts. Even Khadija and Aisha had their moments of irrational behavior. Only Fahmy was exemplary in his self-control. His laughter was a smile and his anger a frown. Yet his profoundly calm character did not diminish the sincerity of his emotions or the steadfastness of his zeal.

Kamal could not remember seeing his brother in such a state. He would never forget Fahmy's condition when they talked privately in the study: eyes wandering, soul troubled, and voice trembling. For the first time in his life Fahmy had spoken to him in a tone of warm entreaty, totally shocking Kamal, who had memorized the message and repeated it over and over again to Fahmy.

From the tenor of the message itself he realized that the affair was closely linked to the strange conversation he had overheard and conveyed to his sisters, stirring up an argument between them. It all related to Maryam, that girl with whom he frequently exchanged taunts. There were times when he liked her and others when she annoyed him, but he did not understand why there should be an important connection between her and his brother's peace of mind and welfare. Maryam! Why was she, rather than any other person, able to do all this to his dear and wonderful brother? He felt there was a mystery to the situation like that surrounding the existence of spirits and ghosts, which had often aroused both curiosity and fear in him. Thus his heart resolved eagerly but anxiously to get to the bottom of this secret.

His anxiety did not prevent him from repeating the message to himself the way he had gone over it with his brother, so he could be sure not to forget a single syllable of it. He was reciting it when he passed the home of the Ridwan family. Then at its corner he turned into the alley where the door was located.

He knew the house well, for he had often slipped into its small courtyard, where a handcart, missing its wheels, was pushed into a corner. He would climb in, relying on his imagination to supply the wheels and make it go wherever he wished. He had often wandered through the rooms uninvited to be greeted and petted by the lady of the house and her daughter. Despite his youth, he thought of them as old friends. He knew the house – its three rooms arranged around a small sitting room that had a sewing machine below a window overlooking Hammam al-Sultan – as well as he knew his own house with its big rooms surrounding the large sitting room where their coffee hour was held evening after evening.

Some aspects of Maryam's house had made a lasting impression on him, like the dove's nest on the roof of the enclosed balcony of her room. Its edge could be seen above the wooden grille at the corner adjoining the wall of the house, looking like a semicircle to which a mat of straw and feathers had been attached. Sometimes the mother dove's tail stuck out, sometimes her beak, depending on how she happened to be sitting. As he looked at it, he would be torn between two desires. One, based on instinct, urged him to destroy it and snatch the babies, and the other, acquired from his mother, would have him sympathetically investigate the life of the dove and her family.

There was also the picture of the Ambassadress Aziza, a flamboyant character from popular literature, which hung in Maryam's room. The colors of the print were brilliant. The heroine's complexion was radiant and her features pretty. She was even more beautiful than the belle whose picture gazed down at him every afternoon at Matoussian's store. He would look for a long time at the picture, wondering about her. Then Maryam would tell him as much of her story as she knew. Even things she did not know would slip easily from her tongue, enchanting and fascinating him.

Thus there was nothing strange about the house for him. He made his way to the sitting room without anyone noticing him. He cast a fleeting glance into the first room and found Mr. Muhammad Ridwan lying in bed as usual. He knew the old man had been sick for years. He had heard him described as "paralyzed" so often that he had asked his mother what the word meant. She had been alarmed and had begun to seek refuge with God from the evil suggested by this term. He had shrunk back in retreat. From that day on, Mr. Muhammad Ridwan had aroused his pity and a curiosity mixed with fear.

He passed by the next room and saw Maryam's mother standing in front of the mirror. There was a doughlike substance in her hand which she was stretching over her cheek and neck. She pulled it off in rapid, successive motions. Then she felt where it had been with her fingers to assure herself that the hair had been pulled out and her skin was smooth. Although she was over forty, she was as extraordinarily beautiful as her daughter. She loved to laugh and joke. Whenever she saw him she would greet him merrily, kiss him, and ask him, as though her patience was exhausted, "When are you going to grow up so I can marry you?" He would be overcome by embarrassment and confusion, but he enjoyed her jesting and would have liked even more.

He was curious about this procedure she carried out in front of the mirror from time to time. He had asked his mother about it once, but she had scolded him, reprimanding him for asking about something that did not concern him. That was the most extreme form of discipline she employed. Maryam's mother had been more indulgent and gracious. Once when she noticed he was watching her with astonishment, she had him stand on a chair in front of her. She stuck on his fingers what he at first thought was dough. She held her face out to him and said laughingly, "Go to work and show me how clever you are."

He had begun to imitate what she had been doing and established his cleverness to her satisfaction and his delight. He had not been content with the pleasure of doing it but had asked her, "Why do you do this?"

She had laughed loudly and suggested, "Why don't you wait ten more years to find out for yourself? But there's no need to wait. Isn't smooth skin better than rough skin? That's all there is to it."

He went by her door softly so she would not know he was there. His message was too important for him to meet anyone except Maryam. She was in the last room, sitting on her bed, her legs crossed beneath her, eating melon seeds. There was a saucer in front of her filled with shells. When she saw him she exclaimed in astonishment, "Kamal!" She was about to ask him why he had come at such an hour, but she did not, for fear that that would frighten or annoy him. "You honor our house," she continued. "Come sit beside me."

He shook hands with her. Then he unfastened the buttons of his high boots. He removed them and jumped onto the bed. He was wearing a striped shirt that went to his ankles and a blue skullcap decorated with red lines. Maryam laughed tenderly and put some seeds in his hand. She told him, "Crack these open, sparrow, and move your pearl-like teeth. . . . Do you remember the day you bit my wrist when I was tickling you . . . like this . . .?" She stretched her hand toward his armpit, but he moved in the opposite direction and crossed his arms over his chest to protect himself.

A nervous laugh escaped him, as though her fingers actually were tickling him. He yelled at her, "Have mercy, Miss Maryam."

She let him alone but expressed her amazement at his fear: "Why does your body shrink from being tickled? Look: I don't mind it at all." She began to tickle herself nonchalantly while giving him a scornful look.

He could not refrain from challenging her: "Let me tickle you and then we'll see."

She raised her hands over her head. His fingers attacked under her arms and proceeded to tickle her as gently and quickly as possible. He fixed his eyes on her beautiful black ones so he could catch the first sign of any weakening on her part. Finally he was forced to give up, sighing with despair and embarrassment.

She greeted his defeat with a gently sarcastic laugh and said, "So you see, you weak little man. . . . Don't claim you're a man anymore." Then she continued as though she had suddenly remembered something important: "What a calamity! You forgot to kiss me. . . . Haven't I repeatedly told you that the greeting when we meet is a kiss?" She moved her face toward him. He put out his lips and kissed her cheek. Then he saw that scraps of melon seeds had escaped from the corner of his mouth and stuck to her cheek. He brushed them away with embarrassment. Maryam grasped his chin with her right hand and kissed his lips time and again. Then she asked him with amazement, "How were you able to get away from them at this time of the day? Maybe your mother's looking for you right now in every room of the house."

"Oh . . . " He had been having such fun talking and playing that he had almost forgotten the message he had come to deliver. Her question reminded him of his mission. He looked at her with a different eye, an eye that wished to delve deep inside her to learn the secret power that was rocking his fine, sober brother. When he realized that he was the bearer of unhappy news, his inquisitive look disintegrated. He said despondently, "Fahmy sent me."

A new, serious look came into her eyes. She searched his face attentively for a clue to his mission. He felt that the atmosphere had changed, as though he had gone from one class to another. Then he heard her ask in a soft voice, "Why?"

He answered her with a frankness that indicated he did not understand the seriousness of the news he brought, even though he felt it instinctively: "He told me, 'Give her my greetings and tell her that Fahmy asked his father's permission to become engaged to her. He did not consent for the engagement to be announced while Fahmy was still a student. He asked him to wait till he completed his studies.' "

She was staring at his face with intense interest. When he fell silent, she lowered her eyes without uttering a word. Their tête-à-tête degenerated into a despondent silence which his young heart found hard to bear. He longed to scare it away no matter what. Kamal continued: "He assures you that the refusal came in spite of him and that he'll hurry to finish his studies so that what he desires may come to pass."

When he found that his words did not help free her from the clutches of silence, his wish to restore her former happiness and good humor increased. He asked her enticingly, "Should I tell you what Fahmy and Mother said when they talked about you?"

She responded in a neutral tone, halfway between interest and disinterest, "So what did they have to say?"

He felt good about this partial victory and recounted to her what he had overheard from beginning to end. It seemed to him that she sighed. Then she commented crossly, "Your father's a harsh, frightening man. Everyone knows he's that way."

Without thinking he agreed: "Yes . . . Daddy's like that."

Fearfully and cautiously he raised his head to look at her, but he found her lost in thought. Remembering his brother's instructions, he asked, "What shall I tell him?"

She laughed through her nose and shook her shoulders. She started to speak but paused to think for a moment. Then she replied with a naughty gleam in her eyes: "Tell him that she won't know what to do if a suitor asks to marry her during this long period of waiting."

Kamal was more concerned about memorizing the new message than he was about understanding it. He sensed at once that his mission had ended. He put the remainder of the melon seeds in his shirt pocket. Then he shook hands with her, slipped to the floor, and departed.

22

WHENEVER AISHA looked at herself in the mirror, she was immensely pleased with what she saw. Who else from her illustrious family, indeed from the whole neighborhood, was adorned by golden tresses and blue eyes like hers? Yasin flirted openly with her, and Fahmy, when he spoke to her about one thing or another, did not neglect to give her admiring glances. Even little Kamal did not want to drink from the water jug unless her mouth had moistened the lip. Her mother spoiled her and said she was as beautiful as the moon, although she did not conceal her anxiety that Aisha was too thin and delicate. For this reason she had encouraged Umm Hanafi to concoct a remedy to fatten her up. Aisha herself was perhaps more conscious of her extraordinary beauty than any of the others. Her intense solicitude for every detail of her appearance made this clear.

Khadija did not let her sister's excessive concern for her beauty pass without comment, rebuke, and criticism. It was not that Khadija would have been pleased if Aisha had neglected herself. She took after her mother more than any of the others when it came to cleanliness and neatness. But it annoyed her to observe her sister greet the day by combing her hair and fixing her attire before doing the household chores, as though Aisha could not bear for her beauty to be left untended for even one hour out of her whole life.

It was not simply interest in her own beauty that caused Aisha to want to fix herself up first thing in the morning. When the men went off to work, she wanted to be ready to repair to the parlor and open the shutters of the window overlooking Palace Walk just the least bit. Then she would stand searching the street, while she waited anxiously and fearfully.

She stood there this morning with her eyes wandering from Hammam al-Sultan to the ancient building that housed the public cistern. Her young heart pounded while she waited for "him." Then he appeared in the distance. He turned the corner, coming from al-Khurunfush, and strutted along in his uniform with the two stars gleaming on the shoulder. As he approached the house, he cautiously began to raise his eyes but not his head. When he was close, the faintest of smiles flickered across his face, one more clearly perceived by the heart than the eyes, like the crescent moon the first night. Then he disappeared beneath the balcony.

She whirled around to continue watching him from the other window overlooking al-Nahhasin but was shocked to see Khadija, standing on the sofa between the two windows, looking over her head at the street. A moan escaped Aisha. Her eyes grew big with unmistakable alarm. She stood rooted to the spot. When and how had her sister come? How had she gotten up on the sofa without Aisha being aware of it? What had she seen? . . . When and how and what?

Meanwhile Khadija fixed her eyes on her sister, slowly and silently narrowing them. She extended the silence as though to prolong Aisha's suffering.

Aisha gained partial control of herself. She lowered her eyes with great effort and turned toward the couch, futilely pretending to have steadied her nerves. She stammered, "Lady, you frightened me!"

Khadija did not show any interest. She remained where she was on the sofa. Her gaze was directed at the street through the crack. Then she muttered sarcastically, "Did I frighten you? . . . May the name of God protect you. . . . I must be the bogeyman."

After retreating a little to escape from Khadija's eyes, Aisha gritted her teeth in rage. In a calm voice she said, "I suddenly saw you, over my head, without knowing you'd come in. Why did you sneak up?"

Khadija jumped down. She sat on the sofa, completely and scornfully at ease. "I'm sorry, sister," she said. "Next time I'll hang a bell around my neck like a fire truck so you'll know I'm here and won't be frightened."

Still terrified, Aisha answered, "There's no need to wear a bell. It would be enough if you'd just walk the way God intended us to. . . ."

Casting her a knowing look, Khadija continued in the same sarcastic tone: "Our Lord knows I walk the way He intended. What's clear is that you, when you stand behind the window,

I mean behind this crack, are so caught up in what's in front of you that you're no longer conscious of what is happening around you and don't act the way our Lord intended."

Aisha snorted and mumbled, "You'll never change."

Khadija was silent again for a moment. She turned her eyes away from her victim and raised her eyebrows as if thinking about a difficult puzzle. Then she pretended to be pleased, as though she had found the right answer. Speaking to herself this time, without looking at her sister she said, "Then this is the reason she frequently sings: 'You there with the red stripe, you who have taken me prisoner, have pity on my humiliation.' Not being suspicious, darling, I just thought it was an innocent song, merely for your amusement."

Aisha's heart beat wildly. What she feared most had happened. It was no use anymore to cling to the phantoms of false hopes. She was afflicted by a disturbance that rocked the very pillars of her being, and she almost choked on her tears. All the same, her despair forced her to risk everything to defend herself. In a voice that shook so much the words were hard to understand, she yelled, "What's this nonsense you're saying?"

Khadija appeared not to have heard her. She continued to herself: "This is also the reason she fixes herself up so early in the morning. I've often asked myself if it made sense for a girl to get all dolled up before she does the sweeping and dusting. But what sweeping and what dusting? Oh, Khadija, you poor dear, you'll live a fool and die a fool. You're the one who'll do the sweeping and dusting, and you won't have time to worry about your appearance either before or after work. You miserable creature, why should you deck yourself out? You could look through the crack of the window day after day, and if even one officer out on patrol took an interest in you, I'd be so surprised I'd chop my arm off."

Upset and nervous, Aisha shouted at her, "Shame on you. Shame."

"She's right, Khadija. You with your muddled mind aren't able to understand these arts. Blue eyes, hair of spun gold, a red stripe, and a gleaming star, these all fit together nicely in a rational way."

"Khadija, you're mistaken. I was looking at the street. That's all. I wasn't trying to see someone or be seen by him."

Khadija turned toward her as though hearing her protest for the first time. She asked apologetically, "Were you talking to me, sweetheart, Shushu? Excuse me, I'm thinking about some important matters. So don't say anything just now." She shook her head thoughtfully again and said to herself, "Yes, it all makes perfect sense, but is this your fault, Mr. Ahmad Abd al-Jawad? I feel sorry for you, sir, you noble and generous man. Come see your women, sir, you whom I honor most of all."

Aisha's hair stood up on end at the mention of her father. Her head whirled. She remembered what he had said to her mother when he was attacking Fahmy's request to get engaged to Maryam: "Tell me: Has he seen her? . . . I didn't know I had sons who were sneaking looks at the respectable women of our neighbors." That was what he thought about his son; so what would he think about his daughter? She nearly choked as she cried out, "Khadija . . . this isn't right. . . . You're mistaken. . . . You're wrong."

Khadija kept on talking to herself without paying any attention to her sister: "Do you suppose this is love? Perhaps! Don't they say, 'Love has penetrated my heart. . . . It won't be long till I'm taken to Tokar Prison'? I wonder where this notorious Tokar Prison is? Perhaps it's in al-Nahhasin; indeed perhaps it's in the home of Mr. Ahmad Abd al-Jawad."

"I can't bear what you're saying. Have mercy on me and spare me your tongue. Oh Lord . . . why won't you believe me?"

"Think carefully about what you're going to do, Khadija. It's not a game. You're the older sister. A duty is a duty, no matter how bitter it may seem. The authorities must be informed. Should you confide the secret to your father? The truth is that I wouldn't know how to tell him such an important secret. Yasin? He might as well not exist for all the help he can provide. The most that can be hoped from him is for him to chant some incomprehensible words. Fahmy? But he's also sweet on the golden-haired wonder who is the source of the whole problem. I suspect the best thing is for me to tell Mother. I'll let her do what she thinks is right."

Khadija moved as though she intended to get up. Aisha rushed at her like a chicken without a head. She grabbed her shoulders and shouted, as her chest heaved, "What do you want?"

Khadija asked, "Are you threatening me?"

Aisha started to speak but all at once choked on her tears. She murmured some words that were mangled by her sobs. Khadija stared at her silently and thoughtfully. Then the mischievous sarcasm of her expression changed to a frown as she listened uncomfortably to the girl's sobs. Speaking in a serious tone for the first time, she remarked, "What you did was wrong, Aisha."

Then she stopped. The frown on her face became more pronounced. Her nose seemed to stick out even farther. She was clearly moved. She started speaking again: "You've got to confess you made a mistake. Tell me how you talked yourself into this mischief, you crazy girl."

Drying her eyes, Aisha mumbled, "You misjudge me."

Khadija snorted and scowled as though she could not stand any more of this lamentable obstinacy. All the same, she abandoned the notion of acting hostilely toward Aisha or of mistreating her. She always knew when and where to stop. She would not let things get out of hand. Her sarcasm had satisfied her rough and hostile tendencies. As usual, she was content to draw the line there. Her other inclinations, as far removed as possible from hostility and harshness, still had not been satisfied. They were impulses arising from the affections of an older sister. Indeed her feelings were almost maternal and embraced every member of the family, no matter how fierce her attack against one of them might be, or his against her.

Impelled by these affectionate urges, Khadija said, "Don't be obstinate. I saw it all with my own eyes. I'm not joking now. I want to tell you frankly that you made a big mistake. Our family has not known this kind of mischief in the past and we don't want to experience it again, now or in the future. It's nothing but recklessness that has landed you here. Listen to me and pay attention to my advice. Don't ever do this again. Nothing remains a secret forever, no matter how long it may be concealed. Imagine the situation for all of us if someone on the street or one of our neighbors noticed you. You know very well how people talk. Imagine what would happen if the news reached Daddy. God help us!"

Aisha bowed her head and allowed her silence to serve as a confession. Her face was stained red with shame in a physical manifestation of remorse that conscience releases inside us when injured by one of our offenses.

Khadija sighed and said, "Beware, beware. Understand?" Then a wave of sarcasm swept across her and her tone changed somewhat: "Hasn't he seen you? What's keeping him from asking for your hand like an honorable man? When that happens, we'll gladly say farewell to you, lady, or even good riddance."

Aisha got her breath back. Her smile resembled the first glimmer of consciousness after a long swoon. The sight of this smile seemed to make Khadija disinclined to let her sister escape from her grasp so soon, after she had enjoyed dominating her for a long time. She shouted at her, "Don't think you're off the hook. My tongue won't be still unless you do a good job of entertaining it."

Aisha asked her cheerfuly, "What do you mean?"

"Don't neglect it. Otherwise it might yield to a malicious urge. Divert it with some candy so it'll be occupied with that and not you, a box of bonbons from Shangarly, for example."

"You can have all you want and more."

Silence reigned while each of them was busy with her own thoughts. Khadija's heart, as it had been from the beginning of the encounter, was a breeding ground for all sorts of different emotions . . . jealousy, anger, sympathy, and affection.

23

MRS. AMINA was busy getting ready for the traditional family coffee hour when Umm Hanafi rushed up to her. The gleam in her eyes suggested that she was bringing good news. She announced importantly, "Three ladies I've never seen before wish to call on you."

The mother set everything down and straightened up quickly in a way that showed the impact of the news on her. She stared at the servant with a look of intense interest, as though it was likely the visitors were from the royal family or even from heaven. Then, seeking confirmation, she stammered, "Strangers?"

Umm Hanafi replied in a tone that had a happy, triumphant ring to it, "Yes, my lady. They knocked on the door and I opened it. They asked me, 'Isn't this the home of al-Sayyid Ahmad Abd al-Jawad?' I said, 'Yes, indeed.' They said, 'Are the ladies in?' I replied, 'Yes.' They said, 'We would like to have the honor of calling on them.' I asked them, 'Shall I say who the visitors are?' One of them told me with a laugh, 'Leave that to us. All the messenger needs to do is carry the message.' So I flew to you, my lady. I've been saying to myself, 'May our Lord make our dreams come true.'"

Her interest still showing in her eyes, the mother said quickly, "Invite them to the parlor . . . hurry."

For a few seconds Amina did not move. She was sunk in these new thoughts, in a happy dream world that suddenly revealed its riches to her, after she had worked for nothing else all these past years. Then she snapped out of her reverie and called Khadija in a voice that made it clear she would not tolerate any delay. The girl came at once. The moment their eyes met she smiled and, unable to restrain her joy, told her daughter, "Three ladies we've never seen before are in the parlor . . . Put on your best clothes and get yourself ready."

When Khadija blushed, Amina blushed too, as though she had caught this contagious embarrassment from her daughter. Then she left the sitting room to retire to her room on the top floor to prepare herself as well to receive the visitors. Khadija was looking vacantly at the door through which her mother had vanished. Her heart was pounding so much it almost hurt. She asked herself, "What's behind this visit?" Then she pulled herself together. Her mind immediately resumed functioning. She summoned Kamal from Fahmy's room and told him, "Go to Miss Maryam and give her my greetings. Tell her that Khadija asks her to send some powder, kohl, and rouge."

The boy jumped at the chance to obey this order and rushed out of the house. Khadija hastened to her room and proceeded to remove her housedress. Aisha looked at her with inquiring eyes. Khadija told her, "Pick out the best dress for me . . . absolutely the best one."

Aisha asked her, "Why are you in such a state? . . . Is there a visitor? Who?"

Khadija replied in a faint voice, "Three ladies. . . . " With special emphasis, she added, "Strangers . . . ."

Aisha drew back her head in astonishment. Then her beautiful eyes grew wide with delight. She cried out, "Oh! . . . Should we understand from this that . . . Oh, what news!"

"Don't get your hopes up . . . for who knows what it really means."

Aisha headed for the armoire to select an appropriate dress. She was laughing and saying, "There's something in the air. . . . A wedding smells like pure perfume."

Khadija laughed to hide her uneasiness. She went to the mirror and looked carefully at herself. She covered her nose with her hand and said ironically, "There's nothing wrong with my face now." Removing her hand from her face, she commented, "Now, like this, only God can save me."

While helping her sister put on a white dress embroidered with lavender flowers, Aisha laughingly remarked, "Don't be so hard on yourself. Can't your tongue spare anything? There's more to a bride than her nose. What about your eyes, long hair, and quick wit?"

Khadija wrinkled her nose as she answered, "All people see are the defects."

"That's true for people with your temperament, but not everyone is like you, thank God."

"I'll answer you when I can find the time."

As Aisha smoothed her sister's dress, she patted her waist and said, "And don't forget your soft, plump body. . . . What a great body you've got."

Khadija laughed happily and said, "If the bridegroom was blind I wouldn't worry about anything. . . . I wouldn't mind a blind one, even if he was a religious scholar from al-Azhar Mosque."

"What's wrong with the religious scholars from al-Azhar? Don't some of them have treasures as boundless as the ocean?"

When they were done with the dress, a murmur of displeasure escaped from Aisha. Khadija asked her, "What's the matter?"

She grumbled, "There isn't a bit of powder, kohl, or rouge in our house, as though there weren't any women living here."

"The best thing would be to take this complaint to Father."

"Isn't Mother a lady? Doesn't she have a right to use cosmetics?"

"She's beautiful just the way she is, without any need for them."

"What about you? Are you going to meet the visitors like this?"

Khadija laughed and replied, "I sent Kamal to Maryam to get the powder, kohl, and rouge. Is my face one to leave bare when I meet matchmakers?"

Since there was not enough time to waste even a minute, Khadija removed her scarf and began to take down her two long, thick braids. Aisha started combing the flowing hair. She remarked, "What long, straight hair you have. What do you think? I'll plait it into a single braid. Wouldn't that be the more beautiful?"

"No, two braids. . . . But tell me: Should I leave on my stockings or have bare legs when I meet them?"

"It's winter and people would normally wear wool stockings, but I'm afraid if you leave them on they'll think there's something wrong with your foot or leg that you're deliberately trying to hide."

"You're right. A court of law is more merciful than the room of women waiting for me now."

"Be brave. Our Lord has promised us . . ."

At that moment Kamal hurried into the room. He was panting. He gave his sister the containers of cosmetics and told her, "I ran all the way and even up the stairs."

Khadija smiled and said, "Bravo! Bravo! What did Maryam say?"

"She asked me if we had company . . . and who they were. I told her I didn't know."

Concern was visible in Khadija's eyes when she asked him, "Was she satisfied with that answer?"

"She asked me to swear by al-Husayn to tell her everything I knew. I swore I'd told her everything."

Aisha laughed. Her hands kept on with their work as she observed, "She'll guess what's happening."

Khadija was spreading powder on her face and said, "She wasn't born yesterday. It's not likely that anything will escape her. I bet you she'll come visit us tomorrow at the latest to conduct a thorough investigation."

Kamal should have left the room then, but he did not want to, and perhaps could not, he was so interested in the scene unfolding before his eyes. For the first time in his life he witnessed his sister's face undergo this transformation into a new face altogether, boasting white skin, pink cheeks, and eyelids with delicate black lines along their edges that enhanced her eyes and made them look splendidly clear. His heart rejoiced at this new face. He shouted with excitement, "Sister, now you're just like those beautiful candy bride dolls Papa buys for the festival of the Prophet's Birthday."

The two girls laughed. Khadija asked him, "Do you like the way I look now?"

He rushed up to her and put his hand out to the tip of her nose, saying, "If only this would go away."

She evaded his hand and told her sister, "Throw out this slanderer."

Although he resisted, Aisha seized his hand, dragged him outside, and bolted the door. Then she went back to her beautifying task. The sisters proceeded with their endeavors seriously and silently. Although it was understood in the family that matchmakers would be allowed to meet only Khadija, she told Aisha mischievously, "You need to prepare yourself to meet the visitors too."

Aisha replied as slyly as her sister, "That won't be until you've been escorted to your bridegroom." Then she corrected herself before Khadija could speak: "Now that the moon is rising how can little stars be seen?"

Her sister cast her a skeptical look and asked, "Which of us is the moon?"

Laughing, Aisha replied, "Me of course."

Khadija gave her a poke with her elbow and sighed: "I wish you could lend me your nose the way Maryam lent me her powder."

"Forget your nose, even if only for this one evening. A nose is like a sore that grows larger every time you think about it."

By then they had practically finished their work as beauticians. Khadija's interest in her appearance waned. Her thoughts shifted fearfully to her pending examination. She was afraid in a new way, not simply because it was a novel situation but because of its serious consequences.

She soon complained, "What's this meeting that's being inflicted on me? Picture yourself in my place, surrounded by strangers. You don't know the least thing about them or their background. Have they come with good intentions or am I just an amusing spectacle for them? What will become of me if they are abusive faultfinders, like me . . . huh?" She laughed briefly. "What can I do but sit beside them politely and submissively while they stare at me from left and right, front and back? I'll have to obey their orders without the slightest hesitation. If they ask me to stand, I stand. 'Walk' – I walk. 'Sit' – I sit. Nothing will slip by them: the way I sit or stand, if I'm silent or speak, my limbs and features. In addition to putting up with all this abuse, we must be nice to them and lavishly praise their kindness and generosity. Afterward we still won't know whether we've won their approval or displeasure. My, oh my . . . I could curse the man who sent them."

Aisha quickly replied in a tone that revealed her personal interest in the subject: "May no evil harm him."

"Don't pray for him till we're sure he's ours . . . Oh, how my heart is pounding. . . . "

Aisha stepped back to be out of range of her sister's elbow before she replied, "Be patient. . . . You'll find many opportunities in the future to get your revenge for today's frightful meeting. How often they'll be roasted by the fire of your tongue once you're the mistress of the house. Perhaps they'll recall today's inspection and say to themselves, 'I wish that had never happened.' "

Khadija confined her response to a smile. There was no time for a counterattack. In any case, she would not have gotten the salutary delight from it she usually derived, or any pleasure at all, because she was dominated by her terror and anxiously wavering between hope and fear.

When they had finished their work, Khadija paused to give her reflection in the mirror a thorough examination. Aisha, who was two steps behind her, looked back and forth from the reflection to the original.

Khadija began to murmur, "Bless your hands. I look good, don't I? This is the true Khadija. Never mind my nose now. O Lord, may Your wisdom be exalted. It took a little effort, but everything turned out all right. So why . . . " Then she realized she had said too much and quickly added, "I ask God's forgiveness. May Your wisdom prevail in everything."

She moved a few steps farther away from the mirror, still examining her image carefully. She recited the opening prayer of the Qur'an to herself. She turned toward Aisha and said, "Pray for me, girl." Then she left the room.

24

WITH THE advent of winter, the coffee hour acquired a new aspect represented by the large stove placed in the center of the room. The family clustered around it, the men in their overcoats and the women wrapped up in their shawls. The coffee hour offered them, in addition to the appetizing refreshments and pleasant conversation, a chance to get warm.

Although Fahmy had been sad and silent for the past few days, he seemed ready to spring some important news on the family. His hesitation and reflection only served to show how momentous and important the news was. After giving the matter a little more thought he decided to reveal it and transfer the burden to his parents and the fates. He said, "I've got some important news for you. Listen."

All eyes were fixed on him attentively. He was known to be such a sensible young man that everyone expected his news would be as important as he claimed. He continued: "Mr. Hasan Ibrahim, an officer in the Gamaliya police station, who is one of my acquaintances, as you all know, came to see me and asked me to tell my father of his wish to become engaged to Aisha."

Just as Fahmy had expected, the news affected people in extremely different ways. That was the reason he had hesitated and thought for so long before revealing it. His mother looked at him with intense interest. Yasin whistled, gazed at Aisha flirtatiously, and shook his head. The young girl bowed her head out of embarrassment and to hide her face from prying eyes that might detect the turmoil of her throbbing heart. Khadija's first reaction was surprise, which soon turned to fear and foreboding. There was no clear reason for either, but she felt like a pupil waiting impatiently for examination results who hears privately of a comrade's success.

The mother asked with an anxiety inappropriate for the topic of a joyous wedding, "Is that all he said?"

Taking care to avoid looking at Khadija, Fahmy replied, "He began by stating he wished to have the honor of asking for the hand of my younger sister."

"What did you tell him?"

"I naturally thanked him for his good intentions."

His mother was not questioning him to find out something. She was attempting to conceal her uneasiness and wished time to mull things over. She began to wonder if there might be a connection between this request and the ladies who had called on them a few days before. She remembered then that one had observed before Khadija had appeared, in the context of a general conversation about the family of al-Sayyid Ahmad, that they had heard the gentleman had two daughters. She had understood then that they had come to see both daughters but had turned a deaf ear to the suggestion. Those ladies had been related to the family of a merchant in al-Darb al-Ahmar. Fahmy had said once that the father of the officer, on the other hand, was an employee in the Ministry of Works. This fact did not decisively rule out the possibility of some link between the two families. It was customary for a family to send marriage scouts selected from one of its branches, not from the bridegroom's immediate family, as a precaution. She dearly wished to ask Fahmy about this point but seemed afraid his answer would confirm her fears, thereby putting an end to the hopes of her elder daughter and bringing her a new disappointment.

It so happened that Khadija posed the question for her mother. She veiled her frustration with a listless laugh as the issue troubling her breast emerged in these words: "Perhaps he's the one who sent those ladies to visit us a few days ago?"

Fahmy replied at once, "Of course not. He told me he'd send his mother to us if his request is approved."

Although he spoke in a way that inspired trust, he was not telling the truth. He had gathered from his conversation with the officer that the ladies were his relatives. Although he loved Aisha and was convinced that his friend the officer was worthy of her, he was unwilling to cause pain to his older sister. He felt a brotherly affection for her and was very upset at her bad luck. Perhaps the disappointment he had suffered played a powerful role in strengthening this affection.

Yasin guffawed and remarked with childish glee, "It seems we'll soon have two weddings."

The mother cried out with heartfelt joy, "May our Lord answer you. . . ."

"Will you speak to Daddy for me?" When the question escaped from Fahmy, he was preoccupied with this engagement, but afterward his words sounded odd to him, as though they came not from his tongue but from his memories. These words plunged into his inner depths, before floating to consciousness again with memories clinging to them. He remembered the comparable question he had addressed to his mother in similar circumstances. His heart became dispirited, and his pains were inflamed. He felt once more the tyranny that had buried his hopes. He began to tell himself, as he had done repeatedly during the preceding days, how happy he would have felt about the present, how hopeful he would have been about the future, how content he would have been with life as a whole, had it not been for his father's stern will. This memory made it impossible for him to be concerned about anything but himself. He surrendered himself to the sorrow gnawing at his heart.

The mother thought for a time and then asked, "Wouldn't it be a good idea for us to think about what I can say to your father if he asks me why the officer requested Aisha specifically and didn't ask for Khadija's hand? Since he hasn't seen either one . . ."

The two girls both focused their attention on their mother's remark. They both remembered their scene at the window. The annoyance Khadija felt at that memory doubled her unhappiness about the current situation. Her heart protested against blind fate, which refused to reward reckless frivolity with anything but good. Aisha felt her flow of delight obstructed by her mother's observation, as if a throat happily swallowing a tasty and delicious morsel had been obstructed by a sharp thorn stuck in the food. Fear quickly sucked the heart out of the happiness that had been making her spirit quiver.

Only Fahmy rebelled against his mother's words. He was not defending Aisha, as it might have seemed, since on such a delicate issue he could not defend Aisha in Khadija's presence. He was angry because of his suppressed sorrow, about which he could not speak openly with his father. Unconsciously addressing his father in the person of his mother, he remarked angrily, "This would be unjust and arbitrary. Reason and intellect provide no support for such an objection. Don't men learn a lot of things about decent

women kept secluded from the street by talking to female relatives, whose only goal is the formation of a legal union between a
man and a woman?"

Their mother had meant nothing by her remark. She was
merely trying to hide behind her husband until she could discover
some way out of the bind she found herself in with Aisha and
Khadija. When Fahmy voiced his objections to her so frankly, she
found herself forced to answer with similar frankness: "Don't you
think it would be best for us to wait till we hear something from
those women who visited us?"

Khadija could not bear to remain silent. Driven by her pride,
which forced her to declare that she cared nothing about
the matter at all, despite the anxiety and forebodings struggling inside her, she said, "This is one thing and that's quite
another. So there's no reason to postpone one because of the
other."

Their mother remarked in a calm but forceful way, "We're all
agreed that Aisha's wedding will be delayed until after Khadija's."

Aisha could only say, gently and submissively, "The matter's not
open to discussion."

Khadija's breast filled with resentment when she heard the
gentle tone of Aisha's voice. Perhaps it was this gentleness that
angered her most of all. It may have suggested to her that she
deserved to be pitied, which she absolutely rejected. It may also
have been that she would have liked for Aisha to declare her
opposition openly so she could attack her sister and find some
outlet for her anger. Aisha had armed herself with that hateful fake
sympathy to defend herself from harm, thus doubling Khadija's
resentment, which was lying in ambush, waiting for a chance to
pop out. Finally she found herself obliged to say, if a bit sharply,
"I don't agree that this matter's not open to debate. It's not fair that
someone's bad luck should cause you to destroy another person's
good luck."

Fahmy noticed the angry sorrow concealed behind the altruism
of Khadija's words. He wrenched himself free from his personal
grief. He regretted what he had said in a moment of anger, fearful
that Khadija would interpret it to mean he sided openly with her
sister. Addressing Khadija, he said, "Telling Papa about Hasan
Effendi's request doesn't mean we agree Aisha should marry
before you. There would be no harm in our making acceptance

of the engagement conditional on postponement of its announcement to an appropriate time."

Yasin was not convinced it was right to require one marriage to precede the other, but he could not muster enough courage to express his opinion. He found some comfort in making a general statement that could be understood in different ways. He said, "Marriage is the fate of every living creature. Anyone not getting married today will marry tomorrow."

Kamal had been following the conversation with interest and at this point his shrill voice rang out, asking unexpectedly, "Mother, why is marriage the fate of every creature?"

His mother ignored his question. The only response he received was a loud laugh from Yasin, who made no other comment. Then the mother observed, "I know every girl will marry today or tomorrow, but there are considerations not to be overlooked. . . ."

Kamal tried asking his mother another question: "And will you be getting married too, Mother?"

They all roared with laughter, and this relieved the tension. Yasin seized the favorable opportunity and found the courage to say, "Present the matter to Father. Whatever he says will be final in any case."

With a curious insistence, Khadija said, "That's the only way. That's the way it has to be."

She meant what she said, because she knew how impossible it was to conceal a matter like this from her father and firmly believed her father would not allow Aisha to marry first. In addition to these reasons, she also wished to continue pretending indifference to the issue. Although she did not know of the connection between the officer and the visitors, her anxious forebodings had not left her for a moment.

25

ALTHOUGH MRS. AMINA had encountered more than one cause for unhappiness during her life, she had had no experience with this unforeseen problem and its unique character, since it seemed to pertain to one of the essential foundations of happiness in this world. Even so, in her household and in her heart in particular, it had turned into a cause for anxiety and distress. How right she was when she asked herself, "Who would have suspected that the arrival of a bridegroom, something we have been avidly awaiting, would cause us all this trouble?" Yet that was what had happened.

Several views struggled for control of her mind without her being comfortable about any of them. For a time she thought that agreeing to let Aisha marry before Khadija would destroy her elder daughter's future. On other occasions she thought that stubborn opposition to destiny would create an extremely dangerous situation, with sinister repercussions for both girls. It also troubled her a great deal to close the door in the face of a bridegroom as splendid as the young officer. It was asking a lot to expect that luck would provide another one as good. But what would Khadija's position be and what kind of luck and future would she have if the agreement was concluded? Mrs. Amina could not make up her mind. It was especially difficult since all the prospects seemed so bleak, leaving her unable to find any solution. She was ready to cast the whole burden on the shoulders of her husband and felt relieved, despite the apprehension that swept through her every time she was about to bring up a topic she feared might upset him.

She waited until he finished his coffee. Then she said in her soft voice clearly intended to be polite and submissive, "Sir . . . Fahmy told me one of his friends asked him to present his request to become engaged to Aisha."

From his place on the sofa he looked down at her on her pallet not far from his feet. His blue eyes were filled with interest and astonishment. He seemed to be asking her, "How can you be talking to me about Aisha when I've been waiting for news about Khadija since hearing about the three women visitors?" He asked, to make sure he had heard correctly, "Aisha?"

"Yes, sir."

Al-Sayyid Ahmad looked straight ahead of him with annoyance. Then, as though addressing himself, he said, "I decided a long time ago which order to follow."

The woman quickly said, so he would not think she was opposing his opinion, "I know how you feel about it, sir, but I have to inform you of everything that goes on here."

He scrutinized her keenly, as though probing to discover how much of her statement was true and sincere, but his scrutiny was interrupted by a new thought that shone in his eyes. He asked her with concern and anxiety, "Do you suppose there's a connection between this and the ladies who visited you?"

Once they were alone, Fahmy had told her that there was a connection. The young man had suggested keeping it from his father when she broke the news to him. She had promised to think about it carefully and had hesitated between accepting and rejecting the idea. Finally she had been inclined to keep it a secret, as Fahmy had suggested, but when her husband's question put her on the spot and she felt his eyes looking at her like blazing sunlight, her resolve crumbled and her conviction melted. She replied without hesitation, "Yes, sir. Fahmy learned they were relatives of his friend."

Al-Sayyid Ahmad frowned in anger. As usual when he was angry, his white complexion became flushed and sparks flew from his eyes. It seemed that anyone who belittled Khadija was belittling him. Whoever questioned her honor attacked his, head-on. Yet the only way he knew to show his anger was through his voice, which grew loud and coarse. He asked angrily and scornfully, "Who is this friend?"

She did not know why, but she was uneasy about mentioning the name. "Hasan Ibrahim, an officer at the Gamaliya police station," she said.

He asked her excitedly, "Didn't you tell me you showed only Khadija to the ladies?"

"Yes, sir."

"Did they visit you again?"

"Certainly not, sir. Otherwise I would have told you."

He scolded her as though she were responsible for this peculiar behavior: "He sent his relatives. They saw Khadija. Then he asks for Aisha! . . . What's the meaning of this?"

The mother swallowed and cleared her throat, which was dry from the give-and-take of their conversation. She murmured, "In a case like this, the matchmakers don't go to the house in question until they have visited many of the neighboring households to make inquiries about matters of concern to them. In fact, they did hint in their conversation with me that they had heard you had two daughters. Perhaps presenting only one instead of both . . ."

She had meant to say, "Perhaps presenting only one instead of both served to confirm for them the rumor they had heard about the beauty of the younger girl." She stopped herself partly from fear of increasing his anger and partly from apprehension at openly stating this fact that was linked in her mind to gloomy anxieties and worries. She caught herself and concluded her statement with a mere gesture of her hand, as if to say, "And so on and so forth."

Al-Sayyid Ahmad glared at her until she lowered her eyes submissively. He became resentful and sad, compressing the anger within his heart. He began to pound his chest, trying to get some relief or company for his sorrow. Then he shouted in a stormy voice, "Now we know everything. Here's a suitor asking for your daughter's hand. So let me hear your opinion."

She felt that his question was dragging her into a bottomless pit. Holding her hands out subserviently, she replied without any hesitation, "My opinion is the same as yours, sir. I have no opinion of my own."

He roared back, "If that was so, you wouldn't have mentioned the matter to me at all."

She said apprehensively and devotedly, "Sir, I mentioned it to you only to keep you informed about the new development, since it's my duty to let you know everything that affects your home, coming from near or far."

He shook his head peevishly and said, "Who knows . . . yes, by God, who knows? You're just a woman, and no woman has a fully developed mind. And the topic of marriage in particular is enough to make you women lose your senses. So perhaps you . . ."

She interrupted him in a trembling voice: "Sir, I seek refuge with God from what you suspect. Khadija is my daughter and my flesh and blood just as much as yours. . . . What's happening to her is breaking my heart. Aisha's still in the first bloom of youth. It won't hurt her to wait till God brings help for her sister."

Her husband was nervously smoothing his thick mustache with the palm of his hand. Then he stopped suddenly as though he had remembered something. He asked, "Does Khadija know?"

"Yes, sir."

He waved his hand angrily and shouted, "How can this officer ask for the hand of Aisha despite the fact that no one has seen her?"

Although her heart was throbbing, she replied heatedly, "I told you, sir, perhaps they heard something about her."

"But he works in the Gamaliya police station – in other words, in our area. It's as though he lived here."

His wife replied very emotionally, "No man has ever seen either of my daughters since they stopped going to school when they were little girls."

He struck his hands together and shouted at her, "Not so fast. . . . Slow down. Do you think I have any doubts about that, woman? If I did, not even murder would satisfy me. I'm just talking about what will go through the minds of some people who don't know us. 'No man has ever seen either of my daughters . . .' God's will be done. Would you have wanted a man to see them? What a crazy prattler you are. I'm repeating what might be rumored by fools. Yes . . . he's an officer in the area. He walks along our streets morning and evening. So it's not out of the question that people, if they learned he was marrying one of the girls, would suspect that he might have seen one of them. I would despise giving my daughter to someone if that meant stirring up doubts about my honor. No daughter of mine will marry a man until I am satisfied that his primary motive for marrying her is a sincere desire to be related to me . . . me . . . me . . . me . . . 'No man has ever seen either of my daughters . . .' Congratulations, Mrs. Amina, congratulations."

The mother listened with her head bowed, not uttering a word. The room was still. Then the man rose, signaling that he was going to put on his street clothes and return to his shop. She quickly got up. Her husband took his arms out of the sleeves of his house shirt and raised it to take it off but stopped before the neck of the shirt had gone past his chin. With the garment folded around his shoulders like the mane of a lion, he asked, "Didn't Mr. Fahmy understand the seriousness of the request his friend was making?" Nodding his head sadly, he continued: "People envy me my three sons. The truth is that all I've got are daughters . . . five daughters."

26

ONCE AL-SAYYID AHMAD left the house, they soon learned
what he thought about Aisha's engagement. Although his opinion
was accepted without opposition by people obliged to agree with
him, it reverberated inside each of them in different ways. Fahmy
was sorry to hear the news. He was unhappy Aisha was going to
lose a fine husband like his friend Hasan Ibrahim. Before his
father's decision, Fahmy had wavered between enthusiasm for
the prospective bridegroom and sympathy for Khadija's delicate
position. When the matter was settled, the part of him pitying
Khadija found relief, while the other part wishing for Aisha's
happiness was sad. This sorrow gave him the courage to state his
opinion openly: "Without any doubt, Khadija's future is of concern to all of us, but I don't agree with the insistence on forbidding
Aisha to take advantage of her opportunities. A person's fortune is
part of the invisible world known only to God. Perhaps God has
stored up an even better fortune for the person forced to wait."

Khadija was possibly the one who felt most uncomfortable,
since this was the second time she had stood in the way of her
sister's getting married. She brooded about her anguish, not while
her future was on the line, but after her father's categorical decision, when the danger threatening her had retreated. Then her
anger and pain faded away, to be replaced by a distressing feeling of
embarrassment and anguish. Fahmy's words did not please her,
because deep inside she wanted everyone to support her father's
decision and leave her the only one opposing it. All the same, she
commented, "Fahmy was right in what he said. That's what I've
thought all along."

Yasin reaffirmed his idea: "Marriage is the destiny of every
living creature. . . . Have no fear. . . . Don't panic."

He contented himself with this general observation, even
though he was very fond of Aisha and indignant over the injustice
that had befallen her. He was afraid that if he stated his opinion
frankly, Khadija might misunderstand and suspect some link

between this and the innocent squabbles that frequently broke out between them. His sensitivity about being a half-brother also prevented him from volunteering an opinion that might offend a family member whenever they confronted a serious matter of delicate family business.

Aisha had not uttered a word but finally forced herself to speak, so her silence would not betray her pain, which she was determined to conceal. She would pretend to have no feelings about the engagement, no matter how much that distressed her, and announce her relief about the outcome, to conform with the atmosphere of the household that did not allow human emotions their rightful place and where the affections of the heart were hidden behind veils of self-denial and hypocrisy. So she said, "It wouldn't be right for me to marry before Khadija. The best thing by far is what my father has decided." She continued with a smile: "Why should you all be in such a hurry to get married? How do you know that we'll enjoy as happy a life in our spouse's home as we do here in our father's house?"

When, as usual, they picked up their conversation around the stove that evening, Aisha did not hesitate to participate in it as much as she was able, given her wandering thoughts and the disintegration of her ego. In truth, she resembled nothing so much as a chicken with its head cut off, darting about with out-spread wings, bursting with vitality and energy at the very moment blood flowed from its neck, draining away the last drops of life.

Aisha had anticipated what would happen even before the matter was presented to her father. All the same, she had nourished a glimmer of hope in her dreams, like one of us tempted by the hope of winning first prize in a major lottery. At first, influenced by the generosity that comes with victory or happiness and by affection for her unlucky sister, she had been willing to object to getting married. Now her generosity had faded away and her affection had dwindled. Nothing remained but resentment, anger, and despair. There was not a thing she could do about it. This was her father's will and she could not criticize it. All she could do was submit and obey. In fact, she had to be happy and content. To be despondent would be an unforgivable offense. To protest would be a sin her conscience and sense of etiquette could not allow. From the intoxication of bounteous happiness that had elated her night and day she awoke to despair. How gloomy the darkness seemed coming immediately after dazzling light. Thus the pain was not limited to the current darkness but was doubled many times over by regret for the light that had vanished. She asked herself why, since light had been able to shine for a while, it could not keep on shining. Why should it die out? Why had it died out? It was a new regret to add to the others – drawn from memories, the present, and dreams of the future – that sorrow was weaving around her heart. Although she was sunk in thought about this and it dominated her feelings, she wondered again, as though for the first time, whether the light had really gone out. The bitter truth seemed to be bombarding her emotions for the very first time.

Had the ties been severed between her and the young man who had filled her heart and imagination? Here was a new question, no matter how often it was repeated, and a new shock even though it had already penetrated her very bones. Her searing regret kept getting buffeted by the despair consuming her and the hopes fluttering in the air. Whenever a hope took flight, regret returned and settled deep inside her, to float back to the surface time and again, until it was firmly established. When her soul had bade farewell to the last of her hopes, regret became an inseparable part of her.

It was over, as though he had never existed. There was no way to get him now. How easy it was for them. They treated it like an everyday affair, as though remarking, "What are we going to eat tomorrow?" or "I had a strange dream last night" or even "You can smell the jasmine all over the roof terrace." A word here and a word there . . . a suggestion to announce and an opinion to explain. They were strangely calm and reserved, offering her smiling condolences and jesting encouragement. Then the topic of conversation would change and branch out.

Everything had ended. It would be incorporated into the family history and forgotten. How did her heart fit in with all this? She did not have a heart. No one imagined she had one. So in reality it did not exist. How alienated she felt. She was lost and abandoned. They were not part of her. She was not part of them. She was alone, banished, disowned. How could she forget that a single word bestowed by her father's tongue would suffice to change the face of the world and turn her into a new person? Just one word, the expression "yes," would be enough to produce a miracle. It would not have cost him a tenth of the effort that went into the long discussion leading to his refusal. Yet he had willed otherwise and had been pleased to let her suffer all this torment.

Although she was hurt, angry, and resentful, these emotions could not touch her father. They fell back impotently like a wild animal stopped by its trainer, whom it loves and fears. Aisha was not able to attack her father, not even in the depths of her heart. She continued in her love and devotion for him. She felt sincerely dutiful to him, as though he were a god whose decree could only be received with submission, love, and loyalty.

That evening the young girl tightened the rope of despair around her delicate neck. Her sensitive heart believed it had dried up and become barren forever. The role of happy indifference she had resolved to assume with her family doubled her nervous tension, as did participation in their conversation, which she imposed on herself. Finally her golden head bowed under the strain and their voices became a dull clamor in her ears. As soon as it was time to withdraw to the bedroom she collapsed there in exhaustion like an invalid. In the security provided by the darkness of the room, her face frowned for the first time, presenting an accurate reflection of the state of her heart.

Someone was still watching her, Khadija, but Aisha had been sure from the start that dissimulation would be useless with her. When they were at the coffee hour, she had avoided her eyes. Now that she was sitting beside her, there was no escape and no place to flee. Aisha expected her sister to pounce on the subject with her customary resolve. She waited from one moment to the next for the sound of her voice. Her heart welcomed the conversation, but not because it would give birth to any new hope. She wished to find some consolation in the excuses and anguish her sister would certainly express truthfully.

She did not have long to wait before Khadija's voice did make its way to her through the darkness: "Aisha, I'm really sorry, but God knows there's nothing I can do. I wish I had enough courage to ask Father to change his mind."

Aisha wondered whether these words were sincere or hypocritical. She reacted immediately to her sister's sad tones with a feeling of annoyance. Even so, she was forced to resume the false voice of happy indifference she had used throughout the coffee hour with her mother. She replied, "What's there to be sad or despondent about? My father wasn't in error. He wasn't unjust. There's no need to be in a hurry."

"This is the second time your marriage has been delayed because of me."

"I'm not sorry at all."

Khadija observed pointedly, "But this time's not like the first."

As quick as lightning Aisha realized what her sister meant. Her heart pounded painfully with love and regret, weeping from passion and love. It was a hidden love, which could be awakened by any hint reaching it from outside, whether intentional or accidental, like a sore or a boil that hurts when touched or pierced. She started to talk, but was forced to stop because she was out of breath. She was afraid her voice would give her away.

Then Khadija sighed and remarked, "That's why you find me so sad and melancholy. But our Lord is generous. There's no distress that's not followed by relief. Perhaps he'll wait and be patient, so he becomes your destiny no matter how unlikely that seems now."

Every part of Aisha's body cried out, "If only that were so!" But her tongue said, "It's all the same to me. The matter's simpler than you think."

"I hope that's the case. I'm very sad and upset, Aisha."

The door opened suddenly, and the form of Kamal could be made out in the faint light slipping in from the crack of the door. Khadija shouted at him crossly, "Why have you come? What do you want?"

The boy answered in a tone that revealed his indignation at her rude reception, "Don't drive me away.... Make room for me."

He jumped onto the bed and knelt between them. He put out a hand to each of them and began to tickle them. He wished to create a better atmosphere for his discussion than that suggested by Khadija's rebuff. They grabbed his hands, however, and said one after the other, "It's time for you to go to bed. Go and sleep."

He shouted angrily, "I won't go until I learn what I've come to ask you about."

"What do you want to ask about at this hour of the night?"

Changing his tone in hopes they would pay attention to him, he asked, "I want to know whether you'll both leave the house when you get married."

Khadija yelled at him, "Wait till the marriage takes place!"

He asked obstinately, "But what is marriage?"

"How can I answer you when I haven't been married? . . . Go and sleep. May God protect you from evil."

"I won't go until I find out."

"My dear, trust in God and leave us."

In a sad voice he said, "I want to know if you'll both leave the house when you get married."

She replied angrily, "Yes, sir. . . . What else do you want?"

He said anxiously, "Then don't get married. That's what I want."

"We hear and obey."

Then he went on, protesting excitedly, "I can't bear for you to go far away from us. I'll pray to God that you never get married."

Khadija shouted, "Straight from your mouth to the portals of heaven. . . . Great . . . wonderful. May our Lord be generous to you. Be kind enough to leave us in peace."

27

A FEELING spread through the household that they would have a day's reprieve from their oppressively prim life. Safe from their guardian's eye, they would be able, if they so desired, to get an innocent breath of fresh air. Kamal was of the opinion that he could do as he wished and spend the whole day playing, inside the house and out. Khadija and Aisha wondered if they might slip over to Maryam's house in the evening to spend an hour there having fun and amusing themselves.

This break did not come as a result of the passing of the gloomy winter months and the arrival of the first signs of spring with intimations of warmth and good cheer. It was not occasioned by spring granting this family liberty they had been deprived of by winter. This respite came as a natural consequence of a business trip, lasting a day or more, that al-Sayyid Ahmad made to Port Said every few years. It so happened that he set out on a Friday morning when the weekly holiday brought the family together. They all responded eagerly to the freedom and the peaceful, relaxed atmosphere the father's departure from Cairo had unexpectedly created.

The mother hesitantly dashed the girls' hopes and the young boy's high spirits. She wanted to make sure the family persisted with its customary schedule and adhered, even when the father was absent, to the same rules it observed when he was present. She was more concerned to keep from vexing him than she was convinced that he was right to be so severe and stern.

Before she knew what was happening, though, here was Yasin saying, "Don't oppose God's plan. . . . Nobody else lives like us. In fact, I want to say something novel. . . . Why don't you have some fun too? What do you all think about this suggestion?"

Their eyes looked at him in astonishment, but no one said a word. Perhaps, like their mother, who gave him a critical look, they did not take what he was saying seriously. All the same, he continued: "Why are you looking at me like this? I haven't contravened any of the directives of the Prophet recorded in the revered collection of al-Bukhari. Praise God, no crime has been committed. All it would amount to is a brief excursion to have a look at a little of the district you've lived in for forty years but never seen."

The woman sighed and murmured, "May God be merciful to you."

The young man laughed out loud. He said, "Why should you ask God to be merciful to me? Have I committed some unforgivable sin? By God, if I were you, I'd go as far as the mosque of our master al-Husayn. . . . Our master al-Husayn, don't you hear? . . . Your beloved saint whom you adore from afar when he's so near. Go to him. He's calling you."

Her heart pounded and the effect could be seen in her blush. She lowered her head to hide how deeply she was affected. Her heart responded to the call with a force that exploded suddenly in her soul. She was taken by surprise. No one around her could have anticipated this, not even Yasin himself. It was as though an earthquake had shaken a land that had never experienced one before. She did not understand how her heart could answer this appeal, how her eyes could look beyond the limits of what was allowed, or how she could consider the adventure possible and even tempting, no − irresistible. Of course, since it was such a sacred pilgrimage, a visit to the shrine of al-Husayn appeared a powerful excuse for the radical leap her will was making, but that was not the only factor influencing her soul. Deep inside her, imprisoned currents yearning for release responded to this call in the same way that eager, aggressive instincts answer the call for a war proclaimed to be in defense of freedom and peace.

She did not know how to announce her fateful surrender. She looked at Yasin and said in a trembling voice, "A visit to the shrine of al-Husayn is something my heart has wished for all my life . . . but . . . your father?"

Yasin laughed and answered, "My father's on his way to Port Said. He won't be back until tomorrow morning. As an extra precaution you can borrow Umm Hanafi's wrap, so anyone who sees you leaving the house or returning will think you're a visitor."

She looked back and forth between her children with embarrassment and dread, as though seeking more encouragement. Khadija and Aisha were enthusiastic about the suggestion. In their enthusiasm they seemed to be expressing both their own imprisoned desire to break free and their joy at the visit to Maryam, which had become, after this revolution, a certainty.

Expressing his heartfelt approval, Kamal shouted, "I'll go with you, Mother, and show you the way."

Fahmy gazed at her affectionately when he saw the expression of anxious pleasure on her face, like that of a child hoping to get a new toy. To encourage her and play down the importance of the adventure, he said, "Have a look at the world. There's nothing wrong with that. I'm afraid you'll forget how to walk after staying home so much."

In an outburst of enthusiasm Khadija ran to Umm Hanafi to get the black cloth she wrapped around herself when she went out. Everyone was laughing and offering their comments. The day turned into a more joyous festival than any they had experienced. They all participated, unwittingly, in the revolution against their absent father's will. Mrs. Amina wrapped the cloth around her and pulled the black veil down over her face. She looked in the mirror and laughed until her torso shook. Kamal put on his suit and fez and got to the courtyard before her, but she did not follow him. She was afflicted by the kind of fear people feel at crucial turning points. She raised her eyes to Fahmy and asked, "What do you think? Should I really go?"

Yasin yelled at her, "Trust God."

Khadija went up to her. Placing her hands on her shoulders, she gave her a gentle push, saying, "Reciting the opening prayer of the Qur'an will protect you." Khadija propelled her all the way to the stairs. Then she withdrew her hands. The woman descended, with everyone following her. She found Umm Hanafi waiting for her. The servant cast a searching look at her mistress, or rather at the cloth encompassing her. She shook her head disapprovingly, went to her, and wrapped the cloth around her again. She taught her how to hold the edge in the right place. Her mistress, who was wearing this wrap for the first time, followed the servant's directions. Then the angles and curves of her figure, ordinarily concealed by her flowing housedresses, were visible in all their details. Smiling, Khadija gave her an admiring look and winked at Aisha. They burst into laughter.

As she crossed the threshold of the outer door and entered the street, she experienced a moment of panic. Her mouth felt dry and her pleasure was dispelled by a fit of anxiety. She had an oppressive feeling of doing something wrong. She moved slowly and grasped Kamal's hand nervously. Her gait seemed disturbed and unsteady, as though she had not mastered the first principles of walking. She was gripped by intense embarrassment as she showed herself to the eyes of people she had known for ages but only through the peephole of the enclosed balcony. Uncle Hasanayn, the barber, Darwish, who sold beans, al-Fuli, the milkman, Bayumi, the drinks vendor, and Abu Sari', who sold snacks – she imagined that they all recognized her just as she did them. She had difficulty convincing herself of the obvious fact that none of them had ever seen her before in their lives.

They crossed the street to Qirmiz Alley. It was not the shortest route to the mosque of al-Husayn, but unlike al-Nahhasin Street, it did not pass by al-Sayyid Ahmad's store or any other shops and was little frequented. She stopped for a moment before plunging into the alley. She turned to look at her latticed balcony. She could make out the shadows of her two daughters behind one panel. Another panel was raised to reveal the smiling faces of Fahmy and Yasin. The sight of them gave her some courage for her project.

Then she hurried along with her son down the desolate alley, feeling almost calm. Her anxiety and sense of doing something wrong did not leave her, but they retreated to the edges of her conscious emotions. Center stage was occupied by an eager interest in exploring the world as it revealed one of its alleys, a square, novel buildings, and lots of people. She found an innocent pleasure in sharing the motion and freedom of other living creatures. It was the pleasure of someone who had spent a quarter of a century imprisoned by the walls of her home, except for a limited number of visits to her mother in al-Khurunfush, where she would go a few times a year but in a carriage and chaperoned by her husband. Then she would not even have the courage to steal a look at the street.

She began to ask Kamal about the sights, buildings, and places they encountered on their way. The boy was proud to serve as her guide and volunteered lengthy explanations. Here was the famous vaulted ceiling of Qirmiz Alley. Before walking beneath it one needed to recite the opening prayer of the Qur'an as a defense against the jinn living there. This was Bayt al-Qadi Square with its tall trees. She might have heard him refer to the square as Pasha's Beard Square, from the popular name for its flowering lebbek trees, or at times also as Shangarly Square, giving it the name of the Turkish owner of a chocolate shop. This large building was the Gamaliya police station. Although the boy found little there to merit his attention, except the sword dangling from the sentry's waist, the mother looked at it with curiosity, since it was the place of employment of a man who had sought Aisha's hand. They went on until they reached Khan Ja'far Primary School, where Kamal had spent a year before enrolling at Khalil Agha Elementary School. He pointed to its historic balcony and remarked, "On this balcony Shaykh Mahdi made us put our faces to the wall for the least offense. Then he would kick us five, six, or ten times. Whatever he felt like."

Gesturing toward a store situated directly under the balcony, he stopped walking and said in a tone she could not mistake, "This is Uncle Sadiq, who sells sweets." He refused to budge until he had extracted a coin from her and bought himself a gummy red candy.

After that they turned into Khan Ja'far Alley. Then in the distance they could see part of the exterior of the mosque of al-Husayn. In the center was an expansive window decorated with arabesques. The façade was topped by a parapet with merlons like spear points bunched tightly together.

With joy singing in her breast, she asked, "Our master al-Husayn?" He confirmed her guess. Her pace quickened for the first time since she left the house. She began to compare what she saw with the picture created by her imagination and based on what she had seen from her home of mosques like Qala'un and Barquq. She found the reality to be less grand than she had imagined. In her imagination she had made its size correspond to the veneration in which she held its holy occupant. This difference between imagination and reality, however, in no way affected the pervasive intoxication of her joy at being there.

They walked around the outside of the mosque until they reached the green door. They entered, surrounded by a crowd of women visitors. When the woman's feet touched the floor of the shrine, she felt that her body was dissolving into tenderness, affection, and love and that she was being transformed into a spirit fluttering in the sky, radiant with the glow of prophetic inspiration. Her eyes swam with tears that helped relieve the agitation of her breast, the warmth of her love and belief, and the flood of her benevolent joy. She proceeded to devour the place with greedy, curious eyes: the walls, ceiling, pillars, carpets, chandeliers, pulpit, and the mihrab niches indicating the direction of Mecca.

Kamal, by her side, looked at these things from his own special point of view, assuming that the mosque served as a shrine for people during the day and the early evening but afterward was the home for his martyred master al-Husayn. The Prophet's grandson would come and go there, making use of the furnishings in much the same way any owner uses his possessions. Al-Husayn would walk around inside and pray facing a prayer niche. He would climb into the pulpit and ascend to the windows to look out at his district surrounding the mosque. How dearly Kamal wished, in a dreamy kind of way, that they would forget him in the mosque when they locked the doors so he would be able to meet al-Husayn face to face and pass a whole night in his presence until morning. He imagined the manifestations of love and submission appropriate for him to present to al-Husayn when they met and the hopes and requests suitable for him to lay at his feet. In addition to all that, he looked forward to the affection and blessing he would find with al-Husayn. He pictured himself with his head bowed, approaching the martyr, who would ask him gently, "Who are you?"

He would answer, before kissing his hand, "Kamal Ahmad Abd al-Jawad." Al-Husayn would ask what his profession was. He would reply, "A pupil in Khalil Agha School," and not forget to hint that he was doing well. Al-Husayn would ask what brought him at that hour of the night. Kamal would reply that it was love for all the Prophet's family and especially for him.

Al-Husayn would smile affectionately and invite him to accompany him on his nightly rounds. At that, Kamal would reveal all his requests at once: "Please grant me these things. I want to play as much as I like, inside the house and out. I want Aisha and Khadija to stay in our house always. Please change my father's temper and prolong my mother's life forever. I would like to have as much spending money as I can use and for us all to enter paradise without having to be judged."

The slowly moving flow of women carried them along until they found themselves near the tomb itself. How often she had longed to visit this site, as though yearning for a dream that could never be achieved on this earth. Here she was standing within the shrine. Indeed, here she was touching the walls of the tomb itself, looking at it through her tears. She wished she could linger to savor this taste of happiness, but the pressure of the crowd was too great. She stretched out her hands to the wooden walls and Kamal imitated her. Then they recited the opening prayer of the Qur'an. She stroked the walls and kissed them, never tiring of her prayers and entreaties. She would have liked to stand there a long time or sit in a corner to gaze at it and then circle around again, but the mosque attendant was watching everyone closely. He would not allow any of the women to tarry. He urged on women who slowed down and waved his long stick at them threateningly. He entreated them all to finish their visit before the Friday prayer service.

She had sipped from the sweet spiritual waters of the shrine but had not drunk her fill. There was no way to quench her thirst. Visiting the shrine had so stirred up her yearnings that they gushed forth from their springs, flowed out, and burst over their banks. She would never stop wanting more of this intimacy and delight. When she found herself obliged to leave the mosque, she had to tear herself away, her heart bidding it farewell. She left very regretfully, tormented by the feeling that she was saying farewell to it forever, but her characteristic temperance and resignation intervened to chide her for giving in to her sorrow. Thus she was able to enjoy the happiness she had gained and use it to banish the anxieties aroused by leaving the shrine.

Kamal invited her to look at his school and they went to see it at the end of al-Husayn Street. They paused there for a long time. When she wanted to return the way they had come, the mention of returning signaled the conclusion of this happy excursion with his mother, which he had never before dreamed would be possible. He refused to abandon it so quickly and fought desperately to prolong it. He proposed a walk along New Street to al-Ghuriya. In order to put an end to the opposition suggested by the smiling frown visible through her veil, he made her swear by al-Husayn. She sighed and surrendered herself to his young hand.

They made their way through the thick crowd and in and out of the clashing currents of pedestrians flowing in every direction. She would not have encountered even a hundredth of this traffic on the quiet route by which she had come. She began to be uneasy and almost beside herself with anxiety. She soon complained of discomfort and fatigue, but his desperation to complete this happy excursion made him turn a deaf ear to her complaints. He encouraged her to continue the journey. He tried to distract her by directing her attention to the shops, vehicles, and passersby. They were very slowly approaching the corner of al-Ghuriya. When they reached it, his eyes fell on a pastry shop, and his mouth watered. His eyes were fixed intently on the shop. He began to think of a way to persuade his mother to enter the store and purchase a pastry. He was still thinking about it when they reached the shop, but before he knew what was happening his mother had slipped from his hand. He turned toward her questioningly and saw her fall flat on her face, after a deep moan escaped her.

His eyes grew wide with astonishment and terror. He was unable to move. At approximately the same time, despite his dismay and alarm, he saw an automobile out of the corner of his eye. The driver was applying the brakes with a screeching sound, while the vehicle spewed a trail of dust and smoke. It came within a few inches of running over the prostrate woman, swerving just in time.

Everyone started shouting and a great clamor arose. People dashed to the spot from every direction like children following a magician's whistle. They formed a deep ring around her that seemed to consist of eyes peering, heads craning, and mouths shouting words, as questions got mixed up with answers.

Kamal recovered a little from the shock. He looked back and forth from his prostrate mother at his feet to the people around them, expressing his fear and need for help. Then he threw himself down on his knees beside her. He put his hand on her shoulder and called to her in a voice that was heartrending, but she did not respond. He raised his head and stared at the surrounding faces. Then he screamed out a fervent, sobbing lament that rose above the din around him and almost silenced it. Some people volunteered meaningless words of consolation. Others bent over his mother, examining her curiously, moved by two contrary impulses. Although they hoped the victim was all right, in case there was no hope for recovery they were grateful to see that death, that final conclusion which can only be delayed, had knocked on someone else's door and spirited away someone else's soul. They seemed to want a rehearsal free of any risks of that most perilous role each of them was destined to end his life playing.

One of them shouted, "The left door of the vehicle hit her in the back."

The driver had gotten out of the car and stood there half blinded by the glare of the accusations leveled at him. He protested, "She suddenly swerved off the sidewalk. I couldn't keep from hitting her. I quickly put on my brakes, so I just grazed her. But for the grace of God I would have run her down."

One of the men staring at her said, "She's still breathing. . . . She's just unconscious."

Seeing a policeman approaching, with the sword he carried on his left side swinging back and forth, the driver began speaking again: "It was only a little bump. . . . It couldn't have done anything to her. . . . She's fine . . . fine, everybody, by God."

The first man to examine her stood up straight and as though delivering a sermon said, "Get back. Let her have air. . . . She's opened her eyes. She's all right . . . fine, praise God." He spoke with a joy not devoid of pride, as though he was the one who had brought her back to life. Then he turned to Kamal, who was weeping so hysterically that the consolation of the bystanders had been without effect. He patted Kamal on the cheek sympathetically and told him, "That's enough, son. . . . Your mother's fine. . . . Look. . . . Come help me get her to her feet."

Even so, Kamal did not stop crying until he saw his mother move. He bent toward her and put her left hand on his shoulder. He helped the man lift her up. With great difficulty she was able to stand between them, exhausted and faint. Her wrap had fallen off her and some people helped put it back in place as best they could, wrapping it around her shoulders. Then the pastry merchant, in front of whose store the accident had taken place, brought her a chair. They helped her sit down, and he brought a glass of water. She swallowed some, but half of it spilled down her neck and chest. She wiped off her chest with a reflex motion and groaned. She was breathing with difficulty and looked in bewilderment at the faces staring at her. She asked, "What happened? . . . What happened? . . . Oh Lord, why are you crying, Kamal?"

At that point the policeman came forward. He asked her, "Are you injured, lady? Can you walk to the police station?"

The words "police station" came as a blow to her and shook her to the core. She shouted in alarm, "Why should I go to the police station? I'll never go there."

The policeman replied, "The car hit you and knocked you down. If you're injured, you and the driver must go to the police station to fill out a report."

Gasping for breath, she protested, "No . . . certainly not. I won't go. . . . I'm fine."

The policeman told her, "Prove it to me. Get up and walk so we can see if you're injured."

Driven by the alarm that the mention of the police station aroused in her, she got up at once. Surrounded by inquisitive eyes, she adjusted her wrap and began to walk. Kamal was by her side, brushing away the dust that clung to her. Hoping this painful situation would come to an end, no matter what it cost her, she told the policeman, "I'm fine." Then she gestured toward the driver and continued: "Let him go. . . . There's nothing the matter with me." She was so afraid that she no longer felt faint. The sight of the men staring at her horrified her, especially the policeman, who was in front of the others. She trembled from the impact of these looks directed at her from everywhere. They were a clear challenge and affront to a long life spent in seclusion and conceal-ment from strangers. She imagined she saw the image of al-Sayyid Ahmad rising above all the other men. He seemed to be studying her face with cold, stony eyes, threatening her with more evil than she could bear to imagine.

She lost no time in grabbing the boy's hand and heading off with him toward the Goldsmiths Bazaar. No one tried to stop her. No sooner had they turned the corner and escaped from sight than she moaned. Speaking to Kamal as though addres-sing herself, she said, "My Lord, how did this happen? What have I seen, Kamal? It was like a terrifying dream. I imagined I was falling into a dark pit from high up. The earth was revolving under my feet. Then I didn't know anything at all until I opened my eyes on that frightening scene. My Lord . . . did he really want to take me to the police station? O Gracious One, O Lord . . . my Savior, my Lord. How soon will we reach home? You cried a lot, Kamal. May you never lose your eyes. Dry your eyes with this handkerchief. You can wash your face at home. . . . Oh."

She stopped when they were almost at the end of the Gold-smiths Bazaar. She rested her hand on the boy's shoulder. Her face was contorted.

Kamal looked up with alarm and asked her, "What's the matter?"

She closed her eyes and said in a weak voice, "I'm tired, very tired. My feet can barely support me. Get the first vehicle you can find, Kamal."

Kamal looked around. All he could see was a donkey cart standing by the doorway of the ancient hospital of Qala'un. He summoned the driver, who quickly brought the cart to them. Leaning on Kamal's shoulder, the mother made her way to it. She clambered on board with his help, supporting herself on the driver's shoulder. He held steady until she was seated cross-legged in the cart. She sighed from her extreme exhaustion and Kamal sat down beside her. Then the driver leaped onto the front of the cart and prodded the donkey with the handle of his whip. The donkey walked off slowly, with the cart swaying and clattering behind him.

The woman moaned. She complained, "My pain's severe. The bones of my shoulder must be smashed." Meanwhile Kamal watched her with alarm and anxiety.

The vehicle passed by al-Sayyid Ahmad's store without either of them paying any attention. Kamal watched the road ahead until he saw the latticed balconies of their house. All he could remember of the happy expedition was its miserable conclusion.

28

WHEN UMM HANAFI opened the door she was startled to see her mistress sitting cross-legged on a donkey cart. Her first thought was that Mrs. Amina had decided to conclude her excursion with a cart ride just for the fun of it. So she smiled but only briefly, for she saw that Kamal's eyes were red from crying. She looked back at her mistress with alarm. This time she was able to fathom the exhaustion and pain the lady was suffering. She moaned and rushed to the cart, crying out, "My lady, what's the matter? May evil stay far away from you."

The driver replied, "God willing, it's nothing serious. Help me get her down."

Umm Hanafi grasped the woman in her arms and carried her inside. Kamal followed them, sad and dejected. Khadija and Aisha had left the kitchen to wait for them in the courtyard, thinking about some joke they could make when the two returned from their excursion. They were terribly surprised when Umm Hanafi appeared, struggling to carry their mother in from the outer hall. They both screamed and ran to her. Terrified, they were shouting, "Mother . . . Mother . . . what's wrong?"

They all helped carry her. At the same time Khadija kept asking Kamal what had happened. Finally the boy was forced to mutter with profound fear, "A car!"

"A car!"

The two girls shouted it together, repeating the word, which sounded incredibly alarming to them. Khadija wailed and screamed, "What terrible news! . . . May evil stay far away from you, Mother."

Aisha could not speak. She burst into tears. Their mother was not unconscious but extremely weak. Despite her fatigue she whispered to calm them, "I'm all right. No harm's done. I'm just tired."

The clamor reached Yasin and Fahmy. They came to the head of the stairs and looked down over the railing. Alarmed, they immediately hurried down, asking what had happened. From fear of repeating the dreadful word, Khadija gestured to Kamal to answer for himself. The two young men went over to the boy, who once again muttered sadly and anxiously, "A car!"

Then he started sobbing. The young men turned away from him, postponing for a time the questions that were troubling them. Together they carried the mother to the girls' room and sat her down on the sofa. Then Fahmy asked her anxiously and fearfully, "Tell me what's the matter, Mother. I want to know everything."

She leaned her head back and did not say anything while she tried to catch her breath. Meanwhile Khadija, Aisha, Umm Hanafi, and Kamal were weeping so loudly that they got on Fahmy's nerves. He scolded them till they stopped. Then he caught hold of Kamal to ask, "How did the accident come about? What did the people there do to the driver? Did they take you to the police station?" Without any hesitation Kamal answered his questions in full, giving most of the details.

The mother followed the conversation, despite her feeble condition. When the boy finished, she summoned all the strength she had and said, "I'm fine, Fahmy. Don't alarm yourself. They wanted me to go to the police station, but I refused. Then I came along as far as the end of the Goldsmiths Bazaar, where my strength suddenly gave out. Don't be upset. I'll get my strength back with a little rest."

In addition to his alarm over the accident Yasin was extremely upset, since he was responsible for suggesting what they would later term the ill-omened excursion. He said they should get a doctor. Without waiting to hear what anyone else thought of his idea, he left the room to carry it out. The mother shuddered at the mention of the doctor just as she had earlier at the reference to the police station. She asked Fahmy to catch his brother and dissuade him from going. She asserted that she would recover without any need for a doctor, but her son refused to give in to her request. He explained to her the need for one.

Meanwhile the two girls assisted each other in removing the wrap. Umm Hanafi brought a glass of water. Then they all crowded around her, anxiously examining her pale face and asking over and over how she felt. So far as she was able, she pretended to be calm. When the pain got bad, the most she said was: "There's a slight pain in my right shoulder." Then she added, "But there's no need for a doctor." The truth was that she did not like the idea of sending for a doctor. She had never had a doctor before, not merely because her health had been good but also because she had always succeeded in treating whatever ailed her with her own special medicine. She did not believe in modern medicine and associated it with major catastrophes and serious events. Further-more, she felt that summoning a doctor would have the effect of highlighting a matter she wanted to hush up and conceal before her husband returned. She did her best to explain her fears to her children, but at that delicate moment they were only concerned about her well-being.

Yasin was not gone more than a quarter of an hour, since the doctor's clinic was in Bayt al-Qadi Square. He returned ahead of the doctor, whom he took to his mother the moment he arrived. They emptied the room of everyone except Yasin and Fahmy. The doctor asked the mother where she hurt and she pointed to her right shoulder. Her throat was dry with fear, but she swallowed and said, "I feel pain here."

Guided by what she said and what Yasin had told him before in general terms, he set about examining her. The examination seemed to take a long time, both to the young men waiting inside and to the women with throbbing hearts who were listening from the other side of the door. The doctor turned from his patient to Yasin and said, "There's a fracture of the right collarbone. That's all there is to it."

The word "fracture" caused dismay both inside and outside the room. They were all astonished that he had said, "That's all there is to it." It sounded as though there was something about a fracture that made it bearable. All the same, they found the phrase and the tone in which it was delivered reassuring. Torn between fear and hope, Fahmy asked, "Is that serious?"

"Not at all. I'll move the bone back where it belongs and fix it there, but she'll have to sleep a few nights sitting up with her back supported by a pillow. It'll be hard for her to sleep on her back or side. The fracture will set within two or three weeks at the most. There's no cause for alarm at all . . . Now let me get to work."

They all breathed a sigh of relief after having been worried sick, especially those outside the door. Khadija murmured, "May the blessing of our master al-Husayn rest with her. The only reason she went out was to visit him."

Kamal asked in astonishment, as though her words had reminded him of something important he had forgotten for too long, "How could this accident happen after she was blessed with a visit to our master al-Husayn?"

Umm Hanafi replied with great simplicity, "Who knows what might have befallen her, we take refuge in God, had she not been blessed by visiting her master and ours?"

Aisha had not recovered from the shock. All the talk was getting on her nerves. She cried out fervently, "Oh, my Lord, when will everything be over, as though it had never happened?"

With sorrow and regret Khadija spoke again: "What was she doing in al-Ghuriya? If she had returned home directly, immediately after the visit, nothing would have happened to her."

Kamal's heart pounded with fear and alarm. In his eyes his offense appeared an abominable crime. Even so, he tried to evade their suspicions. In a disapproving tone he said, "She wanted to walk along the road and I tried in vain to talk her out of it."

Khadija gave him an accusing look. She started to reply, but she stopped out of sympathy and concern for his pale face. She told herself, "We've got enough troubles for the time being."

The door opened and the doctor left the room. He told the two young men, who followed him, "I'll have to see her every day until the fracture sets, but as I told you, there's absolutely no cause for alarm."

They all rushed into the room. They saw their mother sitting on the bed with her back supported by a pillow folded behind her. The only difference was a bulge in her dress over her right shoulder that betrayed the existence of a bandage beneath it. They rushed over to her and called out, "Praise to God."

When the doctor had been treating her fracture, the pain had been intense. She had moaned continually. Had it not been for her natural reserve, she would have screamed aloud. The pain was gone now, or so it appeared. She felt relatively comfortable and peaceful. The diminution of her sharp pain, though, allowed her mind to resume its energetic activity and she was able to think

about the situation from different points of view. She was soon
consumed by fear. With her eyes wandering back and forth
between them she asked, "What can I say to your father when
he returns?"

This question, like a protruding boulder blocking the safe
passage of a ship, mockingly challenged the wisps of reassurance
they had grasped. It did not take their minds by surprise. It had
perhaps insinuated itself into the crowd of painful emotions their
hearts had harbored since they were first confronted by the news,
but it had been lost sight of in the confusion. Consideration of it
had been postponed for a time. Now it had returned to occupy the
place of honor in their souls. They found no alternative to confronting it. They considered it to be more threatening to them and
their mother than the fracture from which she would soon
recover. When her question was greeted by silence, the mother
felt isolated, like a guilty person whose comrades desert him when
an accusation is lodged against him. She complained softly, "He'll
certainly learn about the accident. Moreover, he'll discover I went
outside, because that's what led up to it."

Although Umm Hanafi was no less worried than the family
members and understood the seriousness of the situation just as
well as the others, she still wanted to say something reassuring to
lighten the atmosphere. She also felt it her duty as a longtime and
devoted servant of the family not to keep quiet when calamity
struck. She was afraid they might think she did not care. Even
though she was well aware that her words were remote from
reality, she observed, "When my master learns what happened to
you, he'll have to overlook your mistake and praise God for your
safe recovery."

Her comment was received with the neglect it deserved from
people who could see the reality of the situation quite clearly. All
the same, Kamal believed it. As though completing Umm Hanafi's
statement, Kamal said enthusiastically, "Especially if we tell him
we only went out to visit our master al-Husayn."

The woman looked back and forth from Yasin to Fahmy with
her half-closed eyes, and asked, "What can I say to him?"

Yasin, who was overwhelmed by the weight of his responsibility, said, "What demon led me astray so that I advised you to go
out? A word slipped from my tongue. I wish it never had. But the
fates wanted to cast us into this painful predicament. Even so,

I assure you that we'll think of something to tell him. In any case, you shouldn't trouble your mind about what might happen. Leave the matter to God. The pains and fears you've endured today are enough for you now."

Yasin spoke with intensity and affection. He was pouring out his indignation against himself and his affection for their mother. He was commiserating with her situation. Although his words did not help or hinder anything, they provided some relief for his oppressive feeling of anguish. At the same time he was probably expressing what was going through the minds of those standing there with him. He spared them from having to express it themselves.

He had learned from experience that sometimes the best way to defend one's actions is to attack them. A confession of guilt would promote goodwill as much as an attempt to defend himself would have aroused anger. What he had most to fear was that Khadija would seize this golden opportunity to attack him openly about his responsibility for the consequences of his advice. She could use it to assail him. He had anticipated her plan and pulled the rug out from under her.

He was right about his hunch, for Khadija was just about to demand that he, as the person with primary responsibility for what had happened, should find them some solution. After he had made his little speech, she was ashamed to attack him, especially since she did not usually assail him in anger but only when they were bickering. Thus Yasin's situation was slightly improved, but the overall situation remained bad. Nothing improved it, until Khadija volunteered, "Why don't we claim she fell on the stairs?"

Her mother looked at her with a face that yearned for salvation by any means. She looked at Fahmy and Yasin too. There was a glimmer of hope showing in her eyes. All the same, Fahmy asked anxiously, "What about the doctor? He'll be checking on her day after day. Father will certainly bump into him."

Yasin refused to close the door through which a breath of hope had slipped to hint he might be rescued from his pains and fears. He said, "We can reach an agreement with the doctor about what Father should be told."

They looked back and forth at each other, trying to decide whether to accept or reject this idea. Then the gloomy atmosphere became festive, and a mutual feeling of salvation was evident in their faces. It was like a blue streak appearing unexpectedly in the middle of dark clouds. By an amazing miracle, the blue streak spread in just a few minutes until it covered the entire celestial dome and the sun came out.

Yasin said, "We've been saved, praise God."

After Khadija recovered her normal vivacity in the new climate, she told Yasin, "No, you've been saved. You're the one who thought it all up."

Yasin laughed until his huge body shook. He replied, "Yes, I've been saved from the scorpion sting of your tongue. I've been expecting it would reach out and bite me."

"But it's my tongue that saved you. For the sake of the rose, the thorns get watered."

In their happiness at being saved they had almost forgotten that their mother was confined to bed with a broken collarbone, but she herself had almost forgotten it too.

SHE OPENED her eyes and found Khadija and Aisha sitting on the bed by her feet. They were gazing at her with expressions wavering between hope and fear. She sighed and turned toward the window. She saw bright daylight streaming through the gaps in the shutters. She murmured in disbelief, "I slept a long time."

Then Aisha said, "Just a few hours. It was dawn before you closed your eyelids. What a night! I'll never forget it, no matter how long I live."

The mother was visited once again by memories of the past night dominated by sleeplessness and pain. Her eyes expressed her sorrow for herself and the two girls who had sat up with her all night, sharing her pain and insomnia. She moved her lips as she inaudibly sought God's protection. Then she whispered, almost in embarrassment, "I've really worn you out. . . ."

In a playful tone Khadija answered, "Wearing ourselves out for you is relaxing, but you had better not scare us again." Then she continued in a voice that showed emotion was getting the better of her: "How could that dreadful pain pick on you? . . . I'd think you were sound asleep and in good shape and lie down to get some sleep myself, only to wake up hearing you moan. You kept going 'Oh . . . oh' till dawn."

Aisha's face shone with optimism as she said, "In any case, here's good news. This morning I told Fahmy how you were doing when he asked about your health. He told me the pain troubling you was a sign the broken bone was starting to mend."

Fahmy's name brought Amina back from the depths of her thoughts. She asked, "Did they all get off safely?"

Khadija replied, "Of course. They wanted to speak to you and reassure themselves about you, but I wouldn't let anyone wake you after we'd gotten white hair waiting for you to doze off."

Their mother sighed with resignation, "Praise to God in any case. May our Lord make everything turn out for the best. . . . What time is it now?"

Khadija said, "It's an hour till the noon call to prayer."

The lateness of the hour prompted her to lower her eyes thoughtfully. When she raised them again, her anxiety was reflected in her look. She murmured, "He may be on his way home now. . . ."

They understood what she meant. Although they could feel fear creeping through their hearts, Aisha said confidently, "He's most welcome. There's no reason to be anxious. We've agreed on what has to be said, and that ends the matter."

All the same, his impending arrival spread anxiety through Amina's feeble soul. She asked, "Do you think it will be possible to conceal what happened?"

In a voice that became noticeably sharper as her anxiety increased, Khadija answered, "Why not? We'll tell him what we agreed on, and the matter will pass peacefully."

Their mother wished that Yasin and Fahmy could have stayed by her side at that hour to give her courage. Khadija had said, "We'll tell him what we agreed on, and the matter will pass peacefully," but could what had happened remained a closed secret forever? Would the truth not find some opening through which it could reach the man? She feared lying just as much as she feared the truth. She did not know what destiny lay in wait for her. She looked affectionately at one girl and then the other. She had opened her mouth to speak when Umm Hanafi rushed in. She whispered, as though afraid someone outside the room might hear, "My master has come, my lady."

Their hearts beat wildly. The girls got off the bed in a single bound. They stood facing their mother. They all exchanged glances silently. Then the mother mumbled, "Don't you two say anything. I'm afraid of what might happen to you if you deceive him. Leave the talking to me, may God provide assistance."

A tense silence reigned like that of children in the dark who hear footsteps they think are those of jinn prowling around outside. Then they could hear al-Sayyid Ahmad's footsteps coming up the stairs. As they drew nearer, the mother struggled to break the nightmare silence. She mumbled, "Should we let him climb up to his room and not find anyone?"

She turned to Umm Hanafi and said, "Tell him I'm here, sick. Don't say anything more."

She swallowed to wet her dry throat. The two girls shot out of the room, each trying to escape first. They left her alone. Finding herself cut off from the entire world, she resigned herself to her destiny. Frequently this resignation on her part, since she was deprived of any weapon, seemed a passive kind of courage. She collected her thoughts in order to remember what she was supposed to say, although her doubt that she was doing the right thing never left her. It hid at the bottom of her emotions and announced its presence whenever she was anxious and tense or her confidence dwindled.

She heard the tip of his stick striking the floor of the sitting room. She mumbled, "Your mercy, Lord, and assistance."

Her eyes watched the doorway until he blocked it with his tall and broad body. She saw him come in and approach her. He gave her a searching look with his wide eyes. When he reached the center of the room he stopped and asked in a voice she imagined was more tender than usual, "What's the matter with you?"

Lowering her eyes, she said, "Praise to God for your safe return, sir. I'm well so long as you are."

"But Umm Hanafi told me you're sick. . . . "

With her left hand she pointed to her right shoulder and said, "My shoulder has been injured, sir. May God not expose you to any evil."

Examining her shoulder with concern and anxiety, the man asked, "What injured it?"

It was destined to happen. The crucial moment had arrived. She had only to speak, to utter the saving lie. Then the crisis would be safely concluded. She would receive even more than her share of sympathy. She raised her eyes in preparation for it. Then her eyes met his, or, more precisely, were consumed by his. Her heart beat faster, pounding mercilessly. At that moment all the ideas she had collected in her mind evaporated. The determination she had accumulated in her will was dispersed. Her eyes blinked from dismay and consternation. Then she gazed at him with a bewildered expression and said nothing.

Al-Sayyid Ahmad was amazed to see her confusion. He was quick to ask her, "What happened, Amina?"

She did not know what to say. She did not seem to have anything to say, but she was now certain she would not be able to lie. The opportunity had escaped without her knowing how. If

she renewed the attempt, the words would come out in a disjointed and damning way. She was like a person who after having
walked over a tightrope in a hypnotic trance is asked to repeat the
trick in a conscious state. As the seconds passed she felt increasingly
nervous and defeated. She was on the brink of despair.

"Why don't you speak?" His tone seemed to suggest he was
growing impatient and would soon start shouting angrily. By God,
she certainly needed some assistance. What demon had tempted
her to go on that ill-omened excursion?

"Strange. Don't you want to speak?"

The silence then was more than she could bear. Driven by
despair and defeat, she murmured in a shaking voice, "I have
committed a grave error, sir. . . . I was struck by an automobile."

His eyes widened with astonishment. A look of alarm coupled
with disbelief could be seen in them. It seemed he had begun to
doubt her sanity. The woman could no longer bear to hesitate. She
resolved to give a complete confession, no matter what the consequences. She was like a person who risks his life in a dangerous
surgical operation to get relief from a painful disease he can no
longer endure. Her feeling of the seriousness of her offense and the
danger of her confession doubled. Tears welled up in her eyes. In a
voice she did not attempt to keep free from sobs, either because
she could not help it or because she wanted to make a desperate
appeal to his sympathy, she said, "I thought I heard our master al-
Husayn calling me to visit him. So I obeyed the call. . . . I went to
visit his shrine. . . . On the way home an automobile ran into
me. . . . It's God's decree, sir. I got up without anyone needing
to help me." She spoke this last sentence very distinctly. Then she
continued: "At first I didn't feel any pain. So I thought I was fine. I
walked on until I reached the house. Here the pain started. They
brought me a doctor, who examined my shoulder. He decided it
was broken. He promised to return every day until the fracture is
healed. I have committed a grave error, sir. I have been punished
for it as I deserve. . . . God is forgiving and compassionate."

Al-Sayyid Ahmad listened to her without commenting or
moving. He did not turn his eyes away from her. His face revealed
nothing of his internal agitation. Meanwhile she bowed her head
humbly like a defendant waiting for the verdict to be pronounced.
The silence was prolonged and intense. The oppressive atmosphere was shot through with intimations of fearful threats. She was

nervous about it and did not know what decree was being worked up or what fate would be allotted her.

Then she heard his strangely calm voice ask, "What did the doctor say? . . . How serious is the fracture?"

She turned her head toward him in bewilderment. She had been ready for anything except this gracious response. If the situation had not been so terrifying, she would have asked him to repeat it so she could be sure she had heard him correctly. She was overcome by emotion. Two large tears sprang from her eyes. She pressed her lips tightly together to keep from being choked up by weeping. Then she mumbled contritely and humbly, "The doctor said there's absolutely no reason to worry. May God spare you any evil, sir."

The man stood there for a time, struggling with his desire to ask more questions. He got control of himself and then turned to leave the room, saying, "Stay in bed till God heals you."

30

KHADIJA AND AISHA rushed into the room after their father left. They stopped in front of their mother and looked at her inquisitively. Their expression revealed their concern and anxiety. When they noticed that their mother's eyes were red from crying they were disturbed. Although her heart was fearful and pessimistic, Khadija asked, "Good news, God willing?"

Blinking her eyes nervously, the mother limited herself to replying tersely, "I confessed the truth to him."

"The truth!"

With resignation she said, "I wasn't able to do anything but confess. There was no way the affair could have been kept from him forever. I did the best thing."

Khadija thumped her chest with her hand and cried out, "What an unlucky day for us!"

Aisha was struck dumb. She stared at her mother's face without uttering a word. The mother smiled with a mixture of pride and embarrassment. Her pale face blushed when she remembered the affection he had showered on her when she had been expecting nothing but his overwhelming anger that would blow her and her future away. Yes, she felt both pride and embarrassment when she started to talk about their father's sympathy for her in her time of need and how he had forgotten his anger because of the affection and pity that had seized hold of him.

Then Amina murmured in a soft voice that was barely audible, "He was merciful to me, may God prolong his life. He listened silently to my story. Then he asked me what the doctor had said about the seriousness of the fracture and left. He directed me to stay in bed till God would take me by the hand."

The two girls exchanged astonished and incredulous glances. Then their fear quickly left them. They both sighed deeply with relief, and their faces became bright with joy. Khadija shouted, "Don't you see? It's the blessing of al-Husayn."

Her prediction having come true, Aisha commented proudly, "Everything has its limits, even Papa's anger. There was no way he could be angry with her once he saw her in this state. Now we know how much she means to him." Then she teased her mother, "What a lucky mother you are! Congratulations to you for the honor and affection shown you."

The blush returned to the mother's face and she stammered modestly, "May God prolong his life. . . . " She sighed and continued, "Praise to God for this salvation."

She remembered something and turned to Khadija. She told her with concern, "You've got to go to him. He'll certainly need your help."

The girl was nervous and uncomfortable in her father's presence. She felt she had fallen into a trap. She replied angrily, "Why can't Aisha go?"

Her mother said critically, "You're better able to serve him. Don't waste time, young lady. He may be needing you this very moment."

Khadija knew it would be pointless to protest, since it always was when her mother asked her to undertake a task for which she thought Khadija better suited than her sister. All the same, she was determined to voice her objection as she always did at such times, driven by her fiery temper as well as her aggressive nature that made her tongue its most willing and incisive weapon. She wanted to force her mother to say once more that she was more proficient at this or that than Aisha. That would be an admission from her mother, a warning to her sister, and a consolation for her.

The fact was that if one of these important tasks had been awarded to Aisha instead of her, she would have been even more furious and would have intervened. In her heart she still felt that performing these duties was one of her rights. They set her apart as a woman worthy of her status as second-in-command to her mother in the household. Yet she refused to acknowledge openly that she was exercising one of her rights when she undertook the task. It was, rather, a heavy burden that she accepted only under duress. Thus anyone summoning her to do something would feel uncomfortable about it. If she objected, she would be able to protest with an anger that would provide her some relief. She could make whatever commentary she wished about the situation. Finally, she would be reckoned to be doing the person a favor meriting his thanks.

Therefore as she left the room, she said, "In every crisis you call on Khadija, as though there was no one else at hand. What would you do if I weren't here?"

The moment she left, her pride abandoned her. Its place was taken by terror and agitation. How could she present herself to him? How would she go about serving him? How would he treat her if she stuttered or was slow or made a mistake?

Al-Sayyid Ahmad had removed his street clothes by himself and put on his house shirt. When she stood at the door to ask what he needed, he ordered her to make a cup of coffee. She hastened to fetch it. Then she presented it to him, walking softly with her eyes lowered, feeling shy and afraid. She retreated to the sitting room just outside his door to wait there for any signal from him. Her sense of terror never left her. She wondered how she would be able to continue serving him through all the hours he spent at home, day after day, until the three weeks were over. The matter seemed nerve-racking to her. She perceived for the first time the importance of the niche her mother filled in the household. She prayed for her speedy recovery out of both love for her mother and pity for herself.

Unluckily for her, al-Sayyid Ahmad was of a mind to rest up after the fatigue of his journey and did not go to the store as she hoped. Accordingly, she was obliged to remain in the sitting room like a prisoner. Aisha came up to the top floor and crept silently into the room where her sister was sitting. She came to parade herself before Khadija. She winked at her to ridicule her situation. Then she returned to her mother, leaving her sister boiling with rage. The thing that infuriated Khadija most was for someone to tease her, even though she happily teased everyone else. Khadija regained her freedom, and then just provisionally, only when her father fell asleep. Then she flew to her mother and began to tell her about all the real and imaginary services she had rendered her father. She described to her the signs of affection and appreciation for her services that she had noticed in his eyes. She did not forget to turn on Aisha and rain abuse and reprimands on her for her childish conduct.

She went back to her father when he woke up and served him lunch. After the man finished eating, he sat reading over some papers for a long time. Then he summoned her and asked her to send Yasin and Fahmy to him the moment they got home.

The mother was upset about his request. She was afraid that the man's soul had some concealed anger trapped inside and that he now wished to find a target for his anger – namely, the two young men.

When Yasin and Fahmy came home and learned what had happened and that their father had ordered them to appear before him, their minds entertained the same thought. They went to his room with fearful forebodings, but the man surprised them by greeting them more calmly than usual. He asked them about the accident, the circumstances surrounding it, and the doctor's report. They recounted at length what they knew while he listened with interest. Finally he asked, "Were you at home when she went out?"

Although they had expected this question from the outset, when it came after this unexpected and unusual calm, it alarmed them. They feared it was a prelude to change from the harmony they had enjoyed with relief, thinking they were safe. They were unable to speak and chose to remain silent. All the same, al-Sayyid Ahmad did not insist on his question. He seemed to attach little importance to hearing the answer he had guessed in advance. Perhaps he wanted to point out their error, without caring whether they confessed. After that he did nothing but show them the door, allowing them to depart. As they were walking out, they heard him say to himself, "Since God has not provided me with any sons, let Him grant me patience."

Although the incident appeared to have shaken al-Sayyid Ahmad enough that he was altering his conduct to an extent that amazed everyone, it could not dissuade him from enjoying his traditional nightly outing. When evening came he dressed and left his room, diffusing a fragrance of perfume. On his way out he passed by his wife's room to inquire about her. She prayed for him at length, gratefully and thankfully. She did not see anything rude in his going out when she was confined to bed. She may have felt that for him to stop to see her and ask after her was more recognition than she had expected. Indeed, if he refrained from pouring out his anger on her, was that not a boon she had not even dreamt of?

Before their father had left his room, the brothers had asked, "Do you suppose he'll forsake his evening's entertainment tonight?"

The mother had replied, "Why should he stay home when he's learned there's nothing to be worried about?" Privately she might have wished he would complete his kind treatment of her by renouncing his night out, as was appropriate for a husband whose wife had suffered what she had. Since she knew his temperament well, though, she fabricated an excuse for him in advance, so that if he did rush off to his party, as she expected, she could put a pleasant face on her situation. She would justify his departure with the excuse she had already invented and not let it seem to be caused by his indifference.

All the same, Khadija had asked, "How can he bear to be at a party when he sees you in this condition?"

Yasin had answered, "There's nothing wrong with his doing that once he's satisfied himself that she's all right. Men and women don't react to sorrow the same way. There's no contradiction between a man going out to a party and feeling sad. It may actually be his way of consoling himself so he'll be able to carry on with his difficult life." Yasin was not defending his father so much as his own desire to step out that was beginning to stir deep inside him.

His cunning did not work on Khadija. She asked him, "Could you stand spending the evening in your coffee shop?"

Although he cursed her secretly, he quickly replied, "Of course not. But I'm one thing and Papa's something else."

When al-Sayyid Ahmad left the room, Amina felt again the relief that follows a rescue from genuine danger. Her face lit up with a smile. She observed, "Perhaps he thought I'd already been punished enough for my offense. So he forgave me. May God forgive him and all of us."

Yasin struck his hands together and objected, "There are men as jealous as he is, some of them friends of his, who see no harm in permitting their women to go out when it's necessary or appropriate. What can he be thinking of to keep you imprisoned in the house all the time?"

Khadija glanced at him scornfully and asked, "Why didn't you deliver this appeal for us when you were with him?"

The young man began laughing so hard his belly shook. He

replied, "Before I can do that I need a nose like yours to defend myself with."

Her days in bed passed without a recurrence of the pain that had devastated her the first night, although the slightest movement would make her shoulder and torso hurt. She convalesced quickly because of her sturdy constitution and superabundant vitality. She had a natural dislike of being still and sitting around and that made obedience to the doctor's orders a difficult ordeal. The torment it caused her overshadowed the pains of the fracture at their worst. Perhaps she would have violated the doctor's commands and gotten up prematurely to look after things if her children had not watched her so relentlessly.

Yet her confinement did not prevent her from supervising household affairs from her bed. She would review everything assigned to the girls with a tiresome precision, especially the details of tasks she was afraid they might neglect or forget. She would ask persistently, "Did you dust the tops of the curtains? . . . The shutters? . . . Did you burn incense in the bathroom for your father? . . . Have you watered the hyacinth beans and jasmine?"

Khadija got annoyed by this once and told her, "Listen, if you took care of the house one carat, I'm taking care of it twenty-four."

In addition to all this, her compulsory abandonment of her important position brought with it some ambivalent feelings that troubled her a great deal. She asked herself whether it was true that the house and its inhabitants had not lost anything, in terms of either order or comfort, by her relinquishing her post. Which of the two alternatives would be preferable: for everything to remain just the way it ought to be, thanks to her two girls who had been nurtured by her hands, or that there should be sufficient disturbance of the household's equilibrium to remind everyone of the void she had left behind her? What if it was al-Sayyid Ahmad himself who sensed this void? Would that be a reason for him to appreciate her importance or a reason to become angry at her offense that had caused all this? The woman wavered for a long time between her abashed fondness for herself and her open affection for her daughters. It became clear that any shortcoming in the management of the house disturbed her immensely. On the other hand, if it had retained its perfection as though nothing had happened, she would not have been totally at ease.

In fact, no one did fill her place. Despite the earnest and energetic activity of the two girls, the house showed evidence of being too large for them. The mother was not happy about that, but she kept her feelings to herself. She defended Khadija and Aisha sincerely and vehemently. Even so, she suffered from alarm and pain and could not endure her seclusion patiently.

31

AT DAWN on the promised day, the day for which she had waited so long, she hopped out of bed with a youthful nimbleness derived from her joy. She felt like a king reclaiming his throne after being exiled. She went down to the oven room to resume her routine that had been interrupted for three weeks. She called Umm Hanafi. The woman woke up and could not believe her ears. She rose to greet her mistress, embracing her and praying for her. Then they set about the morning's work with an indescribable happiness.

When the first rays of the rising sun could be seen, she went upstairs. The children greeted her with congratulations and kisses. Then she went over to where Kamal was sleeping and woke him. The moment the boy opened his eyes he was overcome by astonishment and joy. He clung to her neck, but she was quick to free herself gently from his arms. She asked him, "Aren't you afraid my shoulder will get hurt again?"

He smothered her with kisses. Then he laughed and asked mischievously, "Darling, when can we go out together again?"

She replied in a tone that had a ring of friendly criticism, "When God has guided you enough so you don't lead me against my will to a street where I almost perish."

He understood she was referring to his stubbornness that had been the immediate cause of what befell her. He laughed until he could laugh no more. He laughed like a sinner who has been reprieved after having his offense hang over his head for three weeks. Yes, he had been terribly afraid that the investigation his brothers were conducting would reveal the secret culprit. The suspicions entertained by Khadija at one time and Yasin at another had come close to uncovering him in his redoubt. He had been spared only because his mother had defended him firmly and had resolved to bear responsibility for the accident all by herself. When the investigation had been transferred to his father, Kamal's fears had reached their climax. He had expected from one moment to the next to be summoned before his father. In addition to this fear, he had been tormented during the past three weeks by seeing his beloved mother confined to bed, suffering bitterly, unable either to lie down or to stand up. Now the accident was past history. Gone with it was its bad taste. The investigation was terminated. Once again his mother had come to wake him in the morning. She would put him to bed at night. Everything had returned to normal. Peace had unfurled its banners. He had a right to laugh his heart out and congratulate his conscience on its reprieve.

The mother left the boys' room to go to the top floor. When she approached the door of al-Sayyid Ahmad's room she could hear him saying in his prayers, "Glory to my Lord, the Magnificent." Her heart pounded and she stood hesitating, a step away from the door. She found herself wondering whether to go in to wish him good morning or prepare the breakfast tray first. She was less interested in the actual question than in fleeing from the fear and shame rampant in her soul, or perhaps she was interested in both. At times a person may create an imaginary problem to escape from an actual problem he finds difficult to resolve.

She went to the dining room and set to work with redoubled care. Even so, her anxiety increased. The period of delay she had granted herself was worthless. She did not find the relief she had hoped for. The ordeal of waiting was more painful than the situation she had shrunk from confronting. She was amazed that she had been scared to enter her own room, as though she were preparing to enter it for the first time. All the more so because al-Sayyid Ahmad had continued to visit her, day after day, during her convalescence. The fact was that her recovery had removed the protection afforded her by ill health. She sensed that she would be meeting him without anything to hide behind for the first time since her error had been disclosed.

When the boys arrived for breakfast one after the other, she felt a little less desolate. Their father soon entered the room in his flowing gown. His face revealed no emotion on seeing her. He asked calmly as he headed for his place at the table, "You've come?" Then, taking his seat, he told his sons, "Sit down."

They began to consume their breakfast while she stood in her customary place. Her fear had peaked when he came in, but she started to catch her breath after that. The first encounter after her recovery had taken place and passed peacefully. She sensed that she would find no problem in being alone with him shortly in his room.

The breakfast ended, al-Sayyid Ahmad returned to his room. She joined him a few minutes later carrying a tray with coffee. She placed it on the low table and stepped aside to wait until he had finished. Then she would help him get dressed. Her husband drank the coffee in profound silence, not the silence that comes naturally either as a rest, when people are tired, or as a cloak for someone with nothing to say. It was a deliberate silence. She had not given up her hope, however faint, that he was fond enough of her to grant her a kind word or at least discuss the subjects he usually did at this hour of the morning. His deliberate silence unsettled her. She began asking herself again whether he still harbored some anger. Anxiety was pricking her heart once more. Yet the heavy silence did not last long.

The man was thinking with such speed and concentration that he had no taste for anything else. It was not the kind of thought that arises on the spur of the moment. It was a type of stubborn, long-lasting thought that had stayed with him throughout the past days. Finally, without raising his head from his empty coffee cup, he asked, "Have you recovered?"

Amina replied in a subdued voice, "Yes, sir, praise God."

The man resumed speaking and said bitterly, "I'm amazed, and never cease to be amazed, that you did what you did."

Her heart pounded violently, and she bowed her head dejectedly. She could not bear his anger when defending a mistake someone else had made. What could she do now that she was the guilty person? . . . Fear froze her tongue, although he was waiting for an answer.

He continued his comments by asking her disapprovingly, "Have I been mistaken about you all these years and not known it?"

At that she held out her hands in alarm and pain. She whispered in troubled gasps, "I take refuge with God, sir. My error was really a big one, but I don't deserve talk like this."

Nevertheless, the man continued to talk with his terrifying calm, compared to which screaming would have been easy to bear. He said, "How could you have committed such a grave error? . . . Was it because I left town for a single day?"

In a trembling voice, its tones swayed by the convulsions of her body, she replied, "I have committed an error, sir. It is up to you to forgive me. My soul yearned to visit our master al-Husayn. I thought that for such a blessed pilgrimage it was possible for me to go out just once."

He shook his head fiercely as though saying, "There's no point trying to argue." Then he raised his eyes to give her an angry, sullen look. In a voice that made it clear he would tolerate no discussion, he said, "I just have one thing to say: Leave my house immediately."

His command fell on her head like a fatal blow. She was dumbfounded and did not utter a word. She could not move. During the worst moments of her ordeal, when she was waiting for him to return from his trip to Port Said, she had entertained many kinds of fears: that he might pour out his anger on her and deafen her with his shouts and curses. She had not even ruled out physical violence, but the idea of being evicted had never troubled her. She had lived with him for twenty-five years and could not imagine that anything could separate them or pluck her from this house of which she had become an inseparable part.

With this final statement, al-Sayyid Ahmad freed himself from the burden of a thought that had dominated his brain during the past three weeks. His mental struggle had begun the moment the woman tearfully confessed her offense when confined to her bed. At the first instant he had not believed his ears. As he started to recover from the shock, he had become aware of the loathsome truth that was an affront to his pride and dignity but had postponed his wrath when he saw her condition. In fact, it would be correct to say that he was unable to reflect then on the challenge to his pride and dignity because of his deep anxiety for this woman, verging on fear and alarm. He had grown used to her and admired her good qualities. He was even fond enough of her to forget her error and ask God to keep her safe. Confronted by this imminent threat to her, his tyranny had shrunk back. The abundant tenderness lying dormant within his soul had been awakened. He had gone back to his room that day sad and dispirited, although his face had remained expressionless.

When he saw her make rapid and steady progress toward recovery, his composure returned. Consequently he began to review the whole incident, along with its cause and results, with a new eye, or, more accurately, the old one he was accustomed to using at home. It was unfortunate, unfortunate for his wife, that he reviewed the matter when he was calm and all alone. He convinced himself that if he forgave her and yielded to the appeal of affection, which he longed to do, then his prestige, honor, personal standards, and set of values would all be compromised. He would lose control of his family, and the bonds holding it together would dissolve. He could not lead them unless he did so with firmness and rigor. In short, if he forgave her, he would no longer be Ahmad Abd al-Jawad but some other person he could never agree to become.

Yes, it was unfortunate that he reviewed the situation when he was calm and all alone. If he had been able to give vent to his anger when she confessed, his rage would have been satisfied. The accident would have passed without trailing behind it any serious consequences. The problem was that he had not been able to get angry at the suitable moment and his vanity would not let him announce his anger after she had recovered, when he had been calm for three weeks. That kind of anger would have been more like a premeditated reprimand. When his anger flared up, normally it was because of a combination of premeditation and natural emotion. Since the latter element had not found an outlet at the appropriate time, premeditation, which had been provided with plenty of quiet time to review its options, was left to discover an effective method of expressing itself in a form corresponding to the seriousness of the offense. Thus the danger that threatened her life for a time, which protected her from his anger by stirring up his affection, turned into a cause of far-reaching punishment, because the scheming side of his anger had been given so much time to plan and think.

He rose with a frown and turned his back on her. He reached for his garments on the sofa and said, "I'll put my clothes on myself."

She had stayed put, oblivious to everything. His voice roused her. She quickly grasped from his words and stance that he was ordering her to leave. She headed for the door, making no sound as she walked.

Before she got through it she heard him say, "I don't want to find you here when I come back this noon."

32

HER STRENGTH gave out in the sitting room, and she threw herself down on the edge of the sofa. His harsh, decisive words were bouncing around inside her. The man was not joking. When had he ever told a joke? Much as she wanted to flee, she could not leave immediately. If she left before him that would be contrary to the normal routine and arouse the boys' suspicions. She did not want them to begin their day and go off to their jobs digesting the news of her being thrown out of the house. There was another sentiment at work as well, possibly embarrassment, that kept her from wishing to see them when she was in the humiliating status of a discarded wife. She decided to stay where she was until he had left. Better still, she would take refuge in the dining room so he would not see her on his way out. With a broken heart she slipped into that room and, gravely and despondently, sat down on a pallet.

What did he really mean? Was he evicting her temporarily or forever? She did not believe he intended to divorce her. He was more noble and generous than that. Yes, he was irascible and tyrannical, but only extreme pessimism could hide from her his gallantry, chivalry, and mercy. Could she forget how sympathetic he had been when she was confined to bed? He had visited her day after day to inquire about her health. A man like that would not lightly destroy a house, break a heart, or wrest a mother from her children.

She began pondering these ideas as though trying to restore some composure to her shaken soul. She persisted at this task, but her persistence only revealed the fact that composure refused to settle in her soul. Similarly, the weaker some invalids feel, the more they boast of their strength. She did not know what to do with her life or what meaning life would have if her hopes were dashed and the worst did happen.

She heard his stick tapping on the floor of the sitting room as he made his exit. She lost her train of thought and listened intently to the succession of taps, until he had departed. At that moment she felt the enormous pain of her situation and was furious at the iron will that had made no allowance for her weakness.

She rose feebly and left the room to go down to the first floor. At the head of the stairs she could make out the voices of the boys as they descended one after the other. She stretched her head out over the railing and caught sight of Fahmy and Kamal. They were trailing after Yasin on their way to the door that led to the courtyard. Affection rushed through her heart and overwhelmed it. She was amazed at herself. How could she let them go without saying goodbye? She would not be able to see them again for days or even weeks. Perhaps for the remainder of her life, she would see them only infrequently, as though they were strangers. She stood where she was on the stairs, without budging, while affection surged through her heart. Although her heart was filled with emotion, she could not accept the painful thought that this gloomy fate was her destiny. She had a limitless belief in God, who had protected her in the past when she was alone with the jinn. Her trust in her husband also continued undimmed. No evil had yet afflicted her that was serious enough to deprive her quiet life of its confident trust. For all these reasons, she was inclined to consider her ordeal a harsh trial through which she would pass unscathed.

She found Khadija and Aisha embroiled in a quarrel as usual, but they abandoned it when they noticed her sorrow and the dead look of her eyes. They feared, perhaps, that she had left her bed before fully recovering her health. Khadija asked anxiously, "What's the matter, Mother?"

"By God, I don't know what to say. I'm going."

Although the last phrase emerged in a terse and impromptu fashion, it acquired a gloomy meaning from her despairing look and plaintive tone. Both girls were frightened by it and cried out together, "Where?"

She had been apprehensive beforehand about the effect her words would have on them and even on herself. Now she said brokenly, "To my mother."

They rushed to her in alarm and said at the same time, "What are you saying? . . . Don't say that again. . . . What happened?"

She found some consolation in her daughters' dismay, but – as often happens in such circumstances – that only caused her sorrows to burst forth even more. Struggling with her tears, she said in a trembling voice, "He hasn't forgotten anything and hasn't forgiven anything." She said this with an anguish that revealed the depth of her sorrow. She continued: "He was angry with me and postponed doing something about it till I recovered. Then he told me, 'Leave my house immediately.' He also said, 'I don't want to find you here when I come back this noon.'" Then she remarked in a voice that betrayed both disappointment and melancholy censure, "Hear and obey...hear and obey."

Khadija, in a state of nervous agitation, yelled at her, "I don't believe it. I don't believe it. Say something else.... What's happened to the world?"

Aisha shouted in a broken voice, "This will never do! Does our happiness mean so little to him?"

Khadija asked again, angrily and sharply, "What's he got in mind?... What does he plan to do, Mother?"

"I don't know. That's exactly what he said, with no additions or deletions."

At first this was all she would say, perhaps because she wished to increase their sympathy and gather some consolation from their dismay. Then her pity for them and her desire to reassure herself got the better of her and she went on: "I suspect that all he plans to do is separate me from you for a few days to punish me for my misadventure."

"Wasn't what happened to you enough for him?"

The mother sighed sadly and murmured, "The matter's in God's hands.... Now I must go."

Khadija blocked her way. She said in a voice choked by sobs, "We won't let you go. Don't leave your home. I don't think he'll persist in his anger if he returns and finds you with us."

Aisha implored her, "Wait till Fahmy and Yasin get back. Father will think twice about tearing you away from all of us."

In rebuttal, their mother admonished them: "It's never wise to challenge his anger. A man like him becomes softer when people obey him and fiercer if people rebel."

They tried to protest once more, but she silenced them with a motion of her hand and observed, "There's no point in talking. I've got to go. I'll gather my clothes and set off. Don't be alarmed.

We won't be separated long. We'll be reunited again, God willing."

The woman went to her room on the second floor with the two girls at her heels. They were crying like babies. She started to remove her clothes from the armoire, but Khadija seized her hand and asked her passionately, "What are you doing?"

The mother felt that her tears were about to get the best of her. She refrained from speaking for fear her voice would give her away or she would start weeping. She was determined not to cry when her daughters could see her. She gestured with her hand as if to say, "Circumstances require me to get my clothes together."

Khadija said sharply, "You're only going to take one change of clothing with you . . . just one."

A sigh escaped from her. At that moment she wished the whole affair was a frightening dream. Then she said, "I'm afraid he'll be furious if he sees my clothing in the usual place."

"We'll keep it in our room."

Aisha collected her mother's clothes, except for a single outfit, as her sister had suggested. Their mother yielded to them with deep relief. It seemed to her that so long as her clothes remained in the house she retained her right to return there. She got out a bag and stuffed in it the clothing she was permitted to take. She sat down on the sofa to put on her stockings and shoes. Her daughters stood facing her. They looked at her with sad, bewildered eyes. Her heart melted at the sight and, pretending to be calm, she said, "Everything will return to normal. Be brave, so you don't make him angry at you. I entrust the house and family to you with full confidence in your abilities. Khadija, I'm certain you'll find Aisha helpful to you in every way. Do what we used to do together just as though I were with you. Each of you is a young woman fully prepared to found and nurture a home."

She rose to get a cloth to wrap around herself. Then she lowered a white veil over her face with deliberate slowness to delay the painful, frightening final moment as long as she could. They all stood facing each other, not knowing what would come next. Her voice refused to say goodbye. Neither of the girls had the courage to fling herself into her mother's arms as she wished. Seconds ticked by, made heavy by suffering and anxiety. Finally, the woman, who had steeled herself, feared her resolve would desert her. She moved a step closer and bent toward them to kiss them, one after the other. She whispered, "Never lose heart. Our Lord is with all of us."

At that they clung to her. They were sobbing too hard to speak.

The mother left the house, her eyes filled with tears, and the street seemed to dissolve as she looked at it through them.

33

AS SHE knocked on the door of the old house she was thinking with painful embarrassment about the alarm and distress her arrival as a chastised wife would cause. The door was located on a dead-end alley that branched off from al-Khurunfush Street. At the end of the alley there was a little mosque of a Sufi religious order where prayers had been said for a long period before the building was finally abandoned because of its age. The crumbling ruins were left to remind her, each time she visited her mother, of her childhood, when she would wait by the door for her father to finish his prayers and come to her. She would poke her head inside while people were praying. She found it diverting to watch the men bow and prostrate themselves on the floor. At times she would observe members of various mystical Sufi orders who met in the alley next to the mosque. They would light some lamps, spread mats on the ground, and attempt to establish contact with God by chanting His name while swaying back and forth.

When the door was opened, the head of a black servant in her fifties peeked out. The moment she saw who it was, her face shone and she called out to welcome the visitor. She stepped aside to make room for her, and Amina entered. The servant waited there as though expecting a second person. Amina understood what her stance implied. She whispered in a vexed tone, "Close the door, Sadiqa."

"Didn't al-Sayyid Ahmad come with you?"

She shook her head and pretended to ignore the servant's astonishment. She crossed the courtyard, with the oven room in the center and a well in the left corner, and went to the narrow stairway to climb to the first and final floor. Then she passed through the vestibule into her mother's room. When she entered, she saw her mother seated cross-legged on a sofa at the front of the small chamber. She was grasping with both hands a long string of prayer beads that dangled down to her lap, and her eyes were directed inquisitively at the door. She had no doubt heard some-one knock and footsteps approach. When Amina drew near, her mother asked, "Who is it?"

As she spoke, her lips parted in a gentle smile of happiness and welcome as though she had guessed the identity of the visitor. Amina answered her, in a voice made soft by her depression and sorrow, "It's me, Mother."

The elderly woman stretched her legs out. Her feet searched the floor for her slippers. When they were located, she shoved her feet in. She stood up and spread out her arms eagerly. Amina threw her bag on the edge of the sofa and wrapped herself in her mother's arms. She kissed her mother on the forehead and both cheeks, while the other woman planted a kiss wherever her lips landed, on her daughter's head, cheek, and neck. When they finished embracing, the old lady patted her on the back affectionately and stayed where she was, facing the door. The smile on her lips announced a welcome for someone else as she made the assumption Sadiqa had before. Once again, Amina understood what was implied by her posture. With vexed resignation she said, "I came by myself, Mother...."

Her mother turned her head toward her curiously and mut-tered, "By yourself?" Then, affecting a smile to ward off the anxiety that afflicted her, she added, "Glory to God, who never changes."

She retreated to the sofa and sat down. With a voice that revealed her anxiety this time, she asked, "How are you?... Why didn't he come with you as usual?"

Amina sat down beside her. Like a pupil confessing how atrocious his answers were on an examination, she said, "He's angry at me, Mother...."

The mother blinked glumly. Then she muttered in a sad voice, "I take refuge in God from Satan, who deserves to be pelted with stones. My heart never deceives me. I was upset when you told me, 'I came by myself, Mother.' What do you suppose made him angry at a gracious angel like yourself whom no man before him was lucky enough to possess?... Tell me, daughter."

With a sigh, Amina said, "I went to visit the shrine of our master al-Husayn during his trip to Port Said."

Her mother reflected sadly and dejectedly. Then she asked, "How did he learn about the visit?"

From the very beginning, Amina, out of compassion for the old lady and to make her own responsibility seem lighter, had been careful not to refer to the automobile accident. Thus she gave her an answer she had worked up in advance: "Perhaps someone saw me and told on me. . . ."

The elderly woman said sharply, "There's not a human being who would know you except the people in the house with you. Isn't there someone you suspect? . . . That woman Umm Hanafi? Or his son by the other woman?"

Amina quickly intervened to say confidently, "Possibly a neighbor woman saw me and told her husband, without meaning any harm, and the man brought it to al-Sayyid Ahmad's attention, without understanding the dangerous consequences. Suspect anyone you like, but not a member of my household."

The old lady shook her head skeptically and observed, "Your whole life you've been too trusting. God alone can decipher and overcome the schemes of crafty people. But your husband? . . . An intelligent man going on fifty . . . can he find no other way to express his anger than by throwing out the companion of a lifetime and separating her from the children? . . . O Lord, glory to You. Most people get wiser as they get older, while we grow older and become foolhardy. Is it a sin for a virtuous woman to visit our master al-Husayn? Don't his friends, who are just as jealous and manly as he is, allow their wives to leave the house for various errands? . . . Your father himself, who was a religious scholar and knew the Book of God by heart, permitted me to go to neighbors' homes and watch the procession of pilgrims setting out for Mecca."

There was a long period of despondent silence until the old woman turned toward her daughter with a perplexed, critical smile. She asked, "What tempted you to disobey him after that long life of blind obedience? . . . This is what puzzles me the most. . . . No matter how fiery his temper, he's your husband. The safest thing to do is to be careful to obey him, for your own peace of mind and for the happiness of your children. Isn't that so, daughter? . . . I'm amazed because I've never found you needed anybody's advice before . . . ."

A smile appeared at the corners of Amina's mouth, suggesting a slight relaxation of her anxiety and embarrassment. She mumbled, "The devil made me do it."

"God's curse on him. Did the cursed one cause your feet to slip after twenty-five years of peace and harmony? . . . Well, he was the one who got our father Adam and our mother Eve expelled from paradise. . . . It makes me very sad, daughter, but it's just a summer cloud that will disperse. Everything will return to normal." She continued as though addressing herself: "What harm would it have done him to be more forbearing? But he's a man, and men will always have enough defects to blot out the sun." Then, pretending to be happy and welcoming, she told her daughter, "Take off your things and make yourself comfortable. Don't be alarmed. What harm will it do you to spend a short holiday with your mother in the room where you were born?"

Amina's eyes glanced inattentively at the old bed with its tarnished posts and at the shabby carpet, threadbare and frayed at the edges, even though the design of roses had retained its reds and greens. Her breast was too affected by separation from her loved ones to be receptive to a flood of distant memories. Her mother's invitation did not arouse the kind of nostalgia in her heart that memories of this room, of which she was so fond, ordinarily did. All she could do was sigh and confess, "The only thing bothering me is that I'm anxious about my children, Mother."

"They're in God's care. You won't be away from them long, if God the Compassionate and Merciful permits."

Amina rose to remove her wrap while Sadiqa, sad and mournful because of what she had heard, retreated from her post by the entrance to the room, where she had remained as they talked. Amina sat down again next to her mother. They discussed the matter inside and out, backward and forward.

The juxtaposition of the two women appeared to illustrate the interplay of the amazing laws of heredity and the inflexible law of time. The two women might have been a single person with her image reflected forward to the future or back into the past. In either case, the difference between the original and its reflection revealed the terrible struggle raging between the laws of heredity, attempting to keep things the same, and the law of time, pushing for change and a finale. The struggle usually results in a string of defeats for heredity, which plays at best a modest role within the framework of time. It was the law of time that had transformed Amina's elderly mother into a gaunt body with a withered face and blind eyes. There had also been internal changes hidden from the senses. All of the splendor of life that she retained was what is known as "the charm of old age" – that is, a calm manner, a somber new dignity, and a head adorned with white. Although she was descended from generations of people who had lived to a ripe old age and not given up without a fight, her protest against time, once she reached seventy-five, was limited to rising in the morning in exactly the same way she had for the past fifty years and groping her way to the bathroom without any assistance from the maid. There she would perform her ablutions before returning to her room to pray. The rest of the day she passed with her prayer beads, praising God and meditating in total privacy. The servant was usually busy with the housework, but when she was free to sit with her mistress, the old lady enjoyed conversing with her.

The lady's enthusiasm for work and zest for life had definitely not abandoned her. For example, she supervised every detail of the household budget, the cleaning and arranging. She took the servant to task if she spent too long on a job or was late returning from an errand. Not infrequently she made her swear on a copy of the Qur'an to assure herself of the veracity of the maid's accounts of scrubbing the bathroom, washing the pots and pans, and dusting the windows. Her meticulousness verged on paranoia. Her insistence on this may have been a continuation of a custom that became embedded in her when she was young or a flaw introduced by old age.

Her perseverance in staying on in her house in almost total isolation after the death of her spouse and her insistence on remaining there even after she lost her sight could also be attributed to this extremism of her character. She had turned a deaf ear to the repeated invitations of al-Sayyid Ahmad to move to his house, where she could be cared for by her daughter and grandchildren. In this way, she exposed herself to the accusation of being senile. Al-Sayyid Ahmad finally stopped inviting her. The truth was that she did not want to leave her house, because she was so attached to it and because she wished to avoid the unintentional neglect she might find in the new one. Her presence there might also impose new burdens on the shoulders of her daughter, who already had many weighty responsibilities. Nor was she eager to squeeze herself into a home headed by a man known to his family for his ferocity and anger. She might inadvertently fall victim to his comments and thus threaten her daughter's happiness. Finally, the sense of honor and pride she harbored deep inside herself caused her to prefer living in the house she owned, dependent only upon God and the pension left her by her late husband.

There were other reasons for her insistence on remaining in her house that could not be attributed to her sensitivity or common sense, like her fear that if she moved out of the house she would find herself forced to choose between two options. She would either have to allow strangers to live there, even though the house was what she treasured most dearly, after her daughter and grand-children, or leave it deserted and let the jinn appropriate it as their playground, after it had been the home of a religious scholar who knew the Qur'an by heart – her husband. For her to move into al-Sayyid Ahmad's house would also create awkward problems that in her opinion had no easy solution. At that time she had brooded about it. Should she accept his hospitality and give nothing in return – and she certainly would not be comfortable with that – or surrender her pension to him in return for staying in his house? Giving him her pension would upset her instinctive need to own things, which, along with old age, became one of the primary elements of her general paranoia.

At times when he urged her to move to his house she even imagined that he had greedy designs on her pension and the house she would vacate. She chose to refuse him with blind obstinacy. When al-Sayyid Ahmad bowed to her will, she told him with relief, "Don't be offended by my stubbornness, son. May our Lord honor you for the affection you have shown me. You see, don't you, that I'm just not able to move out of my house? It's good of you to humor an old woman with her many shortcomings. All the same, I ask you to swear to God that you'll allow Amina and the children to visit me from time to time, now that it's difficult for me to leave the house."

Thus she had remained in her house as she wished, enjoying her mastery and freedom as well as many of the customs of her cherished past. Some of these, like her excessive concern with her house and her money, were hardly compatible with the serenity and tolerance of wise maturity. Therefore, they appeared to be accidental infirmities of old age. There was another practice she had retained that could adorn youth and lend majesty to maturity. It was worship, which continued to be the central interest of her life and the source of her hopes and happiness. She had absorbed religion as a young girl from her father, who was a religious scholar. It had become deeply ingrained in her through her marriage to another religious scholar, who was no less pious and God-fearing than her father. She had continued to worship with love and sincerity, although in her earnestness she did not discriminate between true religion and pure superstition. She was known to the women of the neighborhood as "the blessed shaykha."

Sadiqa, the maid, was the only person who knew both her good and bad sides. After a tiff had flared up between them, Sadiqa might say, "My lady, wouldn't worship be a better use of your time than quarreling and squabbling over trivial things?"

Her mistress would answer sharply, "Vile woman, you're not advising me to pray out of love for it. All you want is to be left free to mess around, neglect your duties, roll in filth, and loot and plunder. God commands us to be clean and honest. Keeping close track of you is both a form of worship and a reward."

Since religion played such an important role in her life, she had held her father and then her husband in even higher esteem than that required by their relationship. She had often envied them the honor they had of housing the words of God and His prophet in their breasts. She may have remembered this as she consoled and encouraged Amina, "By expelling you from your house, al-Sayyid Ahmad merely intended to show his anger at your failure to obey his command. He will not do more than discipline you. Yes, evil cannot befall a woman who had a father and grandfather like yours."

Amina was cheered by the reference to her father and grandfather. She was like a person lost in the dark who hears the voice of the watchman calling out. Her heart believed what her mother had said, not only because she was eager to be reassured but because she believed in the sanctity of those two departed scholars. She was a replica of her mother in body, faith, and most traits of character. At that moment, memories of her father swarmed into her mind. When she was a girl, he had filled her heart with love and faith. She prayed to God to rescue her from her predicament out of respect for his holiness. The old lady returned to her consoling remarks. With a tender smile on her dry lips she said, "God in His compassion is always looking out for you. Remember the epidemic, may God never repeat it. God spared you and took your sisters. You weren't harmed at all."

A smile triumphed over Amina's gloom and appeared on her lips. She searched back through a twilight region of the past almost obliterated by forgetfulness. Out of a jumble of memories she could discern clearly an image that awakened echoes within her from that terrible era. She was a little girl skipping outside closed doors behind which her sisters were stretched out on beds of sickness and death. She was by the window watching the endless stream of coffins go by as people fled from them. Another time she was listening to the masses of people who, in their terror and despair, sought out a religious leader like her father. They were lamenting and praying fervently to the Lord of the heavens. Despite the serious threat to her and the loss of all her sisters, she had escaped safe and unharmed from the clutches of the epidemic. The only thing disturbing her serenity had been the lemon juice and onion she had been forced to consume once or twice a day.

Her mother started speaking again, in a tender and affectionate voice that revealed she was abandoning herself to her dreams. Memory seemed to have taken her back to a bygone age. She was recalling the life and memories of that time, which were dear and precious because of their association with her youth. With the pains forgotten, they were cleansed of any blemish. She remarked, "It was your good fortune that not only were you saved from the epidemic but you were treasured as the only child left in the family. You were all the family possessed in this world, its hope, consolation, and happiness. You flourished in a nursery formed by our hearts."

After these words, Amina no longer saw the room the way she had before. Now everything had the freshness of youth breathed back into it: the walls, carpet, bed, her mother, and Amina herself. Her father had returned to life and taken his customary place. Once again she listened to his whispered expressions of love and affection. She was dreaming of the stories of the prophets and their miracles, recalling the extraordinary exploits of good people against the infidels, from the Prophet's companions down to the struggle of the nineteenth-century Egyptian patriot Urabi Pasha against the English. Her past life was resurrected along with its magical dreams and promising hopes for happiness.

Then the old lady said, as though drawing a conclusion from the premises she had previously laid out, "Hasn't God preserved and protected you?"

Although the comment was meant to console her, it made her remember her present condition. She awoke from the dream of her happy past to return to her current melancholy. A person who has forgotten his sorrows can be forced to confront them once more when someone with the best intentions favors him with a word of comfort. Amina sat idly and grimly beside her mother. The only time she had felt like this had been during her recent confinement in bed. She disliked it and was uncomfortable. Her continuing conversation with her mother only occupied half her attention. The other half was given over to restless anxiety.

At noon, when Sadiqa brought in a tray with lunch, the old lady told her, mainly to distract her daughter, "A new watchman has come to discover your thefts."

Just then Amina was not interested in whether the maid stole or acted honestly. The servant did not respond to her mistress, out of respect for the guest and because she had grown so accustomed to both the bitter and sweet sides of her mistress that she would have missed one without the other.

As the day wore on, Amina thought even more desperately about her household. Al-Sayyid Ahmad would be returning home for his lunch and siesta. Then after he went back to his store the boys would be arriving, one after the other. Her imagination derived extraordinary power from her pain and homesickness. She could see the house and its inhabitants as though they were present. She saw al-Sayyid Ahmad removing his cloak and caftan without any assistance from her. She was afraid he might have gotten used to that during her long stay in bed. She attempted to read the thoughts and intentions hidden behind his forehead. Did he sense the void she had created by leaving? How did he react when he found no trace of her in the house? Hadn't he made some reference to her for one reason or another? Here were the boys returning home, rushing to the sitting room after waiting impatiently for the coffee hour. They found her place empty. They were asking about her. They were answered by their sisters' gloomy and tearful looks. How would Fahmy take the news? Would Kamal understand the significance of her absence? This question made her heart throb painfully. Were they deliberating for a long time? What were they waiting for? Perhaps they were already on their way, racing toward her.... They must be on their way. Or had he ordered them not to visit her? They must be in al-Khurunfush already.... A few minutes would tell.

"Were you talking to me, Amina?"

This question from the old lady interrupted Amina's train of thought. With a mixture of astonishment and embarrassment she came to her senses. She inferred that some words from her internal dialogue had inadvertently slipped out and been picked up by her mother's sharp ear. She found herself obliged to answer, "I was asking, Mother, if the boys won't come visit me."

"I think they've arrived." The elderly woman was listening intently and leaning her head forward.

Amina listened silently. She heard the door knocker telegraphing quick, consecutive beats like a voice urgently calling out for help. She recognized Kamal's touch in these nervous raps. She knew who it was just as well as when she heard him knock on the door of the oven room at home. She quickly dashed to the head of the stairs and called to Sadiqa to open the door. She looked down over the railing. She saw the boy leaping up the steps with Fahmy and Yasin following him. Kamal clung to her and prevented the others from embracing her for a while.

When they entered their grandmother's room they were all talking at the same time, heedless of the others' comments because their souls were so agitated and their minds so confused. Then they saw their grandmother, standing with her arms spread out and her face beaming in a smile of welcome filled with love, and they stopped talking so they could kiss her, one after the other.

The room was relatively quiet except for the soft noise of their kisses. At last Yasin cried out in a sad voice of protest, "We no longer have a home. We will never have a home until you return to us."

Like a fugitive seeking asylum, Kamal climbed into his mother's lap. For the first time he stated his decision that he had kept secret at home and on the way: "I'm staying here with Mother.... I'm not going back with you."

Fahmy had been gazing at her silently for a long time the way he did when he wanted to tell her something with a look. This silent glance was the best expression for her of what both their hearts were feeling. He was her darling and his love for her was exceeded only by hers for him. When he talked to her, he rarely spoke openly of his feelings, but his thoughts, words, and deeds all revealed them. He had seen a look of pain and embarrassment in her eyes that upset him terribly. He said sadly and painfully, "We're the ones who suggested you should go out. We encouraged you to do it. But here you're the only one getting punished."

His mother smiled in confusion and said, "I'm not a child, Fahmy. I shouldn't have done it. . . ."

Yasin was touched by this exchange. His distress increased because he was so upset at being the proponent of the ill-omened suggestion. He hesitated for a long time between repeating his apology for the suggestion within earshot of their grandmother, who would criticize him or harbor a grudge against him, and keeping silent, even though he wanted to get some relief by expressing his anguish. He overcame his hesitation and chose to repeat Fahmy's comment in different words. He said, "Yes, we're the guilty ones, and you're the one who got accused." Then with special emphasis, as though reacting to his father's stubbornness and rigidity, he continued: "But you will return. The clouds overshadowing all of us shall be dispersed."

Kamal took hold of his mother's chin and turned her face toward him. He showered her with a stream of questions about the meaning of her departure from the house, how long she would stay at his grandmother's house, what would happen if she returned with them, and so on. None of her answers was able to calm his mind. Not even his determination to stay with his mother was able to reassure him, for he was the first one to doubt that he would be able to carry through on it.

After each of them had finished expressing his feelings, the course of the conversation changed. They began to discuss the situation in a new way, for as Fahmy said, "There's no point talking about what has happened. We need to think about what will happen."

Yasin replied, "A man like our father is not willing to let an incident like Mother's excursion pass unnoticed. He will inevitably express his anger in a way that's hard to forget.

But he will never exceed the limits of what he has already done."

This opinion seemed plausible and everyone was relieved by it. Fahmy expressed both his satisfaction and his hopes when he said, "The proof you're right is that he hasn't done anything else. Someone like him doesn't postpone something once he's resolved to do it."

They talked a lot about their father's heart. They agreed that he had a good heart, even though he was severe and easily enraged. They thought it highly unlikely that he would do something to injure his reputation or harm anyone.

At that point the grandmother said, just to tease them, since she knew what an impossible request it was, "If you were men, you would search for some way to touch your father's heart and make him stop being so stubborn."

Yasin and Fahmy exchanged sarcastic glances about this pretense of manliness that would melt at the first mention of their father. The mother for her part was afraid that the discussion between the two young men and the grandmother would lead to some reference to the automobile accident. She motioned to them, pointing to her shoulder and then her mother, to tell them she had kept it a secret from her. As though springing to the defense of the virility of the two youths, she told her mother, "I don't want either of them to expose himself to the man's anger. Leave him alone until he's ready to forgive."

Then Kamal asked, "When is he going to forgive you?"

The mother gestured upward with her index finger and murmured, "Forgiveness comes from God."

As usual in a situation like this, the conversation went full circle. Everything that had been said before was repeated in the same words or different ones. Rosy thoughts continued to predominate. The conversation went on, without bringing up anything new, until night fell and the time came to leave. Their hearts were overwhelmed by the pervasive gloom of departure, and they were too busy thinking about it to have anything to say. A silence reigned, like that before a storm, broken only by words intended to soften its impact or to make it seem it was not yet time to say goodbye. Out of compassion for the other side, no one was willing to take responsibility for saying goodbye.

At this time the old lady guessed what was troubling the people around her. She blinked her sightless eyes and ran her fingers through her prayer beads quickly and devoutly. Minutes passed which, despite their brevity, were unbearably oppressive, like the moments when a dreamer expects, in his nightmare, to fall from a great height. Then she heard Yasin's voice say, "I think it's time for us to go. We'll return soon to fetch you, God willing."

The old lady listened intently to see whether her daughter's voice trembled when she answered, but she did not hear anyone speak. All she heard was the movement of people rising and then the sound of kisses and a hum of farewells. Kamal protested against being forcibly removed and started crying. Now it was her turn to say goodbye to them in an atmosphere fraught with sorrow and foot-dragging. Finally the footsteps went off, leaving her alone and apprehensive.

Amina's light steps returned. The old lady listened anxiously. Finally she cried out to her, "Are you crying? . . . What a dunce you are! . . . Can't you bear to pass a couple of nights with your mother?"

34

OF ALL of them, Khadija and Aisha appeared to be the most distressed by the absence of their mother. In addition to their sorrow, which was shared by their brothers, the two of them had to bear the burdens of looking after the house and serving their father. The household chores did not weigh nearly so heavily on them as serving their father, for that required taking a thousand things into account. Aisha tended to flee from anything having to do with her father. Her excuse was that Khadija had assisted him when their mother was confined to bed. Khadija found herself obliged to return to those terrifying and delicate situations she endured if she was near her father or doing some task for him. The very first hour after her mother's departure, Khadija said, "This situation had better not last long. Life in this house without her is unbearable suffering."

Aisha concurred in what her sister said, but the only way she could respond was by bursting into tears. Khadija waited to explain what she had in mind until her brothers returned from her grandmother's house, but before she could, they began to tell her about their mother in her place of exile. Khadija found their comments strange and objectionable, as though they were telling her about strangers she had never been permitted to meet.

She was overcome by emotion and said sharply, "If we're all content to keep silent and wait, days and weeks may go by while she's separated from her house and consumed by grief. Yes, talking to Papa is an arduous task, but it's no more oppressive than keeping quiet, which wouldn't be right. We must find some way. . . . We must talk."

Although the expression "we must talk" concluding her remarks embraced everyone present, it was naturally understood to refer to one or two individuals, each of whom felt uncomfortable for obvious reasons. Even so, Khadija continued: "The task of speaking to him about matters that came up was no easier for

Mother than it would be for us. She never hesitated to speak to him as a favor to one of us. It's only fair for us to make the same sacrifice for her sake."

Yasin and Fahmy exchanged a glance that revealed they felt they were choking. That sensation was rapidly overwhelming them. Yet neither of them dared to open his mouth for fear his words would lead to his selection as the sacrificial lamb. Like a mouse succumbing to a cat, each waited for the outcome of the discussion. Khadija left the general plane to get specific and turned toward Yasin. She said, "You're our oldest brother. In addition to that, you're an employee – in other words, you're really a man. You're the one best suited for this mission."

Yasin breathed in deeply and then exhaled. He was playing with his fingers in obvious anxiety. He stammered, "Our father has a fiery temper and does not accept corrections for his opinions. I, for my part, am no longer a boy. I have become a man and an employee, as you pointed out. What I fear most is that he'll get angry and I'll lose control of myself and become angry too."

Despite their shattered nerves and sad spirits, they had to smile. Aisha almost laughed and hid her face in her hands. It was possibly their tension itself that helped them smile so they could get some temporary relief from it and their pain. At times people who are extremely sad become lighthearted for the most trivial reasons, merely to obtain the relief furnished by the exactly opposite condition. In other words, the family considered what Yasin had said a joke deserving sarcastic laughter. He himself realized better than anyone else how totally incapable he was of even thinking about getting angry or contending with his father. He was the first to recognize that he had only said that to keep from having to confront his father and out of fear of his wrath. When he saw they were making fun of him, all he could do was smile along with them and shrug his shoulders as though to say, "Leave me alone."

Fahmy was the only one careful not to smile too much. He was afraid he might get tapped even before his smile had faded. His fears were confirmed when Khadija turned away from Yasin with scornful despair and told Fahmy with affectionate entreaty, "Fahmy . . . you're our man!"

He raised his eyebrows in confusion and gave her a look that seemed to say, "You know very well what the consequences will be." He did in fact possess qualities none of the rest of the family had. He was a law student and the most intellectual and influential of the children. He could control himself well in awkward situations and had demonstrated his courage and manliness. To appear before his father, however, was enough to cause all his strengths of character to vanish, leaving blind obedience his only recourse. He seemed not to know what to say. Khadija nodded her head to tell him to speak. In dismay he observed, "Do you think he's going to accept my request? No. He'll rebuff me and say, 'Don't interfere in what doesn't concern you.' That's if he doesn't get angry and say even worse things to me."

Yasin was comforted by this wise statement, which he found could also serve as a defense for himself. As though completing his brother's thought, he commented, "Our meddling might lead to our being examined again about our position on the day she went out. We'll be exposing ourselves to charges we won't know how to rebut."

The girl turned on him, enraged and furious. She said bitterly and sarcastically, "We won't expect any help from you. You've done enough harm already."

Fahmy had derived some new energy from the instinct of self-preservation. He said, "Let's think about this matter in the broadest possible terms. I think he won't accept a request from me or Yasin, since he considers us accomplices against him in this error. The case will be lost if one of us tries to defend her. But if either of you girls spoke to him, perhaps you would succeed in appealing to his sympathies. Even in the worst case you would only meet with a calm rejection free of any violence. Why doesn't one of you speak to him? . . . You, for example, Khadija?"

The girl had fallen into the trap. Her heart sank and she glared at Yasin, not Fahmy. She said, "I thought this was a job more suitable for men."

Fahmy continued his nonviolent offensive, saying, "The reverse is true, if we focus on the success of the endeavor. Let's not forget that all your lives you two have been exposed to his anger only on rare occasions that don't count. He's as used to being gentle with you as he is to being brutal to us."

Khadija bowed her head thoughtfully. She did not try to hide her anxiety. She seemed to fear that if she was silent too long the attack against her would intensify and she would be drafted into the dangerous mission. She raised her head to say, "If you're right, then it would be better for Aisha to talk to him than me."

"Me! ... Why?" Aisha spoke with the alarm of a person who finds herself on the firing line after calmly assuming for a long time the position of a spectator with no special involvement in the case. Since she was young and still something of a pampered child, she was not entrusted with anything important, let alone the most perilous assignment any of them could have. Even Khadija could think of no clear justification for her suggestion, but she insisted on it with an obstinacy overflowing with bitter irony. She replied to her sister, "We need your golden hair and blue eyes for our project to succeed."

"What do my hair and eyes have to do with a confrontation with Father?"

At that moment Khadija was not so interested in being convincing as she was desperate to find a way to escape, even if she had to distract their minds with matters that were almost humorous to prepare for her retreat and escape by the safest possible route. A person in trouble who lacks an adequate line of defense will resort to humor in order to allow himself to escape in happy clamor rather than let himself be subjected to scorn and condescending laughter. Khadija said, "I know they have a magical effect on everyone who comes in contact with you ... Yasin, Fahmy ... even Kamal. Why shouldn't they have the same effect on Father?"

Aisha blushed and said in panic, "How could I speak to him about something like this when my mind becomes a complete blank the moment his eyes light on me?"

Then, after everyone in succession had evaded this dangerous task and no one felt directly threatened, they all found that their salvation had not spared them from feeling guilty. In fact, it was possibly the main reason they felt that way. In a crisis a person will concentrate his thoughts on saving himself. Once he is safe, his conscience will start to give him trouble. Similarly, when a member of the body is ill, the body drains vital energies from other areas to try to heal it. When the diseased member recovers, these energies must be redistributed equally to other, neglected parts of the body. Khadija seemed to be trying to assuage her feeling of guilt when she said, "Since none of us is able to speak to Papa, let's ask Maryam's mother to help us."

The moment she mentioned the name Maryam she noticed

Fahmy's involuntary reaction. Their eyes met for an instant. The young man was uncomfortable with her suggestion. He turned his face away, pretending to be uninterested. No one had mentioned this name in his presence since his idea of getting engaged to her had been renounced. Everyone had either respected his feelings or felt that Maryam had acquired a new significance after Fahmy had admitted his love for her. She had entered the corps of sacrosanct topics that house rules did not permit to be discussed openly in the presence of the person involved. Even so, Maryam herself had continued to visit the family, pretending she did not know what had taken place in secret.

Yasin did not miss the awkward exchange between Fahmy and Khadija. He wanted to blunt the probable outcome by shifting their attention in a new direction. Putting his hand on Kamal's shoulder, he said in a half-sarcastic and half-provocative way, "Here's the right man for us. He's the only one who can beg his father to give him back his mother."

No one took his words seriously, particularly not Kamal. All the same, the next day when the boy was walking across Bayt al-Qadi Square on his way home from school, after spending most of the day thinking about his banished mother, he suddenly remembered what Yasin had said. He stopped going toward Qirmiz Alley and headed back to al-Nahhasin Street. His sad heart was pounding with distress and pain. He proceeded to al-Nahhasin with slow steps. He had not made up his mind about what he would do. He was led forward by the torment he was suffering from the loss of his mother. He was held back by the fear that overcame him when he merely thought about his father, not to mention talking to him or begging him for something. He could not picture himself standing in front of his father to discuss this affair. He was well aware of the fears that would probably overwhelm him if he did. He had not made up his mind about anything, but nonetheless, as though he longed to relieve his tortured heart even if only indirectly, he kept walking ahead slowly until his eyes fell on the door of the shop. He was like a mother kite circling overhead but lacking the courage to attack the predator seizing her chicks. He approached within a few meters of the store and stopped. He paused there for a long time without advancing or retreating. He had not been able to decide what to do. Suddenly a man emerged from the store laughing uproariously. There was Kamal's father, following the man to the threshold to say goodbye. He too was engulfed in laughter. Kamal was stunned. He stood nailed to the spot, taking in his father's relaxed, laughing face with indescribable incredulity and astonishment. He could not believe his eyes. He imagined that a new person had taken over his father's body or that this laughing man, much as he resembled Kamal's father, was a different individual whom he was seeing for the first time. The man laughed. He laughed uproariously. His face beamed with happiness like the sun radiating light.

When al-Sayyid Ahmad turned to go back into the store, his eyes fell on the boy who was looking at him in bewilderment. The father was astonished to see him standing there like that. Al-Sayyid Ahmad's features quickly regained their serious and sedate expression. Scrutinizing his son's face, he asked him, "What brings you?"

At once, despite the boy's bewilderment, his soul was permeated by the instinct of self-defense. He went up to his father and stretched out his small hand. He leaned over and kissed his father's hand politely and deferentially, without uttering a word. Al-Sayyid Ahmad asked, "Do you want something?"

Kamal swallowed but did not find anything to say. Choosing to remain on the safe side, he remarked that he wanted nothing and was simply on his way home.

His father was impatient and noticed the boy's anxious expression. He told him roughly, "Don't stand there like a statue. Tell me what you want."

The roughness of his father's voice penetrated Kamal's heart and he trembled. He was tongue-tied. His words were stuck to the roof of his mouth. Al-Sayyid Ahmad became even more impatient and shouted at him sharply, "Speak. . . . Have you forgotten how?"

The boy summoned all his strength for one purpose and that was to end his silence at any cost and save himself from his father's anger. He opened his mouth to say anything that would come out: "I was on my way home from school. . . ."

"What made you stand here like an idiot?"

"I saw . . . I saw your honor, so I wanted to kiss your hand."

A skeptical look appeared in the gentleman's eyes. Dryly and sarcastically he remarked, "Is that all there is to it? . . . Did you miss me so much? Couldn't you have waited till tomorrow morning to kiss my hand, if that's what you wanted? . . . Listen . . . you better not have done something wrong at school. . . . I'll find out all about it."

Kamal replied quickly and uneasily, "I haven't done anything. I swear by our Lord."

His patience exhausted, the man said, "Then go. . . . You've wasted my time for nothing. . . . Get lost!"

Kamal started off. He was so shaken he was barely able to see where he was putting his feet. Al-Sayyid Ahmad moved to go back into his store. The moment his father's eyes turned away, the boy revived. Afraid the man would leave and the opportunity be lost, without pausing to consider what he was doing Kamal shouted, "Bring back Mama, God help you." Then he sped away as fast as the wind.

35

AL-SAYYID AHMAD was having his afternoon coffee in his room when Khadija entered and said in a voice that was so deferential it was barely audible, "Our neighbour Umm Maryam wishes to see you, sir."

Her father asked in amazement, "The wife of Mr. Muhammad Ridwan? What does she want?"

"I don't know, Papa."

Attempting to curb his amazement, he ordered her to show the woman in. Although it did not happen often, this would not be the first time one of the respectable ladies from the neighborhood came to call on him, either for some matter relating to his business or because he was trying to reconcile her and a husband who was one of his friends. All the same, he thought it unlikely that this lady was coming to see him for one of these reasons. While he was wondering about this, he happened to think of Maryam and his discussion with his spouse concerning a possible engagement; but how could there be any connection between that secret, which would not have gone beyond the limits of his family circle, and this visit? Then he thought of Mr. Muhammad Ridwan and the possibility that the visit had some link to him. Yet he had never been anything more than a neighbor. Their relationship had never been elevated to the rank of friendship. In former times they had visited each other only when it was necessary. Once the other man became paralyzed, he had called on him a few times, but after that he had knocked on his door only during the religious festivals.

In any case, Maryam's mother, Umm Maryam, was no stranger to him. He remembered she had been in his store once to buy some items. On that occasion she had introduced herself to him to assure herself favorable treatment. He had been as generous with her as her thought appropriate for a good neighbor. Another time he had met her at the door of his house when his departure coincided with her arrival. Although accompanied by her daughter, she had astonished him then with her daring, for she had greeted him openly, saying, "Good afternoon, your honor, sir."

His dealings with his friends had taught him that some of them were lenient where he was strict. He was extreme in his insistence on retaining traditional standards for his family. These other men saw nothing wrong with their wives going out to visit or shop. They were not disturbed by an innocent greeting like Umm Maryam's. Despite his ultraconservative, Hanbali bias in religion, he was not one to attack his friends over what they found appropriate for them and their women. Indeed, he saw nothing wrong with the fact that some of the more distinguished ones took their wives and daughters along when they went in a carriage for outings in the countryside or to frequent wholesome places of entertainment. All he would do was repeat the saying "You've got your religion and I've got mine." In other words, he was not inclined to impose his views blindly on other people. Although he could distinguish what really was good from what was bad, he was not willing to embrace every "good" thing. In that respect he was influenced by his sternly traditional nature, so much so that he considered his wife's visit to the shrine of al-Husayn a crime deserving the gravest punishment he had meted out during his second marriage. For these reasons, he had felt an astonishment mixed with panic when Umm Maryam had greeted him, but he had not thought any the worse of her.

He heard someone clearing her throat outside his door. He perceived that the visitor was warning him she was about to enter. When she did come in, she was swathed in her wrap and her face was concealed behind a black veil. Large black eyes enhanced by kohl could be seen on either side of the golden cylinder connecting her veil to her scarf. She brought her ample and corpulent body with its swaying hips close to him. He rose to greet her. Putting out his hand, he said, "Welcome. You honor our house and family."

She held her hand out to him after wrapping it in a corner of her cloth, so she would not nullify his state of ritual cleanliness. She replied, "Sir, your honor, may our Lord hold you in high esteem."

He invited her to have a seat. Then he sat down and asked her for the sake of politeness, "How is al-Sayyid Muhammad?"

As though the question had reminded her of her sorrows, she sighed audibly and responded, "Praise to God who is the only one we praise for adversity. May our Lord be gracious to all of us."

Al-Sayyid Ahmad shook his head as though he were grieved and murmured, "May our Lord take him by the hand and grant him patience and good health."

The exchange of pleasantries was followed by a short silence while the lady began to prepare for the serious conversation that had brought her. She resembled a musician preparing to sing after the instrumental prelude has ended. Al-Sayyid Ahmad lowered his eyes decorously while retaining a smile on his lips to announce his welcome for the expected conversation. She said, "Al-Sayyid Ahmad, you're such a chivalrous person that you're proverbial throughout the whole district. A person who comes to you and appeals to your chivalry is not disappointed."

Although he was wondering to himself, "What's behind all this," he murmured modestly, "I ask God's forgiveness."

"The fact is that I came just now to visit my sister Umm Fahmy. How appalled I was to learn that she's not here in her house and that you're angry with her."

The woman fell silent to gauge the effect of her words and to hear what he might think of them. For his part, al-Sayyid Ahmad took refuge in silence, as though he could not think of anything to say. Although he felt uncomfortable that this topic had been raised, the smile of welcome remained plastered on his lips.

"Is there a lady finer than Umm Fahmy? She is a wise and modest lady, a neighbor for twenty years or more. During that time we have never heard anything but the nicest things about her. What could she possibly have done that would merit the anger of a just man like you?"

Al-Sayyid Ahmad persisted in his silence and ignored her question. Some ideas occurred to him that increased his discomfort. Had the woman merely come to the house by accident or had she been invited to carry out some schemer's plan? . . . Khadija? Aisha? Amina herself? The children would never tire of defending their mother. Could he forget how Kamal had dared to scream in his face and ask him to bring back his mother? That incident had led to a beating so fiery that smoke had poured from the boy's ears.

"What a fine lady she is. She doesn't deserve such punishment. . . . And what a noble gentleman you are. Violence does not become you. It's the work of cursed Satan, may God humiliate him, but your excellence will prevail to spoil his scheme."

At that point, he felt he could no longer remain silent, not even out of politeness to his guest. He muttered with deliberate brevity, "May our Lord remedy the situation."

Encouraged by her success in getting him to talk, Umm Maryam said zealously, "How it hurts me for our fine neighbor to leave her home after a long life of seclusion and honor."

"The streams will return to their banks, but there is a right time for everything."

"You are like a brother to me. Indeed, you're dearer than a brother. I won't add a single word."

A new element had entered the affair and did not escape his attentive mind. He registered it the way an observatory might record a distant earthquake, regardless of how faint it seemed. He imagined that when she said, "You are like a brother to me," her voice had been tender and sweet. When she said, "Indeed, you're dearer than a brother," her voice had revealed a warm affection that lent a pleasant fragrance to the embarrassed atmosphere. He was amazed and wondered about it. Perplexed, he could no longer bear to keep his eyes lowered. He raised them hesitantly. He stole a look at her face. Contrary to his expectations, he found her looking at him with her large black eyes. He was flustered and lowered his again quickly. He was partly surprised and partly embarrassed. To cover up his emotions, he continued the conversation: "Thank you for considering me your brother. . . . "

He wondered whether she had been looking at him that way throughout their conversation or whether he had merely raised his eyes at a moment when she happened to glance at him. What could be said about her not lowering her eyes when their eyes met? He immediately scoffed at these ideas, telling himself that his infatuation with women and experience with them made him especially prone to think ill of them. No doubt the truth was as far removed as possible from what he imagined. She might be one of those women whose nature gushes with affection, so that people who do not know them think they are flirting when they are not. In order to confirm his opinion, since confirmation was needed, he looked up again. How appalled he was to see her still looking at him. He was a little more courageous this time and fixed his eyes on her for a moment. She kept gazing at him submissively but boldly. In total confusion he lowered his eyes. At that time he heard her soft voice say, "After this request I'll see whether I'm truly favored by you."

Favored? If the word had not been spoken in this atmosphere filled with emotion and charged with doubt and confusion, it would have passed without leaving any trace. But now...? With considerable embarrassment he looked at her again. He discerned some hints in her eyes that tantalized his suspicions. Had his feeling been right? Was this possible at the very moment she was interceding for his wife? For a man as experienced with women as he was, that would be no surprise... a playful wife with a paralyzed husband. His consciousness was permeated by surges of delight that filled him with warmth and pride. When had this sentiment begun? Was it an old one that had simply been waiting for an opportunity? Had she not visited him at the store once without doing anything to excite his suspicions? Even so, the store was not a place where a woman like her would feel comfortable revealing a secret passion, as the performer Zubayda had, with no prior preparation for the announcement. Was it a sentiment born of the moment that had arisen along with the golden opportunity when she found herself alone with him? If that was true, then she was merely another Zubayda disguised in a lady's clothing.

Although he knew a lot about passionate women, it was not surprising that he had overlooked her. He was zealous to respect the honor of his neighbors in the most exemplary way. If she was flirting with him, how should he respond? Should he say, "You're more in favor with me than you can imagine"? It would be a pretty phrase, but she might see it as a welcoming response to her invitation. He certainly did not want that. He was completely opposed to it and not merely because he was still enthralled with Zubayda. He would not agree to a situation deviating from his principles, which called for total respect for the reputations of honorable people in general and of friends and neighbors in particular. In spite of all his amorous and sensual excesses, there was not a single blot on his page to embarrass him with a friend, neighbor, or virtuous person. It had always been his custom to fear God as much when he was amusing himself as when he was being serious. He had only allowed himself things he considered licit or within the bounds of minor offenses. This did not imply that he had been endowed with supernatural willpower shielding him from passion. What he did was revel in every passion allowed him and turn his eyes away from respectable women. Throughout his entire life he had never deliberately looked at the face of a woman from his district. He was known to have rejected a promising affair out of concern for the feelings of an acquaintance. A messenger had come one day to invite him to meet the sister of that man, a middle-aged widow, on a night he would name. Al-Sayyid Ahmad had received the invitation silently and shown the messenger out with his customary politeness. Then he had avoided the street where her house was for years afterward.

Umm Maryam was possibly the first person to test his principles face to face. Although he found her attractive, he refused to answer the temptations of passion. The voice of wisdom and sobriety won out, protecting his much-discussed reputation from a world of reproaches. His good reputation seemed to mean more to him than seizing a proffered pleasure. He consoled himself with the opportunities that arose from time to time for romances with no unpleasant consequences.

This will to respect his obligations and act honorably with friends remained with him even in the realms of amusement and desire. He had never been accused of making a pass at the mistress of a companion or of looking lustfully at the sweetheart of a friend. He chose friendship over passion. He would say, "The affection of a friend endures. A girlfriend's passion is fleeting." For this reason, he was content to select his lovers from unattached women or to wait until a woman had ended her previous relationship. Then he would seize his opportunity. At times he would even ask permission from her former companion before beginning to court her. Thus he was able to conduct his amorous adventures with a delight free of regret and a serenity unblemished by ill will. In other words, he had successfully balanced the animal within him that was voracious for pleasure with the man in him that looked up to higher principles. He had succeeded in harmoniously joining these two sides of his personality in a compatible whole. Neither side dominated the other, and each was able to pursue its own special interests easily and comfortably. Just as he had reconciled the opposing forces of sensuality and ethics, he was also able to merge piety and debauchery successfully into a unity free of any hint of either sin or repression.

Yet his good faith was not inspired merely by loyalty to a code of ethics. It was based most of all on his innate desire to continue to be loved and enjoy a fine reputation. The success of his amorous forays made it easier for him to avoid love marred by betrayal or depravity. Moreover, he had never known a true form of love that could have pushed him into succumbing either to emotion, without regard to principles, or to a fierce emotional and moral crisis, in which he could not keep from being burned.

Umm Maryam represented nothing more to him than a delicious kind of food, which, if it threatened his digestion, he could easily turn down in favor of some of the other tasty but wholesome dishes that covered the table. Therefore, he answered her tenderly, "Your mediation is accepted, God willing. You will hear something that will please you shortly."

The woman said as she rose, "May our Lord be generous to you, sir, your honor."

She stretched out her soft hand. He took it, but lowered his eyes. He imagined that she squeezed his hand a little when they were saying goodbye. He began to wonder whether this was the way she usually shook hands or if she had deliberately squeezed it. He tried to remember what her handshake had been like when she arrived, but he could not. He spent most of the time before he returned to the store thinking about the woman, what she had said, her tenderness, and her handshake.

36

"OUR AUNT, the widow of the late Mr. Shawkat, wishes to see you."

Al-Sayyid Ahmad threw Khadija a fiery look and shouted at her, "Why?"

His angry voice and irritated looks proclaimed that he meant more than this "why" implied and that he would have liked to tell her, "I've barely gotten rid of the intermediary who came yesterday when you bring me a new one today. Who told you these tricks would work on me? How can you and your brothers dare to try to put something over on me?"

Khadija's face became pale. In a trembling voice she replied, "I don't know, by God."

He nodded his head as though to say, "Yes, you do know, and I know too. Your cunning will achieve nothing but the most disastrous consequences for you." Resentfully he declared, "Let her come in. I won't be able to drink my coffee with a calm mind after this. My room has turned into a court with judges and witnesses. That's the kind of rest I find at home. God's curse on all of you!"

Before he could finish speaking, Khadija had vanished like a mouse that has heard the floor creak. Al-Sayyid Ahmad glowered angrily for a few moments. Then he remembered the sight of Khadija retreating so fearfully that her foot stumbled in its wooden clog and her head almost collided with the door. He smiled sympathetically. His impulsive fury was wiped away and left him feeling affectionate. What children they were! They refused to forget their mother even for a single minute.

He directed his eyes toward the door and readied a beaming face to greet the visitor, as though he had not just seconds earlier fumed with anger at the thought of her visit. When he got angry at home for the most trifling reason or for none at all, he was not bluffing, but this visitor, as the widow of the late Mr. Shawkat, had a special status and outranked all the women who called at the

house from time to time. Her husband had been a special friend
and the two families had been linked by a bond of affection since
the days of their grandparents. The departed gentleman had been
like a father to him. His widow continued to be a mother to him
and, consequently, to his entire family. It was she who had
arranged his engagement to Amina. She had helped bring his
children into the world. In addition to all of these considerations,
the Shawkat family were people it was a privilege to know. Not
only were they of Turkish origin, but they had a high social
standing and owned real estate in Cairo between al-Hamzawi
and al-Surayn. If al-Sayyid Ahmad was in the middle ranks of
the middle class, they were indisputably members of its top eche-
lon. Perhaps it was the woman's maternal feelings toward him and
his filial feelings for her that made him indignant and uncomfortable about her anticipated intercession.

She was a person who would mince no words when she spoke
to him. She would not weary of appealing to his emotions. Moreover, he knew her to be scathingly frank. Her excuses for it were
her age and her status. Yes, she was not one to . . .

He stopped brooding when he heard her footsteps. He rose to
greet her: "Welcome. It's as though the Prophet himself were
visiting us."

The elderly lady approached him. She was hobbling along,
leaning on her parasol. She looked up at him with a face that
was fair and full of wrinkles. Her transparent white veil did little to
conceal her features. She responded to his greeting with a smile
that revealed her gold teeth. She shook his hand and sat down
beside him casually. She said, "A person who lives a long time sees
a lot. Even you, pride of mankind . . . and even in this house . . .
things are happening that are unpleasant to discuss. . . . By the God
of al-Husayn, you've grown senile. Your dotage has arrived
unexpectedly."

She rattled on, giving her tongue free rein to say whatever it
pleased without allowing al-Sayyid Ahmad an opportunity to
interrupt or comment. She told him how she had come to visit
and had discovered his wife was absent. "I thought at first that she
was out visiting someone. So I pounded my chest in astonishment.
I exclaimed, 'What's become of the world?' . . . How could her
husband have permitted her to leave the house? Does he think so
little of the decrees of God, of human law, and of the edicts of the

Ottoman Empire?" She had quickly learned the whole truth. "I regained my senses and said, 'Praise to God, the world's just fine. This truly is al-Sayyid Ahmad. This is the least one could expect from him.'"

Then she abandoned her mocking tone and began to scold him for his harshness. She was outspoken in her laments for his wife, whom she considered the last woman to deserve punishment. Whenever he attempted to interrupt she would yell at him, "Hush. Not a word. Save your sweet talk that you make so flowery. It won't fool me. I want you to do the right thing, not say something eloquent." She told him frankly that he was excessively conservative in his treatment of his family. It was abnormal. It would be a good thing if he would act in a kindlier, more indulgent way.

Al-Sayyid Ahmad listened to her for a long time. When she allowed him to speak, only after she was exhausted from talking, he explained his point of view to her. Her passionate defense of his wife and his respect for her did not prevent him from asserting to her that his treatment of his family was based on principles he would not abandon. He did promise at the end, as he had promised Umm Maryam earlier, that everything would turn out for the best. He thought the time had come for the meeting to conclude.

Before he knew what was happening she said, "The absence of Mrs. Amina was an unpleasant surprise to me, since I needed to see her for an extremely important reason. Because of my health it's not an easy matter for me to go out. Now I don't know whether it would be better for me to tell you what I was going to tell her or to wait till she returns."

Al-Sayyid Ahmad replied with a smile, "We are all ready to serve you."

"I would have liked her to be the first to hear, even though you leave her no voice in the matter. Since this opportunity has escaped me, I'll console myself by preparing a happy reason for her return."

The gentleman was baffled by her statement. He wondered as he stared at her, "What's behind all this?"

Stabbing the carpet with the point of her parasol, she said, "I won't keep you in suspense. I have chosen Aisha to be my son Khalil's wife."

He was astounded. He was taken by surprise and by something totally unexpected. He felt uneasy and even alarmed for reasons that were hardly secret. He perceived immediately that he would have to drop his long-standing resolve that the younger daughter should not marry before the elder. He could not ignore this precious request announced by a person who was well acquainted with his resolution. She had obviously rejected it in advance and would refuse to be ruled by his judgment.

"Why are you silent as though you hadn't heard me?"

Al-Sayyid Ahmad smiled in confusion and embarrassment. Then, in order to say something pleasant while pondering the issue in all its aspects, he replied, "This is an enormous honor for us."

The lady shot him a look that seemed to say, "Don't use your honeyed phrases on me." She said combatively, "I don't need to be made fun of with empty words. Nothing will satisfy me but total acceptance. Khalil entrusted me with the task of finding a wife for him. I told him, 'I've the best bride you could hope for.' He was pleased by my choice. He had no reservations about becoming your son-in-law.... Has the time come that you meet a request like this, from me, with silence and evasion? My God, my God."

How long would he be tormented by this difficult problem, which he could not resolve without inflicting a rude shock on one of his daughters? He looked at her as though trying to beg her sympathy for his situation. He mumbled, "The matter's not the way you imagine. Your request is my command, but . . ."

"A pox on 'but.' Don't tell me you've decided not to let the younger marry until the elder has. Who are you to decree this or that? Leave God's work to God. He's the most compassionate one of all. If you want, I can give you tens of examples of younger sisters who married before the older ones without their marriages keeping their sisters from excellent matches. Khadija is an extraordinary young woman. She will not go wanting for a fine husband as soon as God wills it. How long will you stand in the way of Aisha's destiny? Doesn't she too deserve your affection and compassion?"

He asked himself, "If Khadija's such an extraordinary young woman, why don't you choose her?" He thought about putting her on the spot the way she had him, but he was afraid she would toss him an answer that would insult, however innocently, Khadija and thus him as well. In a voice that was very serious and earnest he said, "It's just that I feel sorry for Khadija."

She replied sharply as though she was the one making the concession, "Every day things like this happen without upsetting anyone. God dislikes it if His servant is stubborn and proud. Accept my request and trust in God. Don't reject my hand. I haven't made this offer to anyone before you."

The gentleman cloaked his feelings with a smile and said, "This is an enormous honor, as I told you a moment ago. . . . If you would just be patient with me for a short time while I pull myself together and straighten things out, you will find that my opinion corresponds to your wishes, God willing."

She said, in the tone of a person wishing to terminate a conversation, "I won't waste any more of your time than I have. The longer this give-and-take is drawn out, the more I think you're not really accepting my request. A woman like me wants you to say yes at once and not beat around the bush when she asks for something. I'll only add one word to what I've said: Khalil is as much your child as mine and the same holds true for Aisha."

She rose and al-Sayyid Ahmad stood up to say goodbye to her. He was expecting only a word of farewell, but she insisted on reiterating everything she had said. She seemed to fear he might miss some nuance and so repeated it all in detail. Before he knew what was happening, or she did either, she was harking back to corroborate some of her ideas and substantiate others. One idea led to another and she rambled on without interference until she had repeated most of what she had earlier said about the engagement. Nor did she care to conclude her remarks before paying her respects to the subject of the banished mother with a word, or two, or three. Then once more she was overpowered by the association of ideas and carried on until the man had trouble controlling his nerves. He almost laughed when she finally told him, "I won't waste any more of your time than I already have."

He escorted her to the door, apprehensive at each step that she might stop walking and take another shot at conversation. When he could at last sit down again, he was breathing heavily. He was distressed and dejected. He had a sensitive heart, more sensitive than most people would have suspected. In fact, it was too sensitive. How could anyone believe that who had only seen him grinning, bellowing, or laughing sarcastically?... Sorrow was going to scorch his flesh and blood in a way that could spoil his whole life, making it seem ugly to him. How happy it would make him to spare no expense to delight both his daughters, the one in whose beautiful face he could detect a resemblance to his mother's and the other girl who had only received a faint glimmer of good looks. Each of them was a vital part of him.

The husband whom the widow of the late Mr. Shawkat was offering was a catch in every sense of the word. He was a young man of twenty-five with a monthly income of not less than thirty pounds. It was true that, like many members of the elite, he had no occupation and little education, the latter not extending beyond knowledge of reading and writing. All the same, he had many of his father's good qualities. He was pleasant, generous, and polite.

What should he do? He had to make up his mind. He did not usually hesitate or ask for advice. It was not acceptable, even for a brief moment, for him to appear indecisive to his family, as though he did not know what he thought. Could he not consult with his closest friends? He was not ashamed to do that when something serious came up. In fact, their evenings usually began with a discussion of worries and problems before wine transported them to a world where worries and problems were unknown. He realized that he was very opinionated and would not deviate from what he believed. He was the kind of person who requests advice to shore up his opinion, not to undermine it. Even so, that would provide consolation and relief.

When the man was exasperated with thinking he cried out, "Who would believe that the unbearable state I'm in results from a blessing God has bestowed upon me?"

37

AMINA HAD no occupation during her exile other than sitting beside her mother and discussing at length anything that came to mind. They had talks about the distant and not so distant past and the present, ranging from precious memories to the current drama. Had it not been for the painful separation and the specter of divorce, she would have been content with her new life. It was like a restful holiday after the burden of her duties or a voyage to a world of memories.

When days passed with nothing happening to frighten her and when she heard about the mediation by Umm Maryam and Widow Shawkat, she felt less apprehensive and more relaxed. Moreover, the evening visits of the boys continued without interruption and breathed new hope into her breast. She got to spend almost as much time with them in the new house as in the old one. In both instances, she was separated from them until they were free to come to the evening reunion. Even so, she longed for them like an emigrant in a distant land parted by fate from her loved ones. She yearned for them, feeling deprived because she could not breathe the same air, share their memories, and supervise their workaday and leisure activities. Every inch a person's body travels on the road of separation seems like miles to the heart.

When the old lady found her silent or sensed that her daughter's thoughts were wandering, she would tell her, "Patience, Amina. I feel sorry for you. A mother away from her children is a stranger. She's a stranger even if she's staying in the house where she was born."

Yes, she was a stranger. The house might just as well not have been the only home she had known as a child. Her mother was no longer that mother she could not bear to leave for even a moment. So long as the house was her place of exile where she waited regretfully for a word of pardon from heaven, it could not be her home.

After a long interval her pardon did arrive. The boys brought it one evening. When they came, their eyes flashed like lightning. Her heart pounded so hard it shook her whole chest. She was apprehensive about giving this sign a grander interpretation than it deserved, but Kamal ran toward her and put his arms around her neck. Then, beside himself with joy, he yelled to her, "Put on your wrap and come with us."

Yasin roared with laughter and said, "It's all over."

Then he and Fahmy together said, "Father summoned us and told us, 'Go get your mother.'"

She lowered her eyes to hide her overwhelming joy. She could not conceal the emotions rocking her soul. Her face seemed an extremely accurate mirror, registering everything that was inside her, no matter how small. She wanted so much to receive the happy news with a composure befitting her maternal role, but she was transported by joy. The features of her face laughingly expressed her childish delight. At the same time she felt ashamed, although she did not know why. She remained motionless for so long that Kamal's patience was exhausted. He pulled her by the hand, putting his entire weight into it until she yielded and rose. She stood for a little while in a strange confusion. Before she realized what she was doing she turned and asked, "Should I go, Mother?"

This question sounded peculiar and slipped out with an inflection of confusion and embarrassment. Fahmy and Yasin smiled. Only Kamal was astonished and almost alarmed. He affirmed to her once more the news of the pardon they brought.

The grandmother had sensed everything her daughter was feeling and surmised what was going on inside her. Her heart was touched. Taking care not to appear surprised by the question, not even registering so much as a faint smile, she replied seriously, "Go to your house, and may the peace of God go with you."

Amina went to put on her wrap and bundle up her clothes, with Kamal following at her heels. The grandmother asked the young men in a critical tone softened by a tender smile, "Wouldn't it have been more appropriate for your father to come himself?"

Fahmy answered apologetically, "Grandmother, you know very well what my father's like."

Yasin laughed and observed, "Let's thank God for what's happened."

The grandmother muttered something they could not understand. Then she sighed and said, as though replying to her own muttering, "In any case, al-Sayyid Ahmad's not a man like the others."

They left the house with their grandmother's prayers and blessings ringing in their ears. For the first time in their lives they walked along the street together. They found it an extraordinary event. Fahmy and Yasin exchanged smiling glances. Kamal remembered the day he had gone along, as he was now, holding his mother's hand tight and leading her from alley to alley. Then there had ensued the pains and fears that were even worse than a nightmare. He marveled about it for some time but soon was able to overlook the sorrows of the past in favor of the joy of the present. He found himself wanting to jest. He laughingly suggested to his mother, "Come on, let's sneak off to our master al-Husayn."

Yasin laughed and commented allusively, "May God be pleased with him. He's a martyr and loves martyrs."

They could see the protruding wooden balcony of their house and two shapes moving behind the spindles of its latticework. The mother's heart fluttered with affection and longing at the sight of her daughters. Just inside the door she found Umm Hanafi waiting to welcome her and smother her mistress's hands with kisses. In the courtyard she met Khadija and Aisha, who clung to her like little girls.

They climbed the stairs in a tumultuous parade with exhilarating and frenzied happiness. They came to a halt in her room. Each one tried to help her remove her wrap, that symbol of the loathsome separation, as they roared with laughter. When she sat down among them she was breathless from the impact of her emotions. Kamal wanted to tell her how happy he was. The best way he found to put it was: "Today's dearer to me even than the procession with the holy shrine on the camel when the pilgrims leave for Mecca."

For the first time in a long while all the regulars were present at the coffee hour. They resumed their evening chat in an atmosphere of delight. Its splendor was doubled by the days of separation and dejection preceding it, just as the pleasure of a warm day is greater if it follows a frigid week. The joy of the reunion notwithstanding, the mother did not forget to ask the girls about the household affairs, progressing from the oven room all the way up to the hyacinth beans and jasmine. She also asked a lot about their father. She was delighted to learn that he had not allowed anyone to assist him with removing or putting on his clothes. Whatever rest she might have afforded him by her absence, a change had crept into the system of his life, which had without doubt imposed a burden on him that would disappear now that she was back. Her return, and that alone, would guarantee him the kind of life he was accustomed to and comfortable with.

One thing that did not occur to Amina was that some of the hearts happy at her return discovered in this return itself a reason for brooding about their sorrow and pain. Yet this is what happened. These hearts, distracted from their sorrows by their mother's, began to think again about their own worries now they were reassured about their mother's well-being. In the same way, when we have acute but temporary intestinal pain we forget our chronic eye inflammation, but once the intestinal distress is relieved, the pain in the eyes returns.

Fahmy was telling himself, "It appears that every sorrow has an end. My mother's affliction is over. But it seems my sorrow will never end." Aisha resumed her own reflections, to which no one else was privy. Her dreams and memories visited her, although compared with her brother she was considerably calmer and readier to forget.

Amina could not read their thoughts, and nothing disturbed her serenity. When she retired to her room that night it was clear she would not be able to sleep, her mind was so overflowing with happiness. She only dozed off a few times before she got out of bed at midnight. She went to the balcony as usual to gaze through the latticework screens at the wakeful street until the carriage bringing her husband home swayed into sight.

Her heart beat violently, and she blushed with shame and confusion. She might well have been meeting her husband for the first time. Had she not reflected about this moment for a long time . . . the awaited moment of reunion and how she would approach him? How would he treat her after this long separation? What could she say to him, or he to her? If only she could pretend to be asleep. But she had no talent at all for acting and could not bear for him to find her lying down when he came in. Yes, she would not be able to neglect her duty to go to the stairway with a lamp to light the way for him. Over and above all these considerations, after winning the right to return and overcoming his anger at her, she felt good. She forgave everything that had happened and assumed full responsibility for the offense, to the point of thinking that, although her husband had not taken the trouble to go to her mother's house to reach a settlement with her, he deserved to be treated in a conciliatory fashion.

She took the lamp and went to the staircase. She held her arm out over the railing and stood there with a throbbing heart, listening to the sound of his approaching footsteps, until he made his way up to her. She greeted him with her head bowed, so she did not see his face when they met. She did not know if any change had taken place in his appearance since she last saw him. She heard him say in a normal voice that bore no trace of the painful recent past, "Good evening."

She mumbled, "Good evening, sir."

He went to his room. She trailed after him holding up the lamp. He began to remove his clothes silently. She went to assist him. She set to work, privately heaving sighs of relief. She remembered the ill-fated morning of the separation when he had risen to don his clothes and told her harshly, "I'll put my clothes on myself." The memory, though, lacked any of the feelings of pain and sorrow that had overwhelmed her at the time. As she carried out this service for him, which he had not allowed anyone else to perform, she felt she was reclaiming the dearest thing she possessed in all the world.

He took his place on the sofa and she sat cross-legged on the pallet at his feet, without either of them uttering a word. She expected him to put the painful past to rest with some word of advice or admonition. She had prepared herself for that in a thousand different ways. All he did was ask her, "How's your mother?"

Sighing with relief, she answered, "Fine, sir. She sends you her greetings and prayers."

Another period of silence passed before he remarked with apparent disinterest, "The widow of the late Mr. Shawkat disclosed to me her wish to choose Aisha as Khalil's wife."

Amina looked up at him in an astonishment that eloquently revealed the impact of the surprise on her. He shrugged his shoulders as though it was nothing. Fearing she might express an opinion that happened to agree with his decision, which he had kept secret from everyone, and would then suspect he had taken her advice, he quickly added, "I've thought about the matter for a long time and have decided to accept. I don't want to interfere with my daughter's fortune any more than I have already. The matter is in God's hands, both now and later."

38

AISHA RECEIVED the good news with the joy of a girl who since early childhood had cherished the dream of getting married. She could scarcely believe her ears when she was told about it. Had her father actually agreed? Had marriage become an imminent reality and not a dream or a cruel joke? No more than three months had passed since the disappointment she had suffered. Although the impact on her of that experience had been harsh and intense, with the passing days it had become lighter and weaker, turning into a pale memory, which when aroused would excite only a gentle sorrow of no particular significance.

Everything in the house yielded blindly to a higher will with a limitless authority almost like that of religion. Within these walls even love itself had to creep into their hearts timidly, hesitantly, and diffidently. It did not enjoy its normal influence or domi-nance. The only dominant force here was that higher will. There-fore, when her father had said no, his verdict had become lodged in the depths of her soul. The girl had firmly believed that every-thing was really over, since there was no way to escape or to ask for a review. She had no hope that anything would help. It was as though this "no" were one of the processes of nature, like the alternation of night and day. No objection to it would be of any significance, since only obedience was allowed. This belief of hers, whether conscious or not, worked to terminate everything, and terminated it was.

Aisha wondered privately whether her current good fortune did not embrace an incomprehensible contradiction. Less than three months after one rejection, permission had been granted for her to marry. Thus she would not be part of the destiny of the young man for whom her heart had yearned. She kept this thought to herself, and no one learned about it, not even her mother. To announce her happiness with a suitor, even one of whom she had only the vaguest concept, would be a wanton affront to modesty. It would have been inconceivable for her to express a desire for some specific man. In spite of all this and despite the fact that she knew nothing about the new bridegroom except what her mother had mentioned in a general discussion of his family, Aisha was happy beyond words with the good news. Her eager emotions had found a pole toward which to gravitate. Her love seemed to be more a disposition than an attachment to any particular man. Even if one man was disqualified and another took his place, she was satisfied and everything was fine. She might prefer one man over another but not enough to destroy her taste for life or to push her into rebellion and revolt.

Now that she was in good spirits and her heart fluttered with delight, she felt, as she usually did in such circumstances, pure affection and sympathy for her sister. She wished that Khadija had married first. By way of apology and encouragement she told her, "I wish you'd been the first to marry . . . but it's fate and destiny. It will all come soon."

Khadija did not enjoy affectionate words of comfort when defeated. She received Aisha's statement with unconcealed annoyance. Their mother had already apologized to her delicately: "We all wanted your turn to come first. We acted on this assumption more than once, but perhaps it is our stubbornness about something beyond our control that has thwarted your luck until now. Let's allow things to proceed as God wills. Something good comes out of every delay."

Khadija found that Yasin and Fahmy were also full of affection for her, whether they expressed it in words or revealed it by being nice to her, at least for the moment, instead of resorting to the stinging humor customary between them, especially between her and Yasin. The only thing matching Khadija's sorrow at her bad luck was her nervousness about the affection smothering her, but not because of an innate aversion to sympathy. She was like a patient with influenza whose health would be harmed by exposure to the fresh air that would normally invigorate him when well. She discounted this affection as a trifling substitute for lost hope and may well have been suspicious of their motives for showering it on her. Was her mother not always the intermediary between the matchmakers and her father? How could Khadija know whether her mother's mediation had been confined to carrying out the duties of the mistress of the house and had not been influenced by a covert desire for Aisha to get married? Was it not Fahmy who brought the message from the officer at the Gamaliya police station? Could he not have acted deftly behind the scenes to change the officer's mind?

Was it not true that Yasin ... but why should she blame Yasin when a brother even more closely related to her than Yasin had let her down? What kind of affection was this? No, one should ask what kind of hypocrisy and what kind of a lie. Therefore she was impatient with all the sympathy. It reminded her of their ill treatment, not their beneficence. She was filled with resentment and anger but concealed that deep inside her so as not to appear displeased by her sister's happiness. She did not care to expose herself, as her suspicious nature made her think she might, to the abuse of anyone wishing to revile her. In any case, there was no alternative to suppression of her emotions, because in this family that was an ingrained custom and a moral imperative established by threat of paternal terror. Between her hatred and resentment on one side and concealment and pretended delight on the other, her life was a continual torment and an uninterrupted effort.

What about her father? What had made him alter his former opinion? How could she seem so unimportant to him now, after he had cherished her? Had he lost patience waiting for her to get married and decided to sacrifice her, leaving her to her fate? She could not get over her amazement at the way they were abandoning her as though she did not exist. In her rebellious mood, she forgot how they had stood up for her previously. Now all she remembered was their betrayal.

Her anger for everyone in general was nothing compared with the feelings of jealousy and resentment against Aisha that she had packed into her breast. She hated her happiness. Most of all she hated Aisha's attempt to hide her happiness. She hated her beauty, which to Khadija's eyes appeared to be an instrument of torture and oppression. In much the same way, a man stalking prey finds the glistening full moon oppressive. She hated life too. It held nothing for her but despair. The progression of days only added to her sorrows as the presents of the bridegroom were brought to the house along with little tokens of his affection. While the house was filled with an atmosphere of unadulterated delight and happiness, she found herself in a forlorn isolation that was as fertile a breeding ground for sorrows as a stagnant pond is for insects.

Then al-Sayyid Ahmad began to outfit the bride. Talk about the trousseau dominated the family's evening reunions. The bride was shown various styles of furniture and clothing. She would praise one and shun another, comparing one color with a second with such concern that everyone forgot the elder sister and her need for consolation and flattery. Khadija was even forced, since she was pretending to be delighted about everything, to join energetically and enthusiastically in their interminable discussions. This complex emotional situation might have appeared to a stranger to portend only evil, but there was a sudden change when attention was directed to making the wedding gown. Then all eyes were fixed on Khadija with great interest and hope. She had dreaded this task as an inescapable duty she hated to accept but was unable to decline, for fear of revealing her concealed emotions. But her resentment faded away and modesty brought her rebellion under control once their attention was focused on her.

Her mother urged her to do a good job for her sister. Aisha's eyes were filled with embarrassment and entreaty when she gazed at Khadija. Fahmy told Aisha in her hearing, "You won't be a real bride until Khadija makes your wedding gown."

Yasin agreed: "You're right . . . that's a fact."

Khadija's latent good nature came to the surface like a green plant emerging from a seed hidden beneath the mud once sweet water has been provided. She did not suspect the motives of this interest in her the way she had previously. She knew this was genuine and directed at her unquestionable skill. It constituted a general admission of her importance and significance. Although happiness was not hers to enjoy, it would not be fully realized until she contributed to it. She set about this new project with a heart totally cleansed of her hostile emotions. Although members of this family, like most other people, were subject to feelings of anger, they never were so afflicted that their hearts were hostile in a consistent or deep-rooted fashion. Some of them had a capacity for anger like that of alcohol for combustion, but their anger would be quickly extinguished. Then their souls would be tranquil and their hearts full of forgiveness. Similarly in Cairo, during the winter, the sky can be gloomy with clouds and it even drizzles, but in an hour or less the clouds will have scattered to reveal a pure blue sky and a laughing sun.

Khadija had not forgotten her sorrows, but her generosity had purified them of malice and resentment. With each passing day she was less inclined to find fault with Aisha or some family member and more apt to blame her luck. Ultimately she made it the target of her resentment and grumbling. Her luck had been too stingy to make her beautiful. It had delayed her marriage until she was over twenty and clouded her future with fears and anxiety.

Finally, like her mother, Khadija surrendered to the fates. Her fiery side, inherited from her father, and the complex of characteristics arising from her interaction with the environment were both unable to deal with her fortune. She found peace of mind by relying on her tranquil side, which she had inherited from her mother. So she yielded to her destiny. She resembled a commander who, unable to achieve his objective, chooses a naturally fortified location for his remaining forces to make a stand or asks for a truce or peace.

Khadija would express her grief when she performed her prayers or was alone with God the Compassionate. Since childhood she had imitated her mother's piety and observance of religious duties with a persistence that showed an awakened spirituality. Aisha, on the other hand, worshiped in isolated bouts of religious enthusiasm but could not bear to keep it up for long. Khadija was often amazed when she compared her fortune with that of her sister. Why did she achieve such poor results with her religious devotion while Aisha was richly rewarded for being slack?

"I perform my prayers regularly, but she can't do it for more than two days in a row. I fast during the whole month of Ramadan, while she fasts for a day or two and then just pretends. She slips secretly into the pantry and fills her belly with nuts and dried fruit. When the cannon is fired in the evening to mark the end of the daily fast, she rushes to the table ahead of those who have been fasting."

Khadija would not even concede wholeheartedly that her sister was more beautiful. Of course, she did not announce her opinion to anyone and frequently chose to attack herself in order to prevent others from being tempted to do so. But she would look at herself in the mirror for long periods and tell herself, "No doubt Aisha is beautiful, but she's skinny. Being plump is half of beauty. I'm plump. The fullness of my face almost compensates for the size of my nose. All I need is for my luck to improve." She had lost her self-confidence during the recent crisis. Although in the past she had frequently repeated to herself similar observations about beauty, plumpness, and luck, now she made them to ward off her unnerving feeling of being unsure of herself. In the same way, we resort at times to logic to reassure ourselves about matters, like health or illness, happiness or misery, and love or hate, that bear no relationship whatsoever to logic.

In spite of her many chores as mother of the bride, Amina did not forget Khadija. Her happiness for the bride reminded her of her sorrow for her other daughter, just as the relief provided by an anesthetic drug reminds us of the pain that will return eventually. Aisha's wedding reawakened her old fears about Khadija. Searching for reassurance without being too particular about the source, she sent Umm Hanafi with one of Khadija's handkerchiefs to Shaykh Ra'uf at al-Bab al-Akhdar for him to read her fortune. The woman returned with good news. She related that the shaykh had told her, "You'll be bringing me a kilo of sugar soon when my prediction comes true." Although this was not the first augury of glad tidings for Khadija the servant had brought, Amina hoped for the best. She welcomed the news as a sedative to calm the anxiety that had been hounding her.

39

"ISN'T IT time yet, bitch? I've melted away, Muslims. I've dissolved like a bar of soap. Nothing's left but the suds. She knows this and doesn't care to open the window. Go ahead, play the coquette, you bitch. Didn't we agree on a date? But you're right to hold back . . . one of your breasts could destroy Malta. The second would drive Hindenburg out of his mind. You've got a treasure. May our Lord be gracious to me. May our Lord be gracious to me and to every poor rogue like me who can't sleep for thinking about swelling breasts, plump buttocks, and eyes enhanced by kohl. Eyes come last, because many a blind woman with a fleshy rump and full breasts is a thousand times better than a skinny, flat-chested woman with eyes decorated with kohl. You're the performer's daughter and a neighbor of al-Tarbi'a Alley. The performer has taught you to flirt, and the alley has supplied you with its secret beauty potions. If your breasts have grown full and round, it's because so many lovers have fondled them. We agreed on this date. I'm not dreaming. Open the window. Open up, bitch. Open up. You're the most beautiful creature ever to arouse my passion. Holding your lip between mine . . . sucking on your nipple. . . . I'll wait until dawn. You'll find me very docile. If you want me to be the rear end of a donkey cart that you rock back and forth on, I'll do it. If you want me to be the ass pulling the cart, I'll do that. What a mishap, Yasin! Your life is destroyed, you son of Ahmad Abd al-Jawad. How the Australians gloat at your fate. Woe to me, expelled from the Ezbekiya entertainment district, a prisoner in al-Gamaliya. It's all the fault of the war. Kaiser Wilhelm launched it in Europe and I have become its victim here in al-Nahhasin. Open the window, delight of your mother. Open up, my delight. . . ."

This was the way Yasin had begun talking to himself as he sat on a bench in the coffee shop of al-Sayyid Ali. His eyes were gazing at the house of the performer Zubayda through the small window overlooking al-Ghuriya. The more anxious he became, the more he sank into his dreams and musings, which soothed his anxiety but aroused his desires, just as some sedatives deal with insomnia but tire the heart. He had progressed a step forward in his court-ship of the lute player Zanuba. He had advanced from the pre-paratory stage – frequenting the coffee shop of al-Sayyid Ali in the evening, watching for her, walking behind her donkey cart, smil-ing, twisting his mustache, and raising his eyebrows playfully – to the stage of negotiating and getting down to business.

He had taken this step in al-Tarbi'a Alley, which was long and narrow with a canvas roof. There were small stores clustered on either side like the cells of a beehive. He was certainly not unfam-iliar with al-Tarbi'a, a bazaar frequented by women of all classes. They thronged there to purchase something that was light to carry and had much to offer. They were shopping for various types of perfume useful in promoting delight and beauty. He headed for this market whenever he had no other special destination. It was a favorite haunt of his Friday mornings. Going from one end to the other, he would walk along slowly, both because of the congestion and because he wanted it that way. He pretended to examine the shops as though wanting to select something. Actually, he was scrutinizing the faces, visible when veils were momentarily lifted, and the outlines of bodies, discernible where the ladies' wraps were drawn tight. He saw some features in their entirety and others only in part. He took in the charming fragrances here and there as well as the voices that slipped out from time to time or their whispering laughter. He usually kept within the bounds of good manners because of the preponderance of respectable women there. He was content to observe, compare, and criticize. From what he saw he gathered extraordinary pictures with which to decorate his mental museum. Nothing made him so happy as to come upon a clearer complexion than he had ever seen before, an unusual glance from an eye, a breast that was astonishingly round, or buttocks unique in size or build. When he reviewed them later, he would say, "The winner in today's competition for full breasts was the lady standing in front of so-and-so's shop," or "Today's the day of the rump surpassing size five," or "What a full bag, what a bag . . . today's the day for splendid bags."

It was characteristic of him to devote all his attention to a woman's body and neglect her personality. He also tended to concentrate on individual parts of the body and ignore the way they fit together. These investigations allowed him to keep his hopes alive, refreshing them with possible opportunities he could set aside for today or tomorrow. He seemed a man with no goal in the world that took precedence over women. On rare occasions he succeeded in making a good catch on these sexual excursions.

Late one afternoon he was sitting beneath the small window in al-Sayyid Ali's coffee shop when he saw the lute player leave the house alone. He rose at once to follow her. She turned into al-Tarbi'a Alley, and he turned too. When she stopped at a store, he stood beside her. She had to wait while the proprietor of this perfume shop tended to some other customers. So Yasin waited. She did not turn toward him. From her attempt to pretend he was not there, he inferred she was aware of his presence. She must also have guessed from the outset that he was following her. He whispered into her ear, "Good evening."

She continued to look straight ahead of her, but he noticed her mouth move slightly in a smile of greeting or at least of recognition for all the time he had spent following her, evening after evening. He sighed with relief and victory, confident now that he would pluck this fruit he had patiently pursued. Lust surged inside him, the way a ravenously hungry man's mouth waters when his nose smells meat being broiled for him.

He thought the best thing would be to pretend they had come together. So he paid for her purchases of henna and tonic with the good humor of a man who believes he will acquire an enjoyable and entertaining right by rendering this small service. He did not mind when she seemed inclined to purchase several more things once she was sure he was paying. As they returned, he told her, with the haste of a person who fears the end of the road is in sight, "Beautiful and lovely lady, I have spent my whole life following after you, as you have seen. Can't a lover aspire to be rewarded with at least a meeting?"

She cast him a mischievous glance and asked sarcastically, "At least a meeting?"

He was almost consumed by laughter, body and soul, the way he usually was when intoxicated by joy, but he quickly shut his mouth tight to keep from causing a commotion that would attract attention. He answered her with a whisper, "A rendezvous and everything that goes with it."

She observed critically, "Each of you asks for a rendezvous, as though there were nothing to it, but it's an important matter that does not take place for some people until after a proposal, negotiation, recitation of the opening prayer of the Qur'an, a dowry, a trousseau, and the arrival of a religious official to write the contract. Isn't that so, sir . . . you, the gentleman who's as tall and broad as a camel?"

He blushed in confusion and said, "No matter how harsh your rebuke, coming from your lips it's like honey. Hasn't passion always been like this, beautiful lady, since God created the earth and the people on it?"

She raised her eyebrows until they were level with the top of the cylinder connecting her veil to her scarf and resembled the spreading wings of a bee. "My camel, how would I know about passion?" she asked. "I'm just a musician. Do you suppose passion has things that go with it too?"

Trying not to laugh, he replied, "They're the same things that go along with a rendezvous."

"No more and no less?"

"No more and no less."

"Not one more than another?"

"Not more of one thing than another."

"Perhaps that's what they call illicit sex."

"One and the same thing."

A laugh escaped from her. She said, "You've got a deal . . . wait in the coffee shop of al-Sayyid Ali, where you've spent all these evenings. When I open the window, come to the house."

He waited evening after evening after evening. One evening she went in the cart with the troupe. Another evening she went in a carriage with the chanteuse. Still another evening there was no sign of life in the house. Here he was waiting. His head was worn out from looking up at her window for so long. It was past midnight, the shops were closed, the road was deserted, and al-Ghuriya was enveloped in darkness. He found, as he often did, that the darkness and emptiness of the street acted as a strange stimulus for the desire latent in his body. He became more and more agitated.

Yet everything has an end, even waiting that seems endless. He made out a rattling noise coming from the direction of the window, which was lost in the darkness. This breathed a spirit of new hope into his senses just as the drone of an airplane inspires a person lost at the North Pole with hope that people are arriving to search for him in the snow. Light could be seen coming from the opening of the window. Then the musician's silhouette was visible at the center of the opening.

He got up at once and left the coffee shop to cross the street to the performer's house. He pushed against the door without knocking. It swung open as though it had been left unlatched on purpose. He made his way inside, where it was too dark for him to find the staircase. He stayed put in order not to bump into something or trip. A question that made him a little nervous leapt into his head. Did the performer know that Zanuba had invited him? Did she allow the girl to meet her lovers in this house? But he dismissed the thought disdainfully. No obstacle was going to make him abandon this adventure. In any case, there was no need to worry about the consequences of a lover's being caught in a house that depended for its very existence on lovers.

He cut short these reflections when he saw a pale light coming from upstairs. Then he noticed it slowly advancing down the walls. He could make out that he was an arm's length from the bottom step of the staircase. It was not long before he saw Zanuba approaching with a lamp in her hand. He went to her, drunk with desire. He pressed her forearm affectionately with gratitude and lust. She laughed softly. Despite the softness of her laugh, it showed she was not trying to be cautious. She asked mischievously, "Did you have to wait long?"

He touched the hair at his temples and complained, "My hair turned gray while I waited, may God forgive you." Then he whispered, "Is the lady here?"

She jestingly imitated his whisper: "Yes . . . she's alone with a fantastic man."

"Won't she be angry if she learns I've come at this hour?"

She turned around, shrugging her shoulders in disdain. She started up the stairs saying, "Is there a more appropriate hour for a lover like you to come?"

"So she won't see anything wrong with our meeting in her house?"

With a dancing motion of her head, she replied, "Perhaps she would think it very wrong if we didn't meet."

"Long live the lady!"

She resumed speaking, proudly this time, "I'm not just her lute player. I'm her sister's daughter. She's not stingy with me. . . . You can enter in peace."

When they reached the foyer upstairs they could hear some delightful singing accompanied by lute and tambourine. Yasin listened a little and then asked, "Are they alone or is it a party?"

She whispered in his ear, "Alone and a party both. The sultana's lover is a good-humored man who loves music. He wouldn't bear for even an hour of his soiree to pass without lute, tambourine, wine, laughter . . . and you know what else."

She turned to open a door and entered, setting the lamp on a table bracketed to the wall. She stood in front of the mirror to examine her reflection carefully. Yasin forgot about Zubayda and her musical lover. He riveted his greedy eyes on Zanuba's desirable body, which he was seeing for the first time stripped of the wrap. He fixed his eyes on her with force and concentration and moved them deliberately and delightedly from top to bottom and from bottom to top. Before he could act on any of the tens of wishes racing through his breast, Zanuba remarked, as though continuing the same conversation, "He's a man with no equal in his graciousness or sensitivity to music. As for his generosity, we could talk about that from today till tomorrow . . . that's what lovers should be like . . . otherwise . . ."

He did not miss the implications of her reference to the generosity of the performer's lover. He had accepted from the start that his new romance would cost him dearly, but her reference to it seemed in poor taste and offended him. Motivated by an instinct of self-defense, he found himself forced to say, "Perhaps he's a rich man."

Responding to his maneuver, she said, "Wealth is one thing, generosity is another. Many a wealthy man is stingy."

He inquired, not because he wanted to know but merely to avoid silence, which he was afraid would seem to express disapproval, "Who do you suppose this generous man is?"

Turning the knob to raise the wick on the lamp, she answered, "He's from our district. You must have heard of him . . . al-Sayyid Ahmad Abd al-Jawad."

"Who!"

She turned toward him in astonishment to see what had frightened him. She found him in a rigid pose with his eyes bulging out.

She asked him disapprovingly, "What's the matter with you?"

The name she had spoken had come upon him like a hammer falling violently on top of his head. The question had escaped from him unintentionally in a scream of alarm. For some moments he was bewildered and oblivious to his surroundings. When he saw Zanuba's face again and its expression of astonishment and disapproval, he was afraid he would give himself away. He exerted his willpower to defend himself. To conceal his alarm, he resorted to some playacting. He clapped his hands together, as though he could not believe what had been said about the man, because he thought he was so respectable. He muttered incredulously, "Al-Sayyid Ahmad Abd al-Jawad! . . . With a store in al-Nahhasin?"

She gave him a bitterly critical look for alarming her for no reason. She asked him scornfully, "Yes, him. . . . So what made you cry out for help like a virgin being deflowered?"

He laughed in a perfunctory way. Praising God secretly that he had not told her his full name the day they met, he replied with mock astonishment, "Who would believe this of such a pious, respectable man?"

She looked at him with skepticism before asking him sarcastically, "Is this what really alarmed you? . . . Nothing but that? Did you think he was a sinless saint? . . . What's wrong with his doing this? Can a man attain perfection without having an affair?"

He said apologetically, "You're right . . . there's nothing in this world worth being astonished at." He laughed nervously and continued: "Imagine this dignified gentleman flirting with the sultana, drinking wine, and swaying to the music. . . ."

In her same sarcastic tone she said, as though to continue his statement, "And playing the tambourine better than a professional like Ayusha and telling one gem of a joke after another until everyone with him is dying of laughter. It's not surprising, given all of this, that in his store he's seen to be a fine example of sobriety and earnestness. You should be serious about serious things and playful when you play. There's an hour for your Lord and an hour for your heart."

He plays the tambourine better than a professional like Ayusha. . . . He tells jokes that make his companions die from laughter. . . . Who could this man be? His father? . . . Al-Sayyid Ahmad Abd al-Jawad? That stern, tyrannical, terrifying, God-fearing, reserved man who kills everyone around him with fright?

How could he believe what his ears had heard? How, how?... There must be some confusion between two men with similar names. There could be no relationship between his father and this tambourine-playing lover. But Zanuba had agreed he owned a store in al-Nahhasin. There was only one store in al-Nahhasin that bore this name and it was his father's. Lord, was what he had heard true or was he raving? He wanted dearly to learn the truth for himself, to see it with his own eyes. That desire gained control of him. This investigation appeared to him the most important thing in life. He was unable to combat the desire. He smiled to the girl and shook his head sagely as though to say, "What days we live in. Each more amazing than the last." Then he asked her, as if motivated by nothing but curiosity, "Isn't there some way I could see him without being seen?"

She objected, "You're strange! What need is there to spy?"

He entreated her: "It's a sight worth seeing. Don't deprive me of it."

She laughed contemptuously and commented, "You've got the brains of a child in the body of a camel. Isn't that so, my camel? But death to anyone who disappoints one of your requests.... Hide in the foyer while I take them a dish of fruit. I'll leave the door open till I come back."

She left the room and he trailed after her with a pounding heart. He hid in a dark corner of the hall while the lute player continued on her way to the kitchen. She soon returned with a dish of grapes. She went to the door from which the singing came and knocked. She waited a moment and then went in, leaving the door open. There he saw a divan at the end of the room. Zubayda sat in the middle of it cradling a lute. She accompanied herself as she sang, "O Muslims, O People of God."

Sitting next to her was his father, not someone else. When he saw him, his heart pounded harder. His father had removed his cloak and rolled up his sleeves. He was shaking the tambourine and gazing at the performer with a face brimming with joy and happiness. The door was open only so long as Zanuba was in the room, one or two minutes, but during that time he witnessed an amazing sight: a secret life, a long story with many ramifications. He awoke like a person emerging from a long, deep sleep to the convulsions of a violent earthquake. In those two minutes he saw a whole life summed up by one image, like a brief scene in a dream that brings together diverse events that would take years in the real world. He saw his father the way he truly was – his father, not some other man, but not as he was accustomed to seeing him. Never before had he seen him without his cloak, at a relaxed, spontaneous party. He had never seen him with his black hair sticking up as though he had been running around bareheaded. He had never seen his naked leg as it appeared at the edge of the divan, sticking out from his gown, which had been pulled up. He had never seen, by God, the tambourine in his hands as he shook it with a dancing rhythm gracefully interspersed with taps on the skin. Perhaps most amazing of all, he had never before seen his face smile. It was glistening with such affection and goodwill that Yasin was stunned, just as Kamal had been when he saw their father laughing in front of his store, the day he went to see him driven by his desire to get his mother released.

Yasin saw all of this in two minutes. Once Zanuba had closed the door and gone to her room he remained where he was, listening to the singing and the jingling of the tambourine with a spinning head. It was the same sound he had heard when he entered the building, but how differently it affected his soul, what new images and ideas it brought to his mind now. . . . When a child who has not started school yet hears a school bell ring, he smiles, but once he is a pupil it sounds like a warning of the many hardships ahead.

Zanuba rapped on the door of her room to summon him. He awoke from his daze and went to her. He was trying to gain control of himself so he would not appear disturbed or stunned when she saw him. He entered with a broad smile on his face.

"Did you see something to make you forget yourself?"

He replied in a contented and relieved tone, "It was a rare sight, and the singing was excellent."

"Would you like us to do what they're doing?"

"On our first night? . . . Certainly not. . . . I wouldn't want to mix anything else with you, not even singing."

At first he had been forcing himself to talk so he would appear to her, and to himself, to be calm and natural. He got caught up in what he was saying and no longer needed to pretend. He found he had returned to normal faster than he would have imagined. Similarly, a person who pretends to cry at a funeral may end up weeping profusely. Even so, Yasin was suddenly struck with astonishment and told himself, "What an amazing situation! It would never have occurred to me. Here I am with Zanuba and my father's in a nearby room with Zubayda. Both of us in the same house!" He soon shrugged his shoulders and continued to himself: "But why should I bother to be amazed at something that seems incredible when it's an actuality I've observed myself? There it is, so it's silly to wonder with astonishment whether I can believe it. I'll believe it and stop marveling at it. What's wrong with that?"

He felt not only relief but happiness beyond measure. He needed no encouragement to continue his sex life, but like most men indulging in forbidden pleasure, he was interested in the company of a like-minded person. How incredible to have found this person in his father, the traditional role model, who had terrified him for so long, whether consciously or not, because he assumed they held contradictory views. He set aside everything but his joy, which seemed the most precious thing he had achieved in life. He felt new love and admiration for his father, unlike the old types he had previously known, which had a thick coating of awe and fear. This new emotion sprang from the depths of his soul and was intertwined with the roots of his being. It seemed identical to his love and admiration for himself. His father was no longer a man who was distant, hard to reach, a closed door. He was near at hand, a bit of his own soul and heart. Father and son were a single spirit. The man in there shaking the tambourine was not al-Sayyid Ahmad Abd al-Jawad but Yasin himself, the way he would be in the future and the way he should be. Nothing separated them except secondary considerations of age and experience.

"Good health to you, Father," he thought to himself. "Today I've discovered you. Today's your birthday in my soul. What a day and what a father you are. . . . Until tonight I've been an orphan. Drink and play the tambourine even better than Ayusha. I'm proud of you. Do you sing too, I wonder?"

"Doesn't al-Sayyid Ahmad Abd al-Jawad sing sometimes?"

"Are you still thinking about him? Why can't people leave each other alone? . . . Yes, he sings, my camel. . . . When he's drunk, he joins in singing the choruses."

"How's his voice?"

"As full and beautiful as his neck."

"All the singing voices in our family go back to this source," he mused. "Everyone sings. It's a family with deep roots in music.

I wish I could hear you, even just once. The only memory I have of your voice is of yelling and scolding. The only refrain of yours we all know is 'Boy! Ox! Son of a bitch!' I'd like to hear you sing 'Affection's rare with good-looking people' or 'I'm in love, my beauty.' What are you like when you're drunk, Father? What are you like when you get rowdy? I must know so I can follow your example and live according to your traditions. How are you when you're in love? How do you embrace?"

He remembered Zanuba. He saw her in front of the mirror smoothing her hair with her fingers. The armhole of her dress revealed smooth, clear skin sloping down to a breast like a round loaf of unbaked bread. Intoxicating desire swept through his body, and he fell on her like a bull elephant crushing a gazelle.

40

THREE AUTOMOBILES proffered by friends of al-Sayyid Ahmad stopped in front of his house to wait for the bride and her party, whom they were to convey to the Shawkat residence in Sugar Street, or al-Sukkariya. It was late in the afternoon. The rays of the summer sun had withdrawn from the street and were resting on the houses opposite the bride's home. There was no hint of a wedding there, except for the roses decorating the lead vehicle. These caught the eyes of the nearby shop owners and of many of the passersby.

The engagement had been arranged previously. The presents had arrived. The trousseau had been sent. The marriage contract had been signed. At no time during all of this had there been any ululations of joy from the house, any decorations on the door, or any other of the customary signs of a wedding to reveal what was going on inside. Families were usually proud to make a display on such occasions, using weddings as an excuse to express their concealed longing for delight with song, dance, and shrieks of joy.

Everything had been concluded in calm silence. No one knew about the marriage except for relatives and friends and a select group of neighbors. Al-Sayyid Ahmad had refused to budge from his sense of decorum or to allow any member of his family to escape from it even for an hour. Consequently, accompanied by the women of her family, the bride left the house in silence despite the protestations of Umm Hanafi. Aisha dashed for the automobile at breakneck speed, as though she feared that the eyes of the onlookers might scorch her wedding gown or her white silk tiara and veil, which were decorated with different varieties of jasmine. Khadija and Maryam followed her, together with some other girls. The mother and women relatives and neighbors found their places in the other automobiles. Meanwhile Kamal took his seat beside the driver of the bride's car.

The mother wanted the procession to pass by al-Husayn so she could have a fresh look at his shrine, which her desire to see had cost her so dearly once before. She wished to ask al-Husayn's blessing on her beautiful bride. The automobiles went along the streets she had taken that day with Kamal. Afterward they turned into al-Ghuriya at the corner where she had almost met her death. Finally they dropped their passengers at Mutawalli Gate in front of the entrance to Sugar Street, which was too narrow for cars to enter. They all dismounted and entered the alley, where wedding decorations could be seen. The boys of the district rushed toward them while screams and trills resounded from the Shawkat residence, the first house on the right as they entered the alley. The windows of the house were crowded with the heads of people peering down and trilling with joy. The bridegroom, Khalil Shawkat, stood at the entrance with his brother Ibrahim Shawkat as well as Yasin and Fahmy. Khalil smilingly approached the bride and offered her his arm. She did not know what to do and would not have moved if Maryam had not taken her arm and put it around his. Then he escorted her inside. They passed by the crowded courtyard as roses and sweets were showered at the bride's feet and those of the bridal party until the women disappeared behind the door of the women's quarters.

Although the marriage contract for Aisha and Khalil had been signed a month or more earlier, the sight of their arms being intertwined and of them walking side by side affected Yasin and Fahmy, and especially the latter, with an astonishment mixed with embarrassment and a feeling almost of disapproval. The family code did not seem to make any exception for wedding ceremonies conducted in full accord with Islamic law. This reaction was even more pronounced in Kamal, who pulled on his mother's hand in alarm and pointed to the bridal couple preceding everyone else up the stairs. He seemed to be appealing to her to prevent an outrageous evil.

The two young men wanted to steal a look at their father's face to see what effect that rare sight had on him. They quickly looked all around but found no trace of him. He was not at the entrance or in the adjacent courtyard, where benches and chairs were arranged in rows with a platform up in front for the singers. The fact was that al-Sayyid Ahmad had shut himself up with some of his best friends in a reception room opening on the courtyard and had not left it since he had set foot in the house. He was determined to stay there until the evening was concluded. He wanted to keep some distance between himself and the "masses" clamoring around outside. Nothing made him so uncomfortable as to be with his family at a wedding party. He did not want to impose his supervision on them at a time set aside for delight and did not care to observe at close hand their relaxed response to a festive occasion. What he hated most of all was for any of them to see him lapse from the stern dignity to which they were accustomed. If the matter had been left to him, the wedding would have been carried out in complete silence. The widow of the late Mr. Shawkat had met his suggestion with totally inflexible opposition. She had refused for the bride to be welcomed to her home with anything less than a gala evening party. For the entertainment she had hired the female vocalist Jalila and the male vocalist Sabir.

Kamal was so ecstatic with the freedom and enjoyment he was allowed that he could have been the bridegroom. He was one of the few individuals permitted to move freely back and forth between the women's section inside and the men's area in the courtyard by the stage. He stayed for a long time with his mother, gazing at the women's ornaments and jewelry and listening to their jokes and conversations, which were dominated by the topic of marriage. He also heard the performer Jalila there. She sat at the front of the hall, resembling in both her huge size and her ornamentation the ceremonial camel litter sent with the pilgrims to Mecca. She proceeded to sing some popular songs, while openly drinking wine.

The jovial atmosphere was strange and attractive to Kamal, and he felt very comfortable. The most important thing of all to him was Aisha, who was dressed up more magnificently than he had ever dreamed possible. His mother encouraged him to stay with her so she could keep an eye on him. After a time she changed her mind and was forced, for reasons she had not anticipated, to urge him in a whisper to go find his brothers. One reason was his intense interest in Aisha, now with her dress and the next time with her ornaments. Amina was afraid he would spoil her outfit. Then, too, he let some childishly frank observations slip out concerning some of the ladies present. For example, one time he pointed to a woman from the bridegroom's family and called out to his mother, "Look at the nose of that lady, Mother. Isn't it bigger than Khadija's?"

When Jalila was singing he had surprised everyone by joining with the troupe in the chorus: "Beautiful dove . . . where can I find her?" The performer had invited him to sit with the members of her ensemble. In this way and in others he had attracted a lot of attention, and the women had begun teasing him. His mother was not comfortable with the commotion he was causing. Apprehensive that he might upset some people and worried that he might be admired more than was safe for him, she reluctantly chose to have him leave the room to join the men's party.

He wandered among the rows of chairs and then stood between Fahmy and Yasin until Sabir had finished singing "You beauty, why are you already in love?" Then Kamal started roving around again. When he passed by the reception room, his curiosity prompted him to have a look inside. He poked his head in and before he knew it his eyes met his father's. Kamal felt nailed to the spot and unable to turn his eyes away. One of his father's friends, al-Sayyid Muhammad Iffat, saw him and called him. To avoid angering his father, he found himself forced to obey this summons. He approached the man fearfully and reluctantly and stood before him, straight as a ramrod with his arms at his sides, as though a soldier at attention. The man shook his hand and said, "God's will be done . . . what year in school are you, Uncle?"

"Third year, fourth section. . . ."

"Splendid . . . splendid. . . . Did you hear Sabir sing?"

Although the boy was answering Muhammad Iffat, he had been careful from the beginning to answer in a way that would please his father. He did not know how to reply to the last question or at least he hesitated. The man took pity on him and quickly asked, "Don't you like singing?"

The boy said emphatically, "Certainly not."

It was clear that some of the men present planned to make a joke about this response, the last they would have expected from a person related to Ahmad Abd al-Jawad, but their host cautioned them against it with his eyes, and they kept quiet.

Then Mr. Muhammad Iffat asked Kamal, "Isn't there something you like to listen to?"

Looking at his father, Kamal said, "The Holy Qur'an."

Expressions of approval were heard and the boy was allowed to depart. Thus he did not get to hear what was said about him behind his back. Al-Sayyid al-Far laughed out loud and commented, "If that's true, the boy's a bastard."

Al-Sayyid Ahmad Abd al-Jawad laughed and, pointing to where Kamal had been standing, said, "Have you seen anyone craftier than that son of a bitch, pretending to be pious in front of me? . . . One time when I got home, I heard him singing 'O bird, you up in the tree.'"

Al-Sayyid Ali observed, "Oh, you should have seen him standing between his two brothers and listening to Sabir with his lips moving as he sang along, keeping time perfectly, even better than Ahmad Abd al-Jawad himself."

Then Muhammad Iffat addressed an inquiry to al-Sayyid Ahmad: "The important thing is to tell us whether you liked his voice when he sang 'O bird, you up in the tree.'"

Al-Sayyid Ahmad laughed. Pointing at himself, he said, "He's this lion's cub."

Al-Far cried out, "God have mercy on the lioness who gave birth to you."

Kamal escaped from the reception room to the alley. He seemed to be awakening from a nightmare. He stood amid the crowd of boys on the street. He soon recovered his spirits and walked along, proud of his new clothes, delighted with his freedom that allowed him to go anywhere he wanted, except for the frightening reception room. There was no one to restrict or supervise him. What a historic night for him! Only one thing troubled his serenity whenever he thought of it. That was Aisha's moving to this house, which they had begun referring to as her home. This move had been accomplished in spite of him, without anyone being able to convince him that it was right or beneficial. He had asked repeatedly how his father could allow it, since he would not allow even the shadow of one of his women to be seen through the crack of a window. The only answer he received was loud laughter. He had asked his mother critically how she could do something so extreme as giving Aisha away. She had told him he would grow up one day and take a girl like her from her father's house, and that she would be escorted to his house with cries of joy.

Kamal had asked Aisha if she was really happy about leaving them. She had said no, but the trousseau had been carried to the stranger's house. Aisha, whose place on the cup was Kamal's favorite, had followed her trousseau. Although it was true that the present festivities were helping him forget things he had thought he would be unable to forget even for a moment, sorrow veiled his cheerful heart like a small cloud passing in front of the moon on a clear night.

It was interesting that his pleasure in the singing that night surpassed his other pleasures, like playing with the boys, observing the women and the men having a good time, or even eating the "palace" bread pudding and the fancy gelatin dessert at supper. All the men and women who noticed him were astonished at the serious interest he took in listening to Jalila and Sabir. It seemed unusual for a child his age, but no one in his family who knew his background in music as Aisha's student was surprised. He had a fine voice, which was considered second in the family only to Aisha's, although their father's voice, which they had only heard screaming, was the best of all. Kamal listened for a long time to both Jalila and Sabir. He found to his surprise that he preferred the singing of the male vocalist and the music of his troupe. They made a greater impact on his heart. Some lines from their songs stuck in his memory, like "Why are you in love? . . . Because that's the way it is." After the night of the wedding, he frequently repeated these lines in the hyacinth bean and jasmine bower on the roof of their home.

Amina and Khadija also enjoyed some of the same delights and freedom as Kamal. Like him, neither of them had ever witnessed an evening so filled with fellowship, music, and merriment. Amina was especially delighted by the attention and flattery she received as mother of the bride, since she had never before been afforded either. Even Khadija's grief disappeared in the festive lights just as the gloom of night gives way to morning's radiance. She forgot her sorrows under the influence of soft laughter, sweet tunes, and pleasant conversation. It was all the easier for her to forget, because she had a new sorrow, an innocent one that arose from her feeling of regret over Aisha's imminent departure. This feeling engendered sincere love and affection. Her former sorrows were obscured by this new one, just as feelings of animosity may be obliterated by generosity. Similarly, a person who both loves and hates someone may find that the sorrow of parting obscures the hatred, leaving only the love. Moreover, Khadija felt a new confidence in herself from appearing with makeup and fine clothes that attracted the attention of some of the women, who praised her enthusiastically. Their praise filled her with hope and dreams and provided her some happy moments.

Yasin and Fahmy sat side by side, alternately chatting and listening to the music. Khalil Shawkat, the bridegroom, joined them from time to time, whenever he had a break from the duties of his enjoyable but taxing evening. In spite of the atmosphere of celebration and delight, Yasin was rather anxious. There was a lingering, vacant look in his eyes. He would ask himself occasionally whether it would be all right for him to quench his thirst, if only with a glass or two of wine. For that reason, he leaned toward their friend Khalil Shawkat and whispered, "Rescue me before the whole evening is lost."

The young man reassured him with a wink of his eye and said, "I've set aside a table in a private room for friends like you."

Yasin was cheered by that, and his interest in conversation, jokes, and music revived. He did not intend to get drunk, for in a place like this, overflowing with family and acquaintances, even a little wine had to be considered a great victory. Although his father was secluded in the reception room, he was not far away. Yasin's penetration of his father's secrets did not shake the man's traditional authority over him. Al-Sayyid Ahmad continued to occupy his heavily fortified stronghold of awe and reverence, and Yasin had not stirred from his own position of obedience and veneration. He had not even thought of revealing his father's secret, which he had discovered surreptitiously, to anyone, not even to Fahmy. For all these reasons, Yasin was at first satisfied with a glass or two with which to cajole his unruly appetite. It would help prepare him to enjoy the merriment, conversations, music, and other pleasures that lost their savor for him without wine.

Unlike Yasin, Fahmy did not find and doubted he ever would find anything to quench his thirst. His grief had been aroused unexpectedly by the arrival of the bride. He had gone with the bridegroom and Yasin to welcome her with a carefree heart. Then he had seen Maryam walking directly behind the bride. Her mouth was resplendent with a smile of greeting for everyone. Distracted by the trills of joy and the roses, she did not notice him. Her silk veil was so sheer that the clear complexion of her face was visible. He had followed her with his eyes, his heart pounding, until she disappeared behind the door to the women's quarters. He returned to his seat as shaken as a skiff suddenly caught in a violent storm. Before he saw her, he had been calm, apparently distracted enough by conversation to have forgotten everything. In fact, long periods would pass when he was in this oblivious, forgetful state, while his heart became a reservoir for his suffering. The moment a thought occurred to him, a memory stirred, someone mentioned her name, or anything similar happened, his heart would throb with pain and exude one grief after another. It was like a decayed tooth with an inflamed gum. For a time the toothache may die down until the tooth presses against a morsel of food or touches a solid object. Then the pain erupts. Thus Fahmy's love would beat against his ribs from the inside as though craving a breath of air, shouting at the top of its lungs that it was still a prisoner. No amount of consolation or forgetfulness had set it free.

He often hoped she would remain invisible to other suitors until he could get established as a free man, acting and deciding his own fate. As days, weeks, and months passed without a suitor asking for her hand, it seemed his wish had been granted, but he did not enjoy any real peace of mind. He was prey to anxiety and fear, which took turns, time and again, ruffling his serenity, spoiling his dreams, and conjuring up for him many different types of pain and jealousy, which although imaginary were no less ferocious and cruel than if his fears had been realized. Even this desire itself and the delay in the occurrence of the misfortune became incentives for more anxiety and fear and consequently for pain and jealousy. Whenever his torment was severe, he wished the calamity would take place so he could receive his share of grief all in one blow. Perhaps afterward, through his despair, he could attain the tranquillity and repose he had not been able to achieve through his pipe dreams.

He could not yield to his emotions at a musical soiree where he was surrounded by the looks of friends and relatives. Yet the impact the sight of Maryam had made on him as she walked behind his sister could not pass without provoking some noticeable reaction. Since Fahmy was not able to brood about his sorrows or reveal his hidden emotions, he softened their impact by going to the other extreme. He talked, laughed, and pretended to be blissfully happy, but whenever he had even a moment to himself, he felt deep inside the alienation of his heart from everything around him. With the passing of time he realized that the sight of Maryam walking in the bridal court had aroused his love the way a sudden racket decisively arouses an anxious person with a tendency toward insomnia. For that evening at least, Fahmy would be unable to enjoy any peace of mind. Nothing happening around him would be able to remove from his mind her image or the smile with which she responded to the warm welcome composed of trills of joy and roses. It was a pure, sweet smile, suggestive of a carefree heart aspiring to calm and happiness. It was a smile that seemed too pretty ever to be replaced by a grimace of pain. The sight of her ripped into his heart, disclosing to him that only he was suffering. He alone bore his troubles. But had he not been laughing boisterously just now and moving his head to the music as though he was happy and glad? Was it not possible that someone looking at him might be deceived and think the same thing of him that he did of her? He derived some consolation from that thought but was no more convinced than a typhoid patient who asks himself, "Isn't it likely that I'll recover the way so-and-so did?"

Fahmy remembered her message Kamal had brought him some months before: "Tell him that she won't know what to do if a suitor asks to marry her during this long period of waiting." He asked himself, as he had tens of times before, whether any emotion lay behind those words? Indeed, no man, no matter how obstinate, could blame her for a single one of them. Nor could he overlook the good sense and wisdom they contained. Yet, for this very reason, he felt powerless against them and hated them. Good sense and wisdom are seldom happy with the impetuousness of emotion, which characteristically knows no limits.

Fahmy returned to the present, to the musical evening, and his raging love. It was not merely the sight of her that had rocked him so violently. Perhaps seeing her for the first time in a new place had done it. She had been here in the courtyard of the Shawkat residence, far removed from his house. He had never seen her in any other area before. For her to remain put in the old location established her in the mechanical daily routine, whereas her sudden appearance in a new place re-created her before his eyes and gave her a new existence in his consciousness, which in turn reawakened her original, latent presence in his mind. Both old and new visions of her had joined together to create this violent jolt. Moreover, her former existence linked to his house was separated from him by a wall of despair created by the stern rules of his family. Here, far removed from that house, her new existence was attended by a feeling of freedom and liberation as well as a spirit of parade and vivacity unknown to him. Her new existence was in the context of a wedding and thoughts of love and union. All of these circumstances helped to free her from her confinement atop a pedestal. Now his heart could see her as a possible goal. She seemed to be telling him, "Look where I am now. Just one more step and you'll find me in your arms." This hope soon collided with the thorny reality, helping create his violent jolt. Perhaps the sight of her in this new location also worked to establish her even more firmly in his soul, embed her in his life, and fix her in his memories. Images penetrate more deeply into us when they are associated with the different places we know from our experiences. Previously Maryam was associated with the roof of his house, the arbor of hyacinth beans and jasmine, Kamal, listening to his English lesson, the coffee hour, and talking to his mother in the study, and the message Kamal brought back from her. Henceforth she would be associated with Sugar Street, the courtyard of the Shawkat residence, the evening's musical entertainment, the singing of Sabir, Aisha's wedding procession, and everything else that was crowding in through his senses. Such a transformation could not occur without adding to the violent shock that had stunned him.

During one of Sabir's intermissions, the voice of the female vocalist happened to carry through the windows overlooking the courtyard so the men could hear her. She was singing "My lover's departed." Fahmy set about listening eagerly and with enormous interest. He concentrated all of his attention on absorbing the music, not because he particularly liked Jalila's voice, but because he thought Maryam would be listening to her at that moment. The lyrics would be speaking to both of them at the same time. Jalila united the two of them in a single experience of listening and possibly of feeling. She had created an occasion for their spirits to meet. All of these considerations made him revere her voice and love her song. He wished to share this one sensation with Maryam. He tried for a long time to get through to her soul by retreating deep into himself. He sought to contact the vibrations of her reactions by following his own. Notwithstanding the distance and the thick walls separating them, he wished to live for a few moments inside her essence. To accomplish this, he attempted to determine from the lyrics the effect they would have on his beloved's soul. What would her response be to "My lover's departed" or "It's a long time since he sent me a letter"? Had she been lost in a sea of memories? Had not at least one of those waves slipped away to reveal his face? Had not her heart felt a stabbing pain or a piercing grief? Or was she in such a daze throughout that she saw nothing in the song but enjoyable music?

Fahmy imagined her listening attentively to the music, free of her veil, parading her vitality, or her mouth parted in a smile like the one he had glimpsed when she arrived, which had upset him since he had inferred from it that she had forgotten him. She might be talking to one of his sisters as she frequently enjoyed doing. He envied his sisters that privilege, which would daze him to the point of panic, whereas they regarded it as an ordinary conversation like any they conducted with girls in the neighborhood. Indeed, he had frequently been amazed by his sisters' attitude toward her, not because they took an interest in her, for they did love her, but because they loved her exactly the same way they did the other girls in the neighborhood, as though she was just some girl. How could they greet her without getting flustered and do it in an ordinary manner, the way he greeted any passing girl or his fellow law students? How could they talk about her and say, "Maryam said this" or "Maryam did that" and pronounce the name like any other one, Umm Hanafi, for example? Hers was a name he had only pronounced once or twice in someone else's presence. Then he had been amazed by its impact on him. When he was alone, he would only repeat her name as though it were one of the venerable names of Muslim saints engraved in his imagination along with the ornamentation provided by legends. These were names he would not pronounce without immediately adding one of the appropriate religious formulas: "May God be pleased with him" or "Peace on him." How could he explain that not merely the name but even Maryam herself lacked any magic or sanctity for his sisters?

When Jalila finished singing, there were shouts of appreciation and applause. Fahmy concentrated on that with even greater interest than he had given the song, since Maryam's voice and hands were participating. He wished it was possible for him to make out her voice among all the others and to isolate her clapping from all the rest, but that was no easier than distinguishing the sound of one wave from the roar of all those beating against the shore. So he responded lovingly to the cries of applause and the clapping without distinction, as a mother prays for blessings and peace collectively when she hears the voices of pupils from a school her son attends.

Although their reasons differed, no one so resembled Fahmy in his inner isolation as his father, who did not leave the chamber where he was surrounded by some of his very best friends. Some companions had not been able to endure the sober atmosphere in there when music was resounding outside. They had broken away from his circle to scatter among the listeners where they could enjoy the music and have a good time. The only people left with al-Sayyid Ahmad were those who loved his company even more than having a good time. They all observed an unaccustomed solemnity as though performing a duty or attending a funeral. These old friends had understood in advance it would be like this when he had invited them to the wedding. They knew from experience that there were two sides to his character. One was reserved for his friends and the other was for his family. There was a paradoxical contradiction between this somber behavior with which they were celebrating a wedding and their boisterous nightly reunions when they had nothing to celebrate. They did not hesitate to joke about their dignified conduct, but in a calm and delicate manner. When Mr. Iffat's voice was raised in laughter once, Mr. al-Far put his finger to his lips as though warning him to lower his voice. He whispered in his ear to caution and scold him: "We're at a wedding, man."

Another time, when they had been silent for a while, Mr. Ali looked around at their faces and, raising his hand to his head, congratulated them: "May God thank you for your effort."

At that, al-Sayyid Ahmad asked them to join their other friends outside and have fun, but Mr. Iffat told him in a critical tone of voice, "Should we leave you alone on a night like this? Do you know who your friends are until you're in need?"

Al-Sayyid Ahmad could not keep from laughing. He commented, "It will only take a few more wedding nights before God forgives all of us."

A wedding had other ramifications beyond mandatory solemnity at a party devoted to merrymaking and music. There were implications for him in particular as a father with an unusual temperament. He had ambivalent feelings about his daughter's marriage. He was not comfortable about it, even though reason and religion did not support his position. It was not that he did not wish for his two daughters to marry. Like all other fathers, he wished to protect his daughters, but would have preferred that marriage was not the only way to provide this protection. He may even have wished that God had created girls in a manner that made marriage unnecessary or that he had never had any daughters. Since his wishes had not been and could not be fulfilled, he was forced to hope his daughters would marry, like a man who longs for an honorable or painless death, since he knows life cannot last forever.

Al-Sayyid Ahmad had often expressed his reluctance in many different ways, both conscious and unconscious. He would tell some of his loyal friends, "You ask me about fathering females? It's an evil against which we are defenseless, but let us thank God. In any case, it's a duty. This is not to say that I don't love my daughters. In fact, I love them as much as I do Yasin, Fahmy, and Kamal, each equally. But how can my mind be at rest when I know that I will carry them to a stranger one day? However attractive he may seem on the outside, only God knows what's inside him. What can a weak girl do when she's faced by a strange man far from the supervision of her father? What will her fate be if her husband divorces her one day, after her father has died? She must take refuge in her brother's house to endure a life of neglect. I'm not afraid for any of my sons. No matter what happens to one of them, he's a man and is able to confront life. But a girl . . . my God, preserve us."

He might say with apparent candor, "A girl is really a problem. . . . Don't you see that we spare no effort to discipline, train, preserve, and care for her? But don't you also see that after all of this we ourselves hand her over to a stranger and let him do as he wishes with her? Praise to God who alone is praised for adversity."

Al-Sayyid Ahmad's anxious and ambivalent feelings found expression in the critical attitude he adopted toward Khalil Shaw-kat, the bridegroom. It was a harsh, faultfinding attitude that kept searching to discover some defect to satisfy its obstinacy. Khalil seemed not to count as a member of the Shawkat family, which had been bound to his own family by ties of affection and friendship for more than a generation. He seemed not to be the young man whose manliness, good looks, and honor were attested to by everyone who knew him. Al-Sayyid Ahmad was not able to deny the boy's good qualities but hesitated for a long time over his full face and the calm, heavy look of his eyes that seemed indicative of laziness. He was pleased to infer from these signs that he was sluggish. The gentleman told himself, "He's nothing but a bull, living only to eat and sleep." His recognition of the young man's good qualities followed by his search for any defect was an emotional dialectic reflecting al-Sayyid Ahmad's latent emotions. He both desired the girl to get married and detested the idea of marriage. His acknowledgement of Khalil's qualities had made it possible for the marriage to take place. His search for Khalil's defects helped relieve his hostilities toward the marriage. He was like an opium addict, enslaved by its pleasures and terrified by its danger, searching for it by any means, while cursing it. For the moment, al-Sayyid Ahmad ignored his ambivalent feelings. He was surrounded by his best friends and consoled himself alternately with conversing and listening to the distant music. He allowed contentment and joy a place in his heart and prayed that his daughter would be happy and lead a tranquil life. Even his critical attitude toward Khalil Shawkat was reduced to a scornful feeling free of any rancor.

When the guests were invited to the dinner tables, Fahmy and Yasin were separated for the first time. Khalil Shawkat conducted the latter to a special table where wine was in ample supply. Conscious of the possible consequences, Yasin was cautious at first. He announced that two glasses were enough for him. He resisted with courage (or was it cowardice?) the freely flowing wine, until he reached the first stage of intoxication. Then his memories of the pleasures of drunkenness were stirred, and his willpower weakened. He wanted to get more intoxicated without exceeding the limits of safety. He had a third glass and fled from the table, although he took the precaution of hiding a half-filled bottle in a secret place so he could retrieve it if there was a pressing need. He kept one eye on paradise, while the other was peering down at hell. The young men returned to their seats with vibrant new spirits that imparted to the atmosphere a delight freed from restrictions.

In the women's quarters, intoxication had gained firm control over the performer Jalila. She started looking around at the faces of the women in the audience, asking, "Which of you is the wife of al-Sayyid Ahmad Abd al-Jawad?"

Her question attracted their attention and aroused everyone's interest. Amina was too shy to utter a word. She began to stare at the entertainer's face with anxiety and disapproval. When the performer repeated the question, Widow Shawkat pointed to Amina and volunteered, "There she is. Why do you ask?"

The performer examined her with piercing eyes. Then she let out a resounding laugh and said with satisfaction, "A beauty, by the truth of God's house. Al-Sayyid Ahmad's taste is unbeatable."

Amina was so embarrassed she was like a tongue-tied virgin. Embarrassment was not her only emotion. She asked herself with anxiety and alarm what the implications were of the entertainer's question about al-Sayyid Ahmad Abd al-Jawad's wife and of her praise for his taste. She had spoken in a tone that only a person who knew him well would adopt. Aisha and Khadija felt the same way. Khadija glanced back and forth from some of her friends to the performer, as though asking them what they thought of this tipsy woman. Jalila paid no attention to the panic her words had provoked. She turned her eyes to the bride and examined her as she had the mother previously. Then she wriggled her eyebrows and declared admiringly, "As beautiful as the moon, by the Messenger of God! You're really your father's daughter. Anyone seeing those eyes would immediately remember his." She laughed boisterously before continuing: "I see you are all wondering how this woman knows al-Sayyid Ahmad. . . . I knew him before his wife herself did. He was a neighbor and childhood playmate. Our fathers were friends. Do you think a performer doesn't have a father? My father was head of a Qur'anic primary school and a blessed man. What do you think about that, you beauty?"

She directed this question to Amina, whose fear, natural indulgence, and good humor prompted her to answer, as she struggled with her embarrassed confusion, "May God have mercy on him. We're all children of Eve and Adam."

Narrowing her eyes, Jalila began to rock her head left and right. Her memories and expressions of piety seemed to have made a great impact on her, or perhaps her drunken head enjoyed this routine. She began speaking again: "He was a man with a jealous sense of honor. But I grew up with a natural tendency to be playful, as though I had been suckled on coquetry in the cradle. When I laughed on the top floor of our house, the hearts of men in the street would be troubled. The moment he heard my voice, he would rain blows upon me and call me the worst names. But what point was there in trying to discipline a girl who was so gifted in the arts of love, music, and flirtation? His attempts were in vain. My father went to paradise and its delights while I was fated to adopt the epithets he hurled at me as my banner in life. That's the way the world is. . . . May our Lord nourish you with the good things in life and spare you the evil. . . . May God never deprive us of men, whether through marriage or affairs."

Laughter rang out from all sides of the room. It drowned the shocked exclamations of some women here and there. The reaction was perhaps primarily caused by the apparent contradiction between the final, licentious prayer and the expressions preceding it which at least outwardly seemed serious and regretful. The woman had cloaked her expressions with a serious and dignified veil, before finally revealing her joke. Even Amina, uneasy though she was, could not keep from smiling, although she bowed her head so no one would see. At a party like this, women were able to entertain the drunken jokes of the performers and respond to their humor, although the limits of decency were occasionally surpassed. They seemed to enjoy a break from their normal primness.

The intoxicated entertainer continued her discourse: "My father, may God make paradise his final abode, had good intentions. For example, he brought me a fine man like himself one day and wanted to marry him to me." She roared with laughter. "What kind of marriage would that have been, my dear? What was left for a husband after what had already happened? I told myself, 'Jalila, you'll be disgraced. You've fallen into a tar pit.'"

She paused for a time to whet their appetite or to enjoy the attention focused on her, which was even greater than when she was singing. Then she went on: "But God was gracious. I was saved a few days before the anticipated disaster. I ran off with the late Hassuna al-Baghl, a drug dealer. He had a brother who played the lute for the entertainer Nayzak. He taught me how to play it. Since he liked my voice he also taught me how to sing. He coached me until I got into Nayzak's troupe. When she died,

I took her place. I've been singing for ages and have had a hundred lovers, plus. . . ."

She frowned as she tried to remember how many more than a hundred there had been. Then she turned to ask her tambourine player, "How many, Fino?"

The musician quickly responded, "Plus five – like the five fingers of the Prophet's granddaughter Fatima held up to ward off the evil of infidels."

Laughter resounded once more. Some of the women most fascinated by the performer's account attempted to silence the laughing ladies so she would resume speaking, but she rose suddenly and headed for the door. She paid no attention to the women asking her where she was going. Although they received no answer, no one pressed her, because she was notorious for her outbursts, which she made no effort whatsoever to resist.

Jalila descended the staircase to the door of the women's quarters and stepped into the courtyard. When her sudden appearance attracted the attention of nearby eyes, she paused to allow everyone to see her. She wanted to enjoy the interest that the sight of her would arouse in them and use it to challenge Sabir, who had worked his audience to a peak of enthusiasm. Her wish was granted. The contagion of turning to look at her spread as quickly as a yawn from one man to the next. Her name was repeated by every tongue. Although Sabir was carried away by his own singing, he too noticed the sudden rift between him and his audience. He turned to see what was attracting everyone's attention and his eyes came to rest on the chanteuse, who was gazing at him from afar with her head tilted back in a mixture of intoxication and pride. Sabir was compelled to stop singing and motioned to his musicians to cease playing. He raised his hands to his head to greet her. He knew about her outbursts and, unlike most people, also knew how kindhearted she was. Taking into consideration the dangers of antagonizing her, he displayed unreserved affection for her. His ruse succeeded, and the woman's face shone with delight. She called out to him, "Continue singing, Sabir. That's what I've come to hear."

The guests applauded and jubilantly returned to Sabir. Then Ibrahim Shawkat, the bridegroom's elder brother, approached her and asked politely what she needed. His question reminded her of the real reason she had come. She asked him in a voice that carried to many of the men present and most importantly to Yasin and Fahmy, "Why don't I see al-Sayyid Ahmad Abd al-Jawad? Where has the man hidden himself?"

Ibrahim Shawkat took her arm and smilingly escorted her to the reception room. Meanwhile Fahmy and Yasin exchanged an astonished and incredulous glance. Their eyes followed Ibrahim and the entertainer until they disappeared behind the door.

Al-Sayyid Ahmad was no less astonished than his sons to see her strutting toward him. He stared questioningly at her in alarm, while his companions exchanged smiling, knowing looks.

Jalila looked everyone over quickly and said, "A fine evening to you, gentlemen."

She focused her eyes on al-Sayyid Ahmad. She could not keep herself from laughing heartily. Then she asked sarcastically, "Has my visit frightened you, al-Sayyid Ahmad?"

He gestured to caution her about the people outside. He replied seriously, "Restrain yourself, Jalila. What has motivated you to visit me here under the eyes of all the people?"

Although her sarcastic smile never left her, she replied apologetically, "I would have hated to miss congratulating you on the marriage of your daughter."

Al-Sayyid Ahmad responded uneasily, "Thank you, lady, but didn't you think about the suspicions your visit might arouse in the minds of those who saw you?"

Jalila clapped her hands together and said almost as a reprimand, "Is this the best welcome you have for me?" Then she addressed his companions: "Gentlemen, you're my witnesses. Observe how this man, who used to be unhappy if he couldn't stick the tip of his mustache in my belly button, can't bear the sight of me."

Al-Sayyid Ahmad gestured to her as if to say, "Don't make the mud any wetter." He entreated her, "God knows I'm not unhappy to see you. The only problem is, you see, the awkward situation. . . ."

At this point, Mr. Ali tried to remind her of something she should not forget: "You lived together as lovers and parted friends. There's nothing to be revenged. But the women of his family are upstairs and his sons are outside."

Continuing to try to infuriate al-Sayyid Ahmad, Jalila asked, "Why do you pretend to be pious around your family when you're a pool of depravity?"

He threw her a look of protest and said, "Jalila! . . . There's no might or power except with God."

"Jalila or Zubayda, you saint?"

"I rely on God and the blessings of his deputy the Prophet. . . ."

She wriggled her eyebrows at him as she had in honor of Aisha before him, but this time it was sarcastic and not a sign of admiration. In a calm voice as serious as a judge's in pronouncing a verdict, she said, "It's all the same to me whether you're Zubayda's lover or some other woman's, but by the head of my mother it troubles me to see you roll in the dirt after being up to your ears in cream here." She pointed to herself.

Mr. Muhammad Iffat, who was the closest to her, rose at that point. He was afraid her intoxication would lead her to do something with unfortunate consequences. He took her hand and gently pulled her toward the door as he whispered in her ear, "I adjure you by al-Husayn to return to your audience, who are waiting impatiently for you."

After some resistance, she obeyed him, but as she slowly moved off, she turned toward al-Sayyid Ahmad to say, "Don't forget to give my greetings to the filthy bitch, and I'll give you some sisterly advice. Wash yourself off with alcohol after you've been with her, otherwise her sweat will affect your blood."

Al-Sayyid Ahmad saw her off with a furious look. He was cursing his luck which had decreed for him to be disgraced before the eyes of many, including his family, who knew him as a shining example of earnestness and dignity. Well, there was still hope that not everyone in his family had heard about the incident, but it was only a feeble one. There was also a chance that in their innocence they would not really understand if they did hear about it, although that possibility was hardly guaranteed, and for more than one reason.

Even assuming the worst, there was no reason for him to be alarmed. Their subservience to him and his domination over them both assured that no convulsion would shake them, not even this scandal. Moreover, he had never assumed it was out of the question that one of his sons, or even the whole family, might discover the truth about him, but he had not been overly worried about that, because of his confidence in his power and because in rearing them he had not relied on either setting an example or persuasion. There was no need to fear that they would swerve off the high road if they discovered he had. He thought it unlikely they would learn anything about him before they came of age, when he would not care much whether they did uncover his secret. Yet none of this could lighten his regret at what had happened, although the event had also pleased and flattered his pride in his sexual appeal. For a woman like Jalila to seek him out to greet him, tease him, or even to make fun of his new sweetheart was a real event that would have a great impact on the circles where he passed his nights. It was an occurrence with far-reaching significance for a man like him who enjoyed nothing so much as love, music, and companionship. But how much purer his happiness would have been if the beautiful event had taken place at a distance from this family atmosphere.

Yasin and Fahmy had not turned their eyes away from the door to the reception room from the moment Jalila disappeared through it till she emerged again, escorted by Mr. Muhammad Iffat. Fahmy was so astonished his head spun like Yasin's when he had heard Zanuba reply, "He's from our district. You must have heard of him . . . al-Sayyid Ahmad Abd al-Jawad. . . ." Now Yasin was overcome by a voracious curiosity. With a happiness that awakened in his heart a frenzy of the same admiration and feeling of affinity for his father that he had felt in Zanuba's room, he realized that Jalila was another adventure in his father's life, which Yasin had begun to picture as a golden chain of romantic escapades. The man surpassed everything he had imagined about him. Fahmy was still hoping and praying he would eventually learn that the entertainer had merely wanted to meet his father for some reason or other connected with her contract to perform at Aisha's wedding.

Then Khalil Shawkat came and laughingly told them that Jalila had been "teasing" their father and had "treated him affectionately, like a good friend."

With that, Yasin could no longer bear to keep his secret. The intoxication of the wine encouraged him to reveal his information. He waited until Khalil left. Then he leaned close to his brother's ear and, trying not to laugh, told him, "I've kept some things from you that I was uneasy about disclosing at the time. Now that you've seen what you have and heard what you have, I'll tell you." He started narrating to his brother what he had heard and seen in the home of the performer Zubayda.

As Yasin told the story with all its details, Fahmy kept interrupting him in bewilderment with, "Don't say that," or "Have
you lost your senses?" and "How do you expect me to believe
you?" Because of Fahmy's strong faith and idealism, he was not
prepared to understand, let alone digest, his father's secret life,
which was revealed to him for the first time, especially since
his father was one of the pillars of Fahmy's creed and one of
the buttresses of his idealism. There may have been some
similarity between his feelings when he was first experiencing
these revelations and those of a child, if imagination is to
be trusted, when he leaves the stability of the womb for the
chaos of the world. He could not have been more incredulous
or panic-stricken if he had been told that the mosque of
Qala'un had been turned upside down, with its minaret below
the building and the tomb on top, or that the Egyptian nationalist leader Muhammad Farid had betrayed the cause of his
mentor and predecessor Mustafa Kamil and sold himself to the
English.

"My father goes to Zubayda's house to drink, sing, and play the
tambourine. . . . My father allows Jalila to tease him and be affectionate with him. . . . My father gets drunk and commits adultery.
How could all this be true? Then he wouldn't be the father he
knew at home, a man of exemplary piety and resolve. Which was
correct? I can almost hear him now reciting, 'God is most great. . . .
God is most great.' So how is he at reciting songs? A life of
deception and hypocrisy? . . . But he's sincere. Sincere when he
raises his head in prayer. Sincere when he's angry. Is my father
depraved or is licentiousness a virtue?"

"Astonished? . . . I was too when Zanuba mentioned his name,
but I quickly got over it and I asked her what's wrong with it? . . . A
sin? Men are all like this or ought to be."

"This statement is entirely appropriate for Yasin. Yasin's one
thing and my father's something else. Yasin! . . . What about Yasin?
How can I repeat this now, when my father, my father himself
doesn't differ at all from Yasin except in having sunk lower. . . . But
no, it's not depravity. . . . There must be something I don't
know. . . . My father hasn't done anything wrong. . . . He can't
do anything wrong. He's above suspicion. In any case, he doesn't
merit contempt."

"Still bewildered?"

"I can't imagine that anything you've said could have happened."

"Why? . . . Laugh and enjoy the world. He sings. So what's wrong about singing? He gets drunk, and believe me, drinking is even better than eating. He has affairs and so did the Muslim caliphs. Read about it in the ancient poems contained in Abu Tammam's anthology *Diwan al-Hamasa* or see its marginal glosses. Our father isn't doing anything sinful. Shout with me, 'Long live al-Sayyid Ahmad Abd al-Jawad! Long live our father!' I'll leave you for a moment while I visit the bottle I hid under a chair for just such an occasion."

On the return of the entertainer to her troupe, the news of her meeting with al-Sayyid Ahmad Abd al-Jawad spread through the women's quarters. It passed from mouth to mouth until it reached the mother as well as Khadija and Aisha. Although his family was hearing something like this about him for the first time, many of the ladies whose husbands were friends of al-Sayyid Ahmad were hardly surprised by the news and smilingly winked as if to say they knew more than was being said. But none of them let herself be tempted to plunge into the topic. To bring it up publicly in front of his daughters would not have seemed appropriate to them. Courtesy dictated remaining silent about it in the presence of Amina and her two daughters. Widow Shawkat did jokingly tell Amina, "Watch out, Madam Amina. It seems Jalila's eye has strayed to al-Sayyid Ahmad."

Amina smiled and pretended not to be concerned but blushed with shame and confusion. For the first time she had tangible evidence for the doubts she had entertained long ago. Although she had trained herself to be patient and submissive about what happened to her, her collision with this tangible evidence had cut her to the quick. She felt a torment she had never experienced before. Her pride had also taken a beating.

A woman who wished to add a flattering comment appropriate for the mother of the bride said, "Anyone with a face as beautiful as Mrs. Amina's doesn't have to worry about her husband's eyes straying to another woman."

Amina was deeply moved by the praise, and her vivacious smile returned. In any case, it provided her some consolation for the silent pain she was suffering. Yet when Jalila began a new song, filling their ears with her voice, Amina suddenly became angry and felt for a few seconds she was about to lose control of herself. She quickly suppressed her anger with all the force of a woman who did not acknowledge that she had a right to get angry. Meanwhile Khadija and Aisha received the news with astonishment and exchanged an anxious glance. Their eyes were asking what it was all about. Their astonishment was not coupled with panic like Fahmy's nor with pain like their mother's. Perhaps they understood that for a woman like Jalila to leave her troupe and take the trouble of going down to where their father was sitting to greet him and talk to him was something to be proud of. Khadija felt a natural desire to look at her mother's face. She stole a glance at her. Although Mrs. Amina was smiling, her daughter grasped right away the pain and uneasiness she was enduring, which were robbing her of her peace of mind. Khadija felt upset and became angry at the entertainer, Widow Shawkat, and the gathering as a whole.

When it was time for the wedding procession, everyone forgot his personal concerns. No matter how many weeks and months passed, the picture of Aisha in her wedding gown would not leave their minds.

Al-Ghuriya was dark and quiet when the family left the bride's new home to return to al-Nahhasin. Al-Sayyid Ahmad walked alone in front followed a few meters back by Fahmy and Yasin. The latter was exhausting himself by trying to act sober and walk straight, for fear his giddiness would reveal he had drunk too much. At the rear came Amina, Khadija, Kamal, and Umm Hanafi. Kamal had joined the caravan against his will. If his father had not been there to lead them, Kamal would have found some way to free himself from his mother's hand and run back to where they had left Aisha. He was looking behind him at Bab al-Mutawalli from one step to the next to bid farewell sadly and regretfully to the last trace of the wedding, that shining lamp a worker on a ladder was removing from its hook over the entrance to Sugar Street. Kamal was heartbroken to see that his family had relinquished the person he loved best after his mother. He looked up at his mother and whispered, "When will Aisha come back to us?"

She whispered, "Don't say that again. Pray for her to be happy. She'll visit us frequently and we'll call on her a lot."

He whispered to her resentfully, "You've tricked me!"

She motioned toward al–Sayyid Ahmad up in front, who had almost been swallowed up by the darkness. She pursed her lips to whisper, "Hush."

But Kamal was preoccupied with recalling images of things he had happened to see during the wedding. He thought them extraordinarily odd, and they made him uneasy. He pulled his mother's hand his way to separate her from Khadija and Umm Hanafi. Then, pointing back, he whispered to her, "Do you know what's going on there?"

"What do you mean?"

"I peeked through a hole in the door."

The mother felt distressed and alarmed, because she could guess which door he meant, but refusing to trust her intuition, she asked, "What door?"

"The door of the bride's room!"

The woman said with alarm, "It's disgraceful for a person to look through holes in doors."

He immediately whispered back, "What I saw was even more disgraceful."

"Be quiet."

"I saw Aisha and Mr. Khalil sitting on the chaise longue . . . and he was . . . "

She hit him hard on his shoulder to make him stop. She whispered in his ear, "Don't say shameful things. If your father heard you, he'd kill you."

He persisted and told her, as though revealing something to her she could not possibly have imagined, "He was holding her chin in his hand and kissing her."

She hit him again, harder than she ever had before. He realized that he had certainly done something wrong without knowing it. He fell silent and was afraid. When they were crossing the court-yard of their house, straggling behind the others except for Umm Hanafi, who had waited behind to bolt the door, lock it, and latch it, Kamal's anxiety and curiosity overcame his silence and fear. He asked pleadingly, "Why was he kissing her, Mother?"

She told him firmly, "If you start that again, I'll tell your father."

41

YASIN WAS quite intoxicated when he retired to the bedroom. Since Kamal had fallen sound asleep the moment his head touched the pillow, Yasin was alone with Fahmy. Free at last from parental supervision, he felt in the mood for a noisy row as a release from the nervous strain he had been under all evening, especially on the way home when he had struggled to control himself and act right. Since the room was too cramped for rowdiness, he felt like relieving his tensions by talking. He looked at Fahmy, who was getting undressed, and said sarcastically, "Compared with our brilliant father, we're failures. He's truly some man."

Although this statement revived Fahmy's pain and anxiety, he was content to answer with a bitter smile, "You've been blessed too. What an excellent son!"

"Are you sad our father's one of the great skirt chasers?"

"I wish there had been no change in the ideal picture I've had in my soul."

Rubbing his hands merrily, Yasin said, "The real picture is even more splendid and delightful. He's more than a father. He's the ultimate. Oh, if you had only seen him grasping the tambourine, with a glass shining in front of him. Bravo . . . bravo, al-Sayyid Ahmad!"

Fahmy asked uneasily, "What about his prudence and piety?"

Yasin frowned in order to concentrate on the question, but he found it easier to merge opposites than to reconcile them. Motivated by nothing but admiration, he replied, "There's absolutely no problem there at all. Your cowardly intellect's just creating the problem from nothing. My father's prudent, a Muslim, and loves women. It's as simple and clear as one plus one equals two. Perhaps I'm the one who most resembles him, because I'm a Muslim believer and love women, although I'm not too prudent. You yourself are a believer, prudent, and love women, but you base your acts on faith and prudence while shying away from the third alternative: women." He laughed. "It's the third that lasts."

Yasin's final statement was only remotely linked to his admiration for his father that had started him rattling on and was only superficially in defense of him. It was really an expression of a burning feeling Yasin's intoxication had aroused. Once the guardians he respected were out of the way, he experienced a raging lust incited by an imagination charged with alcohol. His body felt a mad craving for love, and his willpower was unable to bridle it or coax it away. But where could he find what he wanted? Did he have enough time? . . . Zanuba? . . . What was keeping him from her? It wasn't far. It wouldn't take long to make love with her. Then he could come home and sleep deeply and calmly. He was delighted by these visions and seemed not to have a brain to make him think twice. He was in a rush to bring them to pass with no further delay. He quickly told his brother, "It's hot. I'm going up to the roof to enjoy the moist night air."

He left the room for the outer hall and groped his way down the steps in total darkness, being extremely careful not to make a sound. How could he get in touch with Zanuba at this hour of the night? Should he knock on the door? Who would open it? What could he say when the person asked him what he wanted? What if no one woke up to answer the door? What if the night watchman, with his knack for arriving at the wrong time, should catch him? These thoughts floated on the surface of his brain like bubbles and then were carried off by the swift current of the wine. They did not seem obstacles with consequences to be taken seriously. They were little jokes to make him smile during this lonely adventure. His imagination flew past them to Zanuba's room overlooking the intersection of al-Ghuriya and al-Sanadiqiya streets.

He pictured her in a diaphanous white nightgown that curved obediently around her breasts and buttocks, with the bottom pulled up to reveal rosy legs with gold bangles. He went wild and would have leapt down the steps had it not been so dark. In the courtyard it was brighter because of the faint light from the stars. After the total darkness of the stairway it appeared almost light. When he had taken two steps toward the outer door at the end of the courtyard, he noticed a feeble glow, which came from a lamp sitting on a meat block in front of the oven room. He looked at it in surprise until he spotted nearby a body flung down on the ground, illuminated by its light. He recognized Umm Hanafi,

who had evidently chosen to sleep out in the open to escape the
stifling atmosphere of the oven room. He started to continue on
his way, but something made him stop. He turned his head once
more toward the sleeping woman no more than a few meters
away, whom he could see with unexpected clarity from where he
stood. He saw her stretched out on her back. Her right leg was
bent, creating a pyramid in the air with the edge of her dress,
which clung to her knee. At the same time, the bare skin of a
section of her left thigh near the knee was revealed. The opening
that was formed where her dress stretched between her raised knee
and the other leg, extended on the ground, was drowned in
darkness.

Although Yasin's feeling of being pressed for time and in a rush
to get what he wanted had not diminished, he kept looking at the
supine body, apparently unable to tear his eyes away. He was
unwittingly drawn into observing it with an interest evident in
the alertness of his bloodshot eyes and the way his full lips spread
open. As he examined the fleshy form, which occupied as much
space as a plump female water buffalo, the alertness of his eyes
turned into unnerving desire. They came to rest on the dark
opening between the raised leg and the extended one. There
was a change of course for the current raging through his veins,
and its momentum directed him toward the oven room. He
seemed to have discovered for the first time the woman with
whom he had rubbed shoulders for years.

Umm Hanafi had not been favored with a single attribute of
beauty. Her gloomy face made her look older than her forty years.
Even her treasure of flesh and fat, because it lacked proportion or
harmony, seemed a bloated swelling. Perhaps also because she was
hidden away in the oven room so much of the time and because he
had lived with her since he was a boy, he had never paid any
attention to her.

Yasin was in such turmoil that he was unable to reason clearly. He
was blinded by lust. What kind of lust was it? A lust kindled by a
woman simply because she was a woman, not because of any of her
qualities or associations. It was a lust that loved beauty but would
not turn away from ugliness. In these crises, everything was equivalent. He was like a dog that eagerly devours whatever scraps it finds.

At this juncture, Yasin's first choice for an escapade – Zanuba –
seemed surrounded by obstacles with unknown consequences. He

no longer considered going to her at this hour of the night, knocking on the door, thinking of something to say when the door was opened, and avoiding the night watchman to be laughing matters. They were real impediments and enough to cause him to shy away from her.

With his mouth hanging open, he advanced gently and cautiously. He was oblivious to everything except the mountain of flesh spread at his feet. To his greedy eyes this body appeared to be preparing itself to receive him. He hesitated before her legs. Then, almost unconscious of what he was doing, little by little he leaned down over her, driven by urgent internal and external stimuli. Before he knew it, he was sprawled out on top of her. He had perhaps not intended to go this far all at once. Perhaps he had intended to indulge in some of the foreplay that ought to precede the final violent motions, but the body on top of which he was sprawled began to heave with terror, and a resounding scream escaped, before his hand could stifle it. The pervasive silence was shattered and his brain was dealt a blow that brought him back to his senses. He put his hand over her mouth as he whispered anxiously and fearfully in her ear, "It's me. Yasin. It's Yasin, Umm Hanafi. Don't be afraid."

He kept repeating these words until he was certain she understood who he was. Then he removed his hand, but the woman, who had never stopped resisting, was finally able to push him off. She sat up straight, panting from her exertion and emotion, and asked him in a voice that was loud enough to alarm him, "What do you want, Mr. Yasin?"

Whispering, he entreated her, "Don't raise your voice like that. I told you not to be afraid. There's absolutely nothing to be afraid of."

Although she lowered her voice a little, she asked sternly, "What brings you?"

He began to caress her hand affectionately and sighed with anxious relief, since he saw in the lowering of her voice an encouraging sign. He asked, "Why are you angry? I didn't mean to hurt you." Then he said amiably, "Come into the oven room."

In a troubled but decisive manner, she replied, "Certainly not, sir. Go to your room. Go. God's curse on Satan. . . ."

Umm Hanafi was not able to weigh her words carefully. They escaped from her in reaction to the situation. Perhaps they did not express her wishes so much as her surprise at a proposition that had not been preceded by any hint but had pounced on her while she slept like a predatory kite swooping down on a chicken. She rejected the young man and scolded him without taking time to think whether she wanted to.

He took her words the wrong way and was filled with resentment. Ideas raged through his head. "What's to be done with this bitch? I can't retreat after revealing my intentions and going far enough to cause a scandal. I must get what I want even if I have to resort to force."

He thought quickly about the best way to overcome any resistance she might display, but before he could reach a decision he heard an unexpected sound, perhaps footsteps, coming from the door of the stairway. He jumped to his feet, totally overcome by panic. He swallowed his lust the way a thief swallows a stolen diamond when caught unawares in his hideout. He turned toward the door anxiously and saw his father crossing the threshold, holding his arm out with a lamp. Yasin stayed nailed to the spot, pale with fear, resigned, stunned, and desperate. He realized at once that Umm Hanafi's scream had not been in vain. The rear window of his father's room had served as an observatory. But what use was hindsight? He had fallen into a snare set by divine decree and destiny.

Trembling with rage, al-Sayyid Ahmad began to examine Yasin's face grimly and silently, dragging out the silence. Without taking his pitiless eyes off Yasin, he pointed with his hand to the door, ordering him inside. Although at that moment disappearing would have been dearer to Yasin than even life itself, he was paralyzed by fear and confusion. The father was outraged, and his scowl showed he was about to explode. His eyes seemed to shoot off sparks as they reflected the light of the lamp, which trembled as the hand holding it shook. He rebuked him loudly, "Go upstairs, you criminal. You son of a bitch."

Yasin became even more paralyzed. Then al-Sayyid Ahmad fell upon him. He grabbed Yasin's right arm roughly and yanked him toward the door. Yasin yielded to this extraordinary force and almost fell on his face. Regaining his balance, he turned around in terror. He fled for his life, leaping up the stairs, heedless of the darkness.

42

BESIDES HIS father and Umm Hanafi, two other people knew about Yasin's scandal, Mrs. Amina and Fahmy. They had heard Umm Hanafi's scream and watched from their windows what transpired between the young man and his father. They were able to guess what had happened without too much thought.

Al-Sayyid Ahmad mentioned his son's blunder to his wife and asked her in some detail about Umm Hanafi's morals. Amina defended her servant's character and integrity, reminding him that had it not been for the woman's scream, no one would have been the wiser. The man spent an hour cursing and swearing. He cursed Yasin and cursed himself for fathering children who would destroy his peace of mind with their evil passions. His anger boiled over, and he damned his house and all the people in it.

Amina remained silent, as she did later, when she pretended to know nothing about it. Fahmy also feigned ignorance of the subject. He pretended to be sound asleep when his brother returned to the room, out of breath after forfeiting the battle. Fahmy never gave any indication that he knew about it. He respected his older brother and would have hated for him to realize he was aware of the shameful depravity to which Yasin had stooped. Fahmy's respect for Yasin was not shattered by this discovery of his reckless antics, by his own superiority to Yasin in education and culture, or even by Yasin's nonchalance about whether his brothers respected him. Yasin would joke with them and let them tease him as though they were his equals. Fahmy still respected him. Perhaps his desire to continue respecting him could be attributed to Fahmy's own manners, seriousness, and sense of dignity, which made him seem older than he was.

Khadija did not fail to observe the morning after the incident that Yasin was not eating with his father. She asked incredulously why. He claimed he had suffered indigestion at the wedding. The girl, by nature acutely suspicious, felt there must be some reason other than indigestion. She asked her mother about it, but did not receive a convincing answer.

When Kamal returned from the dining room, he also asked. He was not motivated by curiosity or regret but by the hope of good news of a prolonged period during which the field would be empty of a dangerous competitor for food like Yasin.

The matter might have been forgotten had Yasin not left the house in the evening without participating in the customary coffee hour. Although he apologized to Fahmy and their mother and claimed he was tied up with an appointment, Khadija said bluntly, "There's something going on. I'm no fool. . . . I'll cut my arm off if Yasin hasn't changed."

The mother was forced to announce that al-Sayyid Ahmad was angry at Yasin for some unknown reason, and the coffee hour was devoted to their conjectures about the cause. Amina and Fahmy guessed along with the others, in order to conceal the truth.

Yasin avoided eating with his father until he was summoned one morning to meet him before breakfast. The invitation did not come as a surprise and yet it alarmed him. He had expected it from day to day. He was certain his father would not feel there had been an adequate response to his offense. His father would return to the subject by one avenue or another. Yasin expected to be treated in a manner inappropriate for a gainfully employed person like himself. At times he thought of leaving the house temporarily or for good. For his father, especially the father he had learned about in Zubayda's house, to make such a catastrophe out of his blunder was not nice. It was also not right for Yasin to expose himself to treatment incompatible with his manly status. The best thing would be for him to leave, but where to? He would have to live alone. That was not out of the question. He considered the matter from every angle, estimated his expenses, and asked himself how much would be left over for his entertainment in al-Sayyid Ali's coffee shop, in Costaki's bar, and with Zanuba. At this point his enthusiasm flagged. Then it was extinguished like the flame of a lamp when a strong gust of wind hits it.

Although he knew he was not being totally honest, he told himself, "If I obey Satan and leave home, I'll create a bad precedent that would be wrong for our family. No matter what my father says or does, he's my father. It's absurd to think his discipline would be unjust." Then he continued with the candor he affected

when in a playful mood: "Have some humility, Yasin Bey.
Spare us the talk about honor, by the life of your mother. Which
do you love more: your honor or Costaki's cognac and Zanuba's
navel?"

Thus Yasin abandoned the thought of leaving home and kept
on waiting for the anticipated summons. When it arrived, he
pulled himself together and set off, reluctantly and apprehensively.
He entered the room, walking softly, his head bowed. He stopped
at some distance from his father and did not dare offer him a word
of greeting. Yasin waited while al-Sayyid Ahmad gave him a long
look. Then the father shook his head in amazement and said,
"God's will be done! So tall and broad . . . a mustache and a wide
neck. If someone saw you on the street he'd comment admiringly,
'What a fine son for some lucky man.' If only he'd come to the
house to see you in your true colors."

The young man became even more distressed and embarrassed
but said nothing. Al-Sayyid Ahmad continued to examine him
angrily. Then in a stern and commanding voice he told him
tersely, "I've decided you're going to get married."

Yasin was so astonished he could scarcely believe his ears.
Curses and rebukes were all he had been expecting. It had never
occurred to him that he would hear an important decision altering
the whole course of his life. He could not keep himself from
raising his eyes to look at his father's face. When they met his
father's piercing blue ones, he looked down, blushed, and kept
silent.

Al-Sayyid Ahmad realized that his son had been expecting
rough treatment and was caught off guard by these blissful tidings.
The father was enraged at the circumstances that dictated this
mild-mannered approach, fearing it would shake Yasin's faith in
his reputation for tyranny. He vented his anger in his voice as he
said with a frown, "I don't have much time. I want to hear your
answer."

Since the man had decided Yasin was to marry, there was only
one possible answer, and there was nothing to prevent him from
hearing the answer he wanted. In this case, Yasin's obedience
to his father was also obedience to his own desire. Yes, no sooner
had his father announced the decision than Yasin's imagination
shot off, depicting his beautiful bride. He would have a woman
entirely to himself, to be at his beck and call. The image delighted

him so much, his voice almost gave him away when he answered, "The decision's up to you, Papa."

"Do you want to marry or not? . . . Speak."

With the caution of a person wanting to get married but financially unprepared, the young man replied, "Since this is your wish, I agree with all my heart."

Al-Sayyid Ahmad softened the roughness of his voice when he said, "I'll request for you the daughter of my friend Mr. Muhammad Iffat, a textile merchant in al-Hamzawi. She's a treasure who's too good for an ox like you."

Yasin smiled delicately and, trying to ingratiate himself with his father, said, "With your help I'll try to be a good husband for her."

His father glared at him as if attempting to pierce through his flattery and said, "No one hearing you would imagine what you're capable of doing, you hypocrite. . . . Get out of my sight."

Yasin started to leave, but his father stopped him with a gesture of his hand. Al-Sayyid Ahmad added, as though he had just happened to think of the question, "I suppose you've saved up enough for the dowry?"

Yasin did not have an answer. He became more upset. His father was enraged and remarked incredulously, "Even after you got a job you continued to live at my expense the way you did when you were a student. What have you done with your salary?"

All Yasin did was move his lips without uttering a word. His father shook his head in annoyance. He remembered speaking to him a year and a half before. When Yasin got his government position, al-Sayyid Ahmad had told him, "If I were to ask you to take care of your own expenses like an adult, I would not be deviating from the norm between fathers and sons, but I will not ask you for a single penny, so you can have an opportunity to put aside a sum of money to have at your disposal when you need it." In this way he had shown his confidence in his son.

He could not imagine that one of his sons, after the stern discipline and training he had meted out, would have an inclination for any of the passions that squander money. He could not imagine that his little boy would turn into a philandering drunkard. The wine and women al-Sayyid Ahmad considered a harmless form of recreation for himself, fully compatible with manly virtue, became an unforgivable crime when they defiled one of his sons. The young man's blunder in the courtyard, which al-Sayyid

Ahmad had discovered, reassured him to the same extent that it angered him. It would have been impossible, in his opinion, for Umm Hanafi to tempt the young man if he had not been struggling to maintain an intolerable level of chastity and rectitude.

He could not imagine that his son had wasted his money on wine and women, but he did remember noticing Yasin was fond of elegance, choosing expensive suits, neckties, and shirts. He had been uncomfortable about that and had warned him against throwing away his money. His warning had been mild, because he did not think elegance a crime and because it was an interest he shared with his son. He saw no harm in his sons imitating him in this manner. It made him feel kindly and well disposed toward them. What had been the result of that lenience? It was clear to him now that Yasin had squandered his money on unimportant luxuries. The man snorted with rage and told his son bitterly, "Get out of my sight."

Yasin departed from the room, leaving his father angry at him for squandering his money, not, as he had anticipated, for his moral lapse. Being a spendthrift had never troubled Yasin before. He had let it happen without any thought or planning. He would spend whatever he had in his pocket until it was gone. He was immersed in the present, turning a blind eye to the future, as though it did not exist. Yasin left the room upset, cowering from his father's scolding, but he felt a deep relief since he realized that this scolding meant he would not be thrown out of the house and also that his father would bear the expenses of his wedding. He was like a child who, having pestered his father for a coin, gets it and is shoved outside. Then the happiness of the boy's triumph makes him forget the strength of the push.

Al-Sayyid Ahmad was still angry and began to repeat, "What an animal he is. He's got a big, strong body, but no brain." He was angry that Yasin had squandered his money, as though he himself never had. He saw nothing wrong with extravagance, any more than he did with his other passions, so long as it did not bankrupt him, make him forget his obligations, or harm his character. But what guarantee did he have that Yasin would be as resolute? Al-Sayyid Ahmad did not forbid his son what he allowed himself merely out of egoism and authoritarianism, but because he was concerned about him. Of course, this concern of his revealed how confident he was of himself and how little he trusted his son, and neither sentiment was entirely free of conceit. As usual, his anger abated as quickly as it had flared up. His peace of mind returned, and his features relaxed. Matters began to appear to him in a new, agreeable, tolerable light.

"You want to be like your father, ox? . . . Then don't adopt one side and neglect the others. Be Ahmad Abd al-Jawad completely if you can, otherwise know your limits. Did you really think I was angry at your extravagance because I wanted you to get married at your own expense? Far from it. . . . I simply hoped to find you had been careful with your money so I could marry you off at my expense and leave you with a surplus. This is the hope you disappointed. Did you suppose I wouldn't have thought about choosing a wife for you until I caught you philandering? What a wretched excuse for sex that was, wretched, like your taste and your mother's. No, you mule, I've been thinking about your married bliss since you became a government employee. How could it be otherwise, since you were the first to make a father of me? You're my partner in the torment to which your damned mother has exposed us. So don't I have the right to give you, in particular, a festive wedding? I'm going to have to wait a long time to marry off the other ox, your brother, who's a prisoner of love. Who knows who'll be alive then?"

The following moment he recalled something directly related to his present situation. He remembered how he had told Mr. Muhammad Iffat about Yasin's "crime" and how he had scolded him and yanked him by the arm in a way that almost made him fall on his face. That revelation had been apropos of his request for the hand of the man's daughter for his son. The fact was that the two men had already agreed on the marriage before he brought it up with Yasin.

Muhammad Iffat had asked him, "Don't you think it would be appropriate to change the way you treat your son, as he grows more mature, especially now that he has a job and has become a responsible adult?" He had laughed before continuing: "It's clear you're a father who doesn't ease up until his sons openly rebel."

Al-Sayyid Ahmad had answered his friend: "It's out of the question that the relationship between me and my sons should change with time." He had felt a boundless confidence and pride in this answer but later had acknowledged that his treatment actually had changed, although he had tried to keep anyone from detecting his hidden intention to change. He had added: "The truth is that I'm no longer willing to lift my hand against Yasin or even Fahmy. I only yanked Yasin like that because I was so angry. I didn't mean to get carried away." Then, reverting to a time in the distant past, he had continued: "My father, God's mercy on him, raised me so strictly that my severity with my sons seems lenient, but he quickly changed the way he treated me once he asked me to help him in the store. Then after I married Yasin's mother, his treatment changed into a father's friendship. My self-esteem became so great that I opposed his final marriage, because he was much older than the bride. All he did was to say, 'Do you oppose me, ox? . . . What's it got to do with you? I'm better able than you to satisfy any woman.' I couldn't keep from laughing, and I apologetically set about conciliating him."

While al-Sayyid Ahmad was recalling all of this, a saying came to his mind: "When your son grows up, make him your brother." Perhaps more than ever before he felt how complicated it is to be a father.

That same week, their mother announced Yasin's engagement at the coffee hour. Fahmy had learned about it from Yasin himself. Khadija instinctively recognized that there was some relationship between the engagement and her father's anger at Yasin. She suspected his anger had arisen from Yasin's desire to get married, going on the analogy of what had happened between her father and Fahmy. She stated her opinion bluntly, but in the form of a question.

Glancing at their mother with shame and embarrassment, Yasin laughed and said, "The truth is that there's a very strong link between the anger and the engagement."

In order to make a sarcastic joke, Khadija pretended to be skeptical. She said, "Papa can be excused for getting angry, because you won't do him much credit with a close friend like al-Sayyid Muhammad Iffat."

Yasin countered her sarcasm: "Father's position will become even more difficult when the aforementioned personage learns the bridegroom has a sister like you."

Then Kamal asked, "Will you leave us, Yasin, the way Aisha did?"

His mother replied with a smile, "Of course not. A new sister, the bride, will join our household."

Kamal was relieved at this answer, which he had not been expecting. He was relieved because his storyteller was staying to entertain him with stories, anecdotes, and conviviality. But then he asked why Aisha had not stayed with them too.

His mother replied that it was customary for the bride to move to the bridegroom's house and not vice versa. Kamal wondered who had established this custom. He dearly wished it had been the other way round, even if he had had to sacrifice Yasin and his droll stories. He was not able to state this desire openly, and so he expressed it with a look directed at his mother.

Fahmy was the only one saddened by the news. Although he was happy for Yasin, marriage had become a subject that awakened his emotions and stirred up his sorrows, just as talk of victory stirs up the sorrows of a mother who has lost her son in a triumphal battle.

43

THE CARRIAGE set off to take the mother, Khadija and Kamal to Sugar Street. Was Aisha's wedding the harbinger of a new era of freedom? Would they finally be able to see the world from time to time and breathe its fresh air? Amina had not let herself get her hopes up or become too optimistic. The man who had forbidden her to visit her mother, except on rare occasions, was equally capable of preventing her from calling on her daughter. She could not forget that many days had passed since her daughter's wedding. Al-Sayyid Ahmad, Yasin, Fahmy, and even Umm Hanafi had visited Aisha, but he had not given her permission to go, and her courage had not been up to asking. She was wary about reminding him that she had a daughter on Sugar Street whom she needed to see. She remained silent, but the image of her little girl never left her mind. When the pain of waiting grew too great to bear, she summoned all her willpower to ask him, "Is my master planning to visit Aisha soon, God willing, so we can be sure she's all right?"

Suspecting that her question was motivated by a hidden desire, al-Sayyid Ahmad got angry at her, but not because he had decided to prevent her visit. It was typical of him in such cases to wish to grant permission as a gift, without a prior request. He did not want her to think her request had had any influence on him. He assumed she was trying to remind him with this sly question. At an earlier time he had thought about this question apprehensively and had been annoyed to realize that such a visit was unavoidable. So he shouted at her furiously, "Aisha's in her husband's house and doesn't need any of us. Besides, I've visited her, and her brothers have too. Why are you anxious about her?"

In her despair and defeat, her heart sank and her throat felt dry. Al-Sayyid Ahmad had decided to punish her for what he considered her unforgivable cunning by remaining silent, as though the subject was closed. He ignored her for a long time, although he glanced stealthily at her sorrowful expression. When it was time for him to leave for work, he said tersely and gruffly, "Go visit her tomorrow."

Her face, which was incapable of hiding any emotion, immediately became radiant with joy. She looked as happy as a child. It did not take long for his anger to return. He shouted at her, "You'll never see her after that, unless her husband allows her to visit us."

She made no reply to this remark but did not forget a promise she had made to Khadija when they discussed bringing up the topic with him. Hesitantly and apprehensively she asked, "Will my master allow me to take Khadija?"

He shook his head as though to say, "God's will be done. . . . God's will be done." Then he replied sharply, "Of course, of course! Since I've agreed to let my daughter get married, my family's got to join the demimonde parading through the streets. Take her! May our Lord take all of you away."

Her joy was even more complete than she had thought possible. She paid no attention to the final curse, which she often heard when he was angry or pretending to be angry. She knew it came from his lips and not his heart, which felt quite the opposite way. He was like a mother cat which appears to be devouring her kittens when she is actually carrying them.

The wish was granted, and the vehicle started on its way to Sugar Street. Kamal seemed happiest of all, for three reasons. He was going to visit Aisha, he was on an excursion with his mother and sister, and he was riding in a carriage. As though he could not keep his joy a secret and wished to announce it to everyone or attract attention to himself sitting in the carriage between his mother and sister, he suddenly stood up and cried out, "Amm Hasanayn, look!" when the vehicle approached the barbershop. The man looked at him. Discovering that Kamal was not alone, he quickly lowered his eyes and smiled. The mother was terribly embarrassed and upset. She grabbed Kamal by the edge of his jacket, so he would not repeat his performance as they passed the other shops, and scolded him for the crazy thing he had done.

The house on Sugar Street appeared to be ancient, a relic. It looked quite different without its decorative wedding lights. The very age and mass of the building and the expensive furnishings all suggested power and prestige. The Shawkats were an old family, although not much was left of their former glory, except their name, especially since the family fortune had been divided up over the years by inheritance. The fact that they shunned modern education had not helped either. The bride had taken up residence on the second floor. Because of her age, Widow Shawkat had difficulty climbing the stairs and moved down to the first floor with her elder son, Ibrahim. The third floor remained vacant. They did not try to use it and refused to rent it out.

When the family entered Aisha's apartment, Kamal wanted to rush off on his own, the way he would at home, in order to scout around until he found his sister all by himself. He looked forward to the pleasure of the surprise and pictured it to himself as he climbed up the stairs, but his mother would not let him escape from her grip, no matter how hard he tried. Before he knew what was happening, the servant had led them to the parlor and left them there alone. Kamal felt they were being treated like strangers or company. He was dejected and depressed and began to repeat with alarm, "Where's Aisha? . . . Why are we waiting here?"

The only answer he received was "hush" and a warning that he would not be allowed to visit again if he raised his voice. His pain quickly left him once Aisha came running in, her face beaming with a smile of such brilliance it outshone her magnificent clothes and dazzling finery. Kamal ran to her and put his arms around her neck. He clung to her all the time she was exchanging greetings with her mother and sister.

Aisha appeared to be ecstatic about herself, her new life, and her family's visit. She told them about the visits from her father, Yasin, and Fahmy and how her desire to see the rest of the family had conquered her fear of her father. She had been daring enough to ask permission for them to call on her.

She said, "I don't know how my tongue obeyed me and let me speak. Perhaps it was his new image that encouraged me. He seemed to be charming, mild-mannered, and smiling. Yes, by God, he was smiling. Even so, I hesitated for a long time. I was afraid he would suddenly revert back to form and scold me. Finally I put my faith in God and spoke."

Her mother asked her how he had replied. Aisha answered, "He said, in as few words as possible, 'God willing.' Then he continued quickly in a serious tone that sounded like a warning: 'But don't think this is a game. There's a limit to everything.' My heart pounded and I proceeded to invoke blessings on him for a long time to try to humor and placate him."

Then she skipped back a little to describe how she had felt when she was told, "The head of your family is in the parlor."

She said, "I raced to the bathroom and washed my face to get off every trace of powder. Mr. Khalil asked me why I was doing that, but I told him, 'Believe me, I can't even meet him in this summer dress, because my arms show.' I didn't go till I wrapped myself in my cashmere shawl."

Then she said, "When Mother . . ." She laughed. "I mean my new mother. When she heard about it, because Mr. Khalil told her what happened, she said, 'I know al-Sayyid Ahmad extremely well. He's like that and worse.' Then she turned to me and said, 'Shushu, you should realize that you're no longer part of the Abd al-Jawad family. Now you're one of the Shawkats. So pay no attention to anyone else.'"

Aisha's splendid appearance and her conversation awakened their love and admiration. Kamal gazed at her as he had the night of the wedding and asked contentiously, "Why didn't you look like this when you were at our house?"

She laughed and immediately answered him, "Back then, I wasn't a Shawkat."

Even Khadija looked at her affectionately. The girl's marriage had eliminated all the reasons for the name-calling that used to break out between them when they were cooped up together. Moreover, only a small trace was left of the resentment Khadija had felt when permission was granted for the younger sister to marry first, since she blamed her misfortune on luck, not her sister. Her heart held nothing but love and longing for her. She missed her frequently, particularly when she needed a companion to confide in.

Then Aisha talked about her new home with the enclosed balcony overlooking Mutawalli Gate, the minarets that shot up into the sky nearby, and the steady flow of traffic. Everything around her reminded her of the old house and the streets and buildings surrounding it. There was no difference except for the names and some secondary features. "And, come to think of it, you don't have anything comparable to the huge gate where you live."

Then, with a trace of disappointment, she admitted, "Although Mr. Khalil told me the procession of pilgrims setting off for Mecca does not pass by our balcony. . . ."

She continued: "Directly under the balcony there's a spot where three men sit all day long until night comes: a crippled beggar, a vendor of red leather shoes, and a fortune-teller who makes his predictions by reading patterns in sand. They are my new neighbors. The geomancer is the most successful. Don't ask me about the droves of women and men who squat in front of him to find out what their fortune will be. . . . How I wish my balcony were a little lower so I could hear what he tells them. The most entertaining sight of all is the Suarès omnibus coming from al-Darb al-Ahmar when it meets a wagon of stones on its way from al-Ghuriya. The entrance of the gate is too narrow for both of them, and each of the drivers gets it into his head to challenge the other and force him to retreat and make way. At first the language is relatively polite, but then it becomes sharp and rude. Their throats bellow out curses and insults. Meanwhile the donkey carts and the handcarts arrive on the scene till the road is choked with them and no one has any idea how to get things back to normal. I stand there at the peephole trying not to laugh as I watch the faces and the sights."

The courtyard of Aisha's new home was quite similar to theirs, with an oven room and a pantry. Her mother-in-law ruled the courtyard with the help of the maid Suwaydan. "I don't have any work to do. If I even mention the kitchen, a tray of food is brought to me."

At that, Khadija could not keep from laughing. She commented, "You've finally got what you always wanted."

Kamal did not find much of interest in this discussion, but its general tone left him with the impression that Aisha was settling here permanently. He was alarmed and asked her, "Aren't you coming back to us?"

The room was filled by a voice answering, "She won't return to you, Mr. Kamal." It was Khalil Shawkat, who entered the room laughing. He strutted in, his medium-sized body arrayed in a white silk house shirt. He had a full, oval face with white skin. His eyes bulged out slightly, and his lips were full. His large head was topped by a narrow brow and thick black hair parted at the crown. The color and styling of his hair resembled that of al-Sayyid Ahmad. There was a good-humored, languid look in his eyes, possibly the result of his life of rest, relaxation, and fun. He bent over his mother-in-law's hand to kiss it, but she quickly withdrew it in embarrassment and discomfort, stammering her thanks. He greeted Khadija and Kamal and sat down – as Kamal put it later – as though he were one of them. The boy seized the opportunity presented by the bridegroom's conversation with the others to scrutinize his face for a long time. It was a stranger's face that had suddenly appeared in their lives, where it occupied a prominent position that entitled the man to be one of their closest relatives – in fact, Aisha's husband. Whenever Kamal thought of this new relationship, he remembered the loss of Aisha, just as surely as the thought of white brings to mind the color black. He looked at Khalil's face for a long time and repeated to himself Khalil's confident words: "She won't return to you, Mr. Kamal." Kamal disapproved of Khalil. He found him repulsive and resented him. These sentiments had almost gained control of Kamal when the man rose suddenly, returning shortly with a silver tray with different kinds of sweets. He gave Kamal a fine selection of the very best varieties. Khalil smiled pleasantly at Kamal, even though two of his teeth overlapped each other.

Then Widow Shawkat appeared, leaning on the arm of a man they assumed to be Khalil's older brother, since he looked so much like him. Their assumption was confirmed when the widow introduced him: "My son Ibrahim . . . don't you know him yet?" She noticed how upset Amina and Khadija were when greeting him and said with a smile, "We've been like a single family for a long time, but some of us are only now seeing each other for the first time . . . never mind!"

Amina understood that the woman was encouraging her and trying to make it easy for her. She smiled but felt anxious. She wondered whether her husband would consent to have her meet this man when she was not wearing a veil, even if he was as much a new member of the family as Khalil. Should she tell her husband about the encounter or avoid mentioning it in the interests of peace?

Ibrahim and Khalil could have been twins except for the difference in age, for their other differences seemed slight indeed. In fact, but for Ibrahim's short hair and twisted mustache, there would have been nothing to distinguish him from Khalil, even though Ibrahim was in his forties. His youthfulness and general appearance seemed not to have been affected by the passing years. Amina remembered what her husband had told her once about the late Mr. Shawkat, that he "looked twenty years or more younger than he really was." He had also said that he, "despite his good nature and nobility, was like an animal in never allowing thought to ruffle his serenity." How strange that Ibrahim looked thirty, even though he had married when young and had had two children by his wife, who had subsequently died along with their children. He had emerged unscathed and unharmed from this grim experience, returning to his mother to live the indolent, calm life of leisure of all the Shawkats.

Khadija amused herself, whenever no one was watching her, by stealing glances at the brothers who resembled each other in amazing ways. Each had a full, oval face and wide protruding eyes. They were both portly and languid. These traits stirred Khadija's sense of irony, and she laughed about them to herself. She began to store up images in her memory that she could make use of at the coffee hour. Because of her propensity for sarcasm, she was prone to mischief and comedy. She searched carefully for a descriptive and critical epithet she could apply to them, like the ones she gave to her other victims, on a par with their mother's nickname, "the machine gun," inspired by the way her spit flew when she talked.

Glancing furtively at Ibrahim, Khadija was terrified to find his wide eyes looking at her. Peering out from beneath his thick eyebrows, they were examining her face with interest. She lowered her eyes in shame and confusion. She asked herself with alarm what he might infer from her look. Then she found herself thinking nervously about her appearance and the impression it would make on him. Would he ridicule her nose the way she had his corpulence and lassitude? She became engrossed in these anxious thoughts.

Even though he had been reunited with Aisha, Kamal was bored. They were being treated like guests. None of his wishes had been realized, except for the sweets he had been given. He sidled up to the bride and gestured to her that he wished to be alone with her. She rose and, taking his hand, left the room. She thought he would be satisfied to sit with her in the central living room, but he pulled her into the bedroom and slammed the door behind them. His face beamed and his eyes shone. He looked at her for a long time and then studied the room from corner to corner. He sniffed the new furniture fragrance which blended with a sweet aroma possibly left from the activities of the wedding perfumers. Then he looked at the comfortable bed and the pair of rose-colored cushions lying side by side at the point where the bedspread covered the pillows. He asked her, "What are they?"

She replied, "Two small pillows."

He asked, "Do you sleep on them?"

She said with a smile, "No, they're just for decoration."

He pointed at the bed and asked, "Where do you sleep?"

Still smiling, she answered, "Inside it."

As though he wanted to make certain whether her husband slept with her, he asked, "What about Mr. Khalil?"

Giving his cheek a gentle pinch, she said, "Outside."

Then he turned toward the chaise longue in amazement and went over to sit on it. He invited her to sit beside him and she did. He was soon lost in his memories. He had to lower his eyes to hide their uneasy look. His disquieting suspicions had been aroused by the intensity of his mother's attack on him after the wedding when he was confiding to her what he had seen through a hole in the door. He was tempted to tell Aisha his secret and ask her about it. This temptation contained an element of cruelty. Embarrassment and doubt prevented him from asking. He suppressed his desire, in spite of himself. He raised his clear eyes to look at her and smiled.

She smiled back and leaned toward him to kiss him. Then she rose. Her face was covered by a sweet smile when she said, "I've got to fill your pockets with chocolates."

44

THE BOYS massed near the door of the house and along the sidewalk by the historic cistern building were all yelling back and forth to each other. Among the screams of joy, Kamal's voice could be heard proclaiming, "I see the bride's car." He repeated that three times. Yasin, splendidly attired in his best clothes, left the group of men waiting at the entrance to the courtyard to stand in front of the door, facing toward al-Nahhasin. He caught sight of the bridal procession, which was advancing slowly, as though on parade.

At that hour so full of both happiness and dread, Yasin appeared steady and resolute, despite the eyes staring at him from inside the house and out, from above and below. He was charged with manliness and virility, and one factor that helped steady him was his sensation of being the focus of attention. He wrestled courageously with his internal discomfort so people would not think him unmanly. He may also have known that his father was out of sight, having withdrawn to a spot behind the group at the entrance composed of the male members of the families of the bride and bridegroom. Thus Yasin was in full control of himself when he saw the automobile decorated with roses that was bringing him his bride. The girl had been his wife for more than a month now, although he had not set eyes on her yet. Yasin's resolve was also strengthened by the hope forged by his dreams, which were thirsty for happiness and would not be satisfied with anything transitory.

The first automobile in the long line came to a halt in front of the house. Yasin prepared for the auspicious arrival. He hoped once more that he could see through the silk veil well enough to get a first look at the face of his bride. The door of the car was opened and out stepped a black maid in her forties. She was powerfully built and had gleaming skin and large eyes. He surmised on the basis of her confident and proud gestures that she was the servant selected to continue serving the bride in her new home. She moved aside to plant herself like a sentry and smile with pearly-white teeth before addressing Yasin in a resounding voice: "Come take your bride."

Yasin approached the door of the automobile and leaned partway inside. He saw the bride in her white garments sitting by two young ladies. He was greeted by the fragrance of a captivating perfume. Dazzled, he lost himself in the beautiful atmosphere. Although his eyes had not adjusted from the light outside and could scarcely discern anything, he held out his arm. The bride's shyness restrained her, and she made no movement. The girl to her right intervened to take the bride's hand and place it on his arm. She whispered merrily to her, "Take heart, Zaynab."

They entered the house side by side, but because of her modesty she held a large fan of ostrich feathers between them to hide her head and neck. Passing between two rows of male guests, they crossed the courtyard. They were followed by the women from her family, who let out their trilling shrieks of joy, paying no attention to the presence nearby of al-Sayyid Ahmad. Thus joyful cries rang out in this silent house for the first time, and the tyrannical master was present to hear them. If the members of his household were astonished, it was an astonishment mixed with delight and even a trace of innocent and merry malice, which revived their spirits after his stern and weighty decree that there would be no shouts of joy, no singing, and no entertainment. The wedding night of his eldest son was to be just like any other night.

Amina, Khadija, and Aisha exchanged smiling but quizzical looks. They crowded up against the peephole in the window grille overlooking the courtyard to observe al-Sayyid Ahmad's reaction. They saw him talking and laughing with Mr. Muhammad Iffat. Amina murmured, "All he can do tonight is laugh, no matter what he notices that he doesn't like."

Umm Hanafi seized this golden opportunity to slip her barrel-like figure in among the ladies doing the trilling. She let loose with a powerful, ringing cry that drowned out all the others. With it, she sought to make up for all the opportunities for merriment and delight during the engagements of Aisha and Yasin that had been lost because of the dread house rules. She came upstairs to be with the ladies and trilled until they were dying from laughter. She told them, "Give a trill of joy even if it's the only time in your life. . . . He won't know tonight who's doing it."

After escorting his bride to the door of the women's quarters, Yasin returned and came upon Fahmy, who had an apprehensive and uneasy smile on his lips, possibly because of this forbidden but splendid racket. He was peeking furtively at his father. Then he looked back at his brother and laughed briefly in a halfhearted way. Yasin reacted indignantly and asked, "What's wrong with enlivening a wedding night with gaiety and cries of joy? How would it have harmed him to hire a female vocalist or a male singer?"

The family had wanted to have a singer, but they had found no way to express this wish, although Yasin had encouraged Mr. Muhammad Iffat to intervene with his father. Al-Sayyid Ahmad had declined. He had refused to allow any music at the wedding. The joys of the evening would be confined to a sumptuous dinner.

Yasin continued sorrowfully: "I won't have anyone to provide music for a real bridal procession tonight. I'll never have another chance. I'll enter the bridal chamber without any send-off, songs, or tambourines. I might as well be a dancer trying to wiggle his torso without a percussion accompaniment."

A naughty, cheerful smile could be seen in his eyes when he added, "There's no doubt that the only place our father can tolerate women entertainers is in their own homes."

Kamal remained for a time on the top floor, which had been prepared to receive the women guests. Then, in search of Yasin, he went down to the first floor, where the male guests were being entertained. He found his brother in the courtyard inspecting the mobile kitchen the caterer had set up. Kamal approached him happily, proud of having carried out the mission his brother had entrusted to him. He told him, "I did just what you said. I followed the bride to her room and examined her after she removed the veil from her face."

Yasin took him aside and asked with a smile, "So? . . . How's she built?"

"Her build's like Khadija's."

Yasin laughed. "Nothing wrong with that. . . . Did you like her as much as Aisha?"

"Of course not. . . . Aisha's much prettier."

"A pox on your house. Do you mean to say she looks like Khadija?"

"Of course not. She's prettier than Khadija."

"A lot prettier?" Yasin shook his head thoughtfully and ordered the lad impatiently, "Tell me what you liked about her."

"Her nose is small, like Mama's. . . . Her eyes are like Mama's too."

"And then?"

"She has a fair complexion. Her hair is black. She has a beautiful fragrance."

"Praise God. May our Lord be gracious to you." Yasin imagined that the boy was struggling with a desire to say something more. He said to him somewhat anxiously, "Tell everything. Don't be afraid."

"I saw her take out a handkerchief and blow her nose." Kamal twisted up his lips in disgust, as though he thought it terrible that a bride at the height of her charms should do such a thing.

Yasin could not keep himself from laughing. He said, "Up to this point, everything's great. May our Lord make everything that follows good too." He cast a despairing look at the courtyard, which was empty except for the caterer and his assistants and a few children. He thought there should have been some decorations and a tent where musicians could perform for the guests. Who had decreed it should be this way? His father . . . the man who devoted his energies to buffoonery, rowdiness, and music. What a strange man he was to sanction forbidden forms of entertainment for himself while denying his family legitimate enjoyments. Yasin began to imagine his father the way he had seen him in Zubayda's room, with his glass of wine and the lute. Before he knew it, a strange thought jumped into his mind. Although it was extremely clear to him now, it had never occurred to him before. He saw a similarity between his father's character and that of his own mother. Both of them were sensual and pleasure-seeking. They recklessly ignored conventions. Perhaps if his mother had been a man she would have been just as enamored of wine and music as his father. The relationship between them had ended quickly, because a man like him could not stand a woman like her, and vice versa. In fact, married life would have been impossible for his father, if he had not happened upon his current wife. Yasin laughed, but his dismay at this strange idea robbed his laughter of any delight. "I know now who I am. I'm nothing but the son of these two sensual people. It wouldn't have been possible for me to turn out any other way."

The next moment he asked himself whether he had been mistaken when he neglected to invite his mother to the wedding. He wondered about it, even though he remained convinced he had done the right thing. His father had probably been trying to ease his conscience when he offered a few nights before the wedding: "I think you ought to inform your mother. If you want to, you can invite her to the wedding party." Yasin assumed he had spoken with his tongue, not his heart. He could not imagine that his father would want him to go to the residence inhabited by that miserable man his mother had married after all her many other spouses. He would not want Yasin to try to ingratiate himself with her, inviting her to his wedding while that man watched. Neither the wedding nor any other happiness he could attain in this world would make him reestablish the link that had been severed between him and that woman . . . that scandal . . . that disgraceful memory.

At the time he had merely replied to his father, "If I truly had a mother she would be the first person I would invite to my wedding."

Yasin suddenly noticed that the children in the courtyard were staring at him and whispering to each other. He singled out some of the little girls and asked them in a jovial but loud voice, "Are you already dreaming of marriage, girls?"

He headed for the door of the women's quarters and remembered Khadija's mocking words from the day before: "Don't let embarrassment get the better of you tomorrow when you're with the guests. Otherwise, they'll realize the bitter truth that it's your father who's paying your wedding costs, your dowry, and all the expenses of the party. Keep circulating and don't stop. Move from room to room among your guests. Laugh with this one and talk to that one. Go upstairs and come back down. Inspect the kitchen. Yell and shout. Perhaps you'll make people think you're really the man of the evening and its master."

Yasin laughed as he went on his way. He intended to follow her sarcastic advice. He strutted among the guests with his tall and massive body. He was exceptionally elegant, attractive, good-looking, and in the prime of his youth. He went back and forth and up and down, even if there was no need for it. All this activity dispelled any doubts he might have had. His soul became immersed in the charms of the evening.

When Yasin thought about his bride, a bestial tremor passed through his body. Then he remembered the last night, a month before, that he had spent with the lute player Zanuba. He had informed her of his impending marriage and told her he was saying goodbye to her.

She had screamed in a sham rage, "You son of a bitch! . . . You kept the news secret until you got what you wanted. The boat you're leaving on is better than the one coming here. You deserve to be beaten a thousand times with a slipper, you bastard." Zanuba no longer meant anything to him, nor did any other woman. He had lowered the curtain on that side of his life forever. He might return to drinking, because he thought his desire for that would not die, but as for women, he could not imagine his eyes straying when he had a beauty at his disposal. His bride was a renewable resource and a spring of water for the wild thirst that had troubled his existence so frequently.

Yasin went on to imagine what life had in store for him that night and the following ones, for the next month and the next year, for the rest of his life. His face was radiant with delight at his good fortune. Fahmy noticed that with an eye filled with curiosity, calm happiness, and not a little regret.

Kamal, who had been into everything, suddenly appeared. With joy at the good news visible in his face, he informed Yasin, "The caterer told me that there's more dessert than will be needed for the guests. There'll be lots left over."

45

WITH THE addition of Zaynab, the coffee hour acquired a new face, one glowing with youth and the joy of being married. The three rooms adjoining the parents' bedroom on the top floor had been outfitted with the bride's furniture. Otherwise, Yasin's marriage brought little change to the general organization of the house in terms of either domestic politics or household management. The residents remained subservient in every sense of the word to the authority and will of al-Sayyid Ahmad. Housekeeping remained a subsidiary department under the direction of the mother, just as it had been before the marriage. The real change was emotional and mental, and it was easily observable. It would have been hard for Zaynab to occupy the position of wife of the eldest son, or for her and her husband to unite together with the other members of the family in a single household, unless there had been a significant development of the family's emotions and sentiments.

The mother regarded Zaynab with a mixture of hope and caution. What sort of person was this girl who was destined to live with her for a long time, possibly for the rest of her life? What was she hiding behind her tender smile? On the whole, she welcomed the girl the way a landlord greets a new tenant, warily hoping for the best.

Khadija, notwithstanding the flattering comments she and Zaynab exchanged, began to focus on Zaynab her penetrating eyes, which were naturally inclined toward sarcasm and suspicion. She probed for defects and shortcomings with an eagerness inspired by her resentment and hidden annoyance against Zaynab for joining the household and marrying her brother. When Zaynab stayed in her chambers the first few days after the marriage, Khadija asked her mother in the oven room, "Do you suppose the oven room isn't good enough for her?"

Although her mother found some relief for her own anxious thoughts in Khadija's attack on Zaynab, she defended the girl and replied, "Be patient. She's still a bride starting out on a new life."

In a tone revealing her disapproval, Khadija asked, "Who decreed that we should be servants for brides?"

Her mother asked, as though putting the question to herself, "Would you prefer her to have her own kitchen?"

Khadija cried out in protest, "If the money were her father's and not my father's, that would be all right. But I think she ought to work with us."

A week after the wedding when Zaynab decided to assume some of the tasks in the oven room, Khadija's heart did not welcome this step toward cooperation. She began to observe the bride's work with critical attention to detail and told her mother, "She hasn't come to assist you but to exercise what she may claim is her right." Khadija would remark sarcastically, "We hear so frequently about the Iffat family and how elite they are. They don't eat what other people do.... Have you found anything extraordinary about her cooking?"

One day Zaynab suggested that she would make a "Circassian" chicken dish with hazelnut sauce, since it was a favorite at her father's table. That was the first time this Circassian dish was served in al-Sayyid Ahmad's home, where it garnered everyone's admiration, and most especially Yasin's. Their mother felt a twinge of jealousy. Khadija became frantic and made fun of it: "They said, 'Circassian,' and we said, 'The longer a teacher lives, the more he learns,' but what did we see? Rice and sauce strategically arranged and a taste that's neither here nor there. It's like a bride who's shown to the bridegroom in her wedding procession, splendidly attired, with glittering jewels, but when she takes off her gown, she's just an ordinary girl predictably composed of flesh, bones, and blood."

Scarcely two weeks after the wedding Khadija said in the hearing of her mother, Fahmy, and Kamal that although the bride had a fair complexion and a moderate share of good looks, she was just as dull as her Circassian chicken. She said that even though she was then mastering the dish with her customary proficiency.

Some comments escaped from Zaynab – innocently, since the time for malice had not yet arrived – that stirred up their thoughts and cast a shadow of doubt over her. Whenever an opportunity arose she bragged about her Turkish origin, although she did so politely and graciously. She also enjoyed telling them what she had seen when she rode in her father's carriage and accompanied him to the gardens or other places of innocent recreation. All this talk startled and alarmed the mother. She was amazed by that kind of life, which she was hearing about for the first time. She had not thought such things possible and privately disapproved of this strange freedom more than words could tell. Zaynab's pride in her Turkish origin, no matter how polite and innocent, displeased Amina a great deal, because despite her humble and unobtrusive character, she was very proud of her father and her husband. She felt that because of them she had attained the highest possible rank, but she suppressed her reactions. Zaynab always received her full attention and a polite smile.

If the mother's desire to keep the peace had not been so strong, Khadija would have exploded angrily with unfortunate results. She revealed her resentment in more covert ways that were not a threat to the peace. For example, since she could not openly state her opinion about the carriage rides, she exaggerated the way she showed her astonishment. Gazing at the face of the speaker, she would cry out, "Oh, my goodness!" She might strike her breast and exclaim, "The men passing by saw you walking in the park?" Again, she might say, "My Lord, I would never have thought that possible," or other similar things. Her words did not express any disapproval, but her dramatic or melodramatic tone implied more than one meaning, like the scolding tone assumed by a father who is reciting from the Qur'an and saying his prayers when he notices that his son nearby has acted improperly or impolitely, for that is easier than breaking off his prayers and scolding his child openly.

To relieve her rage, as soon as Khadija was alone with Yasin she told him, "Goodness gracious, what a promenader your wife is."

He laughingly answered, "That is the Turkish fashion. It's hard for you to understand."

The word "Turkish" reminded her of Zaynab's boasts of her ancestry, which Khadija found hard to bear. She commented, "By the way, the lady of the house brags a lot about her Turkish ancestry. Why? Because the grandfather of the grandfather of the grandfather of the grandfather of her grandfather was Turkish? Watch out, brother. Turkish women end up going crazy."

Countering her sarcasm, he replied, "I prefer insanity to a person who has a nose that would drive anyone with good taste crazy."

The battle brewing between Khadija and Zaynab was evident to members of the family with any ability to predict the future. Fahmy warned Khadija to watch her tongue lest the other girl learn of her rude remarks. He also secretly cautioned Kamal, who kept flitting back and forth between them and the bride like a butterfly carrying pollen from flower to flower. But Fahmy could not have foreseen, no more than anyone else in the family, that fate was at work to separate the two girls.

Widow Shawkat and Aisha paid the house a visit crowned with an ending none of them could have imagined. In the presence of Khadija, the old lady addressed the mother: "Mrs. Amina, I have come to visit you today in order to ask for Khadija's hand for my son Ibrahim."

It was a joy that came with no warning, although they had awaited it for an unbearably long time. The woman's words were beautiful poetry to the mother's ears. Amina could not remember any previous statement ever bringing such a balm of comfort and peace to her breast. She was almost giddy with happiness when she replied in a trembling voice, "Khadija's no more mine than yours. She's your daughter. She will certainly find twice as much happiness in your custody as she has in her father's home."

This happy conversation went on for some time, but Khadija's attention drifted away. She was in a kind of daze. She lowered her eyes from modesty and confusion. The mocking spirit that so often gleamed in her eyes abandoned her. She became uncommonly meek and yielded to the current of her thoughts. The proposal had come as a surprise, and what a surprise. Troublesome when absent, it was incredible now that it had taken place. But her happiness was almost submerged by a wave of consternation. "To ask for Khadija's hand for my son Ibrahim. . . ." What had come over him? Despite his languor, which had aroused her ridicule, he had a handsome face. He was a prince among men. So what had come over him?

"It's fortunate that the two sisters will be united in one home."

The voice of Widow Shawkat confirmed the reality and vouched for it. There was no doubt about it, then. Ibrahim had as much money and status as Khalil. The fates had reserved a fine destiny for her. How unhappy she had been when Aisha married first. She had not known that Aisha's marriage was destined to open the doors of good fortune for her.

"How lovely it is that the sister-in-law will also be a sister. This will remove one of the basic causes for headaches in a family." She laughed and continued: "That leaves only her mother-in-law and I think she'll be easy to deal with."

"Since her sister-in-law is her sister, then her mother-in law will be a mother for her."

The two mothers continued to compliment each other. Khadija loved the old lady who brought her these glad tidings as much as she had hated her when she came to ask for Aisha's hand. Maryam must be told the news today. She could not bear to put it off. She did not know the reason for this insistent desire. Perhaps it was Maryam's comment about Aisha's engagement: "How would it have hurt them to wait until you got engaged?" At the time Khadija had been suspicious of the question's apparent innocence.

When the Shawkat family had left, Yasin wanted to tease and provoke Khadija. He remarked, "As soon as I saw Ibrahim Shawkat I told myself, 'This ox of a man, who looks incapable of distinguishing between black and white, will probably choose a wife like Khadija someday.'"

Khadija smiled briefly but said nothing. Yasin cried out in astonishment, "Have you finally learned manners and modesty?" Even as he teased her, his face revealed his pleasure and delight for her.

Nothing spoiled their good cheer until Kamal asked anxiously, "Is Khadija going to leave us too?"

To console him and herself, his mother replied, "Sugar Street's not far away."

Kamal could not express what he felt with complete freedom until he was alone with his mother that night. He sat on the sofa facing her and asked in a voice of protest and reproach, "What's happened to your mind, Mother? . . . Are you going to give up Khadija the way you abandoned Aisha?"

She explained to him that she was not abandoning either of the girls but was pleased by what would make them happy. As though pointing out something she had overlooked before and was about to overlook again, he warned, "She'll leave us too. Perhaps you think she'll return, the way you did with Aisha. But she won't return. If she visits you, it'll be as a guest. The moment she's drunk her coffee, she'll tell you goodbye. I say quite frankly that she'll never return."

Then, cautioning and preaching at the same time, he continued: "You'll find yourself alone with no companion. Who will help you sweep and dust? . . . Who will assist you in the oven room? Who will keep us company in the evening? . . . Who will make us laugh? You won't find anyone except Umm Hanafi, who will see the way clear to steal all our food."

She explained to him that happiness has a price. He protested, "Who told you marriage brings happiness? I can tell you that there's absolutely no happiness in marriage. How can anyone be happy when separated from his mother?"

He added fervently, "And she doesn't want to get married any more than Aisha did before her. She told me that one night in her bed."

His mother argued that a girl needs to get married. Then he could not keep himself from saying, "Who says a girl's got to go to the home of strangers? What will she do if that other man makes her sit in a chaise longue and takes her chin in his hand too and . . .?"

She scolded him and ordered him not to talk about things that did not concern him. Then he struck his hands together and warned her, "You can do what you want . . . but you'll see."

That evening Amina was kept awake by her happiness as though by brilliant moonlight. She stayed awake until after midnight when her husband returned and she told him the good news. Despite his strange ideas about the marriage of a daughter, he received the news with such delight that it cleared the hangover from his head. But he frowned suddenly and asked, "Has Ibrahim been allowed to see her?"

The woman asked herself why his delight, which was so rare, could not have lasted longer than half a minute. She mumbled anxiously, "His mother . . ."

He interrupted her angrily, "Has Ibrahim been allowed to see her?"

For the first time that evening her happiness deserted her, and she said, "Once when we were in Aisha's apartment he entered the room as a member of the family. I did not see anything wrong with that."

He observed furiously, "But I didn't know about it."

Everything pointed to an evil outcome. Would he deal the girl's future a fatal blow? She could not keep the tears from welling up in her eyes. Ignoring his sullen anger, she said, before she knew what she was doing, "Master, Khadija's life is in your custody. It's hardly likely that fortune will smile at her a second time."

He threw her a harsh look and began to snarl, growl, mutter, and grumble as though his anger had reduced him to communicating with the sounds his first ancestors had used. But he said nothing more. He had perhaps intended from the start to agree but had refused to yield until he had expressed his anger, like a politician who attacks an opponent, even though supporting the same goal, in order to defend his principles.

46

DURING HIS honeymoon Yasin devoted all his energy to his new life as a married man. Since his wedding coincided with his summer holiday, he did not have to depart for work during the day. At night he did not go out in search of entertainment and left the house only for a pressing necessity like buying a bottle of cognac. Otherwise, he found no employment, meaning, or identity outside the conjugal framework. He poured himself into marriage with all the energy, enthusiasm, and optimism of a man who imagined he was carrying out the initial steps of a huge program for carnal enjoyment that would last day after day, month after month, and year after year.

During the final ten days of the month, he realized he had been a little too optimistic in at least one respect. A flaw he did not completely understand had appeared in his life. He was extremely perplexed and for the first time ever suffered from that illness native to the human soul known as boredom. He had not experienced it before when he was with Zanuba or even with the woman who sold doum palm fruit, because they had not been his property the way Zaynab was. She was securely settled in his own home. This secure, peaceful form of ownership inspired a kind of apathy. Marriage's external appearance was beguiling, tempting enough to die for, but inside it was so staid and sedate that a person might become indifferent or disgusted. It was like a trick chocolate presented on April Fools' Day with garlic stuffed inside the sweet coating. What a calamity it was that the intoxication of body and soul should be lost in a self-conscious, mechanical, planned, repetitive, and cold habit that destroyed the emotion and novelty of married love. In the same manner a tranquil, spiritual vision may be transformed into a verbal prayer inattentively repeated by rote.

The young man began to wonder what had happened to his rebellious nature and what had calmed his demons. Why was he satiated? How had that happened? Where had the temptation gone? Where was the old Yasin and where was Zaynab? Where were the dreams? Was marriage itself at fault or was he? What if months went by followed by more months? Yasin had not lost all desire for his wife, but it was no longer the desire of a fasting person for a tasty delicacy. He was appalled to find his desire becalmed when he had expected it to flourish. His perplexity was increased by the fact that the girl showed no comparable reaction. As a matter of fact, her vivacity and desire had increased. When he would think that sleep had become a necessity after such a long period of activity, before he knew it her leg would be flung over his as if of its own accord. So he told himself, "How amazing . . . she's the one who's realizing my dreams for our marriage."

In addition to all this, although he had enjoyed it at first, now when he embraced her he was embarrassed, because it ultimately made him lose himself in memories to which he thought he had said farewell forever. Zanuba and his other women rose from the depths to dominate his mind the way objects thrown into the sea float to the surface when a storm is over. He had entered the nest of matrimony with no leftover desires and a heart full of good intentions, but after comparing, contrasting, and pondering his alternatives, he became convinced that a bride was not the magic key to the world of women. He did not know how he could really be faithful to the good wishes with which he had strewn the path of matrimony. It seemed that at least one aspect of his naïve dreams would be difficult to achieve – namely, his assumption that in the arms of his wife he would have no need for anything else in the world and would be able to remain in her shelter his whole life. That had merely been a dream inspired by his innocent lust. He would find it increasingly difficult to cut himself off from his former world and habits, and what need was there for that? He had to search for some method or other to escape frequently from himself, his thoughts, and his failure. Similarly, when even an excellent singer spends too much time on the instrumental preludes to his vocal improvisations, the listener feels a desire for the main part of the piece to begin.

Liberation from his prison would also give him a chance to meet with some of his married friends. Perhaps they had reassuring answers to the perplexing questions that troubled him, even if not a panacea for every malady. From this moment on, how could he believe a panacea existed? The best thing would be for him to stop trying to make long-range plans that would soon come to naught and mock his vision. He should satisfy himself with proceeding in life a step at a time so that he could see where he was ending up. He would begin by acting on a suggestion that she, his wife, had made for them to go out together.

To the family's amazement, Yasin and his wife left the house without informing anyone of their destination, even though they had both been chatting with them that evening. Because of the lateness of the hour and because they were residents of the home of al-Sayyid Ahmad, their excursion seemed a strange event and aroused various suspicions. Khadija did not hesitate to summon Nur, the bride's servant, to ask her what she knew about her mistress's outing. With great simplicity, the maid answered in her ringing voice, "Lady, they went to Kishkish Bey."

Khadija and her mother both exclaimed at the same time, "Kishkish Bey!"

They were not unfamiliar with that name, which had taken the world by storm. Everyone and his brother were singing the songs about this vaudeville character created by al-Rihani, but all the same he seemed as distant as a legendary hero or the zeppelin, that Satan of the skies. For Yasin to take his wife to see him was an extremely different matter. They might as well have been hauled into court. The mother cast her eyes back and forth between Khadija and Fahmy and asked with apparent fear, "When will they return?"

With an inane smile decorating his lips, Fahmy replied, "After midnight, perhaps a little before dawn."

Their mother excused the servant and waited until her footsteps could no longer be heard. Then she blurted out emotionally, "What's come over Yasin? He sat here with us in full control of his senses. . . . Has he stopped worrying about what his father will think?"

Khadija said resentfully, "Yasin's too smart to plan a trip like this. It's not sense that he lacks, but he's too meek. That doesn't suit a man. I'll cut off my arm if she isn't the one who goaded him into it."

Motivated by a desire to lighten the tense atmosphere, although he instinctively shunned his brother's recklessness, Fahmy said, "Yasin's always liked the theater."

His defense of Yasin increased Khadija's anger. She burst out: "It's not Yasin and his likes or dislikes that concern us. He can love places of amusement all he wants or continue to stay out until dawn whenever he wants, but to take his cloistered wife with him is an idea that could not have originated with him. Perhaps it came up because it was obvious he wouldn't be able to resist, especially now that he's so docile, like a house cat in her arms. So far as I can tell, she would not think twice about this. Haven't you heard her describe her excursions with her father? If she had not inspired him to do it, he wouldn't have taken her with him to Kishkish Bey. What a scandal! . . . In these dark days when grown men hide at home like mice in their holes for fear of the Australians."

The incident had stirred everyone so deeply that, whether they supported it, opposed it, or were neutral, they kept commenting on it. Only Kamal followed the heated discussion with alert silence. He could not grasp the secret that had turned Kishkish Bey into a reprehensible crime meriting all this discussion and distress. Was not Kishkish the model for the little doll sold in the markets with a body that jumped around playfully, a laughing face with a thick beard, a loose gown, and a conical turban? Was he not the figure to whom those jolly songs were ascribed? He had memorized some of them to sing with his friend Fuad, who was the son of Jamil al-Hamzawi, the assistant to Kamal's father. Why were they attacking this pleasant character who was linked in Kamal's imagination with fun and mirth? Perhaps the reason for their distress was the fact that Yasin took his wife with him, not anything about Kishkish Bey himself. If that were so, he agreed with their alarm at Yasin's daring, especially since he could not forget the excursion he had made with his mother to see al-Husayn and the ensuing events. Yes, it would have been better for Yasin to go alone or to take Kamal, if he wanted a companion, particularly since Kamal was on his summer holiday and had done very well in the school examination. Before he knew it, he was moved to voice his thoughts: "Wouldn't it have been better for him to take me?"

His question broke into their conversation like a Western theme incorporated into a purely Eastern piece of music. Khadija commented, "From now on we'll know to excuse you for your lack of sense."

A laugh escaped from Fahmy. He observed, "The son of the goose is a good swimmer."

The proverb did not sound right to him once he said it, and the surprised stares from his mother and Khadija confirmed that it had not been well received. He realized his unintentional slip and, feeling upset and embarrassed, corrected himself: "The brother of the goose is a good swimmer.... That's what I meant to say."

Taken as a whole, their conversation betrayed Khadija's prejudice against Zaynab and the mother's fear of the consequences, although Amina did not divulge everything she felt. That evening she had learned things about herself she had not known before. She had frequently felt disappointed or uneasy with Zaynab but never to the point of hating or disliking her. She had blamed the problem on the girl's pride, whether or not it was justified. Today she was appalled to find Zaynab violating common decency and tradition. In Amina's opinion, Zaynab was arrogating to herself masculine prerogatives. She took exception to this conduct, precisely because she was a woman who had spent her life shut up inside her house, a woman who had paid with her health and well-being for an innocent visit to al-Husayn, the glory of the Prophet's family – not to Kishkish Bey. Her silent criticism was mixed with a feeling of bitterness and rage which she seemed to be rationalizing when she observed to herself, "Either that woman is punished too or life has no meaning."

Thus in one month of living with this new woman, Amina's pure, devout soul was soiled by rancor and resentment after a lifetime of earnestness, discipline, and fatigue during which her heart had known nothing but obedience, forgiveness, and serenity. When she retired to her room, she did not know whether she wished that God would conceal Yasin's crime, as she had stated in front of her children, or whether she hoped that he or, more appropriately, his wife would receive the scolding and punishment she merited. That night nothing in the world seemed to matter to her except preserving the family's traditions from being tampered with and defending them from the attack launched against them. Her moral fervor was keen enough to be cruel. She buried her normal, tender emotions deep inside herself in the name of sincerity, virtue, and religion, as an excuse for ignoring her troubled conscience. A dream may similarly

reveal suppressed drives in the name of freedom or some other
lofty principle.

Amina was in this determined state of mind when her husband
returned, but the sight of him sent shivers of fright up her spine.
She could not bring herself to speak. She listened to what he had to
say and answered his questions absentmindedly. Her heart was
pounding and she did not know how to express the thought raging
through her mind. As the minutes passed and bedtime
approached, a nervous desire to talk troubled her. She wished
with all her heart that the reality would reveal itself. If Yasin and his
wife returned before the father fell asleep, then al-Sayyid Ahmad
would learn firsthand about Yasin's reprehensible deed. The frivolous bride would be confronted by his opinion of her conduct,
without the mother having to interfere. That would no doubt
grieve her but also relieve her mind.

Anxiously and apprehensively, she listened for a long time for
someone to knock on the door. She waited minute after minute
until her husband yawned and told her in a relaxed voice, "Put out
the lamp."

With defeat at hand, she found her voice. In a soft but troubled
tone, she said as though thinking about it to herself, "It's late, and
Yasin and his wife aren't home yet."

Al-Sayyid Ahmad stared at her and asked in amazement, "His
wife? . . . Where did they go?"

The woman swallowed. She was afflicted by fear not only of her
husband but of herself as well. She found herself forced to answer,
"I heard the maid say they went to Kishkish Bey."

"Kishkish!"

His voice sounded loud and petulant. Sparks seemed to fly from
his eyes inflamed by alcohol. He proceeded to ask her question
after question, storming and snarling, until he felt wide awake
again. He refused to go to bed until the two reprobates returned.
He waited, seething with fury. His anger cast a shadow of terror
over her. She was as terrified as if she had been the guilty person.
She was consumed by regret for what she had said, regret that
descended on her immediately after she had revealed her secret.
She almost seemed to have spoken in order to regret it. She would
have given anything then, no matter how costly, to be able to
correct her error. She was merciless and accused herself of being
responsible for the evil that would occur. If she really wanted to

reform them rather than get revenge, should she not have covered up for them and waited till the next day to point out their error to them? She had intentionally yielded to malice. She had wanted something bad to happen. She had prepared for the young man and his bride a calamity they had never dreamed of and had brought down on herself remorse that was savagely eating away at her tormented heart. Although she was ashamed to mention His name, she prayed to God to be merciful to all of them. Each minute that passed made her feel worse.

She was roused by her husband's voice saying with bitter sarcasm, "Mr. Kishkish has arrived."

She listened carefully and looked out the open window to the courtyard. She heard grating as the main door was closed. Al-Sayyid Ahmad rose and left the room. She got up mechanically but remained frozen where she stood from cowardice and shame. Her heart pounded wildly until she heard his loud voice tell the new-comers, "Follow me to my room." She was terribly frightened and slipped away to escape.

Al-Sayyid Ahmad returned to his seat, followed by Yasin and Zaynab. Ignoring Yasin, he gave the girl a penetrating look and said firmly, but not coarsely or rudely, "Listen to me carefully, my little girl. Your father is like a brother to me, or even closer and dearer. You are my daughter just as much as Khadija and Aisha. I would never want to trouble your peace of mind, but there are matters that I cannot be silent about without committing what I consider an unforgivable crime. One of these is for a girl like you to stay out of her house until this hour of the night. Do not imagine that the presence of your husband excuses such perverse behavior, for a husband who demeans his honor to this degree is unfit to steady the person whom he has unfortunately been the first to shove. Since I am certain you are innocent or, rather, that your only offense was complying with his wishes, my hope is that you will assist me in reforming him by refusing to submit to his enticements again."

The girl was speechless and overwhelmed by astonishment. Although she had enjoyed a measure of freedom in her father's care, she could not work up the courage to argue with this man, not to mention oppose him. After living for a month in his home, her character had been infected with the virus of submission to his will, which terrified everyone in the house. Her conscience protested that her father himself had allowed her to accompany him to the cinema more than once. It was not right for this man to forbid her something that her husband allowed. She was satisfied that she had not done anything wrong or disgraceful. Her conscience told her this and more, but she was unable to speak a single word when faced by his eyes, which demanded obedience and respect, and his large nose, which when his head was tilted back looked like a revolver aimed at her. Her internal dialogue was concealed behind a façade of polite agreement, just as sound waves seem to hide inside the wireless receiver once it is turned off.

Before she knew what was happening, she heard him ask her, as though continuing his conversation, "Do you have any objection to what I have said?"

She shook her head in the negative and the word "no" was traced on her lips although she did not say it. So he told her, "We've agreed, then. You may retire to your room in peace."

She left the room with a pale face, and al-Sayyid Ahmad turned toward Yasin, who was looking at the ground. Shaking his head with great sorrow, he said, "The matter is extremely serious, but what can I do? You're no longer a child. If you were, I'd break your head. But, alas, you're a man and an employee and a husband too, even if you don't abstain from frivolous entertainments on account of your marriage. So what can I do with you? Is this the result of the education I've given you?" Then he continued even more sorrowfully: "What came over you? . . . Where's your manhood? . . . Where's your sense of honor? By God, I can scarcely believe what I've heard."

Yasin did not raise his head and did not speak. His father assumed that his silence showed he was afraid and felt he had been in error. He did not imagine that his son might be drunk. Yasin's apparent contrition was no consolation to him. The offense seemed too outrageous to be left without some decisive remedy, even though the former one, the stick, was out of the question. He would have to be firm or the family structure would be destroyed.

He said, "Don't you know that I forbid my wife to leave the house even if only to visit al-Husayn? How could you have given in to the temptation to take your wife to a bawdy show and stayed there with her until after midnight? You fool, you're propelling yourself and your wife into the abyss. What demon has hold of you?"

Yasin thought it best to seek refuge in silence, for fear his voice or his garrulousness would reveal his intoxication. This strategy seemed especially necessary since his mind, scoffing at his serious situation, insisted on stealing out of the room and shooting off to the far horizons, which to his drunken head appeared to be dancing at times and swaying at others. No matter how much his father's voice terrorized him, it could not silence the tunes the comedians had sung at the theater. They leapt to his mind, in spite of himself, like ghosts appearing to a frightened person at night, and whispered:

> I'll sell my clothes for a kiss
> From your creamy cheek, you Turkish delight;
> You, there, sweet as a tart,
> You're a pudding too or even smoother.

The song would be banished by his fear, only to bounce back.

His father became upset by his silence and shouted angrily, "Speak! Tell me what you think. I'm determined that this incident will not slide by."

Afraid that silence would prove harmful, Yasin abandoned it fearfully and uneasily. Making a valiant effort to gain control of himself, he said, "Her father treated her somewhat leniently." Then he added hastily, "But I'll admit I made a mistake."

Overlooking the last phrase, al-Sayyid Ahmad screamed angrily at him, "She's no longer in her father's house. She must respect the rules of the family to which she now belongs. You're her husband and master. It's up to you to make her see things the way you want. Tell me: Who's responsible for her going with you: you or her?"

Despite his intoxication, Yasin was aware of the trap laid for him, but fear forced him to equivocate. He mumbled, "When she learned of my intention to go out, she begged me to let her go too."

Al-Sayyid Ahmad beat his hands together and said, "What kind of man are you? . . . The proper reply to her would have been a blow. Only men can ruin women, and not every man is capable of being a guardian for them." (Qur'an 4:34.)

Then, furious at his son, he said, "You take her to a place where women dance half naked?"

In his imagination Yasin saw once more the scenes his father's appearance at the head of the stairs had spoiled. The tunes rang through his head again: "I'll sell my clothes . . . "

Before Yasin knew what was happening the man was threatening him: "This house has rules which you know. Reconcile yourself to respecting them if you wish to remain here."

47

AISHA TOOK charge of beautifying Khadija for her wedding and accomplished the task with unparalleled zeal and extraordinary skill, as though she felt the adornment of Khadija was in every way the most rewarding accomplishment of her life. Khadija really looked like a bride and prepared herself to move to the bridegroom's house. In keeping with her custom of downplaying the value of services other people performed for her, she claimed that the credit should go to her plumpness more than to anything else. Moreover, her beauty was no longer the focus of her concern, since a man who had happened to see her himself had asked for her hand.

Despite all the manifestations of happiness surrounding her, they were not able to obliterate her pulsing homesickness at the prospect of the impending separation. It was exactly what one would expect of a girl whose heart pounded with love for nothing so much as for her family and house – from her parents, whom she adored, to the chickens, hyacinth beans, and jasmine. Not even marriage itself, for which she had longed and yearned so impatiently, was able to diminish the bitterness of parting. Before anyone had asked for her hand she had seemed oblivious to her love and respect for the house. Any minor vexation would suffice to mask her authentic feelings, for love is like health. It is taken lightly when present and cherished when it departs. With her mind put at ease about her future, her heart refused to make the change from one life to another without intense anguish that seemed an attempt to atone for some offense or a stingy reluctance to part with something of value.

Kamal gazed at her silently. He no longer asked, "Will you return?" He had learned that a girl who marries does not return. He murmured to his sisters, "I'll visit both of you frequently in the afternoon when school lets out."

Although they indicated they would welcome his visits, Kamal was no longer beguiled by false hopes. He had visited Aisha often without ever finding the old Aisha. In her place he found another woman, all decked out, who received him with such exaggerated affection that he felt like a stranger. Even if he was alone with her for a moment, her husband would soon join them. Khalil did not leave the house and amused himself with various pastimes like smoking his cigarettes or water pipe or strumming his lute. Khadija would be no better than Aisha. The only companion he would have left in the house would be Zaynab, and she was not as affectionate to him as she should be, unless his mother was watching. Then she seemed to try to ingratiate herself with Mrs. Amina by being nice to him. Whenever the mother left, Zaynab would ignore him, as though he were invisible.

Although Zaynab did not feel she would be losing a dear friend with the departure of Khadija, she disapproved of the quiet and serious atmosphere enveloping the wedding day. She used that as a pretext for expressing some of the resentment and rage she harbored against the domineering spirit of al-Sayyid Ahmad. She observed sarcastically, "I've never seen a house like yours where what's licit is forbidden.... What's the wisdom of that?" Since Zaynab did not feel like saying goodbye to Khadija without a polite word, she praised her abilities highly and said she was a good homemaker who would be a credit to her husband.

Aisha agreed with that and added, "The only thing wrong with her is her tongue. Haven't you experienced it, Zaynab?"

Zaynab could not help laughing. She replied, "Praise God, I haven't, but I've heard it used against other people."

Everyone laughed, and Khadija was the first. Then they saw suddenly that the mother was trying to listen to something. She said, "Hush." They all stopped laughing immediately. They could hear people shouting outside.

Khadija said at once in alarm, "Al-Sayyid Ridwan has died."

Maryam and her mother had excused themselves from the wedding because of the acute condition of Mr. Muhammad Ridwan. It was not strange, then, that Khadija should infer from the clamor that he had died. The mother rushed out of the room. After a few minutes she returned to say with great sorrow, "Shaykh Muhammad Ridwan has indeed passed away.... What an awkward situation."

Zaynab said, "Our excuse is as obvious as the sun. It's no longer in our power to postpone the wedding or to keep the bridegroom from celebrating his special night in his house, which, praise God, is far away. What more can they expect from you than this profound silence?"

Khadija, though, was lost in other thoughts that cast fear in her heart. She saw an evil portent in this sad news. She murmured as though to herself, "O Gracious Lord. . . ."

Her mother read her thoughts and became upset too, but she refused to yield to this uninvited emotion or to allow her daughter to do so. Pretending to play down the importance of the coincidence, she commented, "We should not second-guess God's decree. Life and death are in His hands. Looking for evil omens is the work of Satan."

Yasin and Fahmy joined the assembled women in the bride's room once they had finished dressing. They told the mother that al-Sayyid Ahmad had gone to represent the family, in view of the pressure of time. He would bear the necessary condolences to the family of al-Sayyid Ridwan.

Yasin looked at Khadija and said with a laugh, "Al-Sayyid Ridwan refused to remain in this world once you decided to move out of our neighborhood."

She responded with a pale smile that gave no indication of her feelings. He began to examine her carefully and nod his head in approval. He sighed and remarked, "Whoever said, 'Dress up a reed and you can make it look like a bride,' was right."

She frowned to indicate she was not prepared to banter with him. She brushed him off: "Be quiet. I don't think it's a good omen that al-Sayyid Ridwan has died on my wedding day."

He laughed and said, "I don't know which of you is more to blame." He laughed some more and continued: "Don't worry about the man's death. What I'm afraid does not augur well is your tongue. My advice for you, which I never tire of repeating, is to soak your tongue in sweet syrup till it's fit for you to converse with the bridegroom."

At that, Fahmy said in a conciliatory way, "Putting aside the question of al-Sayyid Ridwan, your wedding day coincides with a blessing for which the world has been waiting a long time. Don't you know that the armistice has been announced?"

Yasin cried out, "I almost forgot about that. Your wedding isn't today's only miracle. Something happened for the first time in years. The fighting stopped and Kaiser Wilhelm surrendered."

Their mother asked, "Will the high prices and the Australians go away?"

Yasin laughed and replied, "Naturally . . . of course. The high prices, the Australians, and Miss Khadija's tongue."

Fahmy looked thoughtful. He remarked as if to himself, "The Germans were defeated. . . . Who would have imagined that? There's no longer any hope that Khedive Abbas or the nationalist leader Muhammad Farid will return. All hopes of restoring the Muslim caliphate have been lost. The star of the English continues in the ascendant while ours sets. We're in His hands."

Yasin said, "The two who got something from the war are the English and Sultan Fuad. Without it, the former could never have dreamed of getting rid of the Germans and the latter could never have dreamed of ascending the throne of Egypt." He was quiet for a moment and then continued merrily: "And there's a third party whose luck was equal to theirs. She's the bride who never dreamed of finding a husband."

Khadija cast him a threatening glance and remarked, "You insist on provoking me to say something vicious about you before I leave the house."

He backed down, saying, "I'd better ask for an armistice. I'm no mightier than Kaiser Wilhelm or Hindenburg." Yasin looked at Fahmy, who seemed more pensive than was appropriate for such a happy occasion. Yasin advised him, "Put politics behind you and prepare for music, delicious food, and drinks . . . ."

Although many thoughts were running through Khadija's mind and dream upon dream filled her heart, an insistent memory from just that morning almost obliterated all her other concerns because of its intense impact on her. Her father had invited her to a private meeting in honor of the day that was the beginning of a new life for her. He had received her with a graciousness and compassion that were a healing balm for the shame and terror that afflicted her, making it difficult for her to walk without stumbling. He had told her, with a tenderness that made a strange, unprecedented impression on her, "May our Lord guide your steps and grant you success and peace of mind. I cannot give you any better advice than to imitate your mother in every respect, both great and small."

He had given her his hand, which she kissed. Then she had left the room, so moved and touched she could scarcely see what was in front of her. She kept repeating to herself, "How gracious, tender, and compassionate he is . . . ."

With a heart filled with happiness she remembered his words: "Imitate your mother in every respect, both great and small."

Her mother had listened to her with a blushing face and flickering eyelids when Khadija asked, "Doesn't this mean he thinks you're the best model for the best kind of wife?" She had laughed and continued: "What a lucky woman you are! Who could have believed all this? It's like a happy dream. Where was all this beautiful affection stored away?" She had invoked God's blessing for him until her eyes flowed with tears.

Then Umm Hanafi came to inform them that the automobiles had arrived.

48

THE COFFEE hour lost Khadija just as it had previously lost Aisha, but Khadija left a void that remained unfilled. She seemed to have taken with her the session's spirit, plundered its vitality, and deprived it of the qualities of fun, mirth, and squabbling that were so important to it. As Yasin observed to himself, "In our conversations she was like the salt in food. Salt by itself doesn't taste good, but what taste is there to food without it?" Out of consideration for his wife, he did not make his opinion public. Although his hopes for marriage were so disappointed that he no longer sought a remedy at home, he at least worried about hurting her feelings, if only to keep her from growing suspicious of his spending night after night "at the coffee shop," as he claimed.

Yasin preferred mirth to seriousness so much that there was little of the serious about his character. Now he had lost the companion who inspired his jokes and taunted him in return. Thus all he could do was content himself with the few remnants of his traditional observance of the coffee hour. He sat on the sofa with his legs folded under him, sipped some coffee, and looked at the sofa opposite, where the mother, his wife, and Kamal were absorbed in meaningless chatter. For perhaps the hundredth time he was amazed at Zaynab's earnestness. He remembered that Khadija had accused her of being dull and was inclined to accept that opinion. He would open *al-Hamasa*, Abu Tammam's collection of ancient poems, or *The Maiden of Karbala*, a novel by Jurji Zaydan, and read to himself or relate to Kamal some of what he had read.

When he looked to his right, he found that Fahmy wanted desperately to talk. What would it be about? The nationalist leaders Muhammad Farid and Mustafa Kamil? Yasin had no idea, but it was clear that Fahmy was going to speak. Indeed, today, ever since returning from the Law School, he had looked like a sky threatening to rain. Should he stir him up? No, there was no need for that. Fahmy was acknowledging his glance with intense interest and staring at Yasin as though he was about to address him. He asked, "Don't you have any news?"

Fahmy asked him what news he had! "I've got too much news to count," he thought. "Marriage is just a big deception. After a few months as tasty as olive oil, your bride turns into a dose of castor oil. Don't feel sad that you didn't get to marry Maryam, you callow politician. Do you want some other news? I've got a lot, but it definitely wouldn't interest you. Even if I wanted to, I'm not courageous enough to reveal it in my wife's presence."

To his surprise, Yasin found he was reciting to himself a verse from the medieval poet al-Sharif al-Radi:

> *I have passionate messages I won't mention,*
> *But if we weren't being watched,*
> *I would have shared them with your mouth.*

Yasin asked Fahmy in turn, "What news do you mean?"

Fahmy replied excitedly, "Amazing news is spreading among the students. Today it was all we talked about. A delegation or 'wafd' composed of the nationalist leaders Sa'd Zaghlul Pasha, Abd al-Aziz Fahmy Bey, and Ali Sha'rawi Pasha went to the British Residency in Cairo yesterday and met with the High Commissioner, requesting that the British protectorate over Egypt be lifted and independence declared."

Yasin raised his eyebrows to show his interest. A look of astonished doubt appeared in his eyes. The name of Sa'd Zaghlul was not new to him, but there was little he could attach to it except some obscure memories connected with incidents he had forgotten long ago. They had made no appreciable impact on him emotionally, for he paid slight attention to public affairs. He was hearing about the other men for the first time. But the strangeness of their names was nothing compared with their strange action, if what Fahmy had said was true. How could anyone think of requesting independence for Egypt from the English immediately after their victory over the Germans and the Ottoman Empire? He asked his brother, "What do you know about them?"

With the resentment of a person who wished these men were members of the National Party, Fahmy replied, "Sa'd Zaghlul is Vice President of the Legislative Assembly and Abd al-Aziz Fahmy and Ali Sha'rawi are members of it. The truth is, I don't know anything else about the last two. As for Sa'd, I don't see anything wrong with him, based on what many of my fellow students who are nationalists tell me. They disagree about him a lot. Some of them think he has sold out totally to the English. Others acknowledge his outstanding qualities that make him worthy of being ranked with the men of the National Party. In any case, the step he took with his two colleagues was a magnificent act, and he's said to have been the instigator. He may be the only one left who could have done something like that, since the prominent members of the National Party have been banished, including their leader, Muhammad Farid."

Yasin tried to appear serious so his brother would not think he was making fun of his enthusiasm. As though wondering aloud, he repeated the words: "Requesting that the British protectorate over Egypt be lifted and independence declared . . . ."

"We also heard that they requested permission to travel to London to lobby for Egyptian independence. For that reason they met with Sir Reginald Wingate, the British High Commissioner for Egypt."

Yasin could no longer conceal his anxiety. His features revealed it, and he asked in a slightly louder voice, "Independence! . . . Do you really mean it? . . . What do you mean?"

Fahmy replied nervously, "I mean the expulsion of the English from Egypt: what Mustafa Kamil called an 'evacuation' when he advocated it."

What a hope! Yasin was not naturally inclined to seek out conversations about politics, but he would accept Fahmy's invitation in order to avoid upsetting his brother and to amuse himself with this novel form of entertainment. His interest in politics was aroused occasionally, but never to the point of enthusiasm. He may have shared his brother's hopes in a calm, passive way, but he had never demonstrated much interest in public affairs at any time in his life. His only goal was enjoyment of the good things in life and its pleasures. For this reason, he found it difficult to take Fahmy's statements seriously. He questioned his brother again: "Does this fall within the realm of possibility?"

Fahmy replied with a combination of enthusiasm and censure: "So long as there's life there's hope, brother."

This sentence, like the others before it, prompted Yasin's sarcasm, but pretending to be in earnest, he asked his brother, "How can we expel them?"

Fahmy thought for a moment and then said with a frown, "That's why Sa'd and his colleagues asked permission to journey to London."

The mother had been following their conversation with interest. She was concentrating her full attention on it to try to understand as much as she possibly could. She always did whenever the conversation turned to public affairs remote from domestic chatter. These matters intrigued her, and she claimed to be able to understand them. She did not hesitate to participate in such a discussion, if the opportunity arose, and was oblivious to the scorn mixed with affection that her opinions often provoked. Nothing could daunt her or prevent her from taking an interest in these significant matters, which she appeared to follow for the same reasons she felt compelled to comment on Kamal's lessons in religious studies or to debate what he related to her about geography and history in the light of her religious and folkloric information. Because of her serious attention, she had acquired some knowledge of Mustafa Kamil, Muhammad Farid, and "Our Exiled Effendi," the Khedive Abbas II. Her love for those men was doubled by their devotion to the cause of the Muslim caliphate, making them seem in her eyes, which were those of a person who judged men by their religious stature, almost like the saints of whom she was so fond. Thus when Fahmy mentioned that Sa'd and his colleagues were asking permission to travel to London, she suddenly asked, "Where in God's world is this London?"

Kamal answered her immediately in the singsong voice pupils use to recite their lessons: "London is the capital of Great Britain. Paris is the capital of France. The Cape's capital is the Cape . . . ." Then he leaned over to whisper in her ear, "London is in the land of the English."

His mother was overcome by astonishment and asked Fahmy, "They're going to the land of the English to ask them to get out of Egypt? This is in very bad taste. How could you visit me in my house if you're wanting to throw me out of yours?"

Her interruption annoyed the young man. He gave her a look that was smiling and critical at the same time, but she thought she would be able to convince him. So she added, "How can they ask them to leave our lands after they have been here all this long period. When we were born and you as well, they were already in our country. Is it humane for us to oppose them after this time we've spent living together as neighbors and to tell them bluntly, and in their country at that, to get out?"

Fahmy smiled in despair. Yasin guffawed, but Zaynab said seriously, "Where do they get the nerve to tell them that in their own country? Suppose the English kill them there. Who would know what happened to them? Haven't their soldiers made walking in the streets of Cairo far from home hazardous and uncertain? So what will happen to someone who storms into their country?"

Yasin wished he could encourage the two women to keep saying these naïve things in order to satisfy his thirst for fun, but he noticed Fahmy's annoyance and was apprehensive about making him angry. He turned toward his brother to continue their interrupted conversation: "They both have a point, although they might have expressed it more clearly. Tell me, brother, what can Sa'd do against a nation that now considers itself the unrivaled mistress of the world?"

The mother nodded her head in agreement, as though he had been addressing her. She stated: "The revolutionary leader Urabi Pasha was one of the greatest men and one of the most courageous. Sa'd and the others are nothing compared with him. He was in the cavalry, a fighting man. What did he get from the English, boys? They imprisoned him and then exiled him to a land on the other side of the world."

Fahmy could not keep himself from entreating her crossly, "Mother! . . . Won't you let us talk?"

She smiled in embarrassment, for she was anxious not to anger him. She changed her zealous tone, as though announcing by this change of tone a total shift of her opinion, and said gently and apologetically, "Sir, everyone who tries hard deserves some reward. So let them go there in God's safekeeping. Perhaps they'll win the sympathy of the great queen . . . ."

Without thinking about what he was doing, the young man asked her, "Which queen do you mean?"

"Queen Victoria, my son. Isn't that her name? . . . I often heard my father talk about her. She's the one who ordered Urabi banished, although according to what was said she admired his courage."

Yasin commented sarcastically, "If she banished the cavalry knight Urabi, she's even more liable to banish that old man Sa'd."

The mother said, "All the same, she's a woman and no doubt still bears in her chest a sensitive heart. If they speak to her the right way and know how to win her affection, she'll be sympathetic to their views."

Yasin was delighted by their mother's logic and the way she spoke about the historic queen as though she were talking about Maryam's mother or some other neighbor. He no longer felt like conversing with Fahmy. To encourage her to say more he asked, "Tell us what they should say to her?"

The woman, who was delighted by this request recognizing her political acumen, sat up straight. As was appropriate for a "conference," she began to think with an intensity apparent in the way her eyebrows were bunched together, but Fahmy did not give her time to think through the subject to the end. Tersely and indignantly he told her, "Queen Victoria died a long time ago. Don't wear yourself out pointlessly."

Yasin noticed then from the cracks between the shutters that it was starting to get dark outside. He realized it was time to excuse himself from the coffee hour to go off in search of entertainment. Since he was certain that Fahmy's thirst for conversation had not yet been quenched, he sought to apologize for his departure by putting his weight behind the news that had captured Fahmy's interest. Rising, he said, "They are men who doubtless know the danger of their undertaking. Perhaps they've worked out a winning strategy. Let's pray they succeed." He left the group after gesturing to Zaynab to follow and get his clothes ready.

Fahmy watched him depart with a look that was slightly hostile. He was angry that he had not found a partner to share the excitement of his ardent soul. Talk of national liberation excited great dreams in him. In that magical universe he could visualize a new world, a new nation, a new home, a new people. Everyone would be astir with vitality and enthusiasm. The moment his mind returned to this stifling atmosphere of lassitude, ignorance, and indifference, he felt a blazing fire of distress and pain that desired release from its confinement in order to shoot up to the sky. At that moment he wished with all his heart that the night would pass in the twinkling of an eye so he could be surrounded once more by a group of his fellow students. Then he would be able to quench his thirst for enthusiasm and freedom and ascend with their blazing zeal to that great world of dreams and glory.

Yasin had asked what Sa'd could do face to face with a country that now was justly considered the mistress of the world. Fahmy did not know exactly what Sa'd would do or what he could do himself, but he felt with all the power of his being that there was work to be done. Possibly there was no example in the real world, but he sensed it existed in his heart and blood. It had to manifest itself in the light of life and reality. Otherwise, life and reality would be in vain. Life would be a meaningless game and a bad joke.

49

THE STREET in front of al-Sayyid Ahmad's store did not look any different, for it was crowded with pedestrians, vehicles, and customers of the shops crammed along either side. Overhead there was a decorative, misty quality to the light. It was a pleasant November day and the sun was obscured by thin clouds. There were pure white billows resembling pools of light over the Qala'un and Barquq minarets. Nothing in the sky or on the ground seemed to differ from what al-Sayyid Ahmad saw every day, but the man's soul, those of the people connected to him, and perhaps those of everyone else too, had been exposed to a powerful wave of excitement almost making them lose control of themselves. Al-Sayyid Ahmad went so far as to say he had never experienced times like these when people were so united by a single piece of news, their hearts all beating with the same emotion.

Fahmy, usually silent in his father's presence, had initiated a conversation to tell him in great detail what he had learned about Sa'd's meeting with the High Commissioner. That same evening at al-Sayyid Ahmad's musical soiree, some of his friends had confirmed the truth of the information.

In his shop, customers who did not know each other had, on more than one occasion, plunged into a discussion of this meeting. That very morning, to his surprise, Shaykh Mutawalli Abd al-Samad had burst into the store after a long absence. He had not been satisfied to recite some verses from the Qur'an and receive the customary gift of sugar and soap but had insisted on recounting news of the visit as though making the first announcement.

When al-Sayyid Ahmad had asked him playfully what he thought the outcome of the visit would be, the shaykh had replied, "It's impossible! . . . It's impossible that the English will leave Egypt. Do you think they're crazy enough to leave the country without a fight? . . . There certainly would be fighting, and we would lose. So there's no way to expel them. Perhaps our men could succeed in getting the Australians sent away. Then order could be restored. Things would revert to the way they used to be. There'd be peace."

In these days of news and overflowing feelings al-Sayyid Ahmad was intensely receptive to infectious nationalist political aspirations. He was in such an expectant and attentive mood that he read with passionate enthusiasm the newspapers, which for the most part seemed as if they had been published in some other country where there was no passion or awakening. He greeted his friends with an inquisitive look that yearned to discover anything new they had learned.

It was in this fashion that he greeted Mr. Muhammad Iffat when he hurried into the store. The penetrating look and energetic motions of the man indicated that he was not just a casual visitor stopping by the store to drink some coffee or tell an amusing anecdote. The proprietor found that his friend's appearance matched his own anxious feelings, which were full of nationalist aspirations. While his friend was still making his way through the customers being served by Jamil al-Hamzawi, al-Sayyid Ahmad welcomed him: "It's a damp morning. What do you know, you lion?"

Mr. Muhammad Iffat sat down next to the desk. He smiled proudly, as though the proprietor's question, "What do you know?" – the same question he repeated whenever he met one of his friends -- was a recognition of Mr. Iffat's importance during these especially significant days, because of his ties of kinship to some influential Egyptian personalities. Mr. Iffat was also a link between the original group of merchants and those distinguished civil servants and attorneys who had joined them later. Of all these men, al-Sayyid Ahmad held the most cherished spot in his friend's affection because of his personality and disposition. Although the value of Mr. Iffat's connections had never been lost on his old friends who looked up to the civil servants and people with titles, it had increased now that fresh information was more important than water or food.

Mr. Iffat spread out a sheet of paper he had been holding in his right hand. Then he said, "Here's a new step. I'm no longer simply reporting news. I've become a messenger to bring you and other noble people this joyous authorization petition . . . ." Murmuring, "Read it," he offered the paper to him with a smile.

Al-Sayyid Ahmad took it and read aloud: "We, the signatories of this document, authorize Messrs. Sa'd Zaghlul Pasha, Ali Sha'rawi Pasha, Abd al-Aziz Fahmy Bey, Muhammad Ali Alluba Bey, Abd al-Latif al-Makabbati, Muhammad Mahmud Pasha, and Ahmad Lutfi al-Sayyid Bey, and those persons they choose to include in their number, to strive by all legal and peaceful means available to them to achieve the total independence of Egypt."

The proprietor's face was radiant when he read the names of the Egyptian delegation, for he had heard them mentioned when nationalism was discussed. He asked, "What does this paper mean?"

The man replied enthusiastically, "Don't you see these signatures? Put yours below them and get Jamil al-Hamzawi to sign too. This is one of the authorization petitions the delegation has had printed up for citizens to sign. They'll use them to show that they represent the Egyptian nation."

Al-Sayyid Ahmad took a pen and signed with a delighted gleam in his blue eyes. He smiled in a sensitive way that revealed his happiness and pride at having Sa'd and his colleagues represent him. Although those men had not been famous long, they had been welcomed into everyone's heart, arousing deep, suppressed desires. Their encouraging impact was like that of a new cure on a patient with an old malady that has resisted treatment, even though he is trying the medicine for the first time. The proprietor summoned al-Hamzawi, who also signed. Then he turned to his friend and remarked with intense interest, "It seems the matter is serious."

The man pounded on the edge of the desk with his fist and said, "Extremely serious. It's all progressing with forceful determination. Do you know what motivated the printing of these petitions? It's said that 'the man,' the British High Commissioner, asked in what capacity Sa'd and his colleagues had spoken with him on the morning of November the thirteenth. So the delegation has had to rely on these petitions to prove that they speak in the name of the nation."

The proprietor commented emotionally, "If only Muhammad Farid were here with us too."

"Some of the men of the National Party have joined the delegation: Muhammad Ali Alluba Bey and Abd al-Latif al-Makkabati. . . ." He shrugged his shoulders as though to shake away the past and then said, "We all remember Sa'd from the enormous row he stirred up when he was appointed Minister of Education and then Minister of Justice. I still remember that the nationalist newspaper *al-Liwa'* welcomed him when he was nominated to the cabinet, although I can't forget its attacks on him afterward. I won't deny that I was influenced by his critics because of my devotion to the late Mustafa Kamil, but Sa'd has always shown that he merits admiration. His most recent move entitles him to the highest regard."

"You're right. It's a blessed undertaking. Let's pray to God it meets with success." Then he asked with concern, "Do you think they'll be allowed to make the trip? . . . What do you think they'll do if they go there?"

Mr. Muhammad Iffat rolled up the petition. Then as he rose he said, "Tomorrow's not far off . . . ."

On their way to the door, the proprietor's playful spirit got the better of him and he whispered into his friend's ear, "I'm so happy about this petition that I could be a drunkard lifting his eighth glass between Zubayda's thighs."

Muhammad Iffat waggled his head enthusiastically, as though intoxicated by the picture his imagination had conjured up at the mention of a glass of wine and Zubayda. He murmured, "Oh, what we'll soon be hearing. . . ."

Then he left the store and his smiling friend called after him, "And what we'll see after that . . . ."

Al-Sayyid Ahmad returned to his desk. His face showed the happy impact of the jest, even though his patriotic enthusiasm had not subsided in his heart. He was like this in all concerns of life, so long as they had no connection to his home. He could be totally serious when that was called for but would not hesitate to lighten the atmosphere with humor and mirth whenever he felt like it, motivated by an irresistible urge. He had an unusual ability to reconcile seriousness and mirth, without either one suppressing or spoiling the other. His jesting was not a luxury of marginal importance to his life but was as much a necessity as seriousness. He had never been able to achieve total seriousness or to concentrate his energies on it. Consequently, he had been content to limit his patriotism to an emotional and psychic participation, not taking any action that might have altered the life he enjoyed so much that he would not have exchanged it for any other. For this reason he had never thought of joining one of the committees of the National Party, even though he was deeply attached to its principles. He had never even taken the trouble to go to one of their rallies. Would that not have been a waste of his precious time? The nation did not need his time, and he was eager to have every minute of it to spend on his family, on his business, and especially on his amusements with his friends and chums. Thus his time was reserved for his own life, and the nation was welcome to a share of his heart and emotions. It was easier to part with money than time. He was not stingy about contributing to the cause. He did not feel he was neglecting his duty in any way. On the contrary, he was known among his comrades for his patriotism, both because none had a heart as liberal with its emotions as his and because even those with liberal hearts were not as generous with their financial contributions. His patriotism set him apart so that he was known for it. It was added to the rest of the fine qualities on which he secretly prided himself. He could not imagine that the nationalist cause could ask any more of him after he had given so generously. Although his heart was filled with romance, music, and humor, he still found room for patriotism. Even if his nationalist fervor was confined to his heart, it was strong and deep, preoccupying and engrossing his soul.

His patriotism had not come to him accidentally. It had matured with him since childhood, when he had heard the previous generation recount tales of the heroism of the Egyptian revolutionary Urabi. It had been enflamed by articles and speeches printed in the nationalist newspaper *al-Liwa'*. And what a unique sight it had been, arousing both laughter and concern, the day he was seen crying like a baby over the death of Mustafa Kamil. His companions were touched because none of them had been indisposed at all by their sorrow. At their party that evening they had roared with laughter when they recalled the improbable sight of the "Lord of Laughter" sobbing with tears.

Today, after years of the war, now waning, after the death of the youthful leader of the National Party and the banishment of his successor, after all hope for the return of "Our Effendi" Khedive Abbas II had been lost, after the defeat of Turkey and the victory of the English, after all of this or in spite of all of this, there came amazing news, the facts of which seemed like legends: presenting to the Englishman, the High Commissioner, demands for independence, signing nationalist petitions, and wondering about the next step. Hearts were shaking off the dust to separate out what was vital to them. Souls were radiant with their hopes. What was behind all of this? His pacific soul, accustomed to passivity, wondered about this turn of events to no avail. He could hardly wait for nightfall so he could rush to his musical gathering, where political talk had become the appetizer before the drinks and music. It fit in with the other attractions that made him long for his evening's entertainment, like Zubayda, his love for his comrades, the drinking and the music. In that enticing atmosphere, it appeared pleasantly refreshing and induced emotions like enthusiasm and love without asking more of the heart than it could bear.

Al-Sayyid Ahmad was thinking about all of this when Jamil al-Hamzawi came over to him and asked, "Have you heard about the new name that's being given to the home of Sa'd Pasha? . . . They're calling it 'the House of the Nation.'" He leaned toward his employer to tell him how this news had reached him.

50

WHILE THE nation was preoccupied by its demand for freedom, Yasin was likewise resolutely and determinedly striving to take charge of his own destiny. He was struggling for the right to go on his nightly outings, which he had virtuously given up for several weeks following his marriage. An excuse he frequently repeated to himself was that he could not have imagined while intoxicated by the dream of marriage that he would ever return to the life of idling his time away at the coffee shop and Costaki's bar. He had sincerely believed he had set that aside for good, since he harbored only the best of intentions for his married life. When the hopeless and total disappointment of marriage overwhelmed him, his nerves were agitated by enduring the boredom or "the emptiness of life," as he put it. With all the strength of his pampered and sensitive soul, he sought escape through relaxation, entertainment, and distraction at the coffee shop and the bar. This was no longer the temporary life of amusement he had thought it to be when he treasured the hope of getting married. It was all that life had left for him to enjoy after marriage had become a bitter disappointment. He was like a person whose hopes forced him away from his native land but whose failure brought him back repentant.

Zaynab had once experienced his warm affection and greedy flattery. She had even been so cherished by him that he had taken her to the theater to see Kishkish Bey in defiance of the bulwark of stern conventions his father had constructed around the family. Now this same Zaynab had to endure his staying out until midnight evening after evening and coming home staggering drunk. It was a blow she found painful to bear.

She could not keep herself from expressing her sorrows to him. He had known instinctively that a sudden transformation in his married life could not be accomplished peacefully. From the beginning he had expected some form of resistance, whether criticism or a quarrel. He had taken precautions to secure his

position with the same forcefulness his father had employed on
intercepting him the night he returned from Kishkish Bey, when
he had told Yasin, "Only men can ruin women, and not every man
is capable of being a guardian for them."

As soon as she voiced her complaints, he told her, "There's no
reason to be sad, darling. Since antiquity, houses have been for
women and the outside world for men. Men are all like this. A
sincere husband is as faithful to his wife when he's away from her as
when he's with her. Moreover, the refreshment and delight I
derive from my outings will make our life together thoroughly
enjoyable."

When she mentioned his drinking and protested that she was
afraid for his health, he laughed and observed in a tone that
blended tenderness with resolve, "All men drink. Getting drunk
is good for my health." Then he laughed some more and suggested, "Ask my father or yours."

Even so, she tried to drag out the discussion, guided by false
hopes. He was resolute, drawing courage from his boredom,
which made it easier than before to feel indifferent about angering
her. He proceeded to emphasize that men have an absolute right to
do anything they want and women a duty to obey and abide by the
rules. "Look at my father's wife. Have you ever seen her object
to his conduct? . . . In spite of that, they are a happy couple and
a stable family. There will be no need to talk about this subject
again."

Perhaps if he had left it up to his feelings, he would not have
spoken to her so diplomatically, for his disappointment with
marriage made him feel something like a desire for revenge. At
other times, he felt a kind of intermittent loathing for her,
although neither of these sentiments kept him from wanting her.
He was considerate of her feelings out of fear or respect for his
father, who was very fond of Mr. Muhammad Iffat. Nothing
disturbed him so much as his fear that she might complain about
him to her father, who would then complain to al-Sayyid Ahmad.
He had even decided that if something like that happened he
would take a separate house, no matter what the consequences.

His fears were not realized. Despite her grief, the girl proved
that she was "reasonable," as though she were the same type of
woman as his father's wife. She evaluated her position carefully
and resigned herself to the situation. She had to fall back on her

husband's oft-repeated assertions of his fidelity and of the innocence of his nightly excursions. She was content to air her pain and
sorrow within the narrow family circle at the coffee hour, where
she received no real support. How could she in a household that
viewed submission to men as a religion and a creed? Mrs. Amina
disapproved of her complaints and was annoyed at her strange
craving to monopolize her husband. The mother was unable to
imagine women being any different from her or men from her
husband. She saw nothing strange in the enjoyment Yasin derived
from his freedom. What seemed strange to her was his wife's
complaint.

Only Fahmy appreciated her sorrows. He took it on himself to
repeat them to Yasin, although he was certain from the start that he
was defending a lost cause. He may have been encouraged to bring
up the topic because they met frequently at the coffee shop of
Ahmad Abduh in Khan al-Khalili. That coffee shop was situated
belowground like a cave hewn from a mountain. Residences of
this ancient district formed its roof. Its narrow rooms faced each
other around a courtyard with an abandoned fountain, cut off
from the outside world. Its lamps were lit both day and night, and
it had a calm, dreamy, cool atmosphere.

Yasin had chosen this coffee shop because it was close to
Costaki's bar and because he had been forced to abandon al-Sayyid
Ali's coffee shop in al-Ghuriya after breaking up with Zanuba.
The antique look of this new haunt also appealed to his poetic
inclinations. Fahmy had not learned the route to coffeehouses as
the result of any setback to his career as a diligent student. He came
in response to the troubled times, which called on the students and
everyone else to meet and consult. He and some comrades had
chosen Abduh's coffeehouse for the antique characteristics that
made it a refuge from prying eyes. They sat there evening after
evening to talk, scheme, predict, and await forthcoming events.

The two brothers met frequently in one of the small rooms, if
only for a short time before Fahmy's colleagues arrived or Yasin
moved on to Costaki's bar. On one of these occasions, Fahmy
alluded to Zaynab's distress. He expressed his astonishment at his
brother's conduct, which was not compatible with the married life
of a young couple. Yasin laughed as though he felt he had every
right to mock his brother's naïveté in offering advice about something of which he was totally ignorant. He did not wish to justify

his conduct directly, preferring to say whatever came to mind. He told the young man, "You wanted to marry Maryam. No doubt you were deeply saddened when Father prevented that desire from being fulfilled. I tell you, and I really know what I'm talking about, that if you had known then what marriage conceals beneath the surface you would have praised God for your failure."

Fahmy was astonished and even alarmed. He had not expected to be assaulted so abruptly by phrases combining the words "Maryam," "marriage," and "desire," which had played unforgettable roles on the stage of his heart. He may have exaggerated his astonishment to conceal the emotional impact of these memories. Perhaps that was the reason he was unable to say a word.

Gesturing to express his weariness and boredom, Yasin continued: "I never imagined that marriage would be so dreary. In fact, it's nothing more than a false dream. It's a cruel and evil swindler."

These words seemed difficult for Fahmy to stomach and aroused his suspicion. That was only to be expected from a young man whose emotional life was centered on a single goal which could be pictured only in the form of a wife and under the rubric "marriage." Fahmy was disturbed to have his irresponsible brother attack this revered category with such bitter sarcasm. He muttered in evident astonishment, "But your wife's perfect . . . a perfect lady."

Yasin cried out sarcastically, "A perfect lady! That she is. Isn't she the daughter of a respected gentleman? And her stepmother's from a distinguished family. Beautiful? . . . Refined? . . . Yes, but some unknown demon in charge of married life turns these qualities into trivial characteristics of little interest through the sickening boredom of marriage. These noble but meaningless qualities are like the noble and happy expressions we rain down on a poor person when we offer him our condolences for his poverty."

Fahmy replied simply and truthfully, "I don't understand a word you've said."

"Wait till you learn for yourself."

"Why have people kept on getting married, then, since the beginning of creation?"

"Because warnings and caution are as futile for marriage as for death." Yasin continued as though to himself: "My imagination really tricked me. It lifted me up to worlds of delight superior even to those of my dreams. I kept asking myself: Is it actually true that I'll share a house with a beautiful maiden forever? What a dream! . . . But I assure you that there's no disaster more oppressive than being united with a beautiful woman under one roof forever."

With the bewilderment of a person so buffeted by youthful passions that he found it difficult to imagine boredom, Fahmy murmured, "Perhaps you've discovered something else concealed inside a flawless exterior?"

Laughing bitterly, Yasin replied, "I'm not complaining about anything except the flawless exterior. . . . My complaint is actually based on the beauty itself. . . . It's beauty that's made me so bored I'm sick. It's like a new word that dazzles you the first time. Then you keep repeating it and using it until it's no different for you than words like 'dog,' 'worm,' 'lesson,' and other commonplace expressions. It loses its novelty and appeal. You may even forget its meaning, so that it becomes a strange, meaningless word you can't use. Perhaps someone else will come across it in your essay and be amazed at your brilliance, while you're amazed at their ignorance. Don't wonder about the disaster of being bored by beauty. It's a boredom that appears inexcusable and consequently totally condemnable. It's difficult to try to avoid groundless despair. Don't be surprised at what I'm saying. I excuse you because you're looking at the situation from a distance. Beauty is like a mirage that can only be seen from afar."

In spite of his brother's bitter tone, Fahmy doubted it was justified, since from the beginning he had been inclined to blame his brother and not human nature for Yasin's deviant behavior. Was it not possible that his complaint could be attributed to his shameless behavior before he got married? Fahmy held firm to this assumption because he refused to allow his fondest dreams to be destroyed. Yasin was not as interested in what his brother thought as in getting some things off his own chest. Smiling sweetly for the first time, he continued: "I've come to understand my father's position perfectly. I know what turned him into that boisterous man who's always chasing after romance. How could he have put up with a single dish for a quarter century when I'm dying of boredom after five months?"

Fahmy was upset that his father had been dragged into the conversation. He protested: "Even if we suppose that your complaint arises from some misery that's an integral part of human nature, the solution you so cheerfully announce . . ." he was about to say, "is far removed from being harmonious or natural," but to seem more logical he switched to: "is far removed from religion."

Yasin was content to limit his observance of religion to belief and paid no serious attention to its commandments or prohibitions. He responded, "Religion supports my view, as shown by its permission to marry four wives, not to mention the concubines with whom the palaces of the caliphs and wealthy men were packed. Religion acknowledges that even beauty itself, once familiarity and experience make it seem trite, can be boring, sickening, and deadly."

Fahmy observed with a smile, "We had a grandfather who spent the evening with one wife and the morning with another. Perhaps you're his heir."

Yasin murmured with a sigh, "Perhaps."

At that time, Yasin had not yet realized any of his rebellious dreams. Although he had returned to the coffeehouse and the bar, he had hesitated before taking the final step of slipping back to Zanuba or some other woman. What had made him reflect and hesitate . . . some feeling of responsibility toward married life? Perhaps he had not freed himself from respect for the religious view that distinguished between an unmarried fornicator and a married adulterer and punished the latter far more severely? Perhaps until he recovered from the disappointment of the greatest hope he had ever nurtured he would be alienated from worldly pleasures? None of these reasons would have been a serious obstacle capable of restraining him, had he not found an unavoidable and irresistible temptation in the example provided by his father's life.

Yasin associated the reasonableness of his wife with that of his stepmother. His imagination busied itself sketching out a plan for her future with him based on Mrs. Amina's life with his father. Yes, he deeply wished that Zaynab would settle down in the life for which she was destined the way his father's wife had. Then he would embark on a series of daring escapades like his father's. He would come home at the end of the night to a calm house and a compliant wife. In that manner and that alone, marriage appeared bearable. Indeed, it would be desirable, with qualities he would otherwise miss out on.

"What more does any woman want than a home of her own and sexual gratification? Nothing! Women are just another kind of domestic animal, and must be treated like one. Yes, other pets are not allowed to intrude into our private lives. They stay home until we're free to play with them. For me, being a husband who is faithful to his marriage would be death. One sight, one sound, one taste incessantly repeated and repeated until there's no difference between motion and inertia. Sound and silence become twins. . . . No, certainly not, that's not why I got married. . . . If she's said to have a fair complexion, then does that mean I have no desires for a brown-skinned woman or a black? If she's said to be pleasingly plump, what consolation will I have for skinny women or huge ones? If she's refined, from a noble and distinguished family, should I neglect the good qualities of girls whose fathers push carts around in the streets? . . . Forward . . . forward."

51

AL-SAYYID AHMAD was bent over his ledgers when he heard a pair of high-heeled shoes tapping across the threshold of the store. He naturally raised his eyes with interest and saw a woman whose hefty body was enveloped in a wrap. A white forehead and eyes decorated with kohl could be seen above her veil. He smiled to welcome a person for whom he had been waiting a long time, for he had immediately recognized Maryam's mother, or the widow of the late Mr. Ridwan, as she had recently become known. Jamil al-Hamzawi was busy with some customers, and so the proprietor invited her to sit near his desk. The woman strutted toward him. As she sat down on the small chair her flesh flowed over the sides. She wished him a good morning.

Although her greeting and his welcome followed the customary pattern repeated whenever a woman customer worth honoring came into the store, the atmosphere in the corner near the desk was charged with electricity that was anything but innocent. Among its manifestations were the modest lowering of her eyelids, visible on either side of the bridge connecting her veil to her scarf, and the glance of his eyes, which were lying in wait above his huge nose. The electricity was hidden and silent but needed only a touch to make it shine, glow, and burst into flame.

He seemed to have been expecting this visit, which was an answer to whispered hopes and suppressed dreams. The death of Mr. Muhammad Ridwan had made him anticipate it, arousing his desires the way the death of winter excites youthful hopes in creatures. With his neighbor's passing, al-Sayyid Ahmad's chivalrous scruples had vanished. He reminded himself that the deceased man had merely been a neighbor, never a friend, and that he was now dead. Today he could recognize the woman's beauty, which he had previously tried to ignore to help preserve his honor. He could express this recognition and allow it a measure of enjoyment and life.

His affection for Zubayda was starting to go bad, like a fruit at the end of its season. In contrast to the last time, now the woman found him an uninhibited male and uncommitted lover. The unwelcome idea that this might be an innocent visit crossed his mind, only to be banished on the evidence of the tender and exquisitely provocative hints she had let drop at their last encounter. The fact that she was making an unnecessary call on him proved that his doubts were unfounded. An old hand at this game, he finally decided to try his luck. Smiling, he told her tenderly, "What a fine idea!"

Somewhat uneasily she replied, "May God honor you. I was just returning home when I passed by the store and it occurred to me to do my shopping for the month myself."

He considered her excuse but refused to believe it. That it had seemed a good idea to do her shopping for the month was not convincing. There had to be some other motive, especially since she would know instinctively that a second visit after the overtures of the past one would be apt to excite his suspicions and inevitably appear provocative. Her haste to apologize also increased his confidence. He commented, "It's an excellent opportunity for me to greet and serve you."

She thanked him briefly, but he did not give her his full attention. He was busy thinking about what to say next. Perhaps he ought to mention her late husband and ask God's mercy on him, but he abstained for fear it would destroy the mood. Then he wondered whether he should go on the offensive or encourage her advances? Either method had its pleasures, but he could not forget that for her to come alone to see him was a giant step on her part that deserved a warm reception from him. He added to his previous greeting: "Indeed it's an excellent opportunity to see you."

Her eyelids and eyebrows moved in a way that revealed modesty or discomfort, or both at once, but most of all that she understood the hidden meanings behind his flattery. Yet he viewed her embarrassment more as a reaction to her own feelings, which had moved her to visit him, than to his statement. He felt certain his hunch was correct and proceeded to repeat his words tenderly: "Yes, an excellent opportunity to see you."

At that, she replied in a tone with a bite of concealed criticism, "I doubt that you consider seeing me an 'excellent opportunity.'"

Her criticism pleased and delighted him, but he protested, "Whoever said that some forms of doubt are sinful was right."

She shook her head to tell him that such talk proved nothing. Then she said, "It's not merely a doubt. I'm certain of it. You're a man who doesn't lack understanding. Even if you suspect otherwise, I'm that way too. . . . So it wouldn't be right for either of us to try to deceive the other."

He felt scornful and bitter that a woman would say such things only two months after the death of her husband but thought up an excuse for her, something he would not have considered doing in other circumstances, and told himself, "Her patience during his long illness has to be considered on her behalf." Spurning this uninvited feeling, he told her with feigned regret, "You're angry with me? . . . That's an evil fate I don't deserve."

She said somewhat impetuously, perhaps because the restrictions of time and place did not allow much playful repartee, "I told myself when I was on the way here, 'You shouldn't go.' So now I have only myself to blame."

"Why so angry, lady? I ask myself what crime I've committed."

She asked provocatively, "What would you do if you greeted someone and he didn't return your greeting?"

He realized immediately that she was referring to her display of affection on her previous visit, which he had met with silence, but he pretended not to understand the reference. Imitating her allusive style, he said, "Perhaps he wasn't able to hear the greeting for one reason or another."

"His hearing's excellent and so are his other senses."

His mouth opened in an uncontrollable and self-satisfied smile. Like a sinner starting to confess, he said, "Perhaps he was too bashful or pious to return the greeting."

With a candor that pleased and stirred him, she replied, "As for bashfulness, he's not at all bashful, and how could a serious person accept the remainder of the excuse?"

A laugh escaped from him, but he cut it short and glanced at Jamil al-Hamzawi, who seemed engrossed in the business of assisting some customers. Then al-Sayyid Ahmad said, "I would prefer not to rehash the complications troubling me at the time. All the same, I shan't despair so long as regret, repentance, and forgiveness remain."

She asked skeptically, "Who says there's regret?"

In an ardent tone that he had perfected over the years, he replied, "With God as my witness, I have been consumed by regret."

"And repentance?"

Boring deep into her with a flaming look, he said, "The greeting is returned ten times over."

She asked flirtatiously, "How do you know there's forgiveness?"

He answered suavely, "Isn't forgiveness one of the qualities of noble people?" Then he continued with delirious intoxication: "Forgiveness is frequently the secret word granting entry into paradise." Gazing at the sweet smile he detected in her eyes, he concluded, "The paradise I refer to is located at the intersection of Palace Walk and al-Nahhasin. Fortunately, the door opens onto a side alley far from prying eyes and there's no watchman."

It crossed his mind that her late husband, who had been the watchman guarding the terrestrial paradise he was attempting to enter, was now an occupant of the heavenly paradise. His mind was troubled by fear that the woman might have realized the same ironic truth, but he found she was daydreaming. He sighed and secretly asked God's forgiveness.

Jamil al-Hamzawi had finished taking care of his customers and approached to attend to her requests. Al-Sayyid Ahmad had an opportunity to mull things over. He began to remember how his son Fahmy had once wanted to get engaged to Maryam, this woman's daughter, and how God had inspired him to turn Fahmy down. At that time he had believed he was merely acting according to his principles. It had not occurred to him that he was sparing his son the most terrible tragedy that can befall a husband. What course would a girl follow but her mother's? . . . And what a mother! A thoroughly dangerous woman. . . . Although she was a precious jewel to skirt chasers like him, on the domestic front she would be a bloody disaster. What had she been up to during the long years when her husband was as good as dead? All the evidence pointed in one direction. Perhaps many of the neighbors knew. Indeed, if anyone in his home had been skilled at observing these affairs, he would have known all about it, and his wife, who even now believed in her, would not have remained a friend. He felt once more a desire, which had first seized him after her doubt-provoking visit, to separate this wanton woman from his pure

family. He had found no way then to fulfill it without arousing
suspicion. Because of his anticipated liaison with her, he saw that it
was time to act on this desire. He would suggest that she gradually
terminate her friendship with his wife, and thus, without any
damage to her reputation, he would achieve his goal by making
use of a legitimate excuse. The closer this woman got to his heart,
the farther she was removed from his respect.

When al-Hamzawi finished getting what she needed, she rose
and held out her hand to al-Sayyid Ahmad. He accepted it with a
smile and said softly, "Until we meet again."

As she started to leave, she murmured, "We'll be waiting for
you."

She left behind her a man who was overjoyed and intoxicated
by pride at his conquest, but she had also created a problem for him
that would occupy a prominent place among his daily concerns.
He would have to think about the safest way to withdraw from
Zubayda's house, as seriously as he pondered what the military
authority was doing, what the English were up to, and what Sa'd
was planning. Yes, as usual, this new happiness carried a tail of
thought behind it. If he had not craved for people to love him –
and it was this love that brought him his happiest moments – it
would have been easy for him to leave the entertainer. His love
had become threadbare, its bloom had faded, and satiation had
plunged it into a brackish swamp, but he was always apprehensive
about leaving behind an angry heart or a spiteful soul. Whenever
he got bored with a relationship he would hope for his lover to
initiate the separation so that he would be the one left, not the one
departing. How he wished that his relationship with Zubayda
could end like those previous ones when a temporary unpleasant-
ness had been washed away by choice farewell presents. Then this
former liaison would evolve into a solid friendship.

He suspected that Zubayda was as satiated as he was. Would she
accept his apologies graciously? Could he hope that his presents
would adequately compensate for his leaving her, which he was
determined to do? Would she prove to be as bighearted and
generous as her colleague Jalila, for example? He would have to
think about these questions at length to prepare the most satisfying
excuses for himself. He sighed deeply, as though complaining that
love should be so transitory. If it were lasting, it would spare the
heart troublesome passions. Then his imagination wandered off

to nightfall. He could see himself creeping along in the darkness, groping his way to the appointed house where the woman was waiting with a lamp in her hand.

52

"ENGLAND PROCLAIMED the Protectorate of its own accord without asking or receiving permission from the Egyptian nation. It is an invalid protectorate with no legal standing. In fact, it was one of those things necessitated by the war and should end now that the war has ended."

Fahmy dictated these words, one at a time, deliberately and in a clear voice, while his mother, Yasin, and Zaynab followed this new dictation exercise Kamal was tackling. He concentrated his attention on the words without understanding anything he wrote down, whether he got it right or not. It was not unusual for Fahmy to give his younger brother a lesson in dictation or some other subject during the coffee hour, but the topic seemed different, even to the mother and Zaynab.

Yasin looked at his brother with a smile and remarked, "I see these ideas have gained control of you. Has God not inspired you with any dictation for this poor boy except this nationalist address that could get a person thrown into prison?"

Fahmy quickly corrected his brother: "It's an address Sa'd gave in front of the occupation forces in the Legislative and Economic Assembly."

Yasin asked with interest and astonishment, "How did they reply?"

Fahmy said passionately, "Their answer hasn't come yet. Everyone's anxiously and apprehensively wondering what it will be. The speech was an outburst of anger in the face of a lion not known for restraint or justice." He sighed with bitter exasperation and continued: "This angry outburst was inevitable after the Wafd Delegation was prevented from making their journey and Rushdi resigned as Prime Minister. Sultan Ahmad Fuad disappointed our hopes when he accepted the Prime Minister's resignation."

Fahmy hurried to his room, returning with a piece of paper, which he unfolded. He presented it to his brother and said, "The speech isn't all I've got. Read this handbill, which has been

distributed secretly. It contains the letter from the Wafd Delegation to the Sultan."

Yasin took the handbill and began to read:

"Your Majesty,"

"The undersigned, members of the Egyptian Wafd Delegation,
are honored to represent the Nation by presenting these concerns
to Your Majesty:

"Since the belligerents agreed to make the principles of freedom
and justice the basis for the peace treaties and announced that
peoples whose status had been altered by the war would be
consulted about self-government, we have taken upon ourselves
an effort to liberate our country and to defend its case at the Peace
Conference. Since the traditionally dominant power has disappeared from the arena and since our country, with the dissolution
of Turkish sovereignty over it, has become free of every claim
against it, and since the Protectorate, which the English proclaimed unilaterally without any agreement from the Egyptian
nation, is invalid and merely one of the necessities of war, which
ends with the end of the war, based on these circumstances and the
fact that Egypt has suffered as much as could be expected of her
while serving in the ranks of those claiming to protect the freedom
of small nations, there is nothing to prevent the Peace Conference
from acknowledging our political freedom pursuant to the principles it has adopted as its foundation.

"We submitted our request to travel to your Prime Minister,
His Excellency Husayn Rushdi Pasha. He promised to assist us,
confident that we expressed the views of the Nation as a whole.
When we were not permitted to travel and were confined within
the borders of our country by a tyrannical force with no legal
authority, we were prevented from defending the cause of this
distressed nation. When His Excellency the Prime Minister was
unable to bear the responsibility for retaining his post while the
will of the people was obstructed, he resigned along with his
colleague His Excellency Adli Yeken Pasha. Their resignations
were welcomed by the people, who honored these men and
acknowledged the sincerity of their nationalism.

"People believed that these two men in their noble stand in
defense of liberty had a powerful ally in Your Majesty. Therefore
no one in Egypt expected that the final solution to the question of
the journey of the Wafd Delegation would have been acceptance

of the resignation of the two ministers, which will further the
purposes of those desiring to humiliate us and strengthen the
obstacle placed in the path of the delivery of the Nation's plea at
the Conference. It also makes it appear that we consent to the
perpetuation of foreign rule over us.

"We know that Your Majesty may have been forced for dynastic considerations to accept the throne of your illustrious father
when it became vacant on the death of your late brother Sultan
Hasan, but the Nation, for its part, believed that when you
accepted this throne during a temporary, invalid protectorate for
those dynastic considerations, you would not be deterred from
working for the independence of your country. Resolution of the
problem by accepting the resignation of the two ministers who
demonstrated their respect for the will of the Nation is impossible
to reconcile with the love for the good of your country to which
you are naturally disposed or with your respect for the wishes of
your subjects. Therefore, people have been amazed that your
advisers have not sided with the Nation at this critical time. That
is what is requested of you, O wisest of the descendants of our
great liberator Muhammad Ali, so that you will be the mainstay in
the achievement of the Nation's independence, no matter what
the cost to you. Your zeal is too lofty to be limited by the
circumstances. How did it escape the attention of your advisers
that Rushdi Pasha's resignation guarantees that no patriotic Egyptian will agree to replace him? How did it escape them that a
cabinet dedicated to programs contrary to the wishes of the people
is destined to fail?

"Pardon, Your Majesty, if our intervention in this affair seems
inappropriate. In other circumstances perhaps it would be, but the
matter has now gone beyond consideration of any concern other
than the good of the Nation, of which you are the faithful servant.
Our Sovereign holds the highest position in the country and
therefore holds the greatest responsibility for it. The greatest
hopes are placed in him. We will not be misrepresenting our
advice to him if we implore him to take into account the views
of his Nation before reaching a final decision regarding the current
crisis. We affirm to His Majesty that there is no one among his
subjects, from one end of the country to the other, who does not
seek independence. Obstruction of the Nation's request is a
weighty responsibility which Your Majesty's advisers did not

consider with the necessary care. Therefore, our duty to serve our country and our loyalty to Our Sovereign have compelled us to bring to the attention of His Majesty the feelings of his Nation, which hopes fervently for independence now and greatly fears what the agents of the colonial party may do to it. The Nation has a right, which it seeks to exercise, for its sovereign to be angry when it is angry and for him to side with it. This is the goal the Nation has chosen. . . . And God is capable of granting that. . . . "

Yasin raised his head from the handbill. There was an astonished look in his eyes and his heart pounded with a new excitement. He shook his head and exclaimed, "What a letter! . . . I doubt I would be able to send anything like that to the headmaster of my school without being severely punished."

Fahmy shrugged his shoulders disdainfully and said, "The matter has now gone beyond consideration of any concern other than the good of the Nation." He repeated the words from memory, just as they appeared in the handbill.

Yasin could not keep himself from laughing. He observed, "You've memorized the handbill . . . but that doesn't surprise me. You seem to have been waiting all your life for a movement like this in order to throw your whole heart into it. Although I may share your feelings and hopes, I'm not happy about your holding on to this handbill, especially after the cabinet has resigned and martial law has been proclaimed."

Fahmy said proudly, "I'm not just keeping it. I'm distributing it as much as I can."

Yasin's eyes widened in astonishment. He started to speak, but the mother spoke first. She said with alarm, "I can scarcely believe my ears. How can you expose yourself to danger when you're such an intelligent person?"

Fahmy did not know how to answer her. He felt the awkwardness of the situation his recklessness had created. Nothing could be more difficult for him than discussing this matter with her. He was closer to the heavens than he was to convincing her that he had a duty to expose himself to danger for the sake of the nation. In her eyes, the nation was not worth the clippings from his fingernail. The expulsion of the English from Egypt seemed easier to him than persuading her of the necessity of expelling them or inducing her to hate them. Whenever the subject came up in a conversation she would remark quite simply, "Why do you despise them, son? . . . Aren't they people like us with sons and mothers?"

Fahmy would reply sharply, "But they're occupying our country."

She would sense the bitter anger in his voice and fall silent. There would be a veiled look of concern in her eyes that would have said if it could have spoken, "Don't be like that."

Once when he was exasperated by her reasoning, he had told her, "A people ruled by foreigners has no life."

She had replied in astonishment, "But we're still alive, even though they've been ruling us for a long time. I bore all of you under their rule. Son, they don't kill us and they don't interfere with the mosques. The community of Muhammad is still thriving."

The young man had said in despair, "If our master, Muhammad, were alive, he would not consent to being ruled by the English."

She had responded sagaciously, "That's true, but what are we compared to the Prophet, peace and blessings on him? . . . God sent His angels to assist him."

He had cried out furiously, "Sa'd Zaghlul will do what the angels used to."

She had raised her arms as though trying to fend off an irresistible calamity and shouted, "Ask your Lord's forgiveness. O God, Your mercy and forgiveness!"

That was what she was like. How could he answer her now that she had realized the danger threatening him because he was distributing the handbill? All he could do was resort to lying. Pretending to dismiss the matter lightly, he said, "I was just joking. There's nothing for you to be alarmed about."

The woman spoke again entreatingly, "This is what I believe, son. How I would hate for my hopes in the person with the best sense of all to be disappointed. . . . And what business of ours are these affairs? If the pashas think the English should be expelled from Egypt, let them expel the English themselves."

Throughout the conversation, Kamal had been trying to remember something important. When the conversation reached this point, he shouted, "Our Arabic language teacher told us yesterday that nations gain their independence through the decisive actions of their sons."

The mother cried out in annoyance, "Perhaps he meant big pupils. Didn't you tell me once that some of the other pupils already have mustaches?"

Kamal asked innocently, "Isn't my brother Fahmy a big pupil?"

His mother replied with unaccustomed sharpness, "Certainly not! Your brother's not an adult. I'm amazed at that teacher. How could he have succumbed to the temptation of discussing something with you that wasn't part of the lesson? If he really wants to be a nationalist, he should address such talk to his sons at home, not to other people's children."

This conversation would have grown progressively more heated had not a chance remark intervened to change its direction. Zaynab wanted to gain her mother-in-law's approval by supporting her. She attacked the teacher and called him "a despicable mosque student to whom the government gave a responsible position despite the changing times."

The moment the mother heard this insult aimed at students in Islamic universities like al-Azhar, she was distracted from her former concerns. She refused to let the remark slip by unchallenged, even though it had been said to support her. She turned to Zaynab and said calmly, "Daughter, you are disparaging the best thing about him. The religious shaykhs carry on the work of God's messengers. The man is to be blamed for exceeding the boundaries of his noble calling. He should have contented himself with being a student at a mosque and a religious scholar."

Yasin was not blind to the secret behind his stepmother's change of direction. He quickly intervened to erase the bad impression left by his wife's innocent remark.

53

"LOOK AT the street. Look at the people. After all this, who could say that the catastrophe hasn't taken place?"

Al-Sayyid Ahmad did not need to look. Everyone was asking about the event and trembling. His friends plunged into heated discussions in which grief, sorrow, and anger played equal parts. The news was repeated by everyone, friends and customers alike. They all agreed that Sa'd Zaghlul and his closest associates had been arrested and transported to an unknown location, either in Cairo or outside it.

Mr. Muhammad Iffat, his face flushed with anger, said, "Don't question the accuracy of the rumor. Bad news has a stench that stops up the nose. Wasn't this to be expected after the Wafd's letter to the Sultan? . . . And after Sa'd's rejection of the British threats with that stupendous letter to the British cabinet?"

Al-Sayyid Ahmad said despondently, "They arrest the great pashas. . . . What a terrifying event! What do you suppose they'll do with them?"

"Only God knows. The country is stifling under the shadow of martial law."

Mr. Ibrahim al-Far, the copper merchant, rushed in. He cried out breathlessly, "Have you heard the latest news? . . . Malta!" He struck his hands together and proceeded: "Exile to Malta. None of them is left here with us. They've exiled Sa'd and his colleagues to the island of Malta."

They all exclaimed at the same time, "Exiled them!" The word "exile" stirred up sad old memories that had stayed with them since childhood concerning the revolutionary leader Urabi Pasha and what had happened to him. They could not help feeling anxious, wondering if the same fate lay in store for Sa'd Zaghlul and his colleagues. Would they really be exiled from their nation forever? Would these great hopes be nipped in the bud and die?

Al-Sayyid Ahmad felt a kind of grief he had never experienced before. It was a heavy, dull sorrow that spread through his chest like nausea. Under its weight he felt rigid, dead, choked. They began to exchange eloquently somber and gloomy looks that screamed out their feelings soundlessly, inciting each other without a single shout. There was a bitter taste in all their mouths.

On the heels of al-Far came another friend and then a second and a third to repeat the same news, hoping the other men would be able to calm their inflamed souls. All they found was silent sorrow, dejected gloom, and suppressed rage.

"Will today's hopes be for naught like those of yesterday?"

No one answered. The questioner kept looking from face to face, but to no avail. There was no answer to comfort a soul's turmoil, even though they refused to admit publicly the fear that was killing them. Sa'd had been exiled. . . . That was true, but would Sa'd return, and if so, after what length of time? How would Sa'd return? What power could bring him back? If Sa'd did not return, what would become of these vast hopes? From their new hope a profound and fervent life had sprung that was too overwhelming to abandon to despair. Yet they did not know how their souls could justify reviving it again.

"But isn't there any way that the information might be a false rumor?"

No one paid any attention to that suggestion. Even the person making it was not surprised to be ignored. He had only offered his remark in an attempt to find some escape, however imaginary, from the stifling despair.

"The English have imprisoned him. . . . Who is there to stand up to the English?"

"He was a man unlike other men. He inspired our lives for a dazzling moment and vanished."

"Like a dream. . . . He'll be forgotten. Nothing more will be left of him than is left from a dream by midmorning."

Someone exclaimed in a voice hoarse with pain, "God exists!"

They all shouted together, "Yes . . . and He's the most merciful of all who are compassionate." The mention of God's name was like a magnet attracting and assembling around it their roving thoughts which had been scattered by despair.

That evening, for the first time in a quarter century or more, the assembled friends seemed averse to fun and music. They were overwhelmed by gloom. All their comments concerned the exiled leader. Sorrow had subjugated them. Even if one of them was torn between his sorrow and a desire to drink, sorrow would win out over drinking, because of his respect for the feelings of the group and his sense that it was inappropriate under those circumstances. When the conversation had dragged on until they had exhausted all aspects, they took refuge in silence. A covert anxiety afflicted them that revealed the itching addiction to alcohol active within them. They seemed to be waiting for a sign from someone daring enough to lead their forces.

Mr. Muhammad Iffat said suddenly, "It's time for us to return to our homes."

He did not mean what he said. He merely wanted to warn them that they were allowing the time to pass and would soon be forced to go home. Their long familiarity with each other had taught them to understand each other's hints.

Abd al-Rahim, the flour merchant, was encouraged by the hidden content of this warning to say, "Are we to part without a glass of wine to lighten today's suffering?"

His statement cheered them up the way a surgeon's does when he leaves the operating room to tell the family of a sick patient, "Praise God . . . the operation was a success."

Yet a man whose sorrow was struggling with his desire to drink pretended to protest, while concealing the relief gladdening his heart: "Should we drink on a day like this?"

Al-Sayyid Ahmad cast him a knowing look. Then he said ironically, "Let them drink by themselves and we'll go outside, you . . . son of a bitch."

They laughed for the first time, and bottles of wine were brought in. Apparently wanting to apologize for this behavior, al-Sayyid Ahmad said, "A little fun won't alter what's in a man's heart."

They applauded his words. Throughout the evening they had hesitated a long time before answering the call of their physical yearnings. Stirred by the sight of the wine bottles, al-Sayyid Ahmad soon observed, "Sa'd's rebellion was intended to cheer the Egyptians, not to torment them. So don't let your sorrow for him make you feel embarrassed about drinking."

His own grief did not prevent him from joking, although it was not an enjoyable or carefree evening. Al-Sayyid Ahmad described it later as "a sick night which had to be treated with doses of wine."

The family began their coffee hour with unprecedented gloom. Fahmy launched into a long revolutionary speech with tears in his eyes. Yasin listened sorrowfully and sadly. The mother wanted to dispel the despair and lighten their affliction but was afraid she would only make things worse. Then the infectious sorrow soon passed into her heart. She felt sorry for the old man they had taken away from his house and wife to a distant place of exile.

Yasin commented, "It's a sad affair. All our men: the Khedive Abbas II, the nationalists Muhammad Farid and Sa'd Zaghlul . . . all have been driven far from the nation."

Fahmy exclaimed passionately, "What rogues the English are! . . . We address them in the same terms they used to gain sympathy during their ordeal and they answer with military threats, exile, and banishment."

The mother could not bear to see her son so upset. She forgot about the leader's tragedy and said gently and soothingly, "Don't take it so hard, son. May our Lord be gracious to us."

This gentle tone only made him more upset. Without turning to look at her he shouted, "If we don't confront terrorism with the anger it deserves, may the nation never live again. It's unthinkable for the nation to be at peace when its leader who has sacrificed himself for it suffers the torments of captivity."

Yasin commented thoughtfully, "It's fortunate that Hamad Basil Pasha was one of those exiled. He's the chieftain of a ferocious tribe. I doubt that his men will keep quiet about his banishment."

Fahmy replied sharply, "What about the others? . . . Aren't there men behind them too? . . . The case doesn't just concern one tribe, it concerns the whole nation."

The conversation continued without interruption and grew even more bitter and violent. The two women kept still out of anxiety and fear. Zaynab could not understand the reasons for this emotional outburst. It seemed meaningless to her. So what if Sa'd and his men had been exiled? Clearly, if they had lived the way God's children should, no one would have thought of banishing them. But they were not content to live like that. They wanted things it was dangerous to desire. There was no necessity for what had occurred. Regardless of what had happened to them, why was Fahmy so insanely angry, as though Sa'd were his father or his brother? Indeed, what was making Yasin, a man who never retired to bed sober, so sad? Were men like him and the others really saddened by Sa'd's banishment? Did her life need anything else to upset it so that Fahmy had to spoil the serenity of this brief gathering with his tantrum? She thought about this as she observed her husband from time to time with vexed amazement. Her expression seemed to say, "If you're really sincere about your sorrow, then don't go out this evening, just this one evening, to the bar."

She did not utter a word. She was too wise to cast her icy reflections into that fiery stream. Her mother-in-law resembled her in this. Her courage rapidly evaporated when confronted by anger, no matter how trivial. For that reason, she retreated into silence and kept her intense discomfort to herself as she apprehensively followed the raging, unruly conversation. She was better able than Yasin's wife to fathom the reasons for these storms. She remembered Urabi with her mind, and her heart still felt sad about "Our Effendi," the Khedive Abbas II. Yes, the word "exile" was a meaningful concept to her. Indeed, the way she understood the term it lacked the hope that could tantalize a person like Fahmy. In her mind, like those of her husband and his friends, it was not associated with any possibility of return. If it meant something else, where was "Our Effendi"? Who deserved to return to his nation more than he did? Would Fahmy's sorrow last as long as Sa'd's banishment? What was so unlucky about these days that coming and going brought news to shake their security and destroy their peace of mind? How she wished peace would return to its abode and that this gathering would be pleasant again, the way it had been all their lives. She wished Fahmy's face would smile and that the conversation would be amiable. How she wished it. . . .

"Malta! Here's Malta!" Kamal yelled suddenly, raising his head from a map of the Mediterranean Sea. He had set his finger on the outline of the island and now looked at his brother with triumph and delight, as though he had found Sa'd Zaghlul himself. All he saw of Fahmy was a scowling, gloomy face. There was no response to his cry of discovery. His brother paid no attention to him at all. The boy subsided and looked back down at the drawing of the island in confusion and embarrassment. He gazed at it for a long time while he measured with his eyes the distance between Malta and Alexandria and then between Malta and Cairo. He tried to imagine what the real Malta looked like. He pictured the men they had been talking about who had been transported there. Since he had heard Fahmy say the English had taken Sa'd away at spear-point, he could only visualize him being carried on the points of spears. The great leader was not in pain or screaming, as one would expect in such a situation, but "steadfast as a mountain," as his brother had also described him at another stage of the conversation. How Kamal wished he could ask his brother about the essence of that wonderfully magical man who rested as steadfast as a mountain on the points of spears. In view of the outpouring of anger that had destroyed the peace of the entire gathering, Kamal postponed any action on his desire until a more suitable opportunity.

Fahmy finally grew uncomfortable at dominating the session, after he had ascertained that the emotions he felt were too great to be relieved by a conversation with Yasin in this setting, where the latter, even if sympathetic, still played the part of a spectator. Fahmy's soul urged him to join his comrades at the coffee shop of Ahmad Abduh, where he would find hearts as responsive as his own and souls that vied with his to express the perceptions and ideas raging inside. There he would hear an echo of the anger crackling in his heart. He would be able to formulate his daring and unruly impulses in a splendid atmosphere of yearning for total freedom. Fahmy leaned toward Yasin and whispered, "To Ahmad Abduh's coffee shop."

Yasin sighed deeply, because he had begun to wonder with great discomfort about some graceful way of slipping out of the coffee hour to go off in search of entertainment without adding any more fuel to Fahmy's flaming anger. Yasin's grief had not been fabricated, at least not entirely. The momentous news shook his heart, but left to his own devices he would have forgotten it without much effort. In view of the strain on his nerves of trying to keep up with Fahmy, to flatter him and show respect for his unprecedented anger, Yasin left the room saying to himself, "I've done enough for the nationalist movement today. Now it's my body's turn."

54

FAHMY OPENED his eyes when he heard the sound of dough being pounded in the oven room. The shutters were closed, and the room was almost dark except for the pale light coming through the openings between the slats. He could hear Kamal's regular breathing and turned his head toward his brother's nearby bed. Memories of his life, fresh this morning, swarmed through his mind. He was waking up from a deep sleep resulting from his total exhaustion of mind and body. He had not known whether he would wake up in this bed or never wake up again. He had not known, nor had anyone else, for death was roaming the streets of Cairo and dancing along its arcades.

How amazing! Here was his mother making bread as always. Here was Kamal, sound asleep, rolling around as he dreamt. Yasin's footsteps overhead indicated that he had wrenched himself out of bed. His father was probably taking a cold shower. Here was the morning light, both splendid and shy. It first rays were gently seeking entry. Everything was proceeding as usual, as though nothing had happened, as though Egypt had not been turned upside down, as though bullets were not searching for chests and heads, as though innocent blood was not enriching the earth and walls. The young man closed his eyes with a sigh. He smiled at the swelling current of his emotions that carried zeal, sorrow, and belief in successive waves.

During the last four days he had lived a life of far greater scope than he ever had known before. His only comparable experience had been in shadowy daydreams. It was a pure, lofty life, ready to sacrifice itself in good conscience for the sake of something glorious, a goal worthier and more exalted than life itself. It did not care whether it risked death, which it greeted resolutely and attacked scornfully. If it escaped from death's clutches once, it returned to attack again, shunning any consideration of possible consequences. This life always had its eyes fixed undeviatingly on a magnificent light and was driven by an irresistible force. It submitted its fate to God, whom it felt encompassing it like the air.

Life considered as a means to something else was despicable. It was less significant than an atom. Life considered as an end in itself was so exalted it was equal to the heavens and the earth. Life and death were brothers. They were like one hand in the service of one hope. Life strengthened this hope with exertion, and death strengthened it with sacrifice. If the awesome upheaval had not occurred, Fahmy would have perished from grief and distress. He could not have stood for life to have continued on in its calm, deliberate way, treading beneath it the destinies and hopes of men. The upheaval had been necessary to relieve the pressure in the nation's breast and in his own. It was like an earthquake providing relief to the pressures that accumulate inside the earth.

When the struggle began, it found him ready. He threw himself into the midst of it. When and how had that happened? He was riding a streetcar to Giza on his way to the Law School when he found himself in a band of students who were waving their fists and protesting: "Sa'd, who expressed what was in our hearts, has been banished. If Sa'd does not return to continue his efforts, we should be sent into exile with him."

The other passengers, their fellow citizens, joined in their discussion and threats. Even the conductor neglected his work and stopped to listen and talk with them. What a moment! . . . After a dark night of grief and despair, Fahmy's hope shone anew. He was certain that this blazing fire would not grow cold.

When they reached the courtyard of the school, it was swarming with clamorous students creating a great uproar. Their hearts raced ahead of them as they rushed to their colleagues. They sensed that something was brewing. Someone immediately began calling for a strike. . . . That was new and unheard of then. While they were shouting for a strike with their law books under their arms, the head of the Law School, Mr. Walton, came to greet them with unusual graciousness and advised them to enter their classrooms. In response, a young man climbed up the stairway leading to the secretary's office and began to address them with extraordinary zeal. All the dean could do was withdraw.

Fahmy listened to the speech with rapt attention. His eyes were fixed on the speaker, and his heart was beating rapidly. He would have liked to climb up there too and pour out the contents of his raging heart, but he did not have a background in public speaking. He was content for someone else to repeat the outbursts of his own heart. He listened to the speaker attentively and enthusiastically until the first pause. Then Fahmy shouted along with all his comrades at the same time, "Independence!"

He listened to the continuation of the speech with an interest enlivened by the shouting. When the speaker reached a second stopping point, Fahmy cried out with everyone else, "Down with the Protectorate!" Then, his body rigid with emotion and his teeth clenched to hold back the tears inspired by the agitation of his soul, he kept on listening until the speaker reached his third stopping place. With all the others, he shouted, "Long live Sa'd!" That was a new chant. Everything seemed new that day, but this was a ravishing chant. Deep inside him, his heart reverberated to it and kept repeating it with its successive beats, as though echoing his tongue. But the cry on his tongue was actually echoing his heart.

He remembered now that his heart had repeated this chant silently all through the night prior to the uprising. He had spent that night in grief and distress. His stifled emotions, love, enthusiasm, aspirations, idealism, and dreams had been scattered in disarray until the voice of Sa'd had rung out. They had been drawn to him like a pigeon floating in the sky drawn back by its master's whistle.

Before they knew what was happening, Mr. Amos, the assistant British judicial counsel in the Ministry of Justice, was making his way through their midst. They greeted him with a single chant: "Down with the Protectorate!" He was gruff with them and not even civil, advising them to return to their lessons and leave politics to their fathers.

At that point one of them protested: "Our fathers have been imprisoned. We won't study law in a land where the law is trampled underfoot."

The cry from the depths of their hearts resounded like a peal of thunder, and the man quickly withdrew. For a second time, Fahmy wished he were the speaker. How many ideas were swarming through his mind, but other students proclaimed them first. His enthusiasm became even more intense. He was consoled by the fact that what he expected to happen would more than compensate for anything he had missed.

Matters progressed rapidly. Someone called for them to leave the school. They went off in a demonstration, heading for the School of Engineering, where the students joined them at once, and then on to Agriculture, where the students rushed out chanting as though they had been expecting them. They went to Medicine and Commerce. As soon as they reached al-Sayyida Zaynab Square they merged with a mass demonstration of citizens. Shouts were raised for Egypt, independence, and Sa'd. With every step they took, they gained more enthusiasm, confidence, and faith, because of the impulsive participation and spontaneous response of their fellow citizens. They encountered people whose souls were primed, reeling with anger that found expression in their demonstration.

Fahmy's astonishment that the demonstration had occurred almost overpowered his feelings about the demonstration itself. He wondered, "How did all this happen?" Only a few hours had passed since morning, when he had been despondent and dejected. Now here he was a little before noon taking part in a turbulent demonstration where he discovered in every other heart an echo of his own, repeating his chant and imploring him not to hesitate but to persevere to the end. How joyful he was and how enthusiastic. . . . His spirit soared off into the heavens with boundless hope. It regretted the despair that had overcome it and was ashamed of the suspicions it had entertained about innocent people.

In al-Sayyida Zaynab Square he witnessed another of the novel scenes of that amazing day. He was one of those who saw groups of mounted policemen commanded by an English officer advancing on them, trailing plumes of dust behind the horses. The earth shook with their hoofbeats. He could well remember how he had stared at them in dismay. He had never before found himself exposed to such unexpected danger.

He looked around him at faces that glowed with enthusiasm and anger. He sighed nervously, but kept on waving his fist and chanting. The mounted policemen surrounded them. Of the formidable ocean in which he was surging he could only observe a limited area and even there everyone else was craning his head to see. Then they heard that the police had arrested many students, those who had confronted them defiantly or had been at the head of the demonstration. For the third time that day he had an unfulfilled wish. He wished he were one of those arrested, but he could not have extricated himself from the band he was in without extraordinary effort.

That day had been relatively peaceful compared with the next. Monday morning began with a general strike and a demonstration in which all the schools participated, carrying their banners, together with untold throngs of citizens. Egypt had come back to life. It was a new country. Its citizens rushed to crowd into the streets to prepare for battle with an anger that had been concealed for a long time. Fahmy threw himself into the swarms of people with intoxicating happiness and enthusiasm, like a displaced person rediscovering his family after a long separation.

The demonstration, which was thronged by onlookers, passed by the homes of influential politicians, voicing its protests in various terms, until it reached Ministries Street. Then a violent disturbance passed through the swarms of people and someone shouted, "The English!" Bullets immediately started flying and drowned out the sound of the protesters. The first fatalities occurred. Some people continued on with insane zeal, while others seemed nailed to the ground. Many separated off and sought shelter in homes and coffeehouses. Fahmy was in this last category. He slipped into a doorway, his heart beating wildly in alarm. He stopped thinking about anything except his life. He stayed there for he knew not how long until silence prevailed everywhere. Then he stuck out his head, followed by his feet, and set off for home, incredulous that he had survived. He was in a kind of daze when he reached his house. In his sorrowful solitude he wished that he had been one of the departed or at least one of those who had held their ground. In a blaze of harsh self-criticism, Fahmy promised his stern conscience to act more thoughtfully the next time. Fortunately the arena for thoughtful action was vast and near at hand.

Tuesday and Wednesday were like Sunday and Monday. They were comparable in both their joys and sorrows. There were demonstrations and chants, bullets and victims. Fahmy threw himself totally into all of this. Driven by his enthusiasm, he reached far-flung horizons of lofty sentiment. He was troubled that he was still alive and regretted his escape. His zeal and hopes were doubled by the spread of the spirit of anger and revolution. It was not long before the tramway workers, the drivers and street sweepers went on strike. The capital appeared sad, angry, desolate. There was good news that attorneys and civil servants were about to strike. The heart of the nation was throbbing. It was alive and in rebellion. The blood would not have been shed in vain. The exiled leaders would not be forgotten. A self-conscious awakening had rocked the Nile Valley.

The young man rolled over in bed. He turned his mind away from the deluge of memories and began to follow the beats of the dough once more. He looked around the room, slowly becoming visible as the sun rose outside the closed shutters. His mother was making bread! She would continue to knead the dough morning after morning. God forbid that anything should distract her from concentrating her attention on preparing the meals, washing the clothes, or cleaning the furnishings. Great activities would not interfere with minor ones. Society would always be flexible enough to embrace exalted and trivial matters and to welcome both equally. But not so fast . . . . Was a mother not part of life? She had given birth to him, and sons fueled the revolution. She fed him, and nourishment fueled the sons. In fact, nothing about life was trivial. But would not some day come when a great event would rock all the Egyptians, leaving none of the differences of opinion that had been present at the coffee hour five days ago? How remote that day seemed. . . . Then a smile came to his lips when this question leapt into his mind: What would his father do if he learned about his continual struggle, day after day? What would his tyrannical, despotic father do about it and his tender, affectionate mother? He smiled anxiously, because he knew he would be exposed to problems no less significant than if the military authority itself should learn his secret.

He pulled back the covers and sat up in bed murmuring, "It's all the same whether I live or die. Faith is stronger than death, and death is nobler than ignominy. Let's enjoy the hope, compared to which life seems unimportant. Welcome to this new morning of freedom. May God carry out whatever He has decreed."

55

NO ONE could claim any longer that the revolution had not changed at least some aspect of his life. Even Kamal's freedom to go to school and return by himself, which he had enjoyed for a long time, was affected by a development he found obnoxiously burdensome, although he could not prevent it. His mother had ordered Umm Hanafi to follow him on his way to and from school. She was not to let him out of her sight and to bring him home if they ran into a demonstration. He would not have a chance to loiter or obey any frivolous impulses.

The news of the demonstrations and disturbances made the mother's head spin. Her heart trembled at the savage attacks on the students. She spent gloomy days filled with alarm and panic, wishing she could keep her two sons at home until matters returned to normal. She was unable to achieve her goal, especially after Fahmy promised he would definitely not participate in any strike. Her confidence in his good sense had not been shaken. Her husband rejected the idea of keeping Kamal home from school, because he knew the school would prevent the younger pupils from participating in the strike. Reluctantly the mother agreed that the brothers could go to school, but she had stipulated Umm Hanafi's supervision for Kamal, telling him, "If I were able to go out, I would follow you myself."

Kamal had objected as forcefully as he could, because he realized intuitively that this supervisor, who would keep nothing about him secret from his mother, would put a decisive end to all the mischief and tricks he enjoyed in the street. That would destroy this brief, happy time of his day as he went from one of his prisons to the other: home and school. He was also intensely annoyed at walking down the street accompanied by this woman whose excessive weight and faltering step would certainly attract attention. He was forced to submit to her supervision, since his father had ordered him to accept her. The most he could do to comfort himself was to scold her whenever she got too close to him, since he had decreed that she should stay several meters behind him.

In this manner they made their way to Khalil Agha School on Thursday morning, the fifth day of the demonstrations in Cairo. When they reached the door of the school, Umm Hanafi approached the gatekeeper and, acting according to her daily instructions received at home, asked him, "Are the pupils in the school?"

The man answered her indifferently, "Some have gone in and others have left. The headmaster is not interfering with anyone."

This answer was a bad surprise for Kamal. He was prepared to hear the response he had come to expect since Monday – namely: "The pupils are on strike." Then they would return home where he would spend the whole day in freedom. That made him love the revolution from afar. His soul urged him to flee to escape the consequences of this new reply. He told the gatekeeper, "I'm one of those who leave."

He walked away from the school with the woman behind him. When she asked him why he had not gone in with the others who were staying, he implored her repeatedly, for the first time in his life, to deceive his mother by telling her that the pupils were on strike. To strengthen his entreaty and gain her affection, he prayed for her to have a long and happy life when they were passing by the mosque of al-Husayn. Umm Hanafi was unable to keep the truth, as she had heard it, from his mother, who chided him for being lazy and ordered the woman to take him back to school. They left the house again and Kamal treated her to a fierce tongue-lashing and accused her of treachery and betrayal.

In school, he found only boys his age, the youngsters. The others, the overwhelming majority, were on strike. About a third of the pupils were present in his class, which contained a higher percentage of younger students than any other. The teacher ordered them to review the previous lessons. Meanwhile he busied himself correcting their exercises and ignored them as though they actually were on strike. Kamal opened a book. He pretended to read but paid no attention to the book. He did not like staying at school with nothing to do, when he could have been with the strikers or at home enjoying the vacation that these amazing days had unexpectedly granted him. He found school oppressive in a way he had not before.

His imagination flew away to the strikers outside with astonishment and curiosity. He often wondered which view of them
was accurate. Were they "daredevils" as his mother claimed, with
no feeling for themselves or their families, unnecessarily putting
their lives in jeopardy? Or were they "heroes" as Fahmy described
them, sacrificing their lives to struggle against God's enemy and
their own? He was often inclined to agree with his mother because
of his resentment toward the older pupils at his school who were
among the strikers. They had made the worst possible impression
on him and the other young pupils like him with the rough
treatment and contempt they meted out in the school courtyard,
where they challenged the younger boys with their enormous
bodies and insolent mustaches.

Yet he could not totally accept this view, because Fahmy's
opinion always carried a lot of weight with him and was hard to
ignore. Kamal could not deny them the heroism Fahmy ascribed
to them. He even wished he could observe their bloody battles
from a safe place. Something extremely serious was no doubt
underway, otherwise why were the Egyptians striking and band-
ing together to clash with the soldiers? . . . And what soldiers? The
English! The English . . . when a mention of that name had once
sufficed to clear the streets. What had happened to the world and
to people? This amazing struggle was so overwhelming that its
basic elements were engraved in the boy's soul without his having
made any conscious effort to remember them. The terms "Sa'd
Zaghlul," "the English," "the students," "the martyrs," "handbills," and "demonstrations" became active forces inspiring him at
the deepest levels, even if he was only a perplexed bystander when
it came to understanding what they stood for. His bewilderment
was doubled by the fact that the members of his family reacted
differently to the events and at times in contrary ways. While
Fahmy was outraged and attacked the English with lethal hatred,
yearning for Sa'd so much it brought tears to his eyes, Yasin
discussed the news with calm concern and quiet sorrow that did
not prevent him from continuing his normal routine of chatting,
laughing, and reciting poetry and stories followed by an evening
on the town that lasted until midnight. Kamal's mother kept
praying that God would bring peace and make life secure again
by cleansing the hearts of both the Egyptians and the English.
Zaynab, his brother's wife, was the most disconcerting of them all.

She was frightened by the course of events, and the only person she could find to vent her anger on was Sa'd Zaghlul himself, whom she accused of having caused all the evil. "If he had lived the way God's children should, meekly and peacefully, no one would have harmed him in any manner and this conflagration would not have broken out."

Thus the boy's enthusiasm was set on fire by the thought of the struggle itself, and his sorrow overflowed at the thought of death in the abstract, without his having any clear understanding of what was going on around him, locally or nationally. He would have had a fine opportunity to observe a demonstration at close range or to participate in one, if only in the school courtyard, the day the pupils of Khalil Agha School had been called to strike for the first time, had not the headmaster, to Kamal's distress, immediately shut the younger pupils up in their classrooms. He had lost that opportunity and found himself kept indoors, although he could listen to the loud chanting with a mixture of astonishment and secret delight, inspired perhaps by the chaos affecting everything and mercilessly wreaking havoc with the tedious daily routine. He had missed the chance then to participate in a demonstration, just as he had lost the opportunity today to enjoy a holiday at home. He would remain confined to this boring assembly, looking at a book with eyes that saw nothing, cautiously and fearfully exchanging pinches with a friend across a book bag until the end of the long day came.

Then, suddenly, something attracted his attention. It might have been an unfamiliar voice at some distance or a ringing in his ears. He looked around him to determine what he had heard. He found that the pupils' heads were raised and that they were looking at each other. Then everyone stared at the windows overlooking the street. It was a reality, not something imaginary, that had attracted their attention. Different voices were blended together into an enormous, incomprehensible sound. Because of the distance, it seemed like the roaring of waves far away. As it grew closer it could be termed a din, or even an advancing din. There was a commotion in the classroom. Pupils started whispering. Then a voice called out: "A demonstration!"

Kamal's heart pounded. His eyes took on a gleam of joy mixed with dismay. The din came closer and closer until the chanting could be heard clearly, thundering and raging in all directions, surrounding the school. His ears were bombarded by the words that had filled his mind during the past days: "Sa'd," "independ- ence," "protectorate." . . .

The chanting came even nearer and got louder, until it filled the school courtyard itself. The pupils were dumbfounded. They were sure this deluge would flood them, but they welcomed it with a childish delight that shunned any consideration of the consequences, because of their zealous yearning for anarchy and liberation. Next they heard footsteps coming toward them and noisy shouting. The door swung wide open from the impact of a violent shove. Bands of students from the University and al-Azhar poured into the room like water rushing through an opening in a dam. They were shouting, "Strike! Strike! . . . No one can stay here."

In a matter of moments, Kamal found himself swept away by a tumultuous wave pushing him forward so forcefully that resistance was impossible. He was extremely upset. He moved along slowly like a coffee bean revolving in the mouth of the grinder. He did not know where to look. All he knew of the world were bodies crammed together, not to mention the clamor assaulting his ears, until he discerned from the appearance of the sky overhead that they had reached the street. He was being squeezed ever more tightly till he could scarcely breathe. He was so frightened he screamed a loud, continuous, piercing wail. Before he knew what was happening, a hand had grabbed his arm and yanked him forcibly, making a way for him through the crowd until it pushed him up on the sidewalk and against a wall. He started panting and searching around him for a safe place. He discovered that the metal security door of Hamdan's pastry shop had been pulled down until it was close to the ground. He rushed over and got on his knees to crawl under it. When he stood up inside he saw Uncle Hamdan, who knew him quite well, two women, and a few young pupils. He rested his back against the side of the counter with the trays on it while his chest rose and fell repeatedly. He heard Uncle Hamdan say, "Students from al-Azhar and the Uni- versity, workers, citizens . . . all the roads leading to al-Husayn are jammed with people. Before today I wouldn't have thought the earth could support so many people."

One of the women said in astonishment, "How can they keep on demonstrating after they've been fired on?"

The other woman commented sadly, "May our Lord provide guidance . . . they're all good boys, alas."

Uncle Hamdan said, "We've never seen anything like this before. May our Lord protect them."

The chanting burst out from the demonstrators' throats, convulsing the atmosphere, at times so near it resounded in the shop and at other times at a distance in a great, incomprehensible hullabaloo like the roaring of the wind. It continued without interruption, its slow but steady motion revealed by the differing degrees of intensity and loudness between the waves of people as they approached and drew away.

Whenever he thought it had ended, another wave came along. It seemed it would never end. Kamal concentrated his whole being in his ears to listen attentively, although he felt uneasy and anxious. As time passed without anything terrible happening, he was able to catch his breath and regain his composure. Then he was finally able to consider the situation as transitory. It would soon be over. He wondered whether he should tell his mother what had happened to him once he got home: "A demonstration without beginning or end burst into our classrooms, and before I knew it, I was surrounded by the raging current, which swept me out into the street. I shouted along with everyone else, 'Long live Sa'd! Down with the Protectorate! Long live independence!' I was carried from street to street until the English attacked us and opened fire."

She would be so alarmed she would weep, hardly able to believe he was still alive. She would recite many verses from the Qur'an as she shuddered.

"A bullet went by my head. I can still hear its drone ringing in my ear. People were bumping into each other like madmen. I would have perished with the others if a man had not pulled me into a store."

His daydreams were cut short by loud, sporadic screams and footsteps rushing past in confusion. His heart pounded, and he looked at the faces surrounding him. He saw that they were staring at the door with an expression suggesting they expected to be hit on the head. Uncle Hamdan went to the door and leaned down to peer out the gap at the bottom. Jumping back, he quickly lowered the door until it was flush with the ground. He stammered in confusion, "The English!"

Many people were shouting outside, "The English!...The English!"

Others called out, "Stand firm...stand firm."

Someone else yelled, "We die, but the nation lives."

Then for the first time in his short life the boy heard shots fired nearby. He recognized them instinctively and shook all over. When the women let out a scream of terror, he burst into tears.

Uncle Hamdan was saying in a shaky voice, "We proclaim that God is one...one."

Kamal felt afraid, and a deathly chill crept throughout his body from his feet to his head. The shots kept on coming. Their ears were assailed by a clatter of wheels and a neighing of horses. Voices and movement were heard in extraordinarily rapid succession and then they were joined by roars, screams, and moans. To those crouching behind the door, a fleeting moment of combat seemed an eternity spent in the presence of death. Then a frightening silence prevailed, like a swoon following an onslaught of pain.

Kamal asked in a hoarse and trembling voice, "Have they gone?"

Uncle Hamdan put his finger to his lips and murmured, "Hush." Then he recited the Throne Verse from the Qur'an (2:255) about the omnipotence of God.

Kamal recited another verse about God, to himself since he no longer felt able to speak. "Say: He is God, one, only one" (Qur'an, 112:1). Perhaps this verse would drive away the English as effectively as it drove away the jinn in the dark.

The door was not opened until the noon prayer, when the boy ran out into the deserted street and dashed off like the wind. Passing by the steps leading down to Ahmad Abduh's coffee shop, he noticed a person coming up whom he recognized as his brother Fahmy. He rushed to him like a drowning man grabbing at a life preserver. As Kamal grasped his arm, the young man turned in alarm. When he recognized his little brother he shouted at him, "Kamal?...Where were you during the strike?"

The boy noticed that his brother's voice was so hoarse it was hard for him to speak. He replied, "I was in Uncle Hamdan's shop. I heard the shots and everything."

Fahmy told him quickly and hastily, "Go home and don't tell anyone you met me....Do you hear?"

The boy asked him in bewilderment, "Aren't you coming home with me?"

He replied in the same tone, "Of course not... not now.... I'll return at my usual time. Don't forget, you didn't run into me at all."

He pushed him away, leaving him no opportunity for discussion. The boy galloped off until he reached Khan Ja'far Alley. There he saw a man standing in the middle of the road. He was pointing to the ground and addressing several others. Looking in the direction he was pointing, Kamal saw red splotches in the dust. He heard the man say, as though delivering a funeral oration, "This innocent blood screams out to us to continue the struggle. It was God's will that blood should be shed in the sacred precincts of al-Husayn, the Prince of Martyrs, to link our present trials to our past. God is on our side."

Kamal was terrified. He turned his eyes away from the bloody ground and ran off like a madman.

56

IN THE early morning darkness, Amina was groping her way to the door of the room cautiously and deliberately to avoid waking her husband when she heard a strange commotion coming from the street that sounded like the droning of bees. At this, her usual time to arise, she normally heard only the clatter of garbage carts, a cough from someone heading for work early, and the shouts of a man who liked to break the pervasive silence after he returned from the dawn prayer by crying out from time to time, "Proclaim Him one." She had never heard this strange commotion before. She was at a loss to explain it and curious to learn its source. She walked softly to the window in the sitting room that overlooked the street. She raised the cover of the peephole and poked her head out. She found it was dark with a glimmer of light at the horizon, but that was not enough for her to be able to see what was happening below her. The commotion grew louder and more mysterious at the same time. She could hear human voices of unknown origin. As her eyes became slightly more accustomed to the darkness, she looked around. Below the historic cistern building on Palace Walk and near it at the intersection of al-Nahhasin with Qirmiz Alley she could make out indistinct human figures, as well as things shaped like small pyramids and other objects like short trees. She stepped back anxiously and went downstairs to the room Fahmy shared with Kamal. Then she hesitated. Should she wake him up to solve this puzzle for her or postpone it until he woke by himself? She could not bring herself to disturb Fahmy and decided to wait until the normal time for him to awaken at sunrise, which was not far off.

She performed her prayers and then went back to the window, driven by her curiosity. She peered out. Rays from the rising sun were beginning to adorn the gown of night. The light of morning was streaming off the peaks of the minarets and the domes. She was able to see the road much more clearly. Her eyes examined the shapes that had alarmed her when it was dark. She could see what they really were. A moan of terror escaped her, and she stepped back to rush to Fahmy's room. She woke him without any hesitation.

The young man shuddered and sat up in bed. He asked in alarm, "What's wrong, Mother?"

Trying to catch her breath, she replied, "The English are filling the street below our house."

The young man jumped out of bed to run to the window. Looking down, he saw a small encampment on Palace Walk under the cistern building at a vantage point for the streets that branched off there. It consisted of a number of tents, three trucks, and several groups of soldiers. Adjacent to the tents, rifles had been stacked up in groups of four. In each bunch the muzzles leaned in against each other and the butts were separated, forming a pyramid. The sentries stood like statues in front of the tents. The other soldiers were scattered about, speaking to each other in a foreign language and laughing. The young man looked toward al-Nahhasin and saw a second encampment at the intersection of al-Nahhasin with the Goldsmiths Bazaar. There was a third encampment in the other direction at the corner of Palace Walk and al-Khurunfush.

His first impulse was to think that these soldiers had come to arrest him, but he soon decided that was silly. He attributed the idea to his rude awakening, from which he had not quite recovered, and to his sense of being followed that had not left him since the revolution had broken out. Then the truth gradually became clear to him. The district that had frustrated the occupying forces with its continual demonstrations had been occupied by troops. He went on looking through the blind, examining the soldiers, tents, and wagons while his heart pounded with terror, sorrow, and anger. When he turned away from the window he was pale and muttered to his mother, "It's the English, just as you said. They've come to intimidate people and to stop the demonstrations at their source."

He began to pace the room back and forth, while he commented to himself resentfully, "Incredible . . . preposterous."

Then he heard his mother say, "I'll wake your father to tell him about it." The woman made that statement as though it were the only alternative left. She implied that al-Sayyid Ahmad, who solved all the problems of her life, was equally capable of finding a solution for this one and of guiding them to safety.

Her son told her sadly, "Leave him alone until he wakes up at the normal time."

Terrified, the woman asked, "What are we going to do, son, with them stationed outside the entrance of our house?"

Fahmy shook his head anxiously and repeated her question: "What are we going to do?" Then in a more confident tone he continued: "There's no reason to be afraid. They're only trying to frighten the demonstrators."

Swallowing because her mouth felt dry, she remarked, "I'm afraid they'll attack peaceful citizens in their homes."

He thought for a little while about what she had said. Then he murmured, "Of course not . . . If their goal had been to attack the houses, they wouldn't have waited there quietly this long." He was not totally sure about his statement but thought it was the best thing to say.

His mother came back with yet another question: "How long will they stay here with us?"

He replied with a blank stare, "Who knows? . . . They've pitched tents, so they're not leaving soon."

He noticed that she was addressing questions to him as though he were a military commander. He looked at her affectionately and did not let her see the ironic smile that had formed on his pale lips. He thought for a moment about teasing her, but the situation was distressing enough to deter him. He became serious once more. Similarly, when Yasin recounted one of their father's exploits to him, the very nature of the anecdote would make him want to laugh, but the anxiety that afflicted him whenever he learned something about the hidden side of his father's character would restrain him.

They heard footsteps hurrying toward them. Then Yasin, followed immediately by Zaynab, stormed into the room. His eyes looked swollen and his hair was disheveled. He shouted, "Have you seen the English?"

Zaynab cried out, "I'm the one who heard them. So I looked out the window and saw them. Then I woke up Mr. Yasin."

Yasin continued: "I knocked on Father's door until he woke up, so I could tell him. When he saw them himself he ordered that no one should leave the house and that the bolt on the door should not be opened. But what are they doing? . . . What can we do? . . . Isn't there a government in this country to protect us?"

Fahmy told him, "I don't think they'll interfere with anyone except the demonstrators."

"But how long are we going to remain captives in our houses? . . . These houses are full of women and children. How can they set up encampments here?"

Fahmy muttered uneasily, "Nothing's happening to us that isn't happening to everyone else. Let's be patient and wait."

Zaynab protested nervously, "All we hear or see anymore is something frightening or sad. God damn the bastards."

At that point, Kamal opened his eyes. He looked with astonishment at all the people unexpectedly assembled in his room. He sat up in bed and looked inquisitively at his mother, who went to him and patted his large head with her cold hand. Then in a whisper she recited the opening prayer of the Qur'an, while her thoughts wandered off.

The boy asked, "Why are you all here?"

His mother wanted to break the news to him in the nicest way, and so she said gently, "You won't be going to school today."

He asked with delight, "Because of the demonstrations?"

Fahmy replied a bit sharply, "The English are blocking the road."

Kamal felt he had discovered the secret that had brought them all together. He looked at their faces with dismay. Then he ran to the window and looked for a long time through the blind. When he returned, he remarked uneasily, "The rifles are in groups of four." He looked at Fahmy as though pleading for help. He stammered fearfully, "Will they kill us?"

"They won't kill anyone. They've come to pursue the demonstrators."

There was a short period of silence. Then the boy commented, as though to himself, "What handsome faces they have!"

Fahmy asked him sarcastically, "Do you really like their looks?"

Kamal replied innocently, "A lot. I imagined they'd look like devils."

Fahmy said bitterly, "Who knows? . . . perhaps if you saw some devils you'd think they were handsome."

The bolt on the door was not pulled back that day. None of the windows overlooking the street was opened, not even to freshen the air or let in sunlight. For the first time ever, al-Sayyid Ahmad conducted a conversation at the breakfast table. He said, in a voice that implied he knew what he was talking about, that the English were going to take strong measures to stop the demonstrations and that it was for this reason they had occupied the areas where most of the demonstrations had taken place. He said he had decided they would stay home all day until matters became clearer.

Al-Sayyid Ahmad was able to speak with confidence and preserve his customary awesome appearance. Thus he prevented anyone from discerning the anxiety that had afflicted him since he had hopped out of bed in response to Yasin's knocks.

It was also the first time that Fahmy had dared question one of his father's ideas. He remarked politely, "But, Father, the school may think I'm one of the strikers if I stay home."

Al-Sayyid Ahmad naturally knew nothing of his son's participation in the demonstrations. He replied, "Necessity has its own laws. Your brother as a civil servant is in more jeopardy than you are, but you both have a clear excuse."

Fahmy was not courageous enough to ask his father a second time. He was afraid of angering him and found his father's order forbidding him to leave the house an excuse that eased his conscience for not going into the streets occupied by soldiers thirsty for the blood of students.

The breakfast group broke up. Al-Sayyid Ahmad retired to his room. The mother and Zaynab were soon busy with their daily chores. Since it was a sunny day with warm spring breezes, one of the last of March, the three brothers went up on the roof, where they sat under the arbor of hyacinth beans and jasmine. Kamal got interested in the chickens and settled down by their coop. He scattered grain for them and then chased them, delighted with their squawking. He picked up the eggs he found.

His brothers began to discuss the thrilling news that was spreading by word of mouth. A revolution was raging in all areas of the Nile Valley from the extreme north to the extreme south. Fahmy recounted what he knew about the railroads and telegraph and telephone lines being cut, the outbreak of demonstrations in different provinces, the battles between the English and the revolutionaries, the massacres, the martyrs, the nationalist funerals with processions with tens of coffins at a time, and the capital city with its students, workers, and attorneys on strike, where transportation was limited to carts. He remarked heatedly, "Is this really a revolution? Let them kill as many as their savagery dictates. Death only invigorates us."

Yasin, shaking his head in wonder, observed, "I wouldn't have thought our people had this kind of fighting spirit."

Fahmy seemed to have forgotten how close he had been to despair shortly before the outbreak of the revolution, when it took him by surprise with its convulsions and dazzled him with its light. He now asserted, "The nation's filled with a spirit of eternal struggle flaming throughout its body stretched from Aswan to the Mediterranean Sea. The English only stirred it up. It's blazing away now and will never die out."

There was a smile on Yasin's lips when he observed, "Even the women have organized a demonstration."

Fahmy then recited verses from the poem by the Egyptian author Hafiz Ibrahim about the ladies' demonstration:

> Beautiful women marched in protest.
> I went to observe their rally.
> I found them proudly
> Brandishing the blackness of their garments.
> They looked like stars,
> Gleaming in a pitch-black night.
> They took to the streets;
> Sa'd's home was their target.

Yasin was touched. He laughed and said, "I'm the one who should have memorized that."

Fahmy happened to think of something and asked sadly, "Do you suppose news of our revolution has reached Sa'd in exile? Has the grand old man learned that his sacrifice has not been in vain? Or do you think he's overcome by despair in his exile?"

57

THEY STAYED on the roof until shortly before noon. The two older brothers entertained themselves by observing the small British encampment. They saw that some of the soldiers had set up a field kitchen and were preparing food. Soldiers were scattered between the intersections of Qirmiz Alley and al-Nahhasin with Palace Walk in an area otherwise deserted. From time to time many would fall into line at a signal from a bugle. Then they would get their rifles and climb into one of the vehicles, which would carry them off toward Bayt al-Qadi. This suggested that demonstrations were underway in nearby neighborhoods. Fahmy watched them line up with a pounding heart and flaming imagination.

When the two older brothers finally went downstairs to the study they left Kamal alone on the roof to amuse himself as he saw fit. Fahmy got his books to review what he had missed during the past days. Yasin selected Abu Tammam's medieval collection of Arabic poetry, called *al-Hamasa*, and Jurji Zaydan's historical romance *The Maiden of Karbala* and went out to the sitting room. He was counting on these books to help pass the time, which accumulated as plentifully behind the walls of his prison as water behind a dam. Although novels, including detective stories, had the greatest hold over his affections, he was also fond of poetry. He did not like to exert himself too much when he learned a poem. He was content to understand the parts that were easy to grasp and to enjoy the music of the difficult sections. He rarely referred to the margin of the page packed with glosses. He might memorize a verse and recite it, even though he understood very little of its meaning. He might ascribe a meaning to it that bore almost no relationship to the real one or not even try to attribute a meaning to it. Nevertheless, certain images and expressions settled in his mind. He considered them a treasure to brag about and exploit determinedly when appropriate and even more often when not. If he had a letter to write, he prepared for the assignment as though he were a novelist and crammed it full of any resounding expressions he could recall, inserting whatever remnants of the poetic heritage of the Arabs God allowed him to remember. Yasin was known among his acquaintances as eloquent, not because he really was but because the other men fell short of his attempts and were stunned by his unusual accumulation of knowledge.

Until that time, he had never experienced such a long period of enforced idleness, deprived of all forms of activity and amusement for hour after hour. If he had possessed the patience for reading, that might have helped, but he was only accustomed to read when he was with other people and then only during the short periods preceding his departure for his evening's entertainment. Even on those occasions, he saw nothing wrong with interrupting his reading to join in the coffee hour conversations or to read a little and then summon Kamal to narrate to him what he had read. He enjoyed the boy's passionate response to storytelling, typical of children of that age. Consequently, neither the poetry nor the novel was able to brighten his solitude on such a day. He read some verses and then a few chapters of *The Maiden of Karbala*. He choked on his boredom, drop after drop, while he cursed the English from the depths of his heart. He passed the time until lunch in a bad mood, feeling vexed and disgruntled.

The mother served them soup and roast chicken with rice, but there were no vegetables because of the blockade around the house. She ended the meal with cheese, olives, and whey, substituting molasses for the sweet. The only person with a decent appetite was Kamal. Al-Sayyid Ahmad and the two older brothers were not much inclined to eat, since they had spent the day without any work or activity. This nourishment did assist them to escape from their boredom by helping to put them to sleep, especially the father and Yasin, who were able to fall asleep whenever and however they wanted.

Yasin got up from his nap shortly before sunset and went downstairs to attend the coffee hour. The session was short, since the mother was not able to leave al-Sayyid Ahmad alone for long. She had to withdraw to return to his room. Yasin, Zaynab, Fahmy, and Kamal remained behind to chat with each other listlessly. Then Fahmy excused himself to go to the study. He asked Kamal to join him, leaving the couple alone.

Yasin wondered to himself, "What can I do from now till midnight?" The question had troubled him for a long time, but today he felt depressed and humiliated, forcibly and tyrannically separated from the flow of time which was plunging ahead outside the house with its many pleasures. He was like a branch that turns into firewood when cut from the tree.

Had it not been for the military blockade, he would have been in his beloved seat at the coffeehouse of Ahmad Abduh, sipping green tea and chatting with his acquaintances among its patrons. He would have been enjoying himself in its historic atmosphere. He was captivated by its antiquity, and his imagination was stirred by its subterranean chambers buried in the debris of history. Ahmad Abduh's coffeehouse was the one he loved best. He would not forsake it, unless scorched by some desire, for as they say: "Desire's a fire." It was desire that had attracted him in the past to the Egyptian Club, which was close to the woman who sold doum palm fruit. Desire had also been responsible for tempting him to move to al-Sayyid Ali's coffeehouse in al-Ghuriya, situated across the street from the home of the lute player Zanuba. He would exchange coffeehouses according to the object of his desire. He would even exchange the patrons who had offered him their friendship. Beyond satisfying the desire itself, the coffeehouse and his friends there were meaningless. Where were the Egyptian Club and those friends? They had gone out of his life. If he ran into one of them, Yasin might pretend not to know him and avoid him. It was now the turn of Ahmad Abduh's coffeehouse and its regulars. God only knew what coffeehouses and friends the future had in store for him.

In any case, he did not spend too much of his evening at Ahmad Abduh's. He would soon slip over to Costaki's grocery store, or, more exactly, to his secret bar to get a bottle of red wine, or "the usual," as he liked to call it. Where was "the usual" on this gloomy night? At the memory of Costaki's bar, a shudder of desire passed through his body. Then a look of great weariness showed in his eyes. He seemed as fidgety as a prisoner. Staying home appeared to him to be prolonged suffering. The sharpness of the pain intensified when he entertained the images of bliss and memories of intoxication associated with the bar and the bottle. These dreams tormented him and doubled his anguish. They encouraged his ardent longing for wine's music of the mind and the games it played with his head. Those made him warm and happy, over-flowing with delight and joy. Before that evening he had never realized how incapable he was of patiently abstaining from alcohol for even a single day. He was not sad to discover how weak he was and how addicted. He did not blame himself for the overindulgence that had ended up making him miserable for such a trivial reason. He was as far as one could be from blaming himself or being annoyed. The only cause for his pain that he could remember was the blockade the English had set up around his house. He was consumed by thirst when the intoxicating watering hole was near at hand.

He glanced at Zaynab. He found her examining his face with a look that seemed to say resentfully, "Why are you so inattentive? Why are you so glum? Doesn't my presence cheer you up at all?" Yasin felt her resentment in the fleeting moment their eyes met, but he did not respond to her sorrowful criticism. To the contrary, it annoyed and riled him. Yes, he disliked nothing so much as being forced to spend a whole evening with her, deprived of desire, pleasure, and the intoxication on which he relied to endure married life.

He began to look at her stealthily and wonder in amazement, "Isn't she the same woman? . . . Isn't she the one who captured my heart on our wedding night? . . . Isn't she the one who drove me wild with passion for nights and weeks on end? . . . Why doesn't she stir me at all? What's come over her? Why am I so restless, disgruntled, and bored, finding nothing in her beauty or culture to tempt me to postpone getting drunk?"

As usual, he was inclined to find her deficient in areas where women like Zanuba excelled. They were clever at providing him special services, but Zaynab was the first woman who had attempted to live with him in a permanent relationship. He had not spent much time with the lute player or the doum fruit vendor. His attachment to them had not been great enough to prevent him from moving on when he felt like it. Many years later he would recall these anxious moments and his reflections on them. Then he would realize things from his own experience and from life in general that had not occurred to him at the time.

He was awakened from his thoughts by her question: "I guess you're not happy about staying home?"

He was not in a condition to deal with criticism. Her sarcastic question affected him like a careless blow to a sore. He shot back with painful candor: "Of course not."

Although she had tried to avoid quarreling with him from the beginning, his tone hurt her badly. She replied sharply, "There's no harm in that. Isn't it amazing how you can't bear to miss your carousing for even one night?"

He said angrily, "Mention one thing that would make staying home bearable."

She became enraged and said in a voice that showed she was on the verge of tears, "I'll leave. Perhaps then you'll like it better."

She turned her back on him to flee. He followed her with a stony glare. "How stupid she is! She doesn't know that only divine decree keeps her in my house."

Although the quarrel had relieved a little of his anger, he would have preferred for it not to have happened, if only because it served to increase his depressing boredom. If he had wanted to, he could have appeased her, but the listlessness of his mind had overwhelmed all his feelings.

In a few minutes, a relative calm took possession of him. The cruel words he had thrown at her echoed in his ears. He acknowledged that they were harsh and uncalled for. He felt almost regretful, not because he had suddenly discovered some dregs of affection for her in the corners of his heart, but because of his desire to treat her politely, perhaps out of respect for her father or fear of his. He had not exceeded these bounds, even during the nerve-racking period of adjustment when with decisive firmness he had undertaken to make her accept his policies. He had apologized when he got too angry.

Anger was nothing out of the ordinary for this family. The only time they attempted to control their tempers was when the father was present, monopolizing for himself all rights to anger. Their anger was like a bolt of lightning, quick to flare up and quick to die down. They would be left with various forms of regret and sorrow. Yasin was like this, but he was also obstinate. His regret did not motivate him to seek a reconciliation with his wife. He told himself, "She's the one who made me angry.... Couldn't she have spoken to me in a gentler tone?" He wanted her to be consistently patient, forbearing, and forgiving, so that he could shoot off in pursuit of his passions, confident about the home front.

After she got angry and withdrew, he felt even more uncomfortable with his imprisonment. He left the room to go to the roof. He found the air pleasant there. The night was tranquil. It was dark everywhere but more profoundly so under the arbor of hyacinth beans and jasmine. On the other side of the roof, the dome of the sky was visible, studded with stars like pearls. He began to pace back and forth on the roof between the wall adjoining Maryam's house and the end of the hyacinth bean garden with its view of the Qala'un mosque. He gave himself over to contemplation of various mental images.

As he was walking slowly by the entrance to the arbor a rustling sound or perhaps a whisper caught his ear. He could hear someone breathing. Surprised, he stared into the darkness and called out, "Who's there?"

A voice he easily recognized replied in ringing tones, "Nur, master."

He remembered immediately that Nur, his wife's maid, retired at night to a wooden hut containing a few sticks of furniture, next to the chicken coop. He looked across the roof until he made out her figure standing a few feet away, like a condensed and solidified piece of night. He saw the whites of her eyes, as pure white as circles drawn in chalk on a jet-black form. He kept on pacing and said nothing more, but her features were automatically traced on his imagination. She was black, in her forties, and solidly built. She had thick limbs and a full chest. Her rear was plump. She had a gleaming face, sparkling eyes, and full lips. There was something powerful, coarse, and unusual about her, or he had thought of her that way since she had appeared in his house.

Suddenly and unexpectedly, an inclination to assault her exploded within his breast like fireworks going off without any warning. This was a forceful, dominating lust. The whole point of his life seemed to be concentrated in it. It got control of him just as it had the night of Aisha's wedding, when he had seen Umm Hanafi in the courtyard as he was reaching the threshold. His languid being was permeated by a bubbling new life. Restless desire spread through his veins, electrifying him. His ennui and boredom were replaced by an insane, raging, hot interest. All of this happened in the twinkling of an eye. His gait, thought, and imagination all became energetic. Unconsciously he stopped pacing the entire width of the roof. He cut back on the distance by a third and then half. Whenever he passed her, his body was troubled by tempestuous desire. . . . A black maid? . . . A servant? So what? It would not be the first time for him. Women like Zanuba definitely were not the only ones he craved. Just one beautiful feature was enough for him, like the kohl-enhanced eyes of the doum fruit vendor in al-Watawit, which had compensated for the stench of her armpits and the mud caked on her legs. Even ugliness, so long as there was a woman attached to it, was excused by his blind lust, as it had been with Umm Hanafi or with the one-eyed geomancer with whom he had enjoyed some private moments behind al-Nasr Gate.

Nur at any rate had a solid, firm body. Touching it would no doubt inspire him to be virile and active. The very fact that she was a black maid would lend interest to the tryst and novelty to the experience. He would be able to verify the rumor about girls of her heritage, who were said to be hot and passionate.

The circumstances seemed propitious. It was dark and secure on the roof. His desire intensified. His nervous energy was bounding. His heart raced. He cast a piercing glance in her direction and changed course slightly so that he would just happen to rub against her one way or another when he passed her. He would postpone making an open declaration of his intentions until he had a chance to sound out the situation cautiously, for fear that she might be a fool like Umm Hanafi and cause the house to echo with a new scandal.

Staring at her, he advanced with deliberate steps. He wanted to have all the lust raging inside him conveyed to her by the message in his eyes, in spite of the encompassing darkness. When he got close to her, his heartbeats became irregular. He came up beside her and his elbow touched the upper part of her body. He kept on walking, as though it had been an accident. A tremor passed through his body when he collided with her. He was not sure what he had touched, for he was wandering in a trance world. All he could remember as his mind cleared a bit at the edge of the roof was that he had felt something tender and appealing and she had stepped back nonchalantly. His suspicion that she was not worried about him was corroborated by her reaction.

He turned around, determined to attack again. He went back toward her with his arm folded so his elbow would touch one of her breasts. His senses did not mislead him this time. He did not move his elbow away, as one would have expected from a person who had simply lost his way. He left it there to brush gently past the other breast, no longer trying to avoid awakening her suspicions. He walked on, telling himself, "She'll no doubt understand what I'm after. Perhaps she has understood and wanted to step aside but was slow to do it. Perhaps she was taken by surprise and startled. At any rate, she didn't push me away with her hand and she remained still. She won't start screaming suddenly like that other bitch. Let's try a third time."

On this occasion his pace was quick and impatient. He slowed down when he reached her. Then he stretched his elbow out to her breasts that swelled like a full pair of little waterskins. He moved his arm in a hesitant, doubtful manner. He started to walk on, driven by a desire to flee, but found her so yielding or dull that the remnants of his conscious mind were drowned in an insane flood. He stopped. With a voice that emerged from a fog of lust, trembling and fading away, he asked, "Is that you, Nur?"

The maid, who was backing away from him, replied, "Yes, master."

To prevent her from escaping, he pursued her until her back was against the wall and he was almost touching her. He wanted to say anything he could think of to declare his inner turmoil, like a boxer waving his fist in the air while watching for an opportunity to deal a final blow. Breathing on her forehead, he asked, "Why didn't you go into your room?"

Blockaded by him, she stammered, "I was enjoying the fresh air a little."

His greedy appetite overcame his hesitation. He put his hand on her waist. Then he pulled her gently toward his breast. She put up some resistance and kept him from achieving his goal. Putting his cheek next to hers, he whispered in her ear, "Come to the room."

She muttered uneasily, "Shame on you, master."

Her voice rang out in the silence in a way that disturbed him. She had not raised her voice intentionally, but it did not appear easy for her to whisper or her whisper had a resonance to it, even if less pronounced than that of her normal voice. His panic quickly deserted him, both because his lust was fully ignited and because her tone lacked the protest that her words suggested. He took her by the hand as he murmured, "Come along, sweetheart."

She did not attempt to free her hand, either because she was pleased or because she was obedient. He was lavishing kisses on her cheek and neck, swaying from the intense emotional impact, in a delirium of happiness. He began to say, "What's kept you from me all these months?"

She answered him in her normal tone of voice, lacking any ring of protest, "Shame on you, master."

Smiling, he commented, "Your objections are very attractive. Make some more."

She did resist a little when they reached the entrance to the room and said, "Shame on you, master. . . . " Then, as though to caution him, she added, "The room's full of bedbugs."

He pushed her inside, whispering with his mouth at the nape of her neck, "I'd lie among scorpions for your sake, Nur."

She was a servant in every sense of the word. She stood submissively in front of him in the dark while he placed his lips on hers and kissed her in a fiery, passionate manner. She was still and submissive, as though watching a scene in which she had no part. He told her emotionally, "Kiss me!" He put his lips to hers again and kissed her. Then she kissed him.

He wanted her to sit down. She repeated her phrase, "Shame on you, master," which was becoming comic through monotonous repetition.

He sat her down himself and she complied without any resistance. He began to enjoy the juxtaposition of her protests and her obedience. He sought to elicit more. Her verbal resistance continued, combined with her active obedience. He forgot the time.

He imagined that the darkness around him was moving or that there were strange creatures prancing about in it. Perhaps the exertion was beginning to tell on him after he had stayed at it such a long time – if he had been there long. He certainly did not know how much time he had spent with her. Perhaps the raging currents crashing against each other in his head had impinged on his vision, causing him to see imaginary lights. But not so fast . . . the walls of the room were undulating. A faint light flowed over them into which the pitch-black darkness dissolved so thoroughly that the room's secrets were disclosed. He raised his head to stare. He saw a faint light slipping through the cracks in the wooden wall, intruding on his privacy.

Then his wife's voice was raised to call the maid: "Are you asleep, Nur? Nur. . . . Have you seen Mr. Yasin?"

His heart trembled in alarm. He leapt up and quickly and regretfully grabbed his clothes to put them on. With roving eyes he searched the room on the chance that he might find a hiding place among its cast-off furnishings. One look was enough to make him despair of concealing himself. Meanwhile the sound of approaching slippers assaulted his ears. The maid could not keep herself from saying in a tearful voice, "It's all your fault, master. What am I going to do now?"

He hit her hard on the shoulder to make her stop. He stared at the door with terror and despair. Without thinking about what he was doing, he retreated to the corner farthest from the entrance and pressed against the wall. He froze there and waited. The calls were repeated, but no one answered. Then the door was pushed open. Zaynab's arm appeared, holding a lamp in front of her. She was crying, "Nur . . . Nur."

The maid was forced to murmur in a sad, weak voice, "Yes, madam."

She chided her in an angry voice, "How quick you are to fall asleep, old lady. . . . Have you seen Mr. Yasin? My father-in-law sent for him. I looked for him downstairs and in the courtyard. Now I haven't been able to find him on the roof. Have you seen him?"

As soon as she finished speaking, her head poked inside the room. She looked down at the compromised maid in astonishment. Then, instinctively, she turned to her right and her eyes fell upon her husband, whose enormous body was plastered against the wall, looking flabby and weak from shame and disgrace. Their eyes met for an instant before he looked down. Another instant of lethal silence passed. Then a scream like a howl escaped from the girl. She retreated. Beating her breast with her left hand, she cried out, "You scandalous black slut . . . You! You!"

She began to tremble and the lamp in her hand trembled along with her. The light reflected on the wall opposite the door shook. Then she turned and fled. Her wail rent the silence.

Swallowing, Yasin told himself, "I'm ruined. What's done is done." He remained standing where he was, oblivious to everything around him. When he came to his senses, he left the room for the roof, without thinking about going any farther. He did not know what to do. How widely known would the scandal become? Would it be confined to his own apartment or travel to the other one? He began to scold himself for being too stunned and weak to catch up with her in order to contain the scandal in the smallest possible circle. He wondered with intense discomfort how he would deal with this scandal. Would he be resolute? Perhaps he could be if the news did not get through to his father.

He heard movement coming from the direction of the ill-omened room. He turned and saw the figure of the maid leaving it with a large bundle in her hand. She hastened to the door of the stairway and departed. He shrugged his shoulders disdainfully. When he touched his chest he realized he had forgotten to put on his undershirt and quickly returned to the room.

58

SOMEONE KNOCKED on the door early in the morning. It was the shaykh, or supervisor, of the district. He met with al-Sayyid Ahmad and told him that the authorities had instructed him to inform the residents of the occupied areas that the English would not interfere with anyone except the demonstrators. It was incumbent upon al-Sayyid Ahmad to open his store, on the pupil to go to school, and on the civil servant to go to his place of employment. The shaykh cautioned him against keeping pupils home lest they be suspected of striking. He directed his host's attention to the orders strictly forbidding demonstrations and strikes.

In that manner the house resumed the activities with which it normally greeted the morning. The men breathed a sigh of relief after the captivity of the previous day. People felt refreshed, attaining a certain degree of composure and tranquillity.

After the visit from the shaykh of the district, Yasin told himself, "Conditions outside the house have begun to improve, but inside it's nothing but mire and muck."

Most members of the family had passed a hideous night dominated by the scandal. The misfortune had torn the family apart. Zaynab's patience, which had kept her sorrows and grievances confined to her breast, could not stand up to the shocking vision in her maid's room. Her reserve exploded and threw flames in every direction. She deliberately intended for her wail to reach the ears of al-Sayyid Ahmad.

He rushed to her, wondering what was the matter. The scandal was revealed. She told him everything, emboldened by her insane passion. Without it, her courage would not have been up to confronting him with her story, since she still dreaded him more than anyone else. In this manner, she got revenge for her wounded honor and for the patience she had shown, voluntarily at times and resentfully on many other occasions.

"A maid! A servant! Old enough to be his mother! In my house! So what do you suppose he does elsewhere?"

She was not weeping from jealousy, or perhaps her jealousy was temporarily hidden behind a thick veil of disgust and anger, like fire concealed by clouds of smoke. It seemed she would prefer death to staying under the same roof with him, even for a single day, after what had happened. In fact, she abandoned her bed to spend the night in the parlor. She was awake most of it, delirious as though she had a high fever. The short time she slept, her slumber was deep but troubled like an invalid's. When she awoke, she was determined to leave the house. This decision was virtually the only thing that provided any relief from her pains. What could even her father-in-law do? He could not undo the reprehensible act after it had occurred. No matter how tyrannical he was, he could not punish her husband as much as he deserved and heal her wounded heart. The most he could do would be to reprimand and pour out his wrath upon his son. The debauched sinner would listen with head bowed but then continue with his nasty style of life. How preposterous!

Al-Sayyid Ahmad had implored her to leave the matter to him. He had advised her at length to overlook her husband's slip and rely on the patience of virtuous women like herself. But she could not bear to be patient or forgiving any longer. A black servant over forty! No! This time she would leave him without any hesitation. She would tell her father all her sorrows and remain in his custody until Yasin came to his senses. If he then came to her repentant, having reformed his behavior, she might return. Otherwise, this whole life, with its good and bad aspects, could go to the devil.

Yasin was wrong to think she was too reasonable and sensible to reveal her worries to other people. The truth was that from the beginning she had been so apprehensive she had shared her concerns with her mother, who had demonstrated how sensible she was by making sure the complaint did not reach Zaynab's father. She had counseled her daughter to be patient, telling her that men, like her father for example, spent their evenings out and drank. Zaynab should be satisfied if her household was well provided for and if her husband returned to her, no matter how late or how drunk. The girl had heeded her mother's advice grudgingly and had attempted to the best of her abilities to adorn herself with patience. She had spared no effort to content herself with the reality and trim her vast dreams down, to be satisfied with what she actually had, especially since she was pregnant and looking forward to the proud status of motherhood. With her grievances buried deep inside her, she was content to surrender, consoling herself at different times with her mother's example and that of the mistress of her new home.

There was room enough for doubt. Her heart was troubled occasionally about what her husband might be doing at his drinking parties. She confided her fears to her mother. Indeed, she did not conceal from her the man's diminished interest. Her sensible mother explained to her that this decrease in passion was definitely not caused by what she had in mind. It was "something natural," common to all men. She would become convinced of that herself as she became more experienced in life. Even if her suspicions were correct, what did she think she was going to do about it? Should she leave her home just because her husband had sex with other women? Of course not . . . a thousand times no! If a woman renounced her position for a reason like this, households would soon run short of honest women. A man might set his sights on one woman or another, but he would always return home, so long as his wife was worthy of being his last resort and enduring refuge. Patient women would be the winners. She proceeded to remind her daughter of women who had been divorced for no fault of their own and of women whose husbands had more than one wife. Was her husband's fickleness, even if a reality, not a lighter matter than the conduct of those other types of men? Moreover, Yasin was a young man of only twenty-two. It was inevitable that he would become more reasonable in time and return to his home, occupying himself with his children to the exclusion of the rest of the world. The moral of all this advice was that she had to be patient, even if her suspicions were true. What if they were not? What then? The mother had repeated this and other, similar advice until the girl's defiance was tamed. She had come to believe in patience and had resigned herself to it, but with one fatal blow the incident on the roof had completely destroyed the entire structure of patient resignation.

Al-Sayyid Ahmad did not comprehend this distressing fact. He thought the girl had resolved to follow his advice. Even so, his anger was too great to be easily assuaged. The maid had done the right thing when she fled, but Yasin had not left the roof, where he was anticipating with alarm the storm that awaited him. When he heard his father's voice calling him, it sounded like whips cracking. His heart pounded, but he did not answer or obey. Feeling desperate, he stayed put. Before Yasin knew what was happening, the man stormed up to the roof. He stood there snarling for some moments while he searched the area. When he made out his son's shape, he headed toward him, coming to a stop nearby. He folded his arms across his chest and glared at Yasin severely and haughtily. He remained silent for a long time to increase his son's torment and terror. He seemed to want his silence to express his feelings, which words could not convey. He may also have wished it to symbolize the violent kick and punch he would have used to discipline his son had he not been a man and a husband like himself.

When he could not stand to be silent any longer, shaking with anger and rage, he rained down insults and rebukes on Yasin: "You defy me within my hearing and sight. . . . You and your disgrace can go to hell. . . . You've defiled my house, you scoundrel. There's no way this house can ever be pure again so long as you're in it. You had an excuse before you got married, alas. What excuse do you have now? . . . If my words were addressed to an animal, it would behave itself, but they're directed to a stone. . . . A household that includes you is likely to be cursed." He relieved his flaming breast of words like hot lead.

Yasin stood before him still, silent, with his head bowed, as though he were about to melt away into the darkness. When the father had screamed as much as he could, he turned his back on him and left the place, cursing him and his father and mother. In his rage, he thought that Yasin's slip was a crime deserving the ultimate punishment. In his fury, he neglected to remember that his own past was a long and repeated series of slips like Yasin's. He had persisted with this conduct even halfway through his fifth decade, when his children were growing up and some were married. His rage did not really make him forget, but he allowed himself liberties he did not permit any of his family. He had a right to do what he wanted, but they were expected to adhere to the limits he imposed on them.

His anger was possibly greater at the elements present in Yasin's offense of challenge to his will, disdain for his existence, and distortion of the image he wanted to have of his children than at the offense itself. But as usual his anger did not last long. Its flames soon died down and its blaze abated. He slowly became calm,

PALACE WALK 417

although his façade, and just his façade, remained despondent and distressed. He was now able to see Yasin's "crime" from more than one angle. He could contemplate it with a clear head. Its darker side faded to reveal its various comic aspects, which entertained his enforced solitude. The first thing that occurred to him was to look for an excuse for the guilty party. It was not from any love of lenience, for he hated to be lenient at home. He wanted to use this excuse as an explanation for Yasin's apparent violation of his will. He seemed to be telling himself, "My son did not disobey me.... Far from it! His excuse is such and such."

Should his youth be considered an excuse, since it was a time of recklessness and rashness? Certainly not... Youth might be an excuse for the offense, but it was no excuse for defying his will. Otherwise Fahmy and even Kamal would be allowed any extremes in ignoring his instructions. The excuse should be sought, then, in his status as a man. It was his manhood that gave him a right to free himself from his father's will, if only to a limited extent, and spared al-Sayyid Ahmad from bearing responsibility for his son's deeds. The father seemed to be telling himself, "He did not disobey me. Far from it! He's just reached an age when it's not an offense to deviate from my will." Needless to say, he would not admit this truth to Yasin and would never have forgiven his son if Yasin had dared to make this demand. Indeed, he would not admit it to himself unless there was a rebellious act requiring some justification. To reassure himself, he did not forget even under such circumstances to remind himself that he had been unusually hard on his son when he was growing up. Few fathers were so strict. Yasin had submitted totally to this discipline in a way that few sons would have.

He turned his mind thoughtfully to Zaynab, but he felt no sympathy for her. He had tried to comfort her out of respect for her father, who was his dear friend, but he felt the girl was not really worthy of her father. It was not appropriate for a good wife to implicate her husband in a scandal as she had, no matter what the circumstances. How she had wailed! How she had screamed! What would he have done if Amina had surprised him one day in a comparable situation? But what was she compared with Amina? Moreover, how shamelessly she had recounted to him everything she had seen.... Pshaw! Pshaw! If this girl had not been Muhammad Iffat's daughter, Yasin would have been within his rights to discipline her for what she had done. He himself would not have been happy to allow this incident to pass without a scolding to punish her. Yasin had made a mistake, but she had made an even greater one.

Then his thoughts quickly returned to Yasin. With inner joy he thought about the temperament they both shared. They had no doubt inherited it from the grandfather. It might well be blazing in Fahmy's chest behind a veil of culture and morality. In fact, did he not remember how he had come home unexpectedly one day and heard Kamal singing "O bird, you up in the tree"? He had waited outside the door, not merely to pretend he had arrived after the song was completed but also to follow the voice, savoring its timbre and probing its length of breath. When the boy had finished the tune, he had banged the door and coughed when he entered. He had concealed inside his breast his delight, which no one had detected. He was pleased to see himself flourishing once more in the lives of his sons – at least during calm and serene times. But not so fast. . . . Yasin's disposition was peculiar to him and not something they shared. They did not have a single temperament, if the precise meaning of the word was to be respected. Yasin was a blind animal. . . . He had assaulted Umm Hanafi once and had been caught again with Nur. He thought nothing of wallowing in the mud. He himself was not like that!

Yes, he could understand how vexing it had been for Yasin to be forced to spend the night in something like a prison. He understood, because he had endured it too, feeling depressed and sad, as though he had lost a loved one. Suppose he had been strolling around the roof garden like the boy and had come upon a maid – assuming she was to his liking – would he have embarked on this adventure? Certainly not . . . absolutely not! But what obstacle would have restrained him? Perhaps the location? The family! Perhaps his maturity. . . . Oh, he became irritated when this last possibility came to mind. He imagined that he envied Yasin both his youthful appetite and the folly of his slip. . . . No, however that might be, they had two different temperaments.

Al-Sayyid Ahmad was not infatuated with women per se, with no conditions or stipulations. His lust was always distinguished by a taste for luxury. It was propelled by a refined sense of selection. It was concerned about social qualifications, which it lumped together with the customary physical ones. He was infatuated with feminine beauty in all its flesh, coquetry, and elegance. Jalila, Zubayda, Maryam's mother, and tens more like them had all possessed at least some of these characteristics. In addition to that, it was not like him to be comfortable or content without a delightful setting and a congenial gathering, along with the wine, pleasant conversation, and music that went with such occasions. He did not need to spend much time with a new lover before she would realize what he desired and prepare the kind of setting his soul yearned for, with a fragrant atmosphere redolent of roses, incense, and musk.

Just as he loved beauty in the abstract, he loved it in its glittering social framework. He liked to be noticed and to have a widespread reputation. Therefore he enjoyed sharing his love and lovers with his special friends, except on those rare occasions when circumstances required him to be discreet and secretive, as with Maryam's mother. This social use of his love did not require him to sacrifice beauty, for in his circle beauty and reputation went hand in hand, like an object and its shadow. Beauty was most often the magic wand that opened the door to reputation and noteworthy status. He had been the lover of some of the most famous entertainers of his time. Not one of them had disappointed his yearning for beauty or his craving for loveliness.

For these reasons he thought scornfully of Yasin's conquests. He repeated disapprovingly, "Umm Hanafi! . . . Nur! . . . What a beast he is!" He himself was innocent of such abnormal lusts, although he did not need to wonder too long about their source. He had not forgotten the woman who had given birth to Yasin. She had passed on to him her character with its passion for the sordid. He was responsible for the strength of Yasin's lust, but she had to answer for the nature of this lust and its base inclinations.

The next morning he thought seriously about the issue again. He almost summoned the couple to try to reconcile them with each other and with him, but he deferred it to a more appropriate time than morning.

When Fahmy asked Yasin why he stayed away from the breakfast table, he answered tersely, "It's just some trivial thing. I'll tell you about it later."

Fahmy remained in the dark about the secret reason his father was angry with Yasin until he learned that the maid Nur had disappeared. He was then able to guess everything. The morning started off in an unusual way for the family, because Yasin left the house early and Zaynab stayed in her room. Then the other men of the family left the house. They were agitated and careful not to look at the soldiers. Behind the peephole of the window, the mother prayed for God to protect them from any harm.

Amina did not want to become involved in the "incident" on the roof. She went down to the oven room and waited from one moment to the next for Zaynab to join her as usual. She would not admit that Zaynab had a right to be angry about her honor. She considered it a form of coquetry of which she disapproved. She began to ask herself, "How can she claim rights for herself that no other woman has ever claimed?"

It was clear that Yasin had done something wrong. He had defiled a pure house. But he had wronged his father and step-mother, not Zaynab. . . . "I'm an angel compared with that girl. . . ."

As the waiting became protracted, she could no longer pretend to ignore the girl. She convinced herself that it was her duty to go console her. She went up to her apartment and called her. She entered the room and found no trace of her. She went from room to room, calling her until she had searched the whole house. Then she struck her hands together and exclaimed, "O Lord . . . has Zaynab seen fit to leave her home?"

59

AMINA FOUND no relief from her anxiety all day long. The possibility that the soldiers would stop one of her men going or coming never left her head. Fahmy was the first to return. On seeing him, she felt slightly less anxious, but when she noticed he was frowning she asked, "What's the matter, son?"

He complained, "I hate these soldiers."

The woman told him apprehensively, "Don't let them see it. If you love me, don't do it."

Even without her entreaty he would not have. He was not bold enough to challenge them with even a look as he walked along at their mercy. He kept his eyes from turning to gaze at any of them. On his way home he had asked himself sarcastically what they would do with him if they knew he was returning from a demonstration during which a violent confrontation had taken place and that early in the morning he had distributed tens of handbills inciting people to resist the soldiers.

He sat down to pass in review the events of the day. He recalled a few of them as they had actually happened but most as he wished they had been. It was his notion to work during the day and dream in the evening. In both cases, he was motivated by the most sublime and most hideous emotions: patriotism and a desire to kill and devastate. His dreams would intoxicate him for some time and then he would rouse himself, sad that they were impossible to carry out and depressed because they seemed silly. The fabric of these dreams was woven from the battles he would lead like Joan of Arc. Having seized the enemy's weapons, he would attack, achieving the defeat of the English, and then deliver his immortal speech in Cairo's Opera Square. The English would be forced to announce the independence of Egypt. Sa'd would return triumphant from exile. Fahmy would meet the leader, who would address the nation. Maryam would be present at the historic inauguration. Yes, his dreams were always crowned by the image of Maryam, even though, like the moon hidden behind storm clouds, she had been tucked away all this time in a remote corner of his heart that was beset by distractions.

Before he knew what was happening, his mother, tightening the kerchief around her head, told him uneasily, "Zaynab's angry and has left for her father's home."

Oh . . . he had almost forgotten what had happened to his brother and family that morning. His speculations when he learned that the maid, Nur, had disappeared were now confirmed. He avoided his mother's eyes in embarrassment. He did not want her to discern what was passing through his mind, especially since he was sure she knew the truth of the matter. He thought it likely that she realized he knew about it too or at least suspected he did. He did not know what to say, since in his conversations with her he was not accustomed to pretending things he did not feel. He hated nothing so much as having wiles replace candor in their relationship. He limited himself to muttering, "May our Lord remedy the situation."

Amina said nothing more, as though the disappearance of Zaynab was a trivial event to be dismissed with a declarative statement and a pious wish.

Fahmy had to hide a smile, which almost betrayed that he knew more than he was saying. He realized that his mother was suffering too. She was uneasy because she had no natural talent for acting. She was not good at lying. Even if she was forced to prevaricate at times, her temperament, which was too straightforward to allow the veils of deception to cling, would give her away.

Their confusion did not last long, for in a few minutes they saw Yasin heading toward them. From the way he looked up at them, they imagined he did not realize what problems lay in store for him in the house, although even they did not know the extent of the trouble. Fahmy was not surprised, for he knew that Yasin paid little attention to problems other people found oppressive.

Yasin was overwhelmed by the breathtaking sensation of having emerged triumphant from an adventure that had caused him to forget most of his problems, if only temporarily. He had been on his way to the house when a soldier, apparently popping up from nowhere, had blocked his way. Yasin had trembled all over, expecting unprecedented evil or at least a distressing insult that would be observed by the shop owners and passersby. He had not hesitated to defend himself, addressing the soldier gently and ingratiatingly, as though asking permission to pass: "Please, sir."

The soldier had asked for a match and smiled. Yes, he had smiled. Yasin had been so astonished to see him smile that he had encountered difficulty understanding what he wanted until the soldier repeated his request. He had never imagined that an English soldier would smile that way. Even if English soldiers smiled like other human beings, he would not have thought one would smile at him so politely. He had been transported by delight and remained frozen for a few moments, neither offering an answer nor making a motion. Then with all the energy he could muster, he had tackled this simple assignment for the mighty, smiling soldier. Since he did not smoke and did not carry any matches, he had gone at once to al-Hajj Darwish, who sold beans, and purchased a box of matches. Then he had rushed back to the soldier, holding it out to him. The soldier had taken it and said, in English, "Thank you."

Yasin had not yet recovered from the impact of that magical smile. Now here was "thank you." It was like a glass of beer a person drinks to refresh himself when he has had enough whiskey. It filled Yasin with gratitude and pride. His pudgy face blushed and beamed as though the words "thank you" were a high decoration with which he had been publicly invested. It practically guaranteed that he would be able to go and come as he pleased in perfect safety. As soon as the soldier gave the first sign of moving away, Yasin told him in a friendly manner that came straight from his heart, "Good luck, sir."

Yasin proceeded to the house almost reeling with joy. What good luck he had had. . . . An Englishman – not an Australian or an Indian – had smiled at him and thanked him. . . . An Englishman – in other words, the kind of man he imagined to embody all the perfections of the human race. Yasin probably detested the English as all Egyptians did, but deep inside he respected and venerated them so much that he frequently imagined they were made from a different stuff than the rest of mankind. This man had smiled at him and thanked him. . . . Yasin had answered him correctly, imitating English pronunciation so far as his mouth would allow. He had succeeded splendidly and had merited the man's thanks.

How could he believe the brutal acts attributed to them? Why had they exiled Sa'd Zaghlul if they were so gracious? His enthusiasm faded the moment his eyes fell on Mrs. Amina and Fahmy. From their expressions he could grasp that something was wrong. His worries, from which he had been temporarily severed, wound round him like a rope. He realized that he was confronted once more by the problem from which he had fled early that morning. Pointing upstairs, he asked, "Why isn't she sitting with you? Is she still angry?"

Amina exchanged a glance with Fahmy. Then she muttered nervously, "She's gone to her father."

He raised his eyebrows in astonishment or alarm. Then he asked her, "Why did you let her go?"

Amina replied with a sigh, "She slipped out without anyone noticing."

He felt he ought to say something to defend his honor in front of his brother and stepmother. He declared scornfully, "Whatever she wants."

Fahmy decided to resist his urge to keep silent. He wanted his brother to think he knew nothing about his secret and also wished to dispel any suspicion that he had heard it from his mother. He asked simply, "What caused this misfortune?"

Yasin gave him a searching look. He waved his large hand and grimaced as if to say, "Nothing's caused any misfortune." Then he observed, "Girls today no longer have the ability to get along with people." Looking at Mrs. Amina, he asked, "Where are the ladies of yesteryear?"

Amina bowed her head, apparently from embarrassment but actually to hide a smile that got the better of her when her mind tried to reconcile the image of Yasin now – contemplative, hortatory, and victimized – with the Yasin of the previous evening when he had been caught on the roof. All the same, Yasin's discomfort was far greater than the circumstances allowed him to admit. Despite the oppressive disappointment he had sustained in his married life, he had never thought for a moment of terminating it. He found in marriage a secure haven and refuge, not to mention the promise of imminent fatherhood, which he welcomed enthusiastically. He had always hoped to have his marriage waiting for him when he returned from his various sorties like an explorer returning to his homeland at the end of the year. He was not oblivious to the new conflict between him and his father as well as Mr. Iffat that would result from his wife's departure. All of this would be further clouded by the scandal. Its odor would be diffused until it stopped up everyone's nostrils. . . . The bitch! He had been fully determined to bring her around gradually to confessing that her error was more serious than his. Indeed, he may even have been so convinced that he felt it would certainly happen. He had sworn to make her apologize and to discipline her, but she had departed. She had turned his plans upside down and left him in an extremely awkward crisis. The bitch!

He was wrenched from his stream of thoughts by a scream that rent the silence enveloping the house. He turned toward Fahmy and his stepmother. He found they were trying hard to listen, looking concerned and anxious. The screaming continued, and they easily ascertained that it came from a woman. Their eyes showed that they were wondering what direction it came from and what the cause was. Was it announcing a death or a fight or calling for help? Amina began to ask God's protection against all evils.

Then Fahmy said, "It's near . . . perhaps on our street." He rose suddenly, furrowing his brow, and asked, "Could it be that the English have attacked a woman who walked past them?"

He rushed to the balcony with the others trailing behind. The screaming stopped, leaving no indication of the direction from which it had come. The three of them looked through the peephole in the latticework to search the street. Their eyes came to rest on a woman who attracted attention by the strange way she was standing in the center of the street and by the circle of passersby and storekeepers gathered around her. They recognized her immediately and cried out together, "Umm Hanafi! . . ."

Amina had sent the servant to get Kamal from school. She asked, "Why don't I see Kamal with her? What's making her stand there like a statue?"

"Kamal. . . . My Lord . . . where's Kamal?"

Relying on her intuition, the mother said, "She's the one who screamed. I recognize her voice now. . . . Where's Kamal? Save me. . . ."

Neither Fahmy nor Yasin uttered a word. They were busy searching the roadway in general and the English camp in particular for Kamal. They saw people looking toward the soldiers, most notably Umm Hanafi. They were certain that it was Umm Hanafi who had screamed and thus gathered the people around her. They felt instinctively that she was calling for help because some danger was threatening Kamal. Their fears centered on the English. But what was the danger? Where was Kamal? What had happened to the boy?

The mother kept appealing for help. They did not know how to comfort her and probably needed some reassuring themselves.... Where was Kamal? Some of the soldiers were sitting down, others stood or walked along minding their own business. Each was preoccupied with his own activities, as though nothing had happened, as though there was no crowd of people gathered in the street.

Suddenly Yasin punched Fahmy's shoulder and yelled, "Don't you see those soldiers standing in a circle under the cistern building on our street? Kamal's standing in the middle. . . . Look."

The mother could not keep herself from screaming, "The soldiers have Kamal. . . . There he is, O my Lord . . . Lord . . . save me."

Four giant soldiers had linked arms to form a circle. Fahmy's eyes had searched in that direction more than once without discovering Kamal. This time he noticed the boy in the center of the circle, visible through an opening between the legs of a soldier who was standing with his back to them. The family imagined the soldiers were going to kick him back and forth like a ball until they did him in.

Fahmy's fear for his brother made him forget his own safety. He turned around and said excitedly, "I'm going to him, no matter what."

Yasin's hand grabbed his shoulder. Yasin told Fahmy decisively, "Stop." Then with a calm, cheerful voice he told the mother, "Don't be afraid. If they had wanted to harm him, they would not have hesitated. . . . Look. He seems to be involved in a long conversation. And what about this red thing in his hand? I wager it's a piece of chocolate. . . . Calm yourself. They're just having some fun with him." He sighed and continued: "He's frightened us for no reason at all."

Yasin regained his composure. He still remembered his happy adventure with the soldier. He did not think it too unlikely that some of the man's fellow soldiers were as gracious and gentle as he was. Then he thought he would shore up and corroborate what he had said for the sake of the mother's agonized heart. He pointed to

Umm Hanafi, who had not moved, and observed, "Don't you see that Umm Hanafi kept screaming until she realized there was no need for it? The people around her are beginning to move away. They seem reassured."

The mother murmured in a shaky voice, "My heart won't be reassured until he comes to me."

They focused their attention on the boy or what they could see of him from time to time. The soldiers unlinked their arms and relaxed their legs as though they were confident that Kamal would not run away. Now Kamal could be seen in his entirety. He was smiling, and they could tell from the movement of his lips and from the gestures of his hands, which he used to get a point across, that he was talking. The fact that he and the soldiers seemed to understand each other indicated that they could use the Cairo dialect of Arabic to some extent. But what was he telling them and what were they saying to him? None of them could guess that, but they calmed down. Even the mother in her anxious astonishment was finally able to watch silently, without any wail or call for help, the strange scene unfolding before her eyes.

Yasin laughed and said, "It's clear we were far too pessimistic when we assumed that the occupation of our district by these soldiers would create endless problems for us."

Although Fahmy appeared to be grateful that the soldiers were treating Kamal correctly, he did not appreciate Yasin's remark. Without turning his eyes away from the boy, he commented, "The way they treat men and women may differ from their treatment of children. Don't get too optimistic."

Yasin almost burst out with an account of his happy adventure, but he stopped himself in time for fear of enraging his brother. To be polite and ingratiating he said, "May our Lord free us safely from them."

Amina asked impatiently, "Isn't it time for them to let him go, with our thanks?"

It appeared that the circle of men around Kamal were expecting something else to happen. One of the four had gone off to a nearby tent to fetch a wooden chair, which he placed in front of Kamal. The boy immediately jumped on the chair. He stood there erect, with his arms hanging down straight at his sides, as though reviewing a formation of soldiers from an elite guard. His fez had slipped down over the back of his head, probably without his noticing it, to reveal his large, protruding forehead. What was he doing? Why was he standing like that? They did not have long to wonder, for his clear voice soon rang out with this song:

> *I want to go home,*
> *Darling.*
> *They've taken my boy,*
> *Darling.*

He sang it all the way through in his pleasing voice while the soldiers watched, their mouths open and smiling. They clapped their hands in appreciation at the end of each phrase. One of them was touched when he understood part of the meaning of the song and began to shout, "I'm going home. . . . I'm going home."

Kamal was encouraged by the enthusiastic response of his audience. He sang his very best, taking special care with his vibrato and projection. He finished the song to applause and praise, in which his family at the peephole participated, after singing along with him in their hearts, filled with joy and apprehension. Yes, the family participated in praising him after sharing vicariously in the singing, which they had followed anxiously, praying that he would excel and not make any mistakes. They might almost have been singing through him. It was as though their honor, both individually and as a family, was riding on his success.

Amina forgot her fears in the midst of these other feelings. Even Fahmy thought of nothing but the song and his hopes for its success. When the song was concluded successfully they all sighed deeply and wished Kamal would hurry home before anything happened to spoil the impact.

It seemed clear that the party was about to break up, for Kamal jumped down from the chair. He shook hands with each of the soldiers and raised his hand in salute. Then he shot off toward the house. The family rushed from the balcony to the sitting room to be ready to greet him. He arrived flushed and out of breath, with perspiration on his brow, his eyes and features contented, his limbs moving jerkily and aimlessly from his joyful feeling of victory. His young heart was filled to overflowing with happiness, which he could not help but proclaim in every possible way, calling the others to share in it. It was like a swelling deluge the riverbanks cannot retain that floods the fields and valleys. One look would have been enough to show him the impact of his adventure on their faces, but he was blinded by his joy and shouted, "I've got news you won't believe. You couldn't imagine it...."

Yasin laughed loudly and sarcastically, "What news, my darling?"

This phrase lifted the veil from his eyes, like a light suddenly glowing in the darkness, so he could see the eloquent expressions of their faces. His knowledge that they had witnessed his adventure compensated for missing the opportunity to astonish them with his amazing account. He burst into laughter, slapping his knees with his hands. Then, struggling with his giggles, he asked, "Did you really see me?"

At that the voice of Umm Hanafi was heard complaining, "It would have been better if they had seen how I suffered.... What's all this joy about after I was almost undone? ... One more incident like that and it'll be time for God to have mercy on me." She had not removed her black wrap and looked like a sack of coal full to bursting. Her face appeared pale and sickly. There was a strange look of resignation in her eyes.

Amina asked her, "What happened? ... Why did you scream? God was kind to us and we didn't see anything alarming."

Umm Hanafi leaned her back against the door and commenced: "I'll never forget what happened, lady. We were on our way home when a devil of a soldier jumped in front of us and motioned to Mr. Kamal to go with him. Frightened, he ran toward Qirmiz Alley, but another soldier cut him off there. He turned into Palace Walk. He was screaming and my heart plunged from fear. I started to call for help at the top of my lungs. My eyes did not leave him for a minute while he ran from one soldier to another until they surrounded him. I was so afraid I almost died, and I couldn't see straight. I could not see much of anything. Before I knew it, people had gathered around me, but I kept on screaming until Uncle Hasanayn, the barber, told me, 'May God spare him from being harmed by those bastards. Proclaim the oneness of God. They're being nice to him.' Oh, lady, our master al-Husayn was with us and protected us from evil...."

Kamal objected, "I never screamed."

Umm Hanafi beat her hand against her breast and said, "Your screaming was so loud it hurt my ears and drove me crazy."

In a low voice, as though apologizing, he said, "I thought they were going to kill me, but one of them began to whistle and patted my shoulder. Then he gave me a piece of chocolate." Kamal patted his pocket before continuing: "I stopped feeling afraid."

Amina's happiness left her. Perhaps it had been a hasty, spurious joy. The fact she should not lose sight of was that Kamal had been terrified for some minutes. She would need to pray to God for a long time to spare Kamal any evil effects. She did not think of fright merely as a transitory sensation. Certainly not. . . . It was an abnormal state with a mysterious, invisible halo around it. The jinn sought refuge there like bats in darkness. A frightened person, particularly someone young, would be harmed. There would be bad consequences. In her opinion, fear required special care and precautions, whether recitation of verses from the Qur'an, incense, or amulets. She remarked sadly, "They frightened you! May God destroy them. . . ."

Yasin, reading her thoughts, joked, "Chocolate is a useful charm against fright." Then he addressed Kamal: "Did you talk to them in Arabic?"

Kamal embraced the question, because once more it opened for him the doors to imagination and adventure, rescuing him from the vexations of reality. With his face beaming again, he replied, "They spoke to me in a strange kind of Arabic. . . . I wish you had heard it yourself." He went on to imitate the way they talked until everyone was laughing. Even his mother smiled.

Yasin, who envied his brother, asked him, "What did they say to you?"

"Lots of things! . . . 'What's your name?' 'Where's your house?' 'Do you like the English?' "

Fahmy asked sarcastically, "How did you reply to that wonderful question?"

Kamal looked at him and hesitated, but Yasin answered for him: "Of course he said he loves them. . . . What would you have wanted him to say?"

Kamal spoke up again to add fervently, "But I also told them to bring back Sa'd Pasha."

Fahmy could not restrain himself from laughing out loud. He asked Kamal, "Really! . . . What did they say to that?"

Feeling better now that his brother had laughed, Kamal replied, "One of them tweaked my ear and said in English, 'Sa'd Pasha, no.'"

Yasin had another question: "What else did they say?"

Kamal replied innocently, "They asked me if there weren't any girls in our house?"

For the first time since Kamal had arrived they looked at each other grimly. Fahmy asked him with concern, "What did you tell them?"

"I told them my sisters Aisha and Khadija got married, but they didn't understand what I was saying. So I said there's no one at home except 'Nina.' They asked what that meant and I told them 'Mama.'"

Fahmy gave Yasin a look that said, "Do you see how appropriate my suspicions were?" Then he remarked sarcastically, "They didn't give him the chocolate simply for the love of God."

Yasin smiled feebly and muttered, "There's nothing to be worried about." He was not willing to allow this subject to cloud their reunion. So he asked Kamal, "Why did they invite you to sing?"

Kamal laughed. He said, "During the conversation one of them began to sing in a low voice. Then I asked them if they wanted to hear me."

Yasin laughed loudly. He remarked, "What a daring boy you are. . . . Weren't you afraid when you were surrounded by their legs?"

"Not at all," Kamal boasted. Then he said with feeling, "How handsome they are! I've never seen anyone more handsome before. Blue eyes . . . golden hair . . . gleaming white skin. They look like Aisha!"

He suddenly ran off to the study, where he raised his head to see the picture of Sa'd Zaghlul on the wall next to those of the Khedive Abbas II, Mustafa Kamil, and Muhammad Farid. When he returned he said, "They're a lot better-looking than Sa'd Pasha."

Fahmy shook his head sadly and remarked, "What a traitor you are. . . . They bought you with a piece of chocolate. You're not so young you can be excused for saying that. Pupils in your school are dying as martyrs every day. May God grant you failure."

Umm Hanafi had brought in the brazier, coffeepot, cups, and the container with the coffee. Amina began to prepare the coffee for the time-honored session. Everything had returned to normal except that Yasin had begun to think once more of his angry wife. Kamal went off by himself and took the chocolate out of his pocket. He began to remove its gleaming red wrapper. Fahmy's attempt to make him feel bad seemed to have been in vain, for in his heart there was nothing but contentment and love.

60

YASIN'S MARITAL problems became more complex. They were more momentous than anyone had expected. Before al-Sayyid Ahmad knew what was happening, Muhammad Iffat appeared in the store the day after Zaynab had fled. Even before he freed his hand from al-Sayyid Ahmad's handshake of greeting, he said, "Al-Sayyid Ahmad, I've come to you with a request. Zaynab must be divorced today. Before tomorrow, if possible."

Al-Sayyid Ahmad was staggered. Yes, he had been totally disgusted by Yasin's behavior, but he had never thought it would inspire an honorable man like Mr. Muhammad Iffat to request a divorce. He had certainly not imagined that these "errors" would require a divorce. Indeed, it had never occurred to him that a request for divorce would come from the wife. It seemed to him that the world had been turned upside down. He refused to believe the man was in earnest. In the gracious tone that had so often captivated the hearts of his friends, he said, "I wish the brothers were here to observe you hurling this harsh language at me. . . . Listen to me. In the name of our friendship I forbid you to mention the word 'divorce.'"

He examined his friend's face to gauge the impact of his words on him but found Muhammad Iffat frowning glumly in a determined way that boded ill. He began to sense the seriousness of the situation and to feel pessimistic. He invited his visitor to have a seat. Mr. Iffat sat down but looked even glummer. Al-Sayyid Ahmad knew him to be a stubborn, intractable man. When he got angry, affection and kindness were useless. All ties of kinship and friendship were ripped apart by the cutting edge of his wrath.

Al-Sayyid Ahmad said, "Declare the oneness of God . . . and let's talk calmly."

Muhammad Iffat replied, in a tone he seemed to have borrowed from the angry fire of his cheeks, "Our friendship is not in question, so let's leave it out of this. Your son Yasin is not fit to live with. I ascertained this after learning everything. How patient the poor girl has been. . . . She kept her worries to herself for a long time. She hid everything from me. Then she revealed it all after her heart was broken. . . . He stays out all night and returns at dawn so drunk he can't walk straight. He has scorned her and rejected her. What has been the result of all her patience? She catches him in her house with her servant." He spat on the ground before continuing: "A black maid! . . . My daughter wasn't made for this. Absolutely not, by the Lord of Heaven. You know better than anyone else how I feel about her. No . . . by the Lord of Heaven. I would not be Muhammad Iffat if I kept quiet about this."

It was the same old story but with a new element that stunned and shocked him: Mr. Iffat's statement that Yasin "returns at dawn so drunk he can't walk straight." Had he learned his way to the bar as well? When? How? . . . Oh, he did not have time to think about it or to be upset. He needed to control his emotions. The hour required calmness and control. He had to take charge of the situation to ward off any irreparable damage. He observed in a sad voice, "What distresses you distresses me twice as much. Unfortunately, none of the disgraceful actions you have mentioned ever reached me or came to my attention, by God, except the last incident. I have disciplined him more severely for that than any other father would have thought permissible. What can I do? I have subjected him to stern discipline since he was a boy. Beyond our wills, there are the devils and the world of the flesh, which mock our determination and spoil our best intentions."

Avoiding al-Sayyid Ahmad's eyes by looking at the desk, Muhammad Iffat replied, "I have not come to blame you or to criticize you. You are a model father who can be imitated but never equaled. But that does not alter the distressing fact that Yasin has not turned out the way you wished. In his current condition he is not fit for married life."

Al-Sayyid Ahmad protested, "Not so fast, Mr. Muhammad."

The other man corrected himself while remaining resolute: "In any case, he is not a fit husband for my daughter. He will find some woman who accepts him with his faults, but not her. My daughter was not made for this. You know better than anyone how I feel about her."

The proprietor moved his head close to his friend's and said in a low voice and with a hint of a smile, "Yasin's not unusual as husbands go. Lots of them get drunk and boisterous and do things they shouldn't."

Muhammad Iffat frowned to make it clear he would not allow the situation to be turned into a joke. He answered sternly, "If you're referring to our group or to me in particular, it is true that I get drunk, become rowdy, and take lovers, but I refrain from wallowing in the mud. We all do. A black maid. . . . Is my daughter destined to share a husband with her in a polygamous marriage? By the Lord of Heaven, no. She will not be Yasin's wife and he will not be Zaynab's husband."

Al-Sayyid Ahmad perceived that Muhammad Iffat, perhaps like his daughter, might be ready to forgive many things, but not Yasin's attempt to have both the girl and her black maid. He knew Muhammad Iffat was of Turkish descent and stubborn as a mule. He happened to recall the words of his friend Ibrahim al-Far the day he told him he was asking for Zaynab's hand for his son Yasin. The man had observed, "She's a fine girl from a good family. Muhammad is our brother and friend. His daughter is our daughter. But have you thought carefully about the girl's status with her father? Have you considered the fact that Muhammad Iffat does not allow the tiniest speck of dust to settle on her?" Although that was true, al-Sayyid Ahmad had found it difficult to judge matters by any standards but his own and had always boasted that Muhammad Iffat, despite his atrocious temper, had never gotten angry with him even once throughout their long friendship.

He said, "Take it easy. Don't you see we're all made of the same stuff, even if the details differ? A black maid and a female vocalist – aren't they both women?"

Muhammad Iffat flew into a rage. He pounded on the edge of the desk with his fist. He burst out: "You don't mean what you're saying. A servant's a servant and a lady's a lady. Why don't you take servants for mistresses then? Yasin's not like you. I'm sorry my daughter's pregnant by him. I hate for my grandchild to have such filth in his veins."

The last sentence stung al-Sayyid Ahmad and he was enraged, but he was able to suppress his anger by using the forbearance he lavished on his acquaintances and friends, the strength of which was matched only by that of his irascibility with his family. He replied calmly, "I would like to suggest that we postpone this conversation to some other time."

Muhammad Iffat said angrily, "I want my request carried out immediately."

Al-Sayyid Ahmad was extremely vexed. There was nothing unsavory about divorce as a solution, but he was apprehensive about his lifelong friendship, and it was hard for him to admit defeat. Was he not the man whose mediation people requested to settle disputes and mend quarrels between friends and spouses? How could he accept defeat and divorce when he was defending his own son? What good were his forbearance, diplomacy, and finesse?

"I attempted to strengthen our friendship through this marriage tie between our families. How can I accept a weakening?"

His visitor answered disapprovingly, "Our friendship is not in doubt. . . . We're not children, but my honor is not going to be sullied."

Al-Sayyid Ahmad asked gently, "What will people say about a marriage that doesn't even last a year?"

Muhammad Iffat replied haughtily, "No intelligent person will blame my daughter."

Oh . . . once again, a new insult, but he met it with the same forbearance. His annoyance at failing to achieve a reconciliation seemed to have eclipsed that aroused by the angry man's words. He was not nearly so concerned about the blast directed against him as about justifying his own lack of success. He began to console himself with the thought that the divorce was in his hands alone. If he wanted to, he could grant it. If he did not, he could prevent it. Muhammad Iffat knew that perfectly well. It was for this reason he had come to ask for it in the name of their friendship, which was the only mediator he had to fall back on. If al-Sayyid Ahmad said no, that would settle the matter. The girl would return to his son, voluntarily or involuntarily. Their lengthy friendship would be in the past tense. If he said yes, the divorce would take place, but the friendship would be preserved and he would have the credit for doing his friend a favor. In the future, it would not be difficult to bring all these considerations into play to reunite what had been severed. Although the divorce was a defeat, it was a temporary one, which clearly demonstrated his goodwill and nobility. In time it might turn into a victory. Once he was even partially reassured about his position, he felt a desire to criticize his friend for taking him for granted. He warned him, "The divorce will not take place without my consent. . . . Do you disagree? . . . I will not reject your request, if you are still determined to proceed with it, out of respect for you and the friendship you slighted when you spoke to me. . . ."

Muhammad Iffat sighed, either from relief at achieving the desired result or in protest against his friend's criticism, or both. Then with a voice free of the sharp edge of anger for the first time, he said resolutely, "I told you a thousand times that our friendship was not in jeopardy. You haven't wronged me in any way. To the contrary, you have honored me by granting my request, although you didn't want to."

Al-Sayyid Ahmad echoed his words sadly, "Yes . . . I didn't want to."

The moment his visitor passed from sight, al-Sayyid Ahmad's resentment flared up. His suppressed rage exploded, encompassing himself, Muhammad Iffat, and Yasin, especially Yasin. He asked himself whether the friendship would really remain secure and not be muddied by events to come. Oh . . . he would have spared no expense to protect himself from a rude jolt like this. . . . But it was all because of Turkish obstinacy. No . . . the devil, no . . . Yasin . . . Yasin, not anyone else.

He told his son angrily and scornfully, "You have spoiled the purity of a friendship no number of days would have been able to harm, even if they had conspired to that goal."

After repeating to Yasin what Muhammad Iffat had said, he concluded: "You have disappointed my hopes in you so much that only God and His blessings can ever repay me. I raised and disciplined you. I watched over you. . . . Then all my efforts lead to what? . . . An alcoholic wretch who talks himself into raping the most humble servant in his family's home. There is no power or might save with God. I never imagined that my discipline would produce a son like you. Everything is in God's hands, the past and the future. What can I do with you? If you were a juvenile, I'd smash your head in, but time will certainly take care of that. You'll receive your just deserts. Decent families will wash their hands of you and let you go for a song."

He may have been sorry for his son, but his anger got the upper hand. Then all he could feel was contempt. Although Yasin was virile, handsome, and large, he no longer brought delight to his father's eyes. He wallowed in the mud, as Muhammad Iffat (may

God destroy him) had observed. Yasin had been too weak to tame an unruly woman. How callow he was. His recklessness had soon been rewarded by a degrading disaster from which he had been unable to save himself. How contemptible he was! Let him get drunk, carouse, and take lovers, on condition that he remain the unchallenged master of his family. But his shameful defeat made him seem totally contemptible to his father. As Muhammad Iffat (may God destroy him) had also observed: Yasin was not like him.

"I do what I want and still I'm al-Sayyid Ahmad. That's all there is to it. What a fine idea it was for me to try to rear my sons to be outstanding examples of rectitude and purity, since it would be difficult for them to balance my lifestyle with my honor and rectitude. But, alas, my effort was in vain with this son by Haniya."

"Did you agree, Father?" Yasin's voice reverberated like a death rattle.

"Yes," he answered gruffly, "to preserve a long-lasting friendship and because it was the best solution, at least for now."

Yasin's hand began to contract into a fist and then unfold, in a mechanical, nervous gesture. The blood drained from his face until he looked extremely pale. He felt more humiliated by this than by anything else in his life except his mother's conduct. His father-in-law was asking for a divorce! In other words, Zaynab was requesting one or at least consenting to one.... Which of them was the man and which the woman? There was nothing strange about a man casting out a pair of shoes, but shoes were not supposed to throw away their owner. How could his father agree to this unprecedented humiliation for him? He glared at his father harshly but also in a way that reflected the cries for help surging in his breast. In a voice he desperately strove to keep free of any hint of protest or objection, as though trying to remind his father there might be a more appropriate solution, he remarked, "A husband has legal means of forcing a wife to return and obey him if she's rebellious...."

Al-Sayyid Ahmad sensed what his son was going through and was touched. Therefore he shared some of his own thoughts with him. He told him, "I know that, but I've decided we should be generous. Muhammad Iffat has an inflexible, Turkish mentality but a heart of gold. This is not the last word. It's not the end. I'm not forgetting your welfare, even though you don't deserve it. Let me proceed as I wish."

"As you wish," Yasin thought. "Who has ever gone against your wishes? You marry me and divorce me. You give me life and take it away. I don't really exist. Khadija, Aisha, Fahmy, Yasin ... all the same thing. We're nothing. You're everything. No.... There's a limit. I'm no longer a child. I'm just as much a man as you are. I'm the one who is going to decide my destiny. I'm the man who will grant the divorce or have her legally confined to my house until she's ready to obey me. Muhammad Iffat, Zaynab, and your friendship with her father can all lick the dust from my shoes."

"What's the matter? Don't you have anything to say?"

Without hesitation, Yasin answered, "Whatever you want, Father."

"What a life! What a household! What a father!" Yasin reflected. "Scoldings, discipline, and advice.... Scold yourself. Discipline yourself. Give yourself some advice. Have you forgotten Zubayda? Jalila? The music and the wine? After all that, you appear before us wearing the turban of the most authoritative Muslim legal scholar, the Shaykh al-Islam, and carrying the sword of the Caliph, the Commander of all Muslims.... I'm not a child anymore. Look after yourself and leave me and my affairs alone. 'Marry.' Whatever you say, sir. 'Divorce.' Whatever you say, sir.... Curses on your father."

61

THE INTENSITY of the demonstrations decreased in the Husayn district after the British soldiers occupied it, and al-Sayyid Ahmad was able to resume a favorite custom he had temporarily been forced to curtail, that of attending the Friday prayer service at al-Husayn Mosque, accompanied by his sons. It was a practice he had scrupulously observed for a long period. He had invited his sons to join him, when they were old enough, in order to direct their hearts toward religion early in life. He hoped it would be a blessing to him, his sons, and the entire family. Amina was the only one with reservations about this caravan that set out at the end of each week, consisting of her three men, as big as camels, resplendent and virile. She watched them through the balcony peephole and imagined that everyone was staring enviously at them. In her alarm, she prayed to God to spare them the dangers of the evil eye. One day she felt compelled to confide her fears to her husband, who seemed swayed by her warning momentarily but did not yield. He told her, "The blessing of the religious duty we fulfill by attending the Friday prayer service is sufficient protection against any evil."

Since childhood, Fahmy had cheerfully obeyed the summons to attend the Friday service with a heart eager to perform his religious duties. He was motivated not only by his father but by sincere religious sentiment, enlightened by views drawn from the teachings of the influential Egyptian theologian Muhammad Abduh and his disciples. He was the only one in the family to adopt a skeptical attitude toward incantations, charms, amulets, and the amazing deeds performed by saints. His mild temperament kept him from making his doubts public or announcing his disdain for such things. He accepted without protest the amulets from Shaykh Mutawalli Abd al-Samad that his father brought him from time to time.

Yasin complied with his father's request to attend prayers with him because he had no alternative. Left to his own devices he might never have thought of squeezing his huge body in among the masses of worshippers, not from any religious doubt but from laziness and a lack of interest. On Fridays, Yasin suffered from a special distress all morning. When it was time to go to the mosque he grumpily put on his suit. He followed behind his father like a prisoner, but gradually as he approached the mosque his grouchiness decreased. By the time he entered the sanctuary he felt at peace with the world and performed the prayer, asking God to forgive him and pardon his sins. He would not ask for repentance, since he secretly feared his prayer might be granted and he would be turned into an ascetic with no taste for the pleasures of life he loved and without which he thought life would be meaningless. He knew beyond the shadow of a doubt that repentance was a necessity and that he could not be pardoned without it. He just hoped it would come at an appropriate time so he could have full enjoyment of both this world and the next. Therefore, despite his laziness and grumbling, in the end he praised the circumstances that forced him to perform a religious duty as important as the Friday prayer. In the final reckoning, it might erase some of his bad deeds and lighten the burden of his sins, especially since it was virtually the only religious duty he did perform.

Kamal had just recently been invited to join them, when he became ten. He obeyed the summons proudly, cockily, and happily. He sensed that the invitation implied recognition of him as a person and almost put him on a par with Fahmy, Yasin, and even his father. He was particularly pleased to follow in his father's footsteps without having to dread some punishment from him. He stood beside him as an equal in the mosque, where everyone copied the motions of the same imam or prayer leader. At home when he prayed, he was totally absorbed in the experience to a degree he could not attain at the Friday prayer service. There he was nervous about performing his prayers surrounded by so many people and apprehensive that he might slip up in some manner his father would detect. When he was in the mosque, the intensity of his devotion to al-Husayn, whom he loved more than himself, also interfered with giving the kind of total attention to God that a person should when praying.

Thus they appeared on al-Nahhasin Street walking briskly toward Bayt al-Qadi, al-Sayyid Ahmad in front with Yasin, Fahmy, and Kamal following in a line behind him. They found places in the mosque and sat listening to the sermon in total silence, their heads craned to see the pulpit. Although the father listened attentively, he was also praying silently. His heart reached out to Yasin in particular, since he thought the young man deserved compassion after his false steps. He prayed to God at length to reform Yasin, straighten him out, and compensate him for everything he had lost. The sermon directed his attention to his own sins, sweeping aside all other considerations. He found himself directly confronted by them. They were given such terrifying vividness by the penetrating and resonant voice of the preacher that al-Sayyid Ahmad imagined he was singling him out and screaming into his ears at the top of his voice. He would not have been surprised to hear the preacher address him by name: "Ahmad, restrain yourself from evil. Cleanse yourself of fornication and wine. Repent and return to God your Lord."

He was troubled by anxiety and doubt just as he had been the day Shaykh Mutawalli Abd al-Samad had argued with him. He usually was not affected this way by the sermon, for he would become distracted, praying for pardon, forgiveness, and mercy. Like his son Yasin, he did not pray for repentance, or if he did it was only with his tongue and not his heart. If his tongue said, "O God, repentance," his heart limited its request to pardon, forgiveness, and mercy. They seemed to be a pair of musical instruments playing together in a single orchestra but rendering different tunes. He could not imagine viewing life in any other fashion than the way it actually appeared to him. Whenever anxiety and doubt threatened to gain control of him, he would rise to defend himself against them, putting his defense in the form of a prayer or a plea for forgiveness. He would say, "O God, You know my heart, my faith, and my love. God, increase my dedication to the performance of my religious duties and my ability to do good deeds. O God, a good deed outweighs ten others. God, You are forgiving and merciful." With such a prayer he would gradually recover his peace of mind.

Yasin did not have this ability to reconcile his piety and his practice or did not feel in need of it. He never thought about it. He wandered through life just as he wanted, believing in God in exactly the same way he believed in his own existence. He would surrender himself to the flow of life, not opposing or resisting it. When the preacher's words reached his ears, he prayed mechanically for mercy and forgiveness with complete peace of mind, for he felt no real danger. God was too merciful to cause a Muslim like himself to burn in hell for transitory lapses that harmed no one. And there was always repentance. . . . It would come one day and erase everything that had preceded it.

Biting on his lip to suppress his laughter, he looked stealthily at his father and wondered what the man might be thinking while he listened with such evident interest to the sermon. "Is he tormented by every Friday service or do you suppose he's a hypocrite and doesn't admit the truth? . . . No, neither one. . . ." He was like Yasin and believed in the vastness of God's mercy. If matters were as grave as the preacher's description implied, then his father would have chosen one of the two conflicting paths. He stole another glance at al-Sayyid Ahmad. He thought he looked like a noble and handsome stallion among the seated worshippers gazing at the pulpit. The admiration and love he felt for him were pure. There was no trace of resentment left in his soul, although on the day of the divorce he had been so angry that he had revealed his anguish to Fahmy: "Your father has destroyed my household and made me a laughingstock for people." Now he had forgotten his resentment along with the divorce, the scandal, and everything else.

The preacher himself was no better than his father. In fact, he was quite certainly more debauched. One of his friends at Ahmad Abduh's coffee shop had told him, "He believes in two things: God in heaven and adolescent boys on earth. He's such a sensitive type that when he's in al-Husayn, his eye twitches if a lad moans in the Citadel." Yasin felt no rancor toward him because of that. On the contrary, the preacher and his father seemed like a trench at the front lines that the enemy would have to storm across first before reaching him.

Then the call to prayer was given. The men rose all at once and positioned themselves in closely packed lines, which filled the courtyard of the great mosque. They brought the building to life with their bodies and souls. The congestion was so intense that Kamal was reminded of the annual procession along al-Nahhasin, or Coppersmiths Street, of the pilgrims leaving for Mecca. Intermingled in the long, parallel lines were men with all different styles of clothing – suits, cloaks, or floor-length shirts – but they all became a single organism, moving in unison, facing in a single direction for prayer. Their whispered recitations reverberated in an all-encompassing hum until the benediction came.

At that moment, the orderly discipline was abandoned. Freedom drew a deep breath, and everyone rose to go wherever he wished. Some went to visit the sepulcher, some headed for the doors to leave, and others stayed behind to chat or to wait until the crowd thinned out. The streams of traffic in different directions frequently got mixed up with each other. The happy moment Kamal had promised himself was at hand, that of visiting the sepulcher, kissing the walls, and reciting the opening prayer of the Qur'an for himself and on behalf of his mother, as he had promised her. He began to move along slowly, following in his father's footsteps.

Before anyone knew what was happening, a young theology student from al-Azhar University suddenly burst out of the crowd to block their way so violently that people started looking. He spread his arms out to thrust people aside. He stepped back to glare at Yasin, frowning as sparks of anger flew from his sullen face. Al-Sayyid Ahmad was startled by him and began to look back and forth between him and Yasin, who seemed even more startled and began in turn to look questioningly from the theology student to his father. People noticed what was happening and focused their attention to watch with curious astonishment.

Al-Sayyid Ahmad could not restrain himself any longer. He asked the young man indignantly, "What's the matter, brother? Why are you looking at us that way?"

The seminarian pointed at Yasin and cried out in a voice like thunder, "Spy!"

The word ripped into the family like a bullet, making their heads spin. Their eyes were fixed on the man, and their bodies became rigid. Meanwhile the accusation was on everyone's lips, repeated with alarm and resentment. People began to gather around them, warily linking their arms together to form a circle from which they could not escape. Al-Sayyid Ahmad must have been the first to come to his senses, although he understood nothing of what was happening around him. He sensed the danger of remaining silent and of retreating into himself. He shouted angrily at the young man, "What are you saying, Mr. Shaykh? What spy do you mean?"

The seminarian paid no attention to the father. He pointed once more at Yasin and yelled, "Beware, people. This fellow's a traitor, one of the spies for the English who has slipped in among you to collect information he turns over to his criminal masters."

Al-Sayyid Ahmad was furious. He took a step toward the young man and, losing control of himself, shouted, "What you're saying doesn't make any sense. Either you're a troublemaker or you're crazy. This young man is my son. He's no traitor or spy. We're all nationalists. This district knows us as well as we know ourselves."

Their adversary shrugged his shoulders disdainfully and shouted oratorically, "A despicable English spy. I have seen him repeatedly with my own eyes conversing privately with the English at Palace Walk. I have witnesses to that. He won't dare deny it. I challenge him. . . . Down with the traitor."

An angry rumble resounded throughout the mosque. Voices were raised here and there, crying, "Down with the spy." Others called out, "Teach the traitor a lesson."

It was clear from the threatening looks in the eyes of those near them that people were just waiting for some initial gesture or sign before pouncing on them. The only thing holding back the tide may have been the impressive sight of al-Sayyid Ahmad, who was standing beside his son as though offering to absorb the harm threatening him, as well as the tears of Kamal, who was wailing. Yasin was standing between his father and Fahmy, barely conscious from alarm and fear. He began to say in a trembling voice no one could hear, "I'm not a spy. . . . I'm not a spy . . . with God as my witness for what I say."

The crowd's anger was becoming a frenzy. People were converging on the circle of prisoners. They were shoving against each other with their shoulders and threatening to harm the spy.

Then a voice cried out from the center of the mob: "Not so fast, gentlemen. . . . This is Yasin Effendi, the secretary of the school on Coppersmiths Street."

Voices roared back, "Coppersmiths or ironmongers, it doesn't matter. Let's teach him a lesson."

Another man was making his way between the bodies with difficulty but also with invincible determination. As soon as he reached the front, he raised his hands and screamed, "Listen! Listen!" When it was a little quieter he pointed at al-Sayyid Ahmad and said, "This is Mr. Ahmad Abd al-Jawad from a well-known family on al-Nahhasin. There's no way his household could harbor a spy. Be patient until the truth is discovered."

The theology student yelled angrily, "I'm not concerned with whether he's Mr. Ahmad or Mr. Muhammad. This young man is a spy, no matter who his father is. I've seen him joking with the executioners who are filling the tombs to overflowing with your sons."

At once countless people were shouting, "Let's beat him with our shoes."

A violent wave surged through the people packed together there. Eager zealots moved in from every direction waving their shoes and boots. Yasin felt desperate and defeated. He glanced all around him and wherever he looked all he saw was the face of someone looking for a fight, bubbling over with anger and hatred. Al-Sayyid Ahmad and Fahmy pressed close to Yasin in an instinctive gesture as though trying to protect him from harm or at least to share it with him. The two of them felt as choked by desperation and defeat as Yasin. Meanwhile Kamal's sobs had turned into a scream that almost drowned out the voices of the mob.

The seminarian was the first to attack. He threw himself on Yasin and grabbed his shirt. Then he pulled hard to drag him out of the refuge he had created for himself between his father and his brother so the blows would not miss him. Yasin grasped the man's wrist to fight him off and al-Sayyid Ahmad intervened. For the first time in his life, Fahmy saw his father in an alarming situation. He was so outraged that he was oblivious to the danger engulfing them. Fahmy shoved the theology student in the chest hard enough to force him back. He shouted at the man threateningly, "Don't you dare come a step closer."

The seminarian lost his temper and screamed, "Get all of them!"

At that moment a powerful voice commanded, "Wait, Mr. Shaykh. . . . Everyone, wait."

Eyes were turned toward the voice. It was a young effendi who emerged from the crowd heading for the circle with the prisoners. He was followed by three others his age, dressed like him in modern clothing. They marched forward in a confident and resolute manner until they stood between the young shaykh and his victim and the victim's family. Many people whispered to ask each other, "Police . . . police?"

The questioning ceased when the theology student held out his hand to the commander of the group, and the two shook hands warmly. The leader asked the seminarian resolutely, "Where's this spy?"

The young shaykh pointed with scorn and loathing at Yasin. The leader turned to scrutinize him coldly. Before he could say a word, Fahmy took a step forward to attract his attention. When the man noticed him, his eyes quickly grew wide in amazement and disbelief. He muttered, "You . . ."

Fahmy smiled wanly and said somewhat sarcastically, "This spy is my brother."

The leader turned to the seminarian to ask, "Are you certain of what you're saying?"

Fahmy answered first: "He may be correct in saying he saw him talk to the English, but he really misinterpreted what was happening. The English are camped in front of our house and confront us whenever we go in or out. At times we're forced to talk to them, against our wills. That's all there is to it."

The theology student started to speak, but the young leader silenced him with a gesture. Putting his hand on Fahmy's shoulder, he addressed the crowd: "This young man is one of our friends among the freedom fighters. We both work on the same committee, so I'll take his word for it. . . . Let them pass."

No one said a thing. The young shaykh from al-Azhar withdrew without any hesitation and the crowd began to disperse. The young patriot shook hands with Fahmy and then went off, followed by his companions. Fahmy patted Kamal on the head until he stopped crying.

Silence reigned while everyone nursed his psychic wounds. Al-Sayyid Ahmad realized that some of his acquaintances had gathered around him. They began to offer him their condolences and apologies for the grave mistake committed by the theology student and those in the crowd whom he had misled. They assured him that they had spared no effort to defend him. He thanked them, although he did not know when they had arrived or how they had defended him. He renounced the visit to al-Husayn's sepulcher, because he was so overwhelmed by emotion. He headed for the door, frowning, his lips pressed tight together. His sons followed him in total silence.

62

AL-SAYYID AHMAD got his breath back in the street, relieved to be away from the people who had participated in the incident, even if only by watching. He hated everything to do with the misadventure and hurled insults at it. He saw scarcely anything of the street along which he was walking. He exchanged greetings twice with acquaintances in a cursory, formal manner he never used. He concentrated on himself and his wounded soul, which was boiling with anger.

"I would rather die than be humiliated like that: the prisoner of a mob of rabble," he reflected. "This ill-fed, louse-infected theology student claiming to be a patriot attacked me shamelessly. He showed no respect for my age or dignity. I wasn't made to be treated like this. I'm not a person who can be humiliated this way. And when I'm with my sons. . . . Don't be surprised. . . . Your sons are the source of the problem. This ox, born of misery, will never stop causing trouble for you. He has acted scandalously in my home and alienated me from my dearest friend, crowning the year with a divorce. Was that enough? . . . No, Haniya's son feels compelled to chat publicly with the English and let me pay the price of being attacked by riffraff. Take your friends the soldiers to your mother so her museum of lovers can be rounded out with Englishmen and Australians.

"It seems you'll be causing trouble for me as long as I live." This sentence slipped out bitterly, but he resisted the temptation to upbraid his son.

Despite his anger, he could see the state Yasin was in and felt sorry for him. He observed that his son was dazed, pale and ill, and he could not force himself to attack. The trouble Yasin had gotten himself into sufficed for now. He was not the only one giving him trouble. There was the hero. "But let's postpone his case till we recover from the headaches caused by the ox . . . an ox at home and in the tavern, a bull with Umm Hanafi and Nur. But in the battle at the mosque, he was totally useless, a spineless wonder."

What bastards his sons were.... If God would only dispense with children, descendants, and families.... "Oh...why are my feet leading me home? Why don't I get a bite to eat away from the poisoned atmosphere of the house? Amina, for her part, will wail when she hears the news. I don't need to feel any more disgusted. I'll get some kabob at al-Dahan's.... I'll surely find a friend there to whom I can recount my disaster and tell my troubles.... But no, I have other problems that cannot wait that long. The hero...a new calamity we must remedy. On to the disastrous dinner. Wail, lament, and cry, woman, and curses on your father too."

Fahmy had only just finished changing clothes when he was summoned to talk to his father. Despite his depleted energy and his distress, Yasin could not keep himself from muttering, "Now it's your turn."

Pretending not to understand the point of his brother's remark, Fahmy asked, "What do you mean?"

Yasin laughed, finally able to, and said, "The traitors have had a turn, and now the freedom fighters will have theirs."

Fahmy wished dearly that the terms his friend had used to describe him in the mosque had been forgotten in all the commotion of the disturbance and the family's dazed reaction, but they had not been. Now Yasin was repeating them. Without any doubt, his father was summoning him to discuss them. Fahmy sighed deeply and departed.

He found his father sitting on the sofa with his legs tucked under him. He was fiddling with his prayer beads, and the look in his eyes was sad and thoughtful. Fahmy greeted him with great courtesy and stopped, submissively and obediently, about two meters away from the sofa. The man nodded his head slightly to return the greeting but the gesture did more to reveal how upset he was than to greet his son. It seemed to imply: "I'm returning your greeting reluctantly and only for the sake of politeness, but this spurious courtesy of yours no longer deceives me."

Al-Sayyid Ahmad directed a frowning glare at his son, which radiated anxiety and thus resembled a lamp used to search for a person concealed in the darkness. He told the boy resolutely, "I've summoned you, to learn everything. I want to know everything. What did he mean when he said you were on the same committee? Don't hesitate to tell me everything with complete candor."

Although Fahmy had grown accustomed during the past few weeks to confronting various dangers and had even gotten used to having bullets whiz past, it was his prerevolutionary heart that surfaced once his father began interrogating him. He was terrified and felt reduced to nothing. He concentrated his attention on skirting this wrath and trying to escape. He told his father gently and politely, "The matter's quite simple, Papa. My friend probably exaggerated to extricate us from our dilemma."

Al-Sayyid Ahmad's patience was exhausted. He said, "'The matter's quite simple . . .' Great. . . . But which matter is it? Don't hide anything from me."

With lightning speed, Fahmy considered the subject from different perspectives to select something he could say without fear of the consequences. He responded, "He called it a 'committee' when it's nothing more than a group of friends who talk about patriotic topics whenever they get together."

His father cried out furiously and resentfully, "Is this how you earned the title of 'freedom fighter'?"

The man's voice betrayed intense disapproval, as though he was hurt that his son was trying to put something over on him. The wrinkles of his frowning face looked threatening. Fahmy rushed to defend himself by making a significant admission, in order to convince his father that in every other respect he had been obedient to his commands, just as an accused man may voluntarily confess to a lesser offense in an attempt to plea for mercy. He said rather modestly, "It happens sometimes that we distribute appeals on behalf of nationalism."

Al-Sayyid Ahmad asked in alarm, "Handbills? . . . Do you mean handbills?"

Fahmy shook his head no. He was afraid to admit this, since the word was linked in the official pronouncements to the harshest penalties. When he had found a suitable formula to make his confession seem less dangerous, he said, "They're nothing but appeals that urge people to love their country."

His father allowed the prayer beads to fall to his lap. He clapped his hands together. Unable to control his alarm, he exclaimed, "You're distributing handbills! . . . You!"

Al-Sayyid Ahmad could not see straight, he was so alarmed and angry: distributing handbills . . . a friend of the freedom fighters. "We both work on the same committee!" Had the flood reached his roost? He had often been impressed by Fahmy's manners, piety, and intelligence. He would have lavished praise on his son except that he thought praise corrupted, whereas gruffness was educational and corrective. How had all of this peeled away to reveal a boy who distributed handbills, a freedom fighter? "We both work on the same committee . . ."

He had nothing against the freedom fighters, quite the contrary. He always followed news about them with enthusiasm and prayed for their success at the conclusion of his normal prayers. News about the strike, acts of sabotage, and the battles had filled him with hope and admiration, but it was a totally different matter for any of these deeds to be performed by a son of his. His children were meant to be a breed apart, outside the framework of history. He alone would set their course for them, not the revolution, the times, or the rest of humanity. The revolution and everything it accomplished were no doubt beneficial, so long as they remained far removed from his household. Once the revolution knocked on his door, threatened his peace and security and the lives of his children, its flavor, complexion, and import were transformed into folly, madness, unruliness, and vulgarity. The revolution should rage on outside. He would participate in it with all his heart and donate to it as generously as he could. . . . He had done that. But the house was his and his alone. Any member of his household who talked himself into participating in the revolution was in rebellion against him, not against the English. Al-Sayyid Ahmad implored God's mercy for the martyrs both night and day and was amazed by the courage their families displayed, according to what people said, but he would not allow one of his sons to join the martyrs nor would he embrace the courage their families had displayed. How could Fahmy have seen fit to take this insane step? How had he, the best of his boys, chosen to expose himself to certain destruction?

The man was more alarmed than he had ever been before, even more than during the melee at the mosque. In a stern and threatening voice as though he were one of the English police inspectors, he asked Fahmy, "Don't you know the penalty for persons caught distributing handbills?"

Despite the seriousness of the situation, which required Fahmy to concentrate his attention on it, the question aroused a recent memory that shook his soul. He remembered being asked this same question, identical in words and import, by the president of the supreme student executive committee – together with many other questions – when he had been chosen a member of the committee. He also remembered that he had replied with determination and enthusiasm, "We are all ready to sacrifice ourselves for our country." He compared the different conditions under which the same question had been addressed to him and felt the irony of it.

Fahmy answered his father in a gentle and self-deprecating tone: "I only distribute among my friends. I don't have anything to do with general distribution.... That way there's no risk or danger."

Al-Sayyid Ahmad, concealing his fears for his son behind the virulence of his anger, shouted harshly, "God does not protect those who expose themselves to danger needlessly. He, may He be glorified, has commanded us not to put our lives in jeopardy." The man would have liked to cite the verse of the Qur'an that dealt with this but had only memorized those short suras of the Qur'an he recited when he prayed. He was afraid that if he tried to quote it he might overlook a word or get it wrong and thus commit an unforgivable sin. He was content to cite the meaning and repeat it in order to make his point.

Before he knew what was happening, he heard Fahmy reply in his refined way, "But God also urges Believers to struggle, Papa."

Afterward Fahmy asked himself in amazement how he had found the courage to confront his father with this statement, which betrayed the fact he had been trying to conceal: that he was sticking to his ideas. Perhaps he thought the Qur'an would protect him if he took refuge behind one of its phrases. He was confident that his father would refrain from attacking him under such circumstances.

Al-Sayyid Ahmad was shocked by both his son's audacity and his argument. He did not give way to anger, though, which might have silenced Fahmy but not his argument. He would ignore the audacity for a moment while he pounded away at Fahmy's argument with a comparable one from the Qur'an, so that the erring child could be provided with correct guidance. Afterward he could settle the other account with him in any manner he wished. God inspired him to say, "That's struggle 'for the sake of God.'" (Qur'an, 9:20.)

Fahmy took his father's answer to show a willingness to debate with him. Once more he found the courage to speak: "We're struggling for God's sake too. Every honorable struggle advances God's cause."

Al-Sayyid Ahmad privately agreed with this statement, but his agreement itself and the feeling of insecurity it occasioned when he was debating with his son made him fall back on anger. Actually he was motivated not just by anger but by wounded pride and his concern that the youth would go too far in his rebellion and get himself killed. He abandoned the debate and asked disapprovingly, "Do you think I called you here to argue with me?"

Fahmy realized the threat his father's words contained. His dreams evaporated and he became tongue-tied. His father continued sharply: "The only struggle for the sake of God is when I intend to advance God's cause in a specifically religious struggle. There's no argument about that. Now I want to know whether my command is going to be obeyed?"

The young man quickly replied, "Most certainly, Papa."

"Then break every link between you and the revolution.... Even if your role was limited to distributing handbills to your best friends."

No power in existence could come between him and his patriotic duty. He absolutely would not retreat even one step. The time for that had passed, never to return. This passionate, dazzling life, springing from the depths of his heart and illuminating every area of his soul, could not die away. How preposterous to think he would kill it himself. All this was no doubt true, but could he not find some way to please his father and escape his wrath? He could not defy him or openly declare that he disagreed with the command. He could rebel against the English and defy their bullets almost every day, but the English were a frightening and hated enemy, while his father was his father, a frightening and beloved man. Fahmy worshipped him as much as he feared him. It was hard to disobey him. There was also another feeling Fahmy could not ignore. His rebellion against the English was inspired by noble idealism. His disobedience against his father was associated only with disgrace and misery. What reason was there for this quandary? Why not promise to obey and then do whatever he wanted?

Lying was not considered contemptible or shameful in this household. Living in their father's shadow, none of them would have been able to enjoy any peace without the protection of a lie. They openly admitted this to themselves. In fact, they would all agree to it in a crisis. Had his mother intended to admit what she had done the day she slipped off to visit al-Husayn when her husband was out of town? Would Yasin have been able to drink, Fahmy to love Maryam, and Kamal to get up to all sorts of mischief when walking between Khan Ja'far and al-Khurunfush without the protection provided by lying? None of them had scruples about it. If they had been totally truthful with their father, life would have lost its savor. For all these reasons, Fahmy said calmly, "Your command is obeyed, Papa."

This declaration was followed by silence as each of them rested with relief. Fahmy imagined that his interrogation had been safely concluded. Al-Sayyid Ahmad imagined that he had rescued his son from the pit of hell. While Fahmy was waiting for permission to leave, his father suddenly rose and went to the armoire, which he opened. He thrust his hand inside as the young man watched with uncomprehending eyes. The father returned to the sofa with the Qur'an. He looked at Fahmy for some time. Then he held the Book out to him and said, "Swear it on this Book."

Fahmy jerked back involuntarily as though fleeing from the tongue of flame that had suddenly shot out at him. Then he remained nailed to the spot as he stared at his father's face in desperate, alarmed confusion. Al-Sayyid Ahmad kept his hand stretched out holding the Book and looked at his son with incredulous disapproval. His face became flushed, as though on fire, and there was a frightening gleam to his eyes. He asked in astonishment, as though he could not believe his eyes: "Don't you want to swear?"

Fahmy was tongue-tied. He could not utter a word or make a gesture. His father asked in a calm voice, with a shaky quaver suggestive of the raging anger behind it, "Were you lying to me?"

No change came over Fahmy, although he lowered his eyes to escape his father's. Al-Sayyid Ahmad placed the Book on the sofa. Then he exploded and shouted in such a resounding voice that Fahmy felt he was being slapped on the cheek: "You're lying to me, you son of a bitch. . . . I don't let anyone pull the wool over my eyes. What do you think I am and what do you think of yourself? You're a vile insect, vermin, a son of a bitch whose exterior appearance has deceived people for a long time. I'm not turning into an old lady any time soon. Do you hear? Don't mistake me for some old woman. You sons of bitches are driving me crazy. You've turned me into a laughingstock for people. I'm going to hand you over to the police myself. Do you understand? By myself, you son of a bitch. The only word that counts here is mine. Mine, mine, mine. . . ." He picked up the Book again and continued: "Swear. . . . I command you to swear."

Fahmy appeared to be in a trance. His eyes were fixed on some unusual motifs in the Persian carpet but saw nothing. He stared at the motifs for so long they became imprinted on his mind, only to fragment into chaos and emptiness. With each passing second he plunged deeper into silence and despair. He had no alternative to this desperate, passive resistance.

Al-Sayyid Ahmad rose with the Book in his hand and took one step toward him. Then he roared, "Did you think you were a man? Did you think you could do what you like? If I wanted, I'd beat you till your skull caved in."

Fahmy could not keep himself from crying then, but not from fear of the threat, for in his condition he was oblivious to any harm that might befall him. His tears expressed his sense of defeat and helped relieve the struggle raging within him. He started to bite on his lips to suppress his tears. He felt ashamed at being so weak. When he was finally able to speak, he launched into a rambling plea, because he was deeply moved and wished to conceal his embarrassment: "Forgive me, Papa. I'll obey every command of yours more than willingly, but I can't do this. I can't. We work like a single hand. I can't accept shrinking back and abandoning my brothers, and I don't think you would like me to. There's no way that life would be bearable if I did. There's no danger in what we're doing. Others have more exalted tasks like participating in the demonstrations in which many of them have been martyred. I'm no better than those who have been killed. There are funeral processions for tens of martyrs at a time with no lamentation except for the nation. Even the families of the victims shout slogans instead of weeping. What is my life worth? . . . What is the life of any man worth? Don't be angry, Papa. Think about what I'm saying. . . . I assure you that there's no danger in our little, nonviolent job."

Fahmy was so overcome by emotion that he could no longer bear to face his father. He fled from the room, almost colliding with Yasin and Kamal, who were listening behind the door, their dismay visible on their faces.

63

YASIN WAS heading for Ahmad Abduh's coffee shop when he ran
into one of his mother's relatives in Bayt al-Qadi. The man
approached him solicitously, shook his hand, and told him,
"I was on my way to your house to see you."

Yasin guessed that this statement presaged some news about his
mother, who had already caused him so much trouble. He felt
uncomfortable and asked listlessly, "Good news, God willing?"

The man answered with unusual concern, "Your mother's ill,
actually very ill. She's been sick for a month or more, but I only
learned of it this week. At first they thought it was nerves and
didn't worry about it, until it became entrenched. When the
doctors examined her, it was diagnosed as a serious case of
malaria."

Yasin was astonished by this totally unexpected news. He had
anticipated word of a divorce, a marriage, a row, or something
along those lines. He had not considered illness. He scarcely knew
what he felt, since his emotions were so conflicting. He asked,
"How is she now?"

The man replied with a premeditated candor not lost on Yasin,
"Her condition's grave. . . . In spite of the prolonged treatment
there has not been the least hint of progress. To tell the truth, her
condition has continued to deteriorate. She has sent me to tell you
frankly that she feels her end is near and that she wants to see you at
once." He added in a tone that implied Yasin should carefully
consider what he was saying, "You must go to her without any
delay. This is my advice to you and my plea. God is forgiving and
compassionate."

Perhaps there was a certain amount of exaggeration in the man's
words, intended to induce him to go, but they could not be a total
fabrication. So he would go, if only from a sense of duty.

Here he was, once again traversing the curve in the road leading
to al-Gamaliya, between Bayt al-Mal and Watawit Alley. On his
right was al-Tih Street, where the woman who sold doum palm

fruit had her place in shimmering memories of darkness. In front of him lay the road of sorrows. He would shortly see the store of the fruit merchant, lower his eyes, and slink past like a fugitive thief. Whenever he thought he would never return here, misfortune brought him back. No power short of death could have brought him to her this time.... Death! "Has her time really come?" he wondered. "My heart's pounding...with pain? Sorrow? All I know is that I'm afraid. Once she's gone, I'll never return to this place again.... All the old memories will succumb to forgetfulness. What's left of my property will be returned to me, but I'm afraid...I'm angry at these vicious thoughts. O God, preserve us.

"Even if I gain a more comfortable life and greater peace of mind, my heart will never escape from its pains. On her death I will bid farewell to a mother, with a son's heart ... a mother and a son, isn't that the way it is? I'm a person who has suffered a lot, not a beast or a stone. Death is new to me. I've never witnessed it before. I wish the end could come without it. We all die ... really? I've got to resist my fears. Nowadays we hear about people dying all the time, on Ministries Street, in the schools, and at the mosque of al-Azhar. There are victims of the violence in the city of Asyut daily. Even the poor milkman, al-Fuli, lost his son yesterday. What can the families of the martyrs do? Should they spend the rest of their lives weeping? They weep and then forget. That's death. Ugh...it seems to me there's no way out of trouble now. At home there's Fahmy and his stubbornness. In front of me there's my mother. How hateful life is. What if it's all a trick and I find her in the best of health? She'll pay dearly.... She'll certainly have to pay a high price for it. I'm not a toy or an object to be ridiculed. She won't find her son until she dies. Do you suppose there's any money left for me? When I go in the house, will I find that man there? I won't know how to treat him. Our eyes will meet for a dreadful moment. Woe to him! Should I ignore him or throw him out? That's a solution. There are violent alternatives the man won't have considered. The funeral will certainly bring us together. What a joke! Imagine her coffin with her first and final husbands following behind it, while her son walks between them with tears in his eyes. By that time there definitely will be tears in my eyes. Isn't that so? I won't be able to evict him from the funeral. Scandal will accompany me to the very end. Then she'll be buried. Yes, she'll be buried, and everything will end. But I'm afraid, hurt, and saddened. May God and His angels pray for me.... Here's the sinister store.... There's the man. He won't recognize me. Far from it.... I'm disguised by age. 'Uncle ... my mother says ...'"

The servant opened the door for him, the same servant who had received him the year before. At first she did not recognize him and looked up curiously, but the questioning look quickly left her face to be replaced by a flash of recognition that seemed to say, "Oh ... you're the one she's waiting for." Then she made way and pointed to a room on the right as he entered. She said, "Step this way, sir.... No one else is there."

Her final phrase attracted his attention immediately, since it addressed one of his major concerns. He realized that his mother had removed this obstacle. He headed for her room, cleared his throat, and entered. His eyes met his mother's as she looked up from her bed, to his left. Her eyes, known for their clarity, were clouded, so that her gaze seemed faint, as though coming from far away. Despite the feebleness of her eyes and their apparent disinterest, occasioned by their fading strength, she fixed them on him with a look of recognition. The delicate smile of her lips betrayed her feelings of victory, relief, and gratitude. Since she was wrapped in a blanket up to her chin, only her face was visible, a face that was far more changed than her eyes. Once full and round, it now looked withered and elongated, pale instead of rosy. Her delicate skin revealed the outlines of her jaw and protruding cheekbones, giving the pitiable appearance of a face wasting away. He stopped in stunned disbelief, incredulous that any power in existence would dare play such a cruel joke. His heart was seized by alarm, as though he were staring at death itself. He was stripped of his manhood and seemed to have become a child again, searching everywhere for his father. Irresistible emotion drew him to the bed. He bent over her, murmuring in sorrowful tones, "Never mind.... How are you?"

He felt genuinely sympathetic. In the warmth of this emotion his chronic pains disappeared. Similarly, in rare cases the symptoms of a hopeless medical condition, like paralysis, may disappear because of a sudden, overwhelming onslaught of terror. He seemed to be rediscovering the mother of his childhood whom he had loved, before pain had hidden her from his heart. Gazing at her faded face, he clung to this rejuvenated feeling which had also rejuvenated him, taking him back years before the pain, just as an exhausted invalid clings to a moment of lucidity he fears intuitively may be almost his last. Yasin clung to this sentiment with all the intensity of a man fully conscious of the strength of the forces threatening him. The very way he clung to this emotion revealed that those pains still existed deep inside him. He was aware of the sorrow awaiting him if he carelessly allowed this pure emotion to become spoiled by letting it mix with other feelings.

The woman extracted from the covers a gaunt, emaciated hand with dry skin washed with faded black and blue as though it had been mummified for thousands of years. Immensely touched, he took it in his own hands. At that moment he heard her weak, husky voice say, "As you can see, I've turned into a phantom."

He murmured, "May our Lord bring His mercy to bear on you and make you all well again."

Her head, which was covered with a white scarf, nodded prayerfully as if to say, "May our Lord hear you." She gestured to him to sit down. When he sat on the bed, she started talking with renewed strength derived from his presence: "At first I felt strange shivers. I thought it was something that would go away, that it was caused by nerves. People advised me to make a pilgrimage to the shrines and to burn incense. So I went to the mosques of al-Husayn and his sister al-Sayyida Zaynab and burned various different types of incense – Indian, Sudanese, and Arab – but my condition only got worse. Sometimes I was overcome by a constant shaking that wouldn't leave me until I was almost dead. At times my body would feel as cold as ice. On other occasions, fire would go through my body until I screamed, it was so hot. Finally we decided, I and Mi . . ." She stopped herself from mentioning the man's name, realizing at the last moment the error she was about to commit. "Finally I sent for the doctor, but his treatment did not make me any better and may even have set me back some. Now there's no hope."

Gently squeezing her hand, Yasin said, "Don't despair of God's mercy. His compassion is universal."

Her pale lips smiled and she said, "It pleases me to hear that. It pleases me to hear it from you more than from anyone else. You're dearer to me than the world and all its inhabitants. You're right. God's mercy is universal. I've had bad luck for so long. I don't deny that I've slipped up and made mistakes. Only God is infallible."

He noticed, uneasily, that her conversation was verging on confession. He was upset and alarmed that things he could not bear would be repeated in his hearing, even if only with reflective regret. He became tense and jumpy. He implored her, "Don't tire yourself out with talking."

She raised her eyes with a smile and answered, "Your visit has given me back my spirit. I want to tell you that never in my life did I want to harm anyone. Like everyone else, I was seeking peace of mind, but my luck tripped me up. I didn't harm anyone, but many people have harmed me."

Yasin felt that his prayer for the hour to pass peacefully would not be answered and that his pure emotion would suffer a crisis that would spoil it. In the same tone of entreaty he said, "Forget these people, both the good and the bad ones. Your health is more important now than anything else."

She patted his hand, as if asking for his affection and tenderness. She whispered, "There are things I should have done. I haven't done all that I should have for God. I wish I could live longer to make up for some of the things I've neglected. But my heart has always been full of faith, with God as my witness."

As though defending both her and himself, he remarked, "The heart's everything. It's more important to God than fasting and prayer."

She pressed his hand gratefully. Then she changed the direction of the conversation. She told him welcomingly, "You've finally returned to me. I didn't dare ask you to come till the illness brought me to the state you see. I felt I was saying goodbye to life, and I couldn't bear to leave it without seeing you. When I sent for you I was more afraid of your refusal than of death itself. But you've had mercy on your mother and come to bid her farewell. So accept my thanks and my prayers, which I hope God will heed."

He was deeply touched but did not know how to express his feelings. Either because of his shyness or lack of practice, loving words felt awkward and clumsy in his mouth whenever he tried to address them to this woman, whom he had grown accustomed to spurning and treating roughly. He discovered he could most effectively and sensitively express himself with his hand. He gently pressed hers and mumbled, "May our Lord make your destiny a safe one."

She kept referring back to the idea expressed in her previous statement, repeating the same words or finding other ways to put it. She paced her conversation by swallowing with noticeable difficulty or by falling silent for short periods while she caught her breath. For this reason, he repeatedly implored her to refrain from talking, but she would smile to cut him off and then continue her conversation. She stopped as her face showed she had just thought of something significant. She asked, "Have you gotten married?"

He raised his eyebrows in embarrassment and blushed, but she misinterpreted his reaction and hastened to apologize: "I'm not upset.... Of course, I would have liked to see your wife and children, but it's enough for me to know you're happy."

He could not keep himself from responding tersely, "I'm not married anymore. I got divorced about a month ago."

For the first time he noticed an interested look in her eyes. If they had still been able to sparkle they would have, but a dreamy light emanated from them as though coming through a thick curtain. She murmured, "You're divorced, son.... How sorry I am."

He quickly replied, "Don't be sorry. I'm not sorry or sad." He smiled and continued: "She left. Good riddance."

But she asked sadly, "Who chose her for you ... him or her?"

In a manner that suggested he wished to close the door on this subject, he answered, "God chose her. Everything's fated and destined."

"I know that, but who chose her for you? Was it your step-mother?"

"Oh no. My father chose her. There was nothing wrong with his choice. She was from a good family. It was just a question of fate and destiny, as I said."

"Fate, destiny, and your father's choice," she observed coldly. "That's what it was!"

After a short pause she asked, "Pregnant?"

"Yes...."

She sighed and commented: "May God make your father's life difficult."

He deliberately allowed her remark to go unchallenged, as though it were a sore that might not itch anymore if he did not scratch it. They were both silent. The woman closed her eyes from fatigue but soon opened them and smiled at him. She asked him in a tender voice, with no edge of emotion to it, "Do you think you can forget the past?"

He lowered his eyes and shuddered, feeling an almost irresistible urge to flee. He implored her, "Don't go back over the past. Let it depart, never to return."

Perhaps his heart did not mean it, but his tongue had found the right thing to say. The statement may even have accurately expressed his feeling at the moment, when he was totally absorbed by the current situation. His phrase, "Let it depart, never to return," may have sounded odd to his ears and heart, leaving anxiety in its wake, but he refused to ponder it. He fled from that subject and clung to his sincere emotion, which he had been determined not to relinquish from the beginning.

His mother asked again, "Do you love your mother the way you did in the happy days?"

Patting her hand, he replied, "I love her and pray for her safety."

He soon found himself richly repaid for his anxiety and inner struggle by the look of peace and deep contentment that spread over her withered face. He felt her hand squeeze his, as though to tell him of the gratitude she felt. They exchanged a long, dreamy, calm, smiling look that radiated an ambiance of reassurance, affection, and sorrow throughout the room. She no longer seemed to want to talk or perhaps it was too much effort for her. Her eyelids slowly drooped until they closed. He looked at her questioningly but did not move. Then her lips opened a little and a delicate, recurrent snoring could be heard.

He sat up straight and scrutinized her face. Then he closed his eyes for a bit while he conjured up the image of her other face with which she had looked at him the year before. He felt depressed, and the fear that had dogged him on his way over returned. Would he ever be permitted to see this face again? With what emotions would he encounter her if he returned? He did not know. He did not want to try to picture what lay in the world of the unknown, the future. He wanted his mind to stop and to follow events, not to try to anticipate them. He was afflicted by fear and anxiety. It was strange . . . he had wanted to flee when he was listening to her talk, so much that he had thought he would be relieved if she fell asleep, but now that he was alone he felt afraid. He did not know why. He wished she would wake up from her nap and start talking again. How long should he wait? . . . Suppose she stayed sound asleep until morning? He could not spend that much time at the mercy of fear and anxiety. He had to set a limit to his pains. . . . The next day or the day after that congratulations or condolences would be in order. Congratulations or condolences? . . . Which would he prefer? The uncertainty had to end. "Whether it's congratulations," he thought, "or condolences, I mustn't anticipate events. The most that can be said is that if we are fated to part now, we've parted friends. It will be a good ending to a bad life. But if God prolongs her life . . ."

While his mind wandered, his glance roamed about, until his eyes fell on the mirror of the wardrobe that stood opposite him. He could see reflected in it the bed with his mother's body stretched out under the blanket and he saw himself, almost blocking from view the upper half of his mother except for her hand, which she had removed from the covers when she welcomed him. He gazed at it affectionately and placed it under the covers, which he arranged carefully around her neck. Then he looked back at the mirror. It occurred to him that this mirror might reflect the image of an empty bed by the next day. Her life, in fact anyone's life, was no more permanent than these visions in the mirror. He felt even more afraid and whispered to himself, "I've got to limit my pains. . . . I've got to go." Leaving the mirror, his eyes moved around until they fell upon a table with a water pipe on it. The flexible tube was wound around the neck of the pipe like a snake. He looked at it with astonishment and disbelief, at once replaced by a raging feeling of disgust and anger. That man! . . . No doubt he was the owner of this pipe. He imagined the man sitting cross-legged on the sofa between the bed and the table, slumped over the pipe, inhaling and exhaling with pleasure as Yasin's mother fanned its coals for him. Oh . . . where was he? Somewhere in the house or outside? . . . Had the man seen him from some concealed spot? He could not bear to stay any longer with the water pipe. He cast a final look at his mother and found her fast asleep. He gently got up and went to the door. Seeing the servant in the outer hall, he told her, "Your mistress has fallen asleep. I'll return tomorrow morning."

At the door of the apartment he turned to say once more, "Tomorrow morning." He seemed to want to warn the man about the time so he could keep out of sight.

He headed straight for Costaki's bar. He drank as usual, but it did not cheer him up. He was unable to dispel the fear and anxiety from his heart. Although dreams of his mother's fortune and the comfort it would provide him did not leave his mind, he was unable to erase from his memory the image of sickness and ideas of annihilation.

When he got home at midnight he found his stepmother waiting for him on the first floor. He looked at her in surprise. Then with his heart pounding he asked, "My mother?"

Amina hid her face and said in a soft voice, "A messenger from Palace of Desire Alley came an hour before you returned. Have a long life, son."

64

KAMAL'S ASSOCIATION with the British developed into a mutual friendship. Citing Yasin's misadventure in the mosque of al-Husayn, the family attempted to persuade the boy to sever his relations with these friends, but he protested that he was young, too young to be accused of spying. To keep them from stopping him, he went directly to the encampment when he got back from school, leaving his book bag with Umm Hanafi. There was no way to prevent him except by force, which they did not think appropriate, especially since he was having such a good time in the camp, directly under their eyes, and was welcomed and treated generously wherever he went. Even Fahmy showed forbearance and amused himself by watching Kamal move among the soldiers like a "monkey playing in the jungle."

"Tell al-Sayyid Ahmad," Umm Hanafi suggested once when complaining that the soldiers were fresh with her because of the accursed friendship and that some of them had mimicked the way she walked. For that reason, they deserved "to have their heads cut off." No one took her suggestion seriously, not merely out of consideration for the boy but to spare themselves too, fearing an investigation would reveal that they had concealed this friendship for a long time. They let the boy and his concerns alone. They may also have hoped that the reciprocal good feelings between the boy and the soldiers would protect the rest of them from interference or injury they might otherwise expect from the soldiers when members of the family came and went.

The happiest times of Kamal's day were those inside the encampment. Not all the soldiers were his friends in the ordinary sense of the word, but they all knew him. He would shake hands with his special friends, pressing their hands warmly, but limit himself to a salute for the others. When his arrival coincided with the sentry duty of one of his friends, the boy ran up to him cheerfully and happily, putting out his hand, only to be shocked to find that the soldier remained curiously and disturbingly rigid, as though snubbing Kamal or as though he had turned into a statue. The boy only realized this was not the case when the others burst out laughing.

It was not unusual for the alarm siren to sound suddenly when he was with his friends. They would rush to their tents, returning shortly in their uniforms and helmets and carrying their rifles. A truck would be brought out from behind the cistern building. The soldiers would quickly jump into it, until it was packed full. He would realize from the scene in front of him that a demonstration had broken out somewhere and that the soldiers were going to break it up. Fighting would certainly flare up between them and the demonstrators. The only thing that concerned him at these times was to keep sight of his friends until he saw them packed into the truck. He would gaze at them, as though bidding them farewell. When they headed off for al-Nahhasin, he would spread out his hands to pray for their safety and to recite the opening sura of the Qur'an.

He only spent half an hour each afternoon at the camp. That was the longest he could absent himself from home when he got back from school. During that half hour, all his senses were on the alert every minute. He prowled around the tents and trucks, which he inspected piece by piece. Standing in front of the pyramids of rifles, he examined them in detail, especially the barrel muzzles where death lurked. He was not permitted to get too close to them and suffered terribly because he wanted to play with them or at least touch them.

If his visit coincided with teatime, he went with his friends to the field kitchen set up at the entrance to Qirmiz Alley and took his place at the end of the "tea queue," as they called it. Then he would return behind them with a cup of tea and milk and a piece of chocolate. They would sit on the wall of the fountain to drink their tea. The soldiers all sang while he listened with interest, waiting for his turn to perform.

The life of the camp made a deep impression on him, giving an all-encompassing vividness to his flights of imagination and dreams that were engraved in his heart alongside Amina's legends and accounts of the world of mysteries and Yasin's stories and their magical universe, to which Kamal added the phantoms and visions of his daydreams about the lives of ants, sparrows, and chickens, which occupied his mind when he was on the roof surrounded by sprigs of jasmine, hyacinth beans, and pots of flowers. From this inspiration, he created a military encampment, completely equipped and staffed, next to the wall separating their roof from Maryam's. He erected tents of handkerchiefs and pencils. The weapons were twigs, the vehicles wooden clogs, and the soldiers date pits. Near the army camp he had demonstrators, represented by pebbles. He usually began the performance by distributing the pits in groups, some in the tents or by the entrances, others around the rifles. To one side there were four pits surrounding a pebble that stood for himself.

First he imitated the English style of singing. Then it was time for the pebble to sing "Visit me once each year" or "O Darling." He would move over to the pebbles and arrange them in rows as he shouted, "Long live the Nation. . . . Down with the Protectorate. . . . Long live Sa'd." Returning to the camp and giving a warning whistle, he organized the pits in columns, putting a date at the head of each one. He moved a clog as he huffed to imitate the truck's drone. After putting pits on the clog he shoved it toward the pebbles. The battle would break out, and many victims would fall on both sides. He did not allow his personal feelings to influence the course of the battle, at least not at the beginning or even midway through it. His single dominant desire was to make the battle authentic and thrilling. Both sides would struggle, pushing and pulling to try to maintain an equal number of casualties. The outcome would remain in doubt as the advantage passed back and forth, but eventually the battle would have to end. Then Kamal would find himself in an awkward position. Which side should win? His four friends, headed by Julian, were on one side, but on the other side were the Egyptian demonstrators with whom Fahmy was deeply involved emotionally. In the final moment the victory would be accorded to the demonstrators. The truck would withdraw with the few remaining soldiers, including his four friends. One time the battle ended with an honorable armistice, which warriors from both sides celebrated in song at a table set with teacups and different types of sweets.

Julian was his favorite, distinguished from the others by his good looks, gentle temperament, and greater skill in speaking Arabic. He was the one who had issued Kamal a standing invitation to tea. He was also the soldier most touched by Kamal's singing. Almost every day he would ask to hear "O Darling." He would follow the words with interest. Then he would murmur with heartfelt homesickness, "I'm going home to my country.... I'm going home."

Kamal appreciated the man's sensitivity and it made him like the soldier all the more. He felt comfortable enough to tell him once quite seriously that the way to escape from his distress was to "return Sa'd Pasha and go back to your country."

Julian did not receive this suggestion with the good humor Kamal had anticipated. To the contrary, he asked the boy, as he had before in comparable circumstances, not to mention Sa'd Pasha. In English he said, "Sa'd Pasha ... no!" Thus failed the "first Egyptian negotiator," as Yasin dubbed Kamal.

The boy was surprised one day to have one of his friends present him with a caricature he had drawn of him. Kamal looked at it in astonishment and alarm, observing to himself, "My picture? ... This isn't my picture." Deep inside, he felt it did look like him and no one else. He looked up at the men standing around him and found they were laughing. He realized it was a joke and that he should accept it with pleasure. He laughed along with them to hide his embarrassment.

When Fahmy looked at it, he studied the portrait of Kamal with amazement. Then he said, "O Lord, this picture omits none of your defects and exaggerates them ... the small, skinny body, the long, scrawny neck, the large nose, the huge head, and the tiny eyes." Laughing, he continued: "The only thing your 'friend' seems to admire is your neat, elegant suit, and that's no fault of yours. All the credit belongs to Mother, who takes such superb care of everything in the house."

With a gloating look, Fahmy told his little brother, "It's clear what the secret of their fondness for you is.... They like to laugh at your appearance and foppishness. To put it plainly, you're nothing but a comic puppet to them. What have you gained from your treachery?"

Fahmy's rebuke had no impact on the boy, because he understood how hostile Fahmy was to the English. He thought his brother was plotting to separate him from them.

One day he arrived at the encampment as usual and saw Julian at the far wall of the cistern building looking with interest at the alley where the residence of the late Mr. Muhammad Ridwan was situated. Kamal went toward him and noticed that Julian was waving his hand with a gesture the boy did not understand. Kamal stopped, obeying an instinctive feeling he could not explain. His curiosity tempted him to detour around the tents erected in front of the cistern. He crept up behind Julian and looked in the same direction. There he saw a small window in a wing of the Ridwan family residence which blocked off the short alley. Maryam's smiling and responsive face could be plainly seen there. Stunned, Kamal stood looking back and forth between the soldier and the girl, almost refusing to believe his eyes.

How could Maryam have dared to appear at the window? How could she show herself to Julian in this shameless way? He was waving and she was smiling. . . . Yes, the smile was still evident on her lips. . . . Her eyes were so busy looking at the soldier that she was not aware of Kamal's presence. He accidentally moved and attracted Julian's attention. The soldier burst into laughter when he saw the boy standing behind him and made some remarks that sounded like gibberish to Kamal. Maryam, clearly terrified, retreated at breakneck speed. Kamal stared in a daze at the soldier. The way Maryam had fled only increased his suspicions, although the whole affair seemed extremely mysterious to him.

Julian asked him affectionately, "Do you know her?"

Kamal nodded his head in the affirmative and said nothing. Julian went off for a few minutes, returning with a large parcel, which he presented to Kamal, telling him as he pointed toward Maryam's house, "Take it to her."

Kamal jumped back with alarm. He shook his head from side to side stubbornly. That incident lingered in his mind, and although he sensed from the beginning that it was serious, he did not realize just how serious it was until he told the story at the evening coffee hour. Amina sat up straight, drawing away from him, with the coffee cup still in her hand, not bringing it to her lips or putting it back on the tray. Fahmy and Yasin raced over from their sofa to the one shared by the mother and Kamal and began to stare at him with unexpected interest, astonishment, and alarm.

Swallowing, Amina said, "Did you really see that? . . . Didn't your eyes deceive you?"

Fahmy grumbled, "Maryam? . . . Maryam! . . . Do you know for certain who it was?"

Yasin asked, "Was he gesturing to her and was she smiling back at him? . . . Did you really see her smile?"

Replacing her cup on the tray and leaning her head on her hand, Amina said in a threatening voice, "Kamal! Lying about a matter like this is a crime God will not forgive. Think carefully, son. . . . Didn't you exaggerate something?"

Kamal swore his weightiest oaths. Fahmy commented with bitter despair, "He's not lying. No sensible person would accuse him of lying about this. Don't you see that a person his age wouldn't be able to invent such a story?"

The mother asked in a sad voice, "But how is it possible for me to believe him?"

As though to himself, Fahmy observed, "Yes, how is it possible to believe him? . . ." Then in a serious voice he added, "But it happened . . . happened . . . happened."

The word sank into him like a dagger. When he repeated it, he seemed to be deliberately stabbing himself. It was true that events had distracted him from Maryam and that her memory appeared only at the edges of his daydreams, but this blow to her reputation struck deep into his heart. He was dazed, dazed, dazed, not knowing whether he had forgotten her or not, whether he loved or hated her, was angry out of a sense of honor or jealousy. . . . He was a dry leaf caught up in a howling storm.

"How can I believe him? . . . My trust in Maryam has been like mine for Khadija or Aisha for such a long time. Her mother is a virtuous woman. Her father, may God let him rest in peace, was a fine man . . . neighbors for a lifetime, excellent neighbors. . . ."

Yasin, who had seemed lost in thought all the while, replied in a tone not innocent of sarcasm, "Why are you surprised? . . . Since ancient times, God has created evil people from the loins of pious ones."

Amina, as though refusing to believe that she had been taken in for such a long time, protested, "With God as my witness, I've never observed anything discreditable about her."

Yasin agreed cautiously: "Nor has any of us, not even Khadija, the supreme faultfinder. People far more clever than either of us have been deceived about her."

Fahmy cried out in anguish, "How can I penetrate the world of mysteries? It's a matter that defies the imagination." He was boiling with anger at Yasin. Then it seemed to him that everyone was hateful: the English and the Egyptians in equal measure . . . men and women, but especially women. He was choking. He longed to disappear and be alone to inhale a breath of relief, but he stayed where he was, as though tied down with heavy ropes.

Yasin directed a question to Kamal: "When did she see you?"

"When Julian turned toward me."

"And then she fled from the window?"

"Yes."

"Did she notice that you saw her?"

"Our eyes met for a moment."

Yasin said sarcastically, "The poor dear! . . . No doubt she's imagining our gathering now and our distressing conversation."

"An Englishman!" Pounding his hands together, Fahmy shouted, "The daughter of al-Sayyid Muhammad Ridwan. . . ."

Shaking her head in amazement and sighing, Amina mumbled something to herself.

Yasin observed thoughtfully, "For a girl to flirt with an Englishman is no easy matter. This degree of corruption could not have appeared in a single leap."

"What do you mean?" asked Fahmy.

"I mean that her corruption must have proceeded a step at a time."

Amina implored them, "I ask you to swear by God to give up this conversation."

As though he had not heard her entreaty, Yasin kept on with his observations: "Maryam's the daughter of a lady whose art in adorning herself has been witnessed by the women of our family. . . ."

Amina cried out in a voice filled with censure and rebuke, "Yasin!"

Backing down, Yasin said, "I want to say that we as a family live according to such strict standards that we know little of what goes on around us. No matter how hard we try to guess, we imagine that other people live the way we do. We've associated with Maryam for years without knowing what she's really like, until the truth about her was discovered by the last person one would have expected to uncover the facts." He laughed and patted Kamal on the head.

Amina once again implored them fervently, "I beg you to change the topic of this conversation."

Yasin smiled and said nothing. Silence reigned. Fahmy could not bear to stay with them any longer. He responded to the inner voice that was anxiously calling for help and encouraging him to flee far from other eyes and ears, so that he could be all alone and repeat the conversation to himself from start to finish, word by word, phrase by phrase, sentence by sentence, in order to understand and fathom it. Then he could see where he stood.

65

IT WAS after midnight when al-Sayyid Ahmad Abd al-Jawad left the home of Maryam's mother, Umm Maryam, concealing himself in the darkness of the cul-de-sac. The whole district appeared to be sound asleep, enveloped in the gloom. It had been that way every night since the English had set up camp there. No one chatted in a coffeehouse, no vendor roamed about, no shop stayed open late, and no passerby stole along. The only traces of life or light were those coming from the camp. None of the soldiers had ever interfered with him as he came and went, but he felt anxious and apprehensive whenever he approached the camp, especially when returning home late at night exhausted but relaxed and in a daze that made it difficult for him even to attempt to walk safely and steadily.

He went down to al-Nahhasin Street before turning to head back toward his house, glancing stealthily at the sentry until he reached the most dangerous section of the street, where it was illuminated by light from the camp. There he was always seized by the feeling that he was an easy mark for any predator. He quickened his steps to reach the dark area near the entrance to his house but had hardly advanced a step when his ears rang as a rude, gruff voice yelled after him in gibberish. He realized from the violent tone and concision of the words, even though he could not understand them, that an order not subject to debate was being tossed at him. He stopped walking and turned, terrified, toward the voice.

He saw another soldier, not the sentry, heading toward him, armed to the teeth. What new development had brought on this treatment? Was the man intoxicated? Perhaps he had been overcome by a sudden urge to attack someone? Or was he out to plunder and loot? With a pounding heart and a dry throat, al-Sayyid Ahmad watched the soldier approach. The lingering effects of his intoxication fled.

This soldier stopped a few feet away from him and in a commanding voice addressed a few brisk words to him. Al-Sayyid

Ahmad naturally did not understand a single one. The soldier pointed toward Palace Walk with his free hand. Al-Sayyid Ahmad looked desperately and ingratiatingly at him, suffering bitterly from his inability to communicate or to convince the man that he was innocent of his accusations. He wished he could at least discover what the man wanted. It occurred to him that the soldier had gestured down Palace Walk to tell him to move away, thinking he did not live in this neighborhood. He pointed in turn to his house, so the man would understand that he was a resident returning home. The soldier ignored his gesture and snarled at him, pointing persistently in the other direction. He motioned with his head, as though urging al-Sayyid Ahmad to go in that direction. Apparently growing impatient, he seized him by the shoulder, forcibly turned him around, and shoved him in the back. Al-Sayyid Ahmad found himself moving toward Palace Walk with the other man behind him. He surrendered to his fate, but his joints felt like rubber. On his way to an unknown destination, he passed the military camp and the cistern building. After that, the last trace of light from the camp vanished.

He waded into the waves of gloomy darkness and profound silence, seeing nothing but phantom houses and hearing only the heavy footsteps that followed him with mechanical precision, as though counting out the minutes or perhaps seconds left for him to live. Yes, he expected at each moment to be dealt a blow that would finish him off. He walked along, waiting for it, his eyes staring into the darkness, his mouth pursed from worry, his Adam's apple jerking up and down as he tried to swallow to relieve his dry, burning throat. He was startled by a gleam of light that made him look down. He almost screamed from dismay, like a child, as his heart plummeted. He saw a circle of light going back and forth and realized that it was caused by rays of light from a battery-powered lantern that his warder had turned on to see where he was going. He got his breath back after his sudden alarm subsided, but this relief was short-lived. He was once more seized by fear, fear of the death to which he was being led. Once more he expected to die from moment to moment. He was like a drowning man flailing about in the water who thinks he sees a crocodile preparing to attack. When it becomes clear that the beast is just some plants floating in the water, he enjoys a momentary relief at being spared this danger, before choking again under the pressure of the real danger presented by the ocean.

Where was the man leading him? If he could only talk that gibberish, he would ask. It seemed he would be forced to go all the way to the cemetery at Bab al-Nasr. There was no trace of any man or beast. Where was the night watchman? He was alone at the mercy of a merciless person. When had he ever suffered like this? Could he remember? In a nightmare . . . yes, it was a nightmare he had had several times when he was sick. Even in a nightmare the gloom is occasionally brightened by a flash of hope, considerately letting the sleeper feel that his dream is not real and he will be saved from it sooner or later. It was farfetched to assume that destiny would grant him any comparable hope. He was awake, not asleep. This soldier, armed to the teeth, was a reality, not a phantom. The street witnessing his humiliation and captivity was frighteningly tangible, not imaginary. His suffering was real, there was no doubt about that. The least sign of resistance from him would probably result in the loss of his head. There was no doubt of that.

Umm Maryam had told him when she said goodbye to him, "Until tomorrow." Tomorrow? Would that day ever come?

"Ask the heavy feet rocking the earth behind your back. . . . Ask the rifle with its sharp-pointed bayonet."

She had also teased him: "The fragrance of wine coming from your lips is about to intoxicate me." Now both the wine and his mind had flown off. The time for passion was gone, although only a few minutes before it had been all that mattered in life. Now suffering was his whole life. . . . Only a few short minutes separated the two conditions. A few minutes?

When he reached the corner of al-Khurunfush, his eyes were attracted by rays of light flashing in the darkness. He looked along the street and saw a lantern carried by another soldier driving before him an uncertain number of figures. He wondered whether the soldiers had been given orders to capture all the men they came across at night. Where were they leading them? What punishment would be meted out? He wondered about these things for a long time with astonishment and alarm, although the sight of these new victims provided some consolation and relief for his heart. At least he was not the only one, as he had thought. He had found some mates to share his affliction. They would keep him from feeling so lonely and would share his fate. He was a short distance ahead of them.

He began to listen to their footsteps with the relief a person lost in a desert feels on hearing human voices carried to him by the wind. His dearest wish was for them to catch up with him so that he could join their group, regardless of whether he knew them or not. Let their hearts beat in unison as they marched briskly to an unknown destination. These men were innocent. He was innocent. So why had they been captured? What special reason could there be for taking him captive? He was not one of the revolutionaries and was not involved in politics. He was not even young. Were the English privy to the secrets in men's hearts or capable of scrutinizing their emotions? Were they going to arrest members of the general public after arresting all the leaders? If only he knew English so he could ask his captor. . . . Where was Fahmy to interpret for him?

He was stung by painful homesickness. Where were Fahmy, Yasin, Kamal, Khadija, Aisha, and their mother? Could his family imagine his disgraceful state? Their only image of him was one of venerable and exalted power. Would they be able to imagine that a soldier had shoved him in the back almost hard enough to make him fall on the ground and herded him along like livestock? When he remembered his family, he felt such painful homesickness that tears almost came to his eyes.

On the way, he passed shadowy houses and stores whose owners he knew and coffeehouses he had frequented, especially when he was younger. It made him sad to walk past them as a prisoner with no one coming to his aid or even offering their condolences for his situation. He really felt that the most distressing form of humiliation was that suffered in his own district.

He looked up to the heavens to transmit his thoughts to God, who could see into his heart. He sent his prayers to Him without saying anything with his tongue, not even under his breath. He was ashamed to mention God's name when his body had not been cleansed of the vapors of wine and the sweat of lovemaking. His fear increased, because his polluted state might interfere with his salvation. He might meet a fate that suited his debauchery. Pessimism and dejection gained control of his emotions. He was on the verge of despair when, approaching the lemon market, he heard unintelligible sounds, instead of the silence broken only by footsteps. Staring into the darkness, he listened intently, alternating between fear and hope. He could hear a clamor but did not know if it came from men or beasts. Before long he could tell it was shouting. He could not keep from exclaiming to himself, "Human voices!"

As the road turned, he saw lights moving. At first he thought they were more lanterns, but it became clear that they were flaming torches. By their light he saw one side of Bab al-Futuh. There were British soldiers standing under this ancient city gate. Then he caught a glimpse of Egyptian policemen. The sight of them quickened his pulse.

"Now I'll know what they want with me," he thought. "It's only a few more steps. Why are the English soldiers and the Egyptian policemen crowded together at the gate? Why are they rounding up citizens from all areas of the district? I'll know everything shortly. Everything? I'll seek God's protection and submit my destiny to Him. I'll remember this dreadful hour for the remainder of my life, if there is a remainder.... Bullets, the gallows, not to mention the brutal injustice the English inflicted on the villagers at Dinshawai.... Am I going to join the roster of martyrs? Will I become an item of news about the revolution to be passed on by Muhammad Iffat, Ali Abd al-Rahim, and Ibrahim al-Far the way we've been discussing such things at our evening sessions? Can you imagine one of our parties with your place empty? God's mercy on you.... 'He's gone and done for.' How they'll weep for you. They'll remember you for a long time. Then you'll be forgotten. How upset I am. Submit your fate to your Creator. O God, encompass us, don't oppose us."

As he approached the British soldiers they looked at him in a stern, cold, threatening manner. He had a sinking feeling along with intense pain in his chest. Was it time for him to stop? He dragged his feet and hesitated uncertainly.

"Enter," an Egyptian policeman shouted to him, pointing to the area inside the great portal. Al-Sayyid Ahmad looked inside questioningly but also ingratiatingly and pitifully. He passed between the English soldiers, barely able to see what was in front of him, he was so scared. He wished he could hide his head in his arms in response to his instinctive fear. What he saw under the gateway explained, without any need for questions, why he was wanted. He saw that a deep pit like a trench had been dug there to obstruct the road. He likewise saw a swarm of citizens working nonstop to fill the hole under the supervision of the police. They were carrying baskets of dirt, which they emptied into the trench. Everyone was working zealously and quickly while their eyes glanced stealthily and fearfully at the English soldiers stationed at the entrance to the gate.

A policeman came up to him and threw him a basket, telling him in a gruff voice that sounded threatening, "Do what the others are doing." Then he added in a whisper, "Be quick so you don't get hurt."

This final sentence was the first humane expression he had encountered during his terrifying journey, and it felt like air in the throat of a man close to asphyxiation. Al-Sayyid Ahmad bent over the basket to pick it up by the handle and asked the policeman in a whisper, "Will I be set free when the work's completed?"

The policeman whispered, "God willing."

He sighed profoundly and felt like crying. It seemed he had been born anew. With his left hand he lifted the bottom of his cloak and tucked it into the belt of his caftan so it would not impede his work. He took the basket to the sidewalk where dirt was piled. Putting the basket at his feet he filled his hands with dirt and emptied them into the basket. When it was full, he carried it to the hole and threw the dirt in before returning to the sidewalk. He kept on with this, surrounded by groups of men, both old and young, some in modern dress and others wearing traditional turbans. They all worked with a high degree of energy stemming from their desire to live.

He was refilling his basket when an elbow nudged him. He turned to see who it was and recognized a friend named Ghunaym Hamidu, the owner of an olive-oil-pressing firm in al-Gamaliya and a guest at some of al-Sayyid Ahmad's parties. They were delighted to see each other and soon were whispering together.

"So you got caught too!"

"Before you. I arrived a little before midnight. I saw you getting your basket, so as I went back and forth with my basket I began to follow a path that would gradually bring me over to you."

"Welcome . . . welcome. Aren't any more of our friends here?"

"You're the only one I've found."

"The policeman told me they'll let us go when we finish the work."

"I was told that too. May our Lord hear us."

"They've ruined my knees, may God destroy their homes."

"So far as I can tell, I don't even have knees anymore."

They exchanged a quick smile. "How did this pit get here?"

"I was told that a bunch of the boys from al-Husayn dug it at the beginning of the night to prevent the trucks from coming through here. They also say a truck fell in."

"If that's true, then you can say goodbye to us."

The second time they worked beside each other at the dirt pile they were somewhat more resigned to their situation. Their spirits had revived and they could not keep themselves from smiling as they filled their baskets with dirt like construction workers.

Ghunaym whispered, "May God and His blessings repay us for these sons of bitches."

Al-Sayyid Ahmad smiled and whispered back, "I hope they're going to pay us the normal wage."

"Where did they catch you?"

"In front of my house."

"It figures."

"What about you?"

"I had taken some dope, but I got over it fast. The English are stronger than cocaine."

"They're even more effective than throwing up."

By the light of the torches the men went back and forth quickly between the sidewalk with the dirt and the ditch. They stirred up the dust until it spread throughout the vaulted area of the gate, filling the air. They had trouble breathing. Sweat poured from their brows and plastered their faces with mud. They were coughing from inhaling the dust. They looked like ghosts brought to light when the hole gaped open.

In any case, he was no longer alone. There was this friend and the other men from his district. Even the Egyptian policemen were with them in their hearts. The fact that they had been stripped of their weapons was evidence of that. They no longer had swords in metal scabbards dangling from their belts.

"Be patient," he advised himself. "Be patient. Perhaps this suffering will pass. Did you think you'd work until morning or even almost till noon? Buck up. You won't always be carrying dirt and exploited to fill the hole.... The hole refuses to fill up...."

There's nothing to be gained from complaining. To whom would you complain? Your body's powerful and strong and can take it, despite being impaired by the evening's inebriation. What time is it? It wouldn't be prudent to check now. If this had not happened to me, I'd be stretched out in bed enjoying a sound sleep. I would be able to wash my head and face and get a refreshing drink flavored with orange blossoms from the water jug. Congratulations to us for this participation in the hell of the revolution. Why not? The country is in revolt every day. Every hour there are casualties and martyrs. Reading the papers and passing on news is one thing, but carrying dirt at gunpoint is something else. Congratulations to all of you asleep in your beds. O God, preserve us. . . . I'm not meant for this . . . not meant for this. God vanquish those who doubt Your power. We are weak. . . . I'm not meant for this.

"Does Fahmy realize the dangers threatening him? He's reviewing his lessons now, unaware of what is happening to his father. He said no to me for the first time in his life. He said it with tears in his eyes, but it means the same thing. I didn't tell his mother and I won't. Should I reveal my lack of power to her? Should I seek help from her weakness after my power has failed? Certainly not. . . . Let her remain ignorant of the whole affair. He says he's not exposing himself to any danger. Really? God, hear my prayer. If it had not been for that, I wouldn't have been so easy on him. God preserve him. God preserve all of us from the evil of these days. What time is it now? Once it's morning, we'll be safe. They won't kill us in front of the people."

"I spat on the ground to clear the dust from my throat," his friend remarked, "and one of the policemen shot me a look that made my hair stand on end."

"Don't spit. Do like me. I've swallowed enough dirt to fill this hole."

"Perhaps Zubayda cursed you?"

"Perhaps."

"Wasn't filling her hole better than filling this one?"

"It was even more strenuous!"

They smiled quickly at each other. Then Ghunaym said with a sigh, "God help me, my back's broken."

"Me too. Our only consolation is that we're sharing some of the pains of the freedom fighters."

"What do you think? Should I throw my basket in the soldiers' faces and cry out at the top of my lungs, 'Long live Sa'd'?"

"Has the dope started working again?"

"What a loss! . . . It was a piece the size of the pupil of your eye. I stirred it in my tea three times. Afterward I went to al-Tambakshiya to listen to Shaykh Ali Mahmud recite poetry in the home of al-Hamzawi. On my way back, shortly before midnight, I was telling myself, 'Your old lady's waiting for you now. There's nothing to be gained from disappointing her.' Then that monkey popped up and drove me along in front of him."

"May our Lord compensate you."

"Amen."

Soldiers brought in more men, some from al-Husayn and others from al-Nahhasin, who were quickly incorporated into the work force. Al-Sayyid Ahmad looked around. The place was almost packed full of people. They spread out around the trench in every direction, going between the sidewalk and the hole without taking a break, their panting faces illuminated by light from the torches. They looked thoroughly exhausted, humiliated, and afraid. There was blessed safety in numbers. "They won't slaughter this swarm of people," he reflected. "They wouldn't take the innocent along with the guilty. Where do you suppose the guilty ones are? Where are those brave young men? Do they know their brothers have fallen in the hole they dug? May God destroy them. Did they think that digging a hole would bring Sa'd back or drive the English out of Egypt? I'll certainly abandon my nightlife if God grants me a new lease on life. Abandon my nightlife? It's no longer safe to go out at night. Will life retain any savor? Life loses its savor in the shadow of the revolution. Revolution . . . in other words, a soldier takes you captive, you carry dirt in your hands, Fahmy says no to you. No! When will the world return to normal? A headache? . . . Yes, a headache and I want to throw up too. A few minutes to rest. I don't want anything more than that. Maryam's mother, Bahija, is sound asleep. Amina's waiting for me like Ghunaym's 'old lady.' There's no way you could imagine what's happened to your father. O Lord, the dust's filling my nose and eyes. O Master Husayn. . . . Fill, fill . . . isn't all this enough dirt for you? O grandson of the Messenger of God, Husayn. . . . The Battle of the Trench, that's what the revered preacher called it. The Prophet Muhammad, God's peace and blessings on him, fought a Battle of the Trench and worked alongside the other men, digging the dirt out with his own hands. His enemies were pagans back then. Why are the pagans winning today? It's a corrupt age. . . . The times are corrupt. I'm corrupt. Will they remain camped in front of my house until the revolution's over?"

"Did you hear the cock?"

Al-Sayyid Ahmad listened intently and mumbled, "The cock's crowing! Is it dawn?"

"Yes, but the hole won't be filled up until morning. . . . The important thing is that I need to relieve myself, badly."

Al-Sayyid Ahmad's mind thought about the lower part of his body. He realized that he needed to go too. Part of his pain was no doubt related to his swollen bladder. Thinking about it seemed to make it much worse, and the pressure of his bladder was intense. "Me too," he said.

"What can we do?"

"There's no solution at hand."

"Look over there at that monkey pissing in front of Ali al-Zajjaj's store. . . ."

"Oh. . . ."

"Getting a little urine out of my body's more important to me now than getting the English out of Egypt."

"Get the English out of all of Egypt? Let them get out of al-Nahhasin to begin with."

"O Lord. . . . Look. The soldiers are still bringing people in."

Al-Sayyid Ahmad saw a new batch making their way toward the trench.

66

WHEN AL-SAYYID AHMAD awoke it was almost time for the afternoon prayer. News of his mishap had spread among his family and friends. Many of them stopped by the house to congratulate him on his deliverance. Despite the seriousness of the topic, he told them the whole story in a style graced by comic touches and flourishes that inspired their comments.

Amina was the first to hear the story, which he recounted while still psychologically shattered and physically weak, scarcely able to believe he had escaped alive. She heard the terrifying aspects uncensored. Once he fell asleep, she wept profusely and began to pray to God to watch over her family with His care and mercy. She prayed so long she felt she was losing her voice.

Al-Sayyid Ahmad, on finding himself surrounded by friends, especially close ones like Ibrahim al-Far, Ali Abd al-Rahim, and Muhammad Iffat, recovered his spirits and had difficulty ignoring the humorous aspects of the incident, which finally won out over everything else. His rendition turned the episode into a comedy. He might have been telling them about one of his escapades.

While the top floor was crowded with male visitors, the family gathered on the lower floor, except for the mother, who was busy with Umm Hanafi preparing coffee and cold drinks. Once again the sitting room witnessed a reunion of Yasin, Fahmy, Kamal, Khadija, and Aisha for the traditional coffee hour. Khalil and Ibrahim Shawkat had been with them all day long but had gone to the father's room shortly after he had awakened, leaving the brothers and sisters alone. Their sorrow over what had happened to their father vanished as they became reassured. Their hearts were filled with affection, and they jumped at the chance to chat and joke with each other the way they had in the past. They had felt anxious until they had seen their father with their own eyes. They had gone to him, one after the other, kissed his hand, and prayed he would have a long and peaceful life. Then they had left his room with military order and discipline.

Although the father had merely held his hand out to Yasin, Fahmy, and Kamal without saying a word, he had smiled at Khadija and Aisha, asking them tenderly how they were doing and if they were in good health. They had been treated to this tenderness only after they got married. Kamal had noticed it with delighted astonishment, as though he were the recipient. In fact, Kamal was the happiest of anyone whenever his sisters visited. On those occasions he enjoyed a profound happiness tarnished only by anticipation of the visit's end. The warning would come when one of the men, Ibrahim or Khalil, stretched or yawned. Then he would say, "It's time for us to leave." The phrase was a command to be obeyed, not rejected.

Neither of Kamal's sisters was gracious enough, even once, to tell her husband, for example, "You go. I'll join you tomorrow."

In time, Kamal became accustomed to the strange bond linking his sisters to their husbands and accepted its authority. He contented himself with their short visits every now and then and rejoiced without longing for more. Yet he could not keep himself from asking wishfully sometimes, "Why don't you return and live here the way you used to?"

His mother would quickly reply, "May God spare them the evil of your good wishes."

The most amazing thing he had noticed about their married life was the bizarre change that had befallen their bellies and the attendant symptoms, which seemed as frightening as a disease and as exotic as legends. He had learned some new concepts, like pregnancy and cravings, and associated ones like vomiting, malaise, and the consumption of pellets of dry clay.... So what was the matter with Aisha's belly? When would it stop growing? It looked like an inflated waterskin. Khadija's belly too appeared to be undergoing the same transformation. If Aisha with her ivory complexion and golden hair craved mud, what would Khadija crave? As it turned out, Khadija confounded his fears and craved pickles.

Kamal had countless questions but was unable to elicit a satisfactory answer for any of them. His mother told him that Aisha's belly, as well as Khadija's, would produce a tiny baby, who would be the apple of his eye. But where was this baby living? How was it living? Did it hear and see? What did it hear and see? How did it come into existence? Where did it come from? For these significant questions he received answers that deserved to be added to the lore about saints and jinn, amulets and spells, and other such matters he had gleaned from his mother's personal encyclopedia. Therefore he asked Aisha with concern, "When will the baby come out?"

She laughed and replied, "Be patient. It won't be long."

Yasin asked, "Aren't you in your ninth month?"

She answered, "Yes, although my mother-in-law insists I'm in my eighth."

Khadija observed sharply, "It's just that our mother-in-law always wants to have a different opinion. That's all there is to it."

Since everyone knew of the frequent disputes that flared up between Khadija and her mother-in-law, they looked at each other and laughed.

Aisha said, "I want you to move to our house and stay with us until the English evacuate your street."

Khadija said enthusiastically, "Yes. Why not? The house is large. You'll be comfortable and have plenty of space. Papa and Mama can stay with Aisha because she's on the middle floor, and the rest of you can stay with me."

Kamal was overjoyed by the suggestion and to prod them asked, "Who will tell Papa?"

Fahmy shrugged his shoulders and said, "You both know perfectly well that Papa will not agree."

"But he likes to go out at night, and he'll be exposed to interference from the soldiers," Khadija protested. "What criminals they are! To lead him off in the dark and make him carry dirt. . . . My head spins whenever I think about it."

Aisha said, "I waited for my turn to kiss his hand so I could examine him from head to toe, to reassure myself. My heart was pounding and my eyes were blinking away tears. . . . God's curse on those dogs, the bastards."

Yasin smiled. Winking at Kamal, he cautioned Aisha, "Don't insult the English. They have a friend among us."

Fahmy observed sarcastically, "Perhaps it would amuse Papa to know that the soldier who captured him last night was just one of Kamal's buddies."

Smiling at Kamal, Aisha asked, "Do you still love them after what they've done?"

Blushing from embarrassment and confusion, Kamal stammered, "If they had known he was my father, they wouldn't have harmed him."

Yasin could not keep himself from laughing so loudly he had to put a hand over his mouth. He looked up at the ceiling warily, as though afraid the sound of his laughter might reach the upper story. Then he said mockingly, "What you ought to say is: If they had realized that Kamal was Egyptian they would not have tormented Egypt and the Egyptians. They just don't know any better."

Khadija said fiercely, "You should leave this talk to someone else. . . . Are you denying that you have befriended them too?" She addressed Kamal in as biting a tone: "Will you be brave enough to perform the Friday prayer at the mosque of our master al-Husayn now that people know about your friendship with them?"

Yasin understood her allusion and replied with mock regret, "It's permissible for you to give me a hard time now that you're married and have acquired some basic human rights. . . ."

"Didn't I have this particular right before?"

"God's mercy on those bygone years . . . but it's marriage that returns the spirit to wretched girls. Bow down in thanks to the saints . . . and to Umm Hanafi's incantations and prescriptions."

Trying not to laugh, Khadija retorted, "You've gained the right to attack people, whether or not what you say is true, after inheriting from your late mother and becoming a man of property."

With childish glee Aisha said, as though she knew nothing about it, "My brother's a man of property. . . . How lovely to hear that. . . . Are you really rich, Mr. Yasin?"

Khadija said, "Let me enumerate his properties for you. Listen, lady: the store in al-Hamzawi, a residence in al-Ghuriya, the house in Palace of Desire Alley . . ."

Shaking his head and lowering his eyes, Yasin recited, "And from the evil of the envious person when he envies . . ." (Qur'an, 113:5).

Khadija continued her comments without paying any attention to his interruption: "And valuables like jewelry and coins worth even more than the real estate."

Yasin cried out with genuine sorrow, "That all disappeared, by your life. Stolen. That son of a bitch stole them. Father asked him if she had left jewelry or money, but the thief said, 'Search for yourselves. God knows I paid her expenses during her illness from my own money.' What a man! His 'own money' . . . that son of a washerwoman."

Aisha said sympathetically, "The poor dear . . . sick, confined to bed, at the mercy of a man who wanted her money . . . without a friend or a loved one. She left the world without anyone to grieve for her."

Yasin asked, "Without anyone to grieve for her?"

Khadija pointed through the half-open door at Yasin's clothes hanging on a rack. She protested ironically, "And this black bow tie? . . . Isn't that a sign of mourning?"

Yasin said seriously, "I really did mourn for her, may our Lord be merciful to her and forgive her sins. Didn't we become reconciled at our last meeting? May God be merciful to her and forgive her and the rest of us."

Khadija lowered her head a little and raised her eyebrows to gaze at him, as though looking over the top of a pair of spectacles. She said, "Ahem, ahem . . . listen to our revered preacher." She cast him a skeptical look and continued: "But I suspect that your sorrow was not too deep?"

He looked at her furiously and replied, "Praise to God, I did not fall short in my duties to her. I received people and had the Qur'an recited for three nights. Every Friday I visit the cemetery with fragrant herbs and fruit. Do you want me to strike my face, wail, and spread dirt on my head? Men grieve differently from women."

She shook her head as though to say, "You have assisted me. May God assist you." Then with a sigh she remarked, "Oh, the grief of men! . . . But tell me, by my life, didn't the shop, apartment, and house alleviate some of the torment of your grief?"

He grumbled, "The person was right who said, 'An ugly tongue bespeaks an ugly face.'"

"Who said that?"

Smiling, he replied, "Your mother-in-law!"

Aisha laughed. Fahmy laughed too and asked Khadija, "Haven't relations between you improved?"

Aisha answered for her, "Relations between the English and the Egyptians will improve before theirs do."

Khadija for the first time spoke resentfully: "She's a strong-willed woman. May our Lord hold it against her. By God, I'm innocent and falsely accused."

"We all believe you," Yasin commented sarcastically. "There's no need for an oath. We'll testify to that before God on Judgment Day."

Fahmy asked Aisha, "How are you doing with her?"

Glancing apprehensively at Khadija, she replied, "As well as could be hoped."

Khadija shouted, "Fie on your sister Aisha. She knows when to lead and when to bow her head. Fie. . . ."

Pretending to be serious, Yasin said, "At any rate, may God be merciful to your mother-in-law and my sincere congratulations to you."

Khadija observed sarcastically, "God willing, the real congratulations will soon be for you when you're escorted to your second bride. Isn't that so?"

He could not help but laugh. "May God hear your prayer," he said.

Aisha asked with interest, "Really?"

He thought a little. Then he said somewhat seriously, "The Believer does not put his hand back in the lair to be bitten a second time, but who knows what the morrow will bring? Perhaps second, third, and fourth brides."

Khadija exclaimed, "That's what I expect. May God be compassionate to your grandfather."

They all laughed, even Kamal. Then Aisha said sadly, "Poor Zaynab! She was such a fine girl."

"She was . . . and also stupid, with a father as unbearable as my own. If she had been content to live with me the way I wanted, I would never have renounced her."

"Don't admit that. Protect your honor. Don't give Khadija a chance to gloat over your misfortune."

He said scornfully, "She got what she deserves. Let her father brew her up and drink her down."

Aisha muttered, "But she's pregnant, poor dear. Are you pleased that your child will grow up in someone else's custody until returned to you as a boy?"

Oh, she had drawn blood. His child would grow up in the mother's custody the way Yasin had before him. Perhaps he would suffer misery like Yasin's or even worse. He might grow up hating his mother or father. In any case, it was miserable. Frowning, he said, "Let his fate be like his father's. There's nothing that can be done about it."

They were quiet for a time until Kamal asked Khadija, "And you, sister, when will your baby come out?"

Laughing and feeling her belly, she answered, "He's still in his first stage."

Studying her face, he told her innocently, "You've really gotten thin, sister, and your face has become ugly."

They all laughed, covering their mouths with their hands. They laughed so much that Kamal felt embarrassed and confused. Khadija was unable to take offense at Kamal and was inclined to flow with the current. Laughing, she agreed: "I confess that during this time of special cravings I have lost all the flesh that Umm Hanafi worked hard for so many years to create. I've grown thin, my nose sticks out, and my eyes are sunken. I imagine my husband's looking everywhere in vain for the bride he married."

They laughed again. Yasin commented, "The truth is that your husband has been wronged. Despite his obvious stupidity, he's good-looking. Glory to God who united a stallion and a jenny."

Khadija pretended to ignore him. Pointing toward Aisha, she told Fahmy, "Both her husband and mine are slow. They hardly leave the house by night or day. They have no interests or jobs. Her husband squanders his time smoking or playing the lute like those beggars who go to people's houses at the festivals. My husband is always lying around smoking or chattering so much it makes me dizzy."

"Aristocrats don't work," Aisha said apologetically.

Khadija sneered. "I beg your pardon.... It's right for you to defend that life. The truth is that God never united two such identical people as when he united the two of you. When it comes to laziness, mildness, and indolence you're the same person. Mr. Fahmy, by the Prophet, her husband spends the whole day smoking and playing music while she adorns herself and flits back and forth in front of the mirror."

Yasin inquired, "Why not, so long as what she sees in the mirror is pretty?" Before Khadija could open her mouth, he quickly asked, "Tell me, sister, what will you do if your child looks like you?"

She was fed up with his attacks and answered him seriously,

"With God's permission he will resemble his father, grandfather, grandmother, or aunt.... If..." She laughed. "If he insists on resembling his mother, then he'll deserve to be banished even more than Sa'd Pasha."

With the tone of a man of experience, Kamal told her, "The English don't care about beauty, sister. They like my head and nose a lot."

Khadija struck her breast with her hand and cried out, "They claim to be your friends when all the time they're making fun of you.... May our Lord send another zeppelin after them."

Aisha cast a tender look at Fahmy and said, "How your prayer would please some people."

Fahmy smiled and muttered, "How can I be happy when they have gullible friends in our house?"

"What a pity your influence has failed with the boy."

"Some people aren't helped by good influences."

Kamal protested, "Didn't I ask Julian to bring back Sa'd Pasha?"

Khadija laughed and said, "Next time have him swear by that head of yours he likes so much."

More than once Fahmy had felt they were trying to draw him into the conversation and distract him every chance they got, although that did nothing to dissipate his feeling of alienation, which for a long time had come between him and his family whenever he was with them. He would feel alienated or alone no matter how crowded the coffee hour was. He would withdraw into his heart, grief, and zeal when surrounded by giddy, laughing people. When they could, they even made a joke out of Sa'd's banishment.

He glanced stealthily at each of them in succession and found they were all happy. Aisha was flourishing, although a little tired because of the pregnancy. She was happy about everything, even her fatigue. Khadija was bouncy and quick to laugh. Yasin's health was outstanding, and he looked blissful. Who among them cared what was happening nowadays? Who among them was concerned whether Sa'd was in Egypt or in exile and whether the English left or stayed? He felt like a stranger or at least estranged from these people. Although this feeling was usually blunted by his magnanimous spirit, now he felt angry and resentful, perhaps because of what he had been going through over the past few days. He had frequently expected to hear that Maryam was getting married. He had been concerned and troubled about that, even though he had already resigned himself to it in despair. As time passed he had almost accepted the idea. Even his love had retreated from center stage in his emotions while he was distracted by weighty concerns. But the incident with Julian had been like an earthquake. What was the meaning of her flirtation with an Englishman she could not hope to marry? Would anyone but a shameless woman do such a thing? Was Maryam a shameless woman? What had happened to the object of his dreams?

The first chance he had had to be alone with Kamal he had asked his little brother to tell the story again, insisting on all the details. How had he observed what took place? Where was the soldier standing? Where was Kamal standing? Was he certain that it was Maryam herself who was in the little window? Was she really looking at the soldier? Did he see her smile at the man? Where . . .? Was . . .? Did . . . ? Clenching his teeth as though trying to crush the distress that was tormenting him, Fahmy had asked, "Did she act scared and leave when she saw you?"

Afterward Fahmy had visualized the whole episode, gesture by gesture and scene by scene. He imagined her smile at length until he could almost see her lips parting, the way he had seen them the day of Aisha's wedding when the girl was following along after the bride in the courtyard of the Shawkat family residence.

"It seems Mama won't join us today," Aisha said sadly.

Khadija commented, "The house is full of visitors."

Yasin laughingly remarked, "I'm afraid the soldiers will become suspicious of the number of people coming here and think a political rally is being held in our home."

Khadija said proudly, "Papa's friends are so numerous they could hide the sun."

Aisha observed, "I saw Mr. Muhammad Iffat himself at the head of the procession."

Khadija confirmed her sister's statement: "He's been his best friend since before we saw the light of day."

Shaking his head, Yasin said, "Papa accused me falsely of destroying their friendship."

"Doesn't divorce separate even the dearest friends?"

Yasin smilingly replied, "Not your father's friends!"

Aisha boasted, "Who would ever want to oppose Papa? By

God, there's no one in the whole world who's equal to him."
Then with a sigh she continued: "Whenever I think of what
happened to him last night, my hair turns gray."

Khadija had finally had enough of Fahmy's despondency. She
decided to attack it directly, after indirect methods had failed. She
turned toward him and asked, "Brother, do you see how gracious
our Lord was the day you were denied your wish with regard
to . . . Maryam?"

Fahmy looked at her with astonished embarrassment. All eyes
were immediately focused on him with concern, even Kamal's.
Profound silence reigned, revealing the existence of a stifled
sentiment that had been ignored or concealed until Khadija
expressed it so boldly. They looked at the young man as though
awaiting his reply, almost as though he was the one who had asked
the question.

Yasin thought he had better end the silence before it got any
worse and caused more pain. Pretending to be happy, he commented, "The reason is that your brother's a saint, and God loves
His saints."

Fahmy, suffering from anguish and embarrassment, said tersely,
"This is an old issue that's been forgotten."

To shield him, Aisha said, "Mr. Fahmy wasn't the only one to
be deceived by her. We were all taken in."

Khadija defended herself as best she could against this alleged
oversight: "Well, I was never convinced for a moment – even
when I believed she was innocent – that she was worthy of you."

Pretending to dismiss the whole affair, Fahmy said, "This is an
old issue that's been forgotten. An Englishman, an Egyptian, it's all
the same thing. Let's skip all this."

Yasin found himself thinking once again about the "issue" of
Maryam. . . . Maryam? He had never looked at her in the past if she
came into view except in a cursory fashion. Fahmy's attachment to
her had increased Yasin's desire to ignore her, until her scandal had
been broadcast in the family. That had aroused his interest, and he
had wondered for a long time what sort of girl she was. He would
have liked to study her carefully and observe the girl who had
aroused the desire of an Englishman sent to fight, not flirt. Yasin's
anger at her was only a conversational device. He was actually
enraptured by the presence nearby of a daring "fallen woman,"
separated from him by a single wall. His broad, sturdy chest was

pervaded by a bestial intoxication bringing out the hunting instinct in him, but he held back in honor of Fahmy's sorrow, for he loved his brother. He limited himself to a passive, emotional delight, although no one in the whole district so stirred his interest as Maryam.

"It's time to leave," Khadija remarked as she rose. She had heard the voices of Ibrahim and Khalil, who were coming in from the hall. Everyone stood up. Some stretched while others adjusted their clothing. Only Kamal remained seated. He looked at the door of the sitting room mournfully, his heart pounding.

67

AL-SAYYID AHMAD sat at his desk bent over his ledgers, immersing himself in his daily tasks, which helped him forget, if only temporarily, his personal worries as well as the bloody public ones that were in the news all the time. He had grown to love the store as much as his evenings of fellowship and music, because in both situations he successfully freed himself from the hell of thinking. Although the store's atmosphere was full of haggling, selling, buying, making money, and similar concerns of ordinary, daily life, it restored his confidence that everything could return to normal, to the original condition of peace and stability. Peace? Where had it gone and when would it be ready to return? Even in his store there were distressing, whispered conversations about bloody events. Customers were no longer content just to bargain and buy. Their tongues kept belaboring the news and bewailing events. Over the bags of rice and coffee beans he had heard about the battle of Bulaq, the massacres at Asyut, the funeral processions with tens of coffins, and the young man who had wrested a machine gun away from the enemy, intending to bring it back into al-Azhar Mosque, only to be killed before he could get there as swarms of bullets sank into his body. News like this, tinged crimson with blood, assaulted his ears from time to time in the very place where he had taken refuge, seeking to forget.

How miserable it was to live constantly in the shadow of death. Why did not the revolution achieve its objectives quickly before he or any of his family was harmed? . . . He was not stingy with money and did not begrudge it his emotional involvement, but sacrificing a life was another matter. What kind of punishment was God inflicting on His flock? Life had become cheap and blood was flowing. . . . The revolution was no longer a thrilling spectacle. It threatened his security whenever he came or went and menaced the life of his rebellious son. His enthusiasm for it, but not for its goal, had dwindled. He still dreamt of independence and the return of Sa'd, but without a revolution, bloodshed, or terror.

He chanted slogans with the demonstrators and was zealous with the zealots, but his mind was attached to life and struggled to resist this current, like a tree trunk in a flood, its branches torn off by storms. Nothing, no matter how great, would weaken his love for life. Let him keep his love for life to the end of his days. If only Fahmy felt that way too, so that he would not sacrifice his life; Fahmy, the disobedient son who had thrown himself into the stream without a life preserver.

"Is al-Sayyid Ahmad here?"

He heard the voice and sensed that someone was hurtling into the shop like a human projectile. He looked up from his desk and saw Shaykh Mutawalli Abd al-Samad in the middle of the room blinking his inflamed eyes, futilely trying to peer toward the desk. Al-Sayyid Ahmad's spirits rose. With a smile he shouted at the visitor, "Make yourself at home, Shaykh Mutawalli. We are blessed by your presence."

The shaykh appeared reassured. He advanced, his torso swaying backward and forward as though he were riding on a camel. Al-Sayyid Ahmad leaned over his desk, putting out his hand to take his visitor's and press it firmly, saying gently, "The chair's to your right. Please sit down." Shaykh Mutawalli leaned his stick against the desk and took his seat. Putting some of the weight of his shoulders on his hands, which were placed on his knees, he said, "May God preserve you and sustain you."

The proprietor responded wholeheartedly, "How fine your prayer is and how much I've needed it." Turning toward Jamil al-Hamzawi, who was weighing rice for a customer, he advised him, "Don't forget to prepare the parcel for our master the shaykh."

Jamil al-Hamzawi responded, "Who could forget our master the shaykh?"

The shaykh spread out his hands and raised his head, moving his lips in a quiet prayer of which only an intermittent whisper could be heard. Then he returned to his former pose and was silent for a moment. By way of invocation he said, "I begin with a prayer for the Prophet, our guiding light."

Al-Sayyid Ahmad said fervently, "The finest of all blessings and peace on him."

"I ask a double portion of mercy for your father of blessed memory."

"May God have great mercy on him."

"Then I ask God to delight your eyes with your family and offspring for generations to come."

"Amen."

Sighing he continued: "I ask Him to return to us 'Our Effendi' the Khedive Abbas II, Muhammad Farid, and Sa'd Zaghlul."

"May God hear your prayer."

"And devastate the English for their past and present sins."

"Glory to the Omnipotent Avenger."

At that point, the shaykh cleared his throat and wiped his face with his palm before saying, "I saw you in a dream waving your hands. As soon as I opened my eyes I resolved to visit you."

The proprietor smiled somewhat sadly and replied, "That's not surprising, because I'm in desperate need of your blessings, may God multiply them."

The shaykh leaned his face toward al-Sayyid Ahmad affectionately and asked, "Is what I heard about the incident at Bab al-Futuh correct?"

Al-Sayyid Ahmad smiled and answered him: "Yes . . . I wonder who told you."

"I was passing by the oil-pressing establishment of Ghunaym Hamidu when he stopped me and said, 'Haven't you heard what the English did to me and your dear friend al-Sayyid Ahmad?' In alarm I asked him to explain. So he told me, wonder of wonders."

Al-Sayyid Ahmad recounted the whole story with every detail. He never tired of repeating it, even though he had told it tens of times over the past few days.

As the shaykh listened, he recited the Throne Verse about God under his breath (Qur'an, 2:255). "Were you frightened, my son?" he asked. "Describe your fear to me. Tell me about it. There is no power or might save from God. Were you convinced you would be saved? Have you forgotten that fright doesn't just go away? You prayed for a long time and asked God for salvation. That's excellent, but you'll need an amulet."

"Why not! . . . It will bring us added blessings, Shaykh Mutawalli. And the children and their mother – weren't they frightened too?"

"Of course . . . their hearts are weak, inexperienced with brutality or terror. . . . An amulet. . . . An amulet's the remedy."

"You are goodness and blessing, Shaykh Mutawalli. God rescued me from a grave evil, but there's another evil still threatening me that keeps me awake nights."

Once again the shaykh's face leaned toward al-Sayyid Ahmad affectionately. He asked, "May God forgive you. What's troubling you, son?"

The proprietor looked at him despondently and muttered angrily, "My son Fahmy."

The shaykh raised his white eyebrows inquisitively or in alarm and commented hopefully, "He's safe, with the permission of God the Merciful. . . ."

Al-Sayyid Ahmad shook his head sorrowfully and said, "He disobeyed me for the first time. The matter's in God's hands."

The shaykh spread his arms out in front of him as though to ward off affliction and shouted, "I take refuge in God. Fahmy's my boy. I'm certain he's dutiful by nature."

Al-Sayyid Ahmad said with annoyance, "His honor insists on doing just what the other boys are doing at this bloody time."

The shaykh was astonished and incredulous. He protested, "You're a resolute father. There's no doubt about that. I would never have imagined that one of your sons would dare oppose you in anything."

These words cut him to the quick and drew blood. He felt upset and inclined to downplay his son's rebellion in order to defend himself, both to the shaykh and to himself, against the accusation of weakness. He said, "Of course he did not dare do so directly, but I asked him to swear on a copy of the Qur'an that he would not participate in any revolutionary activity. He wept instead of having the courage to say no. What can I do? I can't lock him up in the house. I can't keep him under surveillance at school. I'm afraid that the current of events at this time will be too strong for a boy like him to resist. What should I do? Threaten to beat him? Beat him? But what good is a threat when he doesn't mind risking death?"

The shaykh stroked his face and asked anxiously, "Has he thrown himself into the demonstrations?"

Shaking his broad shoulders, the proprietor answered, "Of course not. But he distributes handbills. When I pressured him, he claimed he only distributed them to his best friends."

"Why is he interested in such activities?...He's the mild-mannered son of a mild-mannered father. These activities are for a different type of man. Doesn't he know that the English are brutes with rough hearts unaffected by mercy who feed on the blood of the poor Egyptians from dawn to dusk? Talk to him amicably. Preach to him. Show him the difference between light and darkness. Tell him that you're his father, that you love him and are afraid for him. For my part, I'll make several amulets of a special type and remember him in my prayers, especially the Dawn Prayer. It's God who is our help from first to last."

The proprietor said mournfully, "Every hour there's more news of fatalities. That should be warning enough for anyone with half a mind. What's happened to his intellect? The son of al-Fuli, the milkman, was lost in an instant. Fahmy attended the funeral with me and offered his condolences to the boy's poor father. The lad was distributing bowls of curdled milk when he ran into a demonstration. He was tempted by fate to join it, without giving the matter any thought. Then in not much more than an hour he was slain in front of al-Azhar Mosque. There's no might or power save with God. We are from God and return to God. When he was late getting back, his father became anxious and went to his customers to ask after him. Some of them said he had brought the milk and departed and others said he had not passed by them as usual. When he reached Hamrush, who sells sweet shredded pasta bars, he found the boy's tray and the remaining bowls that hadn't been distributed. Hamrush told the father that the boy had left them with him while he participated in a demonstration that afternoon. The poor man went crazy and proceeded at once to the Gamaliya police station. They sent him to the Qasr al-Ayni Hospital, where he found his son in the autopsy room. Fahmy heard the story with all the details, just the way al-Fuli related it to us when we were at his house to offer him our condolences. Fahmy learned how the boy had been lost and might just as well have never existed. He witnessed the father's excruciating grief and heard the wails of the family. The poor lad perished, but Sa'd didn't return and the English didn't leave. If Fahmy were a stone, he would have understood something. Still, he's the best of my children, for which I praise and thank God."

In a sad voice, Shaykh Mutawalli said, "I knew that poor boy. He was the oldest of al-Fuli's children, isn't that so? His grandfather was a donkey driver, and I used to hire his donkey to go to Sidi Abu al-Sa'ud. Al-Fuli has four children, but he was fondest of the one who died."

For the first time Jamil al-Hamzawi entered into their conversation: "In these crazy times, people can't think straight, not even the youngsters. Yesterday my son Fuad told his mother he wanted to take part in a demonstration."

Al-Sayyid Ahmad said anxiously, "The young ones participate in demonstrations and the big ones are struck down in them. Your son Fuad's a friend of my son Kamal, and they both go to the same school. Hasn't he, haven't they both been tempted to join in a demonstration? . . . Huh? Nothing seems amazing anymore."

Al-Hamzawi regretted having let that slip out and observed, "It hasn't gone this far, al-Sayyid Ahmad, sir. I disciplined him mercilessly for his innocent wish. Mr. Kamal never goes out unless he's accompanied by Umm Hanafi, may God preserve and watch over him."

They were silent. The only thing that could be heard in the store was the rustling of the paper in which al-Hamzawi was wrapping the present for Shaykh Mutawalli Abd al-Samad. Then the shaykh sighed and commented, "Fahmy's a bright boy. He mustn't let the English threaten his dear soul. The English! . . . May God make it up to me. Haven't you heard what they did in the villages of al-Aziziya and Badrashin? . . ."

The proprietor was so perturbed he did not really wish to inquire what had happened. He expected it would be the same sort of thing he kept hearing about. He merely raised his eyebrows to seem interested.

The shaykh commenced: "The day before yesterday I was visiting the esteemed and noble Shaddad Bey Abd al-Hamid in his mansion in al-Abbasiya. He invited me to have lunch and supper, so I presented him with some amulets for him and the members of his household. There I learned what happened at al-Aziziya and Badrashin."

The shaykh was silent for a bit. Al-Sayyid Ahmad asked, "The well-known cotton merchant?"

"Shaddad Bey Abd al-Hamid is the greatest of all the cotton merchants. Perhaps you knew his son Abd al-Hamid Bey Shaddad? He was closely linked with Mr. Muhammad Iffat once."

Al-Sayyid Ahmad spoke slowly to give himself time to think: "I remember I saw him at one of Mr. Muhammad Iffat's parties before the outbreak of the war. Then I heard he had been exiled following the fall of 'Our Effendi' Abbas II. What news is there of him?"

Shaykh Mutawalli replied quickly in passing, as though putting his words in parentheses so he could return directly to his original topic, "He's still in exile. He lives in France with his wife and children. Shaddad Bey is intensely worried he will die before he sees his son again in this world." He fell silent. Then he began to shake his head right and left, reciting in a musical voice as though chanting the opening of a poem in praise of the Prophet, "Two or three hours after midnight when the people were sleeping, a few hundred British soldiers armed to the teeth surrounded the two towns."

Al-Sayyid Ahmad's attention was rudely awakened. "They surrounded the villages when the people were sleeping? Weren't the besiegers similar to the soldiers camped in front of the house? They began by attacking me. What's the next step they plan?"

The shaykh slapped his knee as though trying to set the rhythm for his recitation as he continued: "In each village they burst into the home of the magistrate, ordering him to surrender his weapons. Then they penetrated the women's quarters, where they plundered the jewelry and insulted the women. They dragged them outside by their hair, while the women wailed and called for help, but there was no one to help them. Have sympathy, God, for Your weak servants."

"The homes of the two magistrates! Isn't the magistrate a government official? I'm no magistrate, nor is my house the home of one. I'm just a man like any other. What might they do to people like us? Imagine Amina being dragged by her hair. Is it fated that someday I'll wish I were insane? . . . Insane!"

Shaking his head, the shaykh continued with his account: "They forced the magistrates to show them where the village elders and the leading citizens lived. Then they stormed those houses, breaking down the doors and plundering everything of value. They attacked the women in a most criminal fashion, after killing those who tried to defend themselves. They beat the men violently. Then they moved out of the towns, leaving nothing precious untouched and no honor undefiled."

"Let them take anything precious with them straight to hell," al-Sayyid Ahmad brooded. "But 'no honor undefiled' . . . where was God's mercy? Where was His vengeance? . . . The flood and Noah . . . the nationalist leader Mustafa Kamil. . . . Imagine! How could a woman remain under one roof with her husband after that? And what fault had she committed? How could he counten-ance it?"

The shaykh struck his knee three times before resuming his account. His voice had begun to tremble and he lamented, "They set fire to the villages, pouring gasoline over the poles and thatch forming the roofs of the houses. The towns awoke in dreadful terror. Residents fled from their homes, screaming and wailing as though they had gone mad. The tongues of flame reached everywhere until both villages were engulfed."

Al-Sayyid Ahmad cried out involuntarily, "O Lord of heaven and earth!"

The shaykh proceeded: "The soldiers formed a ring around the burning villages to wait for the wretched inhabitants, who rushed off in every direction followed by their livestock and dogs and cats, looking for some way to escape. When they reached the soldiers, the latter fell upon the men, beating and kicking them. Then they detained the women to strip them of their jewelry and divest them of their honor. Any woman who resisted was killed. Any husband, father, or brother who lifted a hand to protect them was gunned down."

Shaykh Mutawalli turned to look at the stunned proprietor. He struck his hands together and shouted, "And they led the survivors to a nearby camp, where they forced them to sign a document containing their confessions to crimes they had not committed and their admission that what the English had done to them was an appropriate punishment. Al-Sayyid Ahmad, this is what happened to al-Aziziya and Badrashin. This is an example of the kind of punishment imposed on us, mercilessly and heartlessly. O God, bear witness, bear witness."

A despondent, oppressive silence reigned while each of the men wrestled with his own thoughts and images. Then Jamil al-Hamzawi moaned, "Our Lord exists."

"Yes!" shouted al-Sayyid Ahmad, applauding his statement. Gesturing in all four directions, he said, "Everywhere!"

Shaykh Mutawalli advised the proprietor, "Tell Fahmy that Shaykh Mutawalli counsels him to stay away from danger. Tell him, 'Surrender to God your Lord. He alone is capable of devastating the English as He has devastated those who disobeyed Him in the past.'"

The shaykh leaned over to grasp his stick. Al-Sayyid Ahmad gestured to Jamil al-Hamzawi, who brought the present. He put it in the shaykh's hand and helped him rise. The shaykh shook hands with both men and recited as he left, "'The [God-fearing] Byzantines have been defeated in a nearby land, but after their defeat, they will be victorious' [Qur'an, 30:2–3], and not the friends of the pagans. The words of God Almighty are true."

68

AT DAWN, when darkness was slowly giving birth to light, a servant from Sugar Street knocked on the door of al-Sayyid Ahmad's house and informed Amina that Aisha's labor had begun. Amina, who had been in the oven room, turned her work over to Umm Hanafi and rushed to the stairway.

For perhaps the first time in the long history of her employment in the house, Umm Hanafi appeared to be indignant. Was it not obligatory for her to be present when Aisha gave birth? She had every right to be there, just the same as Amina. Aisha had first opened her eyes in Umm Hanafi's lap. Every child in the family had two mothers: Amina and Umm Hanafi. How could she be separated from her daughter at such a terrifying time?

"Do you remember what it was like when you had your child?" she asked herself. "The apartment in al-Tambakshiya. . . ." The master had been out as usual. She had been alone, although it was after midnight. Umm Hasaniya had been both a friend and a midwife. "Where is Umm Hasaniya now? Is she alive today?" Then her son Hanafi had arrived amid moans of pain. He had departed amid moans of pain too, when he was still in the cradle. If he had lived, he would be twenty. "My little mistress will be suffering, while I'm stuck here preparing food."

Amina's heart was filled with the same apprehensive joy she had felt when she first prepared to give birth. Here was Aisha getting ready to deliver her first child and commence life as a mother, as she herself had begun with Khadija. Thus the life that had sprung from her would continue on endlessly. She went to her husband to announce the good news to him in a quiet, courteous way. She tried her best to appear shy and polite, so her ardent desire to rush off to her daughter would not show. Al-Sayyid Ahmad received the news calmly and then ordered her to go without delay. She got dressed quickly, appreciative of the wonders motherhood could work at times for a weak woman like herself.

The brothers learned the news when they woke up, shortly after the mother's departure. They smiled and exchanged questioning glances.

"Aisha's a mother!"

"Isn't that strange?"

"What's strange about it? Mother was younger than Aisha when Khadija was born."

"Has Mother gone to deliver the baby with her own hands?" Kamal's question was answered by two smiles.

"This is a warning for me," Yasin observed. "The bitch will have her baby soon. . . ."

"Who do you mean?"

"Zaynab."

"Oh, if Papa ever heard you . . . "

"Aisha's a mother and I'm a father."

"And I'm an uncle twice over," Fahmy remarked. "You will be too, Mr. Kamal."

"I'm going to have to stay out of school today to go to Aisha's."

"That's great. Just ask Papa's permission at breakfast, if you're able."

"Oh! We need more births to keep up with the dent the English are making in our population."

"If I stay home from school, that won't be a problem. Three-fourths of the students have been on strike for more than a month."

"Tell Papa that. He'll surely be convinced by your argument. Then he'll hit you in the face with a plate of beans."

"Oh! A new baby. . . . In an hour or two Papa will become a grandfather and Mama a grandmother. We'll all be uncles. This is a significant event. How many children are being born at this moment, do you suppose? And how many people are dying right now? We need to let Grandmother know."

"I can go to al-Khurunfush and tell her, if I stay home from school. . . ."

"We've explained that your school is none of our business. Tell Papa. He'll welcome your idea."

"Oh! Perhaps Aisha's suffering now. The poor darling. . . . Golden hair and blue eyes won't make the labor pains any lighter."

"May our Lord bring her through it safely. Then we'll drink the traditional broth and light some candles."

"A boy or a girl?"

"Which do you prefer?"

"A boy, of course."

"Perhaps she'll begin with a girl, like her mother."

"Why not start with a boy, like her father?"

"Ah . . . by the time school lets out, the baby will already have arrived. Then I won't get a chance to watch him come out."

"You want to see him being born?"

"Of course."

"You'd better postpone this desire until it's your own child."

Kamal was the most deeply affected by the news. It preoccupied his mind, heart, and imagination. Had he not felt that the school disciplinarian was keeping track of him and watching his every move to report in detail to his father, he would have been unable to resist the temptation to go to Sugar Street. He remained in school, but only in body. His spirit was hovering over Sugar Street, inquiring about the new arrival he had been awaiting for months, in hopes of learning its secret.

He had once seen a cat give birth when he was not quite six. She had attracted his attention with her piercing meows. He had rushed to her, finding her on the roof under the arbor of hyacinth beans, writhing in pain with her eyes bulging out. When he saw her body part with an inflamed bit of meat, he had backed away in disgust, screaming as loudly as he could. This memory haunted his mind, and he felt the same old disgust. It was a pesky, distressing memory, encompassing him like a fog, but he refused to let himself be frightened. He could not imagine any connection between the cat and Aisha, except the slight relationship between an animal and a human being, whom he believed to be as far apart as earth from heaven. But what was going on in Sugar Street, then? What strange things were happening to Aisha? These were vexing questions that appeared to have no easy answers. The moment he got out of school that afternoon he dashed off at full speed to Sugar Street.

He was panting when he entered the courtyard of the Shawkat residence. He went to the door of the women's quarters but chanced to peer into the reception room. To his chagrin, he found himself looking straight into his father's eyes. The man was sitting down, grasping with both hands the top of the walking stick held between his legs. Kamal froze, staring as though hypnotized, not blinking or moving. He felt he must have unwittingly done something wrong. He waited for the punishment to fall on him, as the chill of fear spread through his limbs. Then al-Sayyid Ahmad started talking to the person sitting beside him and turned in that direction. Kamal averted his eyes and swallowed. He caught a glimpse of Ibrahim Shawkat, Yasin, and Fahmy in the pavilion before he fled. He leapt up the stairs till he reached Aisha's floor. The door was partway open and he went in. There he found Khalil Shawkat, Aisha's husband, standing in the sitting room. He noticed that the bedroom door was closed. He could hear voices conversing inside. He recognized those of his mother and Widow Shawkat, but there was a third he did not know. He said hello to Khalil and, looking up at him with smiling eyes, asked, "Has Aisha had her baby yet?"

The man put a finger to his lips to caution him and said, "Hush."

Kamal realized that he and his question were not welcome, although Khalil usually greeted him warmly. Kamal was embarrassed and felt uneasy for no particular reason. He wanted to go over to the closed door but was stopped by Khalil's voice yelling at him peremptorily, "No."

Kamal turned toward him questioningly. The man told him quickly and urgently, "Be a good boy and go downstairs and play."

The boy was crushed. Disheartened, he retreated with heavy feet. It hurt him to be rewarded so shabbily for the torment of waiting he had endured all day. Just as he was about to leave, a strange sound coming from the closed room made his ears ring. It began high, shrill, and piercing and then became husky and disjointed, even raucous, before ending as a long, harsh rattle. It died away just long enough for the person to breathe. Afterward there was a deep moan of complaint. At first Kamal did not recognize the voice, but despite its shrillness, huskiness, and rattling, there was something distinctive about its tortured sound that revealed the person's identity. It was the voice of his sister Aisha, without any doubt, or of Aisha exhausted and fading away. When the deep, complaining moan was repeated, he knew he was right. He trembled all over. He imagined her writhing in pain. That reminded him of the cat. He glanced toward Khalil and found him contracting and relaxing his fists as he murmured, "O Gracious Lord."

Kamal imagined that Aisha's body was contracting and relaxing like her husband's hands. He lost control of himself and raced off, unable to say anything because of his sobs. When he reached the door of the women's quarters he heard footsteps behind him. He looked up and saw the servant Suwaydan hurrying down. She passed without paying any attention to him. Stopping at the door, she called her master Ibrahim. When the man hastened to her, she told him, "Praise to God, master." She added nothing further and did not wait to hear his reply. She turned on her heels and rushed back up the steps without any delay.

Ibrahim went to the reception chamber with a beaming face. Kamal stayed where he was, alone, not knowing what to do. In less than a minute Ibrahim returned, followed by al-Sayyid Ahmad, Yasin, and Fahmy in that order. The boy stepped aside to let them pass and then trailed after them with a pounding heart.

Khalil received them at the door of the apartment. Kamal heard his father say, "Praise to God for good health."

Khalil muttered despondently, "Praise to God in any case."

With concern, al-Sayyid Ahmad asked him, "What's the matter?"

In a low voice Khalil said, "I'm going to call the doctor."

Al-Sayyid Ahmad asked anxiously, "For the baby?"

He replied as he shook his head no, "Aisha! . . . She's not in good shape. I'll get the doctor at once."

He departed, leaving behind him undisguised dejection and anxiety. Ibrahim Shawkat invited them into the parlor. They went there silently. Widow Shawkat arrived soon and greeted them. She smiled to reassure them. When she sat down she said, "The poor dear suffered so long that her strength gave out. It's just a temporary condition and will soon pass. I'm sure of what I say, but my son seems to be unusually fearful today. In any case, there's no harm in having the doctor come." Then she commented in a low voice to herself, "The real doctor is our Lord. He's the true physician."

Though surrounded by his sons, al-Sayyid Ahmad was unable to maintain his customary composure. With evident anxiety he asked, "What's the matter with her? . . . Can't I see her?"

The woman smiled and said, "You'll see her shortly, when she's feeling better. It's my crazy son's fault that he alarmed you unnecessarily."

Within his broad, powerful chest that seemed so resolute, dignified, and awe-inspiring was a grievously tormented heart. Inside those grave, despondent eyes was a frozen tear. "What's happened to my little girl? The doctor! Why is the old lady keeping me from seeing her? A tender smile or an affectionate word from me, from me in particular, would certainly lessen her pains. Marriage, husband, pain. . . . She never tasted the bitterness of pain in my house. The beautiful, darling little girl . . . mercy, God. Life's lost its flavor. The taste is destroyed by the least harm threatening them. Fahmy . . . I see he's dejected and in pain. . . . Has he understood the meaning of pain? How could he know what a mother's heart feels? The old lady's calm and confident of what she says. Her son upset us for no reason at all. O God, hear our prayer. You know the state I'm in. You'll save her the way You saved me from the English. My heart can't take this torment. God is merciful. He's capable of saving my children from every evil. Otherwise, life would have no taste. What enjoyment would I get from gaiety, music, and entertainment if there was a sharp thorn planted in my side? My heart prays for their deliverance, because it's a father's heart. It can't enjoy amusements unless it's free from worry. Will I go to the party tonight with a heart at ease? When I laugh, I like it to resound from the depths of my sincere heart. An anxious heart is like a string that's out of tune. Fahmy's enough for me to worry about. He pesters me like a toothache. How hateful pain is! A world without pain . . . nothing is too much for God. A world without pain, even if only for a brief time . . . a world in which my eye's delighted by my children. Then I would laugh, sing, and play. Most Merciful of the merciful. . . . Have mercy on Aisha, O God."

Khalil returned with the doctor after an absence of three-quarters of an hour. They entered the door at once, closing it behind them. When al-Sayyid Ahmad learned they had arrived, he rose and went to the door of the parlor. He stood at the threshold for a little while, looking at the closed door. Then he went back to his place and sat down.

Widow Shawkat said, "We'll see how right I am once the doctor speaks to us."

Al-Sayyid Ahmad raised his head heavenward and murmured, "Pardon comes from Him."

He would soon know the truth and escape from the fog of

doubt, regardless of the outcome. His heart pounded rapidly. Let him be patient. It would not be long. His faith in God was deep, profound, and not easily shaken. He should surrender the affair to Him. No matter how long the doctor stayed inside, he would eventually come out. Then he would ask what it was all about. A doctor? . . . He had not thought about that before. . . . A doctor at a delivery, face to face with her womb. Was not that so? But he was a doctor. . . . What could be done? "The important thing is for our Lord to take her by the hand. We ask him for deliverance."

In addition to being worried, al-Sayyid Ahmad felt embarrassed and annoyed. The examination lasted about twenty minutes. Then the door opened. He rose and went at once to the sitting room, followed by the boys. They gathered around the doctor, who knew al-Sayyid Ahmad. Shaking his hand, he said with a smile, "She's in good health." He continued more seriously: "They brought me for the mother, but I found the one really in need of my care was the baby girl."

Al-Sayyid Ahmad sighed with relief, feeling better for the first time in about an hour. With a gracious smile brightening his face, he asked, "Can I be sure of what you say, then?"

Pretending to be astonished, the doctor said, "Yes, but aren't you concerned about your granddaughter?"

Smiling, he replied, "I'm not familiar yet with the duties of a grandfather."

Khalil asked, "Isn't there any hope she'll live?"

Knitting his brows, the doctor answered, "Lives are in God's hands. I found that her heart's weak. It's likely she'll die before morning. If she makes it safely through the night, she'll be out of immediate danger, but I think she won't live long. In my judgment, she won't live past her twenties. But who knows? Only God controls our lives."

When the doctor had gone off about his business, Khalil turned toward his mother with a sad smile. He told her, "I was intending to name her Na'ima, after you."

The woman gestured with her hand to scold him and observed, "The doctor himself said, 'Lives are in God's hands.' Are you going to have less faith than the doctor? Name her Na'ima. You must name her Na'ima in my honor. God willing, her life will be as long as her grandmother's."

Al-Sayyid Ahmad was thinking to himself, "The fool called a doctor to look at his wife for no reason, no reason at all. What an idiot he is!" Unable to contain his fury, although he disguised it in a gentle tone, he said, "It's true that fear makes men do foolish things, but shouldn't you have thought a little before rushing off to bring an outsider to take such a searching look at your wife?"

Khalil did not respond. He glanced at the people around him and remarked earnestly, "Aisha must not know what the doctor said."

69

"WHAT'S HAPPENING in the street?" al-Sayyid Ahmad wondered as he rose hastily from his desk. He went to the door, followed by Jamil al-Hamzawi and some of their customers. Al-Nahhasin was not a quiet street, quite the contrary. Its strident noise did not abate from one dawn until shortly before the next. There were the loud cries of vendors, haggling of shoppers, pleas of crazed beggars, and wisecracks of passersby. People conversed as though delivering a public oration. Even the most personal discussions ricocheted everywhere, flying up to the minarets. To this general commotion the Suarès omnibus added its clanking and the donkey carts their clatter. In no sense was it a quiet street, but a sudden clamor had arisen, at first heard in the distance like the roar of waves, then growing stronger and more raucous until it sounded like a howling wind. It enveloped the whole district, near and far. Even on this noisy street it was out of the ordinary and exceptional.

Al-Sayyid Ahmad thought a demonstration had broken out, as anyone who had experienced those days would have, but cries of joy were audible in the uproar. Wondering what it was, he went to the door where he bumped into the shaykh, or supervisor, of the district, who had rushed up. He was crying out with a jubilant face, "Have you heard the news?"

Even before he heard any more, the proprietor's eyes began to glow optimistically. "No," he said. "What's it all about?"

The man replied enthusiastically, "Sa'd Pasha has been freed."

Al-Sayyid Ahmad could not restrain himself from yelling, "Really?"

The shaykh affirmed, "Allenby broadcast a bulletin with this good news just now."

The next moment the two men were hugging each other. Al-Sayyid Ahmad was deeply moved. His eyes filled with tears. Laughing to disguise his emotions, he said, "He's known for broadcasting threats, not good news. What's made him change, that old son of a gun?"

The shaykh of the district replied, "Glory to the one who never changes." He shook hands with the proprietor and then left the store shouting, "God is most great. *Allahu akbar.* Victory to the Muslims."

Al-Sayyid Ahmad stood at the door of the shop, looking up and down the street with a heart that had recaptured the delight and innocence of childhood. The effect of the news about Sa'd was evident everywhere. The entries of the shops were jammed with their owners and customers, who were congratulating each other. The windows of the houses were crowded with children, and ululating trills of joy could be heard from the women at the peepholes of the window grilles. Impromptu demonstrations took place between al-Nahhasin, the Goldsmiths Bazaar, and Bayt al-Qadi, with people yelling their hearts out for Sa'd, Sa'd, Sa'd, and then Sa'd. The muezzins went up to the balconies of their minarets to give thanks, pray, and shout. There were tens of donkey carts with hundreds of women, fully covered in wraps, dancing and singing patriotic songs. All he could see were people, or, more precisely, people shouting. The earth had disappeared and the walls were concealed by them. Shouts for Sa'd were heard everywhere. The air seemed to have turned into a tremendous phonograph record, spinning incessantly on a turntable, repeating his name. News bounced along the mass of heads that the English were striking their camps, which had been set up at the street corners, in preparation for redeployment of the soldiers to al-Abbasiya. The enthusiasm increased and delirium reached a fever pitch. Al-Sayyid Ahmad had never seen such a sight before. He looked every which way with sparkling eyes and a bounding heart. Under his breath, he sang along with the women dancers, "O Husayn . . . a burden has been lifted."

Then Jamil al-Hamzawi put his head close to the proprietor's ear to say, "The shops are distributing cold drinks and putting up flags."

Al-Sayyid Ahmad told him enthusiastically, "Do what the others are doing and more. Put your whole heart into it." Then with a trembling voice he added, "Hang Sa'd's picture under the calligraphy of 'In the Name of God.'"

Jamil al-Hamzawi looked reluctant and cautioned him, "In that place it can be seen from outside. Wouldn't it be better for us to bide our time until things return to normal?"

The proprietor replied scornfully, "The era of fear and bloodshed has passed, never to return. Don't you see that demonstrations are going on under the eyes of the English, who aren't making any attempt to interfere with them? Hang up the picture and trust in God."

"The days of fear and bloodshed have vanished. Isn't that so? Sa'd is free and at liberty. He's probably on his way now to Europe. Only a step or a word stands between us and independence. These are demonstrations with trills of joy, not bullets. Those of us who are still alive are happy people, having passed safely through the fires. God's mercy on the martyrs. . . . Fahmy? He's escaped from a much greater danger than he ever imagined. He's escaped, praise and thanks to God. Yes, Fahmy has escaped. What are you waiting for? Pray to God your Lord."

When the family gathered that evening, their hoarse voices revealed that they had spent the day shouting. It was a happy evening. Joy was evident in their eyes, lips, gestures, and words. Even Amina's heart imbibed some of the overflowing happiness. She realized that Sa'd's release brought good news of a return to peace and joy.

"From the balcony I saw something no one has ever seen before," she commented. "Has Judgment Day come with the scales to weigh our sins? Were those women crazy? The echo of their singing still rings in my ears: 'O Husayn . . . a burden has been lifted.' "

Laughingly messing up Kamal's hair, Yasin said, "It was a word of farewell to speed the departing English on their way, just as you see off an unwelcome guest by breaking a jug after him."

Kamal looked at his brother without saying anything. Then Amina had another question: "Is God finally pleased with us?"

Yasin replied, "No doubt about it." Then he asked Fahmy, "What do you think?"

Fahmy, who seemed as happy as a child, said, "The English wouldn't have freed Sa'd if they weren't agreeing to our demands. He'll travel to Europe and then return with independence. This is what everyone says. No matter what else happens, April 7, 1919, will remain the date marking the success of the revolution."

Yasin exclaimed, "What a day! Government employees participated openly in the demonstrations. I didn't think I was capable of walking that distance or yelling for so long."

Fahmy laughed. He said, "I wish I could have seen you shouting zealously. Yasin takes part in a demonstration. He gets excited and yells. What a rare spectacle!"

It truly was an amazing day. Yasin had been swept along by its swelling current and carried by its strong waves like a tiny, weightless leaf, fluttering everywhere. He could scarcely believe that he had been able to regain control of himself and had retreated to a quiet observation tower where, through its glass, he had calmly watched what was happening, without any emotional involvement. In the light of Fahmy's observation, he began to recall the state he had been in while he was in the demonstration. He remarked with astonishment, "A man forgets himself in the strangest way when he's with so many people. He almost seems to become a new person."

Fahmy asked him with interest, "Did you really feel enthusiastic?"

"I shouted for Sa'd so much my throat became sore. I had tears in my eyes once or twice."

"How did you get into the demonstration?"

"We heard the news that Sa'd had been released when we were at school. I was really ecstatic. Were you expecting that? Then the teachers suggested joining the large demonstration outside. I didn't feel like it and thought I'd slip off home but was forced to walk with them until I could get an opportunity to escape. Then I found myself in a swirling sea of people. There was an electric atmosphere of enthusiasm. Before I knew it, I forgot myself and merged with the stream. I was as zealous and optimistic as a person can be. Please believe me."

Fahmy shook his head and murmured, "Amazing. . . ."

Yasin laughed out loud and asked, "Did you think I had lost my sense of patriotism? The thing is, I don't like noise and violence. I don't have any problem reconciling love of country and love of peace."

"What if that reconciliation is shattered?"

Yasin smiled and answered without any hesitation, "I put love of peace first. I come first. . . . Is it impossible for my country to be happy unless it consumes my life? God's deliverance! I'm not taking any chances with my life, but I'll love my country so long as I'm alive."

"That's very wise," Amina commented. Then, looking at

Fahmy, she asked, "Does my master think otherwise?"

Fahmy replied calmly, "Of course not. It's very wise, as you said. . . ."

Kamal was not happy to be left out of the conversation, especially since he was convinced that he had played a vital role that day. He volunteered, "We went on strike too, but the headmaster told us we were still children and would be trampled underfoot if we left school. He gave us permission to demonstrate in the school courtyard. So we assembled there and chanted for a long time, 'Long live Sa'd.'" He repeated the chant in a loud voice. "After that we didn't go back to the classes, because the teachers had left the school to join the demonstrators outside."

Yasin threw the boy a sarcastic look and remarked, "But your friends have gone. . . ."

"To hell," Kamal said, in spite of himself. The comment did not express his true feelings at all, but he felt that circumstances required it and, faced with Yasin's sarcasm, he wished to mask his defeat. In his heart he felt bewildered and slandered. He could not forget how, on his return from school, he had stood in the deserted campsite, casting his eyes in every direction in painful silence as tears welled up in his eyes. It would be a long time before he forgot tea on the sidewalk by the cistern, the admiration his singing had garnered, his affectionate treatment by the soldiers and especially by Julian, and the friendship that linked him to those outstanding gentlemen whom he believed to be superior to the rest of mankind.

Amina said, "Sa'd Pasha's a lucky man. The whole world is chanting his name. Not even 'Our Effendi' Abbas II was treated like that. Sa'd's no doubt a Believer, because God grants real victories only to Believers. Sa'd's been victorious over the English, who even defeated the zeppelin. What greater victory can you ask for? The man was born auspiciously on the Night of Destiny in Ramadan, which commemorates the Qur'an's descent."

"Do you love him?" Fahmy asked with a smile.

"I love him, since you do."

Fahmy spread his hands out and raised his eyebrows disapprovingly. "That doesn't mean anything," he said.

She sighed somewhat uneasily and explained, "Whenever I got some sad news, tearing my heart to pieces with sorrow, I would ask myself, 'Do you suppose this would have happened if Sa'd had not started his rebellion?' But a man loved by everyone must also be loved by God." Sighing audibly, she continued: "I grieve for those who have perished. How many mothers are weeping sorely now? How many a mother finds that today's joy only adds another sorrow to her regrets?"

Fahmy winked at Yasin and told her, "A really patriotic mother would trill with joy at her son's martyrdom."

She put her fingers in her ears and shouted, "May God be my witness to what the young master has said. . . . A mother trills with joy when her son is martyred? Where? On this earth? Not here or even underground where the devils reside."

Fahmy laughed loudly. He thought for a while. Then with twinkling eyes he said, "Mama . . . I'm going to tell you a terrible secret that can be revealed now. I participated in the demonstrations and met death face to face."

She looked at him gravely and incredulously. With a bewildered smile she said, "You? . . . Impossible. You're part of my flesh and blood. Your heart comes from mine. You're not like the others. . . . "

Smiling at her, he declared, "I swear to you by God Almighty that it's true."

Her smile disappeared and her eyes grew wide with consternation. She looked back and forth between him and Yasin, who was also staring inquisitively at Fahmy. After swallowing, she mumbled, "O Lord! . . . How can I believe my ears?" Shaking her head in helpless agony, she exclaimed, "You!"

He had expected her to be upset, but not to the extent that she clearly was. After all, his confession came after the danger had passed. Before she could say anything more, he told her, "That's ancient history. It's over and done with. There's no reason to be alarmed now."

She responded with nervous insistence, "Hush! You don't love your mother. May God forgive you."

Fahmy laughed disconcertedly. With a mischievous smile, Kamal told his mother, "Do you remember the day I was fired on in the pastry shop? I saw him in the deserted street on my way home. He warned me not to tell anyone I had seen him." Then he turned to Fahmy and asked with avid interest, "Tell us, Mr. Fahmy, what you experienced in the demonstrations. How did the battles start? What happened when people fell dead? Were you armed?"

Yasin interrupted the conversation to tell the mother, "It's ancient history, dead and buried. It would be better to thank God he's safe than get alarmed."

She asked him harshly, "Did you know about it?"

He quickly replied, "No, by my mother's grave." For fear that might not be adequate, he added, "And by my religion, faith, and Lord."

He rose to go to her. He put a hand on her shoulder and told her tenderly, "Did you relax when you should have been alarmed only to be alarmed now that you can relax? Declare that God is one. The danger has passed and peace has returned. Here's Fahmy in front of you. . . . " He laughed. "By tomorrow we'll be able to walk the length and breadth of Cairo by day or night without fear or anxiety."

Fahmy said earnestly, "Mama, please don't spoil our good spirits with pointless sorrow."

She sighed and opened her mouth to speak, but no words came out, even though her lips moved. She smiled wanly to announce her compliance with his request. Then she bowed her head to hide her eyes filled with tears.

70

BY THE time Fahmy fell asleep that night he had made up his mind to get back into his father's good graces no matter what it cost him. The next morning he decided to act on his resolve without delay. Although he had never harbored any angry or defiant feelings toward his father during his rebellion, a guilty conscience was a heavy burden for his sensitive heart, which was imbued with dutiful obedience. He had not defied his father verbally but had acted against his will and had done so repeatedly. Moreover, he had refused to swear an oath the day his father had asked him to, announcing with his tears that he would stick to his principles despite his father's wishes. To his unbearable regret, all these acts had put him in the position, regardless of his good intentions, of being wickedly disobedient. He had not attempted to make peace with his father earlier from fear of scraping the scab off the wound without being able to bandage it. He had assumed his father would ask him to take the oath again as penance for what he had done and that he would be forced once more to refuse, thus reviving his rebellion when he wanted to apologize for it.

The situation today was different. His heart was intoxicated with joy and victory, and the whole nation was drunk on the wine of delight and triumph. He could not stand for a barrier of suspicion to separate him from his father a moment longer. They would be reconciled and he would receive the pardon he craved. Then there would be true happiness, unblemished by any defect.

He entered his father's room a quarter of an hour before breakfast and found his father folding up the prayer rug as he mumbled a prayerful entreaty. The man no doubt noticed him but pretended not to and went to sit on the sofa without turning toward his son. He sat facing Fahmy, who stood at the door, looking ashamed and confounded. Al-Sayyid Ahmad stared at him impassively and disapprovingly as though to ask, "Who is this person standing there and why has he come?"

Fahmy got the better of his consternation and quietly walked toward his father. He leaned over his hand, which he took and kissed with the utmost respect. He was silent for some time. Then in a scarcely audible voice he said, "Good morning, Papa."

His father continued to gaze at him silently, as though he had not heard the greeting, until the boy lowered his eyes in confusion and stammered in a despairing voice, "I'm sorry. . . ." Al-Sayyid Ahmad persisted in his silence.

"I'm really sorry. I haven't had a moment's peace of mind since . . . " He found his words were leading him up to a reference to something he wanted with all his heart to skip over. So he stopped.

Before he knew what was happening, his father asked him harshly and impatiently, "What do you want?"

Fahmy was overjoyed that the man had abandoned his silence and sighed with relief as though he had not noticed the harsh tone. He entreated his father, "I want your approval."

"Get out of my sight."

Feeling the grip of despair loosening a little around his neck, Fahmy said, "When I have your approval."

Becoming sarcastic suddenly, al-Sayyid Ahmad asked, "My approval! . . . Why not? . . . Have you, God forbid, done anything to make me angry?"

Fahmy welcomed his father's sarcasm twice as much as his renunciation of silence. Sarcasm with his father was the first step toward forgiveness. When he was really angry, he would slap, punch, kick, curse, or do all at once. Sarcasm was the first sign of a change of heart.

"Seize the opportunity," Fahmy told himself. "Speak. Speak the way a man preparing to be a lawyer should speak. This is your opportunity. Say, 'Answering the call of the nation should not be considered rebellion against your will, sir. I really didn't do much by way of patriotic deeds . . . distributing handbills to friends. . . . What did that amount to? What am I compared with those who willingly gave their lives? I understood from your words, sir, that you were afraid for my life, not that you really rejected the idea of patriotic duties. I simply did a little of my duty. I'm confident that I actually did not disobey your wishes.' . . . And so forth and so on."

Then Fahmy did say, "God knows it never occurred to me to disobey you."

Al-Sayyid Ahmad responded sharply, "Empty words. You pretend to be obedient now that there's no reason to rebel. Why haven't you asked for my approval before today?"

Fahmy said sadly, "The world was full of blood and grief. I was preoccupied by sorrow."

"Too preoccupied to ask for my approval?"

Fahmy replied ardently, "I was too preoccupied to think about myself." In a low voice he added, "I can't live without your approval."

Al-Sayyid Ahmad frowned, not from anger as he made it appear, but to hide the good impression his son's words had made on him. "This is the way a person should speak," he reflected. "Otherwise, forget it. He's really good at using words. This is eloquence, isn't it? I'll repeat what he said to my friends tonight to see what impact it makes on them. What do you suppose they'll say? The boy takes after his father. . . . That's what they ought to say. People used to tell me that if I had completed my education I would have been one of the most eloquent attorneys. I'm quite an eloquent person even without a higher education and a law practice. Our daily conversation is exactly like the law in revealing one's gift for eloquence. How many attorneys and important civil servants have cowered like sparrows before me at our parties. Not even Fahmy will be able to replace me one day. They'll laugh and say the boy's really a chip off the old block. His refusal to swear that oath still troubles me, but don't I have a right to be proud that he participated in the revolution, even if only remotely? Since God has allowed him to live to see this day, I wish he had done something important in it. From now on, I'll say he waded into the midst of the revolution. Do you think he was content just to distribute handbills as he claimed? The son of a bitch threw himself into the bloody stream of events. 'Al-Sayyid Ahmad, we must acknowledge your son's patriotism and courage. We did not wish to tell you this during the danger, but now that peace has come, there's no harm saying it.' Do you disown your patriotic feelings? Didn't the people collecting donations for the nationalist Wafd Party commend you? By God, if you were young, you would have done much more than your son has. But he defied me! He defied your tongue and obeyed your heart. What can I do now? My heart wishes to forgive him, but I'm afraid he'll think then it's okay to disobey me."

He finally spoke: "I can never forget that you disobeyed me. Do

you think the meaningless oration you have delivered this morning, before I even had breakfast, can influence me?"

Fahmy started to speak, but his mother entered at that moment
to announce, "Breakfast is ready, sir."

She was astonished to find Fahmy there. She looked from one
to the other and tarried a little in hopes of hearing part of what was
being said. But the silence, which she was afraid her arrival had
caused, made her leave the room quickly. Al-Sayyid Ahmad rose
to go to the dining room, and Fahmy moved out of his way. The
boy's intense sorrow was evident to his father, who hesitated a few
moments before finally saying in a conciliatory voice, "I hope that
in the future you won't insist on being so stupid when you address
me."

He walked off, and the young man followed after him with a
grateful smile. As they went through the sitting room he heard his
father say sarcastically, "I suppose you put yourself at the head of
those who liberated Sa'd."

Fahmy left the house happy. He went at once to al-Azhar,
where he met with his colleagues on the supreme student committee. They were discussing arrangements for the enormous,
peaceful demonstrations the authorities were allowing so that
the nation could express its delight. It had been decided that
representatives of all segments of the population would participate.

The meeting lasted quite a while. Then the participants separated, each going off about his business. Fahmy rode over to
Ramses Square in front of the central railroad station, after learning of his assignment to supervise the groups of students from the
secondary schools. Although the tasks he was customarily assigned
could be considered rather secondary, compared with those of the
others, he undertook them with precision, care, and joy, as though
each was the happiest moment of his life. Even so, his industry was
accompanied by a slight feeling of discontent, which he did not
share with anyone else, originating from his conviction that he was
less daring and forward than his other comrades. Yes, he had never
hesitated to attend a demonstration the committee supported but
he became discouraged when the trucks carrying soldiers
appeared, especially once shots were fired and victims started to
fall. One time he had sought refuge in a coffee shop, trembling.
Another time he had run so far he ended up in the cemetery for

theology students. What was he compared with the man who had carried the flag in the Bulaq demonstration, or massacre, as it had come to be called? That fellow had died a martyr, clasping the flag with his hands, standing his ground at the head of the procession, shouting at the top of his lungs for everyone to stand firm. What was Fahmy compared with that martyr's companions who had rushed to raise the flag again only to be shot down around him with their breasts decorated heroically by bullet holes? What was he compared with that martyr who had grabbed the machine gun from the hands of the enemy at al-Azhar? What was he compared with all those men and the others whose heroism and martyrdoms were always in the news? Heroic acts appeared to him to be so dazzling and magnificent that they were breathtaking. He frequently heard an inner voice daring him to imitate the heroes, but his nerves had always let him down at the decisive moment. When the fighting started, he would find himself at the rear, if not hiding or fleeing. Afterward he would regain his determination to double his efforts to struggle tenaciously, but with a tortured conscience, an anxious heart, and a limitless desire for perfection. He would console himself at times by saying, "I'm just an unarmed warrior. Even if stunning deeds of heroism have passed me by, it's enough that I've never hesitated to throw myself into the thick of the fray."

On his way to Ramses Square, he began to observe the streets and vehicles. It appeared that everyone was heading his way: students, workers, civil servants, and ordinary folk, riding or walking. They had a relaxed look about them, appropriate for people going to a peaceful demonstration sanctioned by the authorities. He too felt the way they did. It was not the same as when he had searched for the appointed place with an excited soul and a heart that pounded hard whenever he thought about perishing. That was in a former time. Today he went along, feeling secure, with a smile on his lips. Was the struggle over? Had he emerged from it safely with no losses or gains? No gains? . . . If only he had suffered something like the thousands who had been imprisoned, beaten, or wounded slightly by gunfire. Wasn't it sad that security should be the reward for a person with a heart and enthusiasm like his? He was like a diligent student unable to obtain a diploma.

"Do you deny you're happy that you're safe? Would you have

preferred to be a martyr? Certainly not. . . . Would you have liked to be one of those wounded but not killed? Yes. That was in your reach. Why did you recoil from it? There was no way to guarantee that the wound wouldn't be fatal or the imprisonment temporary. You don't regret your current deliverance, but you wish you had been afflicted in some way that wouldn't interfere with this happy ending. If you ever engage in another struggle like this again, you had better have your fortune told. I'm going to a peaceful demonstration with a calm heart and an uneasy conscience."

He reached the square around one o'clock. It was two hours before the demonstration was due to commence. He took his place at the spot assigned to him, the door of the railroad station. There was no one in the square except for supervisory personnel and scattered groups from various religious factions. The weather was mild, but the April sun poured down on those exposed to its scorching rays. He did not have long to wait, for groups began to throng into the square from the different streets leading to it. Each group went to the location where its banner was displayed. Fahmy set to work with pleasure and pride. Although the task was simple, consisting of nothing more than the organization of each of the schools behind its banner, Fahmy was filled with pride and conceit, especially since he was supervising many students who were older than he was. His nineteen years did not seem like much in a mass of students with twisted mustaches going on twenty-two or twenty-four.

He noticed eyes that were looking at him with interest and lips that were whispering about him. He heard his name, accompanied by his title, being repeated by some tongues: "Fahmy Ahmad Abd al-Jawad, representative of the supreme committee." That touched the strings of his heart. He pressed his lips together to keep them from smiling, out of concern for his dignity. Yes, he must look the part of a representative of the supreme committee by being serious and stern, as was only proper for the elite corps of young freedom fighters. He wanted to leave room for the imaginations of those looking at him to guess what deeds of heroism and valor were concealed behind his imposing façade. Let the spectacular deeds he had been unable to carry out in reality be performed in their imaginations. He had no desire to discourage them but was stung by the unvarnished truth. He had distributed handbills and been part of the rear guard. That was all he had been.

Today he was entrusted with supervision of the secondary schools and had a leadership role. Did others think he had played a more important part than he did himself? How much respect and affection they were awarding him. . . . They had not had a meeting without taking time to hear his opinion.

"Oratory? There was no need for you to deliver speeches, isn't that so? You can be great without being an orator, but what a pity it will be for you on the day the supreme committee appears before the great leader if, when the orators try to outdo each other, you take refuge in silence. No, I won't remain silent. I'll speak. I'll say exactly what I feel, whether or not I excel at it. When will you stand before Sa'd? When will you see him for the first time and feast your eyes on him? My heart is pounding and my eyes long to weep. It will be a great day. All of Egypt will come out to welcome him. What we're doing today will be like a drop of water in the sea compared with that time. O Lord! The square's full. The streets feeding into it are full: Abbas, Nubar, al-Faggala. There's never been a demonstration like this before. A hundred thousand people, wearing modern fezzes and traditional turbans – students, workers, civil servants, Muslim and Christian religious leaders, the judges . . . who could have imagined this? They don't mind the sun. This is Egypt. Why didn't I invite Papa? Yasin was right. . . . A person forgets himself in a crowd of people. He rises above himself. What are my personal ambitions? Nothing. How my heart is pounding. I'll talk about this for a long time tonight and after that too. Do you suppose Mama will tremble with fear once again? It's a magnificent spectacle, which humbles a person and calms him. I would like to be able to gauge its impact on those devils. Their barracks overlook the square. Their cursed flag is fluttering in the wind. I see heads in the windows there. What are they whispering to each other? The sentry's like a statue, seeing nothing. Your machine guns did not stop the revolution. Do you understand that? Soon you'll be seeing Sa'd return victoriously to this square. You exiled him by force of arms and we are bringing him back without any weapons. You'll see, before you evacuate."

The enormous parade began to move. Successive waves rolled forward, chanting patriotic slogans. Egypt appeared to be one great demonstration . . . united in one person and a single chant. The columns of the different groups stretched out for such a long distance that Fahmy imagined the vanguard would be approaching Abdin Palace before he and his group had budged from their position in front of the railroad station. It was the first demonstration that machine guns had not interrupted. No longer would bullets come from one side and stones from the other.

Fahmy smiled. He saw that the group in front of him was starting to move. He turned on his heels to direct his own personal demonstration. He raised his hands and the lines moved in anticipation and with enthusiasm. Walking backward, he chanted at the top of his lungs. He continued his twin tasks of directing and chanting until the beginning of Nubar Street. Then he turned the chanting over to one of the young men surrounding him, who had been waiting for their chance with anxious, excited voices, as though they had labor pains that would only be relieved by being allowed to lead the chants. He turned around once again to walk facing forward. He craned his neck to look at the procession. He could no longer see the front of it. He looked on either side to see how crowded the sidewalks, windows, balconies, and roofs were with all the spectators who had begun to repeat the chants. The sight of thousands of people concentrated together filled him with such limitless power and assurance it was like armor protecting him, clinging tightly to him so that bullets could not penetrate.

Now the police force was helping to maintain order, after they had been unable to suppress the demonstrations by their attacks. The sight of these men going back and forth on their horses, like guards associated with the demonstration, delegated to assist it, was the most eloquent proof of the victory of the revolution. The chief of police! . . . Was that not Russell Bey? Of course, he recognized him perfectly. There was his deputy trotting along behind him, looking at everything impassively and haughtily as though protesting silently against the peace reigning over the demonstration. What was his name? How could he forget a name that everyone had been repeating during the bloody, dark days? Did it not begin with a *g* or a *j*? "Ja . . . Ju . . . Ji . . ." He could not recall it. "Julian!" Oh, how did that hated name slip into his mind? It fell on him like dirt, putting out the fire of his zeal. "How can we respond to the call of zeal and victory when the heart is dead? My heart dead? It wasn't dead a minute ago. Don't surrender to sorrow. Don't let your heart become separated from the demonstration. Haven't you promised yourself to forget? In fact, you really have forgotten. Maryam . . . who is she? That's ancient history. We live for the future, not the past. Guise, Mr. Guise, I think that's the name of the deputy police chief, may God curse him. Start chanting again to shake off this dusty cloud of regret."

Fahmy's own part of the demonstration slowly approached Ezbekiya Garden. The lofty trees could be seen over the banners that were displayed all along the street. Then Opera Square was visible in the distance looking like an endless mass of heads that all seemed to spring from a single body. He was chanting forcefully and enthusiastically, and the crowd repeated his chants with a sound that filled the air like the rumble of thunder. When they came near the wall of the garden, suddenly there was a sharp, resounding pop. He stopped chanting and in alarm looked around questioningly. It was a familiar sound that had often assaulted his ears during the past month and had frequently echoed in his memory during the quiet nights, although he had never gotten used to it. The moment it rang out he became pale and his heart seemed to stop pumping.

"A bullet?"

"Incredible. Didn't they sanction the demonstration?"

"Did you forget to allow for treachery?"

"But I don't see any soldiers."

"Ezbekiya Garden is an enormous camp, packed full of them."

"Perhaps the explosion was an automobile tire blowing out."

"Perhaps."

Fahmy listened intently to what was going on around him without regaining his peace of mind. It was only a few moments before a second explosion was heard. "Oh. . . . There could no longer be any doubt. It was a bullet like the one before. Where do you suppose it hit? Isn't it a day of peace?"

He felt the uneasiness moving through the ranks of the demonstrators, coming from the front like the heavy wave that a steamboat plowing down the center of a river sends to the shore. Then thousands of people started to retreat and spread out, creating in every direction insane and unruly outbursts of confusion and consternation as they collided with each other. Terrifying shouts of anger and fear rose from the masses. The orderly columns were quickly scattered and the carefully arranged structure of the parade collapsed. Then there was a sharp burst of shots in close succession. People screamed in anger and moaned in pain.

The sea of people surged and swelled, and the waves thrust through every opening, sparing nothing in its way and leaving nothing behind it.

"I'll flee. There's no alternative. If the bullets don't kill you, the arms and feet will." He meant to run or retreat or turn, but he did not do anything. "Why are you standing here when everyone has scattered? You're in an exposed position. Flee."

His arms and legs began a slow, limp, disjointed motion. "How loud the clamor is. But what are they screaming about? Do you remember? How quickly memories are slipping away. What do you want? To chant? What chant? Or just call out? To whom? For what? There's a voice speaking inside you. Do you hear? Do you see? But where? There's nothing. Nothing. Darkness and more darkness. A gentle motion's pushing with the regularity of the ticking of a clock. The heart is flowing with it. There's a whisper accompanying it. The gate of the garden. Isn't that so? It's moving in a fluid, rippling way and slowly dissolving. The towering tree is dancing gently. The sky... the sky? High, expansive... nothing but the calm, smiling sky with peace raining from it."

71

AL-SAYYID AHMAD Abd al-Jawad heard footsteps at the entrance to the store. He glanced up from his desk and saw three young men approaching him. They looked serious and grave. They stopped just in front of his desk and said, "Peace to you and the compassion of God."

Al-Sayyid Ahmad rose and with his customary politeness responded, "And to you peace and the compassion of God and His blessings." He motioned to the chairs and said, "Please sit down."

They graciously declined his invitation. The boy in the center asked, "Sir, are you Mr. Ahmad Abd al-Jawad?"

The proprietor smiled, although there was a questioning look in his eyes, and replied, "Yes, sir."

"What do you suppose they want?" he asked himself. "It's not likely that they came to purchase anything. Their military gait and serious tone wouldn't be appropriate if they were buying something. Moreover, it's after seven o'clock. Don't they see that al-Hamzawi is putting the bags up on the shelves to show that the store is closing? Are they collecting donations? But Sa'd's been released, and the revolution has concluded. I'm not fit for anything now except my evening party. Fellows, you should understand that I haven't bathed my head and face with cologne, combed my hair and mustache, adjusted my cloak and caftan just to meet you. What do you want?"

When he looked at the young man who had addressed him, the face seemed familiar. Had he seen him before? Where? When? He tried to remember. He was certain this was not the first time he had seen him. Then the proprietor's face relaxed and he asked with a smile, "Aren't you the fine young man who came forward to save us just in time the day people attacked us in the mosque of al-Husayn, may God be pleased with him?"

The youth said in a subdued voice, "Yes, sir."

"So I was right," he thought. "Fools say that wine weakens the memory. But why are they looking at me that way? See! These stares don't look like good news. O God, make it good. I take refuge in God from Satan, who should be pelted with stones. For some reason I feel depressed. They've come about something relating to . . ."

"Fahmy?" he asked. "Have you come looking for him? . . . Perhaps you . . ."

The young man lowered his eyes and said in a trembling voice, "Our mission is hard, sir, but it's a duty. May our Lord grant you endurance."

Al-Sayyid Ahmad suddenly leaned forward, supporting himself on the edge of the desk. He cried out, "Endurance? . . . For what! . . . Fahmy?"

The young man said with obvious sorrow, "We are sad to inform you of the death of our brother freedom fighter Fahmy Ahmad. . . ."

Although there was an unmistakable look of belief and dismay in his eyes, the father rejected the news, shouting, "Fahmy?"

"He fell a martyr in the demonstration today."

The boy on his right said, "A noble patriot and sterling martyr was conveyed to a world of pious souls."

Their words fell on ears deafened by misery. His lips were sealed and his eyes gazed blankly and vacantly. They were all silent for a time. Even Jamil al-Hamzawi was frozen to the spot where he stood beneath the shelves, looking dazed and staring at his employer with sorrowful eyes. Finally the young man murmured, "His loss has deeply saddened us, but we have no choice but to submit to God's decree with the patient endurance of Believers, of whom you, sir, are one."

"They are offering you their condolences," al-Sayyid Ahmad realized. "Doesn't this young man know that I excel in offering condolences in circumstances like these? What meaning do they have for an afflicted heart? None! How could words put out the fire? Not so fast. . . . Didn't your heart feel something was dreadfully wrong even before he spoke? Yes . . . the specter of death appeared before my eyes. Now that death is a reality, as you hear, you refuse to believe it. How can I believe that Fahmy is really dead? How can you believe that Fahmy, who requested your approval just hours ago, when you were short with him –

Fahmy, who was full of health, good spirits, hope, and happiness when we left home this morning – is dead? Dead! I'll never see him again at home or anywhere else on the face of the earth? How can I have a home without him? How can I be a father if he's gone? What has become of all the hopes attached to him? The only hope left is patience. . . . Patience? Oh. . . . Do you feel the searing pain? This really is pain. You were mistaken previously when you occasionally claimed to be in pain. No, before today you've never known pain. This is pain. . . ."

"Sir, be strong and turn your concerns over to God."

Al-Sayyid Ahmad looked up at the young man. Then in a sick voice he said, "I thought the time for killing had passed."

The youth answered angrily, "The demonstration today was peaceful. The authorities had given permission for it. Top men from all walks of life participated in it. At first it proceeded safely, until the middle section reached Ezbekiya Garden. Before we knew what was happening, bullets fell upon us from behind the wall, for no reason at all. No one had confronted the soldiers in any manner. We had even forbidden any chants in English to avoid provoking them. The soldiers were suddenly stricken by an insane impulse to kill. They got their rifles and opened fire. Everyone has agreed to send a strong protest to the British Residency. It's even been said that Allenby will announce his regrets for what the soldiers did."

In the same sick tone, the proprietor complained, "But he will not bring the dead back to life."

"Alas, no."

Al-Sayyid Ahmad, racked by distress, said, "He's never partici-pated in any of the violent demonstrations. This was the first demonstration he took part in."

The young men looked knowingly at each other but did not utter a word. Al-Sayyid Ahmad seemed to be growing impatient with the way they were separating him from Fahmy and the rest of the world. He moaned and said, "The matter's in God's hands. Where can I find him now?"

The young man answered, "In the Qasr al-Ayni Hospital." When he saw that the proprietor was in a hurry to leave, he gestured for him to wait. "There will be a funeral procession for him and thirteen of his fellow martyrs at exactly three o'clock tomorrow afternoon."

The father cried out in distress, "Won't you allow me to begin his funeral procession at his home?"

The young man said forcefully, "No, his funeral will be with his brothers in a public ceremony." Then he entreated the man, "Qasr al-Ayni is cordoned off by the police. It would be better to wait. We intend to allow the families of the martyrs to pay their last respects to them in private before the funeral procession. It would not be right for Fahmy to have an ordinary funeral like a person who dies at home." In parting he held his hand out to the bereaved father and said, "Endure patiently. Endurance is from God."

The others shook hands with al-Sayyid Ahmad, repeating their condolences. Then they all departed. He leaned his head on his hand and closed his eyes. He heard the voice of Jamil al-Hamzawi offering his condolences in a sobbing voice, but he seemed distressed by kind words. He could not bear to stay there. He left his seat and moved slowly out of the store, walking with heavy steps. He had to get over his bewilderment. He did not even know how to feel sad. He wanted to be all alone, but where? The house would turn into an inferno in a minute or two. His friends would rally round him, leaving him no opportunity to think. When would he ponder the loss he had undergone? When would he have a chance to get away from everyone? That seemed a long way off, but it would no doubt come. It was the most consolation he could hope for at present. Yes, a time would come when he would be all alone and could devote himself to his sorrow with all his soul. Then he would scrutinize Fahmy's life in light of the past, present, and future, all the stages from childhood to the prime of his youth, the hopes he had aroused and the memories he had left behind, giving free rein to tears so he could totally exhaust them. Truly he had before him ample time that no one would begrudge him. There was no reason to be concerned about that. Consider the memory of the quarrel they had had after the Friday prayer at al-Husayn or that of their conversation that morning, when Fahmy had appealed for his affection and he had reprimanded him – how much of his time would they require as he reflected, remembered, and grieved? How much of his heart would they consume? How many tears would they stir up? How could he be distressed when the future held such consolations for him? He raised his head, which was clouded by thought, and saw the blurred outline of the latticed balconies of his home. He remembered Amina for the first time and his feet almost failed him. What could he say to her? How would she take the news? She was weak and delicate. She wept at the death of a sparrow. "Do you recall how her tears flowed when the son of al-Fuli, the milkman, was killed? What will she do now that Fahmy's been killed. . . . Fahmy killed? Is this really the end of your son? O dear, unhappy son!. . . Amina . . . our son was killed. Fahmy was killed. . . . What? . . . Will you forbid them to wail just as you previously forbade them to trill with joy? Will you wail yourself or hire professional mourners? She's probably now at the coffee hour with Yasin and Kamal, wondering what has kept Fahmy. How cruel! I'll see him at Qasr al-Ayni Hospital, but she won't. I won't allow it. Out of cruelty or compassion? What's the use, anyway?"

He found himself in front of the door and stretched his hand toward the knocker. Then he remembered the key in his pocket. He took it out and opened the door. When he entered, he heard Kamal's voice singing melodiously:

> *Visit me once each year,*
> *For it's wrong to abandon people forever.*

PALACE OF DESIRE

72

AL-SAYYID AHMAD Abd al-Jawad closed the door behind him and crossed the courtyard of his house by the pale light of the stars. His step was lethargic, and his walking stick sank into the dusty earth whenever he leaned on it wearily. He felt on fire and craved cold water so he could wash his face, head, and neck and escape, if only briefly, from the July heat and from the inferno in his belly and head. Cheered by the thought of cool water, he smiled. When he entered the door leading to the stairway, he could see a faint light coming from above. It flowed along the wall, revealing the motion of the hand that held the lamp. He climbed the steps with one hand on the railing and the other on his stick. Its successive taps had long ago acquired a special rhythm, which identified him as easily as his features. Amina was visible at the head of the stairs with the lamp in her hand. On reaching her, he stopped to regain his breath, for his chest was heaving. Then he greeted her in his customary way: "Good evening."

Preceding him with the lamp, Amina murmured, "Good evening, sir."

Once inside his room he rushed to the sofa and collapsed. Letting go of his stick and taking off his fez, he threw his head back and stretched out his legs. The sides of his cloak fell open, and the caftan underneath rode up to reveal the legs of his long underwear tucked into his socks. He shut his eyes and wiped his forehead, cheeks, and neck with a handkerchief.

After placing the lamp on a table, Amina waited for him to rise so she could help remove his clothes. She looked at him with anxious concern. She wished she had the courage to ask him not to stay out so late — now that his health could no longer shrug off excesses — but she did not know how to express her sad thoughts.

A few minutes passed before he opened his eyes. Then he extracted the gold watch from his caftan and took off his diamond ring to place them both in his fez. When he stood up to remove his cloak and caftan with Amina's assistance, his body seemed as tall, broad, and full as ever, although the hair at his temples had been assailed by gray. When he was putting his head in the neck of his white house shirt, a smile suddenly got the better of him. He remembered how Mr. Ali Abd al-Rahim had vomited at their party that evening and had apologized for his weakness, attributing it to an upset stomach. They had all singled out their friend, upbraiding him and asserting that he could no longer tolerate alcohol, for only a special kind of man could keep on drinking to the end of his life, and so forth. He remembered the anger and vehemence of Mr. Ali in defending himself against this suspicion. How amazing that some people lent importance to such trivial matters. . . . But if it were not important, then why had he himself boasted in the merry hubbub that he could drink a whole tavern of wine without ill effects?

He sat down again and lifted his feet so that his wife could take off his shoes and socks. Then she disappeared briefly, returning with a basin and a pitcher. She poured the water for him while he washed his face and neck and rinsed out his mouth. Afterwards he sat with his legs folded beneath him, enjoying the gentle breeze flowing between the latticed balcony and the window overlooking the courtyard.

"What an atrocious summer we're having this year!"

Pulling the pallet out from under the bed and sitting cross-legged on it at his feet, Amina replied, "May our Lord be gracious to us." She sighed and continued: "The whole world's a blazing pyre, especially the oven room. The roof terrace is the only place you can breathe in summer – once the sun has set."

She sat there as usual, but time had changed her. She had grown thin, and her face seemed longer, if only because her cheeks were hollow. The locks of hair that escaped from her scarf were turning gray and made her seem older than she was. The beauty spot on her cheek had grown slightly larger. In addition to their customary look of submission, her eyes now revealed a mournful absent-mindedness. Her anguish over the changes that had befallen her was considerable, although at first she had welcomed them as an expression of her grief. Then she had begun to wonder anxiously if she might not need her health to get through the remainder of her life. Yes . . . and the others needed her to be healthy too, but how could everything be put back the way it was before? And she was older, if not old enough to warrant such a transformation. Still, her age had to make a difference.

Night after night she had stood on the balcony observing the street through the wooden grille. What she could see of the street had not altered, but change had crept through her.

The voice of the waiter at the coffeehouse echoed through their silent room. She smiled and stole a glance at al-Sayyid Ahmad.

She dearly loved this street, which stayed awake all night keeping her heart company. It was a friend but ignorant of the heart that loved it through the shutters of the enclosed balcony. Its features filled her mind, and its evening inhabitants were live voices inhabiting her ears – like this waiter who never stopped talking, the person with the hoarse voice who commented on the events of the day without getting tired or annoyed, the man with the nervous voice trying his luck at cards with the seven of diamonds and the jack, and the father of Haniya – the little girl with whooping cough – who night after night would reply when asked about her, "Our Lord will be able to cure her." Oh ... the balcony seemed to be her special corner of the coffeehouse. Memories of the street paraded before her imagination while her eyes remained fixed on the man's head, which was leaning against the back of the sofa. When the flow of remembered images stopped, she concentrated her attention on her husband. She noticed that the sides of his face were bright red, the way she had grown accustomed to seeing them of late when he returned home. She was uncomfortable about it and asked him apprehensively, "Sir, are you well?"

He held his head up and muttered, "Well, praise God." Then he added, "But the weather's atrocious."

Clear raisin liqueur was the best drink in summer. That was what they had repeatedly told him, but he could not stand it. For him it was whiskey or nothing. Thus every day he had to put up with summer hangovers, and it was a ferocious summer. He had really laughed hard that evening. He had laughed until the veins of his neck were sore. But what had all the laughter been about? He could hardly remember. There seemed to be nothing to relate or repeat. Yet the atmosphere of their party had been charged with such a sympathetic electricity that a touch had sufficed to set off a flash. The moment Mr. Ibrahim al-Far had said, "Alexandria set sail from Sa'd Zaghlul Pasha today heading for Paris," reversing his words, they had all burst out laughing, since they considered the remark an exquisite example of a slip of the tongue caused by intoxication.

They had been quick to add, "He will continue negotiating until he regains his health, when he will set sail for the invitation in response to the London he received from" or "He will receive Ramsay MacDonald from the independence of the agreement" and "He will return with Egypt for independence." They had begun to discuss the anticipated negotiations, larding their comments with whatever jests they saw fit.

Vast as his world of friends was, it really boiled down to three: Muhammad Iffat, Ali Abd al-Rahim, and Ibrahim al-Far. Could he imagine the world's existence without them? The way their faces lit up with genuine joy when they saw him made him happier than anything else could. His dreamy eyes met Amina's inquisitive ones. As though to remind her of something extremely important, he said, "Tomorrow."

With a beaming face she replied, "How could I forget?"

He did not attempt to conceal his pride when he commented, "It's said that the baccalaureate results were awful this year."

She smiled once more to share in his pride and said, "May our Lord make his efforts successful and let us live long enough to see him obtain his degree."

"Did you go to Sugar Street today?" he asked.

"Yes," she replied, "and I invited everyone. They'll all come except the old lady, who excused herself because she's so tired. Her two sons will congratulate Kamal on her behalf."

Gesturing toward his cloak with his chin, al-Sayyid Ahmad said, "Today Shaykh Mutawalli Abd al-Samad brought me amulets for the children of Khadija and Aisha. His wish for me was: 'God willing, I'll make you amulets for your grandchildren's children.'"

Shaking his head, he smiled and continued, "Nothing's impossible for God. Shaykh Mutawalli himself is like iron even though he's in his eighties."

"May our Lord grant you health and strength."

He reflected for a time while he counted on his fingers. Then he observed, "If my father had lived, may God be compassionate to him, he would not have been much older than the shaykh."

"May God have mercy on all those who have departed this life."

Silence reigned until the impact of the reference to the dead had dissipated. As though remembering something important, the man said, "Zaynab's gotten engaged!"

Amina's eyes grew wide. She raised her head and asked, "Really?"

"Yes, Muhammad Iffat told me tonight."

"Who is it?"

"A civil servant named Muhammad Hasan, who is head of the records office in the Ministry of Education."

She commented despondently, "It sounds as though he's advanced in years."

"Not at all," he objected. "He's in his thirties, thirty-five, thirty-six, forty at the most." He continued sarcastically, "She tried her luck with young men and failed. I mean young men with no backbone. Let her try her luck with mature men."

Amina said sorrowfully, "Yasin would have been better for her, if only because of their son."

Al-Sayyid Ahmad shared her opinion, which he had defended for a long time with Muhammad Iffat. In order to conceal his failure, he did not mention that he agreed and said with annoyance, "Her father no longer trusts Yasin, and in truth he's not trustworthy. That's why I didn't insist on it. I was unwilling to exploit our friendship and make her father accept something that would end badly."

Amina mumbled sympathetically, "A youthful mistake can be forgiven."

Her husband felt he could acknowledge some portion of his unsuccessful effort and remarked, "I didn't neglect Yasin's rights but met with no encouragement. Muhammad Iffat told me, 'My first reason for refusing is my concern that our friendship might be exposed to discord.' He also said, 'I would not be able to refuse a request from you, but our friendship is dearer to me than your request.' So I stopped talking about it."

Muhammad Iffat had actually said that, but only to fend off al-Sayyid Ahmad's insistent urging. Because of his friend's high standing with him and in society, al-Sayyid Ahmad had been very keen to restore his bond with Muhammad Iffat, which was severed when their children were divorced. Although he could not hope to find a better wife for Yasin than Zaynab, he was forced to accept the calamity of divorce and remarriage, especially after his friend had told him bluntly at least part of what he knew of Yasin's private life. Muhammad Iffat had even remarked, "Don't tell me we're the same as Yasin. We differ in several respects, and the fact is that I have higher standards for my daughter Zaynab's husband than for her mother's."

Amina inquired, "Does Yasin know what's happened?"

"He'll learn tomorrow or the next day. Do you think he'll mind? He's the last person to be concerned about honor in marriage."

Amina shook her head sadly and asked, "What about Ridwan?"

Al-Sayyid Ahmad replied with a frown, "He'll stay with his grandfather or go with his mother, if he can't bear to be separated from her. May God embarrass those who have caused the boy this embarrassment."

"My Lord, the poor child – his mother one place and his father another. . . . Can Zaynab really bear to be parted from him?"

Her husband replied with apparent disdain, "Necessity has its own laws." Then he asked, "When will he be old enough to come to his father? Do you remember?"

Amina thought for a bit and said, "He's a little younger than Na'ima, Aisha's daughter, and a little older than Khadija's son Abd al-Mun'im. So he must be five, and his father can claim custody in two years. Isn't that right, sir?"

Yawning, al-Sayyid Ahmad replied, "We'll see when the time comes." Then he went on: "He's been married before. I mean her new husband."

"Does he have children?"

"No. His first wife didn't bear any."

"Perhaps that helped endear him to Mr. Muhammad Iffat."

The man retorted angrily, "Don't forget his rank!"

Amina protested, "If it was merely a question of social status no one could match your son, if only for your sake."

He felt indignant and secretly cursed Muhammad Iffat, despite his love for the man. But then he reiterated the point that consoled him: "Don't forget that had it not been for his desire to safeguard our friendship, he would not have hesitated to honor my request."

Amina echoed this sentiment: "Of course, naturally, sir. It's a lifelong friendship and not something to be trifled with or taken lightly."

He began yawning once more and muttered, "Take the lamp."

She rose to carry out his order. He closed his eyes for a moment before rising in a single bound, as though to overcome his inertia. He headed for his bed to stretch out. Now he felt fine. How good it was to lie down when exhausted. Yes, his head pulsed and throbbed, but he almost always had some kind of headache. Let him praise God in any case. Being totally at ease was a thing of the past.

"When we are by ourselves," he reflected, "we become conscious of something missing that will never return. It looms up out of the past in a pale memory, like the faint light from the little window in the door."

In any case he should praise God. He would enjoy his life, which others envied. The best thing was to reach a decision about whether to accept his friends' invitation or not. Or should he leave tomorrow's problem till the morrow?

Yasin was a problem not only for tomorrow but for yesterday and today.... He was no longer a child, since he was twenty-eight. It would not be difficult to find him another wife, but "God does not change people until they change themselves" (Qur'an, 13:11). When would God's guidance shine forth and encompass the earth so that its light dazzled the eye? Then he would cry out from the depths of his soul: "Praise the Lord." But what had Muhammad Iffat said? That Yasin prowled and patrolled the Ezbekiya entertainment district from top to bottom.... Ezbekiya had been another kind of place when he had prowled and patrolled it himself. He was shaken by longing at times to return to its watering holes and revive some memories. Praise God that he had learned Yasin's secret before setting out. Otherwise Satan would have laughed at his embarrassment from the bottom of his mocking heart.

"Clear the way for the next generation," he told himself. "They've grown up. The Australians kept you away from there once. Now it's this Australian mule of a son who does."

73

THE EARLY-MORNING silence was broken by the repeated
thumps of dough being kneaded in the oven room and by the crowing of a rooster. Umm Hanafi's corpulent body was bent over the
bread bowl. Her face looked full by the light of a lamp atop the oven.
Age had not affected her hair or her plumpness, but her appearance
had taken on an air of gloom and her features seemed coarser. On a
kitchen chair to her right sat Amina, who was spreading bran on the
breadboards. They continued the work in silence until Umm
Hanafi finished kneading the dough, took her hand from the
bowl, and wiped her sweaty brow with her forearm. Then the servant waved her fist, which was covered with dough and looked like
a white boxing glove, as she observed, "It'll be a hard day for you,
ma'am, but a delightful one. May God grant us many happy days."

Without raising her head from her work, Amina murmured,
"We've got to make sure the food's delicious."

Umm Hanafi smiled, gestured toward her mistress with her
chin, and said, "Your skill will take care of that." She planted
her hands in the bowl once more to resume punching the dough.

"I wish we had contented ourselves with distributing stew to
the needy around al-Husayn Mosque."

Umm Hanafi gently scolded her mistress: "No one present will
be an outsider."

Amina muttered somewhat nervously, "But there'll be a banquet and a lot of commotion. Fuad, Jamil al-Hamzawi's son, has
also earned the baccalaureate – without anyone seeing or hearing
anything about it."

But Umm Hanafi kept up her scolding: "It's just an opportunity
for us to get together with our loved ones."

How could joy be free from reproach or forebodings? In former
times she had reckoned up the years, discovering that Kamal
would receive his school certificate at the same time Fahmy
received his law degree. That celebration would never take
place, and her pious vow could never be honored. Nineteen,

twenty, twenty-two, twenty-three, twenty-four . . . the prime of his young life, which she had been prevented from witnessing. Instead, it had been earth's lot to embrace him. How heartbreaking what they termed sorrow was!

"Mrs. Aisha will be delighted by the baklava. It will remind her of the old days, my lady."

Aisha would be delighted. So would Amina, her mother, who experienced the succession of night and day, satiation and hunger, wakefulness and sleep, as though nothing had changed.

"Forget your claim to be unable to live on a single day after he died," she thought. "You have lived on to swear by his grave. When a heart is turned upside down, that does not mean the world is too. He seems totally forgotten, until it's time to visit the cemetery. You filled my eye and soul, son. Now they only think of you during the holidays. What has come over them? Everyone's busy with his own affairs, except for you, Khadija. You have your mother's heart and spirit. I even have had to admonish you to be strong. Aisha's not like that. But not so fast! It's not right for me to find fault with her. She's mourned quite enough. And Kamal can't be blamed either. Have pity on their young hearts. Fahmy was everything to me. Your hair has turned gray, Amina, and you look like a ghost. That's what Umm Hanafi says. You'll never be young and healthy again. You're going on fifty and he wasn't twenty yet. Pregnancy with all its cravings, childbirth, breast-feeding, love, hopes . . . and then nothing. I wonder if my husband's head is free of such thoughts. Leave him out of it! 'The grief of men is not like that of women.' That was what you said, Mother, may God make paradise your abode. It tears me apart, Mother, that he's gone back to his old habits, as though Fahmy had never died or all memories of him had evaporated. He's even critical when grief overwhelms me. Isn't he the father as much as I'm the mother? My mother said, 'Poor dear Amina, don't allow such thoughts into your heart. If we could judge people's hearts by comparison with a mother's, all others would seem to be stones. He's a man, and the grief of men is not like that of women. If men gave way to sorrow, they would collapse from the weight of their burdens. It's your duty to cheer him up if you notice he's sad. My poor daughter, he's your bulwark.'"

That affectionate voice had vanished. Its loss had come when their hearts were already filled with grief, so that hardly anyone had mourned for the old lady. Her mother's wisdom had been demonstrated late one night when he had come home drunk and had thrown himself sobbing on the sofa.

"Then you wanted him to recover, even if he forgot his dead son forever. You yourself, don't you forget sometimes? And there's something even more atrocious. It's your enjoyment of life and desire for it. That's what the world is like, so they say. You repeat what they say and believe it. Then how could you have allowed yourself once to resent Yasin's recovery and continuation of his former way of life? Not so fast . . . rely on your faith and forbearance. Submit to God's will and to whatever He sends you. You'll always be Fahmy's mother and be called Umm Fahmy. So long as I live I'll continue to be your mother, son, and you'll be my child."

The beats of the dough being kneaded continued as al-Sayyid Ahmad opened his eyes to the early-morning light. He stretched and yawned in a loud, prolonged way – the sound rising like a complaint or a protest. Then he sat up in bed, leaning on hands that rested on outstretched legs. His back seemed curved, and the upper part of his white house shirt was damp with sweat. He began to shake his head right and left, as though to clear the weight of drowsiness from his head. He slipped his feet to the floor and made his way to the bath for a cold shower, which was the only remedy he used to restore balance to his mind and poise to his body. He took off his clothes. As the spray of water hit him, he remembered the invitation he had received the day before. His heart pounded from the combined impact of the memory and the invigorating sensation of the cold water.

Ali Abd al-Rahim had said, "Look again at your former sweet-hearts. Life can't go on like this forever. I know you better than anyone else."

Should he take this final step? For five years he had resisted it. Had his repentance been merely that of an afflicted Believer? Had it been kept hidden because he feared making it public? Had it been in good faith, even though he had not committed himself fully to it? He did not remember. He did not want to remember. A man going on fifty-five was no youngster. What was there to disturb and upset his thoughts so? He had felt the same way when he had been invited to return to their drinking parties and had agreed, as well as the time he had been asked to rejoin their musical evenings and had accepted. Would he answer this plea on behalf of his former sweethearts in the same way? When had grief ever brought a dead man back to life?

"Did God order us to slay ourselves when those we love depart?"

Grief had almost killed him during the long year of mourning and self-denial. He had drunk no alcohol and listened to no music. Not a single witty remark had escaped from his mouth, and his hair had turned gray. Yes . . . that year had been the first time that gray had appeared in his hair. Then he had reverted to drinking and music, out of consideration for his close friends who had renounced their entertainments to honor his grief, or at least that had been how he rationalized it. He had started drinking again both because he could not do without it any longer and because he felt sorry for his three friends. They had not been like the others.

"The others are not to be blamed. They shared in your grief, but then they began to divide their evenings between your sober soirees and their drinking sessions. What was wrong with that? But your three best friends refused to allow themselves more of life than you did. Slowly you returned to everything except the women, since you thought adultery a major sin. At first they did not press you. How you resisted and how you grieved! Zubayda's emissary made no impression on you. You rejected Maryam's mother with sad and resolute dignity. You endured unprecedented pains. You were certain you would never go back. Time after time you asked yourself, 'How can I return to the arms of women entertainers when Fahmy's embraced by the earth?' Oh . . . we are so weak and wretched that we desperately need God's compassion.

" 'Let him continue to grieve who can be sure he will not die tomorrow.' Who came up with this pithy saying? It was either Ali Abd al-Rahim or Ibrahim al-Far. Muhammad Iffat Bey's not good at wise sayings. He rejected my request and married his daughter to a stranger. Then he tried to take me in with his display of affection. He did not renounce his anger but took care not to let me observe it again. But what a man he is! What loyalty and affection! Do you remember how his tears mixed with yours at the cemetery? Yet he's the one who later said, 'I'm afraid you'll become senile if you don't do anything. . . . Come to the houseboat.' When he sensed my hesitation, he said, 'Let it be an

innocent visit. . . . No one's going to rip your clothes off and toss
you on a woman.' God knows my grief has lasted a long time.
When Fahmy passed away, a great part of me died. My best hope
in this world vanished. Who can blame me if I'm able to achieve
some peace of mind and consolation? Even if it laughs, my heart's
still wounded. I wonder what the women are like now? How have
five years, five long years, changed them?"

Yasin's snoring was the first thing Kamal noticed when he woke
up. He could not keep himself from calling to his older brother,
more from a desire to pester him than to awaken him on time. He
kept after him persistently until Yasin responded in a complaining
and scolding voice like a death cry and turned his huge body over,
making the bed creak as though it was groaning with pain. He
sighed and opened his red eyes.

In his opinion there was no need for this haste, since neither of
them could venture to the bathroom until their father had left it. It
was no longer an easy matter to get the first turn in the bathroom.
A new regime had been established in the house five years before,
when – except for the reception room and the adjacent sitting
room furnished with simple furniture as a vestibule – everything
from the lower floor had been moved upstairs. Although Yasin
and Kamal had hardly welcomed the notion of sharing a floor with
their father, they had been forced to comply with his wish to
vacate the lower level, where no one set foot, except to entertain a
visitor.

Yasin closed his eyes but did not go back to sleep, not merely
because it would have been futile but also because an image had
flashed through his mind, setting his emotions on fire . . . a round
face with black eyes at the center of its ivory surface. Maryam! He
answered the call of his daydreams and abandoned himself to a
spell even stronger than that of sleep.

A few months back she had meant nothing to him and might
just as well have never existed. Then he had heard Umm Hanafi
tell his stepmother one evening, "Have you heard the news, my
lady? Mrs. Maryam's gotten divorced and returned to her
mother." At that time he had remembered Maryam, Fahmy, and
the English soldier who had been Kamal's friend, although the
soldier's name had escaped him. Then he had remembered in turn
how lively his own interest in her had been after the scandal.
Before he had realized what was happening, a signboard had

suddenly lit up inside him. It was like a billboard illuminated at night with the message: "Maryam ... your neighbor ... separated from you by only a wall ... divorced ... and with quite a history behind her ... Rejoice!" He had tried at once to discourage himself. Her link to Fahmy had deterred and troubled him, prompting him to close the door firmly and repent, if possible, for this passing thought he kept secret.

Later he had run into her and her mother in the Muski. Their eyes had accidentally met, but she had immediately granted him a smiling look of recognition, which could scarcely have been accidental. His heart had been stirred – initially by nothing more than the look but subsequently by the pleasant impression made on him by her ivory complexion, kohl-enhanced eyes, and body pulsing with youth and vitality. She made him think of Zaynab at her prime. He had proceeded on his way with pensive excitement, although after a few steps, as he descended to Ahmad Abduh's subterranean coffeehouse, a sad memory had come to mind and distressed his heart. He recalled Fahmy – what he had looked like and his characteristic ways of speaking and moving. Yasin's passion had subsided and abated, and he had been overcome by a heavy sorrow. He would need to bring everything to a halt ... but why?

An hour later, after several days, or whenever he asked himself this question, the answer was: Fahmy. But what relation was there between the two of them? He had wanted to get engaged to her once. Why had he not done so? "Your father would not agree. Was that all? It was the initial reason. Then what? Next came the scandal with the Englishman when the faint trace of affection remaining in Fahmy's soul had been erased. Faint trace? Yes, because most probably he had forgotten her. So he forgot her first and spurned her afterwards. . . . Yes, so what relationship was there then between them? None. But! . . . But what? I mean, what about my feelings as his brother? Is there any doubt concerning the sincerity of your feelings for him? Of course not! A thousand times no! Is the girl worth it? Yes! Both her face and her body? Yes! So what are you waiting for?"

From time to time he would catch a glimpse of her at the window and then on the roof ... repeatedly on the roof.

"Why had she gotten divorced?" Yasin asked himself. "If it was because of some defect in her husband's character, then she was lucky to be divorced. If it was occasioned by some fault of hers, then you're the lucky one."

"Get up, or you'll fall asleep again."

Yasin yawned as he combed his untidy hair with his thick fingers. Then he remarked: "You're fortunate to have that long school vacation."

"Didn't I wake up before you?"

"But you could have kept on sleeping if you'd wanted to."

"As you can see, I didn't want to."

Yasin laughed for no particular reason. Then he asked, "What was the name of the English soldier who was your friend long ago?"

"Oh . . . Julian."

"Yes, Julian."

"What made you ask about him?"

"Nothing!"

Nothing? What ridiculous things we say! Was he not superior to Julian? At any rate Julian had been a transient, and Yasin was a permanent resident. "There's always a hint of a smile in her face for you. Hasn't she noticed how frequently you appear on the roof? Certainly! Remember Julian. She's not a woman who would miss the significance of such a gesture. She responded to your greeting. . . . The first time she turned her smiling face. The second time she laughed. What a beautiful laugh she has! The third time she gestured to the roofs of the other houses to caution you. 'I'll come back once the sun has set,' that's what I daringly said. Didn't Julian accost her from the street?"

"I really loved the English when I was young. But see how I hate them now."

"Your hero Sa'd Zaghlul has set off to court their friendship."

Kamal exclaimed sharply, "By God, I'll detest them even if I'm the only one who does."

They exchanged a sad look. They could hear the clatter of their father's clogs as he returned to his room, reciting, "In the name of God" and "There is no power or might save with God." Yasin slipped out of bed and left the room yawning.

Kamal rolled over on his side and then stretched out on his back, relaxing. He folded his arms and clasped his hands together under his head. He gazed at his surroundings with eyes that saw nothing.

"Let the summer resort of Ra's al-Barr be happy to have you. Your angelic complexion was not made to roast in the heat of Cairo. Let the sand enjoy the tread of your feet. Let the water and air rejoice in seeing you. You celebrate your summer resort and praise its beauty. Your eyes show your delight and longing for it. I look at them sadly with a yearning heart and an inquisitive eye. What is this place that has enchanted you and proved worthy of your satisfaction? . . . But when will you return and when will your magical voice fill my ears? What's the resort like? I wish I knew. It's said that people there are free as the air, that they meet in the arms of the waves, and that there are as many love affairs as grains of sand on the beach. Many there will get to see your face, but I'm a person whose heartbeats make the walls groan with complaints, since I'm consumed by an inferno of waiting. How impossible it is to forget your face shining with joy when you murmured, 'We're leaving tomorrow. . . . How beautiful Ra's al-Barr is!' How can I forget my dejection at receiving the warning of separation from a mouth sparkling with radiant happiness, as though I was being administered poison in a bouquet of fragrant flowers. Why shouldn't I be jealous of inanimate objects that make you happy when I can't? They win your affection, which is denied to me. Didn't you notice my dejection when you said farewell? Of course not. You noticed nothing . . . not because I was one among many, but, darling, because you didn't notice . . . as though nothing caught your attention or as though you were an exotic and unusual creature hovering over ordinary life and observing us from above with eyes that roam through a divine realm beyond our ken. So we stood there face to face – you a torch of dazzling happiness and I ashes of despondent dejection. You enjoy absolute freedom or yield only to laws beyond our comprehension, while I am compelled by an overwhelming force to revolve in orbit around you as though you were the sun and I the earth. Have you found some freedom at the seashore that you do not savor in the villas of al-Abbasiya? Of course not! By the truth of everything you mean to me, you're not like the others. In the garden of the mansion and on the street your feet leave fragrant prints. In the heart of each friend you leave memories and hopes. A young lady welcoming yet inaccessible, you pass between us but remain aloof – as though the East had requested you as a gift from the West on the anniversary of the Night of Destiny, at the end of Ramadan, when prayers are sure to be answered. I wonder what new favor you might grant where the coast is long, the horizon distant, and the beach packed with admirers. What would it be, my hope and my despair?

"Without you, Cairo's a wasteland exuding melancholy desolation and consisting of only the dregs of life and living creatures. Of course it has sights and features, but none that speak to the emotions or stir the heart, for they seem antiquities, memories of an unopened pharaonic tomb. No place in Cairo offers me any solace, distraction, or entertainment. I imagine myself at different times as choking, imprisoned, lost, or wandering aimlessly. How amazing! Did your presence provide me with a hope that separation has banished? Certainly not, my destiny and my doom, but like that aspiration, so long as I remain under your wing, I feel fresh and safe, even if my hope is groundless. Of what use to a person eagerly searching the dark sky is his knowledge that the full moon is shining on the earth somewhere else? None, even if he does not seek any control over the moon. Yet I desire life to its most profound and intoxicating degree, even if that hurts. If you are present as my heart beats, it's because of that fabulous creature, the memory. Before I knew you, I never realized what a miracle it is. Today, tomorrow, or after a lifetime, in al-Abbasiya, Ra's al-Barr, or at the ends of the earth, my imagination will never lose sight of your dark black eyes, your eyebrows which join in the middle, your elegant straight nose, your face like a bronze moon, your long neck, and your slender figure. Your enchantment defies description but is as intoxicating as the fragrance of a bouquet of jasmine blossoms. I will hold on to this image as long as I live. When I die, may it overcome all obstacles and hindrances to become my destiny and mine alone, since I have loved you so deeply. If that is out of the question, tell me what meaning life has for us to seek or what delight there is to yearn for after death.

"Don't claim to have fathomed the essence of life unless you're in love. Hearing, seeing, tasting, and being serious, playful, affectionate, or victorious are trivial pleasures to a person whose heart is filled with love – and from the first look, my heart. Even before my eyes left her, I was certain that this was to be permanent, not transitory. It was one of those fleeting but decisive moments like conception or an earthquake. Oh Lord, I was no longer the same person. My heart collided with the walls of my chest as the secrets

of the enchantment revealed themselves. My intellect raced so fast
it courted insanity. The pleasure was so intense that it verged on
pain. The strings of existence and of my soul vibrated with a
hidden melody. My blood screamed out for help without knowing where assistance could be found. The blind man could see, the
cripple walked, and the dead man came back to life. I entreated
you by everything you hold dear never to leave . . . You, my God,
in heaven and she on earth.

"I believe that all my past life has been in preparation for the
glad tidings of love. The fact that I did not die young and went to
Fuad I School and not some other one, that the first pupil
I befriended was her brother Husayn, and . . . and that . . . all of
that was just so I would be invited to the mansion of the Shaddad
family. What a memory! My heart is almost torn out by the impact
of it. Husayn, Isma'il, Hasan, and I were busy discussing various
issues when there came to our ears a melodious voice saluting us.
I turned around, totally astounded. Who could be approaching?
How could a girl intrude on a gathering of young men to whom
she was not related? But I quickly abandoned my questions and
decided to set aside traditional mores. I found myself with a
creature who could not possibly have originated on this earth.
She seemed to know everyone but me. So Husayn introduced us:
'My friend Kamal . . . my sister, Aïda.' That evening I learned why
I had been created, why I had not died, and why the fates had
driven me to al-Abbasiya, to Husayn and the Shaddad family
mansion. When did that take place? Unfortunately the date has
been forgotten but not the day. It was Sunday, a regular holiday at
her French school which coincided with a governmental holiday
for state schools, possibly the Prophet's birthday. In any case it was
a day of birth for me.

"Of what importance is the date? The calendar has a magic that
makes us imagine a memory can be resurrected and revived, but
nothing returns. You'll keep on searching for the date, repeating:
the beginning of the second year at school, October or November, during Sa'd Zaghlul's journey to Upper Egypt, and before he
was exiled for the second time. No matter how much you consult
your memory, the evidence, and events of the day, you'll simply
end up clinging desperately to your attempt to rediscover that lost
happiness and a time that has disappeared forever. If only you had
held out your hand when you were introduced, as you almost did,

she would have shaken it and you would have experienced her touch. Now you imagine it repeatedly with feelings of both skepticism and ecstasy, for she seems to be a creature with no physical body. Thus a dreamlike opportunity was lost, which – along with that moment – will never return. Then she directed her attention to your two friends, conversing freely with them while you crouched in your seat in the gazebo, racked by the anxiety of a person fully imbued with the traditions of the Husayn district. At last you asked yourself whether there might not be special rules of etiquette for mansions. Perhaps it was a breath of perfumed air originating in Paris, where the beloved creature had grown up. Then you submerged yourself in the melody of her voice, savoring its tones, becoming intoxicated by its music, and soaking up every syllable that slipped out. Perhaps you did not understand, you poor dear, that you were being born again at that very moment and that like a newborn baby you had to greet your new world with alarm and tears.

"The girl's melodious voice remarked, 'We're going this evening to see *The Coquette*.' With a smile, Isma'il asked her, 'Do you like the star, Munira al-Mahdiya?' She hesitated a moment as was fitting for a half-Parisian girl. Then she replied, 'Mama likes her.' Husayn, Isma'il, and Hasan all got involved in a conversation about the outstanding musicians of the day: Munira al-Mahdiya, Sayyid Darwish, Salih Abd al-Hayy, and Abd al-Latif al-Banna.

"Suddenly I was taken by surprise to hear the melodious voice ask, 'What about you, Kamal? Don't you like Munira?'

"Do you recall this revelation that descended on you so unexpectedly? I mean do you recall the natural harmony of it? It was not a phrase but a magical tune that came to rest deep inside you where it sings on silently to an attentive heart, which experiences a heavenly happiness unknown to anyone but you. How astounded you were when greeted by it. It was like a voice from the heavens singling you out to address you by name. In a single draft you imbibed unparalleled glory, bliss, and grace. Immediately afterwards you would have liked to echo the Prophet's words when he would feel a revelation coming and cry out for help: 'Wrap me up! Cover me with my cloak!'

"Then you answered her, although I don't remember how. She stayed a few minutes longer before saying goodbye and departing. The charming look of her black eyes added to her fascinating beauty by revealing an agreeable candor – a daring that arose from self-confidence, not from licentiousness or wantonness – as well as an alarming arrogance, which seemed to attract and repel you at the same time.

"Her beauty has a fatal attraction. I don't understand its essence and I know nothing comparable. I often wonder if it's not the shadow of a much greater magic concealed within her. Which of these two forms of enchantment makes me love her? They're both puzzles. The third puzzle is my love. Although that moment fades farther into the past every day, its memories are eternally planted in my heart because of its associations with place, time, names, company, and remarks. My intoxicated heart circles through them until it imagines they are life itself, wondering somewhat skeptically whether any life exists beyond them. Had there really been a time when my heart was empty of love and my soul devoid of that divine image? At times you were so ecstatically happy that you grieved over the barrenness of your past. At other times you were so stung by pain that you pined for the peace that had fled. Caught between these two emotions, your heart could find no repose. It proceeded to search for relief from various spiritual opiates, finding them at different times in nature, science, and art, but most frequently in worship. From the innermost reaches of your awakened heart there flared up a passionate desire for divine delights. . . . 'People, you must love or die.' That was what your situation seemed to imply as you proudly and grandly strode along bearing the light of love and its secrets inside you, boasting of your elevation over life and other living creatures. A bridge strewn with the roses of happiness linked you to the heavens. Yet at times, when alone, you fell victim to a painful, sick, conscious reckoning of your shortcomings and to merciless brooding about them. These confined you to your little self, your modest world, and the mortal level of well-being.

"Oh Lord, how can a person re-create himself afresh? This love is a tyrant. It flies in the face of other values, but in its wake your beloved glistens. Normal virtues do not improve it and ordinary defects of character do not diminish it. Such contrasts appear beautiful in its crown of pearls and fill you with awe. In your opinion, was it in any way demeaning for her to have disregarded the customs most people observe? Of course not . . . in fact it would have been more demeaning if she had observed them.

Occasionally you like to ask yourself: What is it you want from her love? I answer simply that I want to love her. When life is gushing through a soul, is it right to question what the point is? There's no ulterior motive for it. It's only tradition that has linked the two words: 'love' and 'marriage.' It is not merely the differences of age and class that make marriage an impossible goal for someone in my situation. It is marriage itself, for it seeks to bring love down from its heaven to the earth of contractual relationships and sweaty exertion.

"Someone insists on making you account for your actions and asks what you have gained from falling in love with her. Without any hesitation I reply, 'A fascinating smile, the invaluable gift of hearing her say my name, her visits to the garden on rare blissful occasions, catching a glimpse of her on a dewy morning when the school bus is carrying her off, and the way she teases my imagination in ecstatic daydreams or drowsy interludes of sleep.' Then your madly yearning soul asks, 'Is it absolutely out of the question that the beloved might take some interest in her lover?' Don't give in to false hopes. Tell your soul, 'It is more than enough if the beloved will remember your name when we meet again.'"

"Quick. To the bathroom. Aren't you late?"

Registering his surprise, Kamal's eyes looked at Yasin, who had returned to the room and was drying his head with a towel. Kamal jumped out of bed. His body looked long and thin. He cast a glance in the mirror as though to examine his huge head, protruding forehead, and a nose that appeared to have been hewn from granite, it was so large and commanding. He took his towel from the bed frame and headed for the bathroom.

Al-Sayyid Ahmad had finished praying. Now he lifted his powerful voice in his customary supplications for his children and himself, asking God for guidance and protection in this world and the next. At the same time Amina was setting out the breakfast. Then she went to invite him in her meek voice to have breakfast. Going to the room shared by Yasin and Kamal, she repeated her invitation.

The three men took their places around the breakfast tray. The father invoked the name of God before taking some bread to mark the beginning of the meal. Yasin and then Kamal followed his lead. Meanwhile the mother stood in her traditional spot next to the tray with the water jugs. Although the two brothers appeared polite and submissive, their hearts were almost free of the fear that had afflicted them in former times in their father's presence. For Yasin it was a question of his twenty-eight years, which had bestowed on him some of the distinctions of manhood and served to protect him from abusive insults and miserable attacks. Kamal's seventeen years and success in school also afforded him some security, if not as much as Yasin. At least his minor lapses would be excused and tolerated. During the last few years he had become accustomed to a less brutal and terrifying style of treatment from his father. Now it was not uncommon for a brief conversation to take place between them. An intimidating silence had previously dominated their time together, except when the father had asked one of them a question and the son would hastily answer as best he could, even if his mouth was full of food.

Yes, it was no longer out of the ordinary for Yasin to address his father. He might say, for example, "I visited Ridwan at his grandfather's house yesterday. He sends you his greetings and kisses your hand."

Al-Sayyid Ahmad would not consider such a statement to be impudent or out of line and would answer simply, "May our Lord preserve him and watch over him."

It was not out of the question at such a moment for Kamal to ask his father politely, "When will custody of Ridwan revert to his father, Papa?" In that way he demonstrated the dramatic transformation of his relationship to his father.

Al-Sayyid Ahmad had replied, "When he turns seven," instead of screaming, "Shut up, you son of a bitch."

One day Kamal had attempted to establish the last time his father had insulted him. He had finally recalled that it had been about two years before, or a year after he had fallen in love, for he had begun to date events from that moment. At the time, he had felt that his friendship with young men like Husayn Shaddad, Hasan Salim, and Isma'il Latif demanded a large increase in his pocket money, so that he could keep up with them in their innocent amusements. He had complained to his mother, asking her to request the desired increase from his father. Although it was not easy for the mother to raise such an issue with the father, it was less difficult than it had once been, because of the change that had occurred in his treatment of her after Fahmy's death. Commending the new ties of friendship to important families with which her son had been honored, she had mentioned the request to her husband. Al-Sayyid Ahmad had then summoned Kamal and poured out his anger on the boy, yelling, "Do you think I'm at the beck and call of you and your friends? Cursed be your father and their fathers too."

Thinking the matter at an end, Kamal had left disappointed. To his surprise, the following day at the breakfast table the man had asked about his friends. On hearing the name Husayn Abd al-Hamid Shaddad, he had inquired with interest, "Is your friend from al-Abbasiya?"

Kamal had answered in the affirmative, his heart pounding.

Al-Sayyid Ahmad had said, "I used to know his grandfather Shaddad Bey. I know that his father Abd al-Hamid Bey was exiled, because of his ties to the Khedive Abbas. . . . Isn't that so?"

Kamal had replied in the affirmative once more, while contending with the strong emotion aroused by this reference to the father of his beloved. He had remembered immediately what he knew of the years her family had spent in Paris. His beloved had grown up in the brilliance of the City of Light. He had been seized by a feeling of renewed respect and admiration for his father along with redoubled affection. He had considered his father's acquaintance with the grandfather of his beloved to be a magical charm linking him, however distantly, to the home from which his inspiration flowed and to the source of everything splendid. Shortly thereafter his mother had brought him the good news that his father had agreed to double his allowance. Since that day Kamal had not been cursed by his father again, either because he had done nothing to merit it or because his father had decided to spare him further insults.

Kamal stood beside his mother on the balcony, which was enclosed with latticework. They were watching al-Sayyid Ahmad walk along the street and respond with dignity and grace to the greetings of Uncle Hasanayn the barber, al-Hajj Darwish, who sold beans, al-Fuli the milkman, Bayumi the drinks vendor, and Abu Sari' who sold seeds and other snacks.

When Kamal returned to his room, he found Yasin standing in front of the mirror, grooming himself patiently and carefully. The boy sat on a sofa between the two beds and studied his older brother's body, which was tall and full, and his plump, ruddy face with its enigmatic smile. He harbored sincere fraternal affection for Yasin, although when he scrutinized his brother visually or mentally he was never able to overcome the sense of being in the presence of a handsome domestic animal. Although Yasin had been the first person to make his ears resound with the harmonies of poetry and the effusions of stories, Kamal, who now thought that love was the essence of life and the spirit, would wonder whether it was possible to imagine Yasin in love. The response would be a laugh, whether voiced or internal. Yes, what relationship could there be between love and this full belly? What could this beefy body know of love? What love was there in this sensual, mocking look? He could not help feeling disdain, softened by love and affection. There were times, though, when he admired or even envied Yasin, especially when his love was troubled by a spasm of pain.

Yasin, who had once personified culture for him, now seemed almost totally lacking in it. In the old days Kamal had considered him a scholar with magical powers over the arts of poetry and storytelling. What little knowledge Yasin had was based on superficial reading confined to the coffee hour, or a portion of it, as he went back and forth, without subjecting himself to effort and strain, between *al-Hamasa*, which was a medieval anthology of poetry, and some story or other, before he rushed off to Ahmad Abduh's coffeehouse. His life lacked the radiance of love and any yearnings for genuine knowledge. Yet Kamal's fraternal affection for his brother was in no way diminished by such realizations.

Fahmy had not been like that. He was Kamal's ideal, both romantically and intellectually, but eventually Kamal's aspirations had reached beyond Fahmy's. He was afflicted by a compelling doubt that a girl like Maryam could inspire genuine love of the sort illuminating his own soul. He was also skeptical that the legal training his late brother had chosen was really equivalent to the humanities he was so eager to study.

Kamal uninhibitedly considered those around him with an attentive and critical eye but stopped short when it came to his father. The man appeared to him to be above any criticism, a formidable figure mounted on a throne.

"You're like a bridegroom today. We're going to celebrate your academic achievements. Isn't that so? If you weren't so skinny, I could find nothing to criticize."

Smiling, Kamal replied, "I'm content to be thin."

Yasin cast a last glance at himself in the mirror. Then he placed the fez on his head and carefully tilted it to the right, so it almost touched his eyebrow. He belched and commented, "You're a big donkey with a baccalaureate. Relax and take time to enjoy your food. This is your vacation. How can you feel tempted to read twice as much during your school holiday as you do during the academic year? My God, I'm not guilty of slenderness or of association with it." As he left the room with his ivory fly whisk in his hand, he added, "Don't forget to pick out a good story for me. Something easy like 'Pardaillan' or 'Fausta' by Michel Zévaco. Okay? In the old days you'd beg me for a chapter from a novel. Now I'm asking you to provide me with stories."

Kamal rejoiced at being left to his own devices. He rose, muttering to himself, "How can I put on weight when my heart never slumbers?"

He did not like to pray except when he was alone. Prayer for him was a sacred struggle in which heart, intellect, and spirit all participated. It was the battle of a person who would spare no effort to achieve a clear conscience, even if he had to chastise himself time and again for a minor slip or a thought. His supplications after the prescribed prayer ritual were devoted entirely to his beloved.

74

ABD AL-MUNI'M: "The courtyard's bigger than the roof. We've got to take the cover off the well to see what's in it."

Na'ima: "You'll make Mama, Auntie, and Grandma angry."

Uthman: "No one will see us."

Ahmad: "The well's disgusting. Anyone who looks in it will die."

Abd al-Mun'im: "We'll get the cover off, but look at it from a distance." Then he continued in a loud voice, "Come on. Let's go."

Blocking the door to the stairway, Umm Hanafi protested, "I don't have any strength left to keep going up and down. You said, 'Let's go up on the roof,' so we did. You said, 'Let's go down to the courtyard,' and we did. 'Let's go up to the roof.' So we came up another time. What do you want with the courtyard? . . . The air's hot down there. Up here we have a breeze, and soon the sun will set."

Na'ima: "They're going to take the cover off the well to look in it."

Umm Hanafi: "I'll call Mrs. Khadija and Mrs. Aisha."

Abd al-Muni'm: "Na'ima's a liar. We won't raise the lid. We won't go anywhere near it. We'll play in the courtyard a little and then come back. You stay here till we return."

Umm Hanafi: "Stay here! . . . I have to follow your every step, may God guide you. There's no place in the whole house more beautiful than the roof terrace. Look at this garden!"

Muhammad: "Lie down so I can ride on you."

Umm Hanafi: "There's been enough riding. Pick some other game, by God. God . . . look at the jasmine and the hyacinth vines. Look at the pigeons."

Uthman: "You're as ugly as a water buffalo, and you stink."

Umm Hanafi: "May God forgive you. I've gotten sweaty chasing after you."

Uthman: "Let us see the well, if only for a moment."

Umm Hanafi: "The well is full of jinn. That's why we closed it."

Abd al-Muni'm: "You're a liar. Mama and Auntie didn't say that."

Umm Hanafi: "I'm the one who's right, me and the lady of the house. We've seen them with our own eyes. We waited until they entered it. Then we threw a wooden cover over the opening of the well and weighted it down with stones. Don't talk about the well. Repeat with me: 'In the name of God the Compassionate, the Merciful.'"

Muhammad: "Lie down so I can ride on you."

Umm Hanafi: "Look at the hyacinth beans and the jasmine! Don't you wish you had something like that? All you've got on your roof are chickens and the two sheep you're fattening up for the Feast of the Sacrifice."

Ahmad: "Baa ... baa ... baa."

Abd al-Muni'm: "Fetch a ladder so we can climb up it."

Umm Hanafi: "May God preserve us. The boy takes after his uncle. Play on the ground, not in the sky."

Ridwan: "At our house we have pots of carnations and of red and white roses on the balcony and in the men's reception room."

Uthman: "We have two sheep and some chickens."

Ahmad: "Baa ... baa ... baa."

Abd al-Muni'm: "I'm going to religious kindergarten. What about all of you?"

Ridwan: "I've memorized 'Praise to God ...'"

Abd al-Muni'm: "Praise to God for lamps and meatballs."

Ridwan: "For shame! You're a heathen."

Abd al-Muni'm: "That's what the teacher's assistant chants when he's walking in the street."

Na'ima: "We've told you a thousand times not to repeat it."

Turning to Ridwan, Abd al-Muni'm asked, "Why don't you live with Uncle Yasin, your father?"

Ridwan: "I'm with Mama."

Ahmad: "Where's Mama?"

Ridwan: "With my other grandfather."

Uthman: "Where's your other grandfather?"

Ridwan: "In al-Gamaliya ... in a big house with a special reception room for men only."

Abd al-Muni'm: "Why does your mother live in one house and your father in another?"

Ridwan: "Mama's with my grandfather there and Papa's with my grandfather here."

Uthman: "Why aren't they in one house like my papa and mama?"

Ridwan: "Fate and destiny. That's what my other grandmother says."

Umm Hanafi: "You've pestered him until he's confessed. There's no power or might save God's. Have mercy on him and go play."

Ahmad: "The water buffalo knows how to talk."

Muhammad: "Get down so I can ride on you."

Ridwan: "Look at the sparrow on the hyacinth vine."

Abd al-Muni'm: "Fetch a ladder so I can grab it."

Ahmad: "Don't raise your voice. It's looking at us and hears every word you say."

Na'ima: "How beautiful she is! I know her! She's the sparrow I saw yesterday on our clothesline."

Ahmad: "The other one was on Sugar Street. How could it find its way to my grandfather's house?"

Abd al-Muni'm: "You donkey. The sparrow can fly here from Sugar Street and return before nightfall."

Uthman: "Her family is there, but she has relatives here."

Muhammad: "Get down so I can ride you. Otherwise I'll cry till Mama hears me."

Na'ima: "Why don't we play hopscotch?"

Abd al-Muni'm: "No, let's have a race."

Umm Hanafi: "Without any quarreling between the winner and the loser."

Abd al-Muni'm: "Shut up, water buffalo."

Uthman: "Moo . . . moo."

Ahmad: "Baa . . . baa."

Muhammad: "I'll ride in this race. Get down so I can ride you."

Abd al-Muni'm: "One, two, three . . ."

Al-Sayyid Ahmad Abd al-Jawad welcomed the guests, for whom he had set aside the whole first part of the day. He took his place in the center at the banquet, surrounded by Ibrahim Shawkat, Khalil Shawkat, Yasin, and Kamal. After the meal, he invited the two guests to his bedroom, where they conversed in an atmosphere of affection and friendship, marked by a certain reserve on the host's part and a special politeness on the part of his sons-in-law, stemming from the etiquette the father observed in his relations with his family, even those who did not reside with him, despite the fact that al-Sayyid Ahmad and Ibrahim Shawkat, Khadija's spouse, were of nearly the same age.

The children were invited to their grandfather's room to kiss his hand and receive precious gifts of chocolate and Turkish delight. They presented themselves in order of seniority: Aisha's daughter Na'ima first, then Yasin's son Ridwan, followed by Khadija's son Abd al-Muni'm, Aisha's son Uthman, Khadija's son Ahmad, and Aisha's son Muhammad. Al-Sayyid Ahmad observed strict impartiality in distributing affection and smiles to his grandchildren but took advantage of the absence of observers, except for Ibrahim and Khalil, to relax his customary reserve. He shook the little hands warmly, pinched their rosy cheeks affectionately, and kissed their brows, while teasing this one and joking with that one. He was always careful not to show favoritism, even with Ridwan, whom he loved best.

When alone with one of them he would examine the child with passionate interest, motivated by paternal feelings and additional ones like curiosity. He took great pleasure in tracing the features of grandparents and parents in the boisterous new generation, who had scarcely learned to respect him, let alone fear him. He was captivated by the beauty of Na'ima, who with her golden hair and blue eyes surpassed even her mother's good looks. She graced the family with her beautiful features, some inherited from her mother and others from the Shawkat family. Her brothers Uthman and Muhammad were also handsome but looked more like their father, Khalil Shawkat. They clearly had his large, protruding eyes with the calm, languid look.

By way of contrast, Khadija's sons Abd al-Muni'm and Ahmad had their mother's and maternal grandmother's beautiful small eyes, although they shared the Shawkat complexion. Their noses were exceptionally similar to their mother's or, to be more precise, their maternal grandfather's.

Ridwan could not help but be handsome. His eyes were identical to his father's and therefore like the black, kohl-enhanced ones of Haniya, Yasin's mother. He had the ivory complexion of his mother's family, the Iffats, and his father's straight nose. Indeed, a captivating grace shone in his face.

It had been a long time since al-Sayyid Ahmad's children had been able to cling to him the way his grandchildren did now, without fear on their part or reserve on his. Oh, what days they had been! What memories! Yasin, Khadija . . . and Fahmy, then Aisha and Kamal. He had tickled every one of them under the arms and carried each on his shoulders. Would they remember that? He himself had almost forgotten.

Na'ima, her bright smile notwithstanding, seemed shy and polite. Ahmad would not stop asking for more chocolates and Turkish delight. Uthman stood waiting impatiently for the response to Ahmad's request. Muhammad rushed to the gold watch and the diamond ring inside the fez and grabbed hold of them. Khalil Shawkat had to use force to pry them from his grip. Al-Sayyid Ahmad spent a few moments beset by confusion and anxiety, not knowing what to do, for he was surrounded and even under attack from every side by his beloved grandchildren.

Shortly before the afternoon prayer, the patriarch left the house for his store. His departure allowed the sitting room, where the remaining members of the family were gathered, to enjoy total freedom. It had inherited the role of the abandoned one down-stairs and was furnished with the same mat, sofas, and large ceiling lantern. It had become the lounge and coffeehouse for those of the family still living in the old house. No matter how crowded, it had remained tranquil all day long. Now that the only trace of their father was the fragrance of his cologne, it could breathe freely. Their talk grew louder and so did their laughter. Everyone became more animated. The coffee hour once more seemed just like the old days. Amina was sitting cross-legged on a sofa by the coffee utensils. On another couch facing her sat Khadija and Aisha. On a third to the side, Yasin and Kamal were ensconced. Once al-Sayyid Ahmad had left, Ibrahim and Khalil Shawkat joined the party. Ibrahim took a place to the right of their mother-in-law and Khalil one to her left.

Ibrahim had hardly settled there when he addressed Amina affectionately: "God bless the hands that prepared such appetizing and delicious food for us." Then he glanced around the assembly with his languid, protruding eyes as though delivering an oration and continued: "Those casseroles . . . what casseroles! They're marvelous in this house. It's not the ingredients, no matter how delicious and excellent, it's the way they're allowed to cook down, more than anything else. It's an art. It's a miracle. Find me another casserole as delicious as those we had today."

Khadija followed his comments attentively. She was torn between applauding his recognition of her mother's skill and arguing against him, because he was ignoring hers. When he paused to allow his listeners an opportunity to agree with him, she could not restrain herself from saying, "No one would contest that verdict. No one needs to testify on its behalf. But I remember and think it worth consideration that you've filled your belly in your own home repeatedly with casseroles no less skillfully prepared than those we ate today."

Aisha, Yasin, and Kamal all smiled knowingly. Their mother was clearly attempting to overcome her embarrassment and say something that would express her thanks to Ibrahim without offending Khadija. But Khalil Shawkat burst out: "Khadija's right. Her casseroles are a blessing to all of us. You better not forget that, brother."

Ibrahim looked back and forth between his wife and his mother-in-law, smiling apologetically. Then he said, "God forbid that I should fail to acknowledge my indebtedness to my wife, but I was discussing the senior chef." Then he laughed and said, "In any case I was praising the merits of your mother, not mine."

He waited until the laughter provoked by his last remark died down. Then turning toward his mother-in-law, he continued lauding her: "Let's return to the casseroles, although why should we confine our remarks to them? In fact all the other dishes were just as delicious and sumptuous. Take, for example, the stuffed potatoes, the mallow greens, the fried rice with giblets, and the assorted stuffed vegetables. God Almighty, what chickens! How meaty! Tell me, what do you feed them?"

Khadija answered sarcastically, "Casseroles! That's what!"

"I'll have to do penance for a long time and give credit where it is due, but God is forgiving and compassionate. In any case, let's pray that God grants us many more days of celebration. Congratulations on your baccalaureate, Kamal. God willing, you'll have the same good success with your university degree."

Blushing with embarrassment and happiness, Amina said gratefully, "May our Lord give you reason to celebrate for Abd al-

Muni'm and Ahmad, for Mr. Khalil to rejoice for Na'ima, Uthman, and Muhammad" – then turning to Yasin – "and for Yasin to rejoice for Ridwan."

Kamal was glancing stealthily at Ibrahim and Khalil. On his lips he had the fixed smile with which he normally concealed his lack of interest in a conversation he did not find to his taste, whenever he felt he ought to participate, if only by paying attention.

The man was talking about food as though still at the table, intoxicated by greed. Food, food, food . . . why did it deserve all this attention? These two strange men did not appear to have changed with time, as though beyond its reach. Ibrahim today was the same as he had been. He was almost fifty, but the only signs of age were the scarcely noticeable wrinkles under his eyes and at the corners of his mouth or his sedate, serious air, which did not give him the appearance of dignity so much as of lethargy. Not a single hair of his head or of his twisted mustache had gone gray. His full body was still powerful, firm, and free of flab. The resemblance between the two brothers in appearance, state of health, and their languid gaze was great enough to be comical or a subject for mockery. There were only inconsequential differences, like the cut of their hair. Khalil's was long and smooth while Ibrahim's was short. They were both wearing white silk suits, and each had removed his jacket to reveal a silk shirt with gold cuff links gleaming through the buttonholes. Their elite status was obvious from their appearance, but nothing else.

In the course of the seven years during which their two families had been joined by marriage, Kamal had been alone with one or the other of the brothers for periods of time but had never had a conversation of any substance with either of them. But what reason was there for criticism? If they had not been like that, would there have been this successful harmony between them and his two sisters? Fortunately scorn was not incompatible with affection, benevolence, and fondness.

Oh . . . it seemed that the conversation about the casseroles had not ended yet. Here was Mr. Khalil Shawkat preparing to have his say: "My brother Ibrahim did not exceed the truth in what he said. May we never be deprived of those hands. The food was certainly worth boasting about."

Amina secretly loved praise and had suffered bitterly because she was so often deprived of it. She was conscious of her tireless exertions, lovingly and voluntarily expended in the service of her house and family. She had often longed to hear a kind word from her husband, but he was not accustomed to bestowing praise on her. If he did, it was brief and limited to a few exceptional occurrences scarcely worth mentioning. With Ibrahim and Khalil on either side of her, she found herself in a pleasant and unusual situation. It truly delighted her but also embarrassed her so much that she felt uncomfortable. To hide her feelings she said, "Don't exaggerate, Mr. Khalil. You have a mother whose cooking would make anyone familiar with it steer clear of all other food."

While Khalil proceeded to reiterate his praise, Ibrahim involuntarily turned his eyes toward Khadija, where they met hers. She was staring at him as though she had expected him to look her way and was prepared for it. He smiled victoriously and told his mother-in-law, "Some people would not concede that to you."

Yasin understood this allusion and laughed out loud. The gathering was quickly engulfed in laughter. Even Amina smiled broadly as her torso shook with suppressed giggles. She concealed her mirth by bowing her head as though to look at her lap. Khadija was the only one whose face remained rigid. She waited until the storm calmed down and then said defiantly, "Our disagreement was not about food and how to cook it. It concerned my right to look after my household myself. And I'm not to be blamed for that."

Those present were reminded of the ancient battle that had flared up during the first year of Khadija's marriage. It had pitted her against her mother-in-law and concerned the kitchen. The issue had been whether there would be a single kitchen for the entire household under the supervision of the Widow Shawkat or whether Khadija would have her own kitchen as she wanted. It had been a serious quarrel threatening the unity of the Shawkat family. News of it had reached her parents' home on Palace Walk, so that everyone knew about it, except al-Sayyid Ahmad. No one dared tell him about it or any of the other disputes that broke out afterwards between the old lady and her daughter-in-law. Khadija had soon realized that she would need to rely on herself alone in the struggle. Her husband was, as she put it, "a slugabed," who was neither for her nor against her. Whenever she prodded him to stand up for her rights, he would entreat her almost playfully, "Lady, spare me the headache." Although he did not come to her defense, he did not silence her either. So she had ventured alone onto the field of battle to oppose the venerable old lady with unexpected daring and stubbornness, which did not disappoint her even in those delicate circumstances.

The old lady had been amazed by the audacity of this girl at whose birth she had assisted. Soon the battle had been joined, and anger had flared up. She had proceeded to remind the girl that had it not been for her own generous interest, Khadija could never have hoped in her wildest dreams to win a husband from the Shawkat family. Although in open rebellion, the daughter-in-law had muzzled her rage and insisted on obtaining what she considered her right, without utilizing her notoriously sharp tongue, for she was restrained by respect for the old lady and by fear that her mother-in-law would complain to al-Sayyid Ahmad.

Her cunning had prompted her to incite Aisha to rebel, but she had found that her lazy sister was cowardly and unwilling to become involved, not from love for their mother-in-law but because she preferred the calm and peace she enjoyed to her heart's content under the tyrannical supervision the old lady imposed on everyone. Khadija had poured out her anger on her sister and accused her of being weak and lazy. Galvanized by her own stubbornness, Khadija had continued her crusade relentlessly and persistently, until the older woman had gotten fed up and grudgingly granted her "gypsy" daughter-in-law an independent kitchen, telling her elder son, "So much for you. You're a weak man, powerless to discipline your wife. You're getting your just reward, which is to be deprived of my cooking forever."

So Khadija had gotten her way, retrieving the copper pots and pans that had been part of her trousseau, and Ibrahim had arranged a kitchen for her according to her specifications. But she had alienated her mother-in-law and severed the ties of friendship that had bound them since Khadija was in the cradle. Amina had not been able to tolerate the idea of a dispute but had waited patiently for everyone to calm down. Then she had set to work on the grande dame with the cooperation of Ibrahim and Khalil until a truce was concluded. Yet what kind of truce had it been? It was a truce that would scarcely come into effect before a new skirmish took place, to be followed by another truce. And so on and so forth. . . . Each of them would hold the other woman responsible. To her dismay, Amina was caught between the two. Ibrahim stood by like a neutral party or an observer, as though the matter did not concern him. Whenever he did choose to intervene, he did so listlessly, contenting himself with repeating some word of advice calmly and even coldly, paying no attention whatsoever to his mother's scolding or his wife's criticism. Had it not been for Amina's dedication and gentleness, the old lady would have complained to al-Sayyid Ahmad. She reluctantly abandoned that notion and set about venting her wrath by complaining at length to everyone she met, whether family or neighbors. She announced for all to hear that her selection of Khadija to be her son's wife had been the biggest mistake of her whole life and that she would just have to bear the consequences.

Smiling as though to lighten the impact of his correction, Ibrahim amended Khadija's statement: "But you weren't satisfied to get what was rightfully yours. You attacked anything you felt like criticizing, if my memory does not mislead me."

Her hair concealed by a brown scarf, Khadija defiantly raised her head. Staring at her husband with scorn and rage, she asked, "Why should your memory mislead you? Do you have any thoughts or concerns to burden it enough to mislead you? If only everyone else could have a memory as calm, contented, and disinterested as yours! Your memory has not betrayed you, Mr. Ibrahim, but it has betrayed me. The truth is that I did not oppose your mother's power. It was of no interest to me, and I had no need for it. Praise God, I know my duties and how to perform them in the best possible way. But I did not like to sit at home while food was carried in from outside, as though we were guests at a hotel. If that weren't enough, unlike someone I know, I could not bear to spend my whole day sleeping or playing, while another person looked after my house."

Aisha realized immediately that she was the target of the comment and laughed before Khadija had finished. As though motivated by compassion, the younger sister commented tenderly, "Do what you think best, and don't worry about other people – or those you know. There's no reason for you to be unhappy now, for you're the mistress of your own destiny – may Egypt achieve that too. You work from dawn to dusk in the kitchen, the bath, and on the roof. At one and the same time you look after the furniture, the chickens, and the children. The maid Suwaydan doesn't dare approach your apartment or pick up one of your children. My Lord . . . why all this exertion when a little would do?"

Khadija responded with a thrust of her chin, while she fought off a smile betraying her pleasure with Aisha's comments. Then Yasin commented, "Some people are born to rule and others to serve."

Revealing his overlapping incisors, Khalil Shawkat smiled and said, "Madam Khadija is a sterling example of a housewife, except that she overlooks her right to relaxation."

Ibrahim Shawkat expressed his total agreement: "That's my opinion exactly. I've told her so repeatedly. Finally I decided to keep quiet to spare myself the headache."

Kamal looked at his mother, who was filling Khalil's cup for the second time. He thought of his father and his dominance. His lips curled up in a smile. Then he looked at Ibrahim with astonishment and commented, "You seem to be afraid of her!"

Shaking his large head, the man replied, "I attempt to avoid trouble whenever I can. Your sister attempts to avoid peace whenever she can."

Khadija shouted, "Listen to this wisdom!" Then pointing at him as though challenging him to disagree, she continued: "You try your best to find a way to sleep."

Giving her a warning look, her mother said, "Khadija!"

Ibrahim patted his mother-in-law on the shoulder and remarked, "This goes on all the time at home . . . but see for yourself."

Yasin was looking back and forth between the powerful, chubby Khadija and the slender, delicate Aisha in a way intended to draw people's attention to them. Then he said incredulously, "You've told us that Khadija works nonstop from dawn till dusk, but where's the evidence of this toil? She looks like the loafer, and Aisha the worker."

To ward off the evil eye, Khadija spread her fingers apart and held up her hand with the palm facing Yasin, reciting, "And from the evil of the envious person in his envy" (Qur'an 113:5).

Aisha was not satisfied with the turn the conversation had recently taken. A look of protest was apparent in her clear blue eyes. Ignoring the point of Yasin's remark and feeling a little jealous, she hastened to defend her slimness: "Plumpness is no longer in fashion nowadays." Sensing that Khadija's head was turning her way, Aisha corrected herself: "Or at least, many think slimness as fashionable as plumpness."

Khadija commented scornfully, "Slenderness is in vogue among women who can't gain weight."

Kamal's heart pounded when the word "slenderness" reached his ears. From his unconscious mind the image of a tall figure with a slender build sprang into his imagination. His heart danced to a spiritual music inspiring raptures. A pure delight captivated him. Within that deep, calm dream he forgot himself, his location, and the time. He did not know how long it was before he became aware of a dark shadow of sadness, which frequently trailed along after his dreams. It did not arrive as an intrusive stranger or an incompatible element but flowed into his splendid dream like one of the threads from which it was woven or a melody forming part of its harmony. He sighed profoundly and then with his dreamy eyes glanced at the faces he had loved for as long as he could remember. They seemed in one way or another to be challenged by her beauty, especially the fair-complexioned one of his sister Aisha. He had once thirsted to drink from the place her lips had touched on the cup. He was embarrassed and almost unhappy to recall that, for he felt he should be devoted to no type of beauty save that of his beloved, even if other varieties might merit his affection and love.

"I don't like slenderness, not even in men," Khadija continued. "Look at Kamal! He ought to gain some weight. Brother, learning's not all there is to life."

Kamal listened to her with a scornful smile. He was examining her body, with its folds of fat and flesh, and her face, which had become so plump that its defects were no longer apparent. He was amazed by the happiness and victory her appearance conveyed but did not feel inclined to debate with her.

Yasin responded with defiant sarcasm: "Then, Khadija, you must like my looks a lot. Don't try to deny it."

His right leg was folded under him while his left one extended to the floor. It was hot and he had opened the collar of his house shirt. Tufts of the thick black hair of his chest could be seen above the wide neck of his undershirt. Khadija cast a penetrating look at him before replying, "But you've overdone it just a tad, and the fat's gone to your brain. So that's an entirely different question!"

As though at a loss for an answer, Yasin sighed and turned to ask Ibrahim Shawkat sympathetically and compassionately, "Tell me how you survive, caught between a wife like this and your mother?"

Ibrahim lit a cigarette, took a drag on it, and exhaled, puffing out his cheeks. He thus joined his brother Khalil, who had not removed his pipe from his mouth except to speak, in polluting the air of the sitting room. Then he responded with apparent disinterest, "I act as though one of my ears was made of clay and the other of dough. This is what I've learned from experience."

Looking at Yasin, Khadija commented in a loud voice that showed how angry she was, "Experience has nothing to do with it. I swear by your life with me that experience hasn't taught you this. The fact is that our Lord gave him a temperament as smooth as Uncle Badr the Turk's ice cream. Even if the minaret of al-Husayn Mosque started shaking, not a hair of his head would be ruffled."

Amina raised her head and gave Khadija a critical, warning look until the daughter smiled and lowered her eyes as if embarrassed. Then Khalil Shawkat said with gentle pride, "This is the temperament of the Shawkat family. It's an imperial one. Isn't that so?"

Although Khadija laughed to lighten the impact of her words, she remarked pointedly, "Unfortunately for me, Mr. Khalil, your mother did not inherit this 'imperial' temperament."

Amina's patience was exhausted, and she shot back, "Your mother-in-law has no equal. She is a lady in every sense of the word."

With a gleam in his protruding eyes, Ibrahim tilted his head to the left to gaze down at his wife. Then, sighing victoriously, he said, "A witness from her own family has testified. God bless you, Mother-in-law." Then he addressed the whole assembly: "You're all aware that my mother's getting on in years. She's at an age when she needs to be treated with consideration and restraint, and my wife knows nothing of the latter."

Khadija was quick to defend herself: "I don't get angry unless there's a reason. I've never been an irritable person. My family's present. You can ask them."

Silence prevailed. The members of her family did not know what to say until a laugh escaped from Kamal. They all looked at him, and he could not keep from saying, "Dear Khadija is the most irritable self-restrained person I've ever known."

Yasin found enough nerve to add, "Or the most self-restrained irritable person, and only God knows for sure."

Khadija waited for the gale of laughter occasioned by these remarks to quiet down before gesturing toward Kamal as she shook her head regretfully. She said, "I've been betrayed by some-one I held on my lap more often than I have my own sons, Ahmad and Abd al-Muni'm."

Kamal replied somewhat apologetically, "I don't think I've revealed a secret. . . . "

Amina changed sides to defend Khadija, who appeared to be in trouble. With a smile she said, "Only God the Exalted is perfect."

With equal suavity, Ibrahim Shawkat remarked, "You're right. My wife has virtues that must not be overlooked. God's curse on anger, which strikes the angry person first of all. In my opinion there's nothing in the world worth getting angry about."

"How lucky you are!" Khadija said with a laugh. "That's why – and I don't envy you – no matter how many years pass, you're impervious to change."

For the first time Amina's serious disapproval was evident. To warn Khadija she said, "May our Lord preserve his youth and that of others like him."

Making no attempt to conceal his pleasure at his mother-in-law's prayer, Ibrahim laughingly asked, "Youth?"

Addressing his remarks to Amina, Khalil Shawkat responded, "In our family, forty-nine is considered young."

Amina said apprehensively, "Don't talk like that. Let's be done with it."

Khadija smiled at her mother's evident anxiety, for she knew what motivated it. Any frank expression of praise for a person's health was disliked in the old house, because it showed an ignor-ance of the dangers of the evil eye. Even Khadija herself would not have referred to her husband's good health if she had not spent the last six years with the Shawkats, who paid little more than lip service to many beliefs, such as the danger of envy and the evil eye. They also delved fearlessly into various subjects, such as the jinn's conduct, death, and ill health, which were not discussed in her old home, because of the residents' anxiety and caution.

The tie between Ibrahim and Khadija was firmer than it appeared on the surface and was not something a casual word or deed would harm. They were a successful couple, and each of them sensed deep inside that he could not do without the other, regardless of flaws. Strangely enough, it was when Ibrahim fell sick once that Khadija was able to reveal the love and devotion she harbored for him.

Yes, there was always some quarrel going on between them, at least from her side. His mother was not her only target. Despite his diplomacy and calmness, she was never at a loss for something to criticize about him – how much he slept, the way he lounged at home instead of going to work, his dismissal of any consideration of a career, his endless chatter, and the way he ignored domestic quarrels and disputes. According to Aisha, days and days would pass when her sister's conversation was totally given over to suspicious and acid remarks about him.

In spite of all this, or perhaps because of it – for an argument may improve a relationship like cayenne pepper, which adds zest to food – their emotional commitment to each other remained strong and uninfluenced by moments of apparent annoyance with each other. It was like a deep current in the water that keeps a steady course, unaffected by surface turbulence or spray. Moreover, it took little effort for her husband to appreciate her exertion, evidence of which was everywhere – in his sparkling residence, delicious meals, smart clothing, and tidy sons.

He would tease her and say, "The truth is that you're a treasure, you gypsy."

His mother's opinion of Khadija's energetic activity was quite different, and she did not hesitate to make it public during their frequent quarrels. She had told her daughter-in-law sarcastically, "This is a virtue for maids to brag about, not ladies."

Khadija had shot back, "The only vocation you people have is eating and drinking. The true master of a house is the person who takes care of it."

In the same scornful tone, the old lady had replied, "If they instilled such ideas in you at home, it was to conceal their opinion that you would never be good for anything except domestic service."

Then the younger woman had screamed, "I know why you're furious with me. I've known ever since I refused to let you push me around in my own home."

The mother-in-law had shrieked, "My Lord, I testify that al-Sayyid Ahmad Abd al-Jawad is a fine man, but he's fathered a she-devil. I deserve to be beaten with a slipper as punishment for picking you."

Khadija had gone off murmuring under her breath so the other woman would not hear, "You certainly deserve to be beaten with a slipper. I won't disagree with that."

Yasin looked at Aisha. Smiling mischievously, he said, "How happy you are, Aisha. You're on good terms with all factions."

Khadija perceived the veiled allusion to her in this remark. Shaking her shoulders disdainfully, she scolded him: "A troublemaker is trying to stir up dissension between two sisters."

"Me? . . . God forbid. God knows my intentions are good."

She shook her head as though in sorrow and replied, "You've never had a good intention."

Commenting on Yasin's remark, Khalil Shawkat said, "We live peacefully. Our motto is: 'Live and let live.'"

Khadija laughed until her gleaming teeth showed. In a tone not free of sarcasm she said, "At Khalil's house, it's one party after another. He's always strumming away on his lute while the lady of the house listens, primps in front of the mirror, or chats with this or that girlfriend through a window or the peephole of the enclosed balcony. Na'ima, Uthman, and Muhammad turn the chairs and pillows into a playground, and if Abd al-Muni'm and Ahmad get fed up with my supervision, they flee to their aunt's apartment, where they join the demolition squad."

Aisha asked with a smile, "In your opinion, is that all there is to our happy home?"

Khadija replied in the same tone, "Or you might be singing while Na'ima dances. . . ."

Aisha said boastfully, "I'm satisfied with the affection of all the neighbors and my mother-in-law."

"I don't see myself confiding in one of these chatterboxes, and as for your mother-in-law, she likes anyone who flatters her and bows down before her."

"We ought to love people. How wonderful it is when people love us too. Then hearts truly speak directly to each other. My friends all fear you. They frequently tell me, 'Your sister doesn't make us feel at home and never tires of putting us down.'" Then, laughingly addressing her mother, Aisha continued: "She still gives people comic nicknames that we joke about at home.

Abd al–Muni'm and Ahmad memorize them and repeat them to boys in the neighborhood. That way they become widely known."

Amina smiled again. Khadija, who appeared to be remembering some awkward situations, laughed uneasily. With unconcealed delight, Khalil said, "When you put all of us together, we're a complete ensemble, with a lute player, a vocalist, and a dancer. We only need some more singers and a chorus, but I have my hopes set on my children. It's just a question of time."

Directing his comments to Amina, Ibrahim Shawkat said, "I can testify that your granddaughter Na'ima is a brilliant dancer."

Amina laughed until her pale face turned red. Then she replied, "I've seen her dance. She's charming!"

With an enthusiasm that revealed her well–known affection for her family, Khadija exclaimed, "How beautiful she is! She looks like a picture in an advertisement."

"What a beautiful bride she'll make for Ridwan," Yasin commented.

With a laugh Aisha protested, "But she was the first of the grandchildren. . . . (Oh, I'll never be able to lie about her age the way a mother should.)"

Yasin asked calmly, "Why do people insist on the bride being younger than the bridegroom?"

No one answered, but Amina observed, "Na'ima won't have to wait long to find a suitable husband."

Khadija added, "My Lord, how beautiful she is! I've never seen anyone as beautiful."

"What about her mother?" Aisha asked with a laugh. "Haven't you seen her mother?"

Khadija frowned to lend dignity to her remarks and said, "She's more beautiful than you, Aisha. You can't contest that." Her ironic spirit returned at once, and she continued: "And I'm more beautiful than either of you."

"These people are talking about beauty," Kamal reflected. "What do they know about its essence? They like certain colors: the whiteness of ivory and the gold of precious ingots. If you ask me about beauty I won't speak of a pure bronze complexion, tranquil black eyes, a slim figure, and Parisian elegance. Certainly not! All those are pretty, but they're nothing but lines, shapes, and colors subject to investigation by the senses and open to comparison. Beauty itself is a painful convulsion in the heart, an abundance of vitality in the soul, and a mad chase undertaken by the spirit until it encounters the heavens. Tell me about this, if you can. . . ."

"Why should the ladies of Sugar Street seek the affection of Mrs. Khadija?" Yasin asked, to stir his sister up again, when he noticed that the conversation was going to leave her in peace. "Perhaps she does have some good qualities, as her husband has testified, but in general people are attracted by a pretty face and a sweet tongue."

Khadija threw him a look as if to say, "If you knew what was good for you, you'd quit." Sighing audibly, she remarked, "What more can I ask than God's protection and blessings. I didn't know I had another mother-in-law here."

Then, to Yasin's surprise, she took up the topic again in a serious vein, explaining, "I don't have time to waste on visits. The house and the children consume every moment, especially since my husband pays no attention to either."

In his own defense, Ibrahim Shawkat said, "Fear God and don't exaggerate your role in everything. The truth of the matter is that a man with a wife like mine must take an active, defensive role from time to time, whether to protect pieces of furniture from being dusted and cleaned so much they're almost worn away or children from being pushed beyond their capacities. The most recent incident of this kind, as you know, is her thrusting Abd al-Muni'm into religious school before he's even five."

Khadija retorted proudly, "If I had taken your advice, I would have let him stay home till he came of age. There seems to be some hostility against learning in your family. No, darling, my children will be raised like their maternal uncles. I review Abd al-Muni'm's lessons with him myself."

Yasin asked incredulously, "You review his lessons with him?"

"Why not? Mother went over Kamal's lessons with him in exactly the same way. I sit with him every evening while he recites what he's memorized at school." She laughingly admitted, "That also helps me remember the principles of reading and writing, which I fear I may eventually forget."

Amina blushed from embarrassment and delight. She looked at Kamal as though begging him for a sign that he remembered those bygone nights. He smiled to show how well he did.

"Let Khadija raise her sons the way their uncles were," Amina told herself. "Let one of them follow in Kamal's footsteps as he makes his way to university. Let one of them emulate . . . oh, broken hearts are too weak to bear such dizzying blows. If he had only lived, today he would be a judge or on his way to becoming one. How often he discussed his hopes with you. Or were they your hopes? What has become of all that? If only he had lived, even as an insignificant member of the thronging masses . . ."

Ibrahim Shawkat told Kamal, "We're not as bad as your sister makes out. I sat for the primary certificate in 1895, as Khalil did in 1911. In those days the primary certificate was a major achievement, unlike now, when no one finds it impressive. We didn't continue our education because we had no intention of pursuing a career. In other words, we didn't need a career."

Kamal felt ironic amazement at Ibrahim's words: "I sat for the primary certificate," but answered politely, "This goes without saying."

"How could learning have any intrinsic value for two happy oxen?" he asked himself. "The two of you have provided me with a valuable lesson, teaching me that it's possible to love a person I despise and to wish only the best for someone whose principles in life excite my aversion and disgust. I instinctively hate man's animal nature from the depths of my heart. This emotion became a reality once the heavenly breeze brushed against my heart."

With comic enthusiasm Yasin cried out, "Long live the old primary certificate!"

"We're in the majority in any case." Yasin was annoyed to hear Khalil thrust himself, and by implication his brother, among the holders of the primary certificate, which they had unsuccessfully attempted to obtain, but found himself forced to play along.

Khadija said, "Abd al-Muni'm and Ahmad will continue their studies until they receive university degrees. It will be a new era in the Shawkat family. Listen carefully to the sound of these names: Abd al-Muni'm Ibrahim Shawkat and Ahmad Ibrahim Shawkat. Don't they have the same ring to them as Sa'd Zaghlul?"

Ibrahim laughingly shouted, "Where do you get such wild ambitions?"

"Why not? Wasn't Sa'd Zaghlul Pasha a student at al-Azhar? He went from the student dole to being Prime Minister. One word from him is enough to make everyone sit up and take notice. Nothing's too much for God to achieve."

Yasin asked ironically, "Wouldn't you be satisfied if they were as important as the politicians Adli Yeken Pasha and Abdel Khaliq Sarwat Pasha?"

As though seeking refuge with God, she shouted back, "Traitors? My sons won't be the kind of politicians people chant about night and day to get them removed from office."

Ibrahim took out a handkerchief from his trousers and wiped his face, which had turned a deeper red from the heat and from the perspiration caused by drinking cold water and hot coffee. As he dried his face he said, "If a mother's severity is a factor in the creation of great men, then you can already announce the glory awaiting your sons."

"Would you want me to let them do anything they wish?"

Aisha remarked gently, "I don't remember Mother ever scolding any of us, let alone striking us. Do you?"

Khadija replied sorrowfully, "Mother never resorted to violence because Papa was there. A mention of him was enough to ensure that his commands were obeyed. But at my house – and yours is just the same – the father is present only in name." She laughed when she made this last comment. "What can I do when the situation's like that? If the father's a mother, then the mother must be a father."

Yasin said with delight, "I'm sure you're successful in your paternity. You a father! I've felt this for a long time without being able to put it into words."

Khadija pretended to be complimented and retorted, "Thank you, Miss Bamba Kashar, you seductive songstress."

"Khadija and Aisha," Kamal thought. "What different types. . . . Consider them carefully. Which do you think better suited to be a model for your beloved? . . . Ask God's forgiveness! No one can be a model for my beloved. I can't picture her as a housewife. How impossible it is to imagine that!" His beloved in a housecoat, restraining a child, or supervising a kitchen? "How alarming! How disgusting! She ought to be at ease, oblivious, promenading in a splendid gown through a garden or a park, riding in a car, an angel on a happy, impromptu visit to earth, a unique exemplar of her species, itself unlike any other and known only to my heart. If she is referred to by the same term as these women, it's simply because I don't know the correct one. If her beauty is called by the same name as Aisha's and all the other varieties, that's because I don't know the real name for it. Here is my life, which I consecrate to learning about you. What other thirst for understanding is there beyond that?"

"What do you suppose Maryam's news is?" Aisha asked when she happened to think of her former friend. The name made visibly different impressions on the various people sitting there. Amina's expression changed to reveal her intense annoyance. Yasin pretended not to have heard the question and busied himself with an inspection of his fingernails. Kamal's head swarmed with disturbing memories. It was Khadija who replied coldly, "What do you expect? She's divorced and has returned to her mother."

After it was too late, Aisha realized that she had inadvertently tumbled into an abyss and hurt her mother through a slip of the tongue. Her mother had long believed that Maryam and her mother had not been sincere in their grief for Fahmy and might have actually gloated over the family's misfortune, because of al-Sayyid Ahmad's opposition to the proposed engagement between Maryam and his late son. Khadija had been the first to suggest the idea, and her mother had not hesitated to embrace it uncritically. Amina's feelings toward her longtime neighbor had quickly changed in a way that had led to an estrangement and then a break.

Attempting to apologize for her question, Aisha said nervously, "I don't know what made me ask about her."

With obvious emotion, Amina said, "You shouldn't think about her."

When suspicions had first been voiced about her friend, Aisha had questioned their accuracy. She had argued that the engagement proposal had been kept secret and could not have reached Maryam's home. Thus the girl and her family would have had no reason to rejoice at their sorrow. Her mother had refused to see it that way, on the grounds that it was impossible for an important matter like an engagement to be kept from leaking to the interested parties. Aisha had not insisted on her opinion for long, fearing she would be accused of partiality for Maryam or indifference toward her late brother.

Confronted by her mother's passion, Aisha found herself forced to make up for her slip. She remarked, "No one save God knows the truth, Mother. Perhaps she's innocent."

Contrary to her daughter's expectations, Amina's displeasure grew more intense. There were visible warning signs of anger that seemed out of character for her, since she was known for her calm and self-restraint. In a trembling voice she said, "Don't talk about Maryam, Aisha."

Khadija, who shared her mother's feelings, shouted, "Let's not have anything to do with Maryam and her goings-on."

Aisha smiled in confusion but said nothing. Yasin continued to be engrossed with his fingernails until this violent conversation was concluded. Encouraged by Aisha's statement, "No one save God knows the truth, Mother," he had been on the point of joining in, but had been silenced by Amina's quick answer in that unusual, trembling voice. Yes, he kept his peace and inwardly expressed his thanks for the blessing of silence.

Kamal had followed the conversation with concern, although his face did not betray his feelings. The period during which his love had weathered delicate and adverse conditions had imparted to him enough of an ability to act so that he could conceal his emotions and, if necessary, make people think he felt quite the opposite way. He remembered what he had heard about the alleged gloating of Maryam's family. Although he had never taken the accusation seriously, he recalled the secret message he had conveyed to Maryam and the answer he had brought back to Fahmy. He had kept that old secret, continuing to guard it to honor his promise to his brother, out of respect for Fahmy's wishes. Kamal was amused and astonished that he had only recently grasped the meaning of that message as its ideas took on a new life within him. He had been a stone with obscure inscriptions carved on it, until love had come and solved the riddle.

He did not fail to notice his mother's anger. It was a new phenomenon, to which she had not been subject before the calamity. She was no longer the same. The change was not dramatic or constant, but from time to time she succumbed to angry spells she had never experienced or at least had never yielded to before. What could he say about that? It must be the wounded heart of a mother, about which he knew nothing except for some few insights he had come across in his reading. He felt intense pain for her. But what explained Aisha's conduct or Khadija's? Was it fair to accuse Aisha of insensitivity toward the memory of Fahmy? He could not imagine or admit that. She was a benevolent person with a heart disposed to friendship and affection. Not without reason, she was inclined to think Maryam innocent. Perhaps since her heart was open to everyone, she felt nostalgic for the time when the girl had been her friend. Khadija had been swallowed up by married life. Her interests were limited to being a mother and housewife. She had no need for Maryam or anyone else. The only part of the past that meant anything to her was her attachment to her family and especially to her mother, in whose footsteps she was following. There was nothing strange in that.

"What about you, Mr. Yasin? How long will you remain a bachelor?" Ibrahim Shawkat asked, motivated by a sincere desire to clear the air.

Yasin jestingly replied, "My youth has left me. It's too late for that now."

In a serious tone, which showed he had not understood that Yasin was joking, Khalil Shawkat said, "I got married when I was about your age. Aren't you twenty-eight?"

Khadija was upset by the reference to Yasin's age, for it indirectly revealed how old she was. She addressed Yasin sharply: "Won't you get married and spare people having to talk about your bachelorhood?"

Aiming to please Amina more than anything else, Yasin answered, "Given our experiences of the past few years, it's been necessary for a person to forget about his own desires."

Khadija drew her head back as though a hand were shoving it. She cast him a glance as if to say, "You devil, you beat me." Then with a sigh she remarked, "You're the limit! If you would just say that marriage doesn't suit you, that would be more truthful."

To show her affection for him, Amina commented, "Yasin's a fine man who stays away from marriage only if he's forced to. The fact is that it's time for you to think about getting married again, if only to comply with the teachings of religion."

He had often thought of perfecting his compliance with Islam in this manner, not merely to try his luck again but out of a desire to wipe his honor clean of the blot it had gained when he had been forced, at the instigation of his father, to divorce Zaynab, because that was what her father, Muhammad Iffat, wanted. Then Fahmy had been slain, and Yasin had put off thinking about marriage. Eventually he had grown accustomed to the free life of a divorcé. All the same he meant every word he said when he told Amina,

"Some situations are unavoidable. There's a right time for everything."

Their reflections were suddenly interrupted by a screaming hullabaloo and din accompanied by rapid footsteps on the stairs. They looked questioningly at the door to the stairway. It was only a moment before Umm Hanafi appeared on the threshold, frowning and gasping for breath. She cried out, "The children, my lady! Mr. Abd al-Muni'm and Mr. Ridwan are fighting. They threw pebbles at me when I tried to separate them."

Yasin and Khadija rose, rushed to the door, and disappeared up the stairs. They were back again in a couple of minutes. Yasin had Ridwan by the hand and Khadija was pushing in front of her Abd al-Muni'm, whom she was halfheartedly punching in the back. The others noisily followed them. Na'ima ran to her father, Khalil, Uthman to Aisha, Muhammad to his grandmother Amina, and Ahmad to his father, Ibrahim. Khadija scolded Abd al-Muni'm and warned him he would never see his grandfather's house again. Pointing accusingly at Ridwan, who was sitting between his father and Kamal, the boy began to scream in a tearful voice, "He said they're richer than we are."

Ridwan shouted back, "He's the one who told me that they're richer. He also said they own all the treasures hidden in the old city gate, Bab al-Mutawalli."

Trying to calm his son, Yasin said with a laugh, "Forgive him, son. He's a spitfire like his mother."

Khadija could not help but laugh and asked Ridwan, "Why quarrel over Bab al-Mutawalli when you have, sir, another ancient city gate, Bab al-Nasr, near your grandfather's house. You take that one and don't quarrel."

Ridwan shook his head to show his dissatisfaction and replied, "It's full of corpses, not treasures. Let him have it!"

Aisha spoke up then to implore and tempt them: "Pray by the Prophet; here's a rare opportunity to hear Na'ima sing. What do you think about that suggestion?"

Approval and encouragement came from every corner of the room, and Khalil took Na'ima in his arms to set her on his lap. He told her, "Let all these people hear your voice. My God . . . my God, don't be bashful. I don't like it when you are."

Na'ima was overcome by shyness and buried her face in her father's chest until all that could be seen of her was a halo of gold.

Aisha happened to glance around and saw Muhammad attempting unsuccessfully to remove the beauty spot from his grandmother's cheek. She went and brought him back against his will before resuming her encouragement to Na'ima to sing. Khalil too kept after the girl until she whispered that she would not sing unless she could hide behind his back. He gave her permission, and she crept behind him on the sofa, crawling on all fours. A pleased and expectant silence fell on the room. The quiet lasted so long that Khalil almost lost patience, but then a charming, delicate voice could be heard, starting as a whisper. Gradually she gained courage and her tones became increasingly fervent as she sang:

> *Turn aside here*
> *And come to me,*
> *You whom I love*
> *As you love me.*

Small hands began to clap to the music.

75

"IT'S TIME for you to tell me which branch of the university you plan to choose."

Al-Sayyid Ahmad Abd al-Jawad was seated on his bedroom sofa with his legs folded beneath him. At the far end, Kamal sat facing the door with his arms crossed in front of him, cloaked in polite submission. The man would have liked his son to reply, "Whatever you think best, Father," but al-Sayyid Ahmad conceded that choice of specialization at the University was not a matter he could dictate. His son's consent would be an important factor in the selection process. His own knowledge of the topic was also extremely limited, being derived for the most part from occasional discussions at his parties with friends who were attorneys or civil servants. They all agreed that a son should be granted the right to choose which branch of learning to pursue, lest he become discouraged and fail. For all these reasons, the father was not averse to discussing the topic, after confiding his lot to God's care.

"I have decided, Papa, God willing and with your approval, of course, to enroll in the Teachers Training College."

Al-Sayyid Ahmad's head moved in a way that revealed his discomfort. His large blue eyes opened wide. He stared at his son strangely. Then in a disapproving tone he said, "The Teachers College! . . . A free school! Isn't that so?"

After some hesitation Kamal replied, "Perhaps. I don't know."

The father waved his hand scornfully. He seemed to want to tell his son, "You must exercise a little patience and not leap to a decision on something you know nothing about." Then he remarked disdainfully, "It's just as I said. For that reason it rarely attracts students from good families. And then there's the teaching profession. . . . Do you know anything about teaching or is your information limited to the Teachers College? It's a miserable profession, which wins respect from no one. I'm well informed about what's said of such matters, but you're young and inexperienced. You know nothing of the ways of the world. It's an occupation uniting people who have modern educations with the products of traditional religious education. It's one utterly devoid of grandeur or esteem. I'm acquainted with men of distinction and with civil servants who have flatly refused to allow their daughters to marry a teacher, no matter how high his rank."

After belching and exhaling heavily, he continued: "Jamil al-Hamzawi's son Fuad, to whom you used to give your old suits, will attend Law School. He's a smart boy who's done well in school, but he's no smarter than you. I've promised his father to help pay his fees until he's been there long enough to get free tuition. How can I pay for other men's children to go to decent schools when my own son is studying free of charge in a worthless one?"

This grave report on the teacher and his mission came as an alarming surprise to Kamal. What reason was there for all this prejudice? It was not possible to attribute it to the teacher's calling, which was to impart knowledge. Was it based on the absence of tuition fees at the college where teachers were trained? He could not understand how money entered into the question of the value of learning. Why should learning have any worth beyond that of knowledge for its own sake? He believed too deeply in its intrinsic value for his faith to be shaken. He was convinced of the inherent merit of the sublime ideas he came across while reading the works of men he loved and respected, such as the Egyptian authors al-Manfaluti and al-Muwaylihi. He threw his whole heart into living in the ideal world reflected in the pages of their books. Thus he did not hesitate to reject his father's opinion as mistaken, no matter how much he revered the man. He excused this error by attributing it to their backward society and the influence of his father's ignorant friends. He was sorry but could only repeat, with all the politeness and delicacy he could muster, a phrase he had picked up in his reading: "Learning's superior to prestige and wealth, Papa."

Al-Sayyid Ahmad looked back and forth between Kamal and the wardrobe, as though appealing to an invisible person for confirmation of the absurdity of the idea he had just heard. Then he said indignantly, "Really? Have I lived long enough to hear drivel like this? You imply there's a difference between prestige and learning! There's no true knowledge without prestige and wealth. And why are you talking about learning as though it's one thing? Didn't I say that you're young and inexperienced? There are many different types of learning, not just one. Some kinds of knowledge are appropriate for tramps and others belong to the pashas of the world. You need to comprehend this, you ignoramus, before you regret it."

Kamal was convinced that his father had a high regard for religion and consequently for those who made it their profession. Thus he craftily said, "The students who do their advanced training at al-Azhar Mosque don't pay tuition. They become teachers, and no one can despise their fields of learning."

His father gestured scornfully toward him with his chin and said, "Religion's one thing and men who make a career of it are something else."

Deriving strength from his despair for this debate with the man whom he had always been accustomed to obey, he replied, "But, Papa, you revere the religious scholars and love them."

In a voice that was a bit sharp, his father said, "Don't mix things up. I revere Shaykh Mutawalli Abd al-Samad and love him. But I would far rather see you a respected civil servant than a man like him, even if you were to spread blessedness among the people, protecting them from evil with amulets and charms. . . . Every era has its men, but you refuse to understand."

He examined his son to gauge the effect of these words. Kamal looked down and bit his lower lip. He began to blink, while the left corner of his mouth twitched nervously.

"How amazing!" al-Sayyid Ahmad thought. Why did people insist on things that were clearly bad for them? He came close to exploding with anger but remembered that he was dealing with an issue outside the realm of his absolute sovereignty. He suppressed his rage and asked, "But why are you so enamored of the Teachers College, as though it had a monopoly on all learning? What do you dislike about Law School, for example? Isn't it the institution that graduates important people and government ministers? Isn't it the institution where Sa'd Zaghlul Pasha and men like him studied?"

Then with a despondent look in his eyes, he continued in a subdued voice: "And it was the school that Fahmy, may God be compassionate to him, chose after serious thought and reflection. If his time had not come so early, he would be a public prosecutor or a judge today. Isn't that so?"

Kamal replied emotionally, "Everything you say is true, Papa. But I don't want to study law."

The man struck his hands together and said, "He doesn't want to! Of what relevance to learning and institutions are likes and dislikes? Tell me what attracts you to the Teachers College. I want to know which of its alluring beauties has caused you to fall for it. Or are you a person who loves worthless things? Speak. I'm all ears."

Kamal squirmed, as though summoning all his forces to help him clarify the point his father found so obscure. He realized he had a difficult task before him. He was convinced that his efforts would only earn him more of the sarcastic comments he had already experienced during their argument. Moreover, he did not see himself as having a clearly defined goal he could explain to his father. What could he say? If he thought a little, he would know what he did not want. He was not interested in legal studies, economics, geography, history, or English, although he appreciated the importance of the last two subjects for his pursuits. If he did not want these, what did he desire? The yearnings of his soul would require careful scrutiny before his goals could be ascertained. Perhaps he was not convinced that he could achieve them at the Teachers College but thought this institution the shortest route to them. These yearnings had been aroused by things he had read that could not be classified under a single heading. There had been literary and social essays, religious ones, the folk epic about Antar – that heroic black poet of ancient Arabia, *The Thousand and One Nights*, a medieval anthology of Arabic poetry called *al-Hamasa*, the writings of al-Manfaluti, and the principles of philosophy. His aspirations were probably connected in some way as well to the realm of fantasy Yasin had disclosed to him long ago and even to the legends his mother had poured into his spirit before that. He was pleased to apply the name "thought" to this mysterious world and the title "thinker" to himself. He believed that the life of thought was man's loftiest goal, rising with its luminous character high above the material world. It was superior to prestige, titles, and all other counterfeit forms of greatness. The life of thought was certainly along those lines even if its features were not clearly delineated. He might find it in the Teachers College or his training there might merely be a means of advancing toward it, but he would never turn away from this goal.

It was only fair to acknowledge the strong link connecting the Teachers College to his heart or more precisely to his love. Why was that? There was no link between his beloved and the law or economics, but there were many ties, no matter how slender and concealed, between her and religion, spirituality, morality, philosophy, and other comparable branches of learning that tempted him to drink from their springs. She had similar secret affinities to singing and music. He could hope to gain insight into them through the transport of a musical performance or an outburst of ecstasy. He was aware of all this within him and totally convinced of its truth, but what could he say to his father? Once again he attempted to outfox his father, saying, "The Teachers College trains people in noble sciences like mankind's history, which is full of lessons, and the English language."

As he spoke, his father scrutinized him. Suddenly al-Sayyid Ahmad's feelings of disdain and anger vanished. As though seeing the lad for the first time, he pondered his son's slender build, huge head, large nose, and long neck. He decided that Kamal looked as strange and eccentric as his ideas sounded. The father's mocking spirit was almost amused by this realization, but his affection and love for the boy restrained his sense of humor. He asked himself, "If his slenderness is a temporary condition and his nose inherited from me, where did he get this amazing head? Isn't it likely that he'll fall prey to someone like me who searches for defects to make the butt of his jokes?"

This upsetting thought increased his affection for his son. When he spoke, his voice sounded calmer, as if he were patiently giving advice: "Knowledge by itself is nothing. The results are what count. The law prepares you for a legal career. All you get from history and its lessons is a miserable job as a teacher. Take time to consider the consequences long and hard." As the tone of his voice became a little sharper, he continued: "All power and might are God's. Lessons, history, and soot like that! Why don't you talk sense?"

Kamal blushed with embarrassment and pain when he heard his father's opinion of the learning and lofty values he cherished. His father had brought them down to the level of soot, comparing them to it. His consolation lay in remembering what he had read in defense of thought and its sanctity and the references to people who disdain learning and prefer to search for profit and status.

Oh! . . . those authors must have been debating with men just like his father. But not so fast . . . his father was not one of those stupid people. He was of a grand, distinguished type. He was simply the victim of his time, place, and companions. Would it do any good to argue? Should he try his luck once more, relying on a new stratagem?

"The fact is, Papa, that these disciplines have won the highest respect in advanced nations. The Europeans cherish them and erect statues in honor of persons who excel in them."

Al-Sayyid Ahmad turned his face away, clearly implying: "O God, have mercy." But he was not actually angry. He presumably thought the whole affair a comic surprise beyond his wildest imaginings. When he looked back, he said, "As your father, I want to feel secure about your future. I want you to have a respectable profession. Is there any disagreement about that? What really concerns me is to see you become an esteemed bureaucrat rather than a wretched teacher, regardless of whether a statue is erected like that of our national leader Ibrahim Pasha with his finger in the air. Glory to God! The longer we live, the more amazing are the things we hear and see. What does Europe have to do with us? You live in this country. Does it set up statues in honor of teachers? Show me a single sculpture of a teacher." Then he asked in a disapproving tone, "Tell me, son, do you want a career or a statue?"

Encountering no response save silence and confusion, al-Sayyid Ahmad said almost sadly, "I don't know how some of the ideas in your head got there. I'm inviting you to become one of the great men who shake the world with their distinctions and rank. Do you have some model you look up to that I don't know about? Tell me frankly what you think so I may set my mind at rest and understand what you're after. The truth is that you bewilder me."

He would take a new step and explain some of his feelings, putting his trust in God. He said, "Is it wrong, Papa, to aspire to be like the author al-Manfaluti someday?"

Al-Sayyid Ahmad said with astonishment, "Mustafa Lutfi al-Manfaluti? May God have mercy on him. I saw him more than once in the mosque of our master al-Husayn, but so far as I know he wasn't a teacher. He was much too distinguished for that. He was one of Sa'd Zaghlul's companions and writers. Moreover, he

studied at al-Azhar, not at the Teachers College. And his education at al-Azhar had nothing to do with his greatness. He was a gift
from God. That's what they say of him. We are discussing your
future and the school you ought to enter. Let's leave God's work
to God. If you're a gift from God and attain the greatness of al-
Manfaluti, why not do so as a prosecutor or a judge?"

In desperate self-defense, Kamal replied, "I don't want to be as
famous as al-Manfaluti. I want to be as cultured as he was. I haven't
been able to find any college where I can better achieve my
objective or at least lay a foundation for it than the Teachers
College. That's why I prefer it. I have no special desire to be a
teacher. Perhaps the only reason for accepting this profession is
that it's the path open to me for the cultivation of thought."

"Thought?" Al-Sayyid Ahmad remembered a verse from a song
composed and performed by al-Hamuli:

> *Thought has strayed.*
> *Aid me, tears.*

He had loved it for a long time and in the past had frequently
recalled it. Was it this kind of thought his son was striving to
develop?

He asked with astonishment: "What is 'the cultivation of
thought'?"

Kamal was overwhelmed by confusion. He swallowed and said
in a low voice, "Perhaps I don't really know." Then, smiling
ingratiatingly, he continued: "If I knew, I wouldn't need to study
it."

His father asked incredulously, "If you don't know what it is,
what grounds do you have for choosing it? . . . Huh? Are you
simply infatuated with a life of humiliation, for no reason at all?"

Kamal mastered his anxiety with great effort and – driven by
desperation – defended his pursuit of happiness: "Cultivated
thought is something too great to be easily comprehended.
Among other things, it searches for the origin of life and its
destiny."

His father studied him for a long time in bewilderment before
saying, "For this you want to sacrifice your future? The origin of
life and its destiny? The origin of life was Adam, and our destiny is
paradise or hellfire. Or has there been some new discovery concerning this?"

"Of course not. I know that. What I meant to say was . . ."

His father quickly interrupted: "Have you gone mad? I ask you about your future and you reply that you want to know the origin of life and its destiny. What will you do with that? Open a booth as a fortune-teller?"

Kamal was afraid that if he became baffled and fell silent, he would lose and be forced to accept his father's point of view. Drawing on every ounce of courage he possessed, he said, "Forgive me, Papa. I haven't expressed myself well. I would like to continue my study of literature, begun after I passed the preparatory exam. I want to study history, languages, ethics, and poetry. The future is in God's hands."

As though filling in gaps that Kamal had left in his list, al-Sayyid Ahmad shouted with angry sarcasm, "And to study as well the arts of snake charming, puppetry, crystal gazing, and soothsaying. Why not? O God, have pity on me. Have you really been storing up this surprise for me? . . . There is no might or power save God's."

Al-Sayyid Ahmad became convinced that the situation was far more serious than he had thought. He was at a loss. He began to ask himself whether he had been wrong to allow his son to speak and think freely on this subject. Whenever he had patiently and tolerantly given his son some rope, the boy had dug his heels in and argued in an even more extreme fashion. The father found himself torn between his tyrannical tendencies and his recognition of a son's right to choose a school for himself. He was solicitous for Kamal's future and reluctant to admit defeat, but in an uncharacteristic way – or, more precisely, one that would have been out of character in the old days – he finally let reason have the upper hand.

Thus he returned to the debate and said, "Don't be naïve. There's something the matter with your mind that's beyond my understanding. I ask God to deliver you from it. The future is not an amusing game. It's your life and the only one you'll ever have. Think about the question for a long time. Law School is best for you. I understand the world better than you do. I have friends from all walks of life, and they all agree about Law School. You're a stupid child and don't know what it means to be a prosecutor or a judge. These are the professions that shake the world. It's within your power to attain one of them. How can you reject all this so cavalierly and choose to be . . . a teacher?"

Kamal was distressed and angry, not merely at the insult to the honor of teachers but first and foremost for the sake of learning itself, for what he felt was true learning. He did not think well of occupations that shook the earth. He had often found that the writers who inspired him applied derogatory epithets to them, referring, for example, to their counterfeit grandeur and ephemeral glory. Basing his opinion on what they had said, he believed that the only true greatness lay in the life of learning and truth. Thus all manifestations of majesty and pomp seemed spurious and trivial to him. He refrained from expressing this belief for fear of increasing his father's wrath. He said in a sweet and endearing way, "In any case, the Teachers College is a form of higher education."

Al-Sayyid Ahmad reflected for a time. Then despondently and disgustedly he said, "If you don't feel inclined toward the law – for some people even enjoy being miserable – choose a respectable school like the Military or Police academies. Something's better than nothing!"

Alarmed, Kamal asked, "Should I go to the Military or Police academies after getting my baccalaureate?"

"What other alternative is there, since you don't have the background for medicine?"

At that moment al-Sayyid Ahmad noticed that light reflected from the mirror was dazzling his left eye. He turned to look at the wardrobe and saw rays of afternoon sunshine slipping into the room via the window, which overlooked the courtyard. They had advanced from the wall opposite the bed to fill a portion of the mirror, showing that it would soon be time to leave for his store. He moved a little to get away from the light. Then he exhaled in a manner revealing how uneasy he was and bringing the bad news – or was it good? – that the conversation was about to conclude. He asked glumly, "Isn't there any other school besides these?"

Lowering his eyes in dismay at being unable to satisfy his father, Kamal said, "There's only Commerce left, and I've no interest in it."

Although al-Sayyid Ahmad was annoyed by his son's speedy rejection of that school, he himself felt at best indifferent toward it. He assumed that it only graduated merchants and did not want his son to be a merchant. He had known all along that an establishment like his, although it supplied him with a good living, would not be able to support as comfortably a son who succeeded him,

for the income would have to be shared with his other benefi-
ciaries. Therefore he had not attempted to groom one of his sons
to take his place.

But this was not the main reason for his lack of interest in the
School of Commerce. The fact was that he looked up to the civil
service and bureaucrats. He perceived their significance and
importance in public life. He had observed this personally with
his friends who were civil servants and through contacts with the
government relating to his business. He wanted his sons to be civil
servants and had prepared them for that career. It was no secret to
him that businessmen received only a fraction of the respect that
government employees did, even if bureaucrats earned less. He
shared this bias, although he would not have admitted it out loud.
He was pleased by the deference civil servants showed him and
fancied himself to have the mind of a bureaucrat or at least one as
good. Who else would be capable of being a merchant and also the
equal of a bureaucrat? Why did his sons not have a personality like
his? Oh, what a disappointment it was! How he had wished in
former times to see one of them become a doctor. He had focused
his hopes on Fahmy, until he had been told that the arts baccalaureate did not prepare for the School of Medicine. Then he had
contented himself with Law School and had looked forward
happily to what would follow. Subsequently he had attached his
aspirations to Kamal, selecting the arts section for him and dreaming once more of the successful career to follow Law School. He
had never imagined that a struggle between his hopes and fate
would result in the death of the genius of the family and in Kamal's
insistence on being a teacher. How disappointed he felt!

Al-Sayyid Ahmad seemed genuinely sad when he said, "I've
given you the best advice I can. You're free to choose for yourself,
but you must always remember that I did not agree with you.
Think the matter over at length. Don't be hasty. You still have
plenty of time. Otherwise you'll regret your bad choice for the rest
of your life. I take refuge with God from stupidity, ignorance, and
folly." The man dropped his foot to the ground with a motion that
indicated he was preparing to rise and get ready to leave the house.

Kamal stood up politely and modestly and then departed.
Returning to the sitting room, he found his mother and Yasin
conversing there. He was distraught and dejected after having
resisted his father so vigorously, even though the man had been

forbearing and lenient. He was also disturbed by the anxiety and sorrow his father showed toward the end of their discussion. He summarized for Yasin the conversation that had taken place in the bedroom. As the older brother listened, his expression was disapproving and his smile sardonic. He wasted no time in advising the teenager that he agreed with their father and was amazed at both the boy's ignorance about the values important in life and his fixation on others that were fanciful or ridiculous.

"You want to dedicate your life to learning? What does that mean? As an insight or maxim in works by al-Manfaluti like his *Reflections* that's brilliant, but in real life it's nonsense that doesn't get you anywhere. You live here and now, not in al-Manfaluti's books. Isn't that so? Books document strange and supernatural matters. For example, you read at times in them a line like Ahmad Shawqi's: 'The teacher is almost like a prophet,' but have you ever encountered a teacher of whom that was true? Come with me to al-Nahhasin School or recall any of your teachers you please. Show me one of them deserving the title 'human being,' let alone that of 'prophet.' What is this learning you desire? Ethics, history, and poetry? All those are beautiful pastimes but worthless in the workaday world. Be careful that an opportunity for a distinguished life does not slip through your fingers. I frequently regret that adverse circumstances prevented me from continuing my education."

Once Yasin followed his father out of the house and Kamal was left alone with his mother, he asked her opinion. She was not normally consulted on a matter like this, but she had followed his conversation with Yasin and knew of al-Sayyid Ahmad's desire for him to go to Law School. She had begun to consider that idea ill-omened, and it made her uncomfortable.

In any case, Kamal knew exactly how to win her approval for his position in the shortest possible time. He told her, "The science I want to study is closely linked to religion. Among its branches are wisdom, ethics, consideration of the attributes of God, and the essence of His revelatory signs and creations."

Amina's face shone as she said enthusiastically, "This is true science, like my father's and your grandfather's. Religious science is the most noble one of all."

She thought for a time as he watched her with a twinkle in his eyes. Then with the same enthusiasm she continued: "Who would ever disparage a teacher? Don't they say, 'I become the slave of anyone who teaches me even a single syllable'?"

Repeating the argument his father had used to attack his choice, as though to elicit her support, Kamal observed, "But they say a teacher has no chance at getting a good position."

She waved her hand disdainfully and replied, "A teacher makes a decent living, doesn't he? What more can you wish for? I ask God that you may have good health, a long life, and sound learning. Your grandfather used to say, 'Learning is more valuable than money.'"

Amazingly, his mother's advice was better than his father's. It was not based on opinion but on sound feelings, which, unlike his father's, had never been corrupted by contact with the realities of worldly life. Her ignorance of the affairs of the world had protected her feelings from corruption. But what value did feelings have, no matter how noble, if they were rooted in ignorance? Was this same ignorance at least partially responsible for his own ideas? He revolted against this kind of logic and to refute it told himself that he knew the good and bad of the world from books. His choice of the good was based on both his beliefs and his thought. Innate and naïve feelings might agree with wise opinions without discrediting the latter in any way. "Absolutely!" he exclaimed to himself.

He did not doubt for a moment that his opinion was correct and noble, but did he know what he wanted? It was not the teaching profession that attracted him. The truth was that he dreamed of writing a book. What book? It would not be poetry. There was poetry in his diary, but it originated with Aïda, who changed prose into poetry, not with any poetic gift of his. Thus the book would be prose. It would be a large, bound volume about the size and shape of the Holy Qur'an, and, like the Qur'an, its pages would have margins filled with notes and commentaries. But what would he write about? The Qur'an embraced everything, did it not? There was no cause for him to despair. He would find his subject one day. It was enough for him to know the size, shape, and style of annotation for the book. Surely a book that would shake the world was better than a civil service position, even if the latter shook the world too. Every educated person knew about Socrates. Who remembered the judges who had presided at his trial?

76

"GOOD EVENING!"

"She's not going to answer," he thought. "That's what I expected. At the beginning, it's always like that . . . has been and ever will be. So she turns her back on you, moving away from the wall beside you to go to the line and check the clothespins. Hasn't she already done that? Of course, but, Maryam, you're trying to be discreet. I understand perfectly. After ten years of chasing women I've become something of an expert. Delight your eyes with her before it gets dark and she's reduced to a shadow. She's put on weight and gotten firmer. She's even more beautiful than when she was a girl. She was pretty as a gazelle back then but did not possess such full hips. Not so fast . . . she still has a maidenlike figure. How old are you, sweetheart? Your family used to claim you were the same age as Khadija, but according to Khadija you're years and years older. My stepmother declares nowadays that you're in your thirties, on the basis of old memories of the type: 'When I was pregnant with Khadija, Maryam was a girl of five,' and so on. What difference does age make? Do you plan to spend your whole life with her? In a few short days, she'll ripen into all the woman you could want – beautiful, alluring, satisfying, and plump. Oh, she looked toward the street and noticed you. Did you see her eyes look at you like a chicken's? I won't budge from here, you beauty. Isn't a young man whose looks, strength, and financial status you know better than that Englishman you once admired?"

"Doesn't your family think a greeting deserves some reply?" he asked.

"She's turned away from you again," he observed. "But wait . . . didn't she smile? Yes, and whatever force allotted beauty to her gave her an enchanting smile. She smiled. You prepared carefully for this final step. No doubt she's been aware of all my previous motions and maneuvers. My time has come . . . and yours too, since luckily you're not a woman afflicted with modesty. That

Englishman . . . Julian! Here's a noble stallion standing before you, and his body's ready to carry you away. Don't you hear him neighing?"

"Does your family have no respect for neighbors?" he inquired. "I beg you for a word of greeting. I certainly deserve that."

A faint, delicate voice, which seemed to come from far away, since her face was turned in the other direction, said, "You don't deserve it . . . not like this."

The man knocking at the door had received a reply. The door latch had been lifted. "You won't be charmed by sweet nothings until you've swallowed her scoldings," he counseled himself. "Be steady and firm . . . steady."

Borrowing a phrase from seminary students, Yasin said, "If I have done anything to offend you, I shall never forgive myself as long as I live."

She replied critically, "The roof terrace of Umm Ali the midwife's house is the same height as ours. What would someone think if he saw you standing there while I'm hanging out the laundry?" Then she added sarcastically, "Or do you want to cause a scandal for me?"

"May nothing evil happen to you," he thought. "Were you so cautious when you gazed at Julian in the old days? But not so fast . . . the beauty of your eyes and rump make up for any former or future misconduct."

"May God not spare my life a moment longer," he protested, "if I intended to harm you. I hid under the jasmine arbor until the sun set and did not approach the wall separating our houses until I was certain Umm Ali's roof was vacant."

Then, sighing audibly, he continued: "I have the added excuse that I've gotten in the habit of coming here to enjoy the solitude. When I found just now that no one else was present I was transported by joy. In any case our Lord will shield us . . . ."

"Amazing! . . . Why all this effort?"

"That's hardly a naïve question," he thought. "Their questions reflect their experience. She has condescended to converse with you. Congratulations on this conversation."

Out loud he said, "I told myself, 'Nothing could be sweeter than greeting her and hearing her answer.'"

The way she turned her head to look at him revealed even in the semidarkness that she was trying not to laugh. She replied, "Your words are more inflated than your body. I wonder what's behind all this talk of yours?"

"Behind it? Why not come closer to the wall? I have a lot to say. For some time now when I chance to look at the ground on leaving the house I've noticed the shadow of a moving hand. If I look up, I see you glancing down from the wall of the roof terrace. That sight is so beautiful it's unforgettable."

She turned to face him but did not move a step closer. Then she said accusingly, "How dare you look up! If you truly were a good neighbor, as you claim, you wouldn't harm a woman this way. Your evil intentions have become clear from your confession and conduct here."

His intentions really were evil. Was fornication the result of good ones? "These are the kinds of evil intentions you love," he reflected. "You women are the limit. In an hour you'll demand it as one of your rights. In two hours' time, I'll be fleeing, while you pursue me. All the same, tonight's as sweet as jasmine."

"God knows my intentions are good," he declared. "I glanced up because I can't keep myself from looking wherever you are. Haven't you understood that? Haven't you felt it? Your longtime neighbor is speaking out, even if it's rather late."

Mockingly she said, "Speak. Give free rein to your hot air. Raise your voice.... What would you do if your stepmother surprised us on the roof like this?"

"Don't change the subject, bitch. It will be a miracle if I ever convince you," he reflected. "Do you really fear my stepmother? Oh ... one night in this woman's embrace will be worth a whole lifetime."

"I'll hear her footsteps first," he explained. "Let's not get distracted from what we're doing."

"What are we doing?"

"Something so exalted that it defies description."

"It doesn't seem that way to me. Perhaps you're doing it alone."

"Perhaps. Then it's thoroughly heartrending. It's devastating when a heart speaks out and finds no one who will respond. I remember the days when you used to visit our house, those days when we were all like a single family, and I sigh with regret."

Shaking her head, she muttered, "Those days!"

"Return to the past?" he asked himself. "I've made a grave mistake. Don't let painful memories spoil your whole effort. Concentrate on setting aside everything but the present."

He said, "When I finally saw you, I beheld a young woman as beautiful as a flower that blooms by night and illuminates the darkness. I seemed to be seeing you for the first time. I asked myself, 'Could this be our neighbor Maryam who used to play with Khadija and Aisha?' Certainly not! This girl has matured into a perfect beauty. I felt that the world around me had been transformed."

Her tone mischievous once more, she replied, "In the old days your eyes did not take such liberties. You were a neighbor in every sense of the word. But what's left of those days? Everything's changed. We've become like strangers, as though we had never spoken to each other and had not grown up as a single family. This is the way your family wants it."

"Let's not think about that. Don't add to my distress."

"Now you allow your eyes to look anywhere . . . through the window, from the street, and here you are accosting me on the roof."

"What's keeping you from leaving if you really want to?" he wondered. "O light of my darkness, your lies are sweeter than honey."

"This is only a small part of it," he told her. "I'm looking at you even when you don't suspect it. I see you in my imagination more often than you could guess. I tell myself, knowing full well what I say, 'Give me life with her or death.'"

The whisper of a suppressed laugh made his heart tremble. "Where do you find such phrases?" she asked.

Gesturing toward his breast, he replied, "In my heart!"

She moved her foot and caused her slipper to scuff the roof as though she were about to depart. Without quitting her post she said, "Since the discussion has reached the heart, I must leave."

In his ardor, his voice grew louder until he caught himself and lowered it: "No! You must come. Come to me. Now and forever." Then he added sneakily, "To my heart. It and all it possesses are yours."

In a tone of mocking admonishment she advised him, "Don't abuse yourself this way. God forbid that I should deprive you of your heart and its possessions."

"How well do you understand what I'm saying?" he wondered. "When I speak to you, I'm addressing the bitch I love. You're no fool. The memory of Julian makes that clear. Come here, girl. You take after your old lady. I'm afraid I'll light up the darkness with the intense fire flaming inside my body."

"I'll gladly give you my heart and all its possessions," he proclaimed. "Its only happiness is for you to accept it and possess it, if you will belong to it alone."

She answered laughingly, "You crafty fellow, don't you see you want to take rather than give?"

"Where did you learn to talk like that?" he puzzled. "Not even Zanuba, when I was seeing her, could compare. What a cursed place the world would be without you."

"I want you to be mine," he said. "And for me to be yours. What's unfair about that?"

Silence reigned as a look was exchanged by two shadows. Then she said, "Perhaps they're asking now what's keeping you."

Artfully attempting to win her sympathy, he replied, "There's no one in the world who cares about me."

At that, her tone changed and she asked seriously, "How's your son? . . . Is he still with his grandfather?"

"What's behind this question?" he wondered.

"Yes," he answered.

"How old is he now?"

"Five. . . ."

"What's become of his mother?"

"I think she's either married or about to be."

"What a pity! Why didn't you take her back, if only for Ridwan's sake?"

"Bitch!" he thought. "Explain what you're getting at."

"Would you really have wanted that?" he asked.

She laughed gently and replied, "How lucky the man is who brings two people together in a moral way."

"Or immoral?" he wondered.

"I don't look back," he stated.

There ensued a strange silence that seemed thoughtful. Then in a voice that was both tender and admonitory she said, "You better not try to catch me on the roof again."

He answered daringly, "Whatever you command. The roof

isn't a safe place. Did you know I have a house in Palace of Desire Alley?"

She called out incredulously, "Your own house! Welcome to the man of property."

He was silent for a time, as though wishing to be cautious. Then he said, "Guess what's on my mind."

"That's no concern of mine."

"Silence, darkness, seclusion . . ." he thought, "what a dreadful effect the gloom has on my nerves. . . ."

"I was thinking," he declared, "of the two adjoining walls of our roofs. What does their image make you think of?"

"Nothing."

"The sight of two lovers clinging together."

"I don't like to hear talk like that."

"The fact that they're next to each other also reminds me that nothing separates them."

"Ha!" This exclamation escaped like an enticing threat.

Laughingly he continued: "It's as though they were telling me, 'Cross over.'"

She retreated two steps until her back touched a sheet hung out to dry. Then she whispered with genuine reproach, "I won't allow this!"

"This! . . . What's 'this'?"

"This kind of talk."

"What of the deed itself?"

"I'm going to leave angry."

"Don't do that. I swear by your precious life . . ."

"Do you mean what you're saying?" he asked himself. "Am I a greater fool than I suspect or are you more clever than I imagine? Why did you mention Ridwan and his mother? . . . Should you allude to marriage? How intensely do you want her? Madly. . . ."

Maryam said suddenly, "Oh . . . what's keeping me here?" She turned around and bent her head down to duck under the wash.

He called after her anxiously, "Are you leaving without saying goodbye?"

She lifted her head high to look back over the laundry and remarked, "Enter 'houses by their doors.' That's my farewell message for you." (Qur'an, 2:189.) She quickly made her way to the stairway door and disappeared through it.

Yasin returned to the sitting room. He excused his long absence to Amina by referring to the heat indoors and then went to his room to don his suit. Kamal watched his older brother with thoughtful amazement, but when he looked back at his mother he found her calm and reassured. She had finished drinking her coffee and was reading the grounds. Kamal wondered how she would react if she knew what had taken place on the roof.

Kamal himself was still perturbed by the scene of the couple conversing privately, which he had accidentally witnessed on following his brother to see what was delaying him. Yasin had done that. Did the memory of Fahmy mean so little to him? He could not imagine that. Yasin had loved Fahmy sincerely and had grieved for him deeply. It was impossible to doubt his sincerity. Moreover, incidents like this were commonplace. Kamal did not know why people always linked Fahmy and Maryam. His late brother had learned of the girl's affair with Julian before it was finished. A long time had passed after that. Fahmy had apparently forgotten her and gone on to loftier and more significant matters. That was all she deserved, for she had never been good enough for him. What Kamal really needed to think about was whether love could be forgotten. He believed it could not, but how did he know Fahmy had loved Maryam in the way Kamal understood and felt the term. Perhaps it had merely been a powerful desire like that currently overwhelming Yasin or even like that outgrown desire Kamal had once felt for Maryam. It had toyed with him when he reached puberty, playing havoc with his dreams. Yes, that had happened. It had afflicted him in two ways: through the equally powerful torments of desire and remorse. Only Maryam's marriage and subsequent disappearance from their lives had rescued him.

Kamal was concerned to know if Yasin was suffering and to what degree remorse was pricking his conscience. No matter what he thought of Yasin's animal spirits and indifference to higher ideals, Kamal could not imagine it had been easy for him. Despite his tolerant view of the whole matter, Kamal felt the annoyance and anxiety of a young man who would not have compromised his ideals for anything in the world.

After putting on his street clothes and grooming himself, Yasin returned from the bedroom. He said goodbye and departed. Before long they heard someone knocking on the door of the sitting room. Certain of the newcomer's identity, Kamal invited him to enter. A young man of his own age appeared. Short and good-looking, he was dressed in a jacket and a floor-length shirt. He went over to Amina and kissed her hand. Then he shook hands with Kamal and sat down beside him. Although he made a point of being polite, his familiar behavior indicated that he was virtually a member of the household. Amina began speaking to him, addressing him quite simply as Fuad and asking about the health of his mother and of his father, Jamil al-Hamzawi. He answered with delighted gratitude for her gracious welcome. Kamal left his friend with Amina to go put on his jacket in his room. When he returned, the two set off together.

77

THEY WALKED along, side by side, toward Qirmiz Alley, avoiding al-Nahhasin Street to keep from passing the store and their fathers. There was enough contrast between tall, skinny Kamal and short Fuad to attract attention.

Fuad asked in a calm voice, "Where are you going tonight?"

Kamal answered excitedly, "Ahmad Abduh's coffee shop."

It was customary for Kamal to pick their destination and for Fuad to acquiesce, even though Fuad was known for his clear, steady mind and Kamal for caprices that seemed ludicrous to his companion. For example, he had repeatedly asked Fuad to accompany him to the Muqattam Hills overlooking the city, to the Cairo Citadel, or to the Tentmakers Bazaar so that they might – as he put it – feast their eyes on the treasures of the past and wonders of the present. The relationship between the two friends was influenced by the difference in class between their families and by the fact that Kamal's father owned the shop where Fuad's father worked. This distinction was accentuated as Fuad grew accustomed to running errands for Kamal's family. In return, he benefited from Amina's generosity, for she did not begrudge him the finest food she had – he often showed up at mealtimes – and the most serviceable clothes Kamal no longer needed. From the beginning, their friendship had been marked by Kamal's dominance and Fuad's subservience. Although amity had supplanted these other feelings, their psychological impact had never been totally extirpated.

Circumstances decreed that Kamal found virtually no other companion but Fuad al-Hamzawi during the whole summer vacation. His former classmates in the area had not continued their studies. Some had begun careers once they finished their elementary or competency certificates. Others had been forced to take menial jobs, as a waiter in the coffeehouse on Palace Walk or as an apprentice at an ironing shop in Khan Ja'far, for example. Those two boys had been his classmates in religious primary school. The three of them still greeted each other as old friends

whenever they chanced to meet. The words of the two appren-
tices would be filled with respect because of the distinction the
pursuit of knowledge gave Kamal. His greeting would be full of
the affection of a modest and unpretentious soul. Kamal's new
friends who lived in al-Abbasiya, like Hasan Salim, Isma'il Latif,
and Husayn Shaddad, spent their holidays in Alexandria or Ra's
al-Barr. Thus Fuad was the only comrade he had left.

They reached the entry of Ahmad Abduh's coffeehouse after
walking for a few minutes. They descended to its strange space in
the belly of the earth beneath Khan al-Khalili bazaar and sought
out an empty alcove. As they sat facing each other at the table Fuad
muttered with some embarrassment, "I thought you would be
going to the cinema tonight."

His words betrayed his own desire. Although he had almost
certainly felt this way even before he stopped by Kamal's house, he
had said nothing about his wishes then. He had known he would
be unable to change Kamal's mind. Since it was Kamal who paid
for their tickets when they saw a film, Fuad's courage was not up to
mentioning what he would like until they were ensconced in the
coffeehouse, where his words could be understood as an innocent
and casual comment.

"Next Thursday we'll go to the Egyptian Club to see Charlie
Chaplin. Now we'll play a game of dominoes."

They removed their fezzes and placed them on the third chair.
Then Kamal summoned the waiter to order green tea and the
dominoes. The subterranean coffeehouse could well have been
the belly of an extinct beast buried by an ancient accumulation of
rubble except for its huge head, which came up to the level of the
earth. Its mouth, gaping wide open, had protruding fangs shaped
like an entry with a long staircase. The interior consisted of a
spacious square courtyard with large, cream-colored tiles from the
village of al-Ma'asara. There was a fountain in the center surrounded by carnations in pots. On all four sides stood benches
covered with cushions and decorative mats. The walls were interrupted at regular intervals by cell-like alcoves, without doors or
windows. They resembled caves carved into the walls and were
furnished with nothing more than a wooden table, four chairs, and
a small lamp, which burned night and day and hung in a niche on
the back wall. The bizarre setting of the coffeehouse contributed
to its character, for there was a sleepy calm about it unusual among

coffeehouses. The light was dim and the atmosphere damp. Each group of patrons was isolated in an alcove or on a bench. The men smoked water pipes, drank tea, and chatted idly and interminably. Their conversations had a pervasive, continuous, and languid melody of desire, broken at lengthy intervals by a cough, a laugh, or the gurgling sound of a water pipe.

In Kamal's opinion, Ahmad Abduh's coffeehouse was a treasure for the dreamer and provided much food for thought. Although initially Fuad had been intrigued by its curious attractions, now all he saw in it was a depressing place to sit and be enveloped by damp, putrid air. Yet he was forced to agree whenever Kamal invited him to go there.

"Do you remember the day we saw your brother, Mr. Yasin, when we were sitting here?"

Kamal smiled and replied, "Yes. Mr. Yasin is gracious and easy to get along with. He never makes me feel he's my older brother. I begged him not to tell anyone at home that we meet here, not from fear of my father, for none of us would dare disclose a matter like this to him, but from concern that it might upset my mother. Imagine how alarmed she would be if she learned we frequent this coffeehouse, or any other. She thinks most patrons of coffeehouses are drug addicts and people of ill repute."

"What about Mr. Yasin? Doesn't she know he's a regular?"

"If I told her, she'd say Yasin's an adult and not at risk, whereas I'm still young. It's clear that I'll be thought a child at home until my hair turns gray."

The waiter brought their dominoes and two glasses of tea on a bright yellow tray, which he placed on the table. Then he departed. Kamal took his glass at once and began to drink before the tea had cooled off. He blew on the liquid, took a sip, and then blew again. He sucked on his lip when he burned it, but that did not prevent him from stubbornly and impatiently resuming his attempt to drink, as though condemned to finish in a minute or two.

Fuad observed him silently or gazed at nothing in particular while leaning back in the chair with a dignity that far outstripped his years. His large handsome eyes had a calm and profound look. He did not reach for his glass until Kamal had finished struggling with his. Then Fuad began to sip the tea slowly as he savored its taste and enjoyed its fragrance. After each swallow he murmured, "My God . . . how good it is!"

Chafing at the bit, Kamal pressed him to finish so they could start playing. He warned his friend, "I'll beat you today. Luck won't always be on your side."

With a smile Fuad muttered, "We'll see," and began playing.

Kamal brought to the match a nervous intensity that suggested he was embarking on a contest in defense of his life or honor. Fuad calmly and skillfully placed his pieces. His smile never left his lips, whether he was lucky or not and whether Kamal was cheerful or glowering.

As usual Kamal became agitated and shouted, "A stupid move, but a lucky one." Fuad's only response was a polite laugh, calculated not to anger or challenge his friend.

Kamal frequently told himself when enraged, "He's always luckier than I am." Kamal did not display the kind of forbearance appropriate for games and recreation. In fact he manifested the same intensity and zeal in both his serious pursuits and his amusements.

Fuad's superiority over Kamal in dominoes was equaled by his success in school, where he was first in his class and Kamal merely in the top five. Did luck have a hand in that too? How could he explain the success of that young man to whom he felt superior, deep inside? He thought his superiority over Fuad should be evident in their respective intellectual gifts. His way of accounting for his friend's achievements was to observe that Fuad studied all the time. If he had really been as bright as they claimed, he would not have needed to study so much. Kamal also told himself that Fuad avoided sports, whereas he was excellent in more than one. He remarked finally that Fuad limited his reading to schoolbooks. If he thought of reading something other than a school text during the vacation, he chose one that would be helpful for his subsequent studies. Kamal did not limit his reading in any way and did not choose books for their utility. Thus there was nothing strange about the other boy being ranked ahead of him in school. All the same, his grudge against Fuad did not weaken their friendship. He loved him and found such delight and enjoyment in his company that he willingly admitted Fuad's strengths and virtues, at least to himself.

Play continued and the game ended, contrary to initial projections, with a victory by Kamal. He beamed and laughed out loud before asking his opponent, "Another game?"

But Fuad replied with a smile, "That's enough for today." Either he was tired of playing or apprehensive that the proposed match would end in disappointment for Kamal, whose happiness would turn to sorrow.

Kamal shook his head in amazement and commented, "You're a cold fish!" Rubbing the tip of his nose with his thumb and index finger, he added critically, "I'm amazed at you. When you're beaten, you're not interested in avenging your defeat. You love Sa'd Zaghlul but shunned the demonstration to salute him when he became Prime Minister. You seek the blessings of our master al-Husayn but are unruffled by the revelation that his remains may not repose in the nearby sepulcher. You astound me!"

Kamal was intensely annoyed by his friend's icy composure. He could not stand what they termed "being reasonable." He would prefer by far to be "crazy." He remembered the day they were told at school, "The tomb of al-Husayn is a symbol and nothing more."

They had walked home together afterwards. Fuad had repeated the words of the Islamic history teacher. Kamal had asked himself in alarm how his friend was able to deal with this news – as though it did not concern him. Kamal did not brood about it, for he was totally unable to think. How did someone in total revolt against an idea think? He was staggered by the frightful blow, which he felt even in the innermost reaches of his heart. He was weeping for a vision that had faded away and a dream that had evaporated. Al-Husayn was no longer their neighbor. He had never been their neighbor. What had become of all those kisses he had pressed against the door of the sepulcher so sincerely and warmly? What had happened to his exultation and pride in being a close neighbor of the Prophet's grandson? Nothing remained but a symbol in the mosque and desolate disappointment in his heart. He had wept that night until his pillow was soaked, but the revelation had stirred nothing in his reasonable friend save his tongue, which had reacted to the event by repeating their teacher's words. How dreadful it was to be reasonable!

"Does your father know you want to go to the Teachers College?"

When Kamal replied, the sharpness of his tone expressed displeasure with his friend's coldness as well as the pain left over from his interview with his father. "Yes!"

"What did he say?"

Kamal found some relief for his emotions by indirectly attacking his companion. "Alas, my father, like most other people, is crazy about sham forms of success like the civil service, the prosecutor's office, being a judge...that's all he cares about. I didn't know how to convince him of the grandeur of thought and the lofty values that truly deserve to be pursued in this life. But he left the decision up to me."

Fuad's fingers were toying with a domino when he asked compassionately, "No doubt these are lofty values, but where are they respected as they should be?"

"It's not possible for me to reject a heavenly creed simply because no one around me believes in it."

Fuad replied with a calmness intended to appease his friend: "You show admirable spirit, but wouldn't it be better to plan your future by the light of reality?"

"If our leader Sa'd Zaghlul had taken your advice," Kamal suggested scornfully, "do you suppose he would have thought seriously about going to the British Residency to demand independence for Egypt?"

Fuad smiled as though to say, "Although your argument's sound, it's not fit to serve as a general principle for life." He remarked aloud, "Study law so you'll be sure to have a respectable job. Afterwards you can pursue your cultural interests to your heart's content."

Defiantly Kamal retorted, "God didn't place 'two hearts in a man's breast' [Qur'an, 33:4]. And I must object to your association between legal studies and a respectable job. Isn't teaching a respectable profession?"

Fuad was quick to defend himself resolutely against this suspicion: "I didn't mean that at all. Who would ever say that gathering and distributing knowledge isn't respectable work? Perhaps I was unwittingly repeating what people say... people, as you suggested, who are dazzled by power and influence."

Kamal shrugged his shoulders in disgust and said with conviction, "A life dedicated to thought is certainly the most exalted type of life."

Fuad nodded his head in agreement but said nothing. He took refuge in silence until Kamal asked him, "What was your reason for choosing Law School?"

He thought a little and then replied, "Unlike you, I'm not in love with thought. I was able to select a branch of the University solely in terms of what it meant for my future. So I chose law."

Was this not the voice of reason? Of course it was, and that infuriated and revolted him. Was it not unfair for him to have to pass the entire summer vacation as a prisoner of this district with no companion besides this reasonable youth? There was another life totally unlike that of this ancient quarter. There were other companions who differed completely from Fuad. His soul yearned for that other life and those other friends . . . for al-Abbasiya and its elegant young people. More than anything else he craved the refined elegance, Parisian accent, and exquisite dream of his beloved. Oh . . . he wanted to go home to be alone and bring out his diary. He would relive a moment, recall a memory, or record a flight of fancy. Was it not time for him to disband this party and leave?

"I met some people who asked about you."

Tearing himself away from the stream of his reflections, Kamal asked, "Who?"

Fuad replied with a laugh, "Qamar and Narjis!"

Qamar and Narjis were the daughters of Abu Sari', who roasted seeds and other snacks. Kamal remembered the vaulted section of Qirmiz Alley after sunset when the alleys were quite dark. They had fondled each other in a way that combined innocence with sexuality, as they feverishly approached puberty. He could remember all that, but why did his lips pucker up in disgust? That was all relatively ancient history, before the holy spirit had descended on him. He could not recall that flirtation without having his heart boil with anger, pain, and shame, since now it was filled with the wine of pure love.

"How did you come across them?"

"In the crowds at the commemoration of the birth of al-Husayn. I walked along beside them without any hesitation or embarrassment, as though we were all one family touring the sights of the festival."

"You have some nerve!"

"Occasionally. . . . I greeted them and they replied. We talked for a long time. Then Qamar inquired about you."

Kamal blushed a little as he asked, "And then?"

"We agreed I'd tell you and that later we'd all get together."

Kamal shook his head to show his distaste for the idea and said tersely, "Certainly not."

Fuad was astonished. " 'Certainly not'? I thought you'd be happy to meet them in the vaulted alley or the courtyard of a deserted house. Their bodies have filled out. They'll soon be women in every sense of the word. By the way, Qamar was wearing a wrap but no veil. I laughingly told her that if she had been veiled I wouldn't have dared speak to her."

Kamal said emphatically, "Of course not!"

"Why not?"

"I can no longer bear depravity." With a sharpness that betrayed his hidden pain: "I can't meet God in my prayers when my under-clothes are soiled."

Fuad suggested innocently, "Then wash and cleanse yourself before you pray."

Shaking his head in exasperation at being taken so literally, Kamal replied, "Water can't wash away sin."

He had wrestled with this issue for a long time. Whenever he had gone to meet Qamar he had been agitated by lust and anxiety, only to return home with a tormented conscience and a grieving heart. At the end of his prayers he would spend a long time fervently requesting forgiveness. Yet he would set off again in spite of himself, to return in torment and beg for forgiveness once more. Those days had been filled with lust, bitterness, and tor-ment, but then the light had burst forth. All at once he had been able to love and pray without any conflict. Why not? Love was a pure drop from the fountainhead of religion.

Fuad said somewhat plaintively, "My encounters with Narjis ended once she was forbidden to play outside."

Kamal asked him with interest, "Didn't that relationship trouble you, since you're a Believer?"

Lowering his eyes in embarrassment, Fuad answered, "Some things can't be helped." Then, as though to conceal his discom-fort, he asked, "Will you really refuse to take advantage of this opportunity?"

"Absolutely!"

"Merely on religious grounds?"

"Isn't that enough?"

Fuad smiled broadly and commented, "You always try to bear intolerable burdens."

Kamal replied emphatically, "That's the way I am. There's no need for me to be any different."

They exchanged a long look, which expressed Kamal's determination and defiance and reflected both Fuad's desire not to quarrel and his smile, which was like the sun's fiery rays sparkling merrily on the water. Then Kamal continued: "In my opinion, lust is a base instinct. I hate the thought of surrendering to it. Perhaps it was implanted in us merely to inspire us to struggle against it and to seek to rise above it, so we'll be fit to ascend to the truly human rank. If I'm not a man, I'm a beast."

Fuad hesitated a little. Then he observed calmly, "I think it's not all bad, for it motivates us to get married and have children."

Kamal's heart pounded violently without Fuad being aware of it. Was this what marriage was all about? He knew it was a fact but felt perplexed that people could reconcile love and marriage. It was a problem he did not confront with his love, because marriage had always seemed, for more than one reason, beyond his highest hopes. All the same, it was a problem requiring a solution. He could not imagine any felicitous link between himself and his beloved not based on her spiritual affection and on his ardent aspirations. It would resemble worship more than anything else. Indeed it would be worship on his part. What connection did marriage have to this?

"People who are really in love don't get married."

Fuad asked with astonishment, "What did you say?"

Even before Fuad's question, Kamal realized he had said something he did not intend to. For an awkward moment his confusion was apparent. He tried to remember Fuad's last words before this strange assertion had popped out. Although he had just heard them, it was with some effort that he recalled what Fuad had said about marriage and children. He decided to cover up his slip by adapting the meaning as best he could. So he said, "People who are really in love with ideals superior to life itself don't get married. That's what I meant to say."

Fuad smiled faintly – or perhaps he was trying not to laugh – but his eyes, like deep pools, betrayed none of his sentiments. He simply remarked, "These are serious matters. Talk about them now is premature. Everything in its own time."

Kamal shrugged his shoulders scornfully but confidently and said, "So let's postpone it and wait."

There was a mountain separating him from Fuad, but nonetheless they were friends. It was impossible to deny that the difference between them attracted him to Fuad, although it had repeatedly caused him anguish. Was it not time for him to go home? Solitude and communion with his soul called him. Thought of the diary slumbering in the drawer of his desk stirred the passions of his breast. A person exhausted from putting up with reality seeks relaxation deep inside himself.

"It's time to go home," he said.

78

THE CARRIAGE made its way along the banks of the Nile until it stopped in front of a houseboat at the end of the first triangle of streets on the road to Imbaba. Al-Sayyid Ahmad Abd al-Jawad descended at once, followed immediately by Mr. Ali Abd al-Rahim. Night had fallen, and darkness blanketed everything. The only exceptions were the widely spaced lights shining from the windows of the houseboats and other vessels lined up along either shore of the river channel downstream from the Zamalek Bridge, and the faint glow of the village at the end of the road, like a cloud reflecting the brilliance of the sun in a sky otherwise dark and heavily overcast.

Al-Sayyid Ahmad was visiting the houseboat for the first time, although Muhammad Iffat had leased it for the last four years, dedicating it to the romantic escapades and parties al-Sayyid Ahmad had denied himself since Fahmy was slain. Ali Abd al-Rahim went ahead to show him the gangplank. When he reached the stairs he warned his friend, "The stairway is narrow and the steps are steep with no railing. Put your paw on my shoulder and come down slowly."

They descended cautiously as the sound of water lapping against the riverbank and the prow of the boat caressed their ears. At the same time their noses were stung by the rank odors of nearby vegetation mixed with the scent of the silt that the floods at the beginning of September were lavishly depositing.

As Ali Abd al-Rahim felt for the doorbell by the entrance, he remarked, "This is a historic evening in your life and ours: the night the old master returns. Don't you think so?"

Tightening his grip on his friend's shoulder, al-Sayyid Ahmad replied, "But I'm no old master. The oldest master was your father."

Ali Abd al-Rahim laughed and said, "Now you'll see faces you haven't glimpsed for five years."

As though wavering, al-Sayyid Ahmad remarked, "This doesn't mean that I'm going to alter my conduct or deviate from my principles." Then after a moment of silence he continued: "Perhaps . . . maybe . . ."

"If you leave a dog in the kitchen with a piece of meat, can you imagine him promising not to touch it?"

"The real dog was your father, you son of a bitch."

Mr. Ali rang the doorbell. The door was opened almost immediately by an aged Nubian servant who stepped aside to allow them to enter and raised his hands to his head in welcome. Once inside they made for the door on the left, which opened on a small vestibule lit by an electric lamp hanging from the ceiling. The walls on either side were decorated with a mirror beneath which a large leather armchair and a small table were placed. At the far end of the room there was another door, which was ajar. Through it could be heard the voices of the guests, and al-Sayyid Ahmad was deeply moved. Ali Abd al-Rahim shoved the door wide open and entered. Al-Sayyid Ahmad followed and had scarcely crossed the threshold when he found himself confronted by his friends, who rose and came forward to greet him joyfully. Their delight was so great it virtually leapt from their faces.

The first to reach him was Muhammad Iffat, who embraced him as he quoted from a popular song: "The beauty of the full moon is shining upon us."

Ibrahim al-Far cited another song title when he hugged him: "Destiny has brought me what I've longed for."

The men then stepped back to let him see Jalila, Zubayda, and a third woman, who stood two steps behind the others. He soon remembered that she was Zanuba, the lute player. Oh . . . his whole past had been assembled in a single setting. He beamed, although he appeared slightly embarrassed. Jalila gave a long laugh and opened her arms to embrace him as she chanted, "Where have you been hiding, my pretty one?"

When she released him, he saw that Zubayda was hesitating an arm's length away, although a happy light of welcome illuminated her face. He stretched his arm out to her and she squeezed it. At that same moment she arched her painted eyebrows reproachfully and, referring to yet another song, said in a tone not free of sarcasm, "After thirteen years . . ."

He could not help but laugh wholeheartedly. Finally he noticed that Zanuba had not budged. She was smiling shyly, as though she thought their past acquaintance too slight for her to be forward. He held his hand out and shook hers. To encourage and flatter her he said, "Greetings to the princess of lute players."

As they returned to their seats, Muhammad Iffat put his arm around Ahmad's and made his friend sit beside him. He laughingly asked, "Did you just happen to drop by or has passion caught hold of you?"

"Passion caught hold of me, so I just happened to drop by."

At first he had been blinded by the warmth of the reunion and the jests of his friends when they welcomed him. Now his eyes could take in his surroundings. He found himself in a room of medium size with walls and ceilings painted emerald green. There were two windows facing the Nile and two on the street side of the boat. Although the windows were open, the shutters were closed. Hanging from the ceiling in the middle of the room was an electric lamp with a conical crystal shade, which focused the light on the surface of a low table holding the glasses and the whiskey bottles. The floor was covered with a carpet the same color as the walls. On each side of the room there was a large sofa divided in half by a cushion and covered with an embroidered cloth. The corners of the room were filled with pallets and pillows. Jalila, Zubayda, and Zanuba sat on the sofa farthest from the street, and three of the men on the one facing them. The pallets were strewn with musical instruments: lute, tambourine, drum, and finger cymbals. He took his time looking around. Then after sighing with satisfaction he said delightedly, "My God, my God, everything's so beautiful. But why don't you open the windows on the Nile?"

Muhammad Iffat replied, "They're opened once the sailboats stop passing. As the Prophet said, 'If you are tempted, conceal yourselves.'"

Al-Sayyid Ahmad quickly retorted with a smile, "And if you conceal yourselves, be tempted."

"Show us you're still as quick as you used to be," Jalila shouted as if challenging him.

He had intended his words to be nothing more than a joke. The truth was that he was anxious and hesitant about taking this revolutionary step and coming to the houseboat after the long

period of self-denial he had observed. There was something more
too. A change had taken place that he would have to unravel for
himself. He would need to look closely and attentively. What did
he see? There were Jalila and Zubayda, each of them as massively
beautiful as the ceremonial camel when it set off for Mecca with
the pilgrims. He had used that image to describe them in the old
days. They had perhaps even added to their mass of fleshly charms,
but something had come over them that was almost more easily
perceived by his emotions than his senses. No doubt it was
associated with the process of aging. Perhaps his friends had not
noticed it since they had not been separated from the women as he
had. Had he not been affected by age in much the same way? He
felt sad, and his spirits flagged. A man's most telling mirror is a
friend who returns after a long absence. But how could he pinpoint this change? Neither of the women had a single white hair,
for no entertainer would ever allow her hair to turn white. And
they had no wrinkles.

"Do you give up?" he asked himself. "Certainly not. Just look at
those eyes. They reflect a spirit that's fading, no matter how they
sparkle and flash. Fatigue disappears from sight momentarily
behind a smile or a jest, but then its full truth is apparent. You
can read in that look the obituary for their youth, a silent elegy.
Isn't Zubayda in her fifties? And Jalila's several years older. She
violently disputes that fact but will never be able to disprove it no
matter how often she denies it."

There was a change in his heart too. He felt aversion and
repulsion. It had not been that way when he arrived, for he had
come in breathless pursuit of a phantom, which no longer existed.
So be it. God forbid that he should willingly submit to defeat. . . .
"Drink, let yourself be transported by the music, and laugh. No
one will ever force you to do something you don't want."

Jalila said, "I didn't believe my eyes would ever see you again in
this world."

He yielded to an overwhelming temptation to ask: "How do
you find me?"

Zubayda intervened: "The same as ever. As big and strong as a
camel. One white hair shows under your fez. Nothing more than
that."

Jalila protested, "Let me answer, because he asked me." Then
she told al-Sayyid Ahmad, "You look the way you always did.

But there's nothing strange about that. We're all still youngsters."

Al-Sayyid Ahmad discerned her goal. Trying to seem serious and sincere, he replied, "You two have only increased in beauty and good looks. I wasn't expecting this much."

Examining him with interest, Zubayda inquired, "What has kept you away from us all this time?" She laughingly advised him, "If your intentions were at all good, you could have had an innocent rendezvous with us. Can't we ever meet unless there's a bed beneath us?"

Waving his arm in the air to toss back the sleeve of his caftan, Mr. Ibrahim al-Far retorted, "Neither he nor we know how to have an innocent rendezvous with you."

Zubayda grumbled, "I seek refuge with God from you men. All you want a woman for is sex."

Jalila laughed out loud and commented, "Mother's pet, you should thank your Lord for that. Could you have grown so splendidly fat if you had not been content to profit from sex?"

Zubayda told her critically, "Don't interfere with my interrogation of the accused."

With a smile al-Sayyid Ahmad said, "I was sentenced to five years of innocence without labor."

Zubayda pounced on him again and said mockingly, "Alas, poor boy! You deprived yourself of every pleasure, all of them, poor baby, so that the only ones to enjoy were food, drink, music, humor, and staying out till daybreak, night after night."

He answered apologetically, "These things are necessary for a grieving heart, but the other ones . . . "

Zubayda gestured toward him as though to say, "You're hopeless!" Then she remarked, "So, I've learned now that you consider us worse than all the other sins and transgressions put together. . . . "

As though remembering an important matter he had almost forgotten, Muhammad Iffat interrupted her by crying out, "Have we assembled from the ends of the earth just to talk? The glasses are staring down at us, but no one's paying any attention to them. Fill the glasses, Ali. Tune your instrument, Zanuba. And you, the accused gentleman, make yourself more comfortable. Do you think you're at school and can't remove any clothing? Take off your fez and cloak. Don't assume that your interrogation is over, but first all the court officials must get drunk. Then we can resume the interrogation. Jalila insisted that we shouldn't get intoxicated until 'the sultan of good times' arrived. At least that's what she said. This woman esteems you as highly as Satan does a chronic sinner. God's blessing on your relationship with her and hers with you."

Al-Sayyid Ahmad rose to slip out of his cloak, and Ali Abd al-Rahim went to serve as bartender, as usual. A few discordant whispers were emitted by the lute strings as they were being tested. Zubayda crooned gently. With her fingertips Jalila smoothed the strands of her hair and the neck of her dress where it fell between her breasts. Eyes watched Ali Abd al-Rahim's hands with longing as he filled the glasses. Al-Sayyid Ahmad sat down again with his legs tucked beneath him. His eyes wandered over the room and the people in it until they chanced to meet Zanuba's. A smiling look of recognition lit up their eyes. Ali Abd al-Rahim presented the first round of drinks. Then Muhammad Iffat said, "To good health and good love."

Jalila said, "To your return, Mr. Ahmad."

Zubayda said, "To right guidance when it follows error."

Al-Sayyid Ahmad said, "To those I love from whom I've been separated by grief."

They all drank. Al-Sayyid Ahmad raised his drink to his lips. Over the base of the glass he could see Zanuba's face. He was touched by its freshness.

Muhammad Iffat told Ali Abd al-Rahim, "Time for the second round."

Ibrahim al-Far added, "And the third should follow immediately so we can lay the groundwork properly."

As he set to work Ali Abd al-Rahim observed, "A group's servant is their master."

Ahmad Abd al-Jawad found himself watching Zanuba's fingers as she tuned the lute strings. He wondered how old she was, estimating that she was between twenty-five and thirty. He also asked himself why she was present. Had she only come to play the lute or was her Aunt Zubayda preparing to launch her in this profitable career?

Mr. Ibrahim al-Far said that just looking at the water of the Nile made him seasick, and Jalila shouted at him that he had made his mother sick in his day.

Ali Abd al-Rahim asked, "If a woman as big as Jalila or Zubayda were thrown into the water, would she sink or float?"

Al-Sayyid Ahmad answered that she would float, unless there was a hole in her. He wondered what would happen if he felt tempted by Zanuba and told himself that at present it would be a scandal, after five glasses it would be awkward, but after a whole bottle it would become a duty.

Muhammad Iffat proposed they drink to the health of the nationalist leaders Sa'd Zaghlul and Mustafa al-Nahhas, who would be traveling at the end of the month from Paris to London for negotiations. Ibrahim al-Far suggested that they drink a toast to the Labour Party leader Ramsay MacDonald, a friend of the Egyptians.

Ali Abd al-Rahim asked what MacDonald had meant by saying he could solve the Egyptian problem before he finished drinking the cup of coffee he had in front of him.

Ahmad Abd al-Jawad answered that he meant it took an Englishman, on average, half a century to drink a cup of coffee.

Al-Sayyid Ahmad remembered how alienated he had felt by the revolution after Fahmy had been slain and how he had gradually returned to his original pro-nationalist feelings because of the respect and esteem people showered on him as the father of a martyr. In time, he had found that Fahmy's tragedy had even become a source of pride.

Jalila raised her glass in the direction of al-Sayyid Ahmad as she said, "To your health, my camel. I've often asked myself whether you had really forgotten us. But God knows I understood and prayed God would grant you endurance and consolation. Don't be surprised, for I'm your sister and you've been a brother to me."

Muhammad Iffat asked mischievously, "If you're his sister and he's your brother, as you claim, then should you two have done what you used to?"

She emitted a laugh that reminded them of the old days, 1918 or before. She retorted, "Ask your maternal uncles about that, love child."

Glancing at Ahmad Abd al-Jawad slyly, Zubayda said, "I've thought of another reason for his long absence. . . ."

More than one person inquired what it was, while al-Sayyid Ahmad murmured pleadingly, "O God who veils our shortcomings, protect me."

"I suspect he's impotent like other men his age and has used his grief as a convenient excuse."

Shaking her head with all the affectation of a performer, Jalila protested, "He'll be the last to grow old."

Mr. Muhammad Iffat asked al-Sayyid Ahmad, "Which of these two opinions is right?"

Al-Sayyid Ahmad replied suggestively, "The first expresses fear and the second hope."

Jalila said with victorious relief, "You're not a man who disappoints a lady's hopes."

He thought about saying, "It's only when he's tested that a man is honored or despised," but was afraid he would be put to the test or that his statement would be understood as an invitation. Yet whenever he looked closely at them, he was overcome by a wish to hold back and to skip this opportunity. Before coming he would never have thought it possible. Yes, it was undeniable that a change had taken place. Yesterday was gone. Today was different. Zubayda was no longer the same, nor Jalila. There was nothing to justify the risk. He would be satisfied with the brotherly relationship Jalila had acclaimed and expand it to include Zubayda too. He said delicately, "How could a man grow senile when surrounded by such beautiful women?"

Looking at each of the men in succession, Zubayda asked, "Which of you is the oldest?"

Al-Sayyid Ahmad answered inaccurately but with apparent innocence, "I am. I was born just after Urabi's rebellion of 1882."

Muhammad Iffat protested, "Say anything but this. I've heard you were one of Urabi's soldiers."

Al-Sayyid Ahmad replied, "I was a soldier in their bellies, so to speak – just as people now call a child at home a pupil, even before he's started school."

Ali Abd al-Rahim pretended to be astonished and asked, "What was your late mother doing while you were inside a soldier going off to battle?"

After emptying her glass, Zubayda shouted, "Don't evade the question with your jokes. I'm asking you how old you are."

Ibrahim al-Far said challengingly, "Three of us are between fifty and fifty-five. Will you disclose your ages to us?"

Zubayda shrugged her shoulders scornfully and said, "I was born . . ."

She narrowed her kohl-enhanced eyes and looked up at the lamp as though trying to remember, but al-Sayyid Ahmad completed her statement before she could: "After the revolution of Sa'd Zaghlul Pasha in 1919."

They laughed for a long time until finally she waggled her middle finger at them. But it appeared that Jalila did not like the topic of conversation. She yelled, "Let's abandon this smear campaign. What difference does it make how old we are? Let the One who's in charge of the matter worry about it in His heavens. For us, a woman is young so long as she finds a man who desires her and one of you men is a boy so long as he can find a woman who wants him."

Suddenly Ali Abd al-Rahim shouted, "Congratulate me!"

When asked why, he shouted, "Because I'm drunk."

Ahmad Abd al-Jawad said that they ought to catch up before their friend was lost in the land of inebriation, whereas Jalila urged them to let him go on alone as punishment for his haste. Ali Abd al-Rahim retreated to a corner with a full glass in his hand, telling them, "Find another bartender."

Zubayda stood up to look for her wraps and check her handbag to make sure that her container of cocaine was still where she had left it. Ibrahim al-Far seized the opportunity provided by her absence to take the seat beside Jalila. He leaned his head on her shoulder, sighing audibly. Muhammad Iffat went to the windows overlooking the Nile channel and thrust the shutters aside. The surface of the water appeared to consist of a flowing pattern of darkness, except for still streaks of light traced on the undulating river by rays coming from the lamps of other boats where people were staying up late. Zanuba plucked the strings of her lute, and a rollicking tune sprang forth. Al-Sayyid Ahmad gazed in her direction for a long time. Then he rose to refill his glass. When Zubayda returned she sat down between Muhammad Iffat and Ahmad Abd al-Jawad, whose back she thumped.

Jalila's voice was raised in song: "One day you took a bite out of me. . . ."

Now it was Ibrahim al-Far's turn to shout, "Congratulate me!"

Muhammad Iffat and Zubayda started singing along with Jalila once she reached the words: "They brought me an antidote." When Zanuba joined the song, al-Sayyid Ahmad began looking at her again. Before he knew what was happening he was one of the singers too, and Ali Abd al-Rahim's voice lent its support from his corner.

His head still on Jalila's shoulder, Ibrahim al-Far called out, "Six performers and an audience of one: me."

Without stopping his singing al-Sayyid Ahmad told himself, "In the end, she'll comply with my wishes most willingly." Then he mused, "Is tonight to be a passing affair or the beginning of a lengthy relationship?"

Ibrahim al-Far rose unexpectedly and began dancing. The others all started to clap in unison. Then they sang together:

> So take me in your pocket,
> Between your belt and sash.

Al-Sayyid Ahmad wondered whether Zubayda would allow the tryst to take place in her house. When the song and dance were concluded, they vied with each other in trading jests and insults in rapid succession. Ahmad Abd al-Jawad began observing Zanuba's face stealthily whenever he came out with a joke, to judge its impact on her. The merry turmoil intensified, and minutes flew by.

"It's time for me to go," said Ali Abd al-Rahim as he rose to get the rest of his clothes.

Muhammad Iffat shouted at him angrily, "I told you to bring her with you, so the evening wouldn't be cut short."

Raising her eyebrows, Zubayda asked, "Who is this woman you're guarding so carefully?"

Ibrahim al-Far said, "A new girlfriend. A whale of a woman. The madam of an establishment in the Wajh al-Birka entertainment district. . . ."

Al-Sayyid Ahmad asked him with interest, "Who is she?"

Ali Abd al-Rahim answered laughingly as he drew his cloak tightly around him, "Your old friend Saniya al-Qulali."

Al-Sayyid Ahmad's blue eyes grew large and a dreamy look was visible in them. With a smile he said, "Remember me to her and convey my greetings to her."

As he twisted his mustache and prepared to depart, Ali Abd al-Rahim answered, "She asked about you and suggested I invite you to spend an evening at her house, after the time set aside for assignations. I told her, 'His eldest son, may the Prophet's name protect him, has reached an age at which it's considered a duty in their family to frequent Wajh al–Birka and other centers of depravity. Thus if his father came here, he would be in danger of bumping into his son.'" He grinned from ear to ear, said goodbye, and exited to the vestibule.

Muhammad Iffat and Ahmad Abd al-Jawad followed to see him out. They kept on chatting and laughing together until Mr. Ali left the houseboat. Then Muhammad Iffat touched his friend's arm and asked, "Zubayda or Jalila?"

Al-Sayyid Ahmad answered simply, "Neither one."

"Why? May God spare us evil."

He replied as though convinced, "A step at a time. I'll be content to pass the remainder of this evening in drinking and listening to the lute."

Muhammad Iffat urged him to take another step but did not press him once al-Sayyid Ahmad excused himself. They returned to the disordered room and resumed their seats. Ibrahim al-Far became the bartender. Signs of intoxication were clearly apparent in their flaming eyes, flowing conversations, and animated gestures. Following Zubayda's lead, they sang together: "Why is the sea laughing? . . ."

It was remarked that Ahmad Abd al-Jawad's voice rose until it almost drowned out Zubayda's. Then Jalila narrated some snatches of her romantic adventures.

"Since my eyes fell on you," al-Sayyid Ahmad reflected, "I've had the feeling that tonight will not pass without an adventure. How pretty the young girl is. Young? Yes, since she's a quarter century younger than you."

Ibrahim al-Far lamented the passing of the copper trade's golden age, during the war. With a thick tongue he told them, "Back then you would kiss my hand to get a pound of copper."

Al-Sayyid Ahmad commented, "When you need something from a dog, call him 'mister.'"

Zubayda complained about how drunk she was and rose to try to walk it off, going back and forth. They began to clap to keep time with her staggering steps. They called out in unison the words used to encourage children to walk: "A step at a time. Cross over the doorstep. . . . A step at a time. Cross over the doorstep." Wine paralyzes the organ that registers sorrow.

Jalila murmured, "That's enough for now." She rose and left the room. She went down the hall to the two cabins, which were opposite each other. She made for the cabin on the Nile side and entered it. Soon they could hear the creaking of her bed as it received her enormous body. What Jalila had done appealed to Zubayda. She followed her lead and headed for the other cabin. The creaking that her bed emitted was even louder.

Ibrahim al-Far said, "The bed has spoken."

From the first cabin a voice made its way to them, singing in imitation of the husky quality of the renowned singer Munira al-Mahdiya: "Darling, come."

Muhammad Iffat got up and answered in song as well: "I'm coming."

Ibrahim al-Far looked questioningly at Ahmad Abd al-Jawad. Quoting a saying of the Prophet, al-Sayyid Ahmad told him, "Unless you're embarrassed, do whatever you want."

The man rose and replied, "There's no need for bashfulness on a houseboat."

The coast was clear. This was the moment for which he had been waiting so long. The young girl put the lute aside. She sat cross-legged with the end of her dress draped over her legs. They silently exchanged a glance. Then she stared off into space. The silence was so charged with electricity that it was unbearable. When she stood up suddenly, he asked, "Where are you going?"

Hurrying through the door, she replied, "The bathroom."

He stood up too and took a seat next to hers. Picking up the lute, he began to strum on it while he wondered whether there was a third cabin.

"Your heart shouldn't pound that way, as though the English soldier were herding you ahead of him in the dark like that night after you'd been with Maryam's mother. Do you remember? Don't dwell on that, for it's a painful memory. She's returning from the bathroom. How fresh she looks!"

"Do you play the lute?"

"Teach me," he answered with a smile.

"You should stick with the tambourine, for you're expert at that."

He sighed and said, "Those days have vanished. How delightful they were. You were just a child! Why don't you sit down."

"She's almost touching you," he noticed. "How sweet the beginning of the chase is."

"Take the lute and play something for me."

"We've had enough singing, performing, and laughing. Tonight I've understood more than ever before why they missed you so much."

He smiled in a pleased way and asked craftily, "But you haven't had enough to drink?"

She agreed and laughed. He sprang like a charger to the table to fetch a half-filled bottle and two glasses. As he sat down he said, "Let's drink together."

"The delightful glutton – her eyes shine with deviltry and magic. Ask her about the third room. . . . Ask yourself whether it's to be just for one night or an affair. Don't wonder about the consequences. Ahmad Abd al-Jawad, no matter how exalted his stature, opens his arms to the lute player Zanuba. She used to serve you platters of fruit. . . . But you have a right to be happy as a reward for your fresh beauty. Conceit has never been one of my failings."

He saw that her palm grasping the glass was near his knee. He reached his hand out to caress it. She silently drew it back to her lap without looking at him. He asked himself whether flirting was in order at this late hour, especially when the host was a man like himself and the guest a girl like her. But he did not abandon his amiable tenderness.

He asked her suggestively, "Is there a third bedroom on the houseboat?"

She gestured toward the vestibule. Ignoring his suggestion, she merely answered, "On the other side."

Smiling and twisting his mustache, he asked, "Wouldn't it be big enough for both of us?"

Politely but without flirtatiousness, she answered, "If you feel sleepy, you'll find it quite large enough for you."

As though astonished, he asked her, "What about you?"

In the same tone she said, "I'm comfortable just the way I am."

He inched closer to her, but she got up and placed her glass on the table. Then she went to the sofa opposite him. She sat there with a serious look of silent protest sketched on her face. The man was amazed at her attitude. His enthusiasm waned, and he felt that his pride was under attack. He looked at her with a forced smile and then asked, "Why are you angry?"

She kept silent for a long time, her only response being to fold her arms across her chest.

"I'm asking why you're angry."

She answered tersely, "Don't ask questions to which you already know the answer."

He guffawed abruptly to proclaim his disdain and disbelief. Then he rose, filled both glasses, and handed one to her, telling her, "Lighten your spirits."

She took the glass courteously but set it on the table. "Thank you," she murmured.

After retreating to his place he sat back down, raised his glass to his lips, and drained it in one gulp. Then he laughed uproariously.

"Could you have anticipated this surprise? If it were possible to backtrack a quarter of an hour... Zanuba, Zanuba, just plain Zanuba... can you believe it? Don't let yourself be flustered by the blow. Who knows? Perhaps this is the fashion in coquetry now in 1924, you provincial has-been. How have I changed?... Not in any way. It's Zanuba. Isn't that her name? Clearly every man meets at least one woman who resists his advances. Since Zubayda, Jalila, and Maryam's mother are all wild about you, who is there but Zanuba, this dung beetle, to resist you? Endure it to overcome it. In any case the matter's not a catastrophe. Oh, look. See how pretty and firm her leg is. What a solid base she has. You don't think she's really rejected you, do you?"

"Have a drink, sweetheart."

In a voice both polite and determined she replied, "I will when I feel like it."

He fixed his eyes on her. Then he asked suggestively, "When do you think you'll feel like it?"

She frowned in a way that showed she understood his allusion but did not respond.

With a sinking feeling al-Sayyid Ahmad asked, "Doesn't my affection meet with any acceptance?"

Bowing her head to hide her face from his eyes, she begged him, "Won't you stop that?"

He was overcome by a surge of anger, which came in reaction to his sense of being rejected. In astonishment he asked her, "Why did you come here?"

Pointing to the lute lying on the sofa not far from him, she protested, "Because of this."

"Only?... There's no conflict between that and what I'm proposing."

Vexed, she asked him, "Against my will?"

Prey to the disquieting feelings of disappointment and annoyance, he said, "Of course not, but I don't see any reason for you to refuse."

She said coldly, "Perhaps I have some reasons."

He laughed loudly and dryly. Then, exasperated, he said sarcastically, "Maybe you're afraid of losing your virginity."

She glared at him for a long time and then said furiously and vengefully, "I only accept a man I love."

He would have laughed again but restrained himself. He was tired of these sad, mechanical laughs. He stretched his hand out to the bottle and impulsively poured himself half a glass. But he left it on the table. He began to look anxiously at the woman, not knowing how to extricate himself from the fix he had created himself.

"That viper and daughter of a viper only accepts a man she loves," he reflected. "Does that mean anything more than that she falls in love with a different man every night? It will be hard for you to save face after this disaster tonight. The gentlemen are inside, and you're at the mercy of this pampered musician. . . . Flay her with your tongue. . . . Kick her. . . . Shove her into the cabin against her will. . . . The best thing would be to turn your back on her and leave this place immediately. Our eyes have looks fierce enough to humble proud necks. . . . How charming hers is. Don't try to dispute her beauty. When a person loses his head, he will surely suffer."

"I didn't expect such harshness," he said.

He frowned and came to a decision. His face was scowling as he rose. Shrugging his shoulders disdainfully, he said, "I thought you would be gracious and charming like your aunt, but I was wrong. I have only myself to blame."

He heard the gentle smack of her lips as she cleared her throat in protest, but he went to get his cloak, which he put on rapidly. He was fully dressed in less than half the time he usually required to satisfy his taste for elegance. He had made his decision and was angry, but his despair was not yet total. Part of him still rebelliously refused to believe what had happened or at least found it easy to doubt. He picked up his walking stick but watched from one moment to the next for something to occur that would prove him wrong and satisfy the hopes of his wounded pride. She might suddenly laugh and thus slip back the veil of her bogus objection. She would rush to him, deploring his anger. She could leap in front of him to prevent him from leaving. When a woman cleared her throat in protest like that it was frequently a maneuver to be followed by her surrender. But none of these possibilities came to pass.

She remained sitting there, staring off into space, ignoring him as though she did not see him. So he quit the room for the vestibule and went from there to the entrance and on to the road, sighing with regret, sorrow, and rage. The fresh autumn air gently flowing through his garments, he walked along the dark road until he reached the Zamalek Bridge. There he got in a taxi and sped away. His intoxication and brooding thoughts made him oblivious to the world around him. When he began to pay attention he was already in Opera Square. As the vehicle circled around it on the way to al-Ataba al-Khadra Square, by the light of the lamps he chanced to see the wall of the Ezbekiya Garden. He fixed his eyes on it until a turn hid it from view. Then he closed his eyes, for he felt a stinging pain deep within his breast. He was conscious of a voice like a moan inside him, crying out in his silent world. It was praying God's mercy for his darling lost son. He did not dare express the prayer with his tongue, lest God's name be mentioned by one soaked in wine.

When he opened his eyes again, two large tears flowed down.

79

HE DID not know if what had gotten hold of him was a devil to be pelted with stones or a noxious disease. He had gone to sleep hoping the evening's foolishness, which he attributed to his inebriation, was finished. There was no question that drinking caused foolish behavior capable of spoiling pleasures and upsetting delights. When the morning light found him, he was tossing about restlessly in bed. The spray of the shower on his naked body dispelled thought from his mind and made his heart pound. He could see her face before his eyes. The whisper of her lips resounded in his ears, and the vibration of pain returned to his heart.

"You dwell on your romantic fantasies like an adolescent. People around you on the street greet you respectfully, saluting your dignity, piety, and neighborliness. If they only knew that you return their greetings mechanically while you dream of a girl who is an entertainer, a lute player, a woman who offers her body's favors for sale every night . . . if they only realized this, they would surely treat you to a scornful and pitying smile instead of a greeting. Once the viper says yes, I'll drop her with disdain and relief. What's come over me? What do I want? Are you getting senile? Do you remember the ravages time has visited on Jalila and Zubayda? That foul havoc was discovered by your heart, not discerned by your senses. But not so fast. Beware of being taken in by your imagination, for it will feed you like a tasty morsel to destruction. . . . It's all a question of that one white hair. What other reason could a lowly lute player have had for scorning you? Spit her out like a fly that slips into your mouth when you're yawning. Alas, you know you won't spit her out, if only because of a desire for revenge. I need to regain my respect, that's all. The girl must say yes. Then you can abandon her with no regrets. She hasn't enough attractions to merit the struggle. Do you remember her legs, her neck, and the carnal look in her eyes? If you had treated your pride with a spoonful of patience, you would have won enjoyment and delight that very evening. What cause is there for all this anguish? I'm in pain. Yes, I'm suffering. I'm oppressed by the humiliation I've encountered. I threaten to scorn her, but when I think of her, my body blazes with desire. Have some shame. Don't make yourself a laughingstock. I ask you to swear by your children, those who remain and the one departed. Your first wife, Haniya, was the only woman to leave you. You chased after her, and what did you gain from that? Don't you remember?

"The brawlers in the wedding procession dance, get drunk, assault people, and rove around. Then they apply their sticks liberally to the lamps, bouquets of roses, oboes, and guests, till shrieks drown out the trills of joy. That's the kind of man you should be. Be the brawler of the houseboat, and slay your enemies with indifference and neglect. How weak your enemies are, yet how powerful. . . . A yielding leg scarcely able to walk can crush immovable mountains. How atrocious September is, if it's hot, because of the humidity. How charming the evenings are, especially on a houseboat. Comfort follows distress.

"Think about your position and consider which way to go. What's fated to happen will become manifest. To advance is bitter and to withdraw terrifying. You used to see her all the time when she was a fresh young thing. She awakened nothing in you then. You passed by her as though she did not exist. What new development has there been to cause you to shun the ones you loved and love the one you shunned? She's no more beautiful than Zubayda or Jalila. If her looks provided her aunt with any competition, she would not let the girl accompany her. Yet you desire her with all your might. Oh! What's the use of being haughty? 'I only accept a man I love.' May you have a lizard for a lover, you bitch.

"Your pain's so great it's almost stifling. No one demeans a man as successfully as he does himself. . . . Will you go to the houseboat? That's not the most scandalous thing you could do. What about her house? Zubayda will be there: 'Welcome, do come in. Have you finally returned to your lair?'

"How should I answer her? 'I haven't returned to you. I want your niece.' What nonsense! Enough of this prattle. . . . Have you lost your mind? Enlist the support of al-Far or Muhammad Iffat. Al-Sayyid Ahmad Abd al-Jawad seeks a go-between for . . . Zanuba! Wouldn't it be better for you to leech this contaminated blood that's drawing you down to disgrace?"

Night had fallen on al-Ghuriya and the doors of its shops were locked when Ahmad Abd al-Jawad walked back toward his store, which was already closed. His steps were slow and his eyes searched the street and the windows. Two windows at Zubayda's house were lit up, but he could not know what was going on behind them. He walked some distance before retracing his steps. Then he continued on to Muhammad Iffat's residence in al-Gamaliya, where the four friends met each evening before heading off to their party together.

Addressing Muhammad Iffat, al-Sayyid Ahmad remarked, "How delightful nights are on the houseboat. My heart is yearning for it."

Muhammad Iffat laughed triumphantly and said, "It's yours for the asking anytime you want."

Ali Abd al-Rahim added, "You're really longing for Zubayda, you pimp."

Al-Sayyid Ahmad shot back earnestly, "Certainly not."

"Jalila?"

"The houseboat. Nothing else."

Muhammad Iffat asked him craftily, "Would you like it to be an evening limited to us men or should we invite our girlfriends from the old days?"

Al-Sayyid Ahmad laughed to admit his rout. Then he said, "Invite the ladies, you crafty son of a bitch. Let it be tomorrow, for it's getting late now. But I won't do anything more than enjoy the company and the fellowship."

"Ahem," said Ibrahim al-Far.

Quoting the words of a favorite song, Ali Abd al-Rahim recited, "I'm an accomplice against myself."

Muhammad Iffat said sarcastically, "Call it whatever you like. There are many names for it, but they all refer to the same act."

The next day he seemed to be discovering the coffeehouse of al-Sayyid Ali for the first time. He felt drawn there late in the afternoon and took a seat on the bench under the little window. When the owner came over to welcome al-Sayyid Ahmad, as though to justify this first visit to the establishment he told the man, "I was returning from some errands and experienced an urge for some of your refreshing tea."

"It appears that it will be anything but easy to repeat this visit. . . . Slowly, not so fast! Do you want to disgrace yourself in front of everyone? What's the use of this anyway? Would you truly like her to see you through the shutters so she can make fun of your downfall? You don't realize what you're doing to yourself. No matter how much you exhaust your eyes and dizzy your brain, she'll never show herself to you. What's even more upsetting is that she's watching you with amusement from the window. Why did you come? You want to feast your eyes on her. Confess. You wish to survey her supple body, see her smile and wink, and watch her hennaed fingers. What's the point of all this? Nothing comparable has ever happened to you before, not even with women superior to her in beauty, splendor, and renown. Have you been condemned to suffering and humiliation for the sake of such a worthless item? She'll never reveal herself, no matter how much you stare. You've attracted attention to yourself . . . al-Sayyid Ahmad Abd al-Jawad at the coffeehouse of al-Sayyid Ali, peeping out through a little window. How you have fallen! Do you think she hasn't divulged your secret? Perhaps all the members of the troupe have heard it. Possibly Zubayda herself is aware of it. Maybe everyone knows.

"'He held out his hand adorned with its diamond ring, but I brushed him aside. When he pleaded with me, I resolutely rejected this Mr. Ahmad Abd al-Jawad whom you praise so highly.'

"How you have fallen. The most appalling ignominy into which you can slip – no, which you insist on sliding into, since you realize better than anyone else the humiliation and disgrace your shameful act will bring – will be for your friends as well as Zubayda and Jalila to learn your secret. So what are you doing? It's a fact that you're skillful at masking your distress behind a joke, but once the waves of boisterous laughter roll away, the bitter reality will be revealed. This is painful, but what's most troubling is that you want her. Don't try to deceive yourself. You want her so badly you could die.

"What do I see?" he asked himself, looking at a wagon that stopped in front of the performer's home. The door opened without delay, and Ayusha the tambourine player came out, dragging behind her Abduh, who played the zitherlike qanun in their ensemble. The others followed. He realized they were going to a wedding. While he watched the door with an eagerness both mournful and passionate, he was painfully aware of the pounding of his heart. He recklessly stretched his head up, ignoring the people around him. Laughter rang out from the house. Then the lute in its rose-colored case appeared moments before its owner burst from the house in a gale of laughter. She placed the lute at the front of the wagon and climbed up with the help of Ayusha. She sat in the middle, so that all he could see of her was a shoulder visible in a gap between Ayusha and blind Abduh.

Al-Sayyid Ahmad clenched his teeth from both longing and annoyance. He followed the wagon with his eyes as, swaying back and forth, it set off down the street. The sight left a profound feeling of despair and humiliation in his breast. He asked himself whether he should get up and pursue them but did not move a muscle. He did nothing more than tell himself, "Coming here was crazy and stupid."

On the appointed evening he went to the houseboat in Imbaba. He had not been able to decide what to do, although he had mulled the matter over at length. He finally resolved to try to deal with his problems by exploiting the circumstances and opportunities that presented themselves. It was enough for him to be sure of seeing her, at first in the company of the others and then alone at the end of the evening. He would be able to size up the situation again and renew his advances, this time calling into play every form of enticement. He entered the boat somewhat timidly and in a condition that would have aroused his laughter and sarcasm had he observed it in someone else and understood the reasons for it.

He found his comrades there with Jalila and Zubayda but saw no trace of the lute player. He was welcomed warmly and had scarcely removed his cloak and fez to sit down when cheerful laughter rang out around him. Because he was habituated to it, he was able to blend into that happy atmosphere. He conversed, jested, and flirted, while combating his anxiety and setting aside his concerns. Yet his fears – like a pain that disappears temporarily when treated with an anesthetic – lay concealed beneath the mirthful current and did not dissipate. He kept hoping that a door would open and she would appear or that one of them would say something to explain her absence or to predict her speedy arrival. As the minutes dragged by wearily, his hopes faded, enthusiasm waned, and serene expectations became clouded.

"Which do you suppose was the chance occurrence: her presence the day before yesterday or her absence today? I won't ask anyone. The evidence suggests that your secret has been safely kept. If Zubayda knew, she wouldn't hesitate to make a disgraceful scandal out of it."

He laughed a lot and drank even more. He asked Zubayda to sing "My mouth laughs, but my heart of hearts weeps." Once he almost closeted himself with Muhammad Iffat to reveal what he sought. Another time he was on the verge of testing the reaction of Zubayda herself but restrained himself and escaped from that crisis with his secret and honor intact.

When Ali Abd al-Rahim rose at midnight to go to his girl-friend's establishment in Wajh al-Birka, he also got up, to every-one's surprise, to return home. They tried in vain to dissuade him or to get him to stay just one more hour. He departed, leaving behind him astonished and disappointed friends, whose hopes, aroused by his arrival at the designated time, had not been realized.

That Friday he set off for the mosque of al-Husayn shortly before the time for communal prayer. As he was walking down Khan Ja'far Street he saw her proceed from Watawit Alley to the street running by the mosque. Oh! . . . his heart had never pounded that way before. That was followed immediately by the total paralysis of all his psychic faculties. In a daze, he imagined incorrectly that he had stopped walking and that the world around him was silent as a tomb. He resembled an automobile that, although vibrationless, continues to move because of its momen-tum after its engine has been turned off and its roar silenced. When he came to his senses, he discovered that she had gotten far ahead of him. Without any deliberation or consideration he followed after her at once. He passed by the mosque without turning in. Staying some distance back, he pursued her to New Street. What did he hope for? He did not know. He was acting blindly and impulsively. Never before had he followed a woman on the street, not even when he was young. He began to feel anxious and wary. Then an idea both ironic and alarming caught him off guard. What if Yasin or Kamal should discover the secret of this surreptitious pursuit?

He took care to keep the distance between them as great as ever. His eyes feasted ravenously on her charming body while he was overcome by successive waves of passion and pain. Then he saw her leave the street to enter a goldsmith's shop belonging to an acquaintance of his named Ya'qub. He slowed his steps to allow time to plan. His feelings of anxiety and wariness increased. Should he not go back the way he had come? Should he walk past the store without paying any attention to her? Should he look inside and see what would happen?

He gradually drew closer to the store, and only a few paces remained when a daring thought occurred to him. Without any hesitation he quickly put it into action, ignoring the seriousness of its possible consequences. He would leave the flow of pedestrian traffic on the street to mount the sidewalk, where he would saunter past the store, anticipating that the owner would see him and, as usual, invite him in. Then he would accept the invitation. He proceeded according to this plan until he reached the store. Then he glanced inside as though by accident. His eyes met those of Ya'qub, who immediately called out to him, "Welcome to al-Sayyid Ahmad. Please come in."

Al-Sayyid Ahmad smiled amiably and made his way inside, where the two men shook hands warmly. The proprietor invited him to have a glass of carob sherbet, which he graciously accepted. He took a seat at the end of a leather sofa in front of the table on which the scales were placed, giving no indication of being aware of the presence of a third person in the store until he sat down. Then he saw Zanuba. She was standing opposite the proprietor and turning an earring around in her hands. He pretended to be astonished, and their eyes met. Since she smiled, he did so too. Then he placed his hand on his breast in greeting and said, "Good morning. How are you?"

Looking back at the earring, she said, "Fine, may our Lord be good to you."

Mr. Ya'qub was proposing to trade her the earrings for a brace-let, with the balance in cash, but they disagreed about the amount. Al-Sayyid Ahmad seized the opportunity provided by her involve-ment in the negotiations to feast his eyes on her cheek. It did not escape his attention that their haggling offered him a chance to intervene on her behalf. Perhaps, maybe . . . But not knowing what he had in mind, she spoiled his plan by returning the earring to the goldsmith and announcing that she had decided definitively against the exchange. She asked him to repair the bracelet instead. Then she said goodbye to him, nodded at al-Sayyid Ahmad, and left the shop. She accomplished all this more rapidly than he thought necessary. He was taken aback and upset. Listless embarrassment gained control of him. He tarried there with the proprietor, exchanging the usual pleasantries until he had drunk his glass of carob sherbet. Then he asked leave of the man and departed.

With profuse shame he remembered the communal prayer service he had almost missed. He was hesitant about going to the mosque, for he lacked the courage to proceed directly there following his pursuit of a woman during the time set aside for prayer. Had not his frolic terminated the requisite state of ritual cleanliness? Did it not render him unfit to stand before his Compassionate Lord? In pain he sadly gave up the idea of going to prayers and walked the streets aimlessly for about an hour. Then he returned home, reflecting once more on his sin. But even in those sensitive moments filled with regret, his mind never closed the door on Zanuba.

That evening he called on Muhammad Iffat early, before the other friends arrived, so that he could speak to him in private. He told his friend, "I have a favor to ask of you. Tomorrow evening invite Zubayda to the houseboat."

Muhammad Iffat laughed and said, "If you want her, why all this beating around the bush? If you had asked for her the first night, she would have opened her arms to you in the warmest possible welcome."

With some embarrassment al-Sayyid Ahmad replied, "I want you to invite just her."

"Only? What a selfish man you are, thinking of no one but yourself. What about al-Far and me? Why not make it a night to remember forever. We'll invite Zubayda, Jalila, and Zanuba too."

With apparent distaste Ahmad Abd al-Jawad asked, "Zanuba?"

"Why not? As a reserve to be tapped in case of need, she's perfectly adequate."

"How much it hurts me to hear that," al-Sayyid Ahmad said to himself. "So how could she, that chip off the old block, reject me and why?"

"Haven't you discerned my aim yet?" he asked his friend. "The fact is that I don't intend to come tomorrow night."

Surprised, Muhammad Iffat exclaimed, "You ask me to invite Zubayda! You say you won't come! What are these riddles?"

Al-Sayyid Ahmad laughed loudly to conceal his confusion. Then he felt forced to say almost desperately, "Don't be a mule.

I asked you to invite just Zubayda so Zanuba would be left alone in the house."

"Zanuba, you son of a gun."

After laughing long and hard he asked, "Why all this trouble? Why didn't you ask for her that first night on the houseboat? If you had moved a finger, she would have flown over and stuck to you like glue."

Despite his painful resentment, he smiled inanely. Then he said, "Carry out my instructions. That's all I want."

Twisting his mustache, Muhammad Iffat appropriated a phrase about idolatry from the Qur'an: "Feeble are the one who seeks and the one sought" (22:73).

With extreme earnestness Ahmad Abd al-Jawad requested, "Let this be a secret between us."

80

THE STREET was empty and pitch black when he knocked on the door at about nine o'clock. It opened after a while, but the person inside remained hidden. Then a voice that made his heart tremble asked, "Who is it?"

He replied calmly, "Me."

Entering without being invited, he closed the door behind him and found himself face to face with her. She stood on the bottom step, holding out her hand with the lamp, and gave him a surprised look before muttering, "You!"

He stood there silently for a time, and his faint smile revealed his apprehension and anxiety. Encountering no objection or anger on her part, he felt courageous enough to ask, "Is this how you welcome an old friend?"

She turned away and started back up the stairs saying, "Come in."

He followed her quietly, concluding from her having opened the door herself that she was alone and that the position of the maid Jaljal, who had died two years before, remained vacant. He accompanied her to the vestibule, where she hung the lamp on a nail near the door. She went on alone into the reception room, where she lit the large lamp hanging from the ceiling. This served to confirm his hunch. She came back out, gestured to him to enter, and vanished.

Proceeding into the room, he took a seat on the middle sofa, where he had been accustomed to sit in the old days. Removing his fez, he placed it on the pillow that divided the seat in half. He stretched his leg out as he cast a questioning look at his surroundings. He remembered the place as though he had only left it a day or two before. There were the three sofas, the arm-chairs, the Persian carpet, the three tables inlaid with mother-of-pearl. . . . Things were much as they had been. Could he remember the last time he had sat there? His memories about the music room and the bedroom were clearer and firmer, but he could not forget the first meeting he had had with Zubayda in this room, in exactly this spot. He could recall everything that had transpired. Back then no one had been more sure of himself and relaxed than he was. When would she return? What impact had his visit made on her? How overbearing would her conceit be? Had she realized that he had come because of her and not her aunt?

"If you fail this time, you can kiss the whole affair goodbye."

He heard the muffled tread of slippers. Then Zanuba appeared at the door in a white dress decorated with red roses. She wore a spangled sash and was bareheaded, and her hair was arranged in two thick braids that hung down her back. He greeted her... erect, smiling, and optimistic because of the care she had taken to adorn herself. She acknowledged his presence with a smile and motioned for him to sit down. She took a place on the sofa halfway down the wall on his right, as she said with mild astonishment, "Welcome. What a surprise!"

Al-Sayyid Ahmad smiled and asked, "What kind of surprise, I wonder?"

Raising her eyebrows enigmatically, with no hint as to whether she was in earnest or in jest, she replied, "Pleasant, of course."

"Since we've allowed our feet to carry us here," he reflected, "we must put up with whatever style of flirtation she chooses, whether delicate or heavy-handed."

He scrutinized her body and face calmly, as though to isolate in them the features that had tormented him and played havoc with his dignity.

They were both silent until she turned to look at him. Although she said nothing, the motion of her head suggested a polite inquiry, as if saying, "We're at your service."

Al-Sayyid Ahmad asked her slyly, "Will we have to wait long for the sultana? Hasn't she finished dressing yet?"

She gave him a strange look, narrowed her eyes, and then said, "The sultana's not at home."

Pretending to be amazed, he inquired, "Where do you suppose she is?"

Shaking her head and smiling mysteriously, she answered, "Your guess is as good as mine."

He thought about her reply a little and then said, "I would have supposed she kept you informed of her whereabouts."

She waved her hand modestly and said, "You think too highly of us." Then, laughing, she continued: "The time of military rule is over. If you want, you're in a much better position to keep abreast of her activities than I am."

"Me?"

"Why not? Aren't you an old friend of hers?"

Treating her to a deep, eloquent, smiling look, he said, "An old friend and a stranger are much the same. I wonder if your former friends keep up with you?"

She raised her right shoulder and made a face, proclaiming, "I have no friends, neither old nor new."

He started toying with one end of his mustache and responded, "Talk like that would only fool a person totally lacking in sense. A man with any wits about him could not imagine men seeing you and not rushing to become your friends."

"That's what gracious men like you might imagine, but that's all it is — figments of your imagination. You provide the evidence that I'm right. Although you're an old friend of this house, were you ever moved to provide me with a share of that friendship?"

He frowned in confusion. After some hesitation he said, "At that time I was . . . I mean, there were circumstances . . ."

She snapped her fingers and said sarcastically, "Perhaps it was those same circumstances, alas, that have kept the others away from me too."

In a quick, theatrical gesture he reared back against the sofa. Then he looked down his large nose at her, shaking his head as though asking God to rescue him. Finally he commented, "You're a puzzle. I hereby confess that I'm helpless before you."

She hid the smile his praise had inspired and pretended to be astonished as she said, "I absolutely do not understand what you mean. It's clear that we're mountains apart. The important thing is that you said you came to see my aunt. Is there any message I can give her when she returns?"

Al-Sayyid Ahmad laughed briefly. Then he replied, "Tell her, 'Ahmad Abd al-Jawad came to complain about me and didn't find you in.'"

"To complain about me? What have I done?"

"Tell her that I came to gripe about the harsh treatment you meted out to me. It's not becoming to a beautiful woman."

"What a perfect remark for a man who makes everything grist for his jokes and banter. . . ."

He sat up straight and said earnestly, "God forbid that I should make you the subject of my jokes or banter. I'm serious about my complaint. I think you understand the allusion perfectly well, but are flirting the way beautiful women do. They have every right to flirt, but they also have a duty to show mercy."

She pursed her lips and said, "Amazing!"

"It's not amazing at all. Do you remember what happened yesterday in the shop of Ya'qub the goldsmith? Was this stiff reception all that a person merits who is as proud of your friendship as I am and who has known you for as long? I wish, for example, that you had appealed to me to assist you in your negotiations with the goldsmith. I would have liked for you to give me a chance to put my expertise to work for you or for you to go even one step further and leave the whole matter to me, as though the bracelet were mine or its owner my good friend. . . ."

She smiled and raised her eyebrows in confusion. Then she said tersely, "Thanks."

He breathed in deeply, filling his wide chest. "A man like me is not satisfied with thanks," he said eagerly. "What good does it do a hungry man you turn away to tell him, 'May God provide'? A hungry man wants something to eat, food that's tasty and appealing."

She folded her arms across her breast and pretended to be astonished. Mockingly she asked, "Are you hungry, my master, sir? We have mallow greens and rabbit that will melt in your mouth."

He laughed loudly and said, "Fine! It's a deal. Mallow greens and rabbit supplemented by a glass of whiskey . . . then we'll amuse ourselves with some lute music and dancing and stretch out together for an hour while we digest the food."

She waved her hand at him as though to tell him to back off. Then she said, "My God! If we don't speak up, he'll try to bring in his donkey too. Keep your distance."

He folded the fingers of his right hand into a fist, which looked like a tightly puckered mouth. He began to raise and lower it deliberately, as he said oratorically, "Girl, don't waste precious time in talk."

Shaking her head, she replied proudly and flirtatiously, "You should say rather, 'Don't waste valuable time with middle-aged men.'"

Al-Sayyid Ahmad rubbed his broad chest with the palm of his hand in a gesture of friendly challenge. She shook her shoulders laughingly and said, "Even if..."

"'Even if'? What a baby you are! I won't rest easy till I teach you what you need to learn. Fetch the mallow greens, rabbit, whiskey, lute, and the sash for your dance outfit. Come on. Let's go!"

Bending the index finger of her left hand, she placed it by her left eyebrow as she wiggled the other one. She inquired, "Aren't you afraid the sultana will take us by surprise?"

"Never fear. The sultana won't return tonight."

She gave him a sharp, suspicious look and asked, "How do you know?"

He realized that he had said more than he should have and for a time almost fell prey to confusion. He rescued himself by saying adroitly, "The sultana would not stay out this late except for an emergency requiring her to stay over till morning."

She gazed at his face for a long time without speaking. Then she shook her head in a clearly ironic way and said with complete assurance, "How cunning middle-aged men are! Everything about them grows weaker except their guile. Do you think I'm a fool? Certainly not, by your life! I know the whole story."

He began playing uneasily with one end of his mustache again. He asked her, "What do you know?"

"Everything!"

She paused a little to increase his discomfort. Finally she continued: "Do you remember the day you sat in the coffeehouse of al-Sayyid Ali and peeked through the window? At that time your eye stared so intensely at the wall of our house that you dug a hole in it. When I got in the wagon with the other members of the troupe I asked myself, 'Do you suppose he'll follow along behind us yelling like a kid?' But you were craftier and waited for a better opportunity."

The man bellowed with laughter until his face grew even redder. Then, announcing his surrender, he said, "God, forgive us."

"But you forgot to be wise yesterday when you saw me at Khan Ja'far. You followed me and even entered Ya'qub's store after I did."

"Were you aware of that too, you niece of Zubayda?"

"Yes, prince of lovers, although I never imagined you would enter the store while I was inside. Before I knew what was happening there you were sitting on the sofa, even more daring than a lustful jinni. When you pretended to be astonished to see me, I almost let you have it with my tongue, but the circumstances forced me to be polite."

Striking his hands together, he laughingly asked, "Didn't I say you're a puzzle?"

She went on speaking, intoxicated by victory and delight: "And one night what do I know but the sultana tells me, 'Get ready, we're going to Muhammad Iffat's houseboat.' So I proceed to get ready. But afterwards I hear her say, 'It's al-Sayyid Ahmad who suggested the party.' So I smell a rat and tell myself, 'Al-Sayyid Ahmad doesn't suggest something merely out of the goodness of his heart.' I understand the trick and stay home, pretending to have a headache."

"How unfortunate I am! I have fallen into the clutches of a merciless person. Is there anything else?"

"Not much more . . . just the invitation for this evening, an invitation solely for the sultana."

"You couldn't have done any better if you were an experienced fortune-teller."

"How sweet your words are! Ape the preachers, you sinner."

"May God forgive you!" He laughed out loud and with gentle delight observed, "You understood what was up this time as well, but you stayed in. You didn't leave the house or hide yourself. . . ."

Before finishing his sentence he rose, went to her, and sat down beside her. He took the edge of her spangled sash and kissed it, saying, "My God, I testify that this beautiful creature is more delightful than the tunes of her lute. Her tongue's a whip, her love's an inferno, and her lover's a martyr. Tonight will have an importance for all of history."

She pushed him away and remarked, "Don't try to take me in with your chatter. Away! Go back to your place."

"From now on nothing will ever separate us."

She abruptly jerked her sash out of his hand and rose to step aside. Standing an arm's length away, she gazed at him curiously and silently, as though to reconsider some important matters. Then she said, "Why don't you ask what made me refrain from going to the houseboat the day Muhammad Iffat invited us, at your suggestion?"

"In order to stoke the flames of passion."

She gave three short laughs in succession and then was silent for a long time. Finally she said, "Not a bad idea, but a bit passé. Isn't that so, prince of sinners? The truth will remain a secret until I decide to reveal it in my own good time."

"I'll offer my life in exchange for it."

For the first time she smiled with genuine pleasure. Following her ironic glances, there was now a tender look in her eyes, like the calm after a storm. Her appearance proclaimed that a new strategy was being unveiled along with a new idea. Drawing a step closer to him, she gracefully stretched her hand out to his mustache, which she began to twist carefully. In a tone he had not heard her use before she said, "If you offer your life in exchange for this, what will be left for me?"

He felt the kind of deep repose he had not experienced since that unsuccessful night in the houseboat. It was as though he was winning a woman for the first time. He removed her hands from his mustache and held them between his large palms. Affectionately and gratefully he said, "I'm more delirious than words can say, mistress of all creation. May you be mine forever and ever. Death to anyone who refuses you anything you hope or ask for. Complete your benefactions to me and prepare our party. Tonight is unlike any other one. It deserves to be celebrated until dawn."

Stroking the palms of his hands with her fingers, she said, "Tonight really is unlike any other, but you'll have to be satisfied with just a little."

"A little! Is there to be a rebuff after all this tenderness? I can't wait patiently for you any longer."

He began to caress her hands. He unfolded her palms and admired the rose color of the henna with which they were decorated. She unexpectedly asked him in a laughing voice, "Do you read palms, old man?"

He smiled and said jokingly, "I'm renowned for my predictions. Would you like me to read your palm for you?"

She nodded in agreement, and he began to ponder her right hand, pretending to think deeply. With great interest he remarked, "I see a man who will be of great significance to you."

Laughing, she asked, "In a licit way, do you suppose?"

He raised his eyebrows as he continued to scrutinize her palm. Without even the slightest indication that he was not totally in earnest he replied, "No, illicitly!"

"I take refuge with God! How old is he?"

Not raising his head but looking up at her, he said, "That's not clear, but judged by his abilities, I'd say he's in the prime of youth."

She said slyly, "I wonder if he's generous."

"Oh!" he reflected. "It wasn't your generosity that pled your case with them in the old days."

"His heart's unfamiliar with stinginess."

She thought a little and then asked, "Would he be happy for me to stay on as a flunky in this house?"

"The calf is down," he told himself. "Go fetch the knives."

"No. He'll make you a lady without a peer."

"I wonder where I'll be living, under his wing."

"Not even Zubayda," he warned himself, "made you do this. There'll be no end of talk about you."

"In a beautiful apartment."

"An apartment!"

He was amazed by her tone of disapproval. Astonished, he asked her, "Wouldn't you like that?"

Pointing to her palm, she asked, "Don't you see flowing water there? Look carefully."

"Flowing water! Do you want to live in a bathhouse?"

"Don't you see the Nile? A houseboat or a sailboat?"

"Four or five pounds a month all in one blow, not to mention the other expenses. Oh," he reflected, "it doesn't pay to fall in love with lowlife."

"Why choose such an isolated place?"

She came so close to him that their knees were touching and said, "Your rank is not inferior to Muhammad Iffat's. And if you love me as much as you claim, then my luck should not be inferior to the sultana's. You would be able to pass your evenings there with your friends. That's my dream. Make it come true."

He put his arms around her waist and stood there, silently enjoying the softness and reassurance of her touch. Then he told her, "Whatever you want is yours, light of my life."

To thank him she placed her hands on his cheeks. Then she said, "Don't think you're going to give and get nothing in return. Always remember that it's for your sake that I'm leaving this house where I've spent my whole life. I won't be able to return. And remember that if I ask you to make me a lady, it's only because it's not appropriate for your mistress to be anything less than that."

His arms squeezed her waist toward him until her breast was pressed against his face. Then he said, "I understand perfectly, light of my eyes. You'll have everything you want and more. I want to see you the way you want to be. Now, prepare our celebration for us. I would like my life to begin with this night."

She grasped his arms. Smiling apologetically, she said gently, "When we're in our houseboat on the Nile."

He cautioned her, "Don't drive me crazy. Can you withstand my assault?"

She stepped back and said in a tone between entreaty and ultimatum, "Not in this house where I've worked as a servant. Wait till we're united in the new home, yours and mine. Then I'll be yours forever. Not before then. . . . I ask it for the sake of our new life together."

81

"GOOD NEWS, God willing," Ahmad Abd al-Jawad repeated to himself when he saw Yasin coming into his store. This visit was unusual and unexpected, reminding him of the time Yasin had come to discuss the intention of his mother, since deceased, to marry for the fourth time. Al-Sayyid Ahmad was sure his son had not called merely to say hello, pass the time of day, or chat about some routine matter he could bring up at home. No, Yasin would not visit him at the store unless the issue was serious.

After shaking hands with his son he invited him to have a seat and said, "Good news, God willing."

Yasin sat down near his father, who was behind the desk. The young man turned his back on the rest of the shop, including Jamil al-Hamzawi, who stood by the scales weighing a customer's goods. The young man looked at his father uneasily, confirming al-Sayyid Ahmad's suspicions. The proprietor closed the ledger in which he had been recording some figures and sat up straight in preparation for what was to come. The half-open safe was visible to his right. Above his head a photograph of Sa'd Zaghlul as Prime Minister was hung on the wall under an old framed inscription reading: "In the name of God."

Yasin's visit to the store was not a random one but the result of thoughtful deliberation. He considered this the safest place to present his proposal to his father. The presence of Jamil al-Hamzawi and of any customers who happened to be there should safeguard and protect him if his father's wrath were provoked. Yasin still took every precaution to avoid angering his father despite the security age afforded him and the good treatment he ordinarily received.

With great courtesy he said, "Please grant me a little of your precious time. Were it not absolutely necessary, I would not have dared to trouble you. But I am unable to undertake a step without your guidance and consent."

Al-Sayyid Ahmad smiled to himself at this extravagant display of courtesy and began to gaze apprehensively at his huge, handsome, fastidious son. He cast a comprehensive glance over him, taking in the young man's mustache, twisted just like his father's, dark blue suit, shirt with starched collar and blue bow tie, ivory fly whisk, and gleaming black shoes. In honor of this interview with his father, Yasin had altered his normal attire in only two respects. He had hidden the tip of his silk handkerchief, which usually peeked out from his jacket pocket, and had straightened his fez, which he ordinarily wore slanted to the right.

"He says he can't take a step without my guidance.... Bravo! Was he guided by me when he learned to drink or when he roved through the Wajh al-Birka entertainment district, which I forbade him? Did he consult me the night he assaulted the maid on the roof? Bravo! Bravo! What's behind this sermon from the pulpit?"

"Naturally, this is the least that one would expect from a reasonable person like you. I hope it's good news, God willing."

Yasin glanced around quickly at Jamil al-Hamzawi and the customers. Then he brought his chair closer to the desk and, summoning all his courage, said, "I've decided, with your consent and approval, to perfect my religious observance by marrying."

This was a genuine surprise, although unexpectedly a happy one. "But not so fast," al-Sayyid Ahmad reflected. It would be a pleasant surprise only under certain conditions. He would have to wait until he heard the most important part of the proposal. Were there no reasons for concern? Yes, there were: that introduction – so profusely polite and ingratiating – and his choice of the store as the setting for their talk. These warning signs could not escape an astute observer. Al-Sayyid Ahmad had long hoped his son would remarry and for this reason had urged Muhammad Iffat to allow Zaynab to return to Yasin. On concluding his prayers he would entreat God each time to grant Yasin good sense and a good wife. If he had not been apprehensive that his son would cause him and his friends embarrassment – as he had with Muhammad Iffat – al-Sayyid Ahmad would not have hesitated to find him another wife. Now he would bide his time to see if his fears were to be realized.

"An excellent decision.... I'm in full agreement with it. Have you selected any particular family?"

Yasin lowered his eyes for a moment. Raising them, he said, "I have found what I was seeking... an honorable family well known to us, because we have long been neighbors. The head of the household was one of your worthy acquaintances."

Al-Sayyid Ahmad arched his eyebrows inquisitively but said nothing. Yasin continued: "The late Mr. Muhammad Ridwan."

"No!" The word escaped from the father before he could gain control of himself. It popped out in a groan of protest, which he felt obliged to justify in order to conceal the true reason for his feelings. He had no trouble in finding an explanation: "Hasn't his daughter been divorced? Are there so few women in the world that you're willing to marry a divorcée?"

This objection did not come as a surprise. He had been expecting it ever since he had resolved to marry Maryam. He hoped he could overcome his father's opposition, which he imagined would focus on the superiority of a virgin over a divorcée or dislike for a woman who might remind them of Fahmy's tragedy. He had faith in his father's good sense and was optimistic that it would ultimately dismiss these two minor objections. Indeed he was relying heavily on his father's approval to defeat the genuine opposition he anticipated from his stepmother. He was at such a loss to counter it that he had thought of leaving his father's house and marrying as he saw fit. He would elope and present them all with a fait accompli. He could not bear the thought of angering his father, or he would have done that, even though it would have been hard for him to ignore the feelings of his second mother, who had been much more of a mother to him than his own. He felt he should do his utmost to sway her and convince her that he was right.

Yasin answered his father, "There are plenty of women in the world, but she's destined and fated to be mine. I'm not looking for wealth or prestige. A good family and an upright character are enough for me."

If al-Sayyid Ahmad found anything to console himself in the midst of these painful and awkward matters, it was having his undisputed opinion of his son confirmed again. How typical this was of Yasin! He was a man, or beast, who brought problems with him, whether coming or going. Had he conveyed good news or glad tidings he would not have been Yasin. Al-Sayyid Ahmad's opinion and estimation of his son would have been overturned.

"Perhaps he can be excused for not seeking a wife with wealth or prestige, but is the girl of good character? The mule is not to be blamed, for he quite naturally appears to know nothing about the conduct of the mother of the girl he wishes to marry."

Al-Sayyid Ahmad knew about her conduct from personal experience. Perhaps other men had preceded and followed him. What could he do? The girl might be well behaved, but it was certain her mother and home environment were less than ideal. It was sad, but he could not state his opinion openly, since he would be unable to provide the evidence needed to support his views, which would presumably be received with disbelief and annoyance by anyone hearing them for the first time. Worse still, he was afraid that allusion to these matters would motivate Yasin to investigate them thoroughly. Eventually the young man would find some evidence implicating him – al-Sayyid Ahmad. The result would be a scandal to end all scandals.

The issue was delicate and awkward. There was also a sharp thorn concealed within it – the old story linking her to Fahmy. Had Yasin forgotten that? How could he overlook the fact that he wanted to marry the girl his late brother had once sought? Surely this was odious behavior. Yes, it was, although he felt confident that Yasin's sentiments for his late brother were sincere. The harsh logic of life provided an excuse for people like Yasin. Desire was a blind and merciless tyrant. Al-Sayyid Ahmad knew that better than anyone.

The father frowned to make his displeasure clear to his son and said, "I'm upset with your choice. I don't know why. The late Mr. Muhammad Ridwan was really a fine man, but his paralysis prevented him from supervising his household for a long time before his death. I don't intend this observation to cast suspicions on anyone. Certainly not! But it's something that has been said and possibly some people have repeated it. So? The most important thing with me is that she's been divorced. Why was she divorced? This is one of many questions for which you must learn the answer. It's not right for you to trust a divorcée until you've investigated everything about her thoroughly. Perhaps that's what I was trying to say. The world's full of girls from good families."

Encouraged by his father's tone, which was one of discussion and counsel, Yasin said, "I've investigated, and others have too. I've discovered that the husband was at fault. He already had a wife and concealed that from them. Besides, he wasn't wealthy enough to support two households at the same time and was of bad character."

" 'Bad character'! Who's talking unashamedly about bad character? The mule's providing you with rare material for a whole evening's worth of jokes."

"So you've concluded your search and investigation," he said.

Evading the piercing eyes of his father, Yasin said with embarrassment, "This was an obvious first step. . . ."

Looking down, the man asked, "Didn't you realize that the girl is associated with painful memories for us?"

Seized by confusion, as his color drained, Yasin said, "It was impossible for me to overlook that, but theirs was an imaginary relationship with no foundation. I know for certain that my late brother was interested in her for only a few days and then forgot all about the affair. I'm almost positive he later felt relieved his efforts had failed, once he became convinced that, contrary to what he had imagined, the girl was not interested in him."

Was Yasin telling the truth or defending himself? His late brother had confided in him. Yasin was possibly the only person who could rightfully claim special knowledge about Fahmy's personal affairs. If only he was sincere! Yes, if only he was telling the truth, then al-Sayyid Ahmad would be delivered from a torment that kept him awake whenever he recalled it. He was afraid he had stood in the way of his deceased son's happiness. He often worried that his son had died brokenhearted or angry at his tyranny and obstinacy. These ideas had long gnawed at his heart. Did Yasin wish to relieve him of that?

With a sorrow deeper than Yasin could have imagined, he asked his son, "Are you really sure of what you're saying? Did he admit that to you?"

For only the second time in his life Yasin observed his father wilt. The first time had been the day Fahmy was killed. Al-Sayyid Ahmad entreated his son, "Tell me the whole truth without any sugarcoating. This matter interests me more than you can imagine." He was about to admit his pain but held the confession back, even though it was on the tip of his tongue. "The whole truth, Yasin!"

With no hesitation, the young man replied, "I'm certain of what I say. He told me himself. I heard it with my own ears. There's absolutely no doubt about it."

In other circumstances, this statement, or even a more eloquent one, would not have sufficed to convince him that Yasin was telling the truth. But he was eager to believe his son. Thus he accepted Yasin's words and believed them. His heart was filled with deep gratitude and a pervasive feeling of peace. At that moment at least, the question of Yasin's marriage no longer troubled him. He was silent for a time, enjoying the tranquillity that overflowed his heart.

Only slowly and gradually did his attention return to his predicament. After being blinded by emotion he could once more see Yasin clearly. Al-Sayyid Ahmad began thinking about Maryam, her mother, Yasin's marriage proposal, his own duty, and what he could and could not say. Then he told his son, "Whether or not that's true, I would like you to treat this question with deep thought and circumspection. Don't be in too great a hurry. Allow yourself time to consider and reflect. It's a question of your future, reputation, and happiness. I'm ready to choose another bride for you, if you promise me as a man of honor that you won't make me regret intervening on your behalf. So? What do you think?"

Yasin was silent as he thought it over. He was discouraged by the conversation's awkward turn, for it was fraught with embarrassing complications. His father was speaking with amazing self-restraint, but his anxiety and dissatisfaction were apparent. If Yasin insisted on having his way, the discussion could well create a lamentable split between them. But should he retreat in order to avoid this eventuality? Certainly not! He was no longer a child. He would marry any woman he wanted. If only God would help him retain the affection of his father. Yasin said, "I don't want to impose another burden on you. Thank you, Papa. All I hope for is your consent and approval."

Al-Sayyid Ahmad waved his hand impatiently. Rather sharply he said, "You refuse to open your eyes to the wisdom of my advice."

Yasin begged him warmly, "Don't get angry, Papa. Swear to God you won't get angry. Your approval's a boon I can't bear to be denied. Let me try my luck. Pray I'll be successful."

Ahmad Abd al-Jawad realized that he would have to accept the situation but did so mournfully and despondently. Perhaps Maryam was an honorable girl who would be a good wife, despite her mother's wildness. But it was beyond doubt that Yasin had not succeeded in choosing the most suitable bride or the finest family.

The matter was in God's hands. He could no longer simply dictate as he saw fit, without fear of rejection. Yasin was a responsible adult. Any attempt to impose his ideas on his son would only make Yasin rebel. Al-Sayyid Ahmad would just have to give in and ask God that it would end well.

He advised and cautioned his son, while Yasin responded with affectionate apologies, until there was nothing more for either of them to say.

Yasin left the shop convinced that he had obtained his father's consent and approval, but he knew the most serious obstacle awaited him at home. He also knew he would be moving. Merely thinking of adding Maryam to that household would be a form of insanity. He hoped to leave peacefully without causing any hard feelings or resentment. It was not easy for him to ignore the wishes of his stepmother or to appear ungrateful for her affection and care. He had never imagined that fate would force him to adopt this strange attitude toward home and family, but the situation was complicated and his options limited. His only viable alternative was marriage. Amazingly, he had grasped intuitively the feminine strategy working to entrap him. It was an ancient one that could be summarized in two words: seduction and evasion. But desire for the girl had gotten into his blood and had to be satisfied by any means available, even matrimony. It was equally astonishing that although he knew as much of Maryam's history as the others in his family – except, naturally, his father – this knowledge did not restrain or discourage him, for he was dominated by lust.

He told himself, "I won't worry about what's over and done with. I wasn't responsible for it. She'll begin a new life with me. That's when my responsibilities commence. I have unlimited confidence in myself. If my hopes turn out to be groundless, I'll cast her away like a worn-out shoe."

His decision had not been based on careful thought. What thinking he had done had been to justify his wild and unruly passions. He was accepting marriage this time as a substitute for the affair he had been denied. This did not mean that he harbored any antipathy to marriage or that he was using it only as a temporary expedient to attain his goal, for his soul, despite its restlessness, longed for wedded life and a stable home.

These ideas passed through his mind when he took his place beside Kamal at the coffee hour, that gathering he was presumably attending for the last time. With great regret he cast his eyes around the room with it sofas, colored mats, and large lantern hanging from the ceiling. As usual Amina was seated with her legs folded under her on the sofa between the doors to al-Sayyid Ahmad's bedroom and the dining room. Despite the heat, she was bent over the brazier, preparing the coffee. Her white scarf came down over her lavender housedress, which revealed how thin she had become. She was cloaked in a stillness at times stained by sorrow – like seawater that during a momentary calm becomes transparent enough to reveal what is beneath the surface.

Yasin felt sad and uneasy as he prepared to reveal his plan, but there was no alternative. After drinking his coffee, which seemed tasteless, he said, "By God, Mother, there's a question for which I want your advice." The glance he exchanged with Kamal revealed that the latter already knew what the subject would be and was equally concerned about its possible outcome.

"Good news, son?" Amina asked.

Yasin answered tersely, "I've decided to marry."

A look of happy interest appeared in her small honey-colored eyes. "That's a fine idea, son," she commented. "You shouldn't postpone it any longer." There was an inquisitive look in her eyes, but instead of voicing her question she said, as though trying to induce him to confess if there was any secret about it, "Speak to your father or let me. He'll be able to find you another wife better than the first."

With more solemnity than his stepmother thought the subject warranted, Yasin replied, "Actually, I have spoken to my father. There's no need for me to impose a new burden on him, for I've selected someone myself. Father has agreed, and I hope I may have your consent as well."

She blushed with embarrassment and delight at the importance he was attaching to her opinion. Then she replied, "May our Lord help you obtain everything good. As soon as you want, set up house on the first floor, which we've abandoned. But who's the fine girl you've decided to take for your wife?"

Yasin exchanged another glance with Kamal. Then with difficulty he said, "A neighbor. Someone you know."

With her eyebrows contracted in a thoughtful frown, she stared off into space, moving her index finger, as though counting out their neighbors to herself. Then she said, "You perplex me, Yasin. Won't you speak up and set my mind at rest?"

Smiling wanly, he answered, "Our closest neighbors. . . ."

"Who?" The word escaped from her in alarmed denial. She stared at his face. With a gloomy expression he lowered his head and pressed his lips together.

Her voice trembling, she asked once more as she pointed behind her with her thumb, "Them? Impossible! Do you mean what you're saying, Yasin?"

His only response was glum silence. She screamed, "What dreadful news! Those people who gloated over our greatest misfortune?"

He could not keep from crying at her, "I entreat you to swear to God you won't repeat that. It's false, imaginary. If my heart felt for a moment . . ."

"Naturally, you defend them. But it's a defense that won't deceive anyone. Don't wear yourself out trying to convince me of such an absurdity. My Lord! Why is a catastrophe like this necessary? They're riddled with defects and vices. Is there one good point to justify this outrageous selection? You said you'd obtained your father's consent. The man doesn't know anything about these matters, so you should say you duped him."

Yasin entreated her, "Calm down. I hate nothing more than making you angry. Calm yourself and let's talk quietly."

"How can I listen to you when you've given me this harsh slap? Say the matter's nothing more than a silly joke. Maryam? The girl's no good. You know that as well as anyone. Have you forgotten her scandalous past? Have you really forgotten that? Do you want to bring that girl into our home?"

Exhaling, as though to rid his breast of its sorrow and turmoil, Yasin said, "That's not at all what I said. Whether we live here or not is unimportant. What's really important to me is for you to examine the question seriously, setting aside your prejudice."

"What prejudice, fellow? Have I accused her falsely? You say that your father consented. Did you tell him about her scandalous flirtation with the English soldier? My Lord, what's come over children from good families?"

"Calm down. Let's have a quiet conversation. What's the use of all this agitation?"

She shouted at him with a sharpness that would have been totally alien to her in the old days, "I can't be calm about a matter threatening our honor." In a tearful voice she continued: "And you're insulting the memory of your precious brother."

Swallowing, Yasin said, "My brother? May God be merciful to him and grant him a spacious abode in paradise. This question doesn't reflect on his memory in any way. Believe me, I know what I'm saying. Don't disturb his repose."

"I'm not the one disturbing him. You are, since you want that girl. You know it, Yasin. You can't deny it." With great emotion she added, "Perhaps you wanted her even back then."

"Mother!"

"I'm no longer sure of anything. How could I be, after this betrayal? Has the world become so small and desolate that the only girl you can find to marry is one who made your brother's heart bleed? Don't you remember how sad he was when we all heard the story of the English soldier?"

Yasin spread his arms out in supplication, saying, "Let's postpone this conversation to another time. I'll prove to you that when my late brother heeded the call of his Lord there was no trace of emotion left for this girl. As for now, the atmosphere is no longer appropriate for a conversation."

She shouted angrily at him, "It's inconceivable that there should ever be an appropriate atmosphere for me to hear talk like this. You have no respect for Fahmy's memory!"

"I wish you could imagine how sad your words make me."

Her wrath reached its ultimate peak as she yelled, "What sadness? You never grieved for your brother! There were strangers who grieved for him more than you did."

"Mother!"

Kamal attempted to intervene, but his mother silenced him with a gesture of her hand. She cried out, "Don't call me 'Mother.' I've been a mother to you, but you never were a son to me or a brother to my son."

It was impossible for Yasin to stay any longer. He rose sadly and dejectedly, leaving the sitting room for his bedroom. Kamal soon joined him there, no less sad and dejected. He asked his older brother, "Didn't I warn you?"

Frowning, Yasin said, "I won't stay in this house another minute."

With alarm Kamal told him, "You've got to excuse her. You know my mother's changed. Even Father occasionally closes his eyes to her failings. It's just a flash of anger that will soon die down. Don't take her words seriously. That's all I ask."

Sighing, Yasin said, "I don't hold it against her, Kamal. I won't forget all the happy years because of one bad hour. As you said, she's to be excused. But how can I show her my face morning and evening when this is what she thinks of me?"

After some moments of gloomy silence, Yasin continued: "Don't think that Maryam broke our late brother's heart. Fahmy asked permission to marry her one day and Father refused. Fahmy set the matter aside and finally forgot all about it. How is the girl to be blamed for that? And why am I to blame if I want to marry her, six years after all that happened?"

Kamal said hopefully, "You haven't said anything that's not true, and Mother will quickly accept it. I trust your talk of leaving the house was merely a slip of the tongue...."

Shaking his head sadly, Yasin said, "I'm the one most distressed by my departure. But I'll leave sooner or later, for it's impossible to move Maryam in here. Don't think of my departure in any light but this. I'll move to my house in Palace of Desire Alley. Fortunately, my mother's apartment is still vacant. I'll stop by to see Father at the store and explain my reasons for leaving, omitting anything that might upset him. I'm not angry. I'm leaving the house most regretfully. I'll miss everyone here, starting with Mother. Don't be sad. The stream will return to its banks shortly. No one in this family has a vengeful heart, and your mother's is the purest of all."

He went to the wardrobe, opened it, and began looking at his clothes and belongings. He hesitated a little before executing his decision. Turning toward Kamal, he said, "I'm going to marry this girl. The fates have decreed that for me. God knows, I'm convinced that I'm not betraying Fahmy's memory. You recall, Kamal, how much I loved him. Why shouldn't I? If anyone gets hurt by this marriage, it will be me."

82

A SERVANT girl led Yasin into the parlor and then disappeared. He was visiting the home of the late Mr. Muhammad Ridwan for the first time ever. Spacious and with a high ceiling, the room was like those in his father's house. Its latticed balcony overlooked Palace Walk, and its two windows opened on the side alley where the door of the house was located. There was a small carpet on the floor. Couches and armchairs were lined up along the walls. The door and windows were hung with gray velvet curtains, which had grown pale with age. In a large black frame on the wall facing the door there was an inscription reading: "In the name of God." At the center of the wall to the right, above the main sofa, was a portrait of the late Mr. Muhammad Ridwan, showing him in the prime of life. Yasin picked the first couch on his right and sat down. He carefully examined the place until his eyes came to rest on the face of Mr. Muhammad Ridwan, who appeared to be looking at him with Maryam's eyes. Yasin smiled contentedly and started to flick his ivory fly whisk at nothing in particular.

A problem confronting him since he had first thought of coming to ask for Maryam's hand was the absence of any men in her house and his failure to obtain a female representative from his family. He had come alone, like "a branch cut from the family tree," as he put it. This embarrassed him a little, since he was a man who had absorbed from his milieu a pride in family and kin. All the same, he was confident that Maryam had prepared the way for him with her mother. The mere announcement of his visit would suffice to reveal the reason for it and to create a fine atmosphere for the performance of his mission.

The maid put in another appearance, carrying a coffee tray, which she placed on the table in front of him. As she retreated, she informed him that the senior mistress was on her way. He wondered if the junior mistress knew of his visit. What impact would it have on her delicate soul? He was going to carry her and her beauty off to Palace of Desire Alley, no matter what. Who would

have thought that Amina could get so angry? She used to be as
meek as an angel. "May God destroy grief!" he thought.

His father had grown angry too when Yasin had confessed at the
store that he had left home. But it had been a compassionate anger,
revealing how upset and sad he was.

"I wonder if Amina will tell him about Maryam's past. The
anger of a bereaved mother is a frightening thing, but Kamal
promised to persuade her to keep quiet about it. Back at Palace
of Desire Alley you encountered the first happy surprise of this
stormy affair . . . the death of your late mother's former lover, the
fruit seller. His place has been taken by a watchmaker. To the
grave!"

He heard someone at the door clear her throat. As he rose he
turned his eyes in that direction. In no time at all he saw Mrs.
Bahija. She was making her entrance sideways, since only one
panel of the door was open and the space would not have been
wide enough for her had she come in straight. Without meaning
to, he observed the lines demarcating the divisions of her vol-
uminous body. He could not help but marvel when her hips came
into view, for their crest almost reached the middle of her back,
while their bottom flowed down over her thighs. They were like
inflated balloons.

She advanced toward him with steps slowed by the extraordinary weight of her flesh and flab. Then she extended a soft white
hand, which emerged from the sleeve of her loose white dress. She
was saying, "Welcome! Welcome! You honor and illumine us."

Yasin shook her hand politely and remained standing until she
had seated herself on the nearest sofa. Then he sat down. He was
seeing her up close for the first time. Her long-standing ties to his
family and the status of matriarch she had acquired over the years
because of her age and prestige had kept him, when he saw her at a
distance in the street, from scrutinizing her the way he did other
women. Thus, it seemed he was making a new discovery. The
dress she was wearing covered her body from her neck down to
her feet, which she had concealed in white socks despite the warm
weather. The sleeves of her dress reached to her wrists, and her
head and neck were enveloped in a white scarf, the ends of which
spread over her breast and back. She presented a modest appearance suiting the occasion and fitting her age, which was close to
fifty, so far as Yasin knew. Yet she also appeared to be in splendid

health, suggesting a mind at rest and a youthful heart. One thing he noticed was that her face was free of makeup, although he knew her reputation for loving to show herself off to advantage. For that reason she had long been the established authority in the whole quarter for everything relating to feminine taste in clothes and cosmetics. He remembered how Amina had once defended this woman whenever anyone criticized her excesses of self-adornment but over the past few years had attacked Bahija for the most trifling reasons, accusing her of immodesty and of disregard for the decorum appropriate to her age.

"A noble step, Yasin Effendi."

"May God be generous to you." He almost ended his words with "Auntie," but at the last minute an instinctive fear prevented him, especially since he had noticed that she had not called him "my son," as he would have expected.

"How are all of you?" she asked. "Your father, Fahmy's mother, Khadija, Aisha, and Kamal?"

Feeling embarrassed because she had inquired about people who were hostile to her for no clear reason, he answered, "They're all fine. It's hoped you're in good health."

No doubt she was thinking of the cold reception she had received in his father's home after Fahmy's death. After a lifelong friendship she had been forced to stop visiting his family. What rude treatment! No, it had been the beginning of a cold war. His stepmother had soon announced her "feeling" that Maryam and her mother had not grieved sincerely for Fahmy. May God not bring any more evil, why? She had said it was inconceivable that they would not have heard back then in one way or another about al-Sayyid Ahmad's refusal to allow Fahmy to ask for Maryam's hand. If they had not heard, they could have deduced it. And if they knew about it, they would inevitably hold a grudge against Fahmy's family. She frequently repeated that she had heard Maryam at the funeral lament Fahmy's passing by saying, "I'm sorry you didn't get to enjoy your youth." Amina interpreted this to mean: "I'm sorry you didn't get to enjoy your youth, because your family stood in your way," adding to that interpretation whatever else her sorrow and grief dictated. No stratagem had succeeded in weaning her from her "feeling." Her behavior toward Maryam and Umm Maryam had quickly been transformed, and relations had been severed.

Still under the influence of his embarrassment and uneasiness, he said, "God curse the devil!"

Endorsing his sentiments, Bahija said, "A thousand curses! I've frequently asked myself what I did to be treated the way I have been by Mrs. Umm Fahmy, but I keep on praying that she may find some consolation, the poor lady. . . ."

"May God reward you magnificently for your noble manners and good heart. She's truly in a pitiful state and in need of consolation."

"But how am I at fault?"

"You're not. It's the devil, God's curses on him."

The woman shook her head as though she were an innocent victim and was silent for a time until she happened to turn to the cup of coffee, which seemed to be sitting forgotten on the tray. Gesturing toward it, she asked, "Haven't you drunk your coffee yet?"

Yasin raised the cup to his mouth and drained it. Putting it back on the tray, he cleared his throat a little and then began his spiel: "I've been distressed by the events ending the friendship between our two families, but there has been nothing I could do. We need to set that aside and let time take care of it. The fact is I didn't mean to arouse sad memories. That's not why I came. My visit has another purpose, one as far removed as possible from sad memories."

Bahija tossed her head as though to drive away sad thoughts. Then she smiled to show she was ready to hear something new. Her toss of the head and smile resembled a musician's change of key to introduce the vocalist and a new section of the song.

Put at ease by her smile, Yasin said, "My own life is not lacking in sad memories from my past. I refer to my first attempt at marriage. God did not grant me success in finding a proper wife. But I don't want to dwell on that. The fact is that I've come as a result of my decision – putting my trust in God – to turn over a new page in my life, anticipating nothing but good from my resolve. . . ."

Their eyes met, and he found a gratifying reception for his words. Had he been well advised to mention his first marriage? Would not news of the real reasons for the failure of that marriage have reached this woman?

"Don't worry," he told himself. "Her beautiful face gives every indication of unlimited tolerance. Her beautiful face! Aren't her features pretty? They certainly are. If it were not for the difference in age, she would be more beautiful than Maryam. Without any doubt she was more beautiful when she was young. No! She's more beautiful than Maryam, despite the difference in age. She really is!"

"I suspect you've guessed what I have in mind. I've come to ask for the hand of your daughter, Miss Maryam."

Her radiant face was illuminated by a smile in which pulsed a new vitality. She answered, "All I can say is: Welcome and welcome again. An excellent family and an excellent man. Last time we were unlucky and fell victim to a person of no character. This time a man seeks Maryam who can truly make her happy. By the grace of God she will be able to make him happy. Regardless of the separation occasioned by that misunderstanding we've been a single family for a long time."

Yasin was so delighted that his fingers began adjusting his bow tie with quick, unconscious strokes. With a blush on his handsome bronze face he said, "I thank you from the bottom of my heart. May God reward the sweetness of your words. As you observed, we are one family in spite of everything, and Miss Maryam is a girl who adorns our whole district with her lineage and character. May God grant each of us consolation with the other for our past misfortunes."

She murmured, "Amen," and sighed. Then she approached the table with her glorious body. She took the coffee tray and called Yasmina. Holding the tray, she turned around to give it to the maid, who was hurrying in. Suddenly Maryam's mother looked back to tell him, "We've enjoyed your visit," and surprised him staring at her massive hips. He was at once aware that he had been caught in a compromising position. He quickly lowered his eyes so that she would assume he had been looking at the floor, but it was too late. . . . He was rattled and began to ask himself what she would think of him.

After she sat down again he peeked at her stealthily and glimpsed her delicate smile, which seemed to say, "I saw you!" To hell with his eyes that did not know how to be modest. . . . He wondered what was going through her head. Yes, she was trying to pretend that she had not seen anything, but her attitude subsequent to her smile also implied: "I saw you!" The best solution would be for him to forget this blunder. But would Maryam become like her mother one day? When would that day come? The mother had qualities fate rarely handed out. What a woman she was! The best way to rid himself of these thoughts and disperse the cloud of suspicion would be to break the silence.

He said, "If my request meets with your approval, you will find me ready to discuss the important details at your convenience."

She laughed briefly but with an incandescence that made her face seem gentle and youthful. She said, "Why wouldn't we accept, Yasin Effendi? As the saying goes: Seek a neighbor with good lineage. . . ."

Blushing, he replied, "You enslave me with your graciousness."

"All I've said is the truth, with God as my witness."

After a brief silence, she asked, "Is your household in agreement?"

A serious look came into his eyes for a moment. Then he laughed listlessly through his nostrils. He said, "Let's not talk about my household and its affairs."

"May God shelter us from evil, why?"

"Not everything at home is as I would like."

"Haven't you consulted al-Sayyid Ahmad?"

"My father has given his consent."

She clapped her hands together and said, "Now I understand. Fahmy's mother? Isn't that so? She was the first to come to mind when you brought up the topic. Naturally, she hasn't agreed. So? Glory to the One who never changes. Your father's wife is a strange woman."

Shrugging his shoulders dismissively, he said, "That's neither here nor there."

She complained, "How often I've asked myself what I did wrong. How have I harmed her?"

"I don't want to abandon our current conversation for one that will only cause headaches. Whatever her doubts are, the important thing is for me to accomplish my goal. The only issue that concerns me is your consent."

"If you don't have room at your house, ours is at your disposal."

"Thanks! I have my own house in Palace of Desire Alley, out of this quarter altogether. As far as my father's house goes, I moved out of it some days ago."

She struck her breast with her hand and cried out, "She evicted you!"

Laughing, he replied, "Not at all. The matter did not reach that pass. It's just that my choice upset her for reasons from the past connected to my late brother." He gave her a look that suggested they both knew what he was referring to. "Since I could never find a truly convincing way to deal with her objections, I thought it appropriate to prepare a new home for my married life."

Raising her eyebrows and shaking her head somewhat dubiously, she asked, "Why didn't you stay at home until the wedding?"

He laughed to acknowledge his defeat and said, "I preferred to move away for fear the disagreement would become worse."

She commented ironically, "May our Lord resolve the dispute. . . ."

Before finishing, she rose again and went to the window overlooking the alley. She opened the shutter to let in the late-afternoon sunshine, for the door of the balcony no longer admitted sufficient light to illuminate the room. Although he was trying to be cautious, he caught himself, despite his good intentions, gazing stealthily at the precious treasure of her rump, which loomed up like the dome of a shrine as she knelt on the sofa and leaned over the window ledge to fasten back the shutters. The amazing sight he witnessed then made a vivid impression on his soul. His throat felt dry, and he wondered why she had not called the maid to open the window. How could she have permitted this unquestionably suggestive vision to appear before his eyes, which she had so recently caught in a suspicious look? Why and how? How and why? When it came to women, Yasin was perceptive and leery. He was aware of a doubt loitering at the threshold of his consciousness, not wanting to come in and not wanting to disappear. Wary because of the seriousness of the situation, he quickly closed his eyes. Either he was crazy or she . . . she was. Was there some other possibility? If only someone would extricate him from this dilemma. . . .

She straightened up, put her weight back on the ground, and then turned away from the window to regain her seat. Before she whirled around, he was quick to raise his eyes to the inscription of "In the name of God," in order to pretend to be engrossed in examining it. He did not turn his head toward her until the creaking of the couch informed him that she was seated. Then their eyes met. The crafty, smiling look of her eyes put him on notice that it was impossible to hide anything from her. She might just as well have told him in so many words, "I saw you!" For a time he felt agitated and confused. Everything seemed a puzzle to him. He was afraid of being unfair to her and of laying himself open to her accusations. He thought the best thing would be to watch his every move, for any slip could precipitate a scandal.

"The weather's still rather warm and humid...." Her voice sounded calm and natural and showed her desire to banish the silence.

He said with relief, "Yes, it certainly is."

He was reassured but in his imagination could still see the vision he had had of her at the window. Against his better judgment, he found himself mulling it over with fascination. He wished he had stumbled across something like that on one of his romantic excursions. If only Maryam had a body like her mother's! Was it not for something like this that the Qur'an said, "Let those who have aspirations compete"? (83:26.)

She assumed that his silence indicated he was brooding over her comment about his disagreement with his stepmother and almost playfully advised him, "Don't trouble your mind about it. There's nothing in the world worth worrying about." Then she waved her hands and head, making her body quiver in a special way, as though she wished to encourage him to spurn his cares.

He smiled obediently and murmured, "That's true."

All the same, he was doing his best to gain control of himself. Yes, something momentous had happened. Although it appeared to be nothing but a movement of her body meant to express her disdain for trivial worries and to encourage him to feel the same way, it was extremely significant, for it was clear evidence of wanton and licentious flirting. This gesture had escaped in a moment of forgetfulness. It interrupted the modest decorum she had observed with him throughout their interview and unintentionally disclosed her true nature. Or was it intentional? He could not decide between the two, but he no longer doubted that he was in the presence of a woman truly worthy of being the mother of a daughter with a past like Maryam's. Nothing could make him change his mind, for this flirtatious, dancing motion was not one a well-behaved woman would ever exhibit. His alarm lasted only for a fleeting moment and was quickly replaced by a sensation of sly and sensuous joy. He began to recall where and when he had

seen this gesture before.... Zanuba?... Jalila, the night she
surprised his father by storming into the men's reception room
at the Shawkat residence during Aisha's wedding. Yes, that
was it!

It occurred to him that despite her age the mother might be
more desirable and delightful than Maryam. Submitting to his
natural drives, he told himself that he should test her out and if
possible not hold anything back. He felt like laughing at the
novelty of the idea. He would be traveling a rugged path he had
never taken before, but he had never been one to restrain his
passions. Where would this conduct lead him? Would it be possible to give Maryam up for her mother? Certainly not! He had no
intention of doing that. But imagine a dog that finds a bone on its
way to the kitchen. Would it be ashamed to take the bone? In any
case, these were all just thoughts, flights of imagination, and
hypotheses. Let him wait and see. They smiled at each other in
the silence that once more had come between them. Her smile
was apparently that of a host greeting a guest, but his was flavored
with whispers of suffocating lust.

"You've brought light to our home, Yasin Effendi."

"Madam, there's no shortage of light in your home. You
illuminate the town and everything in it."

She laughed and threw her head back as she said softly, "May
God be good to you, Yasin Effendi."

He should have returned to the conversation about his proposal
or asked permission to leave, naming a date when they could
continue their discussion, but he began to cast peculiar glances at
her, some long and some short, without cease. The silence was
frightening. His looks conveyed messages that no one with eyes
could miss. He had to convey all his thoughts to her through these
looks alone to discover her reaction.

"Look before you leap, and down with High Commissioner
Allenby. Let her receive my fiery glance and tell me, if she's
sincere, what madman could ignore her naughty intentions and
assert her innocence. See how she raises and lowers her eyes
absentmindedly but at the same time with a suspicious clarity of
understanding. You can now say that the floodwaters have
reached Aswan and that the sluice gate must be opened. While
you're asking for her daughter's hand? After today anyone who
doesn't believe in insanity must be insane. At present I desire you

more than anything else. '*Après moi le déluge.*' The way you look certainly does nothing to discourage my hopes."

"Do you live alone in the Palace of Desire?"

"Yes."

"My heart goes out to you."

It was a phrase that either a devil or an angel might have uttered. Was Maryam listening behind the door?

"You've experienced loneliness here in your house. It's unbearable."

"Truly unbearable!"

She suddenly put her hand up to her scarf and jerked it from her head and neck, saying apologetically, "Excuse me. It's hot."

Her head in its orange kerchief and her spotless neck could now be seen. He gazed at her neck for some time with increasing anxiety. Then he looked at the door as though to ask who might be lurking behind it. God help the suitor who came asking for the hand of the daughter and fell into the clutches of the mother.

In response to her apology he said, "Make yourself comfortable. You're in your own house. There's no stranger present."

"I wish Maryam were home so I could break the good news to her."

His heart pounded as if directing him to attack. He asked, "Where is she?"

"With friends in al-Darb al-Ahmar."

"Farewell, reason!" he thought. "Your daughter's fiancé wants you and you want him. May God be merciful to anyone who thinks well of women. This woman must not have any sense. She's been our neighbor all my life, and I'm only finding out who she is today . . . a madwoman . . . a fifty-year-old adolescent."

"When will Miss Maryam return?"

"Late in the afternoon. . . ."

Wickedly he said, "I feel my visit's lasted too long."

"It's not a long visit, for you're at home."

With equal naughtiness he inquired, "I wonder whether I may hope you'll return my call."

She smiled broadly as though to tell him, "I understand what's behind this invitation." Then she bowed her head with embarrassment, although the theatrics of her gesture did not escape him.

He did not concern himself with that but started to describe the location of his house and of his apartment within that building.

Her head bowed, she smiled silently. Was she not conscious of
wronging and injuring her daughter in the clearest possible way?

"When will you honor me with a visit?"

She mumbled as she raised her head, "I don't know what
to say."

Confidently and firmly he said, "I'll answer on your behalf.
Tomorrow evening. You'll find me waiting for you."

"There are matters we must take into account."

"We'll deal with all of them . . . at my house."

He rose at once and started to go toward her, but she gestured
for him to keep his distance and looked toward the door to caution
him.

"Tomorrow evening," she said, as though her only goal was to
avert his attack.

83

THE HOUSE in Palace of Desire Alley came to know Bahija as a persistent visitor. Once darkness spread its veil, the lady draped herself in her wrap and proceeded to al-Gamaliya, heading for the home that had once belonged to Yasin's mother, Haniya. There she found Yasin waiting for her in the only furnished room of the apartment. They never referred to Maryam, except once when Bahija said, "I wasn't able to keep the news of your visit from Maryam, because our maid knows you. But I told her you had mentioned your interest in asking for her hand once the obstacles blocking your way in the family circle were overcome."

He was too astonished by her remark to care to comment and merely expressed his agreement and approval. Together they embarked on a life of sensual gratification. Yasin found the custodian of the treasured rump submissive to his every whim, and he himself was as free from inhibitions as a wild stallion. The hastily and frugally furnished room was not an ideal location for an affair, but Yasin went out of his way to create an attractive atmosphere by providing an ample supply of food and drinks so that their trysts would go well. He assaulted her repeatedly with an appetite that knew no limit or moderation.

Shortly before the first week had run its course Yasin began to feel bored. His lust was once more acting out the same cycle he had experienced before, as the remedy became an ailment. At least it did not come as a surprise to him. From the beginning he had harbored no good intentions whatsoever for that curious relationship and had not expected it to last. He obviously thought this romance in the parlor was no more than a passing fling but found that the woman was becoming attached to him. She wanted him and hoped he would be so satisfied with her that he would abandon the idea of marrying her daughter. He saw no alternative to humoring her, lest he put his pleasure at risk. He believed that time bore the sole responsibility for returning everything to normal.

Matters quickly sorted themselves out, probably faster than he had imagined possible. He had gone along with her, thinking that the novelty of her charms would be enough to sustain her appeal for several weeks or a month, but he must have miscalculated. Although her appearance was seductive, it had caused him to commit the greatest folly of a life littered with them. Her years lay concealed behind that beauty like a fever disguised by rosy cheeks. The pounds and pounds of flesh treasured in layers under the folds of her clothes were, as he put it, not quite as appealing when seen stripped naked, for nothing records the effects of a sad life so graphically as the human body. He even told himself, "Now I understand why women are crazy about clothes."

Considering all this, it was hardly strange that he referred to her as a "plague" once he tired of her attentions or that he should resolve to end their relationship. As his mad infatuation with her mother faded, Maryam regained her previous place in his affections. In fact, she had never lost it but had been overshadowed by this unexpected outbreak of passion – like the moon obscured by a fleeting cloud. How amazing! His desire for Maryam was no longer merely a response to his insatiable lust for women, even if that was the dominant factor. His interest in her was also furthered by his longing to start a family, an eventuality he considered both desirable and predestined.

Yasin reluctantly counseled himself to be patient until Bahija returned to her senses, assuming that she would tell him one day, "We've had enough fun. Now go to your bride." But his hopes found no echo in her. She visited him persistently night after night, growing ever more overwhelming and intense. He sensed that as time passed she was beginning to believe he was rightfully hers, as though he had become her property and the pivot around which her life revolved.

She did not think of the affair as a trivial or humorous escapade, and the frivolous, fickle, and reckless character she displayed convinced him that her aberrant behavior with him at their first meeting had not been an isolated phenomenon. Feeling that she was cheap, he scorned her. To his critical eyes her defects were magnified until he was totally disgusted with her. He decided to get rid of her at the first opportunity, although he was eager to avoid any rude conduct that would strew the path to Maryam with obstacles.

One time he said, "Doesn't Maryam ask what has become of me?"

With a reassuring toss of her head, she answered, "She knows perfectly well that your family's opposed."

After some hesitation he said, "I'll tell you frankly that we used to converse occasionally on the roof and that I assured her repeatedly of my determination to marry her, regardless of opposition from any quarter. . . ."

She gave him a piercing look and asked, "What are you trying to say?"

With feigned innocence he replied, "I mean she's heard that assurance from me and knows of my subsequent visit. She needs to be offered some convincing explanation for my disappearance."

With a nonchalance that stunned him, she said, "It won't harm her if you don't. . . . Not every discussion leads to a marriage proposal, and not every proposal leads to a marriage. She knows all that perfectly well." Then she continued in a low voice: "It won't hurt her to lose you. She's a young woman in her prime. She'll have a suitor tomorrow if not today."

Bahija seemed to be apologizing for her selfishness or else pointing out that it was she, not her daughter, who would be harmed by losing him. Her statement only made him more uneasy and annoyed. If that were not enough, he began to nourish fears about the effects of an affair with a woman twenty years his senior, because of the notion popular at the time that associating with a mature woman would rob a man of his youth. Thus the hours they spent together were charged for him with such tension and circumspection that he detested them.

He was in this state of mind when he ran into Maryam one day on New Street. He went up to her without any hesitation, greeted her, and walked along beside her as though he was one of her relatives. She frowned nervously, but he told her that he had been working to achieve his father's consent, which he finally had won, and that he was preparing his dwelling in Palace of Desire Alley for them. He apologized for the length of his absence, citing his many chores. Then he told her, "Inform your mother that I'll visit her tomorrow to make arrangements for the wedding."

He went off, happy that he had seized this unexpected opportunity. In his joyful exuberance he was indifferent to Bahija's possible reaction. That evening she arrived at her regular time, but devastated and agitated.

Even before she removed her veil she shouted at him, "You've sold me out, by hook and by crook."

Then she plopped down on the bed and nervously yanked off her veil. She said, "It never occurred to me that you could be so deceitful, but you're a sneaky coward like every other man in the world."

Gently and apologetically Yasin said, "It wasn't the way you imagine. The truth is that I met her by accident."

Scowling, she shouted, "Liar! Liar! By the truth of the One capable of making me see anything desirable in you, do you think I'll ever believe you again after what's happened?" Then she repeated his words in a sarcastic parody: "'The truth is that I met her by accident.' What kind of accident, buster? Let's suppose it really was an accident. Why did you speak to her in the street in front of all the passersby? Wasn't that the act of a wicked traitor?" Returning to her parody, she said, "'The truth is that I met her by accident.'"

Somewhat ill at ease, he said, "I suddenly found myself face to face with her. My hand stretched out to greet her. It wasn't possible for me to ignore her after our conversations on the roof. . . ."

Her face pale with rage, she screamed, "'My hand stretched out to greet her.' A hand doesn't reach out until you extend it. May your hand and you both be struck down. What you're saying is that you stretched your hand out to her to get rid of me."

"I had to greet her. I'm a man with feelings."

"Feelings? Where are they? You traitor and son of a traitor, may you choke on your feelings." After swallowing she continued: "What about your promise to come make all the arrangements for the wedding? Did that slip away from you too like your hand? . . . Speak, Mr. Sensitivity!"

With extraordinary calm he answered, "Everyone in the neighborhood knows I left my father's home in order to marry your daughter. It was impossible for me to ignore that when talking to her."

She yelled sharply, "You could have invented any excuse you wanted, if you'd had a mind to. You're not a person who is short on lies. But you wanted to get rid of me. That's the truth of it."

Avoiding her eyes, he said, "Our Lord knows of my good intentions."

She cast a long look at him and then asked defiantly, "Would you have me believe that you allowed yourself to be coerced into making this promise to her?"

Recognizing the danger of admitting that, he lowered his eyes and took refuge in silence. Panting with rage, she yelled, "You see! You're a liar, just as I said." Then she shrieked, "See? See? Traitor! Son of a traitor!"

After some hesitation he responded, "A secret can't remain hidden forever. Imagine what people will say if they find out about our affair. Indeed, imagine what Maryam will say. . . ."

She ground her teeth in her fury and said, "You swine! Why didn't you mention any of these reservations the day you stood before me slobbering like a dog? Oh, the male sex! Red-hot hell will be too mild a punishment for you."

He smiled a little and would almost have laughed had he not been restrained by cowardice. Then he said gently and affectionately, "We've had a wonderful time. I'll always remember it fondly. That's enough anger and bitterness. Maryam is your daughter and you more than anyone else desire her happiness."

She shook her head scornfully and said, "Are you the one to make her happy? May the walls be my witness: The poor girl doesn't know the kind of devil she's marrying. You're the lecherous son of a debauchee. May our Lord repay her for the mess she's getting herself into."

He said with the composure he had maintained from the beginning, "Our Lord will be able to set everything right. I have a sincere desire for a good marriage with a good wife."

She said derisively, "I'll cut my arm off if you're speaking the truth. We'll see. Don't cast any aspersions on my qualities as a mother. My daughter's happiness is more important to me than any other consideration. If you had not deceived and betrayed me, I would have been glad to hand you to her like a dirty shoe."

Yasin wondered whether the crisis was over. He was waiting for her to put on her veil and bid him farewell, but she did not budge. Time passed. She was sitting on the bed, and he was on the chair facing her. He had no idea how or when this strange and tense meeting would end. He stole a look at her and found her gazing at the floor, so lost and resigned that his fond feelings for her were momentarily revived.

"Will she start raving again? That's not unlikely. But it appears that she's aware of her delicate situation with regard to her daughter and will honor its demands."

Before he knew what was happening she had removed the wrap from around her shoulders and chest, mumbling, "It's warm." Then she scooted along the bed to the end, where she leaned back against the headboard. She stretched her legs out, paying no attention to her shoes, the heels of which were sinking into the folds of the comforter. She still appeared lost in her reflections. Did she simply have nothing more to say?

In a tone notable for its gentleness, he asked her, "Would you permit me to call on you tomorrow?"

She ignored his question for a minute. Then she threw him a look like a curse and replied, "You will be most welcome, you chip off the old block."

He smiled with satisfaction, although he felt her glances scorching his face. After a moment she said, "Don't think I'm a fool. I reconciled myself to this conclusion sooner or later. It's just that you've speeded it up in a way that . . ." Then she finished with a combination of resignation and scorn: "Whatever we have to do. . . ."

He did not believe her but pretended to. He told her that he was sure it was true and hoped she would forgive him and not harbor ill feelings. She did not bother to listen and made her way back to the edge of the bed. Then she threw her feet to the ground, stood up, and began to pull her wrap around her. She said, "I leave you in the hands of God."

He rose silently and went ahead of her to the door to open it. He led the way out but was caught off guard by a blow falling on the nape of his neck. Then the woman passed by him to the stairs, leaving him stunned, his hand spread over the place where she had hit him. Grasping hold of the railing, she turned back and said, "May you live to receive many more. You've hurt me much more than that. Don't I have a right to satisfy my craving for vengeance, even if only with a slap, you son of a bitch?"

84

"AL-SAYYID AHMAD, please excuse me if I tell you frankly that you're spending money recklessly these days."

Jamil al-Hamzawi said that in a tone blending subservient politeness with friendly informality. Although fifty-seven, he was strong and in good health. His hair was speckled with gray, but time had not decreased his energy in any respect. He still spent the whole day in constant motion, looking after the store and its customers, just as he had since he started working there, back when the business was first established. Over the years he had gained secure rights and the respect due him for his industry and honesty. Ahmad Abd al-Jawad considered him a friend. The affection he had shown his employee recently by helping enroll Fuad in Law School had only increased al-Hamzawi's loyalty and inclination to speak up frankly when necessary to avoid some harm or realize some gain.

Referring perhaps to their brisk sales in the frantic market, Ahmad replied in a reassuring tone, "Business is great, praise God."

Smiling, Jamil al-Hamzawi answered, "My our Lord multiply and sanction it. But I repeat what I've said of you, that if you had embraced the mores of the merchant along with his profession, you would be a wealthy man today."

Ahmad grinned with satisfaction and shrugged his shoulders. He earned a lot and spent a lot. How could he regret the pleasures he gained from life? He had never lost track of the need to keep his income and expenditures in balance and always kept a reserve on hand. Aisha and Khadija were both married. Kamal was beginning the final stage of his schooling. Why should he not enjoy some of the good things life had to offer? But al-Hamzawi was not over-stating the case when he accused his boss of squandering money, for in fact he had been anything but economical and judicious of late. His expenses took many forms. Gifts devoured a substantial sum. The houseboat was squeezing him dry. His mistress was demanding sacrifices of him. In short, Zanuba was pushing him to spend money extravagantly, and he was allowing himself to be manipulated, putting up little resistance. He had not been like that in the past. Of course he had spent lavishly, but no woman had ever been able to sway him from a steady course or to force him to spend recklessly. Back then he had been confident of his powers. He had not cared much whether he responded to all his mistress's requests. If she was coy with him, he would pretend to lose interest in her, for he was proudly aware of his youthful virility. Nowadays, desire for his lover had subjected his will to hers and made the expenses appear trivial to him. He seemed to have no object in life beyond retaining her affection and winning her heart. But how vainglorious her affection was! What a refractory heart she had! The truth of his situation was not hidden from him, and he felt saddened and hurt by it. He remembered his salad days with longing and sorrow, although he did not acknowledge that they had departed. Yet he did not lift a finger to make any serious attempt to resist. That was beyond his power.

Al-Sayyid Ahmad told Jamil al-Hamzawi with apparent irony, "Perhaps you're wrong to consider me a merchant." Then with resignation he added, "Only God is well-to-do."

Some people came in, and al-Hamzawi was busy looking after them. No sooner was al-Sayyid Ahmad left to his own reflections than he noticed a person who, after filling the doorway to capacity, was strutting toward him. This was a surprise. He recalled at once that he had not laid eyes on this figure for four years or more. Moved solely by politeness, he rose to greet her, saying, "Welcome to our honored neighbor."

Maryam's mother held out a hand covered with a corner of her wrap as she said, "Thank you, al-Sayyid Ahmad."

He invited her to sit down, and she took the chair she had used on a day that was now part of history. He sat back down wondering about this new development. He had not seen her since she came to call on him at the store a year after Fahmy's death, when she had attempted to get him to resume his visits to her house. He had been amazed at her daring then. Not having recovered from his grief, he had treated her gruffly and bade her farewell coldly. Why was she coming back today? He looked her over and found her unchanged. She was plump and elegant, wearing a fragrant perfume. Her eyes sparkled over the top of her veil. But her finery could not conceal the advance of time and the lines under her eyes. She reminded him of Jalila and Zubayda. How heroically these women risked their lives in the battle for life and youth. . . . Amina had only too quickly fallen prey to her sorrows and allowed her bloom to fade.

Bahija brought her chair close to the desk and said in a low voice, "Excuse me, al-Sayyid, sir, for this visit. Necessity has its own laws."

Looking dignified and grave, al-Sayyid Ahmad immediately replied, "Welcome to you. Your visit is an honor and a favor for us."

Smiling, she answered in a tone that revealed her gratitude, "Thank you. Praise to God I've found you in good spirits and good health."

He in turn thanked her and prayed that she would be well and strong. Then she was silent for a few moments before saying with concern, "I've come for an important reason. I was told he had consulted you in due time and received your consent. I refer to Yasin Effendi's request to marry my daughter Maryam. Was I correctly informed? This is what I've come to discover."

Ahmad Abd al-Jawad lowered his eyes to keep her from reading in them his resentment at her words. He was not deceived by her pretense at concern for his consent. Let her try her wiles on some other man unfamiliar with what lay hidden behind them. He for one knew beyond the shadow of a doubt that it was all the same to her whether he gave his consent or withheld it. Did she not realize why he had not accompanied Yasin on his visit to her? Even so, she had come to force him to proclaim his approval and for some other reason, which would shortly be revealed.

He looked up at her with calm eyes and said, "Yasin told me of his plan and I wished him success. Maryam has always been like a daughter to us."

"May God grant me the blessing of your being favored with a long life. This marriage tie will be a prestigious honor for us."

"I thank you for your compliment."

She said fervently, "I'm pleased to tell you frankly that I postponed announcement of my consent until I could be certain of yours."

"Bitch!" he exclaimed to himself. "She probably announced her approval even before seeing Yasin."

"Mrs. Umm Maryam, I can only repeat my thanks."

"For that reason, the first thing I told Yasin Effendi was: 'Let me be sure your father agrees before anything else, for every other consideration is negligible compared to his wrath.'"

"My God, my God!" She had no sooner stolen the mule than she was busy throwing ropes around his master.

"Coming from you, such a noble statement is hardly unusual."

With triumphant enthusiasm she continued her verbal offensive: "Al-Sayyid, sir, you're a man after our own heart, the best anyone would boast of in our whole quarter."

The guile of women and their coquetry – how fed up he was with both. Could she possibly imagine that he was wallowing in the dust to pursue the affections of a lute player once scorned by drunkards?

He replied modestly, "God forgive me."

In a sad tone, her voice rising enough so that he was afraid those at the far end of the store would hear her, she said, "I was very sad to learn he had left his father's home."

Al-Sayyid Ahmad shook his head to caution her not to speak too loudly. Before she could say anything more, he commented with a frown, "The fact is, his conduct angered me. I was amazed he had done such a stupid thing. He should have asked my advice first, but he carried his belongings to Palace of Desire Alley. Only then did he come to apologize to me! A juvenile prank, Mrs. Umm Maryam. . . . I lectured him, ignoring his alleged disagreement with Amina. That was a silly reason for him to give in an attempt to justify even more foolish behavior."

"By your life, that's exactly what I told him. But Satan is ingenious. I also advised him that Mrs. Amina is not to be blamed. May our Lord console her for her sufferings. In any case, from someone like you, al-Sayyid, sir, pardon can be hoped."

With a flick of his wrist he seemed to say, "Let's drop this."

She commented ingratiatingly, "But I'll only be satisfied with a full pardon and your approval."

"Pshaw!" If only he could tell her frankly how disgusted he was with all of them: her, her daughter, and the great mule.

"Yasin's my son in any event. May God guide him to the right path. . . ."

She leaned her head back a little and left it there while she savored the pleasures of success and victory. Then she continued in a gentle voice: "May our Lord be gracious to you, al-Sayyid Ahmad. On my way over, I asked myself, 'Do you suppose he'll disappoint me and send me away empty-handed? Or will he treat his old neighbor the way he used to, in the past?' Praise God, you always live up to people's expectations. May God extend your life and enjoyment of health and strength."

"She thinks she's pulling the wool over my eyes," he told himself. "And she's entitled to. You're a failure as a father. Your best son has died, the second's a loss, and the third is headstrong. This has all happened over my dead body, you bitch."

"I can't thank you enough," he said.

Bowing her head, she observed, "Whatever I've said of you is far less than you deserve. How frequently I confessed that to you in the past. . . ."

"Oh, the past! Close that door, by the life of the mule whose acquisition you've come to record." He spread his hand across his chest to express his thanks.

She said dreamily, "Why not? Didn't I love you more than any man before or after you?"

This was what she wanted. Why had he not realized it from the first moment? "She hasn't come for Yasin or Maryam but for me. No, you've come for your own sake, you whom time has not changed in any respect save to deprive you of youth. But not so fast. . . . Can you really bring back a day that's over and done with?"

He allowed her remark to pass without comment, limiting himself to a smile of thanks. She grinned so broadly that her teeth were visible through her veil.

Somewhat critically she said, "It seems you don't remember a thing. . . ."

He wanted to apologize for his apparent disinterest without hurting her feelings. He said, "I no longer have a mind in my head capable of remembering anything."

She cried out sympathetically, "You've grieved far more than you should. Life can't tolerate or allow this, when you – if you'll excuse me for saying it – are accustomed to a pleasant life. The grief that would affect an ordinary man one carat has a twenty-four-carat impact on you."

"It's a sermon intended to benefit the preacher," he reflected. "If only Yasin was as easily satiated as I am. Why do I find you repulsive? You're certainly more obedient than Zanuba and incomparably less expensive. It seems my heart has developed a will to suffer."

With a combination of humility and cunning he asked, "How can a grieving heart laugh?"

As though glimpsing a ray of hope she quickly said with enthusiasm, "Laugh so your heart may laugh. Don't wait for it to laugh first. It's out of the question to think it will laugh all by itself after it's suffered from depression for such a long time. Resume your old life. Its joy, now slumbering, will return to you. Search out the things that delighted you in previous times as well as your former lovers. How do you know that there are no hearts that have stayed true to you, yearning for you, despite your long avoidance of them?"

Despite his better judgment his heart was transported by such delight that his thoughts strayed. This really was the way people ought to speak to Ahmad Abd al-Jawad. Words like these, accompanied by the tinkling of glasses, had caressed his ears during their parties. If only the lute player heard praise like this, perhaps she would curb her excesses. "Too bad it's someone you loathe who is praising you," he brooded.

In a tone that gave no hint of his secret delight, he said, "Those days have passed."

She reared back in protest and said, "By the Lord of al-Husayn, you're still a young man. . . ." Smiling modestly, she continued: "You're a camel and as handsome as the full moon. Your time isn't up and never will be. Don't consider yourself old prematurely. Or let others make that decision, for they may see you in a different light than you do yourself."

He replied politely but in a tone that graciously expressed his desire to terminate their conversation: "Rest assured, Mrs. Umm Maryam, that I'm not killing myself with grief. I've found various amusements to distract me from my sorrow."

Her enthusiasm waning a little, she asked, "Does that suffice to raise the spirits of a man like you?"

"My soul aspires to nothing more," he answered contentedly.

He seemed to have flustered her, but she pretended to be at ease as she said, "Thank God I've found you with the peace of mind and tranquillity I wish for you."

Then there was nothing more to say. She rose and held out a hand covered with the end of her wrap. They shook hands and, preparing to depart, she said, "I hope I leave you in good health."

She left, averting her eyes because she was unable to conceal their disappointed look.

85

THE SUARÈS omnibus went down al-Husayniya Street, and then its two emaciated horses began to traverse the asphalt of al-Abbasiya Street, as the driver goaded them on with his long whip. Kamal was sitting at the front of the vehicle at the end of a bench close to the driver. With a slight turn of his head the boy could see al-Abbasiya Street stretching out in front of his eyes. It was wider than the streets he was used to in the old part of town and so lengthy that it appeared to have no end. The surface was level and smooth, and the houses on either side were huge with spacious grounds and lush gardens.

He admired al-Abbasiya greatly, and the love and respect he harbored for that area bordered on reverence. The underlying reasons for his admiration were the district's cleanliness, its careful planning, and the restful calm reigning over its residences. All these characteristics were alien to his ancient and noisy district. His love and respect were attributable to al-Abbasiya's being the homeland for his heart and the residence for his love, since it was the location of his beloved's mansion.

During the past four years he had come this way repeatedly with an alert heart and fine-honed senses. Thus he had everything memorized. Wherever he looked, he found an image that was familiar enough to be the face of an old friend. All of the region's landmarks, sights, side streets, and many of its residents were associated in his mind with thoughts, emotions, and fantasies which in their totality had become the central focus of his life and the hub of his dreams. Wherever he turned he found an invitation for his heart to prostrate itself in prayer.

He removed from his pocket a letter he had received two days earlier. It had been sent by Husayn Shaddad to inform him of his friend's return from the beach. Hasan Salim and Isma'il Latif had also come home. Kamal was invited to meet them at Husayn's house, and the Suarès was taking him there. He looked at the letter with an eye that was dreamy, thankful, loving, reverent, adoring, and devoted, but not merely because it had been sent by his true love's brother. Kamal assumed that before Husayn wrote this letter the paper had been placed somewhere in the house. Her beautiful eye might have seen it as she passed or her fingers could have touched it, even accidentally. His hunch that the paper had lain near her transformed the letter into a symbol of something divine, which his spirit desired and his heart sought.

He read through the letter for the tenth time until he reached the sentence: "We returned to Cairo on the evening of October first." Without his knowing it, she had been in the capital for four days. Why had he not realized that? Why had he not sensed her presence there, whether by instinct, emotions, or intuition? How had the desolation that had enveloped him all summer long been able to spread its dark shadow over these four blessed days? Had his unbroken despair rendered him insensitive and dull? At any rate, his heart was throbbing now, and his spirit was soaring blissfully. He was looking down from a towering pinnacle. From that vantage point the world's features seemed encircled by diaphanous and luminous halos, like reflections of things in the angelic world. His mind was aflame with vital energy, intoxicating delight, and drunken exaltation. But even at this moment he was haunted by pain, which for him was as constant an accompaniment to the happiness of his love as an echo is to sound. In the old days when his heart was empty of love and oblivious, the Suarès had carried him along this same route. What feelings, hopes, fears, and expectations had he experienced then? All he could remember of life before love was a set of bare-bones memories, which seemed worthless to him now that he had recognized the value of love. But he also longed for them whenever the pain was too great. Yet his mind was so overwhelmed by love that these previous memories almost seemed figments of his imagination. He had begun to date his life by love, saying, "That happened before love, or B.L., and this took place after love: A.L."

The vehicle stopped at al-Wayliya, and Kamal put the letter back in his pocket. He got out and headed for Palaces Street, his eyes fixed on the first mansion on the right, at the edge of the desert. Viewed from the exterior, this two-story mansion seemed a massive, lofty structure. It fronted on Palaces Street, and behind it there was a spacious garden. The tops of tall trees were visible over a gray wall of medium height that surrounded both the mansion and its garden, tracing out a vast rectangle, which extended into the desert. This image was imprinted on the pages of his mind, for he was captivated by the residence's majesty and enchanted by its magnificence. Its grandeur appeared to him to testify to the worth of the owner. Some of the windows that he could see were shuttered and others were hidden by curtains. This seclusion and reserve seemed to symbolize his beloved's distinction, purity, inviolability, and mystery, ideas reinforced by the expansive gardens and the desert, which stretched out to the horizon. Set here and there through the garden were towering palm trees. Ivy vines scrambled up the sides of the house, and intertwining jasmine branches sprawled over the garden walls. This vegetation besieged his heart with clusters of memories like fruit on a tree. They whispered to him of ecstasy, pain, and devotion. They were a shadow of the beloved, a breath from her spirit, and a reflection of her features. Joined to what he knew of the family's exile in Paris, they provided an atmosphere of dreamy beauty. They were comparable to his love in their lofty sanctity and allusions to the mysterious world of the unknown.

As he approached the gate of the mansion, he saw the doorman, the cook, and the chauffeur sitting together on a nearby bench, as they usually did in the afternoon. When he reached them, the doorman stood up and announced: "Husayn Bey is waiting for you in the gazebo."

Kamal went in, greeted by the blend of fragrances from the jasmine vines and from the carnations and roses in pots arranged on either side of the steps, which were a short distance inside the gate and led to a large veranda. Kamal veered off to the right on a side path between the mansion and the garden wall. It conveyed him to the top of the garden near the back porch of the house.

The walk through these sacred precincts was an ordeal for his pounding heart. He was treading underfoot a surface her feet had once traversed. His reverence was so great he could scarcely continue. He would have liked to stretch his hand out to the wall of the mansion to seek its blessing, as he had once at the sepulchre of al-Husayn, before he learned it was nothing but a symbol. In what area of the mansion might his beloved be disporting herself at the moment? What would he do if she favored him with one of her fascinating glances? If only he would find her in the gazebo, then his eye would be rewarded for all its forbearance, longing, and sleeplessness.

He looked around the garden and back to the rear wall, where the desert began. From the street side of the house, the afternoon sun was striking the tops of the trees, the palms, the sprays of jasmine covering the walls in every direction, and the circles, squares, and crescents of assorted flowers and roses, which were separated by paths of stone mosaic. Kamal went down the center walk that led to the gazebo in the middle of the garden. Husayn Shaddad was visible in the distance along with his two guests, Hasan Salim and Isma'il Latif. They were sitting on rattan chairs grouped around a circular wooden table on which glasses were set beside a water jug. Hearing cries of joy from Husayn, Kamal realized that they had noticed his arrival. His friends immediately stood up to greet him, and he embraced each of them, for they had been separated all summer long.

"Praise God for your safe arrival."

"We've missed you a lot."

"How brown your faces have gotten. Now there's no difference between you and Isma'il."

"You're the European among us darker types."

"Soon everything will return to normal."

"We were asking ourselves why we don't get tans from the sun in Cairo."

"Who is brave enough to expose himself to the sun in Cairo — except someone wanting to get sunstroke?"

"What's the secret of this tanning process?"

"I remember we had an explanation of it in one of our courses; yes, perhaps in chemistry. Over the years we studied the sun in different subjects like astronomy, chemistry, and physics. In which of those do we find an explanation for tanning?"

"This question is moot. We're done with our secondary studies."

"So give us news of Cairo, then."

"No, you've got to tell me about Ra's al-Barr, and then Hasan and Isma'il need to tell us about Alexandria. Just wait. There's time for every topic."

The gazebo was nothing more than a round wooden roof supported by a massive post. The ground there was covered with sand and encircled by pots of roses. Its furnishings were

limited to the wooden table and the rattan chairs. The young men
sat near the table in a half circle facing the garden. They were
obviously happy to be reunited, as the summer had separated
them, except for Hasan Salim and Isma'il Latif, who usually
spent the summer in Alexandria. They laughed at the slightest
provocation and occasionally just on looking at each other – as if
recalling comic memories. Kamal's three friends were wearing silk
shirts and gray trousers, but he had on his lightweight gray suit. He
considered the visit to al-Abbasiya a formal occasion. In his own
district, he roamed everywhere content to put a jacket over his
ankle-length shirt.

The surroundings spoke to Kamal's heart and shook it deeply.
He had been smitten by love in this gazebo. Only this garden
shared his secret with him. He was fond of these friends both out
of friendship and because they were part of the saga of his love. All
these things talked to his heart of love. He wondered when she
would appear. Could the gathering conclude without his ardent
eyes catching a glimpse of her? To compensate himself, he cast
long looks at Husayn Shaddad whenever he could, regarding him
with more than a friend's eye. The young man's relationship to
Kamal's beloved lent him a mysterious enchantment. In addition
to love, Kamal came to harbor admiration, veneration, and wonder for his friend. There was a marked resemblance between
Husayn and his sister. It was visible in his black eyes, tall slender
build, and thick, straight black hair as well as in his gestures and
postures, which were distinguished by gracious refinement. The
only major differences were his large hooked nose and his fair
complexion, tanned by the summer sun.

Since Kamal, Husayn, and Isma'il had been successful in the
baccalaureate examination that year – although admittedly the first
two were seventeen and the third twenty-one – they discussed the
examination and related issues pertaining to their futures. Isma'il
Latif raised the topic. When he spoke, he craned his head up as
though to conceal his short stature and light build – compared
with those of his three companions. All the same, he was muscular
and sturdy. The caustic, ironic look of his narrow eyes, his sharply
pointed nose, his thick eyebrows, and his strong wide mouth were
sufficient warning to anyone tempted to attack him.

Isma'il said, "We were one hundred percent successful this year.
Nothing like this has ever happened before, at least not where I'm

concerned. I ought to be in my final year at the University like Hasan, who began Fuad I School with me the same day. When my father saw my number listed in the newspaper among the students who passed, he said sarcastically, 'I wonder whether God will let me live long enough to see you graduate from the University.'"

Husayn Shaddad commented, "You're not far enough behind to justify your father's despair."

Isma'il said ironically, "You're right. Two years in each grade is hardly remarkable." Then, addressing Hasan Salim, he continued: "And probably you're already planning what you'll do when you finish University."

Hasan Salim was in the final year of Law School. He realized that Isma'il Latif was inviting him to announce his goals for the future. But Husayn Shaddad answered Isma'il first: "There's no reason for him to worry about that. He'll surely land a position in the judiciary or the diplomatic corps."

Hasan Salim emerged from his haughty silence. His handsome face with its fine features had an argumentative look. He asked defiantly, "Why should I believe you?"

He prided himself on his industry and intelligence and he wanted everyone to acknowledge them. No one disputed that, but likewise no one was forgetting he was the son of Salim Bey Sabry, superior court judge. To have a father like that was a distinction far more significant than intelligence and industry.

Husayn Shaddad avoided any reference that would rile his friend and said, "Your superior success is the guarantee you're seeking."

Isma'il Latif would not let him enjoy this praise. He said, "And there's your father. I reckon he's far more important than good grades."

Hasan met the attack with unexpected nonchalance. Either he had grown tired of Isma'il's teasing, since they had been together almost every day all summer long, or he had started to think his friend a chronic complainer whose comments should not be taken seriously. The friendship linking the young men did not rule out bickering and wrangles, which occasionally became intense but did not weaken their relationship.

Glaring at Isma'il mockingly, Hasan Salim asked, "What about you? What have your agents been able to come up with for you?"

Isma'il laughed out loud, revealing his sharp teeth, yellow from smoking, which he had been one of the first to embrace in secondary school. He answered, "An unsatisfactory result. Medicine and Engineering didn't accept me, because my overall average was too low. That left only Commerce and Agriculture. So I chose the former."

Kamal was upset that his friend had ignored the Teachers College, as though it was not worth considering. All the same, since he could have attended Law School and there was no dispute about its high status, his choice of the other instead seemed so noble that it helped console him for his lonely sorrow.

Husayn Shaddad laughed in a charming way that showed off his attractive mouth and eyes. He said, "Oh, if only you had chosen Agriculture! Imagine Isma'il out in the fields spending his life with farm laborers. . . ."

Isma'il answered with conviction, "That's not for me, not even if the fields were in downtown Cairo, on Imad al-Din Street."

Then Kamal looked at Husayn Shaddad and asked, "And you?"

Husayn looked off into the distance thoughtfully before he replied, granting Kamal an opportunity to scrutinize him. How fascinated he was by the idea that Husayn was her brother – that his friend kept her company in their home the way he had once lived together with Khadija and Aisha. It was hard for him to picture that. Husayn sat with her, conversed with her, spent time alone with her, and touched her.

"Touches her? He has meals with her! I wonder how she eats? Does she make little noises with her lips? Does she eat regional specialties like mallow greens or beans in oil? That's difficult to imagine too. What's important is that he's her brother."

Kamal could touch the hand that touched hers. If only he might inhale the fragrant perfume of her breath at one remove from her brother. . . .

Husayn Shaddad replied, "Law School on a provisional basis."

Was it not conceivable that Husayn would become friends with Fuad Jamil al-Hamzawi? Why not? Law School was no doubt a truly admirable institution, since Husayn was enrolling in it. Attempting to convince people of the value of his own idealism would be foolhardy now.

Isma'il Latif commented sarcastically, "I didn't know some students enroll in school 'on a provisional basis.' Please explain this to us."

Husayn Shaddad answered seriously, "All the schools are the same to me. None has anything that I find especially attractive. Of course I want to learn, but I don't want to work. Nowhere at the University will I get the knowledge I want free from professional ties. Since I haven't succeeded in discovering anyone in our house who agrees with me, I find myself obliged to meet them halfway. I asked them which school they would choose. My father commented, 'Is there anything besides Law?' So I said, 'Let it be Law.'"

Imitating his tone and gestures, Isma'il Latif exclaimed, "On a provisional basis!"

They all laughed. Then Husayn Shaddad continued: "Yes, on a provisional basis, you quarrelsome fellow. For it's possible, if things turn out the way I want, that I may cut short my studies in Egypt and go to France, even if I have to study law there. Then I could sip freely from the springs of culture. There I could think, see, and listen. . . ."

Still imitating his friend's tone and gestures, as though to complete what had been left unsaid, Isma'il Latif added, "And taste, touch, and smell."

After they had laughed, Husayn Shaddad went on: "Rest assured that my intentions aren't what you suspect."

Kamal believed him wholeheartedly and felt no need for any substantiation, not only because he thought too highly of his friend to doubt him but also because he believed that the life Husayn was bent on enjoying in France would by its very nature transport the soul. Obvious as this point was, Isma'il and others like him, who believed only in things countable and visible, could hardly be expected to grasp it. Husayn had long excited Kamal's dreams. Here was another of those dreams, remarkable for its expansive beauty. This was a dream rife with food for the spirit and for the mind, for hearing and seeing.

"How often I've had this dream," Kamal thought, "both waking and sleeping. After all my aspirations and efforts, the dreaming process has led me to the Teachers College." Then he asked Husayn, "Do you really mean what you said about not wanting to work?"

With a dreamy look in his handsome black eyes, Husayn Shaddad answered, "I'm not going to be a speculator on the stock market like my father. I couldn't stand a life that consisted of uninterrupted work for the sake of making money. I will never be a civil servant. A career as a bureaucrat is slavery disguised as earning a living. I have more than enough to live on. I want to live as a tourist in the world. I'll read, see, hear, and think, moving from the mountains to the plains and back again."

After watching him throughout the discussion with a scornful look softened by his aristocratic reserve, Hasan Salim objected, "A civil service career need not be simply a way of earning a living. I, for example, won't need to work to earn a living, but it's important for me to work in a noble profession. A man must have a career. A dignified occupation is a goal worth achieving for its own sake."

Isma'il endorsed Hasan's statement: "This is true. Even the very richest people aspire to careers in the judiciary, the diplomatic corps, and the civil service." Then, turning toward Husayn Shaddad, he added, "Why don't you select one of these careers for yourself, since they're within your grasp?"

Kamal also addressed Husayn: "The foreign service would provide you with a distinguished profession and opportunities for travel."

Hasan Salim said importantly, "It's hard to get into."

Husayn Shaddad replied, "The foreign service no doubt has extraordinary advantages. For the most part it's a ceremonial career. It would accommodate my desire to avoid the servitude of work. It's a form of tourism and provides free time. It would allow me to have my desired spiritual life dedicated to the pursuit of beauty. But I think I won't attempt it, not because it's so selective, as Hasan points out, but because I doubt I'll continue my formal studies through to the end."

Laughing wickedly, Isma'il Latif said, "I can't help thinking that you want to go to France for reasons that have nothing to do with culture. And you're right."

Husayn Shaddad laughed and shook his head to deny the allegation. "Certainly not!" he said. "You're thinking of your own passions. My distaste for schooling has other reasons. The first is that I'm not interested in studying law. The second is that no one branch of the University can provide me with the variety of disciplines and arts I wish to learn – like theater, painting, music, and philosophy. And if you enroll in some branch, you'll have to cram your head with dust in order to come across a few specks of gold, if you find any at all. In Paris you're allowed to attend lectures in all the different areas of learning without being tied down to a schedule or an examination. That way you can have a beautiful, spiritual life."

Then, as though to himself, he added in a low voice, "Perhaps I'll marry there, so I can spend my life as a tourist both in reality and in my imagination."

Hasan Salim's face gave no indication that he was following this discussion with any serious interest. Isma'il Latif raised his bushy eyebrows, leaving it up to his eyes to disclose the sly irony surging within his breast. Only Kamal seemed enthusiastic and touched. He had nourished these same hopes. His differed only in non-essential details. He was not interested in tourism or getting married in France, but how he longed for learning not confined to a schedule or an examination. . . . That would obviously be far superior to the dirt he would cram into his head at the Teachers College in hopes of coming away with a few atoms of gold. Paris? It had been a beautiful dream for him ever since he learned that his beloved had spent part of her childhood there. It still beckoned Husayn with its magic and fascinated Kamal with its diverse promises. But what cure was there for his passionate hopes?

After some hesitation he said apprehensively, "It seems to me that the school coming closest to offering what you want, if only to a limited degree, is the Teachers College."

Isma'il Latif turned toward him somewhat anxiously and asked, "What have you selected? Don't say the Teachers College! My Lord, I'd forgotten that you're almost as foolish as Husayn."

Kamal smiled so broadly that his large nostrils were flexed. He answered, "I've enrolled in the Teachers College for the reasons mentioned."

Husayn Shaddad looked at him with interest. Then, smiling, he said, "No doubt your cultural passions got the better of you while you were wrestling with this choice."

Isma'il Latif told Husayn accusingly, "You bear a great deal of responsibility for encouraging these passions of his. The truth is that you talk a lot and read little, while this poor boy takes the matter seriously and reads himself blind. Look at your evil influence on him. In the end it's driven him to the Teachers College."

Ignoring Isma'il's interruption, Husayn continued: "Are you sure that the Teachers College has what you want?"

Delighted by this first inquiry about his school free of scorn or derision, Kamal said enthusiastically, "It's enough for me to be allowed to study English. Then I use it as a way of learning a limitless number of things. Besides that, I think it will provide an excellent opportunity for studying history, education, and psychology."

Husayn Shaddad thought a little. Then he said, "I've met many teachers and observed them at close range in my tutorial sessions. They were not good models for the cultured man; but the antiquated instructional program's responsible for that."

With undiminished enthusiasm Kamal said, "All I need are the tools. True cultural development depends on the man, not the school."

Hasan Salim asked, "Do you plan to become a teacher?"

Although Hasan phrased this question politely, it made Kamal uncomfortable. Hasan's politeness was deeply ingrained, and he only abandoned it as a last resort or when an adversary attacked. His courtesy was a natural result of his composure and aristocratic upbringing. So it was difficult for Kamal to determine whether his friend's question was really free of scorn and derision.

Kamal shrugged his shoulders as he said, "That's inevitable, since I'm determined to study what I want."

Isma'il Latif was covertly scrutinizing Kamal, looking at his head, nose, long neck, and skinny body. He must have been trying to judge the impact this sight would have on schoolchildren, particularly the naughtiest ones. He could not keep himself from muttering, "By my life, it'll be a catastrophe."

Revealing his affection for Kamal, Husayn Shaddad continued: "The job's a secondary consideration for people with ambitious goals. And we mustn't forget the elite group of prominent figures who graduated from this school."

The University discussion ended there, and the young men were silent. Kamal attempted to fuse his spirit with the encompassing garden, but the discussion had made such a lively impression on him that he had to wait for its effect to wear off. He happened to notice the jug of ice water on the table. An old fantasy came to mind, one that had made him joyous on occasions like this. It consisted of filling a glass and drinking from it while he imagined that his lips were touching a place on the rim brushed by hers. He went to the table, filled a glass from the jug, and drank. As he sat down again, he concentrated on himself, anticipating some change in his state of consciousness, if he were lucky enough to achieve his goal. A magical force he had never experienced would radiate from his spirit. He would succumb to a divine intoxication transporting him to the heavens of bliss. But, alas, he finally had to satisfy himself with the pleasure he received from the adventure and his delicious hope.

Kamal began to wonder anxiously, "When will she come?" Was it possible for this promising moment to be added to the three months of their separation? His eyes returned to the jug. He recalled a conversation he had once had with Isma'il Latif about it, or rather about its ice water, which was the only refreshment they were served at the Shaddad mansion.

During their talk, Isma'il had mentioned the strict economies observed in the mansion from roof to basement and had asked if that was not a form of stinginess. Kamal had refused to allow the reputation of his beloved's family to be questioned or tarnished and had defended them against this accusation. He had cited their luxurious lifestyle, servants, employees, and their two automobiles: the Minerva and the Fiat, which Husayn virtually monopolized. Once all of that had been taken into account, how could they be accused of parsimony?

Never at a loss for an impudent remark, Isma'il had distinguished between different types of stinginess. He thought that since Shaddad Bey was a millionaire in every sense of the word, he had a duty to surround himself with all the trappings of prosperity. Yet Shaddad Bey limited his family to what, in his circle, constituted the bare necessities. The principle observed without deviation by every member of the family was not to tolerate the expenditure of one millieme except when it was appropriate and necessary. The servants received low wages and ate cheap food. If one broke a dish, the price was deducted from his pay. Husayn Shaddad came from the only family that did not provide an allowance for its sons. They did not want him to get used to squandering money. His father might buy some stocks and bonds for him in honor of a holiday but would not give him spending money. And the dear son's visitors were served nothing but ice water. Was this not stinginess, no matter how aristocratic?

Kamal remembered that conversation while looking at the jug. He wondered with alarm, as he had before, whether it was possible for any defect to attach itself to his beloved's family. His heart refused to believe that. It rejected the possibility that perfection could be flawed in any respect, no matter how slight. All the same, he imagined that a feeling close to relief was mischievously whispering to him, "Don't be frightened. Isn't this shortcoming, if it exists, a factor bringing her closer to your level, if only by a little?"

Although skeptical and dubious about Isma'il's claims, Kamal found himself unintentionally reflecting on the vice of stinginess. He classified it into two types. One was despicable, but the other was a wise policy providing an excellent foundation for a person's financial life. To term systematic care in spending stinginess or a vice would be an extravagant exaggeration. Why not proceed in this manner, since it was compatible with the erection of palaces, the acquisition of automobiles, and the display of prestigious luxuries? Why worry when it applied to noble souls cleansed of all wickedness and baseness?

Kamal was roused from his reflections by Isma'il Latif's hand, which grasped his arm and shook it. Then he heard Isma'il tell Hasan Salim, "Watch out! Here's the Wafd Party representative. He'll answer you."

Kamal realized at once that they had begun discussing politics while he was daydreaming. Political discussion . . . how tiresome and yet how pleasant it was. Isma'il called him the Wafd Party representative. Perhaps he was being sarcastic. So let him make fun of anything he wanted. Kamal had imbibed the nationalist ideology of the Wafd Party from Fahmy, and in his heart it was associated with his brother's sacrifice and death as a martyr.

He looked at Hasan Salim and said with a smile, "My friend, since you are dazzled by nothing save true majesty, what have you said about Sa'd Zaghlul?"

Hasan Salim gave no sign of interest in discussing majesty. Kamal had not expected any other reaction. For a long time he had struggled with his friend only to be rebuffed by Hasan's – and perhaps also his father the superior court justice's – stubborn and arrogant view of Sa'd Zaghlul, whom Kamal almost venerated.

In Hasan Salim's opinion, Sa'd was nothing but a populist agitator. Hasan repeated this characterization with provocative disdain and scorn, which were at odds with his normal gentle courtesy. He made fun of Sa'd Zaghlul's policies and rhetorical flourishes. He extolled the majesty of Adli, Tharwat, Muhammad Mahmud, and other members of the Liberal Constitutionalist group, who, in Kamal's eyes, were traitors or Englishmen in fezzes.

Hasan Salim answered calmly, "We were discussing the negotiations, which lasted only three days before being halted."

Kamal said enthusiastically, "That was a patriotic stance truly worthy of Sa'd. Since the demand for our national rights was not negotiable, it became necessary to terminate the negotiations. And Sa'd pronounced his immortal words: 'We were invited here to commit suicide, but we refused. This is all that happened.'"

Finding politics a fit topic for banter, Isma'il Latif observed, "If he had agreed to commit suicide, his life would have been crowned with the most exalted service he could have rendered his country."

Hasan Salim waited for Isma'il and Husayn to stop laughing before he said, "How have we benefited from this bon mot? Patriotism is nothing for Sa'd but a rhetorical device to seduce the masses. 'We were invited here to commit suicide,' and so on and so forth. 'I like to speak the truth,' and so on. . . . Words and more words. There are men who say nothing but work silently. They are the ones who achieved the only boon the nation has won in recent history."

Anger flared up in Kamal's heart, and he would have exploded had he not been restrained by his respect for Hasan and for his age. Kamal was amazed that a young man like Hasan should follow the deviant political views of his father, a member of the old guard.

"You belittle the importance of words, as though they had none. But in fact the most significant and noteworthy events of human history can ultimately be traced back to some statement. The grand phrase contains hope, power, and truth. We proceed through life by the light of words. And Sa'd Zaghlul is not merely a wordsmith. His record is full of achievements and stands."

Husayn Shaddad ran his long thin fingers through his black hair as he said, "Leaving Sa'd out of it, I agree with what you said about the value of language."

Hasan paid no attention to Husayn Shaddad's interjection. Addressing Kamal, he remarked, "Nations survive and advance with brains, wise policies, and manpower – not through speeches and cheap populist agitation."

Isma'il Latif looked at Husayn Shaddad and asked sarcastically, "Don't you think a man who wears himself out talking about the betterment of this country is like a person attempting to inflate a punctured balloon?"

Kamal turned to Isma'il in order to address Hasan indirectly and to tell him things he would otherwise be reluctant to say. Venting his wrath, Kamal said, "Politics means nothing to you, but occasionally your jokes express so clearly the viewpoint of a faction who claim to be Egyptians that you could be their spokesman. They express their despair that the nation will ever progress, but it stems from contemptuous snobbery, not from a zealous ambition for reform. If politics were not an expedient way of satisfying their greed, they would shun it, like you."

Husayn Shaddad laughed pleasantly. He put his hand on Kamal's arm and squeezed it, saying, "You're a stubborn debater. I like your enthusiasm, even if I don't share your faith in politics. You know I'm uncommitted politically. I don't belong to the Wafd Party or the Constitutionalists, not because I scorn them like Isma'il Latif, but because I'm convinced that politics corrupts the mind and heart. You have to rise above it before life can appear to you as an endless opportunity for wisdom, beauty, and tolerance instead of an arena for combat and deceit."

Kamal was reassured to hear Husayn speak out, and his fury abated. He was ecstatic whenever Husayn agreed with him and broad-minded whenever they disagreed. Even so, he felt that Husayn's defense of political neutrality was nothing more than an excuse for his lack of patriotism. Kamal had never resented that in his friend or regarded it as a failing, although he did with Isma'il. If Kamal ever thought of it as a shortcoming, his goodwill, forbearance, and tolerance allowed him to overlook it.

Picking up on Husayn's ideas, Kamal said, "Life is all of that. It's composed of struggle, deceit, wisdom, and beauty. Whenever you neglect one aspect, you lose an opportunity to perfect your understanding of it as well as your ability to influence it in a positive way. Never scorn politics. It's half of life, or the whole of life if you consider wisdom and beauty to be above life."

As though by way of apology, Husayn Shaddad answered, "So far as politics is concerned, I'll tell you frankly that I don't trust any of those men."

Kamal asked him almost cajolingly, "What made you lose confidence in Sa'd Zaghlul?"

"No, let me ask what should make me trust him? Sa'd or Adli, Adli or Sa'd, how silly it all is. . . . Yet even though Sa'd and Adli are equivalent for me politically, I can't say the same of them as men. I can't ignore Adli's distinguished family lineage, prestige, and culture. Sa'd – don't get angry – is nothing but a former seminarian from al-Azhar."

Oh, how it hurt Kamal whenever his friend let slip some hint of his sense of superiority over the Egyptian people. Kamal was extremely sad, for it seemed that Husayn felt superior to him or – and this was even more devastating and bitter – that his words reflected the feelings of the whole family. Yes, when Husayn talked to Kamal, he left his friend with the impression that he was talking about a people to which neither of them belonged. Was that caused by an error of perception on Husayn's part or was it flattery? Strangely enough, this attitude of Husayn's did not anger Kamal in its general implications nearly so much as it saddened him because of what it implied specifically about Kamal. It did not excite a feeling of class hostility or patriotism in him, for these emotions were put to flight by his friend's guileless grin, which revealed his sincerity and benevolence. They were decisively routed by a love uninfluenced by opinions or events.

Despite their friendship, Hasan Salim's attitude toward the common people enraged Kamal's sense of patriotism, even though Hasan's aloofness and haughtiness were no more pronounced than Husayn Shaddad's. Not even Hasan's polite manner of speaking or his reserve in expressing his feelings mediated for him with Kamal, who considered them a form of cleverness serving to double his friend's responsibility and to reinforce his solidarity with the aristocracy in opposition to the people.

Addressing Husayn, Kamal asked, "Do I need to remind you that true majesty is not determined by whether a person wears a turban or a fez and is poor or rich? It seems to me that politics occasionally forces us to debate self-evident truths."

Isma'il Latif commented, "What I admire in Wafdists like Kamal is their intense partisan spirit." Then, looking around at his friends, he continued: "And what I despise about them is also their party loyalty."

Laughing, Husayn Shaddad said, "You're lucky. No matter what political opinion you advance, no critic can ever object to it."

Then Hasan Salim asked Husayn Shaddad, "You claim you're above politics. Do you insist on that even with regard to the former Khedive?"

Their eyes were directed toward Husayn with cheerful defiance, since his father's support for the former Khedive, Abbas Hilmi II, was well known and since it was for this reason that he had spent several years in exile in Paris. But Husayn said nonchalantly, "These matters are no concern of mine at all. My father was and still is a supporter of the Khedive. I'm not required to embrace his views."

His eyes sparkling with amusement, Isma'il Latif asked, "Was your father one of those who shouted, 'God lives! Abbas arrives'?"

Husayn Shaddad said with a laugh, "I've never heard about this, except from you. The indubitable truth is that there was nothing between my father and the Khedive beyond friendship and loyalty. Besides, as you all know, there's not a single party calling for the return of the Khedive today."

Hasan Salim said, "The man and his era have become part of history. The present situation can be put in these few words: Sa'd Zaghlul refuses to allow anyone else, no matter how fine or wise, to speak in the name of Egypt."

Immediately after receiving this blow, Kamal retorted, "The present situation can be summed up in even fewer words: No one in Egypt is able to speak for her except Sa'd. The people's support for him is great enough to achieve our goals in the end."

Kamal folded his arms across his chest and stretched out his legs until the tip of his shoe touched the table leg. He was planning to continue his remarks, but they heard someone close behind them ask, "Budur, don't you want to say hello to your old friends?"

Kamal's tongue was paralyzed. His heart leapt so violently that it shook his chest in a fashion that initially alarmed and almost hurt him. Then, quicker than a flash of lightning, an overwhelming and intoxicating happiness took hold of him. The effect on him was so great that he almost had to close his eyes. He discovered that every notion pulsing through his soul was directed heavenward. He rose with the others and turned around. He saw Aïda standing a step away from the gazebo, holding the hand of Budur, her little sister, who was three years old. The girls were looking at them with calm smiling eyes. After a wait of three months or more, here she was. Here was the original of the portrait that filled his spirit and body during his waking and sleeping moments. Here she was, standing before him, bearing witness to the fact that the limitless pain, the indescribable happiness, the searing periods of wakefulness, and the dreams spinning him through the skies could, in the final analysis, all be traced back to a charming human being whose feet left prints in the garden. He gazed at her, and her personal magnetism attracted his emotions so totally that he lost all sense of time, place, people, and self. He was once more reduced to a spirit swimming through the void toward his beloved. He perceived her – more with his spirit than his senses – in an enchanting intoxication, a musical rapture, and a lofty splendor. His sight grew weak and feeble. The force of his spiritual reaction seemed to have affected all his vital functions. Thus his senses and his faculties were transported to a semiconscious state approaching annihilation. Therefore, his beloved was more easily observed in his memory than in real life. When he was in her presence, he could scarcely see anything. Later she would appear to his memory with her slender figure, bronze face as beautiful as the moon, and thick black hair cut in a boyish bob, the bangs coming down over her forehead like the teeth of a comb. In her dark eyes there was a look as tranquil, gentle, and majestic as the dawn. He saw this picture in his memory, not with his senses. It was like a magical melody that so absorbs us when we hear it that we are unable to recall anything about it, until it comes back to us as a happy surprise in the first instants when we awake or during a moment of contentment. Then it reverberates deep within our consciousness in a perfectly harmonious manner.

Kamal hopefully wondered whether she would change her usual procedure and shake hands with them. Then he would feel her touch, if only for that one time in his whole life. But she greeted them with a smile and a nod of her head.

In her voice, which by comparison made even the most beloved melodies seem worthless, she asked, "How are all of you?"

They vied with each other to greet and thank her and congratulate her on her safe return.

Then, her slender fingers toying with Budur's hair, she told the girl, "Shake hands with your friends."

Budur sucked in her lips and bit them as she looked around shyly. Then she fixed her eyes on Kamal, and they both smiled. Knowing of the affection between them, Husayn Shaddad said, "She's smiling at the one she loves."

"Do you really love this fellow?" Aïda asked. Then, pushing her sister toward the young man, she said, "So greet him."

Blushing with happiness, Kamal held his hands out to her. She approached him, and he lifted her up. He began to kiss her cheeks with longing and emotion. He was delighted by her love and proud of it. In his arms there was a fragment from the body of the family. When he hugged this part of them, he was embracing the whole family. Was it possible for a worshipper to contact his beloved without some mediation like this? The strange resemblance between this child and her older sister was nothing short of magical. The person contentedly nestled against his breast seemed Aïda herself at an earlier stage of life. Once she had been as young, small, and generous with her affections as Budur. "Ponder that," he advised himself.

Let him rejoice in this pure love. Let him find happiness in embracing a body she embraced and in kissing a cheek she kissed. Let him dream until his mind and heart were transported. He knew why he loved Budur, Husayn, the mansion with its garden and servants. He loved them all for Aïda's sake. What he did not understand was his love for Aïda.

Looking back and forth from Hasan Salim to Isma'il Latif, Aïda asked, "How was Alexandria?"

Hasan replied, "Splendid!"

Then Isma'il asked, "What makes you always want to go to Ra's al-Barr?"

In a pleasant voice with a musical ring, she answered, "We've spent several summers in Alexandria, but the only resort we really enjoy is Ra's al-Barr. The one other place as calm, unpretentious, and congenial is your own home."

Laughing, Isma'il said, "Unfortunately we don't care for calm."

How happy this scene made Kamal . . . and this conversation and this voice. "Think about it," he advised himself. "Isn't this happiness? A butterfly, like the dawn breeze, saturated in delight-ful colors, sipping the nectar of the flowers . . . that's what I am." If only this moment could last forever.

Aïda said, "We had an enjoyable trip. Hasn't Husayn told you about it?"

In a disapproving tone Husayn said, "No, they've been arguing about politics."

She turned toward Kamal to say, "Here's someone who wants to talk about nothing else."

"Her attention comes to you as a grace," Kamal reflected. "Her look's so pure it reveals her angelic spirit. I'm revived by it like a sun worshipper soaking up radiant light. If only this moment would last forever."

"I wasn't responsible for initiating the discussion today."

Smiling, she said, "But you seized the opportunity. . . ."

He grinned in surrender. Then she turned her eyes on Budur and cried out, "Are you planning to fall asleep in his arms? That's enough greeting for you."

Budur was embarrassed and buried her head against his chest. He started stroking her back fondly.

But Aïda threatened: "Then I'll leave you and go back alone."

Budur lifted her head and held out her hand to her sister, mumbling, "No." Kamal kissed her and set her on the ground. She ran to Aïda and grasped her hand. Aïda looked at each of them in turn, waved goodbye, and went back the way she had come. They resumed their seats and continued their conversation.

Aïda's visits to the gazebo in the garden were like this. They were brief, happy surprises, but Kamal appeared content. He felt that his patience during the long summer months had not been in vain. Why did not people commit suicide to attempt to hold on to happiness just as they killed themselves to escape from suffering?

"It's not necessary for you to travel around the world like Husayn if you wish to find pleasure for your senses, intellect, and spirit. It's possible for you to acquire all of those in a fleeting moment without stirring. How does a human being obtain the power to effect all this? What's happened to the political feud, the heated debate, the furious quarrel, and the class conflict? They've melted away and vanished at a look from your eyes, O beloved. What distinguishes dream from reality? I wonder which of them I'm roaming through now."

"Soccer season starts soon."

"Last season belonged to the Ahli team. They were unrivaled."

"The Mukhtalat team was defeated, but it's got some outstanding players."

Kamal sprang to the defense of Mukhtalat – much as he defended Sa'd Zaghlul – to block the attacks of Hasan Salim. All four of them played soccer, but they differed in their skill and enthusiasm. Isma'il was by far the best and stood out among them like a professional playing with amateurs. Husayn Shaddad was the weakest player. Kamal and Hasan were in the middle. The exchange between Kamal and Hasan heated up. The former attributed Mukhtalat's defeat to bad luck, the latter thought it showed the superiority of Ahli's new players. The controversy continued, since neither of them would give in.

Kamal wondered why he always found himself on the other side from Hasan Salim, whether they were discussing the Wafd Party and the Liberals or the Mukhtalat team and Ahli. Among musicians Kamal preferred Hijazi, but Hasan liked Mukhtar. In cinema, the former enjoyed Charlie Chaplin, while the latter favored the dapper French comedian Max Linder.

Kamal left his friends shortly before sunset. As he walked along the path beside the house heading for the gate he heard a voice cry, "There he is."

Enchanted, he looked up and saw Aïda at one of the first-floor windows. She was pointing him out as she held Budur, who sat on the window ledge. Kamal stopped below them, looking up with a smiling face at the child, who waved her small hand at him. He also glanced from time to time at the face in whose form and expressions his hopes for life and the afterlife were vested. His heart was colliding drunkenly with his ribs. Budur waved to him once more, and Aïda asked her, "Are you going to him?"

The little girl nodded yes, and Aïda laughed at this wish that would not be realized. Encouraged by her laughter, Kamal examined her carefully, losing himself in the beautiful coloration of her eyes and in the exquisite meeting point of her eyebrows. He recalled the reverberation of her throaty laughter and the inflections of her warm voice until he was sighing with emotion and passion. Since the situation obliged him to speak, he asked his beloved, "Did she think of me at the beach?"

Moving her head back a little, Aïda said, "Ask her yourself. What you two think of each other is none of my business." Then before he could utter a word, she added, "Did you remember her?"

"Oh," he thought. "This is like Fahmy reviewing lessons with me on the roof while Maryam listened."

"She was never absent from my thoughts," he answered fervently.

A voice called to the girls from inside. Aïda straightened up and lifted Budur in her arms. As she was about to leave she made this final comment: "What an amazing love!" Then she disappeared from the window.

86

AMINA AND KAMAL were the only remaining patrons of the coffee hour, and even he left the house before sunset. Then his mother stayed on there by herself or called Umm Hanafi to keep her company until it was time for bed. Yasin had left a void behind him. Although Amina tried not to mention him, Kamal felt isolated by his brother's departure, and the delightful enjoyment he had found in this gathering was spoiled. In the old days coffee had been an excuse for conversation. Now it was everything to the mother. She drank so much that, without her realizing it, preparation and consumption of the coffee became her sole entertainment. She would drink five, six, or even ten cups in succession.

Kamal anxiously kept track of her excesses and cautioned her about the consequences. She answered him with a smile as though to say, "What would I do if I weren't drinking coffee?" In a confident and assured tone she told him, "There's nothing harmful about coffee."

They sat facing each other, she on the sofa between the doors to the bedroom and the dining room, Kamal on one between the entries to his bedroom and his study. She was bent over the coffeepot, which was half buried in the brazier's coals. He was silent and staring vacantly into space. Suddenly she asked, "What are you thinking about, I wonder? You always look as though you're thinking about something important."

He sensed the criticism in her tone and replied, "The mind constantly finds things to occupy it."

She looked up questioningly at him with her small, honey-colored eyes. Then she said somewhat shyly, "It's been ages since we found time for a conversation."

"Really?" he wondered. That past was gone forever – the era of religious lessons and stories about prophets and demons, when he had been insanely devoted to her. That era had come to an end. What would they discuss today? Except for meaningless chatter there was absolutely nothing for them to say to each other. He smiled, as though to apologize for both past and future silences.

Then he said, "We talk to each other whenever we have something to discuss."

She replied gently, "People who want to talk set no limits on their conversations, but you seem always to be absent or absent-minded. . . ."

After reflecting a bit she added, "You read a lot. You read as much during your vacation as when you're in school. You never get enough rest. I'm afraid you've worn yourself out."

In a tone that indicated he did not welcome this interrogation, Kamal answered, "There are many hours in a day. Spending a few of them reading won't wear anyone out. It's nothing but a pastime, even if it's a beneficial one."

After some hesitation she observed, "I'm afraid reading's the reason you seem so quiet and preoccupied. . . ."

"No," he thought. "It's not reading. If only you knew how it distracts me from my discomfort." Something else had been absorbing him, and he could not escape from it even when he was reading. His was a condition without a cure that she or anyone else could provide. He was sick with love, devoted but at his wits' end, not knowing what to wish for beyond his suffering.

Slyly he said, "Reading's like coffee. There's nothing harmful about it. Don't you want me to become a scholar like my grandfather?"

Delight and pride shone in her pale, oval face. She answered, "Of course. I wish that wholeheartedly, but I want to see you in good spirits all the time."

Smiling, he said, "I'm in as good spirits as you could wish. So don't trouble your mind with idle speculation."

He had noticed that her concern for him had increased in recent years more than was necessary or desirable. Her devotion, solicitude, and apprehension about anything that might harm him – or that she imagined might – had begun to engage her mind to a degree that made him uncomfortable, prompting him to defend his freedom and dignity. Yet he never lost sight of this development's causes, which included Fahmy's death and the misery she had endured. Thus Kamal never overstepped the bounds of affection and politeness in defense of his independence.

"I'm happy to hear that from you, if it's really true. All I desire is your happiness. I prayed for you today at the shrine of our master al-Husayn. I hope God may answer my prayer."

"Amen."

He watched her raise the coffeepot to fill her cup for the fourth time. The corners of his mouth spread open in a faint smile. He remembered how a visit to the mosque of al-Husayn had once seemed an impossible dream for her. Now she visited it whenever she went to the cemetery or to see her two daughters on Sugar Street. But what an oppressive price she had paid for this limited freedom. He too nourished impossible dreams. What price would be exacted from him if he was to fulfill them? Yet, any payment, no matter how great, would seem insignificant if he could.

Emitting a forced laugh, he observed, "The visit to al-Husayn is certainly linked to unforgettable memories. . . ."

Smiling, she felt her collarbone, which she had broken during her first trip there, and said, "And to lasting results."

With a modicum of enthusiasm Kamal said, "You're not a prisoner in the house as you once were. You've gained the right to visit Khadija, Aisha, and our master al-Husayn as often as you want. Imagine what you would have missed if Father had not relaxed the rules."

She looked up at him with confused embarrassment, for the reference to a distinction she had won as a result of losing a child troubled her. Then she bowed her head despondently, as if to say, "I wish I had remained as I was and kept my son." She did not air the feelings raging in her breast for fear of upsetting Kamal. Apologizing for the freedom she enjoyed, she said, "My occasional excursions are not for my entertainment. I go to al-Husayn to pray for you. I visit your sisters to reassure myself about them and to resolve the problems no one else seems able to handle."

He had no difficulty guessing which problems she meant. Knowing she had visited Aisha and Khadija that day, he asked, "Anything new at Sugar Street?"

Sighing, she answered, "The usual."

He shook his head sadly. Then with a smile he remarked, "Khadija has a gift for quarreling."

Amina responded sorrowfully, "Her mother-in-law told me that any conversation with her threatens to end badly."

"It seems her mother-in-law is growing senile too."

"Her age is excuse enough. But what's your sister's excuse?"

"Did you side with her or with the truth?"

Amina laughed in a way that suggested she knew only too well what he meant. She sighed again and said, "Your sister has a hot temperament. She is quick to bridle at even the most sincere advice. And woe to me if I'm polite to her mother-in-law out of respect for her age and status. Then she'll ask me with fiery eyes, 'Are you for me or against me?' There is no strength or might save from God. 'For me or against me!' Are we at war, son? Strangely enough, at times her mother-in-law is at fault, but Khadija carries the fight to such extremes that she ends up in the wrong."

It would be impossible for anything to make Kamal angry at Khadija. She had been and still remained his second mother and an inexhaustible source of affection. How did his sister Aisha compare with her – beautiful, giddy Aisha who had absorbed all the characteristics of the Shawkat family?

"What did the investigation reveal?"

"This time the argument began with the husband, and that's unusual. When I entered their quarters, they were having a violent dispute. I was amazed that something had agitated the good man and intervened to make peace. Then I learned the cause for all of it. She had made up her mind to dust the apartment, but he was still sleeping at nine. So she insisted on rousing him, and he woke up angry. Feeling obstinate for once, he refused to get out of bed. His mother heard the row and was quick to come. Then the fires flared. This quarrel was scarcely concluded before another one broke out, because Ahmad returned from playing in the street with mud on his shirt. She hit him and wanted him to take a bath. The boy appealed to his father for help, and the man came to his rescue. So a second fight broke out in one morning."

Laughing, Kamal asked, "What did you do?"

"I tried my best but did not succeed. She scolded me for a long time because I had attempted to mediate. She told me, 'You should have taken my side the way she stood up for him.'"

Sighing a third time, she continued: "I told Khadija, 'Don't you remember how you saw me act when I was with your father?' She answered sharply, 'Do you think there's another man in the whole world like Father?'"

Uninvited, the vision of Abd al-Hamid Bey Shaddad and his wife, Saniya Hanim, popped into Kamal's imagination. They were

walking side by side from the veranda to their Minerva automobile, which was parked by the gate of the mansion. They did
not seem a master and his servant but two equal friends conversing
easily with each other, with her arm draped over his. When they
reached the vehicle, the bey stepped aside to allow the lady to
climb in first.

"Will you ever get to see your parents act like this?" he wondered. "What a silly idea!"

The couple walked with an air of distinction befitting the
parents of his beloved. Although her mother was as old as his,
she was wearing an expensive coat, which was a marvel of taste,
elegance, and style. Her face was unveiled and attractive, although
it did not compare with the angelic countenance of her daughter.
There emanated from her a fragrant perfume and a captivating
elegance. He wished he knew what they discussed and their
manner of agreeing and disagreeing, if they ever did differ. He
was eager to learn about this life, which was linked to his beloved's
by the firmest ties and bonds.

"Do you remember," he asked himself, "how you gazed at her
– like a worshipper viewing great priests and high church dignitaries?"

He told his mother calmly, "If Khadija's character was more like
yours, she would be assured a happy life."

She smiled with delight, although her pleasure ran afoul of a
bitter truth – namely, that her disposition, no matter how mild,
could not always guarantee her happiness. Then with the smile still
on her lips to conceal her gloomy thoughts, which she was
apprehensive he might detect, she said, "God alone is the guide.
May our Lord make you even more sweet-tempered than you are,
so you'll be a person loving others and loved by them."

He quickly asked her, "What do you think of me?"

With conviction she replied, "You're already like that and
better."

"But how can angels love you?" he wondered. "Call up her
blissful image and contemplate it a little. Can you imagine her
unable to sleep or left prostrate by love and passion? That's too
remote even for a fantasy. She's above love, for love is a defect
remedied only by the loved one. Be patient and don't torment
your heart. It's enough that you're in love. It's enough that you see
her. Her image shines into your spirit and her dulcet tones send

intoxicating delight through you. From the beloved emanates a light in which all things appear to be created afresh. After a long silence, the jasmine and the hyacinth beans begin to confide in each other. The minarets and domes fly up over the evening glow into the sky. The landmarks of the ancient district hand down the wisdom of past generations. The existential orchestra echoes the chirps of the crickets. The dens of wild beasts overflow with tenderness. Grace adorns the alleys and side streets. Sparrows of rapture chatter over the tombs. Inanimate objects are caught up in silent meditation. The rainbow appears in the woven mat over which your feet step. Such is the world of my beloved."

"I went by al-Azhar on my way to al-Husayn and ran into a large demonstration with people chanting slogans. It reminded me of the past. Has something happened, son?"

He answered, "The English do not wish to leave peacefully."

With a look of anger sparkling in her eyes she said sharply, "The English . . . those Englishmen! When will God's just vengeance fall on them?" She had felt a similar aversion to Sa'd Zaghlul himself for a long time, until Kamal had finally convinced her it was impossible to detest a person Fahmy had loved. With obvious anxiety she asked, "What do you mean, Kamal? Are we returning to the days of suffering?"

He replied resentfully, "Only God knows!"

Her discomfort was apparent in her facial contractions. She said, "May God preserve us from suffering. We'll leave them to the wrath of Almighty God. This is the best policy. To throw ourselves to destruction is madness. Let us take refuge with God."

"Don't alarm yourself. Death is inescapable. People die for one reason or another – or for none at all."

She responded indignantly, "I don't deny that what you say is true, but I dislike your tone."

"How should I talk?"

With compelling emotion she said, "I want you to state that you agree it's sinful for a man to risk his life."

Trying to hide his smile, he gave in: "I agree."

She looked at him skeptically and begged, "Say that with your heart, not your tongue."

"I'm speaking with my heart."

"What an enormous gap there is between ideal and reality," Kamal thought. "You zealously strive for the ultimate in religion, politics, thought, and love, but mothers think only of their children's security. What mother would want to bury a son every five years? The quest for ideals in life necessarily requires sacrifices and martyrs. Body, mind, and spirit are sacrificed. Fahmy gave up a promising life in return for a magnificent death. Will you be able to meet death as heroically as he did? You would not hesitate to make this choice, even though that would crush your unfortunate mother's heart. A death that would drain blood from one wound to stanch others . . . what a love it would be! Yes, but as you know, Aïda, the love between me and Budur is not of that kind. The truly amazing love is mine for you. It testifies on behalf of the world against pessimistic adversaries. It has taught me that death is not the most atrocious thing we have to dread and that life is not the most splendid thing we can desire. I have learned that some facets of life are so rough and repulsive that death is sought instead and some so smooth and sustaining that immortality is desired. How captivating are the world's appeals to you in its indescribable voice, not too high or low – like a violin playing the middle note of a scale – resonant and pure as a light (if you can imagine this) colored sky blue and pulsing with conviction. These calls are an invitation to the empyrean."

87

"NEXT THURSDAY, putting my trust in God, I'll get married."

"May our Lord grant us success."

"I'll be successful if I please my father."

"Your father isn't angry at you, praise God."

"The only guests will be family members. You won't find anything there to upset you."

"Fine, fine!"

"I wish Mother would come, but . . ."

"It's not our fault. The important thing is for the evening to pass quietly."

"Naturally. That hasn't escaped me. I know your tastes as well as anyone. There will be nothing to the wedding beyond the marriage contract and some refreshments."

"Fine. May our Lord guide you to the right path."

"I've asked Kamal to give my greetings to his mother and to request her not to deprive me of the benefit of her prayers and to forgive me. . . ."

"Of course. Naturally."

"Please let me hear you say again that you're not angry with me."

"I'm not angry at you. By God I hope you're destined to find success and prosperity. God hears our prayers."

Matters did not turn out according to the wishes of al-Sayyid Ahmad. He was forced to go along with his son for fear of jeopardizing their relationship. His heart was too tender for him to quarrel seriously with Yasin, let alone to sever ties with him. Al-Sayyid Ahmad had agreed to hand over his eldest son to Bahija's daughter and to sanction by his presence the wedding that would bring his former mistress into the family circle. He had rejected Amina's attempt at intervention when she had declared her wish that Fahmy's brother and sisters should be prevented from attending Yasin's marriage to Maryam.

He had told her in a peremptory tone, "That's a silly idea. Some men marry their brother's widow, in spite of their love and devotion for him. Maryam wasn't married to Fahmy. She wasn't even engaged to him. It's ancient history, from six years ago. I won't deny that he's made a poor choice, but for a mule he's got good intentions. He's hurting himself more than anyone else. He could have found a better family, and the girl's divorced. It's in God's hands. Yasin bears full responsibility for this."

Amina had fallen silent, as though accepting his arguments. Although she had acquired from her time of suffering some measure of courage about voicing her opinion in front of her husband, she did not have enough nerve to oppose him. Thus when Khadija visited her to say that Yasin had invited her to his wedding and that she was thinking of using ill health as an excuse for declining, Amina had disagreed and advised her to accept her brother's invitation.

Thursday arrived, and al-Sayyid Ahmad Abd al-Jawad went to the home of the late Mr. Muhammad Ridwan, where he found Yasin and Kamal waiting to greet him. They were soon joined by Ibrahim and Khalil Shawkat, who were accompanied by Khadija and Aisha. Maryam's family was represented by only a few women, and al-Sayyid Ahmad felt reassured that the day would indeed pass tranquilly.

On his way to the parlor, he encountered familiar landmarks, ones he had seen previously in radically different circumstances. He was besieged by memories, which provoked various forms of disgust and vexation within him, because of the silent mockery of the new role he had come to perform – that of the dignified father of the bridegroom. He was secretly cursing his son, who had landed him and himself – if he would only realize it – in a fix. The fact that the marriage was actually taking place tempted him to reconsider the situation and to hope that God had created the daughter from another pattern than her mother's and that Yasin would find Maryam an excellent wife, in every sense of the word, and be spared reckless behavior like her mother's. Then he asked God to conceal things best forgotten.

Yasin was handsome in his finery and obviously happy, despite the simplicity of the reception honoring his wedding. The secret of his good spirits was the presence of his brother and sisters. He had been apprehensive that their mother might influence one of them to stay home. Would it have been possible to dispense with Maryam for their sakes? Certainly not . . . He loved her. Since she had offered him no route to her save marriage, this wedding was inevitable. The objections of his father and stepmother were misplaced. Yasin was unimpressed by the threat of dire consequences. Furthermore, Maryam was the first woman he had desired to marry on the basis of a prior knowledge of her character and appearance. For this reason he was optimistic about the prospects for the marriage, hoping that it would establish a lasting conjugal life for him. That much was true. He felt he would be a good husband and that she would make a good wife for him. In time he was sure Ridwan would have a happy home in which to grow up and mature. Yasin had drifted around a lot, and it was time for him to settle down. Had the circumstances attending his wedding been different, he would not have hesitated to celebrate it with a party offering many delights and pleasures. He was not so old, poor, or ill at ease with parties that he would ordinarily be content with this dreary reunion, more like a funeral than a wedding. But one should not judge the situation too hastily, for necessity has its own laws. He would dedicate this abstinence to Fahmy's memory.

Maryam's reunion with Khadija and Aisha, after a separation of several years, was an emotional one, no matter how reserved or awkward. They exchanged kisses and compliments. Their lengthy conversation ranged far and wide but sidestepped the past, as far as possible. The first moments were the most strained. Each of the women expected old memories relating to the rupture and the development of bad feelings between them to be dredged up in a negative or critical fashion. These first delicate moments passed safely, and Maryam adroitly steered the conversation toward Khadija's clothes and Aisha's slender figure, which she had retained even after bearing three children. Maryam and her mother asked about "the mother." They were told that she was well, and nothing more was said about her.

Aisha looked at her longtime friend with an eye filled with tender affection, for her heart was always ready to love. If she had not felt apprehensive about the consequences, she would have turned the conversation to memories of the past, in order to laugh over them to her heart's content.

Khadija stealthily scrutinized Maryam. Although she had not thought of her former friend for years, news of her marriage to

Yasin had inspired a flood of bitter comments. She had reminded
Aisha about the incident with the Englishman, wondering aloud
what could have blinded and deafened Yasin. Yet Khadija's emotional commitment to her family was so intense that it took
precedence over everything else and prevented her from criticizing Maryam within earshot of members of the Shawkat family.
Not even Khadija's husband was exempted. She cautioned her
mother: "Whether we like it or not, Maryam is going to become
part of our family." There was nothing strange in this attitude, for
Khadija, even after giving birth to Abd al-Muni'm Shawkat and
Ahmad Shawkat, still considered the Shawkats strangers, to a
certain degree.

The marriage clerk arrived early in the evening, and the wedding contract was drawn up. Cool drinks flavored with fruit syrup
were passed around and a single whooping trill of joy resounded.
Yasin received their congratulations and good wishes. The bride
was summoned to meet her "senior master," al-Sayyid Ahmad,
and the family of her new husband. Escorted by her mother,
Khadija, and Aisha, she kissed her father-in-law's hand and
shook those of the others. Then al-Sayyid Ahmad presented her
with the wedding gift, a set of gold bracelets studded with small
diamonds and emeralds. The family gathering lasted a long time,
with the guests starting to leave, one after the other, at about nine.
Then the carriage arrived to take the couple to Yasin's house in
Palace of Desire Alley, where he had prepared the third floor to
receive his bride. Everyone thought that, for better or for worse,
the curtain had fallen on Yasin's second marriage.

But two weeks after this wedding the home of the late Mr.
Muhammad Ridwan witnessed another nuptial party, one considered truly bizarre by the residents of al-Sayyid Ahmad's home,
of Sugar Street, of Palace of Desire Alley, and of the whole Palace
Walk neighborhood. Without any prior warning, people learned
to their total amazement that Bahija was marrying Bayumi, who
sold fruit drinks. Everyone was stunned by this. It seemed they
were realizing for the first time that Bayumi's shop stood at the
head of the alley where the Ridwan residence was located and that
it lay directly beneath one of the venerable latticed balconies of the
house. Confronted by this fact, they could only wonder. And
people had every reason to be amazed, for the bride was the
widow of a man known during his lifetime for his goodness and

piety and she was considered one of the respectable ladies of the district, even though she was fond of personal adornment. And she was fifty. The bridegroom was a common fellow who wore unpretentious ankle-length shirts and sold carob- and tamarind-flavored drinks in a small shop. He was only forty. He had also been married for twenty years and had fathered nine children. All these factors provoked gossip. Without any reserve whatsoever people waded into the subject of the events that must have preceded the wedding but which had passed undetected by anyone. When and how did these things happen? How did they develop to the point of culminating in matrimony? Which of the two parties had initiated the relationship and which had accepted the invitation?

Uncle Hasanayn, the barber, whose establishment was on the other side of the street, next to the ancient building housing the public cistern, reported that he had frequently seen Mrs. Bahija standing in front of Bayumi's stall, consuming a carob drink. Perhaps they had exchanged a few words then, but, being a kindly man, the barber had never suspected anything. Asking God's forgiveness, Abu Sari', who sold roasted snacks from a shop that closed later than other ones, said he had occasionally noticed men slipping into her house by night but had not known Bayumi was one of them. Darwish, who sold cooked beans, had some things to say, as did al-Fuli, the milkman. Although they pretended to pity the man with all those children and to criticize him bitterly for being so stupid as to marry a woman old enough to be his mother, they were secretly envious of his luck and resented his ascent from their class by means of this unorthodox ploy. Following those comments there was a great deal of talk about the extent of his expected inheritance from the house and a possible treasure trove of jewelry.

The households of al-Sayyid Ahmad, of Sugar Street, and of Palace of Desire Alley were severely shaken. "What a scandal!" everyone exclaimed. Al-Sayyid Ahmad was so angry that members of his immediate family were too terrified to speak to him for several days running. From that time on, Bayumi the drinks vendor would surely have a right to consider al-Sayyid Ahmad his relative. "Curses on Yasin and his lusts!" Bayumi the drinks vendor had become his "uncle," and everyone's nose had been rubbed in the dirt.

When the information reached Khadija, she shouted, "What awful news!" Then she asked Aisha, "Who could ever fault Mother after this? Her heart is never wrong."

Yasin swore to his father that the event had taken place without his knowledge or his wife's. It had made his wife sadder than anyone could possibly imagine. But what could she do?

The scandal did not stop there, for the moment Bayumi's first wife heard the news, she went berserk and stormed out of her home like a lunatic, pushing her children in front of her. She swooped down on Bayumi in his store, and a fierce battle broke out between them as words, hands, feet, shrieks, and screams were employed within the sight and hearing of their children, who began to howl and implore people at hand and passersby to help. Soon a crowd had collected in front of the store – pedestrians, shop owners, women, and children. When they separated the couple and forced the woman back into the street, she came to rest under Bahija's balcony. Her dress was ripped, her wrap in shreds, her hair disheveled, and her nose bloody. She reared her head back to look up at the shuttered windows before unleashing a tongue like a whip with poisoned, weighted ends.

Worse still, when she left her post there, she headed for al-Sayyid Ahmad's store, because he was the father-in-law of her husband's new stepdaughter. She begged him tearfully and oratorically to use his influence to convince her husband to mend his sinful ways. Although seething with rage and chagrin at his plight, al-Sayyid Ahmad heard her out. Then he delicately tried to make her understand, so far as he was able, that this whole affair was beyond the scope of his influence, contrary to her expectations. He kept at it until he persuaded her to leave his store. He was furious but, even so, thought long and hard about Bahija's motives for this strange marriage, especially since he was certain it would not have been hard for her to find a way to gratify any desire she might have felt for Bayumi the drinks vendor without exposing herself and her family to the disturbing consequences of marriage. Why had she committed this folly, paying no attention to the man's wife and children and wantonly disregarding the feelings of her daughter and her daughter's new family, as if she had gone insane? Was it not a gloomy feeling of growing old that had made her seek refuge in marriage? Indeed she was sacrificing many of her possessions in her pursuit of the happiness that fleeting youth had once secured for her. He brooded over this idea sorrowfully and despondently. He remembered his own humiliation at the hands of Zanuba the lute player. She had refused him so much as an affectionate glance until he had set her up in the houseboat. That humiliation had shattered his self-confidence and had made him, despite his apparent serenity, frown back at time, since it had begun to frown at him.

In any event, Bahija did not have long to enjoy her marriage. By the end of the third week she was complaining of a sore on her leg. When she had a medical examination she was diagnosed as being diabetic and taken to Qasr al-Ayni Hospital. Reports of the gravity of her condition were heard for several days. Then the appointed hour overtook her.

88

HOLDING A small bag under his arm, Kamal stood in front of the Shaddad family mansion. He was wearing an elegant gray suit, and his black shoes were gleaming. With his fez perched securely on his large head, he looked tall and thin. Protruding from his shirt, his neck seemed nonchalant about supporting this large head and huge nose. The weather was pleasant, although occasionally a chilly breeze announced that December was on its way. The scattered, sparkling white clouds moved across the sky languidly, veiling the morning sun from time to time. Kamal stood there expectantly, his eyes directed toward the garage. Then the Fiat emerged, driven by Husayn Shaddad, who turned it around on Palaces Street and came to a halt beside Kamal. He stuck his head out the window and asked his friend, "Haven't they come yet?"

He blew the horn three times. Opening the door, he said, "Come sit next to me."

Kamal was content to put the bag inside. He muttered, "Be patient." Then Budur's voice reached him from the garden. Turning in that direction, he saw her advance at a gallop with Aïda trailing behind. Yes, his beloved was approaching, her exquisite figure clad in a stylish short gray dress. A blue silk smock hid the top part of her dress but revealed the girl's pure, bronze forearms. The black halo of her hair encircled the back of her neck and her cheeks and swung with a flowing motion as she walked. The strands of her bangs were plastered to her forehead. In the middle of the black oval there was a face of moonlike beauty, lovely in a way both chic and angelic. It seemed the serene ambassador of the kingdom of happy dreams.

Kamal felt held in place by an overpowering magnetic force. He was in a state between dreaming and waking, conscious only of a sense of gratitude and a pulsing ecstasy. With light prancing steps she approached, like a beautiful melody in bodily form, until she was near enough for him to inhale her Parisian perfume. When their eyes met, a cheerful smile that was tempered by aristocratic reserve could be detected in her eyes and on her pursed lips. Kamal responded with an anxious grin and a bow of his head.

Husayn told her, "You and Budur sit in the back seat."

Kamal moved to open the rear door of the automobile and stood there at attention like one of the household helps. He was rewarded with a smile and a word of thanks in French. He waited for Budur and his beloved to climb in. Then he closed the door and slipped onto the front seat beside Husayn, who blew the horn once more as he looked toward the mansion. The doorman immediately arrived with a small basket, which he placed next to Kamal's bag in the space between the two young men. Laughingly tapping the basket and the bag, Husayn asked, "What good is an excursion without food?"

As the engine started it emitted a groan of protest. Then the car dashed off along al-Abbasiya Street. Husayn Shaddad was telling Kamal, "I know a lot about you, and today will permit me to add fresh information concerning your stomach. I suspect that despite your slenderness, you're a glutton. Do you think I'm mistaken?"

Smiling and more delighted than one would think humanly possible, Kamal answered, "Wait and see for yourself."

A single automobile was carrying all of them on a shared adventure almost impossible to imagine except in dreams. Kamal could hear his wishes whisper, "If only you were sitting in the back seat and she was in front, your eyes could have watched her all they wanted during the whole trip, free of supervision."

"Don't be greedy and ungrateful," he cautioned himself. "Bow down in praise and thanksgiving. Liberate your head from thought, free yourself from the stream of desires, and devote all your attention to experiencing the present moment. Isn't an hour worth a whole lifetime or even more?"

"I wasn't able to invite Hasan and Isma'il to join us on this excursion."

Kamal did not speak but gave his friend a questioning look. His heart was throbbing with joy and embarrassment at being singled out for this distinction.

Then Husayn continued apologetically: "The car, as you can see, isn't big enough for everyone."

In a faint voice Kamal replied, "That's clear."

Smiling, his friend observed, "When it's necessary to choose, you should pick the person who most resembles you. And there's no doubt that our interests in life are close. Isn't that so?"

Kamal's face reflected the happiness overflowing his heart, and he said, "Of course." Then, laughing, he added, "Except that I'm content with spiritual journeys, whereas it appears that you won't be satisfied until your spiritual trip takes you all around the physical world."

"Don't you long to see the world?"

Kamal thought a little before saying, "It seems to me that I have a natural love of staying put. I flinch at the thought of travel. I mean because of the commotion and upheaval, not because of the sights and the chance to explore. If it were feasible, I would like to have the world parade past while I stand here."

Husayn Shaddad laughed in an endearing way that came straight from his heart. He said, "Stay aloft in a balloon, if you can, and watch the world revolve beneath you."

Kamal savored Husayn's charming laugh for some time. The image of Hasan Salim came to mind, and he compared these two different versions of the aristocracy: one remarkable for charm and cheerfulness, the other characterized by reserve and arrogance. Regardless of these differences, both were distinguished.

Kamal observed, "Fortunately, mental journeys don't require any movement at all."

Husayn Shaddad raised his eyes with apparent skepticism but abandoned the topic. He said joyfully, "What's important for us now is to take a short trip together, united by our tastes, which are so similar."

Before Kamal knew what was happening, a sweet voice behind him said, "In short, Husayn's as fond of you as Budur is."

Perfumed with love and set to music by her angelic voice, this sentence penetrated Kamal's heart and sent him into an inebriated ecstasy. It was like a magical melody emerging suddenly in the middle of a song, rising above customary expectations in an un-imagined way to leave the listener perched between rationality and delirium.

"The beloved is recklessly playing with the vocabulary of love. She sprinkles you with it, little realizing that she is pouring flammable magnesium on a blazing heart." He recalled the sound of her words in order to re-create their resonant love within him. Affection is an ancient melody but seems marvelously fresh in each new rendition. "My God, I'm perishing from an excess of happiness," he thought.

Commenting on his sister's words, Husayn said, "Aïda's able to translate my thoughts into her special feminine language."

The vehicle sped along to al-Sakakini, then down Queen Nazili Street, followed by Fuad I Street. From there it crossed over the Nile to Zamalek at a speed Kamal thought insane.

"There are a few clouds in the sky, but we need even more if we're to have a comfortable day at the pyramids."

The miraculous voice was then heard, apparently addressing Budur: "Wait till we get to the pyramids. Then you can sit with him all you want."

Laughing, Husayn asked, "What does Budur want?"

"She desires, my dear sir, to sit with your friend."

" 'Your friend!' Why not say 'Kamal'? Why not grant that name a happiness beyond the aspirations of its owner?"

Husayn told him, "Yesterday Papa heard her ask me, 'Is Uncle Kamal coming with us to the pyramids?' So he wanted to know who Kamal was. When I told him, he asked her, 'Do you want to marry Uncle Kamal?' She told him quite plainly, 'Yes.' "

Kamal looked around, but the little girl had leaned back to hide her face against her sister's shoulder. Before turning his head away, Kamal fortified himself with a fleeting glance at the superb face of his beloved. He said, "If she's serious, she better not forget her promise."

When their automobile reached the Giza road, Husayn accelerated, and the roar of the engine increased so much that no one felt like talking. Kamal welcomed this opportunity to be alone with his thoughts and to enjoy his happiness. The day before, their family had discussed him, and the head of the household had suggested he should marry the little girl.

"Oh, what a warbling, flowery happiness! Memorize every word said. Replenish your soul with her Parisian perfume. Stock your ears with these calls of doves and gazelles. Perhaps you will be able to return to these experiences if you're troubled again by sleepless nights. The words of the beloved lack the wisdom of philosophers and the glittering insights of fine authors, and yet they shake you to the core and cause springs of happiness to well up in your heart. This is what makes happiness a mystery baffling the most brilliant minds. All you who breathlessly pursue happiness, I've come across it in a casual remark, a foreign phrase, in silence, and even in nothing at all. My Lord, how huge these giant trees are on both sides of the road! Their lofty branches form a canopy overhead, creating a lush green sky. There's the Nile flowing along with a brilliant coat of pearls supplied by the sun's decorative rays. When did I last see this road? On a trip to the pyramids when I was in the third year of secondary school. Each time I promise myself I'll return here alone. Behind you is sitting the person who has inspired you to see everything in a new way, even the traditional style of life in the ancient quarters of the city. Would you wish for anything beyond your present condition? Yes, for the automobile to continue racing along like this forever. . . . O Lord! Is this the aspect that always escaped you when you were wondering what you desired from love? The inspiration of the hour has revealed it to you, impossible though that seems. Rejoice in this preordained moment. There are the pyramids, looking small in the distance. Soon we'll stand at the foot of the largest one, like an ant at the base of a towering tree."

"We're going to visit the tomb of one of our original ancestors."

Kamal laughed. "To recite the opening prayer of the Qur'an in his memory in hieroglyphics," he joked.

Husayn remarked ironically, "A nation whose most notable manifestations are tombs and corpses!" Pointing to one of the pyramids, he continued: "Look at all that wasted effort."

Kamal replied enthusiastically, "Immortality!"

"Oh, as usual, you'll spare no effort to defend Egypt. Your patriotism's chronic. We differ in this. I might actually prefer to be in France instead of Egypt."

Hiding his pain behind a tender smile, Kamal answered, "There you'll find that the French are one of the most patriotic nations in the world."

"Yes, patriotism is an international disease. But I love France itself and I admire qualities of the French people unrelated to nationalism."

This kind of talk really saddened Kamal, but it did not cause resentment, since it came from Husayn Shaddad. He occasionally became vexed with Isma'il Latif on account of his arrogance. Hasan Salim angered Kamal at times with his haughtiness. But Husayn Shaddad always met with Kamal's approval, no matter what.

The automobile stopped near the foot of the great pyramid and at the end of a long line of empty vehicles. Many people could be seen here and there scattered in small groups. Some were riding donkeys or camels and others were climbing the pyramid. There were also the vendors and the donkey and camel drivers. The expanse of land seemed vast and limitless, but the pyramid shot up in the center like a legendary giant. On the far side, beyond the downward-sloping plateau, the city of Cairo was visible with the tops of its trees, a thread of water, and the roofs of its large buildings. Where were Palace Walk and Kamal's ancient house in all of that? Where was his mother, who would be putting out water for the chickens now, near the jasmine arbor?

"Let's leave everything in the car, so we'll be free to scout around."

They got out of the automobile and set off in single file: Aïda, Husayn, Budur, and finally Kamal, who was holding his young friend's hand. They walked around the great pyramid, admiring it from every direction. Then they went into the desert. The sand made it hard to walk and hindered their progress, but the refreshing breeze blew gently. The sun alternately hid and reappeared. Clusters of clouds spread along the horizons, sketching on the celestial canvas spontaneous pictures, which the hand of the wind altered at will.

Filling his lungs with the air, Husayn exclaimed, "Beautiful! Beautiful. . . ."

Aïda said something unintelligible in French. Kamal with his limited knowledge of that language assumed that she was translating her brother's comment. Using foreign words was a common practice for her, one that softened his extreme identification with the national tongue, Arabic, and imposed itself on his taste as a characteristic of feminine beauty.

Looking at everything around him, Kamal was moved and said, "Truly beautiful, praise to God Almighty."

Laughing, Husayn commented, "You always find God or Sa'd Zaghlul in everything."

"I think we have no quarrel concerning the first of those two."

"But your insistence on mentioning Him gives you an especially religious flavor, as though you were a scholar of religion." Then, in a tone of surrender, he continued: "What's strange about that since you're from a religious district?"

Was there any sarcasm lurking behind this statement? Was it possible that Aïda felt the same way? What did they really think of the ancient Islamic district at the heart of Cairo? How did residents of al-Abbasiya view Palace Walk and al-Nahhasin?

"Should you be embarrassed?" Kamal wondered. "Not so fast.... Husayn demonstrates scarcely any interest in religion and the beloved even less. Didn't she say once that she attends classes in Christianity at Mère de Dieu School, goes to mass, and sings their hymns? But she's a Muslim! A Muslim despite the fact that she knows nothing worth mentioning about Islam.... What do you think of this? I love her, I love her to the point of devotion. Despite the pricking of my conscience, I confess that I love her religion, while asking forgiveness from my Lord."

Husayn gestured toward the beauty and splendor surrounding them. Then he said, "This is what really attracts me. You're wildly patriotic, but compare the splendors of nature with demonstrations, Sa'd Zaghlul and Adli, and trucks packed with soldiers."

Smiling, Kamal replied, "Both nature and politics are splendid."

As though the association of ideas reminded him of an important event, Husayn said suddenly, "I almost forgot. Your leader has resigned." Kamal's only response was a sad smile.

Intending to provoke him, Husayn said, "He resigned after losing both the Sudan and the constitution. Isn't that so?"

With a calm attributable solely to the company in which he found himself, Kamal answered, "The assassination of Sir Lee Stack Pasha was a blow directed at Sa'd's government...."

"Let me repeat for you what Hasan Salim said: 'This attack is a manifestation of the hatred that some people, including the killers, harbor for the English. Sa'd Zaghlul is more responsible than anyone else for inciting this hatred.'"

Kamal suppressed the rage ignited within him by Hasan Salim's opinion. With the composure mandatory when he was in the presence of his beloved he said, "This is the English view. Haven't you read the telegrams printed in the newspaper, in *al-Ahram*? No wonder the Liberal Constitutionalists are repeating it. One of Sa'd's proudest achievements is that he aroused hostility against the English."

With a look of criticism or warning in her eyes and a fetching smile, Aïda intervened to ask, "Are we here to picnic or to politick?"

Kamal gestured toward Husayn as he said apologetically, "There's the one responsible for bringing up this subject."

Laughing and combing his silky black hair with his slender fingers, Husayn said, "I thought I'd offer you my condolences for the resignation of your leader. That's all there is to it." Then he asked in a serious tone, "Didn't you take part in the momentous demonstrations that erupted in your district during the revolutionary era?"

"I was too young!"

In a voice not free of gentle irony, Husayn observed, "In any case, the way you hid in that pastry shop during a demonstration must be considered participation in the revolution."

They all laughed. Even Budur imitated the others. Their quartet was composed of two horns, a violin, and a whistle. After a moment of silence, as though coming to Kamal's defense, Aïda said, "It's enough that he lost his brother."

Feeling pride pulsing through his heart because of their sympathy, Kamal said, "Yes, we lost the best of our family."

She asked with interest, "He was in Law School; isn't that so? How old would he be if he were alive today?"

"He'd be twenty-five...." Then he continued in a mournful voice: "He was a genius in every sense of the word."

Cracking his knuckles, Husayn said, "Was! This is what you reap from patriotism. How can you cling to it after that?"

Smiling, Kamal said, "The time will come when we're all referred to in the past tense. But what a difference there is between one form of death and another!"

Husayn cracked his knuckles once more without comment. Kamal's words seemed to mean nothing to him. What had made them discuss politics? It was not fun anymore. Partisan hostilities distracted people from the English. Down with all of it! A person who had caught a whiff of paradise should not trouble himself with terrestrial cares, not even momentarily.

"You're walking with Aïda in the desert near the pyramids. Ponder this ravishing fact and shout it aloud until the pyramid builders hear you. The beloved and her suitor are strolling together over the sand. The lover's rapture is so intense that the breeze might almost carry him off, while the beloved amuses herself by counting pebbles. If love's malady were contagious, I would not mind the pain. The wind is agitating the fringes of her dress, raking the halo of her hair, and penetrating her lungs. How fortunate it is! Spirits of lovers who float over the pyramid, bless this procession. They admire the beloved and pity the lover. They repeat with the voice of time the phrase: 'Nothing save love is stronger than death.' You see her but a few feet from you. Yet in truth she's as far removed as the horizons, which you imagine touching the earth, even though they are part of the sky and soar high overhead. How my soul wishes I could feel her touch on this excursion, but it seems you'll journey through this earthly existence before you experience that. Why aren't you courageous enough to throw yourself on the sand and kiss her footprints? Take a handful of sand from them for use in an amulet to ward off the pains of love during thought-filled nights. But alas! Everything indicates that the only contact with the beloved will be through singing hymns of praise or via insanity. So sing your psalms or go insane."

He felt a small hand tug at his. He looked down at Budur, who held her arms up to him, asking to be carried. He leaned over and lifted her, but Aïda protested: "No. It seems fatigue's getting the best of us. Let's rest a little."

On a boulder at the top of the slope leading to the Sphinx they sat down in the same order they had observed while walking. Husayn stretched his legs out and planted his heels firmly in the sand. Kamal sat with his legs crossed, holding Budur beside him. Aïda, seated to the left of her brother, took out her comb, which she ran through her hair. Then she smoothed her bangs with her fingers.

Husayn happened to notice Kamal's fez and asked his friend critically, "Why are you wearing a fez on this outing?"

Kamal removed it and placed it on his lap, saying, "I'm not used to going anywhere without it."

Husayn laughed and said, "You're a fine example of a conservative!"

Kamal wondered whether he was being praised or faulted and wished to force his friend to clarify the point, but Aïda leaned forward a little and turned toward Kamal to have a look at his head. He forgot what he was up to and anxiously concentrated all his attention on his own head. Now that it was bare, its huge size was obvious, and his short cropped hair, free of any attempt at styling, was exposed. Her beautiful eyes were gazing at him. What impression did he make on her?

The musical voice asked, "Why don't you let your hair grow out?"

It was a question he had never considered before. Fuad Jamil al-Hamzawi had his hair cut just like his and so did all their comrades in the ancient quarter. Yasin had not been seen with hair long enough to brush or a mustache until he had found employment. Could Kamal imagine encountering his father every morning at the breakfast table with long hair?

"Why should I?"

Husayn asked thoughtfully, "Wouldn't it look better?"

"That doesn't matter."

Laughing, Husayn commented, "It seems to me that you were made to be a teacher."

"Praise or blame?" Kamal wondered. "In any case, your head's to be congratulated for receiving this heavenly attention."

"I was created to be a student."

"Good answer. . . ." Then, with a rising inflection of voice to show he was asking a question, Husayn continued: "You haven't told me the whole story of the Teachers College yet. What do you think of it after almost two months?"

"I hope it will be a serviceable introduction to the world I desire. I'm currently trying to learn the meaning of difficult words like 'literature,' 'philosophy,' and 'thought' from the English professors."

"This is the cultural discipline we want. . . ."

Kamal answered apprehensively, "But it seems human culture is a stormy ocean. We need to know the limits. We must learn more clearly what we want. It's a problem. . . ."

Husayn's interest was apparent in his handsome eyes. He said, "For me, there's no problem. I read French stories and plays, with some help from Aïda to understand the difficult passages. I also listen with her to selections from Western music, some of which she plays expertly on the piano. Recently I've been reading a book that summarizes Greek philosophy in an easy way. All I want is mental and physical forms of tourism, but you also wish to write. That forces you to learn boundaries and goals."

"The worst part is that I don't know exactly what I'm going to write about."

Aïda asked pleasantly, "Do you want to be an author?"

Swept by a tidal wave of happiness rarely experienced by human beings, Kamal answered, "Perhaps."

"Poetry or prose?" Then, leaning forward so she could observe him, she added, "Let me see if I can tell by looking at you."

"I've exhausted all the resources of poetry in my intimate exchanges with your dream vision," he reflected. "Poetry is your sacred tongue. I won't try to make a living from it. My tears have drained its wells during dark nights. How happy I am to have you look at me . . . and how wretched! I revive under your gaze – like the earth, which burgeons with life when the sun shines down on it."

"A poet. Yes, you're a poet."

"Really? How do you know?"

She sat up straight, and a laugh like a whisper escaped from her. She replied, "Physiognomy is too instinctive a science to be explained."

"She's bluffing!" Husayn said, laughing.

She retorted, "Not at all. If you don't like the idea of being a poet then don't be one."

"Nature has made the female bee a queen," Kamal reflected. "The orchard is her palace. The flower's nectar is her drink. Honey is her product. And the reward earned by a person passing her throne is . . . a sting. But she denied Husayn's accusation."

She had another question for him: "Have you read any French stories?"

"Some by Michel Zévaco, in translation. You know I can't read French."

She said enthusiastically, "You won't be an author until you master French. Read Balzac, George Sand, Madame de Staël, and Pierre Loti. After that write your story."

Kamal said disapprovingly, "A story? That's a rather marginal art form. I aspire to do serious work."

Husayn said earnestly, "In Europe the story is considered a serious art form. Some writers there concentrate on it to the exclusion of all other types of writing. This is the way they've achieved the status of immortals. I'm not throwing praise around blindly. The French professor confirmed that."

Kamal shook his large head skeptically, and Husayn resumed speaking: "Be careful not to make Aïda angry. She's a reader who delights in French stories. In fact, she's one of their heroines."

Kamal leaned over a little to observe her reaction to Husayn's comment, seizing this opportunity to fill his eyes with the gorgeous sight. Then he asked, "How did that happen?"

"She gets all caught up in the stories, and her head is crammed with an imaginary life. Once I saw her strutting in front of a mirror. When I asked her what she was doing, she said, 'Aphrodite used to walk like this along the beach at Alexandria.'"

Frowning and smiling at the same time, Aïda said, "Don't believe him. He's more immersed in the world of the imagination than I am. But he's not satisfied until he accuses me of things that aren't true."

"Aphrodite?" Kamal wondered. "What's Aphrodite compared with my beloved? By the truth of your perfection, I'm sad to have you imagine yourself in any form but your own."

He commented sincerely, "You're not to blame. The heroes of al-Manfaluti and Rider Haggard have made a big impression on my imagination."

Husayn laughed delightedly and cried out, "How fitting it would be for all of us to be united in a single book. Why should we stay here on the ground, since we're so drawn to the world of the imagination? It's up to you. Bring this dream to reality. I'm not a writer and don't want to be, but you would be able to bring us together, if you so desired, in one book."

"Aïda in a book of which you would be the author . . ." Kamal marveled to himself. "Worship, mysticism, or insanity?"

"And me?" Budur's voice burst out suddenly in protest. The three others roared with laughter.

Husayn cautioned Kamal: "Don't forget to reserve space for Budur."

Hugging the little girl affectionately, Kamal said, "You'll be on the first page."

Aïda looked off to the horizon and asked, "What will you write about us?"

He did not know what to say. He hid his confusion with a feeble laugh, but Husayn replied for him: "Like all the other authors, he'll write a violent love story ending with death or suicide. They kick your heart around, but it's all a game to them."

"I hope only it's the hero who meets this end," Aïda said with a laugh.

"The hero is unable to imagine his beloved perishing," Kamal thought. He asked, "Is it mandatory that it should end with death or suicide?"

"That's the normal ending for a passionate love story."

"When one is fleeing from pain," Kamal reflected, "or trying to hold on to happiness, death seems a valid goal."

Then he said ironically, "A very distressing business!"

"Haven't you learned that? It seems you haven't been in love yet."

"There comes a moment in the lives we lead," Kamal told himself, "when weeping serves the purpose of the anesthetic in a surgical operation."

Husayn continued: "To me the important thing is that you save a place in your book for me, even if I'm out of the country."

Kamal gave him a long look and asked, "Are you still seduced by the notion of traveling?"

A serious note crept into Husayn Shaddad's voice as he said, "Every moment! I want to live. I want to be everywhere, far and wide, high and low. Then let death come, after that."

"What if it came before?" Kamal wondered. "Could that happen? What of the sorrow that's almost killing you? Have you forgotten Fahmy? A life isn't always judged by its length. Your life, Fahmy, was a brief moment, but it was complete. Otherwise, what's the use of virtue and immortality? But you're sad for another reason. It's hard for you to contemplate dispassionately separation from your friend who is so keen to travel. What will your world be like after he's left? What will become of you if his trip separates you from the mansion of your true love? How deceptive today's smiles are. She's at hand now. Her voice tickles your ear, and her perfume your nose. But can you stop the wheel of time? Will you spend the rest of your life circling round her mansion at a distance, like the fabled lunatic lovers of old?"

"If you want my opinion, you should postpone your travels until you've finished your studies."

Aïda said eagerly, "That's what Papa has told him repeatedly."

"It's sound advice."

Husayn asked sarcastically, "Is it necessary for me to memorize civil and Roman law in order to savor the beauty of the world?"

Still addressing Kamal, Aïda said, "Father has heaped scorn on Husayn's dreams. He hopes to see his son in the judiciary or working in finance like him."

"The judiciary, finance! I'm not going to join the judiciary. Even if I get my degree and seriously consider choosing a profession, my interest will be in the diplomatic corps. And as for money, do you want more? We're already unbearably rich."

"How amazing that a man's wealth can be unbearable," mused Kamal. "Long ago you thought you would be like your father and own a safe similar to his. Wealth is no longer one of your dreams, but don't you wish you could liberate yourself from material concerns to embark on spiritual adventures? How wretched life is when it's devoted solely to earning a living."

"No one in my family understands my hopes. They think I'm a spoiled child. My mother's brother once said sarcastically so I could hear, 'Wouldn't you have expected the only boy in the family to turn out better than this?' Why should they feel like this? It's because I don't worship wealth and prefer living to making money. You see? Our family believes that any effort not leading to an increase in wealth is a foolish waste of time, and you find them dreaming of titles, as though they were a lost paradise. Do you know why they love the Khedive Abbas II? Mama has often told me, 'If only Our Effendi Abbas had stayed on the throne, your father would have been named a pasha long ago.' Precious money is scorned and spent with abandon if a prince honors us with a visit." Then, laughing, he added, "Don't forget to record these foibles if you ever get around to writing the book I proposed."

He had scarcely finished speaking when Aïda told Kamal, "I hope you won't be influenced by the prejudices of my disrespectful brother and slander our family in your book."

Kamal replied in a worshipful tone, "God forbid that I should ever say anything against your family. Moreover, there's nothing disgraceful in what he alleged."

Aïda laughed triumphantly, and Husayn smiled with relief, although his eyebrows were raised in mock astonishment. Kamal felt that Husayn was not totally sincere in his attack on his family. He did not question Husayn's statement that he did not worship wealth and preferred living to making money. Yet Kamal imagined that Husayn's comments about the Khedive, titles, and entertaining princes had slipped out as boastful criticism, not just boasts or criticism. Husayn appeared to be bragging about these things with his heart but condemning them with his mind. Or perhaps he resented them but saw nothing wrong in mentioning them to a friend whom they would dazzle and fascinate, even if he deplored them too.

Smiling calmly, Husayn asked, "Which of us is to be the book's central character? Me, Aïda, or Budur?"

Budur cried out, "Me!"

Hugging her, Kamal said, "Agreed." Then he told Husayn, "This will remain a secret until the book is born."

"What title will you give it?"

"*Husayn Around the World!*"

Except for Budur, they all roared with laughter at this parody of the title of a farce, *The Barbarian Around the World*, which was playing at the Majestic.

Inspired by that, Husayn asked him, "Have you found your way to the theater yet?"

"No, the cinema's enough for now."

Husayn told Aïda, "The author of our book is not allowed to stay out after nine P.M."

Aïda replied captiously, "Still, he's better than people who are allowed to circle the planet."

Then she turned toward Kamal and, with a tenderness capable of eliciting his agreement regardless of what she proposed, she said, "Is it really wrong for a father to want his son to grow up to be as vigorous and respected as he is? Is it wrong for us to pursue money, titles, and higher things?"

"Stay as you are," thought Kamal, "and wealth, prestige, and lofty ideals will pursue you. Everyone will want to kiss the ground you walk on. How can I answer, when the response you desire entails my destruction? Alas for your heart, Kamal; it wishes for something you're forbidden."

"There's nothing wrong with that." Then, after a short pause, he added, "On condition that the person's temperament is congenial to it."

"What temperament would not be congenial to that? The strange thing is that Husayn does not renounce this refined life out of an ambition for something superior to it. No, my good man, he dreams of living without any lifework, in idle unemployment. Isn't that amazing?"

Laughing sarcastically, Husayn asked, "Don't the princesses you adore live that way?"

"Because there's no life above theirs to aspire to. What are you compared with them, lazybones?"

Husayn turned toward Kamal and in a voice tinged with anger said, "The precept followed in our family is to work to increase our fortune and to become friends with influential people in hopes of obtaining the rank of bey. Once that is achieved, you need to redouble your efforts to expand your fortune and befriend the elite so you will be promoted to pasha. Finally you make ingratiating yourself with the princes your supreme goal in life. You have to content yourself with that, since joining the royal family is not an objective you attain by effort or ingenuity. Do you know how much the prince's last visit cost us? Tens of thousands of pounds were wasted on buying new furniture and rare curios from Paris."

Aïda protested: "That money was not spent to curry favor with the prince just because he's a prince, but because he's the Khedive's brother. The motive for flattering him was our loyal friendship for him and his brother. It wasn't fawning ingratiation. And it's an honor no intelligent person could reject."

But Husayn obstinately persisted: "At the same time, Papa keeps on consolidating his ties to politicians like Adli, Tharwat, and Rushdi, who cannot be accused of loyalty to the Khedive. Doesn't that show he accepts the prevailing wisdom that the end justifies the means?"

"Husayn!" Aïda shouted her brother's name in a voice Kamal had never heard before. It was full of haughty, disdainful censure, as though she wanted to warn Husayn that such things should not be said, at least not in the presence of an outsider. Kamal's face blushed with embarrassment and pain. The happiness that had momentarily hovered over him at being included in the activities of this beloved family dissipated. Her head was erect, her lips were knit, and her eyes betrayed a frown, which she had not allowed to reach her forehead. The impression she gave was one of anger— the anger of a highborn queen. Kamal had never seen her emotional before. He had not imagined that she had feelings. He gazed at her face with astonishment and relief but felt so uncomfortable he wished he could invent an excuse to avoid continuing this conversation. After a few seconds he recovered and began to observe the beautiful, regal anger on her queenly face. He admired her flaming pride, domineering scorn, and frowning superiority.

As though speaking for Kamal's edification, Aïda proclaimed, "Papa's friendship with the men you mentioned has a long history prior to the Khedive's deposition."

Kamal wished sincerely to drive away this cloud. He playfully asked Husayn, "If that's the way you feel, why do you look down on Sa'd Zaghlul for having been a student at al-Azhar?"

Husayn laughed in his untroubled way and replied, "I hate fawning over the nobility, but that doesn't mean I respect the masses. I love beauty and despise ugliness. Sadly enough, beauty is rarely found among common people."

Aïda interjected in an even voice, "What do you mean by 'fawning over the nobility'? It's contemptible behavior for someone who does not belong to this class. But I think we do. When we attempt to ingratiate ourselves with other members of our class, they reciprocate it."

Kamal volunteered to answer, saying fervently, "That's the indisputable truth."

Husayn rose at once and said, "We've rested long enough. Let's walk some more."

They got up to resume their excursion, heading for the Sphinx. The sky was partly overcast. Groups of clouds spread out from the horizons to meet and veil the sun with a translucent curtain. The sun's light appeared gleaming white through this covering and fell to earth with a graceful purity.

As they walked along they met parties of students and mixed groups of European men and women. Perhaps wishing to placate Aïda indirectly, Husayn told her, "The European women are looking at your dress with great interest. Are you satisfied?"

She smiled with contented pride. Raising her head with charming conceit, she said in a voice that revealed her secure self-confidence, "Naturally!"

Husayn laughed and Kamal smiled. Then the former told the latter, "Aïda is considered an authority on Parisian taste throughout our whole district."

Still smiling, Kamal said, "Naturally."

Aïda rewarded him with a soft, tender laugh, like the cooing of a dove. It cleansed his heart of the residue left behind by the bizarre aristocratic squabble.

"The wise man," Kamal cautioned himself, "is the one who knows where his foot will fall before he moves it. Recognize how far below these angels you are. The beloved, who looks down at you from the clouds, feels superior even to her own relatives. What's strange about that? She should not have relatives or a family. Perhaps she selected them to be intermediaries between her and her devotees. Admire her composure and rage, her humility and arrogance, her forwardness and reserve, as well as her satisfaction and anger. They are all attributes of hers. So quench your heart's thirst with love. Look at her. The sand impedes her steps. She is not so light-footed here. She has lengthened her stride. Her torso sways like a bough intoxicated by a dying breeze. Yet she affords the eyes a new vision of graceful walking so beautiful that it equals in loveliness her normal manner of strolling down the mosaic paths of the garden. If you turn back, you'll see her charming footprints in the sand. Rest assured that they constitute landmarks on the mysterious road, providing guidance toward the heights of love and the illuminations of happiness. During your previous visits to this desert you spent all your time playing and leaping about. You were oblivious to the perfumed scents of the hidden meanings here, because your heart's bud had not yet blossomed. Today, its petals are moist with the dew of longing – those droplets of delight and pain. If you have been deprived of your peaceful ignorance, you have been granted a heavenly anxiety, which brings the heart to life and makes light sing."

"I'm hungry," Budur complained.

Husayn said, "It's time for us to turn back, don't you think? If we keep on this way, it will be so far that anyone who isn't hungry yet will be starved by the end."

When they reached the automobile, Husayn got out the bag and the basket with the food. He placed them on the hood of the car and started to open the lid of his basket, but Aïda suggested that they should eat on one of the blocks of the pyramid. They went there and climbed up on one of the bottom stones. Putting the food in the center of the block, they sat at the edge with their feet hanging over. Kamal spread out a newspaper that was in his bag and placed on it what he had brought – two chickens, potatoes, cheese, bananas, and oranges. Then he watched Husayn's hands remove the angelic picnic from their basket: elegant sandwiches,

four glasses, and a thermos. Although the food Kamal had brought
was more substantial, it appeared – to him at least – to lack the
elegant flourish of theirs. He was beset by apprehension and
embarrassment. Husayn gazed appreciatively at the chickens and
asked if Kamal had brought any silverware. Kamal extracted
knives and forks from the bag and began to slice up the chickens.
Then Aïda removed the stopper from the thermos and started
filling the glasses with a golden liquid.

Kamal was so surprised that he could not keep from asking,
"What's that?"

Aïda laughed but did not reply. Winking at his sister, Husayn
said quickly, "Beer."

"Beer!" Kamal exclaimed fearfully.

Pointing to the sandwiches, Husayn said defiantly, "And ham."

"You're making fun of me! I don't believe this."

"No, believe and eat. What a skeptic you are! We've brought
the best food and the most delicious drink."

Kamal's eyes proclaimed his astonishment and alarm. He was
tongue-tied, for he did not know what to say. What troubled him
most was the fact that this food and drink had been obtained from
their home and thus with the knowledge and consent of their
parents.

"Haven't you ever had these before?"

"That's a question needing no reply."

"Then you'll taste them for the first time, and the credit is ours."

"Impossible."

"Why?"

"Why! . . . Another question needing no reply."

Husayn, Aïda, and Budur raised their glasses and drank some
beer. The first two smiled at Kamal as though to say, "You see. It
didn't do anything to us."

Then Husayn said, "Religion, huh? A glass of beer doesn't
make you drunk, and ham is delicious and good for you. I don't
see the wisdom of letting religion intrude on questions of diet."

Kamal's heart felt bruised by these words, but in a tone as
amiable as ever he said critically, "Husayn, don't blaspheme."

For the first time since they started eating Aïda spoke: "Don't
think ill of us. We only drink beer to whet our appetites. Perhaps
Budur's participation will satisfy you of our good intentions. And
ham's very tasty. Try it. Don't be a Hanbali fundamentalist. There

are enormous opportunities for you to obey religion in more important ways than this."

Although her words did not differ in any essential way from Husayn's, they brought peace and balm to his wounded heart. Her words also found in him a soul totally committed to doing nothing to upset them or hurt their feelings. He smiled with gentle forbearance and, picking up some of his own food, said, "Let me eat the food I'm accustomed to and do me the honor of sharing it."

Husayn laughed. Gesturing toward his sister, he told Kamal, "We agreed at home to boycott your food if you boycotted ours, but it seems we did not properly appreciate your situation. Therefore, in your honor, I'm going to withdraw from that agreement. Perhaps Aïda will follow my example."

Kamal looked hopefully in her direction, and she said with a smile, "If you promise not to think ill of us."

Kamal answered delightedly, "Death to anyone who thinks ill of you."

They ate with great appetite, Husayn and Aïda first. Then Kamal, encouraged by watching them, followed suit. He served Budur her food himself. She was content with one sandwich and a piece of chicken breast. Then she turned her attention to the fruit. Kamal could not resist the temptation to observe Husayn and Aïda surreptitiously as they ate, in order to see how they handled their food. Oblivious to his surroundings, Husayn devoured his food as though he were alone. Even so, he did not lose his distinguished air and thus represented in Kamal's eyes the beloved aristocracy acting spontaneously. Aïda revealed new dimensions of elegance, grace, and refinement whether in cutting the meat, in grasping the sandwiches by the tips of her fingers, or in the movements of her lips as she chewed. All this took place in an easy, relaxed manner, without any affectation or embarrassment. The truth was that Kamal had been looking forward to this moment expectantly and incredulously, as though skeptical that she ate food like other human beings. Although his knowledge of the type of food she was consuming troubled his religious sensibilities greatly, he found in its novel and unusual nature, compared with what people he knew ate, a parallel to the eater herself, and this helped calm his questioning, perplexed imagination. Two contradictory feelings alternated within him. At first he was uneasy to see her undertake this activity in which both men and animals share. Then he felt somewhat relieved, since this activity brought the two of them closer together, if only a little. But he was still not free of questions. He was forced to wonder whether she also participated in other natural human functions. He could not deny that, but it was hard for him to accept. Therefore he refused to answer, although he experienced a sensation he had not known previously, one containing a silent protest against the laws of nature.

"I admire your feeling for religion and your moral idealism."

Kamal looked at his friend cautiously and suspiciously. So Husayn affirmed, "I'm speaking sincerely, not making a joke."

Kamal smiled shyly. Then he pointed at the remaining sandwiches and beer as he said, "Despite all this, your celebrations in the month of Ramadan are beyond description. Lights are lit, the Qur'an is recited in the reception hall, the call to prayer rings out in the gentlemen's parlor. Isn't that so?"

"My father celebrates the nights of Ramadan out of love, respect, and veneration for the traditions my grandfather observed. He and Mama are also scrupulous about fasting."

Aïda said with a smile, "I am too."

With an earnestness he meant to be sarcastic Husayn said, "Aïda fasts one day out of the whole month and sometimes gives up by afternoon."

Aïda retorted in revenge, "Instead of fasting, Husayn eats four meals a day during Ramadan: the three normal ones and then the meal before daybreak reserved for fasters."

Husayn laughed, and food would have fallen from his mouth if he had not reared his head back quickly. He said, "Isn't it strange that we know so little of our religion? What Papa and Mama know about it is hardly worth mentioning. Our nurse was Greek. Aïda knows more about Christianity and its rituals than she does about Islam. Compared with you we can be considered pagans." Then, addressing Aïda, he added, "Kamal reads the Qur'an and works about the life of the Prophet."

In a tone giving a hint of admiration she said, "Really? Bravo! But don't think any worse of me than is absolutely necessary, for I've memorized more than one Qur'an sura."

Kamal murmured dreamily, "Marvelous, extremely marvelous. Which one, for example?"

She stopped eating to try to remember. Then with a smile she replied, "I mean I used to know some chapters by heart. I'm not sure how much I've retained. . . ." Then, raising her voice as though she had found what she was searching for, she continued: "Like the sura which speaks of God's unity and so forth."

Kamal smiled, since the sura she referred to, number one hundred twelve, had only four verses. He handed her a piece of chicken breast, which she took gratefully, although she confessed she was eating more than she normally would.

She said, "If people ate all their meals at picnics, no one would be slender anymore."

Kamal said hesitantly, "The women in my part of town don't want to be slim."

Husayn agreed with him and commented, "Mama herself feels that way, but Aïda considers herself a Parisian."

"God forgive my beloved her scorn," Kamal brooded. "Like the skeptical notions you read, she deeply troubles your believing soul. But will you be able to confront your beloved's scorn for Egypt and Islam with the same criticism and anger you employed against those skeptical ideas? Of course not! Your soul harbors nothing but the purest love for her. You love even her defects. Defects! She has no defects, even if she makes light of religion and does things it forbids. In someone else, those would be defects. What I fear most is that from now on no beautiful woman will be able to please me unless she takes her religion lightly and performs forbidden acts. Does that make you apprehensive? Ask God's forgiveness for yourself and for her. Say that it is all amazing, as amazing as the Sphinx. How much your love and the Sphinx resemble each other. Each of them is an eternal riddle."

Aïda emptied what was left from the thermos into the fourth glass. Then she asked Kamal seductively, "Won't you change your mind? It's just a refreshing drink. . . ."

He smiled with apologetic thanks. Husayn grabbed the glass and raised it to his mouth, saying, "Me instead of Kamal." With a moan he continued: "We've got to stop or we'll die of overeating."

When they concluded their meal, only half a chicken and three sandwiches remained. Kamal, who thought he would distribute the leftovers among the young boys prowling about, saw Aïda put her sandwiches back in the basket along with the glasses and thermos and felt obliged to return the rest of his food to the bag. He happened to recall Isma'il Latif's comments about the parsimonious spirit of the Shaddad family.

Husayn jumped to the ground and said, "We have a pleasant surprise for you. We've brought a phonograph and some records to help our digestion. You'll hear some European music selected by Aïda and also Egyptian pieces like 'Guess What,' 'After Dinner,' and 'Turn Aside Here.' What do you think of this surprise?"

89

DECEMBER WAS half over, and the weather was still relatively mild, although the month had begun with windstorms, rains, and bitter cold. Kamal approached the Shaddad family mansion with happy deliberate steps, his neatly folded overcoat thrown over his left arm. His elegant appearance suggested that he had brought his coat to perfect the splendor and respectability of his attire rather than to guard against a change in the weather, especially since it was so mild. The late-morning sun was brilliant. Kamal thought their gathering would take place in the garden gazebo rather than the parlor, where they met in cold weather, and that consequently he might have an opportunity to see Aïda, who was only allowed to visit them in the garden.

If winter deprived him of a chance to meet her outside, it did not prevent him from seeing her at the window that overlooked the path to the garden or on the balcony surveying the entrance to the mansion when he arrived or left. He might catch a glimpse of her resting her elbows on the ledge or holding her chin in her hand. He would look up and bow devoutly. She would return his greeting with a delicate smile so sparkling that it lit up his dreams both day and night. Hoping to see her, he glanced stealthily at the balcony when he entered the grounds of the mansion and then at the window as he walked along the path. But he did not find her in either spot. Indulging himself in the hope that he would meet her in the garden, he headed for the gazebo, where he saw Husayn sitting unaccustomedly alone. They shook hands, and Kamal's heart rejoiced with delighted affection as he looked at the handsome face, since Husayn was a kindred spirit.

Husayn welcomed him in a merry, untroubled way: "Greetings to the teacher! Overcoat and fez! Next time don't forget your scarf and stick. Welcome, welcome!"

Kamal removed his fez and placed it on the table. Throwing his coat on a chair, he asked, "Where are Isma'il and Hasan?"

"Isma'il has gone to the country with his father. So you won't see him today. And Hasan telephoned me this morning to say he'll be at least an hour late, because he's copying some lecture notes. You know he's a model student like you. He's determined to get his degree this year."

They sat on neighboring chairs, with their backs to the house. The fact that they would be alone presaged for Kamal a quiet conversation with no dissension. It would be a harmonious and thoughtful meeting lacking the tedious but delightful debates unleashed by Hasan Salim and the stingingly sarcastic comments tossed off ad nauseam by Isma'il Latif.

Husayn continued: "I, to the contrary, am a rotten student. I listen to the lectures attentively, since I'm able to concentrate on them, but I can hardly bear to read my textbooks. I've often been told that studying law requires rare cleverness. They should rather say it requires denseness and patience. Like others motivated by ambition, Hasan Salim's a diligent student. I've often wondered what makes him push himself beyond normal human endurance, working and staying up late. As the son of a superior court judge he could have contented himself with doing just enough to pass, confident that his father's influence would guarantee him the kind of position he desires. The only explanation I can find is pride, which makes him want to succeed and drives him on relentlessly. Isn't that so? What do you think?"

Kamal replied sincerely, "Hasan's a fine young man who deserves praise for his character and intelligence."

"I heard my father say once that his father's an extraordinary and fair judge, except when it comes to political cases."

This opinion coincided with Kamal's own prejudice, since he knew that Salim Bey Sabry favored the Liberal Constitutionalists. He said sarcastically, "That means that he has a brilliant legal mind but is unfit to judge."

Husayn laughed loudly and then said, "I forgot I was speaking to a Wafdist."

Shrugging his shoulders, Kamal answered, "But your father isn't one! Imagine Salim Bey Sabry judging conspiracy and murder charges against Wafdists like Abd al-Rahman Fahmy or al-Nuqrashi . . ."

Had his opinion of Salim Bey Sabry been well received by Husayn? Yes, that could be seen clearly in his handsome eyes, to which prevarication and hypocrisy were alien. Perhaps Husayn's appreciation of this criticism could be attributed to the rivalry – no matter how muted by refined manners and decorum – that often arises between peers. Shaddad Bey was a millionaire, a wealthy man with status and prestige, who also had a long-standing relationship with the Khedive Abbas. Salim Bey Sabry, on the other hand, was a superior court judge for the largest judicial circuit in a land where official titles inspired people to veneration. It was inevitable that high rank and vast wealth should occasionally look askance at each other.

Husayn gazed at the vast garden calmly but sadly. The palms had been stripped of their hanging fronds, the rose bushes were denuded, the lush green of the vegetation had faded, and the smiles of the flowers had disappeared from the mouths of the buds. The garden appeared to be plunged in grief over the advent of winter. Gesturing toward the view, he said, "See what winter has done. This will be our last meeting in the garden. But you're one of winter's admirers."

Kamal really was fond of winter, but he loved Aïda more than winter, summer, fall, and spring put together. He would never be able to forgive winter for depriving him of the happy reunions in the gazebo. Yet he agreed: "Winter's a brief, beautiful season. In the cold overcast conditions and the drizzle there's a vitality to which the heart responds."

"It seems to me that winter's advocates are normally energetic and industrious. You're that way, and so is Hasan Salim."

Kamal rejoiced at this praise but wished most of it had been reserved for him. "I only expend half my energy on school assignments," he said. "The life of the intellect ranges far beyond school."

Husayn nodded his head approvingly and commented, "I don't think there's a school that could use up all the hours you devote to study each day. By the way, I think you're overdoing it, although occasionally I envy you. Tell me what you're reading now."

Kamal was delighted by this kind of conversation. Next to Aïda, it was what he loved best. He answered, "I can tell you my reading has become more systematic. It's no longer a question of reading anything I want – stories in translation, selections of poetry, or critical essays. I've begun to proceed in a slightly more enlightened manner. I recently started spending two hours every evening at the National Library. There I look up the meanings of deep and mysterious words in the encyclopedia, terms like 'literature,' 'philosophy,' 'thought,' and 'culture.' As I read, I jot down the names of books I come across. It's an extraordinary world. My soul dissolves in it from eager curiosity."

Husayn listened with attentive interest, leaning back in his rattan chair and putting his hands in the pockets of his dark blue English jacket. On his broad lips there was a pure smile of empathy. He said, "That's really beautiful. Once you asked me what you should read. Now it's my turn to confer with you. Do you see clearly where you're heading?"

"Gradually. . . . It seems I'm moving toward philosophy."

Husayn raised his eyebrows and said with a smile, "Philosophy? That's a provocative word. Be careful not to mention it within Isma'il's hearing. I've thought for a long time that you're destined for literature."

"Don't feel bad about it. Literature's a lofty form of entertainment, but that's not enough for me. My primary goal is the truth. What is God? What is man? What is the spirit? What is matter? Philosophy gathers all these together into a single, luminous, logical synthesis – as I've recently learned. That's what I crave with all my heart. This is the real journey. Compared with it, your trip around the world is secondary. Imagine! It will allow me to find a satisfactory answer to all these questions."

Husayn's face lit up with enthusiasm and desire as he said, "That's really extraordinary. I won't hesitate to accompany you into this magical world. In fact, I've read some chapters about Greek philosophy, even if I didn't get much out of that. I don't like plunging into things the way you do. I pluck one flower here and another there. Then I flit back and forth. Let me tell you frankly that I fear philosophy will terminate your relationship with literature, for you're not satisfied with learning about something. You want to think and to write. I believe it won't be possible for you to be a philosopher and a literary figure at the same time."

"Nothing will separate me from literature. Love of truth is not incompatible with the enjoyment of beauty. But work is one thing and relaxation another. I've determined to make philosophy my work and literature my relaxation."

Husayn laughed suddenly. Then he said, "So that's how you're going to duck out of your promise to write a story uniting all of us inside the covers of a book."

Kamal could not help but laugh too. He answered, "But I hope to write about 'man' one day. So you'll be part of that."

"I'm not nearly as interested in 'man' as I am in our individual personalities. Wait till I report you to Aïda."

When Kamal heard this name, his heart pounded with recognition, affection, and desire. He felt intoxicated, as if overwhelmed by a lively and expressive tune. Did Husayn really think the matter merited Aïda's censure? How ignorant he was! How could it have escaped him that there was no emotion Kamal felt, idea he pondered, or desire he nurtured that did not have the splendor of Aïda and her spirit glistening across its horizons.

"You wait. Time will show that I won't renege on my commitment so long as I live." Then after a moment he asked in a serious voice, "Why haven't you thought about being a writer? Your circumstances leave you free to devote yourself to this art."

Husayn shrugged his shoulders disdainfully and replied, "I should write so people can read? Why shouldn't people write so I can read?"

"Which of the two is of greater importance?"

"Don't ask me which is more important. Ask which is more pleasant. I consider work the human curse, but not because I'm lazy. Certainly not! Work is a waste of time. It imprisons the individual and gets in the way of living. A life of leisure is the happy one."

Kamal gave him a look that indicated he did not take his friend's words too seriously. Then he said, "I don't know what life a man would have if it weren't for work. An absolutely empty hour is certainly more tedious than a year filled with work."

"What wretchedness! The very truth of your statement confirms how miserable things are. Do you think I'm able to enjoy absolute leisure? Certainly not, alas. I still while away my hours with useful and necessary tasks. But I hope one day to achieve a state of total inactivity."

Kamal started to answer Husayn, but a voice behind them asked, "I wonder what they're talking about." Once this voice, this pretty melody, came within earshot his heart began to vibrate. The response came from deep inside him. Her words and his heart seemed to be different harmonious elements of a single tune. His soul was immediately freed of its bounding thoughts, and an absolute emptiness pervaded it. Was this the kind of total emptiness Husayn dreamt of? It was nothing in itself, but happiness pervaded it.

He turned around to watch as Aïda, preceded by Budur, approached from a short distance and came to a halt in front of them. Aïda was wearing a dress the color of cumin and a blue wool jacket with gilded buttons. Her bronze complexion was so clear it had the depth of a cloudless sky and the purity of distilled water.

When Budur rushed to him, he caught her in his arms and hugged her, as though attempting to conceal by that embrace the ecstasy of love he felt. Just then a servant hastened up. He stopped in front of Husayn and said politely, "Telephone."

Husayn rose, excused himself, and retreated to the men's parlor, followed by the servant.

Thus Kamal found himself alone with her for the first time in his life. Budur's presence did nothing to detract from the intimate atmosphere. He wondered apprehensively whether Aïda would remain or depart. But she advanced a couple of steps to stand under the roof of the gazebo, on the far side of the table from him. He gestured for her to sit down, but she smilingly declined with a shake of her head. So he stood up and lifted Budur onto the table. He caressed the young girl's head anxiously as he devoted all his attention to taming his emotions and mastering his feelings. A period of silence ensued, during which the only sounds to be heard were the rustling of the branches, the whispering of the dry leaves scattered about, and the chirping of the sparrows. To his eyes the earth, sky, trees, and distant wall separating garden from desert – not to mention the bangs of his beloved falling over her forehead and the extraordinary sparkle and contrast of her eyes – all seemed a joyous vision from a happy dream. He could not tell for certain whether these things were really before his eyes or if it was an imaginary scene glimmering in his memory – until the melodious voice crooned, "Don't bother him, Budur."

His response was to clasp Budur to his breast as he said, "If this is what it means to be bothered, I love it."

He gazed at Aïda with eyes full of myriad desires, enjoying himself, free this time of any supervision. He studied her carefully as though to grasp her secrets and to print her features and expressions on the surface of his imagination. He so lost himself in the vision's magic that he seemed in a daze or stupor. Before he knew what was happening she asked, "Why are you looking at me like that?"

When he emerged from his daze, his eyes clearly showed his confusion. She smiled and asked, "Do you want to say something?"

Did he want to say something? He did not know what he wanted. He really did not understand what he wanted. He inquired in turn, "Did you see that in my eyes?"

With a mysterious smile on her lips she replied, "Yes."

"What was it you saw in them?"

She raised her eyebrows in mock astonishment and said, "That's what I want to know."

Should he reveal his closely held secret and tell her straight-forwardly, "I love you," without regard to the consequences? But why divulge it? What would become of him if, as was most likely, this confession ended the friendship and affection between them forever? As he pondered this question, he noticed a daring, self-satisfied, and supremely confident look in her eyes. Free of embarrassment or confusion, this glance seemed to fall on him from above, even though their eyes were at the same level. That made him uncomfortable and even more hesitant. He wondered what lay behind it. So far as he could see it was inspired by a feeling of disdain or perhaps by a sense of sport – as though she were an adult looking at a child. There was also evidence of a feeling of superiority that could not be justified merely by the difference in age between them, for she was only two years older at the most. The towering mansion on Palaces Street might look down on the old house on Palace Walk in just this way. But why had he not glimpsed it in her eyes before? She had never been alone with him. This was the first time he had had an opportunity to look at her closely. These ideas hurt and saddened him, causing his intoxication to fade away.

Budur held her hands out to him asking to be picked up, and so he lifted her in his arms. Then Aïda said, "How amazing! Why does my little sister love you so much?"

Looking at her eyes, he answered, "Because I harbor the same amount of love for her, or even more."

Aïda asked skeptically, "Is that a law?"

"The proverb says, 'Hearts communicate directly with each other.'"

She rapped on the table as she inquired, "Suppose a beautiful girl is loved by many men – should she love all of them? What sense would your law make in this case?"

This enchanting discussion made him oblivious to everything including his troubles. He replied, "She should then love the one who loves her most sincerely."

"How can she pick him out from the others?"

"If only this conversation could last forever," he wished.

"I refer you once more to the proverb: 'Hearts communicate directly with each other.'"

Her brief laugh sounded like a string being plucked. She remarked defiantly, "If this were true, no sincere lover would ever be disappointed in love. Is that correct?"

Her statement shocked him, as though reality was catching up with a man who relied on logic alone. If his reasoning was right, he would have been the happiest person alive with his love and his beloved. But was he anywhere near that blissful state? The long history of his love had embraced some moments of deceptive hope. These had illuminated the dark corners of his heart with an imaginary happiness after a sweet smile granted by the beloved, a passing remark open to wishful interpretation, or a cheerful dream concluding a night of pensive insomnia. His fantasies had drawn strength from maxims he revered, like: "Hearts communicate directly with each other." Thus he had been able to cling to his false hope with all the determination of a desperate person, until reality brought him back to his senses with this sarcastic and definitive statement like bitter medicine. With it, he could cure his future of lying hopes and learn exactly where he stood.

When he offered no response to the question with which she had challenged him, his beloved tormentor cried out victoriously, "I win!"

Silence reigned once more. Again he heard the rustling of the branches, the whispering of the dry leaves, and the chirping of the sparrows, but this time they encountered the tepid response of a disappointed heart. He noticed that her eyes were scrutinizing him more keenly than necessary and that her glance was increasingly daring and self-confident, as though she were toying with him. She looked like anything but a woman engrossed in a romantic conversation. He felt a cold, gnawing sensation in his heart. He wondered whether he had been destined to be alone with her like this so his dreams could be demolished in one blow.

She noticed his anxiety and laughed carelessly. Pointing to his head, she teased him: "You don't seem to have started to let your hair grow out."

He said tersely, "No."

"That doesn't appeal to you?"

Grimacing scornfully, he answered, "No."

"We told you it would look better."

"Does a man have to look handsome?"

Astonished, she replied, "Everyone likes people to look nice, whether they're men or women."

He felt tempted to repeat one of the phrases he had memorized, like: "The beauty of men is in their deeds," but realized that a statement of this kind coming from a person resembling him would only meet with sarcastic mockery from his beloved. He attempted to conceal his heart's pain with a forced laugh and said, "I don't agree with you."

"Or perhaps you flee from beauty the way you flee from beer and ham."

He laughed to relieve his despair and grief. Then she continued: "Hair is a natural covering. I believe your head needs it. Don't you realize that your head is very large?"

" 'The two-headed boy!' Have you forgotten that old taunt?" he asked himself. "What misery!"

"Yes, it is."

"Why?"

Shaking his head disapprovingly, he answered, "Ask it yourself. I don't know."

She laughed faintly, and they were silent.

"Your beloved is beautiful, fascinating, and captivating but – as is appropriate – also all-powerful. Taste her power and discover the different varieties of pain."

She gave no sign of having mercy on him. Her beautiful eyes kept climbing up his face steadily until they fixed on . . . yes, his nose. Deep inside he felt a convulsion that caused his hair to stand on end and his eyes to look down. He waited fearfully. He heard her laugh and looked up to ask, "What's so funny?"

"I remembered some hilarious things I came across in a famous French play. Haven't you read *Cyrano de Bergerac*?"

"The best time to scorn pain is when it's boundless," he advised himself.

Calmly and disdainfully he said, "There's no need to be polite. I know my nose is bigger than my head. But I beg you not to ask me why again. Ask it yourself, if you want."

Then Budur suddenly stretched out her hand and grabbed his nose. Aïda burst into laughter. She leaned her head back. He too could not help but laugh. To hide his confusion he asked the little girl, "And you, Budur – does my nose terrify you?"

They heard Husayn's voice as he came down the steps from the porch. Aïda suddenly changed her tone. She warned him entreatingly, "Don't be angry at my little joke."

Husayn returned to the gazebo and sat down again in his chair, inviting Kamal to be seated. After some hesitation Kamal, placing Budur on his lap, followed his friend's example. But Aïda did not stay long. She took Budur and bade them farewell. As she departed she gave Kamal a significant look, as though to stress her warning not to get angry. Kamal felt little appetite for resuming his conversation with Husayn and confined himself to listening or pretending to listen. From time to time he volunteered a question or an exclamation of surprise, appreciation, or disparagement, simply to show that he was present. Luckily for Kamal, Husayn harked back to a familiar topic requiring little concentration: his desire to go to France and his father's opposition, which he hoped to overcome shortly.

Kamal's heart and mind were preoccupied with the new look Aïda had displayed in the minutes they were alone or almost alone together. Her visage had been disdainful, sarcastic, and harsh. How cruel she had seemed! She had toyed with him mercilessly. Like a cartoonist confronting the human form with his brush, she had focused her jests on him to produce a caricature extraordinary for both its ugliness and its accuracy. In a daze, he recalled her appearance. Although pain flowed like poison through his spirit, spreading a dark stain of dejection and despair, he felt no resentment, anger, or contempt. Was this not a new attribute of hers? Certainly! Like her infatuation with French or her taste for beer and ham, it was one of her essential characteristics, no matter how strange, and therefore worthy of her, although in someone else it would be considered a flaw, an indulgence, or a sin. It was no fault of hers if one of her attributes produced pain in his heart or despair in his soul. The guilt was his, not hers. Was she responsible for giving him an enormous head or a huge nose? In her jests had she deviated from the truth and the reality? She had not and therefore was blameless. He deserved to suffer. It was his duty to accept this with ascetic resignation, like a devotee who believes implicitly in the fairness of a divine decree, no matter how harsh it appears, because the decree has been issued by the perfect beloved whose attributes and acts are beyond suspicion.

In this fashion Kamal fought his way out of the brief but violent ordeal that moments before had overwhelmed him. He felt hurt and tortured, but the strength of his fond fascination with the beloved was in no way affected. He had just experienced a new kind of pain, that of bowing to the harsh verdict passed against him. Previously he had learned, also from love, the different pains associated with separation, forbearance, leave-taking, doubt, and despair. He had learned as well that some pains are bearable, some enjoyable, and others constant, no matter how many sighs and tears are sacrificed to them. It seemed that he had fallen in love in order to master the dictionary of pain. By the glow of the sparks flying from his colliding pains he could see himself and make fresh discoveries.

"It's not merely God, the spirit, and matter you need to learn about. What is love? What are hatred, beauty, ugliness, woman, and man? You must learn about all of these too. The ultimate stage of damnation reaches up to the first level of salvation. Laugh as you remember or remember as you laugh that you were about to reveal your secret to her. Recall, as you weep, that the hunchback of Notre Dame terrified his beloved when he leaned over to comfort her. He, the hunchback, never elicited her sincere affection until he was breathing his last. 'Don't be angry at my little joke.' She even begrudges you the consolation of hopelessness. If the beloved would only speak openly, then we might leave the inferno of uncertainty and content ourselves with the tomb of despair. It's out of the question for despair to eradicate love from my heart, but it could save me from lying dreams."

Husayn turned to ask why he was so quiet but noticed someone approaching. Looking back, he exclaimed, "Here's Hasan Salim. What time is it now?"

Kamal twisted around and saw Hasan approaching the gazebo.

90

HASAN AND KAMAL left the mansion of the Shaddad family around 1 P.M. Kamal was going to say goodbye to his friend in front of the gate, but Hasan asked, "Won't you walk a little with me?"

His invitation willingly accepted, Hasan, whose head barely reached his friend's shoulder, set off along Palaces Street with the lanky Kamal, who wondered what the purpose was, especially since the hour was more suitable for dining and resting than a stroll. Before he knew what was happening, Hasan had turned to ask him, "What were you talking about?"

Although the question only increased his curiosity, he answered, "Different subjects as usual . . . politics, culture, and so on."

It was a genuine surprise when Hasan said in his calm, level voice, "I mean you and Aïda."

Kamal was astonished. Seconds passed without his attempting to reply. Then gaining control of himself he asked, "How did you know? You weren't there?"

Without any change of expression, Hasan Salim said, "I arrived while you were talking. It seemed best to leave so I wouldn't interrupt your conversation."

Kamal wondered whether he would have done the same thing if he had found himself in Hasan's position. He felt even more perplexed, sensing that he was on the verge of an animated conversation with many ramifications. "I don't know why you felt you should go off," he said. "If I had noticed, I wouldn't have let you."

"There are standards of polite behavior. I admit I'm very sensitive in this regard."

"Aristocratic etiquette!" Kamal told himself. "How alien it seems!"

"Excuse me," Kamal said, "if I tell you frankly that you're being overly meticulous."

Hasan's delicate smile tarried on his lips for only a second. He seemed to be waiting for something. When the wait became too long he asked, "Yes? What were you talking about?"

How could refined manners sanction such an interrogation? Kamal briefly considered asking Hasan this but elected to use an approach more compatible with his respect for the young man. This respect was based more on Hasan's personality than on their difference in age. Thus he continued: "The matter's too simple to warrant all this, but I wonder how much I'm obliged to say."

Hasan was quick to respond apologetically, "I hope you won't think I'm intruding or poking my nose into your personal affairs. I have reasons that justify my asking this question. I'll tell you things I haven't had occasion to mention before. All the same, counting on our friendship, I believed you wouldn't be offended by my question. I hope you won't misinterpret it."

The tension was eased. Kamal was pleased to hear tender words of this kind from Hasan Salim, the person he had long considered a shining example of aristocracy, nobility, and grandeur. In addition, he was even more eager than Hasan to enjoy an elevated conversation about anything related to his beloved. If it had been Isma'il Latif asking the question, the issue would not have required so much hemming and hawing over what was or was not necessary and was or was not proper. Kamal would have told him everything, as they laughed. But Hasan Salim never dropped his reserve and did not confuse friendship with intimacy. So there was nothing wrong in letting him pay the price for his reserve.

"Thanks for your good opinion of me," Kamal replied. "You can be sure that if there were anything worth telling I would not keep it from you. We just talked for a short time about some ordinary matters. That's all there was to it. But you've aroused my curiosity. May I ask you, if only to expand my horizons, what reasons justify your inquiry? I won't insist, naturally. In fact, I'm prepared to withdraw my question if it's inappropriate."

With customary calm and moderation, Hasan Salim said, "I'll answer your question but ask you to wait a little. It seems you don't care to brief me on your talk with her. And this is no doubt your right. I don't consider it an offense against the duties of friendship. But I would like to direct your attention to the fact that many are misled by Aïda's words and interpret them in a manner bearing no relationship to reality. For this reason, they cause themselves unnecessary problems."

"Go ahead and spit it out, Hasan," Kamal wished. "There are portents of foul weather in the air. A whirlwind's going to carry off the remnants of your stricken heart. You're the one who's been deceived, my friend. Don't you know that nothing but modesty keeps me from telling you everything? If it makes you feel any better, go ahead and strike me with your thunderbolts."

"I haven't understood a single thing you've said," Kamal protested.

Hasan raised his voice a little to explain: "The most gracious expressions flow easily and freely from her. A young man listening to her words assumes that she attaches some special significance to them or that they are prompted by some measure of affection. But they're nothing but pretty phrases she addresses to anyone she's conversing with, privately or in public. Thus many people have been duped. . . ."

"The cat's out of the bag," Kamal reflected. "Your friend's been afflicted by the same malady that has broken you. But who is he to claim he knows the most secret mysteries? He really makes me mad!"

Smiling and pretending to be unperturbed, Kamal said, "You seem very confident of what you're saying."

"I know Aïda extremely well. We've been neighbors for a long time."

The name he was too awestruck to use in secret, let alone to mention to others, had been pronounced carelessly by this infatuated young man, as though it belonged to some member of the swarming masses. This daring of Hasan's lowered him several notches in Kamal's heart while raising the young man by as many in his imagination. The sentence "We've been neighbors for a long time" plunged into Kamal's heart like a dagger, for it excluded him from serious consideration as effectively as distance does a traveler.

In a polite tone but with ironic insinuation, Kamal asked Hasan, "Isn't it possible that you've been deceived like the rest?"

Hasan drew his head back haughtily and said with great certainty, "I'm not like the others!"

How Hasan's arrogance infuriated him. . . . How angry Kamal was at the good looks and self-confidence of this coddled son of the eminent superior court judge whose rulings in political cases were suspect. . . . A "ha" escaped from Hasan, like the tail end of a laugh, although there was nothing in his look to suggest amusement. It was his way of preparing for a change from a haughty voice to a more gracious tone.

"She's an exceptional girl," he said, "without a flaw, although occasionally her appearance, conversation, and amiable nature leave her open to suspicions."

Kamal was quick to respond enthusiastically, "In both appearance and reality she's beyond criticism."

Hasan bowed his head gratefully as though to say, "Well done." Then he remarked, "That's what anyone with sound judgment and insight must see. Yet there are matters that have troubled a few minds. To make myself clear I'll cite examples. People misconstrue the fact that she visits in the garden with friends of her brother Husayn, thus challenging our cultural traditions. Some question her practice of conversing with these young men and befriending them. Still others fancifully imagine that there must be a weighty secret behind her innocent custom of pleasantly trading jokes with them. Do you get my meaning?"

With the same enthusiasm as before Kamal said, "Naturally I understand what you mean, but I fear your suspicions are exaggerated. I mean I've never been suspicious of any of her actions. Her conversation and little jokes are obviously innocent. Moreover, she did not receive a totally Egyptian upbringing. So she shouldn't be expected to observe all our traditions and shouldn't be blamed for deviating from them. I suspect that's what the others think too."

Hasan shook his head as though wishing he believed Kamal's opinion of their friends. Kamal did not bother to comment on Hasan's silent observation. He was happy with his defense of his beloved and delighted by the opportunity to declare his belief in her chastity and innocence. It was true that his enthusiasm was insincere, but not because he harbored reservations he was hesitant to make public. He had long believed his beloved was beyond suspicion. Yet he lamented his happy dreams based on the assumption that there was a secret meaning behind her jests and delicate hints. Hasan was banishing those dreams, much as the recently concluded conversation in the gazebo had. Although Kamal's wounded heart was struggling secretly to cling to them, if only by a slender thread, he went along with Hasan Salim publicly, accepting his friend's opinion in order to cover his own tracks, conceal his sense of defeat, and demolish his rival's claim to be the authority on the beloved's true nature.

Hasan continued: "It's not surprising that you should understand, for you're a bright young man. As you said, the fact is that
Aïda's innocent, but excuse me if I tell you frankly about a trait
that may seem peculiar to you. Perhaps it's her own fault to a great
degree if she's misunderstood. I refer to her penchant for being the
'dream girl' of all the young men she meets. Don't forget that it's
innocent. I tell you I've never encountered a girl more protective
of her honor than she is. But she's crazy about reading French
novels, frequently refers to their heroines, and has her head filled
with an imaginary world."

Kamal smiled to reassure him, wishing to suggest in this fashion
that he was hearing nothing new. Then driven by a desire to
provoke Hasan, he said, "I learned this some time ago when we
had a conversation – she, Husayn, and I – on this very subject."

He was finally able to make Hasan abandon his aristocratic
composure. Hasan's face showed his astonishment, as he asked
with apparent alarm, "When was that? I don't remember being
present! Did someone tell Aïda she wanted to be everyone's
'dream girl'?"

With victorious relief, Kamal gazed at the changes affecting his
friend. Afraid of carrying it too far, he said cautiously, "That wasn't
mentioned in so many words but was implied during a conversation about her infatuation with French novels and her immersion
in the world of the imagination."

Regaining his calm and equilibrium, Hasan was silent for a
time, as though attempting to collect his thoughts, which Kamal
had momentarily succeeded in scattering. He seemed hesitant.
Eventually Kamal realized that Hasan wanted to know everything
about his conversation with Aïda and Husayn. When had it
occurred? What had made them discuss those sensitive topics?
Would he spell out exactly what had been said?

But Hasan's pride restrained him from asking. At last he said,
"So you can vouch for the accuracy of my view. Unfortunately
many people do not understand Aïda's conduct the way you do.
They don't comprehend the important truth that she loves a
person's love for her, not that person."

"If the fool knew what had actually happened," Kamal thought,
"he wouldn't waste all this effort. Doesn't he know I don't even
aspire to have her love my love? Look at my head and nose.
Reassure yourself!"

In a voice not free of sarcasm Kamal said, " 'She loves a person's love for her, not that person' – what a philosophy!"

"It's the truth, and I'm certain of it."

"But you can't know for certain that this is always the case."

"Yes, I can, even with my eyes closed."

Falling prey to his sorrow, Kamal asked with sham astonishment, "Can you be sure that she does not love one person or another?"

Confidently and contentedly Hasan replied, "I can confirm with total certainty that she does not love any of the men who occasionally imagine she does."

"Only two types of people have a right to speak with such confidence," Kamal reflected, "the believer and the fool. And he's no fool. There's nothing new in what you're hearing. So why does it hurt? The truth is that I've felt enough pain today for a full year of love."

"But you can't prove she doesn't love anyone."

"I didn't say that."

Kamal looked at him as though consulting a diviner and then asked, "So you know she's in love?"

Nodding his head in agreement, Hasan said, "I invited you on this walk to tell you."

Kamal's heart sank in his chest – as though in attempting to flee from pain it had drowned in pain's waves. Until then he had suffered because it was impossible for her to love. Now his tormentor was affirming that she was in love, that the beloved loved, that her angelic heart was subject to the laws of passion, affection, desire, and longing – all directed at one individual. Of course, his intellect, but not his emotions, had occasionally allowed for that possibility, but in the way it accepted death – as an abstract thought, not a cold reality affecting his own body or that of a loved one. For this reason the news took him by surprise, as if the concept and its actual existence were being revealed to him at the same time.

"Reflect on these realities," he counseled himself. "Admit that there are pains in this world you never imagined, despite your expertise in pain."

Hasan continued: "I told you at the beginning that I have my reasons for this conversation with you. Otherwise I wouldn't have intruded into your personal affairs."

He would be consumed by the sacred fire to the last speck of ash.

"I'm sure that's true. I'm interested to hear what you have to say."

Hasan's feeble smile revealed that he was hesitant to utter the decisive words. So Kamal tried to be patient but finally, although his heart dimly perceived the distressing truth, he prodded his friend: "You said you know she's in love. . . ."

Flinging off his hesitation, Hasan said, "Yes. Our relationship gives me a right to assert this."

"Aïda's in love, O celestial realms. The strings of your heart contract to accompany a dirge. Does her heart harbor the same feelings for this happy young man that yours does for her? If this truly were possible, the best thing would be for the world to burst asunder. Your companion isn't lying, for handsome young men from distinguished families don't lie. The most you can hope for is that her love is of a different kind than yours. If this catastrophe is inevitable, it's some consolation that Hasan's the one. It's also comforting to find that sorrow and jealousy do not blot out the reality standing before you – this wealthy, enchanting, marvelous fellow."

As though pressing the trigger of a revolver he knew was empty, he remarked, "You seem extremely confident that she's in love this time with the person himself, not with his love for her."

Another "ha" escaped from Hasan to express his certainty. He glanced swiftly at Kamal to see if he was convinced. Then he said, "Our conversation – mine and hers – was definitely not a talk that could be understood in more than one manner."

"What kind of conversation was it?" Kamal wondered. "I'd trade my whole life for a single word of it. I've learned the truth and am quaffing the torment down to the dregs. Do you suppose he heard the ravishing voice tell him, 'I love you'? Did she say it in French or in Arabic? The fires of hell burn with torment like this."

He said calmly, "I congratulate you. It seems to me that each of you is truly worthy of the other."

"Thanks."

"But I wonder what prompted you to reveal this precious secret."

Hasan raised his eyebrows as he said, "When I discovered you talking together, I was afraid you might be taken in, like many others, by some statement of hers. So I decided to tell you the truth quite candidly, because I hated for you of all people to be deceived."

"Thank you," murmured Kamal, moved by the lofty sentiments of the gifted young man whom Aïda loved and who had hated to let Kamal be deceived and therefore had slain him with the truth. Was it not possible that jealousy had been among the motives inducing Hasan to tell Kamal his secret? But had he no eyes to see Kamal's head and nose?

Hasan picked up the conversation again: "She and her mother frequently visit our residence. Then we have opportunities to talk."

"Alone?" This question slipped out unconsciously, and he regretted it. Feeling uneasy, he blushed.

Hasan replied quite simply, "At times."

How he wished he could see her in this role, that of a woman in love. He had never imagined it in his wildest dreams. What did the glow of passion and affection look like in her dark eyes, which cast him patronizing glances? Although fatal to the heart, it would be a vision to light up the mind with a firebrand of sacred truth justifying an eternal curse on any skeptic.

"Your spirit flutters like a trapped bird wishing to fly free. The world is a crossroads of ruins. It would be pleasant to leave it. But even if you're certain their lips have met in a rose-red kiss, you can look forward to the pleasure of absolute freedom in the whirlpool of madness."

Driven by a suicidal desire he could no more resist than understand, he asked, "How can you agree then to let her mingle with Husayn's friends?"

Hasan hesitated a little before replying, "Perhaps I'm not totally comfortable with it, but I find no real reason to take offense. She's always in full view of her brother and all the others. Then there's her European upbringing. I concede that I've occasionally thought of mentioning my annoyance to her, but I'd hate to have her accuse me of jealousy. She'd love to make me jealous! Naturally you know about these feminine wiles. I'll admit I don't relish them."

"No wonder," mused Kamal, "that the demonstration of the earth's revolution on an axis and around the sun swept myths away and left people feeling dizzy."

"As though she's deliberately baiting you," he said.

Hasan replied confidently, "If I ever need to, I can always make her defer to me."

This sentence and the tone in which it was uttered enraged Kamal to the point of insanity. He wished he could think of some pretext to attack Hasan and to roll him in the dust. Kamal would be strong enough to do it. He looked down on Hasan from above, and their difference in height seemed even greater than it actually was. If she could love someone that short, why could she not love someone a little younger than she was? He felt he had forfeited the world. Hasan invited him to dine with his family, but Kamal excused himself with thanks. Then they shook hands and parted.

He returned home feeling listless, dejected, and despondent. He wanted to be alone to brood over the events of the day, pondering them until their implications became clear. Life seemed clad in mourning weeds. But had he not known from the first that this was a hopeless love? What extra nuances had these events supplied? In any case, his consolation was that while other people talked of love, he loved with all his heart. No one else would be capable of the kind of love that illuminated his heart. This was where his distinction and superiority lay. He would not relinquish his dream of long standing to win his beloved in paradise where there were no artificial distinctions. He would not have a large head or a huge nose there.

"In heaven Aïda will be mine, by virtue of celestial law."

91

HE SEEMED not to exist anymore. She ignored him so totally that it could only have been by design. He first realized this a week after he had spoken with Hasan Salim on Palaces Street, when he met his friends Friday morning at the gazebo in the gardens of the Shaddad mansion. They were all conversing when Aïda arrived as usual, accompanied by Budur. She stayed for a while, chatting with this one and joking with that one, without paying any attention to Kamal. Initially he assumed his turn would come. But when he grew tired of waiting and noticed she did not want to look him in the eye or at least was avoiding his glance, he abandoned his passive stance and commented on something she had said in order to force her to address him. But she kept on talking and ignored him. Although no one else appeared to have noticed his abortive maneuver, because they were engrossed in what the beloved was saying, that did not soften the blow he had received without knowing what could have provoked it. Since he was predisposed to deny what had happened to him, he hid his suspicions. He began to watch for opportunities to try his luck again, though he was extremely apprehensive. When Budur attempted to escape from Aïda's grasp and waved her free hand at Kamal, he went to take the little girl in his arms. But Aïda dragged Budur closer to her, protesting, "It's time for us to go." Then she said goodbye and retraced her steps.

Oh, what was the meaning of this? Aïda was annoyed with him and had come for the sole purpose of displaying her anger. But what was she blaming him for? What sin had he committed? What lapse, great or small, was he responsible for? Sneering at logic, anxiety shattered the certainties of his world.

At the time, he was able to gain firm control of himself so that his worries would not be exposed. He knew how to keep his head and played his normal role to perfection, concealing from his friends' eyes the impact of this crushing blow.

After the gathering broke up, he told himself it was best to face the truth, no matter how bitter. He would have to admit that Aïda had deprived him, for one day at least, of the benefits of her friendship. There was a tiny recording device in his loving heart, and no whisper, thought, or glance of the loved one escaped it. This mechanism even detected her intentions and could anticipate events still remote. Let the cause be whatever it was or let there be no cause – as though this was a disease defying medical treatment – in either case he felt like a leaf ripped from the twig by a violent wind and cast into an oozing heap of refuse.

He found his thoughts hovering around Hasan Salim, who had ended their conversation with the words: "If I ever need to, I can always make her defer to me." But she had come today as usual. Kamal had suffered from her snub, not her absence. Moreover, he and Hasan had parted on good terms. There would have been no reason for Hasan to ask her to ignore Kamal. And she was not a person to take orders from any man, no matter who. Besides, Kamal had done nothing wrong. Lord of the heavens, what was the secret behind this censure? At their meeting in the gazebo Aïda had spoken harshly and mercilessly and had mocked Kamal's head, nose, and dignity. But these remarks had not lacked an affection-ate, jesting quality, and the session had ended with something like an apology. Although it had dashed any hope he had nourished for his love, still his love had always been hopeless. When they met today, he had been ignored, ostracized, and condemned to silence and death. It would have been better for the loved one to treat her devotee harshly or cruelly than for her to pass by him as though he did not exist. How wretched! A new entry had been added to the dictionary of pains he carried in his breast. Here was a new levy – imposed by love – and how oppressive its levies were! In this manner he paid for the light that both illuminated and scorched him.

He was enraged. It was very hard to obtain nothing but this haughty cold-shoulder treatment in return for his enormous love. He was painfully aware that the only expression his anger could find was love and loyalty and that the one way to counteract the blow was prayerful supplication. If his soul had stood accused by anyone else, even by Husayn Shaddad, Kamal would not have hesitated to sever ties, but since the plaintiff was the beloved, all the slivers of anger sped back to his chest. His hostility was poured out on a single target, Kamal. A desire for revenge drove him to inflict punishment on the defendant, Kamal. He sentenced himself to a life of renunciation. A pervasive, sad, obstinate feeling directed him to avoid her forever. He had enjoyed her friendship. Indeed he had considered it a blessing beyond his wildest dreams, even though the force of his love overwhelmed heavens and earth. More than all that, he had enjoyed his despair at ever being loved by her and had forced his unruly cravings to be satisfied with a sweet smile or a kind word, even if these came in parting. But to be ignored by her saddened, baffled, and disoriented him, leaving him alienated from the entire world. In this manner he was afforded an opportunity to feel what a dead man might if still conscious.

His thoughts churned away mercilessly during his waking hours that whole week he was separated from the Shaddad mansion. He kept brooding about his failure, which he agonized over repeatedly – in the morning at home having breakfast with his father, walking along the street with senses that only appeared to be functioning, at the Teachers College listening absentmindedly to a lecture, reading in the evening with scant attention, or humbly begging entry to sleep's ideal realm. Early in the morning when he opened his eyes, these thoughts were ready to fight for control of him, as though they had been lying in ambush at the threshold of consciousness or had awakened him out of an insatiable urge to devour him. Yes, how hideous the soul is when it turns on its master.

On Friday he went to the palace of love and torment, arriving slightly ahead of the appointed hour. Why had he been looking forward so impatiently to this day? What did he hope to gain from it? Did he wish to find some indication, even if only a feeble pulse, that would let him think life had not yet departed from hope's body? Did he dream of a miracle that would unexpectedly cause his beloved to be friendly again for no conceivable reason, exactly as she had grown angry? Or was he trying to stoke the fires of hell so that he might taste cold ashes all the sooner?

He proceeded to the garden along the path strewn with memories. Then he saw Aïda seated on a chair, holding Budur on the edge of the table in front of her. There was no one else in the gazebo. He stopped walking and thought of going back outside before she noticed him. But he rejected this idea defiantly and scornfully. He advanced on the gazebo, driven by a strong desire to face his punishment and to strip the veil from the puzzle that had slain his security and peace of mind. This lovely, gracious creature, this ethereal spirit disguised as a woman – did she realize what her harshness had done to him? Would her conscience rest comfortably once he complained about his suffering? Her tyrannical hold over him resembled the sun's over the earth, which was destined to orbit in a prescribed path. If it drew too close to the sun they would fuse together, but if the earth retreated too far, it would be annihilated once and for all.

She could bestow one smile on him, and he would salve all his pains with it. He approached her, deliberately treading heavily so she would hear. She turned her head around inquisitively, but then her face seemed to go blank. He stopped a little more than a meter from where she was sitting, bowed his head humbly, and with a smile said, "Good morning."

She nodded her head slightly but did not speak. Then she looked straight in front of her.

There was no longer any doubt that hope was a rigid corpse. He imagined she would shout, "Take your head and nose away so they don't obscure the light of the sun." Budur waved to him. He glanced down at her beautiful and radiant face and went toward her to mask his defeat with her innocent affection. She grabbed hold of his arms, and he learned over to kiss her cheek warmly and gratefully.

Then the voice that in the past had opened the portals of celestial music for him said roughly, "Please don't kiss her. A kiss is not a hygienic greeting."

A disconcerted laugh escaped from him, he knew not how or why. He became quite pale. At first dumbfounded and in a stupor, he finally responded incredulously, "It's not the first kiss, so far as I remember."

She shrugged her shoulders as if to say, "That changes nothing."

"Oh!" Was he to begin a new week of torture without getting to utter a word in self-defense?

"Allow me to ask what secret is behind this bizarre change? I've been wondering all week long and have been unable to find an answer."

She did not seem to have heard him and consequently did not bother to reply.

With his voice betraying his anxiety and pain, he continued: "What really makes me sad is that I'm innocent. I've done nothing to deserve this punishment."

She still seemed determined to remain silent, but he was afraid Husayn would arrive before she was coaxed into speaking. In a voice combining complaint with entreaty he quickly said, "Doesn't an old friend like me deserve at least to be informed of his offense?"

She raised her head, cast him a sideways look as gloomy as storm clouds, and said angrily, "Don't pretend you're innocent!"

"O Lord of the heavens, can sins be committed unconsciously?" he asked himself as he mechanically patted Budur's hands, with which she was attempting to draw him close to her, for she understood nothing of what was going on.

"Alas, my suspicions are correct," he said jerkily. "This is what my heart told me, but I couldn't believe it. You think I've done something wrong. Isn't that so? But of what offense are you accusing me? By your life, tell me. Don't wait for me to confess, for the simple reason that I've committed no crime against you. No matter how much I search the recesses of my soul, life, and past I can find no intention, word, or deed meant to harm you. I'm amazed that you don't realize how self-evident this is."

She replied scornfully, "I'm not the kind of girl who's taken in by theatrics. Ask yourself what you said about me."

With alarm he asked, "What have I said about you? To whom did I say it? I swear to you . . ."

She cut him off in exasperation: "I'm not the least bit interested in your oaths. Save them for yourself. The oaths of slanderers are not to be trusted. The important thing is for you to remember what you said about me."

He tossed his overcoat on a chair as though preparing to throw himself into the debate and stepped away from Budur to free himself from her innocent attempts to monopolize his attention. Then he said so heatedly that his words had the ring of truth, "I've never said anything about you I would be embarrassed to repeat now in your hearing. I have never said anything bad about you in my whole life. I wouldn't be able to, if you only realized. . . . If one of our friends has told you something about me that's angered you, then he's a despicable liar who doesn't deserve your trust. I'm ready to confront him in your presence so that you can see for yourself whether he's telling the truth or, more precisely, lying. You have no defects, so how could I mention any? You've really been unfair to me."

She commented sarcastically, "Thanks for this praise, which I don't deserve. I don't think I'm that flawless . . . if for no other reason than that I haven't received a totally Egyptian upbringing."

This last phrase skewered his mind, for he remembered saying it in his conversation with Hasan Salim when defending his beloved from the doubts Hasan had raised. Had Hasan repeated it in a manner that had stirred her doubts about Kamal's good intentions? The noble Hasan Salim . . . would he do such a thing? How Kamal's head was spinning. . . .

His eyes eloquently expressing his shock and sorrow, he said, "What do you mean? I admit I said that, but ask Hasan Salim to tell you — he's got to tell you — that I said those words when I was praising your virtues."

She glared at him coldly and asked, "My virtues? And is my wish to be everyone's 'dream girl' a virtue?"

Kamal cried out with panic and rage, "He said that about you, not I. Won't you stay and let me challenge him in front of you?"

She bitterly and ironically pursued her interrogation: "And is my flirting with you another of my virtues?"

Feeling desperately unable to defend himself from this flood of accusations, he said, "You flirt with me? Where? When?"

"In this gazebo! Have you forgotten? Do you deny you left him with that impression?"

He was hurt by the sarcasm with which she asked, "Have you forgotten?" He perceived at once that Hasan Salim — how stupid it all was — had nourished suspicions about their tête-à-tête and had shared his doubts with his sweetheart or had ascribed them to Kamal in order to investigate them by this dirty trick of which he was the victim.

He said sadly and indignantly, "I deny it. I deny it with all my force and sincerity. I only regret trusting Hasan."

She said haughtily, as though she considered this last sentence a dig at her, "He always deserves that."

Kamal was beside himself. He imagined the Sphinx had raised its awesome stone paw, unmoved for thousands of years, to bring it down on him, crushing him and burying him beneath it forever.

In a trembling voice he said, "If it's Hasan who told you these lies, then he's a common liar. He's the one slandering me. It's not me slandering you."

A stern expression was visible in her eyes. She asked sharply, "Do you deny that in his presence you criticized my association with Husayn's friends?"

Was this the way an aristocratic patrician distorted a person's words? Deeply moved, he said, "Absolutely! That never happened. God knows I didn't. But he claimed something quite stupendous. He said . . . he said you love him. He said that if he wanted to, he could prevent you from associating with us. I never meant . . ."

She interrupted him scornfully and rose, proudly holding herself erect as the halo of her black hair fluttered around her uplifted face. "You're raving! It doesn't matter to me what people say. I'm above all this. In my opinion my only error is in bestowing my friendship indiscriminately."

As she spoke she put Budur down on the ground and took her hand. Then, turning her back on Kamal, Aïda left the gazebo.

He called after her entreatingly, "Wait a moment please, so . . ."

But she was already far away, and his voice was louder than it should have been. He imagined that the whole garden had heard him. The trees, the gazebo, and the chairs all seemed to be staring at him scornfully. He closed his mouth and rested his hand on the edge of the table. He leaned over as though his tall torso was bowed by the force of defeat.

He was not alone long. Husayn Shaddad soon appeared with his usual cheerful expression and greeted Kamal in his normal, sweet, innocent fashion. They sat down on neighboring chairs. Isma'il Latif came a little later. Finally Hasan Salim arrived. He made his way to them with unhurried steps and an arrogant bearing.

Kamal wondered anxiously whether Hasan had observed them from a distance as he had that previous time. When and how would Hasan learn what had been said in their stormy final conversation? Kamal's rage and jealousy swelled within him like a ruptured appendix. He promised not to allow any adversary to gloat over him. He would not expose himself to anyone's mockery or feigned affection. He would not let them see any evidence of the turmoil within him. He threw himself into the current of the conversation, laughing at Isma'il Latif's observations,

commenting at length on the formation of the new Ittihad or
Union Party, on the deserters who had left Sa'd Zaghlul and the
Wafd Party, and on the role of Nashat Pasha in all of that. In brief,
he played his part to perfection until the meeting concluded
peacefully.

When Kamal, Isma'il, and Hasan left the Shaddad mansion at
noon, it seemed that Kamal could not restrain himself any longer.
He told Hasan, "I'd like to speak to you."

Hasan replied calmly, "Go ahead."

Kamal looked apologetically at Isma'il and said, "Alone."

Isma'il was ready to leave them, but Hasan gestured for him to
stay, saying, "I keep nothing from Isma'il."

This tactic infuriated Kamal, for he glimpsed behind it a
dubious ploy, which was cause for concern. All the same he said
nonchalantly, "So let him hear us. I don't have anything to hide
from him either."

He waited until their steps had carried them some distance from
the Shaddad mansion. Then he said, "Before you came today,
I happened to meet with Aïda in the gazebo alone. We had a
bizarre conversation from which I gathered that you had com-
municated to her part of the conversation you'll recall we had
on Palaces Street. But my comments had been so distorted and
mutilated that she assumed I had attacked her unfairly and unjustly."

Hasan repeated the words "distorted and mutilated," his lips
deformed by anger. Then, casting Kamal a glance to remind him
that he was addressing Hasan Salim, not just anyone, Hasan
said coldly, "It would be good for you to choose your words
carefully."

Kamal replied passionately, "That's just what I did. The truth is
that her comments left no room for doubt that you wished to cause
trouble between us."

Hasan became pale with anger but did not yield to it. In a voice
he made as cold as possible he observed, "I'm sad I had a good
opinion of your understanding and comprehension of things."
Then he continued sarcastically: "Won't you tell me what I might
gain from this alleged trouble? The fact is you're jumping to
conclusions without any deliberation or thought."

Kamal's anger intensified, and he shouted, "You have allowed
yourself to be tempted into disgraceful behavior."

At this point Isma'il intervened to say, "My suggestion is that you postpone this conversation to another time when you'll both be in better control of your nerves."

Kamal said determinedly, "The matter's too clear for there to be any need for debate. He knows it and so do I."

Isma'il interjected once more, "Tell us what you said to each other in the gazebo. Perhaps we . . ."

Hasan interrupted haughtily: "I refuse to be put on trial."

Even though he knew full well that Hasan would lie, Kamal gave vent to his anger: "Anyway, I told her what happened, so she could see who was telling the truth."

His face pale, Hasan shouted, "We'll let her compare the words of a merchant's son to those of the son of a superior court judge."

Kamal darted toward him with a clenched fist, but they were separated by Isma'il, who was the strongest of the three despite his diminutive build.

Isma'il said resolutely, "I won't allow this. Each of you is a friend and the respectable son of an honored father. Let's renounce foolish conduct like this, which is better suited to children."

Kamal returned home feeling rebellious, agitated, and hurt. He stamped his feet angrily on the pavement. Inside him there was a wild conflagration. He had received potentially lethal blows to his heart and honor with regard to his beloved and his father. What else was there for him in the world? What of Hasan, whom he had respected more than any other comrade, admiring his rectitude? . . . In a single hour Hasan had been transformed into a vituperative slanderer. The fact was that, angry as Kamal was, he could not believe his own accusation wholeheartedly and unequivocally. He still kept reflecting about it, asking himself whether it was not possible that there was some secret explanation for that painful scene? Had Hasan distorted Kamal's words or could Aïda have misconstrued them and read more into them than she should have? Had she surrendered to wrath too quickly? But the comparison between the son of a merchant and the son of a superior court judge cast Kamal into an inferno of anger and pain, which conspired to make his attempt to be fair to Hasan an exercise in futility.

The next time Kamal went to the Shaddad mansion at the customary hour for their weekly reunion, Hasan was absent, having excused himself because something had come up. After the session disbanded, Isma'il Latif informed Kamal that he –

Hasan – was very sorry for what he had blurted out in a moment of pique about "the merchant's son and the son of the superior court judge" and that he believed Kamal had made serious accusations based on fanciful deductions. Hasan hoped that this untoward incident would not end their friendship and had asked Isma'il to convey this message to Kamal orally.

Later Kamal received a letter from Hasan to the same effect, emphasizing the request that they should put the past behind them when they met and forget about it. The letter concluded with the statement: "Remember everything you did to offend me and what I did to offend you. Perhaps you will be as convinced as I am that each of us was in the wrong and that therefore it would not be right for either of us to reject his friend's apology." This letter made Kamal feel better for a while. Yet he noticed the contrast between Hasan's customary arrogance and this delicate and unexpected apology. Yes, it was unexpected, since he had never imagined that Hasan would apologize for any reason. What had made him change? Their friendship would not have had this huge an impact on his comrade's pride. Perhaps he, Hasan, wished to restore his own reputation for civility more than he wished to reclaim their friendship. Perhaps he also wanted to keep the quarrel from growing any more virulent lest news of it reach Husayn Shaddad, for that young man might be indignant at having his sister embroiled in the dispute or angry for his own sake if he heard what had been said about "the merchant's son and the son of the superior court judge," since Husayn was also the son of a businessman. Any of these would have been plausible reasons and more logical, given Hasan's character, than an apology influenced by nothing but their friendship.

Whether he made peace with Hasan or continued to be his enemy seemed insignificant to Kamal. The important thing was to know whether Aïda had decided to conceal herself. She no longer wandered by when they were sitting in the garden. She was not visible at the window. She did not appear on the balcony. Counting on her pride, Kamal had told her what Hasan had said about being able, if he chose, to prevent her from visiting them. Kamal had done that to shore up her determination to visit the gazebo, so he would not be deprived of seeing her. But in spite of that she disappeared as though she had quit the house altogether, indeed the whole district. Why not say the whole world, which had become insipid? Was it possible that this separation would last forever? He hoped it was her intention to punish him for a time and then pardon him. If only Husayn Shaddad would mention some reason for her absence and dispel his fears. . . . He wished with all his heart for one of these eventualities and bided his time, but his wait was long and fruitless.

Whenever he went to visit the mansion he approached it with anxious eyes, as he wavered between hope and despair. He would steal a glance at the front balcony and another at the window overlooking the side path. Then on his way to the gazebo or the men's parlor he would gaze at the rear balcony. As he sat with his friends, his long reveries featured the happy surprise that just did not take place. When they split up after their conversation, he would keep looking stealthily and sadly at the window and the balconies, especially at the window over the side path, for it frequently served as a frame for his beloved's image in his day-dreams. Then he would depart, gulping down his despair and puffing out his distress. He became so despondent that he would have asked Husayn Shaddad the secret behind Aïda's disappear-ance had it not been for the traditions of the ancient quarter, with which his mentality was saturated. Thus he said nothing but began to wonder anxiously about the extent of Husayn's knowledge of the circumstances leading to the disappearance of the beloved.

Hasan Salim made no reference to the past, and his face gave no indication that he thought about it at all. Yet doubtless at each session that brought them together, he saw a living witness to his victory: Kamal. This thought hurt Kamal a good deal. He suffered a lot and felt the torment penetrating his marrow. The delirium of suffering affected his thinking. His worst agonies stemmed from the grief of separation, the bitterness of defeat, and the anguish of despair. Even more atrocious than all of these was his sense of abasement at being expelled from the garden of her good graces and deprived of the beloved's melodies and illuminations. As his spirit shed tears of grief and sorrow, he began to repeat, "You deformed creature, what are you compared with those blissful fellows?" What meaning would life have if she persisted in con-cealing herself? Where would his eyes find light or his heart warmth? What rapture was there for his spirit to enjoy? So let the beloved appear at whatever price she stipulated. Let her appear and love anyone she pleased, Hasan or someone else. Let her appear and mock his head and nose as much as her sense of humor and her playfulness wanted. His craving to contemplate her form and to hear her voice exceeded the human norm – so what then of a pleasant look to remove the resentment, despair, and desolation from his breast and to cheer a heart deprived of happiness as a blind man is deprived of the light? Let her appear even if she ignored him, for in that case, although he would be denied the pleasure of being acknowledged by her, he would not miss the happiness of seeing her and thus of seeing the world her magnificent light revealed. Otherwise, life would be nothing but successive moments of pain racked by insanity. Her withdrawal from his life was equivalent to extracting the spine from a body, which, having once known a balanced perfection, is then reduced to a sentient blob.

His pain and anxiety made him restless. He could not bear to wait for Friday to come, and he would go with friends to al-Abbasiya and circle around the mansion at a distance, on the chance that he might see her at a window, on a balcony, or as she walked when she thought she was far from his eyes. One of the consolations of waiting patiently in his home on Palace Walk was despair. In his feverish condition hovering near the shrine of the beloved was comparable to putting sticks of dynamite around a pillar of flame. He never saw her. Several times he saw one of the servants going or coming on the street. Then he would follow the fellow with amazed and curious eyes, as if asking the fates why they singled out this person to be near the beloved, to associate with her, and to observe her in various different modes – whether lying down, singing, or daydreaming. Why should all this good fortune befall a man who lived in her prayer niche with a heart oblivious to her worship.

On one of his jaunts he witnessed Abd al-Hamid Bey Shaddad and his treasured wife as they left the mansion to get into the Minerva automobile, which was waiting for them at the gate. Thus he saw the two happy individuals whom, more than anyone else in the whole world, Aïda venerated and respected. They occasionally gave her orders, which she had to obey. This precious mother had carried Aïda in her belly for nine months. Doubtless Aïda had once been a fetus and then a newborn, like those creatures Kamal had stared at for a long time when they first appeared in Aisha's and Khadija's beds. No person knew more about the childhood of his beloved than this happy and precious mother.

The pains would remain, or at least their effects would not be erased, so long as he wandered through life's labyrinth. To what avail were those nights in January when he buried his eyes, flowing with tears, in the pillow? He spread out his hands in prayer to the Lord of the heavens, pleading with total commitment, "O God, tell this love to be as cold as ashes, just as You commanded the fire burning Abraham: 'Be cold and safe'" (Qur'an, 21:69). He wished that love was concentrated in one location in the human being, for perhaps then it could be surgically removed the way a diseased limb is amputated. With a humble heart he uttered her beloved name to hear it echo in the silent room, as though someone else had summoned her. To revive a dream of lost happiness, he imitated her voice speaking his name. He ran his eyes over the pages of his diary to confirm that what had happened was a reality, not a figment of his imagination.

For the first time in years he thought regretfully of his life before love, as if he were a prisoner harking back to memories of lost freedom. Yes, he could think of no condition more like his than the prisoner's. Yet prison bars seemed easier to break and less confining than love's invisible shackles, which take total control over the heart's emotions, the mind's thoughts, and the body's nerves and then refuse to let go.

One day he wondered whether Fahmy had experienced this kind of torment. Memories of his late brother haunted him like a mournful song sighing in the hidden recesses of his soul. Kamal remembered how once in Fahmy's presence he had recounted Maryam's flirtation with the British soldier Julian. Kamal had plunged a poisoned dagger into his brother's heart, recklessly and carelessly. He summoned Fahmy's face into his conscious memory, recalling his brother's deceptive composure at the time. Then he re-created the contractions of pain on that handsome face when Fahmy had gone off by himself. He invented the plaintive monologues Fahmy had no doubt indulged in, like Kamal now, with moans and groans. Kamal felt the pain in his own heart and concluded: "Fahmy felt something worse than a bullet in his heart, even before the lead ripped into his chest."

Strangely enough, Kamal found that the political activities of the day presented an enlarged version of his life. When he read

about developments in the newspapers he could have been reading about the events at Palace Walk or on Palaces Street. Like
Kamal, Sa'd Zaghlul was as good as imprisoned and the victim of
outrageous attacks, unjust charges, and the treacherous betrayal of
friends. They had suffered because of contacts with people distinguished both by the loftiness of their aristocratic backgrounds
and by the baseness of their deeds. The personal distress of the
great nationalist leader also resembled the vanquished state of
the nation. Kamal felt the same emotion and passion about the
political situation as he did about his personal condition. He might
just as well have been referring to himself when he asked of Sa'd
Zaghlul, "Is this unjust treatment appropriate for such a sincere
man?" He might easily have meant Hasan Salim when he said of
Ahmad Ziwar Pasha, who replaced Sa'd Zaghlul as Prime Minister, "He has betrayed our trust and resorted to unfair tactics to gain
control." Aïda could have been on his mind when he said of
Egypt, "Has she dismissed the one man she could trust at a time
when he was busy defending her rights?"

92

THE SHAWKAT residence on Sugar Street did not enjoy the blessings of peace and quiet, not merely because the three floors were crowded with members of the Shawkat family but because of Khadija most of all. The elderly matriarch resided on the bottom floor, and Khalil, Aisha, and their children – Na'ima, Uthman, and Muhammad – were on the top one. But the uproar for which they were responsible was nothing compared with that raised by Khadija, whether it came from her directly or was provoked by her. Various changes in the management of the household had been made with an eye to confining the reasons for disputes to the narrowest possible limits. Khadija, who had been given her own living quarters and kitchen, had also ousted her mother-in-law's chickens from the roof so that she could raise chickens there herself and establish a modest garden patterned after the one on the roof of her childhood home. All these steps should have lessened domestic turmoil a great deal, but it had not decreased, or only to an imperceptible degree.

On this particular day Khadija's normally contentious spirit was afflicted by a certain listlessness. There seemed to be no secret about the reason, for Aisha and Khalil had come to help relieve the crisis. Yes, it was a crisis – one Khadija had precipitated. The two brothers sat on a sofa in the living room and the two sisters, their wives, were on the opposite one. They all looked serious, and Khadija was frowning. They exchanged eloquent glances, but no one wished to address the subject that had brought them together.

Finally, in a tone both plaintive and resentful, Khadija said, "Every household has quarrels like these. That's the way the world has been since our Lord created it. But there's no reason to broadcast our troubles to everyone and especially not to people who ought to be spared idle gossip. But she wasn't satisfied until she transformed our private affairs into public scandals. I can only trust in God and His blessings."

Ibrahim shifted around inside his overcoat as though trying to get comfortable on the sofa. Then he laughed briefly in a manner that left the others in doubt as to the exact import. Khadija looked at him suspiciously and asked, "What do you mean, 'ha–ha'? Is there nothing in the world that can make an impression on your heart?"

She turned away as though despairing of any assistance from him. Then, addressing Khalil and Aisha, she continued: "Are you happy that she went to see my father at the shop to complain about me? Is it right to drag men – especially ones like my father – into women's disputes? No doubt he was annoyed by her visit and complaint. If he wasn't so polite, he would have told her that frankly. But she kept at him until he promised to come. What disgusting conduct! My father wasn't made for petty matters like these. Do you approve of this behavior, Mr. Khalil?"

Khalil frowned disapprovingly and said, "My mother made a mistake. I told her so frankly, and she poured out her anger on me. But she's an old lady. You know people her age need to be treated with flattery and discretion, almost like children. Fine . . . ."

Ibrahim interrupted him irritably: " 'Fine, fine'! . . . How many times are you going to repeat 'Fine'? I'm sick of it. As you observed, Mother's an old lady, but her blow has landed on a person who refuses to show any mercy."

Khadija glared at him with a scowling face and flaring nostrils. She exclaimed, "God! God! All that's left is for you to repeat these outrageous comments in front of Papa."

Expressing his regret with a wave of his hand, Ibrahim answered, "Papa isn't here yet. And if he does come, it won't be to listen to me. I'm just stating the truth, which everyone acknowledges and even you can't deny. You can't bear my mother and can't stand the sight of her. I take refuge in God. Why is all this necessary, reverend lady? With a little discretion and cleverness you would be able to hold her in the palm of your hand. But the moon would be easier to obtain than your moderation. Can you deny a word I've said?"

She looked back and forth from Khalil to Aisha in order to draw their attention to this screaming injustice. They seemed to be wavering between truth and personal safety. At last Aisha, although she was apprehensive about the result, muttered, "Mr. Ibrahim means that you might show a little forbearance with her foibles."

Khalil nodded his head in agreement, with all the relief of a man who has reached a fire escape in the nick of time. Then he said, "That's right. My mother has a quick temper but should be shown the same respect as yours. If you'll be a little more understanding, you'll spare your nerves the discomfort of feuding with her."

Khadija huffed and said, "It would be much more accurate to say that she can't bear me or stand the sight of me. She's made me a nervous wreck. We never meet without her volunteering something, either directly or by insinuation, that makes my blood boil and poisons my nerves. Then I'm asked to be forbearing, as though I'm made of ice . . . . Isn't it enough that Abd al-Muni'm and Ahmad try my patience to the breaking point? Hear my prayer: Where can I find someone who will treat me fairly?"

With a smile Ibrahim said sarcastically, "Perhaps you'll find this equitable person in your father."

She shot back, "You're enjoying my bad luck. I understand everything. But our Lord is present."

In a strained voice, suggesting both resignation and defiance, Ibrahim answered, "Calm down so you'll be relaxed when you see your father."

How could she relax? The old lady had devised the most terrible vengeance. Shortly Khadija would be summoned before her father. Her blood ran cold at the thought of this encounter. Then Abd al-Muni'm and Ahmad's screams resounded through the closed door of their room. These were followed by Ahmad's sobs. Khadija, despite her plumpness, jumped up quickly and headed for their bedroom. Pushing the door open, she entered and screamed, "What's the meaning of this? Haven't I forbidden you to fight a thousand times? The one I'm after is whoever started this."

Once she had disappeared behind the door, Ibrahim said, "The poor dear seems to have a deep-rooted antagonism against tranquillity. Beginning first thing in the morning, she wades into a long series of skirmishes lasting the whole day. She doesn't quiet down until she goes to bed. Everything has to yield to her will and design – the servant, the food, the furniture, the chickens, Abd al-Muni'm, Ahmad, and me. Everything must adjust to her system. I feel sorry for her. I assure you that our residence could enjoy the most systematic order without any need for this obsessive behavior."

Smiling, Khalil said, "May our Lord come to her aid."

"And help me too!" Ibrahim added as he smilingly shook his head. Then he took his cigarette case out of the pocket of his black overcoat. He rose to offer it to his brother, who accepted a cigarette.

Ibrahim invited Aisha to have one as well, but she laughingly declined. Pointing to the door behind which Khadija had disappeared, she said, "Let's give the hour every possible chance of going smoothly."

Ibrahim resumed his seat and lit a cigarette. Gesturing toward the same door, he remarked, "A court of law. There's a trial being conducted in there now. But she'll treat the two defendants mercifully, even if that's against her better judgment."

Khadija returned, grumbling, "How can I enjoy any peace in this house? How and when?"

She sat down and sighed. Then, addressing Aisha, she said, "I looked out through the balcony peephole and saw that the mud left behind by yesterday's rain is still covering the road. So tell me, by your Lord, how my father's supposed to walk through it? Why this stubbornness?"

Aisha asked her, "What about the sky? What does it look like now?"

"Overcast! All the alleys will be lakes by nightfall, but is that enough to make your mother-in-law postpone, even for a day, the evil she's hatching? No, she went to the store despite the hardship walking there posed. And then she hounded the man until he promised to come. Anyone hearing her complain about me in the store under such adverse conditions would have thought I was a cold-blooded killer like those dreadful women in Alexandria: Rayya and Sakina."

They all laughed, seizing the opportunity she had provided to release their tension. Ibrahim asked, "Do you think you're less dangerous than the thieving sisters Rayya and Sakina?"

They heard someone knock on their door. When Khadija's servant opened it, the maid Suwaydan's face appeared. She glanced fearfully at Khadija and said, "My senior master has arrived." Then she speedily vanished.

Khadija's color drained from her face, and she said in a faint voice, "Don't leave us alone together."

She waited for Aisha to cast a searching look at her reflection in the mirror to see that her face was free of makeup. Then they left the apartment together.

Directly under a portrait of the late Mr. Shawkat, al-Sayyid Ahmad Abd al-Jawad sat on a couch in the center of a room decorated in the old style. Widow Shawkat, the mother of Khalil and Ibrahim, was sitting in a nearby armchair wearing a thick coat, which despite its bulk did not conceal her scrawniness or her bent back. Her face had grown thin, and her deep wrinkles were surrounded by folds of dry skin. Nothing about her remained the same except her gold teeth.

Al-Sayyid Ahmad was no stranger to this room or its antique furnishings, the age of which detracted in no way from the magnificence. If the curtains had faded and the velvet of some of the chairs and couches had become bald or torn on the arms or backs, the Persian carpet had a lasting splendor and an increasing value. The room was fragrant with a delicate incense of which the old lady was enamored.

Leaning on her parasol, she said, "I told myself that if al-Sayyid Ahmad didn't come as he promised, he's not my son and I'm not his mother."

He smiled and said, "God forbid. I'm obedient to your command. I'm your son and Khadija's your daughter."

She made a face and said, "All of you are my children. Mrs. Amina is a fine daughter to me. You're a prince of a man. But Khadija . . ." She looked at him, and her eyes grew wide as she continued: "Khadija did not inherit a single quality from her excellent parents." Then, shaking her head, she added, "O Gracious One, be gracious to us."

Al-Sayyid Ahmad responded apologetically, "I'm shocked that she's made you so angry. The matter comes as an immense surprise to me. I won't stand for this at all. But won't you tell me what she's done?"

Frowning, the woman said, "This has been going on for a long time. We've kept everything from you out of respect for the pleas of her mother, all of whose attempts to reform Khadija have failed. But I won't say anything behind her back, al-Sayyid, sir, as I declared to you at the store."

At that moment the group arrived. Ibrahim entered first, followed by Khalil, Aisha, and finally Khadija. They shook hands with al-Sayyid Ahmad one by one until it was Khadija's turn.

She leaned over with exemplary politeness to kiss her father's hand. The old lady could not restrain herself from saying in astonishment, "Lord, what is this charade of manners? Are you really Khadija? Don't let appearances deceive you, al-Sayyid Ahmad."

Khalil said to his mother critically, "Won't you give our father a chance to catch his breath? There's really no need for a tribunal."

The woman's voice grew louder as she replied, "Why are you here? What's brought all of you? Leave her with us, and the rest of you can go in peace."

Ibrahim said gently, "Think of God."

She shouted at him, "I'm acting more devoutly than you, you mule. If you were a real man, there would have been no reason for me to call in this fine gentleman. Why are you here? Shouldn't you be sound asleep as usual?"

Khadija was relieved at this opening. She hoped the quarrel would grow so intense that it would eclipse her case. But al-Sayyid Ahmad blocked the road for the anticipated battle between the old lady and her sons by saying in a loud voice, "What's this I've heard about you, Khadija? Is it true that you haven't been a polite and obedient daughter to your new mother? Asking God's forgiveness – she's a mother for all of us."

Khadija's hopes were disappointed, and she lowered her eyes. Her lips moved, but their whisper was indiscernible. She shook her head no.

The old lady waved her hand to get everyone's attention and began to speak: "This has been going on for a long time. I won't be able to recount all of it in one session. From her first day in this house she has opposed me for no reason whatsoever. She speaks to me with the sauciest tongue I've ever encountered in my whole life. I wouldn't like to repeat what I've heard over these five years or more. There have been many, many ugly remarks. She found fault with my management of the house and criticized my cooking. Can you imagine that, al-Sayyid, sir? She kept it up until she separated her living quarters from mine and thus split one home into two apartments. Even the maid Suwaydan was forbidden to enter Khadija's apartment, because Suwaydan is in my employ. Khadija hired a servant of her own. The roof! The roof terrace, al-Sayyid, sir, is very large, but she didn't think it big enough for both of us. I was forced to transfer my chickens to the courtyard. What else should I say, my son? This is a small sample, but we're not to blame. I told myself, 'What's done is done.' I bore it all and was patient, thinking that once she was independent of me the reasons for discord would be removed. But was my assumption correct? By your life, no!" She stopped talking, for she was overcome by a fit of coughing. She coughed so hard her veins swelled. Khadija prayed to God as she watched that He would carry off her mother-in-law before the indictment was finished. But the coughing died away. The old lady swallowed and recited the Muslim credo. Then, raising tearful eyes to al-Sayyid Ahmad, she asked in a voice not without a trace of huskiness, "Al-Sayyid Ahmad, do you have any aversion to calling me 'Mother'?"

Although Ibrahim and Khalil were smiling, their father-in-law put on a grave face as he answered, "God protect us, Mother."

"May God guard you, al-Sayyid Ahmad. Yet your daughter is averse to it. She calls me Auntie, although I've asked her repeatedly to say Mother. She retorts, 'Then what will I call the one at Palace Walk?' I tell her that I'm Mother and that her mother is also Mother. Then she tells me, 'I have only one mother, may our Lord preserve her for me.' Do you see, al-Sayyid, sir – me, the woman who received her with my own hands the moment she emerged from the unseen world."

Al-Sayyid Ahmad leveled an angry look at Khadija and asked her indignantly, "Is this true, Khadija? You must reply."

Khadija had virtually lost her ability to speak, for both her rage and her fear were extreme. In addition, she was anything but optimistic about the outcome of this discussion. Her instinct for self-defense prompted her to resort to humble entreaty. In a faint voice she said, "I'm unjustly accused. Everyone here knows I'm unjustly accused. By God, Papa, unjustly accused."

Al-Sayyid Ahmad was amazed by what he was hearing. Although from the beginning he had been aware of the influence of senility on Widow Shawkat and although the humorous atmosphere had not escaped his attention, since it was visible in the smiling faces of Ibrahim and Khalil, he was still determined to project a stern gravity in order to humor the grande dame and to intimidate Khadija. He was astonished by the disclosure of his daughter's obstinacy and irritability. He had never imagined that she was like this. Had her temper been so fierce when she lived in his home? Did Amina know more about this than he did? Would he eventually unmask a new image of his daughter, running counter to the one he had had of her, just as he had already found it necessary to revise his picture of Yasin?

"I want to know the truth. I want to know the truth about you. The person our mother has described is not the girl I know. Which of them is really you?"

The old lady joined the tips of her fingers together and then shook her hand up and down in a gesture asking him to be patient until she could finish what she was saying. Then she started off again: "I told her, 'I received you with my own hands when you were born.' She replied in a vicious tone I'd never heard before, 'In that case, it's a miracle I survived.'"

Ibrahim and Khalil laughed, and Aisha bowed her head to hide her smile. The matriarch told her sons, "Laugh, laugh! Laugh at your mother."

But al-Sayyid Ahmad was grim-faced, even though he too was secretly amused. Was it possible that his daughters were fashioned after his pattern? Was this not worth relating to Ibrahim al-Far, Ali Abd al-Rahim, and Muhammad Iffat? He told Khadija roughly, "No, no. . . . I'll certainly find ways to hold you strictly accountable for all this."

Relieved, the old lady carried on: "What caused the row yesterday was that Ibrahim invited some of his friends to a luncheon. Among the dishes served was Circassian chicken. Afterwards Ibrahim, Khalil, Aisha, and Khadija passed the evening with me. There was reference to the luncheon and Ibrahim mentioned his guests' praise for the Circassian chicken. Mrs. Khadija was delighted. But she wasn't satisfied. She went so far as to assert that Circassian chicken was the favorite dish in her childhood home. I remarked with the best of intentions that it was Zaynab, Yasin's first wife, who had introduced Circassian chicken to your family and that Khadija must have learned to make it from her. I swear I meant no harm when I said that. I did not mean to injure anyone, may God watch over you, my dear sir. But she jumped up angrily and shouted in my face, 'Do you know more about our house than I do?' I replied, 'I knew your house years before you did.' She screamed, 'You don't really love us. You can't stand for anything praiseworthy to be attributed to us, even if it's only cooking Circassian chicken – the Circassian chicken that was eaten in our house before Zaynab was born. It's disgraceful for a woman your age to lie.' Yes, by God, this is what she hurled at me, al-Sayyid, sir, in front of everyone. So which of us is the liar – before your Lord at prayers?"

Al-Sayyid Ahmad said with furious indignation, "She accused you of lying to your face! O Lord of heavens and earth, this is not my daughter."

Khalil asked his mother disapprovingly, "Is that why you've summoned our father? Is it proper to disturb him and waste his time because of a childish quarrel over Circassian chicken? This is too much, Mother."

The old lady stared him in the eye. She scowled and shouted at him, "Hush! Get out of my sight! I'm not a liar. It's not right for anyone to accuse me of lying. I know what I'm saying. The truth, which no one needs to be ashamed of, is that Circassian chicken was not a dish known in the home of al-Sayyid Ahmad before Zaynab introduced it. There is nothing in that fact to demean or belittle anyone. But it's the truth. Here is al-Sayyid Ahmad. Let him say if I'm lying. The excellence of the casseroles in his home is proverbial and the dishes stuffed with rice are as good, but Circassian chicken was not served at his table before Zaynab arrived. Speak, al-Sayyid, sir. You alone are the judge."

Al-Sayyid Ahmad had been fighting back the temptation to laugh all the time the woman was speaking. But he said in a ferocious tone, "If only her offense were limited to lying and to making a false claim without her having added to it a breach of manners . . . . Were you tempted to act so badly by the thought that you were beyond the reach of my hand? Without any hesitation my hand will stretch as far as necessary. It's really sad when a father finds his daughter needs to be reprimanded and disciplined after she's fully grown and has taken her place among women as a wife and a mother." Waving his hand, he continued: "I'm angry at you. By God, it hurts me to see your face before me."

Influenced by her emotions and by a realistic assessment of her situation, Khadija suddenly burst into tears, for crying was the only means she had available for her defense. In a choked and quavering voice she sobbed, "I'm unjustly accused. By God, I'm innocent. The moment she sees my face, she flings harsh words at me. She never stops telling me, 'If it weren't for me, you would have remained a spinster your whole life.' I've never done her any harm. They can all testify to that."

Her melodramatic performance, half sincere and half counter-feit, was not without its effect. Khalil Shawkat frowned angrily. Ibrahim Shawkat bowed his head. Although al-Sayyid Ahmad's appearance underwent no change, his heart was moved by this reference to spinsterhood, just as it had been in the old days. The lady shot piercing glances at Khadija from beneath her white eyebrows, as if to tell her, "Play your part, crafty girl, but it won't work with me."

When Widow Shawkat sensed that the atmosphere was becom-ing sympathetic to the actress, she said defiantly, "Here's Aisha, your sister. I adjure you, Aisha, by your eyes and the holy Qur'an: Did you not witness what I heard and saw? Didn't your sister call me a liar to my face? Didn't I give a fair account of the Circassian chicken dispute, without any exaggeration or hyperbole? Speak, daughter, speak. Your sister now accuses me of injustice, after calling me a liar yesterday. Speak, so al-Sayyid Ahmad will learn who the unjust aggressor is."

Aisha was terrified at being suddenly dragged into the tumult of this case, which she had thought she could observe safely from the sidelines until the end. She felt danger encompassing her from every direction. She looked back and forth from her husband to his brother, as though begging for help. Ibrahim started to inter-vene, but al-Sayyid Ahmad spoke first. Addressing Aisha, he said, "Your mother is requesting your testimony, Aisha. You must speak."

Aisha was so upset that she turned quite pale. But the only movement of her lips came when she swallowed. She lowered her eyes to escape from her father's stare and kept silent.

Then Khalil protested, "I've never heard of a woman being called on to testify against her sister."

His mother shouted at him, "I've never heard before of sons ganging up against their mother the way you are." Then she turned to al-Sayyid Ahmad and said, "But her silence is enough to prove my point. Aisha's silence bears witness on my behalf, al-Sayyid, sir."

Aisha thought her torment was over at this point, but before she knew what was happening, Khadija, who was drying her tears, entreated Aisha, "Speak, Aisha: Did you hear me insult her?"

Aisha cursed her sister privately from the depths of her heart. Her golden head of hair began to twitch nervously.

Then the old lady cried out, "Now we're getting somewhere. She's the one asking you to testify. You no longer have an excuse, Shushu darling. My Lord, if I really were as unjust as Khadija claims, why haven't I been unjust to Aisha? Why do I get along so well with her? Why, my Lord, why?"

Ibrahim Shawkat rose and went to take a seat next to al-Sayyid Ahmad, telling him, "Father, I'm sorry we've troubled you in this manner and wasted your precious time. Let's set aside complaint and testimony and put the past behind us, so we can see what's truly important and beneficial. Your presence can only be a positive influence and a blessing. Let's impose a truce between my mother and my wife and have them promise to abide by it always."

Al-Sayyid Ahmad was pleased by this suggestion, but, shaking his head, he objected deftly, "No, I won't agree to oversee a truce, for it would have to be concluded between equals. Here one of the sides is our mother and the other our daughter, and a daughter does not have the status of a mother. First Khadija must apologize to her mother for all past incidents. Then her mother, if she is willing, can forgive Khadija. After that we'll talk about making peace."

The old lady beamed so wide that her wrinkles were pressed together, but she glanced cautiously toward Khadija. Then she looked back at al-Sayyid Ahmad without saying anything. He remarked, "It seems my proposal does not meet with your approval."

The old lady answered gratefully, "You always say the right thing. Blessings on your lips and life."

Al-Sayyid Ahmad motioned to Khadija, who stood up without any hesitation and approached him, feeling more forlorn than ever before. When she was directly in front of him, he told her resolutely, "Kiss your mother's hand and ask her, 'Forgive me, Mother.'"

"Oh!" She had never imagined, not even in a nightmare, that she might be put in this position, but her father, her adored father, was the one imposing it on her. Yes, the verdict had been handed down by a person whose verdicts she could never oppose. So this must be God's will. Khadija turned to the old lady and leaned over her. Then she took the hand that was raised to her – yes, by God, raised without any sign of protest – and kissed it, painfully conscious of her disgust and defeat. Then she mumbled, "Forgive me, Mother."

The old lady looked at her for a time, her face flushed with delight. Then she replied, "I forgive you, Khadija. I forgive you for your father's sake and in recognition of your repentance." A childish laugh escaped her. Then she said in an admonitory fashion, "There'll be no quarrel after today about Circassian chicken. Isn't it enough for your family that your casseroles and your dishes stuffed with rice are superior to any others in the world?"

Al-Sayyid Ahmad said joyfully, "Praise to God for this peace accord." Then, looking up at Khadija, he reminded her, "Mother always. She isn't Auntie. This is Mother exactly like the other one."

Then he continued in a low, sorrowful voice: "Where did you get this disposition, Khadija? No one who grew up in my house should be like this. Have you forgotten your mother and her mild, courteous character? Have you forgotten that any evil you cause tarnishes my honor? By God, I was astonished to hear what your mother had to say. It will continue to amaze me for a long time to come."

93

FOLLOWING THE departure of al-Sayyid Ahmad Abd al-Jawad, the group went back upstairs. Khadija led the procession, her face sullen and pale with angry resentment. The others knew that harmony was still nothing more than a remote possibility for their household. They were apprehensive about what was building up behind Khadija's silence. For this reason, Khalil and Aisha accompanied Khadija and Ibrahim to their apartment, although the racket from Na'ima, Uthman, and Muhammad clearly suggested that their parents would soon need to return home. After they had resumed their seats in the living room, Khalil took the pulse of the situation by saying to his brother, "Your final remarks were decisive and brought good results."

For the first time since the tribunal, Khadija spoke out, passionately: "It brought a truce — isn't that so? A truce that humiliated me more than ever before...."

Ibrahim said somewhat critically, "It's not humiliating to kiss my mother's hand or to ask her forgiveness."

His wife answered cavalierly, "She's your mother but my enemy. If Papa hadn't ordered me, I would never have called her Mother. Yes, she's only Mother on Papa's orders. Papa's orders alone!"

Ibrahim leaned against the back of the sofa and sighed dejectedly. Aisha was anxious, for she did not know what impression her failure to testify had made on her sister. Her anxiety was increased by Khadija's refusal to look at her. She decided to speak to prompt Khadija to reveal her true feelings. So she remarked gently, "There is no humiliation in the affair, since you parted friends. You mustn't remember anything but the happy ending."

Her torso rigid, Khadija glared angrily at Aisha. Then she said sharply, "Don't speak to me. You're the last person in the world who deserves to talk to me."

Aisha pretended to be astonished and, looking back and forth between Ibrahim and Khalil, asked, "Me? Why, God forbid?"

In a voice as cold and penetrating as a bullet, Khadija replied, "Because you betrayed me. Your silence testified against me. You chose to placate the other woman instead of helping your sister. This is treachery pure and simple."

"I don't understand you, Khadija. Everyone knows my silence worked to your advantage."

In as vicious a tone of voice or worse, Khadija retorted, "If you had truly had my best interests at heart, you would have testified for me, even if what you said wasn't exactly true. But you preferred the woman who cooks for you over your own sister. Don't speak! Not a word! We have a mother who will have something to say about this."

Shortly before noon the next day Khadija went to visit her mother, even though the roads were muddy, with pools of stagnant water in low-lying areas. She went to the oven room, and her mother rose to greet her warmly and happily. Umm Hanafi approached, jubilantly welcoming her. But Khadija returned their greetings with a only few terse words. Her mother gave her a searching, inquisitive look.

Without any preliminaries Khadija announced, "I've come to see what you think of Aisha, for I don't have the strength to put up with any more."

Amina's expression revealed her interest and her distress. Motioning with her head for Khadija to precede her out of the room, she said, "What's happened, may God requite us? Your father told me about the events at Sugar Street, but what role did Aisha play in them?"

Then, as they climbed the stairs, she continued: "Lord, Khadija, how many times have I asked you to be more understanding? Your mother-in-law is an old lady. You need to respect her age. The very fact that she went to the store alone in the weather we had yesterday is clear proof of her senility. But what can be done about it? How angry your father was! He couldn't believe you would ever say a spiteful word. But what did Aisha do to make you angry? She kept silent, didn't she? It wasn't possible for her to say anything."

They settled down side by side on a sofa in the sitting room where the coffee hour was held. Khadija admonished her, "Mother, please don't join forces with them. My Lord, why is it that I can't find anyone in this world to help me?"

The mother smiled reprovingly and remarked, "Don't say that. Don't even imagine that, my little daughter. Just tell me what you think Aisha did wrong."

Punching the air as though it were an enemy, Khadija answered, "The worst. She testified against me. So I was miserably defeated."

"What did she say?"

"She didn't say anything."

"Praise God."

"The catastrophe was a result of her silence."

Smiling fondly, Amina asked, "What could she have said?"

As though her mother's question was more than she could stomach, Khadija frowned and replied bitterly, "She could have sworn I never attacked the woman. Why not? If she had done that, it wouldn't have been more than a sister's duty. She could at least have said she didn't hear anything. The truth is, she favored that woman over me. She deserted me and let me fall prey to a malicious schemer. I'll never forget this about Aisha so long as I live."

Feeling hurt and apprehensive, her mother said, "Khadija, don't frighten me. Everything should have been forgotten by morning."

"Forgotten? I didn't sleep at all last night. I tossed and turned, and my head seemed to be on fire. Any disaster would have seemed insignificant, had it not come from Aisha. From my sister? She agreed to team up with Satan. Fine! Let her have what she wants. I used to have one mother-in-law. Now I have two. Aisha! Lord, how many times have I shielded her! If I were a traitor like her, I would have told my father about the streak of improper conduct running through her life. She wants to be thought of as a noble angel while I'm cast as a devil deserving to be pelted with stones. Certainly not! I'm a thousand times better than she is. My reputation is spotless." Her tone became increasingly strident as she added, "If it weren't for my father, no power on earth could have brought me to kiss my enemy's hand or to call her Mother."

Amina patted her daughter's shoulder gently as she said, "You're angry, always angry. Calm down. You'll stay here with me and we'll have lunch together. Then we can have a quiet chat."

"I'm in full control of my intellect. I know what I'm saying. I want to ask my father which is better: the wife who stays at home or the one who visits all the neighbors and sings to them while her daughter dances?"

Amina sighed and said mournfully, "There's no need to ask what your father thinks of this. But Aisha's a married woman, and the final word on her conduct is her husband's. If he allows her to visit the neighbors and knows that she sings when she's with her friends who love her and her voice, then what concern of ours is it? God takes care of everything, Khadija. Is this what you term 'improper conduct'? Does it really infuriate you that Na'ima dances? She's going on six, and dancing is a game for her. You're just angry, Khadija; may God forgive you."

Khadija said determinedly, "I mean every word I've said. If you approve of your daughter singing when she visits the neighbors and letting her daughter dance, do you also approve of her smoking — like men? Yes, you're astonished. I repeat in your hearing that Aisha smokes. She's become addicted and can't do without it. Her husband gives her a pack, telling her quite plainly, 'This is your pack, darling Shushu.' I've seen her, myself, take a puff on one and exhale the smoke through her mouth and nostrils. Her nose! Do you hear? She no longer attempts to hide it from me as she did at first. In fact, she suggested I try smoking, on the grounds that it helps calm agitated nerves. This is Aisha. What do you have to say about that? What would my father say? I wonder."

There was total silence. Amina appeared to be perplexed and at a loss. All the same, she decided to continue trying to calm her daughter. She said, "Smoking's a nasty habit even for men. Your father has never smoked. What can I say then about women smoking? But if it's her husband who tempted her and taught her how, what room is there for comment? What can be done about it, Khadija? She belongs to her husband, not to us. All we can do is give her some advice, whether or not it does any good."

Khadija began to gaze at her mother with a silence that betrayed hesitation. Finally she said, "Her husband pampers her so dreadfully he spoils her. He's made her his partner in all his depraved acts. Smoking isn't his only bad habit. He drinks liquor at home without any embarrassment. There's always a bottle in his house, as though it were one of the necessities of life. He'll get her hooked on drink just as he did with tobacco. Why not? The old lady knows her son's apartment's a tavern, but she doesn't care. He'll serve Aisha liquor. Indeed, I can state categorically that he has, for I smelled a strange fragrance on her breath once. When I questioned her, although she denied everything, she was nervous. I tell you, she surely has drunk alcohol and will become as addicted to it as she is to smoking."

The mother exclaimed gloomily, "Anything but this, O Lord! Have pity on yourself and on me: Fear God, Khadija."

"I am a devout person, God knows. I don't smoke and my mouth does not reek with suspicious odors. I don't allow liquor to come into my home. Don't you know that the other mule attempted to stock this sinful bottle? But I waylaid him and told him with the utmost candor, 'I won't remain in this apartment if there's a liquor bottle in it.' Faced by my resolve, he backed down. Now he leaves his bottle with his brother ... in the apartment of the lady who betrayed me yesterday. Whenever I shout insults at alcohol and those who drink it, he asks – may God slice out his tongue – 'Where did you come by such fundamentalist Hanbalism? Your father's a wellspring of conviviality. His parties almost never lack a drink and a lute.' So you hear what they say about my father in the Shawkat household."

A look of sorrow and anguish was visible in Amina's eyes. She began to clench and release her fist with anxious agitation. Then she said in a plaintive, hurt tone, "Have mercy on us, Lord! We weren't meant for this. God, you're forgiving and compassionate. How men make women suffer! I won't keep still about it – that wouldn't be right. I'll take Aisha to task in no uncertain terms. But I can't believe what you've said of her. Your suspicions have tempted you to imagine groundless things about her. My daughter's pure and will remain pure, even if her husband turns into a demon. I'll speak to her quite bluntly. I'll even discuss it with Mr. Khalil himself, if that's necessary. He can drink as much as he wants until God grants him repentance, but I ask God to draw an invisible line between my daughter and Satan."

For the first time Khadija's soul felt a refreshing breeze. She observed her mother's concern with a satisfied eye, reassured that Aisha would soon experience the full impact of the loss her betrayal was destined to bring her. Khadija felt little remorse for having embellished the facts in her exaggerated portrayal of the situation or in its bitter characterization, which had led her to refer to her sister's apartment as a tavern. She knew that Ibrahim and Khalil rarely touched liquor and then only in moderation and that neither had ever been intoxicated, but she was upset and resentful. She repeated the remarks about her father being "a wellspring of conviviality" to her mother with an incredulous tone to make it clear that she rejected them, although long ago she had been forced to accept their accuracy. She had yielded to the testimony of Ibrahim, Khalil, and their aged mother, especially since they had made their comments not in a prejudiced or critical manner but when praising her father's generosity and according him a leading role among the witty people of his era. In the beginning, she had rejected that consensus with a fierce obstinacy. Then slowly, even if she did not admit it openly, doubt crept in. She found it extremely difficult to reconcile these new attributes with the somber and tyrannical person in whom she had believed all her life. All the same, this doubt did not in any respect lessen her regard and veneration, which may have increased, through the addition of wit and liberality to his qualities.

Khadija was not content with the victory she had won. Trying to goad her mother on, she said, "Aisha didn't just betray me. She's betrayed you too." She fell silent to let her words penetrate deep into her mother. Then she went on: "She visits Yasin and Maryam in Palace of Desire Alley."

Staring at her daughter in alarm, Amina cried out, "What did you say?"

Feeling that she had scaled the peaks of victory, Khadija answered, "This is the sad truth. Yasin and Maryam have visited us more than once. They visited Aisha, and they visited me. I'll admit I was forced to receive them. Had it not been for my respect for Yasin, I wouldn't have been able to. But I did it guardedly. Yasin invited me to visit them at Palace of Desire. I don't need to say that I didn't go. They visited again, but that still did not shake my resolve. Finally Maryam asked, 'Why don't you visit us? We've been like sisters since childhood.' I offered various excuses, and she did her best to tempt me. She started to complain about Yasin's treatment, his sneaky behavior, and his neglect. Perhaps she hoped to arouse my sympathy, but I didn't open my heart to her – unlike Aisha, who receives her warmly, kissing her. Even worse, she exchanges visits with Maryam. She took Mr. Khalil with her once and another time Na'ima, Uthman, and Muham-mad. She certainly seems happy to renew her friendship with Maryam. When I cautioned her about carrying it too far, she replied, 'Maryam's only sin was that we refused one day to make her the fiancée of our lamented brother. Is that fair?' I asked her, 'Have you forgotten the English soldier?' She replied, 'The only thing we should remember is that she's the wife of our oldest brother.' Have you ever heard anything like this, Mother?"

Amina yielded to her sorrow. She bowed her head and took refuge in silence. Khadija looked at her for a time. Then she resumed her denunciation: "That's Aisha, nothing added, nothing subtracted . . . Aisha who testified against me yesterday, humiliating me in front of that prattling old woman."

Amina sighed deeply. She gazed at Khadija with tired eyes. Then she said in a faint voice, "Aisha's a child without any mind or substance. She'll always be like that, no matter how long she lives. What else can I say? I don't want to say more and I can't. Does the memory of Fahmy mean so little to her? I can't believe that. Why can't she be stingier with her affections when it comes to that woman, if only for my sake? But I won't let this pass. I'll tell her she's wronged me, that I'm angry and saddened, and then we'll see how see reacts."

Grasping a lock of her hair, Khadija said, "I'll chop this off if she reforms. She lives in a dream world all her own. God knows I'm not prejudiced against her. I've never had a fight with her since I got married, not a single one. It's true I've often inveighed against her neglect of the children, her humiliating flattery of her mother-in-law, and other similar things I've related to you over the years. But my attacks have never gone beyond the limits of resolute advice and frank criticism. This is the first time she's upset me so badly that I'm publicly quarreling with her."

Although still looking vexed, her mother entreated her, "Let me handle this, Khadija. I don't want you ever to be estranged from her by a dispute. It's not right for your hearts to be alienated from each other when you live together in the same home. Don't forget that you're sisters . . . and that you're her big sister. Your heart is not mean, praise God. It's filled with love for all your family. Whenever I have a problem, my one consolation is your affection. Despite her failings, Aisha is still your sister. Don't forget that."

Stung, Khadija cried out, "I'll forgive her everything except her testimony against me."

"She didn't testify against you. She was afraid of making you angry and afraid of angering her mother-in-law. So she kept silent.

She hates to upset anyone, as you well know, even if her heed-lessness frequently annoys people. She never meant to harm you. Don't expect too much from her. I'll come see you tomorrow and settle accounts with her. But I'll make peace between the two of you, and you'd better not object."

For the first time Khadija's eyes had an anxious, apprehensive look. She lowered them to keep her mother from noticing. She did not say anything for a moment. Then in a weak voice she asked, "You'll come tomorrow?"

"Yes, the situation requires my immediate attention."

As though to herself, Khadija remarked, "She'll accuse me of divulging her secrets."

"So!" Then, sensing her daughter's increasing anxiety and apprehension, Amina added, "In any case, I know what to say and what not to."

With relief Khadija concluded, "That's best, for it's unlikely she'll acknowledge that my intentions are good or that all I want is to help her improve."

94

"OH!" HE suddenly exclaimed with warmth and passion on seeing
Aïda emerge from the gate of her mansion. As usual late each
afternoon, he was standing on the sidewalk of al-Abbasiya Street
watching her house from a distance. The most he had been hoping
for was a glimpse of her on a balcony or at a window. He wore an
elegant gray suit, as though wishing to keep pace with the good
weather, which the last days of March had graciously and cheerfully provided. The more hurt and despondent he felt, the more
dapper his attire became. He had not set eyes on Aïda since she had
quarreled with him in the gazebo. But life would not have been
possible without this afternoon pilgrimage to al-Abbasiya, where
he circled the mansion from afar with unflagging zeal. He would
give free rein to his dreams and satisfy himself temporarily with
contemplation of the shrine and a review of his memories.

In the first days of their separation the pain had almost driven
him crazy, leaving him prey to delirious paranoia. Had it lasted any
longer, it would have done him in. He had escaped from that
dangerous initial stage by virtue of the despair long embedded in
his soul. Pain had crept back into its residence deep inside him,
where it carried on its traffic without disturbing his other vital
functions, as though it were an organic part of his body or an
essential faculty of his spirit. His agony was like a severe illness that
lingers on as a chronic malady after its worst symptoms subside. He
was not consoled. How could he find any consolation for love? It
was the most exalted thing life had ever revealed to him. Since he
believed deeply in love's immortality, he realized he would have
to bear it patiently, as if destined to live out the rest of his days with
an incurable illness.

When he suddenly saw her leave the mansion, this moan
escaped him. His eyes watched her graceful gait, which he had
wanted to see for such a long time, and his spirit danced with a
rapture of affectionate excitement. The beloved turned right and
proceeded along Palaces Street. Revolt flared up in his spirit,

sweeping away the sense of defeat his soul had nourished for nearly three months. His heart shocked him into a decision to cast his complaints at her feet regardless of the consequences. Without any hesitation he walked to Palaces Street. In the past he had spoken cautiously from fear of losing her. Now there was no further loss to fear. Moreover, the torment he had suffered during the last three months would hardly allow him to hesitate or retreat. Aïda soon noticed the approaching footsteps and turned to glance back when he was only a few steps behind her. But then she looked ahead again indifferently. He had not expected a gracious reception, but he reproached her, "Is this the way old friends greet each other?"

She responded by quickening her pace without even glancing at him. He lengthened his steps, deriving stubborn resolve from his pain. When he was almost beside her, he said, "Don't pretend you don't know me. That's unbearable. If you had any regard for fairness, there would be no need for this."

What he feared most was that she would ignore him until she reached her destination. But the melodious voice answered, "Please get away from me. Let me go in peace."

With humble determination he told her, "You will go on your way peacefully, but after we settle accounts."

In a voice that resounded clearly in the silence of the aristocratic street, which seemed almost deserted, she replied, "I don't know what accounts you're talking about and don't want to know. I wish you'd act like a gentleman."

With fervent passion he said, "I promise to conduct myself in a fashion exemplary even for a gentleman. I couldn't act otherwise, since you inspire me in everything I do."

Without ever looking his way she retorted, "I mean you should leave me in peace. That's what I want."

"I can't. I can't until you pronounce me innocent of the false charges for which you've punished me without listening to my defense."

"I'm punishing you?"

He paused for a fleeting instant to enjoy the magic of that moment, for she had agreed to debate with him and to slow her happy stride. Did she want to listen to him or was she deliberately giving herself more time to get rid of him before she reached her destination? In either case it was a dazzling fact that they were walking side by side along Palaces Street. The lofty trees there sheltered them and, from beyond the walls of the mansions, calm narcissus eyes and smiling jasmine mouths followed the couple's progress in a stillness profound enough to soothe his burning heart, if he could only have absorbed it.

He said, "You have punished me cruelly by disappearing for three whole months while I, although innocent, have suffered countless torments."

"Let's not rehash that."

Passionately and humbly he replied, "But we must. I'm determined to. I beg you in the name of the agony I've endured for so long that I lack the strength to suffer anymore."

She asked quietly, "How is that my fault?"

"I want to know whether you still consider me an adversary. One thing that's certain is that I could never harm you under any circumstances. If you would just consider my affection for you over the past years you would embrace my viewpoint without any hesitation. Let me tell you the whole story with total candor. After our conversation in the gazebo, Hasan Salim asked me to have a talk with him."

She interrupted him almost imploringly: "Let's drop this. It's over, finished."

This last sentence had the impact on him that laments at a funeral would make on a dead man if he could hear. Then, touched in a way that showed itself in his voice, where it was like a song dropping down an octave to an answering voice, he said, "Finished . . . I know it's finished, but I would like it to have a positive ending. I don't want you to leave thinking me a traitor or a slanderer. I'm innocent, and it's awful when you think ill of a person who harbors for you . . . harbors for you nothing but veneration and respect and whose every reference to you is coated with praise."

Leaning her head in the other direction, she cast him a look as if to ask teasingly, "When did you become so eloquent?" Then almost tenderly she said, "It seems there's been a misunderstanding. But that's all in the past."

Eagerly and hopefully he said, "It seems that you're still a little skeptical."

Giving in, she answered, "No, but I won't deny that I thought ill of you for a time. The truth only became clear afterwards."

His heart floated high over a cloud of happiness and swayed tipsily above it. He asked, "When did you learn that?"

"Quite a while ago."

He gazed at her with gratitude, so moved by love he felt like crying. Then he said, "You learned I'm innocent?"

"Yes."

Was Hasan Salim going to regain his good reputation? "How did you learn the truth?"

She said quickly and in a way that showed she wanted to end this interrogation, "I learned it. That's the important thing."

He did not insist, for fear of annoying her, but a thought crossed his mind. Sorrow clouded his heart, and he said plaintively, "Even so, you continued to hide yourself. You didn't bother to announce the pardon with a sign or a word, although you were able to express your anger most expertly. But your excuse is obvious and I accept it."

"What excuse is that?"

With a sorrowful voice he replied, "That you haven't ever known pain. I ask God most sincerely that you never will."

She said apologetically, "I thought you didn't care whether you were accused."

"May God forgive you. I cared more than you can imagine. It hurt me dreadfully to find the gap between us so vast. The problem wasn't merely your disinterest in the . . . affection I feel for you. It was also the unfair charges lodged against me. So consider your position and mine. But I'll tell you frankly that the unjust accusation was not responsible for my worst pains . . . ."

She smiled and asked, "So there wasn't just one type of pain?"

Encouraged by her smile as if he were a small child, he proceeded to pour out the story of his devotion. He said passionately, "No. Your accusation caused the least of my pains, and your disappearance the greatest. Each hour out of the past three months has witnessed some moment of pain. The way I've lived, I could easily have been considered insane. So I mean and know what I'm saying when I pray that God will not test you with pain. I've learned from my own experience. What a cruel time it's been! It's convinced me that if you're destined to disappear from my life, I might as well search for another existence. It was like a long, odious curse. Don't make fun of me. I'm always afraid you will. But pain's too exalted to be mocked. I don't picture a generous angel like you joking about the afflictions of other people. And of course you're the cause too. But what can a person do? It's been my fate to love you with all the force of my being."

The silence that followed was broken only by his irregular breathing. She was looking straight ahead, and he could not search her eyes. He was comforted by her silence, for it was easier to bear than a careless word. So he considered it a triumph.

"Imagine hearing her voice – soft and sweet – expressing the very same feelings. . . ."

He was crazy. Why had he released the floodwaters dammed up in his heart? He was like a vaulter who keeps trying to go just a foot higher only to find himself soaring high into the heavens. But what force could muzzle him after this?

"Don't remind me of things I hate to hear, for I've had my fill of that. I won't forget my head, for I carry it with me night and day, or my nose, for I see it repeatedly each day. But I've got something no one else comes close to possessing. My love for you is unequaled, and I'm proud of it. You should be too, even if you spurn it. I've felt this way ever since I saw you the first time in the garden. Haven't you been conscious of it? I haven't thought about confessing it before now, because I was afraid of spoiling our friendship and of being expelled from paradise. It was hideously difficult for me to consider risking my happiness. But now that I've been evicted, what do I have to fear?"

His secret flowed out of him like blood from a wound. He saw nothing in all of existence except her extraordinary person. The road, trees, mansions, and the few passers by vanished into a dense fog with only one gap through which his silent beloved could be seen with her slender build, halo of black hair, and a profile that openly revealed its grace while concealing its secrets. In the twilight shadows her face seemed a pure brown, but when they crossed a side street it was radiant and bright from the rays of the setting sun. He could have kept on talking until morning.

"Did I say I'd never considered confessing my love to you before? That's not quite true. The fact is, I started the day we met in the gazebo when Husayn was called to the telephone. I almost told you then, but before I could, you began attacking my head and nose." He laughed briefly before continuing: "I was like an orator who opens his mouth only to be showered with pebbles by the audience."

She was calm and silent. That was fitting. An angel from another world should not converse in a mortal tongue or take an interest in human affairs. Would it not have been nobler of him to guard his secret? Nobler? Pride vis-à-vis the beloved was blasphemy. For the assassin to be confronted with her victim was only proper.

"Do you remember your happy dream that left you in tears when you awoke? Dreams are quickly forgotten, but tears or rather the memory of them may become an immortal symbol."

Here she was saying, "I was only joking when I said those things, and I asked you then not to get angry."

This refreshing sensation deserved to be savored. It resembled the happy delight one feels after a throbbing toothache. The melodies latent within him echoed each other until a beautiful tune emerged. His beloved's features seemed the musical notation from which he was reading a heavenly composition.

"You'll find I'm content with hoping for nothing, because – as I told you – I love you."

With her natural grace she cast him a smiling look but withdrew it too quickly for him to decipher it. What kind of look had it been? Was she pleased, moved, affectionate, responsive, or politely sarcastic? Had she bestowed it on his face as a whole or directed it toward his head and nose?

Then her voice followed this look: "I can only thank you and apologize for unintentionally causing you pain. You're kind and generous."

His soul was ready to convey him to the warm embrace of happy dreams, but she added in a faint voice, "Now let me ask what follows from this."

Was he hearing the voice of his beloved or an echo of his own? This very sentence was soaring somewhere over Palace Walk, borne aloft by his sighs. Had the time come for him to find an answer for this question?

He asked anxiously, "Does something follow from love?"

"She's smiling," he thought. "I wonder what this smile means. But you want something more than a smile."

She answered, "The declaration is the beginning, not the end. I'd like to know what you want."

Still anxious, he said, "I want . . . I want you to give me permission to love you."

She could not hold back her laughter. She inquired, "Is this really what you want? But what will you do if I refuse?"

Sighing, he replied, "In that case, I'll love you anyway."

In a half-joking manner that upset him she asked, "What's the point of the permission then?"

How absurd it was when words betrayed a person and came out wrong. . . . What he feared most was falling back to earth as suddenly as he had risen from it. He heard her say, "You perplex me. It seems to me that you even perplex yourself."

He answered uneasily, "Me . . . perplexed? Perhaps, but I love you. 'What follows from this?' I imagine occasionally that I aspire to things beyond the earth's capacities. But when I reflect a little, I'm unable to ascertain what my goal is. You tell me what this means. I want you to talk while I listen. Can you rescue me from my dilemma?"

She said with a smile, "I don't have anything to offer in this regard. You ought to be the speaker. I'll do the listening. Aren't you a philosopher?"

His face turning red, he commented dejectedly, "You're making fun of me."

She was quick to answer, "No. But I wasn't anticipating a conversation like this when I left my house. You caught me by surprise, telling me things I wasn't expecting to hear. In any case, I'm thankful and grateful. No one would be able to forget your tender and refined affection. It would be out of the question to make fun of them."

It was a captivating tune with sweet lyrics. Yet he did not know whether the beloved was being serious or frivolous. Were the portals of hope opening . . . or closing with the gentleness of a breeze? When she had asked him what he wanted, he had not replied, because he had not known what he did want. Would it be wrong to say that he longed for communion, the communion of one spirit with another? Should he knock at the mysterious closed door with a hug or a kiss? Shouldn't that be the answer?

At the intersection where Palaces Street ended, Aïda stopped and said gently but decisively, "Here!"

He stopped walking too and gazed at her face with astonishment. "'Here' meaning we must part here?" he wondered. "The sentence 'I love you' is not far-reaching enough to rule out questions."

With no deliberation or thought, he exclaimed, "No!" Then, as though he had suddenly seen the light, he cried out, "What's the point of love? Wasn't that what you were really asking? Here's an answer for you: that we don't part."

With a calm smile, she replied, "But we must part now."

He asked fervently, "Without any displeasure or ill feelings?"

"Absolutely not."

"Will you resume your visits to the gazebo?"

"If circumstances permit."

He anxiously reminded her, "Circumstances permitted it in the past."

"Things are different now."

He was deeply hurt by her response and said, "It seems you won't return."

As though to remind him of the necessity of parting, she said, "I'll visit the gazebo whenever circumstances allow it. Have a happy day."

She set off in the direction of School Street. He stood there gazing after her as though she were a dream vision. When a turn in the road was about to hide her, she looked back with a smile. Then she vanished from sight.

What had he said and heard? He would concentrate on all that shortly, after he came to. When would that be? He was walking all by himself. Alone? . . . What of the pounding of his heart, the delirium of his spirit, and the echoes of that melody? All the same, a feeling of isolation shook his heart to its core. The captivating, enchanting fragrance of jasmine overwhelmed him, but what was its special ingredient? This fragrance and love were similar in their mysterious and captivating enchantment. Perhaps penetration of one's secret would lead to discovery of the other's. Yet he would not solve this puzzle until he finished reciting all the anthems of bewilderment.

95

HUSAYN SHADDAD said, "Alas, this is our farewell meeting."

Kamal was peeved by this reference to leave-taking. He glanced quickly at Husayn to see if his face was actually as sorrowful as his words. All the same, Kamal had been aware of a valedictory atmosphere for more than a week, because the arrival of June usually signaled the departure of his friends for Ra's al-Barr and Alexandria. It was only a matter of days until the garden, the gazebo, and his friends would vanish from his horizons. The beloved had been pleased to disappear even before departure necessitated it. She had remained invisible even after reconciliation crowned their conversation on Palaces Street. Was the farewell meeting to conclude without a visit? Did his affection mean so little to her that she would begrudge him a fleeting vision before leaving for three months?

Kamal smilingly asked, "Why do you say, 'Alas'?"

Husayn Shaddad responded attentively, "I wish you would all go with me to Ra's al-Barr. My goodness! What a summer vacation that would be!"

It would be marvelous, no doubt about it. Kamal would be happy, if only because the beloved would not be able to continue hiding there. Isma'il Latif remarked to him, "May God come to your aid. How can you bear the summer heat here? Summer has barely begun, and yet see how hot it is today."

It was very hot, although the sun's rays were no longer shining directly on the garden or the desert beyond it. Even so, Kamal replied calmly, "There's nothing in life that can't be borne."

The next moment he was scoffing at his own words. He wondered how he could have responded that way and to what degree words could be considered a true expression of feelings. Around him he saw people who certainly looked happy. In their short-sleeved shirts and gray trousers, they seemed to be defying the heat. Only he was wearing a suit — a lightweight white one — and a fez, which he had placed on the table.

Isma'il Latif started praising the examination results: "One hundred percent success. Hasan Salim got his degree. Kamal Ahmad Abd al-Jawad, Husayn Shaddad, and Isma'il Latif all were promoted."

Kamal laughed and observed, "You could have skipped all but the final one, for the others were never in question."

Shrugging his shoulders scornfully, Isma'il retorted, "Each of us has attained the same goal – you with fatigue and exertion all year long, me after only one month's effort."

"That proves you're a scholar at heart."

Isma'il asked sarcastically, "Didn't you casually remark that George Bernard Shaw was the worst student of his day?"

Kamal laughingly replied, "Now I'm convinced that we have among us an equal to Shaw, if only in his failures."

Husayn Shaddad said, "I have news I need to disclose before we get carried away by our conversation."

When he found that this statement had not drawn much attention, he stood up suddenly and said in a theatrical tone, "Allow me to announce some fascinating and happy news." Glancing at Hasan Salim, he asked, "Isn't that so?" Then, looking back at Kamal and Isma'il, he continued: "Yesterday an engagement was arranged between Mr. Hasan Salim and my sister Aïda."

Confronted by this revelation, Kamal felt like a man who suddenly finds himself beneath a streetcar, after feeling completely satisfied about his safety and security. His heart pounded violently, as if an airplane were plunging downward in an air pocket. An inner scream of terror seemed trapped in his rib cage, unable to get out. He was amazed – especially when he thought about it later – that he was able to control his feelings and to flash Husayn Shaddad a congratulatory smile for his sister's good fortune. Perhaps Kamal was distracted from his calamity for the time being by the struggle within him between his soul and the stupor threatening it.

Isma'il Latif was the first to speak. He looked back and forth from Husayn Shaddad to Hasan Salim. The latter as usual projected a calm composure, although this time it seemed mixed with some embarrassment or discomfort. Isma'il cried out, "Really? What happy news, happy and sudden . . . happy, sudden, and treacherous. But I'll postpone discussion of the treachery till later. At the moment I'm content to offer my sincere congratulations."

Isma'il rose and shook hands with Husayn and Hasan. Kamal got up immediately to offer his congratulations too. Despite the smile on his face, he was so startled by the speed of events and the bizarre things people were saying that he imagined he was in a strange dream. Rain was pouring down on his head. He was looking everywhere for shelter. As he shook hands with the two young men he said, "Really good news . . . heartfelt congratulations."

When they had settled back in their places, Kamal could not keep himself from glancing stealthily at Hasan Salim, whom he found calm and composed. Kamal had been apprehensive, imagining that his friend would look conceited or gloating. Experiencing some fleeting relief, Kamal proceeded to rally all his strength to hide his bloody wound from their watchful eyes, in order to keep himself from becoming the target of mocking sarcasm.

"Be firm, my soul. I promise we'll return to all this later. We'll suffer together until we perish. We'll think through everything until we go insane. It will be a satisfying moment in the still of the night, with no eye to observe or ear to eavesdrop, when pain, delirium, and tears are unveiled . . . far from any critic or scold. Then there's the old well. I'll remove the cover, scream down it to the resident demons, and confide my woes to the tears collected in the belly of the earth there from sad people everywhere. Don't capitulate. Beware, for the world seems as fiery red to you now as the pit of hell."

Adopting an accusatory tone, Isma'il said, "Not so fast! Both of you owe us an explanation. How did this come about without any advance warning? Or let's put that aside temporarily. How could you have celebrated the engagement without inviting us?"

Husayn Shaddad replied defensively, "There wasn't a party, not even a small one. The gathering was limited to immediate family members. Your time will come when we celebrate the marriage contract. Then you'll be among the hosts, not the guests."

"The wedding day! That could be the title of a funeral dirge. The heart will be conducted in solemn procession to its final resting place surrounded by flowers, as people pay their last respects with shrieking trills. In the name of love, the young woman raised in Paris will bow before the turbaned shaykh as he recites the opening prayer of the Qur'an. In the name of pride, Satan left paradise."

Smiling, Kamal said, "Your excuse is accepted, and your invitation welcomed."

Isma'il Latif objected loudly: "Eloquence like this belongs with the seminarians at al-Azhar Mosque. When some people see food on the horizon, they forget they have any cause for complaint and magnanimously begin singing the praises of their hosts, all for the sake of a hearty meal. You're a true writer or philosopher or some other type of beggar like that, but I'm not."

Then he continued his attack on Husayn Shaddad and Hasan Salim: "You two are a couple of rascals . . . a long silence followed by the announcement of an engagement. Huh? Really, Mr. Hasan, you're the long-awaited successor for Tharwat Pasha, who did such a good job of suppressing information when he was Prime Minister."

Smiling apologetically, Hasan Salim said, "Husayn himself knew nothing of the matter until only a few days ago."

Isma'il asked, "Was this a unilateral engagement, like Great Britain's unilateral declaration of Egyptian independence on February 28, 1922?"

The conquered Egyptian nation as a whole had proudly rejected that declaration, but nominal sovereignty had been thrust upon it, with the inevitable consequences. Kamal laughed out loud.

Winking at Hasan Salim, Isma'il carelessly mangled and misattributed a quotation from the prophet Muhammad: "'To accomplish' – I don't remember what – 'rely on secrecy.' The caliph Umar ibn al-Khattab said that . . . or the poet Umar ibn Abi Rabi'a, or Omar Effendi down at the department store. God only knows."

Kamal said suddenly, "It's customary for matters like these to come to fruition silently, although I must acknowledge that Mr. Hasan once referred to something of this kind in a conversation with me."

Isma'il gazed at him skeptically. Looking at Kamal with wide eyes, Hasan corrected him: "It was more like subtle hints."

Kamal asked himself in amazement how this statement had escaped from his mouth. It was a lie or at best a half-truth. How could he have wished to convince Hasan in this devious manner that he, Kamal, knew about the young man's intentions and had not been surprised or troubled by them? "What stupidity!"

Staring critically at Hasan, Isma'il told him, "But I didn't garner a single one of these subtle hints."

Hasan replied earnestly, "I assure you that if Kamal found anything in my remarks he considered a reference to a forthcoming engagement, he must have relied on his imagination, not my words."

Husayn Shaddad laughed loudly. He said to Hasan Salim, "Isma'il's your lifelong friend. He wants you to realize that even if you have gotten your degree three years ahead of him, that doesn't mean you should begrudge him your secrets or favor others with them instead."

Smiling as though to conceal his discomfort, Isma'il observed, "I don't question his friendship, but I'll keep after him so I'm not forgotten in a similar manner on his wedding day."

Smiling, Kamal said, "We're friends of both parties. If the bridegroom forgets us, surely the bride won't."

He spoke to prove to himself that he was still alive. But he was alive with pain, intense pain. Had he ever imagined his love would end in any other way? Certainly not ... yet belief in the inevitability of death does not diminish our anguish when it arrives. This was a ferocious, irrational, and merciless pain. He wished he could see it, so he might know where it was concealed or the microbe from which it had emerged. Between seizures of pain he was a victim of lethargy and listlessness.

"When will the ceremony take place?" Isma'il asked the question that was running through Kamal's mind, as though he had been delegated to represent Kamal's thoughts.

But Kamal would have to speak too. He commented, "Yes, it's very important for us to know, so we won't be taken by surprise again. When's the wedding?"

Husayn laughingly asked, "Why are you two in such a hurry? Let's give the bridegroom a chance to enjoy what's left of his bachelor days."

With his customary composure Hasan said, "First of all, I need to learn whether I'm to stay in Egypt or not."

Husayn Shaddad explained, "He's going to be appointed either to the attorney general's staff or to the diplomatic corps."

"Husayn seems delighted with this engagement," Kamal reflected. "I can assert that I hated him, if only momentarily, for having betrayed me. Has anyone double-crossed me?

Everything seems such a confusion. But this evening I'll be alone. . . ."

"Which would you prefer, Mr. Hasan?"

"Let him choose whatever he wants . . . judicial service, diplomatic corps, the Sudan . . . Syria if possible."

"Working as a prosecutor somewhere would be an insult. I'd prefer to be a diplomat."

"It would be good if your father understood that clearly, so he can concentrate on getting you into it." This sentence too jumped out of Kamal's mouth. No doubt it was on target. He would have to get control of his nerves. Otherwise he would find himself embroiled in a public dispute with Hasan. He would also have to keep Husayn Shaddad's feelings in mind, for these two now formed a single family. How cruel this stabbing pain was!

Isma'il shook his head sorrowfully and said, "These are your last days with us, Hasan. After a lifelong relationship, this comes as a sad end."

How stupid it was of Isma'il to think that sorrow could influence a heart grazing in the beloved's oasis.

"It really is a sad ending, Isma'il."

"Lie upon lie . . ." Kamal thought, "like your congratulations to him. In this respect the merchant's son and the son of the superior court judge are equal."

He asked, "Does this mean you'll spend your whole life outside the country?"

"That's what I expect. We'll only see Egypt on rare occasions."

Isma'il marveled: "What a strange life! Have you thought about the difficulties it will pose for your children?"

"Alas, my heart! Is it right to toss around ideas like that? Does this wretch imagine that the beloved will get pregnant and endure cravings, that her belly will become distended and round, that she'll suffer through labor and give birth? Remember Aisha and Khadija in the final months of their pregnancies? This is blasphemy. Why don't you join an underground assassination society like the Black Hand? Murder's better than blasphemy and more beneficial. Then you'd find yourself in the defendant's dock one day. Presiding over the court would be Salim Bey Sabry, father of your friend the diplomat and father-in-law of your beloved, just as he presided this week over the trial of those accused of killing the supreme commander, Sir Lee Stack. The traitor!"

Husayn Shaddad laughingly asked, "Should nations cut off diplomatic relations so the children of diplomats may be raised in their own countries?"

"No, cut off their heads! Abd al-Hamid Inayat, al-Kharrat, Mahmud Rashid, Ali Ibrahim, Raghib Hasan, Shafiq Mansur, and Mahmud Isma'il sentenced to die on the gallows along with Kamal Ahmad Abd al-Jawad . . . by the Egyptian judge Salim Bey Sabry and the English judge Mr. Kershaw. Assassination is the answer. Do you want to kill or be killed?"

Isma'il cautioned Husayn, "Your sister's departure will reinforce your father's determination to refuse your request to travel abroad."

Husayn Shaddad replied confidently, "My case is making steady progress toward a satisfactory solution."

Aïda and Husayn in Europe at the same time . . . he was going to lose his true love and his best friend. "Your spirit will search for your beloved and not find her. Your intellect will search for your companion without finding him either. You'll live alone, exiled to the ancient district, like the echo of a yearning on the loose for generations. Ponder the pains lying in wait for you. It's time for you to harvest the fruit of the dreams planted in your gullible heart. Beseech God to make tears a cure for sorrows. If you can, string your body up with a hangman's ropes or put it at the front of a destructive force unleashed on the enemy. Tomorrow you'll find your spirit's empty – as empty as you once discovered al-Husayn's tomb to be. What a disappointment! Sincere patriots are hanged, while sons of traitors are made ambassadors."

As though to himself, Isma'il Latif remarked, "There'll be no one in Egypt except me and Kamal, and Kamal's not reliable, because his best friend – before, after, or besides Husayn – is the book."

Husayn said with confident conviction, "Travel won't end our friendship."

Despite his lethargy, Kamal's heart pounded. He commented, "My heart tells me that you won't be able to endure a permanent separation from your homeland."

"That's most likely. But you'll profit from my trip by the books I send you. We'll continue our conversations with letters and books."

Husayn was talking as though his voyage had become an established fact. Visits with this friend had been a captivating happiness for Kamal. When he was with Husayn, even silence was enjoy-able. But there was some consolation. The departure of his beloved would teach him to minimize other calamities, no matter how great. Thus the death of his adored grandmother had seemed insignificant to his soul when it was scorched by the fire of his grief for Fahmy. But he had to keep in mind at all times that this was the farewell session. He had to fill his eyes with the roses and the other flowers that were tipsy with blooms and heedless of sorrow. There was a problem he had to solve: How could a mortal ascend high enough to live with the beloved or the beloved fall so far that she could coexist with a human being? If he could not find an answer, he would struggle ahead with shackled feet and a lump in his throat. Love was a load with two widely separated handles. It was designed to be carried by two people. How could he bear it alone?

The conversation raced along and branched off in different directions while Kamal followed it with his eyes, nods of his head, and words designed to demonstrate that the calamity had not polished him off yet. He had his hopes pinned on the fact that life's train keeps moving down the tracks, even though death's station certainly lies ahead somewhere.

"It's dusk. A time of dark stillness. You love it as you love the dawn. 'Aïda,' and 'pain' are two words with a single meaning. So you must love pain, even if from now on your rapture comes from defeat. The conversation keeps moving forward, and the friends laugh together and argue with each other as though none of them had ever experienced love. Husayn's laughter is full of healthy good spirits, Isma'il's of mischief and contention, and Hasan's of reserve and superiority. Husayn refuses to talk about anything but Ra's al-Barr. I promise to make a pilgrimage there one day. I'll ask what sand was trod by the beloved's feet, so I can prostrate myself to kiss it. The other two are singing the praises of San Stefano beach in Alexandria and talking about waves like mountains. Really? Imagine a body the waves cast onto the shore after the dreadful sea has sucked out its beauty and nobility. After all this, let us admit that weary vexation encompasses all living creatures. Possibly happiness lies beyond the gates of death."

The talk continued until it was time for them to go home. They shook hands with each other warmly. Kamal squeezed Husayn's hand, and Husayn squeezed his in return. Then, saying, "See you . . . in October," Kamal set off.

At a time like that any previous year he would have begun asking himself fretfully when his friends would return. Now his desires were not tied to anyone's return. They would still be aflame whether or not October arrived and whether his friends returned or not. He would no longer be blaming the summer months for separating him from Aïda; an abyss much more profound than time had come between them. When time was the problem, he had been able to combat it with doses of patience and hope. Today he was fighting an unknown foe and a mysterious, supernatural force. He did not know a single word of the spells or charms used for it. He could only fall back on a wretched silence until God concluded what He had begun. Love seemed to be suspended over his head like destiny, and he was fastened to it with bonds of excruciating pain. It resembled a force of nature more than anything else in its inevitability and strength. He studied it sadly and respectfully.

The three friends said goodbye in front of the Shaddad family mansion. Hasan Salim went on down Palaces Street, while Kamal and Isma'il as usual headed for al-Husayniya together. There they would part, with Isma'il going to Ghamra and Kamal to the ancient district. As soon as the two of them were alone, Isma'il laughed hard and long.

When Kamal asked him what was so funny, he replied mischievously, "Haven't you figured out yet that you're one of the main reasons speeding up the announcement of this engagement?"

"Me?" This slipped out from Kamal, whose eyes were wide with astonishment.

Isma'il said scornfully, "Yes, you. Hasan wasn't comfortable about your friendship with her. I feel certain of this, even though he never breathed a word of it. As you know, he's really stuck-up. But I find out what I want to. I assure you he was unhappy about your friendship. Do you remember that flare-up between you two? It's obvious that he asked her to stop visiting Husayn's friends. It's equally apparent that she reminded him that he had no right to request that. So he took this major step to get the right."

The pounding of his heart almost drowned out his voice when Kamal said, "But I wasn't the only friend. Aïda was friends with all of us."

Isma'il replied sarcastically, "But she chose you to arouse his anxiety, perhaps because she sensed in your friendship a warmth she did not find with the others. In any case, she was not just reacting randomly to the situation. She decided long ago to win Hasan. Finally she's harvesting the fruit of her patience."

" 'Win Hasan'!" Kamal exclaimed to himself. " 'The fruit of her patience'! These phrases are like a fool's statement that the sun rises in the west."

With a sad heart, Kamal said, "How little you think of people! She's not at all the way you portray her."

Without grasping what his friend felt, Isma'il answered, "Perhaps it happened by chance. Hasan may have been imagining things. In any case, it all worked out to her benefit."

Kamal shouted angrily, " 'Her benefit'! What do you think? Glory to God, you speak as though her engagement to Hasan is a triumph for her, not for him."

Isma'il looked at him strangely and then said, "You don't seem to be convinced that men like Hasan are few and far between. He offers family, status, and a future. There are plenty of girls like Aïda . . . more of them than you think. I wonder if you don't have a higher opinion of her than she deserves. In my opinion, Hasan's family agreed to let him marry her because of her father's immense fortune. She's a girl" – he hesitated before continuing – "whose beauty is not extraordinary at any rate."

"Either he's crazy or you are," Kamal thought. He was transfixed by a pain comparable to that he had felt on reading an offensive attack against the Islamic system of marriage. "God's curse on all unbelievers!"

With a calmness that masked his anguish, he asked, "Then why does she have so many admirers?"

Isma'il disdainfully stuck out his lower jaw while tilting up his chin. "Perhaps you count me among them," he said. "I don't deny that she's amusing and elegant. And her Western upbringing has provided her social graces that make her seem particularly charming and attractive. All the same, she's dark and thin. There's nothing especially seductive about her. Come with me to Ghamra and you'll see all types of beauty. They leave hers in the shade, whether taken as a whole or singly. There you'll see true loveliness . . . fair complexions, swelling breasts, and plump hips. If you want beauty, this is it. There's nothing really desirable about Aïda."

"As if she were a female to be craved like Qamar or Maryam!" Kamal told himself. "Swelling breasts and plump hips? How can you describe a spirit using corporeal expressions? What stabbing pain!" It had been decreed that he should swallow the cup of anguish down to its dregs. Since lethal blows were falling in swift succession, death would be a mercy.

At al-Husayniya they parted, and each went his separate way.

96

OVER THE years his love for this street had never waned. Looking sadly at his surroundings, he mused, "If only my love for a woman were as constant as mine for this street, I'd escape many problems. What an excellent street . . . like a labyrinth!"

Every few meters it turned to the right or left. No matter where a person stood, he was always confronted by a curve, behind which an unknown world lay concealed. Narrowness gave the road an unassuming, familiar character, like that of a pet animal. A man sitting in a shop on the right could reach over and shake hands with his neighbor on the other side. Stretched between the tops of the stores, canvas awnings protected the street from the burning rays of the sun. Beneath them the humidity and diffused light created a dreamy atmosphere. Bunched together on shelves and benches were sacks of green henna, red cayenne, and black pepper – along with flasks of rose water and perfume, colored wrapping paper, and diminutive scales. Hanging from the rafters was a decorative fringe of candles of diverse sizes and colors. The fragrance of different perfumes and colognes filled the air like the aroma of a distant dream.

"The black wraps and veils, the gold nosepieces, the kohl-enhanced eyes, the heavy rumps – may He who bestows all blessings save me from them. To walk dreamily through these beautiful visions is one of my favorite sports, but I must acknowledge that it exhausts my heart and eye. If you start counting the women here, you'll never finish. What a blessed place it is that brings all of them together. The only way to protect yourself is to cry out from the depths of your heart, 'Yasin, you house wrecker!' A voice tells me that I should open a shop in al-Tarbi'a Alley and settle down. Your father's a merchant. He's his own boss. He spends much more on his amusements than you get from your salary. Open a store and put your trust in God, even if you have to sell the apartment in al-Ghuriya and the shop in al-Hamzawi. You arrive in the morning like a sultan. You're not bound to any schedule. There's no supervisor to terrify you. You sit behind the scales, and women come to you from every direction. 'Good morning, Mr. Yasin.' 'Stay healthy, Mr. Yasin.' I would have only myself to blame if I let a chaste woman pass without a greeting and a shameless one without a date. What a sweet idea this is, but what a cruel one for someone who will remain an officer of al-Nahhasin School to the end of his days. Love's a disease. Among its symptoms are constant hunger and a fickle heart. Have mercy, God, on one You created with the appetite of a caliph or sultan but gave the job of a school disciplinarian. My hopes have been destroyed. It's pointless to lie to myself. The day you brought her to Palace of Desire Alley you anticipated a happy, contented life. May God destroy boredom. It pervades the soul as totally as the bad taste sickness brings to the mouth. I pursued her passionately for a year but tired of her in a few weeks. What is misery if not this? Your home must have been the first one that ever overflowed with complaints during the honeymoon. Ask your heart what place Maryam has in it now and where the beauty is that drove you crazy. Let it reply with a laugh like a moan, 'We ate till we were full. Then we couldn't even stand the smell of food.' She's clever. It's hard to put something over on her. Nothing escapes her. She's a bitch and the daughter of one. Remember the virtues of your deceased family members. Was your mother any better than hers? The important thing is that, unlike Zaynab, Maryam's not easy to deceive. How hard her anger is to bear when she gets annoyed. . . . She's not willing to close her eyes, and you're not easily satisfied. It's absurd to think that your fiery cravings can ever be met by one woman or that your heart will settle down. Even so, you hoped to achieve a happy married life. How magnificent your father is and how vile you are. . . . You haven't been able to follow his example, even though that would have saved you. O Lord, what's this I see? Is it really a woman? How many hundred pounds do you suppose she weighs? My God, I've never seen a woman so tall and wide. How can you take possession of this fiefdom? I swear if a woman her size fell into my hands, I'd stretch her out naked in the center of the room and circle her ritually seven times, as if she were a shrine, before putting it in her."

"You!"

The voice from behind made his heart quiver. He quickly turned his eyes from the mammoth female and saw a young woman in a white coat. He could not help but exclaim, "Zanuba!"

They shook hands warmly and she laughed. He suggested they should keep walking to avoid attracting attention. So they strolled along side by side as the crowd swarmed around them. Thus they met again after a long separation. She had only rarely and infrequently crossed his mind after various considerations had distracted him. Yet he found her as beautiful as the day he left her, or possibly even more attractive. What was this new style of clothing she was wearing instead of the traditional black wrap? An invigorating wave of delight spread through him.

She asked, "How are you?"

"Great. And you?"

"Like this."

"Superb, praise God. You've changed the way you dress. I hardly recognized you at first. I still remember how you looked in your wrap when you walked."

"You haven't changed. You don't look older, but you've gained a little weight. That's the only thing."

"Now you're something else! You're a European girl!" He smiled cautiously before adding, "Except the hips come from al-Ghuriya."

"Watch your tongue!"

"You scare me. Have you repented or gotten married?"

"Nothing's beyond God's power."

"Your white coat belies a return to God. As for marriage, it's not farfetched to think a lack of sense would lead you to it someday."

"Watch out. I'm as good as married."

He laughed. As they turned into the Muski, he said, "Exactly like me."

"But you really are married. Isn't that so?"

"How did you learn that?" Then, reconsidering, he added, "Oh, I forgot that all our secrets eventually get to you."

He laughed again suggestively. Smiling mysteriously, she said, "You mean at the sultana's house?"

"Or my father's. Hasn't their affection continued?"

"Sort of."

"Everything with you is tentative now. Well, I'm sort of married. I mean I'm married and looking for a girlfriend."

She brushed a fly from her face, and the gold bracelets on her arm jingled. She said, "I'm a girlfriend who's looking for a marriage."

"A girlfriend? Who's the lucky son of a . . ."

She interrupted him, cautioning, "Don't insult people. He's an important man."

Eyeing her sarcastically, he said, "Important! Ha-ha, Zanuba, I wish I could ram my horn into you."

"Do you remember the last time we met?"

"Oh, my son Ridwan's six now. That must have been about seven years ago."

"A lifetime. . . ."

"While still alive, one should never despair of meeting again."

"Or of parting."

"You seem to have shrugged off loyalty with your black wrap."

She frowned at him and said, "Ox, who are you to talk about fidelity?"

He was pleased to see her become this familiar, for it encouraged his ambitions. He replied, "God only knows how delighted I am to see you again. I've thought of you frequently. But that's the way the world is."

"The world of women, huh?"

Pretending to be upset, he said, "The world of death, the world of troubles."

"You seem to bear your troubles well. Mules could certainly envy your health."

"If only the beautiful eye isn't envious. . . ."

"Are you afraid of the evil eye? You're as tall and broad as Abd al-Halim al-Masri."

He laughed conceitedly. After falling silent for a time, he asked in a new, serious tone, "Where were you going?"

"Why does a woman come to al-Tarbi'a Alley if not to shop? Or do you think everyone's like you with only one thought in life – sex?"

"Falsely accused, by God."

"You, innocent? When I caught sight of you, your eyes were assaulting a woman as big as a city gate."

"No. I was lost in thought and totally unaware of what I was looking at."

"You! My advice for anyone wishing to find you is to walk along al-Tarbi'a and look for the largest woman. I guarantee that he'll definitely find you stuck to her like a tick on a dog."

"Woman, your tongue gets more vicious every day."

"May God's holy name protect yours too."

"Never mind that. Let's stick to essentials. Where are you going now?"

"I'm shopping. Then I'll go home."

He fell silent for a moment, as if hesitating. Then he said, "What would you think about us spending some time together?"

She glanced at him with playful black eyes and replied, "I have a jealous man to consider."

Ignoring her objection, he continued: "A nice place where we can have a couple of drinks."

In a louder voice than before she answered, "I told you there's a jealous man in my life."

Paying no attention to that comment, he added, "The Tout-Va-Bien . . . what do you think? It's a charming place and respectable. I'll get this taxi."

A mumbled protest escaped her. Then she asked with a disapproving tone not matched by her facial expression, "By force?" She glanced at her wristwatch, and this new gesture almost made him laugh. In a voice that laid down the law, she said, "Just don't make me late. It's six now, and I must be home before eight."

As the taxi set off, Yasin wondered whether anyone had noticed them in al-Tarbi'a or the Muski. He shrugged his shoulders disdainfully and with the handle of his ivory fly whisk shoved back his fez, which was slanting down over his right eyebrow. What did he care? Maryam was alone in the world. She did not have a savage guardian like Muhammad Iffat, who had wrecked the first marriage Yasin had established. His own father was a suave man who realized that Yasin was no longer an inexperienced child to be punished in the courtyard of the old house.

They took seats opposite each other at a table in the garden of the Tout-Va-Bien. The bar was crowded with men and women. The player piano was belting out its monotonous pieces, and the aroma of grilled meat came with the evening breeze from a far corner. She was so ill at ease that he realized it was the first time she had ever patronized a public establishment. He felt a sharp delight. The next moment he was certain that he was in the grips of a genuine longing, not just a transient lust. Those bygone days with her seemed the happiest of his whole life.

He ordered a bottle of cognac and then some grilled meat. His cheeks were growing flushed, and his black hair, parted in the middle like his father's, was visible when he removed his fez. On noticing the resemblance, Zanuba smiled faintly. He naturally did not understand why. For the first time ever he was sitting with a woman in a tavern outside of the Wajh al-Birka entertainment district. It was also his first amorous adventure subsequent to his second marriage, with the exception of one indiscretion in Abd al-Khaliq Alley. And he did not normally drink good-quality cognac outside his house. He only got first-rate liquor when he purchased bottles to take home for what he termed licit, "medicinal" purposes.

He filled the two glasses with pride and relief. Then, raising his, he said, "To the health of Miss Zanuba Martell."

She answered with sweet arrogance, "I drink Dewar's scotch with the bey."

He grumbled, "I don't want to hear about him. May our Lord put him in the past tense."

"No way!"

"We'll see. Each glass we drink opens up new doors for us and smooths away difficulties."

They both sensed that the time was short and drank quickly. The glasses were filled and drained again and again. The cognac's fiery tongue began to trill in their stomachs, and the mercury of intoxication rose in the thermometer of their veins. The green leaves watching them from pots behind the wooden garden railing revealed glistening smiles. The piano's music fell on more indulgent ears. Faces both dreamy and feisty repeatedly exchanged fond and friendly looks. Waves of cool evening air flowed around them with silent music. Everything seemed pleasant and beautiful.

"Do you know what I felt like saying when I first saw you today – when you were gazing, as if possessed, at that woman?"

"Yes? . . . But finish your glass first, so I can fill it."

Helping herself to a sliver of meat, she continued: "I almost shouted, 'You son of a bitch . . .'"

Laughing fruitily, he asked, "Why didn't you, bitch's daughter?"

"Because I only curse men I love. You were little more than a stranger to me then."

"How about now?"

"A bastard for sixty generations."

"My goodness, an insult's even more intoxicating at times than alcohol. This blessed night will be in all the papers tomorrow."

"Why, God forbid? Do you intend to cause trouble?"

"Lord, be gracious to her, and to me."

Then she inquired with obvious interest, "Why haven't you told me about your new wife?"

Stroking his mustache, he answered, "The poor dear! Her mother died this year."

"May you have a long life. Was she rich?"

"She left a house, the one beside ours – I mean next to my father's. But she left it jointly to her new husband and my wife."

"Your wife must be a beauty, for you always get the best."

He replied cautiously, "She has a certain beauty, but it doesn't compare with yours."

"Shame on you."

"Have you ever known me to lie?"

"You! There are times when I even doubt that your name's Yasin."

"Then let's drink this round too."

"Are you getting me drunk so I'll believe you?"

"If I tell you I want you and long for you, would you doubt me then?"

"You probably talk like this to every woman you meet."

"Say rather that a hungry man desires all kinds of food yet retains a hankering for mallow greens."

"A man who really loves a woman will not hesitate to marry her."

He sighed and then said, "You're mistaken. I'd like to stand on this table and scream at the top of my lungs, 'Any of you men who's in love with a woman – don't marry her.' Yes, nothing kills love so effectively as marriage. Believe me. I've learned from my own experience. I married once and then a second time. I know how true this is."

"Perhaps you haven't yet found the woman who's right for you."

"Right? What kind of woman would that be? Which of my senses will guide me to her? Where is this woman who'll never be boring?"

She laughed lethargically and then commented, "It sounds as if you'd like to be a bull in a pasture full of cows. That's what you need."

Snapping his fingers appreciatively, he said, "God, God! Who used to call me that in the old days? It was my father, may he have a good evening. How I wish I could be like him. He acquired a wife whose obedience and moderation are exemplary and has been able to give free rein to his passions without encountering any problems. He's successful in his marriage and in his affairs. That's what I'd like."

"How old is he?"

"I think he's about fifty-five, but he's stronger than most young men."

"No one can hold out against time forever. May our Lord grant him good health."

"My father's the exception. He's the sweetheart of women other men crave. Don't you see him nowadays at your house?"

Laughing and tossing a bone to a cat meowing at her feet, she said, "I left that house some months ago. Now I have my own home. I'm the lady of the house."

"Really? I thought you were joking. Have you left the troupe as well?"

"Yes. You're speaking to a lady in every sense of the word."

He guffawed contentedly. Then he said, "So drink and let me drink. May our Lord be gracious to us."

He felt temptation inside and outside him. But which was the voice and which the echo? Even more marvelous was the life throbbing in material objects around them. The flowerpots whispered as they rocked back and forth. The pillars exchanged secrets. As the sky gazed down with starry, sleep-filled eyes at the earth, it spoke. He and his companion exchanged messages expressing their inmost feelings while a glow, both visible and invisible, confounded their hearts and dazzled their eyes. Something was at work in the world, tickling people until they were plunged into laughter. A look, word, gesture, anything was enough to induce all of them to laugh. Time fled as quickly as youth. The waiters carrying the fermented germ of exuberance distributed it to all the tables with grave faces. The tunes of the piano seemed to come from far away and were almost drowned out by the clattering wheels of the streetcar. On the sidewalk rowdy boys and men collecting cigarette butts created a commotion like the drone of flies, as night's legions set up camp in the district.

"You seem to be watching for the waiter to come ask, 'Are you too drunk to find your way home?' You're ignoring and avoiding that issue and an even more important one. If only Maryam would kneel before you and whisper, 'All I need is one room where I can busy myself obeying your every command. Fill the rest of the apartment with all the women you want.' If the headmaster at school would only pat you on the shoulder and say, 'How's your father, my son?' If only the government would carve out a new street in front of the store in al-Hamzawi and the residence in al-Ghuriya. If only Zanuba would tell you, 'Tomorrow I'm leaving my lover's house and then I'll be at your service.' If all this would happen, people would gather after the Friday prayer service and kiss each other with sincere affection. Tonight the best thing you can do is to sit on the sofa while Zanuba dances naked in front of you. Then you'll have a chance to monitor the beauty spot over her navel."

"How's the beloved beauty spot?" he asked as he smilingly gestured toward his own belly.

She laughed and replied, "It kisses your hand."

Glancing casually around the place, he said, "Do you see these men? Each is the debauched son of a fallen woman. All drunks are like this."

"We're honored. But my brain is flying off in every direction."

"I hope the part inhabited by your boyfriend soars away."

"Oh, if he knew what's become of us! He'll stab you one day with the tip of his mustache."

"Is he a Syrian with a colossal one?"

"Syrian?" Then she started singing in a loud voice the Syrian dialect word for salve: "*Barhum*, oh *barhum* . . ."

"Hush. Don't attract attention."

"Whose attention, blind man? Only a few people are left."

After rubbing his stomach and sighing, he observed, "Drink's a crazy thing."

"The crazy thing was your mother."

"You're talking louder than you should. Let's go."

"Where?"

"You know more than I do. Our feet will decide."

"Is a person successful when he lets his feet guide him?"

"That's safer at any rate than relying on a disordered brain."

"Think a little about . . ."

He interrupted her by rising tipsily and saying, "We need to act without any thought. Until tomorrow morning there's no point trying to think. Let's go."

97

"THE HOUSES have closed their eyes. The streets are vacant except for an occasional roving breeze or the light from a sleepy lamp. Free from any competition, silence has wandered everywhere, spreading its wings. What good are hotels? The desk clerks look askance at you, as if you've got a dizzying disease they don't want to catch. Yes, you can scoff at their hostility, but you still don't have a place to stay. Other lovers are tucked in bed. How long are you going to wander around? Here's a driver raising his head heavy with sleep. He's looking at you in a welcoming way. God's mercy on anyone who drags a woman around in the wee hours of the night looking for a place to stay."

"Where to?" Yasin asked.

The driver replied with a smile, "Anywhere you want."

Yasin told him, "I wasn't asking you."

The man replied, "At your service, in any case."

"Don't ask me," Zanuba said. "Ask yourself. Why didn't you think about that before you got drunk?"

Encouraged by seeing them stand beside his carriage, the coachman suggested, "The Nile! That's the best place. Shall I take you to the banks of the Nile?"

Yasin asked contentiously, "Are you a coachman or a sailor? What would we do by the Nile at this hour of the night?"

The driver said suggestively, "The light's dim, and no one's around."

"Ideal conditions for thieves."

Zanuba said fearfully, "Terrible! My ears, neck, and arms are weighted down with gold."

Shrugging his shoulders, the driver said, "There's nothing to fear. Every night I go there with fine people like you and we return in top condition."

Zanuba said sharply, "Don't mention the Nile. Talking about it makes my body shudder."

"May evil stay far from your body."

On taking his place in the carriage next to Zanuba, Yasin said, "Talk to me. What's her body to you?"

"Bey, I'm your servant."

"Everything's a mess tonight."

"May our Lord straighten it out. If you'd like a hotel, we'll go to one."

"We've quarreled with the clerks in three hotels. Three or four, Zanuba? Think of something else."

"There's always the Nile."

Zanuba said angrily, "The gold, fellow."

Putting his feet on the other seat, Yasin added, "Besides, there's no place to . . ."

The driver answered, "There's always the carriage."

Zanuba shouted, "Are you trying to humiliate me?"

Twisting his mustache, Yasin said, "You're right. Absolutely. The carriage isn't the place. I'm not going to act like a foolish kid at this stage in my life. Listen. . . ."

The man turned his ear, and Yasin yelled imperiously, "To Palace of Desire Alley."

"Clip-clop, clip-clop . . . you're plunging into the darkness with no friend save the stars," Yasin reflected.

Anxiety loomed on the horizon only to sink back into a sea of forgetfulness, like an elusive memory. His willpower had dissolved in a glass of wine. Then his companion in merrymaking asked him with a drunken stammer where he was heading in Palace of Desire Alley.

He replied, "My house, which I inherited from my mother."

"The fates decreed that she lived for love there and left it in trust to love at her death," he thought. "It has greeted with yearning Umm Maryam and her daughter Maryam. Tonight it will open its arms to a lady from my past."

"What about your wife, drunkard?"

"She's sound asleep."

"Isn't there a reckoning for everything?"

"You're with a man whose heart doesn't know the meaning of fear. Pluck some pearls from the heavens and drape your forehead with them. Sing softly into my ear, 'Bring me my love tonight, Mother.'"

"Where am I going to spend the rest of it?"

"I'll take you anywhere you want."

"You couldn't carry a straw home."

"How about Paris on the Mediterranean?"

"If only I weren't afraid of him."

"Who is he?"

Throwing her head back, she answered despondently, "Who knows? I've forgotten."

Al-Gamaliya was scarcely visible in the darkness. Even the coffee-house had closed its doors. The carriage stopped at the entrance to Palace of Desire Alley. As Yasin stepped down, he belched. Supporting herself on his arm, Zanuba followed. They walked off together with a caution that did not keep them from swaying tipsily. Behind them they heard the cough of the driver and the squeaking shoes of the night watchman, who passed inquisitively by the carriage as it turned around.

She told him, "The ground's uneven. It's rough walking here."

He replied, "It'll be easy going in the house." Then he added, "Don't worry."

Although sporting a silly smile that was lost in the shadows, Zanuba tried in vain to remind him that his wife was in the apartment they were approaching. She almost stumbled twice climbing the stairs. When they reached the door of the apartment they were both panting. Alarm at the situation momentarily lent their scattered wits the impetus to collect the shreds of consciousness.

Yasin carefully turned the key in the lock, gently shoved the door open, and searched for Zanuba's ear in the darkness. Bending over, he whispered for her to remove her shoes. After taking his off, he stepped in front of her, put her hand on his shoulder, and headed for the parlor near the entrance. Opening that door, he slipped inside with her still behind him. They sighed with relief. Closing the door, he led her to the sofa, where they sat down together.

She said uneasily, "It's very dark, I don't like the dark."

Putting their shoes under the sofa, he replied, "You'll get used to it soon."

"My head's beginning to spin."

"Only now?"

Without paying any attention to her response, he rose suddenly and whispered with alarm, "I didn't shut the outside door." Putting up his hand to remove his fez, he cried out, "I forgot my fez too! Do you suppose I left it in the carriage or at Tout-Va-Bien?"

"To hell with your fez! Lock the door, fellow."

Once again he slipped into the hall and over to the outside door, which he shut with extreme care. On his way back a tempting idea struck him. He went to the console table, holding his hand out in front of him to keep from bumping into one of the chairs. Then he returned to the parlor holding a half-empty bottle of cognac.

Placing it in her lap, he said, "I've brought you the remedy for everything."

After feeling the bottle with her hand she exclaimed, "Liquor! . . . Enough's enough. Do you want us to spill over?"

"One sip to help us catch our breath after all this exertion."

He drank until he felt that he was capable of anything and that insanity was a desirable condition. Then the sea of inebriation began to rage. He rode high on a wave only to plunge down again. He spun round in an endless whirlpool. In the corners of the room there were protruding tongues, raving and ranting in the darkness. Boisterous laughter escaped from these throats with a clamor like the commotion of a market, followed by nothing less than singing. The bottle fell to the floor with a warning thump. But he had a lap to finish swimming, even if he had to do it in a sea of perspiration. The time might have been long or short. He was not keeping track. His eyes were closed and oblivious to the passing and graying of the darkness.

Thus he awakened to voices and movement like a happy dreamer just stretching out his hand to pluck a new treat. Opening his eyes, he saw light and shadow dancing together on the walls. He turned his neck and noticed Maryam at the door. She was holding a lamp, and its light clearly revealed scowling features and eyes flashing with anger. The couple sprawled across the sofa exchanged long, extraordinary looks with the woman standing at the door. Theirs were unsteady and confused, hers flaming with outrage. The silence was unbearable. Zanuba revealed her anxiety by opening her mouth to speak without being able to get any words out. Then she was suddenly overwhelmed by laughter for no apparent reason. She was so convulsed that she had to hide her face in her hands.

Yasin shouted at her with slurred diction, "That's enough laughter! This is a respectable home."

Maryam seemed to want to speak, but either her tongue would not cooperate or fury rendered her speechless. Without knowing what he was saying, Yasin told her, "I found this 'lady' in a severely intoxicated condition. So I brought her home to sober up."

Zanuba was not going to keep quiet about this. She protested, "He's the drunk, as you can see. And he brought me here by force."

Maryam made a motion as if she was seriously considering throwing the lamp at them. Yasin tensed his body and gave her a look that showed he was prepared. But she immediately had second thoughts, once she realized the serious implications of such an act. She placed the lamp on a table and clenched her teeth with rage. Then, her voice dry and trembling but coarsened by resentment and anger, she spoke for the first time: "In my house! . . . In my house? In my house, you criminal child of the devils."

Her voice reverberated like thunder as she poured curses upon him and called him the filthiest names. She screamed, raising her voice so loud that it could be heard through the walls. She summoned the tenants and neighbors, swearing to expose him and to awaken people to be witnesses against him.

Yasin tried in various ways to caution her to keep quiet. He waved his hand at her, stared at her, and scolded her loudly. When these methods failed, he rose excitedly. He went toward her with long steps to reach her as fast as he could without actually running, for he was afraid of losing his balance. He pounced on her and spread his hand over her mouth to keep her from talking. But she screeched in his face like a desperate cat and kicked him in the belly. He backed off unsteadily, his face clouded with resentment and pain. Then he fell flat on his face, like a building collapsing.

A resounding scream burst forth from Zanuba. Maryam ran and fell upon her, pulling the intruder's hair with her right hand while digging the nails of the other one into the woman's neck. She began to spit in Zanuba's face and then to curse and insult her. Yasin got up again at once, shaking his head violently, as if to expel his hangover. He went to the sofa and aimed a fierce blow at the back of his wife, who was lying on top of her rival. Maryam screeched and retreated. He pursued her. Blinded by anger, he rained punches on her until she got on the far side of the dining table. Then she took off one of her slippers and hurled it at him, striking him in the chest. He tried to catch her, pursuing her around the hall.

He shouted at her, "I never want to see you again." Then he pronounced the irreversible triple divorce formula: "You're divorced, divorced, divorced!"

There was a rapping on the door, and the woman who lived on the second floor could be heard crying, "Mrs. Maryam, Mrs. Maryam!"

Breathless, Yasin stopped running. Maryam opened the door and in a voice that filled the whole stairwell immediately said, "Come look in this room and tell me if you've ever seen anything like this before. A whore in my house, drunk and disorderly. Come and see!"

The neighbor said timidly, "Calm down, Mrs. Maryam. Come stay with me till morning."

Yasin cried out recklessly, "Go with her. You have no right to stay in my house."

Maryam screamed in his face, "Adulterer! Criminal! Bringing a whore to your wife's home!"

He pounded on the wall with his fist and shouted at her, "You're a whore! You and your mother!"

"You insult my mother when she's with God?"

"You're a whore. I know that for sure. Don't you remember the English soldiers? It's my fault for not paying attention to the warnings of decent people."

"I'm your spouse, the crown of your life. I'm better than your folks and your mother. Ask yourself what kind of man marries a woman he 'knows' is a whore – as you claim. What is he but a despicable pimp?" Gesturing toward the parlor, she suggested, "Marry that woman. She's the type that fits your filthy character."

"One more word and your blood will spill out where you're standing."

But screams and fiery invective kept leaping from her throat. Finally the neighbor got between them to be able to separate them if necessary. She began patting Maryam's shoulder and imploring her to leave the apartment until morning.

Yasin got even more upset and yelled at her, "Take your clothes and leave! Get out of my sight. You're not my wife. I don't know you. I'm going into this room now. You'll be sorry if I find you here when I come out again." He rushed into the parlor, slamming the door behind him so violently that the walls shook. Then he threw himself on the sofa and dried the sweat from his brow.

Zanuba whispered, "I'm frightened."

He replied gruffly, "Shut up. What are you afraid of?" In a loud voice he said, "I'm free! Free!"

As though to herself she remarked, "What could have happened to my mind to make me obey you and come here?"

"Hush! What's done is done. I'm not sorry about anything. . . . Phooey!"

Through the closed door several voices reached them, indicating that more than one of the neighbor women had gathered around the angry wife. Then Maryam's voice was audible, sobbing, "Have you ever heard of anything like this before? A prostitute off the street in a home? I woke up because they were making such a racket. They were laughing and singing. Yes, by God, they were singing shamelessly. They were so drunk they were oblivious to everything. Tell me if this is a residence or a brothel."

Then a woman's voice protested, "Are you packing up your clothes and leaving home? This is your house, Mrs. Maryam. It's not right for you to leave. It's the other woman who should go."

Maryam cried out, "It's not my house anymore. That honorable gentleman has divorced me."

The other woman replied, "He wasn't in his right mind. Come with us now. Let's leave talk for the morning. In spite of everything, Yasin Effendi's a fine man and comes from a good family. God's curse on Satan. Come along, daughter. Don't grieve."

Maryam shouted, "No talking! No settling! May the sun never rise again on that criminal son of a crooked mother."

There were footsteps of people retreating. Finally only an indistinct buzz of voices could be heard. Then the door was closed with a loud bang. Yasin breathed deeply and stretched out on his back.

98

HE OPENED his eyes to find the morning sunshine filling the room. He had the worst hangover of his entire life, although the preceding night had hardly been his first time to get drunk. Rotating his head mechanically, he noticed Zanuba snoring beside him. Then his memory recalled the events of the past night in one fell swoop. Zanuba was in Maryam's bed. And Maryam? . . . With the neighbors. And the scandal? . . . Broadcast everywhere. What a giant leap into the bottomless pit of destruction! What use was there for anger or regret now? What was done was done. Everything might change but not the previous day. Should he wake her up? Why should he? Let her sleep to her heart's content. Let her stay where she was, for she could not leave the house until dark.

He had to revive himself to meet his difficult day. He pulled the light cover from his body, slipped out of bed, and padded out of the bedroom. His hair was disheveled, his eyelids swollen, and his eyes red. He yawned in the hallway with a bovine sound. Looking at the open door of the parlor, he sighed deeply. He closed his eyes and moaned in response to his hangover. Then he headed for the bathroom. He really had a hard day in front of him. Maryam was at the neighbor's, while the other woman occupied the bed. Day had overtaken him before he could conceal the traces of his crime. How crazy! He should have spirited her out before going to bed. How could he have been so negligent? What disaster had befallen him? When and how had he moved her from the parlor to the bedroom? He did not remember anything. He did not even recall how and when he had fallen asleep. The upshot was a colossal scandal with nothing to show for it. It had been a perfectly innocent evening but one now as filled with disgrace as his head was with distress and discomfort. But it was hardly amazing, for the apartment, a bequest from his mother, God forgive her, had long been inhabited by scandalous demons. The mother had passed on, but the son had remained to become the butt of the neighborhood gossip. By the following day the news would have reached Palace Walk.

"Forward, denizen of the abyss of debauchery. If this cold water you're using to wash your body could only cleanse your mind of its evil memories.... Who knows? Perhaps if you look out the window, you'll find a group of people watching at your doorway for the departure of the woman who expelled your wife and took her place. No, you won't allow her to leave today, no matter what. As for Maryam, you've divorced her. You divorced her without wanting to, when her mother's grave is still fresh. What will people say of you, liar?"

He felt a pressing need for a cup of coffee to revive his senses. On his way from bathroom to kitchen he noticed the console table in the front hall and remembered the bottle of cognac that had spilled in the parlor. He wondered for a moment if the rug was damaged but then remembered with ironic regret that the furniture was no longer his property. It would soon go to join the woman who owned it.

In a few minutes he was carrying a glass half filled with coffee to the bedroom, where he found Zanuba sitting up in bed as she stretched and yawned.

She turned toward him and said, "A good morning for both of us! We'll have breakfast at the police station, God willing."

He took a sip and looked at her over the rim of the glass. Then he said, "Pray to God the Omniscient Benefactor."

She waved her hands until the gold bracelets jangled. Then she blurted out, "You're responsible for everything that's happened."

He sat down on the bed near her outstretched legs. He answered uneasily, "A trial, huh? I told you to address God the Omniscient Benefactor."

She rubbed the small of his back with her heels as she moaned, "You've destroyed my home. God only knows what's waiting for me there."

As he crossed one leg over the other, his house shirt rode up to reveal a thigh that was firm and covered with a forest of coal-black hair. He asked, "Your boyfriend?... May God disappoint him! What's he compared with my wife, whom I've divorced? You're the one who's devastated my household. It's my home that's destroyed."

As though addressing herself, she said, "It's been a dark night.

I haven't been able to tell my head from my feet, and the din is still ringing in my head. But it's my fault. I should never have listened to you."

He suspected she actually was pleased, her complaints notwithstanding, or that she was using them to get at him. Had he not known women in the Ezbekiya fleshpots who boasted of the number of bloody battles waged over them? But he did not get angry. Matters had reached such a desperate pass that he was spared the effort of trying to remedy them.

He could not help laughing as he observed, "It's the worst catastrophes that make you laugh. Laugh! You've wrecked my home and replaced my wife. Get up and pull yourself together. Prepare for a long stay . . . till night falls. You won't leave the house until it's dark."

"What dreadful news! Imprisoned! Where's your wife?"

"I don't have a wife anymore."

"Where is she?"

"In divorce court, if my guess is correct."

"I'm afraid she'll attack me when I leave."

"You afraid? Lord have mercy on us! Last night, menacing though she was, you didn't lose a bit of your sly pluck, you niece of Zubayda."

She laughed for a long time. She seemed to be acknowledging the charge against her and to be proud of it too. Then she put out her hand to take the glass of coffee. After drinking a little, she returned the glass and asked, "Now what?"

"As you can see, I'm in the dark too. It hurts to be exposed in front of people the way I was last night."

Shrugging her shoulders disdainfully, she said, "Don't worry about it. There's not a man alive who hasn't more dirty linen than the earth has room to hide."

"Just the same, a scandal's a scandal. Think of the fight, the wailing, the divorce at dawn. Picture the neighbors coming with alarmed curiosity to my apartment. Their eyes took in everything."

She frowned and said, "She started it!"

He could not restrain his sardonic laughter. She persisted: "If she had been wise, she could have worked everything out. Even strangers in the street are considerate to boisterous drunks. She's the one who brought the divorce down on herself. What did you say to her? 'Whore and daughter of a whore'? Huh? And something else about English soldiers?"

He only remembered this now. Giving her a peeved look, he wondered how these phrases had taken root in her memory. He muttered uneasily, "I was angry. I didn't know what I was saying."

"Humbug!"

"Humbug to you!"

"English soldiers? Did you get her from one of their haunts like the Finish Bar?"

"God forbid. She's from a decent family, lifelong neighbors. It was just anger, a thousand curses on it."

"Without anger, secrets would never come to light."

"By your aunt's life, we have enough trouble as it is."

"Tell me about the English soldiers, as if there was anything I didn't know about them. . . ."

In a loud, defiant voice he replied, "I told you it was anger. That'll do."

She groaned sarcastically and then asked, "Are you defending her? Then go get her back."

"Curses on anyone shameless and cold-blooded enough to do that."

"Curses. . . ."

She got out of bed and went to the mirror. Picking up Maryam's comb, she began to fix her hair quickly as she asked, "What will I do if the man breaks up with me?"

"Tell him goodbye. My house is always open to you."

She turned toward him and said sadly, "You don't understand what you're saying. We were thinking seriously about marriage."

"Marriage! Haven't you dropped that idea after you saw what it's like last night?"

She answered shrewdly, "You don't understand. I'm tired of being a kept woman. All it brings is ruin. A woman like me who weds really values her marriage."

"Who's the idiot?" he asked himself. "In the troupe she was never anything more than a lute player. After thirty a prostitute's over the hill, and she'll be thirty soon. So marriage is her best bet. Is she aiming this talk at you? What a delightful devil! I won't deny I want her. I desire her in the strongest possible way. My scandal bears witness to that."

"Do you love him?"

As if angered, she replied, "If I loved him, you wouldn't find me imprisoned here now."

Although skeptical of her veracity, he longed for her. Yes, even if her heart was not sincere, she had clearly shown a weakness for him.

"I can't do without you, Zanuba. To get you, I've done crazy things, not caring about the consequences. You're mine, and I've been yours for a long time."

Silence reigned. She seemed to be waiting impatiently for more. When he did not continue, she asked, "Should I sever my ties with that man? I'm not a woman who can bounce back and forth between two lovers."

"Who is he?"

"A merchant from the Citadel region called Muhammad al-Qulali."

"Married?"

"And he's got children, but he has lots of money."

"He promised to marry you?"

"He's trying to talk me into it, but I've been hesitating. The circumstances and the fact that he's a husband and father suggest there could be problems."

He put up with her deceitfulness for the sake of her beautiful eyes. "Why don't we go back to the way we were. I'm not destitute, in any case."

"I don't care about your money, but I'm sick of living in sin."

"What's to be done?"

"That's what I'm asking."

"Explain."

"I've said more than enough."

What an unexpected attack! Yes, at first glance it seemed ludicrous, but he wanted her. So he was forced to play along. After a pause he said, "I won't try to hide my low opinion of marriage from you."

"I have a low opinion of living in sin."

"That wasn't how you talked yesterday."

"Then I had a husband within reach, but today..."

"With a little flexibility, we can meet each other halfway. There's one thing you must never lose sight of: No matter how long I stay with you, I'll never let you go."

She cried out defiantly, "Your past adventures really bear that out!"

To hide the weakness of his position he replied earnestly, "A man doesn't learn without paying a price."

"Words no longer beguile me. Shame on you men!"

"And on you women too . . . isn't that so?" he thought. "Have mercy, niece of Zubayda. You arrive here drunk after midnight, and in the morning you're tired of living in sin. Perhaps she told herself, 'If his second wife was a whore, why shouldn't I be the third one?' How low Yasin has fallen. Have you forgotten the trouble ready to pounce on you outside? Let those problems wait. Just don't lose Zanuba with an ugly remark the way you did Maryam. Maryam? I'm atoning for my sin now, Fahmy."

He said calmly, "Our relationship must not end."

"It's up to you whether it continues or ends."

"We need to meet a lot and think a lot."

"As far as I'm concerned, I don't need to think anymore."

"So either I convince you of my opinion or you convince me of the wisdom of yours."

"I'll never come around to yours."

She left the room and did not let him see her smile. He gazed after her rounded back with a look of amazement. Yes, everything seemed amazing. But where was Maryam? On her own, wherever she was. He would not get any rest or peace. He would be questioned tomorrow at Palace Walk and the following day at the Islamic court. All the same, their life during the last period had been one long wrangle. She had even told him quite bluntly, "I hate you and I hate living with you."

"I wasn't made to succeed in marriage. Was my grandfather's life like this? I'm the one in the family who most resembles him, so they say. Despite all this, that crazy woman wants to marry me."

99

THE SUN was about to set when al-Sayyid Ahmad Abd al-Jawad crossed the wooden gangplank to the houseboat. He rang the bell, and the door soon opened to reveal Zanuba in a white silk dress sheer enough to show off her body. On seeing him she cried out, "Welcome! Welcome! Tell me what you did yesterday. I imagine you came, rang the bell in vain, and stood there for a time before leaving." She laughed. "And you must have had some awful suspicions. So tell me what you did."

Despite the elegance of his appearance and the fragrance of his cologne, his face looked grim and his displeasure was visible in his staring eyes. "Where were you yesterday?" he asked.

She went into the sitting room ahead of him, pausing in the center of the room near two windows that opened on the Nile. She took a chair between the windows, pretending to be calm, collected, and cheerful. Then she answered, "I went out yesterday, as you know, to do some shopping. On my way I ran into Yasmina the vocalist, and she invited me to her house. But she refused to let me leave and pestered me until I was forced to spend the night with her. I hadn't seen her since I moved to the houseboat. If you could have heard her criticize my disloyalty and ask me about the secret charm of this man who'd been able to make me forget my relatives and neighbors . . ."

Was she telling the truth or lying? Had he actually endured all those pains yesterday and today pointlessly? He knew the reason for every millieme he gained or lost. How could he have suffered those frightful torments for no reason at all? The world was a tricky place, but if this devil was telling the truth, he was prepared to kiss the ground at her feet. He had to determine whether it was true, even if that took the rest of his life. Had the time come for him to return to his senses? "Not so fast . . ." he admonished himself.

"When did you return to the houseboat?"

She lifted a leg and began to study her pink slipper decorated with a white rose and her toes tinted with henna. Then she said,

"Why don't you sit down first and take off your fez so I can see the part in your hair. Sir, I came home a little before noon."

"Liar!" The word shot out like a bullet coated with rage and despair. Before she could open her mouth, he continued violently: "Liar! You didn't return before noon or after noon. I came here twice during the day and didn't find you."

She was speechless for a time. Then she said in a tone of indignant surrender, "The truth is that I got home just before sunset, about an hour ago. There was no reason for me to make up a story, but when I noticed the groundless look of displeasure in your eyes I wanted to dispel it. The fact is that this morning Yasmina insisted I go shopping with her. When she learned I had left my aunt's ensemble, she suggested I join hers, so I could substitute for her occasionally at a wedding. Naturally I didn't agree, because I knew without asking that you wouldn't be happy if I stayed out late with the troupe. What I'm trying to say is that I remained with her because I knew you wouldn't get here before nine. This is the story. So sit down and bless the Prophet."

"A trumped-up tale or the truth?" he wondered. "What if your friends saw you in this fix? The fates are certainly making fun of you. I'd forgive twice as much as this if I could win a little peace of mind. You're begging now. You never had to beg before. You've humiliated yourself for this lute player. She once had the job of waiting on you. She served you fruit at parties and departed in decorous silence. If I can't reassure myself, let the fires of hell flame up."

"Yasmina doesn't live in never-never land. I'll ask her if this story's true."

Waving her hand to show her disdain and disapproval, she answered, "Ask her anything you want."

He got control of his frayed and refractory nerves all of a sudden and said stubbornly, "I'll ask her this evening. I'm going to look for her. Now! I've satisfied all your requests. You must respect my rights completely."

She caught his contagious fury and responded sharply, "Not so fast! Don't insult me to my face. I've been very lenient with you until now, but everything has a limit. I'm a person made of flesh and blood. Open your eyes and pray to Fatima's father Muhammad."

He asked in astonishment, "Is this the tone you use to address me?"

"Yes, since that's how you're talking to me."

The grip of his hand on his stick tightened as he yelled, "I'm entitled to, since I'm the one who made you a lady and prepared a life for you that Zubayda herself would envy."

His statement provoked her, and like a raging lioness she snarled, "God made me a lady, not you. I only accepted a life like this after you pleaded with me fervently. Have you forgotten that? I'm not your captive or your slave. An interrogation and a police report – what do you think I am? Did you buy me with your money? If you don't like the way I live, then each of us can go his own way."

"O Lord of the heavens," he reflected, "is this how manicured nails turn into claws? If you still have any doubts about last night, then consider this impudent tone. You're suffering from tyranny like Nimrod's. Swallow the pain to the dregs. Drink the abuse till you've had your fill. So what's your response? Scream in her face, as loud as you can, 'Go back to the street where I found you!' Scream, yes, scream. What's stopping you? God's curse on the saboteur! The heart's treachery is far worse than a thousand other forms of treason. This is the romantic abasement you've heard about and mocked. How I'll hate myself for loving her!"

"Would you throw me out?" he asked.

In the same belligerent tone she said, "If your understanding of our relationship is that I'm to stay here as your prisoner while you make accusations against me whenever you please, then the best thing for both of us is to break it off."

She turned her face away from him. He studied her cheek and the side of her neck with an unnatural calm that was almost trancelike. "The ultimate happiness I ask of God is casting her aside without a second thought. She has humiliated and angered you, but could you bear to come here and find no trace of her?"

"I have little confidence in you, but I didn't think your ingratitude would reach this point."

"Do you want me to be a stone with no feelings or sense of honor?"

"If you only realized," he reflected, "that you're even less than that. . . ."

But he replied, "No, I want you to be a person who recognizes the rights arising from good deeds and companionship."

Changing from an angry tone to one of complaint, she said, "I've done more for you than you can imagine. I consented to leave my family and my profession to stay wherever you chose. I haven't even complained about it, to avoid troubling your peace of mind. I didn't wish to tell you in so many words that certain people want a better life for me than this, although I haven't paid any attention to them."

"Are there to be more problems, ones I haven't anticipated?" he asked himself.

"What do you mean?" he inquired indignantly.

She toyed with her gold bracelets, spinning them around her left arm. Then she said, "A respectable gentleman wishes to marry me. He won't take no for an answer."

"The heat and the humidity are stifling you," he thought, "and this shrew is opening her mouth to swallow you whole. How lucky that seaman is, trimming his sail outside the window. . . ."

"Who is he?"

"Someone you don't know. Call him any name you want."

He took a step back and sat down on a sofa flanked by two armchairs. Gripping the handle of his stick with both hands, he asked, "When did he see you? How did you learn of his intentions?"

"He saw me often when I lived with my aunt. Recently he's attempted to speak to me whenever he's run into me on the street, but I've ignored him. So he got one of my girlfriends to tell me. That's the whole story."

"How many stories you have!" he mused. "When I found you gone yesterday, a single pain devastated me. At the time I wasn't aware of all these other pains and troubles. Leave her if you can. Break with her. That's the way to find peace. Aren't people wrong to imagine death's the worst thing we face?"

"I want to know whether you wish to accept this proposal."

With a nervous flick of her wrist she stopped playing with her bracelets and stared at him haughtily. Then she asserted grandly, "I told you I ignored him. You should understand what that means."

"You mustn't go to bed tonight with such lethal thoughts," he counseled himself. "You don't need another night like the last one. Shield yourself from these fears."

"Tell me frankly whether any man has visited you on the houseboat."

"A man? What man do you have in mind? You're the only man who enters this houseboat."

"Zanuba, I can ferret it all out. Don't be secretive. Tell me everything, even trivial details. Then I'll forgive you, no matter what."

She protested angrily, "If you keep doubting my truthfulness, the best thing is for us to part."

"Remember the fly you saw die this morning in a spider's web?" he asked himself.

"Enough of that. Tell me if this man met you yesterday."

"I told you where I went."

In spite of himself he snorted, "Why do you torment me? I've never wanted anything so much as to make you happy."

She clapped her hands together, as though finding his suspicions hard to bear. Then she said, "Why won't you understand me? I've sacrificed everything I value for your sake."

What a beautiful song it was! The calamity was that it could easily have come from an empty heart, for a singer can dissolve into a sad and plaintive song while intoxicated with happy triumph.

"With God as your witness, tell me frankly who this man is."

"Why does it matter to you? I said you don't know him. He's a merchant from another district, but he used to frequent the coffee-house of al-Sayyid Ali occasionally."

"His name?"

"Abd al-Tawwab Yasin. Do you know him?"

"I leased this houseboat to have a good time," he reminded himself. "Remember the happy hours? World, do you recall the Ahmad Abd al-Jawad whom nothing fazed? Zubayda, Jalila, Bahija . . . ask those ladies about him. No doubt he's some other man – not this anxious fellow with white ravaging the hair of his temples."

"The devil of unhappiness," he observed, "is the most energetic one."

"No, it's the devil of doubt, because he's able to create something from nothing."

He began to rap the floor with the tip of his stick. Then in a deep voice he said, "I don't want to live like a blind man. Certainly not! And nothing can make me violate my manly sense of honor. In brief, I can't tolerate your absence last night."

"We're back to that again!"

"And again and again and again. I'm not a child, and you're an adult too, a sensible woman. Today you've been telling me about that man. Has his promise of marriage really duped you?"

She answered proudly, "I know he's not deceiving me. His promise not to approach me till we're married is a proof of that."

"Does this marriage tempt you?"

She frowned disapprovingly and then said as if astonished, "Didn't you hear what I said? I'm amazed at how slow you are today. At any rate, you're not your normal self. Shake off this gloom you've needlessly courted and listen to me one last time: I ignored the man and his wish – for your sake."

He wanted to learn how old this man was but did not know how to phrase the question. Youth and age were not matters he had paid attention to before. After some hesitation he said, "Perhaps he's a callow youth who says things without thinking about them."

"He's no child. He's in his thirties."

In other words, the man was a quarter century behind al-Sayyid Ahmad. In everything except age it is bad to be behind. Jealousy is a brazen assassin.

She continued: "I pretended not to know him, even though he promised me the kind of life I dream of."

"What a chip off the old block!" he told himself. "Zubayda could have learned a lot from you."

"Is that so?" he asked.

"Let me tell you bluntly that I can't stand this life any longer."

"Remember the fly and the spider," he reminded himself.

"Really?"

"Yes. I want a secure life and a legal one. Or do you think that's wrong?"

"You came to interrogate her," he reflected, "but where do you stand now? She's the one ready to throw you out. How come you're so forbearing? Reserve some self-respect for what's left of your life. Do you understand what she's hinting at? . . . How lovely the breaking waves are at sunset."

His silence was prolonged, and she calmly started up again: "This won't anger you, for you're a pious man in spite of everything.

How can you obstruct a woman's desire to live according to the teachings of her religion? I don't want to be a mount for every rider. I'm not like my aunt. I have the heart of a Believer: I fear God. This has strengthened my resolve to abandon my sinful ways."

He listened to her last statement with astonishment and alarm. He started to scrutinize her with annoyance, which he hid behind a feeble smile. Then he replied, "You've never mentioned this to me before. Until yesterday we were getting along fine."

"I didn't know how to disclose my feelings to you."

"She's getting away from you with frightening and wicked speed. What a disappointment! I'm prepared to forget last night, ill-omened though it was. I'll forget my doubt and my pain . . . if she renounces this devilish scheme."

"We lived together happily and harmoniously. Does our relationship mean so little to you?"

"No, but I want to make it better. Isn't a godly life better than a sinful one?"

His lower lip tightened into a meaningless smile. Then he said in a faint voice, "For me the situation is quite different."

"How?"

"I'm married, my son's married, and my daughters are married. As you can see, the matter's extremely delicate." Then he added regretfully, "Weren't we blissfully happy?"

She answered testily, "I'm not telling you to divorce your wife and renounce your children. Many men have more than one wife."

He observed apprehensively, "Marriage for a man my a . . . in my situation is not an easy matter. It provokes a lot of comment."

She laughed sarcastically and said, "Everyone knows you have a mistress. That doesn't bother you. How come the possibility of gossip about a legal marriage worries you – if you want to marry me?"

Smiling with uneasy confusion, he said, "Only a few people know my secret. Besides, my family's totally in the dark about it."

She raised her penciled eyebrows in disbelief and said, "That's what you think. Only God knows for sure. What secret's secure from people's tongues?"

Before he could respond, she continued irately: "Or perhaps you don't think I'm good enough to have the honor of belonging to your family?"

"God forgive me," he thought, "the husband of Zanuba the lute player. . . ."

"I didn't mean that, Zanuba."

She said disdainfully, "You won't be able to hide your true feelings from me for long. I'll learn them tomorrow if not today. If marrying me would disgrace you, then goodbye."

"You came to get rid of the other man," he told himself, "but he's tossing you out. You've given up asking her where she was. She's offering you a choice between marriage and the door. What are you going to do? What's paralyzing you? It's your treacherous heart. Having your bones ripped from your flesh would be easier than leaving this lute player. Isn't it sad you're suffering an insane love like this only when you're getting on in years?"

He asked critically, "Is that what you think of me?"

"I don't think much of a person who treats me like spit."

Sadly and calmly he said, "You're dearer to me than my soul."

"Words! We've heard a lot of them."

"But it's the truth."

"It's time to learn that from your actions, not your words."

He looked down in distress and despair. He did not know how he could accept her proposal and yet did not have the strength to reject it, particularly since his desire for her had destroyed his mental concentration and shackled him. In a subdued voice he said, "Give me time to arrange my life. . . ."

Hiding a sly smile, she said smugly, "If you really love me, you won't hesitate."

He quickly retorted, "It's not that. There are other matters. . . ." He gestured as if to explain his words, although even he did not know precisely what they meant.

She smiled and said, "If that's how it is, I'll wait patiently."

He experienced the temporary relief of a collapsing boxer who hears the bell concluding a round other than the final one. A wish for consolation from his cares and reassurance after his anxiety pulsed through him. Holding his hand out to her, he said, "Come to me."

She drew herself back resolutely in the chair and said, "When God sanctions it."

100

HE LEFT the houseboat, made his way along the dark bank of the Nile, and headed down the deserted street toward the Zamalek Bridge. The gentle breeze cooled his hot brow and with a rustling whisper stirred the interlocking branches of the giant trees, which in the gloom resembled dunes or ebony clouds. Whenever he glanced up he found them hovering over him like phantoms of the worry troubling his breast. Did these lights pouring out of houseboat windows come from homes free of cares?

"But no anxiety's comparable to yours," he assured himself. "There's a difference between a man who dies and one who commits suicide. You've unquestionably agreed to commit suicide."

He continued walking, for he could think of no better way to release his nervous tension and to collect his thoughts before joining his friends. He would eventually closet himself with them and tell them everything. He would not take a step like this without consulting them, even though he could already guess what they would say. He would confess it all to them, no matter how painful, since he felt as overwhelming a desire to confide in them as a drowning man does to cry for help when seized by a violent wave.

He was well aware that he had agreed to marry Zanuba. He could hardly deny his abject craving for her but could not imagine that marriage would accommodate his desires. How could he break the "good" news to his wife and children or to other people? Although he wanted to keep walking for as long as possible and had no destination, he quickened his pace, took broad steps, and struck his stick against the ground as if in a great hurry to get somewhere.

She had rejected him and sent him away. These tricks were no novelty to a man of his worldly experience, but a weak person may knowingly fall into a snare. If the walking and the pure air revived him a little, he still remained befuddled and flustered. The flow of thoughts in his mind was so disordered that he could hardly bear it. He felt he would go crazy if a decisive solution, no matter how flawed, was not found.

In the shadows he had no hesitation or embarrassment about talking to himself. The canopy of branches shielded him from the sky, the fields stretching off to his right absorbed his ideas, and the waters of the Nile, flowing past him on the left, swallowed his feelings. But he had to avoid the light. He needed to be careful not to get caught by its bright ring, for fear of having to take off like a circus wagon trailed by boys and curiosity seekers. Then he could kiss his reputation, dignity, and honor goodbye. He had two personalities. One was reserved for friends and lovers, the other presented to his family and the world. It was this second visage that sustained his distinction and respectability, guaranteeing him a status beyond normal aspirations. But his caprice was conspiring against the respectable side of his character, threatening to destroy it forever.

He saw the bridge with its glowing lights ahead of him and wondered where he should go. Since he wanted more solitude and darkness, he did not cross over but continued straight ahead, taking the Giza road.

"Yasin!" he exclaimed. "The thought of your eldest son alarms you. Your forehead burns with shame. Why? He'll be the first to understand you and make allowances for you. Or do you think he'll rejoice at your misfortunes and make fun of you? You've scolded him and criticized him for a long time, but his foot's never slipped into a pit like yours. . . . Kamal! From now on you'll have to wear a mask to keep him from discerning your guilt. Khadija? Aisha? They'll have to hang their heads low in the Shawkat family. 'Zanuba's your father's wife!' A wedding applauded only by buffoons. . . . In your breast live sinful longings. Select some other stage for them than this world. Is there not a kingdom of darkness beyond the mortal realm where you can satisfy your base cravings in peace? Examine the spider's web tomorrow and see what's left of the fly. Listen to the croaking of the frogs and the chirping of the crickets. How happy these creatures are! Burrow underground if you want to be joyous and carefree. On the surface of the earth you can find happiness only as al-Sayyid Ahmad. Spend the next evening with members of your family, all of them – your wife, Kamal, Yasin, Khadija, and Aisha. Then tell them what you plan to do, if you're able. If you can do that, then and only then marry Zanuba.

"Haniya! Do you remember how you cast her out, even though you loved her? You've never loved a woman as much. It seems, alas, that we lose our senses when we become middle-aged. Drink tonight till they have to carry you out. How I long for a drink! It seems you haven't had one since the year of the prophet Muhammad's birth. The bitter pains you've had to swallow this year could easily erase the happy benefits you've enjoyed throughout your lifetime."

He pounded the earth with his stick and stopped walking. Fed up with the gloom, the stillness, and the tree-lined road, he desired the consolation of his friends. He was not a man who could tolerate being alone for any length of time. He was a member of a group, a part of the whole. In his friends' company, his problems would be solved as usual. He turned to go back to the bridge, but then his being rebelled with anger and disgust. In a strange voice racked by protest, pain, and resentment he said, "She spends a whole night out . . . in an unknown location, and then you agree to marry her."

He was afflicted with contempt for himself, like a sharp pain in his chest and heart. "With her friend Yasmina! How absurd! No . . . she spent the night in the arms of a man she only left the next day after noon." She had stayed with that fellow knowing full well when al-Sayyid Ahmad visited the houseboat. So what did that mean? Clearly her infatuation with the other man had made her forget the time.

"Eternal damnation! Or have you slipped so low she doesn't care whether you're upset or not? Spellbound fool! After that, how could you have spoken ingratiatingly to her? How could you have left her with a promise of marriage? You're a disgrace in this world and the next. Worry has put so much pressure on you that you don't seem to have noticed the horn with which you're crowning the family. It will dishonor them for generations to come. What do you expect people to say about this horn on your handsome forehead?

"Anger, loathing, blood, and tears will not atone for your surrender and your weakness. How she must be laughing at you now as she lies on her back in the houseboat. Perhaps she hasn't yet washed away the sweat of that man, who'll soon be laughing at you too. . . . What's the point of getting up tomorrow if everyone's going to be making fun of you? Confess your weakness to your friends and hear their raucous laughter and comments. 'Attribute it to age and senility. Excuse it by saying he's experienced everything except the delight of sporting a cuckold's horns.' Zubayda will say, 'You refused to be my master and agreed to be my lute player's pimp.' Jalila will declare, 'You're not my brother; not even my sister.' I ask the forbidding road, gloomy darkness, and aged trees to bear witness that I'm racing through the shadows, crying like a child. May I not sleep tonight before I humiliate the tyrant. . . . She turned you away! Why? Because she's tired of a life of sin . . . a sin from which she hadn't yet cleansed her body? Say rather that she can no longer bear you. That's sufficient. How hideous the pain is! But I deserve it for having worshipped her. When a person's doing penance for an ungodly deed, he may crush his head by beating it against a wall. Shaykh Mutawalli Abd al-Samad thinks he knows many things, but how ignorant he is. . . ."

Al-Sayyid Ahmad passed the Zamalek Bridge once more and took the Imbaba road. He began to quicken his steps deliberately and stubbornly, for he was determined to wash away the ignominy staining him. Whenever pain bore down on him, he renewed his efforts, striking the ground with his stick as though walking on three legs.

The houseboat came in sight. There was a light shining from the window. His rage intensified, for he had regained his self-confidence along with his feelings of manliness and honor. He felt composed now that he had reached a decision. He went down the steps, crossed the wooden gangplank, and banged on the door with the end of his stick. He rapped violently until he heard a voice ask with alarm, "Who's there?"

"Me!" he answered forcefully.

The door opened, revealing her astonished face. She stepped aside to let him in as she mumbled, "Good news?"

He crossed into the sitting room. Once in the center, he whirled around and stared at her. She approached with a questioning look and stopped in front of him as she anxiously examined his scowling face. Then she said, "Good news, God willing. Why have you come back?"

With alarming restraint he answered, "Good news, praise God, as you'll learn."

She did not speak but let her eyes ask the questions. So he continued: "I've come to tell you not to put any faith in what I said. The whole matter was just a foolish joke."

Her torso slumped with disappointment. Her face expressed disbelief and resentment. Then she cried out, "'A foolish joke'! Don't you know the difference between a silly prank and a binding word of honor?"

His face ever more glowering, he cautioned her, "When addressing me you'd better be polite. Women of your class earn their living in my home as maids."

Staring him straight in the face, she screamed, "Have you returned to favor me with this thought? Why haven't you ever said that before? Why did you make promises to me, attempt to gain my affection, and ingratiate yourself with me? Do you imagine talk like this will frighten me? I don't have time for foolish jokes."

He waved his hand angrily at her to make her keep still and yelled, "I've come to tell you that marrying a girl like you would be disgraceful and nothing but an anecdote for buffs of embarrassing jokes. They'll have fun with it. Since ideas like these fill your head, you're no longer fit to associate with me. It does me no good to frequent lunatics."

As she listened, sparks of anger flew from her eyes, but she disappointed his hopes and did not lose her temper. Perhaps the sight of his fury frightened her.

In a softer tone than before, she said, "I won't force you to marry me. I told you what I was thinking and left the decision up to you. Now you want to go back on your promise. Do whatever you want. But there's no reason to revile and insult me. Let each of us go his way in peace."

"Is this the most she'll do to hold on to you?" he asked himself. "Wouldn't it have been better if she'd dug her fingernails into you attempting to keep you? Recharge your anger from your pain."

"Each of us will go his own way, but first I want to tell you bluntly what I think of you. I don't deny it was my idea to pursue you – perhaps because the soul occasionally feels a desperate craving for filthy things. You left the people you were happily serving so I could lift you up to this style of life. It doesn't surprise me that I haven't found with you the kind of love and respect I won from them, for trash only appreciates trash. The time's come for me to cease stooping down to your level and to return to my proper environment."

Defeat was visible in her face, the defeat of a person afraid to release the fury pent up in her breast. In a trembling voice she muttered, "Goodbye. Go. Leave me in peace."

Struggling with his pains, he said bitterly, "I've lowered and demeaned myself."

At this point she lost control and shouted, "Enough! That'll do! Have mercy on this vile wretch, but beware of her. Remember how once you humbly kissed her hand. 'Lowered and demeaned,' huh? The truth is that you're getting old. I accepted you in spite of your age, and this is my reward. . . ."

He waved his stick and shouted furiously, "Shut up, bitch! Hush, vile creature! Collect your clothes and leave."

Raising her head jerkily, she shouted back, "Listen carefully to what I say. One more word from you, and I'll make such a row it'll resound throughout the houseboat, the road, and the riverfront until the entire police force arrives. Do you hear? I'm not some little morsel that's easily swallowed. I'm Zanuba! . . . May God repay me for my suffering. You go! This is my houseboat. The lease is in my name. Go peacefully before you're escorted out."

He tarried indecisively for a bit, looking scornfully and derisively at her. Eventually, in order to avoid a scandal, he abandoned the idea of attempting anything rough, spat on the floor, and departed with long, steady steps.

101

HE WENT immediately to his friends and found Muhammad Iffat, Ali Abd al-Rahim, Ibrahim al-Far, and some of the others. As usual, he drank until intoxicated, but then he had some more. He laughed a lot and made the others roar with laughter. In the wee hours of the night he returned home and slept soundly. Once morning came, he anticipated a quiet day free from thought. Whenever his imagination conjured up a scene from the near or distant past he resolutely shut it out – except for the one scene he gladly recalled, the final vignette recording his victory over the woman and himself. He asserted, "It's all over, praise God. I'm really going to be careful during what's left of my life."

At first the day was quiet. He was able to reflect on his obvious triumph and to congratulate himself. Yet, as the day progressed, it started to seem dull or even dead. He could not think of any reason for this, unless it was a reaction to his nervous exhaustion of the last two days, in fact of the last months to a lesser degree. The truth was that his affair with Zanuba now appeared to have been a tragedy from start to finish. He had difficulty accepting this first defeat in his long string of romances, and it made a deep impression on his heart and imagination. He was enraged whenever his mind whispered that his youth had fled, for he was proud of his vigor, good looks, and vitality. He clung to the explanation he had provided the woman the previous evening – that she did not love him because trash can only appreciate trash. All day long he yearned for the reunion with his cronies. As the time neared, he grew impatient and rushed off to Muhammad Iffat's house in al-Gamaliya to visit with him before the others trooped in.

Al-Sayyid Ahmad proclaimed at once, "I'm finished with her."

Muhammad Iffat asked, "Zanuba?"

He nodded in the affirmative, and the other man asked smilingly, "So quickly?"

Laughing sarcastically, al-Sayyid Ahmad answered, "Would you believe she demanded I marry her? I got fed up."

Muhammad Iffat laughed scornfully and said, "Not even Zubayda herself would think of that. How amazing! Her excuse is that you pampered her beyond her wildest dreams. So she wanted even more."

Al-Sayyid Ahmad muttered derisively, "She's crazy."

Muhammad Iffat laughed again and said, "Perhaps love for you affected her brain?"

"What a jab," he thought. "Laugh to compensate for the pain."

"I told you she's crazy. That says it all."

"What did you do?"

"I told her bluntly that I was leaving, never to return. Then I left."

"How did she take it?"

"She cursed and threatened me. She said, 'Go to hell.' So I left the lunatic. It was a mistake from the very beginning."

Shaking his head with satisfaction, Muhammad Iffat replied, "Yes. We've all slept with her but never thought of having an affair with her."

"You've pounced and roamed with the lions only to be routed by a mouse," he told himself. "Hide your shame even from your closest friends and praise God that it's all over."

But in fact nothing really was over, for she lived on in his imagination. In the following days he realized that he could not think of her in the abstract. Her image was always linked to a deep pain, which spread and increased. It became clear to him that this pain was not caused merely by anger over outraged honor but by regret and longing. Apparently it was a tyrannical emotion that demanded nothing less than the destruction of the person experiencing it. All the same, he was fiercely proud of the victory he had recently won and indulged himself in the hope of eventually vanquishing his high-handed and traitorous emotions. For whatever reason, peace of mind had left him. He spent his time in thought, mulling over his sorrows, tormented by things he imagined and remembered. He occasionally felt so weak he considered telling Muhammad Iffat about the pains tormenting him. Indeed he went so far as to think once of asking for Zubayda's help. But these moments of weakness were like bouts of fever, and when he recovered from one he would shake his head with perplexed amazement.

His crisis lent a coarseness to his behavior, although he resisted as much as possible, relying on his forbearance and civility. His self-control was lessened only to a limited degree, and that change passed unnoticed except by friends and close acquaintances accustomed to his mildness, understanding, and tact. The members of his family were not aware of any shift, for his conduct with them remained much the same. What differed was the sentiment underlying his behavior. His feigned ferocity became so real that only he was aware of its intensity. Yet he did not escape his own cruelty. In fact, he may have been its primary target. He attacked himself, scolding and railing against his humiliation. Eventually he began to acknowledge his disgrace, wretchedness, and loss of youth.

He consoled himself by saying, "I won't make a move. I won't humiliate myself any further. Let my thoughts wander in all directions. Let my emotions be convulsed repeatedly. I'll stay right where I am, and only the compassionate and forgiving God will know the pain I'm suffering."

He would suddenly find himself wondering whether she was still on the houseboat or not. If still there, did she have enough of his money to make her independent of other men? Or was the other man meeting her there? He frequently asked himself questions like these, and each time the torture he experienced leached from his spirit to his flesh and bones, breaking him down bit by bit. The only time he felt at peace was when he recollected that final scene in the houseboat. He had left her with the impression, which he had almost shared, that he was repudiating and shunning her. But he could not help recalling scenes recording his humiliation and weakness, and others of unforgettable happiness. His imagination also created fresh scenes in which they met again, quarreled, settled accounts, scolded each other, and then were reconciled and reunited. . . . This was a dream he saw frequently in his inner world, which was teeming with countless varieties of sorrow and happiness. . . . But why should he not discover for himself what had become of the houseboat and its resident? After dark he could go there without being seen by anyone.

Concealing himself in the shadows like a thief, he set off. When he passed the houseboat he saw light filtering out from the shutters, but he did not know whether she or some new tenant was benefiting from this light. Yet his heart felt it was her light, not someone else's. Looking at the houseboat, he imagined that he could detect the mistress's spirit and that all he needed to do to see her face to face was to knock on the door. When it opened, there she would be, just as in the old days, both the happy and the miserable ones. But what would he do if a man's face confronted him? She really was close, but how remote. . . . He had been eternally forbidden use of this gangplank. Oh, had this situation appeared in any of his dreams? She had told him to leave. She had said it from her heart and then had proceeded on with her life as though she had never known him and was totally oblivious to his existence. Such a cruel person could not be expected to pay attention to a plea for mercy or forgiveness.

He went there repeatedly. It became a customary pastime for him to loiter in front of the houseboat after night fell and before he went to his friends' party. He did not seem to want to do anything in particular, except satisfy an insane but sterile curiosity.

He was about to go on his way one evening when the door opened and a figure he could not see clearly in the shadows emerged. His heart pounded with fear and hope. He crossed the road quickly and stood beside a tree, his eyes staring into the darkness. The figure crossed the wooden gangplank to the road and set off in the direction of the Zamalek Bridge. He could tell it was a woman. His heart told him it was Zanuba. He followed her at a distance, not knowing how the evening would end. Whether it was his former mistress or not, what did he have in mind? . . . Yet he continued on, concentrating his attention on the figure. When she neared the bridge and got in range of the lights, his hunch was confirmed. He was now certain that it was Zanuba. But she was cloaked in the traditional black wrap, which she had not worn during their affair. He was surprised by that and wondered what it implied. His suspicion was – and how many he had – that there was an incriminating reason for it. He saw her approach the stop for the Giza streetcar and wait there. He walked beside the fields until he passed the point opposite her and then crossed to her side, where he stood out of sight. When the streetcar came, she boarded it. He raced over and clambered up, taking a seat at the end of the bench nearest the steps, so that he could watch people get off. At every stop he looked out, no longer apprehensive about being discovered. Even if he were caught, she would have no way of knowing that he had been waiting for her in front of the houseboat and spying on her. She got off at al-Ataba al-Khadra. Climbing down, he saw her walk toward the Muski. Again he followed her at a distance, rejoicing in the darkness of the street. Had she resumed contact with her aunt? Or was she going to a new gentleman? But why would she go to his place when she had a houseboat for entertaining lovers?

When they reached the Husayn district, afraid of losing her in the crowd of women wearing wraps, he watched her even more closely. The point of this covert pursuit escaped him, but he was driven forward by a painful, futile, and even violent curiosity, impossible to oppose. She walked past the front of the mosque and made her way to Watawit Alley, where the pedestrians were fewer and the beggars more persistent. She continued on as far as al-Gamaliya and turned into Palace of Desire Alley. Although afraid Yasin would run into him or see him from a window, al-Sayyid Ahmad trailed after her. If he met his son he could claim he was going to visit Ghunaym Hamidu, a neighbor of Yasin's in Palace of Desire Alley and the owner of an oil-pressing establishment. Before he knew what was happening she had entered the first cul-de-sac, which had only one house – Yasin's. His heart pounded and his feet felt heavy. He knew the residents of the first two floors. The families that lived there could have no conceivable link to Zanuba. He was so anxious and uneasy that his eyes looked every which way. But he found himself going into the cul-de-sac without worrying about the consequences. He went close enough to the front door to hear her footsteps as she climbed the stairs. Entering the stairwell, he raised his head to listen. He heard her pass the first door and then the second. Then she was knocking on Yasin's door. Breathing heavily, he remained nailed to his spot. He turned his head, feeling weak and on the verge of collapse. He sighed deeply, pulled himself away, and retraced his steps. He could not see the street, his mind was so crowded with jumbled thoughts and ideas.

Yasin was the man! Did Zanuba know he was Yasin's father? He tried to force peace into his heart as though pounding a thick stopper into a narrow opening. He reminded himself that he had never mentioned any of his children in her presence. Besides, it was incredible that Yasin should know about this secret. He remembered how Yasin had come a few days before to tell him of the divorce from Maryam with the troubled look of a person who knew he was at fault. But his expression had also been innocent and sincere, untainted by any suspicion directed against his father. Of all the hypothetical conjectures he might entertain, the one he could never accept was the thought that Yasin would knowingly steal his mistress. Indeed, how would Yasin know his father was having or had had an affair with any woman? There was nothing for him to worry about in this regard. Even if Zanuba knew he was related to Yasin or learned it one day, she would never tell Yasin for fear of ending their relationship. He continued walking along, postponing his visit with his friends. First he needed to catch his breath and to restore calm to his soul. Although tired and exhausted, he walked in the direction of al-Ataba.

"You wanted to know and now you do. Shouldn't you have forgotten the whole matter and been patient? Praise God that circumstances didn't bring you face to face with Yasin in a scandalous way. Yasin's the man. When did she meet him? Where? How many times did she betray you with your son, without your being aware of it? These are questions for which you'll never attempt to find the answers. Assume the worst to allow your aching head to get some rest. Yasin's the man! He said he divorced Maryam because she was impolite. It would have made sense for him to offer an explanation like that when he divorced his first wife, Zaynab – if you hadn't learned the true cause when it all happened. You'll know the truth one day. But what do you care about truth? Are you still eager to chase after it? Your mind's devastated, and your heart's tormented. Is it possible you're jealous of Yasin? No, this isn't jealousy. To the contrary, it's almost a consolation. If it's inevitable that you're to be slain, then let your son be the assassin. Yasin's an extension of you. So part of you was defeated and part of you won. You're both the victim and the victor. Yasin has reversed the outcome of the battle. You were drinking a mixture of pain and defeat. Now triumph and solace have been added to the blend. You won't grieve about losing Zanuba anymore. You've been too confident. Promise not to omit time from your calculations in the future. If only you could pass this advice on to Yasin so he isn't caught off guard when his turn comes. You should be happy. There's no cause for remorse. You'll need to approach life with a new strategy, a new heart, and a new mind. Let Yasin carry the banner. You'll recover from your dizziness, and everything will proceed as though nothing had happened. But you won't be able to transform the events of the last few days into the usual series of anecdotes to be shared over drinks with your friends. These frightening times have taught you that many things need to be hidden away in your chest. Oh . . . how I long for a drink."

In the following days, al-Sayyid Ahmad proved that he was stronger than his misfortunes. His feet firmly on the ground, he looked to the future. The facts of Yasin's divorce reached him by way of Mr. Ali Abd al-Rahim, who had it from Ghunaym Hamidu and others, but these narrators did not know the identity of the woman whose escapade had provoked Maryam's divorce.

Al-Sayyid Ahmad smiled. He laughed a long time over everything. Then, on his way to Muhammad Iffat's house one evening, he felt such a horrible heaviness in his upper back and head that he gasped for breath. It was not an entirely new sensation. Of late he had frequently been afflicted by headaches, but none had been as severe as this. When he complained about his condition to Muhammad Iffat, the latter man ordered some iced lemonade for him. Al-Sayyid Ahmad stayed at the party to the end but awoke the next day in worse shape than before. He was worried enough to consider consulting a physician. The fact was that he never thought of seeing a doctor except in the most dire circumstances.

102

OBJECTS, LIKE words, take on new meanings as circumstances change. The mansion of the Shaddad family was hardly lacking in grandeur for Kamal, but on that evening in December it appeared in a splendid new form suitable for a rite of passage. Lights had been strung over the structure until every segment was brightly illuminated. Each corner and wall wore a necklace of brilliant pearls. Electric lights of different colors sparkled over the surface from rooftop to ground and along the garden wall with its massive entrance. The flowers and fruit of the trees seemed transformed into red, green, and white lamps, and light flowed from all the windows of the house. Everything jubilantly proclaimed a wedding.

When Kamal first saw this as he approached, he felt transported to the kingdom of light. The sidewalk opposite the house was jammed with boys, and the entryway was strewn with golden sand. The gate was wide open, as was the door of the men's reception room, which had been prepared to receive the guests, its big chandelier aglow. The large upper balcony was filled with a resplendent group of young ladies in magnificent evening gowns. Shaddad Bey and men of the family stood at the entrance to the reception hall welcoming the arrivals. The porch was graced by a marvelous orchestra, and the music could be heard as far away as the desert.

Kamal quickly cast an all-inclusive glance around him, wondering whether Aïda was on the upper balcony with the girls who were looking down. Had she seen him enter with the other guests, his large head and celebrated nose introducing his lanky frame, formal attire, and the overcoat on his arm? He felt ill at ease and, unlike the others, did not go to the reception hall. Instead, he took "his" path, which he had followed to the rear garden so often in the past. Husayn Shaddad had suggested this idea to allow their group as much time together as possible in the beloved gazebo. Kamal seemed to be wading into a sea of light, for he found the door of the rear reception room open too. It was all lit up and crowded with guests, and the upper balcony was swarming with beautiful ladies. The gazebo was deserted except for Isma'il Latif, who wore an elegant black suit that lent his pugnacious appearance a charm Kamal had never observed before.

Isma'il Latif glanced at him and said, "Superb! But why did you bring an overcoat? . . . Husayn only stayed a quarter hour with me, but he'll return when he's finished with the receiving line. Hasan spent a few minutes with me. I doubt he'll be able to sit with us, as we had hoped. This is his day, and he has a lot to do. Husayn thought of inviting some of our acquaintances to the gazebo, but I stopped him. It's enough that he's asked them to share our table. We'll have a special room of our own. That's the most important news I have to give you tonight."

"There's more important news than that," Kamal told himself. "It will amaze me for a long time that I accepted this invitation. Why did you accept? To make it seem you didn't care? Or because you've fallen in love with terrifying adventures?"

"That's fine," Kamal said. "But why don't we go for at least a moment to the great hall to see the guests?"

Isma'il Latif replied scornfully, "You won't see what you want, even if we do. The pashas and beys have been given the front room for their exclusive use. If you go, you'll find yourself in the back room with young men from the family and their friends, and that's not what you want. I wish I could sneak us upstairs where the most glorious paragons of beauty are surging back and forth."

"Only one paragon interests me," Kamal thought. "The paragon for all others. I haven't laid eyes on her since I confessed my love. She discovered my secret and disappeared."

"I won't try to conceal my interest in seeing the important people. Husayn told me his father had invited many of the men I read about in the papers."

Isma'il laughed out loud and said, "Do you imagine you'll find some of them have four eyes or six feet? They're men like you and me, although older and not particularly good-looking. But I understand the secret behind your desire to see them. It's part and parcel of your excessive interest in politics."

"I really ought to drop all interests in the world," Kamal told himself. "She's no longer mine and I'm not hers. But my curiosity about famous people is derived from my love for greatness. You'd like to be great. Don't deny it. You have a promising aptitude for looking like Socrates and suffering like Beethoven, but you owe this aspiration to the woman who deprived you of light when she departed. By tomorrow you'll find no trace of her in Egypt. Delirium of pain, there's something intoxicating about you."

Kamal said longingly, "Husayn told me the reception would bring together men from all the different political parties."

"That's true. Yesterday Sa'd Zaghlul invited the Liberals and the Nationalists to a widely publicized tea party. Today Shaddad Bey invites them to his daughter's wedding. Of the Wafd Party politicians you admire I've seen Fath Allah Barakat and Hamad al-Basil. Tharwat, Isma'il Sidqy, and Abd al-Aziz Fahmy are also here. Shaddad Bey has lofty ambitions he's actively pursuing, and that's only right. The era of 'Our Effendi' the Khedive Abbas is over. People used to chant, 'God lives.... Abbas arrives.' The truth is that he's gone, never to return. So it's most judicious of Shaddad Bey to look to the future. To be on the safe side, all he has to do is to travel to Switzerland every few years to assure the Khedive formally but falsely of his loyalty. Then he returns to continue from success to success."

"Your heart abhors this type of judiciousness," Kamal thought. "Sa'd's recent tribulations demonstrate that the nation abounds with such 'judicious' men. Is Shaddad Bey really one of them? The beloved's father? Not so fast . . . the beloved herself has descended from the highest heavens to marry a human being. Let your heart crumble into so many scattered fragments you're unable to collect them."

"Do you think a celebration like this will be complete without singers?"

Isma'il replied sarcastically, "The Shaddad family's half Parisian. They have little respect for our wedding traditions. They wouldn't allow a woman entertainer to perform at one of their parties. And they don't recognize the worth of any of our male vocalists. Remember what Husayn said about this orchestra, which I'm seeing for the first time in my life? Every Sunday evening they play at Groppi's tearoom. After dinner they'll move into the hall to entertain the dignitaries. Forget about the music. You should realize that the high point of the evening's the dinner and the champagne."

"The musicians Jalila and Sabir . . . the weddings of Aisha and Khadija . . . what a different atmosphere!" Kamal thought. "How happy you were back then. . . . Tonight the orchestra will escort your dream to the grave. Remember what you saw through a hole in the door the night Aisha got married? I feel sorry for a goddess who grovels in the dirt. . . ."

"That doesn't matter," Kamal said. "What I really miss is not being able to see the big men up close. I'll regret that for a long time. There are two important things I'd be watching for. The first is to hear what they say about the political situation. After the coalition between the political parties, is there really any hope of having the constitution reinstated and of reviving parliamentary government? The second is to listen to the ordinary small talk of such festive occasions coming from the mouths of men like Tharwat Pasha. Wouldn't it be extraordinary to hear him gossip and crack jokes?"

Affecting disdain, although his scornful gestures betrayed his pride, Isma'il Latif said, "I've had many chances to sit with friends of my father's like Salim Bey and Shaddad Bey. I can assure you nothing there justifies this interest."

"Where's the difference then between the son of a superior court judge and the merchant's son? Why is it the fate of one to worship the beloved while the other marries her? Isn't this marriage a sign that these people are formed of a different clay than normal folks? But you don't know how your father talks to his friends and associates."

"In any case, Salim Bey isn't the kind of dignitary I had in mind."

Isma'il smiled at this last remark but did not comment on it.

The laughter from the men's reception hall was gleeful, that descending from the upper balcony fragrant with the enchanting perfume of femininity. The two types of laughter harmonized with each other like sounds from distant instruments heard at times in chords and then as a bouquet of different melodies. The tuneful laughter formed a rosy setting in which Kamal's sad and desolate heart stood out like a black funeral announcement in a floral arrangement.

Husayn Shaddad soon arrived, his tall, slender body sporting a frock coat. Beaming and radiant, he opened his arms wide, as did Kamal. Then they embraced each other warmly. He was followed by the handsome Hasan Salim, formally attired, his natural arrogance encased in a polite and refined exterior. Even so, he seemed short and insignificant standing next to Husayn. He shook hands heartily with Kamal, who congratulated him from the depths of his tongue if not his heart.

With his usual bluntness, which was often hard to distinguish from malicious wit, Isma'il said, "Kamal's really sad he's not getting to sit with Tharwat Pasha and his colleagues."

In an uncommonly jolly manner that brushed aside his customary reserve, Hasan Salim retorted, "He'll just have to wait until his 'forthcoming' books are published. Then he'll find he's one of them."

Husayn Shaddad protested, "Don't be stuffy. I'd like us to be completely at ease this evening and enjoy ourselves."

Even before Husayn sat down, Hasan excused himself and went off. That evening he flitted from place to place like a butterfly. Husayn stretched his legs out and said, "Tomorrow they leave for Brussels. They're getting to Europe before me, but I won't stay here long. Soon I'll be able to amuse myself by traveling between Paris and Brussels."

"You'll be traveling between al-Nahhasin and al-Ghuriya," Kamal told himself, "without a lover or a friend. This is what you get for gazing at the heavens. You can look everywhere in the city helplessly, but your eyes will never recover from love's anguish. Fill your lungs with this air perfumed by her breath. Tomorrow you'll be pitying yourself."

"I imagine I'll join you there one day."

Husayn and Isma'il both asked, "How?"

"Let your lie be as enormous as your pain," Kamal advised himself.

"My father agreed to let me go there in a student group at my own expense once I've finished my studies."

Husayn cried delightedly, "If only this dream will come true...."

Isma'il laughed and said, "I'm afraid I'll find myself alone in a few years."

The instruments of the orchestra joined together in a tumultuous movement that allowed each to demonstrate its agility and power. They seemed to be participating in a fierce race. The goal had come in sight of their eyes and ambitions. The music reached its climax, indicating that the end was near. Although Kamal was absorbed by his grief, his mind gravitated toward the fiery tunes, racing after them until his heart beat fast and he felt breathless. Soon he was overcome by tenderness and intoxicated by generosity. These sentiments turned his sorrow into tearful ecstasy. When the music ended, he sighed deeply, as its echoes reverberated melodiously in his spirit, making a powerful impression on him. He wondered whether inflamed emotions would not peak and then die away, like the music. If pieces of music – and everything else – had an end, why should not love have one? He recalled listless states he had experienced on rare occasions when he had seemed to recollect nothing about Aïda except her name.

"Do you remember those times?" he asked himself.

At such instants he had shaken his head in bewilderment and wondered whether everything really was over. But he had always imagined or thought of some idea or scene that had awakened him from his slumbers and cast him, bound in fetters, to drown in the sea of passion.

"If you experience one of these moments," Kamal thought, "try to cling to it with all your might. Don't let it slip away. Then you can hope for a cure. Yes, attempt to destroy the immortality of love."

Smiling, Husayn Shaddad said, "For good luck the party began with the recitation of a Qur'an sura."

"The Qur'an!" Kamal exclaimed to himself. "How charming! Even the beautiful Parisian could not get married without an Islamic clerk and the Qur'an. Her marriage will be associated in your mind with both the Qur'an and champagne."

"Tell us the schedule for the party."

Pointing toward the house, Husayn said, "The formalities will be concluded shortly. Dinner will be served in an hour. After the banquet, the party ends. Aïda will spend one last night in our house. Tomorrow morning she leaves for Alexandria, where she'll board the ship for Europe the following day."

"You'll be deprived of many sights that really ought to be recorded to provide sustenance for your insatiable pains," Kamal thought. "Like seeing her beautiful name inscribed on the certificate, her face waiting expectantly for the happy news, the smile with which she greets it, and then the couple meeting. . . . Even your pain needs nourishment."

"Will the marriage contract be drawn up by a Muslim notary?"

"Naturally," Husayn answered.

But Isma'il laughed loudly. "No, a priest," he said.

"What a silly question!" Kamal scolded himself. "Ask also whether they plan to spend the night together. Isn't it sad that a man of no significance like this marriage clerk should impede the progress of your life? But a lowly worm eats the corpses of the most exalted individuals. What will your funeral be like when the time comes? Will it be an overwhelming spectacle that fills the streets or a small gathering that soon disbands?"

Then silence spread through the house. There was light but no music. Kamal felt fearful and uncomfortable. "Now, somewhere, in one room or another, the wedding's taking place," he told himself.

A long resounding shriek of joy rang out. It revived old memories for him, for it was a trill of joy like all the other ones he had ever heard and totally un-Parisian. It was followed by a bunch of shrieking trills like sirens going off. At that time the mansion resembled any other home in Cairo. The shrieks made his heart race, and he felt out of breath. Hearing Isma'il congratulate the bride's brother, Kamal did so too. He wished he were alone but consoled himself with the thought that for days and nights to come he would be. He promised his pain limitless sustenance. The orchestra burst out playing a piece Kamal knew very well, "Your forgiveness, lordly beauty." He summoned his amazing powers of endurance and self-restraint, although every drop of his blood was tapping against the walls of his veins to announce it was all over. History itself had concluded. Life was at an end. Dreams worth more than life itself were terminated. He was faced with nothing less than a boulder studded with spikes.

Husayn Shaddad said reflectively, "A word and a trill, and one of us enters a whole new world. We'll all experience that some-day."

Isma'il Latif said, "I'm going to postpone it as long as I can."

"All of us?" Kamal asked himself. "For me it's the sky or nothing."

"I'll never yield to that day," he said.

The other two did not appear interested in what he had said or at least seemed not to take it seriously. Isma'il continued: "I won't get married until I'm convinced that marriage is necessary and unavoidable."

A Nubian servant brought around glasses of fruit punch. He was trailed by another with a tray loaded with fancy containers of sweets. They were made of crystal and had four gilded legs. The dark blue glass was decorated with silver, and each box was tied with a green silk ribbon. On a crescent-shaped card attached to the knot were inscribed the initials of the couple's first names: A. H.

When Kamal received his box he felt relieved for perhaps the first time that day. The magnificent container guaranteed that his beloved was leaving behind her a memento that would be as long-lasting as his love. While he lived, this souvenir would remain a symbol of an unlikely past, a happy dream, a heavenly enchant-ment, and a spectacular disappointment. He was overcome by a sense of having been the victim of an atrocious assault. Conspiring against him had been fate, the law of heredity, the class system, Aïda, Hasan Salim, and a mysterious, hidden force he was reluc-tant to name. To his eyes he seemed a miserable wretch standing alone against these combined powers. His wound was bleeding and there was no one to bind it. The only response he could muster against this attack was a stifled rebellion he could not proclaim. In fact, circumstances obliged him to pretend to be delighted, as if congratulating those tyrannical forces for torturing him and eliminating him from the ranks of contented human beings. For all of them he harbored an undying rancor, but he postponed the question of pinpointing and directing it. Indeed, he felt that after this decisive trill he would not be so indulgent with life. He would no longer be satisfied with what was at hand. Events would not be met with magnanimous tolerance. His way would be arduous, rough, twisting, and crammed with hardships and problems, but he did not think of backing down in face of this assault and refused to consider a truce. He issued advance warnings and threats but left it up to destiny to choose a foe for him to tackle and his weapons.

Swallowing to clear his throat of the fruit punch, Husayn Shaddad said, "Don't claim to shun marriage. I believe – if you're allowed to travel as you say – that you'll find a wife who pleases you."

"As though you couldn't find anyone you'd like here," Kamal brooded. "Look for a new country, where the fair sex doesn't take

offense at abnormally large heads and noses. Give me heaven or
death."

Then, nodding his head as though in agreement, he said,
"That's what I think."

Isma'il Latif asked sarcastically, "Do you know what it means to
marry a European? In a word, you 'win' a woman from the lowest
classes, one willing to submit to a man she secretly feels only fit for
servitude."

"You've already experienced servitude," Kamal told himself,
"in your own magnificent country, not in Europe, which you'll
never see."

"You're exaggerating!" Husayn protested disapprovingly.

"See how the teachers from England treat us."

Husayn Shaddad responded with an enthusiasm that was almost
pleading, "The Europeans in their countries don't act the way
they do here."

Kamal asked himself, "Where can I find overwhelming power
to annihilate oppression and oppressors? Lord of the universe,
where's Your heavenly justice?"

Dinner was announced, and the three friends went to the
reception hall and from there to a nearby room opening onto
the rear parlor. A buffet dinner capable of serving at least ten was
laid out there. They were joined by other young men, some
relatives of the Shaddad family and others who were school
friends. Even so, there were fewer than ten guests, a fact for
which Kamal was deeply grateful to Husayn. They quickly set
about eating with gusto and vigor, so the atmosphere became
almost as lively as that of a race. They had to keep returning to
the buffet to do justice to all the dishes spread out there, a small
bouquet of roses separating one from another. Husayn signaled to
the waiter to bring whiskey and bottles of soda.

Isma'il Latif called out, "I swear I expected only the best from
this gesture even before I knew what it meant."

Husayn leaned over to entreat Kamal, "One glass, for my sake."

Kamal advised himself, "Drink," not from any desire, since he
had no experience with it, but out of a wish to rebel. Yet his faith
proved stronger than his grief or rebellion. He smilingly said, "As
for that, no, thank you."

Raising a full glass, Isma'il said, "You've no excuse. Even a
pious man permits himself to get drunk at weddings."

Kamal ate the tasty food calmly. He observed the eaters and drinkers from time to time or joined in their conversation and laughter.

"A man's happiness is proportionate to the number of wedding buffets he's enjoyed," Kamal told himself. "But is the pashas' buffet just like ours? We investigate them while devouring their food. Champagne!... This is an opportunity for you to taste champagne. The Shaddad family's champagne.... What did you say? 'Why doesn't Mr. Kamal touch alcohol?' Perhaps his belly's full and can't hold more. The truth is that I'm eating with unmatched appetite, uninfluenced by my sorrow or even encouraged by it. You ate like this at Fahmy's funeral. Keep Isma'il away from the food and drink or it will be exhausted. The deaths of the writer al-Manfaluti and of the musician Sayyid Darwish and Egypt's loss of the Sudan are events crowning our era with sorrow, but the coalition of political parties and this repast are happy news. We've eaten three turkeys, and one hasn't been touched yet. This fellow... O Lord, he's pointing at my nose. They're all convulsed with laughter. They're drunk. So don't get angry. Laugh along with them, merrily pretending you're not offended. But my heart is shaken by anger. If you're ever able to launch an attack on the world, do it. As for the effects of this splendid evening, it's preposterous to think you'll ever recover from them.... People are talking about Fuad al-Hamzawi, discussing his success and brilliance. Are you jealous? When you mention him, you'll gain their respect, even if only a little."

"He's been a diligent student since childhood," Kamal ventured.

"You know him?"

Husayn Shaddad answered for his friend, "Fuad's father's an employee in the store owned by Kamal's father."

"My heart feels comforted," Kamal reflected. "May God curse hearts."

Then he said, "His father's always been an honest and reliable man."

"What business is your father in?"

"The term 'merchant' was always surrounded by an aura of respect in my mind," Kamal reminded himself, "until the merchant's son was compared unfavorably with the son of the superior court judge."

"Wholesale groceries."

"Lying's a cheap dodge," Kamal told himself. "Watch them. Try to see what's going through their heads. But is there any man in this house as good-looking or vigorous as your father?"

After leaving the tables, most of the guests returned to their seats in the reception hall, although a good number went into the garden to stroll about. People felt relaxed but sluggish. When the guests started leaving, the family members went upstairs to congratulate the couple. The chamber orchestra soon joined them and played some ravishing selections in that happy setting. Kamal put on his overcoat and picked up his magnificent box of sweets. Then he left the Shaddad mansion arm in arm with Isma'il.

Casting his friend an inebriated glance, Isma'il said, "It's eleven. What do you think about walking down Palaces Street until I sober up a little?"

Kamal agreed willingly, because he felt this would provide a good opportunity for a scheme he had been plotting. They sauntered along together, over the same ground Kamal had previously covered with Aïda. Then he had confessed his love and revealed his pains. He would never forget the sight of this street with its elegant, silent mansions. It was lined by lofty trees that viewed the evening with the calm of a peaceful soul and the awe of a celestial imagination.

"Your heart will never stop pounding with desire, ardor, and pain," Kamal reflected, "no matter how often your feet tread on it or your imagination appeals to it. Your heart's like a tree that casts down its leaves and fruit when convulsed by a storm. Although your previous walk here was a failure, you'll always treasure the memory of a bygone dream, a disappointed hope, an illusory happiness, and a pulsing life filled with emotion. Even viewed in the most negative fashion, that was far better than the repose of nonexistence, the desolation of exile, or the extinction of emotion. What nourishment will you be able to find for your heart in the future unless it is places you observe with imagination's eye or names you listen for with passion's ears?"

He said, "I wonder what's happening upstairs now."

Isma'il answered, in a loud voice that disturbed the reigning silence, "The orchestra's playing Western music. The bride and groom are on the dais, smiling, and around them are the Shaddad and Salim families. I've seen a lot of gatherings like that."

"Aïda in a wedding gown!" Kamal exclaimed to himself.

"What a sight! Have you seen anything like that even in a dream?"

"How long will the party last?" he inquired.

"An hour at the most, to let the couple get some sleep, since they're leaving tomorrow morning for Alexandria."

"Words like daggers!" Kamal told himself. "Plunge any of them into your heart."

Isma'il asked, "But who's ever slept on their wedding night?" He laughed raucously. Then he belched and emitted a puff of breath reeking of alcohol. He frowned and grumbled with complaint. Then, as his face relaxed, he said, "May our Lord not condemn you to the sleep of lovers. My dear, they don't get any sleep at all. Don't let Hasan's reserve mislead you. He'll be leaping and bouncing like a stallion until the break of day. That's predestined. There's no way to escape it."

"Savor this new form of distilled pain," Kamal told himself. "It's the essence of pain, the pain of pains. Your consolation is that your pain's unique. No man before you has ever experienced it. Hell will seem easy for you by comparison if you're destined to be carried there by demons who dance you over its tongues of fire. Pain! It's not from losing your lover, because you never aspired to possess her. It's because she has descended from heaven and is wallowing in the mud, after living grandly over the clouds. It's because she's allowed her cheek to be kissed, her blood to be shed, and her body to be abused. How intense my regret and pain are. . . ."

"Is what they say about the first night true?"

Isma'il yelled, "By God, don't you know about these things?"

"How can people consecrate something filthy?" Kamal asked himself.

"Naturally I know, but I didn't until recently. There are things I'd like to hear about again."

Isma'il laughed. "At times you seem an idiot or a fool."

"Let me ask you if it would be easy for you to do that to a person you revere."

Isma'il belched again, bringing the accursed smell of liquor to Kamal's nostrils. He replied, "No one deserves to be revered."

"Your daughter, for example, if you had one."

"Not my daughter or my mother. Where did we come from? It's a law of nature."

"Us?" Kamal asked himself. "The truth's a dazzling light. So look away. Behind the curtain of sanctity, before which you've always prostrated yourself, they'll be cavorting like children. Why does everything seem so empty? Mother, Father, Aïda, the tomb of the Prophet's grandson al-Husayn, the merchant's profession, the aristocratic airs of Shaddad Bey. . . . How intense my pain is!"

"How filthy the law of nature is," he observed.

Isma'il belched for the third time. In a merry tone but without audible laughter he said, "The fact is that your heart's in pain. It's singing the same words as the new vocalist Umm Kalthoum: 'I'd give my life for her, whether she treasures my love or abandons it.'"

Alarmed, Kamal asked, "What do you mean?"

Trying to seem more intoxicated than he was, Isma'il replied, "I mean you love Aïda."

"My Lord!" How had his secret gotten out?

"You're drunk!"

"It's the truth, and everyone knows it."

Staring at his friend in the darkness, Kamal yelled, "What are you saying?"

"I'm saying that it's the truth and everyone knows it."

"Everyone? Who? Who spread this rumor about me?"

"Aïda!"

"Aïda?"

"Aïda . . . she's the one who spilled your secret."

"Aïda? I don't believe it. You're drunk."

"Yes, I'm drunk, but it's the truth too. One of the good qualities of a drunk is that he doesn't lie." Isma'il laughed gently before continuing: "Does this make you angry? As you know, Aïda's a charming girl. For a long time she's secretly directed attention to your loving gaze, without your being aware of it – not to be sarcastic but because she's flirtatious and the attention of her admirers goes to her head. Hasan was the first to realize what was happening and pointed it out to me several times. Then he broke the secret to Husayn. In fact, I know that Madame Saniya, Aïda's mother, heard about the 'lovesick suitor,' as they called you. It's quite possible the servants overheard what was said about you by their employers, so that everyone learned the story of the lovesick suitor."

He felt weak. He imagined their feet were heartlessly trampling his honor. His lips were compressed with bitter grief. Were treasured secrets so easily squandered?

Isma'il continued: "Don't get upset. It was all an innocent joke on the part of people who like you. Even Aïda told your secret solely to boast of it."

"Her imagination deceived her!"

"Denying your love's as futile as denying the sun in broad daylight."

Surrendering sadly, Kamal fell silent. Suddenly he asked, "What did Husayn say?"

In a louder voice Isma'il responded, "Husayn? He's your loyal friend. He frequently expressed his unhappiness with his sister's innocent wiles and stressed your good qualities to her."

Kamal sighed with relief. If his hopes had been disappointed in love, friendship still was unaffected. But how could he ever enter the Shaddad mansion again?

In an earnest voice, as though encouraging his friend to face the situation courageously, Isma'il said, "Aïda was as good as engaged to Hasan for years before the engagement was announced. Besides, she's older than you are. You'll forget these feelings after a good sleep. Don't let it trouble or sadden you."

" 'You'll forget these feelings'!" Kamal exclaimed to himself. Then he asked with unconcealed interest, "Did she make fun of me when she mentioned this alleged infatuation?"

"Certainly not! I told you she enjoyed talking about her admirers."

"Your beloved was a cruel, mocking god," Kamal reflected. "It amused her to make fun of her devotees. Do you remember the day she joked about your head and nose? Like the laws of nature, she's cruel and powerful. After all that, how could she hurry jubilantly to her wedding night like any other girl? Your mother's natural modesty indicates that she at least is conscious of the offense involved in marriage."

They had gone a long way down the street. So they turned to retrace their steps silently, as though tired of their conversation and its sorrows. Soon Isma'il burst out singing poorly: "God's blessing on the girl who sells such treasures. . . ."

Kamal did not break his silence, and did not even seem to notice that his friend was singing. How embarrassed he was to have been a topic of conversation. . . . It appeared that the family, his friends, and the servants had all been winking at each other behind his back without his noticing. That was rude of them, and he did not deserve it. Was this how love and devotion were rewarded? How cruel his beloved was and how atrocious the pain. . . . When Nero sang as Rome burned, perhaps he was avenging a similar wrong.

"Be an invading general handsomely mounted on a charger, a leader borne aloft by the crowd, a metal statue on a column, a wizard who can appear in any form he wishes, an angel flying over the clouds, a monk secluded in the desert, a dangerous criminal causing honest citizens to quake, a clown captivating his merry audience, or a suicide upsetting the onlookers."

If Fuad al-Hamzawi learned the story, disguising his irony with his usual courtesy he would tell Kamal, "It's your fault, because you left us for those people. You scorned girls like Qamar and Narcissus, so enjoy being abandoned by the gods."

"My answer's that I wanted heaven or nothing at all," Kamal thought. "Let her marry as she pleases and go to Brussels or Paris. Let her grow old until her beauty fades. She'll never find a love like mine. Don't forget this road, for here you were intoxicated by enchanting dreams and later swallowed enough despair to make you choke. I'm no longer a resident of this planet. I'm a foreigner and must live like an exile."

When they passed the Shaddad mansion on their way back, they found that workmen were busy removing the decorations and strings of lights from the walls and trees. The large house, stripped of its wedding finery, was enveloped in darkness, except for a few rooms that still had light streaming from their balconies and windows. The party was over, and the crowd had dispersed. The scene seemed to announce that everything has an end. Here he was, going home with a box of candy like a child bribed not to cry by a few pieces of chocolate. The two young men walked along slowly until they reached the beginning of al-Husayniya. Then they shook hands and went their separate ways.

Kamal had not gone more than a few meters down al-Husayniya Street before he stopped. Then he turned and went back to al-Abbasiya Street, which seemed deserted and sound asleep. He walked quickly toward the Shaddad mansion. When he got within sight of it, he turned right, into the desert that surrounded the house, and went far enough through it to reach a place behind the back wall of the garden where he could observe the mansion from a distance. The enveloping curtains of darkness were so thick that a spy had nothing to worry about. For the first time that night he felt cold in this exposed and desolate spot. He fastened the overcoat around his tall, slender body. The shadowy house behind its high wall looked like a huge citadel. His eyes scouted around for the precious target until they came to rest on a closed window with light peeping out between the slats of the shutters. It was at the far right on the second floor. That was the bridal chamber, the only room awake on this side of the mansion. Yesterday it had been the bedroom of Aïda and Budur. Tonight it was decorated to host the strangest spectacle the fates provide. He stared at the window a long time, at first like a bird with clipped wings gazing at its nest atop a tree and then with deep sorrow, as though he could see with his own eyes the death lying in wait for him. What was going on behind that window? If only he could climb that tree in the garden and see. The rest of his life would be a small price he would willingly pay for a look through that window. Was it a trivial matter to see the beloved in the privacy of her bridal chamber? How were they situated? What happened when their eyes met? What were they chatting about? Where in the world had Aïda's pride hidden itself now? He was burning with desire to see this and to record the occurrence of each word, gesture, or hint provided by a facial expression. Indeed, he would have liked to pry into every thought, imaginary notion, feeling, and instinctual urge, everything even if frightening, disgusting, or painfully sad. Afterwards he would surrender his life without regret. He stayed put as time fled by. He did not budge, the light was not extinguished, and his imagination did not tire of its questions. What would he have done if he had been in Hasan Salim's place? He was too perplexed to answer. Lacking selfish goals, devotion had no place on a night like this. He had never aspired to have Aïda. Hasan Salim was obviously from a denomination in which devotion was not mandatory.

Kamal suffered torments in the desert while they exchanged kisses in the bridal chamber like any other human beings. There would be sweaty sighs and then swooning as blood trickled out. A nightgown would slip away to reveal a mortal body. Such was the world of human beings with its empty hopes and frivolous dreams.

"Weep to your heart's content over the abasement of the gods. Fill your soul with this tragedy. But what's to become of the astounding, dazzling feeling that's lit up your heart for the past four years? It wasn't imaginary or an echo of something imaginary, but life itself. Even if the force of circumstances can overwhelm the body, what power's capable of taking on the spirit?"

Thus the beloved would remain his. Love would be his torment and refuge, just as bewilderment would be his diversion, until he stood before the Creator and asked about these complicated matters that perplexed him. If he could only see what was behind that window and discover the secrets of his existence. . . . The cold stung him at times, reminding him of his situation and of the reckless passage of time. But why should he hurry home? Did he really hope sleep would visit him that night?

103

THE WHEELS of the carriage that stopped in front of Ahmad Abd al-Jawad's store were spattered with the mud of al-Nahhasin Street and with the water collected in its potholes. Mr. Muhammad Iffat, wearing a wool cloak, stepped down and went into the store. He laughingly commented, "We came in a carriage. It would have been safer to come by boat."

It had been pouring rain for a day and a half. The ground was soaked, and the alleys and cul-de-sacs were flooded. Although the rains had finally abated, the gloomy sky had not cleared yet. Clouds overshadowed the earth in a dark canopy that made the air murky enough to presage a pitch-black night.

Ahmad Abd al-Jawad welcomed his friend and invited him to sit down. Muhammad Iffat had scarcely settled himself in a chair by the corner of the desk when he disclosed the reason for this unexpected visit: "Don't be surprised that I've come in this weather even though we'll meet at our usual party in a few hours. I wanted to talk to you privately." He laughed as though to apologize for these strange words. Al-Sayyid Ahmad laughed too, but his laughter seemed almost more like a question.

Jamil al-Hamzawi, his head wrapped from chin to crown in a scarf, went to the door, where he called to the waiter at the Qala'un coffeehouse to bring some coffee. Then he returned to his chair, since the rain and cold had freed him from waiting on customers.

Al-Sayyid Ahmad sensed in his heart that there was an important reason for this visit, since it came at a time when only dire necessity could justify it. He was more anxious than usual because of the psychological crises he had suffered and the ill health he had experienced of late. All the same, he camouflaged his anxiety with a polite laugh and said, "Just before you arrived I was remembering last night and what al-Far looked like dancing. May God strike him down."

Smiling, Muhammad Iffat said, "We're all your pupils! With regard to this, let me tell you what Ali Abd al-Rahim's been saying about you. He claims the headache you've had for the past weeks results from a lack of women in your life during this time."

"A lack of women? Is there any cause for headaches besides women?"

The waiter appeared carrying a yellow tray with glasses of coffee and of water, placed it on the corner of the desk between the two friends, and then departed.

Muhammad Iffat drank some water and said, "It's pleasant to drink cold water in winter. What do you think? But why should I ask? You're one of winter's admirers and bathe every morning in cold water, even now in February. So tell me: Did you like the news of the nationalist conference held in the home of Muhammad Mahmud? We've lived to see Sa'd, Adli, and Tharwat all in a united front once more."

"Our Lord in His wisdom welcomes repentance."

"I don't trust those dogs."

"I don't either. But what can be done? King Fuad's made things worse. It's sad the struggle's no longer against the English."

They began to drink their coffee silently. This indicated, if anything, that the period for making polite conversation had ended. It was time for Muhammad Iffat to speak his mind. He sat up straight and asked al-Sayyid Ahmad earnestly, "What do you hear from Yasin?"

The anxious concern the question evoked was evident in the man's wide eyes. His heart began pounding at an alarming rate. He answered, "Good news! He visits from time to time. The most recent one was last Monday. Is there something new? A matter relating to Maryam? Her whereabouts are unknown. I learned recently that Bayumi the drinks vendor bought her share of her mother's house."

Trying to smile, Muhammad Iffat said, "The matter doesn't concern Maryam. Who knows? Perhaps he's forgotten her. I won't beat around the bush. It's a new marriage."

His heart was pounding again in a frightening way. He exclaimed, "A new marriage! But he's made absolutely no reference to it in his conversations with me."

Muhammad Iffat shook his head regretfully and said, "He's been married for a month or more. Ghunaym Hamidu told me just an hour ago. He assumed you knew all about it."

Al-Sayyid Ahmad's left hand began to fidget with his mustache nervously. Then, as though addressing himself, he said, "It's gone that far! How can I believe it? How could he have kept it from me?"

"The circumstances dictated secrecy. Listen to me. I wanted to tell you the truth before it came to you as an unpleasant surprise. But don't rail against it more than it deserves. And above all, you mustn't get angry. Anger's not something your health can withstand anymore. Remember how tired you've been and have pity on yourself."

Al-Sayyid Ahmad asked desperately, "Is there a scandal involved? That's what my heart senses. Tell me what you know, Mr. Muhammad."

Muhammad Iffat nodded his head sadly. Then in a low voice he said, "Be the brave Ahmad Abd al-Jawad we've always known. . . . Yasin's married Zanuba the lute player."

"Zanuba!"

They exchanged glances that showed their full grasp of the significance of this news. Ahmad's discomfort was obvious from his face, and his friend looked apprehensive. The question of the marriage itself no longer seemed so important. Al-Sayyid Ahmad asked breathlessly, "Do you suppose Zanuba knows he's my son?"

"I don't doubt it, but I'm almost certain she hasn't revealed your secret to him. Otherwise she would have had more difficulty getting him to fall into her trap. She's succeeded so admirably in this that she deserves our congratulations."

But Ahmad Abd al-Jawad asked again in the same breathless voice, "Or do you think he kept it from me because he knew what had happened?"

"Of course not. I don't believe that. If he had known this in advance he would never have married her. No doubt he's a reckless young man, but he's not depraved. If he kept it a secret from you, it's because he couldn't get up the courage to tell you he'd married a woman entertainer. What a burden headstrong sons are to their fathers. . . . The truth is that it upsets me terribly, but I hope you won't allow yourself to get angry. It's his fault. You're not responsible for what he's done. No one can blame you."

Ahmad Abd al-Jawad sighed audibly. Then he instructed his friend, "Tell me what Ghunaym Hamidu said about this."

Muhammad Iffat waved his hand disdainfully and replied, "He asked if al-Sayyid Ahmad had agreed. I told him, 'The man knows nothing about it.' He expressed his regrets and said, 'See how big a gap there is between the father and his son. May God come to his aid.'"

In a mournful voice Ahmad commented, "Is this the result of the way I've raised them? I'm bewildered, Mr. Muhammad. The disaster is that we lose effective control of them just when they most require our guidance for their welfare. They're old enough to take responsibility for themselves, but they mishandle their affairs and we're not able to straighten them out. We're men, but our sons aren't. What do you suppose has caused this? The ox! Why did he have to marry a woman within reach of every hand? Let's weep for ourselves. There's no power or might save God's."

Muhammad Iffat placed his hand sympathetically on his friend's shoulder. "We've done our duty," he said. "Beyond that each person's responsible for himself. It's impossible for anyone to think you're to blame."

Then al-Hamzawi's sad voice spoke up: "No fair person would blame you for something like this, al-Sayyid, sir. Although it seems to me there's still hope for reform. Give him some advice, al-Sayyid, sir."

"He'll stand before you like an obedient child. He'll certainly divorce her tomorrow or the next day. The best good deed is a quick one."

Al-Sayyid Ahmad asked plaintively, "What if she's pregnant?"

Al-Hamzawi's anxious voice said, "May God not decree or allow that."

Muhammad Iffat seemed to have more to say. He looked at his friend apprehensively and then remarked, "It's really sad that he sold his store in al-Hamzawi to refurnish his apartment."

Ahmad stared at him. He frowned in disgust and yelled resentfully, "As if I didn't exist! . . . He didn't even consult me about that."

Striking his hands together, he continued: "No doubt they robbed him blind. They came upon an easy prey . . . a mule without a groom, wearing a gentleman's clothes."

Muhammad Iffat said compassionately, "Childish behavior! He forgot his father and his son. But what's the use of getting angry?"

Ahmad Abd al-Jawad shouted, "It seems to me that regardless of the consequences I've got to deal with him firmly."

Muhammad Iffat stretched out his arms as though to ward off danger. Then he said imploringly, " 'When your son grows up, be a brother to him.' All that's required of you is some advice. Leave the rest to God and His decree." He lowered his eyes thoughtfully and seemed to hesitate for a few moments. Then he said, "There's something that concerns me as much at it does you . . . the question of our grandson Ridwan."

The two men exchanged a long look. Then Muhammad Iffat continued: "In a few months the boy will be seven. I'm afraid his father will ask for custody, and Ridwan will grow up in Zanuba's home. This evil must be averted. I don't imagine you'd agree to it either. So convince Yasin to leave the boy with us, until God straightens things out."

It was contrary to the nature of Ahmad Abd al-Jawad to agree voluntarily to allow his grandson to remain with the mother's family beyond the period established by law for her custody, but he also did not wish to suggest that the boy become part of his own household, for fear of adding to Amina's burdens another one she could not be considered eager to assume, because of her age. So with sad resignation he answered, "I admit it wouldn't be right for Ridwan to be reared in Zanuba's home."

Sighing with relief, Muhammad Iffat said, "His grandmother loves him with all her heart. Even if unavoidable circumstances in the future forced him to be transferred to his mother's home, he would be in good hands, for his mother's married to a man in his forties or older, deprived by God of the blessing of offspring."

Ahmad Abd al-Jawad said hopefully, "But I'd prefer him to stay with you."

"Of course, of course. I was just speaking about remote possibilities, which I pray that God will never impose on us. Now all I have to say is to be gentle when you speak to Yasin so it'll be easier to convince him to leave Ridwan with me."

Then al-Hamzawi's conciliatory voice said, "Al-Sayyid Ahmad's the wisest man I know. He realizes Yasin's a man who, like other men, is free to act as he pleases and to dispose of his possessions. Al-Sayyid Ahmad knows these things. He simply needs to advise his son. The rest is up to God."

Ahmad Abd al-Jawad gave over the remainder of the day to sorrowful reflection. He told himself, "In a word, Yasin's a loss as a son. There's nothing more miserable than having a son who's a disappointment. Unfortunately, the direction he's heading is only too clear. No particular insight's required to discern it. Yes, he'll go from bad to worse and need all the grace God grants him."

Jamil al-Hamzawi asked him to postpone his talk with Yasin until the next day. He yielded to this request, more from despair than because he valued the advice.

He summoned Yasin to meet him the following afternoon. As was appropriate for an obedient son, Yasin hastened to comply with his father's request. The truth was that Yasin had not severed relations with his family. The old house was the only place he had not had the courage to visit, even though he felt homesick for it. Every time he met his father, Khadija, or Aisha he would ask them to convey his greetings to his stepmother. If he had not forgotten her anger with him or what he termed her obstinacy, he also refused to overlook the old days when she was the only mother he knew. He had not stopped visiting his sisters. Occasionally he met Kamal in Ahmad Abduh's coffeehouse. He would also invite his younger brother to his home, where Kamal encountered Maryam first and then Zanuba. Yasin visited his father at his store at least once a week. This call allowed him to observe another side of his father's personality, the one al-Sayyid Ahmad used to captivate people. A solid friendship and a deep affection flourished between the two men, encouraged both by the ties of blood and by Yasin's joy at discovering his father.

Even so, when Yasin examined his father's face that afternoon, its expression reminded him of the old look, which had so frequently terrified him. He did not ask what was bothering his father, for he was sure he would discover the secret sooner or later. No doubt he was encountering the tempest he had expected ever since acting so rashly.

Before he could speak, his father said, "I'm sad to find myself so humiliated. Why should I have to learn my son's news from third parties?"

Yasin bowed his head but did not breathe a word. His father was outraged by this deceitful veneer of humility, shouting, "Take off that mask. Don't play the hypocrite. Let me hear your voice. You know what I'm talking about."

In a scarcely audible whisper Yasin said, "I couldn't get up the courage to tell you."

"This happens when someone tries to conceal an offense or a scandal."

Yasin knew instinctively that he should not attempt any form of resistance. So he said with resignation, "Yes. . . ."

Aghast, al-Sayyid Ahmad asked, "If that's really what you think, then why did you do it?"

Yasin resorted to silence once more. His father imagined this failure to reply indicated: "I knew it was scandalous, but I gave in to love." He was reminded of his own disgraceful situation with the same woman.

"How shameful!" al-Sayyid Ahmad told himself. "You washed away your humiliation with an outburst of anger, but then you started pursuing her again. . . . And what a loss this ox is!"

"You embraced a scandal without any consideration of the consequences, which you let all the rest of us suffer."

Yasin cried out ingenuously, "All of you? God forbid."

Furious again, al-Sayyid Ahmad shouted, "Don't pretend to be stupid! Don't claim you're innocent. When you're trying to satisfy your lusts, you pay no attention to the damage you're doing to your father's reputation or that of your brother and sisters. You've forced a lute player on the family. She'll be one of us along with her children. I don't imagine I'm telling you anything new. But you ignore everything for the sake of lust. You've disgraced the family's honor. You yourself are collapsing stone by stone. In the end you'll find you're nothing but a ruin."

Yasin lowered his eyes and was silent for so long that his guilt and submission were obvious.

"This scandal will only cost you a certain amount of theatrics, so far as I can see," al-Sayyid Ahmad fumed to himself. "That's all it means to you, but tomorrow I'll be blessed with a grandson who has Zanuba for a mother and Zubayda as his great-aunt . . . a unique relationship linking the well-known merchant al-Sayyid Ahmad to Zubayda the notorious singer. Perhaps we're atoning for sins we're not even conscious of."

"I tremble when I think of your future. I told you that you're falling apart. Your collapse will become more and more evident. Tell me what you did with the store in al-Hamzawi?"

Yasin raised his melancholy eyes and hesitated momentarily. Then he said, "I was in urgent need of money." Looking down, he continued: "Had the circumstances been different, I would have borrowed what I needed from you, sir, but it was an embarrassing situation. . . ."

Al-Sayyid Ahmad replied furiously, "What a hypocrite you are! Aren't you ashamed of yourself? I bet you didn't see anything odd or reprehensible in what you did. I know you and understand you. So don't try to deceive me. I just have one thing to say to you, even though I know in advance it's pointless: You're ruining yourself, and your fate will be grim."

Yasin was silent once more and pretended to be distressed.

"The ox!" his father thought. "She's an attractive devil, but what forced you to marry her? I imagined she asked me to marry her because of my age. But she trapped this bull, even though he's young." He felt some relief and consolation at that. "Her premeditated plan was to get married at any cost, but she preferred another man. And this fool fell for it."

"Divorce her! Divorce her before she becomes a mother and we're disgraced for generations to come."

After hesitating for some time, Yasin mumbled, "It would be wrong for me to divorce her without any cause."

"You son of a bitch!" he exclaimed to himself. "You've presented me with an exquisite anecdote for tonight's party."

"You'll divorce her sooner or later. Do it before she bears a child, who'll be a problem for you and the rest of us."

Yasin sighed audibly, allowing that to serve as his response. His father began to examine him rather anxiously. Fahmy was dead. Kamal was an idiot or insane. Yasin was hopeless. "The sad thing is that he's the dearest to me of them all. Leave the matter to God. O Lord! What would have happened if my foot had slipped and I'd married her?"

"How much did you get for the shop?"

"Two hundred pounds."

"It was worth three hundred. It was an excellent location, ignoramus. Who bought it?"

"Ali Tulun . . . he sells sundries."

"Great! Congratulations! Was the whole sum squandered on the new furnishings?"

"I still have a hundred."

"You've done well," he said sarcastically. "So the bridegroom's not short of cash." Then he continued in a serious and mournful tone: "Yasin, listen to me. I'm your father. Watch out. Reform your conduct. You're a father yourself. Don't you think of your son and his future?"

Yasin protested vehemently, "The monthly support payment gets to him down to the last millieme."

"Is it just a matter of money? I'm talking about his future . . . and about the future of other children still unborn."

"Our Lord creates and provides sustenance," Yasin said with calm assurance.

His father yelled disapprovingly, "Our Lord creates and you fritter away your sustenance. Tell me. . . ." He sat up straight and then, focusing his eyes forcefully on his son, commented, "Ridwan's almost seven. What are you going to do with him? Are you going to take him and have him grow up under your wife's supervision?"

Yasin's plump face looked uneasy. He asked in turn, "What should I do, then? I haven't thought about it."

The man shook his head sadly and ironically. He said, "May God preserve you from the evil of thinking. Do you have any time to waste on it? Let me think for you. Allow me to tell you that Ridwan must stay in the custody of his maternal grandfather."

Yasin reflected for a moment. Then he expressed his agreement by lowering his head. He said obediently, "Whatever you think best, Father. No doubt that's in his best interest."

His father replied sarcastically, "It seems to be in your best interest too. That'll save you from troubling yourself with such trivial matters."

Yasin's only comment was a smile that implied: "I'm sure you're teasing me, but that's all right."

"I thought it would be hard to convince you to surrender custody."

"It's the confidence I place in your opinion that made it so easy to convince me."

With ironic astonishment al-Sayyid Ahmad asked, "Do you really place so much confidence in my opinion? Why don't you act on it in other matters?" Sighing sadly, he continued: "What's the point? . . . May our Lord guide you. The guilt's all yours. I'll speak to Muhammad Iffat tonight about retaining custody of Ridwan, with the understanding that you'll bear all the boy's expenses. Perhaps he'll agree."

Yasin rose then, said goodbye to his father, and headed for the shop door. He had only taken two steps when he heard his father's voice ask, "Don't you love your son like any other father?"

Stopping to look back, Yasin said reproachfully, "Is there any doubt of that, Father? He's the dearest thing in my life."

Al-Sayyid Ahmad raised his eyebrows. Shaking his head cryptically, he said, "Goodbye."

104

AN HOUR before his departure for the Friday prayer service, Ahmad Abd al-Jawad summoned Kamal to his room. He never called a member of his family to see him unless the subject was important, and something was indeed troubling him. He was impatient to interrogate his son about a matter that had disturbed him. The previous evening some friends had directed his attention to an article in *al-Balagh* attributed to "the young writer Kamal Ahmad Abd al-Jawad." The men had not read any of the article except its title, "The Origin of Man," and the credit, but they took advantage of it to congratulate and tease al-Sayyid Ahmad, offering various comments. Concerned that such praise might attract the evil eye, he had seriously considered commissioning Shaykh Mutawalli Abd al-Samad to prepare a special talisman for the young man.

Muhammad Iffat had said, "Your son's name is printed in the same magazine with those of important authors. Take heart! Pray that God will prepare a career for him as dazzling as theirs."

Ali Abd al-Rahim had told him, "I heard from a reliable source that the late writer al-Manfaluti bought a country estate with the profits of his pen. So hope for the best."

Others had mentioned how writing had opened the way for many to find favor with the ruling elite, citing the authors Shawqi, Hafiz, and al-Manfaluti.

Ibrahim al-Far had used his turn to kid him: "Glory to the One who created a scholar from the loins of a fool."

Al-Sayyid Ahmad had cast one glance at the title and another at the reference to the "young writer" before placing the magazine on his cloak, which he had removed because of the June heat and a warm feeling derived from whiskey. He had postponed reading the article until he was alone – at home or in his store – and had continued to feel happy, boastful, and proud throughout the evening's festivities. In fact, for the first time he had begun to reconsider his hostility toward Kamal's choice of the Teachers

College, telling himself it seemed "the boy" would amount to "something," in spite of that unfortunate choice. He started to fantasize about "the pen," gaining favor with the elite, and al-Manfaluti's country estate. Yes, who could say? Perhaps Kamal would not be just a teacher. He might really make a better life for himself than al-Sayyid Ahmad had dreamed possible.

The following morning, after prayers and breakfast, al-Sayyid Ahmad made himself comfortable on the sofa and opened the magazine with interest. He began to read it out loud to get the sense of it. But what did he find? He could read political articles and understand them without difficulty. But this essay made his head turn and agitated his heart. He read it aloud again carefully. He came across a reference to a scientist named Darwin and his work on some distant islands. This man had made tedious comparisons between various different animals until he was astonished to reach the strange conclusion that man was descended from animals; in fact, that he had evolved from a kind of ape. Al-Sayyid Ahmad read the offensive paragraph yet another time with increasing alarm. He was stunned by the sad reality that his son, his own flesh and blood, was asserting, without objection or discussion, that man was descended from animals. He was extremely upset and wondered in bewilderment whether boys were really taught such dangerous ideas in government schools. Then he sent for Kamal.

Kamal arrived, not having the least idea of what was on his father's mind. Since he had been summoned a few days before so his father could congratulate him on his promotion to the third year of the Teachers College, he did not suspect that this new invitation implied anything unpleasant. He had grown pale and emaciated of late. His family attributed this to the exceptional effort he put out before an examination. The real secret was hidden from them. It was the pain and torment he had suffered for the last five months as a prisoner of hellishly tyrannical emotion, which had almost killed him.

Al-Sayyid Ahmad gestured for him to sit down. Kamal sat at the end of the sofa, facing his father politely. He noticed that his mother was seated near the wardrobe, busy folding and mending clothes. Then his father threw the copy of *al-Balagh* down in the space between them on the sofa and said with feigned composure, "You've got an article in this magazine. Isn't that so?"

The cover caught Kamal's eye. His look of astonishment made it clear that he had certainly not been expecting this surprise. Where had his father acquired this new familiarity with literary journals? In a magazine called *al-Sabah*, Kamal had previously published some "reflections," or innocent philosophical specula-tions and emotional laments in both regular and rhymed prose. He was quite sure his father did not know about them. The only member of the family who did was Yasin. Kamal himself had read them to his brother. Yasin's comment had been: "This is the fruit of my early guidance. I'm the one who taught you about poetry and stories. It's beautiful, Professor. But this philosophy's really deep. Where'd you pick that up?" Yasin had teased him: "What pretty girl inspired this delicate complaint? Professor, one day you'll learn that nothing works with women except beating them with a shoe."

But now his father had read the most dangerous thing he had written – this essay that had stirred up the devil of a battle in his breast when he was thinking about it. His mind had almost been incinerated in that furnace. How had this happened? What explanation could there be unless some of his father's friends who were Wafd Party loyalists made a point of buying all the papers and journals affiliated with the party? Could he hope to escape safely from this predicament? He looked up from the magazine. In a tone that did not even begin to convey his inner turmoil, he answered, "Yes. I thought I'd write something to bolster what I was learning and to encourage myself to continue my studies...."

With spurious calm, al-Sayyid Ahmad commented, "There's nothing wrong with that. Writing for the papers has been and still is a way to gain prestige and recognition from the elite. What's important is the topic a person writes about. What did you intend by this article? Read it and explain it to me. It's not clear what you were getting at."

What a disaster this was! The essay had not been intended for the general public and especially not for his father. "It's a long article, Papa. Didn't you read it, sir? I explain a scientific theory in it...."

His father stared at him with an impatient, glinting look. "Is this what they claim is science nowadays?" al-Sayyid Ahmad asked himself. "God's curse on science and scientists."

"What do you say about this theory? I noticed some strange phrases that seem to imply that man is descended from animals, or something along those lines. Is this true?"

Kamal had recently struggled violently with his soul, his beliefs, and his Lord, exhausting his spirit and body. Today he had to contend with his father. In the first battle he had felt tortured and feverish, but this time he was even more frightened and alarmed. God might delay punishment, but his father's practice was to mete out retribution immediately.

"That's what the theory states."

Al-Sayyid Ahmad's voice rose as he asked in dismay, "And Adam, the father of mankind, whom God created from clay, blowing His spirit into him – what does this scientific theory say about him?"

Kamal had repeatedly asked himself this same question, finding it just as dismaying as his father did. The night he had worried about it, he had not been able to get any sleep. He had thrashed about in bed wondering about Adam, the Creator, and the Qur'an. If he had said it once he had said ten times: "Either the Qur'an is totally true, or it's not the Qur'an." Now he thought, "You're attacking me because you don't know how I've suffered. If I hadn't already grown accustomed to torture, I would have died that night."

In a faint voice he replied, "Darwin, the author of this theory, did not mention our master Adam. . . ."

The man yelled angrily, "Then Darwin's certainly an atheist trapped by Satan's snares. If man's origin was an ape or any other animal, Adam was not the father of mankind. This is nothing but blatant atheism. It's an outrageous attack on the exalted status of God. I know Coptic Christians and Jews in the Goldsmiths Bazaar. They believe in Adam. All religions believe in Adam. What sect does this Darwin belong to? He's an atheist, his words are blasphemous, and reporting his theory's a reckless act. Tell me: Is he one of your professors at the college?"

"How ridiculous this comment would seem if my heart were free to laugh," Kamal mused. "But it's crammed with the pains of disappointed love, doubt, and dying belief. The dreadful encounter of religion and science has scorched you. But how can an intelligent person set his mind against science?"

In a humble voice, Kamal said, "Darwin was an English scientist who lived a long time ago."

At this point, the mother's voice piped up shakily: "God's curse on all the English."

They turned to look at her briefly and found that she had put down her needle and the clothes in order to follow their conversation. They soon forgot her, and the father said, "Tell me: Do you study this theory in school?"

Kamal grabbed for this safety rope suddenly thrown to him. Hiding behind a lie, he said, "Yes."

"That's strange! Will you eventually teach this theory to your pupils?"

"Certainly not! I'll teach literature, and there's no connection between that and scientific theories."

Al-Sayyid Ahmad struck his hands together. At that moment he wished he had as much control over science as he did over his family. He yelled furiously, "Then why do they teach it to you? Is the goal to turn you into atheists?"

Kamal protested, "God forbid that it should have any influence on our religious beliefs."

His father studied him suspiciously and said, "But your essay spreads atheism."

Kamal replied gingerly, "I ask God's forgiveness. I'm explaining the theory so the reader will be familiar with it, not so he'll believe it. It's out of the question that an atheistic notion should influence the heart of a Believer."

"Couldn't you find some other subject besides this criminal theory to write about?"

Why had he written this article? He had hesitated a long time before sending it to the journal. He must have wanted to announce the demise of his religious beliefs. His faith had held firm over the past two years even when buffeted by gales coming from two of the great poets and skeptics of Islam: Abu al-Ala al-Ma'arri and Umar al-Khayyam. But then science's iron fist had destroyed it once and for all.

"At least I'm not an atheist," Kamal told himself. "I still believe in God. But religion? . . . Where's religion? . . . It's gone! I lost it, just as I lost the head of the holy martyr al-Husayn when I was told it's not in his tomb in Cairo . . . and I've lost Aïda and my self-confidence too."

Then in a sorrowful voice he said, "Maybe I made a mistake. My excuse is that I was studying the theory."

"That's no excuse. You must correct your error."

What a good man his father was – wanting to get Kamal to attack science in order to defend a legend. He really had suffered a lot, but he would not open his heart again to legends and superstitions now that he had cleansed it of them.

"I've experienced enough torment and deception," Kamal reflected. "From now on I won't be taken in by fantasies. Light's light. Our father Adam! He wasn't my father. Let my father be an ape, if that's what truth wants. It's better than being one of countless descendants of Adam. If I really were descended from a prophet like Adam, reality wouldn't have made such a fool of me."

"How can I correct my error?"

Al-Sayyid Ahmad said with equal measures of simplicity and sharpness, "You can rely on a fact that's beyond doubt: God created Adam from dust, and Adam's the father of mankind. This fact is mentioned in the Qur'an. Just explain the erroneous aspects of the theory. That'll be easy for you. If it isn't, what's the use of your education?"

Here the mother's voice said, "What could be easier than showing the error of someone who contradicts the word of God the Merciful? Tell this English atheist that Adam was the father of mankind. Your grandfather was blessed by knowing the Book of God by heart. It's up to you to follow his example. I'm delighted that you wish to be a scholar like him."

Al-Sayyid Ahmad's displeasure was apparent in his expression. He scolded her, "What do you understand about the Book of God or scholarship? Spare us his grandfather and pay attention to what you're doing."

She said shyly, "Sir, I want him to be a scholar like his grandfather, illuminating the world with God's light."

Her husband shouted angrily, "And here he's begun to spread darkness."

The woman replied apprehensively, "God forbid, sir. Perhaps you didn't understand."

Al-Sayyid Ahmad glared at her harshly. He had relaxed his grip on them, and what had been the result? Here was Kamal disseminating the theory that man's origin was an ape. Amina was arguing with him and suggesting he did not understand. He yelled at his wife, "Let me speak! Don't interrupt me. Don't interfere in things you can't comprehend. Pay attention to your work. May God strike you down."

Turning to Kamal with a frowning face, he said, "Tell me: Will you do what I said?"

"You're living with a censor who's more relentless than any afflicting free thought elsewhere in the world," Kamal told himself. "But you love him as much as you fear him. Your heart will never allow you to harm him. Swallow the pain, for you've chosen a life of disputation."

"How can I answer this theory? If I limit my debate to citing Qur'an references, I won't be adding anything new. Everyone knows them as well as I do and believes them. To discuss it scientifically is a matter for specialists in that area."

"So why did you write about something outside your area?"

Taken at face value, this objection was valid. Unfortunately Kamal lacked the courage to tell his father that he believed in the theory as scientific truth and for this reason had felt he could rely on it to create a general philosophy for existence reaching far beyond science. Al-Sayyid Ahmad considered his silence an admission of error and so felt even more resentful and sad. To be misled on a topic like this was an extremely grave matter with serious consequences, but it was a field where al-Sayyid Ahmad could exercise no authority. He felt that his hands were as tied with this young freethinker as they had been previously with Yasin when he had escaped from paternal custody. Was he to share the experience of other fathers in these strange times? He had heard incredible things about the younger generation. Some schoolboys were smoking. Others openly questioned their teachers' integrity. Still others had rebelled against their fathers. His own prestige had not been diminished, but what had his long history of resolute and stern guidance achieved? Yasin was stumbling and practically doomed. Here was Kamal arguing, debating, and attempting to slip from his grasp.

"Listen carefully to me. I don't want to be harsh with you, for you're polite and obedient. On this subject, I can only offer you my advice. You should remember that no one who has neglected my advice has prospered." Then after a brief silence he continued: "Yasin's an example for you of what I'm saying, and I once advised your late brother not to throw himself to destruction. Had he lived, he would be a distinguished man today."

At this point the mother said in a voice like a moan, "The English killed him. When they're not killing people, they're spreading atheism."

Al-Sayyid Ahmad went on with his remarks: "If you find things in your lessons that contradict religion and are forced to memorize them to succeed in the examination, don't believe them. And it's equally important not to publish them in the papers. Otherwise you'll bear the responsibility. Let your stance with regard to English science be the same as yours toward their occupation of Egypt. Do not admit the legality of either, even when imposed on us by force."

The shy, gentle voice interposed once more: "From now on, dedicate your life to exposing the lies of this science and spreading the light of God."

Al-Sayyid Ahmad shouted at her, "I've said enough without any need for your views."

She returned to her work, while her husband stared at her in a threatening way until sure she would be quiet. Then he looked at Kamal and asked, "Understand?"

"Most certainly," Kamal answered in a voice that inspired confidence.

From that time on, if he wanted to write he would have to publish in *al-Siyasa*. Because of its political affiliation it would never fall into the hands of a Wafdist. And he secretly promised his mother he would consecrate his life to spreading God's light. Were not light and truth identical? Certainly! By freeing himself from religion he would be nearer to God than he was when he believed. For what was true religion except science? It was the key to the secrets of existence and to everything really exalted. If the prophets were sent back today, they would surely choose science as their divine message. Thus Kamal would awake from the dream of legends to confront the naked truth, leaving behind him this storm in which ignorance had fought to the death. It would be a dividing point between his past, dominated by legend, and his future, dedicated to light. In this manner the paths leading to God would open before him – paths of learning, benevolence, and beauty. He would say goodbye to the past with its deceitful dreams, false hopes, and profound pains.

105

HE CAREFULLY considered everything his eyes could soak up as he approached the Shaddad mansion. Once inside its grounds he redoubled the attention with which he scrutinized his surroundings. He understood that this visit would be his last chance to enjoy the house, its inhabitants, and the memories it held for him. What else could he think, since Husayn had finally won his father's approval to travel to France? With keen eyes and emotions he observed the side path leading to the garden and the window overlooking the path. He could almost see her elegant and graceful figure casting him a beautiful look, one as meaningless as the twinkling of a star. It was a tender greeting addressed to no one in particular – like the song of a bulbul so enthralled by its own happiness that it is oblivious to its audience. Next came the magnificent view of the garden, which stretched from the back of the house to the long wall bordering the desert. Scattered through it were trellises of jasmine, clumps of palms, and rosebushes. Finally there was the gazebo, where he had experienced the twin intoxications of love and friendship. He recalled the English proverb "Don't put all your eggs in one basket," and smiled sadly. Although he had memorized it long before, he had found it unconvincing then. Whether through carelessness, stupidity, or predestined decree, he had invested his whole heart in this one house, partly in love and partly in friendship. He had lost his love, and now his friend was packing for a trip abroad. In the future he would find himself without a lover or a friend.

What could console him for the loss of this view, which was imprinted in his breast and attached to his heart? It had become familiar and sympathetic, as a whole and in its individual parts – the mansion, the garden, and the desert. The names Aïda and Husayn Shaddad had been etched in his memory in similar fashion. How could he be deprived of this sight or content himself with glimpsing it from afar, like any other passerby? He was so infatuated with the house that once he had jokingly accused himself of idolatry.

Husayn Shaddad and Isma'il Latif were sitting opposite each other at the table, on which was placed the customary water pitcher with three glasses. As usual in summer, each wore a shirt with an open collar and white pants. They looked up at him with their contrasting faces. Husayn's was handsome and radiant. Isma'il's had sharp features and penetrating eyes. Kamal approached them in his white suit, holding his fez as the tassel swung to and fro. They shook hands, and he sat down with his back to the house . . . a house that had previously turned its back on him.

Laughing naughtily, Isma'il immediately told Kamal, "It's up to us to find a new place to meet from now on."

Kamal smiled wanly. How happy Isma'il was with his sarcasm, which had never been racked by pain. He and Fuad al-Hamzawi were all Kamal had left. They were friends who would keep his heart company but never blend with it. He would rush to them to escape his loneliness. His only choice was to accept his destiny with good grace.

"We'll have to meet in the coffeehouses or streets, since Husayn's decided to leave us."

Husayn shook his head with the sorrow of a person who has won a coveted objective and is trying to humor friends by appearing sad about a separation that means little to him. He said, "I'll leave Egypt with regret in my heart over my separation from you. Friendship's a sacred emotion I cherish with all my heart. A friend's a partner who's a reflection of yourself. He echoes your sentiments and thoughts. It doesn't matter if we differ in many respects so long as our essential characteristics are the same. I'll never forget this friendship, and we'll keep writing each other until we meet again."

A pretty speech was the only consolation offered a wounded heart that was being forsaken . . . as if Kamal had not suffered enough at the hands of Husayn's sister. "Is this how you abandon me, leaving me without any real friends?" Kamal wondered. "Tomorrow the forsaken friend will be slain by a mocking thirst for spiritual companionship."

He asked dejectedly, "When will we meet again? I haven't forgotten your keen desire to be a perpetual tourist. Who will guarantee your departure won't be permanent?"

Isma'il agreed. "My heart tells me the sparrow won't fly back into the cage."

Husayn laughed briefly but in a way that revealed his delight. He answered, "I wasn't able to win my father's consent to travel until I promised to continue my legal studies. But I don't know how long I'll be able to keep that promise. There's no great affection between me and the law. Besides, I imagine I won't have much patience with systematic instruction. I only want things I love. My heart's torn between various different forms of knowledge. No one college deals with all of them, as I've told you time and again. I wish to attend lectures on philosophy of art as well as others on poetry and fiction. I want to tour the museums and recital halls, fall in love, and have a good time. What college or faculty offers all these opportunities? Then there's another fact you both know. It's that I'd rather hear than read. I want someone else to do the explaining while I listen. Then I'll dash off – my senses at their most perceptive and my mind alert – to mountainsides, seashores, bars, cafés, and dance halls. You'll be receiving a series of reports from me on all these unique experiences."

Husayn seemed to be describing the paradise Kamal had ceased believing in. But Husayn's was a negative paradise, full of taking without any giving. Kamal had aspired to a more positive one. Once this rosy life embraced Husayn to her comely bosom, it was absurd to think he would ever long for his old home.

Isma'il expressed some of Kamal's concerns when he told Husayn, "You won't return. Farewell, Husayn! We have approximately the same dream. Leaving aside the philosophy of art, museums, poetry, mountain slopes, and so forth, we could be a single person. I remind you one final time that you'll never return to us."

Kamal cast Husayn a questioning glance, as if to see what he thought about Isma'il's words.

Their friend said, "No, I'll return frequently. Egypt will be on my extensive itinerary so I can see my family and friends." Then he told Kamal, "I'll be waiting for you to visit Europe with such anxious anticipation that I can almost feel it already."

Who could say? Perhaps Kamal's lie would turn out to be the truth. Maybe he would traverse those distant realms. No matter what happened, his heart told him that Husayn would return one day and that this profound friendship would not end. His heart sincerely believed this, just as it had believed love could not be plucked from the heart, roots and all . . . alas.

He entreated his friend, "Travel and do whatever you want, but come back to Egypt to reside here. Then you can leave for trips when you feel like it."

Isma'il added his support to this idea: "If you're really a decent fellow, you'll accept this obvious solution, which reconciles your wishes with ours."

Bowing his head as if convinced, Husayn said, "My travels will eventually lead me to this solution, I believe."

As Kamal listened to Husayn, he gazed at his friend, especially at the black eyes that resembled Aïda's and the gestures, which were both grand and gracious. Husayn's diaphanous spirit was almost a visible and tangible presence for Kamal. If this dear friend disappeared, what would remain of the blessing of friendship and the memory of love . . . that friendship through which Kamal had learned Platonic affection and relaxed happiness . . . and the love that had inspired in him feelings of heavenly joy and hellish torment?

Referring to each of them in turn, Husayn continued: "When I return to Egypt you'll be an accountant in the Ministry of Finance and you'll be a teacher. It's quite possible I'll find you're fathers. What an amazing idea!"

Isma'il asked laughingly, "Can you imagine us as government employees? Try to picture Kamal as a teacher!" Then he told Kamal, "You'll have to put on a lot of weight before you stand in front of your pupils. You'll find the next generation's a bunch of demons. Compared with them we were angels. Although a dedicated supporter of the Wafd Party, you'll find yourself forced by the government to punish students who strike in support of the Wafd."

Isma'il's observation forced Kamal away from the train of thought absorbing him. He found himself wondering how he could face pupils with his notorious head and nose. He felt resentful and bitter, imagining – on the basis of the behavior of odd-looking teachers he had known – that he would treat his pupils harshly in order to protect himself from their mischief. But he also wondered whether he would be able to be as strict with others as he was with himself.

He ventured, "I don't think I'll always be a teacher."

There was a dreamy look in Husayn's eyes as he said, "You'll go from teaching into journalism, I suspect. Isn't that so?"

Kamal found himself thinking about the future. He thought again of the all-inclusive book he had often dreamt of writing. But what was left of the original subject matter? He no longer considered the prophets to have been prophets. Heaven and hell did not exist. The study of man was merely a branch of animal science. He would have to search for a new topic. Speaking impulsively again, he said, "If I could, I'd start a magazine someday to promote modern thought."

Isma'il admonished him, "No, politics is what sells publications. If you want, you can devote a column on the back page to thought. There's room in this country for a new Wafdist satirical writer."

Husayn laughed out loud and said, "Our friend doesn't seem to be very positive about politics. His family's already made a big enough sacrifice for the nation. But thought's a wide-open field for him." Then he told Kamal, "What you mentioned is certainly possible for you. . . . Your rebellion against religion was a sudden leap I didn't expect."

This observation cheered Kamal, for it sanctioned his rebellion and his pride. Blushing, he said, "How beautiful it would be if man could devote his life to truth, goodness, and beauty."

Isma'il whistled three times, once for each of these qualities. Then he said sarcastically, "Listen and take note!"

But Husayn said seriously, "I'm like you, but I'm satisfied with knowledge and enjoyment."

Enthusiastically and sincerely Kamal replied, "The matter's more exalted than that. It's a struggle toward truth aiming at the good of mankind as a whole. In my opinion, life would be meaningless without that."

Isma'il struck his hands together in a way that reminded Kamal of his father and said, "Then life necessarily has no meaning. How you've worn yourself out and suffered to free yourself from religion. . . . I haven't tired myself like that, because religion never interested me. Do you suppose I'm a born philosopher? It's enough for me to live a life that doesn't need to be explained. I'm instinctively drawn to what you achieve only after a bitter struggle. God forgive me, you haven't achieved it yet, for you still – even after renouncing religion – believe in truth, goodness, and beauty. You wish to dedicate your life to them. Isn't this what religion requests? How can you claim to reject a principle when you believe in everything derived from it?"

"Pay no attention to this gentle mockery," Kamal advised himself. But why should the values he believed in always seem to be the object of ridicule? "Suppose you had to choose between Aïda and a righteous life. Which would you choose? . . . But when I think of her, Aïda's always identified with what's most exemplary."

Feeling the silence had lasted too long, Husayn answered for Kamal: "The Believer derives his love for these values from religion, while the free man loves them for themselves."

"O Lord, when will I see you again?" Kamal asked himself.

Isma'il laughed in a manner that revealed his thoughts were shifting to a new direction. He asked Kamal, "Tell me: Don't you still pray? Do you intend to fast as usual during Ramadan?"

"My invocations for her were the most enjoyable parts of my prayers," Kamal mused. "My evenings in this mansion were the happiest moments of Ramadan for me."

"I no longer pray. I won't fast."

"Will you tell people you're not?"

Laughing, Kamal said, "No."

"You prefer to be a hypocrite?"

He answered resentfully, "There's no need to hurt people I love."

Isma'il asked sarcastically, "If you're this softhearted, how do you think you'll ever be able to confront society with unpopular views?"

"What about a satiric fable like the classic 'Kalila and Dimna'?" Kamal asked himself. This splendid thought drove away his resentment. "Lord, have I stumbled on an idea for a book I never thought of before?"

"Addressing readers is one thing; telling parents you're not fasting is something else."

Gesturing toward Kamal, Isma'il told Husayn, "Here's a philosopher who comes from a family deeply rooted in ignorance."

"You'll never be at a loss for companions to play and joke around with, but you'll never gain another friend for your spirit capable of conversing directly with it," Kamal told himself. "So be content with silence or with talking to yourself like a lunatic."

They were all quiet for a time. The garden was silent too, for there was no breeze. Only the roses, carnations, and violets seemed to be enjoying the heat. The sun had withdrawn its luminous gown from the garden, leaving only a hem trailing over the east wall.

Isma'il ended the silence by turning to Husayn Shaddad and asking, "Do you suppose you'll get a chance to visit Hasan Salim and Mrs. Aïda?"

"My God!" Kamal exclaimed to himself. "Is it just my heart pounding or has the end of the world begun in my breast?"

"After I'm settled in Paris, I'll definitely think of visiting Brussels." Smiling, he added, "We received a letter from Aïda last week. It seems she's having morning sickness. . . ."

"So pain and life are twins," Kamal thought. "I'm nothing but unadulterated pain in a man's clothes. Aïda has a swelling belly awash with fluids. . . . Is this one of life's tragedies or comedies? The most blessed event of our lives will be our extinction. I wish I knew the essence of this pain."

Isma'il Latif exclaimed, "Their children will be foreigners!"

"It's agreed that they'll be sent to Egypt when they're old enough."

"Will you find them one day in a class of your students?" Kamal asked himself. "You'll wonder where you've seen those eyes. Your pounding heart will reply that they've been living inside you for a long time. If her little boy makes fun of your head and nose, will you have the heart to punish him? Forgetfulness, are you a legend too?"

Husayn went on: "She wrote at great length of her new life and didn't conceal her delight with it. In fact, she only said she missed her family to be polite."

"She was created for a life like this in one of those dream countries," Kamal reflected. "That she should partake of human nature was one more example of irreverent toying by the fates with things you hold sacred. Do you suppose it didn't occur to her to refer to her former friends in her chatty letter, not even with one word? . . . But how do you know she still remembers them?"

They were silent again. The sunset colors gradually began to turn a calm brown. A predatory kite could be seen circling in the distant sky. The barking of a dog reached them. Isma'il got a drink from the pitcher. Husayn started to whistle, while Kamal stealthily watched him with a placid face and a broken heart.

"The heat this year's dreadful." Isma'il said that and dried his lips with an embroidered silk handkerchief. Then he burped and put the handkerchief back in his pocket.

"Separation from loved ones is even more dreadful," Kamal reflected.

"When are you leaving for the beach?"

"At the end of June," Isma'il said with evident relief.

Husayn said, "We're going to Ra's al-Barr tomorrow. I'll stay there a week with my family. Then I'll go with my father to Alexandria, where I'll board the ship the thirtieth of June."

The history of an era would end, and perhaps a heart would die. Husayn gazed at Kamal for some time. Then he laughed and said, "We leave you with the country happily united in a coalition of political parties. Perhaps news of Egyptian independence will precede me to Paris."

Addressing Husayn but pointing at Kamal, Isma'il exclaimed, "Your friend's not too happy about the coalition. It rubs him the wrong way for Sa'd Zaghlul to hold hands with traitors. It's even harder on him that Sa'd's agreed to avoid conflict with the British by leaving the post of Prime Minister to his longtime foe Adli. So you'll find that his views are even more immoderate than those of his revered leader."

"The truce with former enemies and traitors is one more disappointment you have to swallow," Kamal told himself. "Is there anything in this world that has lived up to your hopes?"

But he laughed out loud and said, "This coalition wants to impose a deputy from the Liberal Party on our district."

The three of them roared with laughter. A frog hopped into sight and then quickly disappeared in the grass. A breeze stirred, announcing the approach of evening. The clamor and commotion of the world encircling them began to diminish. The gathering would soon break up. That fact alarmed Kamal and made him look around to fill his eyes with the sights. Here for the first time he had experienced love. Here the angelic voice had sung out, "Kamal." Here the devastating conversation about his head and nose had taken place. Here the beloved had leveled her accusations against him. Beneath this sky lay memories of emotions, feelings, and reactions. These could not be disturbed by any power weaker than one capable of bringing the desert to life and making it bloom. He soaked up all of this and took pains to remember the date, for events frequently seem not to have happened if the day, month, and year are not fixed.

"We appeal to the sun and moon for help in escaping from time's straight line when we wish to circle back and regain our lost memories, but nothing ever returns," brooded Kamal. "So break down and cry or dispel your worries with a smile."

Isma'il Latif stood up and said, "The time's come for us to leave."

Kamal allowed Isma'il to embrace their friend first. Then his turn came, and they hugged each other at length. Kamal planted a kiss on Husayn's cheek and received one in return. The fragrance of the Shaddad family filled his nostrils. It had a gentle, zesty bouquet rare for a human being, like a puff of air from a dream that had circled in a sky replete with delights and pains. Kamal inhaled this scent until he grew tipsy. He was silent while he attempted to gain control of his emotions. All the same, his voice trembled when he said, "Till we meet again, even if it's not for a while."

106

"THERE'S NO one here but the staff!"

"That's because the day's hardly over. The patrons usually arrive with the night. Does the emptiness of the place upset you?"

"Not at all. It encourages me to stay, especially since it's the first time."

"Bars here have the priceless advantage of being situated on a street frequented only by people in search of forbidden pleasures. No scolding critic will trouble your peace of mind. If someone you respect – like your father or guardian – stumbles upon you, he's more at fault than you are and more apt to pretend he doesn't know you, or even to flee if he can."

"The name of the street itself is scandalous."

"But that makes it safer than any other. If we go to a bar on Alfi, Imad al-Din, or even Muhammad Ali streets, we could be seen by a father, brother, uncle, or some other important person. But they don't come here to Wajh al-Birka, hopefully."

"That makes sense, but I'm still uncomfortable."

"Be patient. The first step's always difficult, but alcohol's the key to joy. I promise you'll find the world a sweeter and more charming place by the time we depart."

"Tell me about the different kinds of drinks. What should I start with?"

"Cognac's strong. If it's mixed with beer, a person drinking it's as good as gone. Whiskey has an acceptable taste and produces excellent effects. Raisin liqueur . . ."

"That should be the most enjoyable! Haven't you heard Salih sing 'He poured me raisin liqueur'?"

"For a long time I've told you the only thing wrong with you is that you live in a fantasy world. Raisin liqueur's the worst drink of all, no matter what Salih says. It tastes like anise and upsets my digestion. Don't interrupt."

"Sorry!"

"Then there's beer, but that's a hot-weather drink, and, praise God, it's September. There's wine too, but its effect is like a slap from a bitch."

"So . . . so . . . it's whiskey."

"Bravo! For a long time I've had great hopes for you. Perhaps you'll soon agree you have an even greater aptitude for fun than for truth, goodness, beauty, nationalism, humanitarianism, and all the other fancy items over which you've pointlessly exhausted your heart." He called the waiter and ordered two whiskeys.

"The wisest thing would be for me to stop after one glass."

"That might be wise, but we didn't come here in search of wisdom. You'll learn for yourself that delirium's more pleasant than wisdom and that there's more to life than books and thought. Remember this day and don't forget who's to thank for it."

"I don't want to pass out. I'm afraid of that."

"Be your own physician."

"For me the important thing is to find the courage to walk down that alley with no hesitation and to enter one of those houses when I need to . . . ."

"Drink till you feel unconcerned about going in one."

"Fine. I hope I won't live to regret what I've done."

"Regret? I asked you repeatedly, but you excused yourself on religious grounds. Then you proclaimed you'd stopped believing in religion. So I renewed my invitation but was amazed to find you refusing in the name of morality. I must admit you finally bowed to logic."

Yes, at last he had . . . after a long period of anxiety and apprehension, when he was torn between the ascetic skepticism of Abu al-Ala al-Ma'arri and the more hedonistic version of Umar al-Khayyam. He was naturally inclined toward the former doctrine, although it preached a stern and sober life, because of its compatibility with the traditions in which he had been raised. But before he had known what was happening, he had found his soul longing for annihilation. A mysterious voice had whispered in his ear, "There's no religion, no Aïda, and no hope. So let death come." At that juncture, al-Khayyam had appealed to him, using this friend as an intermediary, and Kamal had accepted their invitation. All the same, he had retained his lofty principles by broadening the range of meaning for "goodness" to include all the joys of life. He had told himself, "Belief in truth, beauty, and humanity is merely

the highest form of goodness. For this reason, the great philosopher Ibn Sina concluded each day of deep thought with drinks
and beautiful women. In any case, only a life like this offers an
alternative to death."

"I agreed, but I haven't abandoned my principles."

"Well, I'm sure you haven't abandoned your fantasies. You've
lived with them so long they seem truer to you than reality itself.
There's nothing wrong with reading or even writing, if you can
find readers. But make writing a way of obtaining fame and
fortune. Don't take it too seriously. You were intensely religious.
Now you're intensely agnostic. But you've always been intensely concerned, as though you were responsible for all mankind.
Life's not nearly that complicated. Get a government position
you like, one providing an acceptable standard of living, and
enjoy the pleasures of life with a heart free from cares. Be strong
and assertive when you need to, and you'll find your honor
protected, your success ensured. If this life's compatible with
religion, then be proud of that and enjoy it. If it's not, then
religion's at fault."

"Life's too profound and vast to be reduced to one activity, not
excluding happiness," Kamal told himself. "Pleasure's my recreation, but ascending rugged mountains is still my objective. Aïda's
gone. So I must create a new Aïda exemplifying everything she
meant to me. Otherwise you should abandon life with no regrets."

"Don't you ever give any thought to values that transcend
human life?"

"Ha! I've been distracted from all that by life itself, or more
precisely by my life. No one in my family's an atheist, and no one's
overly devout. I'm that way too."

"A friend's as necessary a part of life as time for relaxation,"
Kamal advised himself. "He's odd-looking too and linked to your
memories of Aïda. So his place in your heart's guaranteed. He
knows his way around these lively alleys. A tyrant if you defy him,
he's at home with pleasures and avoids serious issues. He has no
time for spiritual concerns. Your intellectual and spiritual companion has vanished overseas. Fuad al-Hamzawi's bright but has no
taste for philosophy. He's self-centered even in the appreciation of
beauty. From literature, he desires eloquence to use in drafting
legal briefs. Who can ever replace Husayn for me?"

The waiter arrived and placed on the table two tall glasses with polygonal bases. Opening a bottle of soda, he poured some into the glasses, transforming their golden liquid into platinum encrusted with pearls. Then he set out plates of salad, cheese, olives, and bologna before leaving. Kamal looked back and forth from his glass to the smiling Isma'il, who said, "Do as I do. Start with a big swig. To your health!"

Kamal was content to take a sip and savor it. Then he waited expectantly, but his mind did not take flight as he had anticipated. So he took a big drink and picked up a piece of cheese to dispel the strange taste spreading through his mouth.

"Don't rush me!"

"Haste is from the devil. The important thing's for you to be ready for what you want when you leave here."

What did he want? Was it one of those women who inspired disgust and aversion when he was sober? Would alcohol sweeten the bitter sacrifice of his dignity? He had once fought off instinct by appealing to religion and to Aïda. Now instinct was free to express itself. But there was another incentive for this adventure. He wanted to investigate woman, the mysterious species that included Aïda herself. Perhaps this investigation would provide some consolation for sleepless nights when tears were shed secretly. It might give some compensation for bloody torment curable only by despair or by a loss of consciousness. He could now say he had emerged from the confining cell of resignation to take a first step along the road to freedom, even if this road was paved with inebriation and bordered by passions and other reprehensible things. He drank again and waited. Then he smiled. His insides celebrated the birth of a new sensation, one exuding warmth and sensuality. Kamal responded with abandon, as though reacting to a beautiful melody.

Isma'il, who was watching him closely, smiled and said, "If only Husayn were here to witness this."

"Where is Husayn?" Kamal wondered silently. "Where?"

"I'll write him about it myself. Have you answered his last letter?"

"Yes. I sent him a note as brief as his."

Husayn wrote long letters only to Kamal. They were so extensive that every thought was recorded. This great happiness was exclusively Kamal's, but he was obliged to keep it secret, for he did not want to arouse his coach's envy.

"His letter to me was brief too, except for the kind of discussion you know we enjoy but you don't."

"Thought!" Then Isma'il laughed. "What need does he have for it? He'll inherit a fortune big enough to fill an ocean. So why's he infatuated with such gibberish? Is it an affectation or conceit or both?"

"It's Husayn's turn to come in for a pounding," Kamal reflected. "I wonder what you say about me behind my back."

"Contrary to what you think, there's no conflict between thought and wealth. Philosophy flourished in ancient Greece when some gentlemen were able to devote themselves to learning because they weren't preoccupied by earning a living."

"Your health, Aristotle."

He drained the rest of his glass and waited expectantly. He wondered whether he had ever experienced a state like this before. A discharge of psychic heat raced off through his veins. As it progressed, it swept away the crannies where grief's residue had collected. The sorrow sealing his soul's vessel dissolved. Out flew singing birds of gaiety. One was the echo of a moving tune, another the memory of a promising hope, and yet another the shadow of a fleeting delight. Alcohol was the elixir of happiness.

"What would you think of ordering two more drinks?"

"May your life last longer than mine...." Isma'il laughed out loud and summoned the waiter with the flick of a finger. Then he said with relief, "You're quick to recognize a good thing."

"I have my Lord to thank for that."

The waiter brought two more drinks and fresh appetizers. Customers started to flock in, some in fezzes, some in hats, and others in turbans. The waiter welcomed them by wiping off the tabletops with a towel. Since night had fallen and the lamps had been lit, the mirrors on the walls flashed with reflections of Dewar's and Johnnie Walker bottles. Outside in the street laughter reverberated like the call to prayer, but this summons was to debauchery. Smiling glances of tolerant disapproval were directed at the table occupied by the two adolescent friends. A shrimp seller from Upper Egypt entered the bar. He was followed by a woman with two gold teeth who was selling peanuts, a man offering to shine the customers' shoes, and a kabob vendor who was also a pimp, as the greetings he received from the men demonstrated.

Finally there was an Indian palm reader. Soon nothing was heard except "To your health" and scattered laughter.

In a mirror adjacent to his head, Kamal saw his own flushed face and his gleaming, smiling eyes. Behind his reflection, he saw that of an elderly man, who raised his drink and rinsed his mouth with a rabbitlike twitch before swallowing. In an audible voice, this gentleman told a companion, "Rinsing my mouth with whiskey's a habit I acquired from my grandfather, who died drunk."

Turning away from the mirror, Kamal told Isma'il, "We're a very conservative family. I'm the first to taste alcohol."

Isma'il shrugged his shoulders scornfully and said, "How can you offer opinions about something you've never observed? Were you there to see what your father did in his youth? My father has a glass with lunch and another with dinner, but he's stopped drinking outside the house . . . or that's what he tells my mother."

The elixir of the god of happiness stealthily gained entry into the kingdom of the spirit. This strange transformation happened in moments. Unaided, mankind could not have achieved it in countless generations. All in all, it provided a dazzling new meaning for the word "enchantment." Amazingly Kamal did not find it a totally new sensation. His spirit had experienced this briefly once before; but when, how, and where? It was an inner music performed by the spirit. Normal music was like the apple's peel, while this music was the tasty fruit. What could be the secret of this golden liquid that accomplished such a miracle in only a few moments? Perhaps it cleansed life's stream of foam and sediment, allowing the restrained current to burst forth with the absolute freedom and unsullied intoxication life had enjoyed at the very beginning. When liberated from the body's noose, society's shackles, past memories, and fears for the future, this natural feeling of life's forward thrust becomes a clear, pure music, distilled from and exciting emotion.

"I've felt something like this pass through my spirit before," Kamal told himself. "But when, how, and where? Oh, what a memory . . . it was love! The day she called out, 'Kamal,' that intoxicated you before you knew what intoxication was. Admit your long history with inebriation. You've been rowdy for ages, traveling passion's drunken path, which is strewn with flowers and sweet herbs. That was before the transparent drops of dew were trampled into the mud. Alcohol's the spirit of love once love's inner lining of pain is stripped away. So love and grow intoxicated or get drunk and experience love."

"In spite of everything you've said and reiterated, life's beautiful."

"Ha-ha. You're the one who's been doing the saying and reiterating."

The warrior planted a sincere kiss on the cheek of his foe. Then peace settled over the earth. Perched on a leafy bough, the bulbul warbled. Lovers throughout the inhabited world were ecstatic. Stopping at Paris on the way, desires flew from Cairo to Brussels, where they were received with affection and songs. The sage dipped the point of his pen in his heart's ink and recorded a divine revelation. Then the seasoned man retreated into old age, although a tearful memory inspired a hidden springtime in his breast. Like the black cloth covering of the Kaaba in Mecca, the strands of black hair on her forehead sheltered a shrine toward which drunkards in the taverns of love directed their prayers.

"Give me a book, a drink, and a beautiful woman. Then throw me in the sea."

"Ha-ha. The book will spoil the effect of the drink, the beautiful woman, and the sea."

"We don't agree on the meaning of pleasure. You think it's fun and games. To me it's something extremely serious. This captivating intoxication is the secret of life and its ultimate goal. Alcohol's only the precursor and the symbol for it. In a similar fashion, a bird like the kite was the forerunner of the airplane and observation of fish was a first step in the invention of the submarine. Thus wine's a necessary scout for human happiness. The question boils down to this: How can we turn life into a perpetual state of intoxication without resort to alcohol? We won't find the answer through debate, productivity, fighting, or exertion. All those are means to an end, not ends in themselves. Happiness will never be realized until we free ourselves from the exploitation of any means whatsoever. Then we can live a purely intellectual and spiritual life untainted by anything. This is the happiness for which alcohol provides us a representation. Every action could be a way of obtaining this. If it's not, it serves no end."

"May God devastate your home."

"Why?"

"I hoped I'd find you a charming, witty conversationalist when drunk. But you're like a sick man whose malady only becomes more severe with drink. I wonder what you'd talk about if you had a third drink?"

"I won't have another. I'm happy now and feel capable of soliciting any woman I like."

"Shouldn't you wait a little?"

"Not a single minute."

Kamal walked along bravely and resolutely, arm in arm with his friend. They fell in with the flow of men going their way and ran into another stream coming from the opposite direction, for the curving street was too narrow for its pedestrian traffic. The men swiveled their heads from right to left at prostitutes who stood or sat on either side. From faces veiled by brilliant makeup, eyes glanced around with a seductive look of welcome. At every instant a man would break ranks to approach one of the women. She would follow him inside, the alluring look in her eyes replaced by a serious, businesslike expression. Lamps mounted above the doors of the brothels and the coffeehouses gave off a brilliant light in which accumulated the clouds of smoke rising from incense burners and water pipes. Voices were blended and inter-mingled in a tumultuous swirl around which eddied laughter, shouts, the squeaking of doors and windows, piano and accordion music, rollicking handclaps, a policeman's bark, braying, grunts, coughs of hashish addicts and screams of drunkards, anonymous calls for help, raps of a stick, and singing by individuals and groups. Above all this, the sky, which seemed close to the roofs of the shabby buildings, stared down at the earth with unblinking eyes. Every beautiful woman there was available and would generously reveal her beauty and secrets in exchange for only ten piasters. Who could believe this without seeing it?

Kamal commented to Isma'il, "Harun al-Rashid struts through his harem."

Laughing, Isma'il asked, "Commander of the Faithful, hasn't one of the maidens found favor with you?"

"She was standing in that empty doorway. Where do you suppose she went?"

"She's with a customer inside, Commander of the Faithful. Will Your Majesty wait while one of his subjects accomplishes his objective?"

"How about you? Haven't you found what you're looking for?"

"I'm a habitué of the street and its inhabitants, but I won't tend to my interests until I've delivered you to your girlfriend. What did you like about her? There are many prettier."

She had a brown complexion, and makeup did not conceal her color. The sound of her voice was slightly reminiscent of that immortal music of Aïda. After all, an eye might even see some resemblance between the skin coloring of a man being strangled and the pure blue surface of the sky.

"Do you know her?"

"Here she's called Rose. Her real name is Ayusha."

"Ayusha-Rose!" Kamal exclaimed to himself. "If only a person could change his essence as easily as he changes his name. There's something of this Ayusha-Rose combination about Aïda herself, and about religion, Abd al-Hamid Bey Shaddad, and vast dreams. Alas! But wine's raising you to the throne of the gods. So watch these contradictions drown pathetically in waves of uproarious jests."

He felt an elbow nudge him in the side as Isma'il said, "Your turn."

Kamal looked toward the doorway and saw a man leave the house hurriedly. Then the woman returned to her post where he had first seen her. He advanced toward her with firm steps, and she received him with a smile. He went inside, trailed by her. She was singing, "Let down the curtain around us." Finding the narrow stairway, he started climbing it with a pounding heart. At the top was a hallway leading into a parlor. Her voice caught up with him, saying now, "Go right," then, "Go left," and finally, "The door that's partway open."

It was a small room decorated with wallpaper, containing a bed, a dressing table, a clothes rack, a wooden chair, a basin, and a pitcher. Confused, Kamal stood in the center of the room as he examined it. She proceeded to close the door and the window, through which the rattling of a tambourine, whistling, and clapping could be heard. Her face seemed so grave and even glowering and stern that he wondered ironically what she had in mind for him. She confronted him and looked him up and down. When her eyes reached his head and nose, he felt apprehensive. Wishing to quell his anxiety, he moved toward her and put out his arms.

But she brusquely gestured for him to stay back and said, "Wait."
So he stood stock-still where he was.

Determined to overcome all obstacles, he said with an innocent
smile, "My name's Kamal."

Staring at him in astonishment, she replied, "We're honored."

"Call to me. Say, 'Kamal.'"

All the more amazed, she answered, "Why should I call you
when you're staring me in the face like a calamity?"

"I take refuge in God!" he exclaimed to himself. Was she
making fun of him?

Even more resolved to rescue the situation, he said, "You told
me to wait. What am I waiting for?"

"You're right to ask that," she said. Then she removed her dress
with a theatrical gesture and leaped onto the bed, which creaked
from her weight. She stretched out on her back and began to caress
her belly with hennaed fingers. His eyes opened wide with disapproval. He had not been expecting this acrobatic performance
and sensed they were on different sides of a mountain. What a
distance there was between the valley of pleasure and that of work.
In one moment everything he had built up in his imagination over
the past few days was demolished. There was a bitter taste of
resentment in his mouth, but his curiosity was still intense. So he
overcame his dismay and ran his eyes down the naked body until
they reached their target. For a moment it seemed he could not
believe his eyes. With uneasy aversion he looked more closely, but
in the end experienced something close to alarm. Was this what
women really looked like or had he picked a poor example? But
even if he had chosen poorly, would that affect the essential
characteristics?

"We claim to love the truth," he told himself. "People have
been terribly unfair about your head and nose."

His soul instructed him to flee, and he was on the verge of
obeying. But he suddenly wondered why the man before him had
not fled and what Isma'il would say if Kamal returned right away.
No, he would not flee. He would proceed with the ordeal.

"Why are you standing there like a statue?"

"This voice shook your heart," he reminded himself. "Our ears
don't mislead us, but our ignorance may. You'll have a good time
laughing at yourself later, but you're a winner not a deserter.
Suppose life is a tragedy; still, it's a duty to play your role in it."

"Are you going to stand like that till dawn?"

In a curiously calm voice he answered, "Let's turn out the lights."

Sitting up in bed, she said coarsely and cautiously, "On condition that I see you first in the light."

He asked disapprovingly, "Why?"

"So I can be sure you're healthy."

He stripped for this medical examination. The sight seemed ludicrous to him in the extreme. Then it was pitch-black.

When he returned to the street, he took with him a dreary heart filled with sorrow. He imagined that he and everyone else were suffering from a painful decline and that their salvation was remote. He saw Isma'il coming toward him. His friend, who looked satisfied, tired, and sarcastic, asked, "How's philosophy?"

Kamal took his arm and walked off with him, asking earnestly, "Are all women alike?"

The young man cast a questioning glance at him. After Kamal had revealed his doubts and fears in a concise fashion to Isma'il, the latter smilingly said, "In general the essential traits are the same, even if some of the accidental ones differ. You're so laughable, you deserve pity. Should I assume from your state of mind that you'll not be returning here again?"

"To the contrary, I'll come back here more often than you think. Let's have another drink." Then he continued as though to himself: "Beauty . . . beauty! What is beauty?"

At that moment his soul yearned for purification, isolation, and meditation. He longed to remember the tormented life he had lived in the shadow of his beloved. He seemed to believe that truth would always be cruel. Should he adopt the avoidance of truth as his creed? He walked along the road to the bar, so lost in thought that he scarcely paid any attention to Isma'il's chatter. If truth was cruel, lies were ugly.

"The problem's not that the truth is harsh but that liberation from ignorance is as painful as being born. Run after truth until you're breathless. Accept the pain involved in re-creating yourself afresh. These ideas will take a life to comprehend, a hard one interspersed with drunken moments."

107

KAMAL HAD come to the alley by himself this evening. Inebriated, he was singing under his breath as he made his way boldly through the boisterous tide of humanity. Finding Rose's door vacant, he did not hesitate as he would have when first getting to know the alley. Instead, he headed straight for the house and entered without knocking. He climbed the stairs to the hallway and once there glanced at the closed door, where light was visible through the keyhole. He went to the waiting room, which fortunately was empty. He sat down in a wooden chair and stretched his legs out with satisfaction. A few minutes later he heard the door creak open and prepared to stand up. The other man's movements as he left the bedroom and headed for the stairs were revealed by his footsteps. Kamal tarried a few moments before rising to go into the hall. Through the open door of her room he saw Rose, who was remaking the bed. When she noticed him, she smiled and called for him to sit back down a minute. He retraced his steps, smiling with the confidence of a regular customer. He soon heard someone come up the stairs, and that upset him. He hated to have to wait with other clients, but the new arrival headed for Rose's room.

Kamal heard the woman tell this man gently, "I have a customer. Go to the parlor and wait." Then she raised her voice to summon Kamal: "Please come in."

He rose without any hesitation and ran into the new arrival in the hall. He found himself face to face with Yasin. Their stunned eyes met. Kamal immediately looked down, seething with shame, confusion, and discomfort. He was about to run off as fast as he could, but Yasin forestalled that with a laugh so loud it reverberated strangely against the hall ceiling. The youth looked up at his brother, whose arms were opened wide as he yelled delightedly, "A thousand magnificent evenings! A thousand days of imperial splendor!" He roared with laughter as the dazed Kamal stared at him. When life started to flow through the youth again, he emerged from his stupor and a quizzical smile appeared on his lips. He regained his composure but did not lose his embarrassment.

In an oratorical tone, Yasin burst out, "This is a happy night: Thursday, October 28, 1926, a truly joyous evening. We'll have to celebrate it every year, for on this night two brothers discovered each other and it was demonstrated that the baby of the family's grown up. He's bearing aloft the banner of our glorious traditions in the world of pleasures."

Rose walked up and asked Yasin, "Your friend?"

Laughing, Yasin replied, "No, my brother. The son of my father and . . . No, my father's son. That says it all. So you see, you're the darling of the whole family, you nobody."

She murmured, "Swell." Then she told Kamal, "Etiquette dictates that you yield your turn to your older brother, kid."

Yasin roared his mighty laugh and said, "'Etiquette dictates'! Who taught you the manners of sex? Can you imagine a brother waiting outside the door? Ha–ha . . . "

Giving him a warning look, she said, "If you laugh in that alarming way, drunkard, the police will hear. But you're excused, since your kid brother's always tipsy when he gets here."

Yasin looked at Kamal with astonished admiration. "You've learned that too!" he exclaimed. "My Lord, we really are blood brothers, in every way. Bring your mouth up close so I can smell it. But what's the use? A drunk can't detect the smell of liquor on anyone else's breath. Tell me now: What's your opinion of this wisdom you've gained from life instead of from books?" Then he pointed toward Rose and exclaimed, "One visit to this hussy's equivalent to reading ten banned books. So, you get drunk, Kamal. . . . A thousand bright days! We've been friends from the beginning. I'm the one who tau . . . "

"God, God! Am I going to have to wait till daybreak?"

Yasin gave Kamal a shove and said, "You go with her, and I'll wait."

But Kamal fell back, shaking his head in vehement rejection. Then he spoke for the first time: "No way! Not . . . not tonight." Putting his hand in his pocket, he took out ten piasters, which he gave to the woman.

Yasin cried out admiringly, "Long live gallantry! But I won't let you go off alone. . . . " Giving Rose's shoulder a goodbye pat, he took Kamal's arm, and they left the building together.

Yasin was saying, "We must celebrate this evening. So let's spend some time in a bar. I usually do my drinking on Muhammad Ali Street with a group of civil servants and some others, but it's not an appropriate place for you, and besides, it's far. Let's choose somewhere nearby, so we can get home in good time. Since my latest marriage, I'm as eager as you to return home early. Where did you get drunk tonight, hero?"

Kamal stammered with embarrassment, "The Finish."

"Great! Let's go there. Take advantage of this moment and make the most of it. Tomorrow when you're a teacher, visiting this district with its brothels and taverns will be difficult for you." Then, laughing, he continued: "Imagine one of your pupils running into you here. . . . Even so, the field of pleasure's wide open, and you'll soon advance in it to ever more beautiful experiences."

They continued on to the Finish Bar in silence. Fortunately the bond between Yasin and Kamal had not been affected by Yasin's exodus from the old house, and there was no artificial reserve between them. It was typical of Yasin to overlook his prerogatives as the eldest brother. What Kamal knew from firsthand observation of his brother's conduct as well as from other people's comments gave him every reason to believe that Yasin was addicted to women and easily influenced by passion. Even so, meeting his brother at Rose's was a violent shock, for his imagination had never pictured Yasin intoxicated or loitering down this alley. As time passed, Kamal began to recover gradually from the shock, and his alarm began to give way to confidence and even relief. When the brothers reached the Finish, they found it packed. So Yasin suggested they take a table outside, choosing one toward the edge of the sidewalk at the corner of the street, to be as far as possible from other people. Smiling, they sat down opposite each other.

Yasin asked, "How much have you had to drink?"

Kamal answered hesitantly, "Two glasses."

"No doubt our unexpected meeting destroyed their effect. Let's start all over. I only have a few, seven or eight. . . . "

"You don't say! Is that a few?"

"Skip the naïve astonishment, because you're not naïve anymore."

"By the way, two months ago I didn't even know what it tasted like."

Yasin observed disapprovingly, "It seems I've given you more credit than you deserve."

They laughed together, and Yasin ordered a couple of drinks. Then he renewed his questioning: "When did you meet Rose?"

"I was introduced to Rose and whiskey the same night."

"What other experiences have you had with women?"

"None."

Yasin bowed his head slightly and looked at Kamal from beneath eyebrows contracted in a smiling frown as if to protest: "Come on now!" Then he said, "Don't play the fool. I had many opportunities to observe your flirtations with the daughter of Abu Sari', who grills snacks. At times it was a glance, then a gesture. Remember? Pimp, these matters can't be hidden from an expert. No doubt you were content to play with her, so you wouldn't find yourself obliged to make Abu Sari' your father-in-law – unlike my former mother-in-law, who got involved in a marriage with Bayumi the drinks seller. Yes? Now he's a man of property and your next-door neighbor. I wonder where Maryam's hiding. No one's heard anything about her. Her father was a good man. Don't you remember Mr. Muhammad Ridwan? See what's become of his household. But it's all a question of manners. Any woman who neglects them will find herself despised."

Kamal could not help laughing as he asked, "What about men? Can they neglect their manners without getting in trouble?"

Yasin laughed in his forceful way and replied, "Men and women are two different things, smart aleck. Tell me, how's your mother? Is that good woman still angry at me, even after I've divorced Maryam?"

"I think she's forgotten the whole affair. She has a fine heart, as you know."

Yasin endorsed his brother's words and then shook his head sadly. The waiter brought the drinks and the appetizers. Yasin immediately raised his glass and said, "To the health of al-Sayyid Ahmad's family."

Kamal raised his too and drank half, hoping to regain his lost mirth. His mouth full of black bread and cheese, Yasin commented, "I imagined that, like our late brother, you resembled your mother in temperament. I thought you'd be a straight arrow, but you, but we . . ."

Kamal cast his brother a questioning look. Yasin smilingly continued: "But we're both created from our father's mold."

"Our father! He's so serious it's hardly possible to live with him."

Yasin roared with laughter. He hesitated a little before saying, "You don't know your father. I didn't either, but then an entirely different man was disclosed to me, an extraordinary one." He stopped speaking.

With great curiosity and interest Kamal asked, "What do you know that I don't?"

"I know he's a princely wit with a deep appreciation of music. Don't stare at me like an idiot. Don't think I'm drunk. Your father's a master of jests, music, and love."

"My father?"

"I learned that for the first time in the home of the singer Zubayda."

"Zubayda! What are you saying? . . . Ha–ha . . . "

But since Yasin's expression was anything but joking, Kamal stopped laughing even before his face could regain its serious look. His mouth closed gradually, until his lips were pressed together. He gazed silently at his brother's face as Yasin related in exhaustive detail what he had seen and heard of their father.

Was Yasin fabricating lies about his father? How could that be? What motive would justify it? No, he was only telling what he knew. So this was what Kamal's father was like.

"My Lord!" Kamal exclaimed to himself. "The seriousness, dignity, and gravity – what are they? If you hear tomorrow that the earth's flat or that mankind really did spring from Adam, don't be surprised or alarmed."

Finally Kamal asked, "Does my mother know about this?"

Yasin laughingly replied, "She's no doubt aware of the drinking at least."

"I wonder what effect that's had on her," Kamal brooded. "She becomes alarmed for no reason at all. Is my mother like me in presenting a happy front while feeling wretched inside?"

As though marshaling excuses he did not believe in, Kamal observed, "People love to exaggerate. Don't believe everything they say. Besides, his health shows he's a temperate man."

Gesturing for the waiter to bring another round, Yasin said admiringly, "He's a marvel! His body's a miracle. His spirit's another. Everything about him's miraculous, even his glib tongue." They both laughed. Then Yasin continued: "Imagine, in spite of all this, he rules his family with the firm hand you know and maintains his dignity as you can plainly see. How come I'm such a failure?"

"Consider these wonders," Kamal advised himself. "You're drinking with Yasin. Your father's a shameless old man. What's genuine and what's not? Is there any relationship between reality and what's in our heads? What value does history have? What connection is there between the beloved Aïda and the pregnant Aïda? I myself – who am I? Why did you suffer this savage pain from which you've yet to recover? Laugh till you're exhausted."

"What would happen if he saw us sitting here?"

Yasin snapped his fingers and exclaimed, "I take refuge in God!"

"Is Zubayda really beautiful?"

Yasin whistled and wriggled his eyebrows.

"Surely it's unfair that our father gets to enjoy such a sumptuous treat while all we can find are skinny girls."

"Wait your turn. You're still a beginner."

"Hasn't your relationship with him changed since you discovered his secret?"

"Anything but that!"

There was a dreamy look in Kamal's eyes as he said, "If only he had bestowed some of his charm on us. . . ."

"If only. . . ."

"We couldn't be much worse off than we are."

"What's so bad about loving women and drinking? . . ."

"How can you reconcile his conduct with his deep faith?"

"Am I an atheist? Are you? Were those caliphs who indulged their carnal appetites pagans? God's merciful and forgiving."

Kamal asked himself, "What would my father say? I really wish I could discuss these issues with him. Anything's possible, but I can't believe he's a hypocrite. No, he's not that. The only new dimension of his character revealed is love."

Kamal's final swallow left him in a jesting mood. He commented, "It's too bad he didn't go into acting."

Yasin laughed loudly and replied, "If he'd known the opportunities life offers actors to enjoy women and wine, he would have dedicated his life to this art."

"Is al–Sayyid Ahmad Abd al–Jawad really the butt of this joke?" Kamal wondered. "But is he any more exalted than Adam? And even so, you learned the truth of man's origin by accident. Chance occurrences have played a most significant role in your life. If I had not met Yasin by accident in the alley, the veil of ignorance would not have been lifted from my eyes. If Yasin, ignorant though he is, had not gotten me interested in reading, today I'd be in the Medical School, as my father hoped. If I'd enrolled in a different secondary school, like al–Sa'idiya, I wouldn't have met Aïda. In that case, I would be a different person now. I'd see existence in some other fashion. People like to fault Darwin for his reliance on chance in the explanation of the mechanics of his system. . . ."

Yasin observed sagely, "Time will teach you what you haven't learned yet." Of himself he said sarcastically, "It's taught me to get my enjoyment early in the evening, so I don't awaken my wife's doubts." Then he added, "She's the most forceful of my three wives. I imagine I'll never get rid of her."

Pointing toward the alley, Kamal asked with considerable interest, "What takes you there, now that you're on your third marriage?"

Yasin repeated a famous phrase from the song Kamal had first heard at Aisha's wedding: "Because . . . because . . . because . . ." Then, smiling uneasily, he continued: "Zanuba told me once, 'You've never been married. You've always considered marriage a love affair. It's time for you to start taking it seriously.' Isn't it strange that a woman entertainer should say such things? But she seems more dedicated to married life than either of my two previous spouses. She's determined to remain my wife until I die. But I can't resist women. I fall in love quickly and get bored quickly. For this reason, I repair to alleys like this one to satisfy my desires immediately without any need to get involved in a long affair. If it weren't for boredom, I wouldn't look for women in Massage Alley."

With ever-increasing interest, Kamal asked, "Aren't these women like any others?"

"Certainly not. A prostitute's a woman without a heart. For her, love's a commodity."

His eyes sparkling with hope, Kamal asked, "What do you think distinguishes one woman from another?"

Yasin nodded his head proudly because of the status conferred on him by Kamal's questions. With the confident tone of an expert, he responded, "A woman's place within the ranks of females is determined by her moral and emotional qualities, without consideration of family or class. I think more highly of Zanuba, for example, than I did of Zaynab, because Zanuba's more emotional, more sincere, and more dedicated to our marriage. But in the end, you'll find they're all the same. Even if you had an affair with the Queen of Sheba herself, you'd inevitably find she became boring to look at and like a song you're tired of hearing."

The gleam in Kamal's eyes disappeared. Had Aïda become boring to look at and an overly familiar song? "That's really hard to believe," he told himself. "But you are reality's victim. It's even hard to gloat at her misfortune. Learning that time could turn the beloved, whom the soul still misses, into an overly familiar sight and a tired song might drive a person crazy. In fact, if you had a choice, wouldn't you rather regret her loss than come to find her boring? Of course, at times I sigh for boredom because my desire's so strong, just as Yasin longs for desire because he's bored. Raise your head to the Lord of the heavens and ask Him for a happy solution."

"Haven't you ever been in love?"

"So what do you think I'm currently drowning in?"

"I mean genuine love, not passing lust."

Yasin finished his third drink, wiped his mouth with the back of his hand, twisted his mustache, and then said, "Don't hold it against me if love's concentrated for me in certain locations, like the mouth, the hand, and so forth."

"Yasin's handsome," Kamal observed to himself. "She would never have made fun of his head or nose. But his words make him seem truly pitiable. How can a man be a real man without love? But what's the use of it, since all it has brought you is pain?"

Gesturing for Kamal to empty his glass, Yasin continued: "Don't believe what they say about love in novels. Love's an emotion that lasts a few days or at best a few weeks."

"I've stopped believing in immortality, but is it possible to forget love?" Kamal asked himself. "I'm no longer the way I was. I'm escaping from love's hellish suffering. Life occasionally distracts me. But then I slip back. Once I directed my attention toward death. Today I look to life, although a hopeless one. It's amazing that you rebel against the idea of forgetting her. You almost seem to be blaming yourself for something. Or are you afraid you'll discover the most exalted thing you ever reverenced was just a fantasy? Are you refusing to let oblivion carry off this splendid manifestation of life for fear you'll wake up to find yourself of no more significance than if you'd never been born? Don't you remember why you spread your hands out in prayer to ask God to rescue you from torment and grant you forgetfulness?"

"But true love exists. We read about its effects in the papers, not just in novels."

Yasin smiled sarcastically and said, "Afflicted though I am by the love of women, I won't admit that 'true' love exists. The tragedies we read about in newspapers are actually accounts of youthful inexperience. Have you heard of the ancient Arab poet called 'Layla's Fool' because love for her drove him crazy? There are probably others like him in your stories, but he, Majnun, never married Layla. Show me one person who went insane because he loved his wife too much. Alas! Husbands are rational men, very rational, even when it goes against the grain. But a wife's madness commences with her wedding day, because nothing less than devouring her husband will satisfy her. It seems to me that crazy people become lovers because they're crazy. Lovers don't go insane just because they're in love. You'll observe these lunatics talking about a woman as though she were an angel. A woman's nothing more than a woman. She's a tasty dish of which you quickly get your fill. Let those crazy lovers share a bed with her so they can see what she looks like when she wakes up or smell her sweat or other odors. After that are they going to talk about angels? A woman's charm is a matter of cosmetics and other seductive devices. Once you fall into her trap, you see her for the human being she really is. The secret forces holding marriages together aren't beauty or charm but children, the dowry's balance demanded in exchange for a divorce, and the support payments."

"It would only be fitting if he'd change his opinion on seeing Aïda," Kamal told himself. "But you better rethink this question of love. You once considered it an angelic inspiration, but now you deny the existence of angels. So search for it within man's essence. Insert it into the list of theoretical and practical realities you wish to confront boldly. In this way you'll learn the secret of your tragedy and strip the veil away from Aïda's hidden essence. You won't discover her to be an angel, but the door of enchantment will swing open for you. How wretched it makes me to think of things like pregnancy and its craving, Aïda as an overly familiar sight, and body odors."

With distress that Yasin did not notice, Kamal said, "Man's a filthy creature. Couldn't he have been created better and cleaner?"

Although not looking at anything in particular, Yasin reared his head back and said with curious joy, "God . . . God, my soul's so shimmering it's turning into a song. My limbs are turning into musical instruments. The world's sweet and full of creatures dear to my heart. The weather's delightful. Reality's a figment of our imaginations, and what's imaginary's real. Trouble is nothing but a legend. God, God, what a beautiful thing alcohol is, Kamal. May God grant it a long existence, perpetuate it for us, and grant us the health and strength to drink it to the end of our days. May God destroy the home of anyone who tampers with it or fabricates lies about it. Relish this beautiful intoxication. Reflect on it. Close your eyes. Does any other pleasure compare with this? God . . . God . . . God!"

Lowering his head to look at Kamal, he continued: "What did you say, my son? 'Man's a filthy creature'? Were you offended by my comments about women? I wasn't saying that to arouse disgust for them. The fact is that I love them. I love them with all their faults. But I wanted to demonstrate that the angelic woman does not exist. In fact, if she did, I doubt I'd love her. Like your father, I love full hips. An angel with a heavy bottom wouldn't be able to fly. Take care to understand me and don't misinterpret my words, by the life of our father, al-Sayyid Ahmad."

Kamal quickly grew as tipsy as his brother and said, "Once alcohol's circulating through the body, the world certainly seems adorable."

"God bless your mouth! Now even the usual refrain of beggars in the street sounds enchanting to the ear."

"And our sorrows seem to belong to other men."

"But their women seem our own."

"It all amounts to the same thing, my father's son."

"God, God, I don't want to sober up."

"One vile aspect of life is that we can't stay drunk as long as we'd like."

"Please understand that I don't see drunkenness as just an amusement but as the heavenly goal of life on a par with knowledge and our highest ideals."

"In that case I'm a great philosopher."

"You will be, when you believe what I've said; not before."

"May God grant you a long life, Father, for you've begotten philosophers just like you."

"Why should a man be miserable when all he needs is a drink and a woman, since there are plenty of bottles and women too?"

"Why? . . . Why?"

"I'll tell you the answer once I've drunk one more."

"No," Yasin said in a voice that betrayed a fleeting sobriety. Then he cautioned Kamal again, "Don't overdo it. I'm your drinking partner tonight, so I'm responsible for you. What time is it?" He took out his watch and exclaimed, "Twelve-thirty! Hero, we're in trouble. We're both late. You have our father to worry about, and I've got Zanuba. Let's go."

In no time at all they had left the bar and boarded a carriage that rushed off with them toward al-Ataba, circling the fence around the Ezbekiya Garden on a road buried in darkness. Every now and then they saw a pedestrian hurry or stagger by. Whenever the carriage passed an intersection, the fresh breeze carried to them the sound of people singing. Above the buildings and the lofty trees of the Garden, vigilant stars glittered.

Yasin laughingly said, "Tonight I'll be able to swear quite confidently that I've done nothing reprehensible."

Kamal said rather anxiously, "I hope I get home before my father."

"Nothing's more wretched than fear. Long live the revolution!"

"Yes, long live the revolution!"

"Down with the tyrannical wife!"

"Down with the tyrannical father!"

108

KAMAL KNOCKED gently on the door until it opened to reveal the shadowy figure of Umm Hanafi. When she recognized him, she whispered, "My master's on the stairs."

Before entering, he waited to be sure his father had reached the top floor, but then a voice called down the stairs sharply, "Who knocked?"

Kamal's heart pounded. He felt obliged to step forward and reply, "Me, Papa."

By the light of the lamp that Kamal's mother was holding at the top of the stairs, his father's form was visible on the first-floor landing. Al-Sayyid Ahmad looked down over the railing and asked with astonishment, "Kamal? What's kept you outside the house till this hour?"

"The same thing that kept you," Kamal commented to himself.

He answered apprehensively, "I went to the theater to see a play that's required reading for us this year."

His father shouted angrily, "When did people start studying in theaters? Isn't it enough to read and memorize it? What disgusting nonsense! Why didn't you ask my permission?"

Kamal stopped a few steps below his father and replied apologetically, "I didn't expect it to end so late."

The man said angrily, "Find some other way to study and skip the foolish excuses." Grumbling to himself, he resumed his climb up the stairs. Some of these muttered complaints reached Kamal: "Studying in the theaters till all hours ... one A.M. ... just children ... curses on your author and the author of the play."

Kamal ascended to the top story and went into the sitting room, where he took the lamp from a table. Entering his bedroom with a sullen face, he deposited the lamp on his desk and stood there, resting his hands on the desk, while he asked when his father had last insulted him. He could not remember precisely but was sure his years at the Teachers College had passed without a comparable incident. For this reason the curses made a painful impact on him, even though they had not been directed at him. He turned away from his desk, removed his fez, and started to undress. Then he suddenly felt dizzy and nauseous. He fled to the bathroom, where he vomited everything with bitter violence. When he returned to his room he felt exhausted and disgusted with himself, for the pain in his chest was less intense and profound than that in his spirit. He took off his clothes, extinguished the lamp, and stretched out on the bed, exhaling with nervous annoyance.

In a few minutes he heard the door open softly. Then his mother's voice reached him, asking sympathetically, "Asleep?"

Adopting a natural and contented tone to discourage her, so he could confront his ordeal alone, he said, "Yes. . . ."

Her figure approached the bed and stopped near his head. Then she said apologetically, "Don't let it worry you. I know your father better than anyone."

"Of course! . . . I understand."

As though expressing her own reservations, she said, "He knows how serious and upright you are. That's why he couldn't believe you'd stayed out this late."

Kamal was sufficiently enraged to ask, "If staying out late merits so much disapproval, why does he do it so persistently?"

The darkness prevented him from seeing the expression of astonished disapproval on her face, but her nasal laugh showed that she did not take his question seriously. She replied, "All men stay out at night. You'll be a man soon. But right now, you're a student."

He interrupted her as if he wanted to end the conversation: "I understand. Naturally. I didn't mean anything by what I said. Why did you bother to come? Go in peace."

She said tenderly, "I was afraid you were upset. I'll leave you now, but promise you'll sleep soundly and not worry about it. Recite the Qur'an sura about God's absolute and eternal nature until you fall asleep" (Sura 112).

He sensed her move away. Then he heard the door close as she said, "Good night." He exhaled deeply again and began to stroke his chest and belly as he stared into the darkness. Life had a bitter taste. What had become of the enchanting intoxication of alcohol? What was this stifling depression that had taken its place? It resembled nothing so much as the disappointment supplanting his heavenly dreams of love. But if it had not been for his father, the enchantment would have lasted. Kamal feared the man's despotic power more than anything else. He dreaded and loved it at the same time. Why should that be? Al-Sayyid Ahmad was just a man. Except for the geniality other people attributed to him, there was nothing so special about him. Why did Kamal fear him and feel intimidated by this fear? It was all in Kamal's head, like the other fantasies that had afflicted him. But what use was logic in combating emotions?

His hands had pounded on the gate of Abdin Palace during a great demonstration in which people had defiantly challenged the king: "Sa'd or revolution!" Then the king had backed down, but Sa'd Zaghlul had resigned from the cabinet. Faced by his father, though, Kamal was reduced to nothing. The meaning and significance of everything had changed: God, Adam, al-Husayn, love, Aïda herself, immortality.

"Did you say 'immortality'? Yes . . . as it applies to love and to Fahmy, that martyred brother who is annihilation's guest forever. Remember the experiment you attempted when you were twelve in hopes of discovering his unknown fate? What a sad memory! You grabbed a sparrow from its nest and strangled it. Covering it with a shroud, you dug a small grave in the courtyard near the old well and buried the victim. Days or weeks later you dug up the grave and took out the corpse. What did you see and smell? You went weeping to your mother to ask her what became of the dead . . . all the dead and especially Fahmy. The only way she could silence you was by bursting into tears herself. So what's left of Fahmy after seven years? What will remain of love? What else does the revered father have to show us?"

As his eyes grew accustomed to the dark, he could make out the shapes of the desk, the clothes rack, the chair, and the wardrobe. The silence itself receded enough to grant indistinct sounds a hearing. He was troubled by feverish insomnia as the taste of life seemed to grow increasingly bitter. He wondered whether Yasin was sound asleep. How had Zanuba received her husband? Had Husayn retired to his Parisian bed? On which side was Aïda sleeping now? Was her belly round and swollen? What were they doing on the far side of the world where the sun was perched in the center of the sky? What of those luminous planets – were the creatures inhabiting them free of human misery? Could Kamal's faint moan be heard in that infinite orchestra of existence?

"Father! Let me tell you what's on my mind. I'm not angry about what I've learned of your character, because I like the newly discovered side better than the familiar one. I admire your charm, grace, impudence, rowdiness, and adventuresome spirit. That's your gentle side, the one all your acquaintances love. If it shows anything, it reveals your vitality and your enthusiasm for life and people. But I'd like to ask why you choose to show us this frightening and gruff mask? Don't appeal to the principles of child rearing, for you know less about that than anyone. The clearest proof is what you do and don't see of Yasin's conduct and mine. What have you done besides hurt and punish us with an ignorance your good intentions do nothing to excuse? Don't be upset, for I still love and admire you. I'll always feel that way, sincerely. But my soul can't help blaming you for all the pain you've inflicted on me. We've never known you as a friend the way outsiders do. We've known you as a tyrannical dictator, a petulant despot.

"The saying 'An intelligent enemy's better than an ignorant friend' might well have been coined for you. For this reason, I hate ignorance more than any other evil in life. It spoils everything, even the sacred bond of fatherhood. A father with half your ignorance and half your love would be far better for your children. I vow that if I'm ever a father I'll be more a friend to my children than a disciplinarian. All the same, I still love and admire you, even after the godlike qualities my enchanted eyes once associated with you have faded away. Yes, your power lingers on only as a legend. You're not a superior court judge like Salim Bey, rich like Shaddad Bey, a leader like Sa'd Zaghlul, a crafty politician like Tharwat, or a nobleman like Adli, but you're a beloved friend, and that suffices. It's no small accomplishment. If you just wouldn't begrudge us your friendship.

"But you're not the only one whose image has changed. God Himself's no longer the god I used to worship. I'm sifting His essential attributes to rid them of tyranny, despotism, dictatorship, compulsion, and similar human traits. I don't know at what point I ought to limit my thought or whether it's right to limit it at all. In fact, my soul tells me I'll never stop and that debate, no matter how painful, is better than resignation and slumber. This may interest you less than learning that I've decided to limit your tyranny, which envelops me like this all-embracing darkness and torments me like this cursed sleeplessness. I won't drink alcohol again, because it has betrayed me, alas. If alcohol's a deceitful illusion too, then what's left for man? I tell you I've decided to limit your despotism – not by defying you or rebelling, for you're too dear for that – but by fleeing. Yes, I'll surely leave your house as soon as I'm able to support myself. There's plenty of room in the districts of Cairo for all the victims of oppression.

"Do you know what other consequences there were to loving you despite your tyranny? I loved another tyrant who was unfair to me for a long time, both to my face and behind my back. She oppressed me without ever loving me. In spite of all that, I worshipped her from the depths of my heart and still do. You're as responsible for my love and torment as anyone else. I wonder if there's any truth to this idea. I'm not satisfied with it or overly enthusiastic about it. Whatever the reality of love may be, there's no doubt that it's attributable to causes more directly linked to the soul. Let's allow this to ride until we can study it later. In any case, Father, you're the one who made it easy for me to accept oppression through your continual tyranny.

"And you, Mother, don't stare at me with disapproval or ask me what I've done wrong when I've harmed no one. Ignorance is your crime, ignorance . . . ignorance . . . ignorance. My father's the manifestation of ignorant harshness and you of ignorant tenderness. As long as I live, I'll remain the victim of these two opposites. It's your ignorance, too, that filled my spirit with legends. You're my link to the Stone Age. How miserable I am now as I try to liberate myself from your influence. And I'll be just as miserable in the future when I free myself from my father.

"It would have been far better if you had spared me such exhausting effort. For this reason, I propose – with the darkness of this room as my witness – that the family be abolished, for it's nothing but a pit in which brackish water collects, and that fatherhood and motherhood cease. Indeed, grant me a nation with no history and a life without a past. Let's look in the mirror now. What will we see? This enormous nose and huge head. . . . You mercilessly gave me your nose, Father, without consulting me and thus treated me unjustly even before I was born. On your face it has an august majesty, but its shape and size look ludicrous on a narrow one like mine, where it stands out like an English soldier at a gathering of Sufi mystics. Even stranger than that's my head, because it's of a different type than either yours or my mother's. What distant grandfather bequeathed it to me? I'll continue to hold both of you responsible until I learn its true origin.

"Just before we go to sleep we ought to say, 'Farewell,' because we may never wake up. I love life, despite what it's done to me, just as I love you, Father. There are things about life worth loving, and its page is covered with question marks that evoke our wildest affection. But what's useful in life is to no avail in love. And what's most useful in love is still of little importance.

"I probably won't drink again. Say, 'Farewell, alcohol.' But not so fast! Remember the night you left Ayusha's house fully determined never to go near a woman again as long as you lived? Then afterwards you became her favorite customer. It seems to me that all mankind is moaning from hangovers and nausea. So pray they'll have a speedy recovery."

109

AFTER KAMAL left his older brother alone in the carriage, Yasin's zeal dwindled. Although intoxicated, he seemed pensive. It was past 1 A.M., late enough to inspire doubts. If Zanuba was not awake and angrily awaiting him, she would wake when he entered. In either case, the night would not end in an entirely peaceful manner.

He left the carriage at the corner of Palace of Desire Alley and made his way through the profound darkness. Shrugging his shoulders, he whispered to himself, "Yasin's not accountable to any woman." He repeated that statement as he mounted the steps, guiding himself in the darkness by the railing. But this reiteration did not appear totally assured. He opened the door, entered, and made his way to the bedroom by the light from a lamp in the hall. Looking at the bed, he found his wife asleep and shut the bedroom door to keep out the faint light from the hall. He began to undress quietly and cautiously, feeling increasingly confident that she was sound asleep. He sketched a plan in his mind to allow him to slip into bed without making any noise.

"Light the lamp so I can shadow my eyes with the sight of you."

He turned his head toward the bed and smiled with resignation. Finally, with feigned astonishment, he asked, "You're awake? I thought you were asleep and didn't want to disturb you."

"How kind of you! What time is it?"

"Not later than midnight. I left the gathering around eleven and walked straight home."

"Your meeting must have been out of town then, maybe as far as Banha."

"Why? Am I late?"

"Wait a moment till the crowing cock provides your answer."

"Perhaps he hasn't fallen asleep yet."

Stripped to his shirt and underpants, he sat on the sofa to remove his shoes and socks. He saw her shadowy form sit up as the bed creaked. Then he heard her say sharply, "Light the lamp."

"There's no need for that. I've finished undressing."

"I want to settle accounts with you in the light."

"Settling accounts in the dark is more fun."

She snorted angrily and got out of bed. From his nearby seat he put out his arms, grabbed her flank, and pulled her over to the sofa. Sitting her down beside him, he remarked, "Don't make a row."

She escaped from his grip and replied, "What's happened to our agreement? I let you get drunk in bars as often as you want on condition that you return home early. I accepted that against my better judgment, because if you did your drinking at home, you'd save a lot of money that's just wasted. Yet you come home shortly before dawn – in flagrant disregard of our agreement."

"What hope does a man have of fooling a woman who's grown up playing the lute in a troupe of musicians?" Yasin asked himself. "If she can ever prove you've been unfaithful to her, will her response be limited to a quarrel or . . . what? Think it over carefully and don't forget that her loss would not be a laughing matter. I love her best of all my wives. She knows exactly how to help me and takes our marriage seriously. If I just didn't get bored. . . ."

"I was with my usual group and stayed with them until I set out for home. I have a witness you know. Can you guess who he is?" He laughed out loud.

But she answered coldly, "Don't change the topic."

Still laughing, he said, "My companion tonight was my brother Kamal."

Contrary to his expectations, she was not surprised. Her patience exhausted, she asked, "And who's testifying for the girl?"

"Don't be difficult. My innocence is as obvious as the sun." Then he grumbled, "By God, it makes me sad that you're suspicious of my behavior. I've had more than my fill of playing around. All I want now is a quiet life. The bar's simply an innocent pastime. There's nothing objectionable about that. A man has got to see people. . . ."

In a passionate voice she replied, "Shame on you! You know I'm not a child. Putting something over on me is a difficult feat. It would be better for both of us if there were no room for suspicion."

"A sermon or a threat?" Yasin asked himself. "Why can't I have a model life like my father's? The man does what he wants and finds stability, love, and obedience when he returns home. I wasn't able to realize this dream with Zaynab or Maryam, and it seems unlikely I will with Zanuba either. This beautiful lute player must find nothing to regret while she's in my care."

He declared firmly, "If I'd wanted to violate God's laws any further, I wouldn't have married you."

She yelled sharply, "But you'd been married twice before, and marriage didn't prevent you from doing forbidden things then."

He exhaled a puff of breath reeking of alcohol and said, "You're in a different situation from my other wives, dummy. My first wife was chosen by my father, who imposed her on me. My second wouldn't let me touch her unless I married her. So I did. But no one imposed you on me. You didn't lock me out before we got married. Marrying you brought no promise of any novelty I hadn't experienced before. So, dummy, why did I marry you, unless marriage itself – in other words, a settled, stable life – was my goal? By God, if you had a speck of sense, you'd never doubt me."

"Not even when you return at dawn?"

"Not even if I come home in the morning."

She cried out sharply, "Stop! If that's all you have to say, then a most cordial goodbye."

Frowning nervously, he snapped back, "A thousand goodbyes!"

"I'm leaving. God's earth is vast, and God will provide me a living."

With deliberate scorn he commented, "Do what you like."

In a threatening voice she countered, "I'll leave, but you'll find I'm a thorn that's not easily removed."

Still trying to sound scornful, he said, "Nonsense! Ridding myself of you would be like taking off a pair of shoes."

Changing her tune from defiant challenge to complaint, she yelled, "Should I jump out the window so we'll both feel better?"

He shrugged his shoulders. Then, standing up, he said in a lighter tone, "There's a better solution. That's for you to jump in bed. Let's go to sleep and send the devil packing."

He went to the bed and stretched out, sighing as if he'd been wanting to lie down for a long time. She commented to herself, "Anyone living with you is destined to have trouble."

"I'm destined to have trouble too," Yasin complained to himself. "Your sex is responsible. There's not a single one of you who can keep me from wanting others. You're all powerless to conquer boredom. But I won't voluntarily resume a bachelor's life, and

I can't sell a store every year for a new marriage. So let Zanuba stay as long as she doesn't try to control me. A crazy man needs a clever wife . . . clever like Zanuba."

"Are you going to stay on the sofa till morning?"

"I won't close my eyes. Leave me alone and enjoy your sleep."

"Some things are so necessary they're inevitable," he reflected. Stretching out his arms, he took hold of her shoulder. Then he drew her to him as he murmured, "Your bed!"

She resisted a little before yielding. As she climbed in bed she said plaintively, "When will I be granted the peace of mind other women enjoy?"

"Relax. You must have complete confidence in me. I deserve your trust. A man like me isn't happy unless he goes out at night. You won't find any happiness by making me unhappy and giving me a headache. All you need to do is to believe that my evening was spent innocently. Trust me. You won't regret it. I'm not a coward or a liar. Didn't I bring you to this house one night when my wife was here? Would a coward or a liar do that? I've played around enough. You're all I've got left in life."

She sighed audibly as though wishing to say, "If only you were telling the truth. . . ."

He stretched his hand out playfully and remarked, "My goodness! That sigh broke my heart. May God strike me dead."

Responding to the touch of his hand ever so gradually she said prayerfully, "If only our Lord would guide you."

"Who'd believe a lute player would make a wish like that?" Yasin asked himself.

"Don't ever quarrel with me. Quarreling drains our energy."

"The cure is working," he congratulated himself. "But it won't in all situations. If I'd had Ayusha tonight, it wouldn't have been so easy."

"Don't you see that your suspicions were misplaced?"

110

WHEN YASIN entered the store and approached the desk, al-Sayyid Ahmad Abd al-Jawad was absorbed in his work. An examination of his son's face revealed immediately that Yasin had come to ask for help. There was a distracted, glazed look in the eyes of the young man, who smiled politely and leaned down to kiss his father's hand but seemed to perform these ceremonies unconsciously as his mind strayed God only knew where. When al-Sayyid Ahmad gestured for him to have a seat, he moved the chair close to his father's desk before sitting down. He looked at his father, lowered his eyes, and smiled palely. Al-Sayyid Ahmad wondered what had motivated this visit. Concerned about his son's silence, he asked curiously, "Good news? What's come over you? You're not your normal self."

Yasin looked at him for a long time as if appealing for sympathy. Then, lowering his eyes, he said, "They're going to transfer me to the farthest reaches of Upper Egypt."

"The Ministry?"

"Yes."

"Why?"

Shaking his head in protest, Yasin answered, "I asked the head-master, and he mentioned things with no bearing on my work. It's unfair."

The father asked suspiciously, "What things? Explain."

"Vile slander . . . ." After some hesitation he added, "About my wife . . . ."

Al-Sayyid Ahmad's interest was heightened. He asked his son apprehensively, "What did they say?"

Yasin's discomfort was visible in his face as he replied, "Some fools said I'd married . . . a professional entertainer."

Al-Sayyid Ahmad looked around his store anxiously. He saw Jamil al-Hamzawi waiting on customers – a man standing on one side and a woman seated on the other. They were only a few feet away. Suppressing his rage, the father responded in a low voice not without a tremor of anger, "Perhaps they are fools, but I warned you about this. You do anything you want, never considering how scandalous it is, but then the consequences always catch up with you. What can I say? You're a school official, and your reputation ought to be beyond reproach. I've told you this time and again. There's no power or might save God's. It seems I must neglect all my other responsibilities in the world to care for you."

With apparent bewilderment Yasin observed, "But she's my legal wife. How can a man be blamed for obeying religious law? And why is it the Ministry's business?"

Restraining his fury, al-Sayyid Ahmad replied, "The Ministry must be solicitous of the reputations of its employees."

"Shouldn't you leave talk about reputations to someone else?" Yasin asked silently.

"But this is an unfair and unjust way to treat a married man."

Waving his hand angrily, the father retorted, "Do you want me to set the policies for the Ministry of Education?"

Yasin entreated him dejectedly, "Certainly not, but I hope you'll be able to stop the transfer by using your influence."

Preoccupied by his own thoughts, al-Sayyid Ahmad began to twist his mustache as he stared blankly at Yasin, who tried to gain his father's sympathy and apologized for upsetting him. Yasin asserted that, except for God, he relied exclusively on his father. He did not leave the store until his father promised to try to block the transfer.

That same evening al-Sayyid Ahmad went to al-Guindy's coffeehouse in Opera Square to see Yasin's headmaster, who immediately invited al-Sayyid Ahmad to join him and said, "I was expecting you. Yasin's gone too far. I regret the trouble he gives you."

Taking a seat opposite the headmaster, on a balcony overlooking the square, al-Sayyid Ahmad said, "In any case, Yasin's as much your son as mine."

"Of course, but this matter's out of my hands altogether. It's between him and the Ministry."

Although there was a smile on his face, al-Sayyid Ahmad protested, "Isn't it a bit odd to punish a civil servant for marrying a musician? Isn't that a private matter? And marriage is a legal bond. No one should denigrate it."

The headmaster frowned thoughtfully but inquisitively, as though not understanding his friend's words. Then he said, "The only mention of the marriage has been incidental and at the last minute. Don't you know the whole story? I thought you knew everything."

The man's spirits sank. He asked anxiously, "Is there some other offense?"

The headmaster leaned toward him a little and said sorrowfully, "The problem is, al-Sayyid Ahmad, that Yasin had a fight in Massage Alley with a whore. A police report was filed, and a copy reached the Ministry."

The man was stunned. His pupils opened wide, and his face became pale. The headmaster shook his head sadly and commented, "That's the truth. I did my utmost to lighten the punishment and successfully scuttled the idea of handing him over to a disciplinary panel. They agreed to transfer him to Upper Egypt."

Al-Sayyid Ahmad sighed and muttered, "The dog!"

Gazing at him sympathetically, the headmaster said, "I'm very sorry, al-Sayyid Ahmad. But this kind of conduct is not appropriate for a civil servant. I don't deny that he's a fine young man and diligent in his work. In fact, I'll tell you frankly that I like him, not merely because he's your son but because of his personality. Yet people say the strangest things about him. . . . He's got to reform and change his ways or he'll destroy his future."

Al-Sayyid Ahmad was silent for a long time, his anger obvious from his face. Then, as though addressing himself, he exclaimed, "A fight with a whore! Let him go to hell, then."

But he did not abandon his son. Without delay he met with acquaintances who were in parliament or distinguished in other ways and asked them to intercede to stop the transfer. Muhammad Iffat was his chief assistant in this campaign. A barrage of mediating efforts was aimed at top men in the Ministry of Education. Eventually it succeeded and the transfer was rescinded. But the Ministry insisted on assigning Yasin to a job within its secretariat. Then the head of the Ministry's records office – the new husband of Yasin's first wife – announced his readiness to accept Yasin in his department, on the recommendation of his father-in-law, Muhammad Iffat, and that was agreed to. Thus early in the winter of 1926 Yasin was transferred to the records department, but he did not emerge from the scandal scot-free. An entry was made in his file that he was unfit to work in a school, and he was passed over for promotion to the seventh grade in the civil service, although he had more than ten years' service in the eighth rank immediately below it.

By arranging this assignment to his son-in-law's department, Muhammad Iffat had meant to ensure that Yasin was well treated, but the young man was uncomfortable with working for Zaynab's husband. One day he told Kamal, "She's probably delighted by what's happened and thinks it justifies her father's refusal to return her to me. I know how women think. No doubt she's rejoicing over my misfortune. It's too bad that the only decent position I could find was working for this goat. He's so old he has nothing to offer a woman. It's absurd to think he could fill the void I left. So let the stupid woman gloat. I'm rejoicing at her loss too."

Zanuba never learned the secret behind the transfer. The most she could find out was that her husband had been assigned to a better position in the Ministry. Similarly al-Sayyid Ahmad skirted the real scandal in his discussions with Yasin. When the original transfer was rescinded, the father refrained from saying anything more than "The ending won't always be so happy. You've made a lot of trouble for me and embarrassed me. From now on I won't intervene in your affairs. Do what you like, and may our Lord protect me from you."

Al-Sayyid Ahmad could not stop thinking about Yasin. One day he summoned his son to the store and remarked, "It's time you thought seriously about your life and returned to honorable ways. Free yourself from the life of an outcast you're currently enjoying. There's still plenty of time for us to start all over. I can prepare a suitable life for you. So listen and obey me." Then he presented his proposals to Yasin: "Divorce your wife and return home. I'll marry you off again in a suitable fashion, so you can begin an honorable life."

Yasin blushed and said in a faint voice, "I appreciate your sincere desire to improve my life. I'll do my part to try to reform without troubling anyone else."

His father yelled angrily, "A new promise as meaningless as those of the English! It's plain that you won't be satisfied till you end up in prison. Yes, the next time you scream for help it will be from behind bars. I keep telling you to divorce that woman and return home."

Yasin sighed loudly to make sure his father heard and responded, "She's pregnant, Father. I don't want to add another sin to my list of offenses."

"God preserve us!" al-Sayyid Ahmad exclaimed to himself. "Your new grandchild is being formed in Zanuba's belly. Could you possibly have imagined all the problems this young man had in store for you the moment you received him as an infant – on a day you thought one of the happiest of your life?"

"Pregnant?"

"Yes."

"And you're afraid of adding another sin to your list?" Then before his son could answer he exploded, "Why didn't your conscience trouble you when you were mistreating good women from fine families? By the truth of God's Book, you're a curse."

When Yasin left the store, his father looked after him with eyes filled with pity and scorn. He could not help taking some pride in the young man's appearance, inherited from him, but not in Yasin's character, inherited from the mother. He suddenly remembered how once he had almost fallen into this abyss, courtesy of the same Zanuba. But he also recalled restraining himself just in time. Had it really been self-restraint? He felt vexed and anxious. He cursed Yasin and then cursed Yasin again.

111

WHEN THE twentieth of December arrived, he sensed the day was unlike any other, at least for him. On this date he had entered the world and that fact was recorded on his birth certificate, so that no one would be able to fib about it. Clad in an overcoat, he was pacing back and forth in his room. Glancing at his desk, he saw his diary, which was open to a blank page with the date of his birth at the top. He was thinking about what to write for his birthday. He kept moving to stay warm in the biting cold. As he could see through the windowpane, the sky was concealed behind gloomy clouds. The intermittent rain made him pensive and dreamy.

A birthday had to be celebrated, even if the birthday boy was the only one at the party. The old house had no tradition of commemorating birthdays. His mother herself did not know this was a day she should not forget. Of the births of her children all she retained were vague memories of the seasons when they had occurred and of the pain accompanying them. The most she could say of his birth was: "It was in winter and the delivery was difficult. My labor pains and screams lasted two days."

Formerly, when he had thought of his birth, his heart had been filled with pity for his mother. When he had witnessed Na'ima's birth, these feelings had intensified, as his heart pounded painfully with sympathy for Aisha. Today he thought of his birth in a new way, for his mind had drunk so avidly from the fountains of materialist philosophy that in two months he had grasped ideas mankind had taken a century to develop. He wondered about his delivery and whether part or all of its difficulty was attributable to neglect or ignorance. He asked this as though interrogating a suspect who stood before him. He thought about difficult deliveries, the damage they might cause the brain or nervous system, and the profound effect such injuries could have on the life, destiny, and happiness of the newborn. Might not his exaggerated interest in love be the result of shocks to the top or side of his large head in the hidden reaches of the womb nineteen years before? Why not consider his idealism – which had misled him for so long with ignorant fantasies and induced him to shed countless tears on torment's bloody altar – a sad consequence of the clumsiness of an ignorant midwife?

He thought about the prenatal period, including the time before conception, the uncharted territory from which life sprang, the mechanical and chemical equation to which a living creature could be reduced, the scornful rejection this creature accorded his actual origin from the start as he claimed descent from the stars at which he gazed. Kamal had learned that his origin was not nearly so remote. It was something called sperm. Nineteen years and nine months before, he had been nothing but a drop of sperm ejected because of an innocent desire for pleasure, a pressing need for solace, a bout of excitement inspired by an intoxication extinguishing common sense, or even a feeling of obligation toward a wife who was confined to the house. To which of these did he owe his conception? Perhaps duty had caused him to come into the world, for he was haunted by a concern for doing his duty. He had not allowed himself certain pleasures until they presented themselves as a philosophy he ought to follow and a view he should adopt. Even then, he had engaged in a painful struggle with himself first. His approach to life was hardly one of carefree abandon.

Sperm penetrated a living creature, found the ovum in the Fallopian tube, and fertilized it. Then they slid together into the womb, where they changed into a fetus, which developed flesh and bones. This creature then emerged into the light, causing pain it could not appreciate. It started crying even before its features could be seen clearly. The development of its instincts gave rise in time to so many beliefs and ideas that it was crammed with them. It fell in love and as a result claimed to partake of the divine. Then it was badly shaken, its beliefs were destroyed, and its thoughts were turned upside down. Its heart was broken, and it was reduced to a humbler status than its initial one.

In this manner nineteen years had passed . . . what a long period! Youth fled with the speed of lightning. What consolation was left, besides enjoying life hour by hour and even minute by minute until a crow's call heralded the end?

The age of innocence was over. He had reached a stage of life in which he dated things by love: B.L. and A.L. Today he was conscious of many desires, but the identity of his beloved was unknown. The closest he could come to identifying his beloved was through attribution to it of some divine names, like truth, the joy of life, and the light of knowledge. It seemed his journey would be long. His lover appeared to have boarded the train of Auguste Comte and passed by the station of theology, where the password was "Yes, Mother." This train was now traversing the realm of metaphysics, where the password was "Certainly not, Mother." In the distance, visible through a telescope, was the mountain of reality on which was inscribed its password: "Open your eyes and be courageous."

He stopped in front of the desk and fixed his eyes on the diary, wondering whether to sit down and allow his pen to record whatever it chose for his birthday or to postpone that until his ideas had crystallized. Hearing the drone of falling rain, he glanced at the panes of the window overlooking Palace Walk. He noticed pearly drops clinging to the surface of the glass, which was misty from the humidity in the air. A pearl soon slid to the bottom, tracing on the surface a bright line with a curving path like a shooting star's.

Kamal went to the window and looked up at the raindrops pouring from the heavy clouds. The heavens were united with the earth by these glittering threads. The minarets and domes of the district seemed oblivious to the rain, and the horizon behind them resembled a silver frame. The entire scene was washed with a white blended with the brown of teak, a combination suitable for exalted dreams. The cries of children rose from the street. Kamal glanced down and saw the earth streaming with water and mud. Carts were moving with difficulty, their wheels spattering everything in reach. The shops had withdrawn their outdoor displays, and pedestrians sought refuge in shops and coffeehouses or under balconies.

This view of the sky struck a responsive chord in Kamal's mind. What could be more appropriate than drawing inspiration from it as he contemplated his situation at the beginning of another year of his life? Since Husayn Shaddad had left his homeland, Kamal no longer had a companion with whom he could discuss his spiritual secrets. He had to mull them over by himself if he felt a need for discussion. Since his soul mate had left him, Kamal had been forced to make his own soul his companion.

He asked his spirit, "Do you believe in the existence of God?"

When his spirit's turn came, it asked, "Why don't you jump from star to star and planet to planet as you do from one step to another on the stairs?"

It also inquired about the chosen elite among the self-proclaimed descendants of the heavens who had elevated the earth to a central place in existence, making even the angels bow down to Adam's clay. Then their brother Copernicus had returned earth to the status originally granted it by existence as nothing more than the sun's small servant. He was followed by his brother Darwin, who exposed the secrets of man, this bogus prince, announcing for all to hear that man's true ancestor was the ape held captive in a cage in the zoo, where man invited his friends to gawk at it during holiday excursions.

"In the beginning, the universe was one large nebula. Then stars spread out from this center as if spattered into space by the rotating wheel of a bicycle. Through the eternal interplay of gravitational fields, these stars gave birth to planets. The earth itself was flung out like a molten ball trailed by the moon, which teased the earth by frowning at it with one side of its face and smiling with the other. When the earth's fire cooled, its features assumed their permanent shape as mountains, plateaus, plains, and rock formations. Then life crept forth. Crawling on all fours, earth's son arrived, questioning anyone he encountered about high ideals.

"I won't hide my impatience with legends. In the immense raging wave, I discovered a three-sided rock, which from now on I'll call the rock of knowledge, philosophy, and idealism. Don't say that philosophy, like religion, has a mythical character. It rests on solid, scientific foundations and advances systematically toward its objectives. Art is an elevated form of entertainment and enhances life, but my aspirations stretch beyond art. What I want is to draw inspiration only from the truth. Compared with truth, art seems an effeminate pursuit. To attain my goal, you'll find I'm prepared to sacrifice everything except life itself. My qualifications for this important role include a large head, an enormous nose, disappointment in love, and expectations of ill health. Be careful not to mock youthful dreams, for that's a symptom of senility. People affected by this disease term their sarcasm 'wisdom.' There's nothing to prevent a sensible person from admiring Sa'd Zaghlul as much as Copernicus, the chemist Ostwald, or the physicist Mach; for an effort to link Egypt with the advance of human progress is noble and humane. Patriotism's a virtue, if it's not tainted by xenophobia. Of course, hating England is a form of self-defense. That kind of nationalism is nothing more than a local manifestation of a concern for human rights.

"You ask if I believe in love. My response is that love is still in my heart. I must acknowledge this truth of human nature. Although the roots of love were tangled up with those of religion and of other legends, the collapse of the sacred temples did not shake the pillars of love or diminish its importance. Its status remained unchanged even when its ceremonial niche was invaded by study and analysis. Examination of its biological, psychological, and sociological components has not harmed it. None of these investigations can make the heart pound any less fiercely when a special memory or image comes to mind."

"Do you still believe in love's immortality?"

"Immortality's just a myth. Presumably love will be forgotten, like everything else in the world."

"A year has passed since Aïda's wedding; why do you still hesitate to pronounce her name?"

"I've made some progress on the path to forgetfulness. I've traversed stretches of insanity, stupor, intense pain, and then less frequent discomfort. Now a whole day may pass without my thinking of her, except when I wake up or go to bed, and then once or twice during the day. When I remember her, that affects me in different ways. A mild longing is revived, a sorrow flees by like a cloud, or a regret stings but doesn't burn me. At times my soul will suddenly erupt like a volcano, as the earth turns under my feet. In any case, I've come to believe that I'll continue my life, even without Aïda."

"What do you rely on in your search for forgetfulness?"

"I depend on the study and analysis of love, as previously mentioned, and on minimizing my individual pains through speculations that embrace all of existence so that by comparison man's world seems a trivial speck. I also refresh my soul with alcohol and sex. I seek consolation with philosophers who specialize in it – like Spinoza, who thinks that time is unreal, that passions linked to an event in the past or future make no sense, and that we're capable of overcoming them, if we can form a clear and distinct idea of them."

"Did it make you happy to discover love can be forgotten?"

"It did, because that promised me release from captivity, but the experience also saddened me by introducing me to death prematurely. In no matter what context, I'll despise bondage and love absolute freedom as long as I live."

"It's a happy person who has never thought of suicide or longed for death. It's a happy person who has the torch of enthusiasm blazing in his heart. A person's immortal when working or preparing seriously for work. A person's truly alive when he responds to Umar al-Khayyam's invitation to take up a book, a drink, and a sweetheart. A soul full of fervent hopes forgets or is oblivious to marriage in the same way that a glass full of whiskey has no room for soda water. What more can you want if your infatuation with drink continues happily and your encounters with women are not blocked by disgust or aversion. If you long occasionally for purity and asceticism, that could be a holdover from your previous piety."

The rain kept pouring down. Thunder roared, and there was a gleam of lightning. The street was deserted and all its cries silenced. Wishing to look at the courtyard, he left the bedroom and went to the window of the sitting room. Gazing out the peephole, he saw that water was washing away the loose dirt on the surface, eroding it, and then rushing off toward the old well. Water was also flowing out of the well on the other side and flooding a depression between the oven room and the storeroom. In that declivity, where a residue of wheat, barley, and fenugreek seed, accidentally dropped by Umm Hanafi, had collected, a growth like green silk brocade would sprout. For some days it would thrive, until trampled by their feet. In his childhood, that area had served as the setting for his maneuvers and his dreams. That wellspring of memories still supplied his heart with a yearning and a delight shaded by sorrow like a diaphanous cloud veiling the face of the moon.

Turning away from the window to go back to his room, he became aware of the presence of other people in the sitting room. They were the last remnants of the old coffee hour. His mother sat on the sofa with her legs tucked beneath her and her arms spread over the brazier. She had no one to keep her company save Umm

Hanafi, who sat cross-legged on a sheepskin opposite her mistress. He thought of the gathering in its brightest days and of the beautiful memories it had left behind. The brazier was the only survivor not to have undergone changes the viewer wished to reject.

112

AHMAD ABD AL-JAWAD walked slowly along the bank of the Nile on his way to Muhammad Iffat's houseboat. The night was calm, the sky clear, the stars twinkling, and the weather cool. When he reached the gangplank and started across it, he glanced from force of habit at the distant houseboat he had once called Zanuba's. A year had passed since those painful events, and all that was left of them in his heart was resentful embarrassment. One other consequence had been his boycott of parties comparable to his previous ban following Fahmy's death. He had avoided them scrupulously for a year, before becoming exasperated. After a change of heart, he was now seeking out the forbidden bacchanal.

The next moment he was joining the beloved gathering and seeing his three male friends and the two women. The men he had seen as recently as the previous night, but he had not set eyes on the women for about a year and a half – or, to be precise, not since the night Zanuba had been introduced to his life. The party had yet to begin, for the liquor bottles were full and decorum was still being observed. Jalila, who occupied the main sofa, was toying with her gold bracelets as if wanting to make them jingle. Zubayda, who stood beneath the hanging lamp, was examining her appearance in a small mirror she held in her hand. Her back was to the table crowded with whiskey bottles and plates of appetizers.

Bareheaded, the three men, who had removed their cloaks, were scattered around the room. Ahmad Abd al-Jawad shook hands with them and then warmly clasped the hands of the women.

Jalila greeted him, "Welcome, dear brother."

Zubayda cast him a censorious smile as she said, "Welcome to a person who would deserve nothing but goodbye from us, except for common courtesy."

The man removed his cloak and fez and looked around for a vacant place. Zubayda had taken a seat next to Jalila. He hesitated a little before going to their sofa and sitting there. His vacillation did not escape the eyes of Ali Abd al-Rahim, who said, "You almost seem a novice at this."

Jalila tried to encourage al-Sayyid Ahmad by telling Ali Abd al-Rahim, "Leave him alone. There's never been any reserve between us."

Zubayda was quick to laugh and say scornfully, "I'm the one with the most right to say that. Isn't he my in-law?"

Al-Sayyid Ahmad understood her allusion and wondered anxiously how much she knew of the whole affair. But he replied tenderly, "It's my honor, sultana."

Gazing at him suspiciously, Zubayda asked, "Are you really pleased with what's happened?"

He answered suavely, "Only because you're her aunt."

Waving her hand in disapproval, she said, "My heart will never forgive her."

Before al-Sayyid Ahmad could ask why, Ali Abd al-Rahim, who was rubbing his hands together, yelled, "Save the conversation till we've filled our heads." After rising and going to the table, he opened a bottle and poured drinks, which he presented to them, one at a time, with a solicitude that revealed his customary satisfaction with tending bar. Then he waited until everyone was ready before saying, "To the health of our lovers, our brothers, and music. May we never lack these three things."

Smiling, they raised their glasses to their lips. Ahmad Abd al-Jawad looked over the rim of his at the faces of his companions, these friends with whom he had shared affection and loyalty for almost forty years. They almost seemed slivers of his heart. He could not keep his feelings of sincere fraternal affection from agitating his breast. As his eyes turned to Zubayda, he resumed his conversation with her, asking, "Why won't your heart forgive her?"

She cast him a glance that made him feel she welcomed this chance to talk and replied, "Because she's a traitor with no respect for promises. She betrayed me more than a year ago. She left my house without asking permission and disappeared."

Was it possible she really did not know where Zanuba had been during that time? Since he did not care to offer the least comment on her words, she finally asked him, "Didn't you hear about that?"

"I did eventually."

"I've taken care of her since she was a child and have looked after her as though I were her mother. See how I've been rewarded! To hell with her genes!"

Pretending to object, Ali Abd al-Rahim teased her, "Don't insult her family. You're part of it."

But Zubayda replied seriously, "She doesn't have any of my genes."

Al-Sayyid Ahmad inquired, "Who do you suppose her father was?"

"Her father!" This comment emerged from Ibrahim al-Far in a tone that suggested a string of sarcastic remarks was to follow, but Muhammad Iffat headed him off by interjecting, "Remember you're talking about Yasin's wife."

The mirthful look left al-Far's face, and he retreated into an uneasy silence. Then Zubayda spoke up again: "I'm not joking about her. She envied me for a long time. Even when she was in my custody she wanted to rival me. I spoiled her and pretended not to see her defects." Then she laughed and continued: "She wanted to be a soloist, a vocalist." Looking around at her friends, she observed sarcastically, "But she failed and got married."

Ali Abd al-Rahim asked incredulously, "In your opinion, does marriage constitute failure?"

She squinted an eye at him and raised the eyebrow of the other one and then answered, "Yes, fellow. A performer never leaves her troupe unless she's a failure."

Then Jalila sang, "You're the wine, my love. You've cheered us up."

Al-Sayyid Ahmad grinned broadly and greeted the song with a gentle sigh that revealed his delight. But Ali Abd al-Rahim rose once more, saying, "A moment of silence until we finish off this round." He filled the glasses again, redistributed them, and returned to his seat with his own drink.

Grasping his glass, al-Sayyid Ahmad glanced at Zubayda, who turned toward him and smilingly raised her drink as if to say, "To your health." He imitated her and they both drank at the same time. She was gazing at him with a merry look. A year had passed since he had felt like looking for a woman. The harsh experience he had endured seemed to have deadened his enthusiasm, but pride or ill health could also have been responsible. Even so, the combined influence of alcoholic intoxication and this affectionate look stirred his heart. He savored the sweetness of this welcome, which followed a bitter rejection. He considered this a friendly greeting from the entire sex he had been so fond of all his life. It bound up his wounded dignity, which had fallen victim to betrayal and age. Zubayda's eloquent smile seemed to say, "Your day's not finished yet." He kept looking and smiling at her.

Muhammad Iffat brought the lute and placed it between the two women. Jalila picked it up and began to play. Once she was confident of their attention, she sang, "Beloved, I promise you . . ."

As usual when he heard Jalila or Zubayda sing, Ahmad Abd al-Jawad pretended to be moved by the music. He nodded his head appreciatively, as if wishing to induce ecstasy by acting it out. The truth was that all he had left from the world of song was a set of memories. The great performers he had admired, like al-Hamuli, Uthman, al-Manilawi, and Abd al-Hayy, had passed away – just as his youthful era of conquests had vanished. He would have to accustom himself to taking pleasure in what was at hand and in triggering a feeling of ecstasy by going through the motions. His love of song and infatuation with music had led him to visit the theater of Munira al-Mahdiya, but he had not liked the combination of theater and music. Besides, he chafed at sitting in a theater like a school auditorium. At Muhammad Iffat's house he had also listened to records of the new singer Umm Kalthoum but only with a cautious and suspicious ear. He did not enjoy her singing, even though it was said that Sa'd Zaghlul had praised the beauty of her voice.

Yet his appearance gave no hint of his feelings as he gazed at Jalila with happy delight and sang the words of the refrain, "I hold you responsible," with the others in his pleasing voice.

Then al-Far cried out with regret, "Where, oh where is the tambourine? Where is it so we can hear the son of Abd al-Jawad?"

"Ask rather: Where's the Ahmad Abd al-Jawad who used to play the tambourine?" he said to himself. "Oh . . . why has time changed us?"

Jalila ended her song in an atmosphere of receptive approval. But with a grateful smile she said apologetically, "I'm tired."

Zubayda heaped her with praise. The two performers frequently complimented each other either from politeness or from a desire to keep the peace. Everyone realized that as a performer Jalila's star was rapidly setting. One of the most recent indications of that was the desertion of her tambourine player, Fino, to another troupe. This eclipse was only natural, given the withering away of all the qualities on which her past glory had rested: her charm, beauty, and voice. For that reason, Zubayda no longer felt particularly envious of her and was capable of flattering her former rival good-humoredly, especially since Zubayda had reached the pinnacle of her career, one that could only be followed by a decline.

The friends often wondered whether Jalila had prepared properly for this dangerous stage of her life. It was Ahmad Abd al-Jawad's opinion that she had not. He accused some of her lovers of squandering much of her fortune but at the same time proclaimed that she was a woman who knew how to get money one way or another. Ali Abd al-Rahim supported him, saying, "She profits from the beauty of the women in her troupe, and ever so gradually her home's turning into a different kind of house."

Their consensus was less sanguine about Zubayda's future, for despite the freedom with which she helped herself to her lovers' wealth, she spent liberally and was fond of the showy possessions that dissipate money quickly. Moreover, she was addicted to alcohol and narcotics, cocaine in particular.

Muhammad Iffat told Zubayda, "Allow me to express my admiration for the sweet looks you are directing to one of us."

Jalila laughed and said softly, "His infatuation's revealed by his eyes. . . ."

Ibrahim al-Far asked with sham disapproval, "Do you think you're in a charitable institution for the blind?"

With feigned regret Ahmad Abd al-Jawad replied, "If you continue to speak so bluntly, you'll never fulfill your ambition to be pimps."

Zubayda told Muhammad Iffat, "The only reason I'm looking at him, God forgive me, is out of envy at his youth. Look at his black head of hair among your white ones and tell me if you'd think he's a day over forty?"

"I'd give him about a century more."

Ahmad Abd al-Jawad retorted, "From your surplus years."

Jalila sang the opening of the song "The envious eye has a log in it, sweetheart."

Zubayda commented, "He doesn't need to fear my envy, for my eye would never harm him."

Shaking his head suggestively, Muhammad Iffat replied, "Your eyes are the cause of all the trouble."

Ahmad Abd al-Jawad told Zubayda, "Why are you talking about my youth? Haven't you heard what the doctor said?"

As though she could not believe it, she said, "Muhammad Iffat told me, but what's this pressure you're supposed to have?"

"He wrapped a strange sack around my arm and began to pump it up. Then he told me, 'You've got pressure.'"

"Where did this pressure come from?"

Al-Sayyid Ahmad laughingly answered, "I imagine that pump induced it."

Clapping his hands together, Ibrahim al-Far said, "Perhaps it's a contagious disease, because within a month of our friend's attack each of us had a doctor's examination too, and the diagnosis in each case was the same: pressure."

Ali Abd al-Rahim observed, "I'll tell you the secret behind it. This is one of the side effects of the revolution. The proof is that no one ever heard of it before then."

Jalila asked al-Sayyid Ahmad, "What are the symptoms of this pressure?"

"A bitch of a headache and difficulty breathing when I walk."

Smiling somewhat anxiously, Zubayda murmured, "Who doesn't have those symptoms, if only occasionally? Do you think I've got pressure too?"

Ahmad Abd al-Jawad asked, "Above or below your waist?"

They all laughed, including Zubayda herself, and then Jalila said, "Since you're experienced with pressure, why don't you examine her. Perhaps you can discover what ails her."

Ahmad Abd al-Jawad replied, "If she'll bring the sack, I'll supply the pump."

They laughed again. Then Muhammad Iffat protested, "Pressure, pressure, pressure . . . all we ever hear nowadays is the doctor giving us orders as though we were his slaves: Don't drink alcoholic beverages. Don't eat red meat. Beware of eggs."

Ahmad Abd al-Jawad asked scornfully, "What's a man like me to do? I eat only red meat and eggs and drink nothing but alcohol."

Zubayda replied immediately, "Eat and drink in good health. A man should be his own physician, letting our Lord have the last word."

During the time he had been forced to stay in bed he had followed his doctor's orders. When he had been able to get around again, he had forgotten this medical advice completely.

Jalila spoke up again: "I don't believe in doctors, but I'll admit they have an excuse for what they say and do. They make their living from illnesses just as we performers make our living from joyous occasions like weddings. They couldn't get by without their sack, pump, orders, and prohibitions any more than we could survive without the tambourine, lute, and songs."

With enthusiastic relief, al-Sayyid Ahmad said, "You're right. Illness and health, like life and death, arise solely from God's command. Anyone who trusts in God will have no cause for sorrow."

Laughing, Ibrahim al-Far said, "Feast your eyes on this man, folks. He drinks with his mouth, lusts with his eye, and preaches with his tongue."

Between guffaws, Ahmad Abd al-Jawad retorted, "There's nothing wrong with that, so long as I do my preaching in a brothel."

Examining Ahmad Abd al-Jawad and shaking his head with wonder, Muhammad Iffat commented, "I wish Kamal were here to profit from your sermon along with us."

Ali Abd al-Rahim asked, "By the way, is he still of the opinion that man's descended from an ape?"

Striking her hand against her breast, Jalila exclaimed, "How dreadful!"

"An ape?" Zubayda asked with astonishment. Then, as though reconsidering, she said, "Perhaps he was referring to his father, not a forefather."

Al-Sayyid Ahmad cautioned her, "He also showed that women are descended from a lioness."

Bursting into laughter, she replied, "I'd certainly like to see the child of a monkey and a lioness."

Ibrahim al-Far commented, "When Kamal grows up and leaves his family circle he'll observe that normal people are descended from Adam and Eve."

Ahmad Abd al-Jawad shot back, "Or I'll bring him here one day. That will convince him man's descended from dogs."

Ali Abd al-Rahim went back to the table to fill their glasses again and asked Zubayda, "Since you know al-Sayyid Ahmad more intimately than any of us, can you say which animal family you'd place him in?"

She reflected a little as she watched Ali Abd al-Rahim's hands pour the whiskey. Then, with a smile, she replied, "The ass!"

Jalila asked, "Is this a compliment or an insult?"

Ahmad Abd al-Jawad answered, "Only her belly knows for sure."

They drank some more in the best of humors. Zubayda picked up the lute and sang, "Let down the curtain around us."

The body of Ahmad Abd al-Jawad began to sway to the music in an overwhelming intoxication. He raised his glass, which was empty except for a film of whiskey at the bottom, and looked through that at the woman, as though wishing to observe her with a golden spyglass. Whatever private resentment there might have been between them had vanished. It was clear that the bond between Ahmad and Zubayda had been reestablished. They all sang the chorus with Zubayda, Ahmad's voice growing loud with delight and ecstasy. The song concluded to their jubilant applause.

Muhammad Iffat immediately asked Jalila, "Speaking of the song 'His passion's revealed by his eyes,' what do you think of Umm Kalthoum?"

Jalila answered, "Her voice, with God as my witness, is beautiful, but all too often she's as shrill as a child."

"Some people say she'll be the next Munira al-Mahdiya. Others say her voice is even more marvelous than Munira's."

Jalila cried out, "Nonsense! How does this shrillness compare with Munira's magnificently husky voice?"

Zubayda remarked disdainfully, "There's something about her voice that reminds one of a Qur'an reciter – as though she was an entertainer in a shaykh's turban."

Ahmad Abd al-Jawad said, "I don't care for her, but a lot of people are wild about her. The truth is that the vocal era ended with the death of Abduh al-Hamuli."

Muhammad Iffat teased his friend, "You're a reactionary. You always try to cling to the past." Winking, he continued: "Don't you insist on ruling your home by fiat and force, even in the age of democracy and parliament?"

Al-Sayyid Ahmad replied scornfully, "Democracy's for the people, not the family."

Ali Abd al-Rahim said seriously, "Do you think you can rule the young people of today in the old-fashioned way? These youngsters are used to demonstrating in the streets and confronting the soldiers."

Ibrahim al-Far said, "I don't know what you're talking about, but I agree with Ahmad. We each have sons – God help us."

Muhammad Iffat said playfully, "Both of you are strong advocates of democracy, but you're tyrants at home."

Ahmad Abd al-Jawad protested, "Do you really want me to assemble Kamal, his mother, and Yasin to let them vote before I deal with a problem?"

Zubayda burst into laughter. She reminded him, "Please don't forget Zanuba!"

Ibrahim al-Far said, "If the revolution's the cause for the problems our children are causing us, may God forgive Sa'd Zaghlul."

The drinking, chatting, singing, and joking continued. The din became louder, and their voices blended together. The night advanced, oblivious to the world. He would look at her and find her watching him, or she would be the one to glance at him and catch him watching her. He told himself, "In this world there's only one true pleasure." He wanted to express this thought but did not, either because his enthusiasm for sharing it weakened or because he did not feel he could say it. But why should he feel weak?

Once again he asked himself whether this was to be an hour's enjoyment or a long affair. His soul pined for entertainment and consolation, but there was a ringing in his ears, as though the waves of the Nile were whispering to him. He was almost halfway through his sixth decade. "Ask scholars how a lifetime can pass like this. We know it's happening, but at the same time we don't."

"What's silenced you? May God spare us evil."

"Me? A little rest . . ."

"Yes, how sweet it is to rest," he told himself. "A long sleep from which you'll rise in good health. How delightful it is to be healthy. . . . But they're always after you, not leaving you a single moment to enjoy peace. This look is fascinating, but the whispering of the waves is growing louder. How can you hear the singing?"

"Certainly not. We won't leave until we give him a proper wedding procession. What do you think? A procession . . . a procession!"

"Rise, my camel."

"Me? A little rest."

"The procession . . . the procession, like the first time at the house in al–Ghuriya."

"That was long ago."

"We'll revive it. The procession . . . the procession."

"They're merciless. That time's vanished. It's hidden by dark shadows. How thick the darkness is! How my ears are ringing! What an overpowering forgetfulness!"

"Look!"

"What's wrong with him?"

"A little water. Open the window."

"O Gracious One, O Lord . . ."

"It's all right . . . all right. Wet this handkerchief in cold water."

113

DURING THE week after the father's "accident," he was visited every day by the doctor, but his condition was critical enough that no one else was allowed to call on him. Even his children had to tiptoe into the room for a glimpse of his sleeping face. They would carefully note his look of resigned exhaustion before retreating with gloomy expressions and sinking hearts. They glanced with interest at one another but shrank from the sad reinforcement this exchange provided.

The physician said the seizure was a result of high blood pressure. He cupped the patient, filling a basin with blood, which Khadija, trembling all over, described as black. Amina emerged from the room now and again, looking like an aimless phantom. Kamal seemed to be in a daze, as though asking himself how such earth-shaking events could occur in the twinkling of an eye and how this colossus of a man could have succumbed. Whenever he stole a look at his mother's ghostly form, Khadija's tearful eyes, or Aisha's pale face, he wondered again what all this meant. He found himself unconsciously led to imagine the end his heart dreaded. He pictured a world without his father, and this vision chilled his breast and alarmed his heart. He asked himself apprehensively how his mother could possibly survive. She already appeared as good as dead, and nothing had happened yet. Then he thought of Fahmy and wondered whether their father would be forgotten as easily as their late brother. The world seemed lost in gloom.

Yasin learned of the incident the day after it occurred and came to the house for the first time since he had left to marry Maryam. He went directly to his father's room and silently looked at al-Sayyid Ahmad for a long time. Then he retreated to the sitting room in a state of shock. He found Amina there, and they shook hands after their long separation. He was deeply touched, and his eyes filled with tears as he held her hand.

Al-Sayyid Ahmad remained in bed. At first he could not speak or move. The cupping put some life into him, and he was then able to get out a word or a brief phrase to make his wishes known. But at that time, he became conscious of his pain, which he expressed in assorted moans and groans. Once the intensity of his physical pain diminished, he became restless with this compulsory bed rest, which deprived him of the blessings of motion and cleanliness. He was obliged to eat, drink, and do things that disgusted him all in one place – his bed. His sleep was interrupted, but his annoyance was continual. The first thing he wanted to know was how he had been conveyed to the house when unconscious.

Amina replied that his friends – Muhammad Iffat, Ali Abd al-Rahim, and Ibrahim al-Far – had brought him home in a carriage and had gently taken him up to bed. Then they had found a doctor for him, even though it was very late.

After that, he asked if he had had visitors, and the woman told him they had come regularly, although the physician had forbidden them to see him for the time being.

In a weak voice he repeated, "The matter's in God's hands, both first and last," and "We ask God for a good outcome." But the truth was that he did not despair and did not feel his end was near. His confidence in the life he loved was no weaker, despite his pains and fears. Hope came back with the return of consciousness. He favored no one with last words of advice, made no disposition of his effects, said farewell to no one, and did not reveal any secrets of his business or fortune to those involved. To the contrary, he summoned Jamil al-Hamzawi and asked him to arrange some commercial transactions he himself would not have known how to conduct. He sent Kamal to the tailor to collect and pay for some new clothes he had ordered. His only mention of death was in these phrases he repeated as if to mask fate's cruelty.

At the end of the first week the doctor explained that the invalid had successfully survived the critical stage and would regain his health completely and feel as energetic as ever, with a little patience. The physician repeated the previous warning about high blood pressure, and al-Sayyid Ahmad promised to obey. He also vowed secretly to abstain from licentious behavior, for its disastrous consequences were now clear to him and had convinced him that his health was not a joking matter anymore. He consoled himself by saying, "A healthy life with a little self-denial's better at any rate than being sick." Thus the crisis was successfully overcome. The family members caught their breath, their hearts full of gratitude.

By the end of the second week, al-Sayyid Ahmad was permitted to receive visitors. That was a happy day, and his family were the first to celebrate it. His children with their spouses called on him and conversed with him for the first time since he had been confined to bed. The man looked from face to face, from Yasin to Khadija, Aisha, Ibrahim Shawkat, and Khalil Shawkat. With his customary charm, which did not desert him even in such circumstances, he asked about their children: Ridwan, Abd al-Muni'm, Ahmad, Na'ima, Uthman, and Muhammad. They said they had not brought the children for fear of disturbing him and prayed he would have a long life and be totally restored to good health. They told him of their sorrow over his suffering and their delight at his recovery. Khadija's voice trembled when she spoke, and the tear Aisha left on his hand when she kissed it required no explanation. Yasin suavely said that he had felt ill when his father did and had recovered with him when God had granted a cure. The father's pale face was radiant with joy, and he spoke to them at length about God's decrees, mercy, and grace, explaining that it was the Believer's duty to meet his fate with patience and confidence and to trust only in God.

On leaving his bedroom, they went to Kamal's room so the sitting room would be free to serve as a corridor for the anticipated throngs of visitors.

Yasin approached Amina then and clasped her hand in his as he said, "I haven't spoken to you of my feelings during the last two weeks because Papa's illness left me no mind with which to think. Now that God has restored him to health, I want to apologize for returning to this house without first asking your permission. The truth is that you received me with the same affection as in the happy bygone days, but now it's my duty to present my formal apology to you."

Amina blushed as she replied emotionally, "What's done is done, Yasin! This is your home. You're most welcome to stay here whenever you want."

Yasin said firmly, "I don't like to rake up the past, but I swear by my father's head and the life of my son Ridwan that my heart never harbored any grudge against the members of this family. I love you all as much as I do myself. Perhaps Satan prompted me to err. That could happen to anyone. But my heart was never corrupted."

Amina placed her hand on his broad shoulder and said sincerely, "You've always been one of my children. I don't deny I got angry once, but the anger's gone, praise God. All that's left is the previous love. This is your home, Yasin. Welcome home!"

Yasin sat down forcefully. When Amina left the room, he proclaimed to the others, "What a fine woman! May God never forgive a person who wrongs her. God's curse on Satan, who once tempted me into something that hurt her feelings."

Casting him an eloquent look, Khadija remarked, "Scarcely a year goes by without Satan tempting you into a new disaster. You're just a toy in his hands."

The glance he directed at her seemed to plead for mercy from her tongue. Then Aisha said in his defense, "That's all ancient history."

Khadija asked sarcastically, "Why didn't you bring madame your wife to 'entertain' us on this blessed occasion?"

Attempting to sound proud, Yasin answered, "My wife no longer entertains at parties. Today she's a lady in every sense of the word."

In an earnest voice without a trace of sarcasm, Khadija asked, "How can you do such things, Yasin? May our Lord grant you repentance and guide you."

As though to apologize for his wife's bluntness, Ibrahim Shawkat said, "Don't be offended, Mr. Yasin . . . but what am I to do? She's your sister."

Smiling, Yasin replied, "May God assist you, Mr. Ibrahim."

Aisha sighed and said, "Now that God has come to Papa's aid, I'll tell you frankly that I'll never forget, as long as I live, the way he looked in bed the first time I saw him there. May our Lord not condemn anyone to ill health."

Khadija commented sincerely and ardently, "This life wouldn't be worth a fingernail clipping without him."

Yasin responded passionately, "He's our shelter in every adversity, a man like no other . . . ."

"And what about me?" Kamal asked himself. "Do you remember how you stood in the corner of the room overwhelmed by despair? My heart was shattered by the sight of my mother beside herself with grief. We're familiar with the concept of death, but when its shadow looms on the horizon, the earth spins under us. There will be new attacks of pain each time, no matter how many loved ones you lose. You'll die too, leaving your hopes behind you. But life's desirable, even if you suffer from love."

The ringing of a carriage bell could be heard from the street. Aisha ran to the window to look out the peephole. She turned back to say proudly, "Important visitors!"

There was a steady stream of visitors representing the many friends with whom the father's life was filled – civil servants, attorneys, dignitaries, and merchants. All but a few had been to the house before, although some had come only as guests at the banquets al-Sayyid Ahmad hosted on special occasions. There were also some faces frequently seen in the Goldsmiths Bazaar and on New Street. These men were his friends too, but not in the same class as Muhammad Iffat and his cronies.

The visitors did not stay long, as was appropriate for a sick call, but al-Sayyid Ahmad's children found plenty to satisfy their vanity and pride in the distinguished appearance of these guests and in all the carriages with their beautiful horses.

Aisha, who was still watching the street, said, "Here are his pals."

They could hear the voices of Muhammad Iffat, Ali Abd al-Rahim, and Ibrahim al-Far as the men laughed and raised their voices with thanks and praise for God. Yasin said, "There are no other friends left in the world like these."

Ibrahim and Khalil Shawkat agreed with him. Then Kamal observed with a sorrow that passed unnoticed, "It's rare for life to allow friends to stay together for as long as these men."

Yasin marveled, "A day hasn't gone by without their visiting the house. During his crisis, there were tears in their eyes whenever they left."

Ibrahim Shawkat said, "Don't be amazed by that, for they've spent more time with him than you have."

At this point Khadija went to the kitchen to offer her assistance, since the flow of visitors was continuing unabated. Jamil al-Hamzawi came after closing the store. He was followed by Ghunaym Hamidu, who owned an oil press in al-Gamaliya, and Muhammad Ajami, who sold couscous in al-Salihiya. Then, pointing to the street from the window, Aisha cried out, "Shaykh Mutawalli Abd al-Samad! I wonder if he'll be able to climb to the top floor."

Leaning on his stick, the shaykh began to cross the courtyard, clearing his throat from time to time to warn anyone in his way that he was coming. Yasin responded, "He can climb to the top of a minaret." Then, seeing Khalil Shawkat try to figure up the shaykh's age with his fingers, Yasin continued: "Between eighty and ninety! But don't inquire about his health."

Kamal asked, "Did he never marry during this long life?"

Yasin answered, "It's said that he was a husband and a father but that his wife and children passed on to the mercy of God."

Aisha cried out again, not having budged from her post at the window, "Look! This foreigner! I wonder who he could be."

The man crossed the courtyard, casting a cautious, inquisitive glance around. He wore a round straw hat, and visible beneath the rim was a pockmarked, curved nose and a bushy mustache. Ibrahim said, "Perhaps he's a goldsmith from the Goldsmiths Bazaar."

Yasin muttered anxiously, "But he looks Greek. Where do you suppose I've seen that face before?"

A blind youth arrived wearing dark glasses. He was being dragged along by a man in traditional attire with a shawl wrapped around his head, sporting a long black overcoat beneath which could be seen the tail of a striped gown. Yasin recognized them immediately and was utterly astonished. The blind youth was Abduh, who played the zitherlike qanun in Zubayda's troupe. The other man, called al-Humayuni, was the proprietor of a famous coffeehouse in Wajh al-Birka and a gangster, ruffian, pimp, and so on.

Khalil was heard to say, "The blind man's a qanun player for the vocalist Zubayda."

With feigned astonishment Yasin asked, "How does he know Papa?"

Ibrahim Shawkat smiled as he replied, "Your father's a music lover from way back. It's hardly strange that all the musicians know him."

Aisha kept her head turned toward the street to hide her smile. Yasin and Kamal observed Ibrahim's smile and understood what it implied. Finally Suwaydan, the Shawkat family's ancient maid, tottered into view. Pointing to her, Khalil murmured, "Our mother's emissary has come to ask after al-Sayyid Ahmad's health."

The widow of the late Mr. Shawkat had visited al-Sayyid Ahmad once but was unable to repeat that effort because of the pains of rheumatism that had recently been conspiring with old age to cripple her.

Khadija soon returned from the kitchen with a complaint that was actually a boast: "We need a man from the coffeehouse just to serve all the coffee."

Al-Sayyid Ahmad was sitting up in bed, leaning against a pillow that had been folded back, with the covers drawn up to his neck. His visitors sat on the sofa or the chairs arranged in a circle around the bed. He seemed cheerful, in spite of his weakness, for nothing could make him as happy as having his friends gather around him and compete in flattering him and assuring him of their affection. Although the ailment had harmed him, he could not deny the favor it had done him by allowing him to see his brothers' alarm at his suffering and their grief at his absence from their parties, which had seemed desolate during his seclusion. He appeared to want to elicit all the affection he could from them, for he began to recount the pains he had endured as well as the tedium. He allowed himself considerable license to exaggerate and embellish.

Sighing, he said, "During the first days of my illness I was convinced that I was finished. I started reciting our Muslim credo and the Qur'an sura about God's absoluteness [Sura 112], but when I wasn't occupied with those I thought of you a lot, and the idea of leaving you troubled me greatly."

More than one voice was raised to say, "The world wouldn't be the same without you, al-Sayyid Ahmad."

Ali Abd al-Rahim said emotionally, "This illness of yours has made an impression on me that will never be erased."

Muhammad Iffat ventured in a faint voice, "Do you remember that night? My Lord, our hair turned white then."

Ghunaym Hamidu leaned toward the bed a little to say, "You've been saved by the One who rescued us that night the English made us fill in the trench under the city gate at Bab al-Futuh."

"Those happy days . . ." al-Sayyid Ahmad reflected. "Days of health and romance, when Fahmy was so outstanding and showed such promise . . . ."

"Praise to God, Mr. Hamidu," he replied.

Shaykh Mutawalli Abd al-Samad said, "I want to know how much you paid the doctor, who wasn't entitled to anything. You don't need to reply, but I implore you to feed the friends of God who live near the mosque of al-Husayn."

Muhammad Iffat interrupted him to inquire, "What about you, Shaykh Mutawalli? Aren't you one of them? Explain this to me."

Terminating each phrase by a blow to the floor with his stick, the shaykh continued: "Feed the saints of al-Husayn with me at the head of them, whether or not Muhammad Iffat approves. He ought to feed them too in your honor, starting with me. And you ought to perform the pilgrimage to Mecca this year, since it is your religious duty. How grand it would be if you took me with you, so that God would multiply your reward. . . ."

"What a fine man you are, Shaykh Mutawalli, and how dear to me," al-Sayyid Ahmad thought. "You're one of the landmarks of the age."

"Shaykh Mutawalli, I promise to take you with me to the Hijaz and Mecca, if the Compassionate God permits."

At that point, the foreigner, whose fine white hair was visible since he had removed his hat, said, "A little too much agitation. . . . Agitation's the cause of everything. Give it up and you'll be strong as a bomb."

"Manuli's sold you alcohol for thirty-five years – a purveyor of happiness and an agent for the cemetery," al-Sayyid Ahmad mused privately.

"It's the fault of your goods, Manuli."

The foreigner looked at the faces of his other customers and said, "No one's ever said that alcohol's bad for your health. That's nonsense. Is sickness caused by gaiety, laughter, and comfort?"

Training a nearly sightless eye on the foreigner, Shaykh Mutawalli Abd al-Samad cried out, "Now I've recognized you, source of calamities! When I heard your voice the first time I wondered where I'd heard this devil before."

The couscous vendor, Muhammad Ajami, asked Mr. Manuli with a wink in the direction of Shaykh Mutawalli, "Wasn't Shaykh Mutawalli one of your customers once, Manuli?"

The smiling foreigner replied, "His mouth's so full of food, where would he find room for wine, dear friend?"

Gripping the handle of his stick, Abd al-Samad shouted, "Manners, Manuli!"

Then Ajami shouted at him, "Do you deny, Shaykh Mutawalli, you were a big consumer of hashish before age made it hard for you to breathe?"

The shaykh waved his hand in protest, saying, "Hashish is not forbidden by Islam. Have you ever tried performing the dawn prayer under the influence? . . . God is most great. . . . *Allahu Akbar!*"

Noticing that al-Humayuni was silent, Ahmad Abd al-Jawad turned to him with a smile and to be polite said, "How are you, sir? By God, it's been a long time!"

In a voice like an ox's, al-Humayuni responded, "By God, a long time. Ages, by God. It's your fault, al-Sayyid Ahmad. You're the one who left us, but when Mr. Ali Abd al-Rahim told me, 'Your adversary's confined to bed,' I remembered the days of our youthful passions as though they had never ceased. I told myself, 'It would be disloyal not to visit the dear man myself – such a virile, sociable, jolly man.' If it were not for fear of creating problems for you, I would have brought Fatuma, Tamalli, Dawlat, and Naha-wand. The girls are all eager to see you. My goodness, Mr. Ahmad. You're dear to us whether you honor us with a visit every evening or avoid us for years." Looking at the others with his sharp eyes, he continued: "You've all forsaken us. Blessings on Mr. Ali. May our Lord protect Saniya al-Qulali, who keeps him coming to us. Anyone who loses track of his past goes astray. We provide the sincerest form of fellowship. What's drawn you away from us? If it were repentance, we'd forgive you. But it's not time for repent-ance yet. May God keep that far in the future by granting you a long life and many happy times."

Pointing to himself, Ahmad Abd al-Jawad remarked, "If you look at me, you can see I'm finished with all that."

The pimp replied enthusiastically, "Don't say that, master of men. A temporary indisposition that will depart, never to return. . . . I won't leave till you announce you'll return to Wajh al-Birka, even if only once, when God restores you to health."

Muhammad Iffat said, "Times have changed, Master Humayuni. Where's the Wajh al-Birka that we used to know? Look for it in history books. What remains is a playground for today's youngsters. How can we walk among them when our sons are there?"

Ibrahim al-Far said, "Don't forget that we can't trick our Lord when it comes to age or health. As Mr. Ahmad said, we're finished. We're all forced to visit a doctor, who says, 'You have this. You have that. Don't drink. Don't eat. Don't breathe.' And he has many other disgusting prescriptions for us. Haven't you heard of the pressure disease, Master Humayuni?"

Glancing at him, the pimp replied, "Treat a disease with drunkenness, laughter, and sport. If you find any trace of it after that, give it to me."

Manuli shouted, "By your life, that's what I told him."

Muhammad Ajami, as though completing his companion's thought, said, "And don't forget drugs, sir."

Shaykh Mutawalli Abd al-Samad shook his head in astonishment. He asked anxiously, "Tell me where I am, good people: in the home of Abd al-Jawad's son or in an opium den or a tavern? Listen and advise me."

Giving Shaykh Mutawalli a suspicious look, al-Humayuni asked, "Who's your friend?"

"A blessed saint."

The pimp said sarcastically, "If you're a saint, tell my fortune."

Mutawalli Abd al-Samad exclaimed, "Prison or the gallows!"

Al-Humayuni could not keep from laughing out loud. Then he remarked, "He truly is a saint, for this is the end I expect." Then he told the shaykh, "But watch your tongue, or your prophecy may fall upon you."

Bringing his head close to al-Sayyid Ahmad's face, Ali Abd al-Rahim said, "Rise, my dear. The world's not worth the skin of an onion without you. What's happened to us, Ahmad? Don't you think we'll have to take ill health more seriously after this? Our fathers married new wives when they were over seventy. What's changed?"

With enough force that a drizzle of saliva flew from his mouth, Mutawalli Abd al-Samad exclaimed, "Your fathers were Believers. They were pure. They did not get drunk and fornicate. There's the answer for you."

Ahmad Abd al-Jawad told his friend, "The doctor told me that if I ignore my pressure, the result will be paralysis, and then only God can help me. That's what happened to our friend al-Wadini, may God honor him with a suitable end. I ask God, if it's my time, to grant me death. Confinement to bed for years without being able to move.... O God, have mercy on us."

At this point Ajami, Hamidu, and Manuli excused themselves and left, praying that al-Sayyid Ahmad would have a long and healthy life. Muhammad Iffat leaned over al-Sayyid Ahmad and whispered to him, "Jalila sends you her greetings. She would have liked to see you for herself."

The ears of Abduh, the qanun player, overheard that. He snapped his fingers and said, "And I'm the sultana's representative to you. She was ready to dress up in men's clothes to come visit you herself but felt apprehensive about the unforeseen consequences that might have. She sent me to tell you...." After clearing his throat a couple of times he sang in a low voice:

> "Godspeed, my messenger to him.
> Kiss the sweet fellow on his lips
> And tell him, 'Your infatuated slave's
> At your service.'"

Al-Humayuni smiled and revealed his gold dentures. He commented, "An excellent remedy. Try this and pay no attention to the friend of God who predicts the gallows."

"Zubayda?" al-Sayyid Ahmad asked himself. "I don't desire anything. The world of illness is a despicable one. If the worst had happened, I would have died drunk. Doesn't this mean I've got to turn over a new leaf?"

Ibrahim al-Far told him in a low voice, "We all vowed we wouldn't taste alcohol while you're stuck in bed."

"I free you from that oath, and ask forgiveness for what you've already missed."

Smiling, Ali Abd al-Rahim said enticingly, "If only it were possible to celebrate your recovery here this evening."

Addressing his appeal to all the men present, Mutawalli Abd al-Samad said, "I call you to repentance and pilgrimage."

Al-Humayuni retorted angrily, "You're acting like a soldier in an opium den."

At a prearranged signal from al-Far, the heads of Muhammad Iffat, Ali Abd al-Rahim, and Ibrahim al-Far drew close to that of al-Sayyid Ahmad, and the three began to sing softly:

"Since you're not man enough for wine
Why do you get drunk?"

For this, they appropriated the tune of

Since you're not man enough for passion
Why do you fall in love?

Then Shaykh Abd al-Samad started reciting verses from the Qur'an sura called "Repentance" (Sura 9). Ahmad Abd al-Jawad laughed so hard that tears came to his eyes.

Time passed without anyone noticing, until Shaykh Mutawalli Abd al-Samad began to look alarmed. He said, "I want you to understand that I'm going to be the last to leave. I wish to speak privately with Abd al-Jawad's son."

114

AHMAD ABD AL-JAWAD was able to leave the house after two more weeks. The first thing he did was to take Yasin and Kamal on a visit to the tomb and mosque of al-Husayn to perform their prayers and give thanks to God.

At the time, news of the death of the politician Ali Fahmy Kamil was in the papers. After pondering this event at length, on the way out of the house al-Sayyid Ahmad told his sons, "He dropped dead after addressing a great gathering. I'm walking on my own two legs after a stay in bed when I almost saw death face to face. Who can know the mysteries the future holds? Truly our lives are in God's hands."

He had to wait patiently for days and even weeks to regain his lost weight, but despite that fact, his dignified appearance and good looks seemed not to have been affected. He walked ahead, followed by Yasin and Kamal. This weekly parade had been abandoned after Fahmy's death. On the way from Palace Walk to the mosque, the two young men observed the prestige their father enjoyed throughout the district. Every merchant with a shop on the street greeted him with open arms and shook hands while applauding his recovery.

Yasin and Kamal responded to these warm demonstrations of mutual affection with joyful pride and smiles that lasted the whole way. All the same, Yasin asked himself innocently why he did not enjoy the same standing as his father, since they were equal both in their dignified and handsome exterior and in their shortcomings. Kamal, although momentarily touched, reexamined his perceptions of his father's remarkable prestige in a new light. In the past, to his small eyes his father's status had seemed the epitome of distinction and greatness. Now he saw it as nothing special, at least not in comparison with his own high ideals. It was merely the prestige enjoyed by a good-hearted, affable, and chivalrous man. True greatness was something totally unlike that, for its thunder shook sluggish hearts and drove sleep from dozing eyes. It was capable of arousing hatred not love, anger rather than satisfaction, and enmity instead of affection. Before it rebuilt, it forced disclosure and destruction. But was it not happiness for a man to be blessed with such love and respect? Yes . . . and the proof was that at times the greatness of important figures was measured by the amount of love and tranquillity they sacrificed for lofty goals. In any case, his father was a happy man who was to be congratulated on that.

"See how handsome he is," Kamal told himself. "And how charming Yasin is too! What a strange sight I make between the two of them – like a distorted, trick photograph at a carnival. Claim to your heart's content that good looks are the domain of women not men, but that will never erase from your memory that alarming scene at the gazebo. My father's recovered from his high blood pressure. When will I recover from love? Love's an illness, even though it resembles cancer in having kept its secrets from medical science. In his last letter Husayn Shaddad says, 'Paris is the capital of beauty and love.' Is it also the capital of suffering? My dear friend is growing as stingy with his letters as if they were drops of his precious blood. I want a world where hearts are not deceived and do not deceive others."

At the corner of Khan Ja'far, they could see the great mosque. He heard his father say, "O Husayn!" in a heartfelt way, which combined the charm of a greeting with the fervor of a plea for help. Then al-Sayyid Ahmad quickened his steps. Looking into the mosque with an enigmatic smile, Kamal trailed after him and Yasin. Did he suspect for a moment that Kamal was only accompanying him on this blessed visit to please him or that his son no longer shared any of his religious beliefs? To Kamal, this mosque was now nothing more than one of the many symbols of the disappointment his heart had suffered. In the old days when he had stood beneath its minaret, his heart had pounded, tears had come to his eyes, and his breast had throbbed with ardor, belief, and hope. As he approached it today, all he saw was a vast collection of stone, steel, wood, and paint covering a great tract of land for no clear reason.

"Although forced by obedience to my father's authority, respect for the other people present, and fear of what they might do," Kamal reflected, "to play the role of a Believer until the visit to the shrine's concluded, I find my hypocritical conduct an affront to honor and truth. I want a world where men live free from fear and coercion."

They removed their shoes and entered one after the other. The father headed for the prayer niche and invited his sons to perform a prayer in front of it as a way of saluting the mosque. He raised his hands to his head to begin the prayer ritual, and they followed his example. As usual, the father lost himself in his prayers, and his eyelids drooped as he yielded his will to God's. Yasin too forgot everything except that he was in the presence of God the Merciful and Forgiving. Kamal began to move his lips without reciting anything. He bowed, straightened up, knelt, and prostrated himself as if performing insipid athletic exercises.

He told himself, "The most ancient remaining human structures, on the face of the earth or carved inside it, are temples. Even today, no area is free of them. When will man grow up and depend on himself? That loud voice coming from the far corner of the mosque reminds people of the end. When has there ever been an end to time? How beautiful it would be to see man wrestle with his illusions and vanquish them. But when will the struggle cease and the fighter announce that he's happy and that the world looks so different that it might have been created the day before? These two men are my father and brother. Why shouldn't all men be my fathers and brothers? How could this heart I carry within me let itself torment me in so many different ways? How frequently throughout the day I'm confronted by people I don't like. . . . Why should the friend I love have departed to the ends of the earth?"

When they finished praying, the father said, "Let's rest here a little before circling the tomb."

They sat there silently, their legs folded beneath them, until the father said gently, "We haven't been here together since that day."

Yasin replied emotionally, "Let's recite the 'Fatiha' for Fahmy's spirit."

They recited the opening prayer of the Qur'an, and then the father asked Yasin somewhat suspiciously, "I wonder whether worldly affairs have not kept you from visiting al-Husayn."

Yasin, who had not set foot in the mosque all those years except a handful of times, answered, "I don't let a week go by without visiting my master al-Husayn."

The father turned toward Kamal and cast him a glance as if to ask, "And you?"

Feeling embarrassed, Kamal replied, "Me too!"

The father said humbly, "He's our loved one and our intercessor with his grandfather Muhammad on a day when no mother or father can be of any assistance."

He had recovered from his illness this time, but only after it had taught him a lesson he would not forget. He had found its violence convincing and feared a recurrence. His intention to repent was sincere. He had always believed he would repent, no matter how long he waited. He was now certain that postponing it after this sickness would be stupidity and a blasphemous rejection of God's blessings. Whenever he happened to think of forbidden amusements, he consoled himself with the innocent pleasures awaiting him in life, like friendship, music, and jests. Therefore he entreated God to preserve him from the whispered temptations of Satan and to strengthen his resolve to repent. He proceeded to recite some of the Qur'an's simpler, shorter suras that he knew by heart.

When he rose, his sons did too. Then they went to the sepulcher, where they were greeted by the sweet fragrance pervading the place and a murmur of whispered recitations. They walked around the tomb with the throngs of visitors. Kamal's eyes looked up at the great green turban and then rested for a time on the wooden door, which he had kissed so often. He compared the present with the past and his former state of mind with his current one. He remembered how revelation of this tomb's secret had been the first tragedy in his life and then how the succession of tragedies following it had carried off love, belief, and friendship. Despite all that, he was still standing on his own two feet as he gazed worshipfully at truth, so heedless of the jabs of pain that even his bitterness caused him to smile. He had no regrets over his rejection of the blind happiness illuminating the faces of the men circumambulating the tomb. How could he buy happiness at the price of light when he had vowed to live with his eyes open? He preferred to be anxious and alive rather than comfortable and sleepy. He chose wakeful insomnia over restful sleep.

When they had finished walking around the sepulcher, the father invited them to rest for a while in the shelter of the shrine. They went to a corner and sat down next to each other. Some acquaintances noticed al-Sayyid Ahmad and approached to shake hands and congratulate him on his recovery. Some stayed to sit with them. Most of them knew Yasin either from his father's store or from al-Nahhasin School, but hardly anyone knew Kamal. Some of them noticed how thin the boy was and one jokingly asked al-Sayyid Ahmad, "What's wrong with this son of yours? He's skinny as a ramrod."

As if returning the man's compliment with an even nicer one, al-Sayyid Ahmad shot back, "No, you're the ram!"

Yasin smiled. Kamal did too, for this was the first chance he had had to observe his father's secret personality of which he had heard so much. His father was obviously a man who would not miss a chance for a little joke even when he was beside the tomb of al-Husayn in a sacred place devoted to praise of God and repentance. Yasin was inspired to reflect on his father's future, wondering whether al-Sayyid Ahmad would return to his previous joys even after this serious illness.

Yasin told himself, "Knowing this is extremely important to me."

115

UMM HANAFI was sitting cross-legged on a mat in the sitting room while Aisha's daughter Na'ima and Khadija's sons Abd al-Muni'm and Ahmad sat on the sofa opposite her. The two windows overlooking the courtyard of the house were open because of the hot, humid August weather, but scarcely a breeze stirred and the large lamp suspended from the ceiling cast a steady light throughout the room. The bedrooms opening off the sitting room seemed dark and silent. Umm Hanafi's head was bowed, and her arms were folded across her chest. She would look up at the children on the sofa for a moment and then lower her eyes again. She said nothing but her lips never stopped moving.

Abd al-Muni'm asked, "How long will Uncle Kamal stay on the roof?"

Umm Hanafi muttered, "It's hot down here. Why didn't you stay up there with him?"

"It's dark, and Na'ima's afraid of bugs."

Ahmad asked angrily, "How long are we going to remain here? This is the second week. I'm counting every day. I want to go back to Papa and Mama."

Umm Hanafi said hopefully, "God willing, you'll all return and be in the best possible shape. Pray to God, for He answers the requests of pure young children."

Abd al-Muni'm said, "We pray before we go to sleep and when we wake up, just the way you instructed us."

The woman said, "Pray to God all the time. Pray to Him now. He's the only one who can remove our distress."

Abd al-Muni'm spread out his hands in prayer and looked at Ahmad to invite him to join in. The vexed look still on his face, Ahmad complied. Then they repeated together, as they had grown accustomed to during the last few days, "O Lord, cure Uncle Khalil and our cousins Uthman and Muhammad so we can return home with minds at ease."

The impact this made on Na'ima was apparent in her face. Her features had a sad look and her blue eyes were filled with tears. She cried out, "Papa, Uthman, and Muhammad – how are they? I want to see Mama. I want to see all of them."

Abd al-Muni'm turned toward her to say in a consoling voice, "Don't cry, Na'ima. I've told you repeatedly not to cry. My uncle's fine. Uthman's fine. Muhammad's fine. We'll return home soon. Grandmother said so. Uncle Kamal said so too not very long ago."

Na'ima, who was sobbing, said, "I hear this every day. But they don't let us return. I want to see Papa, Uthman, and Muhammad. I want Mama."

Ahmad grumbled, "I want Papa and Mama too."

Abd al-Muni'm said, "We'll go back when they're well."

Na'ima cried out anxiously, "Let's go back now. I want to go home. Why are they keeping us away?"

Abd al-Muni'm replied, "They're afraid we'll catch the disease."

Na'ima answered stubbornly, "Mama's there. Aunt Khadija's there. Uncle Ibrahim's there. Grandmother's there. Why won't they catch it?"

"Because they're adults!"

"If adults can't catch diseases, why is Papa sick?"

Umm Hanafi sighed and said tenderly, "Is something upsetting you? This is your house too. And here are Masters Abd al-Muni'm and Ahmad to play with you. And your Uncle Kamal loves you more than all the world. You'll soon return to Mama, Papa, Uthman, and Muhammad. Don't cry, little lady. Pray for Papa and your brothers to get well."

Ahmad complained, "Two weeks! I've counted the days on my fingers. Besides, our apartment's on the third floor, and the disease is on the second. Why can't we return to our apartment and take Na'ima with us?"

Umm Hanafi put a finger to her lips as though to caution them and said, "Your uncle Kamal will get angry if he hears what you said. He buys you chocolates and melon seeds. How can you say you don't want to stay with him? You're not babies anymore. Master Abd al-Muni'm, you'll be starting primary school in a month. And you will too, dear Na'ima."

Backing down a little, Ahmad said, "At least let us go outside to play in the street."

Abd al-Muni'm seconded that suggestion: "That makes sense, Umm Hanafi. Why don't we go out and play in the street?"

Umm Hanafi replied firmly, "You have the courtyard, which is as big as the universe. And you also have the roof terrace. What more do you want than that? When Mr. Kamal was young, he only played in the house. When I finish my work, I'll tell you stories. Wouldn't you like that?"

Ahmad protested, "Yesterday you told us you'd finished all your stories."

Drying her eyes, Na'ima said, "Aunt Khadija knows more stories. If Mama was here we could sing together."

Umm Hanafi said ingratiatingly, "I keep begging you to sing for us and you refuse."

"I can't sing here. I can't sing when Uthman and Muhammad are sick."

Sighing, the woman said, "I'll fix supper for you, and then we'll go to bed. How about some cheese, watermelon, and canta-loupe?"

Kamal was sitting in a chair on the open side of the roof, next to the arbor of jasmine and hyacinth beans. He was scarcely visible in the darkness except for his loose-fitting white house shirt. His legs stretched out languidly, he looked at the sky studded with stars. He was lost in thought, and the silence encompassing him was broken only by an occasional voice from the street or a cluck from the chicken house. The family's affliction during the last two weeks had left its imprint on his face. During this time the normal household routine had been disrupted, and his mother had dis-appeared except for rare moments. The atmosphere of the house was transformed by the complaints of the three young prisoners who had roamed its expanses asking for Papa and Mama until Kamal had run out of stratagems for cajoling and amusing them.

Over on Sugar Street, Aisha no longer sang or laughed in the way that had once caused so much talk. She stayed up nights with her beloved family of invalids – her husband and her sons. Kamal had yearned for Aisha to return to her old home when he was young. Now he was extremely apprehensive that she would be forced to return, her wing broken and her heart shattered.

His mother had whispered to him, "Don't visit Sugar Street, and if you do, don't stay long." He did go there occasionally and would leave with his hands smelling strangely of disinfectants and his heart overwhelmed by anxiety.

The most amazing thing was that typhoid germs, like other ones, were incredibly tiny and invisible to the naked eye but capable of stopping the flow of a life, deciding the destiny of men, and breaking up a family. Poor Muhammad had been the first to fall ill. Uthman had been next. Finally and unexpectedly, the father had succumbed.

The maid Suwaydan had come to tell Kamal that his mother would spend the night at Sugar Street. Quoting his mother without comment, she had added that there was no cause for concern. If that was so, why was his mother staying over? Why did his breast feel such forebodings? Despite all this, it was always possible that the gloom might disperse in the twinkling of an eye. Khalil Shawkat and his two darling sons might recover. Aisha's face might sparkle and shine. Could he forget how the household had suffered through a similar ordeal only eight months before? And now his father was up and about, his health totally restored. His muscles had regained their strength and his eyes their attractive sparkle. He had returned to his friends and loved ones like a bird to the leafy tree. So who could deny that it was possible for everything to change in the twinkling of an eye?

"You're here alone!"

Kamal recognized the voice. Turning toward the door of the roof, he rose and stretched out his hand to the newcomer, saying, "How are you, brother? Have a seat."

Kamal got a chair for Yasin, who was breathing heavily after climbing up the stairs. Filling his chest with the scent of jasmine, he sat down and said, "The children have gone to sleep and Umm Hanafi has too."

Resuming his seat, Kamal asked, "What time is it? The poor kids won't rest and won't let anyone else rest either."

"It's eleven. The air here's a lot better than on the street."

"Where have you been?"

"Back and forth between Palace of Desire and Sugar Street. By the way, your mother's not coming home tonight."

"Suwaydan told me that. What's new? I've been extremely apprehensive."

Sighing, Yasin said, "We're all anxious. Our Lord is gracious. Our father's there too."

"At this hour!"

"I left him there." After a pause he continued: "I was at Sugar Street until eight this evening. Then a messenger came from Palace of Desire Alley to say that my wife's labor had begun. I went immediately to Umm Ali, the midwife, and took her to my house, where I found my wife was being cared for by some neighbors. I stayed there an hour but could not bear the moaning and screaming for long. I went back to Sugar Street again and found Father sitting with Ibrahim Shawkat."

"What does this mean? Tell me what you think."

In a low voice Yasin said, "Their condition's extremely grave."

"Grave?"

"Yes. I came here to try to calm my nerves. Couldn't Zanuba have picked some other night to have a baby? I'm exhausted from going back and forth between Palace of Desire and Sugar Street, between the doctor and the midwife. Their condition's critical. When Widow Shawkat looked at her son's face she cried out, 'Protect us, Lord. You should have taken me first.' Your mother was very alarmed, but the old lady paid no attention to her and said in a hoarse voice, 'This is what members of the Shawkat family look like when they die. I saw his father and his uncle die, and his grandfather before them.' There's nothing left of Khalil but a shadow, and the children are the same way. There's no power or might save with God."

Kamal swallowed and said, "Perhaps these suspicions are unfounded."

"Perhaps. . . . Kamal, you're not a child anymore. You ought to know at least what I do. The doctor said the situation's critical."

"For all of them?"

"All! Khalil, Uthman, and Muhammad. O Lord! How wretched your luck is, Aisha. . . ."

In the darkness he imagined Aisha's laughing family as he had seen them in the past. They were joyful, happy individuals who pursued life as though it were an innocent entertainment.

"When will Aisha be able to laugh again?" Kamal wondered. "Fahmy was snatched away. The English or typhoid, it's all the same . . . like any other cause. Belief in God makes death seem a bewildering but wise decree, when actually it's nothing but a cruel joke."

"That's the most atrocious thing I've ever heard."

"That it is, but what can anyone do? What has Aisha done to deserve this? O God, forgiveness and mercy. . . ."

"Is there any sublime philosophy that can justify mass slaughter?" Kamal asked himself. "Death follows the rules for jokes precisely. Yet how can we laugh when we're the butt of the joke. Perhaps I'd be able to meet it with a smile if I could always confront it with contemplation, understanding, and impartiality. That would be a victory over both life and death. But what would any of this mean to Aisha?"

"My head's spinning, brother."

In the sagest voice Kamal had ever heard him use, Yasin remarked, "This is the way the world is. You must come to know it as it really is." Then he rose suddenly and said, "I've got to go now."

Kamal implored him, "Stay with me a little longer."

But Yasin answered apologetically, "It's eleven. I must go to Palace of Desire Alley to reassure myself about Zanuba. Then I'll return to Sugar Street to be with them. I won't sleep an hour tonight, it seems. And by God I know what's awaiting us tomorrow."

Kamal stood up and said with alarm, "You talk as though it was all over. I'm going to Sugar Street right away."

"No, you must stay with the children until morning. Try to get some sleep. Otherwise I'll regret speaking so frankly to you."

Yasin left the roof of the house and Kamal accompanied him downstairs to the door. When they passed the top floor, where the children were sleeping, Kamal said sorrowfully, "What poor kids! Na'ima's wept bitterly during the past few days, as though her heart sensed what would happen. . . ."

Yasin replied frankly, "The children will soon forget. Pray for the grown-ups."

As they went into the courtyard, they could hear a voice from the street crying out, "Special edition of *al-Muqattam*!"

Kamal murmured inquisitively, "A special edition for the paper?"

In a sad voice, Yasin said, "Oh! I know what it's about. When I was on my way here, I heard people spreading the news. Sa'd Zaghlul has died."

Kamal cried out from the depths of his heart, "Sa'd?"

Yasin stopped walking and turned toward his brother to say,

"Don't take it so hard. We have enough problems of our own."

Kamal stared into the darkness without speaking or moving. He seemed oblivious to Khalil, Uthman, Muhammad, and Aisha, to everything except the death of Sa'd Zaghlul.

Yasin walked on and remarked, "He died after receiving his full share of life and greatness. What more would you wish for him than that? May God be merciful to him."

Still stunned, Kamal followed him silently. He did not know how he would have received this news in circumstances that were not so grim. When disasters come at the same time, they compete with each other. Thus Kamal's grandmother had died soon after Fahmy had been slain, at a time when no one had tears to spare for her. So Sa'd was dead. The hero of the exile, the revolution, the liberation, and the constitution had died. Why should he not mourn for Sa'd Zaghlul, when the best qualities of his personality came from Sa'd's guidance and leadership?

Yasin stopped once more to open the door. Then he held out his hand to Kamal. After shaking hands with him, Kamal remembered something that had slipped his mind for too long. Embarrassed that he had forgotten, he told Yasin, "I pray to God that you'll find your wife has given birth safely."

Starting to leave, Yasin replied, "God willing. And I hope you sleep soundly."

SUGAR STREET

116

THEIR HEADS were huddled around the brazier, and their hands were spread over its fire: Amina's thin and gaunt, Aisha's stiff, and Umm Hanafi's like the shell of a turtle. The beautiful pure-white ones were Na'ima's. The January cold was almost severe enough to freeze water at the edges of the sitting room, which had retained its time-honored appearance with its colored mats and the sofas distributed around the sides. The old lantern with its oil lamp had vanished, and hanging in its place was an electric light. The location had changed too, for the coffee hour had returned to the first floor. Indeed the entire upper story had moved downstairs to make life easier for the father, whose heart was no longer strong enough for him to climb to the top.

The family members had changed as well. Amina's body had withered, and her hair had turned white. Although barely sixty, she looked ten years older, and her transformation was nothing compared to Aisha's decline and disintegration. It was ironic or pathetic that the daughter's hair was still golden and her eyes blue, when her listless glance gave no hint of life and her pale complexion seemed the symptom of some disease. With a protruding bone structure and sunken eyes and cheeks, her face hardly appeared that of a thirty-four-year-old woman. Although the years had settled on Umm Hanafi, they did not seem to have marked her in any essential way, hardly diminishing her reserves of flesh and fat. Instead, they had accumulated on her skin and around her neck and mouth like crusts or earthy deposits. But her grave eyes glinted from participation in the family's silent sorrow.

Na'ima stood out in this group like a rose growing in a cemetery, for she had developed into a beautiful young woman of sixteen. Her head enveloped by a halo of golden hair and her face adorned by blue eyes, she was as lovely as her mother, Aisha, had been – or even more captivating – but as insubstantial as a shadow. Her eyes had a gentle, dreamy look suggesting purity, innocence, and otherworldliness. She nestled against her mother's side, as though unwilling to be alone even for a moment.

Rubbing her hands together over the brazier, Umm Hanafi said, "The builders will finish the project this week after working for a year and a half. . . ."

Na'ima responded sarcastically, "A building for Uncle Bayumi the drinks vendor. . . ."

Aisha raised her eyes from the brazier to look at Umm Hanafi for a moment but made no comment. They had previously learned that the house once belonging to Mr. Muhammad Ridwan would be torn down to allow construction of a four-story building for Uncle Bayumi the drinks vendor. This project had stirred up many old memories about Maryam and her divorce from Yasin — what had become of Maryam? — and about Maryam's mother and her marriage to the drinks vendor Bayumi, who had gained possession of the house half by inheritance and half by purchase. Back then life had been worth living, and hearts had been carefree.

Umm Hanafi continued: "The most beautiful part of it, my lady, is Uncle Bayumi's new place for soft drinks, ice cream, and sweets. It has lots of mirrors and electric lights, with a radio playing day and night. I feel sorry for Hasanayn the barber, Darwish the bean seller, al-Fuli the milkman, and Abu Sari' with his snack shop. They have to look out of their dilapidated premises at the store and apartments of their former comrade."

Pulling her shawl tighter around her shoulders, Amina said, "Glory to God who gives blessings. . . ."

With her arms around her mother's neck, Na'ima commented, "The building blocks off our roof on that side. Once it's inhabited, how can we spend any time up there?"

Amina could not ignore the question raised by her beautiful granddaughter, if only out of concern for Aisha. She answered, "Pay no attention to the tenants. Do as you like."

She glanced at Aisha to see what impression her gracious reply had made. She was so afraid for her daughter that she was almost frightened of her. But Aisha was busy looking at herself in the mirror above the dresser between her room and her father's. She had not abandoned the custom of examining her reflection, even though it had become a meaningless exercise. With the passing days her face's withered appearance had ceased to alarm her.

Whenever a voice inside asked, "Where is the old Aisha?" she would answer indifferently, "And where are her sons, Muhammad and Uthman, and her husband, Khalil?"

Observing this, Amina was saddened, and her gloom quickly affected Umm Hanafi, who was so much a part of the family that their worries were hers.

Na'ima rose and went to the radio, which stood between the doors to the parlor and the dining room. Turning it on, she said, "It's time for the records, Mama."

Aisha lit a cigarette and inhaled deeply. Amina stared at the smoke, which spread out in a thin cloud over the brazier. A voice on the radio sang, "Companions from the good old days, how I wish you would return."

Na'ima resumed her seat, tucking the robe around her. Like her mother, she loved singing. She listened carefully so she could memorize the song and sing it in her pleasing voice. This interest was not dampened by the religious feelings that dominated her entire emotional life. She prayed conscientiously and had fasted during the month of Ramadan since the age of ten. She frequently dreamed of the mysteries of the spiritual realm and welcomed with limitless delight her grandmother's invitations to visit the mosque of al-Husayn. All the same she had never weaned herself from a love of singing. She sang whenever she was alone, in her room or in the bath.

Aisha approved of everything her one remaining child did, for Na'ima was the only bright hope on otherwise gloomy horizons. As pleased by her daughter's piety as by her voice, Aisha even loved and encouraged the girl's excessive attachment to her, not tolerating any comment on it. In fact, she had no patience for any kind of criticism, no matter how trivial or well-intentioned. Her only occupations at home were sitting, drinking coffee, and smoking. Whenever her mother invited her to help with the housework, not from a need for assistance but to distract Aisha from her thoughts, she was annoyed and uttered her famous phrase: "Oh, leave me alone." She would not let Na'ima lift a finger to help with the work either, since she feared the least exertion for her daughter. If she could have performed the prayer ritual for Na'ima, she would have, to spare her the effort.

Amina frequently chided Aisha about this, telling her that Na'ima was almost old enough to marry and needed to learn the duties of a housewife. Aisha always responded angrily, "Don't you see she's like a specter? My daughter can't bear any exertion. Leave her alone. She's my sole hope in the world."

Then, heartbroken, Amina would abandon the conversation. Gazing sadly at Aisha, she saw the personification of shattered hopes. When she looked at this unhappy face, which seemed to have lost all its vitality, Amina's soul was overcome by sorrow. Apprehensive about distressing her daughter, she had learned to greet Aisha's rude answers and harsh comments with affectionate forbearance.

The voice kept on singing, "Companions from the good old days," while Aisha smoked and listened to the song. She had been fond of singing once, and sorrow and despair had not killed her taste for it. Perhaps they had even enhanced it, since so many of the lyrics were plaintive and melancholy. Of course nothing could ever bring back her companions of the good old days. She wondered at times if that past had been a reality or a dream, a figment of her imagination. Where was that happy home? Where was her fine husband? Where were Uthman and Muhammad? Did only eight years separate her from that past?

Amina rarely liked these songs. The prime attraction of the radio for her was that it allowed her to hear recitations from the holy Qur'an and the news. The sad themes of the songs worried her. She was concerned about their effect on her daughter and remarked to Umm Hanafi one day, "Don't they sound like funeral laments to you?"

She could not stop thinking about Aisha and almost forgot the trouble she was having with high blood pressure. Visits to al-Husayn and to the other saints in their shrines were the only relief she found. Thanks to al-Sayyid Ahmad, who no longer restricted her movements, she was allowed to hurry off to God's sanctuaries whenever she felt the need. Amina herself was no longer the same woman she had once been. Grief and ill health had changed her considerably. With the passing years she had lost her amazing diligence and her extraordinary capacity for tidying up, cleaning, and running her home. Except for services to al-Sayyid Ahmad and Kamal, she paid little attention to the house. Satisfied to supervise, she had turned over the oven room and the pantry to Umm Hanafi and was remiss even in this supervision. Her confidence in their servant was boundless, for Umm

Hanafi was part of the household. A lifelong companion, she had shared Amina's good and bad times and had been absorbed into the family, so that she identified with all their joys and sorrows.

They were silent for a time, as though the song had distracted them. Then Na'ima said, "I saw my friend Salma in the street today. She was in grade school with me. Next year she's going to sit for the baccalaureate examination."

Aisha commented with annoyance, "If only your grandfather had let you stay in school, you would have surpassed her. But he refused!"

The protest implied by Aisha's final phrase did not escape her mother, who said, "Her grandfather has his ideas, which he won't abandon. Would you have wanted her to pursue her studies, despite the effort involved, when she's a delicate darling who can't stand fatigue?"

Aisha shook her head without speaking, but Na'ima said with regret, "I wish I had finished my education. All the girls study today, just like boys."

Umm Hanafi observed scornfully, "They study because they can't find a bridegroom. But a beauty like you . . ."

Amina nodded her head in agreement and said, "You're educated, young lady. You have the grade school certificate. Since you won't need to find a job, what more than that would you want? Let's pray that God will strengthen you, clothe your captivating beauty with health, and put some meat and fat on your bones."

Aisha retorted sharply, "I want her to be healthy, not fat. Obesity's a defect, especially in girls. Her mother was the outstanding beauty of her day, and she wasn't fat."

Smiling, Amina said gently, "It's true, Na'ima, your mother was the most beautiful girl of her day."

Aisha sighed and said, "And then she became the cautionary tale of her day."

Umm Hanafi murmured, "May our Lord bring you happiness with Na'ima."

Patting the girl affectionately on the back, Amina said, "Amen, Lord of the universe."

They fell silent again as they listened to a new voice sing, "I want to see you every day."

Then the door of the house opened and closed. Umm Hanafi said, "My master." She rose and rushed out of the room to turn on the stairway light.

They soon heard the customary taps of his walking stick. When he appeared at the entrance to the sitting room, they all stood up politely. Breathing heavily, he gazed at them a moment before saying, "Good evening."

They replied in unison, "Good evening to you."

Amina went to his room to put on the light, and he trailed after her, exuding an aura of dignified old age.

He sat down to regain his breath. It was only nine o'clock. He was dressed as elegantly as ever. His broadcloth cloak, striped silk caftan, and silk scarf were of the same type as before, but the white in his hair, his gray mustache, his slender, "deserted" body, and his early return were all symptomatic of a new era. Another novel development was the bowl of yogurt and the orange prepared for his supper. He had to avoid alcohol, the appetizers he ate when drinking, red meat, and eggs. Still, the sparkle in his wide blue eyes indicated that his desire for life had not flagged.

He proceeded to remove his clothes with Amina's assistance as usual. Then he put on a wool nightshirt, wrapped up in a robe, donned a skullcap, and sat down cross-legged on the sofa. Amina served him supper on a tray, and he ate without enthusiasm. Afterward she gave him a glass half filled with water, to which he added six drops from a bottle of medicine. He got it down with a frowning expression of disgust. Then he mumbled, "Thanks to God, Lord of the universe."

His doctor had frequently told him that the medicine was a temporary measure but that this new diet would be permanent. The physician had often cautioned him against being reckless or neglectful, for his high blood pressure had become severe, affecting his heart. Experience had taught al-Sayyid Ahmad to heed these instructions, because he had suffered whenever he had ignored them. Every time he had exceeded the limits, he had paid the price. He had finally been forced to give in, eating or drinking only what he was supposed to and coming home by nine. His heart had not given up hope that, by whatever means, he would regain his health and enjoy a pleasant, quiet existence, even though his past life had disappeared forever.

He listened with pleasure to the song coming from the radio. Seated on the pallet, Amina was talking about the cold and the rain that had poured down before noon. Paying no attention to her, he commented happily, "I heard that some of the old songs will be broadcast tonight."

The woman smiled appreciatively, since she liked that kind of music, perhaps most of all because her husband did. Delight sparkled for a few moments in the man's eyes before giving way to listlessness. He could no longer enjoy happy feelings unreservedly without having them suddenly turn sour on him. A confrontation with the facts would awaken him from his happy dream, as reality impinged on him from every direction. The past was nothing but a dream. What occasion was there for joy, when the days of fellowship, musical ecstasy, and health had departed forever? Delicious food and drink had vanished along with his well-being. Once he had strutted across the earth like a camel, his laughter reverberating from deep inside him, and dawn had found him intoxicated with all sorts of delights. Now he was obliged to return home from his soirees at nine so he could be in bed by ten, and the amounts he ate, drank, and walked were carefully prescribed.

He was the heart and the mainstay of this household, which time had afflicted with sorrows. The wretched Aisha was a thorn in his flesh, for he was incapable of mending the shreds of her life. He could hardly feel comfortable about her condition, since the morrow might find her miserably alone, without a father or a mother. He was also anxious about his own health, which was threatened by various complications of high blood pressure. What he feared most was having his strength fail him, so that he would be forced to lie in bed like a dead man. This had happened to many of his friends and loved ones. These thoughts hovered around him like flies, and he sought refuge with God from their evil torment. Yes, he would hear the old songs and fall asleep to their melodies.

"Leave the radio on even after I'm asleep."

She nodded her head with smiling agreement. Then he sighed and continued: "The stairs are really hard on me!"

"Rest at the landings, sir."

"But it's so humid in the stairwell. What cursed weather we're having this winter. . . ." Then he asked, "I bet you visited al-Husayn as usual despite the cold."

She answered shyly and uneasily, "Hardships seem trivial when I visit him, sir."

"It's all my fault!"

Trying to appease him, she added, "I walk around the holy tomb and pray for your health and well-being."

He was in urgent need of sincere prayers. Every good thing in life had been denied him. Even the cold shower with which he always refreshed his body had been forbidden him, since it was said to be dangerous for his arteries. "God have mercy on us," he thought, "when everything good becomes harmful."

They soon heard the door of the house slam shut. Raising her eyes, Amina murmured, "Kamal."

In a few minutes their son entered the room in his black over-coat, which revealed how thin and tall he was. He looked at his father through gold-rimmed glasses. A compact, bushy black mustache lent him a dignified and manly air. He leaned over to greet his father.

Al-Sayyid Ahmad invited him to sit down and as usual asked with a smile, "Where have you been, Professor?"

Kamal loved this gracious, affectionate tone, which his father had only recently adopted with him. Taking a seat on the sofa, he answered, "I was at the coffeehouse with some friends."

What sort of friends would they be? Kamal appeared excep-tionally serious, sober, and dignified for his age, spending most of his evenings in his study. What a difference there was between him and Yasin! Of course, each had his defects. Still smiling, al-Sayyid Ahmad asked, "Did you attend the Wafd Party congress today?"

"Yes. We heard a speech from the leader, Mustafa al-Nahhas. It was a memorable day."

"I was told it would be an important event but wasn't able to go. I gave my ticket to one of my friends. My health's no longer up to the fatigue."

Overcome by sympathetic affection, Kamal stammered, "May our Lord strengthen you."

"Weren't there any incidents?"

"No. The day passed peacefully. For a change, the police were content to watch."

The man nodded his head with relief. Then in a tone of voice that indicated the special significance he attached to the topic, he said, "Let me revert to an old subject. Do you still persist in your mistaken opinion about private lessons?"

Kamal always felt uncomfortable and uneasy when forced to disagree openly with one of his father's ideas. He replied gently, "We've finished discussing that."

"Every day friends ask if you won't give their children private lessons. You shouldn't reject honest work. Private lessons are a source of substantial income for teachers. The men asking for you are some of the most distinguished inhabitants of this district."

Kamal said nothing, but his face showed his polite refusal. His father asked regretfully, "You refuse and waste your time with endless reading and writing for free. Is that appropriate for an intelligent person like yourself?"

At this point Amina told Kamal, "You ought to love wealth as much as you love learning." Then, smiling proudly, she reminded al-Sayyid Ahmad, "He's like his grandfather. Nothing equaled his love of learning."

Her husband grumbled, "The grandfather again! I mean, was he an important theologian like Muhammad Abduh?"

Although she knew nothing about this distinguished modern reformer, she replied enthusiastically, "Why not, sir? All our neighbors came to him with their spiritual and worldly concerns."

Al-Sayyid Ahmad's sense of humor got the better of him. He laughed and said, "There are more religious scholars like him than you can shake a stick at."

The woman's protest was conveyed by her face, not her tongue. Kamal smiled affectionately but uneasily. He asked their permission to depart and left the room. In the sitting room Na'ima stopped him, wishing to show him her new dress. While she went to get it, he sat down beside Aisha to wait. Like the rest of the family, he indulged Na'ima in order to humor Aisha. But he was also as fond of this beautiful girl as he had been of her mother in the old days. Na'ima appeared with the dress, which he spread out in his hands. He examined it appreciatively and gazed at its owner with love and affection. He was struck by her gentle but extraordinary beauty, which purity and delicacy made magnificently luminous.

Kamal left the room with a heavy heart. It was sad to watch a family age. It was hard to see his father, who had been so forceful and mighty, grow weak. His mother was wasting away and disappearing into old age. He was having to witness Aisha's disintegration and downfall. The atmosphere of the house was charged with warning signs of misery and death.

He ascended the stairs to the top floor, which he called his apartment. He lived there alone, going back and forth between his bedroom and his study, both of which overlooked Palace Walk. He removed his clothes and put on his house shirt. Wrapping his robe around him, he went to the study, where a large desk with bookcases on either side stood near the latticed balcony. He wanted to read at least one chapter of Bergson's *The Two Sources of Morality and Religion* and to revise for the final time his monthly column in the magazine *al-Fikr*. This one happened to be about Pragmatism. The happiest part of his day was the period he devoted to philosophy. Lasting until midnight, it was the time – as he put it – when he felt like a human being. The rest of his day spent as a teacher in al-Silahdar School or in satisfying various needs of daily life was the stamping ground of the animal concealed inside him. That creature's goals were limited to self-preservation and the gratification of desires.

He neither loved nor respected his career but did not openly acknowledge his annoyance with it, especially not at home, for he wished to deprive people of the opportunity of rejoicing at his misfortune. All the same he was an excellent teacher who had won everyone's respect, and the headmaster had entrusted some administrative chores to him. Kamal jokingly accused himself of being a slave, for a slave might have to master work he did not like. The truth was that his desire to excel, which had stayed with him from his youth, compelled him to work hard for recognition. From the beginning he had resolved to win the respect of his pupils and colleagues, and he had achieved that goal. Indeed he was both respected and loved, in spite of his large head and prominent nose. Without any doubt, they – or his painful self-consciousness about them – were primarily responsible for his powerful determination to fashion a dignified persona. Realizing that these features would cause trouble, he had steeled himself to defend them against the plots of troublemakers. He did not escape the occasional gibe or taunt in class or on the playground but countered these attacks with an unflinching resolve softened by his innate sympathy for others.

His ability to explain the lessons in a way students could understand and his selection of interesting and engaging topics related to the nationalist movement or to memories of the revolution also swayed public opinion among the pupils in his favor. These factors as well as his firmness when it was necessary nipped rebellion in the bud. At first he had been hurt by the taunts, which were extremely effective at stirring up forgotten sorrows, but he was pleased by the high status accorded him by the youngsters, who regarded him with respect, love, and admiration.

His monthly column in *al-Fikr* magazine had caused him another problem, for he had to worry about the reaction of the headmaster and the other teachers. They might ask if his presentation of ancient and contemporary philosophical ideas that occasionally seemed critical of accepted beliefs and customs was compatible with a teacher's responsibilities. Fortunately none of these colleagues read *al-Fikr*. He realized at last that only a thousand copies of each issue were printed, of which half were exported to other Arab countries. That fact encouraged him to keep writing for the magazine, without fear of attacks or of losing his job.

During these brief nocturnal periods the English-language teacher at al-Silahdar School was transformed into a liberated voyager who traversed the limitless expanses of thought. He read, pondered, and jotted down observations that he later incorporated into his monthly columns. His efforts were motivated by a desire to learn, a love for truth, a spirit of intellectual adventure, and a longing for alleviation of both the nightmare engulfing him and the sense of isolation concealed within him. He escaped his loneliness by adopting Spinoza's notion of the unity of existence and consoled himself for his humiliations by participating in Schopenhauer's ascetic victory over desire. He put his sympathy for Aisha's misery into perspective by devouring Leibniz's explanation of evil and quenched his heart's thirst for love by appealing to Bergson's poetic effusions. Yet this continuous effort did not succeed in disarming the anxiety that tormented him, for truth was a beloved as flirtatious, inaccessible, and coquettish as any human sweetheart. It stirred up doubts and jealousy, awakening a violent desire in people to possess it and to merge with it. Like a human lover, it seemed prone to whims, passions, and disguises. Frequently it appeared cunning, deceitful, harsh, and proud. When he felt too upset to work, he would console himself by saying, "I may be suffering, but still I'm alive. . . . I'm a living human being. Anyone who deserves to be called a man will have to pay dearly in order to live."

117

LOOKING OVER the ledgers, keeping the books, and balancing the previous day's sales were all tasks Ahmad Abd al-Jawad performed as expertly and exactly as ever, but he accomplished them with greater difficulty now that he was old and sick. He looked almost pitiable as he sat hunched over his ledgers, beneath the framed inscription reading "In the Name of God," his gray mustache almost concealed by his large nose, which looked bigger now because of the thinness of his face. The appearance of his assistant, Jamil al-Hamzawi, almost seventy, was even more pathetic, and the moment he finished waiting on a customer, he would collapse, breathless, on his chair.

Ahmad told himself rather resentfully, "If we were civil servants, our pensions would spare us work and effort at our age." Raising his head from the accounts, he announced, "Sales are still off because of the economic crisis."

Al-Hamzawi pursed his pale lips with annoyance and said, "No doubt about it. But this year's better than last year, and that was better than the one before. Praise God in any event."

Merchants called the period commencing with 1930 the days of terror. Isma'il Sidqy had dominated the country's politics, and scarcity had governed its economy. From morning to night there had been news of bankruptcies and liquidations. Throwing up their hands in dismay, businessmen had wondered what the morrow had in store for them. Al-Sayyid Ahmad was definitely one of the lucky ones. Although bankruptcy had threatened him year after year, he had never gone over the brink.

"Yes, praise God in any event."

He noticed that Jamil al-Hamzawi was gazing at him in a strange, hesitant, and embarrassed way. What could be on the man's mind? Al-Hamzawi stood up to move his chair closer to the desk. Then, sitting down again, he smiled uneasily. It was bitterly cold, although the sun was shining brightly. Gusts of wind rattled the doors and windows, making a whistling sound.

Al-Sayyid Ahmad sat up straight and remarked, "Say what you want to. I'm sure it's important."

Lowering his gaze, al-Hamzawi said, "I'm in an awkward position. I don't know how to put it. ..."

His employer encouraged him: "I've spent more time with you than with my own family. ... You should feel free to express yourself frankly."

"Our years together are what make it so difficult for me, al-Sayyid, sir."

"Our years together!" he thought. This possibility had never occurred to him.

"You want to ... really?"

Al-Hamzawi answered sadly, "The time has come for me to retire. God never asks a soul to bear more than it can."

Al-Sayyid Ahmad felt depressed. Al-Hamzawi's retirement was a harbinger of his own. How could he look after the store by himself? He was old and sick.

He looked anxiously at his assistant, who said emotionally, "I'm really sorry. But I'm no longer up to the work. That time has vanished. Still, I've arranged things so you won't be left alone. My place will be taken by someone better able to assist you than I am."

His trust in al-Hamzawi's honesty had relieved him of half of his labors. How could a man of sixty-three start tending a store again from dawn to dusk? He said, "It's when a man retires and sits at home that his faculties begin to fail. Haven't you noticed that in civil servants with pensions?"

Smiling, Jamil al-Hamzawi answered, "In my case, decline has preceded retirement."

Al-Sayyid Ahmad laughed suddenly as if to mask his discomfort and then observed, "You old rascal, you're deserting me in response to your son Fuad's requests."

Al-Hamzawi cried out indignantly, "God protect us! The state of my health is evident to everyone. It is the only reason."

Who could say? Fuad was an attorney in the government judicial service. A person like that would not want his father to continue working as a clerk in a store, not even when the owner had made it possible for him to earn his government post. Yet al-Sayyid Ahmad sensed that his candor had distressed his excellent assistant. So he tried to cover his tracks by asking courteously, "When will Fuad be transferred back to Cairo?"

"This summer, or next summer at the latest. . . ." The moments that followed were heavy with embarrassment until al-Hamzawi, matching his employer's gracious tone, added, "Once he's settled in Cairo with me, I'll have to think about finding a bride for him. Isn't that so, al-Sayyid, sir? He's my only son out of eight children. I've got to arrange a marriage for him. Whenever I think about this, a refined young lady comes to mind – your granddaughter." He glanced quickly and inquisitively at his employer's face before stammering, "Of course, we're not of your class. . . ."

Al-Sayyid Ahmad found himself forced to reply, "May God forgive us, Uncle Jamil. We've been brothers for ages."

Had Fuad encouraged his father to sound out the situation? To have a position as a government attorney was outstanding, and the most important thing about a person's family was that they be good people. But was this the time to discuss marriage?

"Tell me first of all whether you're determined to retire."

A voice called out from the door of the shop, "A thousand good mornings!"

Although annoyed at having this important conversation interrupted, al-Sayyid Ahmad smiled to be polite and answered, "Welcome! Welcome!" Then he gestured toward the chair al-Hamzawi had vacated, saying, "Please have a seat."

Zubayda sat down. Her body seemed bloated, and her face was veiled by cosmetics. There was no trace of the gold jewelry that had once decorated her neck, wrists, and ears, and nothing remained of her former beauty.

As usual, al-Sayyid Ahmad tried to make her feel at home, but he treated her like any other visitor. His heart was displeased by this call, for whenever she came she burdened him with requests. He asked about her health, and she replied that she was not suffering from anything, "Praise God."

After a moment of silence, he said again, "Welcome, welcome. . . ."

She smiled gratefully but seemed to sense the lack of enthusiasm lurking behind his polite remarks. Pretending to be oblivious to the enveloping atmosphere of disinterest, she laughed. Time had taught her how to control herself. She observed, "I don't like to take up your time when you're busy, but you're the finest man I've ever known. Either give me another loan or find someone to buy my house. I wish you'd buy it yourself!"

Ahmad Abd al-Jawad sighed and said, "Me? If only I could. . . . Times have changed, Sultana. I keep telling you frankly how things are, but you don't seem to believe me, Sultana."

She laughed to hide her disappointment and then said, "The sultana's ruined. What can she do?"

"Last time I gave you what I could, but my circumstances won't allow me to repeat that."

She asked anxiously, "Couldn't you find someone to buy my house?"

"I'll look for a buyer. I promise you that."

She answered thankfully, "This is what I expected from you, for you're the most generous of men." Then she added sadly, "The world's not the only thing that's changed. People have changed even more. May God pardon them. In my glory days, they vied to kiss my slippers, but now if they spot me on the street they cross over to the other side."

It was inevitable for a person to be disappointed by something in life, in fact by many things – health, youth, or other people – but where were those days of glory, melodies, and love?

"You're partly to blame, Sultana. You never made any provision for this time of your life."

She sighed sorrowfully and said, "Yes. I'm not like your 'sister' Jalila. She doesn't mind whose reputation is tarnished, as long as she gets rich. She's accumulated a lot of money and several houses. Besides, God has surrounded me by thieves. Hasan Anbar was depraved enough to charge me a whole pound for a pinch of cocaine when it was scarce."

"Curses. . . ."

"On Hasan Anbar? A thousand!"

"No, on cocaine."

"By God, cocaine's a lot more merciful than people."

"No. No, it's really sad that you've succumbed to its evil influence."

With despondent resignation she admitted, "It has sapped my strength and destroyed my wealth. But what can I do? When will you find me a buyer?"

"At the first opportunity, God willing."

She rose, saying reproachfully, "Listen, the next time I visit you, smile as though you really mean it. I can bear insults from anyone but you. I know my requests are a nuisance, but I'm in straits known only to God. In my opinion, you're the noblest man alive."

He told her apologetically, "Don't start imagining things. It's just that I was preoccupied with an important question when you arrived. As you know, a merchant's worries never end."

"May God relieve you of them all."

Escorting her to the door, he bowed his head to show his appreciation for her comment. Then he bade her farewell: "You're really most welcome, any time." He noticed the eloquent look of distress and defeat in her eyes and felt sorry for her. Returning to his seat with a heavy heart, he looked at Jamil al-Hamzawi and remarked, "What a world!"

"May God spare you its evils and treat you to its blessings." But al-Hamzawi's tone grew harsh when he continued: "Still, it's the just reward for a debauched woman."

Ahmad Abd al-Jawad shook his head quickly and briefly as if to protest silently against the cruelty of this moralizing remark. Then resuming the merrier tone of voice he had used before Zubayda's interruption, he asked, "Are you still resolved to desert us?"

The other man answered uneasily, "It's not desertion but retirement. And I'm very sorry about it."

"Words . . . like the ones I used to deceive Zubayda a minute ago."

"God forbid! I'm speaking from my heart. Don't you see, sir, that old age has almost carried me off?"

A customer came into the store, and al-Hamzawi went to wait on him. Then the voice of an elderly man cried out flirtatiously from the doorway, "Who's that person as handsome as the full moon sitting behind the desk?"

Shaykh Mutawalli Abd al-Samad stood there in a crude, tattered, colorless gown and torn red leather shoes, his head wrapped in a camel's-hair muffler. Propping himself up with a staff, he gazed with bloodshot eyes at the wall next to the desk, thinking that he was looking at the proprietor.

In spite of his worries, al-Sayyid Ahmad smiled and said, "Come here, Shaykh Mutawalli. How are you?"

Opening a toothless mouth, the old man yelled, "High blood pressure, go away! Health, return to this lord of men."

Al-Sayyid Ahmad stood up and walked toward him. The shaykh stared in his direction but backed away as if preparing to flee. Then turning around in a circle, he pointed in each of the four directions and shouted, "You'll find relief here . . . and here . . . and here . . . and here." Exiting to the street, he intoned, "Not today. Tomorrow. Or the next day. Say: God knows best." He strode off with long steps that seemed incongruous for a man who looked so feeble.

118

THE EXTENDED family returned to its roots every Friday, and the old house came alive with children and grandchildren. This happy tradition had never lapsed. Since Umm Hanafi now held pride of place in the kitchen, Amina was no longer the heroine of the day. Still, the mistress never tired of reminding her family that the servant was her pupil. Amina's desire for praise became more pronounced as she sensed increasingly that she did not deserve it. Although a guest, Khadija always helped with the cooking too.

Shortly before al-Sayyid Ahmad's departure for the store, he was surrounded by family members: Ibrahim Shawkat and his two sons, Abd al-Muni'm and Ahmad, along with Yasin and his children, Ridwan and Karima. They were all subject to a humility that transformed laughter to smiles and conversation to whispers. The older al-Sayyid Ahmad got, the more he delighted in their company. He was critical of Yasin for curtailing visits to the store in exchange for this Friday gathering. Did the mule not understand that his father longed to see him as often as possible?

Yasin's son, Ridwan, had a handsome face with memorable eyes and a rosy complexion. His good looks suggested many different sources, reminding al-Sayyid Ahmad of Yasin, of Yasin's mother, Haniya, and of Muhammad Iffat, a beloved friend and the young man's other grandfather. Ridwan was al-Sayyid Ahmad's favorite grandchild. The boy's sister, Karima, was a little lady of eight. She would surely grow up to be a marvel, if only because of her black eyes, so like those of her mother, Zanuba, that they stirred within the patriarch an embarrassed smile rich with memories.

The decisive feature in the appearance of both Abd al-Muni'm and Ahmad was a lesser version of their grandfather's huge nose, but he could also recognize the small eyes of Khadija, their mother. They were bolder too than the others in addressing him. All these grandsons were pursuing their studies with a success he was proud of, but they seemed too busy with their own affairs to pay much attention to him. While they consoled their grand-father by showing him that his life was being passed on through new generations, they reminded him as well that he was gradually having to relinquish the dominant position he had reserved for himself in the family. He was not as sad as he might have been about this, since age had brought him wisdom along with illness and infirmity. Yet it would have been absurd to imagine that his new insight could prevent a flood of memories from bursting forth. Back in 1890, when he had been their age, he had studied only a little and played a lot, dividing his time between the homes of musicians in al-Gamaliya and the haunts of Ezbekiya. Even then his loyal companions had been Muhammad Iffat, Ali Abd al-Rahim, and Ibrahim al-Far. His father, who had run the store, had scolded his only son a little and pampered him a lot. Life had been a tightly wound scroll crowded with hopes. Then he had married Haniya. . . . But not so fast. . . he should not allow memories to carry him away.

He rose to prepare for the afternoon prayers. This was a sign he would soon depart. After he had changed clothes and left for the store, they all assembled in a congenial chatty mood around the grandmother's brazier for the coffee hour.

Amina, Aisha, and Na'ima occupied the center sofa. The one on the right was taken by Yasin, Zanuba, and Karima. On the left-hand one were seated Ibrahim Shawkat, Khadija, and Kamal. Ridwan, Abd al-Muni'm, and Ahmad had chairs in the center of the room, beneath the electric light. Following his time-honored practice, Ibrahim Shawkat extolled the dishes he had most enjoyed. Even so, during the past few years he had changed the direction of his praise toward the excellent instruction Amina was providing her outstanding pupil, Umm Hanafi.

Zanuba always echoed his words, for she never overlooked an opportunity to ingratiate herself with a member of her husband's family. In fact, ever since her in-laws had opened their doors to her, permitting her to mingle with them, she had shown extraordinary skill in strengthening her ties to them. She considered their wel-come an acknowledgment of her status, coming as it did after the years she had lived in isolation like an outcast. The death of a baby had been the pretext for the initial visit, when Yasin's family had come to his home to offer their condolences. Those calls had emboldened her to visit first Sugar Street and then – at a time when al-Sayyid Ahmad was quite ill – Palace Walk. She had even ventured into his room, where they had met like strangers with no past history. Thus Zanuba had become part of al-Sayyid Ahmad's family, calling Amina "Auntie" and Khadija "Sister." She was always exceptionally modest. Unlike other women of the family, she dressed simply when she made her calls, so that she seemed older than she was. Neglected, her beauty began to fade prematurely, and Khadija would never believe she was only thirty-six.

Zanuba had succeeded in gaining everyone's respect, and Amina said of her one day, "No doubt she comes from a good family – even if one or two generations back. It doesn't matter, for she's a good girl and the only one who has been able to live with Yasin."

Khadija seemed to surpass even Yasin in the flabby abundance of flesh and saw no reason to claim she was anything but happy about that. She was delighted with her sons, Abd al-Muni'm and Ahmad, as well as with her generally successful marriage, but to ward off the evil eye of jealousy never let a day go by without some complaint. Her treatment of Aisha had undergone a total change. During the last eight years she had not addressed a single sarcastic or harsh word to her younger sister, not even in jest. In fact, she bent over backwards to be courteous, affectionate, and gracious to Aisha, since she was touched by the widow's misery, frightened that fate might deal her a comparable blow, and apprehensive that Aisha would compare their lots. She had generously insisted that her husband renounce his share of his brother's estate, so that it went in its entirety to Aisha and her daughter, Na'ima. Khadija had hoped her action would be remembered in time, but Aisha was in such a state that she forgot her sister's generosity. This oversight did not keep Khadija from lavishing enough affection, sympathy, and compassion on Aisha to seem a second mother for her younger sister. To feel secure about her own God-granted prosperity, Khadija desired nothing more than Aisha's complaisant affection.

Ibrahim Shawkat took out a pack of cigarettes, and Aisha accepted one gratefully. He helped himself, and they both started smoking. Aisha's excessive dependence on cigarettes and coffee had been the subject of many comments, but her normal response to them was a shrug of her shoulders. Amina limited herself to the prayerful remark: "May God grant her endurance."

Yasin offered the most outspoken advice of any member of the family, for he appeared to think that the death of one of his children gave him this right. Aisha considered his loss inferior to her own and begrudged him any standing in the realm of the afflicted, since his son had died during the first year – unlike Uthman and Muhammad. Discussion of disastrous losses often seemed to be her favorite pastime, and her distinguished rank in the world of suffering was a consolation to her.

Kamal listened attentively to the conversation Ridwan, Abd al-Muni'm, and Ahmad were having about their future. Yasin's son, Ridwan, said, "We're all in the arts, not science. So the only college worth choosing in the University is Law."

Shaking his huge head, which made him, of the three boys, most resemble Kamal, Abd al-Muni'm Ibrahim Shawkat replied confidently in his powerful voice, "That's easy to understand. But he refuses to!" He pointed at his brother, Ahmad, who smiled ironically.

Also gesturing toward Ahmad, Ibrahim Shawkat seized this opportunity to remark, "He can go into the College of Arts if he wants to, but first he has to convince me of its value. I understand the importance of Law School, but not of Arts."

Kamal looked down rather sadly, stirred by old memories of a debate about the relative merits of the Law School and the Teachers College. He still nourished many of his former hopes, but life kept dealing him cruel blows every day. A government attorney, for example, would need no introduction, but the author of articles in *al-Fikr* magazine might be in even greater need of one than his obscure articles. Ahmad Ibrahim Shawkat left him no time for anxious musings. Looking at him with small protruding eyes, the boy said, "I'll let Uncle Kamal answer for me."

Ibrahim Shawkat smiled to hide his embarrassment, and with little enthusiasm Kamal said, "Study what you feel is most appropriate for your talents."

Ahmad turned his slender head to look victoriously from his brother to his father, but Kamal added, "Still you ought to realize that Law School opens up a wider range of good career opportunities for you than Arts. If you choose the Arts Faculty, your future will lie in teaching, which is a difficult profession with little prestige."

"I'm planning a career in journalism."

"Journalism!" shouted Ibrahim Shawkat. "He doesn't know what he's saying."

Ahmad complained to Kamal, "In our family, they see no distinction between guiding thought and guiding a cart."

Smiling, Ridwan observed, "The great intellectual leaders in our country have been Law School graduates."

Ahmad replied proudly, "I'm thinking of quite a different type of intellectual leadership."

Scowling, Abd al-Muni'm Shawkat said, "Unfortunately I know what you have in mind. It's frightening and destructive."

Looking at the others as if to ask for their support, Ibrahim Shawkat told Ahmad, "Look before you leap. You're only in the fourth year. Your inheritance won't be more than a hundred pounds a year. Some of my friends complain bitterly that their university-educated children are unfit for any kind of work or else employed as clerks at minuscule salaries. Once you've thought about all this carefully you're free to choose for yourself."

Yasin intervened to suggest, "Let's hear Khadija's opinion. She was Ahmad's first instructor. Who is better qualified to select between the selfish instruction in one's own rights provided by Law and the altruistic and humane influence of Arts?"

They all smiled, including Amina, who was busy with her coffeepot. Even Aisha smiled. Encouraged by her sister's good humor, Khadija retorted, "Let me tell you a cute story. Late yesterday afternoon – you know it gets dark early in winter – I was returning to Sugar Street from al-Darb al-Ahmar when I sensed that a man was following me. Then under the vault of the old city gate he passed me and asked, 'Where are you going, beautiful?' I turned and replied, 'I'm on my way home, Mr. Yasin.'"

The sitting room exploded with laughter. Zanuba directed a telling look at Yasin, one that blended criticism with despair. Motioning for them to be still, he asked, "You don't think I'm that blind, do you?"

Ibrahim Shawkat cautioned, "Watch your tongue!"

Although only eight, Karima grasped her father's hand and laughed as if she had understood the point of her aunt's story.

Zanuba's commentary on the situation was: "It's the worst things that make a person laugh."

Giving Khadija a furious look, Yasin said, "You've gotten me into hot water, girl...."

Khadija replied, "If anyone present is in need of the humane influences of Arts, it's you, not my crazy son Ahmad."

Zanuba agreed, but Ridwan defended his father, claiming he had been falsely accused. Ahmad kept his eyes fixed on Kamal, as though resting his hopes on his uncle.

Abd al-Muni'm glanced stealthily at Nai'ma, who looked like a white rose leaning against her mother. Her pale delicate face blushed whenever she sensed his small eyes looking at her.

Finally Ibrahim Shawkat spoke, changing the course of the conversation: "Ahmad, think how Law School has allowed al-Hamzawi's son to become an important government attorney." Kamal felt that this comment contained criticism directed against him.

Breaking her silence for the first time, Aisha said, "He would like to get engaged to Na'ima."

After the pause that greeted this news, Amina added, "His father mentioned it to her grandfather yesterday."

Yasin asked seriously, "Has Father agreed?"

"It's still early for such questions."

Glancing at Aisha, Ibrahim Shawkat inquired cautiously, "What does Mrs. Aisha think of this?"

Without looking at anyone, Aisha answered, "I don't know."

Studying her sister closely, Khadija remarked, "But it's all up to you."

Kamal wanted to put in a good word for his friend and said, "Fuad's really an excellent fellow."

Ibrahim Shawkat asked circumspectly, "Aren't his folks rather common?"

In his forceful voice, Abd al-Muni'm Shawkat replied, "Yes. One of his maternal uncles is a donkey driver and another's a baker. He has a paternal uncle who is an attorney's secretary." Then he added as a reluctant concession, "But none of this detracts from the man's worth. A person should be judged for what he is, not for his family."

Kamal realized that his nephew wanted to assert two truths no matter how contradictory: first the baseness of Fuad's origins and second the fact that a humble background does not diminish a person's value. He understood that Abd al-Muni'm was both attacking Fuad and repenting for this unfair attack, because of his strong religious convictions. Surprisingly, the assertion of these rival claims relieved Kamal, sparing him the embarrassment of expressing them himself. Like his nephew, he did not believe in the class system. Yet he was as inclined as Abd al-Muni'm to criticize Fuad and to belittle his friend's position, which he knew was far grander than his own.

Amina was clearly uncomfortable with this attack. She said, "His father's a fine man. He has served us honestly and sincerely his whole life."

Khadija found the courage to reply, "But if this marriage takes place, Na'ima may find herself mixing with people who are beneath her. Family origin is everything."

Her opinion was championed by the last person anyone would have expected when Zanuba said, "You're right! Family origin is everything."

Yasin was upset. He looked swiftly at Khadija, wondering how she would react to his wife's endorsement. What would she think of it? Would it remind her of the troupe and its female entertainers? He cursed Zanuba secretly for her empty braggadocio. Feeling obliged to say something to make up for his wife's remark, he observed, "Remember, you're talking about a government attorney. . . ."

Emboldened by Aisha's silence, Khadija said, "It's my father who made him one. Our wealth has made him what he is."

With sarcasm sparkling in protruding eyes that were reminiscent of his late Uncle Khalil's, Ahmad Shawkat retorted, "We're more indebted to his father than he is to us."

Pointing a finger at him, Khadija said critically, "You're always subjecting us to these incomprehensible remarks."

Sounding as if he hoped to terminate this discussion, Yasin commented, "Don't wear yourselves out. Papa will have the final say."

Amina distributed the cups of coffee, and the eyes of the young men gravitated to Na'ima, who sat beside her mother. Ridwan told himself, "She's a sweet and lovely girl. I wish it were possible for us to be friends and companions. If we could walk together in the street, people would have trouble saying which of us was better-looking."

Ahmad thought, "She's very beautiful but seems glued to her mother and has had little education."

Abd al-Muni'm reflected silently, "Pretty, a homemaker, and intensely religious – her only defect is her frailty. But even that's attractive. She's too good for Fuad." Then, breaking out of his internal monologue, he said, "Na'ima, tell us what you think."

The pale face blushed, frowned, and then smiled. Thrust into this awkward situation, the girl pitted a smile against her frown to free herself of both. Then she said shyly, "I don't have an opinion about this. Leave me alone!"

Ahmad remarked sarcastically, "False bashfulness. . . ."

Aisha interrupted him, "False?"

Correcting himself, he said, "This kind of modesty has gone out of style. If you don't speak up, Na'ima, you'll find that your life's over and that all the decisions have been made for you."

Aisha replied bitterly, "We're not used to talk like this."

Paying no attention to his mother's warning look, Ahmad complained, "I bet our family's four centuries behind the times."

Abd al-Muni'm asked scornfully, "Why precisely four?"

His brother answered nonchalantly, "I was being polite."

Khadija shifted the conversation to Kamal by asking, "And you! When are you getting married?"

Kamal was caught off guard by this inquiry, which he attempted to evade by saying, "That's an old story!"

"And a new one at the same time. . . . We won't abandon it until God unites you with a decent girl."

Amina followed this last part of the conversation with redoubled interest. Kamal's marriage was her dearest wish. She hoped fervently that he would turn her wish into a reality. Then she could rest her eyes on a grandchild fathered by her only living son. She said, "His father has proposed brides to him from the best families, but he always finds some excuse or other."

"Flimsy arguments! How old are you, Mr. Kamal?" asked Ibrahim Shawkat with a laugh.

"Twenty-eight! It's too late now."

Amina listened to the figure incredulously, and Khadija said angrily, "You love to make yourself out older than you are."

Since he was her youngest brother, revelation of his age indirectly disclosed hers. Although her husband was sixty, she hated to be reminded that she was thirty-eight. Kamal did not know what to say. In his opinion this was not a subject to be settled with a single word, but he always felt compelled to explain his position. So he said apologetically, "I work all day at school and every evening in my office."

Ahmad said enthusiastically, "What a fantastic life, Uncle ... but even so, a man needs to marry."

Yasin, who knew more about Kamal than any of the others, said, "You shrug off commitments so that nothing will distract you from your search for the truth, but truth lies in these commitments. You won't learn about life in a library. Truth is to be found at home and in the street."

Doing his best to escape, Kamal said, "I've grown accustomed to spending my salary each month down to the last millieme. I don't have any savings. How can I get married?"

Khadija blocked his escape by retorting, "Make up your mind to get married, and then you'll figure out how to prepare for it."

Laughing, Yasin observed, "You spend every millieme so you won't be able to get married."

"As if the two were equivalent," Kamal thought. But why did he not marry? That was what people expected and what his parents wanted. When he had been in love with Aïda, marriage had seemed absurdly out of reach. After that, love had been replaced by thought, which had greedily devoured his life. His greatest delight had come in finding a beautiful book or in getting an article published. He had told himself that a thinker does not and should not marry. He looked aloft and imagined that marriage would force him to lower his gaze. He had been – and still was – pleased to be a thoughtful observer who avoided, whenever possible, entry into the mechanics of life. He was as stingy with his liberty as a miser is with money. Besides, women no longer meant anything to him beyond a lust to be gratified. He was not exactly wasting his youth, since he did not let a week go by without indulging in intellectual delights and physical pleasures. If these reasons were not enough, he was apprehensive and skeptical about everything. Marriage seemed to be something a person should believe in.

Kamal said, "Relax. I'll get married when I feel like it."

Zanuba smiled in a way that made her look ten years younger and asked, "Why don't you want to marry now?"

Almost in exasperation, Kamal replied, "Marriage is an anthill. You're making a mountain out of it."

But deep inside he believed that marriage was a mountain, not an anthill. He was overcome by a strange feeling that one day he would give in to marriage and that his fate would then be sealed.

He was rescued by Ahmad's comment: "It's time for us to go up to your library."

Welcoming the suggestion, Kamal rose and headed for the door, trailed by Abd al-Muni'm, Ahmad, and Ridwan. As usual, they would borrow some books during this visit to the old house.

Kamal's desk in the center of the room under an electric light was flanked by bookcases. He sat down there to watch the young men read the titles of books on the shelves. Abd al-Muni'm selected a book of essays on Islamic history, and Ahmad took *Principles of Philosophy*. Then they stood around his desk as he looked silently at each of them in turn.

Finally Ahmad said irritably, "I'll never be able to read as much as I want until I master at least one foreign language."

Glancing at a random passage in his book, Abd al-Muni'm muttered, "No one knows Islam as it truly is."

Ahmad remarked sarcastically, "My brother discovers the truth of Islam in the Khan al-Khalili bazaar from a man of the people."

Abd al-Muni'm shouted at him, "Hush, atheist!"

Looking at Ridwan questioningly, Kamal asked, "Aren't you going to choose a book?"

Abd al-Muni'm answered for his cousin, "He's too busy reading the Wafd Party newspapers."

Gesturing toward Kamal, Ridwan said, "Our uncle has this in common with me."

His uncle believed in nothing but was a Wafdist all the same. Similarly, he doubted truth itself but worked pragmatically with other people. Looking from Abd al-Muni'm to Ahmad, he asked, "Since you support the Wafd Party too, what's strange about this? All Egyptian patriots are Wafdists. Isn't that so?"

In his confident voice, Abd al-Muni'm answered, "No doubt the Wafd is the best of the parties, but considered in the abstract it's not completely satisfying."

Laughing, Ahmad said, "I agree with my brother on this. To be more precise, it's the only thing we do agree on. And we may even disagree about the extent of our satisfaction with the Wafd Party. But the most important thing is to question nationalism itself. Yes, there is no argument about the need for independence, but afterward the understanding of nationalism must develop until it is absorbed into a loftier and more comprehensive concept. It's not unlikely that in the future we'll come to regard martyrs of the nationalist movement as we now do victims of foolish battles between tribes and clans."

"Foolish battles! You fool!" Kamal thought. "Fahmy did not die in a foolish battle. But how can you be certain?" Despite these reflections he said sharply, "Anyone slain for a cause greater than himself dies a martyr. The relative worth of causes may vary, but a man's relationship to a cause is a value that does not."

As they left the study, Ridwan told Abd al-Muni'm, "Politics is the most significant career open to a person in a society."

When they returned to the coffee hour, Ibrahim Shawkat was commenting to Yasin, "We rear our children, guide them, and advise them, but each child finds his way to a library, which is a world totally independent of us. There total strangers compete with us. So what can we do?"

119

THE STREETCAR was packed. There was not even room left for riders to stand. Although squeezed in among the others, Kamal towered over them with his lanky physique. He assumed the other passengers were also heading for the celebration of this national holiday, the thirteenth of November. He looked around at their faces with friendly curiosity.

Convinced that he believed in nothing, he still celebrated these holidays like the most ardent nationalist. Buoyed by their common destination and mutual Wafdist allegiance, strangers discussed the political situation with each other. One said, "Commemoration of our past struggle is a struggle in every sense of the word this year. Or it ought to be."

Another observed, "It should provide a response to Foreign Secretary Hoare and his sinister declaration."

Aroused by the reference to the British official, a third shouted, "The son of a bitch said, '... we have advised against the re-enactment of the Constitutions of 1923 and 1930.' Why is our constitution any business of his?"

A fourth reminded the crowd, "Don't forget what he said before that: 'When, however, we have been consulted we have advised . . .' and so on."

"Yes. Who asked for his advice?"

"Ask this government of pimps about that."

"Tawfiq Nasim! Have you forgotten him? But why did the Wafd enter into a truce with him?"

"There's an end to everything. Wait for the speech today."

Kamal listened and even took part in the discussion. Strangely enough, he felt just as excited as the others. This was his eighth commemoration of Jihad – or Struggle – Day. Like the others, he felt bitter about the political experiments of the preceding years.

"I experienced the reign of Muhammad Mahmud, who suspended the constitution for three years in the name of modernization, usurping the people's liberty in exchange for a promise to reclaim swamps and marshlands. I lived through the years of terror and political shame that Isma'il Sidqy imposed on the nation. The people placed their confidence in these men and sought their leadership, only to find them odious executioners, protected by the truncheons and bullets of English constables. Conveyed in one language or another, their message for the Egyptian people has been: 'You're minors. We are your guardians.' The people plunged into one battle after another, emerging breathless from each. Finally they adopted a passive stance of ironic forbearance. Then the arena was empty except for Wafdists and tyrants. The people were content to watch from the sidelines, whispering encouragement to their men but not offering any assistance."

His heart could not ignore the life of the Egyptian people. It was aroused by anything affecting them, even when his intellect wandered off into a fog of doubt.

He got out of the streetcar at Sa'd Zaghlul Street and joined an informal procession heading toward the pavilion erected for the holiday celebrations near Sa'd Zaghlul's home, the House of the Nation. At ten-meter intervals they encountered groups of soldiers with stern but dull faces. They were under the command of English constables. Shortly before reaching the pavilion, he saw Abd al-Muni'm, Ahmad, Ridwan, and a young man he did not know standing together, talking. They came up to greet him and stayed with him for some time. Ridwan and Abd al-Muni'm had been law students for about a month, and Ahmad had begun the final year of secondary school.

In the street Kamal could view them as "men." At home he always thought of them as young nephews. Although Ridwan was exceptionally handsome, his companion, whom he introduced as Hilmi Izzat, was equally good-looking. They demonstrated the truth of the saying: "Birds of a feather flock together."

Ahmad was a source of delight for Kamal, who could always anticipate some entertainingly novel observation or action from him. Of all his nephews, he felt closest spiritually to this one. Although he was shorter and plumper, there was a physical resemblance between Abd al-Muni'm and Kamal, who could love the young man for that reason, if for no other. It was this nephew's certainty and fanaticism he found offensive.

Approaching the huge pavilion, Kamal looked around at the swarming crowds of people, pleased by the astonishing numbers.

After gazing at the platform where the people's spokesman would soon deliver an address, he took his seat. His presence at a crowded gathering liberated a new person from deep inside his alienated and isolated soul, a new individual who was throbbing with life and enthusiasm. While his intellect was temporarily sealed up as if in a bottle, psychic forces ordinarily suppressed burst forth, eager for an existence filled with emotions and sensation. They were incentives for him to strive harder and to hope. At times like these, his life was revitalized, his natural impulses were free to express themselves, and his loneliness melted away. He felt linked to the people around him, as if sharing in their lives and embracing their hopes and pains. It would have been unnatural for him to adopt this life permanently, but it was necessary every now and then to keep him from feeling divorced from the daily routines of the people. For the time being he would postpone consideration of the problems of matter, spirit, physics, or metaphysics, in order to concentrate on what these people loved and hated . . . the constitution, the economic crisis, the political situation, and the nationalist cause. There was nothing strange about shouting slogans like "The Wafd creed is the nation's creed!" after having spent the previous night contemplating the absurdity of existence. The intellect can rob a person of peace of mind. An intellectual loves truth, desires honor, aims for tolerance, collides with doubt, and suffers from a continuous struggle with instincts and passions. He needs an hour when he can escape through the embrace of society from the vexations of his life. Then he feels reinvigorated, enthusiastic, and youthful.

In the library he had a few outstanding friends like Darwin, Bergson, and Russell, but in this pavilion there were thousands of friends. If they seemed mindless, they still collectively embodied a commendable natural alertness. In the final analysis, such people were as responsible as intellectual giants for shaping the events of history. In his political life Kamal loved and hated; he felt pleased and annoyed. Yet as an intellectual skeptic, he thought nothing mattered. Whenever he confronted this contradiction, he was overwhelmed by anxiety. No sector of his life was free from contradictions and therefore from anxiety.

For this reason, his heart yearned intensely to achieve a harmonious unity both perfect and happy. Where was this unity to be found? He felt that the life of thought was unavoidable for him so long as he had a mind with which to think. Yet that did not keep him from considering the opposite style of life toward which all his suppressed and ignored vital impulses pushed him as if toward a secure rock surrounded by surging water.

Perhaps for causes like these Kamal found this gathering splendid. The larger the crowd got, the more magnificent everything seemed. He waited for the leaders to appear with as much fervor and impatience as the rest of the audience.

Abd al-Muni'm and Ahmad sat next to each other, but Ridwan and his friend Hilmi Izzat were either strolling back and forth in the central aisle of the pavilion or standing at the entrance, where they chatted with some of the officials in charge of the festivities. The two certainly were influential young men. The crowd's whispers created a general hubbub. From the far seats occupied by young people there rose a clamor punctuated by yells. Then a loud cry was heard from outside, making heads turn toward the entrance. Everyone stood up and released a deafening roar. Mustafa al-Nahhas appeared on the dais, where he greeted the multitudes with his sincere smile and mighty hands.

Kamal watched the Wafd Party leader with eyes that had temporarily lost their skeptical look, although he wondered how he could believe in this man after ceasing to believe in everything else. Was it because the man was a symbol of independence and democracy? In any case, the warm relationship between the leader and the public was obvious and worth seeing. It had doubtless been a significant factor in the formation of Egyptian nationalism.

The atmosphere was charged with enthusiasm and ardor. The officials wore themselves out quieting the audience so that a reciter could chant some appropriate verses from the Qur'an, including "Prophet, goad the Believers to fight" (8:65). People had been waiting for this call, and their shouts and applause rang out in response to it. Some of the more sedate deplored the outburst and demanded that the audience be silent out of respect for God's Book. Their protest awakened old memories for Kamal of a time when he had been numbered among these pious souls. He smiled and immediately was reminded of his special world, so full of pairs of contradictions canceling out each other that it seemed empty.

The leader rose to deliver his address, which was clear, effective, and delivered in a resonant voice. Lasting for two hours, it

concluded with an open call for the use of force and an unambig-
uous appeal for revolution. The crowd's excitement reached a
fever pitch. People stood on the chairs and yelled with wild
enthusiasm. Kamal shouted as passionately as anyone else. He
forgot he was a teacher who was expected to maintain his dignity.
He imagined that he had been transported back to the glorious
revolutionary days he had heard about but had not been privileged
to experience. Had the speeches back then been as forcefully
delivered? Had the crowds received them with comparable enthusiasm? Had death seemed insignificant for those reasons? No doubt
Fahmy had been in a gathering like this once and had then rushed
off to death and immortality or annihilation. Was it possible for a
skeptic to become a martyr?

"Perhaps patriotism, like love," he thought, "is a force to which
we surrender, whether or not we believe in it."

The passionate outbursts were intense. The chants were ardent
and menacing. Chairs rocked with the motion of the men standing
upon them. What would be the next step? Before anyone knew
what was happening, throngs of people were heading outside. As
he left his place, Kamal looked around, searching for his young
relatives, but found no trace of them. He left the pavilion by a side
door and then walked briskly toward Qasr al-Ayni Street to get
there before the crowd. On his way he passed by the House of the
Nation and, as always, gazed at it, moving his eyes from the
historic balcony to the courtyard, which had witnessed such
momentous events in the nation's history. The building had an
almost magical fascination for him. Here Sa'd Zaghlul had stood.
Here Fahmy and his comrades had stood. On this street bullets had
lodged in the breasts of the martyrs. His people were in perpetual
need of a revolution to combat the waves of oppression that
prevented their rebirth. Periodic revolutions were necessary to
serve as a vaccine against this dread disease, for tyranny was the
nation's most deeply entrenched malady.

Kamal's participation in this patriotic holiday had successfully
reinvigorated him. Nothing mattered to him except the need for
Egypt to reply emphatically and decisively to Hoare's declaration.
He held his tall, slender body erect and his large head high as his
feet pounded against the pavement. He had lofty affairs and significant deeds on his mind as he passed by the American University
campus. Even a teacher occasionally had to join a revolution with

his students. He smiled almost in despair. He was an instructor
with a big head, destined to teach the fundamentals of English and
nothing more, even though this language had introduced him to
countless mysteries. His body occupied a tiny space on the swarming surface of the earth, while his imagination spun round in a
whirlpool embracing all the secrets of nature. In the morning he
asked what this word meant and how to spell that one. In the
evening he pondered the meaning of his existence – this riddle that
follows one puzzle and precedes another one. In the morning his
heart was ablaze with rebellion against the English but in the
evening it was chastened by a general feeling of brotherhood for
all mankind as he felt inclined to cooperate with everyone in order
to confront the puzzle of man's destiny.

He shook his head rather forcefully as if to expel these thoughts.
As he approached al-Isma'iliya Square he could hear people
shouting. He realized that the demonstrators had reached Qasr
al-Ayni Street. The combative spirit animating his breast made
him hesitate. Perhaps he would join in the day's demonstrations
after all. For too long the nation had patiently endured the blows it
received. Today it was Tawfiq Nasim, yesterday Isma'il Sidqy, and
before that Muhammad Mahmud. This ill-omened chain of despots stretched back into prehistory. "Every bastard has been
deluded by his own power and has claimed to be the chosen
guardian for us children. . . . Not so fast! The demonstration is
raging ahead furiously, but what's this?"

Disturbed, Kamal turned to look back. The sound he heard
shook his heart. As he listened intently, the noise of shots rang
out once more. He could see demonstrators in the distance, milling
around chaotically. Groups of people were rushing toward the
square, while others headed for the side streets. English constables
on horseback were galloping in the direction of the demonstrators.
The shouting grew louder. Screams mixed with angry voices, and
the firing became more intense. Kamal's heart pounded as, overcome by a troubled rage, he worried with each beat about Abd al-
Muni'm, Ahmad, and Ridwan. Turning right and then left, he
noticed a coffeehouse at the corner nearby and made for it. The
doors were almost closed, and on entering he remembered the
pastry shop in al-Husayn district where he had first heard gunfire.

There was pandemonium everywhere. Initially the rapid firing
was frightening, but then the shots became less frequent. The

sound of breaking glass was audible as well as the neighing of horses. An increase in volume of the furious voices showed that rebellious bands were dashing at breakneck speed from one location to the next. An elderly man entered the café. Before anyone could ask him what he had seen, he exclaimed, "The constables' bullets rained down on the students. Only God knows how many were hit." He sat down, breathing hard, and then added in a trembling voice, "It was treachery pure and simple. If their goal had been to break up the demonstration, they would have fired into the air from their distant positions. But they escorted the demonstration with calculated calm and then stationed themselves at the intersections. Suddenly they drew their revolvers and began firing. They shot to kill, showing no mercy. Young boys fell writhing in their own blood. The English were beasts, but the Egyptian soldiers were no less brutal. It was a premeditated massacre, my God."

A voice called out from the rear of the room, "My heart told me that today would end badly."

Another answered, "These are evil times. Since Hoare announced his declaration, people have been expecting momentous events. Other battles will follow. I promise you that."

"The victims are always students, the most precious children of the nation, alas."

"But the shooting has stopped. Hasn't it? Listen."

"The main part of the demonstration is at the House of the Nation. The shooting will continue there for hours to come."

But the square was silent. Minutes dragged by heavily, charged with tension. Darkness began to fall, and the lamps in the coffeehouse were lit. There was total silence, as if death had overtaken the square and the surrounding streets. When the double doors of the coffeehouse were opened wide, the square – empty of pedestrians and vehicles – was visible. A column of steel-helmeted policemen on horseback circled it, preceded by their English commanders.

Kamal kept wondering about the fate of his nephews. When traffic in the square hesitantly picked up again, he left the coffeehouse and hurried off. He did not return home until he had first visited Sugar Street and Palace of Desire Alley to reassure himself that Abd al-Muni'm, Ahmad, and Ridwan were safe.

Alone in his library, his heart filled with sorrow, distress, and anger, he did not read or write a single word. His mind was still roaming around the House of the Nation, thinking of Hoare, the revolutionary speech, the patriotic chants, and the screams of the victims. He found himself trying to recall the name of the pastry shop where he had hidden long ago, but memory failed him.

120

THE SIGHT of Muhammad Iffat's house in al-Gamaliya was a familiar and beloved one for Ahmad Abd al-Jawad. The massive wooden door looked like the entrance to an ancient caravansary. The high wall hid everything but the tops of lofty trees. Shaded by these mulberry and sycamore trees and dotted with small henna and lemon trees as well as various types of jasmine, the courtyard garden was marvelous. Equally amazing was the pool in the center. And then there was the wooden veranda stretching along the width of the garden.

Muhammad Iffat stood on the veranda steps, waiting to welcome his guest as he pulled his cloak tighter around him. Ali Abd al-Rahim and Ibrahim al-Far were already seated beside each other. Ahmad greeted his chums and followed Muhammad Iffat to the couch at the center of the veranda, where they sat down together. They had all lost their girth, except for Muhammad Iffat, who looked bloated and had a red face. Ali Abd al-Rahim had gone bald, and the others' hair was streaked with white. Wrinkles spread across their faces. Ali Abd al-Rahim and Ibrahim al-Far appeared to have aged more than the other two. The redness of Muhammad Iffat's face seemed almost to suggest a vascular disorder.

Although Ahmad had lost weight and his hair was turning white, he had retained his unblemished good looks. He loved this assembly and admired the view of the garden, which extended all the way to the high wall on al-Gamaliya Street. He leaned his head back a little as if to allow his large nose to inhale the fragrance of jasmine and henna. He closed his eyes occasionally to concentrate on hearing the chirps of the small birds flitting about in the branches of the mulberry and sycamore trees. Still, the most sublime feeling entertained by his heart just then was one of brotherhood and friendship for these men. When his wide blue eyes gazed at their beloved faces, which were masked by age, his heart overflowed with sorrow and sympathy, not only for them but for himself. The most nostalgic of them about the past, he was enthralled by anything he could remember about the beauty of youth, its passionate emotions, and his chivalrous escapades.

Ibrahim went to a nearby table to fetch the backgammon set, asking, "Who will play with me?"

Ahmad, who rarely joined in their games, said disapprovingly, "Wait a bit. We shouldn't lose ourselves in that from the very beginning."

Al-Far replaced the box. Then a Nubian servant brought in a tray with three teas and one whiskey and soda. Muhammad Iffat smiled as he took the whiskey glass and the others helped themselves to tea. This allocation, repeated every evening, often made them laugh. Waving his glass and gesturing toward their tea, Muhammad Iffat said, "May God be merciful to time, which has refined you."

Sighing, Ahmad Abd al-Jawad responded, "It has refined all of us and you more than the others, for you always were an exceptionally coarse fellow."

At approximately the same time one year they had all received identical medical advice to give up alcohol, but Muhammad Iffat's physician had allowed him one glass a day. Back then Ahmad Abd al-Jawad had assumed that his friend's doctor was more lenient than his own. He had gone to see this man, but the physician had advised him firmly and earnestly, "Your condition is different from your friend's." When the others had learned about this visit to Muhammad Iffat's doctor, it had provoked many jokes and comments.

Ahmad laughed and said, "You certainly must have given your doctor a big bribe to persuade him to let you have this one drink."

Al-Far moaned as he stared at the glass in Muhammad Iffat's hand and said, "By God, I've almost forgotten its intoxication."

Ali Abd al-Rahim jested, "You've destroyed your repentance by saying this, ruffian."

Al-Far asked his Lord's forgiveness and then murmured submissively, "Praise God."

"We've sunk to the point of envying one glass. Whatever has become of our ecstatic intoxications?"

Laughing, Ahmad Abd al-Jawad said, "If you repent, let it be of something evil, not of a blessing, you sons of dogs."

"Like all preachers, you have a tongue in one world and a heart in another."

Making his voice loud enough to suggest a change of subject, Ali Abd al-Rahim asked, "Men, what do you think of Mustafa al-Nahhas? This man was not influenced by the tears of an ailing and elderly king. He refused to forget for one second his highest objective, the 1923 constitution."

Muhammad Iffat cracked his fingers and said delightedly, "Bravo! Bravo! He's even more resolute than Sa'd Zaghlul. Although he saw that the tyrannical king was sick and tearful, al-Nahhas stood up to him with rare courage and repeated, with all the authority of the nation behind him, 'The 1923 constitution first.' So the constitution was reinstated. Who would have imagined that?"

Ibrahim al-Far nodded his head admiringly and said, "Picture this scene: King Fuad, broken by age and ill health, places his hand affectionately on the shoulder of Mustafa al-Nahhas and calls for the formation of a coalition government. Al-Nahhas is unmoved. He does not forget his duty as a trusted leader or abandon for one moment the constitution, which royal tears had almost drowned. Unimpressed by any of this, he says resolutely and courageously, 'The 1923 constitution first, Your Majesty.'"

Mimicking his friend's tone of voice, Ali Abd al-Rahim said, "Or impalement, Your Majesty."

Laughing, Ahmad Abd al-Jawad said, "I swear by the One whose fates tantalize us here with whiskey we're not allowed to drink – what a magnificent stand to take!"

Muhammad drained his glass and then said, "This is 1935. Eight years have passed since Sa'd's death and fifteen since the revolution. Yet the English are everywhere, in the barracks, the police, the army, and various ministries. The foreign capitulations that make every son of a bitch a respected gentleman are still operative. This sorry state of affairs must end."

"And don't forget butchers like Isma'il Sidqy, Muhammad Mahmud, and King Fuad's henchman al-Ibrashi...."

"If the English leave, none of these other men will matter and the constant change of governments will cease."

"Yes. If the king wants to make trouble behind the scenes then, he won't find anyone to help him."

Muhammad Iffat added, "The king will be left with two choices. Either he respects the constitution or he says good-bye."

Ibrahim al-Far asked rather skeptically, "Would the English forsake him if he sought their protection?"

"If the English agree to evacuate Egypt, why would they continue to protect the king?"

Al-Far asked, "Will the English really agree to evacuate?"

Speaking with confident pride in his political acumen, Muhammad Iffat replied, "They caught us off guard with Hoare's declaration. Then there were the demonstrations and the martyrs, may God be compassionate to them. Finally there came the invitation to form a coalition government and the 1923 constitution was restored. I assure you that the English now want to negotiate. . . . It's true that no one knows how this sorry situation will be sorted out, under what circumstances the English will leave, or how the influence of resident expatriates can be ended. But we have boundless confidence in Mustafa al-Nahhas."

"Is the exchange of a few words around a table going to end fifty-three years of foreign occupation?"

"The words have been preceded by the shedding of innocent blood. . . ."

"Even so. . . ."

With a wink, Muhammad Iffat replied, "They'll find themselves in an awkward position, given the grave international situation."

"They can always come up with someone to protect their interests. Isma'il Sidqy's still alive."

In a knowing tone, Muhammad Iffat responded, "I've spoken with many informed people and have found them optimistic. They say that the world is threatened by a crushing war, that Egypt is a potential target, and that it's in the best interests of both sides to reach an honorable settlement." After stroking his belly he continued with smug self-assurance: "Here's some important news for you. I've been promised the nomination for al-Gamaliya district in the forthcoming elections. Al-Nuqrashi himself promised me."

The faces of his friends shone with delight. When it was Ali Abd al-Rahim's turn to comment, he said with mock seriousness, "The only thing wrong with the Wafd Party is that they occasionally nominate beasts as deputies."

Ahmad Abd al-Jawad pretended to defend the Wafd against this charge. "What should the Wafd do? It wants to represent the entire nation. Some of the people are good citizens, and others are trash. What better representatives for trash can you have than beasts?"

Muhammad Iffat punched him in the side as he retorted, "You're a sly old fox! You and Jalila are exactly alike. You're a pair of old foxes!"

"I'd be happy to see Jalila nominated. She could sweep the king himself off his feet if she had to."

Smiling, Ali Abd al-Rahim commented, "I ran into her the day before yesterday near her cul-de-sac. She's still as magnificently massive as the ceremonial camel litter bound for Mecca, but age has eaten away at her and relieved itself all over her."

Al-Far added, "She's become a noted madam. Her house is a hotbed of activity, night and day. Even after the piper dies, her fingers keep on playing."

Ali Abd al-Rahim laughed for a long time and then said, "Passing by her house one day, I saw a man slip inside when he thought no one was looking. Who do you think it was?" With a wink in the direction of Ahmad Abd al-Jawad, he continued: "The dutiful Kamal Effendi, instructor at al-Silahdar School."

Muhammad Iffat and al-Far roared with laughter while Ahmad Abd al-Jawad, his eyes wide with astonishment and alarm, asked in a daze, "My son Kamal?"

"Yes indeed. His overcoat wrapped around him, he paraded along in a most genteel manner sporting his gold-rimmed spectacles and bushy mustache. He walked with such sedate dignity that it was hard to believe he was the son of our court jester. He turned into her establishment as solemnly as if entering the holy mosque in Mecca. Under my breath I said, 'Don't wear yourself out, bastard.'"

They laughed loudly. Ahmad Abd al-Jawad had not recovered yet from his stupor but attempted to overcome it by joining in the laughter.

Staring Ahmad in the face, Muhammad Iffat asked suggestively, "What's so amazing about this? Isn't he your son?"

Shaking his head with wonder, Ahmad Abd al-Jawad replied, "I've always thought him polite, refined, and cool. He spends so much time in his library reading and writing that I've been afraid he would become isolated from the world. He expends far too much effort on worthless things."

Ibrahim al-Far joked, "Who knows, perhaps there's a branch of the National Library in Jalila's house."

Ali Abd al-Rahman ventured, "Or perhaps he retreats to his library to read ribald classics like *The Shakyh's Return*. What do you expect from a man who began his career with an essay claiming that man is descended from an ape?"

They laughed again, and Ahmad Abd al-Jawad chuckled along with them. He had learned from experience that if he tried to be serious at a time like this he would become an easy target for jokes and jests. Finally he said, "This must be why the damned fellow has avoided marriage so studiously that I was beginning to have doubts about him."

"How old is your little boy now?"

"Twenty-nine."

"My goodness! You ought to get him married. Why is he so reluctant?"

Muhammad Iffat belched, stroked his belly, and then observed, "It's the fashion now. Girls crowd into the streets, and men don't trust them anymore. Haven't you heard Shaykh Hasanayn sing, 'What startling things we see: the gentleman and the lady both at the barbershop'?"

"Don't forget the economic crisis and the uncertain future facing young people. University graduates accept civil service jobs at only ten pounds a month, if they're lucky enough to find one."

With obvious anxiety, Ahmad Abd al-Jawad said, "I'm afraid that he's learned Jalila was my mistress or that she knows he's my son."

Laughing, Ali Abd al-Rahim asked, "Do you suppose she asks her customers for references?"

With a wink, Muhammad Iffat commented, "If the hussy knew who he was, she'd tell him his father's life story from A to Z."

Ahmad Abd al-Jawad snorted, "God forbid!"

Ibrahim al-Far asked, "Do you think a fellow who can discern that his original ancestor was an ape will have difficulty discovering that his father's a debauched fornicator?"

Muhammad Iffat laughed so loud that he started coughing. After a few moments of silence he remarked, "Kamal's appearance is truly deceptive . . . sedate, calm, prim – a teacher in every sense of the word."

THE CAIRO TRILOGY

In a gratified tone of voice, Ali Abd al-Rahim said, "Sir, may our Lord preserve Kamal and grant him a long life. Anyone who resembles his father can't go wrong."

Muhammad Iffat commented, "What's important is whether he's a Don Juan like his father. I mean, is he good at handling women and seducing them?"

Ali Abd al-Rahim replied, "I doubt it. I imagine he preserves his grave and dignified appearance until the door is closed behind him and the lucky girl. Then he removes his clothes with the same grave dignity and throws himself upon her with grim earnestness. Afterward he dresses and leaves with precisely the same solemnity, as though delivering an important lecture to his students."

"From the loins of Don Juan has sprung a dunce!"

Ahmad Abd al-Jawad asked himself almost resentfully, "Why does this seem strange to me?" He would try to forget about it. Seeing al-Far go to fetch the backgammon set, he proclaimed without any hesitation that it was time for them to play. Even so, his thoughts kept revolving around this news. He consoled himself with the reflection that he had raised Kamal conscientiously and had seen him get a University degree and become a respected teacher. Now the boy could do whatever he wanted. In view of his son's lanky build and enormous head and nose, perhaps it was lucky that he had learned how to have a good time. If there were any justice in the world, Kamal would have married years ago, and Yasin never would have married at all. But who could claim to understand such mysteries?

Then al-Far asked him, "When did you last see Zubayda?"

After thinking it over, Ahmad answered, "Last January. About a year ago. The day she came to the store to ask me to find a buyer for her house."

Ibrahim al-Far remarked, "Jalila bought it. Then that crazy Zubayda fell in love with a cart driver. But he left her destitute. Now she's living in a room on the roof of the house belonging to the performer Sawsan. She's such a ghost of her former self, it's pitiful."

Ahmad Abd al-Jawad shook his head sorrowfully and murmured, "The sultana in a rooftop shack! Glory to the unchanging One!"

Ali Abd al-Rahim commented, "A sad end, but hardly unexpected."

A laugh of lament escaped from Muhammad Iffat, and he said, "God have mercy on people who place their trust in this world."

Then al-Far invited them to play, and Muhammad Iffat challenged him. They quickly turned their attention to backgammon, as Ahmad Abd al-Jawad said, "Let's see whose luck is like Jalila's and whose resembles Zubayda's."

121

KAMAL WAS sitting with Isma'il Latif at Ahmad Abduh's coffee-house in the same alcove Kamal and Fuad al-Hamzawi had used as students. Although the December weather was cold, it was warm inside this subterranean establishment. With the entrance closed, all openings to the surface of the earth were sealed, and the air inside was naturally warmer and more humid. But for his desire to be with Kamal, Isma'il Latif would not have patronized this place. Of the old group, he was the only one who still kept in touch, although exigencies of employment had forced him to move to Tanta, where he had obtained a position as an accountant, following his graduation from the School of Commerce. Whenever he returned to Cairo on holiday he telephoned Kamal at al-Silahdar School and arranged to meet at this historic spot.

Kamal gazed at this old friend, taking in his compact build and the sharp features of his tapering face. He was pleasantly surprised by what he heard about Isma'il's polite, dignified, and upright behavior. The notorious paradigm of reckless and boorish impudence had become an exemplary husband and father.

Kamal poured some green tea into his companion's glass and then served himself. Smiling, he said, "You don't seem to care for Ahmad Abduh's coffeehouse."

Craning his neck in his familiar way, Isma'il replied, "It really is unusual, but why not choose somewhere aboveground?"

"In any case it's an eminently suitable place for a respectable person like you."

Isma'il laughed and nodded his head as if to admit that – after a wild youth – he now deserved recognition for his respectability.

To be polite, Kamal asked, "How are things in Tanta?"

"Great! During the day I work nonstop at the office and in the evening I'm at home with my wife and children."

"How are the offspring?"

"Praise God. Their relaxation always comes at the expense of our fatigue. But we praise Him no matter what."

Motivated by the curiosity any reference to family life inspired in him, Kamal asked, "Have you really found the kind of true happiness with them that advocates of family life forecast?"

"Yes. I have."

"In spite of the fatigue?"

"In spite of everything."

Kamal looked at his friend with even greater interest. This was a new person, quite distinct from the Isma'il Latif he had known from 1921 to 1927, that extraordinary era when he had lived life to the fullest, when not a minute had passed without some profound pleasure or intense pain. It had been a time of true friendship represented by Husayn Shaddad, of sincere love personified by Aïda, and of vehement enthusiasm derived from the torch of the glorious Egyptian revolution. It had also been a time of drastic experiments prompted by doubt, cynicism, desire. Isma'il Latif was a symbol of the former era and a significant clue to it. But how remote his friend was from all that today. . . .

Isma'il Latif conceded almost grumpily, "Of course, there's always something for us to worry about – like the new cadre system at work and the freeze on promotions and raises. You know I enjoyed an easy life under my father's wing. But I got nothing from his estate, and my mother consumes all of her pension. That's why I consented to work in Tanta – to be able to make ends meet. Would a man like me agree to it otherwise?"

Kamal laughed and said, "Nothing used to be good enough for you."

Isma'il smiled with what appeared to be conceit and pride at his memorable life, which he had renounced voluntarily.

Kamal asked, "Aren't you tempted to recapture some of the past?"

"Certainly not. I've had enough of all that. I can tell you that I've never regretted my new life. I just need to use a little cleverness from time to time to get some money from my mother, and my wife has to play the same game with her father. I still like to live comfortably."

Kamal could not keep himself from observing merrily, "You showed us how and then abandoned us. . . ."

Isma'il laughed out loud, and his earnest face assumed much of its mischievous look of the old days. He asked, "Are you sorry about that? No. You love this life with a curious devotion, even though you're a temperate person. In a few playful years I did more than you'll ever do during a whole lifetime." Then he added in a serious tone, "Get married and change your life."

Kamal said impishly, "This matter deserves serious thought."

Between 1924 and 1935 a new Isma'il Latif had come into existence. Curiosity seekers should search out this novelty. Still, he was the one old friend left. France had seduced Husayn Shaddad away from his homeland. Similarly, Hasan Salim had established himself outside of Egypt. Unfortunately Kamal had no contact with either of them anymore. Isma'il Latif had never been a soul mate. But he was a living memory of an amazing past, and for that reason Kamal could glory in his friendship.

"I also take pride in his loyalty. I derive no spiritual delight from his companionship, but he's living proof of the existence of that past. I desire to establish the reality of that era as eagerly as I desire life itself. I wonder what Aïda's doing now. Where is she in this wide world? How was my heart ever able to recover from the sickness of loving her? All those events are marvels of their kind."

"I'm impressed, Mr. Isma'il. You deserve every success."

Isma'il glanced at his surroundings, inspecting the ceiling, lanterns, alcoves, and the dreamy faces of the patrons, who were absorbed in their conversations and games. Then he asked, "What do you like about this place?"

Kamal did not answer but remarked sadly, "Have you heard? It will soon be demolished so a new structure can be built on its ruins. This historic spot will vanish forever."

"Good riddance! Let these catacombs disappear so a new civilization can rise above them."

"Is he right?" Kamal wondered. "Perhaps . . . but the heart feels strongly about certain things. My dear coffeehouse, you're part of me. I have dreamt a lot and thought a lot inside you. Yasin came to you for years. Fahmy met his revolutionary comrades here to plan for a better world. I also love you, because you're made from the same stuff as dreams. But what's the use of all this? What value does nostalgia have? Perhaps the past is the opiate of the Romantic. It's a most distressing affliction to have a sentimental heart and a skeptical mind. Since I don't believe in anything, it doesn't matter what I say."

"You're right. I advocate demolition of the pyramids if some future use is discovered for the stones."

"The pyramids! What's the relationship of the pyramids to Ahmad Abduh's coffeehouse?"

"I'm referring to all historic relics. I mean let's destroy all of them for the sake of today and tomorrow."

Isma'il Latif laughed. He craned his neck, as he had in the past when challenged, and replied, "You've occasionally supported the opposite point of view. As you know, I read *al-Fikr* magazine from time to time, for your sake. I told you frankly once before what I think of it. Yes, your essays are difficult, and the whole journal is dry, may God grant us refuge. I had to stop buying it, because my wife found nothing in it she wanted to read. Forgive me, but that's what she asserted. I say I've occasionally seen you write the opposite of what you're proposing now. But I won't claim to understand much of what you write. Don't tell anyone, but I don't understand even a little of it. Speaking of this, wouldn't it be better for you to write like popular authors? If you do, you'll find a large audience and make a lot of money."

In the past Kamal had rebelliously and stubbornly scorned such advice. Now he despised it but did not rebel against it. Yet he wondered whether he should be so disdainful, not because he thought the disdain misplaced, but because he worried at times about the value of what he wrote. He was even uneasy about this worry. He was quick to confess to himself that he was fed up with everything and that the world, having lost its meaning, seemed at times to resemble an obsolete expression.

"You never did approve of my way of thinking."

Isma'il guffawed and said, "Do you remember? What days those were!"

Those days had passed. Their fires burned no longer. But they were treasured away like the corpse of a loved one or like the box of wedding candies he had hidden in a special place the night of Aïda's marriage.

"Don't you hear from Husayn Shaddad or Hasan Salim?"

Isma'il raised his thick eyebrows and replied, "That reminds me! Things have happened during the year I've been away from Cairo. . . ." With increasing concern he continued: "I learned on my return from Tanta that the Shaddad family has ended."

Oppressive, rebellious interest erupted in Kamal's heart, and he suffered terribly as he struggled to conceal it. He asked, "What do you mean?"

"My mother told me that Shaddad Bey went bankrupt when the stock market swallowed up his last millieme. Destroyed, he could not stand the blow and killed himself."

"What awful news! When did this happen?"

"Some months ago. The mansion was lost along with all his other possessions – that mansion where we spent unforgettable times in the garden. . . ."

What times, what a mansion, what a garden, what memories, what forgotten pain, and painful forgetfulness. . . . The elegant family, the great man, the mighty dream. . . . Was not his agitation more pronounced than the situation warranted? Was his heart not pounding more violently than these once forgotten memories deserved?

Kamal said sorrowfully, "The bey has killed himself. The mansion has been lost. What's become of the family?"

Isma'il replied angrily, "Our friend's mother has only fifteen pounds a month from a mortmain trust and has moved into an unpretentious flat in al-Abbasiya. My mother, who went to visit them, wept upon her return when describing the woman's condition . . . that lady who once lived in unimaginable luxury. Don't you remember?"

Of course he remembered. Did Isma'il think he had forgotten? He remembered the garden, the gazebo, and the felicity of which the breezes there sang. He remembered happiness and sorrow. Indeed he felt truly sorrowful just then. Tears were ready to well up in his eyes. It would not do for him to mourn the threatened destruction of Ahmad Abduh's coffeehouse anymore, for everything was destined to be turned head over heels.

"That's really sad, and it makes me feel even worse that we didn't do our duty and present our condolences. Don't you imagine Husayn returned from France?"

"No doubt he came back after the incident, as well as Hasan Salim and Aïda. But none of them is in Egypt now."

"How could Husayn go off again, leaving his family in this condition? What's he got to live on, now that his father's money is gone?"

"I heard he married over there. It's not unlikely that he's found work during his long stay in France. I don't know anything about that. I haven't seen him since we both said goodbye to him. How much time has elapsed since then? Approximately ten years . . . isn't that so? That's ancient history, but this upset me a lot."

"A lot . . . a lot," the words echoed inside Kamal. His tears were still trying to escape. He had not cried since that era and had forgotten how to. As his heart dissolved in sorrow, he recalled a time when it had chosen sorrow for its emblem. The news shook him so violently that the present dispersed entirely to reveal the person whose life had been pure love and pure sorrow. Was this the end of the old dream?

"Bankruptcy and suicide!" It almost seemed predestined that this family would teach him that even gods fall. "Bankruptcy and suicide . . . if Aïda was still living luxuriously because of her husband's position, what had become of her lofty pride? Had the events reduced her little sister to . . .?"

"Husayn had a young sister. What was her name? I remember occasionally, but it escapes me most of the time."

"Budur. She lives with her mother and shares all the difficulties of the new life."

"Imagine Aïda living in reduced circumstances . . . a life like those of the men sitting here," Kamal thought. "Does Budur have to wear darned stockings? Does she ride the streetcar? Will she marry an employee of some firm?" But how did any of this concern him?

"Oh . . . don't deceive yourself. Today you're sad. Whatever intellectual posture you adopt concerning the class system, you feel a frightening despair over this family's fall. It's painful to hear that your idols are wallowing in the dirt. At any rate, the fact that nothing remains of your love is gratifying. Yes, what's left of that bygone love?"

Although he thought that no trace remained, his heart pounded with strange affection when he heard any of the songs of that age, no matter how trite the lyrics or the tunes. What did this mean?

"But not so fast. A memory of love, not love itself, was at work. We're in love with love, regardless of our circumstances, and love it most when we are deprived of it. At the moment, I feel adrift in a sea of passion. A latent illness may release its poison when we're temporarily indisposed. What can we do about it? Even doubt, which puts all truths into question, stops cautiously before love, not because love is beyond doubt, but out of respect for my sorrow and from a desire that the past should be true."

Isma'il returned to this tragedy, narrating many of its details. Finally he seemed to tire of it. In a tone that indicated he wished to end the saga he said, "Only God is permanent. It's really distressing, but that's enough misfortune for us now."

Feeling a need for silent reflection, Kamal did not attempt to draw him out. What Isma'il had said was quite sufficient. To his own astonishment, Kamal wept silently with invisible tears shed by his heart. Although once afflicted by love's malady, he had recovered completely. He told himself in amazement, "Nine or ten years! What a long time and yet how short. . . . I wonder what Aïda looks like now."

He wished terribly that he could gaze at her long enough to discover the secret of that magical past and even the secret of his own personality. He saw her now only as a fleeting image in a familiar old song, a picture in a soap advertisement, or when in his sleep he whispered with surprise, "There she is!" But what he actually observed was nothing more than glimpses of a film star or an intrusive memory. He would wake up. What reality was there to it then?

He did not feel like sitting here any longer. His soul yearned for an adventuresome journey through the unseen spiritual realm. So he asked Isma'il, "Will you accept my invitation to have a couple of drinks in a nice place where we won't be seen?"

Isma'il chortled and replied, "My wife's waiting for me to take her to visit her aunt."

Kamal was not concerned about this rejection. For a long time he had been his own drinking companion. The two men continued chatting about one thing and another as they left the coffeehouse. In the middle of that conversation, Kamal remarked to himself, "When we're in love, we may resent it, but we certainly miss love once it's gone."

122

"IT'S PLEASANT sitting here . . . although my resources are limited. From this warm spot you can see people coming and going . . . back and forth from Faruq Street, the Muski, and al-Ataba."

But for the stinging cold of January, this Casanova would not have taken shelter behind the coffeehouse window, reluctantly abandoning the excellent outdoor vantage point the establishment claimed on the opposite sidewalk.

"But spring will come. . . . Yes, it will, even though our resources are limited. Sixteen years or more stuck at the seventh grade of the civil service. . . . The store in al-Hamzawi was sold for a minuscule sum. Even though the rental unit in al-Ghuriya is large, it brings in only a few pounds. The house in Palace of Desire Alley is my residence and refuge. Ridwan has a rich grandfather, but Karima's totally dependent on me . . . the head of a household with a lover's heart. Unfortunately my resources are limited."

His roving eyes suddenly came to rest on a lanky young man with a compact mustache and gold-rimmed glasses. Wearing a black overcoat, the fellow was on his way from the Muski to al-Ataba. Yasin straightened up as though preparing to rise but did not stir from his seat. If the young man had not seemed in a such a hurry, Yasin would have stepped out to invite his brother to sit with him. Kamal was an excellent person to talk to when one was feeling low. Although almost thirty, he had never thought of getting married.

"Why was I in such a hurry to marry? Why did I jump right back in before recovering from the first bout? But who doesn't have something to complain of, whether married or single? Ezbekiya was a delightful place for fun, but it's been ruined. Today it's a meeting place for the dregs of society. All you have left from the world of pleasures is the diversion of observing this intersection and then of pursuing some easy quarry, at best an Egyptian maid who works for a foreign family. Usually she'll be clean, with a refined appearance. Yet her dominant characteristic will undeniably be her questionable morals. She's often found at the vegetable market in al-Azhar Square."

His coffee finished, he sat by the closed window, gazing out at the street. His eyes followed all the good-looking women, recording their images, whether they wore the traditional black wrap or a modern overcoat. He observed their individual attractions and their overall appearance with unflagging diligence. Some evenings he sat there until ten. At other times he stayed only long enough to drink his coffee before rising to hurry off in pursuit of prey he sensed would be responsive and cheap – as if he were a dealer in secondhand goods. Most of the time he was content just to watch. He might trail after a beauty without harboring any serious ambitions. Only occasionally was he overwhelmed enough by desire at the sight of a dissolute maid or of a widow over forty to pursue her in earnest. He was no longer the man he had once been, not merely because of the heavy burdens on his income but also because his fortieth year had arrived, an uninvited and unwelcome guest.

"What an alarming fact! White hairs at my temples! I've told the barber repeatedly to deal with it. He says one white hair is nothing to be concerned about, but they keep popping up. Down with both of them – the barber and white hair! He prescribed a reliable dye, but I'll never resort to that. When my father turned fifty, he didn't have a single white hair. What am I compared to my father? And not only with regard to white hair. . . . He was a young man at forty, a young man at fifty. But I . . . My Lord, I've not been more intemperate than my father. . . . Give your head a rest and exercise your heart. Do you suppose the life of Harun al-Rashid was really as filled with sensual pleasures as reports would have it? . . . Where does Zanuba fit into all this? Considered in the abstract, marriage is a bitch of a deception, but it's a powerful enough force to make you cherish the deception as long as you live. Nations will be overthrown, and eras will pass away. Yet the fates will always produce a woman going about her business and a man seriously pursuing her. Youth is a curse, but maturity's a string of curses. Where can a heart find any relaxation? . . . Where? . . . The most wretched thing that could happen in this world would be having to ask in a stupor one day, 'Where am I?'"

He left the coffeehouse at nine-thirty and proceeded slowly

across al-Ataba to Muhammad Ali Street. Then, entering the Star Tavern, he greeted Khalo, who stood behind the bar in his traditional stance. The bartender returned Yasin's greeting with a broad smile, which revealed yellow front teeth with gaps between them. He gestured with his chin toward the interior, as if to inform this customer that friends were waiting for him there. The hall running beside the bar ended in a suite of three connected rooms that resounded with raucous laughter. Yasin went to the last of the three. It had but one window, which offered through its iron bars a view of al-Mawardi Alley. Three tables were dispersed in the corners. Two were empty, and the third was surrounded by Yasin's friends, who greeted him jubilantly, as they did every evening. Despite his complaints, Yasin was the youngest of the group. The oldest was an unmarried pensioner, who sat next to a head clerk in the Ministry of Waqfs, or mortmain trusts. Present also were a personnel director from the University and an attorney whose rental income spared him from having to practice law. The excessive reliance of these men on alcohol was apparent in their bleary gaze and in their complexions, which were either flushed or exceedingly pale. They made their way to the tavern between eight and nine and did not leave it until the wee hours of the morning, after imbibing the nastiest, cheapest, and most intoxicating drinks available. Yasin did not keep them company the whole time or did so only rarely. He normally spent two or three hours with them.

As usual the elderly bachelor greeted him with the salutation "Welcome, Hajji Yasin." The old man persisted in calling him a hajji, or pilgrim, not because Yasin had been to Mecca, but because of his Qur'anic name.

The attorney, the most alcoholic, observed, "You're so late, hero, that we said you must have stumbled upon a woman who would deprive us of your company all night long."

The bachelor commented philosophically, "There's nothing like a woman to come between one man and another."

Yasin, who had taken a seat next to him and the head clerk from trusts, jested, "There's no need to worry about that with you."

Lifting his glass to his mouth, the old man said, "Except for a few devilish moments when a girl of fourteen may tempt me."

The head clerk retorted, "Talking about it in January is one thing, but doing it in February is another."

"I don't understand what you mean by this rude remark."

"I don't either!"

Khalo brought Yasin a drink and some lupine seeds. Accepting the drink, Yasin said, "See what January's like this year!"

The personnel director commented, "God creates many different conditions. This year January has brought cold weather but has removed Tawfiq Nasim for good."

The attorney shouted, "Save us from politics! We always have politics for an appetizer when we're getting drunk and that spoils the effect. Find some other subject."

The personnel director said, "Actually our lives are nothing but politics."

"You're a personnel director in the sixth grade of the civil service. What does politics have to do with you?"

The director answered vehemently, "I've been at the sixth level for a long time, if you don't mind. Since the days of Sa'd Zaghlul."

The elderly bachelor said, "I reached the sixth level years ago in the era of Mustafa Kamil. In honor of his memory I retired at that rank. . . . Listen, wouldn't it be better for us to get drunk and sing?"

On the verge of draining his glass, Yasin said, "First let's get drunk, pop."

Yasin had never experienced a deep friendship, but wherever he went – coffeehouses or bars – he had pals. He made friends quickly and found friends even more quickly. He had frequented these men ever since developments in his financial situation had prompted him to make this bar his regular spot for evening relaxation. He chatted on intimate terms with the others, although he never met any of them outside of this setting and made no effort to do so. Alcoholism and frugality brought them together. The personnel director outranked the others but had many dependents. The attorney had sought out this bar because of its reputation for serving potent drinks, after normal ones had ceased to have much effect on him. Then he had gotten accustomed and habituated to the establishment.

Feeling drunk enough to become talkative, Yasin threw himself into the riotous maelstrom that swept through the place, surging into every corner. The elderly bachelor was Yasin's favorite. He never tired of teasing the old man, especially with allusions to sex, and the bachelor would caution Yasin not to indulge himself too much, reminding him of his domestic responsibilities.

Yasin's boastful retort was: "My family is made for this. My father's like that, and my grandfather before him was as well."

When Yasin repeated this statement now, the attorney jestingly asked him, "And what about your mother? Was she like that too?"

They laughed a lot, and Yasin laughed with them. But his tormented heart plunged in his chest. He drank more than usual and, in spite of his intoxication, imagined that he was collapsing. The place, the drink, the day – nothing felt right to him.

"Everywhere I go people are secretly making fun of me. What am I, compared to my father? Nothing makes a person so miserable as an increase in age or a decrease in wealth. But drinking provides considerable relief. It pours forth gentle sociability and attractive solace, making every mishap seem trivial. So say, 'How happy I am.' The lost real estate will never return nor will my vanished youth. But alcohol can be an excellent lifetime companion. I was weaned on it as a callow youth. Now it's cheering up my manhood. When covered with white hair, my head will quiver with alcohol's ecstatic intoxication. So no matter what hardships I suffer, I will never lose heart. Tomorrow when Ridwan's established as a man and Karima struts off as a bride, I'll drink several toasts to happiness here in al-Ataba al-Khadra Square. How happy I am!"

Then the group was singing, "What humiliations the prisoner of love experiences. . . ." After that they did a loud and tumultuous rendition of "That girl in the neighboring valley." Men in the other rooms and in the lobby took up the song too. When it was finished, the silence was deafening.

The personnel director began discussing the resignation of Tawfiq Nasim and asked about the pact designed to protect Egypt from the danger Italy posed for her as a troublesome neighbor occupying Libya. But the assembly quickly sang in response, "Let down the curtain around us . . . to keep the neighbors from peeking." Although the elderly man had drunk to excess, participating fully in the rowdiness, he protested against this impudent response and accused them of being silly about a serious matter. Their answer was to sing in unison, "Is your opposition real or feigned?" Then the old man was forced to laugh and to join in wholeheartedly once more.

Yasin left the tavern at midnight, reaching his home in Palace of Desire Alley around one in the morning. As usual each night he walked through the rooms of his apartment as though on an inspection tour. He found Ridwan studying in his room, and the young man looked up from his law book to exchange a smile with his father. The love between them was profound. Ridwan also had great respect for Yasin, even though he realized that his father was always intoxicated when he returned home this late. Yasin was extremely appreciative of his son's good looks and also admired his intelligence and industry. He saw Ridwan as a future public prosecutor who would raise his father's status, give him cause for pride, and console him for many things.

Yasin asked, "How are your studies?" Then he pointed to himself as if to say, "I'm home, if you need me." Ridwan smiled, and the eyes he had inherited from his paternal grandmother, Haniya, lit up. His father asked, "Will it bother you if I play something on the phonograph?"

"It won't disturb me, but the neighbors are sleeping at this hour."

As he left the room Yasin said scornfully, "I hope they sleep well."

Passing by the "children's" bedroom, he found Karima sound asleep in her little bed. On the other side of the room Ridwan's bed was empty, waiting for him to finish studying. Yasin thought of waking his daughter up to joke with her but remembered how she grumbled when awakened in the night and gave up the idea. He went toward his room. The most wonderful night of the week in this house was without doubt that preceding the Friday holiday. Each Thursday evening when he got home, regardless of the hour, he would not hesitate to invite Ridwan to keep him company in the sitting room. Then he would awaken Karima and Zanuba. Starting up the phonograph, he would chat and joke with them until early the next morning. He was very fond of his family, especially Ridwan. It was true that he did not make any effort — or did not have the time — to supervise or guide them. He left their care to Zanuba and her instinctive good sense. Even so, he had never wished to play the cruel role with them that his own father had with him. The idea of creating in Ridwan's heart the feelings of terror and fear he had felt for his own father was deeply abhorrent to Yasin. In fact, he would not have been able to do it, even if he had wanted to. When he gathered them around him after midnight he would openly express his warm affection for them in a double intoxication derived from alcohol and love. While jesting and conversing with them he might tell droll anecdotes about the drunks he had encountered at the bar. He paid no attention to the effect these could have on their innocent souls and waved aside Zanuba's discreet attempts to signal him to desist. He seemed unselfconscious and acted spontaneously without reserve or caution.

As usual he found Zanuba half asleep in their room. It was always like this. Before he entered, he could hear her snoring. By the time he reached the middle of the room she was moving and opening her eyes. In her sarcastic voice she said, "Praise God for your safe return." Then she rose to help him take off his clothes and fold them. Unadorned, she appeared older than she was. He frequently thought she looked as old as he did. But she had become his companion, and their lives had become intermeshed. This former entertainer had succeeded in staying married to him, a feat no lady had accomplished before her. His wedded life was firmly anchored. At first there had been fights and loud quarrels, but she had always shown how much she cherished their marriage. In the course of time she had become a mother. When her son had died, leaving her with only Karima, that loss had made her redouble her efforts to safeguard her married life, especially once her beauty began to fade and she was threatened by premature aging. Time had taught her how attractive patience and conciliation are and how to perfect the role of a lady in every sense of the word. She went to such extremes in this regard that she dressed very simply when she went out. Her efforts eventually won a certain degree of respect for her on Palace Walk and Sugar Street. She had the good judgment to treat her stepson Ridwan exactly like Karima, showing both of them great tenderness and affection, even though she did not feel any love for the boy, especially after she lost the only son she bore Yasin. No longer a beauty, she was still careful to wear attractive clothes and to be clean and neat.

Yasin smiled as he watched her fix her hair in front of the mirror. Although she occasionally annoyed him to the point of anger, he sensed that she had truly become a precious part of his life, someone he could never do without.

Since she was shivering, she got a shawl, complaining, "It's so cold! Do yourself a favor and don't spend your evenings out during the winter."

He answered sarcastically, "As you know, alcohol changes the season. Why tire yourself by waking up?"

She fumed, "What you say is as tiresome as what you do."

In his nightshirt he looked like a blimp. Rubbing his hand over his belly, he gazed at the woman with satisfaction. His black eyes sparkled. Then he laughed suddenly and said, "If you could have seen me exchanging greetings with the officers. . . . The ones on the late patrol have become my dear friends."

Sighing, she muttered, "I'm overjoyed."

123

THE SIGHT of Yasin's son, Ridwan, striding through al-Ghuriya at a deliberate pace was really enough to turn heads. Seventeen years old, he had attractive dark eyes and a medium build with a slight tendency to be stocky. His attire was so dapper it attracted attention. His rosy complexion was attributable to his mother's family, the Iffats. He had a radiant charm, and his gestures betrayed the conceit of a person whose good looks were no secret to him. When he passed by Sugar Street, he turned his face with its faint smile in that direction, as his aunt Khadija and her sons, Abd al-Muni'm and Ahmad, came to mind. The thought of them evoked little reaction save apathy. He had never felt tempted even once to take either of his cousins as a friend in the true meaning of the word. Soon he had passed through Bab al-Mutawalli, the ancient city gate. Then turning into al-Darb al-Ahmar, he went down it until he reached an old house, where he knocked on the door and waited.

The door opened to reveal the face of Hilmi Izzat, who was a childhood friend, a colleague in Law School, and a rival in good looks. Hilmi beamed at the sight of him. They embraced and exchanged a kiss, as they always did when they met. On their way up the stairs, Hilmi commended his friend's tie and the way it matched his shirt and socks. They were both known for their elegance and good taste, and their interest in clothing and fashion was matched by their enthusiasm for politics and studying law. Their destination was a large room with a high ceiling. The presence of a bed and a desk in it indicated that it served for both sleeping and studying. Indeed the two young men frequently stayed up late studying there and then stretched out to sleep side by side in the great bed with its black posts and mosquito netting. It was nothing new for Ridwan to spend a night away from home. Since childhood, he had accepted invitations to pass days at a time in various different homes, like those of his grandfather Muhammad Iffat in al-Gamaliya or of his mother, Zaynab – whose only child he remained, even though she had long since married Muhammad Hasan – in al-Munira. Because of this, his father's natural tendency to be nonchalant, and the secret relief his stepmother, Zanuba, took in anything that kept him away from home even temporarily, Ridwan encountered no opposition to his desire to stay overnight with his friend when they were studying for an examination. Eventually the practice became so common that no one paid any attention to it.

Hilmi Izzat had been raised in a similar atmosphere of indifference. His father, a police officer in charge of a station, had died ten years before. Hilmi's six sisters had married, and he lived alone with his aged mother. She had difficulty controlling him, and he soon came to dominate the entire household. The widow lived on her husband's small pension and the rent from the first floor of her ancient house. The family had not had an easy life since the father's death, but Hilmi had been able to continue his studies and to enroll in Law School. All that time he had managed to keep up appearances. For Hilmi there was no pleasure equal to that of seeing his friend, and no period of work or relaxation was truly enjoyable unless Ridwan was present. Then Hilmi would feel a burst of energetic enthusiasm.

Hilmi invited Ridwan to have a seat on the sofa next to the door of the latticed balcony and, sitting down beside him, began to think of a topic of conversation. There were so many subjects to choose from. . . . But the despondent look in Ridwan's eyes cooled Hilmi's fervor. He gazed at Ridwan questioningly. Guessing what was wrong, he muttered, "You've been to visit your mother. . . . I bet you've just been there."

Ridwan realized that his facial expression had given him away. With a vexed look in his eyes, he nodded his head, without speaking.

"How is she?" Hilmi asked.

"Great." Then he sighed and added, "But that man called Muhammad Hasan! Do you know what it means to have a stepfather?"

Hilmi said consolingly, "Many people have stepparents. There's nothing shameful about it. Besides, that happened a long time ago."

Ridwan cried out angrily, "No, no, no! He's always at home. The only time he leaves is to go to his job at the ministry. For once,

I'd like to visit her when she's alone. He takes it upon himself to play the role of my father and adviser. Damn him. He never misses an opportunity to remind me that he's my father's boss in the records office and doesn't hesitate to criticize my father's conduct at work. But I don't let it pass in silence." He was quiet for a minute while he got control of his emotions. Then he continued: "My mother was a fool to agree to marry this man. Wouldn't it have been better for her to return to my father?"

Hilmi knew about Yasin's notorious behavior. With a smile he recited, "How many laments passion has brought me. . . ."

Waving his hand to show his disagreement, Ridwan said, "So what! Women's taste is a frightening mystery. What's even more disastrous is that she seems happy with him."

"Don't dwell on things that upset you."

Ridwan answered sadly, "How amazing! A vast part of my life is miserable. I detest my mother's husband and dislike my father's wife. The atmosphere is charged with hatred. Like my mother, my father made a bad choice. But what can I do about it? My step-mother is nice to me, but I don't think she loves me. How vile this life is!"

An elderly servant brought in some tea. Ridwan welcomed it with relish, since he had been stung by bitter February winds on the way there. They were silent as they dissolved the sugar in the tea. The expression on Ridwan's face changed, announcing the end of his gloomy recital.

Hilmi welcomed this and said with relief, "I'm so used to studying with you that I no longer know how to do it by myself."

Ridwan responded to this affectionate comment with a smile but suddenly asked, "Do you know about the decree that was issued concerning the delegation for the negotiations?"

"Yes. But many people are making a big stink about the atmosphere surrounding the negotiations. It seems that Italy, which poses a threat to our borders, is the real focus of the negotiations. For their part, the English pose a threat if the agree-ment fails."

"The blood of our martyrs is not cold yet, and we have fresh blood to spill."

Hilmi shook his head as he remarked, "What people are saying is that the fighting's over and the talking has begun. What do you think?"

"At any rate the Wafd constitute an overwhelming majority within the delegation. Picture this. When I asked Muhammad Hasan, my stepfather, his opinion of the situation, he replied sarcastically, 'Do you really think the English can leave Egypt?' This is the man my mother consented to marry."

Hilmi Izzat laughed out loud and asked, "Does your father's opinion differ?"

"My father hates the English. That's enough."

"Does he hate them from the depths of his heart?"

"My father does not hate or love anything from the depths of his heart."

"I'm asking what you think. Are you confident?"

"Why not? How long can this situation drag on? Fifty-four years of British occupation? Phooey! I'm not the only one who is miserable."

Hilmi Izzat took a last sip of tea. Then he smiled and said, "I think you were speaking to me with this kind of enthusiasm when he caught sight of you."

"Who?"

Hilmi smiled mysteriously and replied, "When you get excited you blush and that makes you look especially handsome. No doubt he saw you talking to me at one of those happy moments the day our student delegation went to the House of the Nation to call for unity. Don't you remember?"

With an interest Ridwan did not attempt to conceal he said, "Yes. But who is he?"

"Abd al-Rahim Pasha Isa!"

Ridwan thought a little before murmuring, "I saw him once from a distance."

"Well, this was the first time he noticed you."

There was an inquisitive look on Ridwan's face. Hilmi went on: "After you left, he asked me about you, requesting that I introduce you to him as soon as possible."

Ridwan smiled and then said, "Tell me everything you know."

Patting his friend's shoulder, Hilmi said, "He called me over and with his normal effervescence – by the way, he is very entertaining – asked, 'Who was that beauty conversing with you?' I told him you were a fellow student in the Law School, a longtime friend, and named so-and-so. With evident interest he asked, 'When will you introduce him to me?' Pretending not to understand the reason for his interest, I asked in turn, 'Why, Pasha?' He burst out with feigned anger – his lively wit occasionally carries him to such extremes – and said, 'To give him a lesson in religion, you son of a bitch.' I laughed till he put a hand over my mouth."

During the pause that followed they could hear the wind howling outside. A shutter banged against the wall. Then Ridwan spoke up: "I've heard a lot about him. Does he live up to his billing?"

"And more."

"But he's an old man!"

With inaudible laughter sparkling on his face, Hilmi Izzat said, "That's hardly significant, for he's an important man who is debonair and influential. It may well be that his age makes him more useful than if he were young."

Ridwan smiled again and asked, "Where does he live?"

"In a quiet villa in Helwan."

"It must be swarming with petitioners from all classes of society. . . ."

"We'll be his disciples. Why not? He's a senior statesman and we're novices."

Ridwan asked rather cautiously, "How about his wife and children?"

"What an ignoramus you are! He's single. He's never been married and has no taste for that kind of life. He was an only child and lives alone with his servants, like a branch torn from a tree. Once you've met him, you'll never be able to forget him."

They exchanged a long, smiling, conspiratorial look. Finally Hilmi said a bit anxiously, "Please ask me, 'When are we going to visit him?'"

Looking at the tea leaves in his glass, Ridwan repeated, "When are we going to visit him?"

124

LOCATED AT the corner of al-Najat Street in Helwan, the home of Abd al-Rahim Pasha Isa was of exemplary simplicity and elegance. A one-story brown villa three meters high, it was entered through a gentlemen's parlor and was surrounded by a flower garden. The house, the street, and the neighborhood were refreshingly quiet. Seated on a bench by the gate were the doorman – a Nubian with a handsome face and a slender figure – and the chauffeur, an attractive youth with rosy cheeks.

Looking toward the parlor, Hilmi Izzat whispered to Ridwan, "The pasha has kept his promise. We're the only visitors today!"

Hilmi Izzat was known to the doorman and the chauffeur, who stood up to greet him politely. When he joked with them, they showed no embarrassment about bursting into laughter.

Although dry, the weather was bitterly cold. They went into a magnificent reception hall with a large picture of Sa'd Zaghlul in ceremonial attire on the center wall. Hilmi Izzat turned toward a mirror extending all the way to the ceiling on the right-hand wall to cast a long and searching look at his appearance. Ridwan was quick to join him, examining his own reflection with equal care. At last Hilmi Izzat said, "Two splendid moons in suits and fezzes. All those who love the Prophet's handsome appearance should pray for him."

They sat down beside each other on a gilded sofa with a stunning blue cover. After a few minutes they heard something behind the curtain hanging in the large doorway beneath the portrait of Sa'd Zaghlul. His heart beating with excitement, Ridwan turned to look that way. A man wearing a pleasant cologne and an elegant black suit appeared at once. Clean-shaven, slender, and rather tall, he had fine features marked by age, a dark brown complexion, and small languid eyes. His fez was slanted so far forward that it almost touched his eyebrows. Calm and dignified, he came toward them with slow steady steps. He had a reassuring but awe-inspiring impact on the young man's heart. Silent until he stopped before the two boys, who stood up to greet him, he examined them with a penetrating look that rested on Ridwan long enough to make the young man's eyelids twitch. Then the pasha smiled suddenly. The attractive affability shining from his face lessened the distance between them until it was indiscernible. Hilmi held out his hand, which the man took and held. The pasha puckered up his lips and waited. Noticing what he had in mind, Hilmi quickly presented his cheek, which the man kissed.

The pasha looked in Ridwan's direction and said in a delicate tone, "Don't take offense, my son. This is my way of greeting people."

Ridwan held out his hand shyly. The man took it and laughingly asked, "And your cheek?"

Ridwan blushed. Pointing to himself, Hilmi cried out, "Your Excellency, you need to negotiate that with his guardian."

Abd al-Rahim Pasha laughed and contented himself with a handshake. After inviting them to have a seat, he sat down in a large armchair nearby. With a smile he said, "You have a damn fool for a guardian, Ridwan – isn't that your name? Welcome! I noticed you fraternizing with this naughty boy. I wanted to meet you, because I was enchanted by your manners. And you've been good enough not to begrudge me this pleasure."

"I'm happy to have the honor of meeting you, Your Excellency."

Turning a large gold ring around the finger of his left hand, the man said, "Asking God's forgiveness, my son...don't use any titles or honorific expressions. I don't like that at all. An endearing spirit and a soul that's sincere and pure are what really interest me. This business of 'Pasha' and 'Your Excellency,' well...we're all descended from Adam and Eve. The fact is that your manners pleased me, and I wanted to invite you to my home. So you're most welcome. You're Hilmi's classmate in Law School. Isn't that so?"

"Yes, sir. We've been classmates since Khalil Agha Elementary School."

The man raised his white eyebrows in admiration and said, "Childhood friends!" Then, nodding his head, he continued: "Excellent, excellent! Perhaps like him you're from al-Husayn district?"

"Yes, sir. I was born in the home of my grandfather, Mr. Muhammad Iffat, in al-Gamaliya. I live now with my father in Palace of Desire Alley."

The man said with a joy that was almost delirious, "Cairo's ancient districts . . . grand places! Would you believe that I lived there for a long time with my late father – in Birguwan. I was my parents' only child and a rascal. I frequently got the boys together in a procession, and we'd go from neighborhood to neighborhood, leaving a trail of devastation behind us. Woe to any poor soul whom fate sent our way. My father would get extremely angry and chase after me with a stick. . . . Son, you said that your grandfather is Muhammad Iffat?"

Ridwan replied proudly, "Yes, sir."

The pasha thought for a moment before saying, "I remember seeing him once at the home of the deputy for al-Gamaliya. He's an outstanding person and a sincere nationalist. He was almost nominated to run in the forthcoming elections, but his friend the former deputy beat him out at the last minute. The recent coalition necessitates a certain amount of goodwill so that our brothers in the Liberal Constitutionalists can win a few seats. You're with Hilmi in Law School. . . . Beautiful! Law is the master of all the other disciplines. Its study requires true brilliance. To have a fine future, just strive to do your best."

When he made these last remarks, his tone was encouraging and even promising. Ridwan's heart pulsed with lofty and fervent aspirations as he responded, "We've never failed an exam during our academic careers."

"Bravo! That's the foundation. Then comes a position as a government attorney, to be followed by a judgeship. There will always be someone to open closed doors for industrious young men. A judge's life is an excellent one. Its mainstays are a lively intelligence and a wakeful conscience. By the grace of God I was an honest judge. I left the bench to enter politics. Patriotism occasionally forces us to give up work we love. Yet even today you will find people who swear by my fairness and integrity. Set your sights on being industrious and fair. Then you'll be free to do what you want in your private life. Do your duty and act as you please. If you fail to do your duty, people will see only your faults. Haven't you observed the pleasure some busybodies take in saying that such and such a minister has this defect and that the poet so-and-so has the following disease? Fine . . . but not all the victims of these slanders are cabinet ministers or poets. So be a minister or a poet first, and then do what you want. Don't overlook this lesson, Professor Ridwan."

Quoting the medieval poet al-Mutanabbi, Hilmi said mischievously, " 'The noble man is the one whose faults can be counted.' Isn't that so, Your Excellency?"

Leaning his head toward his right shoulder, the man said, "Of course. Glory to the One who alone is perfect. Man is very weak, Ridwan. But he must be strong in the other parts of his life. Do you understand? If you want, I'll tell you about the great men of our nation. You won't find any without some failing. We'll discuss this at length and study the lessons we can derive from it, in order to have a life amply endowed with achievement and happiness."

Hilmi looked at Ridwan, saying, "Didn't I tell you that the pasha's friendship is a limitless treasure?"

Abd al-Rahim Isa told Ridwan, who could hardly keep his eyes off the man, "I love learning. I love life. I love people. My practice is to offer a young man a hand until he grows up. What is there in the world that's better than love? If we run into a legal problem, we must solve it together. When we think about the future, we shall do that together. If we feel like resting, we should rest together. I've never known a man as wise as Hasan Bey Imad. Today he's one of a select group of prominent diplomats. Never mind that he's one of my political enemies. When he concentrates on a subject, he masters it. Yet when music makes him ecstatic, he dances nude. The world can be a delightful place, if you're wise and broad-minded. Aren't you broad-minded, Ridwan?"

Hilmi Izzat immediately answered for him, "If he's not, we're prepared to broaden it for him."

The pasha's face beamed with a childlike smile that revealed his insatiable appetite for pleasure. He said, "This boy's a rapscallion, Ridwan! But what can I do? He's your childhood friend, the lucky fellow. I'm not the one who invented the saying 'Birds of a feather flock together.' You must be a rapscallion too. Tell me about yourself, Ridwan. Oh! You've let me say more than I intended while remaining silent – like an astute politician. Yes? Tell me, Ridwan. What do you love and what do you hate?"

Then the servant entered, carrying a tray. He was a clean-shaven youth like the doorman and the chauffeur. As they drank the water flavored with orange blossoms, the pasha asked, "Water like this is what the people of al-Husayn district drink, isn't it?"

Ridwan smilingly murmured. "Yes, sir."

Nodding his head ecstatically, the pasha said, "People of al-Husayn, help us!"

They all laughed. Even the servant smiled as he left the chamber. Then the pasha resumed his questioning: "What do you love? What do you hate? Speak frankly, Ridwan. Let me make it easier for you to answer. Are you interested in politics?"

Hilmi Izzat said, "We're both members of the student committee."

"This is the first reason for us to be close. Do you like literature?"

Hilmi Izzat replied, "He's fond of Shawqi, Hafiz, and al-Manfaluti."

The pasha chided him, "You be still. Brother, I want to hear his voice."

They laughed. Smiling, Ridwan said, "I could die for Shawqi, Hafiz, and al-Manfaluti."

"'I could die for'... What an expression! You only hear it in al-Gamaliya. Is the name of your district derived from *gamal*, or beauty, Ridwan? You must be a fan of verses like 'Silver gold,' 'In the still of the night,' 'Who is it?' and 'Removing one branch, he lays down another....' My God, my God! This is another reason for us to be close friends, beautiful Gamaliya. Do you like singing?"

"He adores..."

"You be still."

They all laughed once more. Ridwan said, "Umm Kalthoum."

"Excellent. I may prefer the older style of singing, but all singing's beautiful. I love both 'the profound and the witty' as that medieval skeptic al-Ma'arri put it. Or, I could die for it, as you would say, sir. Very fine. What a delightful evening!"

The telephone rang, and the pasha went to answer it. Putting the receiver to his ear, he said, "Hello.... Greetings, Your Excellency the pasha.... What's so amazing about that? Didn't Isma'il Sidqy himself sit on a negotiating team once as one of the nation's leaders?... I told the leader my candid opinion. It's also that of other Wafdists like Mahir and al-Nuqrashi.... I'm sorry, Pasha. I can't. I haven't forgotten that King Fuad once opposed my promotion. He's the last person to talk about ethics. In any case I'll see you at the club tomorrow. Goodbye, Pasha."

The man returned with a frown but on seeing Ridwan's face almost immediately cheered up and continued their conversation: "Yes, Mr. Ridwan. We've gotten acquainted, and it's been beautiful. I advise you to be industrious. I advise you not to lose sight of your duty or your ideals. Now let's talk about music and having a good time."

Ridwan looked at his watch. The pasha appeared alarmed and said, "Anything but that! The clock is an enemy of friendly reunions."

Ridwan stammered rather uneasily, "But we're late, Your Honor the pasha."

"Late! Do you mean late for me, at my age? You're mistaken, son. I still love to enjoy talk, beauty, and singing until one in the morning. We haven't begun the soiree yet. We've only recited the preliminary blessing: In the name of God the compassionate, the merciful. Don't object. The automobile is at your command until morning. I've heard that you stay out all night when you're studying for an examination. So let's study together. Why not? I'd find it delightful to review an introduction to general law or some Islamic law. By the way, who teaches you Islamic Shari'a law? Shaykh Ibrahim Nadim – may God grant him a good evening – was a very sporting fellow. Don't be astonished! One day we'll write the history of all the important men of the age. You must understand everything. Our night will be a loving, friendly one. Tell me, Hilmi, what's the most appropriate drink for a night like this?"

Hilmi replied confidently, "Whiskey and soda with grilled meat."

The pasha laughed and asked, "Scoundrel, how can you drink grilled meat?"

125

EVERY THURSDAY after lunch Khadija's entire family gathered in a fashion that scarcely ever changed. Assembled in the sitting room were the father, Ibrahim Shawkat, and the two sons, Abd al-Muni'm and Ahmad. It was rare for Khadija to be without some project, and she embroidered on a tablecloth while she sat with them. After a prolonged and heroic struggle against time, Ibrahim Shawkat had finally begun to show his age. His hair was turning white, and he looked a little bloated. Except for this, his health was still enviably good.

Smoking a cigarette, he took his place between his sons with calm assurance. His protruding eyes had their customary look of languid indifference. The two boys kept up a stream of conversation with each other, their father, or their mother, who participated without looking up from her work. She seemed a massive chunk of flesh. There was nothing in the domestic atmosphere to ruffle Khadija's peace of mind. Since the death of her mother-in-law, there had been no one to challenge her control over her home. She performed her chores with unflagging zeal. As plumpness was the key to her beauty, she took extraordinary care to maintain her weight. She attempted to impose her guidance on everyone, especially her husband and their two sons. The man had given in, but Abd al-Muni'm and Ahmad each went his own way, appealing to her love to free themselves from her domination. Some years before she had succeeded in convincing her husband to respect the precepts of Islam. The man had begun praying and fasting and had become accustomed to this. Abd al-Muni'm and Ahmad had grown up with these observances, but for the past two years Ahmad had ceased to perform his religious duties. He would dodge his mother's attempts to interrogate him or excuse himself on some pretext or other.

Ibrahim Shawkat loved and admired his sons greatly. He seized every opportunity to praise the string of successes that had brought Abd al-Muni'm to Law School and Ahmad to the final stage of his secondary education. Khadija also boasted about these achievements, saying, "This is all the fruit of my concern. If I had left the matter up to you, neither of them would have amounted to anything."

It had recently been established that, from want of practice, Khadija had forgotten how to read and write, and this discovery had made her the target of Ibrahim's jests. Finally her sons had suggested that they should teach her what she had forgotten in order to repay her for the helping hand she boasted of giving their education. Their proposal had made her a little angry but had also made her laugh a lot. She summed up her feelings about the situation in one sentence: "A woman does not need to read or write unless she's exchanging letters with a lover."

She appeared to be happy and content with her family, although she did not think that Abd al-Muni'm and Ahmad ate enough. Their thinness enraged her, and she said disapprovingly, "I've told you a thousand times to use chamomile to improve your appetites. You must eat properly. Don't you see how well your father eats?"

Looking at their father, the two young men smiled. Ibrahim said, "Why don't you use yourself as the example? You eat like a food grinder."

Smiling, she replied, "I'll let them decide which of us to imitate."

Ibrahim protested, "Lady, your envious eye has injured me. That's why the dentist suggested I have my teeth extracted."

With a tender look in her eyes, she said, "Don't be upset. Once they're out, you won't have any more problems or pain, God willing."

Ahmad told her, "Our neighbor in the second-floor apartment would like to postpone payment of his rent until next month. He met me on the stairs and made that request."

Frowning at him, she asked, "What did you tell him?"

"I promised I'd speak to my father."

"And did you speak to your father?"

"I'm speaking to you now."

"We don't share the apartment with him. Why should he share our money? If we give him a break, the tenant in the first-floor apartment will follow his lead. You don't know what people are like. Don't get involved in things that don't concern you."

Glancing at his father, Ahmad asked, "What do you think, Papa?"

Ibrahim Shawkat smiled and said, "Spare me the headache. Talk to your mother. . . ."

Ahmad addressed his mother again: "If we're lenient with a man in difficult circumstances, we won't go hungry."

Khadija said resentfully, "His wife has already spoken to me, and I agreed to let them pay later. So don't trouble your mind about it. But I explained to her that paying the rent is as obligatory as paying for food and drink. Is there anything wrong in that? I'm occasionally criticized for not making friends with women in the neighborhood, but when you know people the way I do, you praise God for solitude."

With a wink of his eye Ahmad asked, "Are we better than other people?"

Scowling, Khadija replied, "Yes . . . unless you know something about yourself that would make me think otherwise."

Abd al-Muni'm commented, "In his opinion, he's the best possible man, and his opinion is the only one that counts. All wisdom has been granted to him."

Khadija said sarcastically, "It's also his opinion that tenants should be able to lease apartments without paying the rent."

Laughing, Abd al-Muni'm said, "He's not convinced that some people should have absolute ownership rights to houses."

Shaking her head, Khadija remarked, "I pity such worthless ideas."

Ahmad glared at his brother, but Abd al-Muni'm shrugged his shoulders scornfully and said, "Straighten your mind out before you get angry."

Ahmad protested, "It would be better if we didn't try to debate each other."

"Right. Wait till you grow up."

"You're only a year older than me. No more than that. . . ."

"A person a day older than you is a year wiser."

"I don't believe in that saying."

"Listen, there's only one thing that concerns me. It's for you to start praying with me again."

Khadija nodded her head sadly as she said, "Your brother's right. Usually when people grow up they grow wiser, but you . . . I seek refuge with God from you. Even your father prays and fasts. How could you have done this to yourself? I worry about it night and day."

In a powerful and profusely self-confident voice Abd al-Muni'm said, "To be blunt, his mind needs a thorough cleansing."

"It's just that..."

"Listen, Mother. This young man has no religion. This is what I've begun to believe."

Ahmad waved his hand as if angered and asked loudly, "Where do you get the right to judge a man's heart?"

"Your acts betray your secret thoughts." Then, hiding a smile, he added, "Enemy of God!"

Without abandoning his assured composure, Ibrahim Shawkat said, "Don't make false accusations against your brother."

Looking at Ahmad but addressing Abd al-Muni'm, Khadija said, "Don't deprive your brother of the dearest thing a person can have. How could he be anything but a Believer? If only his mother's relatives wore turbans, they would be recognized as religious scholars. His maternal great-grandfather had a career in religion. When I was growing up everyone around me prayed devoutly and served God, as if we were living in a mosque."

Ahmad said sarcastically, "Like Uncle Yasin!"

A laugh escaped from Ibrahim Shawkat. Pretending to be annoyed, Khadija retorted, "Speak respectfully about your uncle. What's wrong with him? His heart is filled with belief, and our Lord guides him. Look at your grandfather and grand-mother."

"And Uncle Kamal?"

"Your uncle Kamal is watched over by al-Husayn. You don't know anything."

"Some people don't know anything...."

Abd al-Muni'm asked defiantly, "Even if everyone else neglected their religion, would that be any excuse for you?"

Ahmad replied calmly, "In any case, you shouldn't worry about it. You won't ever be held responsible for my sins."

Then Ibrahim Shawkat said, "Stop your quarreling. I wish you could be like your cousin Ridwan."

Khadija stared at him disapprovingly. It was more than she could bear that anyone would prefer Ridwan to her sons. To explain himself, Ibrahim said, "That young man has contacts with top politicians. He's bright and seems guaranteed a glorious future."

Khadija said furiously, "I don't agree with you. Ridwan's an unlucky boy, like anyone else who has been deprived of his mother's care. The fact is that 'Mrs.' Zanuba thinks nothing of him. I'm not deceived by her good treatment of him. It's simply a political stratagem like those of the English. For this reason the poor boy has no real home. He spends most of his time away from the apartment. And his contacts with important men are meaningless. He's a student in the same year as Abd al-Muni'm. What's the point of this weighty remark? You don't know how to pick your examples."

Ibrahim gave her a look, as if to say, "It's impossible for you ever to agree with me." Then he continued with his explanation: "Things aren't the same for young people today. Politics has changed everything. Each important figure surrounds himself with young protégés. An ambitious youth wishing to make his way in the world must find a patron he can rely on. Your father's status is based on his close ties to important men."

Khadija said haughtily, "My father is sought out by people eager to get to know him. He doesn't curry favor with people. As for politics, it doesn't concern my boys. If they had known their uncle who sacrificed his life for the nation, they would learn for themselves what I mean. It's 'Long live so-and-so' or 'Down with someone else,' while people's sons are perishing. If Fahmy had lived, he would be one of the greatest judges today."

Abd al-Muni'm said, "Everyone has to find his own way. We won't imitate anyone. If we wanted to be like Ridwan, we could be."

Khadija said, "That's right!"

Ibrahim told Abd al-Muni'm, "You're just like your mother ... no difference at all between you."

There was a knock on the door and the servant came to announce the tenant from the first floor. As she started to rise, Khadija said, "I wonder what she wants. . . . If she wishes to put off paying her rent, it will take all the policemen from the Gamaliya station to separate us."

126

THE MUSKI was very congested. Already teeming with more than its normal pedestrian traffic, it was being flooded by currents of human beings from al-Ataba. The April sun cast fiery rays from a cloudless sky, and Abd al-Muni'm and Ahmad were sweating profusely as they made their way through the throngs with more than a little effort.

Taking his brother's arm, Ahmad said, "Tell me what you feel."

Abd al-Muni'm thought a little and then replied, "I don't know. Death is always terrifying, especially a king's death. The funeral procession was more crowded than any I'd seen before. Since I didn't witness Sa'd Zaghlul's funeral, I can't compare the two. But it seems to me that most of the onlookers were mourning. Some of the women were weeping. We Egyptians are an emotional people."

"But I'm asking about your own feelings."

Abd al-Muni'm thought again while trying to keep from bumping into people. Finally he said, "I didn't love him. None of us did. So I wasn't sad. Yet I wasn't happy either. I followed the bier without feeling anything one way or the other about the man, but the thought of such a mighty person in a coffin affected me. A sight like that was bound to move me. God's sovereignty is universal. He is alive and eternal. I wish people would realize that. If the king had died before the political situation changed, great multitudes would have rejoiced. And you – what are your feelings?"

Smiling, Ahmad said, "I have no love for tyrants, no matter what the political situation."

"That's excellent. But what about the sight of death?"

"I don't care for sick romanticism."

Abd al-Muni'm asked angrily, "Then were you pleased?"

"I hope to live long enough to see the world cleansed of all tyrants, no matter what the title or description."

They were silent for a time, fatigue having gotten the best of them. Then Ahmad asked, "What happens next?"

With the confident tone for which he was known, Abd al-Muni'm answered, "Faruq is just a boy. He's not as crafty or as vindictive as his father. If all goes well, with successful negotiations and a return of the Wafd to power, things will calm down and the era of conspiracies will vanish. It seems that the future will be good."

"And the English?"

"If the negotiations are successful, they will become our friends and, consequently, the alliance between the palace and the English against the Egyptian people will be terminated. Then the king will be forced to respect the constitution."

"The Wafd Party is better than the other ones."

"No doubt . . . but it hasn't governed long enough to demonstrate its abilities fully. Experience will soon reveal its true potential. I agree it's better than the others, but our ambitions don't stop there."

"Of course not! I believe that rule by the Wafd Party is a good starting point for much greater developments. That's all there is to it. But will we really reach an agreement with the English?"

"If there isn't an agreement, then we'll return to a situation like that under Sidqy. Our nation has an inexhaustible supply of traitors. Their main task is always to discipline the Wafdists whenever we say no to the English. They are certainly watching for another opportunity, even if they're aligned with the nationalists at present. Sidqy, Muhammad Mahmud, and men like them are just waiting. That's the tragedy."

On reaching New Street they suddenly found themselves facing their grandfather, Ahmad Abd al-Jawad, who was heading toward the Goldsmiths Bazaar. They went over and greeted him respectfully.

He smiled and asked, "From where, to where?"

Abd al-Muni'm answered, "We were watching the funeral of King Fuad."

The smile still on his lips, the man said, "Thank you for your thoughtful condolences."

After shaking hands, they went their separate ways. Ahmad watched for a moment as his grandfather walked off. Then he said, "Our grandfather's charming and elegant. His cologne has a pleasant fragrance."

"Mother recounts amazing tales about his tyranny."

"I don't think he's a tyrant. That's incredible."

Abd al-Muni'm laughed and said, "Even King Fuad himself by the end of his days seemed pleasant and charming." They both laughed and proceeded on to Ahmad Abduh's coffeehouse.

In the room opposite the fountain, Ahmad saw a shaykh with a long beard and penetrating eyes. He sat in the center of a group of young men, who watched him attentively. Ahmad stopped and told his brother, "Your friend Shaykh Ali al-Manufi.... 'The earth casts out its burdens' [Qur'an, 99:2]. So I must leave you here."

Abd al-Muni'm invited him: "Come sit with us. I'd love for you to get to know him and to hear him speak. Dispute with him as much as you want. Many of the fellows around him are students from the University."

Freeing his arm from his brother's, Ahmad said, "No, sir. I almost got into a fight with him once. I don't like fanatics. Goodbye."

Abd al-Muni'm stared at him critically and said sharply, "Goodbye. May our Lord guide you." Then he joined the assembly presided over by Shaykh Ali al-Manufi, head of al-Husayn Primary School. The man stood up to greet him, and the young people sitting there also rose and embraced him. When the shaykh sat down, they all resumed their seats. Examining Abd al-Muni'm with piercing eyes, the shaykh commented, "We didn't see you yesterday."

"Studying."

"Industry is an acceptable excuse. Why did your brother leave you to go off by himself?"

Abd al-Muni'm smiled but did not reply. Shaykh Ali al-Manufi remarked, "Our Lord is the guide. Don't wonder about him. Our founder, Hasan al-Banna, encountered many skeptics who today are some of his sincerest disciples. When God wants to guide a people, Satan has no power over them. We are God's soldiers, spreading His light and combating His enemies. More than others, we have given our spirits to Him. Soldiers of God, how happy you are!"

One of the congregation observed, "But the kingdom of Satan is large."

Shaykh Ali al-Manufi scolded, "Look at this fellow who's afraid of Satan's world when he's in God's presence.... What shall we say to him? We are with God, and God is with us. So what should we fear? What other soldiers on earth enjoy your power? What weapon is more effective than yours? The English, French, Germans, and Italians rely primarily on their material culture, but you rely on true belief. Belief can dent steel. Faith is stronger than any other force on earth. Fill your pure hearts with belief, and the world belongs to you."

Another young man commented, "We believe, but we're a weak nation."

The shaykh clenched his fist as he cried out, "If you feel weak, then your faith has decreased without your being aware of it. Faith creates power and induces it. Bombs are made by hands like yours. They are the fruit of power, not its cause. How did the Prophet conquer the whole Arabian peninsula? How did the Arabs conquer the entire world?"

Abd al-Muni'm answered fervently, "Faith and belief."

Then someone else asked, "But how can the English be so powerful? They're not Believers."

The shaykh smiled and ran his fingers through his beard as he said, "Anyone strong believes in something. They believe in their nation and in 'progress.' But faith in God is superior to any other kind of belief. It's only fitting that people who believe in God should be stronger than those believing in the physical world. We Muslims have at our disposal a buried treasure. We must extract it. We need to revive Islam and to make it as good as new. We call ourselves Muslims, but we must prove it by our deeds. God blessed us with His Book, but we have ignored it. This has brought down humiliation upon us. So let us return to the Book. This is our motto: a return to the Qur'an. That was what our leader called for at the beginning in Isma'iliya, and from that time on his message has been sinking deep into people's spirits, winning over villages and hamlets, filling every heart."

"But wouldn't it be wise for us to stay out of politics?"

"Our religion consists of a creed, a code of law, and a political system. God is far too merciful to have left the most troublesome aspects of human affairs devoid of any regulation or guidance from Him. Actually, that's the subject of our lesson for tonight. . . ."

The shaykh was ebullient. His approach was to affirm some truth, which they would then discuss, as disciples asked questions and he replied. Most of his remarks centered on quotations from the Qur'an and from the collections of hadith reports of the Prophet's words and deeds. He spoke as if preaching, indeed preaching to all the patrons of the coffeehouse.

From his seat at the far end of the room, where he was drinking green tea, Ahmad could hear the shaykh. There was a sarcastic smile on the young man's lips, as he incredulously attempted to measure the gulf separating him from this zealous group. Angry and scornful, he grew so irritated that he thought of asking the shaykh to lower his voice and to stop disturbing the other patrons. But he abandoned that idea as soon as he remembered his brother was one of the shaykh's disciples. Finally, he saw no alternative to leaving the coffeehouse, rose resentfully, and left.

127

ABD AL-MUNI'M returned to Sugar Street around eight. The fury of the weather had abated, making for a pleasant evening with some of the freshness of spring. The lesson was still ringing in his head and heart, but he felt mentally and physically exhausted. As he crossed the courtyard in the darkness, heading for the stairway, the door of the first-floor apartment opened. By the light escaping from inside he saw a figure slip out, close the door, and precede him up the stairs. His heart pounded, and his blood pulsed through him like tiny insects inflamed by hot weather. Even in the shadows he could see her waiting for him at the first landing. She glanced at him as he stared up at her, not averting his gaze.

It was amazingly easy for young people to deceive their parents. This young girl had stepped out of her apartment on the pretext of visiting the neighbors. And she would visit them, but only after participating in a dangerous flirtation on the dark landing. He found that his head was empty of ideas, for all the thoughts he had been wrestling with had disappeared like a puff of smoke. He was transfixed by a single desire – to satisfy the craving that would not leave his nerves and limbs alone. His sincere faith seemed to have fled in anger or to have taken refuge deep inside him, where it snarled resentfully, although the sound of its complaints was drowned out by the hissing of lust's flames.

Was she not his girl? Of course she was. The alcoves of the courtyard, the stairwell, and the corner of the roof overlooking Sugar Street could all testify to this. No doubt she had been watching for him to return so that she could meet him at just the right moment. She had taken all this trouble for his sake. He hurried on cautiously until he stood facing her on the landing. There was hardly any distance separating them. The fragrance of her hair tantalized him, and her breath tickled his neck.

He gently caressed her shoulder as he whispered, "Let's go to the second landing. It's safer than here."

She made no reply but headed up the steps, and he cautiously followed behind. At the second landing, halfway between the two floors, she stopped, leaning her back against the wall, and he stood right in front of her. When he put his arms around her, she resisted for a second out of force of habit before warming to his embrace.

"Darling. . . ."

"I was waiting for you at the window. Mother has been busy getting ready for the Shamm al-Nasim holiday."

"Best wishes for our spring festival. Now let me taste spring on your lips."

Their lips met in a long, famished kiss. Then she asked, "Where were you?"

With wrenching suddenness he remembered the lesson on politics in Islam. But he answered, "With some friends at the coffeehouse."

In a tone of protest she said, "The coffeehouse! When there's only a month before the examination?"

"I know what I have to do to prepare for it. . . . But now I'll kiss you again to punish you for thinking ill of me."

"Your voice is too loud. Have you forgotten where we are?"

"We're in our home, in our room. The landing is our room!"

"This afternoon, when I was going to my aunt's, I glanced up in hopes of seeing you at the window, but your mother was looking down at the alley, and our eyes met. I trembled with fear."

"What were you afraid of?"

"I imagined that she knew I was looking for you and that she had discovered my secret."

"You mean 'our secret.' It's the same bond that links both of us together. Aren't we now a single entity?"

Racked by unruly desire, he hugged her violently to his chest as if, in his desperate capitulation to lust, he was attempting to flee the faint voices of protest lodged deep inside him. Blazing fires seared him. He was seized by a force capable of dissolving the two of them into a single swirling vortex.

The silence was broken by a sigh and then by heavy breathing. He finally became aware that he and she were separate beings and that the darkness sheltered two figures. Then he heard her ask shyly in a gentle whisper, "Shall we meet tomorrow?"

With a resentment he did his best to conceal, he replied, "Yes . . . yes. You'll find out when. . . ."

"Tell me now."

As his annoyance grew increasingly hard to bear, he said, "I don't know when I'll have time tomorrow."

"Why not?"

"Goodbye for now. I heard a sound."

"No! There wasn't any sound."

"Nobody should find us like this."

He patted her shoulder as if it were a dirty rag and freed himself from her arms with affected tenderness. Then he quickly climbed the stairs. His parents were in the sitting room listening to the radio. The door of the study was closed, but the light shining through its little window indicated that Ahmad was studying. Saying, "Good evening," to his parents, he went to the bedroom to remove his clothes, bathe, and cleanse himself in the manner prescribed by Islam, before returning to his room to pray. Afterward he sat cross-legged on the prayer rug and lost himself in deep meditation. There was a sad look to his eyes, his breast was aflame with grief, and he felt like crying. He prayed that his Lord would come to his aid to help him combat temptation and to drive Satan away, that Satan he encountered in the shape of a girl who inspired a raging lust in him.

His mind always said, "No," but his heart, "Yes." The fearful struggle he experienced invariably ended with defeat and regret. Every day was a test and every test an experience of hell. When would this torment end? His entire spiritual effort was threatened with ruin, as though he were building castles in the sky. Sinking into the mud, he could not find any secure footing. He wished his remorse could bring back the past hour.

128

IN GHAMRA, Ahmad Ibrahim Shawkat finally found his way to
the building of *al-Insan al-Jadid* (The New Man) magazine. Situated halfway between streetcar stops, the structure had two stories
and a basement. From the wash hanging on the balcony, he
realized at once that the top floor was an apartment. There was a
sign with the magazine's name on the door downstairs. The basement was the printshop, for he could see its machines through the
bars of the windows. He climbed the four steps and asked the first
person he met – a worker carrying proofs – for Mr. Adli Karim,
the magazine's editor. The pressman pointed to the end of an
unfurnished hall and a closed door with a sign reading: "Editor in
Chief." Ahmad walked that way, thinking he might see a recep-
tionist, but reached the door without finding one. After a
moment's hesitation he knocked gently. Then he heard a voice
inside say, "Come in." Ahmad opened the door and entered.
From the far end of the room, two wide eyes stared at him
questioningly from beneath bushy white eyebrows.

Closing the door behind him, he said apologetically, "Excuse
me. One minute. . . ."

The man replied gently, "Yes. . . ."

Ahmad went up to the desk, which was stacked with books and
papers, and greeted the gentleman, who rose to welcome him.
When the editor sat down again, he invited Ahmad to have a seat.
The young man felt relief and pride at being able to view the
distinguished master from whose magazine and books he had
gained so much enlightenment during the past three years.
Ahmad gazed at the pale face, which seemed even whiter because
of the man's white hair. Age had left its mark on this visage. The
only remaining traces of youth were deep eyes that sparkled with a
penetrating gleam. This was his master, or his "spiritual father," as
Ahmad called him. Now the young man was in the chamber of
inspiration with its walls hidden behind bookshelves that stretched
all the way to the ceiling.

The editor said curiously, "You're welcome. . . ."

Ahmad answered suavely, "I've come to pay for my subscription." Reassured by the favorable impression his words had made, he added, "And I'd like to find out what happened to the article I sent the magazine two weeks ago."

Mr. Adli Karim smiled as he inquired, "What is your name?"

"Ahmad Ibrahim Shawkat."

The editor frowned as he tried to place the name and then said, "I remember you. You were the first subscriber to my magazine. Yes. And you brought three other ones. Isn't that so? I remember the name Shawkat. I think I sent you a letter of thanks on behalf of the magazine."

This pleasant memory made him feel even more at home, and Ahmad said, "The letter I received referred to me as 'the magazine's first friend.'"

"That's true. *The New Man* is devoted to principle and needs committed friends if it is to compete with all the picture magazines and the journals controlled by special interests. You are a friend of the magazine and most welcome. But haven't you honored us with a visit before?"

"Of course not. I only got my baccalaureate this month."

Adli Karim laughed and said, "You assume a person must have the baccalaureate to visit the magazine?"

Ahmad smiled uneasily and replied, "Certainly not. I mean I was young."

The editor commented seriously, "It's not right for a reader of *The New Man* to judge a person by his age. In our country there are men over sixty who have youthful minds and young people in the spring of life with a mentality as antiquated as if they had lived a thousand years or more. This is the malady of the East." Then he asked in a gentler tone, "Have you sent us other articles before?"

"Three that were ignored and then this last article, which I was hoping you would print."

"What's it about? Forgive me, but I receive dozens of articles every day."

"Le Bon's theories of education and my comments on them."

"In any case, if you look for it in the adjoining room where the correspondence is handled, you'll discover its fate."

Ahmad started to rise, but Mr. Adli gestured for him to remain seated and said, "The magazine's more or less on vacation today. I hope you'll stay and talk a little."

Ahmad murmured with profound gratitude, "I'd be delighted, sir."

"You said you got the baccalaureate this year. How old are you?"

"Sixteen."

"Precocious. Excellent. Is the magazine widely read in the secondary schools?"

"No, unfortunately not."

"I realize that. Most of our readers are at the University. In Egypt, reading's considered a cheap entertainment. We won't develop until we accept that reading is a vital necessity." After a pause he asked, "What's the attitude of secondary-school students?"

Ahmad looked at him inquisitively, as if wanting clarification of the question, and the man said, "I'm asking about their political affiliation, since that's more obvious than other things."

"The overwhelming majority are Wafdists."

"But is there any talk of the new movements?"

"Young Egypt — Misr al-Fatat? It's insignificant. You could count its supporters on your fingers. The other parties have no followers except for relatives of the leaders. Then there is a minority that's not interested in any of the parties. Some, and I'm among them, prefer the Wafd to the others but hope for a more perfect one."

With satisfaction the man said, "This is what I wanted to know. The Wafd is the people's party and represents an important and natural step in our development. The National Party is Turkish, religious, and reactionary. The Wafd Party has crystallized and purified Egyptian nationalism. It has also been a school for nationalism and democracy. But the point is that the nation is not and must not be content with this school. We want a further stage of development. We desire a school for socialism. Independence is not the ultimate goal. It's a way to obtain the people's constitutional, economic, and human rights."

Ahmad cried out enthusiastically, "What a fine statement!"

"But the Wafd must be the starting point. Young Egypt is a criminal, reactionary, Fascist movement. It's just as dangerous as the reactionary religious groups. It's nothing more than an echo of

German and Italian militarism, worshipping power, demanding
dictatorial control, and disparaging human values and human
dignity. Like cholera and typhoid, reactionary movements are
endemic to this region and need to be eradicated."

Ahmad said zealously, "We in the *New Man* group believe this
firmly."

The editor nodded his large head sorrowfully and said, "That's
why the magazine is a target for reactionaries of every stripe. They
accuse me of corrupting the young."

"Just as they once denounced Socrates."

With a gratified smile, Mr. Adli Karim said, "What's your goal?
I mean, which college of the University are you heading for?"

"Arts."

The editor sat up straight and remarked, "Literature is one of
the greatest tools of liberation, but it can also be employed for
reactionary ends. So watch your step. From the mosque university
of al-Azhar and from the Dar al-Ulum teachers college have come
a sickening type of literature that has left generations of Egyptians
with rigid minds and broken spirits. But no matter what, science is
the foundation of modern life. . . . Don't be surprised that a man
who is considered a literary figure should tell you this frankly. We
must study the sciences and absorb the scientific mentality.
A person who doesn't know science is not a citizen of the twentieth century, even if he is a genius. Artists too must learn their
share of science. It's no longer just for scientists. Yes, the responsibility for comprehensive and profound knowledge of the field as
well as for research and discoveries in it belongs to the scientists,
but every cultured person must illuminate himself with its light,
embrace its principles and procedures, and use its style. Science
must take the place that prophecy and religion had in the ancient
world."

Ahmad endorsed his master's statement: "That's why the message of *The New Man* is the development of a society based on
science."

Adli Karim replied with interest, "Yes. Each of us must do his
part, even if he finds himself alone in the arena."

Ahmad nodded his head, and the other man continued: "Study
literature as much as you want, but pay more attention to your
own intellectual development than to the selections you're asked
to memorize. And don't forget modern science. In addition to

Shakespeare and Schopenhauer, your library must contain Comte, Darwin, Freud, Marx, and Engels. Be as zealous about this as if you were religious, and remember that each age has its prophets. The prophets of this era are the scientists."

The editor's smile indicated that the conversation was coming to an end. Ahmad rose and stretched out his hand. He said good-bye and left the room, feeling joyously alive. Outside, in the hall, remembering his subscription and the article, he looked for the other room, knocked on the door to announce himself, and entered. He saw that there were three desks in the room. Two were empty, and a girl was sitting at the third. He had not been expecting this and stopped in his tracks. He looked at her inquisitively and apprehensively. She was around twenty, with a dark brown complexion, black eyes, and black hair. There was a resolute look about her delicate nose, pointed chin, and thin lips, but that did not detract from her beauty.

Scrutinizing him, she asked, "Yes?"

To justify his presence he said, "My subscription." He paid the amount and took the receipt. Then, overcoming his nervousness, he said, "I sent an article to the magazine, and Mr. Adli Karim told me it would be here."

She invited him to have a seat in front of her desk and asked, "The title of the article, please?"

Still uncomfortable about dealing with this girl, he replied, "Education According to Le Bon."

She opened a file and flipped through some papers until she pulled out the essay. When Ahmad glimpsed his handwriting, his heart pounded. From where he sat he tried to read the red notation upon it, but she saved him the trouble, remarking, "The note says, 'To be summarized and published in the section for readers' letters.'"

Ahmad was disappointed. He looked at her for a few moments without saying anything. Then he asked, "In which issue?"

"The next one."

After some hesitation he asked, "Who will summarize it?"

"I will."

He felt annoyed but asked, "Will it bear my name?"

She laughed and answered, "Naturally. There is usually a statement to the effect that we have received a letter from the writer..." She looked at the signature on the article and continued: "Ahmad Ibrahim Shawkat. Then we provide a full summary of your ideas."

He hesitated a little before saying, "I would have preferred for you to publish it in its entirety."

Smiling, she replied, "Next time, God willing."

He looked at her silently and asked, "Are you an employee here?"

"As you can see!"

He was tempted to ask what her qualifications for the position were, but his courage failed him at the last moment. So he inquired, "What is your name, please, so I can ask for you by telephone, if I need to."

"Sawsan Hammad."

"Thank you very much."

He stood up and bade her farewell with a wave of his hand. Before departing, he turned back to say, "Please summarize it carefully."

Without looking up she replied, "I know my job."

Regretting his words, he left the room.

129

KAMAL WAS in his study wearing a loose-fitting house shirt when Umm Hanafi came to tell him, "Mr. Fuad al-Hamzawi is with my master." He rose and hurried downstairs.

So Fuad had returned to Cairo after a year's absence. The distinguished public prosecutor from Qena district was home again. The friendship and affection that filled Kamal's heart were marred by an uncomfortable feeling. His relationship with Fuad was still marked by a struggle between loving affection and jealous aversion. No matter how hard he tried to elevate himself intellectually, his instincts always forced him back down to the petty mundane level. As he descended the stairs he sensed that this visit would awaken happy memories but also rub the scabs off wounds that had almost healed. When he passed through the sitting room, where the coffee hour – consisting of his mother, Aisha, and Na'ima – was in session, he heard his mother whisper, "He'll ask for Na'ima's hand."

Sensing his presence, she turned to tell him, "Your friend's inside. He's so charming. . . . He wanted to kiss my hand, but I wouldn't let him."

Kamal found his father sitting cross-legged on the sofa and Fuad in a chair opposite. The old friends shook hands, and Kamal said, "Praise God for your safe return. Welcome, welcome! Are you on vacation?"

Smiling, al-Sayyid Ahmad answered, "No, he's been transferred to Cairo. He's finally been moved back here after a lengthy absence in Upper Egypt."

Sitting down on the sofa, Kamal said, "Congratulations! Now we hope to see you more often."

Fuad answered, "Naturally. As of the first of next month we'll be living in al-Abbasiya. We've leased an apartment near the Wayliya police station."

Fuad's appearance had not changed much, but he looked healthier. He had filled out, his complexion was rosier, and his eyes still had the familiar sparkle of intelligence.

Al-Sayyid Ahmad asked the young man, "How is your father? I haven't seen him for a week."

"His health isn't as good as we'd wish. He's still sad about leaving the shop. But hopefully the person he found to take his place is doing a good job."

Al-Sayyid Ahmad laughed and said, "The shop now requires my constant attention. Your father, may God grant him a complete recovery and good health, took care of everything."

Fuad sat up and placed one leg over the other. This gesture attracted Kamal's attention and distressed him, for he considered it disrespectful to his father, even though al-Sayyid Ahmad gave no sign of having noticed. Was this how things were developing? Yes, Fuad was a prominent member of the judicial service, but had he forgotten who it was who sat facing him? Lord, as if that was not enough, he took out a cigarette case and offered it to al-Sayyid Ahmad, who graciously declined. Fuad's judicial career had really made him forget himself, but it was sad that his forgetfulness should extend to the person who had financed his career. Fuad's grateful memories seemed to have vanished in thin air as quickly as the smoke from his fancy cigarette. His gestures appeared quite natural and unaffected, for he was an executive who had grown accustomed to taking charge.

Al-Sayyid Ahmad told Kamal, "Congratulate him on his promotion too."

Smiling, Kamal said, "Congratulations! That's great. I hope I'll soon be able to offer you my best wishes for being named a judge."

Fuad answered, "That's the next step, God willing."

Once a judge he might allow himself to piss in front of the man who sat before him now. The grade-school teacher would remain just that. Kamal would have to content himself with his bushy mustache and the tons of culture weighing down his head.

Looking at Fuad with great interest, al-Sayyid Ahmad inquired, "How is the political situation?"

Fuad answered with satisfaction, "The miracle has happened! A treaty has been signed in London. I could not believe my ears when I heard the radio announce Egypt's independence and the termination of the four restrictions Britain had placed on our independence in the last treaty. Who would have anticipated this?"

"Then you're happy with the treaty?"

Nodding his head as though personally responsible for the decision, Fuad replied, "On the whole, yes. Some oppose it for legitimate reasons and others do so in bad faith. When we consider the circumstances in which we find ourselves and remember that despite the bitterness of the Sidqy era our people endured it without rebelling against him, we must consider the treaty a positive step. It abolishes the 'reserved points' limiting Egyptian independence, prepares the way for an end to the capitulations granting special privileges to foreigners, limits the future presence of foreign troops, and restricts them to a certain region. Without any doubt, it's a great step forward."

Al-Sayyid Ahmad was more enthusiastic and less knowledgeable about the treaty than Fuad. He would have liked the young man to agree more decisively with him, and when that did not happen, he insisted, "In any case, we must remember that the Wafd have restored the constitution to the nation and brought us independence, even if this has taken some time."

Kamal reflected that Fuad had always been lukewarm about politics. Perhaps he still was. But he did seem to favor the Wafd.

"For a long time I was politically engaged in a most emotional way," Kamal reflected. "But now I don't believe in anything. Not even politics is exempt from my insatiable doubt. Yet no matter what my intellect does, my heart pounds with nationalist fervor."

Fuad laughingly remarked, "In periods of unrest, the judicial system quails, and the police take precedence. Thus times of unrest are also times of police power. If the Wafd returns to rule, the judicial system will regain its rightful place and activities of the police will be limited. The natural state of affairs is for the law to have the final say."

Al-Sayyid Ahmad commented, "Can we forget the Sidqy era? Soldiers used truncheons to assemble citizens on election days. Many of our distinguished friends were ruined and went bankrupt as a result of their loyalty to the Wafd. And then we see this 'devil' become a member of the negotiating team, posing as a nationalist liberal."

Fuad replied, "Circumstances required a united front, one that would have been incomplete had it not included this 'devil' and his supporters. It's the end result that counts."

Fuad lingered there for some time, sipping coffee, while Kamal examined his friend, noticing the elegant white silk suit, which had a red rose decorating its lapel, and the forceful personality that he had acquired to match his position. Deep inside, Kamal felt that, in spite of everything, he would be happy to have this young man ask for Na'ima's hand, but Fuad did not touch on this subject. He seemed ready to depart and soon told al-Sayyid Ahmad, "It must be time for you to leave for the store. I'll stay and chat with Kamal, but I'll visit you before going to Alexandria. I've decided to spend the rest of August and part of September at the beach." Then he rose, said goodbye to his host with a handshake, and left the room, preceded by Kamal.

They climbed the stairs to the top floor and settled themselves in the study. Fuad smiled as he looked around at the books on the shelves. He asked, "May I borrow a book from you?"

Hiding his lack of enthusiasm, Kamal answered, "I'd be delighted. What do you normally read during your free time?"

"I have the poetry collections of Shawqi, Hafiz Ibrahim, and Mutran as well as some books by al-Jahiz and al-Ma'arri. I'm especially fond of al-Mawardi's *Culture for This World and the Next*, not to mention works of contemporary authors. This, along with a few books by Dickens and Conan Doyle . . . but my commitment to the law consumes most of my time."

Fuad rose to walk around and inspect the books, reading their titles. Completing his circle, he snorted, "A purely philosophical library! There's nothing to interest me here. I read *al-Fikr* magazine and have followed your essays in it over the years. But I don't claim to have read all of them or to remember anything from them. A philosophical discussion is heavy reading, and a public prosecutor is burdened with work. Why don't you write on popular topics?"

Kamal had heard his works belittled so often that he had almost grown accustomed to it and felt little distress about it. For him, doubt devoured everything, including any sorrow over such criticism. What was fame? What was popularity? Kamal was actually pleased to hear that Fuad found the articles useless for diversion in his spare time.

Kamal asked, "What do you mean by 'popular topics'?"

"Literature, for example."

"I've read many charming works since we were together, but I'm not a novelist or a poet."

Fuad laughed and said, "Then stay in philosophy, all by yourself. Aren't you a philosopher?"

"Aren't you a philosopher?" This expression had been etched into his mind ever since Aïda's lips had tossed it at him on Palaces Street. He shuddered from the terrifying impact it still made on his heart but concealed his emotional turmoil by laughing loudly. He remembered the days when Fuad had been devoted to him, following him around like a shadow. Now Kamal was looking at an important man, who deserved his affection and loyalty.

"What have you done with your life?" he asked himself.

Fuad was examining his friend's mustache. Suddenly he laughed and said, "If only..." When Kamal's eyes inquired what this meant, Fuad continued: "We're both almost thirty, and neither of us has married. Our generation is rife with bachelors. It's a crisis generation. Are you still resolutely opposed to marriage?"

"I haven't budged."

"I don't know why, but I believe that you will never marry."

"You've always been very perceptive."

Smiling warmly as though to apologize in advance for what he was going to say, Fuad commented, "You're an egotistical man. You insist on maintaining total control over your life. Brother, the Prophet married, and that did not prevent him from having a sublime spiritual life." Then, laughing, he emended his statement: "Excuse me for using the Prophet as an example. I almost forgot that you . . . But not so fast. You're no longer the same old atheist. Now you even doubt atheism. This represents a gain for belief."

Kamal replied calmly, "Let's skip the philosophizing. You don't enjoy it. Tell me why you haven't married yet, since this is what you think of the single life."

He immediately sensed that he should not have brought up this topic, for fear his friend would consider it a hint to ask for Na'ima's hand. But Fuad gave no sign of having understood his words in this manner. Instead, he laughed aloud – although without abandoning his dignified demeanor – and answered, "You know, I've only recently started to enjoy the seamy side of life.

Unlike you, I wasn't corrupted early in life. I haven't had enough fun yet."

"Will you marry when you have?"

As if to brush aside the temptation to prevaricate, Fuad waved his hand backwards through the air and confessed, "Since I've waited this long, I need to be patient a little longer, until I become a judge, for example. Then I'll be able to marry the daughter of a cabinet minister if I want."

"You son of Jamil al-Hamzawi!" Kamal exclaimed to himself. "The bridegroom of a cabinet official's daughter . . . her mother-in-law would be from the working-class district of al-Mubayyada. Even though he justified the presence of evil in the world, I defy Leibniz to justify this."

Kamal said, "You consider marriage a . . ."

Before he could complete this statement, Fuad laughingly interrupted: "At least that's better than not considering it at all."

"But happiness . . ."

"Don't philosophize! Happiness is a subjective art. You may find bliss with the daughter of a cabinet minister and nothing but misery with a girl from your own background. Marriage is a treaty like the one al-Nahhas signed yesterday. It involves haggling, realistic appraisals, shrewdness, perspicacity, gains and losses. In our country this is the only door to advancement. Last week a man not yet forty was appointed a senior judge for the appeals court, while I could devote a lifetime of diligent and tireless service to the judicial system without ever attaining such an exalted position."

What was the primary-school teacher to say? He would spend his entire life at the sixth level of the civil service, even if philosophy did fill his head to overflowing.

"Your position should save you from having to resort to such stratagems."

"If it weren't for strategic alliances of this kind, no prime minister would ever be able to assemble a cabinet."

Kamal laughed lifelessly and observed, "You're in need of some philosophy. You would benefit from a spoonful of Spinoza."

"Sip as much of it as you want, but spare us. Tell me where a man can have a good time and find something to drink. In Qena I had to take my pleasures cautiously, on the sly. A position like mine forces a man to be discreet and private. The constant struggle between us and the police means that we must be extra careful. A public prosecutor has a tedious and sensitive job."

"We're returning to talk that threatens to make me explode with bitterness," Kamal noted to himself. "Compared to yours, my life seems disciplined and refined, but it's also the greatest possible test in life for my skeptical philosophy."

"My circumstances," Fuad continued, "bring me together with many important people, and they invite me to their mansions. I feel obliged to refuse their invitations in order to avoid any possible conflict of interest in the performance of my duties. But their mentality is such that they don't understand this. All the leading citizens of the region accuse me of being a snob, although I am entirely innocent of the charge."

Although saying "Yes" agreeably to his friend, Kamal thought, "You're a conceited snob who is solicitous about his position."

"For similar reasons I lost favor with the police force. Dissatisfied with their crooked procedures, I attempted to entrap them. I had the law on my side, while they had the brutality of the Middle Ages on theirs. Everyone hates me, but I'm right."

"You're right," Kamal reflected. "That's what I've always known about you. You're shrewd and honest. But you don't and can't love anyone. You don't cling to what's right simply because it is right but out of conceit, pride, and a feeling of inferiority. This is what men are like. I run into people like you even in lowly callings. A man who is both pleasant and forceful is a myth. But what value does love have? Or idealism? Or anything?"

They talked for a long time. When preparing to leave, Fuad leaned toward Kamal and whispered, "I'm new in Cairo. You naturally know of an establishment – or probably several . . . one that's very private, naturally. . . ."

Smiling, Kamal replied, "A teacher, like a public prosecutor, must always take care to be discreet."

"Excellent. We'll get together soon. I'm busy arranging the new apartment now, but we'll have to spend some evenings together."

"Agreed."

They left the room together, and Kamal accompanied his friend all the way to the street. Passing by the first floor on his return, he met his mother, who stood waiting for him at the door. She inquired anxiously, "Didn't he say anything to you?"

He understood what she meant, and that tormented him terribly. But he pretended not to understand and asked in turn, "About what?"

"Na'ima?"

He answered resentfully, "Absolutely not."

"Amazing!"

They exchanged a long look. Then Amina continued: "But al-Hamzawi spoke to your father about it."

Concealing his fury as best he could, Kamal said, "Perhaps he spoke without having consulted his son."

Amina retorted angrily, "What a silly idea. Doesn't he know how lucky he would be to get her? Your father should have reminded him who he is."

"Fuad's not to blame. Perhaps his father, with all the best intentions, spoke rashly, without thinking it over."

"But he must have told his son. Did Fuad refuse . . . that boy who was transformed into a distinguished civil servant by our money?"

"There's no need to talk about that."

"Son, this is unimaginable. Doesn't he know that accepting him into our family does us no honor?"

"Then don't be upset if it doesn't happen."

"I'm not upset about it. But I'm angered by the insult."

"There has been no insult. It's just a misunderstanding."

He returned to his room, sad and embarrassed, telling himself, "Na'ima's a beautiful rose. Yet, since I'm a man whose only remaining merit is love of truth, I must ask whether she is really a good match for a public prosecutor. Although he comes from a modest background, he will be able to find a spouse who is better educated, from a more distinguished family, wealthier, and prettier too. His good-natured father was too hasty. But he's not to blame. Still, Fuad's remarks to me were impudent. He certainly is impertinent. He's bright, honest, competent, insolent, and conceited, although it's not his fault. It's the result of the factors dividing men from each other. They infect us with all these maladies."

130

AL-FIKR MAGAZINE occupied the ground floor of number 21 Abd al-Aziz Street. The barred window in the office of its proprietor, Mr. Abd al-Aziz al-Asyuti, overlooked the tenebrous Barakat Alley, and therefore the light inside was left on both night and day. Whenever Kamal approached the magazine's headquarters, the gloomy premises and shabby furniture reminded him of the status of thought in his land and of his own position in his society. Mr. Abd al-Aziz greeted him with an affectionate smile of welcome. This was hardly surprising, for they had known each other since 1930, when Kamal had begun sending the magazine his essays on philosophy. During the past six years his collaboration with the editor had been mutually supportive, if unremunerated. In fact, the magazine paid none of its writers for their efforts, which were undertaken solely for the advancement of philosophy and culture.

Abd al-Aziz welcomed all volunteer contributors, even specialists in Islamic philosophy, which was his own field. After receiving an Islamic education at al-Azhar university, he had traveled to France, where he spent four years doing research and auditing lectures without obtaining a degree. His real estate holdings, which provided him with a monthly income of fifty pounds, spared him from having to earn a living. He had founded *al-Fikr* magazine in 1923 and had kept publishing it, even though the profits were not commensurate with the labor he poured into it.

Kamal had scarcely taken a seat when a man his own age entered. Wearing a gray linen suit, he was tall and thin, although less so than Kamal, and had a long profile, taut cheeks, and wide lips. His delicate nose and pointed chin lent a special character to his full face. Smiling, he came forward with light steps and stretched out his hand to Mr. Abd al-Aziz, who shook it and presented the visitor to Kamal: "Mr. Riyad Qaldas, a translator in the Ministry of Education. He has recently joined the group writing for *al-Fikr*, infusing fresh blood into our scholarly journal with his monthly summaries of plays from world literature and his short stories."

Then he introduced Kamal: "Mr. Kamal Ahmad Abd al-Jawad. Perhaps you've read his essays?"

The two men shook hands, and Riyad said admiringly, "I've read them for years. They are essays of value, in every sense of the word."

Kamal thanked him cautiously for this praise. Then they sat down on neighboring chairs in front of the desk of Mr. Abd al-Aziz, who remarked, "Mr. Riyad, don't wait for him to return your compliment and say that he has read your valuable stories. He never reads stories."

Riyad laughed engagingly and revealed gleaming regular teeth with a gap between the middle incisors. "Don't you like literature?" he asked. "Every philosopher has a special theory of beauty arrived at only after an exhaustive examination of various arts − literature included, naturally."

Rather uneasily, Kamal ventured, "I don't hate literature. For a long time, I've used it for relaxation, enjoying both poetry and prose. But I have little free time."

"That must mean you've read what short stories you could, since modern literature consists almost entirely of short stories and plays."

Kamal replied, "Over the years I've read a great number, although I . . ."

Smiling in a knowing way, Abd al-Aziz al-Asyuti interrupted: "It's up to you, Mr. Riyad, to convince him of the truth of your new ideas. For the moment it will suffice if you realize that he's a philosopher whose energies are concentrated on thought." Then, turning toward Kamal, he asked, "Do you have your essay for this month?"

Kamal brought out an envelope of medium size and silently placed it in front of the editor, who took it. After extracting the article and examining it he said, "On Bergson? . . . Fine!"

Kamal explained, "The idea is to give an overview of the role his philosophy has played in the history of modern thought. Perhaps later I'll follow up on it with some detailed studies."

Riyad Qaldas was listening to the discussion with interest. Gazing at Kamal in an endearing way, he asked, "I've read your articles for years, starting with the ones you did on the Greek philosophers. They have been varied and occasionally contradictory, since they have presented rival schools of philosophy. I realize that you're a historian of ideas. Yet all the same I've tried in vain to discover your own intellectual position and the school of philosophy with which you're affiliated."

Abd al-Aziz al-Asyuti observed, "We're relative newcomers to the field of philosophical studies. So we must commence with general presentations. Perhaps in time Professor Kamal will develop a new philosophy. Possibly, Mr. Riyad, you'll become one of the adherents of Kamalism."

They all laughed. Kamal removed his spectacles and began to clean the lenses. He was capable of losing himself rapidly in a conversation, especially if he liked the person and if the atmosphere was relaxed and pleasant.

Kamal said, "I'm a tourist in a museum where nothing belongs to me. I'm merely a historian. I don't know where I stand."

With increasing interest Riyad Qaldas replied, "In other words, you're at a crossroads. I stood there for a long time before finding my way. But I wager there's a story behind your current posture. Usually it's the end of one stage and the beginning of another. Haven't you believed strongly in various different causes before reaching this point?"

The melody of this conversation revived the memory of an old song that was rooted in Kamal's heart. This young man and this conversation. . . . The previous barren years had been completely devoid of spiritual friendship. Kamal had grown accustomed to addressing himself whenever he needed someone to talk to. It had been a long time since anyone had been able to awaken a spiritual response like this in him . . . not Isma'il Latif, not Fuad al-Hamzawi, not any one of the dozens of teachers. Had the time come for the place vacated by Husayn Shaddad's departure to be filled?

He put his glasses on again. Smiling, he said, "Of course there's a story. Like most people, I began with religious belief, which was followed by belief in truth. . . ."

"I remember that you discussed materialist philosophy with suspicious zeal."

"My enthusiasm was sincere, but later I was troubled by skeptical doubts."

"Perhaps rationalism was the answer."

"I quickly felt skeptical about that too. Systems of philosophy are beautiful and tranquil castles but unfit to live in."

Abd al-Aziz smiled and said, "These are the words of one of their denizens."

Kamal shrugged his shoulders to dismiss that remark, but Riyad continued questioning him: "There's science. Perhaps it could save you from your doubts."

"Science is a closed world to those of us who know only its most obvious findings. Besides, I've learned that there are distinguished scientists who question whether scientific truth matches our actual world. Some find the laws of probability perplexing. Others are averse to asserting that there is any absolute truth. So I became even more tormented by doubt."

Riyad Qaldas smiled but made no comment. Then Kamal continued: "I've even plunged into modern spiritualism and its attempts to contact the other world. That made my head revolve in a frightening emptiness, and it's still spinning. What is truth? What are values? What is anything? Occasionally when I do the right thing I feel the prickings of conscience that I normally experience on doing something wrong."

Abd al-Aziz laughed out loud and said, "Religion has taken its revenge on you. You fled it to pursue higher truths only to return empty-handed."

Apparently more from politeness than conviction, Riyad Qaldas commented, "This skeptical stance is rather delightful. You observe and ponder everything with total freedom, acting like a tourist."

Addressing Kamal, Abd al-Aziz said, "You're a bachelor in both your thought and your life."

Kamal noted this chance phrase with interest. Was his single status a consequence of his philosophy or vice versa? Or were both a product of some third factor?

Riyad Qaldas said, "Being single's a temporary condition. Perhaps doubt is too."

Abd al-Aziz replied, "But it seems he's averse to ever getting married."

Amazed, Riyad asked, "What's incompatible about love and doubt? What's to prevent a lover from getting married? A persistent refusal to marry cannot be justified by doubt, which admits no persistence in anything."

Without believing it himself, Kamal asked, "Doesn't love require a certain amount of faith?"

Riyad Qaldas answered laughingly, "Of course not. Love is like an earthquake, rocking mosque, church, and brothel equally."

"An earthquake?" Kamal asked himself. "What an appropriate comparison! An earthquake destroys everything and then drowns the world in deathly silence."

"What about you, Mr. Qaldas?" Kamal inquired. "You have praised doubt. Are you a skeptic?"

Abd al-Aziz laughed and said, "He's doubt incarnate."

They roared with laughter. Then Riyad, as though to introduce himself, commented, "I was a skeptic for a long time before renouncing it. I no longer have any doubts concerning religion, because I've abandoned it. But I believe in science and art. I always shall, God willing."

Abd al-Aziz asked sarcastically, "The God you don't believe in?"

Smiling, Riyad Qaldas answered, "Religion is a human artifact. We know nothing about God. Who can really say he doesn't believe in God? Or that he does? The prophets are the only true Believers. That's because they see and hear Him or converse with messengers bringing His revelations."

Kamal inquired, "Yet you believe in science and art?"

"Yes."

"There's some basis for belief in science. But art? I'd rather believe in spiritualism than in the short story, for example."

Riyad stared at him critically but said calmly, "Science is the language of the intellect. Art is the language of the entire human personality."

"What a poetic statement!"

Riyad received Kamal's sarcasm with an indulgent smile and replied, "Science brings people together with the light of its ideas. Art brings them together with lofty human emotions. Both help mankind develop and prod us toward a better future."

"What conceit!" Kamal exclaimed to himself. "He writes a two-page short story every month and imagines that he's helping mankind progress. But I'm as nauseating as he is, for I summarize a chapter from Høffding's *History of Modern Philosophy* and then deep inside claim to be the equal of Fuad Jamil al-Hamzawi, public prosecutor for al-Darb al-Ahmar. But how would life be bearable otherwise? Are we insane, wise, or merely alive? To hell with everything!"

"What do you say about scientists who do not share your enthusiasm for science?"

"We should not interpret the modesty of science as weakness or despair. Science provides mankind with its magic, light, guidance, and miracles. It's the religion of the future."

"And the short story?"

For the first time it became clear that Riyad was offended, even though he attempted not to let it show. Kamal corrected himself almost apologetically, "I mean art in general."

Riyad Qaldas asked emphatically, "Can you live in absolute isolation? People need confidential advice, consolation, joy, guidance, light, and journeys to all regions of the inhabited world and of the soul. That's what art is."

At this juncture Mr. Abd al-Aziz said, "I have an idea. Let's get together with some of our colleagues once a month to talk about intellectual concerns. Then we can publish our discussion under the title 'Debate of the Month.'"

Looking at Kamal affectionately, Riyad Qaldas said, "Our debate will continue. Or that's what I hope. Shall we consider ourselves friends?"

Kamal replied with sincere enthusiasm, "Most certainly! We must meet as often as possible."

Pervaded by happiness because of this new friendship, Kamal sensed that an exalted side of his heart had been awakened after a profound slumber. He was more convinced than ever of the important role friendship played in his life. It was vital and indispensable for him. Without it, he was like a thirsty man perishing in the desert.

131

THE NEW friends parted at al-Ataba, and Kamal returned by the Muski. Although it was nearly 8 P.M., the air he breathed in was hot enough to be stifling. He slowed down on reaching al-Gawhari Alley, which he entered. Then he stepped into the third house on the right, climbing the stairs to the second floor. After he rang the bell, a little window in the door opened, revealing the face of a woman over sixty. She welcomed him with a smile, which showed off her gold teeth, and admitted him.

"Welcome to my lover's son!" she exclaimed. "Welcome to my brother's son!"

He followed her to a sitting room surrounded by bedrooms. The two sofas were placed opposite each other. Between them were a small carpet gleaming with gold and silver thread, a table, and a water pipe. The fragrance of incense permeated the room.

The woman was plump, but old enough to be fragile, and her head was wrapped in a spangled kerchief. Although decorated by kohl, her eyes had a heavy look indicative of drug abuse. The wrinkles of her face revealed traces of her former beauty and of an enduring wantonness. Sitting down cross-legged on the sofa near the water pipe, she gestured for him to sit beside her.

Obeying her, he smiled and asked, "How is Mrs. Jalila?"

She protested, "Call me 'Aunt.'"

"How are you, Auntie?"

"Superb, son of Abd al-Jawad." Then she shouted in a harsh voice, "Girl! Nazla!"

In a few minutes the maid brought two full glasses, which she placed on the table. Jalila directed: "Drink! ... How often I said that to your father in those sweet bygone days...."

As Kamal picked up a glass he remarked jovially, "It's really sad that I arrived too late...."

She gave him a punch that made the gold bracelets covering her arm jangle. "Shame on you! Would you have wished to ravage what your father adored?" Then she added, "But what are you

compared to your father? He had already married a second time
when I met him. He married young, as was the custom then. But
that did not prevent him from keeping me company for a period
that was the sweetest of my life. Then he left me for Zubayda, may
God take her by the hand. And there were dozens of other women
besides us, may God be indulgent with him. But you're still a
bachelor, and even so you only visit my house once a week, Thursday evenings. Shame on you! What ever happened to virility?"

The father he heard about from her was not the one he knew
personally. This was not even the father Yasin had described to
him. Jalila's lover had been a passionate and impetuous man with a
heart untroubled by qualms. What was Kamal compared to that
man? Even when he visited this brothel each Thursday, only
alcohol could release him from his worries long enough for him
to enjoy "love" here. Without its intoxication, he would have felt
the brothel's atmosphere to be devastatingly grim. That first night,
when fate had led him to this house, had been unforgettable. He
had seen this woman for the first time, and she had invited him to
sit with her until a girl was ready. When he had revealed his full
name during the course of the conversation, she had cried out,
"Are you the son of al-Sayyid Ahmad Abd al-Jawad whose store is
in al-Nahhasin?"

"Yes. Do you know my father?"

"A thousand welcomes to you!"

"Do you know my father?"

"I know him far better than you do. We were lovers, and
I performed at your sister's wedding. In my time, I was as famous
a singer as Umm Kalthoum in your gray days. Ask anyone about
me."

"It's an honor to meet you, ma'am."

"Pick any of my girls you like. Benevolent folks like us don't bill
each other."

So his first girl in this house had been a gift from his father. That
evening Jalila had looked at his face for so long he had felt
embarrassed. Only fear of being rude had kept her from expressing
her astonishment, for what resemblance was there between this
boy's bizarre head and amazing nose and his father's exquisite and
ruddy face? During a lengthy conversation with her he had learned
about his father's secret history, peculiarities, amazing deeds,
romantic adventures, and hidden qualities.

"I'm so bewildered," Kamal reflected. "I've always wavered between instinct's searing flame and mysticism's cool breeze."

He replied, "Don't exaggerate, Auntie. I'm a teacher, and teachers like to be discreet. Don't forget that during the vacation I visit you several times a week. Wasn't I here the day before yesterday? I visit you whenever ..."

"Whenever I'm tormented by anxiety," he confessed to himself. "Anxiety drives me to you far more often than lust."

"Whenever what, my dear?"

"Whenever I don't have to work."

"Say anything but that. Down with this age of yours. Our coins were made of gold. Yours are nickel and copper. We had live entertainment. You have the radio. Our men were descended from Adam's loins. Yours come from Eve's womb. What do you have to say about that, you teacher of girls?"

She took a drag on the water pipe and then sang:

> *Teacher of girls, show them how*
> *To play instruments and sing.*

Kamal laughed, leaned toward her, and kissed her cheek, half affectionately and half flirtatiously.

She cried out, "Your mustache pricks. God help Atiya!"

"She loves pricks."

"By the way, yesterday we had the honor of a visit from a prominent police officer. I'm not bragging. All our clients are distinguished gentlemen. Or do you consider your visits here to be charitable contributions?"

"Madam Jalila, your very name means 'glorious,' and you certainly are that."

"I love it when you're drunk. Intoxication liberates you from your schoolmasterly earnestness and makes you a little more like your father. But tell me. Don't you love Atiya? ... She loves you!"

How could these hearts, hardened by the coarseness of life, love anyone? Yet what experience did he have of hearts generous with love or eager for it? The daughter of the snack shop owner had been in love with him, but he had ignored her. He had loved Aïda, but she had spurned him. In his living dictionary, the only meaning for love was pain ... an astonishing pain that set the soul on fire. By the light of its raging flames amazing secrets of life became visible, but it left behind only rubble.

He commented ironically, "May you find health and love too!"

"She's only been in this line of work since her divorce."

"Praise God! He alone is praised for hateful things."

"Praise to Him in all circumstances."

He smiled sardonically. Grasping what his smile implied, she protested, "Do you begrudge me my enthusiasm for praising God? That's enough from you, son of Abd al-Jawad. Listen, I don't have a son or a daughter. I'm fed up with the world. Forgiveness is from God."

It was interesting that the woman's conversation was so frequently interspersed with this melody celebrating asceticism. Kamal glanced at her stealthily as he drained his glass. For him, alcohol's magic effect began with the first drink. He found himself recalling a bygone age when drinking had brought him a heavenly bliss. How many of his joys had vanished.... At first lust had been both a rebellion and a victory for him. Then it had eventually been transformed into a whore's philosophy. Time and habituation had extinguished its delirium. It was also frequently marred by the agony of a man wavering between heaven and earth – before doubt had reduced heaven to earth's level.

The doorbell rang, and Atiya entered. Her body was full, supple, and fair. Her shoes and her laughter both resounded noisily. She kissed the madam's hand. Casting a smiling glance at the two empty glasses, she teased Kamal, "You've been unfaithful to me!"

She leaned down to the madam's ear and whispered to her. Then, giving Kamal a laughing look, she vanished into the bedroom on the madam's right. Jalila punched Kamal and told him, "Go along, light of my eye."

Picking up his fez, he headed for the bedroom. Nazla immediately caught up with him, carrying a tray with a bottle, two glasses, and some appetizers. Atiya instructed her, "Bring us two pounds of kebab from al-Ajati's restaurant. I'm hungry!"

He took off his jacket and made himself comfortable by stretching out his legs. As he sat watching her, she removed her shoes and dress. Then at the mirror she straightened her chemise and combed her hair. He loved her body, which was so full, supple, and fair. What did Aïda's body look like? Frequently when he remembered her, it seemed that she had no body. Even when he recalled her grace, slenderness, and brown skin, these physical characteristics took their place in his spirit as pure ideas. As for the customary kind of memories concerned with bodily attributes like breasts, legs, or buttocks, he could not remember his senses ever having paid attention to them. Today, if a beautiful woman whose only attractions were a graceful slenderness and a swarthy complexion was presented for his admiration he would not even offer twenty piasters for her. So how had his love for Aïda been possible? Why was his memory of her so firmly protected by veneration and adoration, even though he scorned all her qualities?

"It's hot. Darn it."

"Once the alcohol gets into our systems, we won't care if the weather's hot or cold."

"Stop eating me with your eyes. Take off your glasses!"

"A divorced woman with children," he brooded. "She masks gloomy melancholy with boisterous behavior. These greedy nights carelessly swallow her femininity and her humanity. Her every breath blends together fake passion and loathing. It's the worst form of bondage. Thus, alcohol provides an escape from suffering as well as from thought."

She plopped down beside him and prepared to pour their drinks, reaching her soft hand out to the bottle, which was sold in this establishment for twice what it was worth. Everything here was expensive except women, except for human beings. Without alcohol to distract one from humanity's disdainful glare, reunions like this would be impossible. But life is full of prostitutes of various types. Some are cabinet ministers and others authors.

As his second drink went to work inside him the harbingers of forgetfulness and delight arrived. "I've craved this woman for a long time, even without being conscious of it. Lust is a tyrannical master. Love is something entirely different. When liberated from lust, it appears in the most amazing garb. If one day I'm permitted to find love and lust united in a single human being, a desirable stability will be achieved. I still see life as a set of mismatched parts. I'm searching for a marriage that will affect both the private and public aspects of my life. I don't know which is more basic, but I'm certain that I'm miserable, despite having created a life that assures me both intellectual pleasures and bodily delights. A train, too, rolls forcefully down the tracks without having any idea of where it has been or where it is going. Lust is a tyrannical beauty readily felled by disgust. The heart cries out as it vainly searches in agonizing despair for eternal bliss. Complaints are endless. Life is a vast swindle. To be able to accept this deception gracefully, we must assume that life contains some secret wisdom. We're like an actor who, while conscious of the deceit implicit in his role onstage, worships his craft."

He downed his third drink in a single gulp, sending Atiya into gales of laughter. She loved to get drunk, even though it had a bad effect on her. If he did not stop her in time, she would become rowdy, twitch, weep, and throw up. The liquor had gone to his head, and he quivered with excitement. He gazed at her with a beaming face. She was simply a woman now, not a problem. Problems no longer seemed to exist. Existence itself – the most troublesome issue in life – had stopped being a problem.

"Just drink some more and lose yourself in her kisses," he thought.

"You're so charming," he told her, "when you laugh for no reason at all."

"If I seem to laugh for no reason, I hope you'll understand that some reasons are too important to be mentioned."

132

WRAPPED UP in his overcoat, Abd al-Muni'm returned home to Sugar Street, bracing himself against the bitter winter cold. Although it was only six, darkness had fallen. When he reached the entry to the staircase, the door of the first-floor apartment opened and out slipped the lithe figure that had been waiting for him. His heart pounded and his fiery eyes watched her advance as he climbed the stairs with light steps, taking care not to make any sound. He was torn between his desire, which tempted him to yield, and his will, which urged him to take control of a nervous system apparently bent on betraying and destroying him. He remembered, only then, that she had made a date with him for this evening and that he could have come home earlier or later, thus avoiding the encounter. He had forgotten all about it. How forgetful he was! There was no time for deliberation and reflection. He would have to wait until he was alone in his room, until a moment that would mark triumphant victory or miserable defeat.

Nothing could make him forget his endless struggle. Throwing himself into this trial, he mounted the stairs behind her without having reached any decision. At the landing, he imagined her figure had swelled so large that it filled space and time to bursting.

With some difficulty, he concealed his anxiety and hid his determination to resist temptation when he said, "Good evening."

The voice replied affectionately, "Good evening. Thank you for heeding my advice to wear your overcoat."

He was touched by her tenderness, and the words he was about to cast at her melted in his mouth. Trying to mask his confusion, he said, "I was afraid it might rain."

She raised her head as though to look at the sky and remarked, "It will rain sooner or later. You can't see a single star in the sky. I had trouble recognizing you when you turned into our street."

He collected his unruly faculties and observed as if to caution her, "It's cold and extremely humid in the staircase."

With a directness the girl had learned from him, she replied, "I don't feel the cold when I'm near you."

The heat welling up inside him made his face burn. His condition suggested that he was going to err again, his best intentions notwithstanding. He summoned all his willpower in an effort to master the tremor sweeping through his body.

"Why don't you speak?" she asked.

Sensing her hand gently squeeze his shoulder, he could not stop himself from putting his arms around her. He began with one long kiss and then showered her with more, until he heard her say breathlessly, "I can't bear to be apart from you!"

He kept on hugging her, as he warmed to her embrace. She whispered in his ear, "I wish I could stay like this forever."

Tightening his grip on her, he said in a trembling voice, "I'm sorry!"

In the darkness she drew her head back a little and asked, "About what, darling?"

He replied hesitantly, "The mistake we're making."

"By God, what mistake?"

He gently freed himself from her and removed his overcoat, which he folded and started to place on the railing. But at the last terrifying moment he changed his mind, draped it over his arm, and took a step backwards, breathing heavily. His willpower was able to halt his progressive surrender to lust, and that changed everything. When her hand sought to return to his neck, he grabbed hold of it. Then he waited until his breathing had returned to normal and said calmly, "This is a great error."

"What error? I don't understand."

"A young girl not yet fourteen," Abd al-Muni'm chided himself, "and you're toying with her to satisfy a merciless desire. This flirtation will lead to nothing. It's merely an amusement that will draw down God's wrath and anger on you."

"You must try to understand," he said. "Would we be able to tell everyone what we're doing?"

"Tell everyone?"

"Don't you see you would be forced to deny it? If we can't talk about it, then it must be a despicable error."

He felt her hand search for him again. He climbed the first step of the next flight of stairs, confident that he had passed safely out of the danger zone. "Admit that we're doing something wrong. We mustn't continue to make this mistake."

"I'm amazed to hear you talk like this."

"Don't be. My conscience can no longer tolerate this mistake. It torments me, making it hard for me to pray."

"She's silent," he thought. "I've hurt her, may God forgive me. How painful! But I won't give in. Praise God that desire didn't lead you to commit an even greater error."

"What's happened must teach us not to do anything like this in the future. You're young. You've made a mistake. Don't ever yield to temptation again."

In a sobbing voice she protested, "I haven't done anything wrong. Are you planning to desert me? What are your intentions?"

In full command of himself now, he answered, "Go back to your apartment. Don't do anything you would have to conceal. Don't ever meet anyone in the dark."

The shaky voice asked, "Are you deserting me? Have you forgotten what you said about our love?"

"Those were a fool's words. You were mistaken. Let this be a lesson for you. Beware of the dark, for it could be your ruin. You're young. How come you're so daring?"

Her sobs reverberated in the gloom, but that made no impression on his heart. He was intoxicated by the stern delight of victory.

"Heed my words. Don't be angry. Remember that if I were really a scoundrel I wouldn't have been satisfied with anything less than ruining you. Goodbye."

He bounded up the stairs. The torment was over. Remorse would no longer be able to sink its teeth into him. But he should remember what his mentor Shaykh Ali al-Manufi said: "You cannot conquer the devil by ignoring the laws of nature." Yes, he had to remember that. He quickly changed into his house shirt. Then as he left the room he told his brother, Ahmad, "I want to talk privately with Father in the study. Please give us a little time to be alone."

When Abd al-Muni'm asked his father to join him there, Khadija raised her head to inquire, "Good news?"

"I want to talk to Father first. Then it will be your turn."

Ibrahim Shawkat trailed after his son silently. The man had recently gotten a new set of dentures. His languid complacency had returned, after he had been forced to confront life in a toothless condition for six whole months. They sat down beside each other, and the father asked, "Good news, God willing?"

Without any hesitation or introduction, Abd al-Muni'm said, "Father, I want to marry."

The man stared at his son's face and then knit his brows jovially as though he had not understood. After shaking his head in a baffled way, he remarked, "Marriage? There's a right time for everything. Why are you speaking about this now?"

"I want to get married now."

"Now? You're only eighteen. Won't you wait until you get your degree?"

"I can't."

Then the door opened, and Khadija entered. "What's happening behind this door?" she asked. "Are there secrets you can tell your father but not me?"

Abd al-Muni'm frowned nervously. Ibrahim, who scarcely understood the meaning of his own words, answered, "Abd al-Muni'm wants to get married."

Khadija scrutinized her husband as though fearing he had gone insane. She cried out, "Get married! What do I hear? Have you decided to leave the University?"

In an angry, forceful voice, Abd al-Muni'm responded, "I said I want to marry, not that I'm dropping out of school. I'll continue my studies as a married man. That's all there is to it."

Looking back and forth from one to the other, Khadija asked, "Abd al-Muni'm, are you really serious?"

He shouted, "Absolutely!"

The woman struck her hands together and riposted, "The evil eye has struck you. What's happened to your brain, son?"

Abd al-Muni'm stood up angrily. He asked, "What brings you here? I wanted to speak privately with my father first, but you don't know what patience is. Listen! I want to get married. I have two more years before I finish my studies. Father, you can support me for these two years. If I weren't sure of that, I would not have made this request."

Khadija said, "God's grace! They've destroyed his mind."

"Who has?"

"God knows best who they are. I'll let Him take care of them. You shouldn't have any doubts as to their identity, and we'll soon learn."

The young man told his father, "Don't listen to her. Even now I have no idea what girl will be mine. Choose her yourselves. I want a suitable bride, any bride."

Flabbergasted, she asked him, "Do you mean there's not some special girl who is the cause of this whole calamity?"

"Absolutely not. Believe me. Choose for me yourself."

"Why are you in such a hurry then? I'll select someone for you. Give me a little time. Say a year or two?"

Raising his voice, he said, "I'm not joking. Leave me alone. He understands me better than you do."

His father asked him calmly, "Why the rush?"

Lowering his gaze, Abd al-Muni'm answered, "I can't wait any longer."

Khadija inquired, "How come thousands of other young men like you can?"

The boy told his father, "I'm not willing to do what they do."

Ibrahim thought a little. To put an end to this scene he said, "That's enough for now. We'll continue this discussion another time."

Khadija started to say something, but her husband stopped her and took her by the hand. The couple left the study to resume their places in the sitting room, where they went over the topic, considering it from every angle. After a lot of give-and-take, Ibrahim felt inclined to support his son's request. He took it upon himself to convince his wife. Once she had accepted the notion in principle, Ibrahim said, "We have Na'ima, my niece. We won't need to tire ourselves out searching for a bride."

Capitulating, Khadija said, "I'm the one who persuaded you to renounce your share of your late brother's estate for Aisha's sake. So I have no objection to the choice of Na'ima as a bride for my son. I'm very concerned about Aisha's happiness, as you know. But I'm afraid of her melancholy brooding and am very apprehensive about her eccentric behavior. Haven't you hinted to her repeatedly that we would like Na'ima to marry Abd al-Muni'm? All the same I think she was ready to accept Jamil al-Hamzawi's son when al-Hamzawi proposed it."

"That's ancient history. A year or more has passed since then, and praise God nothing has come of it. No matter how good a position he has, it would have done me no honor to have a young man like that marry my niece. As far as I'm concerned, a man's family origin is everything, and Na'ima is very dear to us."

Sighing, Khadija agreed, "Very, very dear. What do you suppose my father will say about this foolishness when he learns of it?"

Ibrahim replied, "I'm sure he'll welcome it. Everything about it seems like a dream, but I won't regret it. I'm positive that it would be an unforgivable error to ignore Abd al-Muni'm's request, so long as it's within our power to grant it."

133

NO CHANGES worth mentioning had taken place at the old house on Palace Walk, but the neighbors – Hasanayn the barber, Darwish the bean seller, al-Fuli the milkman, Abu Sari', who ran the snack shop, and Bayumi, who sold fruit drinks – had all learned in one way or another that al-Sayyid Ahmad's granddaughter was to marry her double first cousin Abd al-Muni'm today. Al-Sayyid Ahmad did not break with his time-honored traditions, and the day passed like any other one. Only members of the family were invited, and the day's major activity was preparation of the dinner banquet.

It was at the beginning of summer, and they were all assembled in the parlor: al-Sayyid Ahmad Abd al-Jawad, Amina, Khadija, Ibrahim Shawkat, Abd al-Muni'm, Ahmad, Yasin, Zanuba, Rid-wan, and Karima. The only two family members missing were Na'ima, who was adorning herself on the top floor, and Aisha, who was helping her. Sensing that his presence might dampen their spirits at this festive family reunion, al-Sayyid Ahmad went off to his room shortly after welcoming everyone and waited there for the religious official to arrive.

He had liquidated his business and sold the store, choosing to retire, not merely because he was sixty-five but also because Jamil al-Hamzawi's resignation had forced him to assume much of the work at a time when he was no longer up to it. Thus he had decided to retire, contenting himself with his savings and what he had gotten from closing out his store. He calculated that this amount would suffice for the rest of his days. His retirement had been an important milestone in the life of the family. Kamal had begun to wonder whether they had not underestimated the role Jamil al-Hamzawi had played in all their lives and especially in their father's.

Alone in his room, al-Sayyid Ahmad silently pondered the events of the day, as if he could not believe that the bridegroom was his grandson Abd al-Muni'm. He had been amazed and incre-dulous the day Ibrahim Shawkat had raised the matter with him.

"How could you allow your son to speak to you so bluntly and to impose his will on you?" he had wanted to know. "Fathers like you are spoiling the next generation."

He would have said no, had it not been for the delicacy of the circumstances. Out of consideration for Aisha's misery, he had renounced his customary stubbornness, since he could not bear to disappoint her, especially after all the little comments provoked by Fuad al-Hamzawi's silence. If Na'ima's marriage would lessen the anguish of Aisha's heart, then welcome to it. His distress had prompted him to grant his consent, and he had allowed children to force their wishes on adults and to marry before finishing their education. He had summoned Abd al-Muni'm and had made him promise to complete his studies. Citing passages from the Qur'an and from reports of the Prophet's life, Abd al-Muni'm had offered an eloquent defense, setting his grandfather's mind at ease, while arousing in the patriarch feelings of both admiration and contempt. So today the schoolboy was getting married, while Kamal had not yet thought of it – although al-Sayyid Ahmad had once refused even to announce the engagement of his late son Fahmy, who had died before enjoying the prime of his youth. The cosmos seemed to have turned upside down. Another extraordinary world had sprung up in its place.

"We're strangers even among our own kinsfolk," he thought. "Today, schoolboys marry. Who knows what they'll do tomorrow?"

In the parlor, Khadija was concluding a lengthy monologue: "And that's why we moved everyone out of the second floor. Tonight it will look its best when it receives the newlyweds."

Yasin told her impishly, "You have everything it takes to be an outstanding mother-in-law. But you'll be unable to exploit your extraordinary talents with this bride."

Although she fully understood his allusion, she ignored it and said, "The bride is my daughter and my sister's daughter."

To soften the impact of Yasin's jest, Zanuba commented, "Mrs. Khadija is a perfect lady." Khadija thanked her. Despite a secret dislike for this sister-in-law, Khadija responded thankfully and respectfully to her ingratiating remarks, for Yasin's sake.

Karima at ten was already pretty enough for Yasin to make proud forecasts about her future feminine charms. Abd al-Muni'm was conversing with his grandmother, Amina, who was always impressed by his piety. She would occasionally interrupt his comments to invoke God's blessings on him.

Kamal teased Ahmad: "Are you getting married next year?"

"Unless I follow your example, Uncle."

Zanuba, who was listening, said, "If Mr. Kamal will give me permission, I promise to have him married off in a matter of days."

Pointing to himself, Yasin said, "I'm ready to let you find a bride for me."

Shaking her head scornfully, she replied, "You've been married more than enough. You've had your share of brides and your brother's share too."

Attracted by the topic of this conversation, Amina told Zanuba, "If you get Kamal married, I'll trill with joy for the first time in my life."

When he tried to picture his mother trilling joyfully, Kamal laughed. Then he imagined himself in the place of Abd al-Muni'm, waiting for the Islamic notary, and fell silent. The thought of marriage stirred up a whirlpool of emotions deep inside him as surely as winter's humidity troubles the breathing of an asthmatic. Although he categorically rejected the idea of marriage, he could not ignore it. His heart was free, but he found this emptiness as nerve-racking as being in love. If he did decide to marry now, his only recourse would be the traditional process beginning with a matchmaker and ending with a household, children, and immersion in the mechanics of daily life. After that, no matter how much a person wanted to, he would scarcely be able to find time for reflection. Kamal would always view marriage with a strange mixture of longing and aversion.

"The end of your life will be nothing but loneliness and despair," he warned himself.

The truly happy person that day was Aisha. For the first time in nine years she had put on a pretty dress and had braided her hair. Now with dreamy eyes she was looking at her daughter, who was as beautiful as a moonbeam. As her tears began to flow, Aisha hid her own pale withered face from her daughter. At that moment, finding her weeping, Amina gave Aisha a critical look and said, "It's not right for Na'ima to leave the house with a sad heart."

Aisha sobbed, "Don't you see that she's alone today, without a father or a brother?"

Amina replied, "That makes her mother all the more important. May our Lord grant the mother a long life, for the girl's sake . . . and she's going to her aunt and uncle. Besides, she has God, the creator of the whole universe, to watch over her."

Drying her eyes, Aisha said, "From daybreak on, I'm inundated with memories of my departed loved ones. I can see their faces. Once she's gone I'll be all alone."

Amina scolded her, "You're not alone!"

Na'ima patted her mother's cheek and asked, "How can I leave you, Mama?"

Aisha smiled and answered sympathetically, "Your new household will show you how."

Na'ima said anxiously, "You'll visit every day. You've avoided going anywhere near Sugar Street, but from now on you'll have to change that."

"Of course. Do you doubt it?"

Then Kamal came to tell them, "Get ready. The marriage clerk has arrived."

His eyes fastened on Na'ima admiringly. "How beautiful, delicate, and ethereal," he thought. "What role can animal desires and needs play in this exquisite creature?"

On learning that the marriage contract had been executed, they all exchanged congratulations. Then a shrieking trill of joy shattered the somber decorum of the household and reverberated through its still reaches. Their astonished faces discovered Umm Hanafi standing at the end of the sitting room.

When it was time for the dinner banquet and the guests started making their way to the table, Aisha found that she had no appetite and felt depressed, for she could think of nothing but the imminent separation.

Umm Hanafi announced that Shaykh Mutawalli Abd al-Samad was sitting on the ground in the courtyard and that he had asked for some supper, especially for a good selection from the different meat dishes. Al-Sayyid Ahmad laughed and ordered her to prepare a tray and carry it to him. Immediately thereafter, they heard the shaykh's voice calling up from the courtyard, praying that his beloved Ahmad ibn Abd al-Jawad would have a long life. He could also be heard asking the names of al-Sayyid Ahmad's children and grandchildren so he could offer prayers on their behalf too.

Smiling, al-Sayyid Ahmad commented, "What a pity! Shaykh Mutawalli has forgotten your names. May God be indulgent with the infirmities of old age."

Ibrahim Shawkat said, "He's a hundred, isn't he?"

Ahmad Abd al-Jawad agreed. Then the shaykh's voice cried out, "In the name of the martyr al-Husayn, be generous with the meat."

Al-Sayyid laughed and said, "His holy powers are concentrated on meat today."

When it was time to say farewell, Kamal went down to the courtyard before the others to avoid the spectacle. Although Na'ima was only moving to Sugar Street, that deeply troubled her heart and her mother's. Kamal himself felt skeptical about this wedding, for he doubted that Na'ima was strong enough for married life. In the courtyard he saw Shaykh Mutawalli Abd al-Samad sitting on the ground under the electric light attached to the wall of the house to illuminate the area. The old man's legs were stretched out, and he had removed his sandals. Wearing a discolored white shirt that went down to his ankles and a white skullcap, he leaned against the wall as if sleeping off his meal. Kamal noticed water flowing down the man's legs and realized that he was incontinent. Resounding like a whistle, the man's breathing was clearly audible. Kamal stared at him with a mixture of disdain and disgust. Then a thought made him smile in spite of himself. He reflected, "Perhaps in 1830 he was a pampered child."

134

THE VERY next day Aisha went to call at Sugar Street. During the nine previous years, except for a few visits to Palace of Desire Alley when Yasin had lost a child, she had left the old house only to visit the cemetery. She stopped for a moment at the entrance to look around, and her eyes filled with tears. Uthman's and Muhammad's feet had frequently run and skipped there by the doorway. The courtyard had once been decorated for her glorious wedding. That was the reception room where Khalil had smoked his water pipe and played backgammon or dominoes. Here the sweet fragrance of the past was redolent of lost love and tenderness. She had been so joyful that her happiness had been proverbial. Called the merry soprano, she had been accused of flirting with her mirror and of consorting with her dressing table. Her husband had uttered sweet nothings and the children had scampered about . . . in those bygone days. She dried her eyes so she would not meet the bride that way. These eyes were still blue, even though the eyelashes had fallen out and the eyelids seemed withered. She found the apartment newly outfitted and painted, resplendent with the bride's furnishings, on which a considerable amount had been spent. Wearing a diaphanous white frock, her golden hair hanging down to her knees, Na'ima greeted her mother. The bride was serene, charming, and immaculate, and her perfume had a haunting fragrance.

Their long affectionate embrace lasted until Abd al-Muni'm, calmly waiting his turn in a blue-green robe that enveloped his silk house shirt, protested, "That's enough! Just say hello to each other. A nominal separation like this merits nothing more."

Then he embraced his aunt and escorted her to a cozy chair. As she sat down, he remarked, "We were just thinking of you, Aunt. We have decided to invite you to come live with us."

Aisha smiled as she answered, "Anything but that. I'll visit you every day. This will give me an excuse for a walk. I really need more exercise."

With his customary candor, Abd al-Muni'm said, "Sweet Na'ima has told me that you can't bear to stay here for fear of being overcome by memories. But a Believer need not fall prey to sad thoughts. What happened was God's will, and it was a long time ago. God has sent us as a consolation for you."

"Though this young man," Aisha reflected, "is frank and good-hearted, he is cavalier about the impact of his words on wounded hearts."

"Of course, Abd al-Muni'm," she said. "But I'm comfortable at home. It's better this way."

Then Khadija, Ibrahim, and Ahmad entered and shook hands with Aisha. Khadija told her sister, "If I had realized this would make you start visiting us again I would have had them married even before they were old enough."

Aisha laughed. Reminding Khadija of distant times, she asked, "A single kitchen? Or does the bride demand to be independent of her mother-in-law?"

Khadija and Ibrahim both laughed. In a tone that was not free of insinuation, Khadija answered, "Like her mother, she isn't concerned about such silly things."

For his sons' sake, Ibrahim explained Aisha's obscure reference: "The battles between your mother and mine began with the kitchen, which my mother monopolized. Your mother demanded one of her own."

The bridegroom asked in amazement, "Mother, did you fight over a kitchen?"

Laughing, Ahmad said, "Do the struggles between nations have grander causes than that?"

Ibrahim remarked ironically, "Your mother is as powerful as England. While mine . . . well, may God have mercy on her."

Kamal arrived. He was wearing an elegant white suit, but his face was distinguished as always by his protruding forehead, enormous nose, gold spectacles, and thick but compact mustache. He was carrying a large package that promised to be a fine present. As she smilingly examined it, Khadija cautioned him, "Watch out, brother. If you don't go ahead and marry, you'll always be taking presents to other people without getting anything in return. There's a whole family of young people about to get married. We have Ahmad, and Yasin has Ridwan and Karima. Start making plans now to do what's right."

Ahmad asked his uncle, "Has the school vacation begun?"

Removing his fez and gazing at the beautiful bride, Kamal replied, "There's only a short period left while we monitor and correct the elementary-level examination."

Na'ima disappeared and returned shortly with a silver tray filled with sweets of various different types and flavors. For a time nothing was heard but the noise of lips smacking and mouths sucking. Then Ibrahim started to recount what he remembered of his own wedding, the reception, and the male and female vocalists. Aisha listened with a smiling face and a sad heart. Kamal also followed this narrative with great interest, since it reminded him of things he remembered and of others he had forgotten and wanted to learn about.

Laughing, Ibrahim said, "Al-Sayyid Ahmad was just the same as he is today or even more severe. But my mother, may God be compassionate to her, declared decisively, 'Al-Sayyid Ahmad can do anything he wishes at his house. But in our home we'll celebrate as much as we want.' And that's what happened. Al-Sayyid Ahmad was accompanied to the wedding by his friends, may God be gracious to them all. I remember that Ridwan's grandfather, Mr. Muhammad Iffat, was one of them. They sat in the reception room, far removed from the commotion."

Khadija added, "Jalila, the most renowned performer of her time, entertained that evening."

As he thought of the aged madam, who still boasted of her successes in his father's era, Kamal felt like smiling.

Stealing a look at Aisha, Ibrahim remarked, "We used to have our own private singer in the house. Her voice was more beautiful than that of any professional musician. She made us think of Munira al-Mahdiya at her prime."

Aisha blushed and replied quietly, "Her voice has been silent for a long time. She's forgotten how to sing."

Kamal said, "Na'ima sings too. Haven't you heard her?"

Ibrahim answered, "I understand she does, but I haven't heard her yet. The truth is that we've had more opportunities to observe her piety than her singing. Yesterday I told her, 'Your husband is one of the most pious Believers, but you must postpone your prayers and devotions for a while.'"

They all laughed. Then Ahmad taunted his brother, "The only thing your bride hasn't done yet is join the followers of Shaykh Ali al-Manufi."

The bridegroom retorted, "It was our shaykh who first advised me to marry."

Ahmad continued to tease his brother: "It seems the Muslim Brethren have made marriage a plank in their political platform."

Turning to Kamal, Ibrahim said, "You were very young then – I mean when I got married. And you had a lot more hair than today. You accused me and my brother of stealing your sisters and never forgave us."

"I was a blank page then," Kamal thought. "My struggles of conscience were not yet recorded there. They speak of married bliss. Haven't they heard what grumbling spouses say about it? I cherish Na'ima too much for me to tolerate a husband's growing tired of her. What is there in life that doesn't turn out to be a fraud?"

Commenting on her husband's statement, Khadija said, "We thought you were accusing our bridegrooms because you loved us. But eventually it became clear that you spoke from a hatred for marriage that you've had since you were a child."

Kamal laughed along with the others. He loved Khadija, and his affection was strengthened by his knowledge that she loved him dearly. Although upset by the young bridegroom's fanaticism, he liked and admired Ahmad. Kamal was fleeing matrimony but rather enjoyed having Khadija remind him of it at every opportunity. Profoundly influenced by the conjugal atmosphere that surrounded him, intoxicating his heart and senses, he felt a longing, although not for anyone or anything in particular. He wondered, as if for the first time, "What's keeping me from getting married? . . . My intellectual life, as I once claimed? Today I doubt the worth of both thought and the thinker. Is it fear, vengeance, masochism, or some reaction to my former love? My life provides evidence to support any of these hypotheses."

Ibrahim Shawkat asked Kamal, "Do you know why I'm sorry you're a bachelor?"

"Yes?"

"I'm convinced you'd be an exemplary husband if you did marry, for you're a family man by nature. You're organized, upright, and a respected civil servant. No doubt somewhere on this earth there's a girl who deserves you, and you're depriving her of her opportunity."

Even mules occasionally spoke words of wisdom . . . a girl somewhere in the world, but where? Yet he was unfairly accused of being upright, for he was nothing but a sinful and hypocritical pagan inebriate. A girl somewhere on the earth, presumably not in Jalila's brothel on al-Gawhari Alley. . . . Why were pains struggling with each other in his heart? How could one describe the kind of perplexity from which the only refuge was drink and lust? It was said that if you marry and have children, you will be immortal. He yearned in the worst possible way for all forms and varieties of immortality. In his despair would he finally resort to this trite and instinctual method? There was always hope that death would bring no pain to disturb his eternal repose. Death appeared frightening and senseless, but with life having lost all meaning, death seemed the only true pleasure left. How extraordinary it was that scholars devoted themselves to the advancement of science in their laboratories. How amazing it was that leaders jeopardized their careers for the sake of the constitution. But people who wandered aimlessly in their anxious torment – God's mercy on them.

Kamal looked from Ahmad to Abd al-Muni'm with a mixture of admiration and delight. The new generation was making its difficult way to well-defined goals without doubt or anxiety. He asked himself, "What's the secret of my enervating disease?"

Ahmad said, "I'm inviting the newlyweds, my parents, and my aunt to join me in a box at al-Rihani's theater this Thursday."

Khadija asked, "Al-Rihani?"

Ibrahim explained, "The actor who plays Kishkish Bey!"

Khadija laughed and said, "Yasin was almost thrown out of our house soon after he was first married because he took Ridwan's mother to see Kishkish one night."

"That's the way things were back then," Ahmad said, dismissing the implicit criticism. "Nowadays my grandfather wouldn't object to my grandmother's going to see Kishkish Bey."

Khadija replied, "Take the newlyweds and your father. The radio's enough for me."

Aisha said, "And coming to your house is sufficient entertainment for me."

Khadija launched into a rendition of the tale of Yasin and Kishkish Bey. Kamal happened to glance at his watch and remembered his appointment with Riyad Qaldas. So he rose and asked their permission to leave.

135

"ARE YOU really able to enjoy the beauties of nature only a few days before the examination?" one student asked another in a group sitting spread out in a semicircle on a green hill at the top of which stood a wooden pavilion occupied by more students. As far as the eye could see there were clusters of palms and flower beds separated by mosaic walks.

The second student answered, "Just as surely as Abd al–Muni'm Shawkat can get married shortly before it."

Abd al–Muni'm, who was seated toward the center of the semicircle near Ahmad Shawkat, said, "Contrary to what you think, a married student has the best possible chance of passing."

Sitting next to Ridwan Yasin at the other side of the semicircle, Hilmi Izzat remarked, "That's if the husband is one of the Muslim Brethren."

Ridwan laughed and revealed his pearly teeth, although this discussion depressed him. The whole subject of marriage awakened his anxieties, for he did not know whether he would embark on this adventure. The apparent necessity of marriage made it all the more terrifying, since it did not correspond to either his physical or his spiritual longings.

A student asked, "Who are the Muslim Brethren?"

Hilmi Izzat replied, "A religious group with the goal of reviving Islam, intellectually and practically. Haven't you heard of their circles that have been established in all the districts?"

"Does it differ from the Young Men's Muslim Association?"

"Yes."

"How?"

Pointing to Abd al–Muni'm Shawkat, he answered, "Ask the Muslim Brother."

In his powerful voice, Abd al–Muni'm said, "We're not merely an organization dedicated to teaching and preaching. We attempt to understand Islam as God intended it to be: a religion, a way of life, a code of law, and a political system."

"Is talk like this appropriate for the twentieth century?"

The forceful voice answered, "And for the hundred and twen-tieth century too."

"Confronted by democracy, Fascism, and Communism, we're dumbfounded. Then there's this new calamity."

Laughing, Ahmad observed, "But it's a godly calamity!"

There was an outburst of laughter, and Abd al-Muni'm glared at his brother angrily. Ridwan Yasin thought his cousin's words ill chosen and said, "'Calamity' isn't the right word."

The same student asked Abd al-Muni'm, "Do you stone people who disagree with you?"

"Young people are given to deviant views and dissolute behav-ior. They deserve far worse than stoning, but we don't stone anyone. Instead we provide guidance and direction through moral suasion and example. There is a fine illustration in my own household, for I have a brother who is ripe for stoning. Here he is laughing about it in front of you and showing disrespect to his Creator, may He be glorified."

Ahmad laughed, and Hilmi Izzat told him, "If you feel threat-ened by your brother, I invite you to live with me in al-Darb al-Ahmar."

"Are you as bad as he is?"

"Certainly not. But we Wafdists are a tolerant bunch. The senior adviser to our leader is a Coptic Christian. That's what we're like."

The other student continued to question Abd al-Muni'm: "How can you advocate nonsense like this in the same month that the foreign capitulations have been abolished?"

Abd al-Muni'm asked in return, "Should we give up our religion in order to please foreigners?"

Approaching the same topic from a totally different angle, Ridwan Yasin remarked, "The capitulations were abrogated. I wonder what critics of the treaty can say now?"

"Those critics are insincere," Hilmi Izzat declared. "They're just envious and spiteful. True and total independence can only be seized by armed combat. How could they hope to achieve more by negotiating than we have?"

A voice remarked angrily, "Allow us to wonder about the future."

"What point is there in discussing the future in May with

the examination staring us in the face? Spare us. After today to give myself time to study I'm not coming back to the college."

"Not so fast. There aren't any positions waiting for us. What future is there for Law or Arts students? You can either loaf around or take some job as a clerk. Go ahead and wonder about your futures, if you want."

"Now that the capitulations favoring foreigners have been abolished, doors will start to open."

"Doors? There are more people than doors!"

"Listen: Al-Nahhas broadened the system of admissions to the University after many had been arbitrarily excluded. Won't he also be able to find jobs for us?"

Then tongues fell silent and faces looked off toward the far end of the park, where a flock of four young women approached from the University en route to Giza. It was hardly possible to identify them, but as they were advancing with deliberate speed there was hope of a closer look. The path they were following circled around the spot where the young men sat before it turned off to the left. When the women came into plain view, their names and those of their faculties were on the boys' lips. There was a woman from Law and three from Arts.

Looking at one of them, Ahmad said to himself, "Alawiya Sabri." The name galvanized him. She was a young woman with an Egyptian version of Turkish beauty. Slender and of medium height, she had a fair complexion and coal-black hair. Her wide black eyes had lofty eyelids, and her eyebrows met in the center. She was distinguished by her aristocratic demeanor and refined gestures. Moreover, she was a classmate in the first university year. He had learned – and there is no end of information that an inquiring mind may acquire – that she had put her name down for sociology, just as he had. Although he had not yet had a chance to exchange a single word with her, she had aroused his interest at first sight. For years he had gazed admiringly at Na'ima, but she had never shaken him to the core. This girl was truly remarkable, and he looked forward to a platonic and possibly a romantic relationship with her.

Once the flock was out of sight again, Hilmi Izzat said, "Soon the Arts Faculty is going to resemble a women's college."

Looking from one to another of the Arts students in the semi-circle, Ridwan Yasin warned, "Don't trust the friendship of law students who visit you frequently in your college between lectures. Their intentions are quite reprehensible." He laughed loudly, even though he was anything but happy then. Talking about the girls made him uneasy and sad.

"Why are girls so interested in the Arts Faculty?"

"Because the teaching profession offers them more opportunities than most others."

Hilmi Izzat said, "That's true, but there's also something feminine about instruction in the arts. Rouge, manicures, kohl for eyes, poetry, and stories all fall into one category."

Everyone laughed, even Ahmad, and despite their vigorous protests the other Arts students joined in. Ahmad retorted, "This unfair judgment applies equally to medicine. For a long time nursing has been considered a woman's job. The truth not yet firmly established in your souls is that men and women must be believed to be equal."

Smiling, Abd al-Muni'm said, "I don't know whether we praise or censure women when we call them our equals."

"If it's a question of rights and duties, then it's praise, not blame."

Abd al-Muni'm continued: "Islam holds men and women to be equal except with regard to inheritance."

Ahmad responded sarcastically, "Even in slavery it has treated them equally."

Abd al-Muni'm protested furiously, "You don't know anything about your religion. That's the tragedy."

Turning to Ridwan Yasin, Hilmi Izzat smilingly inquired, "What do you know about Islam?"

Another student asked Hilmi, "And how about you?"

Abd al-Muni'm asked his brother, Ahmad, "What knowledge of yours lets you blather on so?"

Ahmad replied calmly, "I know it's a religion, and that's enough for me. I don't believe in religions."

Abd al-Muni'm asked disapprovingly, "Do you have some proof that all religions are false?"

"Do you have any proof they're true?"

Raising his voice enough to make the young man sitting between the two brothers look from one to the other of them with some agitation, Abd al-Muni'm said, "I do. Every Believer does. But allow me to ask you first what you live by."

"My own personal beliefs . . . in science, humanity, and the future. These beliefs entail various duties intended to help establish a new order on earth."

"You destroy everything that makes man a human being."

"Say rather that the survival of a creed for more than a thousand years is not a sign of its strength but of the degradation of some human beings, for this flies in the face of life's normal process of renewal. Conduct and ideas appropriate for me when I was a child should change now that I am a man. For a long time people worshiped nature and other human beings. We can overcome our servitude to nature through science and inventions. Slavery to other human beings should be opposed by progressive theories. Anything else is a brake obstructing the free movement of humanity's wheel."

Disgusted by the thought that Ahmad was his brother, Abd al-Muni'm remarked, "It's easy to be an atheist. It's a simple, escapist solution, allowing you to shirk a Believer's responsibilities to his Lord, to himself, and to other people. No proof for atheism is any stronger than those for faith. Thus we do not choose by our intellects but by our conduct."

Ridwan interjected, "Don't let yourselves get carried away by the fury of your debate. Since you're brothers, the best thing would be for you to take the same side."

Hilmi Izzat, who was afflicted at times by inexplicable moments of rebelliousness, burst out, "Faith! Humanity! The future! . . . What rubbish! The only possible system is one based entirely on science. There is only one thing we need to believe in, and that is the extermination of human weakness in all its manifestations, no matter how stern our science seems. The goal is to bring humanity to an ideal condition, pure and powerful."

"Are these the new principles of the Wafd Party, subsequent to the treaty?"

Hilmi Izzat laughed, and this restored him to his normal good humor. Ridwan explained, "He's really a Wafdist but occasionally entertains bizarre and alien notions. He advocates killing everyone, when it may simply mean that he didn't sleep well the night before."

The reaction to this fierce quarrel was universal silence, which pleased Ridwan. His eyes roamed around, following some kites that circled overhead or gazing at the groups of palm trees. Everyone else felt free to express his opinion, even if it attacked his Creator. Yet he was compelled to conceal the controversies raging in his own soul, where they would remain a terrifying secret that threatened him. He might as well have been a scapegoat or an alien. Who had divided human behavior into normal and deviant? How could an adversary also serve as judge? Why were wretched people so often mocked?

Ridwan told Abd al-Muni'm, "Don't be angry. Religion has a Lord to protect it. As for you, in nine months at the most, you'll be a father."

"Is that so?"

Trying to appease his brother, Ahmad joked, "It's easier for me to confront God's wrath than yours."

Ahmad told himself, "Whether he's angry or not, when he returns to Sugar Street he'll find a sympathetic breast waiting for him. Is it ridiculous to think I'll return one day to find Alawiya Sabri waiting for me on the first floor of our house?"

He laughed, but no one suspected the true reason for his mirth.

136

THERE APPEARED to be an unusual flurry of activity at the home of Abd al-Rahim Pasha Isa. Many people were standing in the garden or sitting on the veranda, and there was a constant flow of men arriving or departing. Hilmi Izzat nudged Ridwan Yasin's arm as they neared the house and observed with relief, "Contrary to the claims of their newspapers, we are not without our supporters."

As the two made their way inside, some of the young men shouted, "Long live solidarity!" Ridwan's face became flushed from excitement. He was as zealous a rebel as the others but wondered anxiously whether anyone suspected the nonpolitical side to his visits. Once when he had confided his fears to Hilmi Izzat, the latter had said, "Only cowards get suspected. Proceed with head held high and resolute steps. People preparing for public life shouldn't pay too much attention to what others think of them."

Sitting in the reception room was a crowd of students, workers, and members of the Wafd organization. Abd al-Rahim Pasha Isa, looking uncustomarily grim, serious, and stern, sat at the front of the room with the aura of an important statesman. When the two young men approached, he rose to greet them gravely. After shaking hands, he gestured for them to be seated.

One of the men sitting there resumed a discussion he had interrupted when the two arrived: "Public opinion was shocked to learn the names of the members of the new cabinet, for they did not find al-Nuqrashi's among them."

Abd al-Rahim Pasha Isa replied, "We suspected something as soon as the cabinet resigned, especially since the dispute had become so well known that it was even the talk of the coffee-houses. But al-Nuqrashi is not like other members of the Wafd. The party has sacked many, but no one with so much support. Al-Nuqrashi is entirely different. Don't forget that al-Nuqrashi implies Ahmad Mahir too. They are the Wafd – the Wafd Party that has struggled, disputed, and fought. Ask the gallows, prisons, and bombs. This time the disagreement is not one that will dishonor those who leave the Wafd, for the regime's integrity and the bombing case are both in question. If the worst happens and the party is split, those who remain will be the deserters, not al-Nuqrashi and Mahir."

"Makram Ubayd has finally shown his true colors."

This statement sounded odd to Ridwan. It was hard for him to believe that such a prominent leader would be attacked this way by stalwart Wafdists.

Someone else remarked, "Makram Ubayd is the source of all this trouble, Your Excellency."

Abd al-Rahim Pasha replied, "The others are just as guilty."

"But he's the one who can't abide his rivals. He wants to control al-Nahhas all by himself. Once Mahir and al-Nuqrashi are out of the way, there will be no one to oppose him."

"If he could get rid of al-Nahhas, he would."

An elderly man sitting there said, "Please, don't exaggerate. The streams may return to their banks."

"After a cabinet has been formed without al-Nuqrashi?"

"Everything is possible."

"That would have been possible in Sa'd Zaghlul's era, but al-Nahhas is an obstinate man. When he's made up his mind. . . ."

At this point a man rushed in. The pasha greeted him at the center of the room. As they embraced each other warmly, the pasha asked, "When did you return? How's Alexandria?"

"Great . . . great! Al-Nuqrashi was welcomed at the Sidi Gabir station by unprecedented popular acclaim. Swarms of educated people shouted their heartfelt greetings. In their fury, they called rebelliously for integrity in government. They cried out, 'Long live al-Nuqrashi, the honest leader. Long live al-Nuqrashi, Sa'd's true successor.' Many shouted, 'Long live al-Nuqrashi, leader of the nation.' "

The man was speaking in a loud voice, and several of those listening repeated his slogans until Abd al-Rahim Pasha had to gesture for them to be calm. Then the man continued: "Public opinion is angry about the cabinet, outraged that al-Nuqrashi has been ousted from it. Al-Nahhas has done himself irreparable harm by consenting to support the devil against this pure angel."

Abd al-Rahim Pasha observed, "We're in August now. The University reopens in October. The showdown should come then. We must start preparing for the demonstrations. If al-Nahhas doesn't return to his senses, he can go to hell."

Hilmi Izzat said, "Rest assured that a great number of student demonstrations will converge on al-Nuqrashi's home."

Abd al-Rahim Pasha commented, "Everything needs to be organized. Meet with your student supporters and make your preparations. Moreover, according to my information, an incredible number of deputies and senators will side with us."

"Al-Nuqrashi was the founder of the Wafdist committees. Don't forget that. Telegrams of support pile up in his office from dawn to dusk."

Ridwan wondered what was happening to the world. Would the Wafd Party be divided again? Was Makram Ubayd truly responsible for this? Were the best interests of the nation really compatible with a split in the party that had represented it for eighteen years?

The exchange of views lasted a long time as the men assembled there discussed how to make their views known and how to run the demonstrations. Then they started to leave. At last only the pasha, Ridwan, and Hilmi Izzat remained. Invited by their host to move to the veranda, they followed him outside. The three sat around a table and were immediately served lemonade. Shortly thereafter a man in his forties appeared at the door. From previous visits Ridwan recognized him as Ali Mihran, an aide to the pasha. The man's appearance showed a natural inclination toward frivolity and mirth. He was accompanied by a young fellow in his twenties with a handsome countenance. Unruly hair, long side curls, and a broad necktie suggested that this stranger was an artist by profession. With a smile on his lips, Ali Mihran advanced, kissed the pasha's hand, and shook hands with the two visitors. Then he introduced the newcomer: "Mr. Atiya Jawdat, a young but gifted singer. Your Excellency, I've mentioned him to you before."

Putting on his glasses, which he had laid on the table, the pasha examined the young man carefully. Smiling, he said, "Welcome, Mr. Atiya. I've heard a lot about you. Perhaps we'll hear you yourself this time."

The singer invoked God's blessings on the pasha and sat down, while Ali Mihran leaned over the pasha to ask, "How are you, Uncle?" That was what he called the pasha when formalities could be ignored.

Grinning, the man replied, "A thousand times better than you are."

With uncustomary earnestness, Ali Mihran said, "At the Anglo Bar people are whispering about a possible nationalist cabinet headed by al-Nuqrashi. . . ."

The pasha smiled diplomatically and murmured, "We're not in line for the cabinet."

With anxious interest Ridwan inquired, "What grounds are there for these rumors? I naturally can't imagine that al-Nuqrashi would plot like Muhammad Mahmud or Isma'il Sidqy to bring down the government."

Ali Mihran said, "A plot? No. At present it's merely a question of convincing a majority of the senators and deputies to join us. Don't forget that the king is on our side. Ali Mahir goes about his work deliberately and wisely."

Ridwan asked dejectedly, "Will we end up being the king's men?"

Abd al-Rahim Pasha observed, "That sounds bad, but the expression means something different now. Faruq is quite un-like his father, King Fuad. Circumstances have changed. The present king is an enthusiastic young nationalist. He's the one wronged by al-Nahhas's unfair attacks."

Ali Mihran rubbed his hands together gleefully as he said, "When do you suppose we'll be congratulating the pasha on his cabinet post? Will you choose me to assist you in the ministry just as you've had me help you with your other affairs?"

Laughing, the pasha said, "No, I'll appoint you director general of prisons, for that's your natural milieu."

"Prison? But they say it's for brutes."

"It takes in other types too. Don't worry about it." Suddenly overcome by annoyance, he cried out, "That's enough politics! Change the mood, please." Turning toward Mr. Atiya, he asked, "What are you going to sing for us?"

Ali Mihran interjected, "The pasha is a connoisseur who delights in music and good times. If your singing appeals to him, you'll find the way open for you to have your songs broadcast."

Atiya Jawdat said gently, "I've recently set to music some lyrics entitled 'They bound me to him,' composed by Mr. Mihran."

Staring at his aide, the pasha asked, "How long have you been writing songs?"

"Didn't I spend seven years at the seminary of al-Azhar, immersed in the study of Arabic and its meters?"

"What's the relationship between al-Azhar and your naughty songs? 'They bound me to him'! Who is he, my dear seminarian?"

"The answer's hiding behind your beard, Your Excellency."

"You son of an old hag!"

Ali Mihran summoned the butler, and the pasha asked, "Why are you calling him?"

"To set up for the music."

Rising, the politician said, "Wait till I perform the evening prayers."

Mihran smiled wickedly and asked, "When we touched in greeting, didn't that end your state of ritual cleanliness?"

137

LEANING ON his stick, Ahmad Abd al-Jawad left his house with slow steps. Things had changed. Since the liquidation of his store, he left home but once a day, for he tried to spare himself the stress that climbing the stairs put on his heart. Although it was only September, he had chosen wool garments. His thin frame could no longer bear the brisk weather his plump and powerful body had once enjoyed. The stick, which had been his companion since he was a young man, when it had been a symbol of virility and of elegance, now helped support him as he plodded along slowly. Even this level of exertion was a trial for his heart. All the same he had not lost his dapper good looks. He still dressed quite splendidly, used a fragrant cologne, and took full advantage of the charm and dignity of old age.

When he drew near the store, his eyes glanced toward it involuntarily. The sign that had borne his name and his father's for years and years had been removed, and the appearance and use of the establishment had changed. It had become a fez shop, where new ones were sold and old ones blocked. The copper forms and the heating apparatus were up in front. He imagined he saw a placard, invisible to everyone else, informing him that his time had passed . . . his time for serious endeavors, hard work, and pleasure. Retreating into retirement, he had turned his back on hope, finding himself face to face with old age, ill health, and the need to idle his time away. He had always been full of love for the world and its pleasures. Often he still was, but now his spirits sank. He had considered faith itself one of the joys of life and a reason for embracing the world. He had never – not even now – pursued the kind of ascetic piety that turns its back on the world and concerns itself solely with the afterlife. The store was no longer his, but how could he erase its memory from his mind, when it had been the hub of his activities, the focus of his attention, the meeting place for his friends and lovers, and the source of his renown and prestige?

"You may console yourself by saying, 'We've found husbands for the girls and reared the boys. We've lived to see our grand-children. We have enough money to keep us till we die. We've experienced life's delights for years.' Has it really been years? 'Now the time has come for us to show our gratitude, and it is our obligation to thank God always and forever.' But oh how nostalgic I feel. . . . May God forgive time – time, which by the mere fact of its uninterrupted existence betrays man in the worst possible way. If stones could speak, I would ask this site to inform me about the past, to tell me if this body could really crush mountains once. Did this sick heart beat regularly then? Did this mouth do anything but laugh? Was pain an unknown emotion? Was this the image of me treasured by every heart? . . . Again, I ask God to forgive time."

When his deliberate pace finally brought him to the mosque of al-Husayn, he removed his shoes and entered, reciting the open-ing prayer of the Qur'an. He made his way to the pulpit area, where he found Muhammad Iffat and Ibrahim al-Far waiting for him. They all performed the sunset prayer together and then left the mosque, heading for al-Tambakshiya to visit Ali Abd al-Rahim. Each of them had retired due to ill health, but they were in better shape than Ali Abd al-Rahim, who was bed-ridden.

Sighing, al-Sayyid Ahmad said, "I imagine that soon the sole way I'll be able to get to the mosque is by riding."

"You're not the only one!"

Then al-Sayyid Ahmad added anxiously, "I'm dreadfully afraid I'll be confined to bed like Mr. Ali. I pray that God will favor me with death before my strength gives out."

"May our Lord spare you and the rest of us every misfortune."

As if frightened by the thought, he commented, "Ghunaym Hamidu lay paralyzed in bed for about a year. Sadiq al-Mawardi suffered the same kind of torment for months. May God grant us a speedy end when the time comes."

Muhammad Iffat laughed and said, "If you let gloomy thoughts get the better of you, you'll be nothing but a woman. Declare that there is only one God, brother."

When they reached the home of Ali Abd al-Rahim, they went to his room. Before they could say anything, he blurted out unhappily, "You're late, may God forgive you."

The vexation of the bedridden man was visible in his eyes. The only time he ever smiled was when they were with him. He complained, "All day long my only occupation is listening to the radio. What would I do if it had not yet been introduced to Egypt? I enjoy everything that's broadcast, even lectures I can barely understand. All the same we're not so old that we should be suffering like this. Our grandfathers married new wives at this age."

Ahmad Abd al-Jawad's sense of humor got the better of him, and he observed, "That's an idea! What do you think about us taking another wife? Perhaps that would bring back our youth and cure what ails us."

Ali Abd al-Rahim smiled but refrained from laughing for fear he would break into a fit of coughing that would strain his heart. "I'm with you!" he said. "Select a bride for me. But tell her frankly that the bridegroom can't move and that it's all up to her."

As though suddenly remembering something, al-Far told him, "Ahmad Abd al-Jawad will see a great-grandchild before you do. May our Lord prolong his life."

"Congratulations in advance, son of Abd al-Jawad."

Al-Sayyid Ahmad frowned as he replied, "Na'ima is pregnant, but I have some misgivings. I still remember what was said about her heart when she was born. I've tried without success to forget that for a long time."

"What an ungrateful soul you are! Since when do you put your faith in the prophecies of physicians?"

Laughing, al-Sayyid Ahmad answered, "Since I'm kept awake till dawn whenever I eat anything they've forbidden me."

Ali Abd al-Rahim asked, "What about our Lord's compassion?"

"Praise to God, Lord of the universe." Then he added, "I'm not oblivious to God's mercy, but fear spawns fear. Ali, the fact is that I'm more worried about Aisha than Na'ima. All my anxieties in life converge on Aisha, that miserable darling. When I leave her, she'll be alone in the world."

Ibrahim al-Far commented, "Our Lord is always present. He is the ultimate guardian for everyone."

They were silent for a time. Finally Ali Abd al-Rahim's voice curtailed the silence: "It will be my turn after yours to see a great-grandchild."

Al-Sayyid Ahmad laughed and said, "May God forgive girls for making parents and grandparents old before their time."

Muhammad Iffat cried out, "Old man, admit you're old and stop being so obstinate."

"You mustn't raise your voice for fear my heart will hear you and act up. It's like a spoiled child."

Shaking his head sorrowfully, Ibrahim al-Far said, "What a year we've had. . . . It's been rough. It hasn't left any of us in good shape – as if ill health had booked an appointment with us."

"In the words of Abd al-Wahhab's song, 'Let's live together and die together.'"

They all laughed. Ali Abd al-Rahim changed his tone and asked seriously, "Is it right? I mean what al-Nuqrashi did?"

Ahmad Abd al-Jawad frowned as he answered, "I hoped so much that things would return to normal. . . . I ask the forgiveness of God Almighty."

"A fraternal bond developed through a lifetime of shared struggle went up in smoke."

"Nowadays all good deeds go up in smoke."

Ahmad Abd al-Jawad continued: "Nothing has made me so sad as al-Nuqrashi's departure from the Wafd. He should not have carried the dispute that far."

"What fate do you suppose awaits him?"

"The inevitable one, for where are rebels like al-Basil and al-Shamsi today? This valiant leader has sealed his own fate and taken Ahmad Mahir down with him."

Then Muhammad Iffat said nervously, "Spare us this story. I'm about ready to renounce politics."

Al-Far had an idea and asked with a smile, "If we were forced – God forbid it – to take to our beds, like Mr. Ali, how would we meet and converse with each other?"

Muhammad Iffat murmured, "God's will be done – not yours!"

Ahmad Abd al-Jawad laughed and replied, "If the worst happens, then we'll talk to each other by radio, the way Papa Soot talks to the children when he does his show."

They laughed together. Muhammad Iffat took out his watch to consult it. Ali Abd al-Rahim became alarmed and said, "You'll stay with me until the doctor comes, so you can hear what he has to say – may he and his days be cursed."

138

THE SHOPS in al-Ghuriya were closing. There were few people in the street, and the cold was intense. It was the middle of December, and winter had arrived early. Kamal had no difficulty tempting Riyad Qaldas to visit the district of al-Husayn. Although not a native of the area, the young man loved strolling through it and sitting in its coffeehouses. More than a year and a half had passed since their first meeting at *al-Fikr* magazine, and not a week had gone by without their seeing each other once or twice. During the school vacation they got together almost every evening at either the magazine, the house on Palace Walk, Riyad's home in Manshiya al-Bakri, the cafés of Imad al-Din Street, or the grand coffeehouse of al-Husayn, to which Kamal had retreated after Ahmad Abduh's historic one had been destroyed and permanently erased from existence.

They were both happy with this friendship, and Kamal had once told himself, "I missed Husayn Shaddad for years. His place remained empty until Riyad Qaldas took it." When he was with Riyad, Kamal's spirit came to life and was filled with an explosion of energy sparked by their intellectual exchange. This was true despite their marked – if complementary – differences from each other. They were both conscious of a mutual affection but never referred to it openly. Neither said to the other, "You're my friend" or "I can't imagine life without you," but this was the truth of the matter. The cold weather did not diminish their desire to walk, and they had decided to proceed on foot to their favorite café on Imad al-Din Street.

Riyad Qaldas was upset that evening. He said passionately, "The constitutional crisis has concluded with the rout of the people. Al-Nahhas's removal is a defeat for the nation in its historic struggle with the palace."

Kamal answered sorrowfully, "It's clear now that Faruq's as bad as his father."

"Faruq's not the only one responsible. The traditional enemies of the people have engineered this debacle. It's the work of Ali Mahir and Muhammad Mahmud. Lamentably Ahmad Mahir and al-Nuqrashi, these two populist leaders, joined ranks with the enemies of the people. If the nation were cleansed of traitors, the king would not find anyone to help him suppress the rights of the people." After a short silence he continued: "The English aren't playing an active role now, but the people and the king are at loggerheads. Independence isn't everything. There is also the people's sacred prerogative to enjoy their rights and their sovereignty – to live as free men, not slaves."

Unlike Riyad, Kamal was not deeply engaged in politics, but his doubts had not been able to destroy it for him, as they had so many other interests. It retained an emotional vitality for him. His heart believed firmly in the rights of the people, no matter how divided his intellect was on the subject, espousing at times "the rights of man," and on other occasions proclaiming, "It's all a question of the survival of the fittest. The masses are the common herd." It might also wonder, "Isn't Communism an experiment worth exploring?" His heart had not been purged of the populist sentiments with which he had grown up, and these were mixed with memories of Fahmy.

Politics was an essential element of Riyad's intellectual activity. He asked, "Is it possible for us to forget the humiliating reception Makram Ubayd got in the square in front of Abdin Palace or al-Nahhas's criminal ouster, that insulting calumny, like spit in the face of the nation? Blind hatred makes some applaud it, alas."

"You're just angry because of what happened to Makram Ubayd," Kamal teased.

Without any hesitation Riyad replied, "All of us Copts are Wafdists. That's because the Wafd Party represents true nationalism. It's not a religious, Turkish-oriented bunch like the National Party. The Wafd is a populist party. It will make Egypt a nation that provides freedom for all Egyptians, without regard to ethnic origin or religious affiliation. The enemies of the people know this. That's why the Copts were targeted for barefaced oppression throughout the Sidqy era. Now we'll be experiencing that again."

Kamal welcomed this candor, which demonstrated the depth of their friendship. All the same he felt like teasing Riyad some more:

"Here you are, talking about Coptic Christians, when you believe in nothing but science and art. . . ."

Riyad fell silent. They had reached al-Azhar Street, where the cold wind gusted rather fiercely. As they walked along they came to a pastry shop, and Kamal invited Riyad to have some with him. They each got a modest plateful and stepped to the side of the shop to eat. Then Riyad said, "I'm both a freethinker and a Copt. Indeed I'm both a Copt and a man without any religion. I frequently feel that Christianity is my community, not my faith. If I analyzed this feeling, I might entertain some reservations about it. But not so fast . . . isn't it cowardly to ignore my people? There's one thing that can help me overcome this quandary, and that is to devote myself to the kind of sincere Egyptian patriotism envisaged by Sa'd Zaghlul. Al-Nahhas is a Muslim by way of religion, but he's also a nationalist in every sense of the word. He makes us think of ourselves as Egyptians, whether we are Muslims or Copts. I could lead a happy life with an untroubled mind by focusing on thoughts like these, but a real life is at the same time a responsible one."

Kamal's breast was agitated by emotion and his thoughts wandered as he smacked his lips over the pastry. Riyad's appearance, which was so purely Egyptian that it reminded him of a pharaonic portrait, stirred various reflections: "Riyad's point can't be denied. I'm torn between the dictates of my intellect and of my heart, and so is he. How can a minority live in the midst of a majority that oppresses it? Different sacred scriptures are commonly compared according to the level of happiness they provide to human beings, and that is most clearly represented by the amount of aid they give the oppressed."

Kamal said, "Forgive me. I've never had to deal with racism. From the very beginning my mother trained me to love everyone, and I grew up in the revolutionary atmosphere that was free of ethnic prejudices. So I have had no experience with this problem."

As they resumed their walk, Riyad said, "One would hope there wouldn't be any problem at all. I'm sorry to have to tell you bluntly that we grew up in homes with plenty of gloomy memories. I'm not a Coptic chauvinist, but anyone who neglects human rights, whether at home or at the ends of the earth, has neglected the rights of all mankind."

"That's beautifully put. It's not surprising that truly humanitarian manifestos originate frequently in minority circles or with people whose consciences are troubled by the problems of minorities. But there are always some fanatics."

"Always. Everywhere. Men have only recently evolved from animals. Your fanatics consider us cursed infidels. Our fanatics consider you infidel usurpers. They call themselves descendants of the kings of ancient Egypt and people who were able to preserve their religion by paying the poll tax levied on non-Muslims."

Kamal laughed out loud. Then he said, "That's precisely what the two sides say. Do you suppose the origin of this dispute is religion or a human proclivity for dissension? Muslims don't all agree with each other and neither do Christians. You will find that there have long been disagreements between Shi'i Muslims and Sunni Muslims, Hijazi Muslims and Iraqi Muslims, Wafdists and Constitutionalists, students in the humanities and in the sciences, and supporters of the rival Ahli and Arsenal soccer teams. But in spite of this contentious streak in human nature, we are deeply upset when we read newspaper accounts of an earthquake in Japan. Listen, why don't you treat this subject in your stories?"

"The problem of Copts and Muslims. . . ." Riyad Qaldas was quiet for a time. Then he said, "I'm afraid it would be misunderstood." After another period of silence he added, "And don't forget that, in spite of everything, we're enjoying our golden age. At one time Shaykh Abd al-Aziz Jawish suggested that Muslims should make shoes from our hides."

"How can we eradicate this problem?"

"Fortunately it has been absorbed by the problems of the people as a whole. Today the Copts' problem is the people's problem. We are oppressed when everyone else is. When the people are free, we are."

"Happiness and peace," Kamal thought. "That's the goal we dream of. Your heart lives by love alone. When will your mind find its proper way? When will I be able to say, 'Yes, yes!' with the certainty of my nephew Abd al-Muni'm? My friendship with Riyad has taught me to read his stories. But how can I believe in art at the very time that I find philosophy inadequate and inhospitable?"

Glancing stealthily in his direction, Riyad suddenly asked Kamal, "What are you thinking about now? . . . Tell me the truth."

Understanding the reason for his friend's question, Kamal answered candidly, "I was thinking about your stories."

"Weren't you distressed by my bluntness?"

"Me! God forgive you."

Riyad laughed a bit apologetically and then inquired, "Have you read my latest story?"

"Yes. It's nice. But I can't help thinking that art isn't serious work. Of course, I need to point out that I don't know whether work or play is more significant in life. You have advanced training in the sciences and perhaps know as much about them as anyone who is not actually a scientist, but all your efforts are squandered on writing stories. I wonder occasionally how science has helped you."

Riyad Qaldas replied vigorously, "I have transferred from science to art a sincere devotion to the truth, a willingness to confront the facts no matter how bitter they are, an impartiality of judgment, and finally a comprehensive respect for all creatures."

These were grand words, but what relationship did they have to comic stories? Riyad Qaldas looked at him and, reading the doubt in his expression, laughed aloud. Then Riyad said, "You have a low opinion of art. My only consolation is that there's nothing on earth that escapes your doubts. We understand with our minds but live with our hearts. Despite your skeptical stance, you love, work together with other people, and share in the political life of your nation. Whether we are conscious of it or not, behind each of these initiatives there is a principle that is no less powerful than faith. Art is the interpreter of the human world. Besides that, some writers have produced works forming part of the international contest of ideas. In their hands art has become one of the weapons of international progress. There is no way that art can be considered a frivolous activity."

"Is this a defense of art or of the artist?" Kamal asked himself. "If the man who sells melon seeds had a talent for debating, he would prove that he plays a significant role in the life of mankind. It's quite possible that everything has an intrinsic merit. Similarly, it's not out of the question that everything, without exception, is worthless. Millions of people are breathing their last at this moment, and yet a child's voice is raised to bewail the loss of a toy and a lover's moans resound throughout existence to broadcast the torments of his heart. Should I laugh or weep?"

Kamal remarked, "With regard to what you said about the international competition of ideas, let me tell you that it's being played out on a small scale in our family. One of my nephews is a Muslim Brother and one a Communist."

"Sooner or later this struggle will be reflected in some form everywhere. We don't live in a vacuum. Haven't you thought about these issues?"

"I read about Communism when I studied materialist philosophy, and similarly I've read books about Fascism and the Nazis."

"You read and understand. You're a historian with no history. I hope you observe the day you emerge from this condition as your true birthday."

Kamal was offended by this remark, not only because of its stinging criticism but also because of the truth it contained. To avoid commenting on it, he said, "Neither the Communist nor the Muslim Brother in our family has a sound knowledge of what he believes."

"Belief is a matter of willing, not of knowing. The most casual Christian today knows far more about Christianity than the Christian martyrs did. It's the same with you in Islam."

"Do you believe in any of these ideologies?"

After some reflection, Riyad replied, "It's clear that I despise Fascism, the Nazi movement, and all other dictatorial systems. Communism might be able to create a world free from the calamities of racial and religious friction and from class conflicts. All the same, my primary interest is my art."

In a teasing tone, Kamal asked, "But more than a thousand years ago Islam created this ideal world you've mentioned."

"But it's a religion. Communism is a science. Religion is nothing more than a myth." Then, smiling, he added, "The problem is that we interact with Muslims, not with Islam."

They found Fuad I Street very crowded despite the cold weather. Riyad stopped suddenly and asked, "What would you think about having macaroni with an excellent wine for supper?"

"I don't drink in places where a lot of people will see me. If you want, we could go to Ukasha's café."

Riyad Qaldas laughed and said, "How can you bear to be so sedate? Spectacles, mustache, and traditional mores! You've liberated your mind from every fetter, but your body is bound with chains. You were created—at least your body was—to be a teacher."

Riyad's reference to his body reminded Kamal of a painful incident. He had attended the birthday party of a colleague, and they had all become intoxicated. Then a guest had launched a verbal attack on him, pointing out his head and nose, and everyone had laughed. Whenever he thought of his head and nose he also remembered Aïda and the past – Aïda, who had first made him self-conscious about his features. It was amazing that when love receded, nothing came to take its place. All that remained were bitter dregs.

Riyad pulled at his arm and said, "Let's go drink some wine and talk about literature. Then afterward we'll go to Madam Jalila's house in al-Gawhari Alley. If you call her 'Auntie,' I will too."

139

THERE WAS a flurry of activity at Sugar Street, or more precisely in the apartment of Abd al-Muni'm Shawkat. Gathered in the bedroom around Na'ima's bed were Amina, Khadija, Aisha, Zanuba, and a nurse-midwife. In the parlor, sitting with Abd al-Muni'm were his father Ibrahim, his brother Ahmad, Yasin, and Kamal. Yasin was teasing Abd al-Muni'm: "Arrange things so that the next birth doesn't come when you're preparing for an exam."

It was the end of April. Abd al-Muni'm was tired, delighted, and anxious in equal measure. Screams provoked by labor pains carried through the closed door, and the entire spectrum of pain was present in these shrill cries.

Abd al-Muni'm remarked, "Pregnancy has exhausted her and has left her incredibly weak. Her face is so pale that all the blood seems to have drained away."

Yasin belched contentedly and then said, "This is normal. It's always this way."

Smiling, Kamal observed, "I still remember when Na'ima was born. It was a difficult delivery, and Aisha suffered terribly. I was very upset and stood here with her late husband, Khalil."

Abd al-Muni'm asked, "Do you mean to tell me that difficult deliveries are hereditary?"

Gesturing heavenward with his finger, Yasin said, "He can make everything easy."

Abd al-Muni'm said, "We got a nurse-midwife who is known throughout the entire district. My mother would have preferred to have the woman who delivered us, but I insisted on having a trained professional. There's no doubt that she is cleaner and more skillful."

Yasin replied, "Naturally. Although, as a whole, childbirth is in God's hands. He controls it."

Lighting a cigarette, Ibrahim Shawkat said, "Her labor pains began early in the morning. Now it's almost five P.M. The poor dear is as insubstantial as a shadow. May our Lord come to her aid."

Then glancing with languid eyes at the other men, particularly at his sons, Abd al-Muni'm and Ahmad, he said, "Oh, if only you would remember the pain a mother endures. . . ."

Laughing, Ahmad said, "How can you expect a fetus to remember anything, Papa?"

The man scolded his son: "When it's a question of gratitude, there's no need to depend solely on memory."

The screams stopped. The bedroom was silent, and everyone looked in that direction. After a few moments, his patience exhausted, Abd al-Muni'm rose, went to the door, and knocked. The door was opened just enough to reveal Khadija's plump face. He gave her a questioning look and tried to poke his head inside. But she blocked him with the palms of her hands and said, "God hasn't granted a delivery yet."

"It's taking a long time. Could it be false labor?"

"The midwife knows better than we do. Calm down and pray for a safe delivery."

She closed the door. The young man resumed his seat next to his father, who justified Abd al-Muni'm's anxiety: "You'll have to excuse him. This is his first time."

Wishing to distract himself, Kamal took out *al-Balagh*, the newspaper that had been folded up in his pocket, and started to leaf through it. Then Ahmad said, "The results of the last election were announced on the radio." Smiling scornfully, he added, "How ridiculous they were. . . ."

His father asked casually, "How many Wafdists were elected?"

"Thirteen, if I remember correctly."

Addressing his uncle Yasin, Ahmad said, "I guess you're happy, Uncle, for Ridwan's sake?"

Yasin shrugged his shoulders and replied, "He's not a cabinet minister or a deputy. So how does that affect me?"

Laughing, Ibrahim Shawkat said, "The Wafdists thought the age of rigged elections was over, but the reformers are more corrupt than the sycophants they replaced."

Ahmad said resentfully, "It's clear that in Egypt the exception is the rule."

"Even al-Nahhas and Makram were defeated. Isn't that a joke?"

At this point Ibrahim Shawkat said rather sharply, "But no one can deny they were rude to the king. Kings have a certain stature. That wasn't the right way to do things."

Ahmad responded, "To wake up from its long torpor, our country needs a strong dose of disrespect for kings."

Kamal remarked, "But these dogs are returning us to a form of absolute rule hidden behind a counterfeit parliament. At the end of this experiment, we'll find that Faruq's as powerful and tyrannical as Fuad, or worse. And all this is the fault of some of our compatriots."

Yasin laughed. As if to clarify and explain the point, he said, "Although when Kamal was a boy he loved the English as dearly as Shahin, Adli, Tharwat, and Haydar did, afterward he turned into a Wafdist."

Looking at Ahmad most of all, Kamal said earnestly, "The elections were rigged. Everyone in the country knows that. All the same they have been recognized officially, and the country will be governed according to their results. What this means is that people will become convinced that their representatives are thieves who stole their seats in parliament, that the cabinet ministers also stole their posts, that the whole government is bogus and fraudulent, and that theft, fraud, and deception are legitimate and officially sanctioned. So isn't an ordinary man to be excused if he renounces lofty principles and morality and believes in deceit and opportunism?"

Ahmad replied enthusiastically, "Let them rule. There's a positive side to every wrong. It's better for the people to be humiliated than for them to be intoxicated by a government they love and trust, if it does not fulfill their true wishes. I've often thought about this, and as a result I have more appreciation for the reign of despots like Muhammad Mahmud and Isma'il Sidqy."

Kamal noticed that Abd al-Muni'm was not taking his usual part in the conversation. Wishing to draw him out, Kamal said, "Why don't you tell us your opinion?"

Smiling vacuously, Abd al-Muni'm answered, "Let me listen today."

Yasin laughed and said, "Pull yourself together. If the baby finds you looking so glum, it will think twice about staying." He shifted restlessly, and Kamal interpreted this as a prelude to an excuse for leaving. Yes, it was time for Yasin to take up his post at the coffeehouse. His evening adventures followed a schedule that nothing could alter.

Kamal thought he would depart with his brother, since there was no reason for him to stay either. Ready to make his move,

Kamal watched Yasin carefully. Then a harsh and violent scream burst forth from Na'ima's room, conveying the deepest form of human emotion. One fierce shriek followed another in rapid succession. All eyes were fixed on the door, and the men fell silent. Finally Ibrahim whispered hopefully, "Perhaps it's the end of the labor, God willing."

Was that it? But the screaming continued, and the men felt disheartened. Abd al-Muni'm looked quite pale. Na'ima's room was silent once more, although only for a time. When the screams resumed they sounded hollow, as though expelled by a hoarse throat and an exhausted chest in the throes of death.

Since Abd al-Muni'm clearly needed encouragement, Yasin told him, "You're not hearing anything you wouldn't at any other difficult delivery."

"Difficult! Difficult! But why should it be difficult?"

The door was opened by Zanuba, who came out, closing it behind her. They stared at her. Walking over to Yasin, she stopped in front of him and said, "Everything's fine, but as a precaution the midwife wants you to ask Dr. Sayyid Muhammad to come."

Jumping to his feet, Abd al-Muni'm said, "Then no doubt her condition requires it. Tell me what's wrong."

In a calm, confident voice, Zanuba replied, "Everything's fine. If you want to reassure us, hurry to get the doctor."

Wasting no time, Abd al-Muni'm went immediately to his room to finish dressing. Ahmad followed him, and they went off together to fetch the doctor. Then Yasin asked his wife, "What's going on in there?"

Her face betraying her anxiety for the first time, Zanuba said, "The poor dear's very tired, God help her."

"Hasn't the midwife said anything?"

In a resigned tone, Zanuba answered, "She says she wants the doctor."

Leaving a heavy cloud of anxiety behind her, Zanuba returned to the bedroom. Yasin wondered aloud, "How far is this doctor?"

Ibrahim Shawkat replied, "In the building over your coffee-house in al-Ataba."

A scream rang out and struck them dumb. Had the labor pains resumed? When would the doctor arrive? There was another resounding scream. The tension increased. And then Yasin cried out in alarm, "That's Aisha's voice!"

Listening intently, they recognized Aisha's shriek. Ibrahim went to the door and knocked. When Zanuba opened it, her face exceedingly pale, he asked apprehensively, "What's the matter? What's the matter with Mrs. Aisha? Wouldn't it be best for her to leave the room?"

Swallowing, Zanuba replied, "Absolutely not. The situation is extremely serious, Mr. Ibrahim."

"What's happened?"

"All of a sudden . . . she . . . look . . ."

In less than a second the three men were at the door of the room, looking in. Na'ima was covered to her chest. Her aunt, her grandmother, and the midwife were around the bed. Na'ima's mother stood in the center of the room, staring at her daughter from afar with eyes that did not seem to focus on anything, as if she was in a daze. Na'ima's eyes were closed, and her breast was heaving up and down as though it had slipped free of its ties to her still body. Her face was white, with a deathly pallor.

The midwife shouted, "The doctor!"

Amina began to exclaim, "Lord! . . ."

In a terrified voice, Khadija called out, "Na'ima . . . answer me."

Aisha said nothing, as if the matter had no relationship to her whatsoever.

"What's happening?" Kamal wondered. Stunned, he asked his brother. But Yasin did not reply.

"What a difficult delivery!" Kamal thought. He glanced around at Aisha, Ibrahim, and Yasin, and his heart sank. Their expressions could mean only one thing.

They all went into the room. It was no longer a delivery room, or they would not have entered. Aisha was in an extreme state, but no one said anything to her. Na'ima opened her eyes, which seemed glazed. When she moved as if wanting to rise, her grandmother helped her sit up and embraced her. The girl gasped and moaned. Suddenly, she cried out as if appealing for help, "Mama . . . I'm going . . . I'm going." Then her head fell on her grandmother's breast.

The room came alive with a noisy commotion. Khadija slapped her cheeks. Directing her words to the girl's face, Amina recited the Muslim credo: "There is no god but God, and Muhammad is the Messenger of God."

Aisha gazed out the window overlooking Sugar Street, focusing her eyes on some unknown spot. Then her voice rang out like a death rattle: "What is this, my Lord? What are You doing? Why? Why? I want to understand."

Ibrahim Shawkat went to her and stretched out his hand, but she pushed it away with a nervous gesture and said, "Don't any of you touch me. Leave me alone. Leave me. . . ." Glancing around at them, she said, "Please leave. Don't say a word. Is there anything you could say? Words won't help me. Na'ima's dead, as you can see. She was all I had left. There's nothing for me in the world now. Please go away."

It was pitch-black when Yasin and Kamal returned to Palace Walk. Yasin said, "It will be very hard for me to break the news to your father."

Drying his eyes, Kamal replied, "Yes."

"Don't cry. My nerves can't take any more. . . ."

Sighing, Kamal said, "She was very dear to me. Brother, I'm sad. And poor Aisha!"

"That's the ultimate calamity. Aisha! We'll all forget in time, but not Aisha."

" 'We'll all forget'?" Kamal asked himself. "I think her face will stay with me to the end of my days, although I've already had one extraordinary experience with forgetting. . . . It can be a great blessing, but when will its balm arrive?"

Yasin continued: "I had my reservations when she got married. Don't you know? When she was born, the doctor predicted that her heart was not strong enough for her to live past twenty. Your father almost certainly remembers."

"I don't know anything about this. Did Aisha know?"

"Certainly not. It's ancient history. There's no escaping God's decree."

"How unfortunate you are, Aisha!"

"Yes. The poor dear is really unlucky."

140

AHMAD IBRAHIM SHAWKAT sat in the reading room of the University library concentrating on the book in front of him. Only a week was left before the examination, and he had exhausted himself studying for it. He heard someone enter and sit down behind him. Turning around curiously, he saw Alawiya Sabri. Yes, it was the girl herself. Perhaps she was sitting there to wait for the book he had. At that moment his eyes met two black ones. He turned his head back to its original position, with heart and senses in a state of intoxication. There could be no doubt that she had begun to recognize him. And she must have realized he was in love with her. Things like that could not be hidden. Besides, wherever she turned, in a class or in al-Urman Gardens, she would often find him glancing at her stealthily.

Her presence distracted him from his reading, but his delight was too great to be measured. Ever since he had learned that, like him, she would be majoring in sociology, he had hoped they would get acquainted the next year. There were too many students in the first university year for him to meet her then. Whenever he had been this close to her before there had been many people watching. He would go to the reference shelves, pretend to look at a book there, and greet her on the way. He cast a glance around him and found some students scattered around the room, but not more than he could count on the fingers of one hand. He rose without any hesitation and walked down the aisle between the seats. As he passed her, their eyes met, and he bowed his head in a polite greeting. The impact of the surprise was apparent in her expression, but she nodded to acknowledge his greeting and looked back at her work.

He wondered whether he had made a mistake, but concluded he had not, since she had been his classmate all year long. It was his duty to greet her when they met face to face like this in a place that was almost deserted. He proceeded on to the bookcase containing the encyclopedia. Choosing a volume, he turned the pages without reading a word. His joy at her having returned his greet-ing was enormous. The fatigue left him, and he felt full of energy. How beautiful she was! He felt such admiration for her and was so attracted to her that she was all he could think of. Everything about her indicated that she came from a "family," as people said. What he was most afraid of was that her gracious manners might conceal some snobbish pride. He could truthfully claim that he too came from a "family," if he had to. Weren't the Shawkats a "family"? Of course . . . and they had properties. One day he would have both a salary and a private income. His mouth parted in a sarcastic smile. A private income, a salary, and a family! What had become of his principles? He felt rather embarrassed. In its passions the heart is oblivious to precepts. People fall in love and get married in ways that are incompatible with their principles, without stopping to wonder about it. They are forced to reshape their ideals, just as a foreigner is forced to speak a country's language to achieve his ends. Besides, class and property were two existing realities that he had not created himself, no more than his father or grandfather had. He bore no responsibility for them. A combination of struggle and science could wipe out these absurdities that separated people from each other. It might be possible to change the class system, but how could he change the past that had decreed he would come from a family with a comfortable private income? It was absurd to think that socialist principles should interfere with love for an aristocrat when Karl Marx himself had married Jenny von Westphalen, whose grand-father, a chief aide to the Duke of Brunswick, had married into a family of Scottish barons. They had called her the "Enchanted Princess" and "Queen of the Ball." Here was another enchanting princess, who – if she danced – would be queen of the ball.

After returning the volume to the shelf, he walked back toward his place, filling his eyes with her figure, upper back, delicate neck, and the braided hair that adorned the rear of her head. What a beautiful sight! He passed by her quietly and regained his seat. In only a few minutes he heard her light footsteps. Assuming that she was leaving, he looked back regretfully but saw her approaching. When parallel with him, she stopped somewhat nervously. He could not believe his eyes.

"Excuse me," she said. "Could I get the history lectures from you?"

He rose and stood at attention like a soldier, blurting out, "Certainly."

She said apologetically, "I couldn't follow what the British professor was saying as well as I should have. I'm unclear about many of the most important points. I don't look up the sources for the subjects I'm not going to major in. I don't have time. . . ."

"I understand. I understand."

"I was told that you have a complete set of notes and have lent them to students, who get what they missed from them."

"Yes. I'll bring them for you tomorrow."

"Thank you very much." Then, smiling, she added, "Don't think I'm lazy, but my English is mediocre."

"Never mind. I'm mediocre in French. Maybe we'll have some opportunities to cooperate. But forgive me. Please sit down. You might want to see this book: *Introduction to the Study of Society* by Hankins."

She replied, "Thanks, but I've gone over it several times. You say your French is mediocre. Perhaps you need my psychology notes?"

Without any hesitation he responded, "I'd be grateful, if you don't mind."

"So tomorrow we'll exchange notes?"

"With pleasure. But forgive me . . . won't you find that most of the instruction in sociology is in English?"

"You know I've chosen sociology?"

He smiled as if to hide his embarrassment, although he felt none, and answered simply, "Yes."

"How did you happen to find that out?"

He said boldly, "I asked someone."

She pressed her crimson lips together. Then she continued as if she had not heard his reply: "Tomorrow we'll exchange notes."

"In the morning."

"See you then, and thanks."

Before she could depart he said, "I'm happy to have met you. See you tomorrow."

He remained on his feet until she had disappeared out the door. When he sat back down, he noticed that some of the young men were looking at him curiously. But he was tipsy with happiness. Had the conversation been a response to his obvious admiration for her or had it been occasioned by a pressing need for his notes?

He had never had a chance to get acquainted with her before. Whenever he had seen her, she had been with a group of friends. This was his first opportunity, and almost miraculously he had obtained what he had wanted for so long. A word from the lips of a person we love is apt to make everything else seem insignificant.

141

NO MATTER how hard he tried to stay calm, Yasin seemed anxious. To both his colleagues and himself he had pretended for a long time that he did not care about anything – not his rank, his salary, or even which party was in power. If promoted to the sixth level, he would only get two pounds more a month, and he spent so much. . . . They said that an increase in his rank would mean a promotion for him from review clerk to head of section. But when had Yasin ever shown any interest in administration? All the same, he felt worried, especially after Muhammad Effendi Hasan, head of the bureau and husband of Ridwan's mother, Zaynab, was summoned to a meeting with the deputy minister to give his opinion of his employees one final time before the list of promotions was signed. Muhammad Hasan? The man was vengeful by nature and would have treated Yasin badly from the beginning had it not been for Mr. Muhammad Iffat. Could such a man give Yasin a good report? Taking advantage of his supervisor's absence to hurry to the telephone, Yasin called the Law School for the third time that day and asked for Ridwan Yasin.

"Hello, Ridwan? It's your father."

"Hello. Everything's great." The boy's voice was confident. He had been working on his father's behalf.

"All that remains is for the promotions to be signed?"

"Have no fear. The minister himself recommended you. Some deputies and senators spoke to him, and he promised that everything would be fine."

"Doesn't the affair require one last recommendation?"

"Not at all. As I told you, the pasha already congratulated me on your promotion this morning. You have every reason to be confident."

"Thanks, son. Goodbye."

"Goodbye, Papa. Congratulations in advance."

He put down the receiver, left the room, and ran into his colleague and competitor for this promotion, Ibrahim Effendi

Fath Allah, who approached carrying some files. They greeted each other circumspectly. Then Yasin said, "Let's be good sports about this, Ibrahim Effendi. Whatever the result is, let's receive it with good grace."

The man said angrily, "On condition that you play fair."

"What do you mean?"

"The selection should be based on merit, not influence."

"What strange ideas you have! Isn't influence necessary to obtain any kind of position in this world? You do your best, and I'll do mine. Whoever is destined to receive the promotion will get it."

"I have more seniority than you do."

"We've both been in the civil service for a long time. One year more or less won't make any difference."

"In one year many people are born and many others die."

"Whether a person is born or dies is all a question of his destiny."

"What about qualifications?"

"Qualifications? Are we constructing bridges or building power plants? What qualifications are required for our clerical work? We both have the elementary certificate. In addition to that, I'm a man of culture."

Ibrahim Effendi laughed sarcastically and replied, "Culture? Greetings to the cultured gentleman! Do you think the poems you've memorized make you cultured? Or is it the style you use in drafting letters for the bureau . . . the kind a person would employ when retaking the elementary certificate examination. I'll leave my fate to God."

The two men parted on bad terms, and Yasin returned to his desk. The room was large. On both sides there were rows of desks that faced each other. The walls were lined with shelves crammed with files. Some of the clerks were busy with their papers, but others chatted or smoked. Meanwhile messengers carrying files came or left.

Yasin's neighbor told him, "My daughter will do the baccalaureate examination this year. I'll sign her up for the Teacher Training Institute, and then I'll be able to stop worrying about her. It doesn't cost anything, and there will be no difficulty finding her a job after she graduates."

Yasin said, "You've done the best thing."

The man asked him argumentatively, "What do you have planned for Karima? By the way, how old is she?"

Although irritated, Yasin relaxed his face into a smile and said, "Eleven. She'll take the elementary-school certificate examination next summer, God willing." After counting out the months on his fingers, he continued: "We're in November, so there are seven more months until it's over and done with."

"If she does well in elementary school, she'll succeed in secondary school too. Girls today are a safer bet in school than boys."

Secondary school? . . . That was what Zanuba wanted. Certainly not . . . he could not bear to have a daughter stroll off to school with bouncing breasts . . . and what about the fees?

"We don't send our girls to secondary school. Why not? Because they're not going to take jobs."

A third man asked, "Does talk like this make sense in 1938?"

"In our family, they'll be saying it in 2038."

A fourth clerk laughed as he said, "Admit you'd have to choose between spending money on her and on yourself. The coffeehouse in al-Ataba, the bar on Muhammad Ali Street, and 'Love for young women has sapped my strength.' That's the true story."

Yasin laughed and then said, "May our Lord protect her. But as I said, we don't educate girls beyond the elementary certificate."

A cough resounded from the corner of the room closest to the entrance. Yasin turned in that direction and then stood up, as if he had remembered something important. He went over to the cougher's desk. Sensing Yasin's presence, the man looked up, and Yasin leaned down to say, "You promised to tell me how to make the elixir."

The man moved his ear closer to Yasin, asking, "What?"

Since he was afraid to raise his voice, Yasin was distressed by the man's difficulty in hearing him. A loud voice from the middle of the room announced, "I bet he's asking you about the prescription for the aphrodisiac that's going to send all of us to the grave."

Yasin retreated to his desk in disgust. Paying no attention to his embarrassment, the man said in a voice everyone could hear, "I'll tell you how to make it. Get the peel of a mango, boil it rapidly until the mixture attains the consistency of honey, and take a spoonful of it before breakfast."

They all laughed, but Ibrahim Fath Allah remarked sarcastically, "That's swell, but wait till you're promoted to the sixth level. See if that doesn't perk you up."

Laughing, Yasin asked, "Does a man's rank help him in this area?"

His neighbor, who was laughing too, replied, "If this theory was correct, then Uncle Hasanayn, our office boy, should be the Minister of Education."

Ibrahim Fath Allah clapped his hands together and, pointing to Yasin, asked, "Brothers, this man is nice and pleasant, a good fellow, but does he do a millieme's worth of work? Give me your honest opinion."

Yasin said scornfully, "A minute of my work is equivalent to a day's work by you."

"The real story is that the director goes easy on you and that you rely on your son's intervention in this bleak era."

Determined to infuriate his rival, Yasin said, "By your life, I'll have an advocate in every era. Now it's my son. If the Wafd returns to power, you'll find I have my nephew and my father. Tell me what advocates you have."

Looking up toward the ceiling, the other man answered, "I have our Lord."

"Glory to Him, I have Him too. Isn't He everyone's Lord?"

"But He's not fond of patrons of drinking establishments on Muhammad Ali Street."

"Does that mean He likes dope addicts?"

"There's no more revolting creature than a drunkard."

"Cabinet ministers and ambassadors drink. Don't you see pictures in the papers of them drinking toasts? But have you ever seen a diplomat at an official party offer opium to someone in celebration of the signing of a treaty, for example?"

Trying to stop laughing, Yasin's neighbor said, "Hush, fellows, or the rest of your civil service will be performed in prison."

Pointing to his adversary, Yasin shot back, "By your life, even in prison he would loathe me and brag about his seniority."

Then Muhammad Hasan returned from his meeting with the deputy minister. There was universal silence as all faces watched him go to his office without pausing to look at anything. The clerks exchanged inquisitive glances. Probably one of the rivals was now head of his section. But which was the lucky one? The door of the director's office opened. The director's bald head appeared, and he called out in an emotionless voice, "Yasin Effendi." Yasin rose and directed his huge body toward the office as his heart pounded.

The director scrutinized him with a strange look and then said, "You've been promoted to the sixth level."

Relieved and delighted, Yasin replied, "Thank you, sir."

In a rather dry tone the man continued: "It's only fair to tell you frankly that someone else deserves it more than you do. But strings were pulled on your behalf."

Yasin was annoyed, as he often was when with this man. He retorted, "Strings! So what? Is anything big or small accomplished without the use of influence? Does anyone get promoted in this bureau or this ministry, yourself included, without influence?"

The other man restrained his rage and said, "You're nothing but a headache for me. You get promoted without deserving it and then resent the least remark, no matter how appropriate. Don't blame us. Congratulations. Congratulations, sir. I just hope you'll pull yourself together. You're head of your section now."

Encouraged by the way the director had backed down, Yasin, without modifying his own sharp tone, replied, "I've been a civil servant for more than twenty years. I'm forty-two. Do you think the sixth level is too good for me? Boys are appointed at this rank merely because they've graduated from the University."

"The important thing is for you to pull yourself together. I hope I'll find you as reliable as the others. When you were the school disciplinarian at al-Nahhasin School, you were a diligent and exemplary employee. Had it not been for that incident long ago . . ."

"That's ancient history. There's no need to mention it now. Everyone makes mistakes."

"You're a mature adult. If you play around, it will be hard to carry out your duties. When you stay out late every night, what condition is your brain in the next morning when you're supposed to work? I want you to shoulder your responsibilities. That's all there is to it."

Yasin was offended by the reference to his conduct and said, "I won't let anyone comment on my private life. Once I'm outside the ministry I'm free to do what I want."

"And inside it?"

"I will do as much work as any other section head. I've toiled enough over the years to suffice for the rest of my life."

When Yasin returned to his desk, despite the anger raging in his breast, he sported a smile. As the news spread, he was showered with congratulations.

Ibrahim Fath Allah leaned over to whisper spitefully to his neighbor, "His son! That's the whole story. Abd al-Rahim Pasha Isa . . . you understand? Disgusting!"

142

SEATED IN a large chair on the latticed balcony, al-Sayyid Ahmad Abd al-Jawad gazed alternately at the street and at *al-Ahram*, the newspaper spread across his lap. The gaps between the spindles of the latticework allowed patches of light to fall on his ample house shirt and on his skullcap. He had left the door to his room open so he could hear the radio from the sitting room. He appeared gaunt and wasted, and the dull look in his eyes suggested sorrowful resignation. From his perch on the balcony, he seemed to be discovering the street for the first time. In the past, he had never experienced it from this angle. Back then, he had slept most of the time he was at home. Nowadays the only amusement he had left, except for the radio, was sitting on the balcony and peering out between the spindles to the north and the south. It was a lively, charming, and entertaining street. Moreover, it had a special character distinguishing it from al-Nahhasin, which he had observed for roughly half a century from his shop, the one he had owned. Here were the establishments of Hasanayn the barber, Darwish the bean seller, al-Fuli the milkman, Bayumi the drinks vendor, and Abu Sari', who grilled snacks. Known for their location on this street, they were also the features by which Palace Walk was identified.

"What good companions and neighbors . . . I wonder how old these men are. Hasanayn the barber has a good build, the kind that rarely shows a man's age. Almost nothing about him has changed except his hair, but he's certainly over fifty. God's grace has preserved these men's health. And Darwish? Bald . . . he always was. But he's in his sixties. What a powerful body he has! I was like that when I was sixty, but now I'm sixty-seven. That's old! I've had my clothes cut down to fit what's left of my body. When I look at the photo hanging in my room, I can't believe I'm that same person. Poor blind al-Fuli is younger than Darwish. Without his apprentice, he wouldn't be able to make his rounds. Abu Sari' is an old man. Old? But he's still working. None of them has given up

his shop. It's a shattering experience for a man to abandon his
store. Afterward all you have left is sitting in your house, staying
home day and night. If only I could go out for an hour every day!
I have to wait for Friday and then I need both my stick and Kamal
to assist me. Praise God, Lord of the universe, in any case. Bayumi's the youngest of them and the luckiest. His prominence began
with Maryam's mother, and mine ended with her. Today he owns
the most modern building in the neighborhood. That's what
became of Mr. Muhammad Ridwan's home. Where it once
stood, Bayumi has built a juice shop lit by electricity. A man's
good fortune may start with a woman's treachery. Glory to God
who gives all things. May His wisdom be exalted. Everything's
been modernized. The roads have been paved with asphalt and
illuminated with streetlights. Remember how pitch-black the
nights were when you used to return home? What a long time
it's been since you did that! Every shop has electricity and a radio.
Everything's new, except me, an old man of sixty-seven who can
only leave his home once a week. Even then I'm short of breath.
My heart! It's all the fault of my heart that loved, laughed, rejoiced,
and sang for so many years. Today it dictates calm, and there's no
way to reject its decree. The doctor said, 'Take your medicine,
stay home, and keep to the diet I've prescribed.' I told him, 'Fine.
But will that make me strong again? Or give me back at least some
of my strength?' He replied, 'Warding off further complications
is the most we can hope for. Any exertion or movement puts
you at risk.' Then he laughed and wanted to know, 'Why do you
want to regain your strength?' Yes, why? It's ridiculous and
pathetic."

All the same, al-Sayyid Ahmad had answered, "I want to be able
to come and go."

The physician had commented, "Every condition has its own
special pleasures – like sitting quietly. Read the newspapers, listen
to the radio, enjoy your family, and on Friday ride to the mosque
of al-Husayn. That's enough for you."

"The matter's in God's hands," he thought. "Mutawalli Abd al-
Samad is still stumbling about in the streets. . . . He says, 'Enjoy
your family.' Amina no longer stays home. Our roles have been
reversed. I'm confined to the latticed balcony while she roams
around Cairo, going from mosque to mosque. Kamal sits with me
for fleeting moments, as if he were a guest. Aisha? Alas, Aisha, are

you alive or dead? And then they want my heart to recover and to feel contented."

"Master . . ."

He turned around and saw Umm Hanafi carrying a small tray with a bottle of medicine, an empty coffee cup, and a glass half filled with water.

"Your medicine, master."

Kitchen fragrances wafted from the black dress of this woman who in the course of time had become one of the family. Picking up the glass, he poured out enough water to fill the cup halfway and then, after removing the medicine bottle's stopper, added four drops to the water in his cup. In anticipation of the taste, he made a face and then swallowed.

"May it bring you health, master."

"Thanks. Where's Aisha?"

"In her room. May God grant her forbearance."

"Call her, Umm Hanafi."

In her room or on the roof . . . what difference did it make? The radio's cheerful songs were in ironic contrast to the mournful atmosphere of this otherwise silent dwelling. Al-Sayyid Ahmad had been confined to the house for only the last two months. A year and four months had passed since Na'ima's death. When the man had asked to listen to the radio in view of his urgent need for entertainment, Aisha had replied, "Of course, Papa. May God find ways to console you for being forced to stay home."

Hearing the rustling of a dress, he turned and saw Aisha approaching in her black attire. Although the weather was warm, she had a black scarf wrapped around her head. Her fair complexion had a strange blue cast to it. "That's a symptom of her depression," he thought. Then he said tenderly, "Get a chair and sit with me a little."

But she did not budge and replied, "I'm comfortable like this, Papa."

The recent past had taught him not to try to make her change her mind about anything. "What were you doing?"

A blank expression on her face, she answered, "Nothing, Papa."

"Why don't you go out with your mother and visit the blessed shrines? Wouldn't that be better than staying at home alone?"

"Why should I visit shrines?"

He seemed astonished by her response but said calmly, "You could entreat God for solace."

"God is with us here in our house."

"Of course. I mean you shouldn't spend so much time alone, Aisha. Visit your sister. Visit the neighbors. Find some amusements for yourself."

"I can't bear to see Sugar Street. I have no friends. I don't know anyone anymore. I can't stand to visit people."

Turning his face away, the man said, "I want you to be brave and to take care of your health."

"My health!" she exclaimed almost incredulously.

He persisted: "Yes. What's the point of sorrow?"

In spite of her agitated condition, she did not abandon the decorum she observed with him and replied, "What's the point of life, Papa?"

"Don't say that. God's reward for you will be great."

Bowing her head to hide the tears in her eyes, she replied, "I want to go to Him to receive my reward. It won't come in this world, Papa." She started to withdraw quietly but before leaving the balcony stopped a moment as if she had remembered something and asked, "How's your health today?"

He smiled and answered, "Fine, praise God, but what's important is your health, Aisha." Then she was gone.

How could he relax in this house? He glanced down at the street again, and finally his eyes came to rest on Amina, who was returning from her daily circuit. Modestly attired in a coat and a white veil, she proceeded at a slow pace. How she had aged! Since he remembered that her mother had lived to a ripe old age, he was not especially concerned about his wife's health. But here she was at sixty-two looking at least ten years older than that.

It was quite a while before she arrived and asked him, "How are you, master?"

Raising his voice loud enough to allow the desired sharpness to reverberate in it, he said, "How are you yourself? God's will be done! You've been out since early this morning, lady."

She smiled and replied, "I visited the shrines of al-Sayyida Zaynab and of al-Husayn. I prayed for you and for everyone else."

Now that she was home, his composure and peace of mind returned, for he sensed he could request anything he wanted without hesitation. "Is it right for you to leave me alone all this time?"

"You gave me permission, master. I haven't been gone long. It's necessary, master. We're badly in need of prayer. I entreated my master al-Husayn to give you back your health so you can go and come as you wish. And I also prayed for Aisha and the others."

She got a chair and sat down. Then she asked, "Have you taken your medicine, master? I told Umm Hanafi . . ."

"I wish you had told her to do something nicer for me than that."

"It's for your good health, master. At the mosque I heard a beautiful talk by Shaykh Abd al-Rahman. Master, he spoke about atonement for sin and how misdeeds can be wiped away. His words were very beautiful, master. I wish I could remember as well as I once did."

"Your face is pale from your walk. It's just a matter of time before you become one of the doctor's regular patients."

"Lord protect us! I only go out to visit the tombs of members of the Prophet's family. So how could any harm befall me?" Then she added, "Oh, master, I almost forgot. They're talking about the war everywhere. They say that Hitler has attacked."

The man asked with interest, "Are you certain?"

"I heard it not once but a hundred times. 'Hitler attacked. . . . Hitler attacked.'"

To make her think she was not telling him anything he did not already know, the man observed, "People have been expecting this from one moment to the next."

"God willing, it won't affect us, will it, master?"

"Did they say only Hitler and not Mussolini? Didn't you hear that other name too?"

"Just Hitler's name."

"Will it affect us?" he asked himself. "Who knows?"

"May our Lord be gracious to us," he said. "If you hear someone selling a special edition of *al-Balagh* or *al-Muqattam* newspapers, buy one."

"It's like the days of Kaiser Wilhelm and the zeppelin. Do you remember, master? Glory to God the everlasting."

143

AS KHADIJA later observed, it was a "momentous" family reunion. When the door of her apartment opened, Yasin, wearing a white linen suit with a red rose in the lapel and brandishing an ivory handled fly whisk, filled the aperture. His huge body almost created a draft of air as he advanced, followed by his son, Ridwan, who had on a silk suit of exemplary elegance and beauty. Then came Zanuba in a gray dress, radiating the modest decorum that had become an inseparable part of her. Finally there was Karima in an exquisite short-sleeved blue dress that revealed the uppermost part of her chest. Although she was only thirteen, her virginal femininity had blossomed and she seemed outrageously attractive. In the parlor they were received by Khadija, Ibrahim, Abd al-Muni'm, and Ahmad.

Yasin wasted no time in asking, "Have you ever heard anything like this? My son is secretary to the chief of the ministry where I'm employed as a section head in the records office. The very earth rises to greet him when he passes, while people are barely aware of my existence."

Although his words were couched in the language of protest, his proud satisfaction with his son was obvious to everyone. After receiving his degree in May, Ridwan had been appointed a secretary to the cabinet minister in June, starting out in the civil service at the sixth level, when most college graduates joined at the eighth as clerks. Abd al-Muni'm, who had received his degree at the same time, still did not know what the future held in store for him.

Feeling a bit jealous, Khadija smiled and said, "Ridwan is a friend of the men in power, but children are only as good as their parents."

With a delight he did not succeed in concealing, Yasin asked, "Didn't you see the photograph of him and the minister in *al-Ahram* yesterday? It's gotten so we don't know how to address him."

Pointing to Abd al-Muni'm and Ahmad, Ibrahim Shawkat said, "These boys are a disappointment. They waste their lives in bitter but meaningless debates, and their best contacts are Shaykh Ali al-Manufi, who runs the al-Husayn Primary School, and that scum of the earth Adli Karim, publisher of a journal called *Light* or *Smut* or who knows what."

Even though he tried to appear calm, Ahmad was infuriated. His uncle Yasin's conceit upset him as much as his father's slighting remarks. Abd al-Muni'm's anger, which under different circumstances might easily have flared up, was dampened by the expectations this family visit had aroused. Glancing surreptitiously at Ridwan's face, he wondered what his cousin was thinking. His heart felt that this visit was an auspicious one, for his relatives would probably not have come unless they were bearing good news.

Responding to Ibrahim's comments, Yasin remarked, "If you ask my opinion, I think you have fine sons. Isn't there a proverb that says, 'The sultan is the one person you don't find waiting by the sultan's door.'"

Yasin's attempt to hide his delight was a complete failure, and he convinced no one that he actually believed what he was saying. All the same, pointing to Ridwan, Khadija remarked, "May our Lord grant him any good that comes to them and spare him whatever misfortunes they experience."

At last, Ridwan turned to Abd al-Muni'm and said, "I hope to be able to offer you my congratulations soon. . . ."

Blushing, Abd al-Muni'm looked inquisitively at his cousin. Ridwan added, "The minister promised to give you an appointment in the Bureau of Investigations."

The members of Khadija's family were impatient to hear all the details and fixed their eyes on Ridwan in hopes of discovering further substantiating signs. The young man continued: "Most probably at the beginning of next month."

Expanding on his son's words, Yasin said, "It's a judicial position. In our records office two young men with university degrees have been appointed to clerical jobs at the eighth level with salaries of only eight pounds a month."

It was Khadija who had asked Yasin to talk to his son about Abd al-Muni'm. So she said gratefully, "Our thanks to God and to you, brother." Turning to Ridwan, she added, "And it goes without saying that we are very appreciative of the favor Ridwan has done us."

Ibrahim added his own thanks to hers, saying, "Absolutely! Ridwan is Abd al-Muni'm's brother and a fine one too."

To remind them of her presence, the smiling Zanuba remarked, "Ridwan and Abd al-Muni'm truly are brothers. There's no question about that."

Abd al-Muni'm, who for the first time felt bashful in Ridwan's presence, asked, "Was he serious about it?"

Yasin answered importantly, "The minister's word! I'm following up on it."

Ridwan said, "I'll take care of any problems that might arise in the personnel office. I have many friends there, even though it's said that employees of the personnel office don't have a friend in the world."

Ibrahim Shawkat sighed and observed, "Praise God who spared us from embarking on a career and from dealing with personnel officers."

Yasin said, "You live like a king, as is only right for a person named after God's friend, the prophet Abraham."

But Khadija retorted scornfully, "May our Lord never decree that a man should stay home."

Zanuba, as usual, intervened with a pleasant word: "To be forced to stay home is a curse, but a man with a private income has a sultan's life."

A mischievous gleam in his eyes, Ahmad said, "Uncle Yasin has a private income and a civil service position too."

Yasin laughed out loud and replied, "I have a civil service post and that's all, if you please. My private income! That's over and done with. How can anyone with a family like mine hold on to his fortune?"

Khadija cried out in dismay, "Your family!"

To end this conversation, which was beginning to get on his nerves, Ridwan turned to Ahmad and said, "God willing, you'll find us ready to serve you next year when you get your degree."

Ahmad answered, "Thank you very much, but I'm not entering government service."

"How so?"

"A civil service job would kill a person like me. My future lies outside the government."

Khadija wanted to remonstrate with her son but chose to postpone the argument to another time. Smiling, Ridwan said, "If you change your mind, you'll find me at your service."

To show his gratitude, Ahmad raised his hand to his head. Then the maid brought in glasses of cold lemonade. During the moment of silence as they began to sip their drinks, Khadija happened to glance at Karima. She seemed to be noticing the girl for the first time since reassuring herself about Abd al-Muni'm. She asked her niece tenderly, "How are you, Karima?"

In a melodious voice the girl replied, "Fine, thanks, Auntie."

Khadija was about to extol her niece's beauty, but caution restrained her. This was not the first time Zanuba had brought her daughter to visit them since the girl had been staying home after finishing her elementary certificate. Khadija told herself that there was something suspicious about it. Karima was Zanuba's daughter, but Yasin was her father. That fact made the matter a delicate one.

Abd al-Muni'm was too engrossed with his future position to give Karima the attention she deserved, although he was well acquainted with her. Moreover, he had not yet recovered from the death of his wife. And there was no space left in Ahmad's heart.

Yasin said, "Karima's still sorry she didn't go to secondary school."

Frowning, Zanuba said, "I'm even sorrier than she is."

Ibrahim Shawkat commented, "The effect the exertion of studying has on girls concerns me. Besides, a girl is going to end up at home. It's only a year or two before Karima will be married off to some lucky fellow."

"You should have your tongue cut out," Khadija observed silently. "He brings up dangerous topics without paying any attention to the consequences. What a situation! Karima is Yasin's daughter and sister to Ridwan, who has done us this important favor. Perhaps there are no grounds for this anxiety, and I'm just imagining things. But why does Zanuba visit us so often, bringing Karima along with her? Yasin's too busy to think up plots, but that woman was raised in a troupe of performers. . . ."

Zanuba responded, "That's what people used to say. But now all girls go to school."

Khadija said, "In our district there are two girls who are studying for advanced degrees, but God knows they are no beauties."

Yasin asked Ahmad, "Aren't some of the girls in your department beautiful?"

Ahmad's heart pounded as the image nestling in his heart appeared before his mind's eye. He answered, "The love of learning is not restricted to ugly girls."

Looking toward her father with a smile, Karima said, "It's all a question of who a girl's father is."

Yasin laughed and said, "Bravo, daughter! That's how a good girl talks about her father. That's how your aunt used to speak to your grandfather."

Khadija said sarcastically, "It really does make a difference who your father is."

Zanuba quickly replied, "Don't blame the girl. Oh, if you could hear the way he talks to his children. . . ."

Khadija said, "I know."

Yasin commented, "I'm a man with his own ideas about child rearing. I'm their father and their friend. I wouldn't want any of my children to tremble from fear when they're with me. Even now I'm ill at ease in my father's presence."

Ibrahim Shawkat said, "May God strengthen him and console him for having to stay home. Al-Sayyid Ahmad is a generation all by himself. There's not another man like him."

Khadija said critically, "Tell him!"

As if to apologize for not being like his father, Yasin agreed, "My father is an entire generation all by himself. Alas, he and his friends are now confined to their homes – men for whom the whole world wasn't big enough."

Ridwan said in an aside to Ahmad, "With the entry of Italy into the war, Egypt's situation has become extremely grave."

"Perhaps these mock air raids will turn into real ones."

"But are the English strong enough to turn back the expected Italian advance? No doubt Hitler will leave the task of taking the Suez Canal to Mussolini."

Abd al-Muni'm asked, "Will America just stand by and watch?"

"Russia holds the true key to the situation."

"But she's allied with Hitler."

"Communism is the enemy of the Nazis, and the evil threatening the world from a German victory is greater than that from a victory by the democracies."

"They have darkened the world," Khadija complained. "May

God darken their lives. What are all these things we never knew before? Air-raid sirens! Anti-aircraft guns! Searchlights! These calamities could turn a man's hair white before his time."

With mild sarcasm, Ibrahim retorted, "At any rate, in our family nobody goes gray prematurely."

"That's only true of you."

Ibrahim was sixty-five now, but compared to al-Sayyid Ahmad, who was only three years his senior, he seemed decades younger.

When the visit was ending, Ridwan instructed Abd al-Muni'm: "Come see me at the ministry."

Once the door was closed behind the departing guests, Ahmad told Abd al-Muni'm, "Be careful not to barge in on him un-announced. Find out how to behave when visiting a minister's secretary."

His brother did not reply or even look his way.

144

AHMAD HAD little trouble finding the villa of his sociology professor, Mr. Forster, in the Cairo suburb of al-Ma'adi. On entering, he realized that he was a bit late and that many of the other students had already arrived for this party, which the professor was giving before he returned to England. Ahmad was welcomed by the host and his wife, and the professor introduced Ahmad to her as one of the best students in the department. Then the young man joined the others, who were sitting on the veranda. All levels of the sociology program were represented. As one of the small group promoted to the final year, Ahmad shared with those peers a sense of excellence and of achievement. None of the women students had appeared yet, but he was confident that they would come or at least that his "friend" would, since she also lived in al-Ma'adi. Glancing at the garden, he saw a long table set on a grassy lawn, which was bordered on two sides by willow and palm trees. Lined up on the table were teapots, containers of milk, and platters of sweet confections and pastries.

He heard a student ask, "Shall we observe British manners or swoop down on the table like vultures?"

Another replied rather sadly, "Oh, if only 'Lady' Forster weren't present."

It was late afternoon, but the weather was pleasant, June's reputation for sultriness notwithstanding. In no time at all the eagerly awaited flock was at the door. As if by design, the only four women students in the department all came together. Wearing a fitted pure-white dress that seemed one with the rest of her charming person – except for her coal-black hair – Alawiya Sabri came into view, striding jauntily forward. At that moment Ahmad, whose secret had long since gotten out, felt a teasing foot rub against his to alert him to her presence, as if there were any need for that. He kept his eyes on the women until they found seats on the veranda in a corner that had been vacated for them.

Mr. Forster and his wife appeared, and, pointing to the girls, Mrs. Forster asked, "Would you like to be introduced?"

Their response was resounding laughter. Extraordinarily lively although nearly fifty, the professor said, "It would be far better if you'd introduce them to me."

The guests laughed noisily once more, and Mr. Forster continued: "At about this time each year we leave Egypt for a holiday in England, but this year we don't know whether we'll see Egypt again or not. . . ."

His wife interrupted: "We don't even know if we'll manage to see England!"

They realized that she was referring to the danger posed to shipping by submarines, and more than one voice called out, "Good luck, ma'am."

The host added, "I'll carry away with me beautiful memories of our life at the Faculty of Arts and of this tranquil and lovely area of al-Ma'adi. I'll always remember you fondly, even your tomfoolery."

To be polite, Ahmad replied, "The memory of you will stay with us forever and will continue to develop as our intellects do."

"Thank you." Then, smiling, the professor told his wife, "Ahmad is an academic at heart, even though he has ideas of a kind that often cause trouble in this country."

One of Ahmad's fellow students explained, "That means he's a Communist."

The smiling hostess raised her eyebrows, and Mr. Forster commented in a tone that conveyed more than his words themselves, "I'm not the one who said that. Your comrade did." Then, standing up, he announced, "It's time for tea. We mustn't let the moment slip away from us. Later there will be an opportunity for conversation and entertainment."

The tea party was catered by Groppi's, a famous Cairo establishment, and its waiters stood nearby, ready to serve the guests. "Lady" Forster sat between the girls on one side, and the professor was at the center on the other. To explain the seating arrangement, he said, "We would have liked to mix you up more but decided to respect Eastern etiquette. Isn't that right?"

Without any hesitation, one of the male students answered, "This, unfortunately, is what we've noticed, sir."

A servant poured tea and milk, and the feast began. Ahmad

observed furtively that Alawiya Sabri was the most proficient of the girls in Western table manners and the most relaxed. She seemed accustomed to social life and as much at ease as if in her own home. Watching her eat pastries was even sweeter than eating them himself. She was his dear friend who reciprocated his friendship without encouraging him to cross its boundaries.

He told himself, "If I don't seize the opportunity that today offers, I may as well give up."

Mrs. Forster raised her voice to advise them, "I hope you won't let the thought of war rationing make you shy about eating the pastries."

A student commented, "It's a lucky break that the authorities haven't restricted tea yet."

Mr. Forster leaned over toward Ahmad, who was sitting to his left, and inquired, "How do you spend your holidays? I mean, what do you read?"

"A lot of economics and a little politics. I write some articles for magazines too."

"I'd advise you to go on for a master's degree when you finish this one."

After chewing what was in his mouth, Ahmad replied, "Perhaps later on, but I'll start out working as a journalist. That's been my plan for years."

"Excellent!"

His dear friend was conversing easily with Mrs. Forster. How quickly she had perfected her English! The roses and other blooms were as saturated with red and their other colors as his heart was with love. In a world that was truly free, love would blossom like a flower. Only in a Communist country could love be a totally natural emotion.

Mr. Forster said, "I'm sad I won't be able to continue my study of Arabic. I would like to read Majnun's poems in praise of Layla without having to rely on one of you."

"It's a pity that you won't be able to study it anymore."

"Unless circumstances permit, later on."

"You may find yourself obliged to learn German," Ahmad reflected. "Wouldn't it be amusing if London were the scene of demonstrations calling for the evacuation of foreign forces and you took part in them? The seductive charm of the English can be attributed to their manners, but that of my dear friend is unique.

The sun will soon set, and night will find us together in an isolated spot for the first time. If I don't seize this opportunity, I may as well give up."

He asked his professor, "What will you be doing once you return to London?"

"I've been invited to work in broadcasting."

"Then we won't be deprived of hearing your voice."

"A polite statement," Ahmad told himself, "is excusable at a party ornamented by my friend, but we only listen to the German broadcasts. Our people love the Germans, if only because they hate the English. Colonialism is the final stage of capitalism. The situation created by our professor's party merits some thought. Although we justify it in the spirit of intellectual inquiry, there is a conflict between our love for this professor and our loathing for his nationality. Hopefully the war will polish off both the Nazi movement and colonialism. Then I can concentrate entirely on love."

They returned to their seats on the veranda, where the lamps had been lit. "Lady" Forster said at once, "Here's the piano. Won't someone play for us?"

A student entreated her, "Won't you please perform for us?"

She rose with the graceful agility of youth, which was many years behind her, and sat down at the piano. Opening some sheet music, she started to play. None of them had any particular familiarity with Western music or a taste for it, but wishing to be polite and courteous, they listened attentively. From his love, Ahmad attempted to extract a magical power to unlock the obscure passages of the music. But he forgot all about the song when he glanced stealthily at the girl's face. Their eyes met once, and they exchanged a smile seen by many of the others.

In an intoxicated delight, he told himself, "Yes, if I don't seize my opportunity today, I may as well give up."

When "Lady" Forster had finished, one of the students played an Eastern tune. Then they conversed for quite a long time. At about eight o'clock, the students said goodbye to their professor and set off. On this night, which seemed remarkably beautiful and compassionate, Ahmad lingered under the canopy of towering trees at a bend in the road until he saw her approach on her way home alone. Then he popped out in front of her.

She stopped in astonishment and asked, "Didn't you go off with the others?"

Exhaling as if to relieve his breast of its turmoil, he replied calmly, "I let the caravan go on ahead so I could meet you."

"What do you suppose they'll think?"

He answered scornfully, "That's their problem."

She walked slowly forward, and he kept pace with her. Then his long days of patience bore fruit as he said, "Before I leave you I want to ask if you will allow me to request your hand in marriage."

Her beautiful head shot up in reaction to this surprise, but no sound escaped her, as if she could not think of anything to say. The street was empty and the streetlights were dim from the blue paint applied as a precaution for air raids. He asked her again, "Will you give me permission?"

In a faint voice with a hint of censure to it she said, "This is the way you talk, but what an approach. . . . The fact is that you've stunned me."

He laughed gently and then said, "I apologize for that, although I would have thought the long history of our friendship would have prevented my words from coming as a startling surprise."

"You mean our friendship and our academic collaboration?"

He was not comfortable with her choice of words but said, "I mean my obvious affection that has taken the form of 'friendship and academic collaboration,' as you put it."

In a jolly but shaky voice she inquired, "Your affection?"

With stubborn sincerity he replied, "I mean my love, my un-concealed love. Usually we do not announce it merely to proclaim it but to rejoice at hearing it proclaimed."

To string him along until she could regain her composure, she said, "The whole thing comes as a surprise to me."

"I'm sad to hear this."

"Why? The truth is that I don't know what to say. . . ."

Laughing, he responded, "Say, 'You have my permission.' Then leave the rest to me."

"But, but . . . I don't know anything about . . . No offense, we really have been friends, yet you've never spoken of . . . I mean there has never been an occasion for you to tell me about your-self."

"Don't you know me?"

"Of course I know you, but there are other things one has to know."

"You mean the traditional things? Those questions are best suited to a heart that has never been a prisoner of love." He felt annoyed but this only made him more obstinate. He continued: "Everything will become clear at the proper time."

Regaining control of herself, she asked, "Isn't this the proper time?"

He smiled wanly and replied, "You're right. Are you referring to the future?"

"Naturally."

This "naturally" exasperated him. He had hoped to hear a song and instead had been subjected to the drone of a lecture, but no matter what happened it was important for him to retain his self-confidence. The icy darling did not know how happy it would make him to make her happy.

"Once I graduate, I'll get a job." Then after a few moments of silence he added, "And one day I'll have a substantial private income."

She stammered in embarrassment, "That's not very specific."

Trying to mask his pain with a calm exterior, he replied, "The salary will be in the normal range, and the income will be around ten pounds."

Silence reigned. Perhaps she was weighing matters and thinking them over. This was the way a materialist would understand love. He had dreamt of a sweet intoxication but had not achieved anything close to that. It was amazing that in this country where people allowed emotion to guide their politics they approached love with the precision of accountants.

At last the delicate voice replied, "Let's leave aside the private income, for it's not nice to plan your life around the death of loved ones."

"I wanted to let you know that my father is a man of property."

With a burst of energy to make up for the vacillation preceding it, she said, "We need to be realistic."

"I told you I'd find work. And you'll get a job too."

She laughed in an odd way and replied, "Certainly not. I won't work. Unlike the other women students, I haven't enrolled in the University to obtain a government position."

"There's nothing wrong in having a job."

"Naturally. But my father . . . The fact is that we're all agreed on this. I won't work."

As his emotions cooled down, he became pensive. He commented, "So be it. I'll work."

In a voice that she seemed deliberately to be making more tender than usual she said, "Mr. Ahmad, let's postpone this discussion. Give me time to think it over."

He laughed dispiritedly and responded, "We have looked at the question from every angle. Don't you really need more time to draft your rejection?"

She said bashfully, "I must talk to my father."

"That goes without saying. But it should have been possible for us to reach an understanding first."

"I need some time, even if it's not very long."

"It's June now, and you'll be going off to your summer resort. We won't meet again until next October at school."

She insisted, "I must have time to think about it and to consult my family."

"You just don't want to commit yourself."

Then she suddenly stopped walking and remarked with determined resolve, "Mr. Ahmad, you're trying to force me to speak. I hope you'll take my words the right way. I've thought about marriage frequently, not with regard to you but in general terms. I've concluded – and my father agrees with me – that my life won't be successful and that I won't be able to maintain my standard of living unless I have no less than fifty pounds a month."

He swallowed this disappointment, which hurt more than he could ever have expected, even allowing for the worst possible outcome. He asked, "Does any working man, I mean one of an age to marry, make a salary that vast?" When she did not respond, he declared, "You want a rich husband!"

"I'm very sorry, but you have forced me to be blunt."

He answered gruffly, "That's better, at any rate."

"Sorry," she murmured.

Although furious, he made a sincere effort to stay within the bounds of polite behavior. Feeling an overwhelming desire to be blunt with her, he asked, "Would you allow me to give you my frank opinion?"

She shot back, "Certainly not! I know many of your ideas. I hope that we can stay friends."

In spite of his anger, he pitied her condition, an inevitable one for a life that had not been transformed by love. A lady who eloped with one of her servants acted naturally but by traditional standards was judged a deviant. In an imperfect society, a healthy man seems sick and the sick one healthy. He was angry, but his unhappiness was greater than his anger. At any rate she would guess what he thought of her, and there was some consolation in that. When she stretched out her hand to take leave of him, his hand took hers and kept hold of it until he had said, "You claimed you didn't enroll in the University to obtain a job. That's a lovely notion in and of itself. But how have you benefited from the University?"

She raised her chin inquisitively. In a slightly sarcastic tone he concluded, "Forgive my foolish behavior. Perhaps the problem is that you haven't fallen in love yet. Goodbye."

He turned on his heels and walked away rapidly.

145

ISMA'IL LATIF SAID, "Perhaps bringing my wife to Cairo to have the baby was a mistake. The air-raid siren goes off every night. In Tanta we know almost none of the terrors of this war."

Kamal replied, "These are just symbolic raids. If they really wanted to harm us, no force would be able to stop them."

This was the second meeting for Riyad Qaldas and Isma'il Latif after their introduction the year before. Riyad laughed and told Isma'il, "You're talking to a man who doesn't know what it means to be responsible for a spouse."

Isma'il asked Riyad sarcastically, "And do you know what it's like?"

"I am a bachelor too, but at least I'm not a foe of matrimony."

They were walking along Fuad I Street early one evening. The darkness was relieved only by the meager amount of light escaping from the doors of commercial establishments. Even so, the street was crowded with Egyptians and British soldiers from different parts of the Empire. There was the damp breath of autumn in the air, but people were still wearing summer clothes.

Riyad Qaldas saw some Indian soldiers and commented, "It's sad that a man should be transported such a long distance from his homeland to kill for someone else's sake."

Isma'il Latif mused, "I wonder how these wretches can laugh."

Kamal answered resentfully, "The same way we can – in our bizarre world that reeks of liquor, drugs, and despair."

Riyad Qaldas chuckled and observed, "You're going through a unique crisis. Your whole world is coming apart at the seams. It appears to consist of nothing but a vain grasping at the wind, a painful debate between life's secrets and the soul, ennui, and ill health. I pity you."

Isma'il Latif advised Kamal with great directness, "Get married. I felt the same kind of ennui before I married."

Riyad Qaldas exclaimed, "Tell him!"

As though to himself, Kamal remarked, "Marriage is the ultimate surrender in life's losing battle."

"Isma'il was mistaken in thinking our situations comparable," Kamal mused. "He's a well-behaved animal. But not so fast. . . . Perhaps you're just conceited, and what's there to be conceited about when you're resting on a dunghill of disappointment and failure? Isma'il knows nothing of the world of thought, only the happiness a man derives from his work, spouse, and children. But isn't happiness right to mock your disdain for it?"

Riyad commented, "If I eventually decide to write a novel, you'll be one of the main characters."

Kamal turned toward him with boyish excitement and asked, "What will you make of me?"

"I don't know, but try not to get angry. Many of the readers who find themselves in my stories become irate."

"Why?"

"Perhaps because each of us has an idea he has created of himself. When a writer strips us of that self-image, we object angrily."

Kamal inquired anxiously, "Are you holding back some secret opinions about me?"

His friend immediately reassured him: "Certainly not. But a writer may begin with someone he knows and then forget all of that person's characteristics in creating a new specimen of humanity. The only relationship between the two may be that the first inspired the second. You seem to be an Easterner teetering uncertainly between East and West. He goes round and round until he's dizzy."

"He speaks of East and West," Kamal thought. "But how could he know about Aïda? It may well be that misery has many faces."

Isma'il Latif said as bluntly as before, "All your life, you've made problems for yourself. In my opinion, books are the source of your misfortunes. Why don't you try living a normal life?"

They reached the corner of Imad al-Din Street and, on turning down it, almost ran into a large group of British nationals. Isma'il Latif said, "To hell with them! Why do they look so optimistic? Do you suppose they actually believe their own propaganda?"

"It seems to me," Kamal observed, "that the outcome of the war has already been determined. It will be over by next spring."

Riyad Qaldas said resentfully, "The Nazi movement is reactionary and inhumane. The world's suffering will increase dramatically under their iron rule."

Isma'il replied, "Be that as it may, what's important is to see the English subjugated in the same manner that they subjugated so many of the weaker areas of the world."

Kamal commented, "The Germans are no better than the English."

Riyad Qaldas said, "We have learned to live with the English, and British imperialism is well into its dotage. It is tempered, perhaps, by some humane principles. With the Germans tomorrow, we'll have to deal with a youthful, greedy, conceited, wealthy, and bellicose imperialism. What will we do then?"

Kamal laughed in a way that suggested a change of mood and suggested, "Let's have a couple of drinks and dream of a united world ruled by a single just government."

"We'll definitely need more than two drinks for that."

They found themselves in front of a new bar they had never seen before. It was probably one of those infernal establishments that spring up overnight during a war. Glancing inside, Kamal noticed the proprietor was a woman with a fair complexion and a voluptuous Eastern body. Then his feet froze to the pavement. He was unable to move, and his companions had to stop to see what he was looking at.

"Maryam!" Kamal whispered to himself. "It's Maryam, no one but Maryam. Maryam, Yasin's second wife. Maryam, the lifelong neighbor. Here, in this bar, after a long disappearance. Maryam, who was thought to have gone to join her late mother. . . ."

"Do you want to go in here? Let's do. There are only four soldiers inside."

He hesitated, but his courage was not adequate for the occasion. When he had recovered from his astonishment, he said, "Absolutely not."

He cast a parting glance at the Maryam who reminded him now of her mother toward the end of that woman's life, and they proceeded on their way. When had he last seen her? It had not been for at least thirteen or fourteen years. She was a landmark of his past, and he would never forget her. His past, his history, and his essence – they were all a single entity. She had received him in the apartment in Palace of Desire Alley one last time before Yasin divorced her. He could still remember how she had complained about his brother's deviant behavior and reversion to a life of shameless wantonness. On that occasion he had not foreseen the consequences this complaint would have, for it had landed her in this hellish tavern. She had once been the darling daughter of Mr. Muhammad Ridwan and Kamal's friend, as well as a source of inspiration for boyish dreams. His old house had then appeared to be a setting that overflowed with tranquillity and delight. Maryam and Aisha had been roses, but time is an indefatigable enemy of flowers. He could easily have bumped into her at one of these brothels, just as he had first encountered Madam Jalila. If that had happened, he would have found himself in an indescribable quandary. Maryam, who had begun her flirtations with the English, had ended up with them.

"Do you know this woman?"

"Yes."

"How?"

"She's one of those women . . . Perhaps she's forgotten me."

"Oh, the bars are full of them: old whores, rebellious servants, every kind of woman."

"Yes. . . ."

"Why didn't you go in? She might have welcomed us warmly for your sake."

"She's no longer young, and we have better places."

He had grown old without noticing it. He was halfway into his fourth decade. He seemed to have squandered his share of happiness. When he compared his current misery to that of the past, he did not know which was worse. But what importance did life have, since he was fed up with living? Death truly was the most pleasurable part of life. But what was this sound?

"Air raid!"

"Where shall we go?"

"To the shelter at the Rex Café."

Since there was no place to sit in the shelter, they remained standing in the crowd of Egyptian gentlemen, foreigners, women, and children. People were speaking a number of different languages and dialects. Outside men from the civil defense forces shouted, "Turn off your lights!" Riyad's face looked pale. He hated the ringing sound of the anti-aircraft guns.

Kamal teased him, "You may not get a chance to play with my character in your novel."

Laughing nervously as he gestured toward the other people, Riyad answered, "There's a representative sample of humanity in this shelter."

Kamal observed sarcastically, "If only they would band together in good times the way they do when they're frightened. . . ."

Isma'il cried out nervously, "Right now my wife must be groping her way down the stairs in the dark. I'm thinking seriously of returning to Tanta tomorrow."

"If we live that long."

"The people of London are really to be pitied."

"But they're the source of all the trouble."

Riyad Qaldas's face grew even paler, but he tried to hide his discomfort by asking Kamal, "I once heard you inquire the way to death's station, so that you could disembark from life's boring train. Will it really seem so trivial to you now if a bomb blasts us to bits?"

Kamal smiled. He was listening with increasing anxiety, for he expected, from one moment to the next, to hear the anti-aircraft guns fire with a deafening sound. He answered, "Of course not." Then he continued in a questioning tone: "Perhaps from fear of pain?"

"Is there still some obscure hope for life stirring within you?"

Why did he not kill himself? Why did his life wear a façade of enthusiasm and faith? For a long time his soul had been torn between the two extremes of hedonism and asceticism. He would not have been able to bear a life devoted entirely to the tranquil satisfaction of his desires. Inside him there was also something that made him shy away from the notion of a passive escape from life. Whatever that thing was, perhaps it was what kept him from killing himself. At the same time, the fact that he clung to the agitated rope of life with both hands contravened his lethal skepticism. The resulting condition was a tormented anxiety.

Suddenly the anti-aircraft guns burst forth with a continuous volley that scarcely left the chest time to breathe. People did not know what they were seeing or saying. Yet, by the clock, the shooting lasted only two minutes. Afterward everyone awaited the odious return of the frightful noise.

Terror gripped their souls, and there was a heavy silence. Isma'il Latif asked, "When do you suppose the raid will be over? I can imagine all too well the state my wife is in now."

Riyad Qaldas asked, "When will the war end?"

Shortly thereafter the all-clear siren sounded, and the shelter's denizens voiced a profound sigh of relief. Kamal said, "The Italians were just teasing us."

They left the shelter in the dark, like bats, as doors emitted one ghostly figure after another. Then a faint glimmer of light could be seen coming from windows, and the world resumed its normal commotion.

In this brief moment of darkness, life had reminded careless people of its incomparable value.

146

OVER THE course of time, the old house assumed a new look of decay and decline. Its routine disintegrated, and most of the coffee-hour crowd was dispersed. These two features had been the household's soul and lifeblood. During the first half of the day, when Kamal was away at his school, Amina was off on her spiritual tour of the mosques of the Prophet's grandchildren al-Husayn and al-Sayyida Zaynab, and Umm Hanafi was down in the oven room, al-Sayyid Ahmad would stretch out on the sofa in his room or sit in a chair on the balcony while Aisha wandered aimlessly between the roof terrace and her bedroom. The radio's voice was the only one heard in the sitting room until late in the afternoon, when Amina and Umm Hanafi met there. Aisha would either stay in her room or spend part of the coffee hour with them. Al-Sayyid Ahmad did not leave his room, and even if Kamal returned home early, he retreated to his study on the top floor. At first, the confinement of al-Sayyid Ahmad had been a source of unhappiness, but then he and the others had become accustomed to it. Aisha's grief had been most distressing, but eventually she and the others had grown used to it too.

Amina was still the first to wake. After rousing Umm Hanafi, she performed her ablutions and her prayers. The maid, who was by and large the healthiest of them all, headed on rising for the oven room.

Opening heavy eyes, Aisha would get up to drink successive glasses of coffee and to light one cigarette after another. When summoned to breakfast, she would take only a few morsels. She had allowed her body to waste away to a skeleton covered with a faded skin. Her hair had started to fall out, and she had been forced to consult a doctor to avoid going bald. She had fallen victim to so many ills that the physician had advised having her teeth removed. All that remained of the old Aisha was her name and the habit of looking at her reflection in the mirror, although not to adorn herself. It was simply a custom allowing her to scrutinize her

sorrows. Occasionally she seemed to have resigned herself gracefully to her losses, as she sat for longer periods with her mother,
took part in the conversation, allowed her withered lips to part in a
smile, visited her father to ask after his health, or strolled around
the roof garden, tossing grain to the chickens.

On one such occasion her mother said hopefully, "It does my
heart good, Aisha, to see you like this. I wish you were always so
cheerful."

Drying her eyes, Umm Hanafi said, "Let's go to the oven room
and make something special."

But at midnight the mother awoke to the sound of weeping
from Aisha's room. She rushed to her daughter, taking care not to
wake al-Sayyid Ahmad, and found Aisha sitting up and sobbing in
the darkness. Sensing her mother's presence, Aisha grabbed hold
of Amina and cried out, "If only I had the baby from her belly as a
reminder of her . . . a bit of her! My hands have nothing to hold.
The world is empty."

Embracing Aisha, the mother said, "I know more about your
sorrows than anyone else. They are so great that any attempt at
consolation is meaningless. I would gladly have given my life for
theirs. But God's wisdom is lofty and exalted. What point is there
to this sorrow, my poor dear?"

"Whenever I fall asleep, I dream of them or of my life in the old
days."

"Proclaim that God is one. I've had my own taste of suffering
like yours. Have you forgotten Fahmy? Even so, an afflicted
Believer asks God for strength. What has happened to your faith?"

Aisha exclaimed resentfully, "My faith!"

"Yes, remember your religion and entreat God for merciful
relief, which may come from some totally unexpected source."

"Merciful relief! Where is it? Where?"

"His mercy is so vast it encompasses everything. For my sake,
visit al-Husayn with me. Put your hand on the tomb and recite the
opening prayer of the Qur'an. Then your fiery suffering will be
changed into a refreshing peace just as Abraham's fire was"
(Qur'an, 21:69).

Aisha's attitude toward her health was equally mercurial. She
would visit doctors diligently and regularly for a time, leading
people to think that she had regained her interest in life. Then she
would neglect herself and scornfully disregard everyone's advice in

a virtually suicidal fashion. Visiting the cemetery was the only custom from which she never once deviated. With happy abandon she spent the income from her husband's and her daughter's bequests on the grave site, transforming it into a lush garden of flowers and fragrant herbs. The day Ibrahim Shawkat came to complete the formalities of the bequest, she had laughed hysterically, telling her mother, "Congratulate me on my inheritance from Na'ima."

Whenever he sensed that she was calm, Kamal would visit her and stay for lengthy periods, humoring her affectionately. He would gaze at her silently for a long time, sadly remembering the exquisite form God had bestowed upon her and examining what had become of it. She was emaciated and sickly, to be sure, but also heartbroken in every sense of the word. The striking similarity between their misfortunes did not escape him. She had lost her offspring, and he had lost his hopes. If she had ended up with nothing, so had he. All the same, her children had been flesh and blood, and his hopes had been deceptive fictions of the imagination.

One day he suggested to them, "Wouldn't it be better if you all went to the air-raid shelter when the siren goes off?"

Aisha replied, "I won't leave my room."

His mother said, "These raids don't harm anyone, and the guns sound like fireworks."

His father called out from the bedroom, "If I were able to go to the shelter, I would go to the mosque or to Muhammad Iffat's house instead."

On another occasion, Aisha rushed down from the roof, all out of breath, to tell her mother, "Something amazing has happened!"

Amina looked at her with hopeful curiosity, and Aisha, who was still panting, explained, "I was on the roof, watching the sun go down. I felt more wretched than ever before. All of a sudden a window of glorious light opened up in the sky. At the top of my lungs I shouted, 'O Lord!'"

The mother's eyes grew wide in amazement. Was this the desired merciful relief or a new abyss of sorrows? She murmured, "Perhaps it's our Lord's mercy, daughter."

Her face radiant with joy, Aisha said, "Yes. I shouted, 'O Lord!' and light filled the whole world."

They all brooded about this event and, with obvious anxiety, kept careful track of developments. Aisha stood for hours at her post on the roof, waiting for the light to break through again. Kamal finally asked himself, "I wonder if this is a finale compared to which death would seem trivial." But fortunately for all of them, she appeared to forget the matter in time and stopped mentioning it. Then she became ever more deeply involved with a private universe of her own creation. She lived there by herself, a solitary figure, whether in her room or sitting beside them, although at infrequent intervals she would come back to their world, as if returning from a voyage. Shortly thereafter she would resume her imaginary travels. She developed a new habit of speaking to herself, especially when no one else was present. This made her family quite nervous, but when she spoke to the dead she recognized that her loved ones had passed away. She did not think that they were present as specters or ghosts. This compromise with reality was a source of some comfort to those around her.

147

"HOW COLD it is this winter! It reminds me of the one people used as a point of reference for years after. I wonder which it was? My Lord, where is the memory for it, where? My old heart yearns for that winter – even though I can't remember the date – since it's part of the past and such memories coax my tears from their hiding places."

In those days he had awakened early, taken a cold shower even in winter, filled his belly, and then burst forth into the world of people, activity, and freedom. He knew nothing of that world today, except for the reports people gave him, and even these seemed to refer to life on the far side of the planet.

More recently, when he had been able to sit on the sofa in his room or in a chair on the balcony, confinement to the house had seemed irksome. Although he had been free to go to the bathroom when it was necessary and to change his clothes by himself he had cursed staying home. One day a week he had been permitted to leave the house – supported by his stick or riding in a carriage – on a visit to al-Husayn or to the home of a friend. Still, he had often prayed for God to deliver him from this house arrest.

Now he could not get out of bed. The boundaries of his world extended no further than the edges of his mattress. The bathroom came to him, instead of the other way around. He had never imagined such a squalid eventuality, and having to cope with this left a resentful pout on his lips and a bitter taste in his mouth. On the same mattress he stretched out during the day and slept at night. He took his meals on it and answered the calls of nature there, he who had once been proverbial for his neatness and fragrant cologne. This household, which had always yielded to his absolute authority, now looked askance at him, granting him pitying looks when he asked for something or scolding remarks fit for a child. His beloved friends had departed from life in rapid succession, as if by prior arrangement. They had gone, leaving him alone.

"God's compassion on you, Muhammad Iffat!"

Al-Sayyid Ahmad had seen him for the last time one night during Ramadan at a party held in the men's parlor overlooking the garden. After bidding Muhammad Iffat farewell, he had started off, accompanied to the door by his friend's noisy laughter. He had scarcely made it back to his room when someone had knocked on the door. Ridwan had rushed in, saying, "Grandfather has died, Grandfather."

"Glory to God . . . When? . . . And how? . . . Wasn't he laughing with us just a few minutes ago? . . . But he fell flat on his face as he headed for bed. That was how a lifelong friend disappeared. It took Ali Abd al-Rahim three whole days to die. His repeated bouts of coughing were so severe that we had no choice but to pray that God would grant him a peaceful end and relieve our friend of his pain, and thus my soul mate Ali Abd al-Rahim vanished from my world."

He had been able to say farewell to these beloved friends but not to Ibrahim al-Far. The severity of his own ailments had kept him in bed, preventing him from paying a sick call on al-Far, whose servant had eventually come to announce his master's death. Al-Sayyid Ahmad had not even been able to attend the funeral. Yasin and Kamal had paid last respects to the man for him.

"To the compassion of God, you most charming man!"

Even before them, Hamidu, al-Hamzawi, and tens of other friends and acquaintances had died, leaving him alone, as though he had never known anyone. No one visited him. No one paid him a sick call. There would not be a single friend to see him off at his funeral. He was prevented even from praying, for he could maintain the necessary state of ritual purity for only a few hours after a bath, and his guardians granted him one very infrequently. He was denied access to prayer when, plunged into oppressive solitude, he was in the greatest need of communion with God the Compassionate.

His days passed in this manner. The radio played, and he listened. Amina came and went. She was very feeble but had never developed the habit of complaining. She acted as his nurse, and what he feared most was that she would soon need someone to care for her. She was all he had left. Yasin and Kamal would sit with him for an hour and then depart. He wished they would stay with him all the time, but this was a wish he could never express and they could never grant. Only Amina never tired of him. If she went to al-Husayn, it was solely to pray for him. In every other respect, his was an empty world.

For him, the day of Khadija's visit was definitely worth the wait. She would bring Ibrahim Shawkat, Abd al-Muni'm, and Ahmad. They would fill the room with life and dispel its desolation. He would not have much to say, but they would.

Once Ibrahim had requested, "Give the master a rest from your chatter."

But al-Sayyid Ahmad had scolded him: "Let them talk.... I want to hear them!"

He prayed that his daughter would have good health and a long life and made similar invocations to God on behalf of her husband and sons. He knew that she would have liked to supervise his care herself. The affection he could see in her eyes defied description.

One day, with jovial curiosity and avid interest, he asked Yasin, "Where do you spend your evenings?"

Yasin answered bashfully, "Today the English are everywhere. It's like the old days."

"The old days!" he mused. "The days of power and strength, of laughter that shook the walls, of convivial evenings spent in al-Ghuriya and al-Gamaliya, and of people of whom nothing is left but their names. Zubayda, Jalila, and Haniya.... I wonder if you remember your mother, Yasin.... Here's Zanuba and her daughter, Karima, sitting beside Karima's father.... You'll never be able to ask for God's mercy and forgiveness often enough."

"Of the people we used to know, who is still at the ministry, Yasin?"

"They've all retired. I no longer have any news of them."

"Nor do they have any of us," he thought. "All our close friends are dead. Why should we ask about acquaintances? But how lovely Karima is! She's more beautiful than her mother in her day. And she's only fourteen. Na'ima was outstandingly beautiful too."

"Yasin, if you're able to persuade Aisha to visit you, do. Rescue her from her solitude. I'm afraid of its effect on her."

Zanuba responded, "I've asked her time and again to visit

Palace of Desire Alley, but she . . . May God come to her aid."

There was a gloomy look in the man's eyes when he asked Yasin, "Don't you ever run into Shaykh Mutawalli Abd al-Samad when you're on the street?"

Smiling, Yasin replied, "Occasionally. He hardly recognizes anyone. But he's still walking around on two sturdy feet."

"What a man! Doesn't he ever feel the urge to visit? Or has he forgotten me, just as he forgot my children's names?"

Deserted by his friends, he had befriended Kamal. This late-blooming friendship probably surprised the son, but al-Sayyid Ahmad was no longer the father he had once known. The man became a friend who shared confidences with him and who looked forward to their chats. Al-Sayyid Ahmad said of him regretfully, "A bachelor at thirty-four, he spends most of his life in his study. May God come to his aid." He no longer felt responsible for what became of his son, for from the beginning Kamal had refused to accept anyone's advice. As a result, he had ended up an unmarried teacher and an emotionally crippled recluse. Al-Sayyid Ahmad avoided annoying references to marriage or to the money that could be made from private lessons. He asked God to make his own savings last until his final breath, so that he would never be a burden on his son.

He asked Kamal once, "Do you like this age?"

Kamal smiled nervously and was slow to reply. So the father continued: "Our times were the real ones! Life was easy and pleasant. We had our health and strength. We saw Sa'd Zaghlul and heard the supreme vocalist, Abduh al-Hamuli. What do your days have to offer?"

Fascinated by the implications of the words themselves, Kamal answered, "Every age has its good and bad points."

Shaking his head, which rested against the folded pillow, the father said, "Pretty words, nothing more. . . ."

Then after a period of silence he announced without any pre-amble, "My inability to perform the prayers hurts me badly, for worship is one of the consolations of solitude. All the same I experience strange moments when I forget all deprivations of food, drink, freedom, and health. I feel such an amazing peace of mind I imagine that I'm in contact with heaven and that there is an unknown happiness compared to which our life and everything about it will seem insignificant."

Kamal murmured, "May our Lord prolong your life and restore your health."

Nodding his head meekly, al-Sayyid Ahmad said, "This has been a good hour. No pain in my chest, no difficulty with breathing . . . the swelling in my leg has started to disappear, and it's time for the listeners' request show on the radio."

Then Amina's voice asked, "Is my master well?"

"Praise God."

"Shall I bring your supper?"

"Supper? Do you call yogurt supper? Oh, bring me the bowl."

148

KAMAL REACHED his sister's home on Sugar Street at about the time for afternoon prayers and found the whole family gathered in the sitting room. He shook hands with them and said to Ahmad, "Congratulations on your degree!"

In a tone that was anything but jubilant, Khadija replied, "Thank you very much. But come hear the latest. The bey doesn't want to enter the civil service."

Ibrahim Shawkat explained, "His cousin Ridwan is ready to find a position for him, if Ahmad will agree. But he insists on refusing the offer. Talk to him, Mr. Kamal. Perhaps your opinion will sway him."

Kamal removed his fez and, because of the heat, took off his white jacket, which he draped over the back of the chair. Although he had expected a fight, he smiled and said, "I thought today would be reserved for congratulations. But this house can never stop quarreling."

Khadija said self-pityingly, "That's my fate. We're just not like other people."

Ahmad told his uncle, "The matter's quite simple. The only kind of position I could get now would be a clerical one. Ridwan informed me that he could get me appointed to a vacant secretarial post in the records office where Uncle Yasin works. He suggested that I should wait three months until the new school year begins, when I might get a job as an instructor of French in one of the schools. But I don't want a civil service position of any kind."

Khadija cried out, "Tell him what you do want."

The young man answered with straightforward determination, "I'm going to work in journalism."

Ibrahim Shawkat snorted and exclaimed, "A journalist! We used to hear him say this but thought it a harmless joke. He refuses to become a teacher like you and strives to become a journalist."

Kamal said sarcastically, "May God spare him the evil of teaching."

Alarmed, Khadija said, "Would you like to see him employed as a journalist?"

To improve the mood, Abd al-Muni'm remarked, "Government service is no longer everyone's first choice."

His mother retorted sharply, "But you're a government employee, Mr. Abd al-Muni'm."

"In an elite unit. I wouldn't want him to accept a clerical position. And here's Uncle Kamal asking God to save my brother from becoming a teacher like him."

Turning toward Ahmad, Kamal asked, "What type of journalism do you have in mind?"

"Mr. Adli Karim has agreed to accept me provisionally on the staff of his magazine. At first I'll prepare translations. Later on I'll help with the editing."

"But *The New Man* is a cultural journal with limited resources and scope."

"It's a first step. I'll get experience that will make it easier for me to get a more important job. In any case, I won't go hungry even if I have to wait."

Looking at Khadija, Kamal suggested, "Let him do what he wants. He's an educated adult and knows better than anyone else what he should do."

But Khadija would not accept defeat so easily. She kept on trying to convince her son to accept a civil service position, and their voices grew loud and acrimonious. After Kamal intervened to separate them, a heavy silence reigned, and the party's atmosphere was spoiled. Laughing, Kamal said, "I came to drink some punch and celebrate, but instead I've found a somber gathering."

Ahmad was already putting on his coat to leave the house, and, excusing himself, Kamal left with his nephew. As they walked along al-Azhar Street, Ahmad informed his uncle that he was going to the offices of *The New Man* to start work, as he had promised Mr. Adli Karim.

Kamal told him, "Do whatever you want, but avoid offending your parents."

Ahmad laughed and commented, "I love them and revere them, but . . ."

"But what?"

"It's a mistake for a man to have parents."

Laughing, Kamal asked, "How can you say that so glibly?"

"I don't mean it literally, but insofar as parents represent bygone traditions. In general, fatherhood acts as a brake. What need do we have of brakes in Egypt when we're hobbling forward with fettered legs?" After reflecting for a moment he added, "A person like me will not know the bitter meaning of struggle as long as he has a home and a father with a private income. I don't deny that I enjoy it, but at the same time I feel embarrassed."

"When do you expect to start getting paid for your work?"

"The editor hasn't set a date. . . ."

They parted at al-Ataba al-Khadra Square, and Ahmad continued on to *The New Man*. Mr. Adli Karim greeted him warmly and took him into the editorial offices to introduce him: "Your new colleague, Mr. Ahmad Ibrahim Shawkat."

Presenting the other members of the staff to Ahmad, he said, "Miss Sawsan Hammad, Mr. Ibrahim Rizq, and Mr. Yusuf al-Jamil."

They shook hands with Ahmad and welcomed him. Then, to be polite, Ibrahim Rizq said, "His name is well known here at the magazine."

Smiling, Mr. Adli Karim observed, "He was our first subscriber and has grown up with the magazine." Pointing to the desk of Yusuf al-Jamil, he added, "You will use this desk, for its occupant spends little time here."

When Adli Karim left the room, Yusuf al-Jamil invited Ahmad to sit down near his desk. He waited until the young man was seated and then said, "Miss Sawsan will allocate your work. You might as well have a cup of coffee now."

He pressed a buzzer, and Ahmad began to study their faces and the room. Ibrahim Rizq, a middle-aged man of decrepit appearance, looked ten years older than he actually was. Yusuf al-Jamil was a mature young man whose looks suggested an alert intelligence. Glancing at Sawsan Hammad, Ahmad wondered whether she remembered him. He had not seen her since that first encounter in 1936. Their eyes met. Wishing to escape from his silence, he mentioned with a smile, "I saw you here five years ago. . . ." Detecting a look of recognition in her eyes, he continued: "I asked what had happened to one of my articles that had not been published yet."

Smiling, she said, "I can almost remember that. In any case, we've published many of your articles since then."

Yusuf al-Jamil commented, "Articles that reveal a fine progressive spirit."

Ibrahim Rizq said, "People have a heightened awareness today. Out on the street wherever I look I see the phrase 'Bread and liberty.' This is the people's new slogan."

Sawsan Hammad remarked with interest, "It's a most beautiful one. Especially at this time when gloom encompasses the world."

Ahmad understood what her words implied, and with enthusiastic delight his soul responded to this new environment. He replied, "The world certainly is cloaked in darkness, but until Hitler attacks Britain, there's still hope of salvation."

Sawsan Hammad said, "I see the situation from another angle. Don't you suppose that if Hitler attacks Britain, it's probable that both giants will be destroyed or at least that the balance of power will shift to Russia?"

"What if the opposite happens? I mean, what if Hitler subdues the British Isles and achieves an uncontested supremacy?"

Yusuf al-Jamil said, "Napoleon, like Hitler, took on all of Europe, but Russia was his downfall."

In this pure atmosphere, with these liberated comrades and this enlightened and beautiful colleague, Ahmad felt more alive and vigorous than ever before. For some reason he thought of Alawiya Sabri and the tormented year during which he had wrestled with unrequited love until he had finally emerged the victor. From the depths of his heart he had cursed that love morning and evening until it had dispersed into thin air, leaving behind enduring traces of rebellious resentment. She was now home in al-Ma'adi, waiting for a husband with an income of at least fifty pounds a month. The girl here was calling for a Russian victory. What was she waiting for?

Then Sawsan waved a sheaf of papers in his direction as she said gently, "Would you mind?"

He rose and walked over to her desk to begin his new career.

149

YUSUF AL-JAMIL came into the office only once or twice a week, since most of his energies were directed toward soliciting advertising and subscriptions. Similarly, Ibrahim Rizq remained in the editorial department for no more than an hour a day before he left for one of the other magazines he helped edit. Most of the time they were alone: Ahmad and Sawsan. Once, when the chief pressman from the printshop came to get some copy, Ahmad was astounded to hear her call him "Father." Afterward, he learned that Mr. Adli Karim himself was related to the man, and this information was a thrilling surprise.

Even more stunning than Sawsan was her diligence. She was the heart of the editorial department and its dynamo. She did far more work than the mere editing of the magazine required, for she was always reading and writing. She seemed serious, bright, and extremely intelligent, and from the very first he was conscious of her forceful personality. So much so that in spite of her attractive black eyes and charmingly feminine body he occasionally imagined himself in the presence of a well-disciplined man with a strong will. Her industry motivated him to work with an assiduous zeal impervious to fatigue and boredom. He had assumed responsibility for translating excerpts from international cultural magazines as well as some significant articles.

One day he complained, "The censors watch us like hawks."

In an irritated and scornful tone, she replied, "You haven't seen anything yet! To its credit, our journal is deemed 'subversive' by the ruling circles."

Smiling, Ahmad said, "Naturally you remember the editorials Mr. Adli Karim wrote before the war."

"During the reign of Ali Mahir, our magazine was closed down once because of an essay commemorating the Urabi rebellion. In it the editor had accused the Khedive Tawfiq of treachery."

One day, in the midst of a conversation on another topic, she asked, "Why did you choose journalism?"

He reflected a little. How much of his soul should he bare to this girl, who, compared to the other women he knew, was one of a kind?

"I didn't go to the University to obtain a government job. I had ideas I wanted to express in print. What better vehicle could there be for that than journalism?"

Her interest in his response delighted him. She countered, "I didn't go to the University. Or, more precisely, I didn't have the opportunity."

He was also enthralled by her candor, which by itself sufficed to show how different she was from other girls. She went on: "I'm a graduate of Mr. Adli Karim's school, an institution no less distinguished than the University. I've studied with him since I finished my baccalaureate. Frankly, I think you've given a good definition for journalism, or the kind of journalism we're engaged in. Yet so far you have expressed your thoughts by relying on others, I mean by translating. Haven't you thought of selecting a genre that suits you?"

He was silent for a time, groping for an answer, as if he had not understood her words. Then he asked, "What do you mean?"

"Essays, poetry, short stories, plays?"

"I don't know. The essay comes to mind first."

In a tone that said more than her words did, she observed, "Yes, but in view of the political situation, it's no longer an easy endeavor. Freethinkers are forced to speak their mind in clandestine publications. An essay is blunt and direct. Therefore it is dangerous, especially when eyes are scrutinizing us. The short story is more devious and thus harder to restrict. It's a cunning art, which has become such a prevalent form it will soon wrest leadership from all the others. Don't you see that there is not a single prominent literary figure who hasn't tried to make a name for himself in this genre, if only by publishing one short story?"

"Yes, I've read most of these works. Haven't you read some of the stories Mr. Riyad Qaldas publishes in *al-Fikr* magazine?"

"He's one of many and not the best."

"Perhaps not. My uncle Kamal Ahmad Abd al-Jawad, who writes for that same magazine, drew my attention to his stories."

Smiling, she asked, "He's your uncle? I've frequently read him, but . . ."

"Yes?"

"No offense, but he's a writer who rambles through the wilderness of metaphysics."

A bit anxiously he asked, "Don't you like him?"

"Liking is something else. He writes a good deal about ancient notions like the spirit, the absolute, and the theory of knowledge. That's lovely, but such topics provide intellectual entertainment and mental enrichment without leading anywhere. Writing should be an instrument with a clearly defined purpose. Its ultimate goal should be the development of this world and man's ascent up the ladder of progress and liberation. The human race is engaged in a constant struggle. A writer truly worthy of the name must be at the head of the freedom fighters. Let's leave talk about mysterious forces like *élan vital* to Bergson."

"But even Karl Marx began as a budding philosopher who rambled through the labyrinth of metaphysics."

"And he ended up with a scientific understanding of society. That's where we should commence – not from his starting point."

Ahmad was uncomfortable at hearing his uncle criticized in this fashion. Motivated more by a desire to defend his uncle than by anything else, he said, "It's always worthwhile to know the truth, no matter what it is or what effects people think it has."

Sawsan responded enthusiastically, "This thought contradicts what you've written. I bet you're just saying it out of loyalty to your uncle. When a man's in pain, he concentrates on eradicating its causes. Our society is in deep pain. So first and foremost we must stop this pain. After that we can play around and philosophize. Imagine a man musing happily about abstruse points of philosophy while his life's blood drains away. What would you say of a man like that?"

Was this really a fair description of his uncle? He had to admit that her words struck a responsive chord inside him, that her eyes were beautiful, and that despite her strange earnestness she was attractive . . . very attractive.

"Actually, my uncle doesn't pay enough attention to these matters. I've discussed them with him many times and have found him to be a man who studies the Nazi movement as objectively as democracy or Communism, without being for or against any of them. I can't figure out his stance."

With a smile, she said, "He has none. A writer can't conceal his convictions. Your uncle is like all those other bourgeois intellectuals who enjoy reading and pondering things. When considering the 'absolute' they may feel such distress that it hurts, but on the street they nonchalantly walk past people who really are suffering."

He laughed and replied, "My uncle's not like that."

"You know best. The stories of Riyad Qaldas are not what we need either. They are descriptive analyses of reality but nothing more. They provide no guidance or direction."

Ahmad thought a little before remarking, "But he often describes the condition of laborers, both farmers and factory workers. This means that in his stories the proletariat is in the spotlight."

"But he limits himself to description and analysis. Compared to real struggle, his work is passive and negative."

This girl was a firebrand! She appeared to be extremely serious. Where was her feminine side?

"What would you want him to write?"

"Have you read any modern Soviet literature? Have you read anything by Maxim Gorky?"

He smiled but did not reply. There was no reason for him to feel embarrassed. He was a student of sociology, not of literature. Besides, she was several years his senior. How old was she? She might be twenty-four, or older.

She said, "This is the type of literature you should read. I'll lend you some if you want."

"I'd be delighted."

She smiled and said, "But a liberated man must be more than a reader or a writer. Principles relate primarily to the will . . . the will above all other things."

Even so, he was aware of her elegance. Although she did not use makeup, she was as fastidious about her appearance as any other girl and her lively breasts were as attractive and fascinating as any other ones. But not so fast . . . didn't the principles that he espoused distinguish him from other men?

"Our class is perverse," he thought. "We're unable to see women from more than one perspective."

"I'm delighted to have met you and predict that we will have many opportunities to work together closely."

Smiling in a way that was quite feminine, she said, "You're too kind."

"I really am delighted to have a chance to get to know you."

Yes, he was. But it was important that he not misinterpret his feelings, which might simply be the natural response of a young man like him.

"Be cautious," he advised himself. "Don't create a dilemma for yourself like that one in al–Ma'adi, for the sorrow it provoked has yet to be erased from your heart."

150

"GOOD EVENING, AUNT."

He followed Jalila to her preferred spot in the parlor, and once they were installed on the sofa, she called her maid, whom she watched fetch the drinks, prepare the table, and then depart after finishing these tasks. Turning toward Kamal, Jalila said, "Nephew, I swear that I no longer drink with anyone but you, when you come every Thursday night. I used to enjoy having a drink with your father in the old days. But back then I drank with many others too."

Kamal commented to himself, "I'm in dreadful need of alcohol. I don't know what life would be like without it." Then he told her, "But whiskey has disappeared from the market, Auntie, along with all other wholesome drinks. They say that one of the last German air raids on Scotland scored a direct hit on the warehouse of an internationally known distillery and that rivers of the best whiskey flowed out."

"What I wouldn't give for a raid like that! But before you get drunk tell me how al-Sayyid Ahmad is."

"No better and no worse. Madam Jalila, I hate to see him confined to bed. May our Lord be gracious to him."

"I'd love to visit him. Can't you summon the courage to give him my best wishes?"

"What an idea! That's all we need to provoke Judgment Day."

The old lady laughed and asked, "Do you suppose that a person like al-Sayyid Ahmad is capable of thinking any man pure, especially one of his own brood?"

"Even so, most beautiful of women. . . . To your health."

"And yours. . . . Atiya may be late, since her son is sick."

"She didn't mention that last time."

"No. Her son fell ill this past Saturday. The poor darling – her son is the apple of her eye. When anything happens to him, she loses her head."

"She's a fine woman who has had rotten luck. I've long felt her character convincing evidence that only dire necessity could have forced her to enter this profession."

In a jovial but sarcastic tone Jalila replied, "If a man like you is embarrassed by his honorable profession, why should she find hers satisfying?"

The maid passed back through the room with an incense burner wafting a pleasant scent. The moist autumn breeze entered through a window at the rear of the parlor, and the alcohol was bitter but potent. Jalila's comment about his profession reminded him of something he might otherwise have forgotten to tell her, and he said, "I was almost transferred to Asyut, Auntie. If the worst had happened, I would be packing my bags now to go there."

Striking her hand against her breast, Jalila exclaimed, "Asyut! How do you like those dates! May your worst enemy be sent there. What happened?"

"It has turned out all right, praise God."

"Your father knows more people in the government ministries than there are ants."

He nodded his head as if in agreement but did not comment. She still pictured his father in his old glory and had no way of knowing that when Kamal had informed his father of the transfer al-Sayyid Ahmad had lamented, "No one knows us anymore. What has become of our friends?"

Before telling his father, Kamal had gone to see his old friend Fuad Jamil al-Hamzawi, thinking he might know one of the top men in the Ministry of Education. But the illustrious judge had told him, "I'm very sorry, Kamal. Since I'm a judge, I can't ask anyone for favors."

With enormous embarrassment, Kamal had finally contacted his nephew Ridwan, and that same day the transfer had been rescinded. What an illustrious young man he was! They were both employed by the same ministry at the same rank, but Kamal was thirty-five and Ridwan only twenty-two. But what could a teacher in an elementary school expect? It was no longer possible for him to find consolation from philosophy or from claiming to be a philosopher. A philosopher is not a parrot who merely repeats what other philosophers have said. Any current graduate of the Arts Faculty could write as well as or better than he did. He had once hoped a publisher would bring out a collection of his essays, but those didactic works were no longer of any particular value. How many books there were nowadays.... In that ocean of learning he was an invisible drop. He had grown so weary that boredom oozed from every pore. When would his carriage reach death's station? He looked at the glass in his aunt's hand and then at her face, which clearly revealed her considerable age.

He could not help marveling at her and asked, "What does drinking do for you, Auntie?"

Displaying her gold teeth, she answered, "Do you call what I'm doing now 'drinking'? That time has passed. Liquor no longer has any taste or effect. It's like coffee. Nothing more or less. Toward the beginning of my career I once got so drunk at a wedding party in Birguwan that the members of my troupe were forced to carry me to my carriage at the end of the evening. May our Lord spare you anything like that!"

"Liquor's still the best thing a bad world has to offer," he reflected. Then he asked, "Have you experienced total intoxication? I used to reach it in two glasses. Today it takes me eight. I don't know how many I'll need tomorrow. But it's an absolute necessity, Aunt. Once intoxicated, the wounded heart dances with joy."

"Nephew, you have a sensitive heart that responds joyfully to music, even without any alcohol."

His heart ... joyful? What of his sorrow ... that constant companion? What of the ashes left from the bonfire of his hopes? ... As a bored man, he had no goal beyond filling himself with liquor, in either this parlor or that bedroom, once the woman tending her sick son arrived. He and his favorite prostitute had reached the same point in life – that of a person whose life was not worth living.

"I'm afraid Atiya won't come."

"She'll come. When someone's ill, there's even more need for money."

"What a response!" he thought. But she did not give him a chance to brood about it, for, turning toward him, she examined him with interest for a time. Then she said in a low voice, "It's only a matter of days."

Without understanding what she actually meant, he replied, "May God grant you a long life and never deprive me of you."

Smiling, she said, "I'm going to give up this life."

Astonished, he sat up straight and cried out, "What did you say?"

She laughed and then answered in a mildly sarcastic tone, "Never fear. Atiya will take you to another house as safe as this one."

"But what's happened?"

"I've grown old, nephew, and God has given me more riches than I need. Yesterday, the police raided a nearby brothel and took the madam to the station. I've had enough. I'm planning to repent. I must change my ways before I meet my Lord."

He finished his drink and refilled the glass. Then, as if he did not believe what he had heard, he remarked, "All that's left is for you to board the boat to Mecca and perform the pilgrimage."

"May our Lord give me the power to do what's right."

After wondering about this for a while, he roused himself from his stupor to ask, "Did all this happen suddenly?"

"Of course not. I don't reveal a secret until I'm ready to act on it. I've been thinking about this for a long time."

"You're serious?"

"Absolutely. May our Lord be with us."

"I don't know what to say. But in any case may our Lord give you the strength to do the right thing."

"Amen." Then, laughing, she added, "Relax. I won't close this house until I've made provisions for your future."

He laughed out loud and asked, "Isn't it absurd to think that I could ever find a house where I would feel as much at home as here?"

"You can depend on me to pass you on to a new madam, even if I'm in Mecca."

"Everything seems ridiculous," Kamal thought. "But alcohol will always be the direction toward which sorrowful people turn their prayerful attentions. Circumstances have changed. Fuad Jamil al-Hamzawi's star has risen, and that of Kamal Ahmad Abd al-Jawad has declined. Yet alcohol will always bring a smile to the face of a grieving person. Kamal once amused Ridwan by carrying the young boy on his shoulder. Now the day has come for Ridwan to grasp Kamal in order to keep him from stumbling. Still, alcohol remains a lifeline for melancholy men."

Even Madam Jalila was planning to repent at the very time that he was searching for a new brothel. But liquor would continue to be his last resort.

"An invalid," he concluded, "finds everything boring, even boredom, but alcohol will always be the key to a happy release."

"Whenever I hear good things about you it makes me happy," he told her.

"May God guide you and bring you happiness."

"Perhaps I had better go? . . . "

She placed a finger in front of his mouth to silence him and exclaimed, "God forgive you! This is your house so long as it is mine. And whatever house I settle in will be yours, nephew."

Was he expiating some ancient curse of unknown origin? How could he escape from the anguish engulfing his life? Jalila herself was thinking seriously about transforming her life. Why should he not follow her example? A drowning man either finds a boulder to cling to or drowns. "If life has no meaning, why shouldn't we create a meaning for it?" he asked himself. "Perhaps it's a mistake for us to look for meaning in this world, precisely because our primary mission here is to create this meaning."

Jalila gave him a peculiar look, and he realized too late that he had unconsciously spoken these last words. Laughing, Jalila inquired, "Have you gotten drunk so fast?"

He masked his discomfort with a loud laugh and replied, "Wartime liquor's like poison. Forgive me. When do you suppose Atiya's coming?"

151

KAMAL LEFT JALILA'S house at one-thirty in the morning. The world was veiled in a darkness tempered by silence as he slowly made his way to New Street and then turned toward al-Husayn. How long would he live in this sacred district that had lost all of its spiritual significance for him? He smiled wanly. The only remaining vestige of the liquor was a hangover. His blazing desires had died away, and he plodded along lethargically. Often at a time like this when lust had been satisfied, something – not regret or a wish to repent – would scream from his inner depths, imploring and urging him to cleanse and free himself from the grip of physical appetites once and for all, as if the receding waves of desire had laid bare submerged boulders of asceticism. When he raised his head skyward to commune with the stars, an air-raid siren ripped through the stillness of the night. His heart raced fiercely, and his sleepy eyes opened wide. He headed instinctively for the nearest wall, to walk along beside it. Looking up at the sky once more, he saw that searchlights were sweeping across the heavens at great speed. They met at times, only to veer off wildly on separate paths. Still hugging the walls, he increased his pace. He had an oppressive sense of being alone, as though he were the only person left on the face of the earth.

A shrill whistling sound, unlike anything he had ever heard before, plummeted from the sky, and it was followed by an enormous explosion that rocked the earth beneath his feet. Was it near or far? He did not have time to review his information about air raids, since the explosions came in such rapid succession that it took his breath away. There were repeated bursts of anti-aircraft fire, and mysterious unidentifiable flashes of light streaked the air like lightning. It seemed to him that the whole earth was flying apart in a burst of sparks. Heedless of his surroundings, he shot off at a gallop toward Qirmiz Alley to shelter under its historic vaults. The guns were firing with an insane rage, as bombs pounded their targets and made the earth shake. After a few terrifying seconds he reached the passageway, which was packed with a multitude of people, whose bodies gave substance to its gloom. Panting, he slipped in among them. In the pervasive darkness, the prevailing sense of terror was voiced by little moans of alarm. From time to time, the entrance and exit to the vaulted section were illuminated by light reflected from the streaks in the sky.

The bombs had stopped falling – or so it seemed – but the anti-aircraft guns kept on firing as wildly as before, and their impact on the soul was no less distressing than that of the bombs. There was a babbling confusion of shrieks, sobs, and scolding reprimands from various men, women, and children.

"This raid's not like the others."

"Our ancient district can't take this new kind of raid."

"Spare us your chatter. Say, 'O Lord!'"

"We are saying, 'O Lord!'"

"Be quiet. Be quiet! May God be compassionate to you."

While watching flashes of light illuminate the exit, Kamal saw a new group approach. He thought he recognized his father among them, and his heart pounded. Was it really his father? How could the man have gotten all the way to the alley? Indeed, how could he have gotten out of bed? Kamal pushed through the agitated throngs of people until he reached the end of the vault. In a glimmer of light, he saw the whole family – his father and mother, Aisha, and Umm Hanafi. He made his way to them and then, standing beside them, whispered, "It's Kamal. Are you all right?"

His father did not answer. Utterly exhausted, he was leaning against the wall, between Kamal's mother and Aisha. The mother said, "Kamal? Praise God. This is atrocious, son. It's not like before. We thought the house was going to tumble down on our heads. Our Lord gave your father enough strength to get out of bed and come with us. I have no idea how he made it or how we got here."

Umm Hanafi muttered, "Compassion is from Him. What is this terror? May our Lord be gracious to us."

Suddenly, Aisha cried out, "When will these guns be still?"

Fearing that her voice suggested her nerves were at the breaking point, Kamal went to Aisha and took her hand between both of his, for he had recovered some of his presence of mind on finding himself with people who needed his support. The guns were still firing with a wild rage, but their fury started to abate by barely perceptible degrees. Kamal leaned toward his father and asked, "How are you, Father?"

The man replied in a feeble whisper, "Where were you, Kamal? Where were you when the raid started?"

To set the man's mind at ease, Kamal said, "I was near the alley. How are you?"

In a shaky voice the father said, "God only knows ... how I got out of bed and rushed along the street. God knows ... I wasn't conscious of what I was doing. . . . When will things return to normal?"

"Shall I take off my jacket for you to sit on?"

"No. I can stand, but when will things calm down?"

"The raid seems to have ended. Don't worry about getting up so suddenly. Surprises often work miracles in an illness."

He had hardly finished speaking when the ground trembled from three explosions in a row, and the anti-aircraft guns went on the rampage again. The passageway was filled with screams.

"It's right over our heads!"

"Declare the unity of God."

"Don't make things worse than they are with your talk."

Kamal released Aisha's hand to take both of his father's in his grasp. It was the first time in his life he had done that. Al-Sayyid Ahmad's hands were trembling, and Kamal's were too. Umm Hanafi, who had thrown herself on the ground, wailed noisily.

An agitated voice called out irritably, "I've had enough screaming! I'll kill anyone who screams."

But the screaming grew louder, and the gunfire continued. Nervous tension increased as they waited for the next shock wave. This expectation of more explosions had a stifling effect on them, as the firing of the guns went unanswered.

"The bombing's over!"

"It only stops to start up again."

"It's far away. If it were close, the houses around us would not have survived."

"The bombs fell in al-Nahhasin."

"It seems that way to you, but they may have fallen on the ordnance depot."

"Listen, will you? Hasn't the gunfire started to die down?"

It had. Soon firing was audible only in the distance. Then it was intermittent, coming at intervals – of a whole minute eventually.

Finally silence descended, spread, and became firmly entrenched. People felt free to talk again, and whispered expressions of tearful hope could be heard. They had so many things to remember as they came back to life and sighed with cautious but anxious relief. Kamal tried in vain to inspect his father's face, for the flashes of light had disappeared and the world was dark.

"Father, things will calm down now."

The man did not answer but wiggled his hands, which his son still grasped, to show that he was alive.

"Are you all right?" Kamal asked. The hands moved once more, and the son felt so sad that he was on the verge of tears.

A siren went off to mark the end of the raid. Afterward, the jubilant shouts heard on all sides were reminiscent of the cries of children after the cannon fires to mark the start of a holiday or to signal the hour for feasting during Ramadan. The alley and the neighboring area were the scene of unlimited commotion as doors and windows banged open, agitated conversations grew loud, and the people packed into the vaulted part of the alley began to move out in waves.

Sighing, Kamal said, "Let's go home."

Placing one arm over Kamal's shoulder and the other over Amina's, al-Sayyid Ahmad walked along between them, a step at a time. They began to wonder how he was and what effect this grim outing would have on him. . . . But he stopped walking and said in a weak voice, "I've got to sit down."

Kamal suggested, "Let me carry you."

The exhausted man protested, "You won't be able to."

Putting one arm around the man's back and the other under his legs, Kamal picked him up. It was not a light load, but little was left of his father in any case. Kamal walked along very slowly, and the others followed him apprehensively.

Aisha suddenly started sobbing. When her father said in a tired voice, "There's no call for a scene," she put a hand over her mouth.

When they reached the house, Umm Hanafi helped Kamal carry the master. They took him upstairs slowly and cautiously. Although he submitted gracefully to this treatment, his stream of mumbled pleas for God's forgiveness betrayed his grief and discomfort. They deposited him carefully on the bed. When the light was turned on, they could see that his face was very pale, as if the exertion had drained his blood. His chest was heaving violently up and down, and his eyes were closed from his exhaustion. He began moaning and moaning. Eventually he got the better of his pain and sank into silence. They stood in a row beside his bed, watching him with apprehensive dread. At last Amina inquired in a trembling voice, "Is my master well?"

He opened his eyes, and took his time looking at the faces, which he did not always seem to recognize. Then he sighed and said in a scarcely audible voice, "Praise God."

"Sleep, master. Sleep to regain your strength."

They heard the ring of the bell outside, and Umm Hanafi went to open the door. They exchanged questioning glances, and Kamal suggested, "Probably someone from Sugar Street or Palace of Desire Alley has come to see if we're all right."

His supposition was confirmed, for Abd al-Muni'm and Ahmad soon entered the room, and they were followed by Yasin and Ridwan. Approaching al-Sayyid Ahmad's bed, they greeted those present. The man glanced at them listlessly. As though speech were beyond him, he contented himself with raising a thin hand to them in greeting. Kamal recounted in an abbreviated form what his father had experienced that alarming night. Then Amina whispered, "An atrocious night – may our Lord never repeat it."

Umm Hanafi remarked, "The movement has tired him, but with some rest he'll recover his strength."

Yasin leaned over his father to say, "You need to sleep. How do you feel now?"

The man gazed with dull eyes at his eldest son and mumbled, "Praise God. My left side doesn't feel good."

Yasin asked, "Should I call a doctor for you?"

The father waved his hand testily and then whispered, "No. It's better if I sleep."

Starting to retreat, Yasin gestured for the family to leave the room, and the man raised his scrawny hand again. They walked out, one after the other, leaving only Amina. Once they were assembled in the sitting room, Abd al-Muni'm asked his uncle Kamal, "What did you do? We hurried down to the reception room in the courtyard."

Yasin volunteered, "We went downstairs to our neighbors' apartment on the ground floor."

Kamal said anxiously, "Fatigue has sapped Papa's strength."

Yasin asserted, "But he'll regain his health by sleeping."

"What can we do if there's another raid?"

No one answered, and there was a heavy silence, until Ahmad complained, "Our houses are ancient. They won't stand up to these raids."

Wishing to dissipate the lingering cloud of despair, since it was upsetting him, Kamal coaxed a smile from his lips and said, "If our houses are destroyed, they'll have the honor of being demolished by the most advanced inventions of modern science."

152

KAMAL HAD barely reached the stairway door after showing out the last visitors of the evening when an alarming din reached his ears from above. His nerves were still on edge, and he feared the worst as he bounded up the steps. The sitting room was empty, but through the closed door of his father's chamber he could hear the loud voices of several people, who were all speaking at once. Rushing to the door, he opened it and entered, expecting something unpleasant but refusing to think what it might be.

His mother's hoarse voice was exclaiming, "Master!"

Aisha was calling curtly for "Papa!"

Mumbling to herself, Umm Hanafi stood riveted to her spot by the head of the bed. When Kamal looked in that direction, he was overcome by desperate alarm and mournful resignation, for he saw that the bottom half of his father's body lay on the bed while the upper half rested on Amina's breast. The man's chest was heaving up and down mechanically as he emitted a strange rattling sound not of this world. His eyes had a new blind look, which suggested that they could not see anything or express the man's internal struggle. Kamal, near the end of the bed, felt that his feet were glued to the floor, that he had lost the ability to speak, and that his eyes had turned to glass. He could think of nothing to say or to do and had an overwhelming sense of being utterly impotent, forlorn, and insignificant. Although aware that his father was bidding farewell to life, Kamal was in all other respects as good as unconscious.

Glancing away from her father's face long enough to look at Kamal, Aisha cried out, "Father! Here's Kamal. He wants to talk to you."

Umm Hanafi abandoned her murmured refrain to say in a choking voice, "Get the doctor."

With angry sorrow, the mother groaned, "What doctor, you fool?"

The father moved as if trying to sit up, and the convulsions of his chest increased. He stretched out the forefinger of his right

hand and then that of the left. When Amina saw this, her face
contracted with pain. She bent down toward his ear and recited in
an audible voice, "There is no god but God, and Muhammad is
the Messenger of God." She kept repeating these words until his
hand became still. Kamal understood that his father, no longer able
to speak, had asked Amina to recite the Muslim credo on his behalf
and that the inner meaning of this final hour would never be
revealed. To describe it as pain, terror, or a swoon would have
been a pointless conjecture. At any rate it could not last long, for it
was too momentous and significant to be part of ordinary life.
Although his nerves were devastated by this scene, Kamal was
ashamed to find himself snatching a few moments to analyze and
study it, as if his father's death was a subject for his reflections and
a source of information for him. This doubled his grief and his
pain.

The contractions of the man's chest intensified and the rattling
sound grew louder. "What is this?" Kamal wondered. "Is he trying
to get up? Or attempting to speak? Or addressing something we
can't see? Is he in pain? Or terrified? . . . Oh. . . ." The father
emitted a deep groan, and then his head fell on his breast.

With every ounce of her being Aisha screamed, "Father! . . .
Na'ima! . . . Uthman! . . . Muhammad!" Umm Hanafi rushed to
her and gently shoved her out of the room. The mother raised a
pale face to look at Kamal and gestured for him to leave, but he did
not budge.

She whispered to him desperately, "Let me perform my last
duty to your father."

He turned and exited to the sitting room, where Aisha, who
had flung herself across the sofa, was howling. He took a seat on
the sofa opposite hers, while Umm Hanafi went back into the
bedroom to assist her mistress, closing the door behind her. But
Aisha's weeping was unbearable, and rising again, Kamal began to
pace back and forth, without addressing any comment to her.
From time to time he would glance at the closed door and then
press his lips together.

"Why does death seem so alien to us?" he wondered. Once his
thoughts were collected enough for him to reflect on the situation,
he immediately lost his concentration again, as emotion got the
better of him. Even when no longer able to leave the bedroom, al-
Sayyid Ahmad had defined the life of the household. It would

come as no surprise if on the morrow Kamal found the house to be quite a different place and its life transformed. Indeed, from this moment on, he would have to accustom himself to a new role. Aisha's wails made him feel all the more distraught. He considered trying to silence her but then refrained. He was amazed to see her give vent to her emotions after she had appeared for so long to be impassive and oblivious to everything. Kamal thought again of his father's disappearance from their lives. It seemed almost inconceivable. Remembering his father's condition in the final days, he felt sorrow tear at his heartstrings. When he reviewed the image of their father at the height of his powers and glory, Kamal felt a profound pity for all living creatures. But when would Aisha ever stop wailing? Why could she not weep tearlessly like her brother?

The door of the bedroom opened, and Umm Hanafi emerged. During the moment before it was shut again, he could hear his mother's lamentations. He gathered that she had finished performing her final duty to his father and was now free to cry. Umm Hanafi approached Aisha and told her brusquely, "That's enough weeping, my lady." Turning toward Kamal, she remarked, "Dawn is breaking, master. Sleep, if only a little, for you have a hard day ahead of you."

Then she suddenly started crying. As she left the room, she said in a sobbing voice, "I'll go to Sugar Street and Palace of Desire Alley to announce the dreadful news."

Yasin rushed in, followed by Zanuba and Ridwan. Then the silence of the street was rent by the cries of Khadija, whose arrival caused the household's fires of grief to burn at fever pitch, as wails mixed with screams and sobs. It would not have been appropriate for the men to mourn on the first floor, and they went up to the study on the top floor. They sat there despondently, overwhelmed by a gloomy silence, until Ibrahim Shawkat remarked, "The only power and strength is God's. The raid finished him off. May God be most compassionate to him. He was an extraordinary man."

Unable to control himself, Yasin started crying. Then Kamal burst into tears too. Ibrahim Shawkat said, "Proclaim that there is only one God. He did not leave you until you were grown men."

With morose sorrow and some astonishment Ridwan, Abd al-Muni'm, and Ahmad gazed at the weeping men, who quickly dried their tears and fell silent.

Ibrahim Shawkat said, "It will be morning soon. Let's consider what has to be done."

Yasin answered sadly and tersely, "There's nothing novel about this. We've gone through it repeatedly."

Ibrahim Shawkat responded, "The funeral must suit his rank."

Yasin replied with conviction, "That's the least we can do."

Then Ridwan commented, "The street in front of the house isn't wide enough for a funeral tent that can hold all the mourners. Let's put it in Bayt al-Qadi Square instead."

Ibrahim Shawkat remarked, "But it's customary to install the tent in front of the home of the deceased."

Ridwan replied, "That isn't so important, especially since cabinet ministers, senators, and deputies will be among the mourners."

They realized that he was referring to his own acquaintances. Yasin commented indifferently, "So let's erect it there."

Thinking about the part he was to play, Ahmad said, "We won't be able to get the obituary in the morning papers. . . ."

Kamal said, "The evening papers come out at about three P. M. Let's have the funeral at five."

"So be it. The cemetery's not far, at any rate. There'll be time to have the burial before sunset."

Kamal considered what they were saying with some amazement. At five o'clock the previous day his father had been in bed, listening to the radio. At that time the following day . . . next to Yasin's two young children and Fahmy. What was left of Fahmy? Life had done nothing to diminish Kamal's childhood desire to look inside his brother's coffin. Had his father really been preparing to say something? What had he wanted to say?

Yasin turned toward Kamal to ask, "Were you there when he died?"

"Yes. It was shortly after you left."

"Did he suffer much?"

"I don't know. Who could say, brother? But it didn't last more than five minutes."

Yasin sighed and then asked, "Didn't he say anything?"

"No. He probably wasn't able to speak."

"Didn't he recite the credo?"

Looking down to hide his tearful expression, Kamal replied, "My mother did that for him."

"May God be compassionate to him."

"Amen."

They were silent for a time until finally Ridwan remarked, "The funeral pavilion must be large, if there's to be room for all the mourners to sit."

Yasin said, "Naturally. We have many friends." Then, looking at Abd al-Muni'm, he added, "And there are all the Muslim Brethren." He sighed and continued: "If his friends had been alive, they would have carried his coffin on their shoulders."

The funeral went off according to their expectations. Abd al-Muni'm had the most friends in attendance, but Ridwan's were higher in rank. Some of them attracted attention because they were well known to readers of newspapers or magazines. Ridwan was so proud they were there that his pride almost obscured his grief. The people of the district, even those who had not known al-Sayyid Ahmad personally, came to bid farewell to their lifelong neighbor. The only thing missing from the funeral was the deceased man's friends, who had all preceded him to the other world.

At Bab al-Nasr, as the funeral cortege made its way to the cemetery, Shaykh Mutawalli Abd al-Samad materialized. Staggering from advanced age, he looked up at the coffin, squinted his eyes, and asked, "Who is that?"

One of the men from the district told him, "Al-Sayyid Ahmad Abd al-Jawad, God rest his soul."

The man's face trembled unsteadily back and forth as a questioning look of bewilderment spread across it. Then he inquired, "Where was he from?"

Shaking his head rather sadly, the other man replied, "From this district. How could you not have known him? Don't you remember al-Sayyid Ahmad Abd al-Jawad?"

But the shaykh gave no sign of remembering anything and after casting a final glance at the casket proceeded on his way.

153

"NOW THAT my master has left this house, it's no longer the place I called home for more than fifty years. Everyone around me weeps. I receive the unflagging attentions of Khadija, who is my heart filled with sorrow and memories as well as the heart of everyone who has a heart. In fact, she's my daughter, sister, and, at times, my mother. I do most of my crying surreptitiously, when I'm alone, for I have to encourage them to forget. Their grief is hard for me to bear. God forbid that one of them should be tormented by sorrow. When I'm by myself, my only consolation comes from weeping, and I cry till I exhaust my tears. If Umm Hanafi disturbs my tearful solitude, no matter how unobtrusively, I tell her, 'Leave me and my affairs alone, may God have mercy on you.' She complains, 'How can I when you're in this state? I know how you feel. But you're the mistress and a Believer, indeed the mistress of all women Believers. From you we learn forbearance and submission to God's decree.'

"That's a beautiful thought, Umm Hanafi, but how can a grieving heart hope to comprehend it? This world is no longer any concern of mine. I have no further tasks to perform here. Every hour of my day is linked to some memory of my master. He was the pivot of the only life I've ever known. How can I bear to live now that he has departed, leaving nothing behind him? I was the first to suggest changing the furniture in the dear room. What could I do? Their eyes would gaze at his empty bed, and then they would break into tears.... My master is certainly entitled to the tears shed for him, but I can't stand to see them cry. I worry about their tender hearts. I attempt to console them with the same ideas you use on me, Umm Hanafi. I ask them to submit to God and His decree. That's why after the old furniture was taken out I moved into Aisha's room. To keep that room from being abandoned, I transferred the sitting-room furniture and the coffee hour in there. When we gather around the brazier we talk a lot and our conversations are interrupted by tears.

"Nothing preoccupies us so much as getting ready to visit the cemetery, and I myself supervise the preparation of the food we distribute to the poor there. That's just about the only task I don't entrust to Umm Hanafi, to whom I have relinquished so many of my duties . . . that dear loyal woman who has certainly earned her place in our family. We both prepare this mercy offering. We cry together. We remind each other of the beautiful days. She's always with me, assisting me with her spirit and her memory. Yesterday when the evening celebrations of Ramadan were mentioned, she launched into a description of what my master did during Ramadan from the time he woke up late in the morning until he returned to have breakfast with us before sunrise the next day. For my part, I mentioned how I used to scurry to the latticed balcony to watch the carriage bring him home and to listen to the laughter of the passengers, those men who have departed to God's mercy, one after the other – just as our sweet days have departed, along with youth, health, and vigor. O God, grant the children a long life and comfort them with its joys.

"This morning I saw our cat under the bed. She was sniffing around where she had nursed her beloved kittens that I gave away to the neighbors. The sight of her, so sad and bewildered, broke my heart and I cried out from the depths of my soul, 'God grant you patience, Aisha.' Poor dear Aisha. . . . Her father's death has awakened all the old sorrows, and she weeps for her father, her daughter, her sons, and her husband. How hot tears are. . . . I, who once found the loss of a child such a bitter experience that I seemed to weep away my heart's blood, am today afflicted with the death of my master. My life, which he once filled completely, is empty. Of all my duties, the only one left is preparing the mercy offering I give on his behalf or collecting it from Sugar Street or Palace of Desire Alley. This is all I have.

"No, son. You should find yourself some gathering other than our mournful one, for I fear it will depress you. . . . Why are you so despondent? Grief is not for men. A man can't bear his normal burdens and sorrow too. Go up to your room and read or write the way you used to. Or get out of the house in the evening and see your friends. Since God created the world, loved ones have left their kin. If everyone fell victim to sorrow, no one would remain alive on the face of the earth. I'm not as forlorn as you think. A Believer should not feel dejected. If God so wills, we'll live and forget. 'There's no way to catch up with the dear one who has gone on ahead until God decrees it.' That's what I tell him, and I go out of my way to appear composed and collected. But when Khadija, the living heart of our household, turns up and weeps with abandon, I can't keep from bursting into tears.

"Aisha told me she'd seen her father in a dream. He was grasping Na'ima's arm with one hand and Muhammad's with the other. Uthman was sitting on his shoulders. He told her he was fine, that they were all fine. She asked about the secret meaning of the window of light she had once seen in the sky only to have it disappear for good. His sole response was the look of censure in his eyes. Then she asked me what the dream meant. How helpless you make your mother feel, Aisha.... All the same, I told her that the dear man, although dead, was still concerned about her and, for that reason, had visited her in a dream and had brought her children from paradise so that the sight of them would cheer her. 'So don't spoil their peace of mind by clinging to your sorrow.' I wish the old Aisha would come back, even for an hour.... If the people around me would get over their grief, I could devote myself entirely to my duty to grieve profoundly.

"I got Yasin and Kamal together and asked, 'What shall we do with these dear items?' Yasin said, 'I'll take the ring, for it fits my finger. Kamal, you take the watch. And, Mother, the prayer beads are for you.... What about his cloaks and caftans?' I immediately mentioned Shaykh Mutawalli Abd al-Samad, the only survivor from the dear man's friends. Yasin said, 'He's as good as dead, for he's oblivious to the world and has no fixed abode.' Frowning, Kamal remarked, 'He no longer knew who Father was. He had forgotten his name and nonchalantly turned away from the funeral procession.' I was shocked and said, 'How amazing! When did that happen?' Even in his last days, my master asked about him. He always loved the shaykh and had seen him only once or twice since his visit to our house the night of Na'ima's wedding. But, my Lord, what's become of Na'ima and of that whole portion of our lives? Then Yasin suggested giving the clothes to the messenger boys in his office and the janitors at Kamal's school because no one deserved the clothes more than poor people like them who would pray for him. And the beloved prayer beads will not leave my hands until I leave this life.

"The tomb is such a pleasant place to visit, even though it stirs my grief. I've frequented it ever since my precious martyred son was taken there. From that time on, I've considered it to be one of the rooms of our house, even though it's at the outskirts of our district. The tomb brings us all together just as the coffee hour once did. Khadija weeps until she's exhausted. Then we're instructed to be silent out of respect for a recitation of the Qur'an. After that they converse for a time. I'm pleased by anything that distracts my loved ones from their sorrow. Ridwan, Abd al-Muni'm, and Ahmad become embroiled in a long argument. Occasionally Karima joins them. That tempts Kamal to participate and brightens the gloomy atmosphere of the grave site. Abd al-Muni'm asks about his martyred uncle. Yasin recounts various stories concerning him. The old days come to life, and forgotten memories are revived. My heart pounds, because I'm at a loss to know how to hide my tears.

"I frequently find Kamal looking despondent. When I ask him about it, he replies, 'His image never leaves me, especially the vision of his death. If only he had had an easier end!'

I told him tenderly, 'You must forget all this.' He asked, 'How can I?' I suggested faith, but he smiled sadly and remarked, 'How I feared him when I was young ... but in his later years he revealed to me a totally different person, indeed a beloved friend. How witty, tender, and gracious he was ... unlike any other man.'

"Yasin weeps whenever he happens to remember his father. Kamal's sorrow takes the form of silent dejection, but huge Yasin weeps like a child and tells me, 'He was the only man I ever loved.' Yes, my master was Yasin's father and mother too. The boy was never treated to affection, care, or concern anywhere but under his father's wing. Even the man's fierceness was compassionate. I'll never forget the day he forgave me and invited me back to his house, confirming my mother's hunch, may God be compassionate to her. She kept telling me, 'Al-Sayyid Ahmad is not a man who will permanently ban the mother of his children.' His love united us in the past, just as his memory does now. Our house does not lack for visitors, but my heart is not at rest unless I have Khadija and Yasin around me with their families. Even Zanuba's grief is quite sincere. Beautiful young Karima suggested, 'Grandmother, come home with us. It's time for the celebrations in honor of al-Husayn. You can hear Sufi groups chanting below our house. I know you like that.' I gave her a grateful kiss and told her, 'Daughter, your grandmother's not used to spending the night away from home.' The girl knows nothing of the customs of her grandfather's house in the old days. How beautiful it is to remember them. . . . The latticed balcony was the outer limit of my world. I waited there for my master to return late at night. At the time, he was so mighty that the earth almost shook when he stepped out of the carriage. Vigor virtually leaping from his face, he would fill the room on entering it, he was so big and tall. He won't come home tonight. He'll never come home. Even before his passing, he withered away, stopped going out, and stayed in bed. He grew thin and lost so much weight you could pick him up with one hand. I'll never recover from my grief.

"Aisha said angrily, 'These children haven't grieved for their grandfather and don't grieve for him.' I told her, 'They did grieve, but they're young. It's part of God's compassion for them that they don't get bogged down in their grief.' She retorted, 'See how Abd al-Muni'm can't stop arguing. He never mourned for my daughter. He quickly forgot all about her, as if she had never existed.' I reminded her, 'No, he mourned her for a long time and wept a great deal. Men's grief differs from that of women. A mother's heart is unlike any other one. Who doesn't forget, Aisha? Don't we take comfort in conversation? Aren't we occasionally surprised by a smile? There will come a day when not a tear is shed. Besides, where is Fahmy? What about him?'

"Umm Hanafi asked me, 'Why have you stopped going to al-Husayn?' I replied, 'My soul is indifferent to all the things I used to love. I'll visit my master al-Husayn once the wound is healed.' She inquired, 'What will heal the wound if not a visit to your Master?' This is how Umm Hanafi takes care of me. She is the mistress of our household. If it were not for her, we would not have a home. My Lord, You who are the lord of all creation, You who issue all the ineluctable decrees, to You I pray. I wish you had allowed my master to keep his strength to the end. Nothing caused me so much pain as his confinement to bed – a man for whom the whole world was hardly big enough. He wasn't even able to pray. I regret the suffering endured by his weak heart and the way he was carried home like a child after the raid. These things cause my tears to flow and dam up my grief."

154

"PUTTING MY trust in God, I shall ask for the hand of my cousin Karima."

Ibrahim Shawkat glanced up at his son with some astonishment. Ahmad bowed his head but smiled in a way that showed the news came as no surprise to him. Khadija set aside the shawl she was embroidering to cast a strange look of disbelief at her son. Then, staring at her husband, she asked, "What did he say?"

Abd al-Muni'm repeated: "Putting my trust in God, I shall ask for the hand of your brother's daughter Karima."

To show her bewilderment Khadija spread her hands out and asked, "Has good taste gone out of fashion in this world? Is this an appropriate time to discuss an engagement, regardless of the identity of your intended?"

Smiling, Abd al-Muni'm said, "All times are appropriate for betrothals."

Shaking her head to express her bafflement, she inquired, "And your grandfather?" Then, as she looked from Ahmad to Ibrahim, she continued: "Have you ever heard of anything like this before?"

Abd al-Muni'm remarked a bit sharply, "An engagement . . . not a marriage or a wedding. And my grandfather's been dead four whole months . . . ."

Lighting a cigarette, Ibrahim Shawkat said, "Karima's still young. She looks older than she is, I think."

Abd al-Muni'm answered, "She's fifteen, and the marriage contract would not be signed for a year. . . ."

Khadija asked with bitter sarcasm, "Has Mrs. Zanuba shown you the birth certificate?"

Ibrahim Shawkat and his son Ahmad laughed, but Abd al-Muni'm said earnestly, "Nothing will happen for a year. By that time almost a year and a half will have passed since Grandfather's death, and Karima will be old enough to get married."

"So why are you causing us a headache now?"

"There wouldn't be any harm in announcing the engagement at present."

Khadija inquired scornfully, "Will the engagement go sour if it's postponed for a year?"

"Please don't jest."

Khadija shouted, "If this happens, it will cause a scandal."

With all the composure he could muster, Abd al-Muni'm replied, "Leave Grandmother to me. She'll understand me better than you do. She's my grandmother and Karima's too."

His mother observed gruffly, "She's not Karima's grand-mother."

Abd al-Muni'm fell silent, but his expression was sullen. Before he could answer, his father interjected, "It's a question of good taste. It would be better to wait a little."

Khadija cried out furiously, "You mean your only objection is to the timing?"

Pretending not to understand, Abd al-Muni'm asked, "Is there some other objection then?"

Khadija did not answer. When she started embroidering the shawl again, Abd al-Muni'm protested, "Karima's the daughter of your brother Yasin, isn't she?"

Dropping the shawl, Khadija said bitterly, "She truly is my brother's daughter, but you ought to remember as well who her mother is."

The men exchanged apprehensive glances. Abd al-Muni'm burst out acerbically, "Her mother's also your brother's wife."

Raising her voice, she proclaimed, "I know that and regret it."

"That forgotten past! Who remembers it now? She's no longer anything but a respectable lady like you."

In a surly voice she retorted, "That woman's not like me and never will be."

"What's wrong with her? Since we were little children we've known her to be a lady in every sense of the word. When a person repents and lives righteously, his former misdeeds are erased. After that, the only people who would remind him of them are . . . "

He stopped. Shaking her head sorrowfully, she challenged him, "Yes? . . . Tell me what I am! Insult your mother for the sake of this woman who has successfully ensnared you. I've long wondered what lay behind those repeated dinner invitations to Palace of Desire Alley. You've been taken in by it."

After looking angrily from his father to his brother, Abd al-Muni'm inquired, "Is this the way we talk? I'd like to hear what you two think."

Yawning, Ibrahim Shawkat said, "There's no need for all this discussion. Abd al-Muni'm will get married again, if not today then tomorrow. You want that to happen. Karima's our daughter and a lovely, charming girl. There's no need to become agitated."

Ahmad remarked, "Mother, you're always the one who thinks first about pleasing Uncle Yasin."

Exasperated, Khadija replied, "You're all against me, as usual, but the only argument you can think of is 'Uncle Yasin.' Yasin is my brother. His primary fault was not knowing how to pick a bride, and his nephew has inherited this strange defect from him."

Abd al-Muni'm asked in amazement, "Isn't my uncle's wife a friend of yours? Anyone watching the two of you exchange secrets would think you are sisters."

"What can I do when the woman's as shrewd a diplomat as Allenby? But if it had been up to me and I had not been concerned about Yasin, I would not have allowed her to enter my home. What has been the result? Against your better judgment you have been won over by the dinners given to promote her own interests . . . God help us."

Then Ahmad told his brother, "Ask for her hand whenever you want. Mother has an active tongue but a fine heart."

Laughing nervously, she said, "Bravo, son. You two differ about everything – beliefs, religion, politics – but you're united against me."

Ahmad said gleefully, "Uncle Yasin is a favorite of yours, and you'll accord Karima the warmest welcome. The thing is that you would like a bride who isn't a relative so that you, as her mother, can dominate her. Fine . . . it'll be up to me to fulfill this dream for you. I'll bring you a bride you've never heard of so your craving can be satisfied."

"I wouldn't be at all surprised if you brought home a dancer tomorrow. Why are you laughing? This devout young shaykh wants to marry into the family of a professional entertainer. So what should I expect from you, whose religious beliefs are suspect, so help me God?"

"We really do need a dancer in the family."

Then, as though she had just remembered a terribly important matter, Khadija asked, "And Aisha? My Lord, what do you suppose she'll say about us?"

Abd al-Muni'm objected, "What should she say? My wife died four years ago. Does she want me to remain a widower for the rest of my life?"

Ibrahim Shawkat said irritably, "Don't turn an anthill into a mountain. The question is far simpler than you suggest. Karima is Yasin's daughter. Yasin is the brother of both Khadija and Aisha. That suffices. Pshaw! You argue about everything, even weddings."

A smile on his face, Ahmad glanced stealthily at his mother. He continued to observe her until she rose, as if infuriated, and left the room. He told himself, "This bourgeois class is nothing but an array of complexes. It would take an expert psychoanalyst to cure all of its ills, an analyst as powerful as history itself. If luck had given me any kind of break, I would have married before my brother, but that other bourgeois woman stipulated a salary of at least fifty pounds a month. This is how hearts are wounded for considerations that have nothing to do with the heart. I wonder what Sawsan Hammad would think if she knew about my abortive adventure?"

155

THE WEATHER was bitterly cold and the dampness of Khan al-Khalili in winter made it a less than ideal destination, but that evening Riyad Qaldas himself had suggested going to the Khan al-Khalili coffeehouse constructed above the site of the old one of Ahmad Abduh. Or, as he put it, "Kamal has finally taught me to appreciate quaint places." From its doorway, which opened out to al-Husayn, this small café, like a corridor with tables lining the two sides, extended back to a wooden balcony that overlooked the new Khan al-Khalili. Drinking tea and taking turns with a water pipe, the friends sat on the right-hand side of the balcony.

Isma'il explained, "I have a few days to pack and then I'll be traveling there."

Kamal asked sadly, "We won't see you for three years?"

"That's right. This is one gamble I have to make. The position offers an enormous salary I couldn't ever imagine getting here, and, besides, Iraq is an Arab country. It's not that different from Egypt."

"I'll miss him," Kamal thought. "He's not a soul mate, but he's my lifelong friend."

Laughing, Riyad Qaldas inquired, "Doesn't Iraq need any translators?"

Kamal asked, "Would you leave home if you had an opportunity like Isma'il's?"

"In the past I wouldn't have hesitated, but not now."

"What distinguishes the present from the past?"

Riyad Qaldas replied merrily, "For you, nothing. For me, everything. It seems I'm soon to join the fraternity of married men."

Astonished by the news, which came without any warning, Kamal felt anxious in a way he could not pinpoint precisely.

"Really? You've never alluded to this before."

"No. It's come about suddenly . . . at the last meeting. When the two of us last met, it wasn't even under consideration."

Isma'il Latif laughed triumphantly. Attempting to smile, Kamal asked, "How did this happen?"

"How? The way it happens every day. A woman teacher came to visit her brother in the translation bureau. I liked her and, on exploring my prospects, found myself invited to proceed."

As he accepted the hose of the water pipe from Kamal, Isma'il asked jovially, "When do you suppose this fellow will get around to exploring his prospects?"

Isma'il never missed a chance to bring up this stale topic. But there was a more serious side to the matter. All of Kamal's friends who had tried marriage maintained that it was a cage. If this wedding took place, he would probably see Riyad only on rare occasions and his friend might change into a different person, a kind of pen pal. The writer was so gentle and tender, it would not take much to subdue him. But how would Kamal's life be possible without him? If marriage transformed Riyad as radically as it had Isma'il, Kamal could bid farewell to the joys of life.

"When are you getting married?" Kamal asked.

"Next winter, at the latest."

It seemed that the tormented Kamal was fated to lose a best friend time and again. "At that moment, you'll become a different Riyad Qaldas."

"Why? . . . You have a fantastic imagination."

Masking his anxiety with a smile, Kamal asked, "A fantastic imagination? Today Riyad Qaldas is a man whose spirit always wants more while his pocket is happy to go empty. Once you're a husband, your pocket will always need more money and you'll have no opportunity for spiritual fulfillment."

"What an offensive description of the husband! But I don't agree with you."

"How about Isma'il, who is being forced to migrate to Iraq? I'm not making fun of that decision, for it's not only natural but heroic. Yet, at the same time, it's hideous. Picture yourself up to your ears in the problems of daily life, thinking only of how to make ends meet, reckoning your hours by piasters and milliemes. Then the poetic side of life can only seem a waste of time."

Riyad replied scornfully, "Imagination's fantasies inspired by fear. . . ."

Isma'il Latif said, "Oh, if only you would experience marriage and fatherhood.... Even today, you have no idea of the true meaning of life."

This view might well be correct, in which case Kamal's life was a silly tragedy. But what was happiness? What exactly did he desire? Even so, the main cause of his distress was the fact that he was once again threatened by a terrifying isolation of the kind he had suffered when Husayn Shaddad had disappeared from his life. What if it were possible for him to find a wife with the body of Atiya and the spirit of Riyad? That was what he really wanted: Atiya's body and Riyad's soul united in a single person whom he could marry. In that way, he would free himself from the threat of loneliness for the rest of his life. This was the challenge.

Riyad remarked impatiently, "Let's not talk about marriage. I've made my decision, and, Kamal, I hope your turn is next. Still there are important political events that demand our attention today."

Although Kamal shared his friend's sentiments, he was unable to shake off his surprise and appeared indifferent to the suggestion, offering no comment.

Isma'il Latif said cheerfully, "Al-Nahhas knew how to avenge his forced resignation of December 1937. He stormed Abdin Palace at the head of a column of British tanks."

To give Kamal a chance to comment, Riyad hesitated briefly. But when his friend was slow to respond, he asked gloomily, "Vengeance? There is little resemblance between the facts and your imagination's depiction of them."

"So what are the facts?"

After glancing at Kamal in a fruitless attempt to induce him to speak, Riyad continued: "Al-Nahhas is not a man who would conspire with the English in order to get returned to power. Ahmad Mahir's crazy. He's the one who betrayed the people and joined ranks with the king. Then he strove to hide the weakness of his position by making a stupid declaration and calling in the press to hear it." Riyad looked at Kamal to see what he thought. This political discussion had finally begun to attract some of his attention, but he felt inclined to disagree with Riyad, if only a little.

"It's clear that al-Nahhas has saved the situation," Kamal said. "I have no doubts whatsoever about his patriotism. A man his age doesn't turn traitor to obtain a position he's held five or six times before. But has he behaved in the ideal manner?"

"You're a skeptic, and there's no end to your doubts. What behavior would have been ideal?"

"He should have persisted in his rejection of the British ultimatum for him to become prime minister. Regardless of the outcome, he should not have yielded."

"Even if the king had been deposed and a British military government had taken control of the country?"

"Yes."

Huffing furiously, Riyad exclaimed, "We're having a pleasant chat over a water pipe. But a statesman has to shoulder tremendous responsibilities. In these delicate wartime conditions, how could al-Nahhas have agreed to let the king be deposed and the country be ruled by an English soldier? If the Allies are victorious – and we must realize that this is possible – then we would be counted among the defeated enemies. Politics isn't poetic idealism. It's realist wisdom."

"I still believe in al-Nahhas, but perhaps he's made a mistake. I don't say he's a conspirator or a traitor . . . ."

"The responsibility rests with those troublemakers who supported the Fascist cause behind the backs of the English – as if the Fascists would respect our independence. Don't we have a treaty with the English? Doesn't honor oblige us to keep our word? Besides, are we not democrats who should be interested in seeing the democratic nations triumph over the Nazis, since they place us at the bottom level of the world's peoples and races and stir up antagonism between the different races, nationalities, and religious groups?"

"I'm with you on all that, but when he yielded to the British ultimatum our independence was reduced to a legal fiction."

"The man protested the ultimatum, and the British deferred to him."

Isma'il laughed out loud and then said, "How admirable the protest was!" But he soon added in earnest, "I agree with what he did. If I had been in his place I would have done the same thing. He was humiliated and forced out of power, even though he had a majority. And he's known how to exact revenge. The fact is that our independence is nothing but a fiction. What purpose would be served by having the king deposed and our country governed by an English military ruler?"

Riyad's expression looked even glummer. But Kamal smiled and said with odd detachment, "Others have made mistakes, and al-Nahhas is having to deal with the consequences of those errors. No doubt he has saved the situation. He's saved the throne and the country. Moreover, all's well that ends well. If, after the war, the English remember appreciatively what he did, no one will bring up the ultimatum of the fourth of February."

After clapping his hands to order more charcoal for the water pipe, Isma'il scoffed, "If the English remember his good deed! I tell you right now they'll sack him long before that."

Riyad said with conviction, "The man has stepped forward to assume the greatest responsibility in the most trying circumstances."

Smiling, Kamal replied, "Just as you will step forward to assume the greatest responsibility of your life."

Riyad laughed. Rising, he said, "If you'll excuse me," and headed off toward the rest room. Then Isma'il leaned in Kamal's direction and gleefully remarked, "Last week a bunch you surely remember visited my mother."

Looking at him inquisitively, Kamal asked, "Who?"

Smiling in a knowing way, the other man answered, "Aïda."

For Kamal this name had an odd ring that eclipsed all the emotions it might otherwise have evoked. At first this name appeared to have emerged from deep inside him, not from his friend's lips. Nothing could have been more unexpected, and for some moments the name seemed meaningless. Who was Aïda? Which Aïda was it? That was all ancient history. How many years had passed since he had heard that name? Since 1926 or 1927 . . . sixteen years . . . long enough for a boy to reach the prime of adolescence, fall in love, and experience heartbreak. He really had grown old. Aïda? How did this memory affect him? It had no impact on him – aside from a sentimental interest mixed with emotions like those of a person who remembers a former painful and critical condition as his hand probes the scars of a surgical operation. He murmured, "Aïda?"

"Yes. Aïda Shaddad. Don't you remember her? The sister of Husayn Shaddad."

Becoming nervous under Isma'il's scrutiny, he said evasively, "Husayn! I wonder what's new with him."

"Who knows?"

He was conscious of how ridiculous his subterfuge was, but what could he do when he sensed that his face was starting to burn in spite of the intensely cold February weather? Although the comparison was a bit odd, love seemed to him to resemble nothing so much as food. "When it's on the table," he mused, "we are intensely aware of it. We are still conscious of it to a lesser degree as we digest it. But when it has been incorporated into our blood, our relationship to it is quite different. Then it is absorbed into the cells, and they are renewed. Eventually no trace of it remains, except perhaps for an inner echo we term 'forgetfulness.' A person may unexpectedly encounter a familiar voice, which will move this forgetfulness toward the level of consciousness. Then somehow he will hear this echo." If this was not correct, then why was he so shaken? Of course, he might pine for Aïda, not because he had once loved her – for that relationship had vanished never to return – but because she represented love, which he had often sorely missed over the years. She was nothing but a symbol, like a deserted ruin that evokes exalted historic memories.

Isma'il continued: "We talked for a long time – Aïda, my mother, my wife, and I. She narrated for us how she and her husband – in fact, all the other diplomats – retreated from the advancing German forces until they ended up taking refuge in Spain. They are finally being transferred to Iran. Then we reviewed the past and laughed a lot."

No matter how dead his love was, his heart felt an intoxicating longing. Inside him, chords once silent reverberated softly and sadly. He asked, "What does she look like now?"

"She's possibly forty. No, I'm two years older than she is. Aïda's thirty-seven. She's filled out a little but is still slender. Her face looks just about the same, except for the earnest and serious expression of her eyes. She said she has a son of fourteen and a daughter who is ten."

So this was Aïda then. She was not a dream, and he had not imagined his time with her. There had been moments when that part of his past had seemed an illusion. She was a wife and a mother. She remembered the past and laughed a lot. But what was her true image? How much of it did he still retain in his memory? Impressions might easily be transformed during their stay in one's memory. He would have liked to get a good look at this person, in order to discover the secret that had enabled her to exert such enormous influence on him in the past.

Riyad returned to his seat. Although Kamal feared that Isma'il would drop this topic, he continued: "They asked about you!"

Looking from one friend to the other, Riyad realized that they were involved in a private conversation and turned his attentions to the water pipe.

Kamal felt that the phrase "They asked about you" posed as great a threat to his immune system as the most virulent germs. Doing his utmost to appear natural, he inquired, "Why?"

"They asked about one and another of their friends from the old days. Then they asked about you. I said, 'He's a teacher in al-Silahdar School and a great philosopher who publishes articles that I don't understand in *al-Fikr* magazine, which I don't even open.' They laughed and then asked, 'Has he gotten married?' And I answered, 'Absolutely not.'"

Kamal found himself asking, "What did they say then?"

"Something – I don't remember what – diverted us from this topic."

The dormant disease threatened to flare up again. Anyone who has had tuberculosis must beware of catching a cold. The phrase "They asked about you" resembled a children's song, for its meaning was as simple as its impact on the soul was profound. Circumstances may arise for a soul to relive in all its fury a former emotional state that then dies away again. Thus, for a fleeting moment Kamal felt he was that lover from the past, resonating with love's joyous and mournful melodies. But he was not in serious jeopardy, for he was like a sleeping man who is distressed by a dream and yet senses with relief that what he sees is not real. All the same, he wished at that moment for a heavenly dispensation allowing him to meet her, if only for a few minutes, so she could confess that she had reciprocated his affection for a day or even part of one and that what had kept them apart had been the difference in their ages or something similar. If this miracle ever came to pass, it would repay him for all his pains, past and present, and he would consider himself a happy person, aware that his life had not been in vain. But wishful thinking like this was as false an awakening as that of death. He should content himself with forgetfulness. That would be a victory, even if tinged with defeat. He should let his consolation be the fact that he was not the only person to suffer failure in life.

He asked, "When are they leaving for Iran?"

"They were to leave yesterday, or at least that's what she said during her visit."

"How did she take her family's disaster?"

"I naturally avoided the subject, and she did not refer to it."

Pointing straight ahead, Riyad Qaldas exclaimed, "Look!" Glancing toward the left-hand side of the balcony, they observed a strange-looking woman in her seventh decade. Skinny and barefoot, she was attired in an ankle-length shirt like a man's and wore a skullcap from which no wisp of hair protruded. Her scalp was either bald or diseased, and her face was so coated with makeup that it appeared ridiculous and disgusting. Her front teeth were missing, and her eyes radiated beaming messages of affectionate ingratiation in all directions.

Riyad asked with interest, "A beggar?"

Isma'il replied, "A crazy woman, more likely."

She stood looking at the empty chairs on the left. Then choosing one, she sat down. When she noticed that they were looking at her, she smiled broadly and said, "Good evening, men."

Riyad responded warmly to her greeting, "Good evening, my good woman."

She emitted a laugh that, as Isma'il said, reminded him of the Ezbekiya entertainment district in its days of glory. Then she answered, "'Good woman'! Yes, I am that, if you mean 'good' as in 'good times.'"

The three men laughed. Encouraged by this reaction, she said enticingly, "Treat me to tea and a pipe, and God will make it up to you."

Riyad clapped his hands together energetically to place her order. Leaning toward Kamal's ear, he whispered, "This is the way some stories begin."

The old woman laughed delightedly and said, "What old-fashioned generosity! Are you members of the wartime rich, my sons?"

Laughing, Kamal replied, "We're members of the wartime poor, in other words civil servants, my good woman."

Riyad asked her, "What is your distinguished name?"

Raising her head with ludicrous pride, she responded, "The celebrated Sultana Zubayda, in person."

"The Sultana?"

"Yes," she continued jovially. "But my subjects have all died."

"May God have mercy on them."

"God have mercy on the living. It's enough for the dead that they're in the presence of God. Tell me who you are."

A smiling waiter brought her a water pipe and tea. Then, approaching the three friends, he asked, "Do you know her?"

"Who is she?"

"The entertainer Zubayda, the most famous vocalist of her time, but age and cocaine have reduced her to the state you see today."

It seemed to Kamal that he had heard the name before. The interest of Riyad Qaldas intensified, and he urged his friends to introduce themselves as she had requested, in order to encourage her to talk.

Isma'il presented himself: "Isma'il Latif."

Giggling and sipping her tea before it could grow cold, she remarked, "Long live names! Even when a charming one like this doesn't fit the person . . . ."

They laughed, and Isma'il cursed her in a low voice she could not hear. But Riyad said, "Riyad Qaldas."

"An infidel? I had one of you for a lover. He was a merchant in the Muski, and his name was Yusuf Ghattas. He was a world-beater. I used to crucify him on the bed till dawn."

She laughed along with them, her pleasure obvious from her face. Then she turned her eyes to Kamal, who said, "Kamal Ahmad Abd al-Jawad."

She was bringing the glass of tea to her lips. Her hand stopped in midair as she experienced a fleeting moment of lucidity. Staring at his face, she asked, "What did you say?"

Riyad Qaldas answered for him, "Kamal Ahmad Abd al-Jawad."

She took a drag on the water pipe and said as if to herself, "Ahmad Abd al-Jawad! But there are lots of people with the same name, as many as there once were piasters." Then she asked Kamal, "Is your father a merchant in al-Nahhasin?"

Kamal was astonished and replied, "Yes."

She stood up and walked toward them. Coming to a stop in front of him, she roared with a laughter that seemed to exceed by far the powers of her emaciated skeleton. Then she exclaimed, "You're Abd al-Jawad's son! O son of my precious companion! But you don't resemble him! This really is his nose, but he was as handsome as the full moon shining by night. Just mention the Sultana Zubayda to him, and he'll tell you more than enough about me."

Riyad and Isma'il burst into laughter. Kamal smiled as he tried to conquer his disquiet. Only then did he remember that long ago Yasin had told him the story – in fact the many stories – about his father and Zubayda the entertainer.

She asked Kamal, "How is al-Sayyid Ahmad? It's been ages since I moved out of your neighborhood, which spurned me. Now I'm one of the people of Imam al-Shafi'i. But I get homesick for al-Husayn and visit on rare occasions. I was ill for so long that the neighbors got disgusted with me. If they had not been afraid of censure, they would have thrown me into the grave alive. How is my master?"

Kamal replied rather despondently, "He passed away four months ago."

She frowned a little and said, "To God's mercy . . . what a pity! He was a man unlike any other."

She returned to her seat and suddenly laughed loudly. Shortly thereafter the proprietor of the coffeehouse appeared at the entry to the balcony and warned her: "That's enough laughter! 'When we did not scold him the first time, he brought in his jenny.' The gentlemen are to be praised for their generosity to you, but if you're rowdy again, I'll show you the door."

She kept quiet until he left and then smiled at the men. "Are you like your father or not?" she asked Kamal as she made a lewd gesture with her hand.

The friends laughed, and Isma'il said, "He's not even married yet!"

In a bantering tone of disbelief, she said, "It's clear that you're trying to make a sucker out of me."

They laughed. Riyad rose and went to sit beside her. He remarked, "We're honored by your company, Sultana. But I want to hear about the days of your reign."

156

TWENTY MINUTES before the lecture was to begin, Ewart Hall at the American University was almost full. According to Riyad Qaldas, Mr. Roger was a noted professor and especially memorable when discussing Shakespeare. There had been a suggestion that the lecture would contain political allusions, but that was hardly worth considering when the speaker was Mr. Roger and the topic William Shakespeare. Even so, Riyad was glum and despondent. Had he not invited Kamal, he would have stayed away. His distress was entirely natural for a man as preoccupied by politics as he was. With obvious passion, he whispered to Kamal, "Makram Ubayd has been expelled from the Wafd! Why are all these outrageous things happening?"

Kamal, who also still felt stunned by the news, shook his head dejectedly without any comment.

"It's a national catastrophe, Kamal. Things should not have deteriorated this far."

"Yes, but who was responsible?"

"Al-Nahhas! Makram Ubayd may be high-strung, but the corruption that has infiltrated the government is a fact that should not be hushed up."

Smiling, Kamal replied, "Let's not talk about corruption in government. Makram's revolt was less about corruption than about his loss of influence."

With a trace of resignation, Riyad asked, "Would a committed nationalist like Makram abandon the struggle on account of a transitory emotion?"

Kamal could not restrain his laughter as he replied, "You've abandoned your struggle for the sake of a transitory emotion."

Without smiling, Riyad insisted, "Answer me!"

"Makram has an emotional personality like a poet's or a singer's. If he can't be everything, he'd rather be nothing at all. He discovered that his authority was shrinking and rebelled by openly criticizing instances of favoritism and by making an issue of it in the cabinet. So he precluded any chance for reconciliation and cooperation. It's regrettable."

"And what's the result?"

"No doubt the palace blesses this new split in the Wafd Party and will embrace Makram at an appropriate time, just as it has embraced other rebels in the past. From now on, we will see Makram playing a new role with the minority parties and palace agents. Otherwise, he will be out of the picture. They may hate him as much as they do al-Nahhas, or worse, and there are some who hate the Wafd because of Makram. But they will embrace him in order to destroy the Wafd. What happens then is anybody's guess."

Frowning, Riyad said, "A hideous picture! Both men were at fault, al-Nahhas and Makram. My heart senses that no good will come of this." Then in a lower voice he continued: "The Copts will have no one to turn to. Or they will seek protection from their archenemy, the king, and his defense of them will not last long. If the Wafd is now treating us as unfairly as the other parties have, what is to become of us?"

Pretending not to understand, Kamal inquired, "Why do you exaggerate the importance of this incident? Makram is not all the Coptic Christians, and the Copts aren't Makram. He's a political figure who has lost power, but the nationalist principles of the Wafd Party will never be abandoned."

Riyad shook his head sadly and answered sarcastically, "The papers may assert this, but what I'm saying is the truth. The Copts feel that they have all been expelled from the Wafd. They are searching for security, and I fear they will never find it. Politics has recently handed me a new puzzle similar to the one I've had with religion. I have spurned religion with my intellect and yet from ethnic loyalty have felt sympathetic to it with my heart. In exactly the same way, I will spurn the Wafd with my heart and feel sympathetically inclined toward it with my intellect. If I say I'm a Wafdist, I betray my heart. If I say I'm opposed to the Wafd, I cheat my intellect. It's a catastrophe I never dreamed of. Apparently Copts are destined to live forever with split personalities. If all of us were a single individual, he would go mad."

Kamal felt vexed and hurt. It seemed to him that all the different ethnic groups into which humanity was divided were acting out an ironic farce that would have a dreadful ending. In a voice betraying little conviction he said, "The problem ceases to exist if you think of Makram as a politician and not as the entire Coptic community."

"Do the Muslims themselves think of him merely as a politician?"

"I do."

Despite Riyad's despair, a smile flickered across his lips as he said, "I'm talking about Muslims. How does this relate to you?"

"Aren't our situations identical, yours and mine?"

"Yes, but with one difference: you don't belong to a minority." Smiling, he continued: "If I had lived when Egypt was first conquered by the Muslims and had been able to foretell the future, I would have urged all Copts to convert to Islam." Then he protested, "You're not listening to me!"

Kamal was not. His eyes were fixed on the entrance to the auditorium. Looking in that direction, Riyad saw a girl in the bloom of youth wearing a simple gray dress, apparently a student. She took a seat at the front, in the section reserved for women.

"Do you know her?"

"I'm not sure."

They had to stop talking, for the speaker had appeared on the stage and hearty applause resounded through the hall. Then the ensuing silence was so profound that a cough would have seemed an outrage. The president of the American University gave an appropriate introduction, and the professor began to speak. Kamal spent most of his time gazing at the girl's head inquisitively. He had noticed her by accident when she entered, and the sight of her had surprised him, wrenching him away from the train of his thoughts. After propelling him twenty years into the past, she had brought him back, breathless, to the present. At first he had imagined he was seeing Aïda, but there was no way this girl could be Aïda, for she was certainly not much over twenty. He had not had enough time to examine her features, but her overall appearance sufficed: the shape of her face, her figure, her spirit, the expressive look of her eyes. . . . Yes, he had never seen anyone with eyes like this, except for Aïda. Could she be Aïda's sister? That was the next person he thought of: Budur. This time he recalled her name. He immediately remembered how fond she had been of him long ago. But it was highly unlikely – if it truly was Budur – that she would know him. The important fact was that her image had awakened his heart and restored to it, at least for the time being, the full rich life it had once enjoyed. He felt agitated and, though he listened to the speaker for a few minutes, spent the rest of the time staring at the girl's head. Inundated by a wave of memories, he patiently savored all the assorted feelings that collided and wrestled with each other inside his psyche.

"I'll follow her to find out who she really is," he told himself. "There's no particular reason for doing it, but a bored man should be a good walker. I long for anything capable of wiping away the accumulation of rust from my spirit."

With this design in mind, he waited for his opportunity. Was the lecture long or short? He had no idea. When it ended, he confided his plan to Riyad, said goodbye, and set off after the girl, carefully pursuing her graceful step and slim figure. He could not compare the gaits of the two women, for he no longer remembered Aïda's clearly. He thought the girl's build was the same. Aïda's hair had been cut in a boyish bob, but this girl's hair was long and braided. Still, the black color was no doubt identical. Because of the crowd of people from the lecture, he was not able to scrutinize her face at the streetcar stop. She boarded number 15 for al-Ataba and squeezed into the women's section. Climbing aboard after her, he wondered whether she was on her way to al-Abbasiya or if his suppositions were merely confused dreams. Aïda had never ridden a streetcar in her entire life. She had two automobiles at her beck and call. But this poor girl . . . He felt as disconsolate as he had on first hearing the story of Shaddad Bey's bankruptcy and suicide.

The streetcar emptied out most of its load at al-Ataba. He picked a spot on the pavement near her and observed the long slender neck of that former era as she watched for the connecting streetcar. He noticed that her complexion was wheat-colored, verging on white . . . not the bronze of the vanished image. For the first time since he had begun his pursuit, he felt regretful. It seemed he had followed her to see the other woman. The streetcar for al-Abbasiya pulled up, and she prepared to board it. Finding the women's compartment full, she got into the second-class car. He did not hesitate but followed right behind her. When she sat down, he took the seat beside her. The places on both sides filled up and then the area in the middle was occupied by standing passengers. Although he derived immense satisfaction from his success in obtaining a seat next to hers, he was sorry to see her sit among the teeming masses of the second class, perhaps because of the contrast between the two images – the former immortal one and this present one beside him. His shoulder brushed gently against hers whenever the streetcar moved suddenly, especially when it started or jerked to a stop. He gazed at her at every opportunity, examining her as best he could. The coal-black eyes, the eyebrows meeting in the center, the regular and charming nose, the beautiful face.... It was just as if he were looking at Aïda. Was that really true? No, there was the contrast between their complexions, and a smidgeon of difference here and there. He could not say whether it was more of this or less of that. Even though the discrepancies were slight, they seemed as significant to him as the one degree that separates the temperature of a healthy person from an invalid's. All the same he was in the presence of the closest possible likeness to Aïda. He imagined that he could remember his former sweetheart more clearly than ever by the light of this lovely face. The girl's body was possibly just like Aïda's, about which he had wondered so often. Perhaps he was seeing it now. This one was svelte and slender. The girl's chest was only modestly developed, as was the rest of her body, which bore no relationship to Atiya's soft and full one to which he made love. Had his taste deteriorated over the years? Had his former love been merely a rebellion against his latent instincts? In any case he felt a happy, dreamy love that made his heart tipsy with inebriating memories. The occasional contact with her shoulder heightened his intoxication and his penetration into the private world of his thoughts. He had never touched Aïda, always considering her beyond his grasp. Yet this young woman walked through the markets and sat demurely among the crowds in the second-class section. He felt very sad. The contrast between the two women, although trifling, appeared critical. It exasperated him, disappointed his hopes, and decreed that his old love would remain a riddle forever.

Calling out, "Tickets and passes," the conductor appeared. The girl opened her handbag and took out her season pass to have it ready for the conductor. Looking stealthily at the pass, Kamal discovered that the girl's name was Budur Abd al-Hamid Shaddad and that she was a student in the Arts Faculty of the University.

"There's no longer any doubt. My heart is beating faster than it should. If only I could filch her pass . . . to preserve the closest likeness to Aïda. Oh, if only this were possible. . . . '36-year-old schoolteacher robs Arts Faculty student'? What a temptingly sensational headline for the papers! A failed philosopher close to forty! I wonder how old Budur is. She wasn't more than five in 1926, so she's in the twenty-first year of her happy life. Happy? No mansion, no automobile, no servants, no retinue. . . . She was at least fourteen when her family's disaster struck. That's old enough to understand the meaning of a catastrophe and to taste the pain. The poor child must have suffered horribly and felt terrified, experiencing the cruel feeling I'm so familiar with. Pain, although visiting us at different times, unites us now, much as our old but forgotten friendship once did."

When the conductor reached her, Kamal heard Budur say, "Here it is," as she handed the man her pass. The voice struck his ears like a beloved but long-forgotten melody, spreading a great sweetness through him and evoking many memories. It brought back to life a heavenly period of his past, and his senses circled for a long time in the divine realm of ecstasy, where dreams of a bygone era were plainly visible.

"This warm, melodious tune so full of the magic of musical delight . . . let me hear your voice. It's not your voice, my unlucky friend from the past. Fortunately, the mistress of that voice still enjoys a life as luxurious as her old one. The sorrows submerging her family have not reached her. But you have descended to us in the second class. Don't you remember your friend whose neck you would cling to while trading kisses with him? How do you live today, my little one? Will you end up like me, teaching in an elementary school?"

The streetcar passed the former site of the mansion, which had been replaced by an enormous new structure. Kamal had seen it a few times before during visits to al-Abbasiya – after his historic break with the area – especially of late when calling at the home of Fuad Jamil al-Hamzawi.

"Al-Abbasiya itself has changed as much as your house, my little one. The mansions and gardens from the time of my love have disappeared to make way for shops, cafés, cinemas, and huge apartment buildings crammed with occupants. Let Ahmad, who is fascinated by observing the class struggle, rejoice, but how can

I gloat over the misfortunes of this mansion and its inhabitants when my heart is buried in its rubble? And how can I despise that extraordinary creature, who has never tasted the adversities of life or the crowded living conditions of the people, when the thought of her is a beautiful idea before which my heart falls prostrate?"

The streetcar paused at the stop beyond the Wayliya police station, she got out, and he followed. Standing on the pavement there, he watched her cross the road to Ibn Zaydun Street, which was directly opposite. This narrow street was lined by old houses inhabited by the middle class, and its asphalt surface was covered with dirt, stones, and scattered bits of paper. She entered the third house on the left through a small door adjacent to an ironing establishment. He stood there, gazing at the street and the house in gloomy silence. This was where Madam Saniya, the widow of Shaddad Bey, resided. An apartment like that would not rent for more than three pounds a month. If only Madam Saniya would come out on the balcony, he could catch a glimpse of her and measure the changes that had affected her. No doubt they were significant ones. He had not forgotten the precious sight of her leaving the men's parlor of her former home, arm in arm with her husband, as they headed for the waiting car. She had sauntered forth grandly, wearing her fluffy coat and glancing about in a regal and self-assured fashion. "Man will never suffer from a more lethal enemy than time," he reflected. Aïda had stayed in this apartment during her visit to Cairo. Perhaps she had passed part of an evening on this shabby balcony. She had quite possibly shared a bed with her mother and sister, for they certainly had only one.

"I wish I had learned she was here in time. I wish I had seen her again after our long separation. Now that I am liberated from her tyranny, I need to see her so I can learn the truth about her and thus the truth about myself. But this priceless opportunity has been lost."

157

KAMAL SAT with students from the English Department, listening to a lecture by the British professor. It was not the first time he had attended the course, and he assumed it would not be the last. He had encountered little difficulty in obtaining permission to audit the course, which met three nights a week. In fact, the professor had welcomed him on learning that Kamal taught English. It was, of course, a bit odd for him to think of auditing this class only at the end of the academic year, but he had explained he was engaged in research that made it imperative for him to attend these lectures, even though he had missed the previous ones. Through Riyad Qaldas, who was a friend of the Arts Faculty secretary, Kamal had learned that Budur was a student in this department. In his dapper suit and gold-rimmed glasses, with a bushy mustache under his large nose and a few gray hairs at the temples of his huge head, Kamal looked different enough to attract attention, especially when he sat in the company of a few young men and women. Most of them seemed to be wondering about him. They gazed at him in a way that made him so uncomfortable he imagined he could hear what they were thinking about him. He knew better than anyone else the type of comments his appearance inspired. He himself was amazed at the unusual step he had taken without any regard for the effort and discomfort it entailed. What really lay behind it and what was its goal? He did not know precisely, but the moment he had seen a ray of light in his gloomy life, he had raced off recklessly in pursuit of it, driven by the overwhelming forces of despair, passion, and hope. He paid no attention to the obstacles looming on this road, which was threatened on one side by prim tradition and on the other by the proclivity of students for sarcasm. After his long immersion in despair and ennui, he now chased eagerly after this adventure, which he did not doubt would prove exceptionally entertaining and invigorating. It was sufficient excuse that he had developed an interest in time, that he had hope in view, and that he now aspired to be happy. Indeed, his heart, which had previously been as good as dead, pounded with life. He felt the pressure of time, since the academic year was fast approaching its prescribed end.

His efforts had not been in vain, for Budur, like the other students, had noticed him. Perhaps she had participated in the whispered exchanges about him. Her eyes had met his more than once. She had possibly read in them the interest and admiration flaming within him. Who could say? As if this was not enough, they rode home on the same streetcars – Giza and then al-Abbasiya – often sitting near each other. She certainly recognized him, and that was no mean accomplishment for a total stranger to her neighborhood, particularly since he was a schoolteacher who avidly sought to preserve appearances, acting with the propriety and dignity demanded by this profession. As for his goal in all this, he had not troubled himself to identify it. Life pulsed through him after a period of stagnation, and that made him feel enthusiastic. With all the strength his tormented soul could muster, he yearned to become once more that man in whose psyche feelings squirmed, from whose intellect ideas soared, and to whose senses visions were manifest. He longed for this magic to supplant his peevishness, ill health, and perplexity at being confronted by unanswerable riddles. Love was like wine, but its enjoyment was profounder and the hangover less objectionable.

During the previous week, an event had made a considerable impact on his heart. Obliged to supervise athletics at al-Silahdar School, he had been unable to reach the Arts Faculty on time. When he had entered the classroom late, tiptoeing in to avoid making a sound, their eyes had met for a magical, fleeting moment. She had immediately lowered her eyelids rather shyly. It had not been merely a look exchanged between neutral eyes. She probably did feel a bit embarrassed. Would she have looked down so quickly if his previous glances had been in vain? The young woman had become bashful about his attentions. Perhaps she had perceived that his looks were not innocent ones directed her way by accident. That realization by Kamal awakened a mass of memories within him and conjured up many images. He found himself remembering Aïda and dreaming about her, for no apparent reason. Aïda had never lowered her gaze in embarrassment when she was with him. Something else must have reminded him of her . . . a little gesture, a look, or that enchanting secret entity we call "spirit."

Another memorable incident had occurred two days before. "See how she's brought you back to life," he reflected. In the past, nothing had been of any significance whatsoever, or importance had been ascribed only to sterile puzzles, like the will in Schopenhauer, the absolute in Hegel, or the *élan vital* in Bergson. Life as a whole was inanimate and unimportant. "See how a glance, a gesture, or a smile can make the earth tremble today?"

This significant encounter had taken place shortly before 5 P.M. as he was cutting through al-Urman Gardens on his way to the Arts Faculty. He had suddenly found himself being observed by Budur and three other girls, who were waiting on a bench until time for class. His eyes had met Budur's as memorably as in the classroom. He had wanted to greet the girls when he drew closer to them, but the path had veered away, as if refusing to participate in this improvised romantic plot. When he had gone a short distance beyond them, he had looked back and seen that the other girls were smiling and whispering to Budur, whose head was resting in her hand, as if to hide her face.

What was he to make of this exquisite scene? If Riyad had been there, he would have been able to describe and analyze it perfectly. But Kamal had no need for his friend's professional skills. They were surely whispering to her about him, and she had hidden her face in embarrassment. Was any other explanation possible? In the words of a popular song, "Had his eyes revealed his love?" Perhaps he had unwittingly gone too far and made himself the target of gossip. Where would he be if the whispering graduated into insinuating remarks voiced by fiendish male students?

He had seriously considered ending his visits to the Arts Faculty, but that evening he found her sitting next to him on a streetcar bound for al-Abbasiya. The only time this had happened before had been the very first night. He waited for her to look his way so he could greet her, no matter what that led to, but when he felt the waiting had lasted a bit too long, he turned to glance at her himself. Affecting surprise at seeing her seated beside him, he whispered politely, "Good evening."

He had no memory of Aïda ever employing any feminine wiles, but Budur glanced at him as if she too was astonished and then whispered, "Good evening."

Two colleagues had exchanged greetings. There was nothing objectionable about this. He had not been so bold with her sister, but Aïda had been his senior. He had been the young innocent.

"I believe you're from al-Abbasiya?"

"Yes."

"She's not going to take an active role in this conversation," he reflected.

"Unfortunately I missed most of the lectures, since I started to attend so late."

"Yes."

"I hope that in the future I can make up what I missed."

Her only response was a smile. "Let me hear your voice some more," he begged silently. "It's the one bygone melody that time has not altered."

"What do you plan to do once you have your degree? Study at the Teacher Training Institute?"

Displaying some enthusiasm about the conversation for the first time, she answered, "I won't have to go on for further training since the Ministry of Education needs teachers – in view of wartime conditions and the expansion of the school system."

He had craved a single tune but had been granted an entire song.

"So you're going to be a teacher!"

"Yes. Why not?"

"It's a hard profession. Ask me about it."

"I've heard that you teach."

"Yes. Oh! I forgot to introduce myself: Kamal Ahmad Abd al-Jawad."

"I'm honored."

Smiling, he observed, "But I haven't had the honor yet."

"Budur Abd al-Hamid Shaddad."

"The honor's all mine, miss." Then he added, as if astonished by something, "Abd al-Hamid Shaddad! From al-Abbasiya? Are you the sister of Husayn Shaddad?"

Her eyes gleamed with interest as she replied, "Yes."

Kamal laughed as if amazed at the odd coincidence and exclaimed, "Merciful heavens! He was my dearest friend. We spent an extremely happy time together. My Lord – are you the little sister who used to play in the garden?"

She cast an inquiring look at him. It was absurd to think that she would remember him. "Back then you were as wild about me as I was about your sister."

"Of course, I don't recollect any of that."

"Naturally. This story goes back to 1923 and continues to 1926, the year Husayn left for Europe. What is he doing now?"

"He's in the South of France, in the area to which the French government retreated following the German occupation."

"How is he? I haven't had any news or letters from him for a long time."

"He's fine. . . ." Her tone indicated that she did not wish to pursue this subject any further.

As the streetcar passed the site of her former mansion, Kamal wondered whether it had been a mistake to mention his friendship with her brother. Would that not limit his freedom to continue what he had begun? When they reached the stop beyond the Wayliya police station, she said goodbye and left the streetcar. He stayed put, as if oblivious to his own existence. Throughout the ride he had examined her at every opportunity in hopes of detecting the secret quality that had once enchanted him. But he had not discovered it, however close he might have been on several occasions.

She seemed charming, meek, and within his grasp. He now felt a mysterious disappointment and a sorrow that had no discernible causes. If he should wish to marry this girl, no serious obstacles would bar his way. In fact, she seemed responsive and receptive, in spite of or because of the appreciable age difference between them. Experience had taught him that his looks would not prevent him from marrying if he chose to. If he married Budur, he would willy-nilly become a member of Aïda's family. But what substance was there to this ludicrous dream? And what was Aïda to him now? The truth was that he no longer wanted Aïda. But he still wished to learn her secret, which might at least convince him that the best years of his life had not been wasted. He was conscious of the desire, which he had frequently experienced during his life, to look again at his diary and at the candy box presented to him at Aïda's wedding reception. Then his breast filled with so much longing that he wondered whether a man with a thorough understanding of the biological, societal, and psychological components of human affection could still fall in love. But did a chemist's knowledge of poisons prevent him from succumbing to them – like any other victim? Why was his breast so agitated by emotions? Despite the disappointment he had experienced, despite the vast difference between then and now, despite the fact that he did not know whether he belonged to the past or to the present – all these considerations notwithstanding – his breast churned and his heart pounded.

158

HERE AT the tea garden, boughs and verdant branches formed the roof, and a duck could be seen swimming in an emerald pool with a grotto behind it. Employees of *The New Man* magazine had the day off, and Sawsan Hammad looked stunning in a lightweight blue dress that revealed her brown arms. Discreetly and cautiously, she had begun using cosmetics. The two had been colleagues for a year, and as they sat across from each other a smile of mutual understanding lit up their faces. On the table between them stood a water carafe and two ice-cream dishes containing only a milky residue colored pink by strawberries.

"She's dearer to me than anything else in the world," he thought. "I owe her all my happiness. All my hopes are pinned on her. We are devoted partners. We have never openly agreed to be in love, but I have no doubt that we are. Our cooperation is perfectly harmonious. We began as comrades in the struggle for freedom, working together like one person – each of us a candidate for incarceration. Whenever I praise her beauty, she stares at me in protest, frowns, and reprimands me – as if love were beneath us. Then I smile and return to the work at hand. One day I told her, 'I love you! I love you! Do whatever you want about it.' She replied, 'Life's an extremely serious matter, but you wish to treat it as a joke.' I said, 'Like you, I think that capitalism is in its death throes, that it has served its purpose, that the working class has a duty to exert its will to guide the process of development – since the fruit will not pluck itself – and that we have an obligation to create a new consciousness. But after all that, or before it, I love you.' Her frown was at least partly feigned as she remarked, 'You keep subjecting me to talk I dislike.' As there was no one else in the office, I felt courageous enough to swoop down on her cheek to plant a kiss there. She glared at me sternly and busied herself with completing the eighth chapter of a book we were translating together on family structure in the Soviet Union."

"If June is this hot, what will the weather be like in July and August, my dear?"

"It seems that Alexandria wasn't created for people like us."

Laughing, he replied, "But Alexandria is no longer a summer resort. Before the war it was, but today rumors of a German invasion have left it deserted."

"Professor Adli Karim reports that most of its inhabitants have fled and that its streets are filled with cats roaming about freely."

"That's what it's like. Soon Rommel will enter it with his troops." Then after a short silence he added, "At Suez, he'll join forces with the Japanese armies, which will have completed their march through Asia. Then the Fascism of the Stone Age will return."

Sawsan responded rather emotionally, "Russia will never be defeated. Mankind's hopes are still secure behind the Ural Mountains."

"Yes, but the Germans are at the gates of Alexandria."

She inquired with a snort, "Why do the Egyptians love the Germans?"

"Out of hatred for the English. It won't be long before we loathe the Germans. The king seems a captive of the British today, but he will break free from them to receive Rommel. Then those two leaders will drink a toast to the interment of our fledgling democracy. Ridiculously enough, the masses of farm laborers expect that Rommel will distribute land to them."

"We have many enemies. Outside of Egypt the Germans and inside it the Muslim Brethren and the reactionaries, who hardly differ from each other."

"If my brother Abd al-Muni'm heard you, he'd be incensed by your words. He considers the Brethren's message a progressive one that is far superior to materialist forms of socialism."

"There may be a socialist aspect to religion, but it's a utopian socialism comparable to doctrines advanced by Thomas More, Louis Blanc, and Saint-Simon. Religion searches in man's conscience for a remedy to human ills, while the solution lies in the development of society. Paying no attention to social classes, it looks instead at the individuals comprising them. Naturally, it has no concept of scientific socialism. Besides all this, the teachings of religion are based on a legendary metaphysics in which angels play an important part. We should not seek solutions to our present-day problems in the distant past. Tell your brother this."

Ahmad laughed with obvious delight and said, "My brother is an educated man and a clever lawyer. I'm amazed that people like him are strongly attracted to the Brethren."

She replied scornfully, "The Brethren have conducted an appalling campaign of misinformation. When conversing with educated people, they present religion in contemporary garb. With uneducated folk, they talk about heaven and hell. They gain adherents in the name of socialism, nationalism, and democracy."

"My darling never tires of talking about her beliefs," Ahmad reflected. "Did I say 'my darling'? Yes, since I stole a kiss from her, I've made a point of calling her that. She protested with words and gestures but eventually started pretending not to notice – as if she had given up hope of reforming me. When I told her I yearned to hear words of love from her mouth, which speaks of nothing but socialism, she scolded me contemptuously: 'This is the traditional, bourgeois view of women, isn't it?' I told her apprehensively, 'My respect for you is beyond words, and I admit that I've been your pupil in the noblest achievements of my life. But I also love you, and there's nothing wrong with that.' I sensed that her anger evaporated then but observed that she did not abandon her vexed look. As I approached with the secret design of kissing her, she somehow guessed my intent. She put a hand on my chest to push me away, but I managed to kiss her cheek. Since what she was trying to avoid did occur, even though she could have taken more serious measures to prevent it, I assumed that she had consented. Although preoccupied by politics, she's an extraordinary individual with a beautiful mind and a beautiful body. When I invited her for an excursion to the tea garden, she said, 'Only if we take the book with us so we can continue translating it.' I replied, 'No, the idea is to relax and chat. If you decline, I'll renounce socialism altogether.' Perhaps what upsets me most about myself is that – steeped as I am in the conventions of Sugar Street – I still occasionally look at women with a traditional bourgeois eye. During hours of lethargic backsliding, I fancy that socialism in the progressive woman is simply another captivating characteristic comparable to playing the piano or to presenting a fine appearance. But it must also be admitted that the year I have worked with Sawsan has changed me a great deal, cleansing me to a commendable degree of the bourgeois attitudes implanted in me."

"It's distressing that our comrades are being arrested in droves."

"Yes, my darling. Imprisonment becomes fashionable in times of war and in periods of terrible repression – although the law sees nothing wrong with standing up for your cause, if you do not combine that with a call to violence." Then Ahmad laughed and continued: "We'll be arrested sooner or later, unless . . ."

While she stared at him curiously, he concluded, "Unless marriage makes us settle down."

Shrugging her shoulders scornfully, she replied, "What makes you think that I'll agree to marry a fraud like you?"

"Fraud?"

She thought a little and then with genuine interest observed, "Unlike me, you're not from the working class. We both struggle against a single enemy, but you have not had my experience with it. I've endured poverty for a long time, and its hateful effects have touched my family. One of my sisters attempted to fight back, but it defeated her and she died. You . . . you're not . . . you're not from the working class!"

He answered calmly, "Neither was Engels."

Her brief laugh brought her feminine side to the fore, and she asked, "What shall I call you? Prince Ahmadov? It's not that I doubt your dedication to the cause, but you still retain deeply embedded bourgeois traits. It seems to me that you're delighted at times to be a member of the Shawkat family."

He replied a bit stridently, "You're wrong and unfair about that. I'm not to blame for my inheritance. I'm no more responsible for my 'wealth' than you are for your poverty. I am referring to the meager income that has supported our lives of indolence. No one should be blamed for a bourgeois background. One is faulted only for backsliding inertia out of keeping with the spirit of our age."

Smiling, she said, "Don't get annoyed. We're both scientific curiosities. Let's not ask where we began. What we're responsible for is our convictions and our actions. I apologize to you, Engels. But tell me: Are you prepared to keep on delivering talks to workers, regardless of the consequences?"

He answered proudly, "As of yesterday, I had given five talks. I've drafted two important manifestos and distributed tens of handbills. I owe the government more than two years in prison."

"I owe them many more years than that!"

He deftly stretched out his hand to place it affectionately and appreciatively on her soft brown one. Yes, he loved her, but his efforts for the cause were not motivated by this love. Did she not seem at times to doubt his sincerity? Was she teasing him or did she feel apprehensive about the bourgeois characteristics she suspected he still harbored? His belief in the cause was as firm as his love for her. He could not sacrifice either.

"What is happiness if not the discovery of a person who truly understands you and whom you truly understand?" he asked himself. "Particularly one from whom you're not separated by artifice of any kind. I worship her when she says, 'I've endured poverty for a long time.' This candid statement elevates her above all the other members of her sex and makes her seem part of me. But we are reckless lovers, and prison lies in wait for us. We could marry and elude these difficulties, contenting ourselves with the pursuit of happiness. But such an existence would lack spirit. How strongly I've felt at times that the cause is a curse cast upon us by an irrevocable decree. . . . Part of my blood and my spirit, it makes me feel responsible for all mankind."

"I love you."

"What's the pretext for saying this?"

"It's true with or without a pretext."

"You talk about the struggle, but your heart is singing of contentment."

"Separating those two things would be as silly as separating the two of us."

"Doesn't love imply contentment, stability, and an aversion to prison?"

"Haven't you heard about the Prophet, whose struggle for the cause by night and day did not prevent him from marrying nine times?"

Snapping her fingers, she exclaimed, "You've borrowed your brother's mouth! What prophet are you referring to?"

Laughing, he answered, "The Muslims' Prophet!"

"Let me tell you about Karl Marx, who devoted himself to writing *Das Kapital* while his wife and children were exposed to hunger and humiliation."

"At any rate, he was married."

"The pool's water could be liquid emeralds," he mused. "This gentle breeze comes to us without any authorization from June. The duck is swimming around with its bill cocked to pluck bits of bread from the water. You're very happy, and your infuriating sweetheart is even more delightful than the rest of the natural world. I think she's blushing. Perhaps she has set aside politics for the time being and begun to think about...."

"What I was hoping, my dear comrade, was that we would have a chance for a sweet conversation in this garden."

"Sweeter than our talk so far?"

"I mean a discussion of our love."

"Our love?"

"Yes, and you know it too."

There was a long silence. Then, lowering her eyes, she asked, "What do you want?"

"Tell me that we want the same thing."

As if merely trying to humor him, she answered, "Yes. But what is it?"

"Let's stop beating around the bush."

She appeared to be reflecting. Although his wait was short, he found it extremely bitter. Then she said, "Since everything is so clear, why do you torment me?"

Sighing with profound relief, he replied, "How glorious my love is!"

The ensuing silence resembled a musical interlude between two songs. Then she said, "One thing is important to me."

"Yes?"

"My honor."

Shocked by the very suggestion, he protested, "Your honor and mine are identical."

She said resentfully, "You are well acquainted with the conventions of your people. You'll hear a lot of talk about family and breeding...."

"Meaningless words.... Do you think I'm a child?"

She hesitated a little before saying, "There's only one thing threatening us and that's the bourgeois mentality."

With a forcefulness reminiscent of his brother Abd al-Muni'm's, he responded, "I have nothing to do with that!"

"Do you comprehend your statement's serious implications,

both personal and social, for the basic relationship between a man and a woman?"

"I understand them perfectly."

"You'll need a new dictionary for old terms like 'love,' 'marriage,' 'jealousy,' 'faithfulness,' and 'the past.'"

"Yes!"

This interrogation might imply something or it might not. He had often brooded about these ideas, but the situation demanded extraordinary courage. Both his inherited and acquired mentalities were on trial in this frightening inquisition. He imagined that he had caught her drift, but perhaps she was merely testing him. Even if she was serious, he would not retreat. Although gripped by pain as jealousy pulsed through him, he would not back down.

"I consent to your conditions. But let me tell you frankly that I was hoping to win an affectionate woman, not merely an analytical mind."

As her eyes followed the swimming duck, she asked, "To tell you that she loves you and will marry you?"

"Yes!"

She laughed and inquired, "Do you think I'd discuss the details if I had not agreed in principle?"

He squeezed her hand gently, and she added, "You know it all. You just want to hear it."

"I'll never grow tired of hearing it."

159

"IT CONCERNS the reputation of our entire family. If nothing else, he's as much your son as he is mine. But you're free to hold your own opinions."

As Khadija spoke, her eyes glanced swiftly and anxiously from face to face, from her husband, Ibrahim, who was sitting on her right, to her son Ahmad in the opposite corner of the sitting room, not omitting Yasin, Kamal, and Abd al-Muni'm on the way.

Imitating his mother, Ahmad said playfully, "Pay attention, everyone. The family's reputation is at stake, and I'm your son, if nothing else."

She complained bitterly, "What is this ordeal, son? You won't listen to anyone, not even your father. You refuse advice, even when it's for your own good. You're always right, and everyone else is wrong. When you stopped praying, we said, 'May our Lord guide him.' You refused to go to Law School like your brother, and we said, 'The future's in God's hands.' You said, 'I'm going to be a journalist.' We replied, 'Be a cart driver if you want.'"

He replied jovially, "And now I want to get married. . . ."

"Get married. We're all delighted. But marriage has certain conditions. . . ."

"Who sets these conditions?"

"A sound mind."

"My mind has chosen for me."

"Hasn't time shown you yet that you can't rely only on your own intellect?"

"Not at all. Asking advice from other people is possible in everything but marriage, which is exactly like food."

"Food! You don't just marry a girl. You marry her entire family. And consequently, we marry along with you."

Ahmad laughed out loud and exclaimed, "All of you! That's too much! Uncle Kamal doesn't want to marry, and Uncle Yasin would like my bride for himself."

Everyone laughed except Khadija. Then before the smile vanished from his face, Yasin commented, "If that would remedy the situation, I am more than ready to make the sacrifice."

Khadija cried out, "Go ahead and laugh! This just encourages him. It would be far better if you'd give him your frank opinions. What do you think of a person who wishes to marry the precious daughter of a printshop employee who works for the girl's own magazine? It's hard for us to bear your working as a journalist. How can you want to marry into the family of a pressman? Don't you have an opinion about this, Mr. Ibrahim?"

Ibrahim Shawkat raised his eyebrows as if he wanted to say something but kept quiet. Khadija continued: "If this disaster takes place, the night of the wedding your home will be jammed with press operators, artisans, cabdrivers, and God knows what else."

Ahmad responded passionately, "Don't talk like that about my family."

"Lord of heaven – do you deny that her relatives are people like this?"

"She's the only one I'm marrying, folks."

Ibrahim Shawkat said in exasperation, "You won't marry just her – may God give you as much trouble as you're causing us."

Encouraged by her husband's protest, Khadija said, "I went to visit their home, as custom dictates. I said, 'I'll go see my son's bride.' I found them living in a cellar on a street inhabited almost entirely by Jews. Her mother's appearance differs in no respect from that of a maid, and the bride herself is at least thirty. Yes, by God! If she had even a hint of beauty, I would excuse him. Why do you want to marry her? He's bewitched. She's cast a spell on him. She works with him at that ill-omened magazine. Perhaps she put something in his coffee or water when he wasn't looking. Go and see her yourselves. You be the judge. I've met my match. I returned from the visit scarcely able to see the road because of my chagrin and sorrow."

"You're making me angry. I won't forgive you for saying such things."

"Sorry!" Then, quoting the title of a wedding song, she continued: "'Sorry, sovereign beauty!' I'm in the wrong! All my life I've been overly critical of other people, and now our Lord has afflicted me with children who suffer from every known defect. I ask the forgiveness of God Almighty."

"No matter what allegations you make about her family, unlike you they don't make false accusations about other people."

"Tomorrow, after it's too late, when you've heard everything," you'll understand that I was right. May God forgive you for insulting me."

"You're the one who has done an outstanding job of humiliating me."

"She's after your money. If she had not come upon a failure like you, the most she could have hoped for would have been a newspaper vendor."

"She's an editor at the magazine with a salary twice the size of mine."

"So she's a journalist too! God's will be done! What kind of girl works outside the home except an old maid, a hag, or a woman who apes men?"

"God forgive you."

"And may He forgive you, too, for all the suffering you're causing us."

Yasin, who had followed the conversation attentively while twisting his mustache, said at this point, "Listen, sister. There's no reason to squabble. Let's give Ahmad the candid advice he needs, but arguing won't help matters."

Ahmad stood up angrily, saying, "Please excuse me. I'm going to get dressed and go to work."

Once he was out of the room, Yasin went to sit beside his sister and, leaning toward her, said, "Quarreling won't do you any good. We can't rule our children. They think they are better and cleverer, than we are. If there's no way to avert the marriage, let him get married. If he's not happy with her, it will be entirely his fault. As you know, I was never able to settle down until I married Zanuba. It's just possible that he has made a wise choice. Besides, we gain understanding from experience not from words." Then he laughed and corrected himself: "Although I haven't been enlightened by either words or experience."

Kamal agreed with Yasin. "My brother's right."

Giving him a reproachful look, Khadija asked, "Is this all you have to say, Kamal? He loves you. If you would talk to him in private...."

Kamal answered, "I'll leave when he does and have a word with him. But we've had enough quarreling. He's a free man. He has a right to marry any woman he wants. Can you stop him? Are you planning to break off relations with him?"

Smiling, Yasin said, "The matter's quite simple, sister. He'll get married today and divorced tomorrow. We're Muslims, not Catholics."

Narrowing her small eyes and speaking through half-closed lips, Khadija said, "Of course. What attorney does he need to defend him besides you? Whoever said that the son takes after his maternal uncle was right."

Yasin roared out his mighty laugh and said, "God forgive you. If women were left at the mercy of other females, no girl would ever get married."

Pointing to her husband, she observed, "His mother, God rest her soul, chose me for him herself."

Sighing cheerfully, Ibrahim said, "And I've paid the price... may God have mercy on her and pardon her."

Khadija ignored his comment and continued regretfully: "If only she were pretty! He's blind!"

Laughing, Ibrahim remarked, "Like his father!"

She turned toward him angrily and snapped, "You're an ingrate, like all men."

The man replied calmly, "No, we're just patient, and paradise belongs to us."

She shouted at him, "If you ever enter it, that will be thanks to me, because I taught you your religion."

Kamal and Ahmad left Sugar Street together. The uncle was skeptical and undecided about this proposed marriage. He could not fault himself for adherence to foolish traditions or for indifference to the principles of equality and human dignity, but still the hideous social reality, which he could not change, was a fact a person could not ignore. In the past he had been infatuated with Qamar, the daughter of Abu Sari', who sold grilled snacks. Despite her charms, she had almost repulsed him with the disagreeable odor of her body. Kamal admired the young man, envying Ahmad's courage, decisiveness, and other qualities that he himself lacked – particularly belief, diligence, and a will to marry. Ahmad could almost have been awarded to the family in compensation for Kamal's stolid negativism. Why did marriage seem so significant to him while for other people it was a normal part of everyday life like saying "Hello"?

"Where are you going, my boy?"

"To the magazine, Uncle. What about you?"

"*Al-Fikr* magazine to meet Riyad Qaldas. . . . Won't you think a little more before taking this step?"

"What step, Uncle? I'm already married."

"Is that true?"

"It's true. And I'm going to live on the first floor of our house . . . because of the housing crisis."

"How provocative!"

"Yes, but she won't get home until after my mother has gone to bed."

After recovering from the impact of the news, Kamal asked his nephew jovially, "Did you marry in the manner prescribed by God and His Messenger?"

Ahmad laughed too and replied, "Of course. We marry and bury according to the precepts of our former religion, but we live according to the Marxist faith." Then, as they parted, he added, "You'll like her a lot, Uncle. Once you see her, you can judge for yourself. She's a wonderful personality, in every sense of the word."

160

WHAT APPALLING indecisiveness. . . . It might just as well have been a chronic disease. Every issue seemed to present a multitude of equivalent sides, making it almost impossible to choose between them. Neither metaphysical questions nor the simple operations of daily life were exempt. Perplexity and hesitation posed an obstacle everywhere. Should he marry or not? He needed to make up his mind but fluctuated so much that he felt dizzy. The normal balance between his spirit, intellect, and senses became disrupted. When the maelstrom finally calmed down, no progress would have been made, and the question – to marry or not – would still lack an answer. Occasionally he felt distressed by his freedom and by his loneliness or resented a life spent in the company of dreary mental phantoms. Then he would yearn for a companion, and the loving family instincts imprisoned inside him would groan for release. He would picture himself a husband, cured of his introspective isolation, his fantasies dissipated . . . but also preoccupied by his children, wholly absorbed in earning a living, and oppressed by all the concerns of everyday life. Then, dreadfully alarmed, he would decide to stay single, no matter how much tormented loneliness he suffered. But indecision would soon rear its head again as he started to wonder about marriage once more, and so on and so forth. How could he make up his mind?

Budur really was a wonderful girl. The fact that she rode the streetcar today did not detract from her charms, for she had been born and raised in the paradise of those angels who had inflamed his heart in the old days. She was a meteor that had fallen from the sky, a truly outstanding girl, and an educated beauty of good character. She would not be difficult to obtain. If he chose to proceed, she would be a promising bride in every respect. All he had to do was to get on with it.

In addition to these considerations, he had to admit that she occupied a central place in his consciousness. Hers was the last image of life he saw on falling asleep and the first he greeted on waking. During the day, she was rarely far from his thoughts. The moment he saw her, the rusty strings of his heart began to vibrate with poignant songs. His world of lonely and confused suffering had been transformed. Breaths of fresh air had penetrated it, and the water of life flowed through it. If this was not love, what was it? For the last two months he had sought out Ibn Zaydun Street late each afternoon, traversing it slowly and training his eyes on the balcony until they met hers. Then they would exchange a smile, as was only appropriate for two colleagues. That had started as if by chance, but the continuation could only have been deliberate. Whenever he turned up at the appointed hour, he found her seated on the balcony, reading a book or glancing around. He was certain that she was waiting for him. Had she wished to erase this idea from his mind, she would have needed only to avoid the balcony for a few minutes each afternoon. What must she think of his visit, smile, and greeting? But not so fast. . . . Instincts are rarely mistaken. Each of them wished to encounter the other. This realization sent him into transports of joy and left him drunk with delight. He was filled with a sense of life's value. But this happiness was marred by anxiety. How could it help but be, when it had not yet been coupled with a determination to proceed? A current swept him along, and he yielded to it, not knowing where it would carry him or where he would land. A little reflection might have forced him to be more circumspect, but the joy of life sympathetically diverted him. He was intoxicated with gaiety but not free of anxiety.

Riyad had told him, "Get on with it. This is your chance." Ever since starting to wear an engagement ring, Riyad had spoken of marriage as if it was man's original and ultimate objective in life, saying conceitedly that since he was boldly embarking on this unique experience, he would be granted a new and more accurate understanding of life, one that would create opportunities for him to write about children and couples. "Isn't this what life is all about, you high-soaring philosopher?"

Kamal had answered evasively, "Today you've gone over to the other side, and so you're the last person from whom to expect a fair judgment. I'll miss having you as my sincere adviser."

Viewed from another perspective, love seemed to him a dictator, and Egypt's political life had taught him to hate dictatorship with all his heart. At his aunt Jalila's house, he surrendered his body to Atiya but then quickly reclaimed it, as if nothing had happened. This girl, shielded by her modesty, would be satisfied with nothing less than possessing his spirit and his body, forever. Afterward, there would only be one course for him to pursue: the bitter struggle to earn a living to support his wife and children properly – a bizarre destiny transforming an existence rife with exalted concerns into nothing more than a means of "gaining" a living. The Indian sadhu might be a fool or a lunatic but was at least a thousand times wiser than a man up to his ears in making a living.

"Enjoy the love you once yearned for," he advised himself. "Here it is, resuscitated in your heart, but bringing lots of problems with it."

Riyad had asked him, "Is it reasonable for you to love her, to have it in your power to marry her, and then to decline to take her?"

Kamal had replied that he loved her but not marriage.

Riyad had protested, "It's love that consoles us to marriage. Since you're not in love with marriage – as you say – you must not be in love with the girl."

Kamal had insisted, "No, I love her and hate marriage."

Riyad had suggested, "Perhaps you fear the responsibility."

Kamal had said furiously, "I already shoulder far more responsibilities at home and at work than you do."

Riyad had snapped, "Perhaps you're more selfish than I had imagined."

Kamal had inquired sarcastically, "What inspires an individual to marry if not latent or manifest egotism?"

Smiling, Riyad had retorted, "Perhaps you're sick. Go to a psychiatrist. He may be able to cure you."

Kamal had remarked, "It's amusing that my forthcoming article in *al-Fikr* magazine is 'How to Analyze Yourself.'"

Riyad had told him, "I admit that you puzzle me."

Kamal had answered, "I'm the one who is always puzzled."

Once, walking down Ibn Zaydun Street as usual, he had encountered his sweetheart's mother on her way home. He had recognized her at first glance, although he had not seen her for at least seventeen years and she was no longer the lady he had once known. She had withered in a most distressing way, and worry had marked her even before age could. A person would hardly have imagined that this emaciated woman scurrying by was the lady who had sauntered through the garden of the mansion, a paragon of beauty and perfection. Nonetheless the shape of her head had reminded him of Aïda, and the sight of her had affected him deeply. Fortunately, he had already exchanged a smile with Budur before seeing her mother. Otherwise, he would not have been able to. Then, for no particular reason, he had found himself remembering Aisha and the ill-tempered fit she had thrown that morning when searching for her dentures, after forgetting where she had deposited them before going to sleep the previous evening.

Then one day he noticed that, contrary to her usual practice, Budur was standing on the balcony. He perceived that she was preparing for an excursion. He asked himself, "Will she go out alone?" She immediately disappeared from view, and he proceeded on his way, slowly and reflectively. If she really did come out alone, she would be coming to see him. Perhaps this intoxicating victory would wash away the humiliation he had suffered years before. But would Aïda have done this, even if the moon had split apart? When he was halfway down the block, he turned to look back and saw her coming . . . by herself. He imagined that the pounding of his heart was audible to the neighbors and sensed immediately the gravity of the developing situation. One side of his personality strongly advocated flight. Their previous exchanges of smiles had been an innocent sentimental entertainment, but this encounter would be of unparalleled significance, bringing with it new responsibilities and the need to make a decisive choice. If he fled now, he would give himself more time for reflection. But he did not run away. He continued on with deliberate steps, as if drugged, until she caught up with him at the corner of al-Galal Street. As he turned, their eyes met, they smiled, and he said, "Good evening."

"Good evening."

Conscious of the ever mounting dangers, he asked, "Where to?"

"To see a girlfriend. She lives in that direction." She pointed toward Queen Nazli Street.

He replied recklessly, "That's the way I'm going. May I accompany you?"

Hiding a smile, she said, "If you want. . . ."

They walked along side by side. She had not decked herself out in this lovely dress to visit a girlfriend. It was for him, and his heart welcomed her with passion and affection. But how was he to conduct himself? Perhaps she had wearied of his inaction and had ventured out herself to provide a propitious opportunity for him. He would have to avail himself of it out of respect for her or ignore it and lose her forever. It had come down to a word that if spoken would affect the entire course of his life or if withheld would have consequences he would rue for the remainder of his days. Thus, against his better judgment, he found himself put on the spot.

They had gone quite a distance, and she presumably expected something. She seemed ready and responsive – as if she did not belong to the Shaddad family. In fact, she was not a Shaddad at all. The Shaddad family was finished. Its time had passed. "The person walking along with you is just one of many unlucky girls," he reflected.

She turned toward him with a tentative smile and said gently, "It's been nice to see you."

"Thanks."

Then what? . . . She seemed to be waiting for a further step on his part. The end of the street was approaching. He had to make up his mind to commit himself or to say goodbye. She had probably never imagined that they would part without even a hopeful word. The intersection was only a few paces ahead. He was painfully aware of the disappointment she would suffer, but his tongue refused to cooperate. Should he say something, no matter what the consequences? She stopped walking, and her smile, which appeared more deliberate than natural, seemed to say, "It's time for us to part." His confusion reached a climax. Then she held out her hand, and he took it. He said nothing for a terrible moment and then finally murmured, "Goodbye."

She withdrew her hand and turned into a side street. He almost called out after her. For Budur to depart in this manner, spattered with failure and embarrassment, was an unbearable nightmare. "You're a past master of miserable situations," he chided himself. But his tongue was frozen. Why had he been following her for the past two months?

"Is it in good taste to spurn her when she comes to you herself? Is it nice to give her the same dismissive treatment meted out to you by her sister? When you love her? Will she pass a night similar to the one that, though long behind you, still lights up the gloomy past like a burning coal with its smoldering pain?"

He walked on, wondering whether he really wanted to remain a bachelor so he could be a philosopher or whether he was using philosophy as a pretext for staying single.

Riyad told him later that what he had done was incredible and that he would regret it. His inaction really was unbelievable, but did he also regret it?

Riyad asked, "How could breaking off with her have seemed so trivial to you after you had been talking of her as the girl of your dreams?" She was not the girl of his dreams, for that girl would never have come to him.

Finally Riyad told Kamal, "You won't be thirty-six much longer. After that, you won't be fit for marriage." Angered by this remark, Kamal succumbed to despair.

161

CLAD IN a wedding gown, Karima came by carriage with her parents and her brother to Sugar Street, where Ibrahim Shawkat, Khadija, Kamal, Ahmad, and Ahmad's wife, Sawsan Hammad, were waiting to receive them. There was nothing to suggest a wedding reception except the bouquets of roses lining the sitting room. The men's parlor, which opened on the courtyard, was filled with bearded young men, in the midst of whom sat Shaykh Ali al-Manufi. Although a year and a half had passed since the death of al-Sayyid Ahmad, Amina did not attend the reception, promising instead to offer her congratulations later.

When Khadija had invited her to this low-key wedding, Aisha had shaken her head in amazement, replying nervously, "I only attend funerals." Although she was offended by this remark, Khadija had grown accustomed to observing exemplary restraint with Aisha.

The upper floor at Sugar Street had been furnished for a second time with a bride's trousseau. Yasin had outfitted his daughter properly and, to finance this expenditure, had sold the last of his holdings, except for the house in Palace of Desire Alley.

Karima, who looked exceptionally beautiful, resembled – especially in the warmth of her gaze – her mother, Zanuba, at her prime. The girl had only reached the legal age of consent during the last week of October. Khadija, as was only appropriate for the mother of the groom, seemed happy. Availing herself of a moment alone with Kamal, she leaned toward him to say, "At any rate, she is Yasin's daughter and, no matter what, a thousand times better than the workshop bride."

A small buffet dinner had been set out in the dining room for the family and another in the courtyard for Abd al-Muni'm's bearded guests, from whom he differed in no respect, since he too had let his beard grow. At the time, Khadija had commented, "Religion's lovely, but what need is there for this beard, which makes you look like Muhammad al-Ajami, the couscous vendor?"

Members of the family sat in the parlor, except for Abd

al-Muni'm, who kept his friends company. After helping his brother welcome them for a time, Ahmad returned to the parlor, where on joining his family he said jovially, "The gentlemen's parlor has reverted a thousand years back into history."

Kamal asked, "What are they discussing?"

"The battle of El Alamein . . . loudly enough to make the walls rattle."

"What's their reaction to the British victory?"

"Anger, naturally. They are enemies of the English, the Germans, and the Russians, too. And so they don't spare the bridegroom even on his wedding night."

Seated next to Zanuba, Yasin, who in his finery looked ten years her junior, said, "Let the armies eat each other alive, so long as they don't do it here. It's our Lord's mercy that He has not made Egypt a war zone."

Smiling, Khadija remarked, "You probably want peace so you'll be free to do as you like." Then she cast Zanuba a sly look that made everyone laugh, for it had recently been reported that Yasin had flirted with the new tenant in his building and that, having caught him in the act, or almost, Zanuba had hounded the woman until she had vacated the apartment.

To hide his discomfort, Yasin said, "How can I do as I like when my home is under military rule?"

Zanuba protested resentfully, "You're not embarrassed – not even in front of your daughter?"

Yasin replied plaintively, "I'm innocent and the woman wrongly accused."

"I'm in the wrong? I'm the one who was caught knocking on her door at night and who then excused himself by saying he had lost his way in the dark? Huh? You spend forty years in a building and then can't find your apartment?"

They roared with laughter, but Khadija said ironically, "He often loses his way in the dark."

"And in the daylight as well."

Then Ibrahim Shawkat asked Ridwan, "How are you getting along with Muhammad Effendi Hasan?"

Yasin corrected his brother-in-law: "Muhammad Effendi Scum!"

Ridwan replied furiously, "He's now enjoying my grandfather's fortune, which went to my mother."

Yasin said argumentatively, "It's a considerable inheritance, but whenever Ridwan approaches her for assistance with some small purchase or other, her insolent husband makes problems for the boy and interrogates him about his expenses."

Khadija told Ridwan, "You're her only child. It would be better if she'd let you enjoy her money while she's still alive." Then she added, "And it's time for you to get married, isn't it?"

Ridwan laughed feebly and answered, "When Uncle Kamal does."

"I've given up on your uncle Kamal. There's no need for you to imitate him."

Kamal listened resentfully to these remarks, but did not allow it to show on his face. If she had despaired of him, so had he. In order to acknowledge consciousness of his guilt, he had stopped walking along Ibn Zaydun Street. He would stand near the streetcar stop, where he could watch her on the balcony without being seen. He could no more overcome his desire to see her than he could deny his love for her or ignore his alarmed aversion to the thought of marrying her. Riyad had told him, "You're sick and refuse to recover."

Ahmad Shawkat asked Ridwan in a knowing tone, "Would Muhammad Hasan interrogate you about your expenditures if your Sa'dist Party were in power?"

Ridwan laughed bitterly and answered, "He's not the only one who calls me to account nowadays. But patience . . . it's only a matter of a few more days or weeks."

Sawsan Hammad asked him, "Do you think the days of the Wafd Party are numbered, as its foes suggest?"

"The length of its rule depends entirely on the English. In any case the war won't drag on forever. Then it will be time to settle accounts."

With great earnestness, Sawsan said, "Primary responsibility for the tragedy lies with the people who helped the Fascists stab the English in the back."

Khadija gazed at Sawsan scornfully and disapprovingly, astonished that her daughter-in-law would join the conversation in such a manly fashion. She could not keep from remarking, "We're supposed to be at a wedding party. Let's talk about more suitable things."

To avoid a clash, Sawsan fell silent, while Ahmad and Kamal

exchanged a smiling look. Ibrahim Shawkat laughed and remarked, "Their excuse is that our weddings aren't what they used to be . . . May God be compassionate to al-Sayyid Ahmad and provide him with a fine dwelling in paradise."

Yasin said regretfully, "I've been married three times, but I've never had a proper procession with a shivaree."

Zanuba asked acidly, "You blab about yourself and forget your daughter?"

Laughing, Yasin replied, "We'll have the proper festivities the fourth time, God willing."

Zanuba remarked sarcastically, "Postpone that until you've escorted Ridwan to his bride."

Ridwan was annoyed but said nothing. "God's curse on all of you and on marriage too," he thought. "Don't you realize that I'll never marry? I'd like to kill anyone who brings up this damn subject."

After a short silence, Yasin said, "I wish I could stay at the ladies' buffet, to avoid mingling with those bearded fellows, who frighten me."

"If they knew what you've done, they'd stone you," Zanuba taunted him.

Ahmad said scornfully, "Their beards will get in the food. It will be more like a battle than a dinner. Does my uncle Kamal like the Brethren?"

Smiling, Kamal answered, "I like one of them at least."

Turning to the silent bride, Sawsan asked affectionately, "What does Karima think about her husband's beard?"

Karima hid her laughter by ducking her crowned head but said nothing. Zanuba answered for her, "Few young men are as pious as Abd al-Muni'm."

Khadija remarked, "I admire his piety, which is a characteristic of our family, but not his beard."

Laughing, Ibrahim Shawkat said, "I must acknowledge that both my sons – the Believer and the apostate – are crazy."

Yasin roared his mighty laugh and commented, "Insanity is also a characteristic of our family."

Khadija gave him a look of protest. Before she could say anything, he attempted to humor her by adding, "I mean I'm crazy. I think Kamal's crazy too. But if you want, I'm the only crazy one."

"That is the unvarnished truth."

"Does it make sense for a man to condemn himself to bachelor-hood so he can have time to read and write?"

"He'll marry sooner or later and be eminently sensible."

Ridwan asked his uncle Kamal, "Why don't you marry, Uncle? I'd like to know at least the basis for your objections so I can defend myself in a similar way if I need to."

Yasin asked, "Are you planning to boycott marriage? I'll never give you permission to do that so long as I live. Just wait until your party is in power again. Then you can have a spectacular political wedding."

But Kamal told his nephew, "If there's nothing to prevent it, you ought to get married at once."

"How handsome this young man is," Kamal mused. "And he has expectations of status and of wealth. If Aïda had seen him when she was young she would have fallen in love with him. If he favored Budur with a glance in passing, she would become wildly infatuated with him." Kamal went around in circles while the whole world advanced. He kept asking himself, "Are you going to get married or not?" Life seemed to offer nothing but gloomy confusion. His opportunity was neither ideal nor worthless. Love was difficult. It was characterized by controversy and suffering. If only she would marry someone else so he could free himself from this confusion and torment.

Then Abd al-Muni'm, preceded by his beard, came to announce, "Please help yourself to the buffet. Our festivities today are limited to the stomach."

162

AT ABOUT ten o'clock one Friday morning Kamal was strolling along Fuad I Street, which was crowded with pedestrians. The weather was pleasant, as it normally is for most of November. He was very fond of walking and had grown accustomed to assuaging his emotional isolation by plunging into crowds of people on his day off. He would wander about aimlessly, entertaining himself by observing people and places.

On his way, he had run into more than one of his young pupils, who had greeted him with a salute. He had returned their greetings politely and cheerfully. How many pupils he had! Some had already found employment. Others were at the University. Most of them were in either elementary or secondary school. Fourteen years of service to learning and education was quite a substantial contribution. Kamal's traditional appearance was little altered: neat suit, glistening shoes, fez planted squarely on his head, gold-rimmed spectacles, and bushy mustache. Not even his civil service rank – the sixth – had changed in fourteen years, although there were rumors that the Wafd was thinking about rectifying such inequities. One visible change was the gray spreading through the hair at his temples. He seemed delighted by the salutations of these pupils, who loved and respected him. No other teacher had garnered a comparable popularity, and he had accomplished this in spite of his huge head and nose and the unruly deviltry in vogue among students.

When his meanderings brought him to the intersection of Fuad I and Imad al-Din streets, he suddenly found himself face to face with Budur. His heart pounded as if a siren had gone off inside. The paralyzed stare of his eyes lasted for a few moments, and then he started to smile in an attempt to obviate some of the awkwardness of the situation. But she turned her eyes away, clearly pretending that she did not know him. She did not soften her expression at all as she walked past him. Then, and only then, did he notice that her arm was around a young male companion's.

Kamal stopped and followed her with his eyes. Yes, it was Budur, in an elegant black coat. Her escort, who was just as dapper, was probably not yet thirty. Kamal did his best to control himself, but the surprise had given him a jolt. He wondered with interest who the young man might be . . . not her brother or her lover, for lovers do not parade their relationship down Fuad I Street, especially not on Friday morning. Could he be? . . . Kamal's heart beat apprehensively. Then without any hesitation he started after them. His eyes never left them, and his attention was fixed so keenly on them that he sensed his temperature rising, along with his blood pressure. The pounding of his heart sounded like a death knell. He saw them pause before the display of a store selling suitcases. He slowly drew closer, directing his eyes toward the girl's right hand until he could see the gold ring. He felt scorched by a burning sensation that seemed a symptom of his profound pain.

Four months had passed since the incident on Ibn Zaydun Street. Had this young man been spying on him from the end of the street, just waiting to take his place? There was no cause for astonishment. Four months was a long time, long enough for the world to be turned upside down. Kamal stood in front of a toy store a short distance away, as if examining the toys. She seemed prettier today than ever before . . . the spitting image of a bride. But what was the black color that had transformed all her garments? A black coat was nothing unusual. Although that was quite fashionable, why was her dress black too? Was it attributable to style or mourning? Had her mother died? He was not in the habit of reading through the obituaries, and how did it concern him? What really mattered was that Budur's page in the book of his life had been turned. Budur was finished. The anxious question, to marry or not, had a conclusive answer. After all his anxiety and suffering, he should be happy. He had often wished she would marry someone else, so his torment would end. Lo and behold, she had. He should be delighted to be released from his suffering. He imagined that a person being executed might experience the sensations he was feeling then as the gates of life closed in his face and he was expelled beyond its walls.

He saw them turn and move his way, passing by him non-chalantly. He followed them with his gaze and considered trailing after them but changed his mind almost irritably. He loitered by the toy display and gazed at it without seeing anything. Then he looked after them one last time, as if to bid her farewell. She got ever farther away, vanishing at times behind other people only to appear again. He saw one side of her once and then the other. All the strings of his heart were murmuring, "Farewell." The tormented feeling that gripped him was accompanied by mournful melodies, which were no strangers to him. He was reminded of a comparable situation in the past. This emotion pulsed through him, carrying with it various associated memories. It could have been a mysterious tune, evoking the most sublime pain but at the same time bringing veiled hints of pleasure. It was a single emotion in which pain met pleasure, just as night and day encounter each other at dawn. Then she disappeared, perhaps forever, exactly as her sister had before her.

He found himself wondering who her fiancé was. Kamal had not been able to scrutinize the young man, although he would have loved to. He hoped – if the man was in the civil service – that his rank was inferior to that of a teacher. But what were these childish thoughts? It was embarrassing. As for the pain, a person as experienced with it as he was should not worry, since he would know from experience that its fate – like that of all things – was death. For the first time, he noticed the toys that were spread before his eyes. The display was beautiful and well arranged. Included in it were all the kinds of toys that children adore: trains, cars, cradles, musical instruments, and dollhouses with gardens. He was so drawn to this sight by the strange force welling up in his tortured soul that he could not take his eyes off the shop window. In his childhood, he had not been allowed to enjoy the paradise of toys. He had grown up harboring this unsatisfied longing, and now it was too late to gratify it. People who spoke of the happiness of childhood – what did they know? Who could declare authoritatively that he had been a happy child? How foolish this wretched and unexpected desire was – to become a child again, like that wooden one playing in a beautiful make-believe garden.... The impulse was both absurd and sad. By their very nature children tended to be unbearable creatures. Perhaps it was only his vocation that had taught him how to communicate with them and how to guide them. But what would life be like if he returned to his childhood while retaining his adult mind and memories? He would play once more in the roof garden but with a heart filled with memories of Aïda. He would go to al-Abbasiya in 1914 and see Aïda playing in the yard. Yet he would be aware of the treatment he would receive at her hands in 1924 and thereafter. Speaking to his father with a lisp, he would disclose that war would break out in 1939 and that al-Sayyid Ahmad would die following an air raid. What foolish thoughts these were.... All the same, they were better than focusing on this new disappointment, which he had just encountered on Fuad I Street. They were better than thinking about Budur, her fiancé, and Kamal's relationship to her. Perhaps unconsciously he was atoning for some past error. How and when had that mistake occurred? Whether an act, a word, or a situation, it was the cause of the torment he was suffering. If he came to know himself thoroughly, he could easily separate the cause from the pains it brought. The battle was not over. The capitulation had not yet taken place. Nor should it. Perhaps this was the reason for the infernal vacillation that had left him biting his fingernails while Budur strolled by arm in arm with her fiancé. He would have to think twice about this torment that concealed within it a mysterious delight. Had he not experienced it once before, when he was in the desert at al-Abbasiya, looking at the light from the window of Aïda's bridal chamber? Had his hesitation with Budur been a trick to put himself into a comparable situation so that he could revive the old sensations, reliving their pleasure and their pain? Before lifting a hand to write about God, the spirit, and matter, he ought to know himself, his individual personality, that of Kamal Effendi Ahmad . . . Kamal Ahmad . . . no, just plain Kamal. Then he would be able to create himself anew. He should start that night by reviewing his diary in order to examine the past very carefully. It would be a night without sleep, but not his first. His collection of them could be put into a single album under the title "Sleepless Nights." He should never say that his life had been in vain, for he would leave behind some bones future generations could play with. Budur had vanished from his life forever, and this truth was as doleful as a funeral dirge. She had left behind not a single affectionate memory, not an embrace or a kiss, not even a touch or a kind word.

He no longer feared insomnia. In the past he had faced it alone. Today he had countless ways of diverting his mind and heart. He would go to Atiya in her new house on Muhammad Ali Street. They would continue their endless conversation.

Last time he had told her with a diction slurred by drink, "We're perfect for each other."

With resigned irony she had answered, "You're very sweet when you're drunk."

He had continued: "What a happy couple we'll make if we ever get married."

Frowning, she had said, "Don't make fun of me. I've been a lady in every sense of the word."

"Yes. Yes. You're more delectable than ripe fruit."

She had pinched him mischievously, observing, "That's what you say, but if I asked you for an extra twenty piasters, you'd flee."

"What we have goes way beyond money."

Giving him a look of protest, she had remarked, "But I have two children who prefer money to talk about a loving relationship."

His sorrow and intoxication having reached their climax, he had said sarcastically, "I'm thinking of following Madam Jalila's example and repenting. When I become a Sufi, I'll leave you my entire fortune."

Giggling, she had said, "If repentance catches up with you, that will be the end of us."

He had laughed loudly and answered, "If repentance would harm women like you, I'll certainly forget about it."

This was his refuge from insomnia. Realizing that he had tarried by the toy display long enough, he turned and walked away.

163

KHALO, THE proprietor of the Star Tavern, asked, "Is it true, my dear, that they're going to close all the bars?"

With confident self-assurance, Yasin replied, "Inconceivable, Khalo! The deputies say all sorts of things when the budget is being debated, and the government complacently promises to investigate the deputies' requests at the earliest opportunity. But this has a way of never arriving."

The members of Yasin's group in the bar on Muhammad Ali Street vied with each other to offer their comments.

The personnel director said, "For as long as anyone can remember they've been promising to throw the British out of Egypt, to open a new university, and to widen al-Khalig Street. Have any of these pledges been kept, Khalo?"

The honorary dean of pensioners observed, "Perhaps the deputy proposing that had drunk some of the lethal wartime liquor and was attempting to get even."

The attorney said, "No matter what, bars on streets visited by foreigners won't be touched. So, Khalo, if the worst happens, just buy into some saloon or other. Like buildings that stand cheek by jowl, dramshop owners support each other."

The head clerk from mortmain trusts remarked, "If the English advanced on the Abdin Palace with their tanks over a trivial question like returning al-Nahhas to power, do you think they'd stand for having the bars closed?"

In addition to Yasin's group, some local merchants were in the room. All the same, the head clerk suggested blending song with drink: "Let's sing 'Prisoner of love.'"

Khalo scurried back to his place behind the counter, and the friends began to sing, "What humiliations the prisoner of love experiences." Inebriation's tune rang out more clearly than any other one, and the grimaces of the merchants showed their disdain for this performance. But the singing did not last long. Yasin was the first to drop out, and the others followed suit, leaving only the head clerk to finish the piece. The ensuing silence was interrupted only by slurping and smacking noises or by the handclap of a patron ordering a drink or a snack.

Then Yasin asked, "Is there some proven way to induce pregnancy?"

The aged civil servant protested, "You keep harping on that question and repeating it. By God, have patience, brother."

The head clerk observed, "There's no cause for alarm, Yasin Effendi. Your daughter's going to get pregnant."

Smiling fatuously, Yasin said, "She's a blooming bride and the belle of Sugar Street. But she's the first girl in our family not to get pregnant during the first year of marriage. That's why her mother is concerned."

"And her father too, it seems."

Laughing, Yasin responded, "When a wife is upset, her husband is too."

"If a man recalled how nasty children are, he'd detest pregnancy."

"So what! People usually get married to have children."

"That's right! If it weren't for children, no one would ever tolerate married life."

Yasin finished his drink and said, "I'm afraid my nephew may hold this opinion."

"Some men want children so they can regain a bit of their lost freedom while their wives are busy with the kids."

Yasin exclaimed, "How absurd! A woman may be nursing one child and rocking another, but she'll still glare at her husband and ask, 'Where were you? Why did you stay out so late?' All the same, even the best minds have been unable to improve on this universal system."

"What's stopping them?"

"Their wives, who don't let them have time to think about this issue. . . ."

"Have no fear, Yasin Effendi. Your daughter's husband can't forget your son's favor in getting him a government job."

"Anything can be forgotten." The alcohol had begun to addle his brain. Laughing, he continued: "Besides, my darling son's out of power right now."

"Oh! This time it seems that the Wafd has settled in for a long stay."

The attorney said grandiloquently, "If things follow their natural course in Egypt, the Wafd will stay in power forever."

"This idea would be more palatable," Yasin replied cheerfully, "if my son had not left the Wafd."

"Don't forget the traffic accident at al-Qassasin. Had the king lost his life, the enemies of the Wafd would have been finished."

"The king's fine."

"But Prince Muhammad Ali has his ceremonial uniform ready, just in case. He's always been sympathetic to the Wafd."

"Whoever is on the throne – no matter what his name is – will be an enemy of the Wafd by virtue of his position, just as surely as whiskey and sweets don't go together."

Laughing drunkenly, Yasin said, "Perhaps you're right. They say that a man even a day older than you is a year wiser, and some of you have reached your dotage while others are almost there."

"God protect you! You're forty-seven!"

"At any rate I'm the youngest."

Swaying back and forth drunkenly but proudly, he snapped his fingers and added, "One's real age shouldn't be measured by years but by the level of intoxication you attain. During the war years, alcoholic beverages have deteriorated in quality and in taste, but the effect is still the same. Waking up the next morning you have a pounding headache, you need pincers to pry open your eyes, and your breath reeks of alcohol when you belch. But I tell you that any side effects of inebriation are trivial compared to its pleasures. Often a brother will ask, 'What of its impact on your health?' Yes, my health isn't what it was. A man of forty-seven today would be no match for one that age back in the old days. This is a sign that everything has become more valuable during the war except age.... In these trying times, a man of forty asks experts for prescriptions to fortify him and a bridegroom on his honeymoon is barely strong enough to stay afloat."

"The good old days! The whole world is nostalgic for them."

With the melodies of intoxication reverberating in his voice, Yasin continued: "The good old days – God have mercy on my father! He frequently beat me to keep me from joining the violent demonstrations of the revolution. But a fellow who can't be frightened off by English bombs is not going to be scared away by a scolding. We met at the coffeehouse of Ahmad Abduh, where we planned the demonstrations and the bombings."

"This same old recording! Tell me, Yasin Effendi: Were you as heavy then as you are today?"

"Yes, or even heavier . . . but in the heat of the struggle, I was as energetic as a bee. The day of the great battle, I walked at the head of the demonstration with my brother, who was the first martyr of the nationalist movement. I heard the whine of the bullet as it sailed past my ear and landed in my brother. What a memory! If he had lived, he would have been one of the select group of cabinet ministers who first rose to prominence during the revolution."

"But you're the one who survived!"

"Yes, but it wasn't possible for me to become a cabinet minister with only the elementary certificate. Moreover, in our struggle, we fought expecting death, not high office. Sa'd Zaghlul marched in my brother's funeral procession, and the leader of the students introduced me to him. That's another momentous memory."

"In view of your dedication to the revolutionary cause, how did you find time to raise cain and fall in love?"

"Listen to that, will you! Aren't the soldiers who screw women in the streets here the same ones who routed Rommel? Armed struggle has no distaste for fun. Don't you realize that alcohol is an essential part of heroism? The combatant and the drunkard are brothers, you genius."

"Didn't Sa'd Zaghlul say anything to you at your brother's funeral?"

The attorney answered for Yasin: "Sa'd told him, 'I wish you'd been the martyr and not your brother.'"

They laughed, for they had reached the point of laughing first and asking why later. Yasin joined in the laughter magnanimously and then continued his lecture: "He did not say that, God rest his soul. He was polite, unlike you, and knew how to have a good time. For this reason, he was broad-minded. He was a politician, a freedom fighter, a man of letters, a philosopher, and a jurist. One word from him could mean life or death."

"May God be compassionate to him."

"And to everyone else. All the dead deserve God's mercy, by the very fact that they've lost their lives . . . even the prostitute, the pimp, and the mother who sent her son to fetch her boyfriend."

"Would a mother do that?"

"Everything you can imagine and lots that you can't exist in this life."

"Wouldn't she find someone to send besides her son?"

"Who takes better care of a woman than her son? And aren't you all products of sexual intercourse?"

"Legal intercourse."

"A mere formality... it comes down to the same thing. I've known unfortunate prostitutes whose bed didn't entertain a lover for a week or more. Show me any of your mothers who went that long without a visit from her husband."

"I've never known any people besides the Egyptians to be so interested in discussing their mothers' reputations."

"We're not very polite."

Yasin laughed and replied, "Time has disciplined us too often. When excessive emphasis is placed on something, the opposite occurs. That's why we're rude but generally good-natured. In the end, most of us repent."

"I'm a pensioner, and I haven't repented yet."

"Repentance doesn't follow the civil service structure. Besides, you're not doing anything wrong. You get drunk several hours every night, and there's no harm in that. One day ill health or the doctor – they amount to the same thing – will prevent you from drinking. By nature we're weak. Otherwise we would not have developed a taste for liquor and we would not put up with married life. With the passing days we grow ever weaker, but our desires remain limitless. How absurd: We suffer and then get drunk again. Our hair goes gray, betraying our age, and some insolent oaf accosts you on the street, saying, 'You shouldn't be chasing women now that your hair is white.' Glory to God! 'What difference does it make to you whether I'm young or old and chasing a woman or a donkey?' You may imagine at times that people are conspiring with your wife against you. Add to that, the officer's truncheon and the aggravations of coquetry, for even the serving girl struts flirtatiously through the vegetable market. You find yourself in a quarrelsome world without a friend to your name save the bottle. Then along come mercenary physicians to tell you as bluntly as possible: 'Don't drink!'"

"Even so, do you deny that we love this world with all our hearts?"

"With all our hearts! Even evil has some good in it. Even the English have redeeming qualities. I once knew some of them intimately. I had some English friends during the revolutionary era."

The attorney cried out, "But you were fighting against them! Have you forgotten?"

"Yes . . . yes. There's a time and place for everything. I was once suspected of being a spy, but the leader of the students rushed to my aid in the nick of time to tell the crowd who I really was. Then they cheered me. That was in the mosque of al-Husayn!"

" 'Long live Yasin! Long live Yasin!' But what were you doing in the mosque of al-Husayn?"

"Answer him! This is an extremely important point."

Yasin laughed and replied, "We were at the Friday prayer service. My father used to take us with him to the Friday prayers. Don't you believe it? Ask the people at al-Husayn."

"You prayed to butter up your father?"

"By God . . . don't think ill of us. We're a religious family. Yes, we're dissolute inebriates, but we all plan to repent eventually."

Moaning, the attorney asked, "Shouldn't we sing a bit more?"

Yasin shot back, "Yesterday when I left the bar singing, a policeman stopped me and cried out to warn me: 'Mister!' I asked him, 'Don't I have a right to sing?' He answered, 'Screeching after midnight is forbidden.' I protested, 'But I'm singing!' He said sharply, 'As far as the law's concerned it's all the same thing.' I asked, 'What about bombs that explode after midnight – shouldn't that be considered screeching?' He answered threateningly, 'It's plain that you want to spend the night at the station.' I backed away, saying, 'No, I'd rather spend the night at home.' How can we be a civilized nation when we're ruled by soldiers? At home you find your wife on the lookout for you, at the ministry there's your boss, and it's said that even in the grave two angels with truncheons will be waiting to examine you."

The attorney suggested again, "Let's have a tidbit of singing to go with our drinks."

The dean of all pensioners cleared his throat and began to chant:

My husband took a second wife
When wedding henna still was fresh
Upon my hands. The day he brought
Her home, her presence seared my flesh.

With savage enthusiasm they took up the refrain. Yasin was laughing so hard that tears came to his eyes.

164

KHADIJA OFTEN felt lonesome. Ibrahim Shawkat tended to stay home all winter long – especially now that he was approaching seventy – but his presence did little to drive away her loneliness. Performing her household chores hardly lessened it either, for they were no longer arduous enough to absorb all of her energy. Although over forty-six, Khadija was still strong and active – and even plumper. Worst of all, her career as a mother had ended before she could assume that of a mother-in-law. It appeared that she would be permanently denied this opportunity, since one of her daughters-in-law was also her niece and the other worked outside the home and thus was visible only on rare occasions.

In a conversation with her husband, who was wrapped up in his cloak, she voiced her buried feelings: "Our sons have been married for more than a year, and we haven't lit any candles for a baby yet."

The man shrugged his shoulders but did not reply. She continued: "Perhaps Abd al-Muni'm and Ahmad consider having children a fad as outmoded as obeying their parents."

The man answered irritably, "Calm down. They're happy, and that should be enough for us."

She asked sharply, "If a bride doesn't get pregnant and have children, what use is she?"

"Perhaps your sons don't share that opinion."

"They disagree with me about everything. All my efforts and hopes have been in vain."

"Are you sad you're not a grandmother?"

She retorted even more acidly, "I'm sad for them, not for me."

"Abd al-Muni'm has taken Karima to the doctor, who said everything would be fine."

"The poor boy spent a lot of money, and he'll have to spend more in the future. Brides – like tomatoes and meat – are expensive today."

When the man's only response was laughter, she added, "As for the other girl, I'm imploring God's assistance with her by way of the saint at Bab al-Mutawalli."

"You'll have to admit that her words are as sweet as honey."

"That's just shrewd cunning. What do you expect from a laborer's daughter?"

"Fear God, my good woman."

"When do you suppose the 'professor' will take her to the doctor?"

"They refuse."

"Naturally.... She has a job. How could she find time to become pregnant and have a baby?"

"They're happy together. That can't be doubted."

"There's no way a woman who works can be a good wife. He'll realize that when it's too late."

"He's a man and can handle it."

"No other pair of young men in this district are as big a loss as my sons."

With the crystallization of Abd al-Muni'm's character and orientation, he established himself as a capable civil servant and an energetic member of the Muslim Brethren. Leadership of their branch in al-Gamaliya devolved upon him. Named a legal adviser to the organization, he helped edit its journal and occasionally delivered sermons in sympathetic mosques. He had turned his apartment into a meeting place where the Brethren talked till all hours of the night under the guidance of Shaykh Ali al-Manufi. The young man was extremely zealous and more than prepared to place everything he possessed – his industry, money, and intelligence – at the service of the cause, which he believed wholeheartedly to be, as its founder put it, "a pure revivalist mission, a brotherhood based upon the Prophet's example, a mystic reality, a political organization, an athletic association, a cultural and scientific league, an economic partnership, and a social concept."

Shaykh Ali al-Manufi said, "The teachings and precepts of Islam provide a comprehensive answer to the problems people confront in reference to this world and the next. Those who assume that its doctrines apply only to the spiritual and devotional aspects of life are mistaken. Islam is a creed, a way of worship, a nation and a nationality, a religion, a state, a form of spirituality, a Holy Book, and a sword."

One of the young men present commented, "This is what we believe, but we're slowed down by inertia. Pagan secularism rules us with its laws, traditions, and people."

Shaykh Ali declared, "We must spread the word and gain zealous adherents. After that, it will be time to act on our teachings."

"How long must we wait?"

"We will wait until the war ends. Then the audience will be ready for our message. People will have lost confidence in the political parties. When the right moment comes for the leader to raise the call, the Brethren will revolt, armed with Qur'ans and weapons."

In his deep and forceful voice, Abd al-Muni'm said, "Let us prepare for a prolonged struggle. Our mission is not to Egypt alone but to all Muslims worldwide. It will not be successful until Egypt and all other Islamic nations have accepted these Qur'anic principles in common. We shall not put our weapons away until the Qur'an has become a constitution for all Believers."

Shaykh Ali al-Manufi continued: "I bring you the good news that by the grace of God our message is reaching every area. Each village has a branch today. It is God's message, and God will not forsake those who assist Him."

Meanwhile, on the lower floor of the building, another operation with totally different objectives was in full swing, although there were fewer participants. Ahmad and Sawsan frequently entertained a limited number of friends from different sects and ethnic groups, most of them in journalism.

Aware of the theoretical nature of the discussions being held there, Mr. Adli Karim, who visited them one evening, commented, "It's fine that you are studying Marxism, but remember that the historical determinism it preaches is different from the inevitability of astronomical events and arises only as a consequence of the volition and effort of human beings. Our primary obligation is not to theorize at length but to raise the proletariat's level of awareness about the historic role they are to play in saving themselves and the world as a whole."

Ahmad answered, "For the educated elite we are translating the most valuable books about this philosophy. We are also giving inspirational talks to rebellious laborers. Both of these endeavors are unavoidable necessities."

The publisher said, "A corrupt society will be transformed only by the worker's hand. When the consciousness of the workers has been filled with the new faith and when people in general share a united will, then neither repressive laws nor cannons will stand in our way."

"We all believe that, but winning over the minds of the intelligentsia will bring control over the group from which leaders and rulers are chosen."

Then Ahmad said, "Sir, there's something I would like to mention. I've learned from experience that it's not hard to convince educated people that religion is a cultural artifact and that the supposed mysteries of the afterlife are a distracting opiate. But it is dangerous to address such ideas to ordinary people. The most serious charge that our enemies can employ against us is that our movement is composed of atheists and infidels."

"Our primary task is to combat the temptation to settle for the status quo, lethargy, and hopelessness. The destruction of religion will be possible only after political liberation has been achieved by revolution. In general, poverty is stronger than belief. It's always wise for us to speak to people at their level of understanding."

The publisher smiled at Sawsan as he said, "You once believed in direct action. Has marriage convinced you of the value of theoretical discussions?"

Although she sensed that he was teasing her and did not mean it, she replied earnestly, "My husband gives talks to workers in dilapidated and out-of-the-way buildings, and I never tire of handing out pamphlets."

Ahmad said glumly, "The weak point of our movement is that it attracts many insincere opportunists. Some work in hopes of a future reward and others are trying to advance the interests of a political party."

Mr. Adli Karim shook his large head with evident disdain as he answered, "I realize this all too well. But I also know that without seeming to believe in Islam the Umayyad clan inherited political power over the Islamic world and, nevertheless, spread Islamic rule through vast stretches of the ancient world, including what is today Spain. So we have a right to make use of these opportunists if we also caution them. Remember that time will favor us if we make every effort and sacrifice we can."

"What about the Brethren, sir? We're beginning to feel that they are a serious obstacle to our progress."

"I don't deny it, but they're not as dangerous as you think. Don't you see that they use our language when appealing to the mind and speak of socialism in Islam? Even reactionaries feel obliged to borrow our vocabulary. If they pull off a revolution before we do, they will realize at least some of our objectives. They will not be able to stop time's progressive motion to the prescribed goal. Besides, the spread of learning is as liable to banish them as light is to discourage bats."

Khadija observed the manifestations of this strange fervor with an astonishment mingled with anger and resentment. She finally complained to her husband, "I've never seen homes like Abd al-Muni'm's and Ahmad's. Perhaps, without telling me, they've converted their apartments into coffeehouses. Not an evening passes without the street being crowded with visitors, some bearded and some who probably aren't even Muslims. I've never heard the likes of this."

The man shook his head, remarking, "The time has evidently come for you to hear it."

She snapped back, "Their salaries aren't big enough to pay for all the coffee they serve."

"Have they complained to you about being short of money?"

"What about the neighbors? What will they say when they see these droves of people going in and out?"

"Everyone's free to do what he wants in his own home."

She huffed: "The sound of their interminable discussions is loud enough at times to be heard in the street."

"So let it be heard down on the street or up in the sky."

Khadija sighed profoundly and struck her hands together.

165

AT ABD AL-RAHIM Pasha Isa's villa in Helwan, they were seeing out the last wave of the visitors who had come to say goodbye to him before his departure for the holy places of the Hijaz.

"Pilgrimage is an aspiration I've long nourished. God curse politics, for that's what has kept me from going, year after year. But a man my age must think about preparing for his forthcoming encounter with his Lord."

Ali Mihran, the pasha's deputy, said, "Yes, God curse politics!"

The pasha's feeble eyes looked thoughtfully at Ridwan and Hilmi. He commented, "Say what you like, but it has done me a favor I shall never forget. It has distracted me from my loneliness. An old bachelor like me would seek companionship even in hell."

Raising his eyebrows playfully, Ali Mihran asked, "Haven't we distracted you, Pasha?"

"Of course you have, but a bachelor's day is as long as a winter's night. A man needs a companion. I admit that a woman is an important necessity. I think often of my mother now. A woman is necessary, even for a person who does not desire her."

Thinking about quite different issues, Ridwan suddenly asked the pasha, "Suppose that al-Nahhas Pasha falls from power. Wouldn't you change your mind about leaving then?"

Waving his hand indignantly, the pasha replied, "Let that disgrace stay in power, at least until I get back from my pilgrimage." Then, shaking his head, he added, "We are all to blame, but pilgrimage washes away sins."

Hilmi Izzat laughed and observed, "You're a Believer, Pasha, even if that fact perplexes many people."

"Why? Belief is broad-minded. Only a hypocrite claims to be absolutely pure. It's foolish to suppose that a man commits sins only when belief is dead. Besides, our sins are more like innocent child's play."

Sighing with relief, Ali Mihran said, "What a beautiful statement! Now let me tell you frankly that I've often felt your determination to perform the pilgrimage to be a sinister omen. I've asked myself, 'Do you think this means repentance? Will it put an end to our pleasures?' "

The pasha laughed so hard that the upper half of his body shook. "You're a devil and the son of one. Would all of you really be sad to learn that I have repented?"

Hilmi groaned: "Like a woman whose newborn babe is slain in her arms."

Abd al-Rahim Pasha laughed again and exclaimed, "Shame on you! Bastards! If a man like me were truly to repent, he would have to prevent himself from seeing beautiful eyes and rosy cheeks and dedicate himself instead to visiting the tomb of the Prophet, may God bless him and grant him peace."

Mihran gloated: "In the Hijaz? Do you know what things are like there? I've heard from people who know. It will be out of the frying pan and into the fire for you."

Hilmi Izzat protested, "Perhaps it's just false propaganda like that spread by the English. In all of the Hijaz is there a face like Ridwan's?"

Abd al-Rahim Isa cried out, "Not even in paradise!" Then, as if experiencing a change of heart, he added, "But, you naughty boys, we were discussing repentance."

Ali Mihran said, "Not so fast, Pasha! You told me once about a mystic who repented seventy times. Doesn't this imply that he sinned seventy times?"

"Or a hundred?" Ridwan interjected.

Ali Mihran said, "I'm satisfied with seventy."

The pasha's face beamed with joy as he asked, "Will we live long enough for that?"

"May our Lord grant you a long life, Pasha. Set our minds at ease and tell us it's your first repentance."

"And the last!"

"Vain boasting! If you provoke me, when you return from the pilgrimage I'll meet you with a moon-faced beauty, or several of them, and then we'll see how long your repentance lasts."

Smiling, the pasha said, "The result will be as ugly as your face, you jinx. You're a devil, Mihran — an indispensable devil."

"I praise God for that."

Almost in unison, Ridwan and Hilmi added, "We praise Him too."

The pasha said with proud delight, "You're my favorite companions. What value would life have without affection and friendship? Life is beautiful. Beauty is beautiful. Musical ecstasy is beautiful. Forgiveness is beautiful. You're young and look at the world from a special perspective. Life will teach you a lot. I love you and the world. I'm visiting God's sanctuary to give thanks, to ask forgiveness, and to seek guidance."

Ridwan observed merrily, "How handsome you are! You exude such serenity."

Ali Mihran remarked slyly, "With only a little friction, he'd exude something quite different. Pasha, you truly have been the mentor of an entire generation."

"And you're Satan himself, you son of a crone. My God – if I'm ever called to account, I'll point to you and that will be an adequate excuse."

"Me! Unjustly accused, by God! I'm just an obedient servant."

"No, you're a devil."

"But an indispensable one?"

Laughing, the pasha answered, "Yes, you scoundrel."

"In your busy life I have represented – and still do – a touching melody, a pretty face, and constantly renewed happiness, your perfidious excellency."

The pasha moaned: "The old days! Children, why do we grow old? May your wisdom be exalted and glorified, my Lord. A poet said:

> *My lance was not deflected by a foe's taunts.*
> *Auspicious times for it were dawn and dusk both.*"

Wiggling his eyebrows, Mihran said, " 'By a foe's taunts'? No, you should say, 'By Mihran.' "

"You son of a bitch – don't spoil the mood with your nonsense. It's not right to joke around when we're reminiscing about those beautiful days. At times tears are more becoming than a smile, more humane, and more respectful. Listen to this too, by al-A'sha:

> *She rebuffed me, but the*
> *Events she rejected*
> *Were baldness and white hair.*

What do you think of the poet's use of 'events'?"

Imitating a newspaper vendor, Mihran called out, "*Events of the Day*, the *Egyptian, al-Ahram . . .*"

Despairingly the pasha said, "It's not your fault but . . ."

"Yours!"

"Mine? I'm not to blame for your depravity. When we first met, you were so debauched that Satan would have envied you. But I won't allow you to spoil the ambiance created by these memories. Yes, hear this as well:

> Just as a stalk is ravished of
> Its leaves, so I was stripped of youth."

Pretending to be shocked by the sexual allusion, Mihran asked, "A stalk, Pasha?"

Looking at Ridwan and Hilmi, who were dissolved in laughter, the pasha said, "Your friend is a corpse with no feeling for poetry. But soon he'll reach the age of regrets, when the only beauties he encounters will be referred to in the past tense." Turning toward Mihran, he asked, "What about our friends from the old days, son of a crone – have you forgotten them?"

"Oh! May God preserve them. They were coy paragons of beauty."

"What do you know about Shakir Sulayman?"

"He was a Deputy Minister of the Interior and a pet of the English until prematurely pensioned off during the second or third government of al-Nahhas . . . I don't remember which. I think he has now retired to his estate at Kom Hamada."

"What marvelous days those were! What about Hamid al-Najdi?"

"He's had the worst luck of any of our dear friends. He lost everything and now tours the public lavatories by night."

"He was witty and charming but a gambler and a boisterous fellow. And Ali Ra'fat?"

"Through his 'exertions' he managed to become a member of the boards of directors of various corporations, but it's said that his reputation cost him a chance at a cabinet post."

"Don't believe what people say. Men whose notoriety has extended far beyond our kingdom have been appointed to the cabinet, but as I have often advised you, I think it is more important for us to develop a virtuous character than for others. If you can manage this, you won't need to worry about censure. The Mamluk sultans, recruited from a corps of military slaves, ruled Egypt for generations, and their descendants still enjoy high status and wealth here. What is a Mamluk? Nothing but a man who can be bought. Let me tell you a story of great import."

The pasha was silent for a time, as if collecting his thoughts. Then he said, "When I was the presiding judge of a court, a civil case concerning a contested inheritance was scheduled to be heard by us. Beforehand, some of the people involved introduced me to a beautiful young man with a face like Ridwan's, a build like Hilmi's, and..." He gestured toward Mihran as he continued: "The grace of this dog in his glory.... We saw each other for a time without my learning that he had a secret connection to the case. Then the day the case was heard, what did I know but he was representing one of the parties to the dispute. What do you think I did?"

Ridwan murmured, "What a situation!"

"I withdrew from the case, without any hesitation."

Ridwan and Hilmi displayed their admiration, but Mihran protested, "You didn't reward him in any way for his efforts?"

Paying no attention to Mihran's kidding, the pasha said, "But that's not all. Out of contempt for his morals, I ended my relationship with him. Yes, a man without morals is worthless. The English aren't the brightest people. The French and the Italians are smarter. But the English have mastered morality and this has made them masters of the world. That is my reason for spurning superficial, decadent beauty."

Ali Mihran asked merrily, "May I assume that my morals are satisfactory, since you've kept me on?"

Giving him a cautionary wave of the hand, the pasha replied, "There are many different moral qualities. A judge should be upright and just. A cabinet minister should have a sense of duty and a respect for the public welfare. A friend should be loyal and sincere. Without doubt you are a troublemaker and frequently a rogue. But you're honest and faithful."

"I hope I'm blushing."

" 'God does not impose more on a soul than it can bear.' In fact I'm content with the amount of good that's in you. Besides, you're a husband and a father, and those are virtues too. The happiness they bring can be appreciated properly only by people who must put up with silent homes. Even so, a silent residence is one of the torments of old age."

Somewhat disapprovingly, Ridwan observed, "I thought old people loved peace and quiet."

"The notions young people have about old age are erroneous. The ideas old people cherish about youth are vain regrets. Tell me, Ridwan, what do you think about marriage?"

Ridwan's face fell, and he answered, "You already know what I think about it, Pasha."

"There's no hope you'll change your mind?"

"I don't think so."

"Why not?"

Ridwan hesitated a little and then said, "It's an amazing thing . . . . I don't really understand it. But I find women revolting."

The expression of the man's feeble eyes was sad as he commented, "What a pity! Don't you see that Ali Mihran is a husband and a father? Your friend Hilmi advocates marriage. I feel doubly sorry for you, since I also pity myself. I have often been perplexed by what I've read and heard about the beauty of women. Out of respect for the memory of my mother, I've kept my opinion to myself. I loved her dearly, and she died in my arms as my tears fell on her brow and cheeks. I hope ever so much, Ridwan, that you can overcome your problems."

Looking frightened and somber, Ridwan said, "A man can live without a woman."

The pasha replied, "That's not so difficult, and you may be able to ignore the doubts of other people. Yet what about your own questions? You can say you find women disgusting, but why don't other men feel that way? You fall prey to a feeling that's almost like a disease, an incurable one. It leads you to withdraw from the world and is the worst possible companion for your solitude. Then you may be embarrassed to despise women without having any choice about it."

Ali Mihran snorted cynically and complained, "I had promised myself a cheery evening together for our farewell party."

Laughing, Abd al-Rahim Pasha said, "But it's a farewell party for a pilgrim. What do you know about seeing off pilgrims?"

"I'll see you off with prayerful invocations and welcome you back with rosy-cheeked beauties. We'll find out what you do then."

Clapping his hands together, the pasha answered jovially, "I entrust my fate to God Almighty."

166

IN FRONT of the Ritz Café at the intersection of Sharif and Qasr al-Nil streets, Kamal found himself face to face with Husayn Shaddad. They both stopped and stared at each other. Then Kamal cried out, "Husayn!"

Husayn exclaimed in turn, "Kamal!"

Laughing with gleeful delight, they shook hands warmly.

"What a happy surprise after such a long time!"

"A very happy surprise! You've changed a lot, Kamal. But not so fast.... Perhaps I'm exaggerating.... The same build and general appearance. But what's this dignified mustache? These 'classic' spectacles and this walking stick? And this fez that no one else wears anymore?..."

"You've changed a great deal too. You're heavier than I would have imagined. Is this the Parisian fashion? Where's the Husayn I once knew?"

"Where's the Paris I once knew? Where are Hitler and Mussolini? Well, let's not worry about it. I was on my way to the Ritz to have some tea. Do you have any objection to joining me?"

"Of course not."

They went into the Ritz and took a table by the window overlooking the street. After Husayn ordered tea and Kamal coffee, they resumed their smiling examination of one another. Husayn had become huge, expanding vertically and horizontally. But what had he done with his life? Had he toured the earth and the heavens as he had once hoped? Despite their friendly expression, his eyes had a coarse look, as if they had undergone a transformation following childhood. A year had passed since Kamal's encounter with Budur on Fuad I Street. During that time he had recovered from his relapse into love, and the Shaddad family had retreated into a forgotten corner of his mind. Now the sight of Husayn awakened Kamal's soul from its slumbers, and, stretching sleepily, the past reappeared to spread its joys and torments before him.

"When did you return from abroad?"

"It's been about a year."

He had made absolutely no attempt to contact Kamal . . . . But why blame Husayn when he himself had forgotten his former friend and written off their friendship?

"If I had known you were back in Egypt, I certainly would have looked you up."

Showing no confusion or embarrassment, Husayn answered quite simply, "When I came back, I found many problems awaiting me. Haven't you heard about us?"

Kamal frowned as he replied briefly and sadly, "Yes, of course . . . from our friend Isma'il Latif."

"My mother tells me he left for Iraq two years ago. . . . As I was saying, I found a lot of problems waiting for me. And then I had to start working. I've had to work night and day."

This was the 1944 edition of Husayn Shaddad, who had once considered work a crime against humanity. Had that past really existed? Perhaps the only clue to its existence was the pounding of Kamal's heart.

"Do you remember the last time we saw each other?"

"Oh! . . ."

The waiter arrived with their tea and coffee before Husayn could complete his response. But he hardly seemed eager to relive those memories.

"Let me remind you. It was in 1926."

"What a fantastic memory!" Then he said absentmindedly, "Seventeen years in Europe!"

"Tell me about your life there."

Shaking his head, which had gray hair only at the temples, Husayn replied, "Leave that for another time. Content yourself now with these headlines: dreamlike years of travel and happiness, love followed by marriage to a Parisian girl from a good family, the war and exodus to the South, my father's bankruptcy, work in my father-in-law's business, a return to Egypt without my wife in preparation for settling here – what more do you want to know?"

"Do you have any children?"

"No."

Husayn seemed reticent. But what remained of their old friendship to make Kamal regret this? All the same, feeling a powerful urge to knock on the doors of the past, he asked, "What about your former philosophy of life?"

Husayn reflected for a time and then, laughing sarcastically, replied, "For years and years my life has been devoted to work. I'm nothing but a businessman."

Where was Husayn Shaddad's spirit, which Kamal had once employed to put himself into contact with the comforting repose of spiritual bliss? It no longer resided in this bulky person. Perhaps it had come to rest in Riyad Qaldas. Kamal did not know the man sitting across from him. The sole tie linking them was an unknowable past, which he would have liked to recapture at that moment in a living image, not in a dead photograph.

"What line of work are you in now?"

"One of my father's friends got me a position in the press censorship office, working from midnight till dawn. Besides that, I translate for some European newspapers."

"When don't you work?"

"Almost never. What makes all the effort less objectionable is my determination to provide my wife with a style of life appropriate to her before I invite her to join me in Egypt. She's from a good family, and when I married her I was considered wealthy." Saying that, he laughed as if to poke fun at himself.

Kamal smiled to encourage Husayn and told himself, "It's lucky I stopped thinking about you a long time ago. Otherwise, I would be weeping now from the depths of my heart."

"And you, Kamal – what are you doing?" Then he added, "I remember that you were wild about culture."

Husayn was certainly to be thanked for this recollection, since Kamal was as dead to him as he was to Kamal. "We die and return to life several times a day," Kamal reflected. "I teach English," he replied.

"A teacher! Yes . . . yes. I'm starting to remember now. You wanted to be a writer."

"What aborted hopes!" Kamal exclaimed to himself.

"I publish essays in *al-Fikr* magazine. In the near future I may collect some of them into a book."

Husayn smiled despondently and remarked, "You're lucky. You've seen your youthful dreams come true. I haven't." And he laughed again.

Kamal felt that the sentence "You're lucky" had a strange

ring to it. The only thing stranger was the envious tone in which it was spoken. He was envied and considered fortunate. By whom? . . . By the leading member of the Shaddad family. All the same, to be polite, Kamal responded, "Your career is more distinguished."

The smiling Husayn said, "I've had no choice. My one hope is to be able to regain some of my former status."

They were silent for a long time as Kamal's eager scrutiny of Husayn triggered images of the past. Finally he found himself asking, "How's your family?"

Husayn replied noncommittally, "Fine."

Kamal hesitated a little and then said, "You had a young sister, whose name I can't recall. What's become of her?"

"Budur! She got married last year."

"God's will be done! Our children are getting married."

"Haven't you married?"

Wondering whether Husayn had forgotten everything, Kamal said, "No."

"Hurry up. Otherwise you'll miss the train."

Laughing, Kamal replied, "It's already miles ahead of me."

"You may end up getting married without actually intending to. Believe me. Marriage wasn't part of my plan, but I've been a husband for more than ten years."

Shrugging his shoulders, Kamal suggested, "Tell me how you find life here after your long stay in France."

"Following the German occupation, life in France was not much fun. Compared to that, life here is easy." Then he added nostalgically, "But Paris – where, where is Paris now?"

"Why didn't you stay in France?"

Husayn answered disapprovingly, "And live entirely at my father-in-law's expense? No. . . . When wartime conditions made it impossible to travel there was an excuse for staying. After that I felt obliged to leave."

Did this smack of the old arrogance? Feeling driven to embark on a painful and dangerous adventure, Kamal asked slyly, "What news do you have of our friend Hasan Salim?"

After staring uneasily at Kamal for a moment, Husayn replied coldly, "None."

"How so?"

Looking out at the street through the window, Husayn said,

"We haven't had any contact with him for about two years."

Unable to hide his astonishment, Kamal started to ask, "You mean . . .?" But he did not finish the question. The shock was too much for him. Had Aïda returned again to al-Abbasiya as a divorcée? He would have to postpone consideration of all this to some other time. He remarked calmly, "His trip to Iran was the last thing Isma'il Latif mentioned."

Husayn said morosely, "My sister spent only a month with him there. Then she returned alone." In a hushed voice he added, "God rest her soul."

"What?" This word escaped from Kamal in a verbal outburst audible at nearby tables.

Husayn looked at him in amazement and said, "You didn't know! She died a year ago."

"Aïda?"

The other man nodded his head, and Kamal felt embarrassed about blurting out her name in such a familiar manner. But his thoughts immediately raced beyond this moment of embarrassment. Words no longer seemed to mean anything. He felt a maelstrom of oblivion whirling around in his head. He was afflicted by astonishment and dismay, not by sorrow and pain. When he could speak again, he exclaimed, "What distressing news! May you have a long life."

Husayn recounted: "She came home from Iran alone and stayed with my mother for a month. Then she married Anwar Bey Zaki, the chief inspector for English-language instruction. But she lived with him for only two months before falling ill. She died in the Coptic Hospital."

How could his head keep up with revelations that came at such breakneck speed? Husayn had said, "Anwar Bey Zaki." He was the chief supervisor of Kamal's own instructional division. Kamal had perhaps met the man several times during his marriage to Aïda. "Oh Lord. . . ." He remembered then that during the past year he had walked in the funeral procession of the supervisor's wife. Had that been Aïda? But how could he have missed seeing Husayn?

"Were you here when she passed away?"

"No. She died before I returned to Egypt."

Shaking his head in amazement, Kamal said, "I was at her funeral but didn't know that the deceased woman was your sister."

"How could that be?"

"I heard at school that the wife of one of the chief inspectors had passed away and that the funeral reception would be in al-Isma'iliya Square the same day. I went with some of my fellow teachers without ever seeing the announcement in the papers. We walked with the other mourners as far as the Sharkas mosque. That was a year ago."

Husayn smiled sadly as he said, "We thank you for taking the trouble."

Had this death occurred in 1926, Kamal would have gone insane or killed himself. Today it seemed like any other piece of news to him. That he should have walked in her funeral procession without knowing it was in her honor was bizarre. At the time, he had still been subject to the bitterness aroused by Budur's marriage and might actually have thought of the deceased when images of Budur and her family passed through his mind. He remembered the day of the funeral. He had offered his condolences to Anwar Bey Zaki and then had taken a seat with the other mourners. When they had called out, "All rise, the coffin's here," he had looked that way, glimpsing a beautiful casket covered in white silk. Some of his colleagues had whispered that she was the inspector's second wife, that they had only recently married, and that she had died of pneumonia. He had paid his final respects to the coffin without knowing he was bidding farewell to his past. A married man over fifty with children . . . how could the angel of that bygone age have consented to this?

"You assumed she was above marriage," Kamal thought. "But she had to accept divorce and then the fate of being a second wife. A long time will pass before the agitation of your breast settles down – not out of grief or pain, but from your shock and astonishment, from the disappearance of the world's splendid dreams, and from the eternal loss of that enchanting past. If there is any reason for regret in all this, it's that you didn't grieve as much as you should have."

"But what changed Hasan Salim?"

Husayn shook his head scornfully and said, "The scoundrel fell in love with an employee at the Belgian legation in Iran. My late sister was outraged at the damage to her honor and demanded a separation."

"In a situation like mine," Kamal mused, "a man's only

consolation may be that even Euclid's self-evident axioms are no longer thought quite so self-evident."

"What about her children?"

"With their paternal grandmother."

"And where is Aïda herself?" Kamal wondered. "What surprises has the year brought her? Is it possible that Fahmy, al-Sayyid Ahmad Abd al-Jawad, or Na'ima has made her acquaintance?"

Then Husayn Shaddad rose, saying, "It's time for me to go. Let's see more of you. I usually have supper here at the Ritz."

Kamal stood up too, and murmured as they shook hands, "God willing...."

They parted this way. Kamal sensed that he would never see Husayn again and that neither of them would have anything to gain from a future encounter. As he left the establishment, he told himself, "I'm sad, Aïda, that I didn't mourn enough for you."

167

LATE ONE night the silence of the Shawkats' residence on Sugar Street was broken by a rap on the door. The knocking continued, waking everyone up. The moment a servant opened the door, heavy footsteps invaded the house, pounded through the courtyard and up the stairs, laying siege to all three apartments. Weak with age, his head still clouded by sleep, Ibrahim Shawkat went to the sitting room, where he found an officer surrounded by policemen and detectives.

The astonished man asked in alarm, "God spare us evil, what's happening?"

The commanding officer asked gruffly, "Are you not the father of Ahmad Ibrahim Shawkat and of Abd al-Muni'm Ibrahim Shawkat, who reside in this building?"

As his face lost its color, he replied, "Yes."

"We have orders to search the entire building."

"Why, your honor?"

Paying no attention to him, the officer turned to command his men, "Search the place!"

As the policemen fanned out into the adjoining rooms in response to this directive, Ibrahim Shawkat asked, "Why are you searching my apartment?"

The officer ignored him. At this juncture Khadija was forced out of the bedroom by the detectives who stormed into it. Wrapping a black shawl around herself, she cried out furiously, "Have you no respect for women? Are we thieves, Mr. Police Chief?"

Glaring angrily at his face, she suddenly sensed that she had seen the man before or, to be more precise, the original version of this countenance before time had marched across it. When and where had that been? "Good Lord!" she thought. It was the same man, without any doubt. He had not changed much. What was his name? Not hesitating, she remarked, "Sir, twenty years ago you were an officer in the police station for al-Gamaliya. No, it was thirty years – I don't remember the year exactly."

The officer looked up at her with curious eyes, as Ibrahim Shawkat gazed from one to the other just as inquisitively. Then she continued: "Your name is Hasan Ibrahim. Isn't that right?"

"Do you know me, ma'am?"

She said imploringly, "I'm the daughter of al-Sayyid Ahmad Abd al-Jawad and the sister of Fahmy Ahmad Abd al-Jawad, who was killed by the English during the revolution. Don't you remember him?"

The officer's astonishment was clearly visible in his eyes. Using a civil tone for the first time, he muttered, "May God be most compassionate to him."

She entreated him even more determinedly, "I'm his sister! Do you enjoy abusing my house like this?"

The officer looked away and replied almost apologetically, "We're just following orders, lady."

"But why, Officer? We're good people!"

He answered gently, "Yes, but I can't say as much for your two boys."

Khadija cried out in dismay, "They're the nephews of your old friend!"

Without looking at either of them, the officer responded, "We're acting on orders from the Ministry of the Interior."

"They haven't done anything wrong. They're good boys. I swear it."

The policemen and the detectives returned to the sitting room without having discovered anything. The commanding officer ordered them to leave the apartment and then, turning toward the couple, said, "We've been informed that suspicious gatherings are held in their apartments."

"A lie, your honor!"

"I too hope this is the case. Even so, I have no choice but to arrest them now. They will be held until the inquiry has been concluded. It's possible that they'll be cleared."

In a trembling voice embellished by sobs, Khadija wailed, "Are you really taking them to the station? This defies the imagination! By the lives of your own children, I beg you to set them free."

"I don't have the power to do that. I have clear orders to arrest them. Have a pleasant evening."

The man left the apartment. Heedless of everything she passed, Khadija rushed down the steps after him, trailed by her elderly husband. Karima, who was standing in front of her apartment in a terrified frenzy, saw them and shouted, "They've taken him, Auntie! They took him to prison!"

Khadija cast a stony glance her way and then sped down to the first-floor apartment, where she found Sawsan at the door as well, observing the courtyard with a gloomy face. Glancing in that direction, Khadija saw Abd al-Muni'm and Ahmad surrounded by policemen, who were taking them out of the house. She could not keep herself from screaming her heart out. She started to rush off in pursuit of them, but Sawsan's hand grabbed hold of her. As she turned furiously on her daughter-in-law, Khadija heard the girl say in a sad but tranquil voice, "Calm down. They didn't find anything suspicious. The police won't be able to pin a charge on them. Don't run after them – out of respect for your sons' honor."

Khadija yelled at her, "Your calm is enviable!"

Gently and patiently Sawsan replied, "They'll come home safe and sound. Don't be alarmed."

Her mother-in-law asked sharply, "What makes you so sure?"

"I'm confident of what I say."

Paying no attention to this remark, Khadija looked toward her husband, clapped her hands together, and said, "Loyalty is dead! I tell him they are Fahmy's nephews, and he says, 'We're just following orders.' My Lord, why do they seize good people and leave the rogues alone?"

Sawsan glanced at Ibrahim and said, "They'll search the family home on Palace Walk. I heard a detective tell the commanding officer he knew their grandfather's house on Palace Walk. The deputy suggested that it should be searched too, so they would be in full compliance with their orders and to make sure that the two boys had not hidden subversive tracts there."

Khadija shouted, "I'm going to my mother's. Perhaps Kamal can do something. Oh, my Lord, I'm on fire."

She got her coat and left Sugar Street with quick and agitated steps. It was cold and still quite dark, but roosters were defiantly crowing back and forth at each other. She shot down al-Ghuriya and traversed the Goldsmiths Bazaar on her way to al-Nahhasin. She found a detective at the door of the house and another in the courtyard. She climbed the stairs breathlessly.

The family had awakened uneasily to the ringing of the door-bell. Then Umm Hanafi had come up to say fearfully, "Police!"

Kamal had rushed down to the courtyard. There he found the commanding officer, whom he asked in alarm, "Can I help you?"

The officer inquired, "Do you know Abd al-Muni'm Ibrahim Shawkat and Ahmad Ibrahim Shawkat?"

"I'm their uncle. . . ."

"What do you do?"

"I'm a teacher at al-Silahdar School."

"We have orders to search the house."

"But why? What charges are you bringing against me?"

"We are searching for subversive tracts belonging to the two young men. We think they may have hidden them here."

"Sir, I can assure you that there are no subversive tracts in our house. But you can search all you want."

Kamal noticed that the commanding officer stationed his men on the roof and the staircase and was the only one who actually entered the living quarters. Instead of turning the house upside down in his search, the officer was content to survey the rooms, casting a superficial glance at Kamal's desk and bookcases. Regaining his composure, Kamal felt enough at ease with the officer to ask, "Did you search their home?"

"Naturally." Then, after a brief moment, the man added, "They are currently being detained at the station."

Kamal asked in consternation, "Has anything been proven against them?"

The man replied with unexpected delicacy, "I hope matters won't reach that point. But the inquiry will be conducted by the prosecutor's office."

"I'd like to thank you for your thoughtfulness."

The officer smiled and replied quietly, "Don't forget that I didn't ransack your house."

"Yes, sir. I don't know how to thank you."

Turning toward Kamal, the man asked, "Aren't you the brother of the late Fahmy?"

Kamal's eyes grew wide with astonishment as he asked, "Yes. Did you know him?"

"We were friends, God rest his soul."

Kamal said hopefully, "What a happy coincidence!" Offering the man his hand, he added, "Kamal Ahmad Abd al-Jawad."

The officer shook the proffered hand and said, "Hasan Ibrahim, commanding officer of the Gamaliya station. I started there as a second lieutenant and have rotated back to it as the commanding officer." Shaking his head, he continued: "Our orders were unequivocal. I hope the boys won't be found guilty of anything."

The sound of Khadija's voice carried to them as she wept and then narrated to her mother and Aisha the events of the evening. The officer remarked, "That's their mother. With her amazing memory she recognized me and reminded me of your late brother – but only after a thorough search of the house had already been conducted. See what you can do to put her mind at ease."

They walked down the stairs side by side. As they passed the second floor, Aisha exploded from the door in an obvious rage. Glaring harshly at the officer, she railed at him, "Why do you arrest people's children for no reason at all? Can't you hear their mother weeping?"

Shocked by this attack, the officer glanced quickly at her, before lowering his gaze politely. He replied, "They'll be set free soon, God willing."

After they were some distance beyond the apartment, he asked Kamal, "Your mother?"

Smiling sadly, Kamal replied, "No, my sister! She's only forty-four, but the misfortunes she's suffered have broken her."

The officer turned toward him as if stunned. Kamal felt the man was about to ask something. But after hesitating for a moment, he apparently changed his mind. They shook hands in the courtyard, and before the officer departed, Kamal asked, "Would it be possible for me to visit them in jail?"

"Yes."

"Thank you."

Kamal returned to join his mother and sisters in the sitting room. He said, "I'm going to visit them tomorrow. There's no reason to be afraid. They'll be released once they've been questioned."

Khadija did not seem to be able to stop crying. Aisha shouted hysterically, "Don't weep! That's enough! They'll come back to you. Didn't you hear?"

Khadija moaned: "I don't know. I don't know. My dear boys are in prison!"

Amina's sorrow had evidently struck her dumb. In a reassuring tone Kamal observed, "The officer in charge knows us. He was

one of Fahmy's friends and was incredibly restrained when searching our house. He'll certainly treat them kindly."

The mother raised her head inquisitively, and Khadija snarled
resentfully, "Hasan Ibrahim! Don't you remember him, Mother?
When I told him I was Fahmy's sister, what did he say but 'We're
just following orders, lady.' Orders, my eye!"

The mother glanced at Aisha, who gave no sign of recognizing
the name. Taking Kamal aside, Amina said with obvious anxiety,
"I don't understand anything, son. Why were they arrested?"

After pondering what to say Kamal replied, "The government
mistakenly suspects that they have been working against it."

Shaking her head anxiously, she remarked, "Your sister says
they arrested Abd al-Muni'm because he's a Muslim Brother.
Why are they arresting Muslims?"

"The government thinks they are working against it."

"And Ahmad? She said he's . . . I've forgotten the word, son."

"A Communist? Like the Muslim Brethren, Communists are
suspected by the government."

"Communists? What community is this? The Shi'ah community of Ali?"

Hiding his smile, Kamal answered, "The Communists aren't a
religious community like the Shi'ah. They're a political party
opposed to the government and the English."

Perplexed, she sighed and inquired, "When will they be set
free? Look at your poor sister. The government and the English –
can't they find some other place to search besides our afflicted
house?"

168

THE DAWN call to prayer was reverberating through the otherwise silent city when the commanding officer of the police station for al-Gamaliya summoned Abd al-Muni'm and Ahmad to his office. Escorted by an armed policeman, they appeared before his desk. After ordering the policeman to leave, the officer examined the young men with interest. Looking at Abd al-Muni'm, he asked, "Your name, age, and profession?"

Abd al-Muni'm replied calmly and resolutely, "Abd al-Muni'm Shawkat, twenty-five, an investigator in the Ministry of Education's Bureau of Investigations."

"How can you, a lawyer, break the laws of the state?"

"I haven't broken any law. We work publicly – writing in the papers and preaching in the mosques. People who spread God's word have nothing to fear."

"Haven't suspicious meetings been held at your house?"

"Certainly not. There have been some ordinary gatherings, when friends assemble to exchange opinions and advice in order to gain a deeper understanding of our religion."

"Is agitation against allied nations a goal of these meetings?"

"Do you refer to Britain, sir? That deceitful enemy? A state that crushes our honor with its tanks cannot be considered an ally."

"You're an educated man. You should have realized that wartime conditions justify certain restrictions."

"I realize that Britain is our principal enemy in the world."

Turning to Ahmad, the officer asked, "You?"

With the suggestion of a smile on his lips, Ahmad replied, "Ahmad Ibrahim Shawkat, twenty-four, an editor with *The New Man* magazine."

"I have alarming reports here about your extremist articles. Besides, it is generally accepted that your magazine has a bad reputation."

"My articles have never exceeded the bounds of a defense of the principles of social justice."

"Are you a Communist?"

"I'm a socialist. Many deputies in parliament support socialism. The law itself does not censure a Communist for his ideas, as long as he does not resort to violent means."

"Should we have waited until the meetings held at your apartment every evening erupted into violence?"

Wondering whether the authorities had unearthed the secret of his tracts and nighttime talks, he replied, "I entertain only close friends in my home. There are never more than four or five visitors a day. Violence has been the furthest thing from our thoughts."

The officer looked from one to the other. After some hesitation he said, "You're educated and cultured . . . and you're both married – aren't you? Fine. Wouldn't it be best if you attended to your personal affairs and kept out of trouble?"

Abd al-Muni'm replied in his forceful voice, "Thank you for your advice, which I shall not follow."

A brief laugh took the officer by surprise and escaped from his lips. Then he admitted, "During the search, I learned that you are grandsons of the late Ahmad Abd al-Jawad. Your lamented uncle Fahmy was a dear friend of mine. I assume you know that he died in the spring of his life and that those of his comrades who survived now hold some of the most important posts."

Discerning the secret reason for the officer's courtesy, which had baffled him, Ahmad said, "Allow me to ask you, sir, what condition Egypt would be in if my uncle and others like him had not sacrificed their lives."

Shaking his head, the man remarked, "Think long and well about my advice. Abandon this lethal philosophy." As he stood up he added, "You will be our guests in this jail until the inquiry is conducted. I wish you luck."

On leaving the office, they were taken into custody by a corporal and two armed policemen. The entire group descended to the ground floor, turned into a dark and extremely damp hall, and walked along it a short distance until the jailer greeted them with his flashlight, as if to show them the door to the jail. Opening the door, the jailer let the new prisoners in and then directed his light inside to guide them to their mats. The torch provided enough illumination for them to see the high ceiling of the medium-sized room as well as the small, barred window at the top of the exterior wall. The chamber had several guests: two youngsters, who looked like students, and three men with bare feet and a repulsive, battered appearance. The door was immediately closed, leaving them in darkness, but the light and the new arrivals had awakened some of the sleeping prisoners. Ahmad whispered to his brother, "I'm not going to sit down, for fear this dampness will be the death of me. Let's remain standing till morning."

"We'll have to sit down sooner or later. Do you have any idea when we'll get out of this jail?"

Then a voice – clearly belonging to one of the young men – said, "There's no way to avoid sitting down. It's not pleasant, but standing up, day after day, is worse."

"Have you been here a long time?"

"Three days!"

The room was silent again until the voice asked, "Why did they arrest you?"

Abd al-Muni'm replied tersely, "For political reasons, apparently."

The voice said cheerfully, "Political prisoners now form the majority in this cell. Before you honored us with your presence, we were in the minority."

Ahmad asked, "What are you accused of?"

"You speak first, for we have seniority here. Although there's probably no need to ask, since we saw that one of you has the beard of a Muslim Brother."

Smiling in the dark, Ahmad asked, "What about you?"

"We're law students. They say we were distributing subversive pamphlets."

Incensed, Ahmad asked, "Did they catch you red-handed?"

"Yes."

"What was in the pamphlets?"

"A report on the redistribution of Egypt's agricultural resources."

"Newspapers have published comparable material even under martial law."

"There were also a few enthusiastic exhortations."

Ahmad smiled once more in the gloom, feeling for the first time that he was not alone. Then the other voice continued: "We're not afraid of the law so much as of being detained without a trial."

"There are promising signs of change."

"But we'll always be targets, no matter who is in power."

A gruff voice barked rudely, "That's enough talk out of you. Let us get some sleep."

But these words awakened a companion, who yawned and asked, "Is it morning yet?"

The first man responded scornfully, "No, but our friends think they're in a hashish den."

Abd al-Muni'm sighed and whispered so softly that only Ahmad could hear, "Am I cast into this hole merely because I worship God?"

Ahmad whispered merrily in his brother's ear, "What could my offense be then, since I don't?"

After that, no one felt like speaking. Ahmad asked himself why the three older men had been arrested. Had the charges been theft, fighting, drunkenness, or rowdy behavior? Clad in his overcoat, he had often written about "the people" in his beautiful study. Here they were – cursing or snoring in their sleep. For a few seconds by the light of the torch he had seen their wretched sullen faces, including that of the man who was scratching his head and armpits. At this very moment his lice might be advancing resolutely toward Ahmad and his brother.

"You are devoting your life to people like this," he told himself. "Why should the thought of contact with them worry you? The person on whom mankind's hopes for salvation are pinned should stop snoring and awake to his historic role. Let him rear up and rescue the entire world."

Ahmad advised himself, "Without regard to the differences of taste between us, our common human condition has united us in this dark and humid place: the Muslim Brother, the Communist, the drunkard, and the thief. Despite dissimilarities in our luck and success at looking after ourselves, we are all human beings."

He wondered, "Why don't you busy yourself with personal affairs as the officer suggested? I have a beloved wife and plenty of money. The truth is that a man may be happy with his niche as a spouse, an employee, a father, or a son and yet be condemned to suffer various travails or even death by virtue of the fact that he is a man."

Whether Ahmad was sentenced to prison this time or released, the heavy, glowering prison gates would always hover at the horizons of his life. He asked himself again, "What is pushing me down this dazzling and dangerous road unless it is the human being that lurks deep inside of me, the man who is conscious of himself and aware of his common, historic, human condition? What distinguishes a man from all other creatures if not his ability to condemn himself to death by his own free will?"

Ahmad felt dampness coursing through his legs and weakness penetrating his joints. Snores echoed through the room with a regular rhythm. Then, between the bars of the small window, the first feeble rays of delicate light were visible.

169

KAMAL DESPONDENTLY followed the physician out of the bedroom. Catching up with the man in the sitting room and gazing at him with questioning eyes, Kamal heard him say calmly, "I'm sorry to inform you that the paralysis is total."

Feeling miserable, Kamal asked, "Is that serious?"

"Of course! And she's also suffering from pneumonia. I'm prescribing an injection so she can get some rest."

"Isn't there any hope she'll recover?"

The doctor was silent for a time and then replied, "Our lives are in God's hands. For what it's worth, my judgment as a physician is that she has three days at the most."

Kamal received this prediction of death resolutely and escorted the physician to the door of the house before returning to the bedroom. His mother was asleep or so it seemed. The thick blanket revealed only a pale face with lips closed but slightly awry. Aisha, who was standing by the bed, walked toward him, asking, "What's wrong with her, brother? What did the doctor say?"

From her station by the head of the bed, Umm Hanafi observed, "She's not speaking, master. She hasn't said a single word."

Kamal reflected, "Her voice will never be heard again." Then he told his sister, "An attack of high blood pressure combined with a slight cold. The injection will help her rest."

Aisha commented, perhaps to herself, "I'm afraid. If she lies in bed like this for a long time, life in our house will surely be unbearable."

Turning from her to Umm Hanafi, he inquired, "Have you told the others?"

"Yes, master. Mrs. Khadija and Mr. Yasin will be here at once. What's wrong with her, master? This morning she was hale and hearty."

She had been! He could attest to that. As always each morning, he had passed by the sitting room before rushing off to al-Silahdar

School. Taking the cup of coffee she had handed him, he had said, "Don't go out today. It's very cold."

Showing him her gentle smile, she had replied, "How can I have a good day if I don't visit your master al-Husayn?"

He had protested, "Do as you like. You're stubborn, Mother."

She had murmured, "Your Lord preserves us." When he was leaving, she had said, "May our Lord make all your days happy ones."

That was the last time he would see her conscious. The news of her illness had reached him at school this noon, and he had returned home, accompanied by the doctor who had just predicted her death. Only three days were left. How many more did he have?

Going over to Aisha, he asked, "When and how did this happen?"

Umm Hanafi answered for her: "We were in the sitting room. She rose and started toward her room to put on her coat prior to going out. She told me, 'When I finish my visit to al-Husayn, I'll call on Khadija.' She went to the bedroom, and the moment she entered I heard something fall. Rushing inside, I found her stretched out on the floor between the bed and the wardrobe. I ran to her, calling for Mrs. Aisha."

Aisha said, "I came as fast as I could and discovered her here. We carried her to the bed, and I started asking her what was the matter. But she didn't respond. She didn't say anything. When is she going to speak, brother?"

He answered uneasily, "When God wills."

Retreating to the sofa, he sat down and began to look sorrowfully at the pale, silent face. Yes, he should gaze at it for a long time. Soon he would be unable to. This very room would no longer be the same, and the characteristics of the whole house would change as well. There would be no one in the building to call "Mother." He had not imagined that her death would cause his heart such pain. Was he not already well acquainted with death? Of course he was. He was old enough and experienced enough not to be frightened by death, but the sting of an eternal separation was agonizing. Perhaps his heart could be criticized for suffering like a novice's despite all the pain it had experienced. How much she had loved him! How much she had loved all of them! How much she had loved everything in existence!

"But your soul only pays attention to such fine qualities when losing someone," Kamal thought. "At this critical moment your memory is crowded with images of places, times, and events having a profound impact on you. Light overlaps darkness as the blue of early morning blends with the roof garden, the glowing brazier of the coffee hour mingles with religious legends, and the dove's cooing mixes with sweet songs. Heart of an infidel, this was a magnificent love. Tomorrow you may truly declare that death has claimed the person you loved most. Perhaps your eyes will fill with tears until old age reproves you. The tragic vision of life is not free of an infantile Romanticism. It would be far worthier of you to view life courageously as a drama with a happy ending called 'death.' But ask yourself how much longer you will continue wasting your life. Your mother dies after concluding a lifetime of achievements. What have you done?"

He was roused by footsteps as Khadija entered the room in a state of shock. She made straight for the bed, calling to her mother and asking what had happened. His pain was compounded by this scene, and fearing that his sangfroid would desert him, he fled to the sitting room. Yasin, Zanuba, and Ridwan arrived almost immediately. After shaking hands with them, Kamal told them about his mother's condition without going into details. They went into the bedroom, leaving him alone until Yasin emerged to ask, "What did the doctor tell you?"

Kamal answered despondently, "Paralysis and pneumonia. Everything will be over in three days."

Yasin bit his lip and said mournfully, "There is not any power or might save God's." Taking a seat, he muttered, "The poor woman – the whole thing comes so suddenly. Hadn't she complained of feeling poorly of late?"

"Not at all. As you know, she never complained. But she did seem tired at times."

"Shouldn't you have called the doctor earlier?"

"She detested nothing so much as consulting a physician."

Ridwan joined them after a while and told Kamal, "I think she should be moved to the hospital, Uncle."

Shaking his head sadly, Kamal answered, "It wouldn't do any good. The pharmacist will send a nurse he knows to administer the injection."

They fell silent, their concern evident on their faces. At this moment Kamal remembered a matter that courtesy required he should not neglect. So he asked Yasin, "How is Karima?"

"She'll have her baby this week, or that's what the woman physician says."

Kamal murmured, "May our Lord take her by the hand. . . ."

Yasin lamented, "The baby will come into the world while the father is in detention."

The doorbell rang. It was Riyad Qaldas. After greeting his friend, Kamal escorted him to the study. On the way up, Riyad explained, "I asked for you at the school, and the secretary gave me the news. How is your mother?"

"She's paralyzed, and the doctor says it will all be over in three days."

Riyad looked glum and inquired, "Can't anything be done?"

Kamal shook his head disconsolately and remarked, "Perhaps it's lucky that she's unconscious and knows nothing of the destiny awaiting her." When they were seated, he added in an ironic tone, "But who among us knows what destiny awaits us?"

Riyad smiled without replying. Then Kamal continued: "Many think it wise to make of death an occasion for reflection on death, when in truth we ought to use it to reflect on life."

Smiling, Riyad answered, "I think that is better. So let's ask ourselves when anyone dies what we are doing with our lives."

"As for me, I'm not doing anything with my life. This is what I was thinking about."

"But you're only halfway down the road. . . ."

"Perhaps yes, perhaps no," Kamal thought. "Although it's always good for a person to ponder the dreams that tempt him. Mysticism is an evasion of responsibility and so is a passive faith in science. There is no alternative to action, and that requires faith. The issue is how we are to mold for ourselves a belief system that is worthy of life."

He asked, "Do you think I've done my duty to life by sincerely pursuing my vocation as a teacher and by writing my philosophical essays?"

Riyad answered affectionately, "There's no doubt that you have."

"But like any other traitor, I live with a guilty conscience."

"Traitor?"

Sighing, Kamal said, "Let me share with you what my nephew Ahmad told me when I visited him at the jail before his transfer to the prison camp."

"By the way – any new developments concerning them?"

"They've gone with many others to the prison camp at al-Tur in Sinai."

Riyad inquired jovially, "The one who worships God and the one who doesn't?"

"You must worship the government first and foremost if you wish your life to be free of problems."

"In any case, being detained without trial is, I think, a lesser evil than being sentenced to prison."

"That's one way of looking at it. But when will this affliction be removed? When will martial law be lifted? When will the rule of natural law and the constitution be restored? When will the Egyptians be treated like human beings again?"

Riyad started to fiddle with the wedding ring on his left hand. He remarked sadly, "Yes, when! Well, never mind. . . . What did Ahmad say in jail?"

"He told me, 'Life consists of work, marriage, and the duty incumbent upon each person claiming human status. This is not an appropriate occasion to discuss an individual's responsibilities toward his profession or spouse. The duty common to all human beings is perpetual revolution, and that is nothing other than an unceasing effort to further the will of life represented by its progress toward the ideal.' "

After reflecting a little, Riyad said, "A beautiful thought . . . but one open to all kinds of interpretations."

"Yes, and that's why his brother and antagonist, Abd al-Muni'm, accepts it too. I have understood it to be a call to adopt some set of beliefs, regardless of its orientation or goal. So I attribute my misery to the guilty conscience of a traitor. It may seem easy to live in a self-contained world of egotism, but it's difficult to be happy this way if you really are a human being."

In spite of the gloomy nature of the occasion, Riyad's face lit up and he replied, "This is the harbinger of an important upheaval that is about to occur in your life."

Kamal cautioned his friend: "Don't make fun of me. The choice of a faith has still not been resolved. The greatest consolation I have is the fact that the struggle is not over yet. It will be raging even when, like my mother's, my life has only three more days remaining." Sighing, he added, "Do you know what else he said? He told me, 'I believe in life and in people. I feel obliged to advocate their highest ideals as long as I believe them to be true, since shrinking from that would be a cowardly evasion of duty. I also see myself compelled to revolt against ideals I believe to be false, since recoiling from this rebellion would be a form of treason. This is the meaning of perpetual revolution.'"

As he listened, Riyad nodded his head in agreement. Since Kamal was clearly exhausted and tense, his friend said, "I must go now. What would you think about accompanying me to the streetcar stop? Perhaps the walk would help you relax."

They both rose and left the room. Finding Yasin, who had met Riyad a few times, at the entrance to the first-floor apartment, Kamal invited him to join them but asked to be excused for a few minutes to look in at his mother again. On entering her bedroom, he found her still unconscious.

Her eyes red from crying, Khadija was seated on the bed by her mother's feet. The despair that had never left her face since the government had laid hands on her sons was plainly visible. Zanuba, Aisha, and Umm Hanafi sat silently on the sofa. Aisha was smoking a cigarette quickly and anxiously. Meanwhile her eyes scouted the room with nervous agitation.

Kamal asked, "How is she?"

Aisha replied in a loud voice that suggested a worried protest, "She doesn't want to wake up!"

He chanced to turn toward Khadija, and they exchanged a long look of mournful understanding and shared sorrow. Sensing that he might lose control of himself, Kamal darted from the room to rejoin his companions.

They walked slowly down the street and traversed the Goldsmiths Bazaar without saying much of anything. On reaching al-Sanadiqiya, they ran into Shaykh Mutawalli Abd al-Samad, who was hobbling along unsteadily with the help of his cane. He was blind, and his arms trembled as he turned from side to side asking in a loud voice, "Which way to paradise?"

A passerby laughingly suggested, "First turn on your right."

Yasin asked Riyad Qaldas, "Would you believe that this man is almost ten years over a hundred?"

Smiling, Riyad answered, "He's hardly a man now, whatever his age."

Kamal looked fondly at the shaykh, who made him think of his father. He had once considered this man a landmark of the neighborhood – like the ancient fountain building, the mosque of Qala'un, and the vault of Qirmiz Alley. The shaykh still encountered many who were sympathetic to him, but there were always boys to plague him by whistling at him or by following him and imitating his gestures.

The two brothers escorted Riyad to the streetcar stop and waited with him until he boarded. Then they returned to al-Ghuriya. Kamal suddenly stopped and told Yasin, "It's time for you to go to the coffeehouse."

Yasin replied sharply, "Certainly not! I'll stay with you."

Knowing his brother's temperament as well as anyone, Kamal said, "There's absolutely no need of that."

Yasin pushed Kamal along ahead of him, protesting, "She's my mother as much as yours."

All at once Kamal felt fearful for Yasin. It was true that he was brimming with life and as huge as a camel, but how much longer could he endure an existence so dominated by passion's impulses? Kamal's heart filled with sorrow, but his thoughts suddenly flew to the detention camp of al-Tur.

"I believe in life and in people." That was what Ahmad had said. "I feel obliged to advocate their highest ideals as long as I believe them to be true, since shrinking from that would be a cowardly evasion of duty. I also see myself compelled to revolt against ideals I believe to be false, since recoiling from this rebellion would be a form of treason."

Kamal had long wondered what was true and what was false, but perhaps doubt was as much of an evasion of responsibility as mysticism or a passive belief in science.

"Could you be a model teacher, an exemplary husband, and a lifelong revolutionary?" he asked himself.

When they reached al-Sharqawi's store, Yasin stopped and explained, "Karima asked me to get some things she needs for the baby, if you don't mind."

They entered the small shop, and Yasin selected the items his daughter had requested: diapers, a bonnet, and a nightgown. Then Kamal remembered that the black necktie he had worn for a year following his father's death was threadbare and that he would be needing a new one when the mournful day arrived. He told the man, when Yasin was finished, "A black necktie, please."

Each one took his package, and they left the store. The setting of the sun was washing the world with a sepia tint as side by side they walked back to the house.

Acknowledgments

I want to thank Mary Ann Carroll
for being the first reader,
Jacqueline Kennedy Onassis
for her sensitive editing,
Riyad N. Delshad for assistance
with some obscure vocabulary and expressions,
and Sarah and Franya Hutchins
for their patience.
Although others have contributed
to this translation, I am happy
to bear responsibility for it.

– William Maynard Hutchins

This book is set in BEMBO which was cut
by the punch-cutter Francesco Griffo
for the Venetian printer-publisher
Aldus Manutius in early 1495
and first used in a pamphlet
by a young scholar
named Pietro
Bembo.